DATE DUE

DEMCO 38-297

PALMERSTON
The Early Years
1784–1841

PALMERSTON
The Early Years
1784–1841

By
Kenneth Bourne

MACMILLAN PUBLISHING CO., INC.
NEW YORK

Macmillan Publishing Co., Inc.
866 Third Avenue
New York, N.Y. 10022

Collier Macmillan Canada, Inc.

Printed in the United States of America

printing number

1 2 3 4 5 6 7 8 9 10

Library of Congress Cataloging in Publication Data

Bourne, Kenneth.
    Palmerston, the early years, 1784–1841.

    Includes bibliographical references and index.
    1. Palmerston, Henry John, Viscount, 1784–1865.
2. Great Britain—Foreign relations—1837–1901.
3. Great Britain—Politics and government—1837–1901.
4. Prime ministers—Great Britain—Biography.
I. Title.

DA536.P2B68   941.081'092'4   [B]   81-18582

ISBN 0-02-903740-9   AACR2

FOR ELEANOR

CONTENTS

LIST
OF
PLATES

ILLUSTRATIONS
IN THE
TEXT

The author and publishers are grateful to the Broadlands Collection for permission to reproduce nos. 1, 2, 3, 4, and to the British Library of Political and Economic Science for nos. 5, 7, 8, 9, 10.

PREFACE

There is no satisfactory biography of Palmerston and there probably never will be. Among the modern biographies, that by Herbert Bell is probably the best of the two-volume studies and that by Donald Southgate the best of the single-volume ones. But neither had access to the family papers. Apart from monographs of diplomatic history (notably by Sir Charles Webster), the only works based on much familiarity with the family papers were those by the official Victorian biographers and by Philip Guedalla. But Bulwer and Ashley's *Life*, though full of valuable original material, was necessarily too discreet, and Guedalla's, though brilliant and fascinating, was infuriatingly allusive rather than solidly informative. Confronted with a vast mass of material and with the impossibility in present times of being allowed to contrive more than two volumes, I cannot expect to have accomplished all that many might have wished. This first volume covers Palmerston's background and education, his early parliamentary elections, his neglected administration of the War Office, his emergence into the political limelight, and his first two periods at the Foreign Office. On all of these there are many new details, including revelations about his private financial affairs and his varied love life. However, in view of Webster's magisterial study of Palmerston's foreign policy in 1830–41, I have tried so far as possible to avoid the details of diplomacy and to confine myself to the formulation of policy in Cabinet (which Webster neglected) and its administration in the Foreign Office (which he covered only incompletely). Palmerston's estate business, both in England and in Ireland, will be dealt with in the second volume.

For all this I owe an immense debt to many archivists, librarians, and private owners. To the last, in particular, a visit from an L.S.E. teacher may these days sometimes seem an unpleasant prospect. Yet only once, to my knowledge, have I been treated on this account with prejudice and discourtesy. To the rest, who have welcomed or at least tolerated me with courtesy and kindness, I hope I have made due acknowledgement in the Key to the Sources. But I must make special mention of Mrs (Felicity) Strong, formerly of the National Register of Archives, who put the Palmerston Papers in Chancery Lane in such magnificent order and helped and encouraged me so unstintingly throughout. To Lord Brabourne and the Broadlands Trustees, who have so generously given me free access to the mass of Palmerston's family papers, still largely unexplored by any other than diplomatic historians, I am of course particularly indebted. I have also benefited more than I can say from the kindness of the descendants of Palmerston's sister, Elizabeth Sulivan, who gave me free use of their small but important collections of family papers and, on visits stretched over several years, treated me more as a friend than an intruder. To James Wade (formerly of Collier Macmillan), who first suggested I tackle Palmerston, I owe unfailing encouragement, and to Peter Carson (of Allen Lane), who has had to put up with the results, I owe equally unfailing patience. My colleague Roger Bullen has kindly read the typescript and made many helpful comments. Lastly, in addition to help from the Research Committees of the L.S.E. and the University of London, I have received years of unpaid labour from my wife; her reward will come, I hope, earlier than in heaven.

K.B., March 1977

Since the above was written there has been a further long delay in publication. That delay has at least given me the opportunity of consulting additional material, in particular the Lamb papers and additional Hobhouse journals in the British Library.

January 1981

PALMERSTON
The Early Years
1784–1841

I

ORIGINS
AND
EDUCATION

Henry John Temple, third Viscount Palmerston (1784 - 1865), was an Irish peer but an Englishman. Tradition had it, and the eagles on the first quarter of their coat of arms proclaimed it, that the Temples were descended from Earl Leofric of Mercia. Nothing could have been more appropriate for the man described in his *Daily Telegraph* obituary as 'the most English minister that ever governed England'. But all that is reasonably certain is that from Peter Temple of Stowe, who died in 1577, had descended by his elder son the Dukes of Buckingham (of the fourth and last creation) and the Temples of the Nash, and by his younger the Viscounts Palmerston. But by the end of the eighteenth century only the last could claim an unbroken descent in the male line. The first Viscount Palmerston acquired his Irish name and peerage after some property his family had in Dublin. He also made two marriages into the City of London, and no doubt with the proceeds improved his two principal houses in England: one at East Sheen, which his uncle or his father had bought, and the other, which he purchased himself in 1736, at Broadlands, near Romsey. His elder son, Henry, also made a useful City marriage, but died soon after. Fortunately his wife had given birth a few months before to a son, also called Henry, who therefore succeeded his grandfather in 1757.

Henry, second Viscount Palmerston (1739 - 1802), was not a particularly rich man by the standards of his class; he enjoyed an income of about £7,000 a year throughout most of his adult life. Nor did he ever become exactly eminent in public life, though he was a member of Parliament for some forty years and briefly held lordships of both the Admiralty and Treasury. Rather it was as a dilettante of the arts and sciences that he was known. A devoted clubman, he knew Garrick, Gibbon and Johnson, and was the friend of Count Rumford and Sir Joseph Banks and patron of Joshua Reynolds and Angelica Kauffman. He married in 1767 a lady who was rather older than himself and who died less than two years afterwards. Then fourteen years later, on 7 January 1783, he was married in Bath to Mary Mee. Mary, at twenty-nine, was a good deal younger than her viscount; but she had evidently known and admired him for some years. She was, in fact, not only a family friend but also a distant relative, her mother being descended from a Dutch family called

1

Godschall, who had connections by marriage with the City of London and were still in business there. Her father, Benjamin Mee, had come from Gloucestershire to establish himself as a merchant in London. The notion that he was a Dublin merchant was a fanciful error of his grandson's first official biographer. He was also dead before his daughter's marriage. Her brother, also called Benjamin, was a Governor of the Bank of England and a Director of the Royal Exchange, and her elder sister, Sarah, was married to a banking partner and brother-in-law of Andreas Grote, William Culverden. The second viscount therefore appeared to be strengthening the tradition developed by his forebears. In this he was to be disappointed; his wife's relations brought financial burdens rather than relief. But they made a moral contribution to the spirit of Broadlands; for the Mees were also related, by marriage as well as business, with the saintly Raikeses and Thorntons.[1]

Mary, Viscountess Palmerston (1754 - 1805) seems to have been a lively and affectionate person. She was clearly much loved by her family and among her friends and acquaintances was generally spoken of as a good-natured and obliging woman. She was, if anything, rather too agreeable. Even close friends thought that she fussed over them too much and in her anxiety to surround her family with agreeable company, particularly perhaps of the sort her husband liked, she could be rather undiscriminating. But no breath of scandal ever really touched her name and the only unpleasant thing ever known to have been said about her came from the mouth of a most malicious and unreliable gossip. But it is also clear that she lacked self-confidence and in her early widowhood she became rather a pathetic figure. As the daughter of a merchant and a second wife she seems to have felt unequal to her husband's rank and to his recollection of his first wife. But she must have felt very proud when at seven in the evening of Wednesday, 20 October 1784, she gave him at last – for the viscount was then forty-five – a son and heir. The Palmerstons had come up to town only a fortnight before for his lordship's sitting to Reynolds, and so the baby came to be born not at Broadlands but at a rented house in Westminster, No. 4 Park Street, now No. 20 Queen Anne's Gate. A month later, at St Margaret's, Westminster, he was baptized Henry John. The following year his first birthday was celebrated 'with great magnificence'; a German singer was engaged for a grand concert and there was a ball late in the evening in Winchester, which was considered more convenient for the many guests than the Palmerstons' country house near Romsey.[2]

Although the third viscount improved the park and outlook and built a few additions in the Gothic style, Broadlands must have looked at the time of his first birthday much the same from the outside as it does today. Still basically an Elizabethan house in external appearance when his father inherited it, it was given a classic façade under the direction of 'Capability' Brown in the 1770s and enlarged and completed by his partner Henry Holland during the next decade. It was, and is now again, an almost perfect gem of a house and Lady Palmerston set about making it a very happy home for her husband and his heir. 'There', reported a fashionable visitor, 'you would have seen a very beautiful Place, a comfortable House, a good-natured poetical, stuttering Viscount, & a pleasing unaffected woman who, tho' she *did* squeeze through the City Gates into a Viscountess, wears her blushing honours without shaking them at you every moment. There you would have seen Waterworks by Day & Fireworks by Night.' Young Harry, who had evidently not been well, certainly got 'much improved' at Broadlands and was soon reported to be 'a fine, eager, lively, good-humoured boy'. He remained 'very white & a little pinched in the face' and indeed throughout his childhood he was constantly afflicted with erysipelas, or, as they called it, St Anthony's Fire, which sometimes produced irritating blotches and even large blisters, on his face especially. But according to his mother he never ceased chattering and soon he was given a partner in a 'jig everlasting and dance without end'. His sister, Frances, was born on 18 February 1786. Two years after that, on 17 January 1788, he was presented with a brother, William. Two more sisters followed in rapid succession, Mary on 15 January 1789 and Elizabeth on 30 March 1790. Their mother seems to have spent much of this period at Broadlands; but her bucolic bliss was not to last much longer. The two eldest children had both been safely inoculated against smallpox by Baron Dimsdale in May 1787, though Harry was in 'indifferent' health for some time afterwards with an intermittent fever and an inflammation of the eyes. But when three years later his parents decided that the other children should also be inoculated little Mary reacted very badly and died within a month. About the same time Lady Palmerston was also troubled by the misadventures of her brother, of whom she was evidently very fond indeed. According to a friend he made later, Benjamin Mee was 'a man of the most insinuating and engaging manners' who had continually to be rescued by his friends and relatives from the consequences of 'unlucky speculations' and 'a gay and extravagant life'. Lord Palmerston had already bailed him out of trouble in 1784-5 and helped him on his way to a partnership in the Bengal Bank. But this venture proved no wiser than the last and in January 1792 he had to make a hurried escape from India in disguise, and then, after spending a few hours only in England, again to the Continent in order to keep out of gaol. This time his brother-in-law was unable to bail him out, but obtained for him the appointment of commissary with the Duke of York's army in the Netherlands. His health, however, had been ruined and he died without seeing England again at Bad Pyrmont on 2 August 1796.[3]

Although it may have been with the intention of giving his wife an invigorating change of scene that Palmerston had initially decided to take all his family off for a grand tour of Europe beginning in the summer of 1792, it was probably because of Ben's disgrace that they stayed away for nearly two and a half years. But Lady Palmerston was very far from being enthusiastic about it and in truth it suited her husband more than it did her. 'Lord Palmerston', a close friend said, 'has not got to his second childhood, but only as far as his second boyhood; for no schoolboy is so fond of a breaking-up as he is of a junket and pleasuring.' His life was an apparently endless round of salons and soirées, clubs, dances and opera parties. But he was, it is clear, as fidgety a man in middle age as ever his children were in infancy. His friend once said that 'one cannot conceive how Lord Palmerston would get through Lent without the oratorios'. Indeed, he had observed as long ago as 1788, for a 'sensible' man Palmerston was strangely dependent for his amusement on the 'external assistance' of 'sights, prints, parties, etc.' Lady Palmerston made a great effort to keep up with him, and not least in his intellectual activities; among her own friends she counted the Berry sisters and their bluestocking acquaintances Miss Carter and Mrs Cholmeley. But she liked to act his gay companion in every other way as well.[4]

Lord Palmerston's oldest friends were Hans Sloane, a Hampshire neighbour, and Thomas Pelham (afterwards second Earl of Chichester), who shared an aunt with him and was also related to his first wife. But in their later years the Palmerstons' closest friends outside the family were the two Amyand sisters and their husbands, Sir Gilbert Elliot and Sir James Harris; their 'oldest, fastest, safest friend', Elliot called Lady Palmerston. Both Elliot and Harris outstripped Palmerston in politics, becoming the first Earls respectively of Minto and Malmesbury. Elliot (1751-1814) was Viceroy of Corsica in 1794-6, minister at Vienna in 1799, President of the Board of Control in 1806 and Governor-General of India in 1807-13. Harris (1746-1820) was regarded as England's pre-eminent diplomat and when deafness forced his retirement he continued as close adviser to Pitt, Portland and Canning. According to Walter Scott, who knew him well, Elliot was 'a man among a thousand', 'pleasing and amiable' with the 'mildest manners', but 'very tenacious of his opinions'. Scott also described Elliot's wife as a 'delight to see, she is so full of spirit and intelligence'. But not everyone had such a good opinion of her. According to Lady Holland she was 'a sprightly, prating, gossiping woman, with a large share of vanity and a moderate one of sense. Parsimonious and ill-tempered (as may be seen from her thin lips) & méchante without wit, she is the only woman . . . Lord H[olland] absolutely cannot endure.'[5]

But it was Anna Maria Elliot's sister, Harriet Malmesbury, whom Lady Palmerston described as her most intimate friend, and Malmesbury who came to exercise the most important influence on the political emergence of the third Viscount Palmerston. The Mintos by no means approved, but probably on personal as much as political grounds. Harriet Malmesbury was considered by the poet Tom Campbell to be 'a shrewd and liberal-minded woman'; but others described her simply as 'a disagreeable old woman' and Minto doubted that she genuinely reciprocated Lady Palmerston's feelings. Evidently he disliked both the Malmesburys; he even shared the common notion that on his famous mission to The Hague Harris had lined his pockets with secret service funds. The uncharitable Lady Holland thought equally unwell of Elliot; 'a hypocrite in private life & . . . a rogue in public' was what she called him. But while both husbands at one time or another had gained reputations as lady-killers, Elliot had made much the happier marriage. The Mintos could therefore only look on with distaste and dismay as the Malmesburys quarrelled violently through the years. Yet there appears not even a whisper of all this in Lady Palmerston's papers. Instead the Malmesburys at Park Place and the Culverdens nearby in Henley formed with other friends and family connections a very 'junkety' throng around the Palmerstons at Sheen.[6]

Minto thought that the Culverdens' villa, Lavender House, was about 'the prettiest and most charming little settlement' he had ever seen, but the sort of company the Palmerstons kept in their later years somewhat fast and even rather seedy. Once he remarked: 'I never saw any two people make such toil of pleasure, as both he and she. She seems completely worn down by her raking, but is always eager for the next labour.' Lady Palmerston was probably much less eager than she seemed; but she hated being separated from her husband or interfering with his pleasures. He was always anxious to be on the move and was probably rather irritated to be tied down at all in her childbearing years. They had got away together for a tour of the West Country in the summer of 1787 but he had to go alone to Ireland in the following year and, in view of Elizabeth's expected arrival, substituted for a winter in Italy a mere six weeks' tour of the Rhine in the autumn of 1789. Two years later the excitement of the French Revolution, which had already touched their Rhineland tour, took him back alone for nearly three months to Paris itself. His second visit with his wife and children in August 1792 nearly proved their undoing. But they escaped in the nick of time and made their way to Switzerland and Italy. In Italy they spent most of their time, sightseeing apart, in buying pictures and having others painted. In Naples they mixed a good deal with Sir William Hamilton and his wife and in Rome they had Angelica Kauffman do a portrait of their daughter Elizabeth. It is strange that they do not seem to have had one made of Harry too; but he acquired something much more useful in Italy – a tutor.[7]

Harry was very fortunate in the choices his parents made for his education. He had of course already had some sort of domestic instruction at home, although his eyes were often so bad that he could not read and had to 'play with maps' instead. But when he was six and his father was away in Paris, Lady Palmerston had a Mr Williams read to him for a couple of hours each morning; 'it was a sad thing', she said, that 'so clever a boy should waste all his hours, and without some obligation to attend it is impossible to expect children will prefer learning anything to playing about.' Earlier still, from the end of 1788, he also had a French governess. Thérèse Mercier was one of two nieces in English service of a man said to be 'justly eminent in French literature' – probably Louis Sébastien Mercier. Certainly she was very well thought of, and she stayed with the family until all the children had grown up. It was therefore she who laid the first foundations of the future Foreign Secretary's famous fluency in French. She went with the family to France and Italy in 1792-4 and it was there that she met her future husband, although they did not marry until May 1800. We know almost nothing about Gaetano Ravizzotti's earlier life beyond his own advertisement as a former teacher of languages in Naples and his son's suggestion that he was originally from Rome. He was later credited with being a refugee, presumably of radical inclinations. But there is no sign that he ever influenced Harry in that direction even though he became his tutor in Italy and stayed close to him for many years. On the other hand it is clear that it was he who built an academic superstructure on the foundations laid by Mlle Mercier and when Sir Gilbert Elliot met the Palmerstons in Florence in May 1794 he reported that the nine-year-old boy was already speaking French and Italian well, although he had not yet begun Latin. The Palmerstons made their way back slowly through Germany and Holland and did not get back to England until October 1794. M. Gaetano, as they usually called him, accompanied them all the way and by January the following year Harry was taking lessons from him in the 'Book Room' at Broadlands. By the end of February he was writing what appears to be his first letter in French; by early May his first in Italian too. But Gaetano was a linguist of wide ability; in 1797 he published an Italian grammar and dedicated it to his young pupil. Two or three years later he published a collection of Spanish poems, and shortly after that a series of translations from Greek and Latin. It was probably under him, therefore, that Harry began to learn these languages too. He was given a Christmas present of *Don Quixote* to get him started on Spanish early in 1798. But he did not proceed very far, probably because by that time he had begun at Harrow school.[8]

Harrow in those days had only recently begun to build its reputation as one of England's leading schools. But it had survived a famous rebellion against the severe régime of Benjamin Heath and in 1795 was riding the peaks of success as Joseph Drury entered his second decade as headmaster. It was to be one of the most brilliant of the school's existence. In 1796 there were still only 139 boys; by 1803 there were 345. Much of this success seems to have been due to Drury himself. He made a special effort to get to know all the boys and in later life Harry Temple acknowledged that it was a positive pleasure even to be reprimanded by him. Certainly, where Heath aroused resentment, Drury appears to have inspired affection. One of the changes he made was to abolish birching for the older boys. He persisted, however, with the system of boarding houses that Heath had extensively overhauled and expanded. Harry was placed in that kept by one of the assistant masters, Thomas Bromley.[9]

Very little is known about Dr Bromley, but he seems to have been a quiet, scholarly man, though proud by the time he retired in 1808 to have contributed so much to Harrow's most aristocratic era. His wife, a sister of Mrs Drury's, was a bustling and, as befitted her position, motherly sort of woman. She told Lady Palmerston that Harry should be provided with '2 suits of clothes, a great coat, 10 shirts, 10 pocket handkerchiefs', and enough linen to change three times a week. There was some debate about nightshirts, since his father thought the other boys might laugh at him; but two other boys were found who wore them, so Harry was allowed to keep his, for a time at least. His room was small and, what with bureau, bookshelves and two lock-up cupboards, rather a tight squeeze. But he was lucky enough to have a folding bed so that there was little danger of it being messed up in the daytime and upsetting the servants.[10]

Harry seems to have been delayed from going to Harrow by an outbreak of scarlet fever there. But he filled up the time in London with private studies and the theatre until his father handed him over to the Bromleys on the evening of 25 May 1795. He was only ten and a half but he seemed in good spirits and very happy to stay. When his father returned a week later, he found him 'quite at home and at his ease' and Dr Bromley told him that 'he never saw a boy become a schoolboy so immediately'. Indeed, 'he spoke very handsomely of him . . . in every respect', 'very quick at his book' and making 'good progress'. So he would keep him unplaced and under his 'immediate inspection' for a while longer so as to become more certain where his 'age and parts' best fitted him to be. The following February Harry was placed in the fourth form, and delighted to have escaped fagging. He was evidently very happy at Harrow. In the first place his health seems to have been much better, though he did have all the usual childish diseases and Mrs Bromley complained that he would overload his stomach with the plum cake his mother sent him. 'The cake was very good, and very much liked,' he reported of an evidently imperfect first delivery, 'but what I liked best in it was that at the top it was plain, and at bottom plumb [sic] and then the sugar was so nice.' But he really frightened Mrs Bromley with his fondness for bathing. He and his elder sister had both got used to the water quite early on when at the age of two and three they had 'bathed' at the seaside as part of the treatment for their St Anthony's Fire. Harry became rather keen on his swimming and eventually it formed an important part of his regimen. But if Mrs Bromley was frightened that he would catch cold, a Harrow song still celebrates 'Temple's frame of iron'. Unfortunately we know little of his cricketing prowess, the records even of the early matches with Eton being lost. But he was writing home in the summer of 1796 for 'two pair of cricket stumps and a good bat' and later talked in a mixture of mock contempt and trepidation about a visiting team of Westminsters. He also played tennis and skated; and he bought himself a half interest in a ferret for catching rats. Riding and shooting had to be reserved for the holidays: he had been given his first pony when he was six, though he did not begin to shoot until 1798. But archery was all the rage at Harrow and he acquired his first crossbow almost as soon as he got there. It was in fact something of a family tradition; for his uncle Ben had been at Harrow and had carried off the much-prized Silver Arrow in 1764. Dr Heath had suppressed the competition in 1772, apparently as part of his campaign to reassert discipline, and it may not have been irrelevant that Ben Mee was a great friend of Samuel Parr, who led an exodus from Heath's régime. Dr Bromley was evidently not very happy about the resurgence of this illicit acivity in his house; and when Harry ordered a crossbow for his brother, it was perhaps in order to vent his own passion more safely in the holidays. When he had been at Harrow a year he also asked his mother to bring him on Speech Day 'a burning-glass . . . and a large one'. But there is no sign that he ever got into any serious trouble. In March 1798 he was joined at Harrow by his brother and not long afterwards he reported to his mother that they were 'both very well in health, tho' not in beauty, Willy's lip being rather swelled by a lick with a ball, and my two blue eyes being exchanged for two black ones in consequence of a battle'. Perhaps this was the occasion recalled two-thirds of a century later by an aged schoolfellow, Augustus Clifford, when Harry fought ' "behind school" a great boy called Salisbury, twice his size and he would not give in, but was brought home with black eyes and a bloody nose, and Mother Bromley taking care of him'. It is more than doubtful that the other boy was twice his size; Salisbury was in the same form, and Harry, his mother reported in December 1799, was already as big as his father. But it is clear that he was popular with both boys and masters. The Bromleys always talked of him as 'a most charming boy' and Clifford of his being 'reckoned the best-tempered' as well as the 'most plucky' boy in the school; and as one of their fags Clifford could vouch for Harry Temple being 'by far the most merciful and indulgent' among his messmates. These latter were the future Earls of Bessborough and Spencer, Lords Duncannon and Althorp. But neither gets much mention in Harry's letters home. Duncannon was rather older and was possibly being confused in Clifford's recollection with his younger brother, Fred Ponsonby, who was certainly in the same form and a close friend.[11]

It was shortly before he left school that Harry was first exposed to the practice of public declamation that was to be so important a part of the career he chose. Like most young men and women of his time and class, he not only attended the theatre a good deal, he also indulged in amateur theatricals. But the only record we have of any performance of his – in a masque called *Cupid's Cure* written by Lord Minto to mark the hurt suffered by his youngest son upon falling from a tree and performed before the Princess of Wales in 1799 – is as a mute. At Harrow, however, Dr Heath had established in place of archery contests annual declamations from the classics. Whatever else might have been said of the practice, it was supposed to develop both the memory and the voice. Certainly many valued it at the time; and it was thought impressive enough to attract an audience of admiring parents. The Palmerstons went to hear Harry give his first oration from Tacitus on 8 May and his second from Cicero on 5 June 1800. He was not supposed to speak again, since there was time for only two or three at the head of the fifth form in addition to the monitors and sixth. But he was disgusted to find that another boy, who stood below him in the fifth form, was going to be included on the flimsy grounds that he was going on his holidays and would not have the chance again. Fortunately someone else dropped out and so Harry did perform again on 3 July, and this time, at his father's wish, with a rendering in English from 'The Bard' by Thomas Gray. He had clashed once before with his rival, though only in a triumphant pillow fight; but his dislike for Dr Drury's favourite stands out very clearly in the letters that he wrote at this time. It was Lord Haddo, the future Earl of Aberdeen and Pam's rival as Foreign Secretary.[12]

Palmerston always looked back with great affection on his days at Harrow, and often revisited the school for some good work or interesting ceremony. His private secretary records how when he was nearly seventy-seven he rode down in the pouring rain to lay the foundation stone of the Vaughan Library and, as always turning adversity to advantage, stayed to pay a charming tribute to the men who had raised up five Prime Ministers in his own time. 'We ought', he told the assembled boys,

to pay due respect to those who form the character of the rising generation; who instruct them that self-control is better than indulgence; who tell them that labour is to be preferred to pleasure; and that whereas mere amusements may be compared to the southern breezes, which, though pleasant to be enjoyed, yet pass away and leave no trace behind them, honourable exertion on the contrary, may be compared to the fertilizing shower which, though it may, as you all know at the present moment, not be agreeable to those who are exposed to it, yet nevertheless leaves, by enriching and improving the soil on which it falls, solid marks behind it by the ample and abundant harvest which it helps to create.

Nor was this merely an old man's maudlin recollection. Only six months after leaving school he was writing with warm approval of the public school as 'a Nation in miniature' where 'a boy who puts himself at the head of his associates in all their games and enterprizes, whether for mischief or amusement, would most likely equally distinguish himself at the head of an army or a council'; and with contempt of the 'Genteel or Polite Academy for young gentlemen' to which boys go in order to avoid the dangers to which at public schools 'his members and his morals' are exposed, but leave with 'worse health and little less ignorance'. In later life he told his brother that the trouble with the third Earl Grey, whose petulant objections kept him from returning to the Foreign Office in 1845, was that he had never had 'the wholesome buffeting of a public school'. At the same time, according to his earlier essay, it was also in such institutions that a boy might be most 'easily taught that subordination and obedience to his superiors, which is so necessary in any station he may afterwards fill. He learns to consider as a chimerical scheme, that doctrine of equality, which has proved so fatal to the peace of Europe.' On the other hand, no school should be 'blamed for not making a genius of a blockhead, any more than the people who could not scrub the blackamoor white'. Nor should too much be made of the public schools' almost exclusive concentration on the classics: 'Mathematics . . . would not be the worse understood, by being delayed a little longer, for . . . nothing is so foolish as attempting to crowd a great deal of knowledge on a young mind . . . Not to mention that children naturally take an aversion for every study which is peculiarly hard and dry, and therefore . . . by bothering their brains with mathematics too early we give them a rooted dislike to the study.'[13]

The second Viscount Palmerston took a rather different view of his son's situation. Harry, he fully acknowledged, had during his whole time at school given him 'uniform satisfaction with regard to his disposition, his capacity and his acquirements'. By the summer of 1800, indeed, he had risen to third place beneath the head boy and towards the end of June Dr Drury had made him a monitor. But his father disapproved of boys staying on too long at school just as much as he did their arriving too early and he felt that at fifteen and a half his son was now 'coming to that critical and important period when a young man's mind is most open to receive such impressions as may operate most powerfully on his character and his happiness during the remainder of his life'. It was therefore of 'the greatest consequence that he should be judiciously directed through such a course of studies as may give full exercise to his talents and enlarge his understanding, and that he should converse as much as possible with persons to whose opinions he must look up with deference, and in whose society his manners would be improved, and his morals secured'. But he had always thought those objects 'unattainable by boys remaining in the upper class of a public school, who can only pursue the common routine of classical instruction, and who must associate principally with companions from whom they can derive no improvement'. It is interesting to note that Lord Palmerston and his successor as Harry's mentor, Lord Malmesbury, both felt that the main benefits of the classics were for effect and pleasure. 'Nothing', his father shortly afterwards wrote to him, 'contributes more to set off and ornament natural talents than a ready acquaintance with the classics; and the being known to be a good scholar gives a young man a reputation even beyond its real value, which is however very considerable.' On the other hand, Malmesbury argued that their limited number made them render the most valuable return on a 'frugal employment' of time and effort, and, as the son of a classical scholar nicknamed 'Hermes', deemed them 'edifying' as well as 'amusing'. 'The classics never should be forgotten,' he was shortly to write to Harry, 'besides the taste and elegance they give to our habits of thinking and modes of expressions, they are an inexhaustible and constant fund of invaluable reading and late in life when other studies fatigue too much, you will find in the reverting to them the most pleasant of all resources . . .'[14]

It is very unlikely that once out of college Harry ever had much time to read the classics, least of all 'late in life' when he was Prime Minister. At Harrow, however, there was very little room in the classroom curriculum for anything else, even though Dr Drury 'spared his hearers any long philological dissertations' and tried instead to imbue the boys with a love of ancient literature. According to a timetable of the period there was also some map-drawing in the lower forms; and Harry had already taken to that as a pleasure before coming up to school. In the upper forms there was a little time set aside for what was vaguely described as 'reading'. Perhaps it was under this heading that Harry learnt the very little he did about both light and arithmetic. At his father's urging he also managed to find an hour on alternate days for French and Italian and he continued to write some of his letters home in one or the other. But by his own acknowledgement he made most progress in the holidays under M. Gaetano. So given all his own many-sided interests in arts and sciences, it is hardly surprising that Lord Palmerston was not content with his son's prizes for some Latin verses in praise of Nelson's victory on the Nile or in mockery of John Gilpin's ride to Ware, and should have looked after the summer speeches of 1800 to speed him on his way through life by another route.[15]

In ordinary times Harry would no doubt have been sent off on a grand tour of Europe in the company of some learned but poor young man; and indeed even in the heat of Bonaparte's invasions there had been some thought of his joining his father's friend Lord Minto, who was at Vienna on a special mission. Minto urged upon them that there was 'no safer or better place for young men . . . the manners, conduct, and character of . . . society [being] uncommonly good'. But Harry himself already had it on very good authority, from Minto's own children in fact, that it was really rather 'a bore'; and his parents simply pleaded his extreme youth. And so it was that in his search for 'an intermediate situation between school and an English university' the second Viscount Palmerston sent his son to Edinburgh.[16]

Harry was peculiarly fortunate in the time and place of his first spell at a university, for Edinburgh was then at the height of its fame and regarded by many as the leading institution of its kind in the world. It was in 1800, as it had been a decade or so earlier, difficult 'to conceive a university where industry was more general, where reading was more fashionable, where indolence and ignorance were more disreputable', and where 'every mind was in a state of fermentation'. So while the inspiration of the French Revolution remained and Napoleon continued to shut them out of Europe the liberal youth of Britain flocked to Edinburgh. But the particular attraction was the Professor of Moral Philosophy. Dugald Stewart (1753-1828) had previously shared the Chair of Mathematics with his father but in 1785 had exchanged with the Professor of Moral Philosophy and by the beginning of the nineteenth century had established himself as the leading exponent of philosophical subjects in the British Isles. The professors at Scottish universities, however, were not very well paid: their stipends were usually only between £50 and £100 a year and even then the chairs and their emoluments were sometimes divided. Apart from whatever some of them might earn from their writings, the greater part of the professors' income, therefore, was derived from lecture fees. In addition, as there was no organized system of student residences and no provision whatever for discipline or even the regulation of their studies, some of the professors occasionally took young men of the wealthier class into their homes. Two future Cabinet ministers had preceded Harry at Dugald Stewart's: Lord Henry Petty, who was to succeed as third Marquess of Lansdowne, and John Ward, who was as Earl of Dudley to become Foreign Secretary in the late 1820s. Another future Foreign Secretary who came up shortly after Palmerston to study under Stewart but lived with Professor Playfair was Lord John Russell. The only other British Prime Ministers, in addition to Palmerston and Russell, to have attended a Scottish university were Melbourne and Campbell-Bannerman, who both went to Glasgow. In 1800, apparently, Stewart was the only professor in Edinburgh taking such young men into his house. He would take on two or three at a time and supervise their studies and their social life both during term time and, if their parents wished it, through the whole of the vacations except for the months of July and August. For board and lodging (including, probably, the stabling of a horse) and for Stewart's own lectures and tuition (though not those of the other professors or the expenses incurred in taking classes with junior teachers) the Palmerstons paid the very substantial sum of £400 a year. It was claimed for Sydney Smith that he was the first to match such a charge in Edinburgh, and one can get some idea of how large a sum it was from the fact that at that time a 'good' student room in Edinburgh could be had for about thirty-five pence a week. In Glasgow the professors charged their boarders only from £80 to £120 for the session.[17]

Since what Stewart called his 'academical business' did not begin until November and he preferred not to receive his new pupils till then or in October at the earliest, Harry spent part of the late summer of 1800 visiting the homes of some of his Harrow friends and then on 11 September began a leisurely journey northwards from London with his parents. It was typical of his father to turn the whole affair into a cultural tour and pleasure trip. Count Rumford went along with them and their visits to the grand residences of Burghley, Clumber and Worksop were all carefully recorded in their diaries along with trips to Glasgow, Loch Lomond and the ironworks in Stirling. They arrived in Edinburgh on 11 October and there his parents stayed another whole month to see something of their Scottish friends and Harry safely settled in. 'At ten o'clock', wrote his mother on 10 November, 'Lord Palmerston, Count Rumford and myself set off from Edinburgh, having bid farewell to my dear Harry. The pain I felt at bidding him adieu made me so wretched that I had no spirits to enjoy a very fine drive, for I wept the whole way. It is impossible to leave so amiable a being without regret, and when that being is one of the most affectionate sons, the pain must be acute.' Harry, however, was in very good hands.[18]

Lothian House, which the Stewarts rented at this time from its namesake, was a large place located in St Andrews Square at the bottom of the New Town and a good distance from the college. It was surrounded by a garden, and Harry, who had a room looking towards Arthur's Seat, thought it all 'perfectly quiet and pleasant'. In addition to his younger children George and Mary, Stewart's elder son by his first wife, Matthew, who was almost exactly Harry's own age, and a nephew of about twenty also lived in the house. But the only other 'young gentleman' was Richard, Lord Ashburton. The only child of the famous politician, John Dunning, the second Lord Ashburton at eighteen was evidently a very queer fish. He struck Harry from the first as 'the most singular compound of oddities' he had ever seen. In appearance he resembled 'a young Hippopotamus or seacow', his legs being hardly one-third of his height; in personality pleasant and in conversation good-humoured enough, but quick to take offence and in Harry's opinion 'on the verge of madness'. He also kept all sorts of animals in the attics, suffered terribly from the attentions of a widowed mother, and eventually ran off with Mrs Stewart's niece. Mrs Stewart was very upset by this, but she at length forgave him and, indeed, held in very close affection all her young charges.[19]

A well-known song-writer whom even Lady Holland called 'clever, well-informed, and pleasing', Helen d'Arcy Stewart was a cheerful, comfortable-looking woman who maintained her contacts with her 'children' throughout her life and in the case of Lord Dudley preserved for posterity his only surviving collection of worthwhile private correspondence to have been printed. Harry had much less need than Ward of a surrogate mother, but though less regular his correspondence too is full of warmth and gratitude and it is clear that Mrs Stewart played an important part in his happiness at Edinburgh. She struck Harry from the start as 'a very pleasant agreeable woman'; indeed, they both seemed 'excessively good natured'. According to another well-informed account, Stewart was 'about the middle size, weakly limbed, and with an appearance of feebleness which gave an air of delicacy to his gait and structure'. Harry reported that he did 'not prepossess one much in his favour at first sight', but within the month he had to acknowledge that he improved 'amazingly on acquaintance'. This was all just as well, since it was Professor Stewart who was to have such an important role in this new stage of his education and development. It was in fact owing to his specific requirements that Harry went up to Edinburgh as early as he did; for he did not take boys after they had turned sixteen since he found that then they did not easily knuckle under to his rules. But although that age was rather close Lord Palmerston assured Stewart that he would find his son 'perfectly tractable and disposed to conform himself with cheerfulness to all such regulations as you shall think fit to prescribe to him; and though he is forward enough in all good points, he is still a boy, and has not assumed the airs and manners of a premature man.' Harry indeed strikes one as all too docile and obedient in these early years. The Mintos, who spent a good deal of time in Edinburgh while Harry was there, and lavished their praises on him, certainly detected something lacking in him. 'He is charming,' Lady Minto reported, 'having no fault or failing, unless it be a want of the spirits belonging to his age.' However, if he displayed a curious lack of rebelliousness for a teenager, it must be admitted that Professor Stewart's régime was systematic rather than severe.[20]

The classes at the college began on Tuesday, 11 November 1800. The principal courses at that time were in mathematics, algebra, natural philosophy (physics), chemistry, botany, history and moral philosophy, and it was Stewart's intention that Harry should attend such of these as he profitably could during the two years or so he might stay at Edinburgh. In the first year, therefore, it was arranged that he should go to the great Professor Playfair's 'second class' on algebra from nine to ten in the mornings, to Stewart's own lectures on moral philosophy from twelve to one, and to Alexander Fraser Tytler's on 'universal history' from two till three. So, soon after breakfast, Harry would make the long haul up the Mound in company with young George Stewart who though 'an amazingly nice little fellow' did not like going to the high school and cried so much that Harry would try to raise his spirits with 'a few bad jokes' at breakfast and then make him laugh all the way. But he did find his own programme 'rather awkward' as no two lectures came together. It was part of Stewart's 'plan' that he should write up the substance of his lectures afterwards and as he had not taken Playfair's first course, in geometry, coach him himself in that subject in the evenings. In addition, in order that his classics should at least not get too rusty in an institution that so neglected them, he was to do Latin and Greek three times a week from three to four with a Mr Williamson, who came to attend Matthew Stewart for the same purpose. Since there was not time enough to get back to Lothian House between Stewart's and Tytler's lectures he also began to go two or three times a week to the riding school from one till two. But he soon found that riding round in small circles gave him sick headaches preceded by a dazzling in the eyes. His father, who had suffered the same sort of thing in his youth, suspected that it was a case of over-indulgence in food and drink. But this, Harry hastened to assure him, was quite a false impression. He never drank anything at dinner, which was at four, and, since they hardly ever stayed in the dining-room for more than an hour and a half, rarely more than one or two glasses afterwards. Then he would go for a walk and return for an hour of geometry with Mr Stewart before tea at eight. He then read in his room till ten, when indeed he did come down for supper. This last was 'a great nuisance' but he thought he ought to come down since everyone else did and then it was difficult to avoid accepting a potato and a glass of ale. But he promised to give these up just in case and, what with rhubarb pills and camomile, seems to have got rid of his headaches, for a while at least. As an extra precaution he also abandoned riding in the manège and on Tuesdays and Thursdays filled up the time instead with drawing lessons. His first instructor was a man called Walker, possibly the engraver John Walker, who made him 'begin from the beginning' by drawing 'half a sheet full of straight lines' but soon gave him some outlines of ruins to do at home, and by February 1801, when they had doubled the number of lessons, had let him move on from landscapes to figures. Harry was very pleased: 'He is a very good master', he reported, 'and most of his scholars draw well.' But the next month he was advised to return to landscapes. From the surviving evidence of childish castles and abbeys in Harry's travel journals of the period, one can only sympathize with Walker. However, although he was allowed to progress to water-colours, by the next session he had discovered that Walker was 'a bad master and a rogue' and as these were 'two very material defects' he had enrolled instead under 'a man . . . called Naesmith'. Apparently Lord Palmerston had noted and admired some scenery painted by Alexander Nasmyth for the theatre at Inverary and presumably Harry was among the small group of pupils who at this time are known to have paid two guineas each for twelve lessons at his house. Harry thought him 'the best teacher in Edinburgh' and spent four hours with him every Wednesday and Saturday, but whether he did Harry much good is another matter. The lessons continued until the spring of 1803 when Nasmyth decided to concentrate on a coming exhibition and a pupil of his called Carlisle took over. A few years later Harry also took lessons from the famous water-colourist, Thomas Heaphy, who was making a whole series of family portraits at Broadlands. But the only evidence of any lasting improvement lies perhaps in the careful lines of the Cupid that he eventually pencilled, along with a suggestive couplet, in Lady Cowper's album.[21]

Harry could have devoted still more time to art if he had been prepared to give up more of his Saturdays or Sundays. But, during the first year at least, these were left entirely free for his pleasure. He took Scottish dancing lessons three times a week and continued as at Broadlands and Harrow to play chess. But he was disappointed in the spring to find that he could not 'muster up a sufficient number of fellows to have a game at cricket', so he took up golf, 'a poor game compared to cricket, but better than nothing'. In the winter he went skating, shooting or walking at the weekends. He also bought a terrier 'who, among his other numerous good qualities (such as drawing badgers, killing cats, etc.), was recommended as a good one for finding rabbits'. Since he was inordinately fond of puns he called it 'Seizer' and kept it in the loft with Ashburton's. He was much less fortunate in an attempt to indulge his fondness for the stage. London had rather spoiled him for Edinburgh's humbler fare; in the north he heard even *Macbeth* 'murdered in every sense' and of a thing called *Life and the Lying Valet* he wrote home that 'if Life was so bad even with the good actors at London, can you have any idea what it was here?' It was in Edinburgh, he also reported home, that he was first made to appreciate that he was, as he put it, 'a Paddy', when an Irish surgeon in the infirmary invited him round to celebrate St Patrick's day. But he was himself so unaware of the fact that he did not till too late realize that he should have bought a shamrock. Moreover the Irish in Edinburgh, he thought, were all blackguards. He exempted one family only from the accusation, the Edgeworths, of whom he saw a little and liked a good deal more. In such a house as Stewart's he was bound to meet with interesting company from time to time. No sooner had his parents left him, indeed, than the famous African explorer, Mungo Park, came to dine. 'He is', he reported in November 1800, 'about five foot ten, not very strongly made, and to look at him one would not think him fitted to undergo the hardships he suffered. His countenance is rather handsome, and very intelligent, with a great deal of good nature expressed in it. . . . his features are not so expressive of a determined character as I expected, [but] I never saw any eye like his. It is of a dark colour, and so very sharp and watchful, that one would think he thought some wild beast was just about to spring on him. He is always looking about him, as if he was distrustful of some treachery. Some say that he contracted that habit in his journey, but I should rather think it was natural.' Harry did not in fact lack at all for 'good' company in Edinburgh. In the winter of 1801-2 the Mintos took a house at the opposite end of town so that their eldest son, Gilbert, could spend a couple of years at the college before going up to Oxford. He was only two years older than Harry and they seem to have got on very well together. Then there were his two sisters, 'Cathan' and Anna Maria, for Harry to flirt with. Gradually he gathered around him a more numerous band of young men friends. Many of them were old schoolfellows, neighbours and family acquaintances following his example. One of the first to come, in January 1801, was Francis Cholmeley, the son of Lady Palmerston's bluestocking friend and the nephew of a rakish crony of his father's, Sir Henry Englefield; according to Harry, he was so far 'not very well educated' and as a Catholic had little future at an English university. The following winter there arrived three old Harrovians he knew. There was also a notion that he would be joined in Edinburgh in 1802 by an even earlier acquaintance he had made, Francis Hare. The eldest son of a friend of Fox and one of four famous brothers who were all to become rather precious literati, Francis Hare had met Harry Temple when they were but four or five years old and somehow this unlikely pair had formed an apparently warm relationship. A few years later, when Hare was still only twelve and Harry but one year more, they had exchanged a precocious correspondence between Bologna and Harrow on education, sausages and marriage. It had been hoped that Hare would join Harry at Dugald Stewart's, but there was no room and he went instead to Aberdeen. Had he joined Harry during these years at Edinburgh the effect might have been interesting. 'The Silent Hare', as he came to be nicknamed on account of his extreme loquacity, was said to be remarkable for 'his leanness, his appetite, and his conversational powers'. Like Harry he gained an early reputation for fluency in foreign languages and although he published the least of all the brothers, he was the most respected as 'a monster of learning'. Unlike Harry, however, he was hopelessly disorganized; Ward, who found him a charming travelling companion in Italy a few years later, said of him: 'To be sure this walking library wants a librarian; the accuracy of the arrangement is not so much to be admired as the abundance of the materials.' But although it was claimed that their 'childish friendship was . . . never laid aside', and he took the trouble to look up Harry on his way to Aberdeen in July 1802 and again at Cambridge in November 1804, he spent most of his life in Italy, where he died in 1842.[22]

Harry's friends obviously made Edinburgh much less grave a place for him than it otherwise would have been and gave him, too, youthful companions on the many visits he made to parties at the grand houses belonging to his father's and his tutor's aristocratic friends. He was, on the whole, also very satisfied with his work at Edinburgh. A timetable clash made it impossible for him to go to Playfair's first course, on geometry, so he began with the second, on algebra. He found it 'rather inconvenient' to have left Harrow with so little arithmetic, but Playfair went slowly for the sake of the 'stupid boys' and Harry, to his own relief, also discovered that algebra was really 'another sort of arithmetic' and mathematics, as a result, 'very easy'. But when Playfair got on to spherical trigonometry, Harry had to drop out for a while. Stewart had been coaching him in geometry every evening and Harry conceded that he was a lucid instructor: '. . . as Mr Stewart does not take half an hour like Monsieur Chantaloup to prove that two things which are equal to the same thing, are equal to each other, I like it much better than I thought I should, only', he added for Lilly's information, 'it is a devilish bore to be obliged to be ten minutes demonstrating a proposition in Euclid's way, which I understand perfectly without the demonstration.' To Fanny he was blunter still: 'I am not far enough yet to admire the *beauty* of a demonstration. My idea of a beautiful demonstration is one that is very short and easy, and in which the letters of the alphabet are not as big as plums in a pudding.' So, although his progress had been too slow to keep up with Playfair's trig, Stewart's instruction was still effective enough for him to enlist in Playfair's geometry class in the middle of April when Stewart's own lectures on moral philosophy finished. Harry was sorry that these latter had come to an end since he found them 'very entertaining'. He thought at first that he was also going to enjoy Fraser Tytler's history course and, when he got as far as the eighth century B.C., that it promised to be 'more interesting' as he approached 'nearer to the modern history'. But when in March the professor resigned his chair in favour of his son, Harry was far from being sorry, 'for perhaps his son may give something like a course of universal history, as I am sure one cannot dignify the father's course by that name. He was two months lecturing about the Ancient Greeks and Romans, whom everybody reads at school . . . and when he comes to the modern part of it he goes off like wild fire and skips on to the Revolution in England under James 2nd and there ends.' However, Tytler's course in any case concluded at the end of that month and so Harry decided instead to fill the time with German.[23]

It has usually been assumed that Palmerston never learned any German at all. But he made several quite serious efforts to do so. In the first, at Edinburgh, he seems to have been encouraged, not by Stewart, who, sadly for a philosopher, had no German and made it clear the language was not in his opinion 'of most essential importance', but by his father's friend, Count Rumford, and challenged by the feebler attempts of his companion Ashburton. Ashburton had been taking lessons from a man they nicknamed 'Yudo', which was possibly some anti-Semitic slur, but he was evidently no good, and Rumford recommended instead a certain Robertson. From the few clues of identity scattered in Harry's letters home this was almost certainly the mysterious James Robertson (1758-1820), a Benedictine who at this time had been sent by his monastery in Ratisbon on a religious mission to Galloway but was a few years later to be sent by Canning and Wellington on secret missions abroad. Perhaps it was Harry who recommended him to his colleagues, but it is in any event interesting to note this early connection with the seamy side of foreign affairs. It is interesting too to learn, regarding the early ambitions of both Palmerston and his brother, that their mother should comment that German would serve to train Harry in diplomacy in case Willy should fail in that line. Robertson, foreshadowing perhaps his third career as teacher of the deaf and dumb, was evidently a good instructor. Harry thought his only disadvantage was that he lived in a fifth-floor flat; but he continued, three times a week and on alternate days with dancing lessons, to struggle up ten flights of stairs for about eighteen months. He began with a novel called *The Knight of Death* and with his flair for languages claimed to be 'going on famously'. It was much easier than French (which, however, he kept up with the same teacher), he reported, and perhaps even as easy as Italian. But before long he found he was hampered by difficulties in getting German books and then in November 1802 Robertson was recalled to Ratisbon and forbidden to return to Edinburgh. With Yudo out of the question as a substitute, Harry seems to have given up; but only for a while. After he had finished his formal education he resumed private lessons in London early in 1806 with a man called Wille, and if he was rather irregular in his attendance he was at least persistent. He was still taking lessons just before he entered the Government in April 1807, and although these seem to have been suspended while he remained in office, he nevertheless maintained his interest and resumed them when he resigned twenty years later. After his brother's appointment as Secretary of Legation at Frankfurt in 1818 he went out of his way to encourage him in German as well as in keeping up his classics. Yet for his own part he evidently found some mental block to really mastering German, of the sort that never seemed to hinder him with Latin tongues. 'I have made considerable progress in Dutch in spite of the people who will all talk English to me,' he wrote from a trip to Amsterdam in 1823, 'but the provoking thing is that though I can never remember a word of German when I want to talk it, it is always coming to my tongue's end when I try to speak Dutch, but by walking about with a little dictionary always in one's hand one manages to get on capitally.' With German, however, he evidently never did get on. He was again taking lessons in 1824 and during his short freedom from administrative duties in 1828-30: 'I have been setting to at German', he wrote, 'and have made considerable progress; I am determined to have a decent knowledge of that useful language.' It seems, however, that he must have given up when the strain of politics again became too great.[24]

At Edinburgh, in the meantime, he had found the pace of his first session slackening as he entered the summer term. He even began riding again and suffered no return of his headaches in consequence. According to Stewart the summer courses were 'much more imperfect' than usual because the Professor of Natural History had become too blind and the Professor of Botany too gouty. But although the latter began late in the term and very early in the morning, Harry managed to attend his lectures; Stewart in any case thought that the long walk from Lothian House to the Botanical Gardens would be good for him. Stewart also filled some spare time by reading to him and his son the lectures he had himself given on physics during the previous year when the Professor of Natural Philosophy was ill. These only covered the elementary part of the course but they would be very good preparation for the regular course in the following session because, so Harry understood, Professor Robison had 'a turn so happily perverse, that he contrives to render the most simple subjects abstruse, and unintelligible to those who are not very good mathematicians'. Stewart also intended to work on Harry's weakness in mathematics during the holidays. It was usually part of his plans that his pupils should accompany him on some summer expedition. A scheme for them to take a house by the seaside in May and June so that Harry could combine bathing with 'some operations of practical geometry' fell through. Harry was glad of that as he rather thought he would miss his holidays at home. Stewart was able to secure for him and Ashburton an invitation to spend a part of the summer at Lord Selkirk's place in Galloway, which, he said, had 'the advantage of an excellent library'. But as he was already engaged to take Ashburton on a private tour of the Highlands he had to leave Harry at Carlisle to make his own way home at the beginning of August 1801.[25]

Although the plans for Harry's first year did not therefore work out quite as had been hoped, everybody seems on the whole to have been very pleased indeed with what had been accomplished. The Stewarts wrote back regularly in fulsome praise of their young charge. He had hardly been among them a month than Mrs Stewart reported that he was 'the idol of the whole family', blessed with the finest of dispositions, and with 'no fault but being sometimes not quite well'. Early in the following year her husband wrote to Lord Palmerston to explain that he too would have written if he 'had had anything to mention of Mr Temple, but the uniform and exemplary propriety of his conduct'. And what else could be expected from one of such 'good sense and . . . uncommon steadiness of . . . character'? 'It is equally unnecessary', he concluded, 'for me to say that his abilities are excellent, his temper most amiable and his industry unremitting. Indeed, I don't know any young man of whom I am disposed to think more highly, or who unites in one greater degree all the qualities to be wished for at his age.' Although Lady Minto rather doubted that he had quite enough of 'the zest that belongs to youth', the Mintos too were unstinting in their praise and very glad to have such a companion at college for their own son. 'Harry is as charming and as perfect as he ought to be,' reported Lord Minto on a visit to Edinburgh; 'I do declare that I never saw anything more delightful. . . . Diligence, capacity, total freedom from vice of every sort, gentle and kind disposition, cheerfulness, pleasantness, and perfect sweetness, are in the catalogue of properties by which we may advertise him if he should be lost.' Harry also had the approval of his peers: 'Temple', Francis Cholmeley reported, 'is [in contrast to other students at Edinburgh] a proof that it is possible to unite the manners of a perfect gentleman, with the utmost attention to science.'[26]

In general the Palmerstons were delighted with the reports they had already received and would continue to receive from Edinburgh. 'Every day', wrote Harry's mother to her husband, 'I feel more & more satisfied with your choice respecting Harry's present situation.' Lord Palmerston felt much the same, but one thing bothered him a little; for although he had deliberately removed his son from Harrow because he did not want his education to be too limited, he did not want him either to neglect the classics too much. Harry tried to reassure him that his private tutor, Mr Williamson, was 'a very tolerable scholar' who took the trouble to go over things with him individually, and Stewart explained that while he did not think Harry had really fallen behind with his classical studies, he had rather assumed that Palmerston would prefer him to concentrate during what he had assumed would be 'a short stay' at Edinburgh on those subjects he would not find it so easy to follow at an English university. He promised, however, that in view of Palmerston's concern he would next year see to it that Harry did not crowd so many inessential things such as German and drawing into too short a time and would place him under the care of the same excellent classical scholar who had earlier looked after Viscount Dudley's son. So when Harry returned to Edinburgh the following winter he devoted two hours every Friday alternately to Latin and Greek with a master from the High School called Christison. Yet at first sight his programme seems to have been as crowded as ever and his father again expressed concern. He certainly kept up with his German and drawing and was riding again between eight and nine in the morning as many as three or four times a week. In addition he began in November 1801 to take lessons in handwriting from a man called Paton. But although he took the same number of courses at the university as he had the previous year, he was nothing like so regular in attendance. He stuck cheerfully to his new course in chemistry. Professor T. C. Hope was considered a very ordinary sort of scholar by discriminating observers, but Harry found his lectures, even with their prolific 'Scotticisms, Irishisms, & nonsensisms', very entertaining and joined in the experiments, burning 'fingers and tables with acids most delightfully'. But he was evidently repeating Playfair's course on algebra and therefore attended only those parts he had skipped before for lack of trigonometry. At the same time he still found Robison so 'abstruse & difficult' that he went only to his first few, elementary lectures 'for curiosity's sake' and then went instead to Stewart's second course in moral philosophy while continuing to study physics with a less demanding tutor at home. Stewart's second course of lectures also finished at the beginning of April, but what with an hour of physics and still more of geometrical exercises every evening afterwards, Harry did have a pretty full time of it throughout the session of 1801-2. Yet he managed during the summer term to fit in an hour of fencing as well.[27]

It was during this session, however, that fate made a major change in Harry Temple's life. His father had been going on much as usual, entertaining his friends at Broadlands and pursuing his junkets in London. But in March 1802 he caught a very bad cold and by the end of the month had become very ill with what was called at the time 'ossification of the throat'. He struggled to keep his spirits up but on 14 April it was decided that his elder son must be called home to the house in Hanover Square that had been bought a decade earlier. Gilbert Elliot came down with him and they stopped at Minto's on the way early in the morning of 19 April. There a servant who knew neither of them by sight took Gilbert quietly upstairs in error for the other and baldly told Harry that his father had died three days before. Apparently Harry had still hardly appreciated that his father was so dangerously ill and the brutal manner in which it was now revealed must have added to the shock. But there were more shocks to come; and if he had been unnerved at first, these soon sobered him. He found that his mother was almost hysterical in her grief, blaming herself for not realizing how ill her husband had been and also for not sending for Harry in time. Then, a few days later, she recovered her composure enough to give him details of his father's estate. The late Lord Palmerston had been having money troubles for some time, what with his expensive way of life, extensive house improvements, distress in Ireland and the fall in the funds. In addition there were the unexpected burdens from the continuing failures of his wife's relations.[28]

It is not clear how much Benjamin Mee's second failure had cost Lord Palmerston; but from the will he made at the time it is clear that he had given up all hope of recovering the £2,000 he had lent him on the first occasion. Originally Culverden had helped in trying to straighten out his brother-in-law's affairs; but in 1797 Culverden's own had also become 'entirely deranged' and subsequently the Grotes decided he was an 'undesirable colleague' and in 1802 he left their partnership. So another burden fell upon the viscount. By this time the Culverdens had only a little while to live – Sarah died in 1810 and her husband the following year – and as they had no children they cannot have been a long-term liability. There was, however, a certain Amelia Elizabeth Godfrey who lived either with them or the Palmerstons. She was the daughter of William Godfrey (formerly Mackenzie) of Woodford and the sister of Peter and Thomas Godfrey of Old Hall in Suffolk. After the death of his wife William Godfrey had wanted to make Mary Mee their stepmother, and though she had refused him, she had promised to treat them as her own. Emma Godfrey never married and remained a dependant of the Palmerstons until her death in 1840. As a companion to Lady Palmerston and her children (who always treated her like a sister), Emma was hardly a burden. But in his last years Lord Palmerston's affairs were in no condition to bear even a small expense. At one time he had even considered selling not only Sheen but also Broadlands. Lady Palmerston, however, had dissuaded him from selling the home she loved so much and they had kept going instead by disposing of other properties and raising loans.[29]

At the second viscount's death there was an outstanding mortgage of £10,000 on the Hampshire properties and legacies of over £71,000 that brought the estate's total indebtedness to about £90,000. Against this there was only £60,000 in stock, some £4,000 in cash at the bank and a year's rental due – probably about £75,000 in all. To meet the shortfall of annual demands upon the capital there was a net income from the estates of rather less than £10,000, more than half of it from Ireland. But from this had to be deducted Lady Palmerston's marriage jointure of £1,200 a year and annuities to her and others of about another £1,500. It was reckoned therefore that the net annual income remaining would be only about £3,500 and out of this were set aside £500 each for the maintenance and education of the three younger children and £1,000 for Harry himself. It was the large sums granted as legacies that most reduced his fortune. In the circumstances it was odd perhaps that his father had so increased the portions of the younger children over the years from ten to fifteen and then to twenty thousand pounds. But what was most surprising of all was that in addition to an annuity of £300 a year to a certain Mary Anne Campbell, otherwise Moore, of Eaton Square, Pimlico, there was a bequest of £10,000 to her son.[30]

Henry Campbell was a young cleric of Methodist persuasions and about ten years older than Harry. He had been an undergraduate at Oxford with the poet Robert Southey, in whose correspondence he appears from time to time in the ridiculous guise of 'Horse' Campbell. Apparently he was rather fat, yet overfond of hunting. Although his mother was still living and was occasionally visited by Lady Palmerston and the other children, he evidently lived quite often as a member of the family at Broadlands, and they were all rather sorry when at last, in the summer of 1801, Lord Lavington, who was an old family friend and Governor of the Leeward Islands, got a living for him in Antigua. It was supposed to be worth as much as £1,800 a year, but the West Indies were a long way off. 'I shall feel a mother's sorrow when I part with him', Lady Palmerston wrote, 'for there never was a kinder or more affectionate son.' And at his father's death Harry for the first time discovered that Campbell was, if not literally his mother's son, then certainly his brother. Their father, as well as giving him £10,000, had even written him and his heirs into the entail after his own legitimate children. Yet faced with the difficult task of informing Campbell both of their father's death and that he now knew all, Harry began his letter simply with 'My Dear Brother'. In its good taste the letter obviously owed much to the example displayed by Lady Palmerston in her attitude to both Campbell and his mother; and in its simple and straightforward style probably no less to Harry's academic instructors.[31]

Lady Palmerston, in a sort of testament written immediately before her husband's funeral, asked Harry to have copies of his father's portrait made for Campbell and 'poor Mrs Campbell' and committed both the Campbells to his 'benevolence and affection'. Harry seems to have done the best he could. Mrs Campbell of course had her annuity; payments were continued until July 1816, when presumably she died. But Palmerston voluntarily continued the payment to her son, who cannot have been very well endowed with talents since it proved very difficult to gain preferment for him even after Palmerston's own influence had grown very considerably.[32]

Apparently the living in Antigua turned out to be worth only £300, and with Lavington fast declining in health Campbell took advantage of his inheritance to return to England by the autumn of 1802. He obtained a curacy near Shrewsbury early in 1805 and on the strength of it married in May that year Anne, daughter of Thomas Rose of Chipping Wycombe. As Secretary at War, Palmerston was enquiring in 1813 about the value of a domestic chaplaincy at Dublin Castle. But in spite of strong and persistent appeals to the Prime Minister – 'there is nothing which interests me more than the success of this suit of mine' – he never obtained more than a £100 curacy for Campbell. In the 1820s Campbell was curate of Nailsworth in Gloucestershire and a local J.P. In 1827 he wrote that he had heard of Palmerston's ill-luck with his investments and he therefore proposed to give up his mother's £300 a year even though this would force him to move into a smaller house. But because of this and because he had never got a curacy worth more than £100 he would have to make a new will. It had always been his intention, he said, to return the whole £10,000 to the family estate; hence his frequent applications to Palmerston for patronage. But now he would reduce it to £4,000. Apparently they had not seen each other for about seven years and, indeed, they can have had little in common by this time, although Palmerston sent him Christmas gifts of game from time to time. He also wrote at the end of 1839 to tell him of his marriage but received in reply a complaint that Campbell had just been 'promoted' by the Bishop of London from a living worth £40 to one with 'nothing at all'. As usual, Campbell exaggerated: the church at Cowley was a new one and the bishop himself was going to pay something out of his own funds until a patron could be found. Campbell died in Cowley in February 1846, shortly before his wife. They had no children, but he left nothing to Palmerston. His heirs were his wife's brother and nephew, both named William Rose and both army surgeons living in Buckinghamshire. Probably, however, Palmerston himself had urged him not to include him in his will. He had intended to visit Campbell during his last illness, but was put off by Campbell's wife because her husband was so very unwell; and he failed to attend the funeral only because he was told it was Campbell's wish that it should be a simple one. He was no doubt much more grateful at that stage of his life to receive shortly after from his sister-in-law's executor (another brother, Philip Rose, later first Baronet of Rayners), various Heaphy water-colours of the family and the offer of the miniature of his father's portrait.[33]

Although it would never have occurred to him to think so, Palmerston, as the third viscount should now be called, was in some ways rather fortunate in the time of his father's death. In the first place the second Irish viscount might, had he lived only a little longer, have closed the door forever to his son's great House of Commons career. For he had several times during the last decade of his life approached Pitt for an English peerage, and although he had not been successful, another attempt with Addington as recently as November 1801 had left him with more than a little hope. The second viscount's unexpected death also endowed the third, more securely than would surely have otherwise been the case, with the important patronage of the first Earl of Malmesbury. Malmesbury's crucial political assistance still lay a little in the future. But as the dominating figure among Palmerston's trustees – the others were Culverden, Sir Ferdinand Poole, who was probably too old and ill to act, and his father's friend Tom Pelham, newly made Lord Pelham by the elevation of his father as Earl of Chichester – Malmesbury was important enough from the beginning, and not least in reinforcing Lady Palmerston's wishes about the continuation of his education.[34]

Palmerston's father was buried at Romsey on 24 April; by the end of the next month Palmerston himself was back at his books in Edinburgh. On the way he stopped a while at the Mintos' place in Hawick, but in spite of Gilbert's company he remained 'very low, silent & in bad spirits'. It was natural enough that he should be, but Lord Minto also thought that while 'his heart and disposition, and indeed capacity' were 'good', his very dejected state now confirmed that he had 'too little spring for his age'. But he seems soon to have recovered his composure after his return to Edinburgh a few days later; within a fortnight he began to fence between twelve and one every day with Matthew Stewart, reporting to his mother that he liked it 'very much'.[35]

Palmerston's mother had had the unwise notion of going with the girls to set up house for him in Edinburgh as a measure of economy; but she was persuaded that they should go and stay instead with her sister in Lavender House. For the summer she had mapped out for her son the first of a new series of instructive journeys in sentimental emulation of what she thought would have been her husband's plans, even though he would not be able to have for friend and companion the 'one whose judgment was so perfect, whose taste so refined'. 'In the long vacation I could wish he would make some tour with some intelligent clever man to point out all that is worthy of observation, to improve his knowledge, open his mind to the advantages his country possesses and give him an insight into the manufactory and the various excellence of England.' Then, after first seeing Ireland, he should choose 'some amiable friend' – perhaps Gilbert Elliot or Malmesbury's son James – and pass two years abroad 'seeing with the eyes of a traveller who wishes to improve by viewing other nations and other countries . . . When he returns I hope he will come into Parliament . . .'[36]

Palmerston managed to fulfil only part of this plan. During that summer there is no record that he managed to travel at all; probably his mother's troubled state kept him all the while at Lavender House and Broadlands. In the autumn he was back in Edinburgh. There had been some thought before his father died that he might go up to Cambridge in October 1802, but it was decided otherwise, perhaps as Lady Minto said because it would be 'much safer' to wait another year before going to a place where 'a young nobleman with a considerable fortune is a prey to every sort of art'. His programme in Edinburgh was fuller than ever, with forty hours a week of formal lessons. There were two hours a week each of riding and fencing, three of dancing and no less than seven with Nasmyth; and in addition there were three of double-entry bookkeeping with his former writing master. He also did more academic work, taking four courses of lectures instead of three. Since he enjoyed chemistry so much he continued to go to Hope's lectures six times a week. But he persisted too with advanced mathematics. He even went to Robison again for five lectures a week, although he took the precaution to have a tutor called Jardine come in especially a couple of hours a week to elucidate them afterwards. Jardine also helped him with Playfair's third course on 'fluxions and the higher branches of mathematics', which he now decided he was pretty well up to. At the same time he reassured his guardian, as he had his father, by continuing to brush up his Latin and Greek with Christison two hours a week. Malmesbury, indeed, fully approved his programme and while insisting on the stylistic benefits of the classics, also welcomed his ward's persistence with maths. 'I am a very great friend to mathematics,' he wrote, 'they accustom the mind to get at and to demonstrate truth; while logic teaches it to reason and argue. Separate, they are but dry pursuits, but united are the best strengtheners of the understanding. . . . Political economy', he also added, 'is a very important and interesting subject.' Stewart's second course on political economy was the shortest that Palmerston undertook in 1802-3; it was only three hours a week at 3 p.m. and it began late and ended early in the session. But it must have been among the most significant experiences of his life.[37]

Dugald Stewart was an enthusiast and a perfectionist, who sometimes had literally to be carried home from his scholarly labours; and there was eloquence, it was said, 'even in his spitting'. Certainly the style, at least as

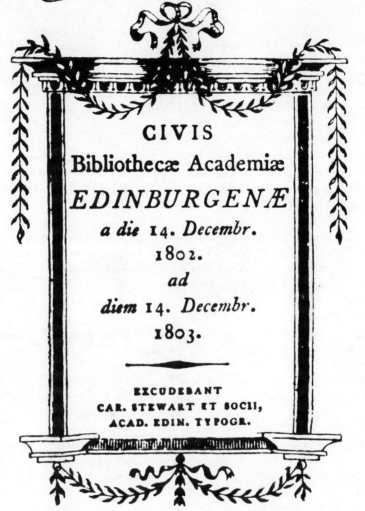

Henricus
Vce Comes Palmerston.

CIVIS
Bibliothecæ Academiæ
EDINBURGENÆ
a die 14. *Decembr.*
1802.
ad
diem 14. *Decembr.*
1803.

EXCUDEBANT
CAR. STEWART ET SOCII,
ACAD. EDIN. TYPOGR.

Palmerston's Edinburgh University Library Ticket

much as the substance, of his lectures seems to have been his great attraction as a teacher. Although, according to a contemporary, 'without genius, or even originality of talent, his intellectual character was marked by calm thought and great soundness. His training in mathematics . . . may have corrected the reasoning, but it never chilled the warmth, of his moral demonstrations [and] a strong turn for quiet humour was rather graced, than interfered with, by the dignity of his science and habits.' His effectiveness, too, was enhanced by his physical appearance: a large, bald forehead, bushy brows, and 'eyes grey and intelligent, and capable of conveying any emotion, from indignation to pity, from serene sense to hearty humour; in which they were powerfully aided by his lips, which, though rather large perhaps, were flexible and expressive'. His voice, too, was 'singularly pleasing', with a slight burr that only made its tones softer; his ear, both for music and for speech, 'exquisite'; and his gestures 'simple and elegant, though not free from a tinge of professional formality'. In short, his whole manner was that of 'an academical gentleman'. The result was that his lectures were

uniformly great and fascinating. The general constitution of moral and material nature, the duties and the ends of man, the uses and boundaries of philosophy, the connection between virtue and enjoyment, the obligations of affection and patriotism, the cultivation and the value of taste, the intellectual differences produced by particular habits, the evidences of the soul's immortality, the charms of literature and science, in short all the ethics of life – these were the subjects, in expatiating on which he was in his native element; and he embellished them all by a judicious application of biographical and historical illustration, and the happiest introduction of exquisite quotation. Everything was purified and exalted by his beautiful taste; not merely by his perception of what was attractive in external nature or in art, but by that moral taste which awed while it charmed, and was the chief cause of the success, with which . . . he breathed the love of virtue into whole generations of pupils.[38]

Stewart made his greatest sensation with his lectures on political economy, which he gave for the first time early in 1800 and then in an improved and expanded form in the session of 1800-1. It was a repeat performance of the latter that Palmerston attended in 1802-3. Stewart's main themes were population, the theory of national wealth, free trade and the circulation of money, the poor law, and the education of the lower classes. Apparently he considered these as more immediately connected with 'the public happiness' than theories of government and comparative constitutions, which he avoided. There was nothing strikingly original in the substance of these lectures; in a large part they were a simplified version of Adam Smith. But they created a sensation at the time because of the popular manner and the exciting eloquence with which Stewart tackled potentially dangerous issues and ideas in an era of revolution and war. There can hardly be any need to emphasize here the importance for Palmerston's career of these topics which he distilled so efficiently into notes. But he got rather more from Stewart than a potted version of Adam Smith or the admittedly important arts of orthography and bookkeeping. Without the habits of hard work instilled in Stewart's home and without the example of logical power and precise analysis displayed there and in the lecture-room, Palmerston probably could never have composed the vast numbers of private letters he did or personally have drafted so many thousands of Foreign Office dispatches. And while, as is well known, the number of those dispatches increased dramatically while he was Foreign Secretary, they were almost always marked by their logical exposition and lucid style. Unlike Castlereagh or Malmesbury's grandson as Foreign Secretaries, Palmerston was hardly, if ever, accused of ambiguity. But if Palmerston owed his systematic style of writing to Dugald Stewart, it must be admitted that he probably owed him too his singular lack of interest in abstract thought or metaphysics. Given that this obedient and even docile youth liked order and simplicity, Stewart offered him only rational convenience, not intellectual challenge or inspiration. This seems to have been as true in the home as in the lecture-room. 'The general conversation after dinner', observed a disappointed visitor, Francis Horner, 'was of that rambling, light, literary kind, which Stewart seems studiously to prefer: he never will condescend in company to be original or profound, . . . but shuns the least approach towards discussion.' John Ward, too, commented in similar vein about both Stewart and his beloved 'Ivy'. 'He has the fault of over-caution, and consequent unwillingness to talk,' he once wrote; and to match her husband's 'almost unconquerable reserve', Mrs Stewart, although she had 'as much knowledge, understanding, and wit as would set up three foreign ladies as first-rate talkers', was 'almost as desirous to conceal, as they are to display their talents'. In Stewart's lectures even an admirer would admit that: 'He dealt as little as possible in metaphysics, avoided details, and shrunk, with a horror which was sometimes rather ludicrous, from all polemical matter. Invisible distinctions, vain contentions, factious theories, philosophical sectarianism, had no attractions for him; and their absence left him free for those moral themes on which he could soar without perplexing his hearers, or wasting himself, by useless and painful subtleties.' This was what 'constituted the very charm of his course. A stronger infusion of dry matter, especially metaphysical, would have extinguished its magic.'[39]

The fact of the matter was that Stewart was not a philosopher but a lecturer in philosophy, and in particular an exponent of Thomas Reid, whose pupil he had once been in Glasgow. Stewart gave to Reid's ideas – which were based mainly on a rejection of Hume's scepticism – what Reid himself was unable to give: system and eloquence. But in so doing he unfortunately overlooked the more positive, if more obscure, aspects of Reid's work and through promoting what became known as the 'common-sense' school of philosophy, advanced an essentially negative point of view and, as the *D.N.B.* avows, ultimately contributed to the decline and death of the Scottish school.

Certainly philosophy was still-born in Palmerston; no one ever called him an intellectual. But he was very strong on common sense; and Stewart's 'system' of rational enquiry undoubtedly provided some of the foundations for his own variety of Liberal Toryism. Most of Stewart's pupils, like Lord Henry Petty, the future Marquess of Lansdowne, and Lord John Russell, indeed moved further to the left; and some of the Palmerstons' political friends thought that Edinburgh University in general, and Stewart, who was a staunch Whig, in particular, were tainted with radical and even revolutionary tendencies. But Harry had soon reassured his parents that the professors he heard were not 'at all inclined to be *Demo's,* but . . . rather the contrary if anything', and that he could not trace anything insidious even in Stewart's ordinary conversation. This seems even to have applied to the 'debates' he conducted for his pupils at home.[40]

The debating societies that flourished in Edinburgh in Palmerston's time were among the brightest and most prominent features of intellectual life. To the famous Speculative Society, for example, belonged no less a congeries of dazzling talents than Francis Horner, Henry Brougham, Henry Cockburn, Francis Jeffrey, Lord Henry Petty and the brothers Charles and Robert Grant. Palmerston came to know most and perhaps all of these while he was at Edinburgh, mainly through Stewart, who was himself a member. Yet he never seems to have joined any organized society himself. Possibly this was because the Speculative in particular was associated at this time with notions then thought to be extreme and in its 'recent discussions had turned away many of the good Tory youths'. Yet his brother William was to become a member only a few years later. In view therefore of the contemptuous opinion Brougham was shortly to express about Palmerston, perhaps it was the combination of his powerful prejudice and position in the society that effectively excluded him. Whatever the reason, Palmerston's debating activities appear to have been confined to domestic affairs in company with Ashburton, the Stewarts and their children, and to the session of 1800-1 alone. They were usually held on a Friday evening or, if there were visitors or someone was not ready, on the following Saturday, and the sessions lasted from 8 till 9.30 p.m. Palmerston prepared five addresses in all, and since they were read as essays and his mother asked to see them they have all been preserved. The subjects, ranging from Mary, Queen of Scots to the advantages of printing, are all quite as innocuous as the sentiments they inspired. Harry himself was evidently disappointed. After the first, led off by Ashburton, he looked forward to the next, by Matthew Stewart on suicide, as 'sure of producing a great deal of arguing afterwards which is what we want'. But before the end of the following January he reported of another: 'Our debate about ghosts ended exactly as all our debates have as yet and I fancy always will, when we had exhausted all our arguments on each side of the Question, the debate was over, & we each retired more strongly than ever confirmed in his own opinion, and more convinced that the other was wrong.' But no doubt it all served also to confirm and convince his mother of the reassuring truth of what Lady Malmesbury had heard in general of the political dangers of Edinburgh: 'As to Jacobinism, it is all stuff everywhere. A boy of nineteen may be seduced by a fair face, or led into gaming, or drinking, or racing, but nobody at that age cares about politics that is worth a farthing. It is, like the love of money, belonging to those who have exhausted or left behind them the light and cheerful pleasures of life.'[41]

Palmerston hardly drank, gamed, or raced much in Edinburgh, though he may have flirted a good deal. In May 1803 he left his classes at Edinburgh forever, and though he managed at last to make his tour of the Highlands in company with Cholmeley and Stewart and then returned to Edinburgh and Minto for a sentimental holiday with his mother and sisters, and possibly an abortive spell of drill with the Edinburgh volunteers, his main thoughts were already turning once more to the south. His father had been at Clare College, Cambridge, but since nothing was too good for Harry, in his case only the two largest and leading colleges, Trinity and St John's, were considered. It was not easy to choose between them, however. St John's had been the leading college for most of the previous century, and between 1749 and 1775 it had had eight Senior Wranglers to Trinity's one and between 1752 and 1780 eighteen Chancellor's medals (for classics) to Trinity's nine. But in the last part of the eighteenth century Trinity had caught up in Senior Wranglers (each had had seven) and eclipsed its rival in medals by sixteen to nine. Palmerston himself spent a day looking around Cambridge late in May 1802 on his way to Edinburgh. But the following spring still found him undecided where to go. For his own part Dr Bromley's recommendation would have been enough, but his mother thought it best to consult in addition two family friends from Cambridge who were also old Harrovians and future Prime Ministers. Inevitably each recommended his own college, and St John's therefore won by two to one. In any case Lady Palmerston was inclined to accept Fred Robinson's judgement as superior to Spencer Perceval's, and so was Palmerston. 'As for Perceval,' he wrote, 'he is a very good humoured fellow but not very remarkably bright.' It also weighed with him that there were more Harrovians at St John's and, perhaps, that he would be allowed to keep a horse there. So, with the approval of Malmesbury and Pelham, Palmerston was admitted at St John's on 4 April.[42]

Palmerston was delivered to St John's personally by Dr Bromley on the evening of Saturday, 22 October 1803, and introduced by him to his private tutor. Edmund Outram (1765-1821), who had been Second Wrangler in 1788 and an assistant master at Harrow in 1791-5, had forfeited his fellowship at St John's by getting married in 1801 and was afterwards eking out his ecclesiastical benefices and his emoluments as Public Orator of the University by private tutoring. He had been personally recommended by Bromley but since he had left Harrow before Lady Palmerston or her son could have known him there, she had gone off to have a look at him and St John's earlier in the summer. About this time Outram's widowed sister-in-law described him as 'a churchman of nervous habits and unused to business', a rather unsatisfactory guardian for her son, the future 'Bayard' of India. Lady Palmerston, however, was glad to be able to report that he was 'the very sort of man I would wish . . . perfectly unaffected, about 35 [he was 37] – open – good humoured, gentlemanlike and possessing a very sensible manner'. Palmerston too was very pleased with him; so, indeed, he was with everyone at St John's. The day after his arrival he dined with the Master, William Craven, and the President, James Wood. Neither of them thereafter gets much mention in his letters home, but there can be little doubt that Wood, who (nominally with Joshua Smith) was his college tutor and had also been dubbed by Lady Palmerston's inspection 'a very pleasing man', had some significant influence on his way of life at Cambridge. For Wood had not risen from very humble origins to Senior Wrangler and a considerable reputation as mathematician and administrator without an almost total dedication to scholarship and, although unimpressive as a lecturer or conversationalist, was credited long before he succeeded Craven with inculcating at St John's an atmosphere of systematic if unobtrusive learning. But even more than Dugald Stewart – though on a distinctly lower level of fame – Wood was 'better known for his mathematical and philosophical knowledge than for his social and convivial qualities'.[43]

Palmerston's other companions were therefore more important to him at Cambridge than they had been at Edinburgh. No one seems to have taken Mrs Stewart's place. There was very near at Madingley Hall a sister-in-law of Emma Godfrey's, Lady Cotton. The young wife of Admiral Sir Charles Cotton, this lady was in Palmerston's opinion a 'remarkably clever, well-informed woman' and her house 'a very pleasant variety to the sameness of college parties'. But although he was evidently there a good deal, she does not figure very prominently in his letters. Nor does the shadowy Mrs Outram; but rather his fellow students. 'I like Cambridge extremely,' he reported in the middle of his second week; 'there is remarkably good society at present at St John's, I believe the best in the University.' Among his first friends at St John's were: Lord John FitzRoy, the youngest son of the Duke of Grafton; Lord Henry Seymour Moore, the second son of the Marquess of Drogheda; Edward Clive, grandson of Clive of India and heir to the future Earl of Powis; and no less than two Percys, one a younger son of the Earl of Beverley and the other, his cousin Lord Percy, heir to the Duke of Northumberland. Of these only FitzRoy had been at Harrow, and he seems soon to have moved over to Trinity. There was, perhaps, a slight note of snobbery when Palmerston asked his mother especially for the sort of wine that Clive and Moore produced for their guests. But it must be said at once that among his early friends there appeared also such humbler folk as Laurence Sulivan and George Shee. Shee (1784-1870) was the eldest son and heir of a recently created baronet from Ireland who had been a minor official in India and subsequently held second-rank offices of state in the British Isles. Sulivan (1783–1866) was the grandson of a Chairman of the East India Company and son of a private secretary to Warren Hastings; he too had studied in Edinburgh at Dugald Stewart's feet and lodged in Lothian House, but had left at the end of 1799 before Palmerston arrived. At Cambridge, however, Sulivan, Shee and Clive soon laid the basis of a lifelong friendship with Palmerston.[44]

Palmerston had to pay quite heavily for this company, as well as for his other pleasures and privileges. As a nobleman, for example, he had to pay a quarterly tuition fee of eight or ten pounds, which was ten times as much as that of an ordinary undergraduate. But this was but a tiny part of the total cost, which can hardly have been less than the £400 a year his family had paid to Dugald Stewart. Whatever it was, there appeared in his first letter home the inevitable 'extras': 'plate money' of about £25 and 'caution money' of no less than £100. That he should have had to pay both is curious, since the nominal gift of plate was supposed to take the place with noblemen of the caution money levied on lesser mortals. Perhaps St John's had found so many noble-men more of a risk than others; or perhaps Palmerston had merely been misled. However, he reported, the caution money 'is afterwards returned but kept while I stay here, lest I should in a mad freak take it in my head to set the college on fire'.[45]

On his first Tuesday in college he also found that there was a gala dinner to celebrate the anniversary of the King's accession, and that as a nobleman he was obliged on such occasions, and there were some six or seven of them a year, to wear 'a grand gown' of 'blue silk embroidered in a most magnificent manner with gold, and a black cap and gold tassel'. A new gown of this sort would have cost him the astonishing sum of £40 or £50, but fortunately he was able to get a second-hand one from a departing Harrovian. He also had to spend a good deal of time and money (about £200, he later reckoned) on getting his rooms ready for occupation. They not only had to be furnished, but also painted, papered and even glazed; he also installed one of Rumford's 'smokeless' fireplaces. He was very pleased with the effect, the paper in his opinion being 'by far the prettiest in the college', the rooms comparatively 'light and airy' with two windows overlooking a small garden, and adjoining a wall on which hung a vine he thought might occasionally provide dessert. According to Willy, who succeeded to them when he went up in 1806, they were 'the warmest and most comfortable in college'. When they were finished, Palmerston – and his servant, George, who slept in a 'closet' – unpacked into them an imposing but by no means unfamiliar list of goods dispatched by his harassed mother: 'tea things, tea chest, china candlestick, pen tray and paper stand, toasting fork, pair of plated candlesticks, 6 silver teaspoons, trays and teaboards, tea and sugar, coffee, chocolate, cocoa, and sugar candy, wax candles, 3 doz. port, 2 doz. white wine . . . , 1 doz. of madeira . . . , Godwin's *Chaucer*, and Mitford's *Greece*.'[46]

The inclusion of these last two items fooled no one; Palmerston and his guardian both felt that the serious part of his education was over. 'It is the leading fault in both our [English] universities', Malmesbury wrote, 'that they concentrate themselves too much in themselves, get too *commonroomish* and do [not] allow their talents and science space to spread and thrive – not so Scotch professors, they have more activity of mind, more growing power in them. They are young plants, which can extend and Cambridge scholars are old trees and sometimes even pollards.' So he expected that Palmerston would find himself at St John's 'with nothing to learn' from his tutors. Still, 'if it should only prove a quiet and comfortable residence for a year or two which you may dedicate to reading, it will answer the going there perfectly'.[47]

During the eighteenth century the deterioration in examining standards at Cambridge had been checked and even put into reverse, notably by the Senate House tests, which were gradually taking precedence over the older 'exercises' or disputations in Latin. 'The candidate for a Bachelor's degree', had written a graduate of 1757, 'is directed to give the maidservant of the Master of the college, to which he belongs, half-a-crown for ... pins ... which he takes with him to the Senate House, where these candidates . . . are assembled for three days, and where they wait ... to be examined ... by any master of arts present. Whilst there waiting, they amuse themselves on the benches at push pin. Some few are examined in classical and mathematical knowledge, but scarce one in ten, and these only pointed out as young men who can stand the test.' By the end of the century the examinations had become a little more searching. Even then, however, the amount of knowledge required for an ordinary degree was almost unbelievably slight: 'two books of Euclid's *Geometry*, Simple and Quadratic Equations, and the early parts of Paley's *Moral Philosophy*, were deemed amply sufficient.' No doubt the candidates at Cambridge, as was said of their contemporaries at Oxford, even then 'contrived to have a friend ready, lest too much might be expected'; yet in the year 1800 three failed to pass even this test. Still, it was no longer merely a random sample of the better candidates, while the examinations for honours were a good deal more onerous and every candidate's performance was classed. One Scots visitor about Palmerston's time even asserted that to be classified a Wrangler required reading that there was hardly any notion of in his native universities.[48]

None of this, however, applied to Palmerston. He had left Edinburgh without taking a degree. But there was nothing unusual in that. In Scotland a degree was a necessary qualification only for those seeking to enter a profession, and hardly anyone else, least of all a gentleman, ever bothered to acquire one. And at Cambridge one category of undergraduate was still exempted from any such arduous and humiliating test – noblemen, including peers' sons and certain relations of the King. The origin of this exemption seems to have been in a statute designed to provide for the award of honorary degrees to distinguished men; and by the end of the eighteenth century it was widely recognized as having fallen into abuse. But an attempt at reform in 1774 was defeated largely by the argument that any noblemen who did not distinguish themselves in such examinations 'would conceive a disgust against the University and be its enemies for ever after' – a very unpleasant prospect when it is remembered that even academically retarded noblemen were in those days more likely than not to achieve positions of power in the land. Although he was not permitted to sit the university degree examinations, Palmerston was nonetheless able to write home to assure his mother that he would have to subject himself to the college examinations at St John's. The college itself had pioneered these in the university about the year 1770 and so far had been imitated only by Trinity. Although it would seem reasonable to believe that at Trinity these had already played some part in raising the college in competition with St John's, with noblemen, perhaps, they had not served so effectively to induce an interest in study. At Trinity, it appeared, all those who were not obliged to take *university* examinations were given what one of them about this time described as an 'acknowledged licence . . . to abstain from all lectures', and apparently everyone took advantage of it. At St John's, however, Lady Palmerston understood that the efforts of Wood and others had through this device created an atmosphere of 'the most studious character'. Some years later Palmerston himself avowed that, although he had 'gone further at Edinburgh in all . . . branches of study' than was required at Cambridge, these examinations did make it 'necessary to learn more accurately at Cambridge what one had learned generally at Edinburgh. The knowledge thus acquired of details at Cambridge was worth nothing, because it evaporated soon after the examinations were over'; but 'the habit of mind acquired by preparing for these examinations is highly useful'.[49]

The St John's examinations – which appear to have been entirely oral – were held twice a year, in December and June, and for each of them there were four tests in mathematics, classics, morality and divinity. For his first December examination Palmerston had to prepare only two books of Euclid, one of Xenophon, a sermon of Dodridge's, and 'an essay in the Jewish antiquities', the two last being the most onerous since he had to learn '160 close octavo' pages by heart in order to answer questions. He thought the examinations were quite easy at first, but they increased in difficulty and the candidates' performances were classed in three divisions on each occasion and also ranked in order of merit at every attempt except the first. To get into the first class, Palmerston asserted, a man had to make himself thoroughly master of what was set and could find his time completely preoccupied. If, on the other hand, he did not wish to try for the first class he might be 'nearly as idle as he pleased' and some, he admitted, did soon become reconciled to 'ranking in the awkward squad, hunt, shoot, etc., and seldom open a book'. These would find themselves in the third class. But at St John's, he assured his mother, it was 'the fashion, not to be sure to read through brick walls, but at least to study a good deal'. Palmerston got consistently into the first class on all the four occasions he took these college examinations, and although he never headed the list, he was placed equal second on one occasion. This was in June 1804 when he was tested in algebra and Euclid and on Hannibal and Locke. He was supposed then to have lost first place by making a 'slip' in algebra; the man who took it later became a Fellow and one of the two who were equal second with Palmerston was Senior Wrangler in 1807. But all fifteen who were placed in the first class of his year received college prizes. For the next examination in December 1804 he had to prepare Euripides' *Medea*, Paley's *Principles of Moral and Political Philosophy* and part of Wood's *Mechanics.* He was again expected to come first and his mother fidgeted at the thought of his getting another prize. But he found himself only tenth out of thirteen in the first class. He had known almost as soon as he had begun the examination that he stood little chance. Considerable concern for his mother's health had delayed his return to college that year, but he expected Wood to blame a picnic he attended on the Saturday on which he took his second test, while he himself thought that his preparation had been 'thrown out' by the time he had recently had to spend on preparing a Latin 'speech'. This last was also a part of the college's formal requirements, every undergraduate having at some time or other to give a prepared 'declamation' in Latin in chapel one Saturday evening. He spent nearly a week writing and learning by heart a 'speech' on the East India Company monopoly and as so often in the future rather overdid it, taking twenty minutes or about twice as long as was normally expected.[50]

Although Palmerston evidently took his exercises and examinations very seriously, he admitted that they required more elementary material than he had generally absorbed at Edinburgh and that he had very much less formal instruction at Cambridge than he had had at Edinburgh. One major difference at Cambridge was the emphasis ostensibly placed on chapel-going. Twenty years later, when speaking in the Commons in favour of the admission of dissenters to the honours examinations and their proposed exemption from compulsory attendance at chapel, he would ask: '. . . how many Dissenters, I should like to know, have been brought over to the doctrines of the Established Church by three years daily attendance at the chapels of their college; or, is the respect of the Dissenters for the service of the Church likely to be much increased by seeing, every day, students rushing in the morning from their beds to chapel; in many cases, unwashed, unshaved, or half-dressed; or running in the evening from wine to prayer, impatient only for the moment when they may return from prayer to wine?' In fact, as an undergraduate, Palmerston used to get up at 7 a.m. and, having skipped chapel, which he was 'never obliged or even expected to attend', he would have in his first term only one lecture a day from eight to nine, alternately on Greek and mathematics; then, after breakfast from nine till ten, he and Outram would spend an hour or an hour and a half going over his next day's lecture work and doing algebra.

After that the day was almost completely his own. From twelve till two he would ride or amuse himself with other exercise, dine from two-fifteen to three, and for the next two hours 'walk, read, or drink wine' – though he later reassured his mother, who was probably well aware of the reputation St John's had at the end of the eighteenth century, that 'nobody is ever pressed to drink a drop more than they chuse'. At five he was obliged at least four times a week to attend chapel for a service of twenty or thirty minutes. But after that he was again entirely free between drinking tea at six and supper parties at nine-thirty or ten-thirty, though these, he again hastened to assure his mother, were 'always over before 12'. He also told his sister that he was always careful to get to bed by 1 a.m. In his second term he proposed to add lecture courses on 'the arts and manufactures' and on law. The first, by the Professor of Chemistry, William Farish, he found 'very excellent' and 'very entertaining'; but he was rather disappointed with law. He had selected courses on both civil law and common law, but while pleased enough with the 'very excellent' lectures on the first by Joseph Jowett, the latter he thought was simply 'time thrown away'. Edward Christian, a former Fellow of St John's, the first Downing Professor of English Law, and brother of the *Bounty*'s Fletcher Christian, was evidently one of those lawyers who, having failed at the bar, failed no less ostentatiously as a lecturer; he died, a Cambridge wit records, 'in the full vigour of his incapacity'. However extreme Christian's case may have been, it confirmed the comparatively low opinion both Malmesbury and Palmerston had of the Cambridge professors. Moreover, Palmerston's judgement, which produced his guardian's reflections on the 'commonroomish' introspectiveness of Cambridge, was, in such a young and inexperienced man, remarkably percipient of the importance of a balance between 'teaching' and 'research'. 'There are certainly a great many very learned and scientific men here,' he reported,

and they are I believe perfectly masters of every branch of science they have turned their attention to, but from what I have seen of them, they seem to be much inferior to the Edinburgh Professors in activity and application. The Cambridge men appear to be satisfied with what they know, and to devote their whole time to teach others what they themselves have acquired, while the Scottish dedicate only a certain portion of their time to instruction, and are in the meantime constantly pursuing their favourite studies, and by constantly corresponding with all the Savants on the Continent, they keep pace with all the discoveries, many of which are either unknown, or disregarded by the Cambridge Professors.[51]

Although Palmerston's academic obligations at Cambridge were much less onerous than they had been at Edinburgh, and there is no mention of those 'bilious headaches' which had marked his introduction into Stewart's régime and had briefly returned in the spring of 1803, family tragedy once again intruded to disturb his otherwise peaceful progress. Lady Palmerston had never completely recovered from the shock of her husband's death. Her devotion to her family made her keep up a brave front, but even in this respect her closest friends detected a note almost of desperation in her behaviour. Far from retreating, she pushed her children forward into the 'gay world' and in doing so seemed to her friends to be overstepping the bounds of prudence. The Mintos reflected in some distaste on the company she kept in the vicinity of Lavender House and complained of being 'driven away early' after dinner, 'literally by the herd of toadies, abigails, & dependants' among whom she now passed her life. It was no doubt in this period that this 'good natured, obliging woman, loving to draw agreeable society to her house, and, probably thinking women of equivocal character might attract gay young men, [was thought to have become] a great protectress of the class of demi-rips'. Ward had no doubt what she was up to: 'I detested that woman,' he said. 'She was so fawning and mean. There was no sort of *bassesse* she was not guilty of in order to get that monster Ashburton to marry her ugly daughter.' It was this remark that brought the well-deserved rebuke from Lady Glenbervie: 'Upon my word you have a very long and very sharp scythe. You have just mown down three at one stroke.'[52]

Sadly, Lady Palmerston had very much more reason than her daughter's ill-favoured looks to justify her haste. In May 1804 she found that she had cancer of the womb. She at once made arrangements to isolate herself at Broadlands with Mrs Culverden and Emma Godfrey. But the dreadful news was kept completely from the younger children and even Palmerston was not told that it was cancer. Instead he was encouraged to go ahead with his plans for a tour of Wales with Sulivan. He suspected more than he liked to think and wondered if he ought to put it off, but Minto, who knew the truth, advised him to go and Malmesbury advanced £300 from the estate for the purpose. Perhaps they thought it would at least divert him from his rather too ostentatious flirtations; they had noticed especially his admiration at Broadlands of the Russell of Swallowfield girls and his escorting Minto's cousins, the Carnegie girls – all ten of them perhaps! – to Vauxhall. But he wrote home from Wales threatening his mother with a red-haired daughter-in-law. During the summer his mother became more and more dependent on opiates, and those in the know found 'her cheerfulness . . . almost more melancholy than depression would be'. In the autumn she kept up her show of spirits and made a great effort to get out and about at Broadlands in a wheelchair; and when Palmerston returned he indulged as gaily as ever in parties, balls and concerts. He may have lingered a little at Broadlands on account of his mother, but people in general thought she was letting her children go about rather too freely. 'It is impossible to say anything about her children's going so much out,' Malmesbury commented, 'but it is a fault people in her situation often fall into, to forget everything, but the *great* end *they* have in view, & not to consider that the gossiping, pecking, vulgar construe & comment just as they like.' But she seems to have been simply over-anxious not to burden her children's salad days with care: 'there is something to me quite wicked in repining at whatever may be our lot in this world', she wrote, 'and I have had my share of happiness and health.' So it was much the same as usual at Christmas even though, as Minto put it, 'the bad time & all its horrors' were 'approaching fast'. 'We have been excessively gay', Palmerston innocently reported early in January 1805, 'and have had nothing but balls.' He had already been to three since arriving from Cambridge on 20 December and that very evening he was off to another 'magnificent assembly' in Romsey. 'The rooms to be sure are not the most splendid in the outward appearance. They are at one of the inns, and upon entering the house you descend into a kitchen from which having mounted a ladder the rooms open full on your view, and . . . if the blaze of beauty displayed by the apothecary's daughter and attorney's wife, etc. or the still more dazzling lustre of six tallow candles stuck in tin chandeliers, did not at first overpower one's imagination, it would not be difficult to conceive oneself in Elysium, to which deception the harmonious scrapings of the rheumatic fidler (who by the by is barber and hairdresser) and the ambrosial exhalation of gin punch and tobacco would much contribute.' But in little more than a week these harmless 'Hampshire Gaieties' were brought to a sudden end by his mother's death. Once again the children clung together for mutual support: the girls were already at Broadlands, Willy hurried down from Edinburgh, where he had been spending his first Christmas with Dugald Stewart, and Harry assumed 'all the dearest ties of parent, brother, and friend'.[33]

These ties, even with Malmesbury's help, seem to have kept Palmerston rather longer than he had planned at Broadlands and in London. One rather annoying problem was the misfortune which overtook the Ravizzottis. This had already involved him as head of the family even before his mother died. In the summer of 1804, when Lady Palmerston needed all the help she could get, the Ravizzottis had finally left Broadlands to set up a boarding school for twelve young ladies in Kensington while Mrs Ravizzotti's unmarried sister came to look after Fanny and Lilly. Since, as Minto put it, the Ravizzottis were 'excellent in every respect' and Mlle Mercier a 'sensible pleasing woman' who had served with other friends, everything seemed to augur well. But on Lady Palmerston's death the new governess went 'raving mad', and long before that the Ravizzottis too had begun to be a serious nuisance. When the school was about to get under way in May 1804, Lady Palmerston had urged her son to do 'something handsome' for the Ravizzottis in view of their 'kindness, unwearied attention, & long service'. He evidently made them over a considerable sum of money, probably £500, for towards the end of July Ravizzotti sent a charming letter in Italian to his 'Carissimo Sigr Enrico', thanking him for all that he had done to make the new venture a success. But less than three months later he was pestering the dying Lady Palmerston for more. Apparently he had spent wildly on luxurious furnishings and finding himself £500 in debt urged on Lady Palmerston that she had promised him £1,000 altogether and rather unwisely compared his trifling debt with what had been spent on Palmerston's rooms at St John's. Palmerston was abso-lutely furious when he found out, but he sent £50 to hold off the upholsterers in Kensington, while he arranged with his trustees to provide further help. Pretending that it was his mother who had sent the £50, he asked that he be permitted to send another £200 for fear that otherwise Ravizzotti's establish-ment would utterly collapse and land Palmerston with the care of the whole family. Yet this was virtually the responsibility he did assume and for more than forty years! Malmesbury and Pelham both suggested that Palmerston make Ravizzotti an annuity in order to keep him under some sort of restraint and sense of obligation and Palmerston agreed. Probably the arrangement had not been completed when Lady Palmerston died and her son found in her testamentary letter the desire that he pay Ravizzotti £300 a year and even continue it after his death to the widow and her daughter. But by this time Mrs Ravizzotti had produced another daughter and soon two or more sons as well. Ravizzotti's affairs were evidently in such a state that Malmesbury suspected his honesty; possibly he also felt that he had dealt unscrupulously with the dying Lady Palmerston's affections. For he forbade Palmerston's sisters to have anything to do with him; and even Palmerston limited the annuity to £200 instead of £300. The school itself was certainly under way in London in 1805, but by the end of December 1817 it had been translated to Paris, where it evidently collapsed. Shortly after that Ravizzotti must have died, but his widow continued to receive gifts of money from other members of the family as well as the annuity from Palmerston. This annuity, indeed, continued to be paid even after Mrs Ravizzotti's death to her eldest son, Gaetano. Shortly before 1840, however, Palmerston must have decided to withdraw it in stages, though in response to Gaetano Junior's pleas about his being orphaned at an early age, marrying early, and burdening himself with four children, he continued it at a reduced rate until the end of 1846 or 1847. However great the sense of personal and family obligation, this was a story of remarkable generosity, extending as it did through a period of very serious financial strain for Palmerston.[34]

It is not clear when Palmerston was able to get back to Cambridge after his mother's death, but although he was certainly late, he nevertheless managed once again to appear in the first class in the college examinations, coming eighth out of twelve. He seems to have gone down as quickly as he could, however, and to have moved about a good deal during the summer of 1805. This was natural enough now that both his parents were dead. There was also nowhere convenient for him and the other children to stay in town since, to relieve the burden on the estate, the house in Hanover Square, as well as the mansion in Sheen, had been let ever since his father's death. But Broadlands, also, was probably still too full of sadness and too empty of friends to attract him that year and so, in addition to a dutiful visit or two to the Malmesburys at Park Place near Henley and a sentimental trip to Harrow early in July, he spent much of the summer visiting his friends. At the end of July, while

William went off with Ashburton to Wales, he left Park Place to pick up Sulivan at Ponsborne Park, his father's place in Waltham Cross, and together they went to visit Minto and Edinburgh, and then spent the latter part of August and most of September shivering with Percy on the grouse moors at Kielder Castle or sheltering more comfortably in Alnwick. As they afterwards went to stay with Cholmeley at Brandsby near York, Palmerston did not get back to Lavender House until early in October and with only a month to idle away before he could return to Cambridge.[55]

St John's in November 1805, however, was not what it had been in 1803 or 1804. 'This place is *very dull,*' he wrote back to his sister. 'You have no idea how melancholy it is to look up to the windows of the rooms of Sulivan, Shee, and Percy.' Of his old cronies, indeed, only Clive remained, though before long he was able to report the arrival of a good fellow in the shape of Michael Bruce (1787–1861), the son of a banker from the East Indies. He also lacked for the first time any real inducement to work. He seems to have returned in the first place only because he thought it was necessary in order to qualify for his degree, being under the impression that he had lost so much time at Cambridge by his mother's illness that he would not be deemed to have completed the six terms required before even a nobleman could take his degree. He was no sooner back, however, than he found that he would have been allowed to take it in July and that St John's would not therefore insist on his attending lectures or taking any more examinations. So he decided to pursue an independent course of study, reading Tacitus and Thucydides with Outram. But he obviously had more time on his hands than ever – at least in the weekdays when there were no parties at Lady Cotton's or evening hops.[56]

A favourite daytime activity in his first year had been with the university volunteers. The resumption of war against Napoleon in May 1803 and the consequent rebellion in Ireland and fears of invasion in England had revived enthusiasm for the militia, and the young gentlemen of the universities this time were determined not to be left out. In Edinburgh 'a large body of gentlemen' of between twenty and thirty-five, not so far attached to any volunteer regiment and 'certainly not keen to die with the levy *en masse*', had formed a regiment at their own expense in August 1803. The attempt was abortive, since the Government preferred to ignore them, but for some six weeks in the summer they marched up and down trying to impress the citizens and themselves. According to Brougham, who with such as Horner and Playfair took an active part, about two-fifths of them were English and included many students from the university. Whether Palmerston was among them is not at all certain. But there are several later clues to suggest that both he and Cholmeley took part on returning from their tour of the Highlands. Certainly when he first arrived in Cambridge Malmesbury attributed his very rapid promotion in the corps recently formed there to his having 'been an old soldier'. He had doubted at first if he could spare the time to drill every day but he evidently persuaded the commanding officer that he had already, as he put it, made such 'great progress . . . in the military art' as to let him compromise on three times a week from twelve till two. He turned out for the first time on 2 November 1803; nine days later, 'having gone through the intermediate steps from the awkward squad to the front rank of the grenadiers', he was promoted to be 'covering serjeant', and a few days after that to be captain of the fourth, or 'light company' of the University Rangers. Malmesbury approved of his amateur soldiering as much as he did his academic studies. 'In these times', he wrote, 'a little military knowledge is indispensable; it may be your lot to pass many years of your life in wars and tumults and as it is becoming to be prepared for everything, the drill makes a very essential part of education.' The heads of colleges, on the other hand, were not at all so sure of this. They feared that an organized corps would interfere in some way with the discipline of the university (though no colleges ever seem to have been blown up, they did catch fire mysteriously from time to time) and it was only with reluctance and under the combined pressure of a committee of fellows and the Government (who clearly distinguished between students in England and Scotland) that they agreed to allow the undergraduates to drill together for limited periods and on the understanding that in the event of invasion they would disperse to join their local county militia regiments. In addition, 'to give as little offence as possible', they adopted a 'grave uniform' of dark blue jacket, black stock, grey trousers and short black gaiters. Fifty years later Palmerston, as Prime Minister, would also go out of his way to discourage the formation of rifle associations in industrial towns, where they might be infiltrated by Chartists and socialists, and to encourage them in country districts, where they would be under the closer watch of the gentry. But there is no doubt that as an undergraduate he thoroughly enjoyed it all. They usually drilled on Sidney Piece, now enclosed in the Master of Trinity's garden, and sometimes on Parker's; and on a 'grand field day' they went to Cherry Hinton Chalk Pits. 'We perform the light infantry manoeuvres and run about in the fields scrambling over hedges and ditches, and every thing that comes in our way,' he reported. 'It is amazingly good fun, and is the only way to teach us our business, for we learn more by this means in one hour, than we should in six on parade or a bowling green.'[57] ·

After the excitement of his first winter, Palmerston seems never again to have mentioned the volunteers in his letters home. Perhaps he did not wish to alarm the family, for there may have been something in the tradition that he was nearly blinded in 'a sham fight' over Clare Hall Gardens: early in 1804 the news reached Edinburgh that a powder horn had blown up in his face. But the volunteers certainly continued their existence: Sedgwick records that upon the news of Trafalgar they were drawn up in the market place to fire three *feux de joie*. In any case Palmerston had other exercise and 'social' activities to amuse him. He joined the Harrow Club, of course, and in November 1804 formed, with a few close friends such as Sulivan, Shee and Clive, a Saturday evening club, probably in imitation of the Beefsteak in London. 'It is a very pleasant thing, will be very agreeable while at College, and be an additional tye between us afterwards,' he reported to his sister. 'We have not yet made any regulations as to the quantity of wine to be allowed each person but have some thoughts of copying the rules of the beefsteak club by which no man is allowed in *common* to exceed his two bottles, upon extraordinary occasions of course a little excess is permitted.' But apart from occasionally coursing hares, the horse-riding he regularly alternated with military drill, and possibly rowing, there is no evidence that he indulged as he had at Harrow in any other physical sport, not even cricket. According to a near contemporary the Cantabs of that period 'regarded boating as a mere pastime, and almost ignored cricket'. Field sports, stagecoach and tandem driving, and the horse races at Newmarket trenched more on college discipline and reading. And, it is stated by a usually well-informed biographer, Palmerston in 1803 joined 'a kind of sporting club of a dozen members'. But the word Palmerston really wrote, thank goodness, was 'spouting'.[58]

In spite of the disappointment Palmerston had felt with the Friday evening debates in Edinburgh, he was immediately attracted on coming up to Cambridge in November 1803 by the thought of joining a similar debating club he discovered there. Consisting of only about a dozen members, it was 'quite private' and possibly even in some sense a secret society, since the university authorities, as always fearful of French Revolutionary influences and bowing to wartime conceptions of loyalty, had severely checked political discussion among the students and driven it underground. Named the 'Speculative' after its more famous predecessor in Edinburgh and possibly nicknamed the 'Fusty' by Palmerston, this society met in term-time once a week, usually on Wednesdays, when one member would read an 'essay', more often than not on an historical topic, and then all the others would be obliged to deliver an opinion in turn. This last regulation particularly pleased Palmerston as ensuring that everyone had to read up in advance and thereby acquired at least 'a good deal of general information'. A year or two earlier two other future politicians from Magdalene, Charles Grant, who afterwards also joined the Edinburgh Speculative, and his brother Robert, had been leading members, and so, shortly afterwards, was George Canning's cousin Stratford of King's. But in Palmerston's time the membership seems to have been confined to students from St John's and Trinity. In his second year there were only six members in addition to himself, including Shee and Sulivan from St John's and Henry Goulburn (Peel's future Chancellor of the Exchequer) from Trinity. In subsequent years, however, they were joined by Clive and Bruce from St John's and J. C. Hobhouse (Byron's friend) among several more from Trinity. But Palmerston evidently remained the dominating figure during his last two years; perhaps he was president, as was a couple of years later another Johnian, Edward Law, subsequently Earl of Ellenborough. The meetings were usually held in his rooms and, as at Edinburgh, he read five essays. But although harmless enough by any reasonable standards, the subjects were distinctly more political than had been the case at Edinburgh. The first, delivered 'to a select party of literati' on 22 February 1804, approved in passing of the moral restraint exerted by the voice of public opinion and, in anticipation of Palmerston's impatience with metaphorical notions about the inevitable decline of Turkey, disapproved of comparisons between the moral and material world. The second, on the advisability of opening India to free trade, so aroused his interest that he enlarged and translated it as his required 'declamation' in chapel. 'One thing only seems clear,' he reflected the day after reading it to the society, 'that the possession of such immense territories at so great a distance from the Mother Country, however it may add to her military glory, can hardly be productive of any real and permanent advantage to Great Britain. All commercial purposes would certainly have been as well answered by a more moderate line of conduct.' But he added in an increasingly characteristic vein: 'There is but one thing to be said in favour of our devouring system which is that by occupying the country ourselves, we exclude the French which is undoubtedly a great object.'[59]

Palmerston clearly valued very highly his membership in the Fusty; years later he noted its absorption into the Cambridge University Union, though not, so far as is known, its early suppression as a political society in 1817 by the Vice-Chancellor, who was none other than his old tutor, James Wood. There is no record that he ever performed in the Union, though he and his friends had been in the habit of returning for debates in the meetings of their own smaller circle.[60]

Palmerston made something like an official farewell to Cambridge on the morning of 13 March 1806. But in addition to the many visits he made on account of political business, for some years he came back regularly for Commencement Week and the Festival of St John's immediately after Christmas. He particularly enjoyed the common-room whist, the punch and turkey pie. But in spite of what he had said about the utility of examinations, he did not regard the education he had received at Cambridge very highly. It was, rather, in his years at Edinburgh, as he would later recall, that he 'laid the foundation of whatever useful knowledge and habits of mind' he possessed. He used very similar language in a House of Commons debate on 8 March 1855: 'He was bound in frankness to say that any information which he might have acquired at Edinburgh was infinitely more useful and general than at Cambridge; and that the two years [*sic*] which he spent at Cambridge he passed very much in forgetting what he had learned at Edinburgh.' Of course he exaggerated. He may not have made much progress with German, but the grasp of mathematics and the skills in bookkeeping and handwriting that he acquired in Edinburgh proved throughout his political and private life to be an immensely useful complement to the French and Italian he had learned as a child. He evidently also owed to Stewart much of the lucidity of style and systematic method in his work. Rather less deep-seated was his intellectual curiosity. Although he later claimed that, like his father and his guardian, he valued an English public school education solely for its inculcating in 'a period during which, perhaps, the human mind is most susceptible of improvement' the classical instruments with which 'men intended for a liberal position in life' might study 'the noblest compositions, perhaps, that ever emanated from the human mind', his Greek was always poor, his Latin tags jejune, and there is no sign that after early manhood he ever read much else than protocols and dispatches. In her testamentary letter his mother had also urged him in this as in other respects to follow his father's example, to 'catch his taste . . . study painting, and be as attached to arts and sciences as he was'. On his travels he did the rounds of the galleries dutifully and added to the family collections a little. But, unlike his father or his brother William, who left an important collection of sculpture to the British Museum, his interest in art as well as science seems to have been quite superficial. The most serious flaw in the young Palmerston, however, was one that Edinburgh could never have made good.[61]

There was always more caution in Palmerston's foreign policy than he has usually been allowed; and for a long time, perhaps even until his marriage, he distinctly lacked self-confidence. Lady Minto and her husband had noticed it in his days in Edinburgh; her sister would too, as she analysed his early efforts in the House of Commons and added a certain 'coldness' to his faults. So the youthful Palmerston not only lacked confidence, he also lacked any outward expression of warmth of feeling. As Cockburn said of Dugald Stewart: 'Knowledge, intelligence, and reflection . . . will enable no one to reach the highest place in didactic eloquence. Stewart exalted all his powers by certain other qualifications which are too often overlooked by those who are ambitious of this eminence, and wonder how they do not attain it – an unimpeachable personal character, devotion to the science he taught, an exquisite taste, an imagination imbued with poetry and oratory, liberality of opinion, and the loftiest morality.' Palmerston could match his old Scots professor in none of these, and though he learned to take his chances and developed as even adult men commonly will, it was personal and political boldness, not moral or intellectual passion, that marked the change.[62]

In spite of their political differences, which lasted, as Mrs Stewart noted, until he made his famous speech on Portugal in 1828, Palmerston kept up a most friendly correspondence and connection with the Stewarts and defended them against their troubles and their enemies. During the brief Fox-Grenville Administration of 1806-7 a new office of Printer of the *Edinburgh Gazette* was created to give Stewart a salary of £300 and more. This gave great offence to the Tories. Yet after bad health compelled his giving up his chair in 1820 they nevertheless added a Civil List pension to his Printer's sinecure and as his death approached in 1828 extended the Printer's patent to him and his heirs for a further term of twenty years. Palmerston may well have had something to do with both of these later favours; the Stewarts certainly credited him with the last. It was also he who, when the income from the *Gazette* temporarily fell off, arranged in 1836 a new Civil List pension of £200 a year for Mrs Stewart. Ten years later Matthew Stewart was reported as receiving a 'large income' from the revived *Gazette.* Palmerston continued to have occasional contacts with the Stewarts, but these probably did not survive the 1830s. Matthew, apparently, had become very odd long before his infamous destruction of his father's papers in what was afterwards called a fit of sunstroke. Even in his father's lifetime, it seems, his family had fled from place to place before his threats to visit them.[63]

Whatever Palmerston's relations with the Stewarts had been, Cambridge touched him a little with the warmth of fellowship as Edinburgh never had. Forty years later he would maintain that while the Scottish system was 'equally good for purposes of instruction', the collegiate system of the English universities contributed 'the greatest degree of discipline'. But he might have added that it also inspired in him affection and regard, even for those who applied the discipline. He got Malmesbury to approach Pitt on Outram's behalf when the Regius Chair of History fell vacant in 1805 and although he was unsuccessful on that occasion it may well have been owing in part to his own intervention as a minister that Outram became Canon of Lichfield and Archdeacon of Derby in 1809. It was certainly with Palmerston's support that Wood became Dean of Ely in 1820. He even endeavoured, though without success, to obtain a Welsh judgeship for Edward Christian, referring as he did so to his having had 'the pleasure & advantage' of knowing the professor from the time he first arrived in Cambridge. But this was surely a case of political discretion: Christian was at least a loyal Pittite if little more, and by 1819 Palmerston might well have reckoned that the day was not far off when he would need all the support he could get for the parliamentary elections at Cambridge. In any case he was always conspicuously loyal to his college. When Bishop Mansel died in 1820 Palmerston compared his régime at Trinity unfavourably with St John's under Wood and urged that he be replaced by a more active head: 'Trinity College has notoriously suffered much for many years past from the absolute practical inefficiency of its Head.' Personally he favoured Professor J. H. Monk, but he had nothing against the actual suc-cessor, Christopher Wordsworth, and was glad enough on personal and politi-cal grounds to see him triumph over Dr Tavel. But when, six years later, Peel approached him about candidates for a commission of enquiry into the Scottish universities, he was still echoing the doubts of his guardian. 'Fellows of Colleges', he replied, 'get their minds so contracted by perpetually revolving in the narrow circle of their local avocations that there really are very few of them whom you would wish to select for such enquiries or whom one would wish to be sent to our acute north countrymen as specimens of the instructors of the youth of England.' He managed to come up with only four names, though one was that of the Master of Corpus who, being about the same age as his proposer, was 'in the prime of life & free therefore from the rust & prejudice which grow later in life upon men confined to a narrow sphere of action'.[64]

While Palmerston kept up, so far as fate and circumstances allowed, the friendly relations he had formed among his contemporaries at Harrow and Edinburgh, it was in the collegiate life of St John's that he made his closest and lifelong friends – Sulivan, Shee and Clive. Bruce would probably also have qualified among them had he not drifted away along another path. In his early letters Palmerston signed himself 'yours affectionately'; but Bruce seems to have been a restless and dissatisfied young man. He interrupted his course at Cambridge with trips to Russia and to Spain and before he was thirty he had had great love affairs with both Lady Hester Stanhope and Madame Ney. This last affair, and his own distinctly leftward inclinations, also involved him in the plot to get some escaped Bonapartists out of France early in 1816 and earned him the name of 'Lavallette Bruce'. Bruce, Palmerston thought, had shown much 'want of judgment & discretion . . . in his public conduct; however he has a good heart & that is a main point'. Little correspondence between them has survived, but in spite of their differing political views Bruce appears frequently in Palmerston's diaries as a dinner guest, and in 1818 Palmerston was best man at his friend's belated wedding to the widow of Captain Sir Peter Parker. He thought the bride 'a pleasing & amiable person & really sensible enough to be of some use to him who is so deficient in ballast'. In the 1826 election at Cambridge, when circumstances had forced them a little closer together in politics, Bruce even served on Palmerston's committee; and in 1831 Palmerston secured for Bruce, who had been admitted to the bar, the valuable appointment of Commissioner of Claims. But soon afterwards their friendship seems to have been brought to a sudden end, perhaps by the part Palmerston had played in stopping Lady Hester's pension shortly before her death in 1839.[65]

None of Palmerston's other close friends was of much more note in later life. 'Lazy Laurence' (as Ashburton habitually called Sulivan) perhaps did best, with all his mediocre talents, as a senior civil servant; Shee gained a very doubtful reputation under Palmerston's régime at the Foreign Office; and Clive, utterly reliable but 'deaf as a post and not very bright', achieved little more than tinsel honours before an accidental shot from his son's gun carried him off in 1848. Even in his relations with these, moreover, there was always some reserve on Palmerston's part. He outlasted Clive, with whom in any case he came to differ politically; and both Sulivan and Shee he considerably outpaced in society and in politics. With Sulivan he did appear to maintain a uniformly close relationship throughout, but then Sulivan had a special qualification in becoming by marriage an actual member of that small but very intimate family circle of Broadlands. Yet even if the friendships he made there were not really so important to him, that Cambridge made at least one vital contribution is indisputable. He may have mixed up Harrow and Cambridge when, having taken the helm in a rough sea crossing from Osborne in December 1847, he explained: 'Oh! one learns boating at Cambridge, even though one may have learnt nothing better.' But his companion was nonetheless well justified in observing the connection between *'steering the vessel of the State,* and steering a common boat'. For it was most certainly Cambridge that launched him into politics.[66]

II

INTO
PARLIAMENT,
1806–7

It is not clear when Palmerston decided that he would try for a career in politics. But it was the obvious role for a man of his rank and in all probability this still very complaisant young man never questioned the desire of his mother and guardian that Parliament should be his destination. Soon after her husband's death Mary Palmerston had written to Harry and to his guardian saying that she hoped he would go into Parliament and Malmesbury had certainly had this in mind when he urged him to persist with the study of law at Cambridge. Nor, in spite of Edinburgh and Dugald Stewart, does there seem to have been any doubt about his adherence to the Tories.[1]

Although he liked to boast that he was a man of independence, the second Viscount Palmerston had departed life a patriotic supporter of the war against France and a convinced follower of Pitt. In September 1799 he had taken his boys 'to show them Mr Pitt, whom they were very curious to see and Harry had the pleasure of shaking hands with him'. Subsequently Malmesbury guided the young man along the same path, in spite of the resentment of Minto, who was an adherent of Grenville, and in spite of the efforts of his Edinburgh acquaintance, Sydney Smith, who could not seduce him either with his wit or with a dinner party of Foxites at the King of Clubs. It must be admitted, moreover, that Malmesbury had all the aid of Palmerston's natural inclinations. Even in his debating 'exercises' he rarely deviated from a line of cautious orthodoxy and on the martial and political events of the day he recorded the purest Pittite Toryism. Thus when his friend Sulivan compromised and supported Grenville in his refusal to join Pitt's Ministry without Fox in 1804, Palmerston replied: 'I differ with you with respect to the pilot [Pitt] . . . , whose vessel seems I think going on very prosperously. If some of his crew, deceived by the appearance of a fat old whale [Fox] floating on the surface, perversely trusted themselves on his back, and have been carried down by it, the fault is surely not in the pilot, who could not prevent them.' The attack on Melville in April 1805, moreover, he feared would lead to the admission to power of 'Fox and all his Jacobine set'.[2]

Palmerston was due to come of age in the autumn of 1805, but there is no sign that he made any active attempt on his own behalf to find a parliamentary seat. Instead he spent a good deal of the summer visiting his young friends around the country. But he had certainly discussed the matter with his guardian, and the word evidently got around that Malmesbury was on the lookout for a vacancy, for early in October there came an anonymous and unsolicited suggestion from 'an Old Burgess of Southampton' that Palmerston stand there as a Pittite candidate. This was a 'scot and lot' constituency with several hundred voters which by the skilful management of a considerable amount of official patronage had recently been brought 'into the vortex of government boroughs'. Palmerston's father had once held a seat there and Malmesbury still figured among the political bosses of Hampshire, where in 1795 he had inherited a house, Heron Court, near Christchurch. But the gratitude of the voters was rather unstable and in 1794 George Rose, Malmesbury's senior partner in the management of government patronage in that part of the world, had been unable even with 'his host of non-resident burgesses' to prevent a severe contest against his own son. Palmerston was by no means keen to take up the offer because Southampton was a mere seven miles from Broadlands; he probably did not much fancy the idea of being so vulnerable to the pressures and importunities of his constituents. In addition Lord Lansdowne had already begun an active canvass there for the Opposition and Palmerston and Malmesbury were both inclined to think that it might become, as 'the Old Burgess' with a vote for sale no doubt hoped and intended, a very expensive contest. In fact they might even have lost, for at the next election the 'independent interest' secured one of the seats. In the meantime, however, Malmesbury had continued to look around for a 'cheaper and more agreeable seat'.[3]

There was probably no 'cheaper or more agreeable' constituency in the entire country than one of the English universities. Certainly university contests tended to be among the least expensive since the electorate was limited to M.A.s who had kept their names on the college registers and could be bothered to come and vote in person. Some six hundred Cambridge M.A.s were to turn out for this purpose in February 1806. The electors were therefore too many to have a direct pecuniary and proprietary interest in the two seats the universities each had, and too few and too respectable to provoke a rowdy contest. Instead a university contest called for a carefully organized campaign, backed by implied if not explicit promises of patronage among the interconnected legions of dons, lawyers and ecclesiastics and sustained by a modest outlay on providing transport for non-resident voters between London and the university. And not only was the election comparatively inexpensive; the rewards of success were unusually large. The successful candidate, who had also to be a Master of Arts of the university, thereby earned considerable prestige and, what was even more useful, some expectation of political security, for the universities were conspicuously loyal to their members.

This was particularly true of Palmerston's university. The two sitting members for Cambridge, Pitt, the Prime Minister, and Lord Euston, the heir of the Duke of Grafton and the brother of Palmerston's St John's acquaintance Lord John FitzRoy, had both been elected for the first time in 1784. But by the end of 1805 Grafton had turned seventy and Euston must soon expect to be called to the House of Lords. Palmerston himself later stated that his tutor, Outram, had 'more than once' suggested to him that his examination performance and the 'general regularity' of his conduct would justify his offering himself in the event of a vacancy. But Grafton in fact lived on until 1811 and the vacancy that first occurred was caused by the less expected but more significant demise of the Prime Minister himself.[4]

Pitt died at half past four in the morning of 23 January 1806. Palmerston had been at a ball until half an hour earlier, but Malmesbury packed him off from London the same day; by the following morning the young man was in St John's canvassing votes. But he was not quick enough. Evidently when he left London he was uncertain whether or not to stand: he already knew there were at least two other candidates from Trinity and possibly a third from his own college. So he wanted to keep his interest secret until he was sure it was worth while standing and even then, he told his sister, it would be 'not with any view to present success so much as by way of future introduction in case of the Duke of Grafton's death'. At Cambridge he found both Wood and Outram rather more encouraging because no one else from St John's had come forward, while he could qualify by taking his M.A. after the weekend on 27 January. He even seemed a little more optimistic: 'I have I think some chance', he wrote, 'if not of success at least of a respectable minority.' But that chance was not enhanced by the fact that the two Trinity graduates, both Opposition men and both already Members of Parliament, had begun to canvass the seat the evening before Pitt had died. To be fair Pitt's death had been expected at any moment; but his devotees nonetheless thought such haste was quite indecent. One of the candidates, Lord Henry Petty, who already held a family seat, had thought it 'more proper' till Pitt's death was actually announced to confine his canvass to London – where a university address of congratulation upon the King's victories in the war at sea had luckily brought the Vice-Chancellor and several Heads of College so that they could be conveniently canvassed together at the Thatched House Tavern in St James's. Fox, however, thought it best that Petty should for the time being withdraw altogether. But the other candidate, who had gone straight off to Cambridge on the evening of the 22nd, did not. Instead, Laurence Sulivan reported from London, while Palmerston hesitated and conferred his friend's vote was being solicited by a mutual Johnian acquaintance for the present member for Okehampton. This was Palmerston's old Harrovian messmate, Lord Althorp, whose father, Earl Spencer, had been Pitt's First Lord of the Admiralty but had now gone over to Fox in company with the Grenvilles.[5]

Palmerston's family and friends went to work at once to make up for lost time and to turn to his advantage every line of contact with political influence and ecclesiastical patronage. Their first task was to secure his position as the only Pittite candidate in the university and the sole contender from St John's. Malmesbury, of course, was particularly useful and he secured the support of several leading politicians, including that of Lord Hawkesbury (later Earl of Liverpool), who was expected to succeed Pitt as Prime Minister. He believed, too, that he had the approval of Windsor Castle, though not of course of the Prince of Wales, who was then firmly committed to the Opposition. But he had also some important failures, especially among the higher clergy. He organized approaches to both archbishops and to the Bishops of Hereford and of Bath and Wells. He tried particularly hard with Tomline, the Bishop of Lincoln, who had been Pitt's tutor at Pembroke and had a good deal of influence among his friends. But in spite of pressure from George Canning and George Rose, Tomline kept Malmesbury and Palmerston on tenterhooks. He had attended Pitt's deathbed and was evidently very upset. Very probably he never did declare in favour of anyone. This was disappointing, but nothing like as damaging as it would have been if Palmerston had had any serious rival as the Pittite candidate. There was at the beginning some thought that Pitt's Attorney-General, Spencer Perceval, might offer to stand and then, when he did not come forward, some five Pittites at Trinity, in order 'to give the College an opportunity of showing its respect for the memory of Mr P.', proposed setting up another Irish peer, Lord Headley, not because he was any older or more promising than Palmerston, but because he was one among themselves. But Headley withdrew when he heard that Palmerston was already in the field.[6]

It was soon to become apparent, however, that Pitt's memory was less effective in holding men together than was his death in making new combinations in politics. Indeed, when in the following year Fox followed Pitt to the grave, the two party system of Foxites and Pittites was soon replaced by what has been aptly described as 'a chaos of personal groups'. But that *system* had always been a 'false dawn', quite incapable of glossing over the personal and political strains between, for example, Pitt and Addington (Lord Sidmouth). Now, without an acknowledged leader, the Government fell apart and succumbed to an unholy alliance of 'All the Talents' – of Foxites, Grenvilles and Sidmouths. In these circumstances the backing of his college became for Palmerston even more important. As the two largest colleges by far St John's and Trinity would dominate the election. In fact between them they turned out more than half the votes on this occasion. Trinity had the larger number of voters, but, as one of Petty's supporters noted, the Johnians were 'more thoroughly disciplined to act together': in the election of 1784 they had brought their candidate within a handful of votes of success against Euston with all his vast support from Pittites and anti-slavery 'Saints'. Palmerston's emergence as the college's favourite son was not automatic, but it was only briefly put in doubt.[7]

The threat came from the Yorkes, who were a powerful family in the county and the University of Cambridge as well as in national politics. The family seat was near by at Wimpole and sons of the house had represented the county in Parliament for more than half a century. Thus Philip Yorke had been M.P. for a decade until he succeeded as third Earl of Hardwicke in 1790, when his half-brother Charles took over for two more. Both these last had generally supported Pitt but Hardwicke, who was a notorious grumbler, liked to think himself an independent and to exercise a considerable restraint upon his brother. Hence, although like Pitt a convinced supporter of concessions to the Catholics, he and his brother had both served under Addington, as Lord Lieutenant in Ireland and Home Secretary respectively; and later, when the fall of the Ministry of All the Talents was engineered, Hardwicke was to be so upset by all the intrigue that he went with them into opposition in 1807. So while in 1806 some might suggest Charles Yorke as an acceptable leader of the Pittites in the House of Commons, he would not have been able to act against his brother's inclination, and no one knew which way Hardwicke, who was still in Ireland, would go. However, both Charles Yorke and Hardwicke's heir, Lord Royston, were Johnians and as soon as news of Pitt's death arrived one Fellow of the college wrote to urge Yorke to stand and another to press for Royston. These suggestions would have made things very awkward even for Palmerston's most enthusiastic sponsors, since Wood had once also commended Royston to his father as a future candidate and Outram, who had also been Royston's tutor, was relying at least as much upon Hardwicke as upon Malmesbury and Palmerston in his pursuit of the Regius Chair. Here, however, Palmerston had some good fortune. Royston had only recently set off to join his father in Ireland and with both of them too far to be consulted before the writs were issued Yorke could not put forward his nephew's claim nor dare to throw up his own county seat. With this danger out of the way, moreover, Johnian solidarity even operated to move a substantial portion of this powerful family into positive support for Palmerston: by 26 January Charles Yorke had already been prevailed upon to secure a vote or two for him.[8]

The Yorkes' anxiety to keep in well with St John's and therefore to appear to be quite loyal to Palmerston was further strengthened by another lucky stroke. This was the coincidence of a contest for the high stewardship of the university. Hardwicke had never intended to become involved in such a contest and risk the indignity suffered by his late uncle, the second earl, when he secured election by a single vote. But while her husband was away in Ireland the mistress of Wimpole committed him before she had made sure of the undivided support of all the Heads of Houses, and so Hardwicke found himself involved after all in a distant contest with the Duke of Rutland. The duke's family, the Mannerses, divided with the Yorkes the aristocratic leadership of the county and after a long and sometimes bitter rivalry they now habitually shared the parliamentary seats. In the city, however, the duke dominated through his association with the leading burgess and local banker,

John Mortlock. All these local interests, moreover, were too intricately inter-woven with those of the university to be neglected. From the very first, therefore, Sulivan had been urging that Palmerston try and enlist Rutland and through him the 'vast influence' of Thomas Mortlock, the banker's son and senior partner, who was a Fellow of St John's and held many in his debt among his college cronies. But Rutland, as he explained to Lady Malmesbury, had already promised whatever 'trifling interest' he had, 'if he interfered *at all*, in another quarter'. Palmerston guessed that Rutland also wished to stand for High Steward and needed therefore to make some bargain with Petty or Althorp.[9]

Rutland announced he would stand as Steward on 28 January and before the end of the month he was canvassing for Althorp 'to the right & left', even though Althorp would not openly declare for him. Spencer was supposed to be interested in running for Steward himself, and this no doubt helped to explain why Rutland chose to make his bargain with Althorp. But once faced with a real contest, Hardwicke had no option but to support Palmerston if he wanted to be sure of the whole-hearted backing of St John's and of fending off the gross indignity of defeat. Still, the support of the Yorkes was never as strong or as united as had been hoped. Given the uncertain state of political alignments and his family's own erratic past, Charles Yorke had no wish, with the prospect of a General Election not far off, to antagonize either Rutland or the Grenvilles. His support of Palmerston, moreover, can hardly have been made more enthusiastic by Rutland's decision to drop out of the race and Hardwicke's unopposed election on 5 February. In any case Palmerston thought the Yorke interest was being mismanaged by his main contact with the family, Herbert Marsh, the St John's divine and opponent of the Evan-gelicals. This was probably because he resented the failure to gain Hardwicke's uncle, the Bishop of Ely, who on 29 January startled St John's by declaring in favour of Althorp.[10]

Palmerston met also with some serious disappointments from his close contemporaries and acquaintances at St John's. One of them, Frank Primrose, the Earl of Rosebery's second son, gave his support to Petty; worse still was the defection – as Palmerston saw it – of Lord Percy. Palmerston was helped by Percy's cousins, Lord Lovaine (the Earl of Beverley's heir) and, in spite of the fact that he was shortly to make a marriage alliance with Rutland, Hugh Percy, his contemporary at St John's. But the Duke of Northumberland himself refused his support. Palmerston believed that Petty had written to the duke before Pitt was actually dead – the Prince of Wales's secretary certainly had – and that the duke must have forbidden his son to stand forward in his friend's support. In fact Lord Percy, who was very soon to emerge again as a more direct threat to Palmerston, did actively canvass St John's for Petty. But Petty did not believe he wrested many votes from Palmerston.[11]

Although Palmerston was at first plainly inclined to exaggerate the support he had among the residents of St John's – at the end of the first day's canvass on 24 January he believed he had secured all their votes save one – he did nevertheless get a great deal of support from the college. Among the non-residents, however, even the most strenuous efforts of his college friends fell short of what was needed. For Petty and his friends at the Foxite headquarters in Holland House had already made a vigorous start outside Cambridge. John Allen, seconded by Francis Horner and J. A. Murray, wrote off to Dugald Stewart to drum up support among those others of Petty's old Edinburgh friends who were now Cambridge men and it is unlikely that they had many rebuffs. William Temple, who had now taken his brother's place as a student in the professor's house, later wrote to say that although Stewart had origi-nally intended to support Petty he had 'desisted' on hearing of Palmerston's intervention. But he probably misunderstood some sort of polite dissimulation on Stewart's part, for it is very unlikely that any inroads were made upon the Foxite sympathies in that part of the world. Palmerston certainly fared badly in another key area, among the many Cambridge voters of the Inns of Court. Palmerston's liaison there was Sulivan, now reading for the bar in Lincoln's Inn. Sulivan apparently began canvassing openly among the lawyers late in the evening of 23 January, before he had heard from Cambridge that Palm-erston would definitely stand. But it was already too late, for Petty and his friends had got off to such a good start that Palmerston never stood a chance of catching up. On 23 January they held a meeting of sympathetic Cambridge lawyers at which, Horner reported, 'several unexpected ones appeared', and the next day Whishaw, the 'Pope of Holland House', reported the establish-ment of a committee working for Petty at the British Coffee House near Charing Cross. According to Horner the canvass in London seemed from the very first, therefore, 'as promising as possible'. The Chief Justice, Lord Ellen-borough, and a 'great many' other 'turncoats' among these 'base worshippers of sunshine', he reported, had declared for Petty as soon as they heard that Pitt was dead. No wonder then that in spite of all his efforts Sulivan had sadly to report on 28 January that while Palmerston could rely on no more than eight or nine supporters among the lawyers there was a 'host' against him. He therefore advocated some rather dubious measures, such as attempting to register new voters who had not kept their names on the college boards or who were under age. Palmerston was tempted at first but eventually concluded that it was too risky. If his opponents found out they would cancel the advantage by resorting to the same tactic; and if the dons found out it would give them 'incalculable offence' and condemn him as 'a most profligate fellow'. All that he could suggest therefore was that Sulivan should imitate Petty's friends and with Shee and another Johnian lawyer, Robert Remmet, who also was a Fellow of the college, organize a committee among their legal friends. Its first task, he suggested when it had been established at Gray's Inn Coffee House, would be to engage as many places as possible for his prospec-tive voters on the 'publick conveyances' from London to Cambridge.[12]

If Palmerston's ill-success among the London lawyers was due initially to Petty's head-start, it continued because the balance of prospective patronage afterwards moved decisively against him. As the Pittite and Government candidate Palmerston's advantages of sentiment and influence should have served him well. But unfortunately Pitt's death brought down the Government and dissolved the union of his friends. So long as there remained any prospect of some of them continuing in power under the Duke of Portland or in a coalition, there was every reason for Malmesbury to go on exercising a special influence among those hoping for preferment, especially as there was some thought of his taking office himself. But this prospect, too, evaporated as Pitt's following broke up and Grenville coalesced with Fox. Before the end of January, indeed, it was widely known that Petty was to be Chancellor of the Exchequer and Lord Spencer Home Secretary, with the virtual gift of a seat on the Treasury for his son, Althorp. The Exchequer in 1806 was by no means the important office that it is now, but it had patronage enough and when the Lord Chief Justice handed Petty his Seals on 5 February he is supposed to have remarked: 'There are a matter of some hundred votes for you.' Malmesbury had already warned his protégé: 'I fear there are votes with you as in every body made up of human beings, which will vary with and follow power.'[13]

Horner was convinced that Petty's promotion would work to his advantage at least as much in Cambridge as among the London lawyers. 'I have unbounded faith in the effect of his new dignity,' he wrote. 'You can easily suppose the instances that have occurred in the course of this canvass of the meanness & undisguised servility of various persons, but particularly the priests and college monks, who are "of all mankind who can read or write" the most selfish and shameless.' But both Sulivan and Palmerston believed that their best prospects of success remained among the residents of Cambridge, where St John's had given him such a good start; Althorp, indeed, confessed to his father that he understood that 'the Johnians stand firm, which most probably will entirely take away my chance'. For Palmerston to win, however, he needed to beat both Althorp and Petty. His main hope was that Althorp and Petty would split both the university and the Trinity vote. 'I never felt more partial to the balance of power,' he quipped. The candidacy of either Perceval or Headley would have split the Trinity vote even more since both were Trinity men: Horner referred to the initial rumours about Perceval as 'our terror'. But even with that particular 'terror' removed Petty's supporters were still not confident. Indeed, when Whishaw first heard of Palmerston's entry into the contest he acknowledged him as 'a formidable competitor' and forecast that as the apparent Government candidate he 'must without all question be completely successful, if the two other parties do not agree to unite'. John Ward and Althorp came to a similar conclusion. In Palmerston's camp an equivalent 'terror' therefore remained, that one of the Opposition candidates would step down in the other's favour. Sulivan thought that it was 'by no means *impossible*' that Petty would be the one to give way. But no one else seems to have had any doubt that Petty was the more dangerous of Palmerston's opponents. No one among his friends and followers apparently discerned the flaws that were to make his political career such a disappointment to them. Horner suspected that his abilities were overrated, but still predicted he would become an eminent statesman. A few years earlier Fox had commented that he had never seen a young man he liked so much and Lady Holland that he united 'a sound, strong understanding [and] a pleasant vein of cheerful humour, with talents and advantages far beyond his years'. Lady Holland did notice that he had 'less vivacity' than her own husband – who was also to prove a disappointment – but evidently Petty's stultifying indolence and lack of ambition were not yet clearly apparent. She had even heard that he could have 'beat Pitt hollow' in the General Election of 1802.[14]

Althorp, for his part, was always very shy – preoccupied in youth as much with horses and gambling as he was later with boxing. He had, when strongly pressed by his parents, displayed his real intellectual ability by taking first place in the college examinations at Trinity in 1801. But he had soon relapsed again into bad habits, so that he had to be withdrawn from Cambridge and sent on his travels abroad. Since 1804 he had been M.P. for Okehampton, but his attendance had been very irregular, and although he owed his seat to Pitt he used to recall in later years 'how gratifying a reflection' it was that he had never given a vote against Fox. Perhaps, therefore, it is not surprising that Althorp was always trailing behind Petty and was generally thought to be behind Palmerston as well. Certainly, after the first three days of canvassing, Petty thought so. 'All goes on well,' he reported to Lady Holland, 'but Lord Palmerston is active & keeps us on the alert. The contest must be between him & me for I do not believe Althorp has as yet more than 10 or 15 votes certain.' There were good grounds therefore for the apprehension in the Palmerston camp that Althorp might withdraw. When Althorp proved stubborn, Petty threatened him with 'a formal proposal to compare strength, which discomposes him a good deal'. On 28 January Petty formally proposed that they compare strengths and agree for the weaker candidate to withdraw. But although Althorp also believed that if they both persisted neither would win, he felt that he owed his supporters a contest and that it might even be a close one. He already had the impression that the Methodists in the university were 'decidedly' with him and his notion was that if only Palmerston would withdraw, the St John's vote would carry him to victory over Petty. It was with this in mind, therefore, that his father approached Malmesbury on the same day as Petty approached Althorp. Malmesbury indignantly refused to entertain any such idea and Althorp finally accepted that Palmerston was determined to persist. But by this time Althorp knew that the Bishop of Ely had declared against Palmerston and even though he doubted that he could get the bishop's active support for himself, he did calculate that the Johnians might well desert Palmerston and vote instead for him in order to defeat Petty.

When he found out that the bishop was going to give him his active support, he must therefore have felt as confident of winning as his lugubrious personality allowed. So he rejected Petty's approach even though he thought he could rely on no more than three resident votes in Trinity itself.[15]

Palmerston for his part was confident of putting up at least a good showing and in spite of the misgivings of his friends he was not so sure himself that he would suffer much from the manoeuvrings of his opponents. He even believed that if Althorp withdrew, some of his votes would come over to him, since it would 'excite great indignation' among the M.A.s, who did not like 'to be turned over like Fen sheep from one hand to another'. For many of the voters from other colleges resented Trinity's prominent role in university affairs, and not least the apparent attempt of its graduates to monopolize every honour – the high stewardship for the Duke of Rutland, and the chancellorship for the Duke of Gloucester when Grafton died, as well as one parliamentary seat for Euston and the other for Petty or Althorp. While, therefore, Palmerston left Trinity as the enemy camp to the very last, he very quickly moved out from his own supposed position of strength in St John's and was already tackling the other colleges on the morning of 24 January. At first, though he met with only two refusals, he got very few distinct promises of support. But he pressed on and soon appeared to be gaining important successes among the Heads of Houses – particularly pleasing news for Malmesbury, who had been anxious that Palmerston's standing should not appear as the 'act merely of sanguine young men'. By 28 January, it seemed, Palmerston had got, in addition to Mansel of Trinity's promise not to oppose him, the actual support of Sumner of King's, Turner of Pembroke and Pearce of Jesus, who happened also to be the Master of the Temple. But, as Horner had suggested, with a change of Government imminent these 'promises' were not perhaps very firm. Petty thought that Mansel's caution was entirely due to self-protecting uncertainty about which side would turn out to be the Government's; and though Pearce, as an old Johnian, was very much under the influence of Craven, the Master of St John's, he was in Horner's view 'an intriguer . . . who does not quite overlook opportunities of doing his own business'. Procter of St Catherine's apparently got out of Cambridge altogether rather than make a compromising declaration. But worst of all, Milner of Queens', whose support Palmerston had earlier thought to have gained, he found was wavering still.[16]

The 'wavering' of the President of Queens' was probably the crucial symptom of the campaign. For Isaac Milner, who was also Lucasian Professor of Mathematics and Dean of Carlisle, was the intimate friend of William Wilberforce and, with Charles Simeon, the Vicar of Holy Trinity, leader of the Saints in Cambridge. In spite of all his mother's friends and relations Palmerston was orthodox rather than devout and his 'church politics' leaned him rather to the opposing wing of the Anglican Church. Hence – after the elimination of a Yorke family candidate – the clear support he received from

Herbert Marsh, who was a bitter opponent of Simeon and Milner. But while Petty was written down in St John's as 'a lurking dissenter', Palmerston had no wish to forfeit any votes by being categorized as anything but conventional. 'I have no qualms about the religious tenets of my voters,' he wrote, '& if they will but support me care not whether they are Simeonites or Atheists, or, what may happen, both.' So while Palmerston, having been promised the support of Lord Headley's 'Wilberforcian friends', canvassed Milner and Simeon in Cambridge, his friends and family strained every connection – save that of Henry Campbell, who was probably closest to the Saints but was passed over on account perhaps of some sense of delicacy about his parentage – to win over Wilberforce himself in London. Sulivan 'set 3 people' at him, while Malmesbury and the family tackled Wilberforce's close friends and above all Lady Palmerston's distant relatives, Henry Thornton, the leader of the Clapham sect, and Samuel Thornton, his brother. Yet in spite of all their efforts and in spite of Palmerston's initially encouraging reports about Milner in Cambridge, Malmesbury was puzzled to find that he could not quite hook Wilberforce himself.[17]

The fact of the matter was that on this occasion religious differences had not succeeded in keeping Wilberforce and the 'godless Whigs' apart. 'The Saints & Sinners are I am sorry to say united, & I hear that Wilberforce supports Petty manfully,' Palmerston reported on 26 January. 'This is unfortunate & unexpected.' He did not apparently think that this included Milner but it is clear that Wilberforce was already putting pressure on the dean and that this had, in Wilberforce's own words, 'produced a sad degree of rufflement' at Cambridge. Milner later wrote that he was uncertain right up to the eve of the election whether or not to vote for Palmerston, though he had no doubt that he could not support Petty. What made him hostile to Petty was the young man's support of Catholic emancipation. On this and on the Test Act, apparently, Palmerston had 'spoken decidedly' and satisfied Milner – but on one other crucial issue had 'not been quite so explicit'. This crucial issue was the question of Negro slavery. It was what had tied Wilberforce to Pitt, more than hatred of Foxite Jacobinism, and it was what now united him with Petty, in spite of doubts about his religious orthodoxy. In this respect it was a conscious political decision of his to change. For Wilberforce had been a devoted follower of Pitt and, a short while after the election, he was to carry the banner at the Prime Minister's funeral. But the abolition campaign had made no headway even with Pitt's help in Parliament and his death removed Wilberforce's hopes of the Tories. Petty, on the other hand, was now an avowed abolitionist and after the failure of Wilberforce's total abolition bill had taken a leading part in organizing meetings at Lansdowne House to promote the attack on the foreign slave trade. But if Wilberforce seemed inclined as early as 23 January to favour Petty, it was, as Petty himself acknowledged by trying to play down his *party* affiliations in the hearing of the Saints, owing to a personal preference over Althorp alone. It was by no means impossible, therefore, that Wilberforce, who was after all a Johnian himself, would change his mind when he heard of Palmerston's entry into the arena and when Milner and Simeon reminded him that Petty was not only a 'lurking dissenter' but had also recently proposed to introduce a motion for Pitt's impeachment. It is obvious therefore why the story was soon put about that Palmerston was unsound on the slavery question. Who began it is much less clear. Perhaps it spread from a letter written by Henry Brougham to Zachary Macaulay, the editor of the abolitionist *Christian Observer*:

> The Government candidate is Lord Palmerston, a young man who only left college a month ago and is devoid of all qualifications for the place. I remember him well at Edinburgh, . . . and what I know of his family and himself increases a hundredfold my wish for Petty's success. The family are enemies to Abolition in a degree that scarcely ever was exceeded. I presume that he is so himself.
>
> His maxim is that of all the objects of ambition in the world the life of a courtier is the most brilliant. Don't you think that the friends of the cause have the more reason to support Petty the more strenuously?[18]

As Horner for one already knew, few commentators ever introduced so much exaggeration and prejudice as Brougham did when his own personal interests and ambitions were involved. It seems quite likely, too, that he had had some personal clash with Palmerston at Edinburgh. Perhaps, indeed, it had been that which had kept even Stewart's protégé out of the Speculative. It is interesting that on his part Palmerston should write to Sulivan a few months later: 'So Brougham is gone out envoy to Lisbon [as secretary to a special mission]. I am glad he is getting on, his talents are certainly very great if he contrives to keep himself out of a strait waistcoat.' And a few years later in a game at a country-house party he would write:

> Beware of the party, whatever the creed,
> Whom this bonny Brougham is permitted to lead,
> For a broom at the head, as by sailors we're told,
> Is a sign understood that the ship's to be sold.

Brougham, certainly, was already angling for a brilliant political opening and he seems to have cared little where he found it. In October 1805 he got Wilberforce to commend him to Pitt; in April 1806 he launched a vigorous attack on Pitt's foreign policy in the *Edinburgh Review*. But whatever the character of the source there was enough superficial plausibility in his accusation to do Palmerston real harm. For unlike both Pitt and Fox Palmerston's father had indeed voted against Wilberforce's abolition motion in 1791, condemning it as 'blind enthusiastic zeal'. The 'dreadful history' revealed by Wilberforce he believed was 'much exaggerated'; an 'unqualified and unprepared abolition' likely to be 'ineffectual and ruinous'. The gradual 'reform' which the second viscount advocated instead had no appeal to abolitionists. Even Brougham admitted that the third viscount might not share the opinions of the second and Wilberforce shortly afterwards confessed that he probably did not. But the mud stuck long enough to do Palmerston fatal harm.[19]

According to Wilberforce himself, as well as to Palmerston's brother William, the slave-trade issue was decisive. Palmerston realized that harm had been done. He had always appreciated that Petty might win and about the end of January he and his friends tried to warm up party spirit and undermine Petty's personal appeal by stressing his character as a Foxite. But he hardly seems to have appreciated how great the harm was. Instead he hoped that the admittedly 'great' loss of Rutland and the Saints would be made up by the Bishop of Lincoln and Charles Yorke both coming out openly in his support. The bishop never did and Yorke only belatedly. But as late as 28 January he was still entertaining 'strong hopes of success', and as his committee's 'travel bureau' began to operate from London – they had staging posts arranged for horses at the Falcon Inn, Waltham Cross, and at the Sun Inn in Cambridge – Palmerston reported on 4 February that his supporters were 'increasing rapidly, . . . Johnians are dropping in incessantly'. The next evening he wrote: 'Our voters are dropping in from all quarters. Cambridge will be as full as it can hold.'[20]

Wood, who was Palmerston's 'manager' in Cambridge, seems to have outsmarted his opponents in regard to travelling arrangements for the voters. According to Althorp he first complained separately to each of Palmerston's opponents about the other 'stopping up the road' and then hired all the available coaches and carriages from under their noses. It was not too difficult to bring in new ones from outside; but it was annoying and it might have been more serious if the election had come on early. In fact the committee's arrangements were rather premature, as the Cambridge writ had been deliberately delayed by Petty's Government friends lest he be elected before receiving the Seals of the Exchequer and, according to the rule of that time, incur the liability of having to be elected all over again on the grounds of his assumption of an office of profit under the Crown. Indeed, they rather overdid it and risked offending the university's considerable sense of propriety. Unlike most parliamentary contests the university poll was confined to a single day and Petty wanted it to be a Thursday, so as to allow his many clerical supporters from the north of England time to vote and return to their livings for the Sunday services. The other candidates were approached and they agreed. But there was a hitch in the formation of the Fox-Grenville coalition and the writ did not arrive in time for due notice to be given. The election therefore had to be postponed until Friday, 7 February. All this delay, although designed originally, as Palmerston realized, to help his opponents, at least gave him a chance to wake up to the seriousness of his position. When Simeon had told him on 3 February that he could not vote against Althorp because of his 'great respect' for Lord Spencer and that he would therefore not vote at all, Palmerston's private reaction was notably flippant. His alternative explanation of Simeon's conduct had nothing to do with respect or religion. 'Perhaps', he wrote to Sulivan, 'he does not wish to appear much in publick after the unfortunate mistake made the other day by one of his parishioners who would come into his [the parishioner's] wife's room while Simeon's curate was proving to her in a most zealous manner his partiality for *works* as well as for faith.' On 4 February he still hoped to get the wavering Milner in the end. But a few days later he thought he had better tackle him again.[21]

The evening before polling day the President of Queens', who had been looking forward to some private conversation, found himself canvassed first by a series of Foxites, then by Robert Grant (to say that his friends had convinced him that Palmerston was sound after all on the abolition question), and finally by Palmerston himself. 'We conversed a full hour on the subject of the Slave Trade,' Milner reported to Wilberforce, 'and I can assure you, a more ingenuous appearance I never saw. The young man's conscience seemed hard at work for fear, not of saying too little, but of saying too much, viz. of saying more than he could justify to his mind, from the little consideration which he had given to the subject. He is but a lad; – but I could not discover the most latent hostility, or ground for suspecting hostility, and he must be a deceiver, indeed, of a very deep cast, if he deceives at all in this instance.' When challenged to say what his attitude would be if confronted in the Commons with the direct question, 'Is it expedient that the slave trade should be abolished', Palmerston gave what Milner described as an 'explicit declaration'. It was not so unreservedly in favour as to bring Milner over to his side at once. But Milner was deeply impressed with the young man's 'very candid explanations' and after Palmerston had left and Milner had thought long and hard about him, he came to the conclusion that such an 'ingenuousness of mind' was bound with better knowledge and experience to make him 'a warm & active abolitionist'. So the next morning he wrote at nine-thirty to say that he had decided after all 'to appear today in your Lordship's favor' (although, he hastened to add, he must not be considered as pledged to him on any future occasion). Within an hour it was reported that this had already brought Palmerston another thirty-four votes. But Milner himself was very sceptical; and he was right to be so for by now the Saints were hopelessly confused. The poll began at midday; by the evening Milner had to acknowledge that his candidate was 'in a woeful minority'. Palmerston indeed did much worse than he had ever expected, coming last even after Althorp. 'Victory, & triumph beyond all hope,' reported Horner to Edinburgh the next day; 'for Ld Henry 331—Althorpe 145—Palmerstone, 128.'[22]

In later years Palmerston averred that 'I stood at the poll where a young man circumstanced as I was could alone expect to stand; that is to say, last, and by a large interval the last of the three'. But the result was certainly worse than he expected at the time. He had, after all, collected little more than half the votes even of the supposedly solid and disciplined Johnians. But this was probably not through any fault of his but because of a number of unfortunate accidents. His being last in the field had lost him a number of hastily committed votes, probably even some Pittite ones to the ambiguous Althorp. Then there was the loss of prospective patronage through the change of Government and above all the unfortunate misunderstanding with the Saints. But Palmerston no doubt agreed with Malmesbury and Minto that, considering his youth and inexperience and the relative political weight of his opponents, he had mustered a very respectable support and not merely among the 'sanguine young men' in the university but also among the senior members and in particular the Heads of Houses. Certainly he was not dispirited. The campaign itself had been neither bitter nor expensive. The candidates were all personally known to each other, and this made things 'less awkward' when they ran into each other during the canvass. It was also the custom at the university elections to forego any public speaking, and when the rival candidates did meet 'it only furnished the occasion of some good-humoured pleasantry, or an amicable discussion of their respective prospects of success. Lord Althorp used to say that it was the most agreeable fortnight that he had ever passed at Cambridge.' Tradition, apparently, frowned upon any over-zealous canvassing. 'I cannot urge too strongly', Petty had written from Cambridge, 'that all unnecessary show of electioneering bustle, etc., should be avoided even in town, & upon the road, & much more here, for the grave people here are nice [i.e., fussy], & perhaps not improperly so upon that subject.' Nor could it have been at all an expensive election, compared, that is, with the thousands, sometimes tens of thousands of pounds that usually changed hands in both popular and proprietary constituencies. Palmerston certainly offered to pay the travelling expenses of his voters and these were probably more than he had hoped, since Hardwicke's election as High Steward was not in the end opposed and so brought no one to Cambridge at the expense of the Yorkes to vote for Palmerston as well. The record shows that he spent £341. 5s. 0d. on horses and carriages in Cambridge and between Cambridge and London. This probably did not include other amounts paid out for similar purposes in London and there must also have been some entertainment expenses. He probably paid for beds for non-residents in Cambridge and there were also the advertisements in the newspapers as well as a hefty bill for post. But in total he had certainly suffered neither a moral nor a material blow sufficient to crush his spirits or put him off politics.[23]

Palmerston had raised the question of what he should do in the event of defeat even before the day of the poll. What he particularly had in mind was the possibility that Petty might be elected before he was appointed minister and therefore have at once to seek re-election. It was not clear indeed until after the election that this was not going to be the case. Malmesbury thought it was a 'nice legal question' and in the end a second election was avoided only on the rather controversial grounds that although the poll had been com-

pleted before the patent of office was sealed, it was after it had been signed and
Petty had kissed hands. While the matter remained in doubt Palmerston
envisaged making a contest out of any new election, presumably on the
assumption that Althorp would drop out and that he would collect enough of
Althorp's votes to win. But the final figures must have shattered that dream; to
persist in forcing an unnecessary contest, Malmesbury pointed out, would be
so futile as to earn him not votes but only reproaches and abuse.[24]

Whatever the doubts and difficulties of the situation Palmerston had done
well enough at Cambridge for him to go on nursing his strength in St John's
for the next vacancy in the university. That Euston would be called to the
House of Lords was likely at any time; in any case, it was thought, the new
Government would probably want to strengthen its position with a General
Election either this year or next although one was not due until the summer of
1809. As a newly appointed minister, the other defeated candidate, Althorp,
had to find a seat as soon as possible. Fortunately for him there was a family
seat available. But Althorp apparently still cast longing eyes in the direction of
the university. As the sitting, Government candidate, moreover, Petty's position in any future General Election would make it difficult to envisage beating
him. On the other hand, if Palmerston made any arrangement for Petty's
support against Euston, he would forfeit the latter's help in gaining the
succession upon the Duke of Grafton's death. All these concerns, however,
Palmerston mixed with a little 'desultory dissipation'. Soon after the end of
the February election he took a house by the quarter in Pall Mall where, in
between hurried lessons in dancing and in German, he played bachelor host to
his college friends from Edinburgh and Cambridge and at the same time big
brother to his sisters. Fanny was presented at court early in March and both
she and Lilly were said, by Minto of course, to be coming out 'beauties at last'.
But politics were never far from the young man's mind. About the middle of
February, having taken the trouble to pay courtesy calls on his voters in
London, he returned to Cambridge for a meeting of the Fusty. On 13 March
he was back again to receive an 'official' letter of farewell from the Harrow
Society's secretary and, as he supposed, to say goodbye for good. But he was
back in June for Commencement week, now taking the Malmesburys with
him, while their son Fitzharris borrowed Broadlands for a month-long honeymoon. The purpose of the visit was all too obvious, even to a prospective
undergraduate on a tour of inspection: 'Lord Palmerston and Lord Henry
Petty were there, as rival M.P.'s for the University, dancing themselves into
favour in the country dance with the daughters and sisters of their constituents. Lord Althorpe was there too.' Palmerston evidently got the impression
that Petty had only come because of his own appearance; that he considered 'a
great compliment'. He also believed that he scored over Petty by being made
steward at the ball which took place on 30 June. This must have been a rather

heavy burden if all the bills and receipts surviving under this heading among his papers really belong together. Still, he concluded, he must have gathered a vote or two on the dance-floor.[25]

It was precisely at this time that Palmerston began his first political journal. The surviving version is marked with the author's customary caution; but no more so than were the letters he wrote about the same time to his closest friends. He told Shee, for example, that he had always been willing to give the new Government a chance. Had he been elected he would not have gone into 'systematic opposition', by which he meant an opposition to all measures regardless of their merits because they came from a particular set of men. That would have been 'factious' – like Fox's own behaviour in opposition. But his hopes of Grenville moderating the coalition had been disappointed and by now, he felt, Fox was clearly in the lead. So, 'from a state of suspended judgment', he had 'become . . . *decidedly* hostile to a Ministry, who in their financial exertions have stumbled out of the path chalked for them by their predecessors only to make two such notable blunders as the iron & beer taxes; who in their military maneuvres [*sic*] have disorganized the Army, changed the constitution of the Militia and disgusted if not dissolved the Volunteers; and who in their management of our foreign relations are endeavouring to restore to their conduct that uniformity of character, which a spirited interference about Hanover had for a time destroyed, by involving us in a Peace with Buonaparte'. He himself held 'an advantageous peace to be a contradiction in terms' and his patriotism was plainly outraged by the Administration's efforts in that direction. He acknowledged to Sulivan that 'peace will always & under any circumstances find a certain number of advocates in a commercial & heavily taxed country'. But he relied on the counter-balancing effects of Petty's budget which, among other things, proposed to raise the property tax from 6.5 to 10 per cent and also to levy a new tax on private brewing. Certainly he believed the Chancellor had lost ground at Cambridge. 'He wrote a foolish letter to Trinity about the beer tax against which the College remonstrated,' Palmerston reported, '& offered to allow them the same exemptions as were to be enjoyed by schoolmasters.'[26]

Parliament was prorogued on 23 July and by this time it hardly seemed likely there would be a General Election until the following year. Palmerston therefore felt free to leave any electioneering at Cambridge until he took his brother up to St John's early in October and in the meanwhile to go off on one of his long summer trips. 'The sort of retired uniform life which a person usually leads at home, is to a quiet mind as pleasant as any other,' he wrote to a lovelorn Sulivan in sanctimonious imitation of Dugald Stewart, 'but when anything presses upon the spirits nothing is so good as change of scene, which by a rapid succession of objects affords the only amusement of which perhaps the mind is capable, and prevents it from preying upon itself and increasing its own disorder.' By the beginning of August he had picked up Willy in Edinburgh and gone to Minto to say farewell to the newly appointed Governor-General of India. Then, after a short visit to his father's picture-collecting friend, Lord Douglas, at Bothwell, he passed southward through the Lakes and Liverpool and after the customary sight of the 'Ladies of Llangollen' went in mid-September to meet up with his sisters at Walcot Park, Clive's home in Shropshire. There they all stayed until the beginning of October. Before going off on this jaunt, however, Palmerston had spent a few days at Park Place, where Malmesbury had suggested to him that they open negotiations for a pocket borough in case Cambridge seemed too unpromising.[27]

About two years earlier Malmesbury had found an apparently comfortable seat for his own son, Fitzharris, at a by-election in Horsham, Sussex; now it appeared the borough's other seat would also become available at the next General Election. Horsham at that time had a population of about 3,200 but a mere handful of voters. The franchise was by burgage tenure, a sort of feudal property whose physical possession brought a vote with it. No man could exercise more than one vote for each seat no matter how many burgages he owned. On the other hand, it was by no means clear whether the vote was vested in the tenant or in the landlord and whether or not additional voters could be created by subdivision. These uncertainties had not long before in 1790 exposed the borough to a challenge from the Duke of Norfolk, who happened to be Lord of the Manor, but he had been repulsed and in 1806 Horsham still appeared, as it had for about a hundred years, in effect to be the pocket borough of the Ingram family. The present 'owner' was Lady Irvine or Irwin, as she was usually known, a widow who was old and ill and lived far away at Temple Newsam near Leeds. She had no sons but five married daughters who must inherit before long. The eldest was Lady Hertford and it was quite possibly she who had first suggested the borough to Malmesbury. In 1806, however, the actual negotiations were left in the hands of her younger sister's husband, Lord William Gordon, the brother of the agitator of 1780. Such however was the sensitivity of the family about the preservation of its property and of both sides about the nature of their dealings that the whole affair was conducted through the medium of a third party, the Earl of Pembroke, and its details concealed even from Lady Irwin's agent in Horsham. 'These are certainly transactions', Palmerston noted, 'in which one can be neither too cautious or too explicit with the other party, as the whole affair is strictly speaking illegal and one rests entirely upon his honour.' The sale of seats was not made expressly illegal until 1809; but it was clearly only another sort of bribery and too flagrant advertisements had already been rebuked, though ineffectively, as breaches of parliamentary privilege. The sum demanded for each seat was 4,000 pounds or guineas, which according to Palmerston was the common price for such boroughs, though occasionally as much as £5,000 was asked. For this they would have the seats for the duration of one Parliament, which might be as much as seven years though in recent times dissolutions had tended to come a year or so earlier. The catch was the old age of others. Fitzharris might very soon find himself forced into the House of Lords by the death of his father – Malmesbury was now sixty – or, still more likely, an expensively early General Election might be forced by the death of the King, as George III was now nearly seventy and of course very far from well. And even if the parties could come to some arrangement of these difficulties there was then the danger that Lady Irwin herself would shortly die – she did the following year – and that the bargain, which was personal and unenforceable in the courts, would not be continued by her heirs, even though the husband of one heir had himself negotiated it. Palmerston and Malmesbury therefore hoped that they might arrange to make over the seven years annual payments of somewhat more than one-seventh of the total, with the outstanding payments continuing only so long as they retained their seats. But this was not an acceptable proposal and at the beginning of October the negotiations were broken off. In the meantime, on 13 September, Fox had died and now there came the news that Parliament would be dissolved before the end of October.[28]

Palmerston had never completely given up his hopes of Cambridge and when he went to install Willy in his old rooms at St John's in the middle of October he decided also to see how the land lay there. He was rather inclined to think that it would be better for him 'to lie quiet at present and make the grand push at ye Duke of Grafton's death'. He would however be guided by the opinion of his friends at Cambridge. Malmesbury suspected that the M.A.s would urge him on simply for the sake of having a contest. But he was quite wrong. Petty might have lost by his budget some sympathy in the university, they told Palmerston, but he still had the great advantage of Treasury influence and, as the sitting members, he and Euston (who was now supporting Grenville's Government) were more likely to co-operate against any intruder than to help him. Malmesbury concluded that he had no chance of success and Palmerston therefore addressed a public letter to Cambridge announcing his withdrawal on the present occasion. He did not neglect to express his 'determination' to try again at the first opportunity; but in the meantime he and Fitzharris hurriedly closed the deal for Horsham after all.[29]

The bargain finally concluded with Lord William Gordon was a little better than had at first been feared. It promised in writing that 'should the Duke of Norfolk create any trouble at the election of course no payment will be expected until they are securely seated' and that for £4,000 each they were to be 'brought in with all re-elections *gratis* on all vacancies in the ensuing parliament during Lady Irwin's life'. Palmerston had specifically asked for this latter part of the agreement. It reserved to him for about a year the possibility of again making an attempt on Cambridge with a free re-election guaranteed at Horsham if he failed. The wording also covered the case of re-election after taking office under the Crown, but there is no sign that the thought had entered Palmerston's head though it certainly would have entered Fitzharris's. This was not all that they had wished but it was an important gain, and in all the new excitement of an imminent General Election, they were assured, they had made 'a very advantageous bargain', the lowest sum so far heard of for such a seat being 4,000 guineas.[30]

Although the dissolution was fixed for 24 October and the election for the first week in November Palmerston made no haste to appear in Horsham and dawdled fondly in Cambridge. Almost at the last moment he was further delayed by the unexpected arrival of his fellow Johnian, Lord Percy. The Duke of Northumberland had felt insufficiently courted by the Foxites when the new Government was formed and during the summer he had moved over to the Grenvilles, securing for his son one of their pocket boroughs at Buckingham. But this was a rather irksome role for such a grandee and when Fox died it was decided that Percy, who in February had been too young to contest Pitt's seat at Cambridge, should compete for Fox's at Westminster. He stood again in the Grenville interest and the Foxites had found it discreet not to oppose him. But the electors of this popular constituency were plainly furious, and when Sheridan was allowed to step forward at the General Election it was thought wise for Percy not to repeat the endeavour, even as Sheridan's colleague.[31]

It was for this reason that on 24 October Percy had turned up in Cambridge just as Palmerston was about to leave and upset him with the announcement that he intended to offer himself for the university. Percy was not likely to succeed but with all his father's wealth and influence behind him he might do well enough to establish a claim as Euston's successor when Grafton died. All this provoked some sort of public 'scene', but Palmerston kept his head and Percy undertook to consult his father again. Palmerston also put it all in writing for the duke, but in case he should prove 'obstinate' he thought he had better stay on for a while at Cambridge to secure his future prospects. Among other things he went to dine with Hardwicke at Wimpole. He suspected, no doubt, that the Yorkes still thought of putting Royston up one day; in any case he could not neglect their patronage. The duke, indeed, had already opened the canvass for his son and approached the Prince of Wales. But on 27 October Percy left Cambridge as suddenly as he had arrived. In fact he had given up the idea of the university seat and was off in pursuit of another in the West Country. 'The University is also quiet,' Euston congratulated himself. So he and Petty (who had withdrawn his beer tax) could now look forward to re-election unopposed. But Percy did not bother to tell Palmerston, and even though Palmerston felt he could safely leave Cambridge the next day, he had to take the precaution on reaching London of dispatching another long letter of warning to Alnwick. He asked that Percy (and by implication the duke) should clearly understand in the first place that it was 'impossible' for Percy to return to the contest; that would be unjust to Palmerston and his supporters. For if Percy were to stand, it would have to be against Palmerston – and what would be the result of that? Percy would not be able to overtake Palmerston either at St John's or in the smaller colleges, but would divide their votes solely to the advantage of the candidates from Trinity. In this way Palmerston would be brought down in Percy's fall. Moreover, to raise 'a point of delicacy' between them, what would people say when they saw two old friends so competing? Might they not 'indulge their propensity to see men's actions in the worst light' and attribute to Percy 'motives and sentiments' which, Palmerston was sure, were really the farthest from his mind? Surely, then, Percy ought 'to consider, whether as the son of the Duke of Northumberland commanding so many Borough seats, & able if willing to sit for either of the two great counties of Middlesex and Northumberland', he ought really to expose himself 'to the certainty of defeat in such a voluntary contest'. Palmerston got no reply to this letter, from either Percy or the duke. But the whole affair had probably done his future prospects at Cambridge no harm, if only by contrast with his rival's. From London Francis Horner wrote with scorn about the 'conduct of a diseased capricious old peer, who has nothing in his head but gout, & whose conduct nobody ever relied on. The scene that followed at Cambridge and the night journey to Launceston have completed the ruin of his son's character in public life.'[32]

Palmerston had so far taken his hypothetical contest for Cambridge much more seriously than he had his actual candidacy at Horsham. But this was natural enough: Horsham, after all, was bought if not yet paid for. In any case borough-mongers did not like the wretched candidates poking about among their valuable possessions. A personal appearance would be necessary, Palmerston was told, but only on the day of the election. 'You & James will live in Lady Irwin's house and at her expense at Horsham,' Malmesbury wrote, 'all you are required to do is to eat, drink & dance with I believe by no means disagreeable constituents male or female.' Evidently neither Fitzharris nor Palmerston had the least inkling right up to the day itself that they would have a real fight on their hands. The Duke of Norfolk's attempt in the General Election of 1790 had after all ended in disaster. As Lord of the Manor he had selected the returning officers who repaid him by declaring his candidates elected. But this had been challenged by petition to Parliament and in 1792 Norfolk's candidates had been unseated and the returning officers forced to pay substantial damages. The failure therefore seemed both expensive and decisive; none of the four general or by-elections between 1793 and 1804 was contested. But the duke was a determined as well as a rich man and he had not finally given up. Rather, while Lady Irwin's advisers had concluded that the decision of 1792 had merely confirmed the burgage character of the franchise, his had noticed that she had been allotted a majority of valid votes by allowing those based on divided burgages. So in the quiet interval of 1793–1806 he had been dividing his and his supporters' holdings while Lady Irwin consolidated hers. When therefore the election day came on 3 November 1806 and Fitzharris and Palmerston were declared elected on a show of hands, Norfolk's men at once demanded and secured a poll.[33]

The poll took the better part of two days, with every elector's title to a vote being closely scrutinized by sponsors, agents and solicitors, as well as by the returning officers. At this time there were only eleven outright burgage-owners, two of whom took no part in the election. But Norfolk and his six satellites had sub-divided their holdings, while Lady Irwin and her single ally had conveyed life interests in undivided burgages to nominees. On one side therefore almost every vote was challenged as 'split' and on the other as 'occasional and fraudulent'. Palmerston and Fitzharris got off to a bad start when for a while their formal nominator, the vicar, could not recall either the location of his burgage property or ever having paid for it or received any rent during his supposed thirteen years of possession. Fortunately Lady Irwin's agent, William Troward, who was a well-known borough-broker from Pall Mall, had at hand a 'snatch-bag' from which he produced in turn the necessary deeds of all the nominees; and when the returning officers seemed ready to accept all the opponents' votes and hinted that they would not object even to burgages cut up into square inches, he avowed that he would 'go and get a wheelbarrow full of new conveyances'. No wonder, then, that at the end of the first day's poll only seventeen votes had been cast, eight for Fitzharris and Palmerston against nine for their opponents, Francis John Wilder and Love Parry Jones. 'We are to be in the Hall at 9 o'clock and to continue there till 4,' wrote Fitzharris early the next day, 'and I much fear that we shall not have *finished being beaten* till tomorrow evening.' It did not take so long; at 3 p.m. they ended up with only twenty-nine to forty-four. Inevitably, as only nine of their opponents' to twenty-seven of their own were supposed by their reckoning to be 'good' votes, Lady Irwin's agents challenged the result. But the bailiffs, Norfolk's 'creatures' according to Fitzharris and in any event anxious to avoid paying damages again, declared all four candidates elected and left it to the House of Commons to decide between them.[34]

The 'defeated' candidates had to put a brave face on it and along with the 'victors' stay for the dinner and ball on the final night of the election. But privately they were furious. Fitzharris complained bitterly about the 'hornets' nest' he had got into and talked darkly of betrayal. 'More knavery on the part of one's adversaries, or *treachery* on the part of one's *friends* was seldom exhibited,' he wrote to his father. 'Do you remember my telling you that Troward was a *slippery chap?*' Troward, apparently, had an interest in a soap factory; in addition it was he who had suggested to the bailiffs that they absolve themselves from blame by making a double return. Malmesbury tried hard to cheer the young men up, recalling that Lady Irwin had won her case the last time it was taken to a House of Commons committee and that until they were safely seated they had nothing whatever to pay. In the meantime 'it is *entirely* Lady Irwin's affair, . . . you need do nothing'. If her agents fail 'she loses £8,000 now and the borough *for ever* – you in fact nothing but what may be got at nearly the same price'. And while they waited they might both enjoy the valuable privilege of franking their letters free and, if the occasion arose, even vote for the Speaker, though once he were chosen they would have to leave the chamber until the committee had upheld their election.[35]

Palmerston, though whisked away at once into another and equally disappointing contest for a party friend at Winchester, tried hard to take it all in the right spirit. 'Now that I can frank', he apologized to Sulivan, 'there is no inducement for me to write; when I could make my friends pay for a thumping double letter there was some fun in corresponding. . . . Our double return will be productive I fancy of no other bad consequence than putting several guineas into the pockets of some of your brother lawyers, a misfortune to which, as they will not come out of my pocket, I submit with Christian fortitude. . . . It is fortunate in the meantime that Members of the Commons are not restricted to the same limited seat as the Peeresses in Westminster Hall, for in a crowded debate eighteen inches would be a narrow allowance [even] for two Members.' To his sister he wrote in more sober terms that he was 'pretty well satisfied with the result' since he had 'not the smallest apprehension as to the decision . . . the only effect of the opposition will have been to keep Fitzharris & myself two days in a hot *high-flavoured* court-room'.[36]

Although double elections were scrutinized first – perhaps to end as soon as possible the expensive concession of twice the due amount of franking – they still had to wait for the necessary committee to be formed and that could not be done until after the new Parliament met on 15 December. In fact it did not start work until after the New Year and then took more than ten days. In the meantime the candidates kept well out of the way, partly out of deference to their patron's interest but more to emphasize that the responsibility for the whole business, and in particular for its costs, did not belong to them. They did have to sign the actual petition and to guarantee the costs but all this, Malmesbury breezily assured them, was merely a matter of form. Lord William Gordon was by the bargain bound in honour to pay the costs on their behalf and also not to seek the agreed price until they were safely seated. Palmerston therefore kept out of the way at Broadlands and Park Place until after Christmas, when he went up to town, ostensibly to have his dentist replace the front teeth he had just lost in a collision with his horse, but mainly to confront Troward. That 'slippery chap' continued to give them uncomfortable moments, and seemed so casual while the Duke of Norfolk engaged big legal guns that even Malmesbury wondered if he were not only double-faced but also double-feed. So he should not be paid one farthing yet awhile. Troward evidently made out some sort of case to Palmerston, who with Fitzharris advanced him money to get their counsel going. But it was all to no avail. The committee which assembled at last on 8 January 1807 was a 'motley choice', according to Malmesbury – the chairman was Lord Walpole and among the twelve members there was Lord Percy once again to harass Palmerston – and from the first began to show a bias in favour of Norfolk. So he expected Palmerston to be 'more sorry than surprised' when he reported on

20 January that the committee had that morning unanimously decided in favour of Jones and Wilder.[37]

Palmerston later recalled:

Harris and I paid about £1500 each for the pleasure of sitting under the gallery for a week in our capacity of petitioners. We thought ourselves unlucky in being unseated; but in a short time came the change of Government, and the dissolution in May, 1807, and we rejoiced in our good fortune in not having paid £5,000 for a three-months' seat.

It was indeed a narrow shave. After the next election in May, when Norfolk's candidates were again returned with precisely the same vote and their opponents' petition produced the same evidence and the same arguments, the House of Commons Committee declared for Lady Irwin. But Palmerston exaggerated about the costs. The price, had they been seated, would have been four, not five, thousand pounds each. But in view of all the difficulties and misunderstandings Gordon and Troward may very well have overlooked their 'obligation of honour' and passed on quite heavy legal costs. The committee had sat for eleven days and as several of the witnesses were very old they must have been paid handsome travelling and accommodation expenses. Norfolk's costs on this occasion were apparently £2,000. So perhaps the experience had cost Palmerston £1,000 or even the £1,500 he later recalled. Still he was far from downhearted. Indeed, he would have had much more cause to be so had he landed himself, as he very nearly did immediately afterwards, with a one month's seat.[38]

After the setback in Horsham Fitzharris soon obtained another seat, in Heytesbury. But Malmesbury had suggested to Palmerston that he ought perhaps to take his time. Vacancies would be hard to find so soon after a General Election and when a session or two of the new Parliament had passed the price would inevitably come down. Palmerston was far too impatient to wait so long; and the price after all would only fall in proportion to the period of tenure left. He was in fact less interested in economy than in assured success. 'Having failed once at Cambridge, besides being again talked of for it at the dissolution, and having been turned out of Horsham,' he wrote on 26 February, 'I feel most particularly desirous of not encountering a third defeat, which could not fail to place me in a ridiculous light; as indeed it does not look respectable for a man to run about the country starting and being beat in places with which he has no connection or interest.'[39]

Palmerston had not the least connection with the constituency that Fitzharris had mentioned to him the previous evening. Great Yarmouth in Norfolk was a corporation borough with a population of nearly 15,000 and an electorate of 800. The Marquess Townshend had the patronage of one seat and it was usually held by a member of his family; the other was a government seat. In the General Election of November 1806, however, the corporation had shown serious signs of an unwonted independence and the situation was further complicated by misunderstandings between the Townshends and the Treasury and by the continuation of a long-standing difference between two other local magnates, Coke of Norfolk and Lord Suffield. In the end Suffield's second son, Edward Harbord, and Stephen Lushington were returned unopposed; but a petition was then got up against the return on the grounds of corruption. The intention was probably to persuade the sitting members to compromise by surrendering one seat. But if they held out and then lost they would be barred under the Treating Act from running again and so new candidates would have to be found. In that event Sir Henry Lushington was to supply his brother's place, but the Suffield family coffers were already severely strained and rather than endure a second contest their place was offered up for sale at 3,000 guineas.[40]

The offer to Palmerston probably came via Viscount Castlereagh, who was a close connection of Harbord's by marriage, but the sum asked was so much below the market price that Palmerston suspected that the family doubted their own ability to deliver the goods. 'The demand for money before the election looks as if they foresaw a chance of defeat,' he wrote. 'I had rather give more on the terms of no cure no pay.' On the other hand they were a very respectable family and he was very doubtful that anything better would come his way at this late stage. In any case he was soon reassured by the information that Harbord commanded a large majority among the voters and concluded that if the committee should turn Harbord out his own election in his place was pretty well a certainty. So some arrangement was evidently made, probably for payment only after the committee had handed its decision down.[41]

Palmerston thought that it was as likely as not that the decision would be to seat Harbord, but regardless of that he quickly plunged whole-heartedly into a sort of informal canvass. The campaign was also kept as secret as possible, probably with a view to making his position so secure beforehand that the opposition would decide to withdraw if and when the committee unseated Harbord. Most of Harbord's supporters resided in or around Yarmouth itself and these were secured without a visit. But there were some 300 voters working at the time in the dockyards along the Thames. These were probably skilled artisans rather than rough workmen, but it was still Palmerston's first experience of a campaign among the lower orders. 'Whatever may be your fate,' Malmesbury commented, 'it truly has introduced you into places & society, you never would have seen otherwise.' Palmerston, as usual, treated it all very cheerfully. He and Harbord spent one day from 9 a.m. till 5 p.m. 'trotting about' Thames Street and the Minories where they 'canvassed about forty votes & got them all'. Then, after a weekend's break, he spent four days or so visiting Deptford – 'at twelve we assembled about 25 in the Inn, and harangued them for a short time' – Woolwich, Chatham, Northfleet and Sheerness. He was pretty pleased with the result, coming away with another 119 firm promises and feeling certain of success if it ever came to a real contest.[42]

'It is but fair that as a petition threw me out a petition should in return contribute to bring me in', Palmerston wrote as soon as his canvass was over and the committee's inquiry began. But it was not to be. The committee opened its proceedings on 4 March and soon Harbord was cheerfully reporting that his opponents' evidence was quite damning and that he was therefore bound to be turned out to make a vacancy for Palmerston. Palmerston, on the other hand, recalling his earlier suspicions and noticing that Coke's interest had made no attempt to answer his informal canvass, began to wonder if it was not really a compromise that both sides had in mind, with Lushington surviving while Harbord gave his seat up, not to Palmerston but to his opponents. As it happened no such compromise was ever reached; but he still did not get a seat. On 11 March the committee reported against the petition and so seated both Lushington and Harbord.[43]

Presumably Palmerston did not have to pay Suffield a penny for such a result as this; but after all the constant disappointments he had suffered in the last year it would not have been surprising if his spirits had failed at last. But they were not to have the chance. For Malmesbury was also dabbling in high politics and the Yarmouth affair was already being overtaken by a national crisis that was to bring Palmerston a better opportunity and even compensation.

The Ministry of All the Talents had struggled on for more than a year through constant failures and disasters so that when at last at the beginning of 1807 it managed to accomplish the abolition of the British slave trade, it was tempted to overreach itself by proposing to the King to nibble away at the prohibitions on his Catholic subjects. But after a tangled and tortuous series of manoeuvres on both sides, the King demurred and, encouraged by the Opposition, cunningly exploited the exposure of his ministers' sharp practice and followed up his victory by demanding their promise not to touch the subject again. When they refused he dismissed them and on 31 March sent for the Duke of Portland. There was some suspicion that Malmesbury had put the King and Portland up to this. If he did, then it was but the first of a rapid series of new obligations that Palmerston owed him. For three days later there came to Malmesbury the offer for Palmerston of his father's old place at the Admiralty. Palmerston was at Broadlands at the time but when he heard from Malmesbury he came up to town at once in order to accept in person. What was now really urgent, however, was for the new junior minister to find a parliamentary seat. Fortunately the Portland Government soon discovered that it had insufficient support in the present House of Commons and dissolved it on 29 April. Naturally, with a General Election in view and this time with the certain backing of Government patronage, Palmerston's thoughts turned once again to Cambridge.[44]

As one of the new Government's 'confidential friends', Palmerston got advance news of the dissolution on Saturday, 25 April, and he rushed down to

Cambridge the same day. The coach lost its way in the dark and he did not arrive until seven-thirty the next morning. But little was lost since that day was a Sunday and no open canvass would have been considered decent. But this did not preclude testing the opinion of his 'particular friends' and from them he gathered that 'things in general look well'. Sulivan was again left behind in London to form a committee, based this time at the Crown and Anchor in the Strand, while in Cambridge another was formed from a number of sympathetic Fellows under the chairmanship of James Wood. In Cambridge Palmerston also had at hand his brother William to help among the students of St John's, while his old tutor Outram acted as courier between that place and London. So once again they scanned the lists of dons and lawyers in Cambridge and London and with Malmesbury set all their friends and connections on the track of scattered and floating votes.[45]

Among the resident voters Palmerston seemed better placed than ever. Euston's seat was considered pretty safe, though he had gone over to Grenville. But to the damage done by his budget Petty had now added much more from his involvement in the attempt to raise the Catholic question. At first Palmerston was inclined to avoid that tricky subject altogether, feeling that any too 'explicit allusion' would lose him as many votes as might be gained. He was very probably wrong. His opponents certainly thought so. 'The yell of "No Popery" has been heard even at Cambridge,' one of their supporters afterwards complained; 'and on the walls of our senate house, of Clare Hall chapel, and of Trinity Hall, I saw the odious words in large characters.' Evidently Palmerston saw them too, for he quickly revised his opinion and adopted Sulivan's suggestion of adding in his election circular at least a simple affirmation of his adherence to the existing constitution of both Church and State. No doubt this helped gain in the first few days firm promises from the heads of Jesus, Corpus Christi and Emmanuel, and, no doubt to his great relief, unhesitating ones this time from Milner of Queens' and even Mansel of Trinity. Presumably there was no difficulty on Craven's part either, for this time no rival appeared from the ranks of the Johnians, and so, according to an observer from Trinity, they were soon 'exerting themselves to the utmost grunting out the praises of their brother Palmerston'. Palmerston had been worried about Percy, but he soon heard that Percy did not intend to oppose him; instead he appeared in Northumberland to turn out Lord Howick, the future Earl Grey. On the other hand, although Royston was further away than ever, there was this time no coincidental contest at Cambridge to alarm Lord Hardwicke's sense of dignity or to restrain the indignation he felt at the supposed anti-Catholic intrigue which had triumphed so recently over the Whig-Grenville alliance. In compensation, however, Malmesbury secured Rutland and with him the Mortlocks and their 'vast influence'. But the major difference for Palmerston on this occasion derived from his being a Government candidate. Unfortunately this turned out to be a very mixed blessing.[46]

Being a Government candidate certainly seemed to bring Palmerston sub-

stantial benefits. It may even have saved him some expense, though the
Treasury's offer of transport for his voters was at first refused because the
candidates' committees had agreed not to supply any; evidently they already
had some reason to apprehend the sort of overcharging that was to mark the
contests of the 1820s. The Government's support definitely placed in
Palmerston's hands the writ for the election; but he was not able to make even
as much use of it as Petty had in 1806. Both Sulivan and Palmerston were
agreed that it would be dangerously offensive to delay for long, but the old
familiar problem of finding a suitable day still obtruded. Allowing for the
necessary notice, the earliest it could have been was Wednesday, 6 May; but
that would not have given enough warning to the more distant voters. The
next day, however, was also 'out of the question being Ascension Thursday,
with two sermons in St Mary's'. So it had to be Friday, 8 May, which, with the
committees agreeing to modify their arrangement so as to allow *return* transport, gave just enough time to get the country parsons back to their homes for
the Sunday services. On the other hand, while Palmerston's association with
the Government must have brought him a good deal of support from those
who looked forward to official patronage, it also brought him a colleague with
whom he had to share it. This was the new Attorney-General, Sir Vicary
Gibbs.[47]

Although Palmerston had appeared at Horsham in harness with Fitzharris,
that had not really been a contest at the *canvass*, and his second attempt at
Cambridge was the first to confront him with the peculiar problems of
fighting for a seat in a two-member election. If it had been a question of either
the Government or the Opposition candidates succeeding together there
would have been no problem. But things were not then as simple as that, least
of all perhaps at one of the universities: party lines were too weak and college
and personal attachments too strong. With four candidates competing for two
seats the strong possibility was that each side might gain a seat. In the present
case few doubted that Euston would come at the head of the poll and Petty at
the bottom. Of Gibbs and Palmerston, therefore, only one could gain the
second seat. With each elector having two votes, however, the peculiar irony of
the situation was that in a close fight for this other seat the second votes of one
candidate's supporters might seat his colleague at his own expense. In these
circumstances it was sometimes arranged among the most determined partisans not to give any second votes at all but to 'plump', as it was called, for a
single candidate. But clearly this could only be done on the basis of the most
reliable information about the prospects and tactics of all sides and at the risk
of quarrelling with one's colleague.

In a situation fraught with such danger it is not surprising that the appearance of a ministerial colleague badly upset Palmerston. If, as had at first been
suggested, Perceval had come forward, things might have been different.
Perceval, after all, was the new Chancellor of the Exchequer and Leader of the
House of Commons, and his cooperation with any young man would have

been highly prized. But it was far otherwise with the new Attorney-General. He was, according to others besides the biased Brougham, narrow-minded, vain and conceited, and so lacking in humour and so bitter in manner that he acquired the name of 'Vinegar Gibbs'. Sulivan, as Palmerston's principal adviser among the lawyers of London, was from the first convinced that he would do his colleague on the hustings more harm than good. But Malmesbury and Palmerston's friends at Cambridge were inclined to think the opposite. As a King's man Gibbs might get a fair number of votes from that medium-sized college but nothing like the number that would be given to the other candidates by Trinity and St John's. All in all, they thought, he was too late and too insignificant to take away from Palmerston the role of leading Government candidate; instead he would provide a harmless and convenient repository for the second votes of those of Palmerston's supporters who were loath to waste them and might otherwise be tempted to give them to Euston.[48]

Palmerston went on writing in this vein even after Gibbs (and also Petty) arrived in Cambridge on 28 April. Two days later, however, all his calculations were known to be upset. It is not clear exactly what had happened, but from Palmerston's later recollections it would seem that he had discovered that the Government had a very different conception of its candidates' respective roles and had instructed those of its supporters who would give but a single vote to bestow it upon Gibbs. Malmesbury was too intimate with Portland for the Prime Minister himself to have been guilty of such behaviour but this does seem to have been the line adopted at Cambridge by the new Lord President of the Council, Earl Camden. According to Lady Malmesbury it reflected the personal and political differences already existing within the Cabinet between Hawkesbury and Castlereagh on the one hand and Canning on the other. Camden, whose family and Castlereagh's were closely connected by marriage, she considered a 'block . . . merely fashioned' by the hands of Canning's enemies. Since her husband was at this time still an ally of Canning's presumably Palmerston was thought to be one too. Whatever the cause, the Government's preference for Gibbs so far as Palmerston was concerned completely upset any notion of a joint canvass, and he evidently wrote at once to tell Malmesbury and Sulivan so. But in London his decision created consternation. For Sulivan, ironically enough, had already been led by Palmerston's initial reaction to begin not only a joint canvas but even a joint committee. To drop it all now would be to demonstrate publicly the lack of cooperation between the Government candidates and to play into their opponents' hands. Word that they were not acting together had, indeed, already got to the enemy and to the Government. 'Perceval', reported Malmesbury, 'expresses great uneasiness that the idea of your each acting separately is so industriously circulated by your antagonists who I fear are conducting themselves with great art and management'; and, he went on to wheedle Palmerston, Gibbs was bound to trail behind and so cooperation could only end in Gibbs throwing all his support in Cambridge to Palmerston's side.[49]

For a few days there hurried urgent letters between London and Cambridge and as Gibbs passed back and forth seeking votes in the colleges of the university and among the Inns of Court, Outram pursued him with proposals and counter-proposals. Palmerston insisted that he had only meant to keep apart in Cambridge, where a joint canvass would have been questioned from the first because of the known lack of any personal connection between the candidates and was now rendered impossible by the fact that his canvass was nearly completed before Gibbs had even begun; but these objections did not apply to London, and since the joint canvass had already begun there it had better continue. But the pressure from London forced him not only to continue the cooperation there but also to restore it in Cambridge. When Outram arrived back in Cambridge at midnight on 1 May, Palmerston dragged Wood and another of his committee from their beds and with their agreement drafted a formal undertaking for Sulivan to show to Gibbs. So far as he could ascertain at so late an hour, his supporters would not be 'averse to making common cause with Sir V. Gibbs, particularly were they assured that the same cordiality prevailed among his friends. . . . With regard to myself I am quite willing to make it at once a matter of honour between Sir V. & myself that each shall use his best endeavours to promote the success of the other.' By the morning of 2 May, therefore, they presumed that the outward semblance of a 'cordial co-operation' had been restored in Cambridge; less sympathetic observers, however, could see that all was 'now in confusion and uproar'. For the fundamental dilemma of the two-member fight remained: what form of cooperation was helpful rather than fatal? Palmerston frankly did not expect to gain as many second votes from Gibbs's supporters at King's as Gibbs would gain from his at St John's, but in an exchange of second votes among the non-resident electors he agreed with Malmesbury that he ought to gain much more from Gibbs's extensive legal connection. All this, however, left unsettled the vital question of plumpers.[50]

According to Palmerston's own recollection it was not until the evening immediately before the poll that he and Gibbs went over their calculations with the chairmen of their committees. The result confirmed the impression that Euston would come top of the poll and that therefore only one of them could get elected. In certain votes Palmerston was reckoned to have 288 to Gibbs's 283, but the difference was not enough to give him a decisive lead and to suggest that Gibbs should give up in order to help him beat Petty. They therefore agreed that on the following day each should persuade his plumpers after all to give their second votes to the other. But the next morning Palmerston made a vital tactical error. Hoping that he could win over a number of 'waverers' by demonstrating his strength he decided to bring the major part of his supporters to the poll early in the day. This merely alerted Petty to the certainty of his defeat and induced him to throw his plumpers over to Euston. So it was made doubly certain that Euston would be elected and that there would be room for only Gibbs or Palmerston.[51]

A miscalculation of policy had spoiled Palmerston's chances in the morning of the poll on 8 May; his sense of personal honour was finally to ruin them in the evening. The poll that day went on till ten o'clock, and just before it closed Gibbs came up to him in the Senate House to say that in spite of their agreement four men still insisted on plumping for Palmerston. Palmerston therefore undertook to post himself at the entrance and 'beg' each man to give his second vote to Gibbs. However, when he got there, he found Outram standing by and was urged by him to leave well alone. For his committee was watching the situation carefully and, having calculated that Gibbs was running him close for second place, they and a 'few more stanch friends' had kept back their votes to see whether or not they needed to plump for Palmerston to seat him over Gibbs. Apparently they had not been present at the meeting of the previous evening and they did not consider themselves bound by his agreement with Gibbs. Palmerston, however, insisted that he was 'bound in honour' and 'with much ill humour and grumbling' they gave way. A short while later the declaration gave the first place, as expected, to Euston and the second to Gibbs by the narrow margin of two votes over Palmerston; Petty came last. The figures were: Euston, 324; Gibbs, 312; Palmerston, 310; Petty, 265.[52]

To have come so near and failed yet again was, as he admitted, a bitter blow to Palmerston. Without Gibbs's intervention he probably would have won. But Gibbs himself, he knew, had behaved 'most honourably', and if there had been any treachery anywhere it was more likely to have been on the part of his own committee since, when the poll was published and the recalcitrant plumpers counted, he found that he himself had had twelve to Gibbs's seven. However, he consoled himself with the thought that it was 'a real victory to have a majority of 45 over a man who a year ago beat me by upwards of two hundred'. So while the disconsolate Petty hurriedly left for London, Palmerston made himself obvious at the May Ball, and with an eye to the future began to count and scrutinize the voting lists, more especially of Gibbs's men at King's. But for the present that was enough. For the ever-calculating Malmesbury had even before the Cambridge poll was ended secured for Harry the safe alternative of a proprietary seat elsewhere.[53]

Malmesbury had probably begun to look for an alternative seat as soon as he heard from Cambridge that the Government seemed to be helping Gibbs in preference to Palmerston. The next day he reported: 'At all events I have reason to hope if Cambridge fails that I have secured a seat for you for £4,000 – but of this I shall not be quite sure until Monday and you had better keep it to yourself – but a *seat* you *shall* have, happen what may.' He was as good as his word, for on the Monday he wrote to Palmerston asking him to deposit the £4,000 at Drummonds the bankers. It would have been returned to him if he had been successful at Cambridge, but as he was not the transaction was completed, and the very next evening after the failure at Cambridge Malmesbury wrote to say that he was M.P. after all. The seat was one of the two at Newport in the Isle of Wight.[34]

The borough of Newport was the principal town on the Isle of Wight and it had a population of between three and four thousand. But the members were 'elected' by a self-perpetuating corporation of a mere twenty-four individuals, many of them non-residents, and they in turn were completely under the influence of a local family called Holmes. Palmerston's father had paid two hundred pounds more for the same seat in 1790. His father's colleague at the election then was the first Viscount Melbourne (he did not become an English baron until 1815) and they had both moved out from their base at Holmes's house to ask the votes of 'about a dozen shopkeepers who looked as if they thought we might as well have saved ourselves the trouble. The evening concluded with a rubber at whist and a supper of which Mrs Holmes and two other Isle of Wight ladies, tolerably vulgar, did the honours.' Since then, however, the family had become perhaps less vulgar but certainly more cautious, and by 1807 so jealous of their interest that it was made a condition of Palmerston's nomination that he should never set foot in the place. Clearly Palmerston would not in any case have been able to get from Cambridge in time for the election at Newport. But it is no wonder that with Malmesbury conducting the negotiations through the Treasury manager, Charles Long, both he and Palmerston hardly ever got the name of the borough right. Malmesbury at the time and Palmerston in his recollections habitually confused it with Newtown, a rotten borough on the island in which the Holmeses also had an interest; and in announcing the election to Palmerston, Malmesbury actually called it 'Winton'.[35]

III

ADMIRALTY
AND
WAR
OFFICE,
1807–28

On 6 April 1807, a month before the electors of Newport made him a Member of Parliament at last, Palmerston had entered upon the duties of a Junior Lord of the Admiralty. In offering the post the First Lord, Mulgrave, had written: 'He has a sort of hereditary claim to a seat there, & I have no doubt that he would also bring to it all the advantages of hereditary abilities.' Malmesbury, who had apparently asked the Prime Minister for the offer, must have been more ambitious for his former ward than that; Lady Malmesbury certainly hoped that Palmerston would be 'much more of a public man' than his father. And, indeed, where the second viscount had spent more than a decade the third stayed a mere two and a half years, but in that short time he both made the beginnings of a real reputation and laid the foundations of an immensely more distinguished career. Yet from the first this reputation was strangely enigmatic. Since he still lacked a town house to his satisfaction, he lived at first at the Admiralty itself, and there, apparently, this 'pattern of industry and virtue' impressed a senior colleague as a 'model young man' who must one day rise to the top, but that colleague's daughters as a 'very pedantic and very pompous' person, whom they nicknamed 'Sir Charles Grandison because he was so priggish and so sedate'. How like the docile but earnest son and ward of Edinburgh and Cambridge days; and, as one of the daughters would herself laughingly recall, how unlike the Pam of later years. But in 1807 the beginning of the transformation was at hand.[1]

Palmerston lived at the Admiralty for only a short while; by November 1807 he had moved into bachelor quarters in Albany and by March 1808 into a house in Lower Brook Street, which would suit his sisters when they came up for the season. William used to join him in Albany during part of his university vacations and when he came down from Cambridge in the summer of 1808 he also moved into Lower Brook Street. William was already thinking of the diplomatic service, but as the war made the prospects of foreign employment so remote he embarked instead on a three-year apprenticeship at the bar. In London, as at Broadlands, the young viscount played his role as head of the family very seriously indeed, though beyond any doubt he saw to it that life continued very happily for them all. He told Sulivan that he wanted to ensure that Willy entered chambers under the eye of someone who would instil 'habits of regular attendance'. Out of office hours and under Palmerston's own eye, Willy also followed his example. Willy himself wrote this account of one brief period:

[Last Tuesday] Harry . . . came home from the opera at one o'clock . . . and . . . at three . . . from Lady Castlereagh's . . . Wednesday we went to Vauxhall and supped afterwards at Mrs Pigou and danced after supper. Thursday we went to see Plot & Counterplot at the little theatre which is extremely laughable. We then went to Lady Shaftesbury who gave a dance & supper . . . ; dancing did not begin till one nor supper till four. Last night we went to Vauxhall . . . tonight we sup at Lady Heathcote's after the opera. . . . On Tuesday . . . Lord Palmerston intends giving a grand dinner . . .[2]

It was no wonder then that Palmerston's London life was reported as 'very gay and dancing at a great rate'. Out of London he continued his family's customary combination of business and pleasure no less vigorously. He made a first inspection of his Irish estates in company with his brother in the autumn of 1808. In the following year Malmesbury, as Lord Lieutenant of the county, gave him command of one of the newly raised regiments of local militia, the South West Hampshire Regiment. So, every year or two until the regiment was reduced in 1816, Lt Col. Lord Viscount Palmerston could advance in summer camps around its Romsey headquarters the military career he had begun as an undergraduate, reducing to the ranks in the daytime sergeants unwilling to 'volunteer' into the regulars and dancing away the evenings with his junior officers' wives. There were, too, the visits to Park Place for Christmas fare and political intrigue, the reminiscence and informal canvass of mid-summer balls in Cambridge and winter festivities at St John's, and the autumn shooting and hunting at Broadlands, together with a little 'administration of farm and garden' and the distribution of prizes among the young ladies of the local school in Romsey. Above all there were the attendances at Devonshire House and the visits to Brocket that spread rumours of marriage prospects and commenced his liaison with a certain discontented countess.[3]

This, however, is not yet the place to dwell upon the more intimate undercurrents of Palmerston's life. In any case his pursuit of pleasure was no more assiduous than his devotion to official duties. The duties of a lay lord of the Admiralty, indeed, were not exactly onerous. They literally consisted of taking his turn during the mornings as one of the three commissioners (out of six) whose signature was necessary to legitimize the board's commands. But the appointment did give him 'opportunities of . . . learning the general routine of business and of acquiring a general information of the management of every Department of the State'. Palmerston certainly gathered a good deal of

information and his short time at the Admiralty was probably more important to him than has usually been granted. He also had his House of Commons
duties, sitting in the mornings in committees to investigate the commerce of
the West Indies or the scandalous patronage exercised at the Horse Guards by
the Duke of York's mistress, and in the evenings getting 'uncommonly occupied . . . with long debates'. It must be admitted, however, that he spoke
very rarely indeed in the House. It was not in fact until 3 February 1808,
almost a year after his election, that he rose to speak for the first time.[4]

Palmerston told no one but his brother in advance, but he prepared very
carefully, pointing out afterwards that the lightness of his duties at the Admiralty gave him plenty of leisure to study the relevant papers and to put his
speech together. He had also planned to speak when he could expect the
subject to attract a full House. But as it turned out the weather was bad on the
night of the debate and there were hardly more than 350 present. 'I was
tempted by some evil spirit to make a fool of myself for the entertainment of
the House,' he reported next day to his sister; 'however, I thought it was a good
opportunity of breaking the ice, although one should flounder a little in doing
so, as it was impossible to talk any very egregious nonsense upon so good a
cause.' The cause was that of defending the Navy's attack on neutral Copenhagen. To demand papers, as the Opposition had done, he argued was unwise
and unnecessary. They would be sure to betray the source of the intelligence
about Napoleon's plans; and the expedition could be justified without them.
It was clear that Napoleon intended to seize the Danish fleet and that Den-
mark was both unable and unwilling to resist. This, Palmerston believed, was
'proved' by her refusal of an English alliance.[5]

Palmerston's first parliamentary speech made no great impression, although the Leader of the House kindly reported to the King that he spoke
'very well'. As he himself complained, the newspapers were not 'very liberal in
their allowance of report' to him and other speeches occupied nearly all their
space. At best Palmerston could only say with reference to a young rival in the
House: 'Robert Milnes . . . had made a splendid speech on the first night of the
discussion. He chose to make a second speech on a following night . . . His
[second] speech was a bad one, and mine was luckily thought better than his
bad one.' Palmerston was only on his feet for half an hour and though he
afterwards claimed to have been less alarmed than he had feared, he was
naturally glad when it was over, but rather afraid that he had 'exposed'
himself.[6]

Palmerston's speech, apparently, was fluent and even elegant in the parts
that he had memorized, but elsewhere he paused too much to find the best
expression and filled his stammering gaps with histrionic gestures of the hand.
Lady Holland wrote: 'Ld Palmerston's maiden speech was not attended either
with the bad or good qualities of a young beginner; he had practised in
debating societies, and formed an unimpressive, bad manner.' Gilbert Elliot
rather grudgingly acknowledged that the subject was an 'unamiable' and

'unfortunate' one for a young beginner. In general, however, his family and friends were much more kind about it. Willy, naturally, was unstinting in his praise, but Mulgrave also sent a polite note of congratulation and even Sir Vicary Gibbs wrote a note of commendation to James Wood in Cambridge. But Lady Malmesbury, while emphasizing that he 'made an excellent speech which was approved by all sides', also shrewdly noted shortly after: 'I think Harry looks sadly – his constitution is not strong enough for this terrible session of parliament added to other business & pleasure.' Palmerston in fact had a recurrence not only of the childish 'fire' that had so often marked his eyes and cheeks but also within two weeks of joining the Admiralty, of the 'bilious headaches' that always seemed to coincide with mental strain.[7]

It is unlikely that anyone outside Palmerston's immediate circle of family and friends would have thought enough about the infrequency and hesitation of his parliamentary performances to spot the flaws that Lady Malmesbury detected. Instead, when another occasion for general comment occurred towards the end of 1809, the opinions of his immediate colleagues at the Admiralty were uniformly favourable; and in general the Government must have thought of him as a competent young man of business and, as his letters to Sulivan show, a loyal and optimistic supporter of their policies in Europe and America. So, with Malmesbury's constant backing, advancement was always probable in the early years both before and after his maiden speech.[8]

Palmerston had been at the Admiralty only a few months when Malmesbury's connections and intrigues brought the first possibility of change. When Canning had taken the Foreign Office in Portland's Government in March 1807, he had chosen Fitzharris as an undersecretary, thinking that this would 'soothe' Malmesbury's supposed disappointment at not getting the Foreign Seals for himself. On the same day as the offer arrived Fitzharris became the father of another, future Foreign Secretary. But he soon dashed Malmesbury's hopes for himself. Canning thought well enough of him at the office, but Fitzharris's temperament was evidently not well suited to political life. At the time it was said simply that he did not like the 'fatigue and constant sedentary life'; later that he was too sensitive to accustom himself to the dissimulation and deceit of politics. The Copenhagen affair was apparently the last straw, though Canning thought that the grind of the office would in any case soon have driven him out. He agreed to stay on a while to help out with some minor problem in the diplomatic service, but early in August 1807 he quit the Foreign Office for the greener pastures of the Government of the Isle of Wight.[9]

Malmesbury, of course, did all he could to save his son's career. Eighteen months earlier he had evidently persuaded him not to give up Parliament altogether; and before the Isle of Wight vacancy upset his schemes, he had written to the Prime Minister to suggest an exchange that would give Fitzharris a less fatiguing lordship of the Treasury or Admiralty. His favourite idea was an exchange with the Prime Minister's son, but Portland was not willing to give up Titchfield's secretarial assistance. Malmesbury did not even mention the Foreign Office to Palmerston until after Fitzharris had accepted the Isle of Wight, so when he wrote on 7 August offering to suggest Palmerston's name to Canning he must by then have been attracted by the notion, not of an exchange, but of replacing in his hopes his ward for his son. Clearly he knew that Palmerston was not so sensitive about Copenhagen. He warned him, however, that if it was a 'very interesting office', it was also 'very laborious' and 'not fit for a married young man'. This last suggests that the rumours of marriage plans about this time were by no means unfounded. But Palmerston simply answered the next day that if Malmesbury thought him up to it, he would willingly undergo the fatigue, as the office was 'so good a trainer'.[10]

It is idle, though very tempting, to speculate on what might have been had Palmerston succeeded in joining Canning at the Foreign Office in 1807 and, consequently, had left with him in 1809. The *fact* is that he did neither; for the undersecretaryship went instead to Charles Bagot. Indeed, it does not seem that the opportunity was ever really there. Malmesbury wrote to Canning on 9 August; but Canning had already written to Bagot the night before. A few days later, on 13 August, Canning walked over to Palmerston in the House to say 'in a very handsome manner' how much he regretted he was already engaged to Bagot and to suggest that Bagot might welcome a proposal from Palmerston for an exchange. But probably neither the excuse nor the suggestion was sincere. Palmerston himself seems to have sensed as much. He did not know Bagot well enough to propose such an arrangement, he wrote to Malmesbury, and did not therefore think it 'very practicable'. Nor was Canning entirely honest about his avowed commitment to Bagot. He told Malmesbury that he had 'long ago' promised the vacancy to Bagot; but he had written to his wife on 6 August discussing Bagot merely as one of several candidates and a definite offer in writing had been sent only on the evening of 8 August. He told Palmerston that he would have had the office had he known of his interest in time; but among the names he had already mentioned to his wife was that of Palmerston himself. It was Fitzharris, of course, who had suggested Palmerston, though at the same time also another Johnian, Lord Lovaine, who was a Commissioner at the Board of Control; either of them, he had said, would 'jump at it'. Malmesbury's notion of Palmerston was supposed to be a secret even from his son, but Fitzharris had evidently been led to suggest such names by doubts that Canning had about Bagot. Bagot had wanted the post when Canning first arrived at the Foreign Office in March. His application had come in too late, but Canning had written then: 'I doubt whether he would have done for me.' He was no keener in August: 'Charles Bagot is very desirous indeed – but I think he would hardly go through with it.' His offer to Bagot, to say the least, was also rather unenthusiastically phrased. How unimpressed he must therefore have been with Palmerston to take Bagot after all![11]

Canning's opinion was not, however, to be of vital importance to Palmerston at this early stage, for Canning himself did not stay very long at the Foreign Office. Instead, his bitter criticism of his colleague Castlereagh's conduct of military policy culminated in a duel and their resignations in September 1809 precipitated the fall of the Portland Government. Portland died almost at once and, an attempt at making coalitions with Grey and Grenville having failed, the task of forming a new Tory administration passed to Spencer Perceval. Perceval's personal position was far from strong. Somehow or other he had to form an administration in the face of an extraordinary combination of difficulties. In particular, he had to tempt Canningites without bringing back Canning, the powerful lobby of Scots without the disgraced Melville, and Sidmouth's group without the despised 'Doctor' himself. The need to attract followers from such camps as these made sport of loyal juniors. But their prospects were improved by the loss of Castlereagh and Canning and by the failure of the approaches to Grey and Grenville since these forced Perceval to look rather lower among the ranks of Government supporters than he would otherwise have done. On this occasion Malmesbury was probably not responsible for putting forward Palmerston's name. For once, indeed, there was no need. Canning's behaviour in 1809 marked the beginning of a serious rift with Malmesbury, who for some time had nursed a deep resentment of Canning's supposedly inordinate ambition, and Palmerston, still following his guardian's lead, was therefore excused the calumny of isolated Canningite. Even so, the offers that consequently came the way of a relative political nonentity of not quite twenty-five were really quite astonishing – to him and to others.[12]

Having, as he usually did during the long parliamentary recess of those days, gone down to the country for the autumn, Palmerston returned to Broadlands from a three days' sailing party on the evening of 14 October 1809 to find a summons from the new Prime Minister. He came up to town on the 16th and saw Perceval at 11 a.m. What the Prime Minister wanted, he found, was to offer him the chancellorship of the Exchequer or, if he preferred it, possibly the situation of Secretary at War.[13]

The chancellorship of the Exchequer was then neither as important nor as well paid as it is now. Moreover, when, like Perceval, the Prime Minister was in the House of Commons, he was usually (indeed, *always*, until the formation of Peel's first Administration in 1834) Chancellor of the Exchequer as well as First Lord of the Treasury. When Portland had been Prime Minister in the House of Lords Perceval, as his Chancellor, had had in the Commons powerful support from such other Lords of the Treasury as Huskisson and Sturges Bourne. With these two gone with Canning, however, 'he felt much in need of some one to take off his shoulders part of the labour of his offices in and out of the House'. He therefore proposed to separate the offices of Chancellor and First Lord.[14]

Perceval told Palmerston that he was not his first choice for the Exchequer and that he had had 'great difficulty in finding any one to take the situation'; the Canningite 'Orator' Milnes was the only other possibility. He had
offered it to Vansittart, but he would not come in without Sidmouth and
Sidmouth was anathema to the friends of Pitt; Palmerston himself wrote to a
colleague at the Admiralty, 'that would indeed be draining the cup to the
dregs'. Perhaps Perceval also mentioned that he had offered the Exchequer to
Charles Yorke as well, for the fact was well known at the time. Portland and
Perceval had for some time been trying to entice Yorke away from the
Grenvilles with a variety of offices in order to strengthen their administrations.
But his brother had constantly thrown obstacles in the way. It was not until
May 1810 that Hardwicke softened enough to let him take the Admiralty. But
Yorke would not in any case have taken the Exchequer, and what he said of
Perceval's offer puts Palmerston's opportunity in much better perspective: 'I
would not entertain the idea for a moment. In truth, it will become a mere
office of detail & subordination under a First Lord of the Treasury in the
House of Commons, of details too of an irksome & unpleasant description just
now'.[15]

Although Perceval more than hinted at the reduced status of the office – he
acknowledged that he would still 'of course take the principal share of the
Treasury business, both in and out of the House' – this was not what made
Palmerston hesitate. It was timidity, not pride, that drew him back. He did
mention to Malmesbury his feeling that if Perceval could find no one better
than himself for the Exchequer then it was clear his government would be too
weak to survive. But what he emphasized to both Perceval and Malmesbury
was his own inexperience in office and, still more, in parliamentary speaking.
He was, indeed, too honest to disguise that what he feared most was failure.
'Of course one's vanity and ambition would lead to accept the brilliant offer,'
he wrote after his first interview with Perceval; 'but it is throwing for a *great
stake,* and where much is to be gained, *very much* also may be lost. I have always
thought it unfortunate for any one, and particularly a young man, to be put
above his proper level, as he only rises to fall the lower.' He knew little of
finance and had spoken but once in the Commons. Yet the approaching
session would be one of 'infinite difficulty', with the state of the country's
finances made 'very embarrassing' by war and the verbal assaults on the
Government certain to be 'very severe' in view of recent events. He hardly
knew which prospect made him more alarmed. 'By fagging and assistance' he
might get on in office, but he doubted that he could act his part properly in the
House:

A good deal of debating must of course devolve upon the person holding the
Chancellorship of the Exchequer; all persons not born with the talents of Pitt
or Fox must make many bad speeches at first if they speak a great deal on
many subjects, as they cannot be masters of all, and a bad speech, though
tolerated in any person not in a responsible situation, would make a Chan-

cellor . . . exceedingly ridiculous, particularly if his friends could not set off against his bad oratory a great knowledge and capacity for business; and I should be apprehensive that instead of materially assisting Perceval, I should only bring disgrace and ridicule upon him and myself.[16]

All this Palmerston told the Prime Minister at their first meeting. Perceval must have been pretty desperate to persist in trying to advance such a nervous youngster on his front bench. Perhaps, he suggested, Palmerston should first feel his way by taking a lordship of the Treasury now and the chancellorship only when he had proved his capacity for 'fagging' and speaking. But that idea was not much liked by either of them, Palmerston because he did not think he would be given long enough to become sure of himself and Perceval because he thought he might have to bear his double burden for too long without effective help. So the Prime Minister made his third suggestion, that he might be able to offer Palmerston the office of Secretary at War.[17]

Unlike the chancellorship, this curious office did not usually take its incumbent into the Cabinet, though the precedent had been created for William Windham in 1794 and the outgoing Canningite Secretary had also been a member. Years afterwards Palmerston recalled that Perceval had told him the War Office would not give him a seat in the Cabinet. But in his recent approaches to others (including Yorke, Bragge Bathurst, Charles Long and Lord William Bentinck, who had all refused it), Perceval had certainly offered the Cabinet with the office and it is probable that in Palmerston's case he always intended to leave him free, whether as Chancellor or Secretary at War, to enter the Cabinet or not as he chose. In any case, Palmerston avowed to Malmesbury, that would not affect his decision. What he pretty frankly admitted would do so was the lesser degree of risk he saw in the routine of the War Office. 'From what one has heard of the office,' he wrote, 'it seems one better suited to a beginner, and in which I might hope not to fail, or in which one would not be so prominent if one did not at first do as well as one ought to do.' If the Government should not last long, 'the ground of the War Office is, I think, *quite* high enough for me to leave off upon'; and, as he told his sister, if it did last, the War Office, though 'a very great confinement & fag' and 'not much less laborious than the Exchequer', would not, after he had learned the business, require so much 'preliminary preparation' or his taking 'so prominent a part' in the House of Commons. [18]

Perceval gave Palmerston until Wednesday, 18 October, to make up his mind. In the meantime Palmerston hurriedly gathered advice, from his colleagues at the Admiralty, from his brother and from Malmesbury. Mulgrave talked about it 'in the kindest and most handsome manner' and advised him to take it if he was 'not nervous about it'. He received almost precisely similar advice from his colleague at the Admiralty, Robert Ward (later Plumer Ward), with whom he walked up Hyde Park discussing the subject. But William, who had not been specifically asked for advice but had intercepted his brother's letter to Malmesbury, reacted in a rather unflattering manner.

'Your letter certainly surprised and pleased me very much,' he wrote, 'as it is extremely flattering that these offers should be made to you who are so young, and wholly dependent on yourself, having no great connexions or interests to push you forward. At the same time it is I am sorry to say a great proof of the weakness of the present administration that Perceval should have so many things to dispose and no old stagers of weight to offer.' He was, moreover, glad that Harry had refused the Exchequer as it was 'too high' for a young man; it would have required too much speaking in the House for him to have done the office work properly and have invited comparisons with Pitt and Petty. Perhaps Malmesbury was beginning, like his wife, to sense the flaws in the young man's character, for, though much more discreetly phrased, his reply also expressed doubts about the Exchequer and a preference for the War Office. More probably, however, it was the weakness of Perceval's position rather than of Palmerston's qualifications that checked his vicarious ambitions. So on Wednesday Palmerston went again to Perceval's in order to accept the War Office. But it turned out then that the Prime Minister was still not in a position to make a definite offer and that there was a distinct prospect that Palmerston might end up after all with nothing better than a mere lordship of the Treasury.[19]

Perceval had written to Milnes as well as to Palmerston on 14 October, and while he waited for Milnes, who had much further to come, he had perhaps reflected on Palmerston's reticence and developed an even more decided preference for the other. In any case he frankly told Palmerston at their second meeting that he was very attracted by the prospect of including Milnes in his Administration and so detaching a rising star from the Canningites. Palmerston's disappointment, however, was not to last for long, for Milnes, though perhaps a better speaker, was certainly more nervous still. 'One morning, while we were at breakfast,' wrote his wife, 'the King's messenger drove up . . . with a despatch from Mr Perceval, offering Mr Milnes the choice of a seat in the Cabinet, either as Chancellor of the Exchequer or Secretary of War. Mr Milnes immediately said, "Oh, no, I will not accept either; with my temperament I should be dead in a year".' Mrs Milnes 'knelt and entreated that he should . . . but all was to no purpose.' But he came down all the way from Scarborough and only after a long weekend of agitated consultations in London did he finally decline. He had a 'long conference' with Perceval on the Saturday and at the Prime Minister's urging another of an hour's length with Canning on the same day. He was supposed to give his reply to Perceval the next day at dinner; instead he wrote on the Sunday evening to ask Palmerston for an interview the next morning, at which he surprised Palmerston 'exceedingly' by his refusal of office from 'real and unaffected diffidence'. Milnes then went with Palmerston to Perceval's and told the Prime Minister that after hearing both sides he had decided that he could 'heartily' support the Government but definitely not join it. At the same Downing Street meeting, however, Palmerston found that the way was still not entirely clear for him. For in the meantime, at Malmesbury's suggestion, the Exchequer had been offered to his old rival and neighbour, George Rose. But Rose dithered and meanwhile Robert Dundas, who had accepted the Colonial Office, had found that he might have to withdraw on account of the jealousy of his father, Lord Melville. So when Palmerston went with Milnes to Downing Street on Monday and had the War Office once again dangled before him he found that it was still 'conditional' on Perceval's delicate and incomplete arrangements working out, and that even if Rose were to accept the Exchequer it might be more 'convenient' to the Government then for Palmerston to take one or both of Rose's present offices as Treasurer of the Navy and Vice-President of the Board of Trade. Inevitably, in view of the complaisant line he was now taking with the Prime Minister, Palmerston agreed to do whatever Perceval wished.[20]

Fortunately for Palmerston, Perceval soon found in the Earl of Liverpool a substitute for Dundas at the Colonial Office – and when first Rose and then Charles Long, though neither was an unequivocal Canningite, refused the Exchequer he decided that he had better keep that office after all. So, at last, on 26 October, Palmerston's appointment was finally settled with the King. But he did not take the seat in the Cabinet which had been provisionally offered him again on the 23rd, and positively refused. Since it was unusual for the Secretary at War to sit in the Cabinet, he explained to Malmesbury, it was 'consequently not an object to me for appearance' sake; and considering how young I am in office, people in general, so far from expecting to see me in the Cabinet by taking the War Office, would perhaps only wonder how I got there. . . . the business of the Department will, I take it, be quite sufficient to occupy one's time.'[21]

It would appear from such comments as have survived that the reaction of Palmerston's immediate colleagues at the Admiralty was generally favourable to his promotion. Robert Ward, of whom he seems to have made something of a friend, commented at the time on 'the talents and excellent understanding, as well as the many other good qualities as well as accomplishments, of this very fine young man'. And in addition to the recommendation of his chief, Mulgrave, Palmerston was also commended to the Prime Minister by the Secretary of the Admiralty, William Wellesley-Pole (Wellington's brother), who wrote to express his 'very high opinion of his sense and judgment' and his confidence in his future success in office. Indeed, only one junior minister is known to have said anything to the contrary. This was Lord Lovaine, Palmerston's old Johnian acquaintance and Cambridge supporter, who wrote to Perceval to resign from the Board of Control since he felt he had a better claim to advancement. Perceval replied: '. . . I certainly do think that I have brought forward into a more prominent and useful situation a young man of considerable parliamentary promise, and one who in my judgment has given proof of such talents as I conceive will be of great use to His Majesty's service.' Lovaine decided to stay. But when word of Palmerston's appointment got

about it was greeted generally with surprise and in some cases with contempt.
Most merely listed him among several of what the Chief Justice called the
'infinitesimals of the 2nd order' with whom Perceval was compelled to fill up
his 'Babyhouse'. Canning reacted similarly, referring to Palmerston as
'another younker'. But some picked out Palmerston's appointment as
especially surprising. William Huskisson, who as Canning's lieutenant could
hardly be expected to be kind, was reported as thinking it 'a very bad
appointment', and even worse than Croker's. Still more preoccupied with
damning Croker's appointment as Secretary of the Admiralty, Brougham
scarcely bothered to mention Palmerston's in his letters to Grey; but he did
find time to make a sideswipe at this 'feeble young courtier' in one to Holland
House. This, however, was an expression he broadcast rather indiscriminately,
and another Edinburgh acquaintance, John Ward, whose spite was equal to
Brougham's jealousy, also revealed more about himself than Palmerston when
he wrote to their old professor's wife: 'This appointment will perhaps be a
subject of criticism, but with very little reason, for he surely is as fit for that
office – as much pointed out for it by public opinion – as Lord Mulgrave . . . is
for the Admiralty, or Robt Dundas for the conduct of the war.' Malmesbury,
on the other hand, forecast great things: 'I enjoy in prospective the vision of
your being the leading man in the Country.' And so it turned out, but not in
Malmesbury's time – nothing like it. Instead Palmerston was to stay at the
War Office for almost nineteen years; and having refused the Cabinet in 1809,
he had to wait nearly another eighteen before he got the chance again and
took it. In retrospect, therefore, the War Office appeared less a stepping-stone
than a dead end. Indeed, he made of it almost precisely what he had told
Malmesbury he would – an office of routine.[22]

Palmerston kissed hands on 1 November; but his predecessor, Granville (as
it is convenient to call Granville Leveson-Gower, even though he did not
assume that style till 1815), had introduced him to the office on the afternoon
of 26 October, and he had already entered on his duties on the morning of
Friday, 27 October. 'There appears to be full employment in the office,' he
wrote, 'but at the same time not of a nature to alarm one, and I think I shall
like it very much.'[23]

This bland comment of Palmerston's disguises a good deal of uncertainty.
The office of Secretary at War (which in 1855 was absorbed by the new
Secretary for War) is not merely difficult, it is almost impossible to describe. It
was not responsible for military policy; that was the business of the Secretary
of State for War and Colonies. It was not in charge of personnel and discipline;
they were the sphere of the Commander-in-Chief. It did not control the supply
of arms and equipment; these were the functions of the Ordnance and
Commissary-General. It did not even pay the Army; that was the job of the
Paymaster-General. But it was concerned primarily with finance and with
acting as a sort of constitutional buffer between the Army and the public, and

the complex nature of these responsibilities, together with the curiously complicated structure of Army organization, deeply involved the War Office one way or another in virtually all aspects of military policy and administration, and its interference and authority therefore overlapped in widely varying degrees with responsibilities that supposedly centred elsewhere.

At the beginning of the nineteenth century the more strictly *military* aspects of policy and command, especially the conduct of war and training, promotion and discipline, were vested in the Secretary of State for War and Colonies and the Commander-in-Chief acting for the Crown. The *civil administration* of the Army, however, was vested in the Treasury and its subordinate, 'expending' departments of pay and supply. These latter were respectively those of the Secretary at War and the Paymaster-General on the one hand and of the Master-General of the Ordnance and the Commissary-in-Chief on the other. But neither the functions nor the responsibilities of any of these departments were quite so distinct as reason would appear to suggest. The Horse Guards (by which name the C.-in-C.'s establishment was commonly known), for example, jealously guarded its grip on purchase and promotion; but it was the Secretary at War (operating from the same set of buildings) who was the channel for publishing commissions in the *Gazette* and recording promotions. Then again, the Commissariat usually acted as an aid to, not a substitute for, the regimental organization, providing supplies only when the regiments' own means were unlikely to be adequate, for example when serving overseas; while the Ordnance, which supplied both Army and Navy with armament and came under the Treasury for purposes of accounting, directly controlled the corps of Artillery and Engineers, commanding them independently of the Horse Guards and paying them independently of the War Office. Moreover, while the heads of all four departments were responsible to Parliament – the Commissary-in-Chief indirectly through the Treasury, but the two other civilians, Secretary at War and Paymaster-General, always as M.P.s, and the Master-General, though like the C.-in-C. a distinguished soldier, usually as a member of the Cabinet – a complicated system of crosschecks and balances endlessly confused an already complex situation.[24]

This was most apparent in the War Office's role as buffer between public and Army. In addition to its special concern with finance it was the medium for correspondence on all subjects between the general public and the Horse Guards, and the Secretary – along with the Judge-Advocate-General – was the spokesman in Parliament for the C.-in-C., whose personal relationship to the monarch was reinforced by carefully excluding him from the Cabinet. This made the Secretary spokesman, for example, in matters of discipline, for which he had no responsibility and perhaps no liking. As a matter of convenience as much as constitutional theory, it also made him responsible for the annual enactment of the Mutiny Bill and Articles of War and, indeed, for all the legislation relating to the Army. On the other hand, as Parliament's watchdog against the evils of a standing army, he was also 'especially charged with the protection of the civil subject from all improper interference on the part of the military'. This obliged him, for example, to supervise the apprehension and escort of *alleged* deserters, the billeting of forces within the United Kingdom, and the removal of troops from the vicinity of elections.[25]

The complicated consequences of checks and balances also obtruded into the War Office's major responsibility in matters of finance. In theory Parliament exerted an ultimate check upon the whole system of finance through an independent Board of Audit Commissioners. But in practice this was a very slow and imperfect process. It was uncertain whether it was intended to re-examine in detail accounts already passed by other departments of state or accept, for example, the War Office's clearance of regimental accounts. The board was quite unable to check properly the so-called 'extraordinaries' of wartime expenditure, which were 'contingent' and therefore ill-defined; and in a long-drawn-out war it fell far behind even with the 'ordinary' expenditure. To curb abuse in the resort to 'extraordinaries' and to prevent fraud in the interval between payment and final audit of the 'ordinaries', therefore, the Treasury had its own Comptrollers of Army Accounts to authorize any extraordinary expenditure and to examine the accounts of the Paymaster-General and the Commissary-in-Chief, together with the latter's contracts and the regimental muster-rolls on which the gross amounts of pay were based. Perhaps inevitably, as the Commissioners' tasks continued to increase in wartime, from 1806 they had to be more selective in their methods, while the three Treasury Comptrollers (a fourth was added in 1814 to accompany the Army abroad) also expanded their activities and took over direct charge of the Commissariat. These direct parliamentary and Treasury checks, however, overlapped with those separately exerted by the War Office.[26]

The Secretary at War was supposed to exercise 'a direct control' over all the arrangements by which any charge was made additional to or different from those sanctioned by Parliament. That is to say, he was to check in detail that the ordinary expenditure corresponded to what Parliament had voted and the extraordinary to what the Treasury had authorized as made necessary by circumstances arising in the intervals between the annual estimates. This implied a general concern with both the consolidation and the audit of accounts. Given also his practical concern with accounts and his special responsibility to Parliament, it was natural enough that one of his principal duties was, on behalf of the Colonial Secretary and the C.-in-C., to prepare the annual Army (but not Ordnance or even Irish Army) estimates for the approval of the Treasury and to present them to the House of Commons.[27]

The greater part of the amounts included in these estimates provided for the pay of the Army and its pensioners. It is important to remember, however, that given the English prejudice against making mercenaries of their own nationals, the 'pay' of the officers was not intended to be much more than a sort of 'honorarium' for gentlemen of independent means; and given the social conditions of the time, that of common soldiers was to be no more than was necessary to maintain an organized force in existence. Recruits came forward through the inducement of bounty money; they were retained by the threat of severe punishment. Any more generous treatment by way of increased pay would, in the view of a man like Wellington, have made expenditure on the Army intolerable to public opinion or, in the view of one like Windham, habitual drunkards of its soldiers. Much of what was voted as 'pay' and allowances, therefore, was really intended to maintain a man as a useful soldier, not as compensation. A considerable portion was allocated to cover the cost of his food ('subsistence') and of his clothing and accoutrements ('off-reckonings'), while smaller sums were absorbed by charges for hospital services and fees ('poundage') for running the whole incredible system.[28]

The pay of the private soldier had been fixed in 1797 at 1/- a day (though the Foot Guards received a little more in recognition of their behaviour in 1688), and that shilling notionally included 6d. for rations (1½d. for a pound of bread and 4½d. for three-quarters of a pound of meat). There was no further increase of pay, as such, until 1867. But long-service increments were introduced by Act of Parliament in 1806. Hitherto the periods of enlistment had varied considerably in the case of wartime volunteers; but for the regulars it was for 'life', though in practice the limit appears to have been thirty years and a man of good character could purchase an early discharge. However, in order to encourage enlistment during the prolonged French wars, the 1806 Act made provision not only for long-service pensions as a matter of right, but also for short periods of enlistment and increments of pay on re-enlistment. Originally intended as a substitute for life enlistment but an optional alternative to it from 1808 until 1829, the new arrangements gave the private soldier two increments of 1d. a day after each of seven and fourteen years in the infantry and ten and seventeen in the cavalry. A further change was made in 1822 with the hope of achieving economy at the same time as encouraging longer enlistment by arranging that those recruited after 24 January 1823 should forego the first increment and receive the extra 2d. a day only after the full fourteen or seventeen years. From time to time various 'contingent allowances' were added or deductions waived or increased according to market conditions. In 1808 the following extra allowances were approved: 1d. a day for beer money; ½d. a day innkeepers' billeting; 1d. a day lodging allowance for married men; 11d. a day for innkeepers' victualling when on the march; a variable allowance of from ¼ to 1½d. a day for the inflated cost of meat; and (save for the cavalry who, however, received extras for the inflated cost of forage) 2/6d. a year for cleaning materials for arms and 2/9d. a year for altering clothing.[29]

The means by which regimental monies were paid out was both curious and chaotic, its historical justification obscured by an irrational process of change and its practice exposed to the constant peril of abuse. Theoretically, and as a direct inheritance from the old system by which private gentlemen were 'commissioned' to raise and equip a force in return for a lump sum, the provision of subsistence and clothing was the immediate responsibility of the regimental colonels, each of whom was issued with a gross amount based partly on the muster-roll of his regiment and partly on an official establishment deliberately inflated with numbers of fictitious or 'warrant' men. In practice this meant that while the full 'stoppage' of 6d. would be made from each man's pay so as to meet the cost of his basic subsistence, no deductions were made in respect of clothing and accoutrements since these were covered by the 'off-reckonings' or difference, after certain deductions, between the gross sum received for the notional establishment and the outgoings in respect of pay and subsistence. An attempt was made in 1803 to simplify the system by laying down specified scales for 'off-reckonings'; but the payment for fictitious men, who might be as many as ten per cent, was continued in spite of criticism. With the aid of the sums received the colonels contracted individually for the supply of subsistence, clothing and accoutrements, privately when at home but usually through the Commissariat when on foreign service. The men were, however, fitted out with clothing and equipment on patterns approved and inspected by a Board of General Officers. At the beginning of the century there appear to have been *ad hoc* boards to approve clothing and to consider the claims of officers for losses (including regimental clothing and equipment). But in 1803 a permanent Clothing Board was established and in 1810 a permanent Board of Claims; in 1816 they were united in one Consolidated Board.[30]

The details of this financial system consequently varied from time to time and even from regiment to regiment. But in general the intention was to get new units started with twenty-four months' off-reckonings for cavalry and twenty for infantry and thereafter to provide new uniforms every year for the infantry and every two years for the cavalry; greatcoats were to be provided every three years. In spite of the supervision from headquarters, however, there were frequent complaints that the cloth did not match the clothiers' promises and that greatcoats in particular were rarely satisfactory for service in such cold places as North America. So a central greatcoat fund was set up from which the regimental off-reckonings might be supplemented and, when this did not resolve the problem, the system was reversed so that the colonels paid an annual contribution of 1/10d. per man into the fund and the Commissariat supplied the coats. In 1808 the Commissary-in-Chief entered into a general contract for this purpose with John Trotter & Co., and in March 1810 Trotter's position was made official by appointing him Storekeeper-General, under the War Office at first but under the Commissariat from about 1815 and under the Ordnance from 1822. There appears to be some conflict of opinion about the benefits of this new system so far as the public purse and efficiency were concerned; but it does not seem to have made any significant inroads upon the profits traditionally accruing to the regimental colonels. For it continued to be the case that any surplus surviving after the proper provision of pay, clothing and subsistence was considered a legitimate part of the colonels' remuneration. The amounts of such profits varied widely, in particular according to the discrepancy between the establishment and effectives; but in 1808 one well-informed estimate was that the average profit made by a colonel at home was £500 to £700 a year, rather less in Ireland, perhaps £200 to £300 more in India.[31]

Since 1797 the monies voted annually by Parliament for all these purposes were held by the Bank of England and drawn as necessary, by the Paymaster-General for issue to the colonels' agents in the case of regiments on home service, and by the General Officer Commanding for issue to the agents and Commissariat in the case of foreign service. The agents then made issues to the regimental paymasters and the paymasters in turn paid both the tradesmen and, after the deduction of 'stoppages', the soldiers. The paymasters dealt with the tradesmen direct, but the soldiers' net pay was handed over to the company captains for distribution. For any balance or 'profit' left over from all this the agent was of course responsible to the colonel. The War Office, however, intruded both at source and at regimental level: they alone could authorize the Paymaster-General's applications to the bank or certify the final settlement of the annual accounts between him and the colonels' agents. At the same time the War Office also communicated directly with the regimental paymaster. For in 1798 it had been decided that paymasters should not be serving officers, lest other military responsibilities divide their attention and military discipline intrude to subject them to the undue influence of their immediate, and interested, superiors. It was acknowledged that military experience would be a considerable asset and it was hoped that paymasters would be drawn chiefly from reduced and half-pay officers attracted by remuneration at the rate, in the case of a regiment of 500 men, of 15/ - a day plus expenses and the assistance of a sergeant-clerk. But, while nominated by the colonel, the paymaster was vetted by the War Office and commissioned by the King. He could therefore be dismissed only by the King or removed like any other commissioned officer by court martial. He was not answerable to the colonel (or to the colonel's agent) and the colonel in turn was responsible only for the paymaster's character at the time of his nomination and not for his subsequent conduct. Consequently it was to the War Office that the paymaster rendered his periodic, provisional accounts (quarterly after 1806) upon which they would authorize the issues made by the Paymaster-General as advances to the agents. He was subject to a fine and suspension without pay if he failed to render them on time. He was also personally answerable to the public for any disallowance in his accounts and for that reason he was required to give a personal bond of £2,000 and two sureties of £1,000 each. But while the paymaster was bonded, the agent, through whose hands passed even larger sums, was not.

By the strict letter of the law the regimental colonel was undoubtedly responsible for the failure of his agent and he was therefore advised that he ought to obtain private security from him. But few agents seem to have failed about this period and most colonels did not bother to demand security. In the few cases of failure the colonels had accepted their liability and paid up. But the Horse Guards argued that such was now the interference of the War Office between the regimental paymaster on the one hand and the colonel and his agent on the other that it was doubtful if the colonel should any longer be held responsible. A Commission of Military Enquiry, which had been set up by Act of Parliament in 1805 and kept Palmerston on his toes and historians well-informed by probings and reports it made for almost a decade, felt in 1808 that the law remained clear on this point; but to obviate all possibility of liability falling upon the public it urged that the War Office deal with paymasters only through the agents and that colonels be required, rather than merely advised, to take security. But neither recommendation was adopted, the former because it did not suit the War Office and the latter because the agents said it would make the business unattractive. There seems to have been some truth in the agents' case. It was the agent's duty to present annual accounts so as to enable the War Office to issue 'clearing warrants' for the final account to be adjusted and settled between him and the Paymaster-General. In spite of considerable paring down by the War Office and widespread suspicion that agents usually profited from the temporary enjoyment of large overpayments, it was demonstrated that any subsequent adjustment had usually to be made in favour of the agent. There were some difficulties, more especially arising out of the failure of agents who had been authorized to receive the pay of officers serving overseas. In these cases, where the paymaster was bypassed, it was necessarily unclear whether, at the time of his failure, the agent had issued the pay officially on behalf of the colonel or received it privately on behalf of the officer. Still, in Palmerston's time there was apparently only one failure that brought large losses upon the public, and that was in the unusual case of an agent for recruiting services. Consequently, even after nearly twenty years' experience he would still deem the whole system the best that could be devised.[32]

As Secretary at War, then, Palmerston found himself in 1809 representative of the Army in Parliament and at the same time watchdog for Parliament over the Army. Neither role was at all likely to make him popular. The one made him the target of the constant criticism of the tyranny and expense of standing armies; the other the object of the bitter distrust and resentment of disappointed officers. Given that the administrative organization of the Army was so incredibly complex, its distribution of authority chaotic and the lines of responsibility obscure, his situation was fraught with great difficulty and even danger. Given, moreover, that in a decade and more of war the army of regulars and militia had expanded rapidly to over a quarter of a million men and that the Peninsular campaign had barely begun, the War Office hardly seemed up to its task. It had, indeed, already proved itself incapable of keeping up with its business. Little more than a week after taking up his duties Palmerston wrote:

> I continue to like this office very much. There is a good deal to be done; but if one is confined it is some satisfaction to have some real business to do; and if they leave us in long enough, I trust much may be accomplished in arranging the interior details of the office, so as to place it on a respectable footing.
>
> Its inadequacy to get through the current business that comes before it is really a disgrace to the country; and the arrear of Regimental Accounts unsettled is of a magnitude not to be conceived.[33]

Apparently there were about 40,000 regimental accounts in arrears, some of them dating back as far as 1783. To put such a sorry state of affairs to rights would be, as Malmesbury acknowledged, a 'Herculean labour'. Yet the War Office had several times been expanded and reorganized in order to grapple with it. Underneath the minister and his Deputy Secretary, the work of the office was arranged in two branches, the Correspondence, or General, Department under the First Clerk and the Accounts Department under the Chief Examiner. In December 1797, when payment of War Office personnel by 'fees' deducted from disbursements was abolished and the new system of regimental paymasters introduced, the establishment was set at three 'principal' clerks and sixteen others in the Correspondence Department and three Assistant Examiners and eighteen clerks in the Accounts Department. In addition there was a small number of messengers, office-keepers and domestic staff. The total burden of salaries was £16,070 per annum. But by 1808 the pressure of more than a decade of war and military expansion had forced a very considerable increase in actual numbers and expense. The number of messengers alone had risen to twenty-three and the clerical establishment to over one hundred at an annual cost in salaries of very nearly £30,000. And to this had to be made the addition – or rather, since it had been established in 1796 and carelessly omitted in the establishment of 1797, the 'discovery' – of the Foreign Department. This handled the accounts of foreign corps in British pay and being therefore temporary had been entirely reduced on the peace of 1802. But on the recommencement of war in 1804 it had had to be re-formed in separate and, indeed, rather independently run offices at No. 13 Duke Street. It too had doubled in size over the years, and in 1809, even though the two senior posts were held by the same man, had a clerical staff of eight or nine paid out of the general parliamentary vote for foreign contingencies. There were also a 'Paymaster of Widows' Pensions' and a 'General Agent for Volunteers and Disembodied Militia'. The first was a 'perfect sinecure', what few duties there were being performed by a deputy, and following a recommendation of 1797 it was due to be abolished on the death of the last incumbent, General H. E. Fox. On the other hand, the General Agency, which had been set up in June 1803 to provide a centralized service for the reserve units whose permanent cadres were too small and periods of training too short for it to be worth-while to have proper regimental agents, had by 1810 swelled to an establishment of ten clerks, working as a virtually independent department from its chief's house in Great George Street.[34]

In spite of almost doubling in size, the Accounts Department in particular proved incapable of keeping up with its business. As early as December 1797 a separate division had been set up specifically to deal with arrears, but the current accounts continued to fall behind, partly because of the calling out of the militia in 1798 and partly because of a deterioration in the quality of regimental paymasters as the army expanded. The addition of nine clerks in 1799-1800 apparently had no great effect and only a change at the top by the replacement in 1801 of an old and inefficient Chief Examiner and a subsequent rearrangement of the office made any appreciable difference. Everyone evidently relied most on catching up after the end of the war. Yet when peace came, in 1802, it proved very short-lived, and soon after the war had recommenced another ten clerks were added, in 1803-4, and another new branch was set up – in Parliament Street, and later Duke Street, as the Horse Guards was full – to deal with the arrears accumulated since 1797. Soon afterwards, in 1805-6, some regimental accounts were also changed from a monthly to a quarterly basis. But still the number of unsettled accounts continued to mount in the 'Current' Department, while neither of the special Arrears Departments managed to finish its share of the work.[35]

Some of the factors contributing to this sorry state of affairs were readily brought to light when the Parliamentary Commission of Military Enquiry questioned the War Office people in 1807-8. In the first place it turned out that although there was a six-day working week and no established holidays beyond Christmas Day and Good Friday, Saturdays were usually free during the long parliamentary recess and the regular office hours lasted only from eleven till four, instead of the minimum of six hours usually worked by other government departments, or the seven or eight by the War Office itself twenty years earlier. Yet at the same time a good deal of extra payment was made, without proper check it was suspected, for overtime put in either in the office or at home. And this applied to senior as well as junior clerks. The three principal assistants to the Chief Examiner, for example, each in this way added £200 to their salaries of £800, £900 and £1,000. Moreover, although there was some notion of a scale of salaries and it was not expected that large sums would be granted without Treasury approval, it appeared that in practice the Secretary still had almost complete freedom with both appointments and remunerations. Consequently, in spite of the abolition of the fees system in 1797 and further Treasury instructions in 1807, sinecures, pluralism and nepotism persisted. It was no longer possible, as it had been a decade earlier, for the Deputy Secretary – then Matthew Lewis, father of the author, 'Monk' Lewis – to combine his post with that of First Clerk so as, through the latter's customary right of distributing the fees collected in the office, to award himself in 1796 – year of extraordinary military activity – the immense sum of £18,000 or, with the abolition of that system in the following year, thereafter to receive salaries of £2,000 and £1,200 for each of his respective posts. But it was possible, when he resigned in 1803 after more than thirty years' service, for him to retire on an annual allowance of £2,000 and in addition to collect a gratuity of £2,500 in token compensation for the loss of fees of over £40,000 since 1796.[36]

Other abuses obtained from top to bottom. For example, William Merry, whose salary as Chief Examiner was £1,500 a year, also enjoyed a life interest, worth about £750 p.a., in the supply of coals to the garrison of Gibraltar; it was a perquisite given him as long ago as 1783 when he was private secretary to Sir George Yonge. But perhaps the most remarkable case was that of one of the principal clerks, Richard Brown, who in addition to his salary of £750 received, by the suspension of regulations, an allowance of £266.18s. 0d. a year in lieu of his half-pay as a retired Deputy Commissary-General and, for fourteen months' personal service to a previous Secretary at War, another £150 as a retired private secretary. The usual emolument for an acting private secretary was £300. According to his chief it was reduced to a special allowance of £100 for extra duty if the private secretary also held a regular appointment in the office. Brown, however, admitted to the Commissioners that he had been authorized to receive the full £300 in addition to his regular salary of £750. Moreover, to collect a government pension at the same time as an official salary was specifically forbidden; but for Brown the regulations had been suspended in both instances.[37]

Among the personnel at the humbler end of the scale the office-keeper, Joseph Foveaux, though appointed as recently as 1806, was too old or ill even to send in written evidence to the Commission. Instead it was done for him by the Examiner's first assistant, who was evidently his son, Michael. The Foveaux had each in turn, but the son before the father, been recruited into the office during General Fitzpatrick's two brief periods as Secretary at War and they had some suspiciously close family connection with him. Michael Foveaux was one of those who collected both perquisites and overtime; but he may well have worked hard for them. Joseph Foveaux, however, performed no duties whatever, but out of his salary of £62 paid £40 to a female substitute, and out of perquisites of £356 paid £100 as a pension to one of his predecessors. Moreover, among the many messengers appointed by earlier Secretaries at least two also never put in an appearance, one getting paid as a retired butler of Yonge's and the other as an actual valet de chambre of Lord Liverpool's. Still worse, the areas penetrated by the appointees of a more recent minister virtually required reports all to themselves. William Windham, as Secretary at War in 1794-1801, had left behind a highly paid and underemployed official in charge of the so-called Miscellaneous Accounts, which after investigation in 1808 were reduced to the portion of a junior clerk; and the Commission more than hinted that two of Windham's close relations, whom he had introduced into quite senior positions, were very loosely supervised in the handling of very large sums of money in the Foreign Department. Yet neither ill-health nor incompetence seems to have earned dismissal. Col. Z. R. Tayler, Merry's predecessor as Chief Examiner, had succumbed to both apparently, and long before he retired in 1801. Indeed it seems that not even the most junior clerk was ever tested for his competence at the point of entry into the office or ever dismissed from it afterwards for anything but 'inattendance'. At worst the discovery of his utter ignorance of simple arithmetic would lead merely to his transfer from the Accounts to the Correspondence Department. Provided therefore that he was regularly there to sign on at ten-forty-five in the morning and his presence was generally in evidence till four o'clock, he was pretty well assured for the rest of his working life of a yearly salary of £90 rising by increments of £10 or £20 to at least £250.[38]

Although the Commission made several recommendations and warnings designed to correct all these abuses – and probably others too delicate even for them to mention – it was really quite clear that the main problems were the amount and complexity of the regimental accounts to be checked. Most of those consulted were inclined to ask for more staff but generally sceptical about the possibility of getting young men with arithmetic enough to cope. One departmental head frankly admitted that he would always need to check everything and therefore himself remain an unclearable bottleneck. Unfortunately they were far from agreed about the virtues of a rational overhaul of the system. One gave the opinion that it was the frequent changes in the recent past that had really slowed down the training of new personnel and thus delayed improvement so far; and this played straight into the hands of the Commander-in-Chief and his staff, who resisted most changes, vaguely on the grounds that they would 'produce a derangement in the military system' and specifically as an interference with the monetary interest that the colonels had in the present arrangements. Consequently the Commission, too, advised against any great disturbance in the status quo, more especially since the return of peace and the consequent reduction of the Army might make any new scheme of short-lived utility and of disproportionate expense. Nor were they convinced that it was practical, as the Comptrollers of Army Accounts had suggested in order to cover the cost of any expanded system, for the agents to take a cut of a quarter or even a third in their rates; they ought indeed to give security, but, if anything, the agents for infantry regiments, if not for cavalry, were already no more than adequately paid for their services. So far as off-reckonings were concerned, they did consider that there should be some tightening-up of assignments made to clothiers and that colonels should not be allowed to claim for fictitious men. But in the latter case there would have to be full compensation, of course, and in general they were satisfied (as previous parliamentary enquirers had not been) that the colonels were the best qualified to see to the clothing of their men.[39]

On only a single matter in the Commissioners' long-drawn-out series of reports did they appear seriously to disagree with the Horse Guards. One rather ingenious proposal from the War Office had aimed at reducing the number of the private soldier's allowances from eight to one. The scheme depended on transferring to the Commissary-in-Chief the whole of the supply and payment for bread, normal and inflated. The transfer of the extra allowance was straightforward enough in appearance; but it would have made no sense from the point of view of simplifying accounts if it had been separated in this way from the basic cost met by a stoppage from the soldier's pay. But the beauty of the scheme was that the stoppage of 1½d. a day happened to be the same as the total value of six out of the other seven allowances. It was proposed therefore to abolish all the allowances except that made to innkeepers for victualling on the march, and in return to issue the soldier with his one pound of bread a day free of all stoppages, transferring the whole charge for that commodity to the Commissary-in-Chief. The soldier would have to meet any 'inflated' cost of his meat, however, without the benefit of an extra allowance. The Horse Guards had had no objection to the transfer as such of bread (and, in the case of cavalry, of forage too); but they were mean enough to assert that the effect of the proposals in the long term would be to raise the income of the soldier beyond its already more than 'ample' level by replacing temporary cost of living allowances with a permanent reduction of stoppages. But the economizing instinct of the Commissioners was attracted by the scheme and, with regard to the remuneration of the soldier, they pointed out that the price of bread might fall and under the proposal benefit the public purse accordingly, while that of meat might also rise and at the expense solely of the soldier.[40]

The Commission also recommended simplifying the accounts, by separating those connected with the recruitment which took place in the United Kingdom from those of the regiments which though nominally concerned might actually be serving overseas. But otherwise they proposed only very minor improvements in the system, such as transferring to the Commissary-in-Chief, instead of sharing with the War Office, the whole of the accounts for each individual cavalry horse. And so far as the size of the War Office establishment was concerned, they rather accepted the notion that more staff would not help and concentrated instead on criticizing the lingering evidence of pluralism and on recommending entrance tests in arithmetic and longer hours of attendance. They did, however, take advantage of the criticism of frequent changes to suggest that in view of the way in which the political character of the Secretary at War produced a certain instability at the very top, the examination of the regimental accounts might best be passed over entirely to the Comptrollers of Army Accounts who, after all, already had a good deal of experience with checking the 'extraordinaries'.[41]

These various recommendations were evidently still in process of review and piecemeal application when Palmerston entered the War Office in October 1809. A mere two or three additional clerks had been recruited earlier in the year and the Treasury was also thinking of adding one more to prevent the current accounts falling even further behind. Within the office little seems to have changed save for the introduction of a very limited probationary system; certainly the office hours remained a mere five a day. This was in part because Palmerston's two immediate predecessors, Sir James Murray Pulteney and Granville, had each had rather a short time in office after the report had been made, and, as Palmerston said, because 'perpetual reference' was necessary to both Treasury and Commander-in-Chief. But it was also because with all their entrenched self-interest, the War Office personnel had no intention of tamely retreating in the face of criticism; they even contemplated turning the pressure for reform into an opportunity to be exploited. First, Pulteney disposed of the proposal to transfer the examination of regimental accounts to the Comptrollers by employing the same arguments that the Commissioners of Enquiry had used against a proposal of Merry's that a War Office Board should take over the greater part of the agents' work (and rewards): that it was the opposite of efficiency to transfer work from experienced into inexperienced hands. Nor, he pointed out, would any better check be obtained by transferring even experienced personnel from one office to another; on the contrary, it should continue to be done in the War Office where the relevant warrants were also issued. So, he concluded, the most obvious improvement to make would be in the means available within his own office. To this the Treasury could only reply that he was absolutely right and at their invitation he moved over to the counter-offensive. What was wanted in order to cope with the current accounts, he urged,was 'a separate establishment' supervised by three commissioners acting pretty independently under regulations laid down by the Secretary at War. He had three people in the office in mind and they had drawn up a comprehensive scheme for the new department.[42]

The submissions of the putative commissioners revealed luxurious dreams of power, patronage and pay. These were natural enough for men brought up in the office traditions of such seniors as Matthew Lewis. Equally natural were the suspicion and caution of the Treasury. But the Treasury was mollified by the intention of the new department to extend the office hours by one and tempted by the Secretary's suggestion that if the agents' role, and therefore the gross sums they handled, were not to be reduced then they might well afford a cut in their fees. Certainly it seemed utterly convinced of the necessity of a radical reform of the War Office and even of its considerable expansion. In principle, therefore, it had approved of Pulteney's notion of a separate department for the regimental accounts and authorized preliminary steps to this end being taken 'as soon as possible'. However, what it did not approve, in addition to some of the over-generous provisions for pay and promotion, was Pulteney's putting the cart before the horse. Before proposing a large new establishment he ought to have his 'commissioners' fix more precisely what was to be their new 'system' for settling the current accounts; to have made definite proposals about the size and scope of the remaining part of the War

Office; and not least to have indicated how the arrears were to be dealt with. By this time Pulteney had given way to Granville, but the response of the new minister, though comprehensive, showed that he was just as much under the influence of his departmental advisers.[43]

Although preparations for the wholesale reorganization of the War Office were therefore well-advanced when Palmerston took over, none of the details had actually been settled. Consequently he soon found himself up to his ears in work. 'I am leading a reformed life,' he wrote to his sister. 'I am up at a little after seven, breakfast between eight & nine, & go to bed at a little after twelve. This morning I have been fagging for 7 hours without stirring.' However, he did not expect again to have to work so hard in order, as he put it, to get the nomination of 'a few new clerks'. It was just as well he prepared himself so thoroughly, for on 23 November the Treasury pronounced at last. It reflected adversely on the ill-defined responsibilities of the 'commissioners', refuted the financial calculations made in support of the size of the new establishment, and refused to sanction some of the crucial features of the salary proposals. Above all, it declared the proposals for the general reorganization of the War Office to be 'wholly inadequate' and those for dealing with the arrears to be 'objectionable in other respects'. It strongly recommended that the minister give his *immediate* attention to devising a new system for tackling the current accounts and that he recognize the impossibility of applying it to any accounts earlier than those for 1810. And before they actually adopted it, the heads of the new department and some of their clerks should actively apply themselves to the clearing up of the arrears. Finally, the Treasury admonished, the increase in numbers should not be considered permanent, but clerks should be transferred to other work as the arrears were cleared off and no vacancy should be filled automatically and without reference to the Treasury. Indeed, at the end of 1810 the minister should report on the progress of the new system and reconsider the establishment with a view to either reducing or increasing it.[44]

Palmerston seems to have been more sensible or simply more cautious than his immediate predecessors. Instead of arguing too much with the Treasury he immediately promised to adopt or consider its points and pleaded the grounds of urgent necessity only for some indulgence in respect of the numbers in the rump of the old War Office. By adopting at least the main features of the methods advocated by the Treasury and by framing his pleas for men and money more modestly, Palmerston finally got most of what he wanted by the middle of February 1810. The Treasury insisted on several minor reductions and modifications of salaries (though it agreed to the Deputy Secretary having a single increment of £500 after five years), but was relatively liberal as regards numbers. The Correspondence Department was established at forty-nine in addition to the Secretary and his deputy; this was a notional increase of nine over the original establishment and five more than Granville had asked for. He did not do quite so well for the Foreign Department. He had asked for three additional clerks but he was probably never very confident of getting them, since he made his initial approach to the Treasury privately through Perceval. In the event he got an increase of only one. But the separation of the regimental accounts did make it possible to dispose of the lease on No. 13 Duke Street and to bring back the nine members of the Foreign Department into the main office.[45]

A short while before these changes, in December 1809, the Deputy Secretary, Francis Moore, decided to retire and was replaced by Merry. It is not at all clear why Moore should have gone; he had filled the post only for about six years and was still no more than forty-three years of age. Perhaps he had some reason to fear he would fall victim to the Tory prejudice against his family's Foxite connections and decided to quit in the afterglow of his brother's death at Corunna. But his going did make it possible to give Merry's former place of Chief Examiner to the old hand, George Collings, who since 1797 had been at work on the arrears accumulated up to that date. It had originally been proposed that the rest of the arrears should be consigned to the neglect of a few clerks' overtime, but in response to the Treasury, who maintained that this was inadequate and commented on the stark contradiction to the promise to abolish overtime allowances, Palmerston agreed that all the rest of the regimental accounts, current and arrear, should come under the three new Superintendents of Military Accounts, as they were now to be called. For them, too, Palmerston did rather well, with an establishment in addition to themselves of seventy-eight, one more than they had originally sought from Pulteney. Although the Treasury cut down some of the salary scales proposed and in particlar refused to countenance the 'unprecedented' notion of merit increments, the response was still fairly generous. The Treasury admitted the necessity of the scales extending high enough to absorb the present rates of pay of individuals, and since the office hours were to be increased to six and allowances for overtime discontinued, consented to the former 'allowances for extra business' also being absorbed by placing individuals at an appropriately high or even off-scale point.[46]

As a result, then, of the major expansion and reforms of 1809-10, Palmerston found himself with a staff of no less than 144 beneath him. Of these, 63, including the Correspondence, Foreign and Chief Examiner's Departments, stayed with him in the Horse Guards. The rest were to form the new Department of Military Accounts in the premises engaged by Granville at Numbers 10 and 11 Duke Street. The three superintendents – Michael Foveaux, Thomas Dods and John Stuart – were formally appointed by Palmerston on 7 December 1809; ten days later about two-thirds of their staff were made up by transfer from the old office; and the rest were recruited by new appointments shortly after.[47]

Following the several suggestions of the Treasury and with a view to their reporting on the various reforms proposed by the Commissioners of Military Enquiry and others, Palmerston directed the superintendents to examine the arrears up to the end of 1809 as well as the current accounts for the first quarter of 1810. But he had to wait a good deal longer for any substantial result than either he or the Treasury seems at first to have envisaged. Little if any direct saving had been made on agents' fees, because it turned out that their percentage was based only on the soldier's old gross rate of pay of 8d. a day; and that, in their own opinion, was already insufficient reward for their services, and in that of the Commander-in-Chief the minimum necessary to attract competent individuals to the job. If a cut of a quarter were to be made, the Horse Guards argued, agencies would fall still more into the hands of the 'great houses' (such as Greenwood & Cox, presumably) who lacked the personal relationship to the colonel and would start charging for all the many extras so far provided free. So it was agreed to leave the agency for infantry at its existing rate, and to make a cut in that for the cavalry, which, taking into account the new forage arrangements, would be the equivalent of one quarter in the old rate. About all, therefore, that Palmerston was able to report by the middle of 1810 was that the safety of the new premises in Duke Street had become endangered by the great weight of papers deposited in the attic, and that, as these had had to change places with the clerks on the ground floor, the superintendents were compelled to ask for an additional messenger.[48]

Palmerston made his first general report to the Treasury in March 1811 and it too hardly reflected any of the revolutionary improvement expected. Rather, he reported, the addition of another nine was needed to the staff of seventy at present working on the current accounts. This was in spite of the fact that the labour of ten examining clerks had been saved by the adoption in the first quarter of 1811 (and with respect to accounts dating from 25 June 1810) of a simplified system on the lines recommended in the 1808 report and with particular reference to recruiting. According to one of the two superintendents in charge of current accounts the saving made in this way was still being more than lost in the extra work occasioned by the 1808 allowances. For the attempt to simplify the system by transferring the charges for bread and forage had run into apparently endless difficulties. On the one hand, the Horse Guards suspected that the War Office was overstepping its proper sphere of authority; on the other, the Commissariat that it was attempting to unload an unfair share of the work. The Commissary-in-Chief, Colonel (later Sir) James Willoughby Gordon, seems to have been perfectly willing to take over the charge not only for bread and forage but also for meat; after all, the Commissariat already handled these items and supplied them under contract to the Army abroad. But he got it into his head that the War Office was trying to unload upon him the examination as well as the handling of the necessary accounts. Gordon, whose job had been created only the previous year in order to overhaul the Commissariat under the Treasury, was an energetic and ambitious man, but possibly not up to the task and evidently suspicious by nature. In addition he upset Palmerston by presuming to tell him the nature of the minister's own job (to which, in truth, he hoped very soon to succeed by favour of the court). 'Depend upon it', Palmerston wrote to one of his super-intendents, 'the less you tell him & the fewer things you put into his hands the better. He knows very little of the matter, [but] has I dare say very decided opinions on the subject, which nothing that you can say on them will at all alter, & will notwithstanding tell all the world that *he* has new modelled the War Office. He is a devilish clever active fellow, but inordinately vain, & self-opinionated.' In October 1811 Gordon was transferred to the Horse Guards as Quartermaster-General to the Forces and was succeeded in the Commissariat by the financier, J. C. Herries. The Prime Minister and the Paymaster-General then made a valiant effort to resolve this petty dispute. 'Here was a business', wrote the Paymaster, 'which the Secretary at War was willing to give up, & the Commissary-in-Chief to undertake & as the former had more upon his hands than he could easily manage & the latter was supposed to get through his business with great facility, the transfer seemed to be an obvious improvement.' So a scheme drawn up by Herries was com-mended as allocating to the Commissariat and War Office what belonged to their proper spheres of expenditure and examination. Yet still the matter did not end. From the tangled and incomplete papers it seems now impossible to discover quite why not. But it is not difficult to sense what had happened. Both offices had no doubt grown obstinate; and so too had Headquarters.[49]

The Horse Guards were already worried that the soldier was going to end up overpaid; and the notion of including meat in the transfer to the Com-missariat upset the delicate balance of advantages between public purse and private soldier in the fine calculations that lay behind the original plan. Still worse, at a time when the issuing by the War Office of circular instructions which had not first been cleared by the Horse Guards was already building up into a major conflict of constitutional principle between them, the War Office were similarly caught out in this affair as well. What seems to have happened was that in the interminable exchange of proposals and counter-proposals on this complicated matter, the War Office had presented to the Treasury as a positive solution what the Horse Guards had really meant to set up as an Aunt Sally. Colonel Torrens, the C.-in-C.'s military secretary, had written to Merry in December 1809 that the transfers proposed would require alterations in the pay structure and detailed what these might involve. Presumably he really meant to underline the difficulties of the scheme, but the following June Palmerston got the Treasury to approve a new procedure on the basis of Torrens's letter. When the draft of a circular intended to apply it was sub-mitted to him Torrens naturally vetoed it. But somehow a revised version was issued the next month without being resubmitted first to Torrens. A blast of rage came from the Horse Guards shortly after, and Palmerston's bland explanations a few days after that. Some blame seems to have attached to the Horse Guards for the carelessness with which Torrens had drafted his original objections; but even after getting Treasury approval and revising the proposals to suit objections from Headquarters, the War Office would have done well to check the final form of circular with the Horse Guards. It would have seemed a natural precaution in what had already become a sensitive matter of principle concerning circulars; and it would have had the added advantage in this case of exposing in better time the misunderstanding of substance between them. As it was the matter dragged on and on.[30]

The change of Commissary-in-Chief does not for some time seem to have helped much. The Horse Guards very much resented losing the Commissariat to a civilian; and Gordon's presence at Headquarters no doubt stimulated that resentment a good deal. But in the summer of 1812 he went out at last as Wellington's Q.M.G. in the Peninsula. There he amply confirmed Palmerston's ill-opinion of him: his behaviour as Q.M.G. was so arrogant, and his role as the 'particular friend and confidential informant' of the Whig Opposition in England so disloyal, that he had to be sent back home at the end of 1812. By that time the knotty question of the transfer to the Commissariat had still not been resolved and the allowances continued to rise and fall in accordance with the market and much to the irritation of the accountants. But the change in the Corn Laws in 1814 and the rapid fall in prices thereafter did lead to a 'natural' disappearance of the old allowances, and this seems (for from the imperfect state of the surviving papers it is impossible to be sure) to have enabled at last a transfer of meat, as well as bread and forage, without all the evil effects feared so by the Horse Guards. Henceforth in Great Britain (but not in Ireland for some reason) the soldier would continue to contribute 6d. from his pay for bread and meat and the Commissariat would supply them as he did overseas. But if the soldier thought he could do better on his own account, it still appears to have been possible for him to keep his 6d. and buy not from the official contractors but wherever else he liked. Indeed, although costs varied a great deal across the country from Cumberland to Kent, in 1822 it was calculated that the soldier's notional ration in Great Britain cost him on average only 4¼d. This seems to have upset the Duke of York, who was responsible for discipline, more than it did Palmerston, who was responsible for pay. The Horse Guards whined that the standard of 6d. had been set when prices were artificially high and that subsistence ought rather to be supplied in kind; then the public and not the profligate soldier would benefit from falling prices. The new system, however, survived both the duke's lifetime and Palmerston's period at the War Office.[31]

In his battle over the Commissariat Palmerston had been helped by continued pressure from the House of Commons. The Committee on Public Expenditure had endorsed the transfer of forage in 1811 and it had further suggested the abandonment of the ineffective muster checks. Palmerston welcomed this latter too. Indeed, for some time he harried the doomed Muster-Master-General with awkward questions about the emoluments of his clerks, their efficiency and their practice of subletting residential apartments in the office. In 1816 the office of Commissary-in-Chief was abolished and his department merged more closely under the Treasury; the following year the Muster-Master also disappeared. But the House of Commons Committee had at the same time, and without consulting the minister, also proposed a half-yearly instead of quarterly system of regimental accounts, biennial reports from the Secretary at War to Parliament, and, not least, the appointment of agents by him. Yet it was just such continual experiments and the consequent changes in blank forms, according to one of the superintendents, that constantly confused inferiors. 'Paymasters and others', he pointed out, 'have had a new lesson to learn every two or three months.' By this time Palmerston had also come to appreciate that such meddling threatened upheaval rather than reform. So he resisted the committee's proposals and for real improvements in the office looked instead to changes in personnel.[52]

This applied to the arrears as much as to the current accounts. When in December 1810 Palmerston had asked the superintendent in charge when he reckoned on clearing the arrears away, the reply was, with his present staff, in forty-five years. According to the later recollections of his closest colleague, Palmerston soon found that the 1809 reforms had proved 'a most inconvenient and dilatory mode of proceeding', the semi-separation of the military accounts in particular creating a vast amount of internal correspondence where little had existed before. It was difficult at first for him to discover quite what to do. But in January 1811 one of the junior superintendents was forced to retire on account of ill-health. Thomas Dods was unfortunately the best of the bunch; but his going gave Palmerston the opportunity of replacing him by his old friend Laurence Sulivan. Sulivan had been in the War Office for little more than a year and merely as Palmerston's private secretary; but he afterwards claimed that his new post soon gave him 'a thorough insight' into what was wrong and made him press urgently for radical changes. Such advice, coming even from this source, was not entirely welcome. 'I can assure you I feel as strongly as you do the necessity of making some arrangement for the accounts, current & arrear,' Palmerston wrote in the spring of 1811; 'but I am quite sensible that no good can be done unless the thing is taken up in good earnest & my days consist but of 24 hours, & my head is of a limited capacity & cannot apply to very many things at once; & for some time past the addition of Estimates, militia bill, election, canal bills, thankings, etc., to the ordinary business of attendance of office & the House has rendered it ridiculous to think of doing anything effectual with the office accounts & if you think otherwise all I can say is, you are as unreasonable as Lady Malmesbury herself.'[53]

Sulivan was 'unreasonable' for the rest of his working life. On the eve of his retirement in 1851 he rather unfairly suggested that Palmerston had never had more than nominal responsibility for applying the reforms of 1809, and implied that he had obstinately resisted suggestions from outside and was slow to give his 'deliberate attention' even to those of his friend. Yet Palmerston really does seem to have moved with reasonable speed and with some effect to reorganize the work of the Department of Military Accounts. First, and as early as June 1811, he added to the superintendents' load of work by transferring to them the task of settling the agents' as well as the regimental accounts. They were obviously best equipped to do it speedily, and in this way a partial examination, hitherto undertaken in order to facilitate the authorization of funds in good time, could be dispensed with. To this end he proposed to the Treasury that as an interim measure paid overtime should be reintroduced, but as a sweetener pointed out that the earlier settlement of the accounts would recover equally early for the Exchequer the overpayments which necessarily (as he asserted, in ignorance perhaps of previous evidence to the contrary) had to be made to the agents. Later in the year he got approval for an increase of eleven in the department. Two years later he came to grips with another internal problem. This was the tendency of the superintendents to act as an independent board. This had evidently been the original intention of Pulteney's nominees when they proposed to take an oath like the Commissioners of Audit and to assume full power to appoint and promote their subordinates. Their pretensions had not passed unnoticed by the Treasury, who had warned both Granville and Palmerston against them. So one of the superintendents had been named 'senior' instead of 'chairman', their patronage made subject to the Secretary's approval and their powers hedged about with detailed advice that they should devote only one day a week to so-called board business and be allowed to make no major changes without reference to him. But these precautions evidently did not quite serve and in the autumn of 1813 Palmerston put an end to any notion of a board by making each superintendent individually responsible to him for the work of his section. Finally, in 1815, Palmerston made the senior superintendent, Foveaux, take over the British arrears from 1804 to 1810, leaving his colleague Stuart with those up to 1803 and Chief Examiner Collings with those prior to 1798, but putting Sulivan in charge of the current accounts and those outstanding from 1811.[34]

All this may have been accomplished rather more slowly than Sulivan wished; but it was probably no more slowly than minimum discretion and some sense of office morale required. No one ever seems to have doubted, moreover, that the reforms achieved substantial success. If Palmerston made no other radical changes of principle in the 'system' of 1809, the abolition of the informal board in 1813 suggests the sort of vital contribution he did nevertheless make. It was intended, according to Sulivan's recollection, 'to throw more of the minor responsibility upon individuals' and to enable the minister himself to give 'a minute personal attention to the various important questions which arose'. This meant making his authority felt and getting better results from those employed rather than constantly seeking to reduce their number. Thus when, at the end of 1814, he had to report that the Department of Military Accounts had 'considerably exceeded' its estimated expenditure and the Treasury awakened to the fact that overtime allowances had been revived, he was able to crush their complaints not merely with the observation that they had sanctioned the practice, but by pointing out that by this means 1,243 agents' accounts had been settled since March 1812 and £93,000 disallowed and so recovered (or retained) for the State at a cost in salaries of less than £8,000. He also did not hesitate to apply for temporary and even permanent increases in his staff from time to time. Even so the peak of about 170 reached in 1815, the last year of war, was only fifteen or so above the original figure in 1810-11. Thereafter, with the restoration of peace, the figure dropped pretty steadily until, by the time Palmerston left in 1828, it was a mere seventy-five. Yet at the same time the arrears were rapidly cleared up, as the reduction of the Army allowed more and more clerks to be transferred from current accounts and as the disbanding of foreign corps converted the work of the Foreign Department wholly to arrears. At the end of 1814 there had been only eight men working on the arrears and nearly ninety on the current accounts, but by the end of 1815 the former had risen to thirty and the latter was under sixty-five; by 1817 there were nearly forty at work on the arrears and only just over fifty were left on the current accounts. So while in 1817 the House of Commons Select Committee on Finance could still find some traces of the eighteenth century to complain of, it could also note with warm approval that 'in the current accounts the arrear is inconsiderable, and by the more modern and judicious arrangement' of the office 'nearly the whole of the outstanding accounts from the year 1784 to the year 1797 have been settled'. At the end of 1817, when Collings retired, the separate department dealing with the pre-1798 arrears could be closed down and his post of Chief Examiner suspended. In 1819, when Superintendent Stuart retired, there was insufficient work outstanding in his section to warrant the appointment of a successor, and so the whole of the British arrears, from 1798 to 1810, were united under Foveaux. By October 1825 the work on the British arrears had advanced so much that eight or ten clerks could be transferred to the Foreign Department and shortly afterwards the whole of the arrears, British and foreign, were concentrated once more in a single department. And at last in 1826 the arrears were completely cleared up and the Duke Street branch virtually closed down; a few clerks remained, presumably as an overflow, but most of the premises were turned over to the Board of General Officers. So, when Joseph Hume sought in 1827-8 to fill the gap left by the demise of the Commission of Military Enquiry in 1819 and devoted an entire session to laying bare the condition of the War Office, Palmerston was able to make a very convincing defence.[55]

Obviously the restoration of peace in 1815 was an enormous aid to the clearing up of the mess in the War Office; but the achievement was still a great personal triumph for Palmerston and his assistants. For it is undeniable that even while the war lasted they had for the first time in over twenty years stopped the arrears from accumulating and so made their post-war task much easier. All this, moreover, was done despite both increased responsibilities and constant pressure from the Treasury for economy after the end of the war. As a responsible minister, well aware of the economic and financial difficulties of the post-war period and specifically charged with the perennial defence of the Army Estimates in the House of Commons, Palmerston fully acknowledged his duty to cooperate. But at the same time, in battling with the Treasury over the actual or prospective 'peace' establishment of his office, he constantly defended its cost and sought always to preserve a salary and career structure that would encourage effort and reward merit. In 1813 he made several requests for considerable improvements in both salaries and status: an increase in the number of senior clerks in the Correspondence Department so that several juniors might be given the rank and salary appropriate to the work they were actually doing; a general improvement to bring the salaries and status of the clerks in the Accounts Department into line with their colleagues in the Correspondence Department; increases for deserving supernumeraries; and both increases and an incremental wage structure for the messengers. Palmerston seems to have obtained most, if not all, of these.[56]

Once the war ended it became more a case of defending what he had than of demanding wholesale improvements. For, at the same time as congratulating the War Office on its progress with the accounts, the 1817 Select Committee mounted a new attack. It complained that several of the old abuses persisted, in particular that 'retired' allowances were still being paid to two former private secretaries currently employed in the office, that unnecessary extra allowances were being paid to clerks working on the Army Estimates, and that the number of messengers was still too high. It noted that the office hours were now ten till four, but suggested nine to four would be better. It also recommended sweeping reductions in the salaries of the higher officers. The minister's own salary of £2,480 was left alone; it was, after all, modest enough by the standards of the day. But for the Deputy Secretary's starting salary it proposed a cut of £500 from the present figure of £2,000 and for the other senior officials a maximum of £1,000 instead of £1,200 or £1,400. Palmerston warmly defended his department. He cut out the allowances to the estimates clerks and got rid of another twelve clerks and seven messengers (making twenty-eight and ten respectively since June 1815). But so far as the office hours were concerned he pointed out that these were purely nominal and that a good deal of overtime, now unpaid, was both expected and performed. And having carefully demonstrated that the salaries of the more senior members of his office compared unfavourably with those in similar departments, he successfully held up the proposed reductions, while agreeing for the time being to withhold increments for those newly promoted only until a new scale was finally settled. Evidently this had considerable effect, for when it turned again to the War Office in the following year the Select Committee adopted a rather neutral tone on these matters. After all, even though Palmerston had to admit that the total charge for his department in 1817 was about the same as it had been in 1813, it was nonetheless considerably less than the peak of over £70,000 exclusive of pensions reached in 1815. It continued, moreover, to decline steadily until by 1821 it was only just over £52,000. But if the House of Commons seemed mollified by all this, it was certainly not satisfied. The estimates of 1821 went more easily than usual, but the following year still found Palmerston having vigorously to defend the War Office establishment, for example by pointing out that since 1810 twenty-six of his clerks had died in the prime of life from pulmonary and other disorders, attributable, in his opinion, to their sedentary habits of work. In addition, in view of the pressure from the House of Commons, and after what Palmerston later called 'a sort of self-denying committee' of ministers had consulted together in August 1821, the Treasury had decided that unless it could show 'adequate cause' to be treated otherwise, every department should by January next return to the situation in which it stood in 1797; and that even if increases of staff could be justified by increased business, the emoluments involved should also correspond as far as possible to those of 1797. So that same month there had come to Palmerston a letter from the Treasury 'requesting' him to make more reductions and a minute drawing his attention to the War Office establishment of 1797.[57]

The actual number of employees in the War Office in 1821 was 136; the establishment of 1797, even with the addition of the then rudimentary Foreign Department, was only 51. Moreover, as Palmerston pointed out, even leaving the arrears aside, the work of the office had increased in the interval in ways that were likely to be permanent. There had been considerable changes in the system of accounting, especially in the year immediately after 1797, and a considerable part of the work of two minor departments – those of the Agent-General of Volunteers and the Commissary-General of Musters – had been absorbed in 1817. And was it really in the public interest, he shrewdly inquired, so to disrupt a department that had at last managed to get on top of its work of controlling expenditure and checking fraud? Nor was it any fairer to press so hard on the Correspondence Department. In 1797 the whole office had issued only 14,253 letters and warrants; in 1820 it was no less than 112,239. In the interval printing and lithography had been introduced wherever possible, but the many new allowances granted since 1797 and the better system of internal administration he himself had introduced had considerably increased the amount of paper work, while the growth of education among the lower classes had created many more people capable of making claims. So he proposed only a limited reduction from 136 to 122 in the actual establishment for 1822, at an estimated saving of £6,800. At the same time he proposed that when the arrears were finished there should be a permanent clerical establishment, including Secretary and Deputy Secretary, of 77 rather than 51, but by rearranging the salary scales and cutting down the number of senior posts on lines approved by the Treasury, the total cost be reduced by another

£11,800 to roughly £26,380. However, even in the prospective permanent establishment, he strongly resisted the higher salaries being cut as drastically as the Select Committee of 1817 had wished. Thus future First Clerks and Chief Examiners were to have theirs reduced from £1,400 to £1,200, not £1,000, and the Deputy Secretary was to have a fixed salary of £2,000 rather than serve for his first five years at £1,500. For the rest of the clerks the maximum would be reduced from £1,000 to £800, but the minimum remain at £90 and the scale in between be merely rationalized and consolidated. For the majority of the existing personnel the application of this new structure would clearly make little or no immediate difference, but, as Palmerston pointed out, the reductions at the top would make their long-term prospects rather less favourable than at present. But he had framed his proposals as a compromise that would have a 'due regard to Public Economy' at the same time as 'provide encouragement to the various classes of clerks'. And as far as the immediate changes for 1822 were concerned, it had been his 'endeavour to ascertain, not what appointments could be retained with demonstrable advantage to the Service, but what could be spared without paralysing the Dept.'[58]

Palmerston's proposals were evidently accepted as a reasonable compromise between retrenchment and efficiency and the next year, 1822, the Treasury approved his scheme for the permanent establishment. Only about some of the off-scale pensions he had proposed for reduced clerks did they demur as being too generous. Yet having, as he said, 'laid about . . . with a vigorous & unsparing pruning knife,' he subsequently found that his colleagues had been less conscientious, while his own department had afterwards collected still more business. In 1822 the War Office had taken over the accounts of the militia recruiting districts and had had transferred to them from Dublin all of the financial business of the regulars, militia and yeomanry in Ireland; the latter Palmerston estimated to be about one quarter of the whole British Army outside India. This new business forced him to ask for ten temporary clerks for six months in 1825. Then, later that year, the division of regiments into service and reserve battalions had added another set of accounts for every regiment that happened to have a service battalion abroad; in 1826 the number was no less than fifty-two. So when the winding up of the arrears drew near in the summer of 1826 and the time came to start putting into practice the new permanent establishment, Palmerston applied for a small increase. He also took the opportunity to press for other minor changes that would improve the chances of promotion. He proposed small increases in the number of the two highest grades of clerk, and in the second grade also an increase in the maximum salary, to bring them into line with their peers in other departments. In the two lowest grades he frankly admitted that his present arrangement did not provide sufficient encouragement; so while he proposed to raise the maximum salary of the fourth class up to the minimum of the third, he also wanted to increase the number of the latter at the expense of the former, so making it easier to adhere to his established principle of promotion by merit rather than seniority. He still had to get rid of twenty-two clerks, chosen firstly from those about to retire and secondly from those least useful to the public service. But he reckoned that all these changes would give the War Office an establishment of eighty-two in addition to himself and his deputy, at an annual cost of about £32,260. Following his usual habit he sounded out the Chancellor of the Exchequer privately in the first instance, for fear that it might not all be agreed and that even if it were the whole arrangement might tumble down with him, as he was just off to a very uncertain parliamentary election. But he survived and he got what he wanted from the Treasury.[59]

Over the whole period of his tenure of the War Office Palmerston could have boasted a proud record of economy. The reductions of 1821 had brought the total charge down by a further £10,000, and then, apart from a small increase in 1825 to cope with newly acquired business, it dropped steadily until by 1827 it was less than £35,000. These figures excluded the provision for retirement allowances, which in the circumstances of such massive reductions as Palmerston had had to make shot up dramatically from £3,711 in 1814 to £22,582 in 1827. But even counting these the total charge still fell from £72,412 in 1814, the last full year of war, to £57,938 in 1827. All in all it does seem, too, that Palmerston walked very well the tightrope between efficiency and retrenchment. Certainly he always recognized the necessity of encouraging effort and rewarding merit. From his attempts to reorganize the staffing structure of his office it would appear that he did not approve the Treasury's refusal to introduce the notion of special merit increments into the new Department of Military Accounts in 1809; and with the prospective reorganization of the establishment and the consolidation in one career structure of all its branches in 1821-2, he finally got the Treasury to agree that henceforth all vacancies were to be filled, not by seniority but according to merit and qualifications. At no point did he ever recommend a wholesale reduction of salaries. Instead he successfully resisted the full force of House of Commons criticism. The lowest point on the new scales he proposed for clerks in 1821 and 1826 was £90, precisely what it had been since 1803 and £10 more than in 1797; and that was a pretty tidy sum at any of those dates. The fact of the matter was that in 1821 no one was in receipt of a salary of less than £100, and when the new scales came into force in 1826 they were broad enough to accommodate the existing salaries of all but the two most senior clerks, and these appear, in accordance with Treasury policy in such cases, to have remained at their old salaries until retirement or promotion. Similarly, the revised rates of £2,000 and £1,200 for the Deputy Secretary and Chief Examiner were applied at this same time only because new appointments to these posts were made, while the First Clerk remained at his old salary of £1,400 though his successor was due to get only £1,200. It does not appear therefore that anyone, except a pluralist Law Clerk, whose salary was cut from £500 to £400 a year, suffered an actual drop in salary. Of course the contraction in numbers inevitably damaged the chances of promotion but, as has been seen, Palmerston did try to improve the situation. And considering the number of the reductions he was forced to make, he was always very generous, within the limits of discretion permitted him, in his recommendations for pensions, even with the relatively undeserving and when under great provocation to be otherwise. Thus when ordered to make the large reduction of posts in 1817, he used his wide discretion to make recommendations for an established clerk with ten years' service and on a salary of £225 to receive a pension of £112 p.a., for a clerk of twenty years to be rewarded with about two-thirds pension, and for a messenger with a salary of £90 p.a. and only six and a half years' service to get a gratuity of one year's pay, £80. When the Treasury tightened up the rules in 1821 and made such generous provision impossible, Palmerston still tried to stretch them and in especially deserving cases urged their relaxation. After fifty years of service, even under the new rules, a man might retire on full pay; and when Deputy Secretary Merry, at his own wish apparently, sought retirement two years short of that, Palmerston recommended and got for him a full rate of pension.[60]

Clearly Palmerston did a great deal of good work in the War Office. He certainly worked harder than some of his predecessors; Windham, for example, was reported on good authority to Fanny Temple 'never' to have attended the office in person. Yet it was commonly believed that Palmerston was not popular in or out of the office. When he finally left it in May 1828 Mrs Arbuthnot noted that it was 'quite extraordinary how he was detested' there and that the clerks would have liked had they dared to burn candles in the windows. By that date she was no longer a friendly or reliable witness. But there does seem to be something in it. He certainly did not (as was also said with equal unfairness of his régime at the Foreign Office) merely amuse himself while overworking his subordinates. On the contrary, he worked as hard in office as at play; he occasionally missed his holidays at Park Place or even Broadlands. On the other hand, though he never lost overall control, he did immerse himself too much in detail. Palmerston, indeed, was something of a bureaucrat. The attention to detail and the concern for system and regularity mark these years at the War Office just as they do those at the Foreign and Home Offices.[61]

One can get a pretty good idea of Palmerston's essential attitude to the administrative process from the reaction he made when in 1825 the Consolidated Board of General Officers proposed to tackle their work of settling claims for losses on a purely *ad hoc* basis. He maintained that the board could never do their work in a satisfactory manner 'unless they had fixed and determined the general principles according to which those claims were to be admitted or rejected, and that to enter into an investigation of a multitude of individual cases with the intention of trying each by its own circumstances without having previously ascertained and settled some general principles to which each case might on succession be referred, would involve any public officer or department who should engage in such an undertaking in an inextricable labyrinth of inconsistency and error.' He admitted that it was 'perfectly true' that no regulations could ever be so framed as to provide for every possible circumstance, but it then became the duty of the administrator to make his decision according to their 'spirit and true meaning'. 'When such rules are previously laid down decisions become consistent and satisfactory; without such rules they are necessarily uncertain and arbitrary.' It was also important that they should be published, because that 'prevents persons from preferring claims which are obviously inadmissible and thus saves them from disappointment, and because a decision is much more likely to be considered just when it is founded upon a principle previously made known'. On the other hand there ought to be a time limit for making claims, especially in the interests of having as fresh evidence as possible: 'there can be no hardship in requiring that an individual who has sustained a loss should immediately apply for compensation tho' there might be some in compelling him to wait.'[62]

Certainly Palmerston made a substantial effort to bring the same lucidity of purpose and practice to his own office. Although most of the internal working papers of the office (as well as many of its files and books of correspondence) have been lost or destroyed, enough have survived to show how much he made his authority felt at every level. While he endeavoured to leave mere routine to his underlings, he was ever alert to matters of principle and precedent, such as the appropriate rate of pension for the first widow of any surgeon-major in the Guards. He paid a good deal of attention as well to the tidying up of administrative detail. Many years later he would still recall with pride that it was he who had established an up-to-date system of registration in the War Office. 'I think I am not saying too much in affirming that it turned night and chaos into light and order,' he claimed when someone suggested some changes in 1852; 'I should be fearful that any alteration which tended to impair the accuracy and regularity of the registration might bring night & chaos back again.' Such objectives presented no mean task for the early nineteenth-century bureaucrat confronted with an accumulation of antique practices. They were also of no small importance, not only to economy but also to natural justice. One irritating discrepancy was the administrative separation of the Army in Ireland from that in the rest of the British Isles. As early as the beginning of 1811 Palmerston was suggesting that the estimates for the Barrack and Commissariat Departments in Ireland, which were prepared by the War Office, and those in the United Kingdom, which were prepared by the Treasury, be united in the same office. It was not, however, until ten years later that all the barrack establishments were brought together under the Ordnance Office. As late as the September of that same year, 1822, he was also drawing the attention of the Horse Guards to the totally unnecessary existence of a separate Medical Department in Ireland and the extraordinary exemption of Irish medical officers from service elsewhere. In this case he successfully pressed for their absorption for general service under the Director-General in London, although there had to be the usual transitional exceptions for favoured protégés. The following year he turned his attention to the equalization of the rates of pay and allowances of the British and Irish Militia. Not only were the local currencies different in value; the clothing rates had been different since 1817, when a reduction was made in the British case but the Irish, then under a different department, was apparently overlooked.[63]

In many cases Palmerston personally drafted or amended outgoing correspondence or general regulations, such as the restrictions that were imposed on half-pay officers undertaking additional employment. Some of these drafts look as if his hectic way of life occasionally compelled him to write them on his knee in a horse-drawn carriage, but it seems to have been during this period at the War Office that his hand acquired that famous clarity of his. Hitherto, while usually legible enough, it had had little of the character of his father's, which it came closely to resemble, and could earn him on occasion from his sister the return address of 'Harry Scribble'. It would appear to have been, therefore, not the academic lessons at Edinburgh but the practical pressures of the War Office that forced him to develop that magnificent boldness of line. Moreover, just as he evidently loathed, in his sister as in others, the execrable if economical habit of finishing letters by writing at right angles across an already ink-filled page, so he would minute alongside the composition of some unfortunate clerk: 'This first sheet to be rewritten without interlineation & the breaks to be more distinct & wider – a letter without breaks is as confused to the eye, as discourse without pauses wd be to the ear & I am constantly finding fault with the copies of the office on this point.' It must be admitted that for this effect he himself persistently resorted to semicolons, a fondness for which neither War nor Foreign Office ever cured in him. His official biographers, Bulwer and Ashley, rather discreetly reduced their number in the letters they printed. So they did his still more redundant capital letters. In the latter case at least they deserve everyone's approval. Palmerston's capitals seem to have no stylistic or philological significance. Possibly they have some deep psychological meaning; but if so it is too deep for this writer to fathom and he has therefore as ruthlessly suppressed them as any Victorian precursor.[64]

Palmerston's intervention in the bureaucratic process was not always speedy; often the internal minutes of his senior advisers would accumulate on little slips of paper in the office and sometimes over long periods of time. Once he peremptorily ordered: 'Let the information on the chaos of slips be reduced to light & order & the slips to ashes.' But when at last all seemed ready to his satisfaction, he would move with a clarity, boldness and decisiveness of purpose as well as hand. Sometimes he was too quick, and it must be said in fairness to him that his subordinates were not then too frightened to suggest that his facts be checked. But he would always go right to the heart of the matter, and indeed so concoct a draft as often to offend by its directness. The behaviour of other offices, with which he was obliged to cooperate, could often be very trying. When in 1823 Palmerston suggested to the Paymaster-General that they abolish a warrant he thought unnecessary and received an overtly positive response, he at once detected that the offer was to replace one form with two and extend this multiplication to a large area of business which had not hitherto been burdened even with the one. He was himself by no means unresponsive to genuine and sensible suggestions for administrative improvement, even from rival offices. He welcomed without hesitation, for example, that of the Army Pay Office in 1823 that it was unnecessary and, in the case of aged and infirm females, unfair to require officers' widows to produce a certificate signed by a priest and *two* churchwardens every time they wrote off for their quarterly pensions. But he could be very fierce indeed with anything he deemed to be impertinent interference. In 1819-20, when the Audit Office complained of some petty irregularity in the issues made by one of his more valued clerks as agent to some retired chaplains, Palmerston sent back an angry letter referring to their 'groundless objections' as a 'waste of time' and an 'unwarranted interference'.[65]

Palmerston's pride of place contributed more than anything else, as will be seen, to undermine his relations with the Horse Guards. Within the War Office also the bureaucrat too often triumphed over the politician. There was, for instance, a good deal of the hardness of the autocrat in the tone of his office instructions. Of these there was probably an almost unceasing stream and, perhaps because of some disappointment of his initial hopes of an early reformation, the choicest samples are not necessarily those of his first days at the office. In October 1814, for example:

Having lately had occasion to notice several mistakes in official letters . . . which appear to me to have arisen from carelessness & inattention, I wish it to be understood that the superintending clerks are responsible for the correctness of the letters prepared in their respective subdivisions, and . . . I shall deem it necessary very strongly to notice such inattention on their part.

If they should have occasion frequently to correct such errors made by the clerks . . . or find the clerks to be otherwise inattentive or inefficient, they are to report them.

In August 1816:

Having occasion perpetually to observe the loss of papers in the office, which is disgraceful to the office and injurious to the business of the Public, I desire that it may be notified that if any paper is lost after the 29 Instant, I shall mark my displeasure in an effectual manner on the Clerk at the head of the subdivision.

And in May 1817:

Inform the subdivisions that I *insist* upon obedience to my repeated orders . . . and let them take care that I have no further occasion to take notice of any further neglect.

On the other hand he was equally direct in issuing compliments: 'Inform Mr Hamilton that I have received with great satisfaction Mr Hamilton's report . . . which is made with proper attention to what I consider to be the duty of gentlemen superintending subdivisions.' And if his instructions were severely expressed, so were those issued about the same time to the Irish Office by his friend Peel.[66]

Palmerston, after all, was only continuing the work, whose necessity had been so heavily underlined by the Commissioners' report of 1808, of cleansing the War Office stables. Moreover, the discontinuance of first Christmas and then New Year presents for messengers was offset by his interest in getting for them an incremental salary structure and in the case of the head messenger at the time a special allowance in lieu until his retirement. He applied the same standard to his own affairs. The King habitually presented his ministers with venison from the royal parks and by ancient tradition the fees levied on these 'gifts' were usually met out of office contingencies. But this Palmerston would not accept. It had also been the custom for the retiring minister to take away the office plate free of any charge and his silver inkstand at about half price. Even the wealthy Pulteney had not neglected to take his plate though he had distributed his salary among what were recorded in the office as 'distressed objects'. But Palmerston left both plate and inkstand behind him, and in the hands of the housekeeper a taper stand and pair of candlesticks as well. His behaviour was not deemed to have created any precedent and his inkstand, which had cost £67, was removed by his successor, Henry Hardinge, on payment of £37.10s.0d. What is more, if Palmerston's own hours were irregular, they were certainly longer and probably more onerous than those of any clerk. The imposition, too, of a six-hour day, restrictions on private visitors, and a ban on unsupervised extra employment could hardly be called tyrannous. Nor could his placing of merit above seniority as the essential criterion for promotion or his interest in a system of probation for recruits.[67]

Probation seems to have existed before Palmerston's time, but it was he who made it a matter of routine as early as January 1810. At the end of a new man's first month each of two supervising clerks would answer a list of thirteen questions concerning such things as his arithmetic and grammar, his handwriting and health, and at the end of a second month the Secretary would decide whether to dismiss him or make him permanent. Between 1810 and 1828, no less than thirty-three probationers were rejected. On the other hand Palmerston does not appear to have been an unbending taskmaster. The surviving record shows that he was confronted with a variety of faults and inadequacies in his office staff, from absence without leave to bankruptcy and mental derangement. It is hardly surprising or discreditable to Palmerston that he found it necessary to order or approve a number of dismissals. But he was not by any means always unkind or unfeeling about them. One young man whom Pulteney had had to sack in 1807 after twelve years' service was twice temporarily re-employed in 1809, and when his continued 'low &

nervous state' finally made it necessary to let him go for good, Palmerston wrote to ask the Treasury to give him a pension of £50 a year as his mother was destitute and himself unable to work from 'nervous debility of body & mind'. He was on principle very sympathetic about genuine illness, often referring to the peculiar risks of a 'sedentary occupation' and the need for periods of recuperation and country air. According to Monk Lewis he was very patient even with a junior clerk whom his own friends or relations thought both ungrateful and disgraced. Nor was he so coldly distant as not to have some of his senior people home from time to time; his diary for 19 December 1819 records, for example, a dinner party attended by several of his senior men. But he would not for very long tolerate much slackness or incompetence at any level. One senior examiner he made an enemy for ever by locking him in his office when there was 'a very long affair' he wished to be given his 'immediate and undivided attention'. Senior and established people were certainly not exempted from the consequences of his reform; rather, as the relics of the eighteenth century, they were especially vulnerable to his assault on the sinecures and pluralism of which the 1808 report had complained so much.[68]

Given that, once they had been granted, most perquisites were regarded as legitimate properties, the usual method of dealing with them by Government was probably the most effective and least objectionable that could be found. The simplest method was to wind them up on the death of an incumbent. But minor ones were often eliminated upon promotion. In this way many of the allowances for overtime and other extra payments made to individuals in the War Office had been absorbed into the additional appointments and new scales of pay approved in the summer of 1809. Palmerston did not find it convenient to stick rigidly to an absolute prohibition on the old practice and overtime payments were occasionally revived, though never without seeking the specific authority of the Treasury. At the same time he resisted attempts to regularize the special exemptions from the prohibition on half-pay officers acting as War Office clerks. In debates on the Estimates in 1817 and 1818 suggestion was made that it was unfair; but Palmerston successfully retorted that while half-pay was in part a retainer for further service, other em-ployment tended to make half-pay officers less fit for future military duties and more unwilling to be recalled. However, he did not like being attacked in such a manner, and as it seemed improbable that many of those concerned would ever be recalled he suggested to the Prime Minister that they do something to anticipate the renewal of the attack the following year. So in 1819 the regulations were relaxed so as to permit such officers to receive as much as three times their half-pay. For the time being Palmerston succeeded in retaining the 'reservist' principle inviolate by making the payments in these cases technically 'military allowances' and not half-pay at all. But in the following year the law was changed in spite of him so as to extend the favour openly – a relaxation much disapproved of by the Finance Committee of 1828 as being 'ill-advised' with a view to economy and 'opposed to the very prin-ciple' of half-pay.[69]

It was more clearly undesirable to have perquisites held in the same office as was supposed to oversee them, even if care was taken to ensure that a single individual did not, as a War Office clerk, 'check' his own accounts as private agent. Palmerston therefore went out of his way to extend the reforming innovations of his predecessors by making the relinquishment of agencies and other perquisites a regular condition of promotion. In this way, for example, he got one of his men in 1817 to give up the agency of a half-pay regiment on promotion to senior clerk. On the other hand, when the Treasury had pointed in 1811 to another junior getting paid privately for acting as clerk to one of his seniors who ran a profitable sideline as agent for chaplains, Palmerston replied that he did not interfere as the man was 'zealous and diligent' in his official duties.[70]

One case that did give Palmerston a good deal of trouble was that of Christopher Holland. When Palmerston took over the War Office he found that Holland acted as agent to a considerable number of half-pay officers, widows and orphans. He objected, as he said, very strongly to such plurality, but he allowed it to continue in this instance because permission had been given by one of his predecessors and because Holland had a large family and a small income. In February 1815 Holland, though still under sixty, was forced by ill-health to retire. But his pension, after fifteen years at the War Office and twelve at India House before that, was at £450 a year insufficient to meet his creditors. Shortly afterwards, therefore, he was declared bankrupt, leaving many poor pensioners with large claims upon him. On investigation it turned out that a single debt to Holland more than covered the whole of his liabilities. This was a sum of over £3,000 that he had advanced to Maj. Gen. John Wood. Wood's expectation of a 'lucrative appointment', however, had not materialized and he had not paid back what he owed to Holland. When he heard of this, Palmerston stopped both Holland's retirement allowance and Wood's unattached pay (i.e., the special rate of pay laid down in 1814 for general officers who did not hold regimental appointments) in order to rescue something for the unfortunate creditors. He also privately reported the general's 'discreditable' behaviour to the C.-in-C. and in 1817 Wood was dismissed from the Army.[71]

Moore's fortuitous retirement as Deputy Secretary in December 1809 made it possible for Palmerston to carry through a plan for disembarrassing the Chief Examiner of his contract for the supply of Gibraltar coals. Merry's original proposal was that advantage should be taken of the separation of the regimental accounts and the reorganization of the Correspondence Department to drop his misleading title of Chief Examiner for that of Joint Under-secretary with Moore. In that case, he had gone on to say, he would be prepared to surrender the Gibraltar contract in return for an allowance of £750 p.a. while his salary was £2,000 and £250 when his salary rose after five years to £2,500. But while Granville had adopted the idea of a new senior post, the Treasury had not; after all, it was pointed out, Matthew Lewis had proved long ago that it was quite unnecessary to have even the existing posts of

Deputy Secretary and First Clerk in separate hands. Moore's determination to retire, however, gave Palmerston an opportunity in December 1809 to contrive a means of compensating Merry for the relinquishment of the contract through promotion instead of a new post. Some meaning was given again to the title of Chief Examiner by giving it to the man in charge of the old pre-1797 arrears and, in return for giving up a contract which everyone conceded was worth at least £750 a year, the new Deputy Secretary got a salary of £2,500 from the start instead of after five years at £2,000. Palmerston also tried but failed to get the Treasury to agree to a further increment of £250 after three years. This however allowed him, when urging an unusually generous pension on Merry's retirement in 1826, to argue that Merry had after all taken a mere £500 a year for five years and surrendered £700 to £800 a year for life. The decision of the Treasury in 1822 to fix the salary of future deputies at £2,000 was made in response to parliamentary pressure and applied to Merry's successor in 1826 simply because a transitional phase prolonged by special circumstances had ended. There is no reason to believe that it had anything to do with the fact that the minister's own salary had hitherto been less than that of his immediate subordinate. As long ago as 1798 Windham had contemplated the Secretary's salary being raised to £4,000 and his deputy's lowered to £2,000 or even £1,800. Granville, on going out of office in 1809, had urged upon the Treasury that the salary of the minister did not have 'a just proportion either to the extent of his personal duties & responsibility, or to his relative rank with the heads of other Public Departments' and also recommended that his successor should have at least £4,000. About the same time a shrewd and discriminating observer from France declared after looking at the War Office: 'The Minister is the only one who is not overpaid.' Yet while Palmerston's salary remained unchanged through all the Treasury's reforms at a mere £2,480, he saved his deputy's from being reduced, as the Select Committee of 1817 had recommended, to a mere £1,500 rising to £2,000 only after ten years. There may, however, have been some sort of personal antagonism between Palmerston and Merry nonetheless.[72]

Merry seems to have been unnecessarily fussy about the War Office's scope of authority – he persisted, for example, in attending the routine meetings of the Chelsea Hospital Board long after Palmerston had found more pressing things to do – and he probably had a good deal to do with precipitating his chief into his initial confrontation with the Horse Guards. There is no evidence that Palmerston ever blamed Merry for leading him into that affair; on the contrary, he adopted the battle as his own. But there were occasional signs of irritation, as when what Palmerston called Merry's 'officious care' led to his getting no post from England during a three weeks' pleasure trip in France in the summer of 1816. After Merry's retirement in 1826 *The Times* also carried suggestions that he had been forced to make way for Palmerston's brother-in-law, and although he was asked to refute them several times he never did so. On the other hand he never denied Palmerston's assertion that he had himself asked to retire, and if he did nurse some resentment it is odd that his son should have stayed on as Palmerston's private secretary and left only in his master's wake in 1828. In any case his behaviour contrasts very unfavourably with the generosity with which Palmerston had always treated him and would continue to treat his son. Yet, however considerate Palmerston may have tried to be, he could hardly have made so many reductions – no less than ninety in all – and disturbed the comforts of others so much without making some enemies. And what really must have embittered them was for Palmerston to make their prospects even worse by bringing in his cronies over their heads. At least one man in the office, it would seem, for years supplied an Opposition newspaper, the *Morning Chronicle*, with detailed denunciations of the favours Palmerston supposedly handed out.[73]

Nepotism was no novelty in the War Office. At the turn of the century there were several cases of father and son being in the office together, and of special favour being shown to the friends and relations of various ministers. In addition to Fitzpatrick's Foveaux, for example, Merry's second son, William, entered the War Office as a junior clerk in February 1810 and his daughter married an accountant in the Foreign Department, J. W. Lukin. Lukin, moreover, was one of at least two among his numerous nephews whom Windham – who was said himself to be 'very fond of money', taking his Secretary's salary 'regularly *every half* quarter' – had placed in well paid and laxly supervised posts; according to contemporary information they netted thus between them a total of £8,000 a year. These connections did not prevent Palmerston wielding his axe and saving £1,095 a year by dispensing with James Lukin's services in 1817. He also complained that it was difficult to get Merry to admit any faults in the First Clerk, Robert Lukin; but although this Lukin never was promoted, Palmerston kept him on and shortly before he himself resigned was warmly recommending the ageing clerk for generous treatment as the time of his retirement drew near. Palmerston was no less generous with his last private secretary, William Merry, junior. This young man seems to have decided to retire with his master in 1828. But instead of simply letting him resign, Palmerston contrived on his last day in office to abolish his established post as a third-class clerk so as to make him eligible for a more generous pension than Treasury regulations would have permitted upon an avowedly voluntary retirement.[74]

By doing such a favour for William Merry's son, Palmerston really took a step backwards into the eighteenth-century system he had done so much to dismantle. But in the case of new appointments it is difficult to see what else he could have done than exercise personal patronage. The days of entry by competitive examination still lay far in the future and recruitment could therefore be made only through personal recommendation and, when presented with candidates of equal merit, by giving the preference to one's personal or political friends. Palmerston himself certainly thought such a practice perfectly proper. As early as November 1809, for example, he made his distant relative, Godschall Johnson, Paymaster of the Bedford Militia District. The job was worth £300 a year and the only sort of patronage the Secretary at War had outside the office. Militia paymasterships were, however, for life and therefore rarely became available. Palmerston told his sister that neither Pulteney nor Granville had ever had the opportunity to fill one. Unfortunately Godschall Johnson again got into financial trouble and found it necessary to flee his debtors; in 1828 he was writing from St Omer to beg the help of another influential friend. Palmerston also sent him money; no less than £320 in 1820. Eventually the Foreign Office would provide him with cheaper means of helping out his family.[75]

Inside the War Office Palmerston had just as much discretion and much more power of manoeuvre. But the men already there, whatever the manner of their own beginnings, must always have been resentful of the introduction into senior posts of outside people, however well qualified, and hardly less so of those thereafter promoted over their heads. After all, as Palmerston would one day put it, 'selection by merit' usually meant 'selection of the men whom I like'. In most cases we simply cannot know what the others may have thought, for example of the appointment to relatively humble positions of William Osborne Rich, a poverty-stricken connection of one of Palmerston's Hampshire neighbours, or, had they been able to appreciate his connection with their minister, of William Thomas Rose, who must surely have been a relative of Henry Campbell's wife. Rose and Rich both entered the War Office along with the younger Merry during the great expansion of February 1810, as junior clerks at £100 a year. Rich was still a third-class clerk when Palmerston resigned in 1828 and had reached only the second class by 1841. Rose, on the other hand, had become an assistant examiner by 1819 and retired five years later on a pension in his early thirties. Palmerston's second private secretary did even better. Henry Elliot (1789-1848) was the grandson of Samuel Glasse, a chaplain to the Dukes of Cumberland and Cambridge and friend and collaborator of Palmerston's maternal relatives, Robert Raikes and William Man Godschall. His father, the Rev. George Henry Glasse, a scholar but a spendthrift, dissipated a fortune, had his name connected with the affair of the Duke of York and Mrs Clarke, and hanged himself at a public house in October 1809. The son assumed the name of the benefactor whose fortune had presumably been squandered and entered the War Office as Palmerston's private secretary in January 1811. In 1819 his clerical post was 'reduced', perhaps with the same intention as was that of his successor, Merry; in addition he turned up in the 1820s as Secretary to the Office of Military Boards. He also continued a close connection with Palmerston. He was an occasional visitor at Broadlands and he helped Palmerston with his canvass at Cambridge in 1826. But what must have raised their eyebrows in the War Office was that Elliot seems to have been able from the remnant of his benefactor's estates, to assist Palmerston in 1828 in pensioning off a former mistress. Perhaps, when actually in the office, Elliot had performed other services often thought to be among the peculiar duties of a private secretary. But even if the other clerks had heard nothing of the sort when Palmerston was still their chief, there was more than enough for them to notice about two of the others Palmerston had placed among them – Sulivan and Shee.[76]

It is not entirely clear what Shee had been about since leaving Cambridge. He seems to have thought most of India and marriage; but his father evidently kept him too short of cash to cope with both, and so in February 1808 he had chosen marriage. Mrs Shee, however, did not enjoy good health and before long her husband evidently began to tire of her. Palmerston had not been at the War Office for a year when he heard that his friend 'was dying for employment' and, it was suspected, for 'some excuse for seeing a little less of dear Mrs Shee'. No doubt, then, it was he who approached Palmerston, probably late on Tuesday, 23 October 1810. For at 3 p.m. on that day Palmerston asked the Agent-General for Volunteers and Disembodied Militia to delay his resignation for a month, but at 11 a.m. the next day introduced Shee to him as his successor. George Hassell, who according to Palmerston was 'rich and idle', was probably not much put out; however, one of his two assistants, Henry Longlands, who had hoped to succeed him and had already canvassed Perceval and Yorke, certainly was. Longlands complained bitterly to Yorke, who regretted he could not help, and repeated his claims to Palmerston, who made it clear he should resign if he could not bring himself to work under Shee. He stayed; but this 'job' did not go unremarked in the world. 'Sir Geo. Shee's son made a college-friend of Ld Palmerston, the new War Minister, who has given him an easy place of £1,000 a year', wrote Lady Charleville to her aspirant son. ' "English connections are certainly efficient to get on, & forget it not".' Shee's father had a few years before been richly rewarded for his active support of the scandalously managed abolition of the Irish Parliament; and Shee seemed now to be getting only a little less well rewarded for his friendship with Palmerston.[77]

Shee's was indeed a rather comfortable office, even by past standards; but the Commissioners of Military Enquiry had been very impressed with it and unlike the regimental agents the Agent-General was required to give substantial security, namely a bond of £10,000 and two sureties of £5,000 each. When the militia regiments were embodied their colonels were expected to appoint their own agents, but Palmerston came to think that the security given by the Agent-General offered a much more satisfactory system. So he tried to get Shee's work continued when the militia was embodied and ran afoul of the Horse Guards in the process by appearing to reduce still further the responsibility of colonels for their agents. After the war, when economy pressed hard upon all his arrangements, he also endeavoured to persuade the Treasury to keep the office in being. After all, he pointed out, in the absence of regimental agents, some office in Whitehall would have to do the work; and in his view Shee had run his office 'like clock-work'. But he did not manage to save Shee's job or even, as it had always been regarded as a temporary office, to get him a pension. The best that he could do was to arrange in 1817 that his own office, and not the Pay Office, should take over the bulk of the work. Shee had to wait for his friend to change saddles before he could surface again in Whitehall.[78]

Considering Palmerston's failure to save anything for him in 1817 and the unsavoury reputation he had on his reappearance over a decade later, it is difficult to believe that Shee was looked on with approval by anyone in the War Office. Laurence Sulivan's appointment, it is quite clear, was deeply resented – though probably with much less justification. By the end of 1809 Sulivan was well embarked on his career at the bar, though it is not at all clear with what success or happiness. Lady Malmesbury did protest that he was sacrificing his profession, but presumably he had conveyed some doubt or even discontent, for Palmerston discussed with him the possibility of making him his private secretary on 24 October, even before he was himself safely made the minister. The next day Sulivan wrote to say that the situation would be 'peculiarly agreeable . . . on all accounts'. When, however, Palmerston arrived in the office he was told by his deputy, Francis Moore, that the post was worth only £300 as a part-time appointment and was usually offered at the reduced rate of £100 to someone already in the office, so that the minister might have immediately and constantly at hand the benefit of informed advice. In addition the private secretary ought to have the experience neces-sary to the proper performance of his incidental special duty of dealing with applications for pensions from the compassionate fund. But Moore must have been prevaricating, for the evidence given to the Commissioners of Military Enquiry shows that it had been by no means uncommon, during the preced-ing decade at least, for a man to enter the War Office as private secretary. So Merry, who was the second man in the office but had himself begun in this manner, told Palmerston that he could see no objection to a new man coming in and that in any case the minister had a perfect right to choose whomsoever he pleased. 'Now Moore's opinion', Palmerston wrote to Sulivan with all the administrative grasp of a one-day-old minister, 'although entitled to weight from his long experience in the office, must yet be taken with the allowance arising from one's knowledge of the force of habit upon geniuses of that sort – a man gets a sort of set of official ideas & whatever is new is to him *therefore* objectionable & difficult.' Perhaps the clerks did not like a new man coming in; 'yet when they found he was on a footing of intimacy with the Sec. at War, they would soon understand that it was their interest *to be civil.*' So it was agreed that Sulivan should at least try out the job, and as it happened both Deputy Secretary and outgoing private secretary seemed to take it very well. Fourteen months later, however, Sulivan – like Lukin before him – was suddenly advanced upon a chance vacancy from very near the bottom to somewhere near the top, as Junior Superintendent of Accounts at a salary of £1,000. Then, when the new accounts section was rearranged in 1815, he was given sole charge of current business. This apparently lit some smouldering resentment even if his original appointment had not.[79]

From the moment of his appointment as junior superintendent, Sulivan many years afterwards recalled, he exerted his 'most zealous endeavours . . . to sift the whole system to the bottom' and 'very soon became convinced that it was calculated to perpetuate every mischief which it professed to remedy'. He may have exaggerated in claiming the exclusive invention of all the improvements subsequently applied; but he was involved enough in them to be faced with what he called 'the inveterate prejudice of those who had been brought up in a vicious school'. Although his family fortunes had never completely recovered from the blows and disappointments suffered by his grandfather, and Sulivan always afterwards resented being the first to suffer the reduced rates of salary on his promotion to the two most senior posts in the office, he must have been well off enough not to have depended on his War Office pay. But most of his colleagues probably had nothing but their salaries to depend on and faced the imminent prospect of losing the perquisites and special allowances condemned by the 1808 report.[80]

The senior superintendent, Michael Foveaux, had evidently conceived a very special grudge against both Palmerston and Sulivan. Foveaux's aged father seems to have survived Palmerston's arrival; for the post of office-keeper was abolished only at Joseph Foveaux's death on 1 January 1814. But Palmerston was certainly involved in recovering from Michael Foveaux a sum of £400 overpaid to him as agency fees for 1805 and 1807. Perhaps, too, he forced him to give up his agency altogether when he was promoted to superintendent at the end of 1809. If so, Palmerston would only have been acting as the House of Commons wished. But what Foveaux certainly did resent was being forced in 1815 to give up the current accounts that he had taken over in 1803. No doubt he disliked being put in charge of a temporary task and a disappearing department; perhaps he sensed, especially after 1819, when Palmerston gave him Stuart's work instead of making a new appointment, that with the final winding up of the arrears he would be retired as well. But what must have rankled all along was the implication that he was in some way personally responsible for the perpetual failure hitherto to keep up with current business. Then, as senior superintendent, he must also have been the principal target of Palmerston's 1813 directive to break up the 'board' in Duke Street. There is in any event no doubt whatever that he nursed a deep resentment against both Palmerston and Sulivan; and this must have been considerably reinforced when Sulivan married his chief's younger sister.[81]

Laurence Sulivan and the Honourable Elizabeth Temple were married on 6 December 1811 in St George's Hanover Square, and by the Malmesburys' second son, Alfred. 'It is good nick with respect to collateral,' Lady Malmesbury reported; for the bride had a dowry of £20,000 and Sulivan had the same amount with expectations of considerably more to come. But while only twenty-one, Lilly was evidently no great catch. 'You must have been surprised with Lilly Temple's marriage,' wrote Lady Minto to her husband. 'She is nearly the foremost in ugliness in the present age, deformed, & with a considerable perfume in her breath. However it is said to be love on both sides . . . I think Sulivan is in love with Harry, & as he cannot marry him takes Lilly.' Lady Minto was too catty and too unkind to be quite truthful. But Lady Malmesbury had also been violently opposed to her protégée marrying such a 'nobody', and though now determined to make the best of a bad job she agreed that Sulivan was rather too inclined to ape Palmerston's mannerisms. And if Lady Minto exaggerated in describing Lilly as a hunchback, the new Mrs Sulivan was clearly no beauty. In short, Lady Minto reported to her husband, she was 'frightful'. 'I trust they will not multiply,' she added.[82]

Sulivan's marriage appears to have been very happy. He lived until 1866; but his wife died in 1837 and Sulivan's tear-stained report to Palmerston is touching testimony to his affection. Meanwhile, they had multiplied. Their elder son, Stephen Henry, was born in 1812 and entered Palmerston's service in the Foreign Office; but being less discreet in his amours than was his uncle he wrecked both his private life and his career, and having been exiled to a diplomatic post in South America was murdered in Lima in 1857. His younger brother, Henry William, was born in 1815 and became a cleric; but he was a sensitive soul and suffered frequent bouts of mental collapse. He died unmarried in 1880, and quite insane, some said. There were also three daughters. The youngest, Mary, upset the family by marrying their local vicar in Fulham. The Reverend Robert Baker was seventy-seven at the time; but she died before him in 1871 and without leaving any children. Her sister, Charlotte Antonia, inherited the family home, Broom House in Fulham, and died there unmarried in 1911. The eldest sister, Elizabeth, married as his second wife Henry Hippisley of Lamborne Place in Berkshire and died in 1886. She alone of Palmerston's immediate relations has left legitimate descendants of the Temples.[83]

Sulivan had become engaged to Elizabeth Temple in July 1811, some six months after his first promotion in the War Office. But Lady Malmesbury avowed that they had been attached for 'several years'. During the first Cambridge election campaign of February 1806, Lilly had written: 'I do *like* Mr Sullivan [sic] *so much* now *really* & *seriously*. He is so warmhearted & has been so zealous in your cause.' It was then an initial refusal perhaps that led Palmerston to urge upon his lovesick friend a change of scene later that summer. Perhaps, too, Palmerston expected Lilly might one day consent and had it all along in mind to provide, if not wealth, then at least additional comfort and employment for a prospective brother-in-law as well as a friend. But he clearly could not have given such promotion to someone whose ability he despised. Lady Malmesbury on Sulivan's engagement naturally described him as 'most admirable, in principles, in right feelings, & understanding, & I have seen him tried in various ways, & always come out of the fire'. Even her sister could say no worse than that he was 'really what one calls a *very good sort of man*, & without any burthen of talents'. Moreover, it was Sulivan who in the early years had pressed Palmerston most on the necessity of reforming the War Office, and it was Sulivan whom Palmerston publicly credited with much of the subsequent improvement. Such at any rate was the reply Palmerston made in the Government newspaper, the *Courier*, when the anonymous informer in the War Office fed the hostile *Morning Chronicle* with dirt with which to smear the minister. Such too was the reply Palmerston made when Foveaux complained of favouritism at his own expense.[84]

Foveaux had evidently held a personal grudge against Palmerston and Sulivan for a very long time; probably he was the *Chronicle*'s anonymous informer. When therefore he discovered in 1821 that he was to be offered up to the Treasury as one of the sacrifices to the economy drive, it is not surprising that he should have sent a strong complaint. But its language was more than that; it was downright impertinent, and, since his presumed protectors were now all dead, very indiscreet. Claiming that it was he who had first suggested the means by which they might most effectively deal with the current accounts, he accused Palmerston directly of injustice to himself and of an unbecoming anxiety to promote Sulivan in his place. Already, he complained, Sulivan had been appointed junior superintendent over the heads of more 'deserving clerks', and if Palmerston now really had economy in mind he would do better not to promote but to sack his protégé. But he had little hope of that, he said, because the minister no doubt harboured the intention of making Sulivan Chief Examiner at £1,200 or even £1,500 a year once he, Foveaux, was safely out of the way. This was an extraordinary missive from a clerk, however senior, to his minister, let alone to one such as Palmerston was supposed to be. Yet proud Lord Palmerston, while objecting to the 'tone' of the letter, wrote out a polite, if curt, reply. He defended Sulivan's record and bluntly observed that no such result could have been expected under Foveaux, who had, he said, displayed integrity, zealousness and labour, but not 'that activity of mind which presses forward to the attainment of results'. 'However sedulous your application to business,' he went on, 'you have not the faculty of disposing of it with perspicuity & dispatch; & ... your want of arrangement & method not only mars your own labours, but defeats to a considerable degree those of the persons under you.'

Before Palmerston had had an opportunity of sending off this very frank rebuke, moreover, there came another proof of Foveaux's unfitness in the form of his further accusation that his successor in charge of arrears, Richard Brown, in 'the last five years ... has had a very small share of necessary public duty at the centre and has therefore had more leisure to cultivate your interest in his behalf '. This time Palmerston merely replied that the style of Foveaux's letter was 'improper & unbecoming' and declined to give any further explanations. When, therefore, another vituperative missive came a few days later, Palmerston abruptly informed him he was dismissed. Mrs Foveaux then put her pen to paper in order to chide the viscount with ignoble feelings if he really intended to deprive her husband of both job and pension. But Palmerston had no such intention. He admitted to a 'just anger', but not to spite. On the contrary it was Foveaux who had offered him 'coarse abuse & gross personalities'. Palmerston indeed had all along intended to treat him generously. When he first wrote to the Treasury with his list of proposed reductions, he went out of his way to urge generous treatment for those with 'long & excellent service' and for Foveaux, who had served for thirty-eight years, a pension of £900 in lieu of his salary of £1,200. Since Foveaux had sent copies of his complaints to the Treasury, Palmerston now did the same with his replies; but at the same time he stressed that he had no wish to have Foveaux's pension withdrawn.[85]

That Foveaux was unfit for his place seems proved, if not by his handling of the accounts, at least by his final correspondence with his chief and in particular by his unpleasant accusations against his successor. But there may have been some truth in his assertion that Palmerston wanted him out of the way in order to promote Sulivan to Chief Examiner. After Sulivan no more superintendents were appointed. When Stuart had retired in 1819 Palmerston had left his place unfilled; Foveaux was not replaced in 1821; and in the prospective establishment Palmerston had the Treasury approve at the time of Foveaux's departure, the position of third superintendent (Sulivan's) was also to be eliminated. But in that same establishment there reappeared instead the old Chief Examiner, at a salary, not of £1,500 as had formerly been the figure, but of £1,200 – which was exactly the saving on Foveaux's former post of senior superintendent. In 1823 the chief examinership was revived for Sulivan and two years later, when Merry decided to retire, Sulivan succeeded him as Deputy Secretary, though at the new salary of £2,000. A few months later, when Palmerston agreed to serve in Wellington's Administration, *The Times* dug up the story that he had dislodged Merry for Sulivan's benefit. Foveaux, perhaps, supplied it.[86]

These attacks did not cease with Palmerston's departure from the War Office in May 1828. In 1831 a number of aggrieved clerks had the nerve to address their protests directly to the Treasury. Apparently they had it plainly made known to them that their action had incurred official 'displeasure', but their spokesman persisted with private letters to influential friends and even one to a Cabinet minister – probably the Chancellor of the Exchequer, Althorp. This letter was almost worthy of Foveaux. It complained of the unfair career structure and promotions policy in the office and bitterly bewailed the loss of morale and efficiency among the clerks who were 'sacrificed to the caprice and iltemper [*sic*] of a scion from the East Indies, & to the will of a member of the British Cabinet, who determines to support the arrogance of his brother in law'. But the writer went on to undermine his case against Sulivan and Palmerston by avowing that there was 'not a more efficient Dept under Govt'. 'To bring the W.O. to its present efficiency', he inadvertently admitted, 'has taken above twenty years.' Indeed, from his earlier letter it would appear that his resentment had really been aroused not in Palmerston's time at all but during the restless but abortive tenure of Sir Henry Parnell. But the writer probably singled out Sulivan and Palmerston as better targets for an incoming minister who, as a radical of the old school, might have been expected to attack tyranny and nepotism. When Hobhouse took over the War Office in February 1832 he did indeed regard himself as committed to radical reform, but he was also an old Cambridge friend of both Palmerston and Sulivan and, as will be seen, there was some reason for him to feel a certain amount of guilt about Palmerston and the War Office. Moreover, his reforming zeal was aimed principally at the Horse Guards and the Army and in this attack he had Palmerston as a powerful ally.[87]

Whether Sulivan really agreed or not with all of Hobhouse's proposals, it was the Deputy Secretary whom Windsor Castle and the Horse Guards both believed to be behind them. 'Sulivan', they said, was 'a kind-hearted man, an amiable member of society and an excellent father and husband', but he had 'unfortunately imbibed a feeling of hostility & jealousy towards the military departments'. Prejudiced or not, Sulivan undoubtedly worked hard on any question of administrative reform. Palmerston, indeed, chided him in characteristic fashion in 1832 when Sulivan, with his 'anxious & susceptible temperament', threatened to return too soon from his sick-bed to the 'harassing squabbles' of the War Office. He would do better to take the country air for a while. 'Be advised. Take care of your health in the first place; make that your first object, and office arrangements your second; and if the consequence should be that you do not carry all your points, what then? At least you preserve that health which is in every point of view, of much more importance.' In 1828, shortly after Palmerston had left the War Office, he told Sulivan how much he missed their daily talks, which he had found as useful as they were agreeable.[88]

Hobhouse, as Secretary at War, had a very high regard for his deputy's efficiency. So must many others. Otherwise Sulivan could hardly have survived Palmerston's departure in May 1828 and the succession of no less than twelve different ministers before his voluntary retirement in July 1851 at the age of sixty-eight. Since nearly half these ministers served for less than a year at a time and only three in addition to his brother-in-law for as many as two, he probably gave the office whatever internal stability it had. There is no doubt, however, that Sulivan was a self-important man, bitterly resenting his own unpopularity in the office and begrudging the credit Palmerston was given for the reforms they had carried through together. Palmerston's immediate successor, General Sir Henry Hardinge, seems to have found Sulivan a difficult subordinate from time to time. After only a few months of the new régime the Deputy Secretary was complaining that he was both degraded and overworked. He was no longer the channel of communication between the minister and the rest of the office, but was being treated like any other clerk and even being given directions by his juniors. He continued to make similar complaints from time to time, even under other ministers, but especially when General Hardinge returned to the War Office in 1841-4. Palmerston obviously thought he was inclined to fuss unnecessarily and in the end told him so pretty bluntly. Moreover, unless Hardinge was an utter hypocrite he must have thought better of his deputy than Sulivan did of him. For when Hardinge's turn came to retire in 1830 he also paid a very warm tribute to Sulivan. On entering the War Office, he reported, he had found it 'in a state of great efficiency, under the very able superintendence of the Dep. Secretary at War, whose arrangements for the detail of business have been such as most justly to entitle him during the whole course of my administration, to my implicit confidence in this as well as in every other matter'. He also wrote in such glowing terms of the diligence and cooperation of the clerks as strongly to suggest that their morale as well as their efficiency must have been reasonably high at the time Palmerston left in 1828. In that year Parliament again turned its attention to the Army, but it was at its behest with abuses in regimental finances and not in the War Office that Hardinge became preoccupied. Perhaps he would not have been so popular as he is reputed to have been among the clerks, if he had announced his plans to reduce the office by one-seventh rather earlier than the month of his own departure.[89]

The grievances of clerks are boundless, but it was probably in periods of reduction and consequent restrictions on promotion that they would most revile the minister whose responsibility it was to root out incompetence and neglect, and the deputy whose task it no doubt was to advise upon the choice of victims. The late 1820s, both immediately before and immediately after Palmerston left, were relatively stable ones in the office. Probably, therefore, when Mrs Arbuthnot reported the clerks' rejoicing at his going she got her impression not so much from those actually *in* the office but from those who were already *out*.

THE ARMY
AND
THE NATION

If Palmerston's reputation among his immediate subordinates is difficult to assess, it is no less difficult to estimate the general impression he made upon the public or even upon the Army. It was the House of Commons, of course, in which he was most publicly exposed and in which, in spite of his reluctance to speak, he was frequently compelled to explain and defend the Government's military policy. In particular he was obliged by his constitutional position between the people and the military to present the Army Estimates and the Mutiny Bill every February or March. He first had to do so in February 1810 and Malmesbury and his friends were as usual very complimentary. But so were many others. Perceval reported to the King that he had done it 'in a very able and perspicuous manner, giving great satisfaction to his friends and extorting commendation from his adversaries'. Whitbread went out of his way to congratulate him, but, then, while he was an opponent he was also a Johnian. George Rose wrote to Malmesbury to say that Palmerston had 'distinguished himself most remarkably. I assure you', he went on, 'I never heard statements made with more precision and clearness in the House of Commons, nor more ably supported; the ability with which that was done drew marked approbation as well as applause from both sides of the House. This was very different from a set speech on any particular question, and holds out *great promise.*'[1]

Inevitably Lord Malmesbury concluded that the young Palmerston had ensured his 'political consequence throughout life'; but it is interesting to discover that both Lady Malmesbury and her sister now expressed a rather different view. Lady Minto reported to her husband, who was away in India, that 'Harry did himself incalculable credit by his speech . . . which was plain, clear, & unpresuming . . . He never will boast of shining talents, or great views, but he is painstaking, & gentlemanlike to the greatest degree, & will always swim where greater talents might sink.' This was a remarkably prescient judgement; so was Lady Malmesbury's, in spite of her being much more biased in his favour:

Harry spoke extremely well on the Army Estimates. On such subjects where clearness & perspicacity are the requisites & time is given for preparation, he will always succeed, but where *opinions* are to be given & *effect to be produced* by *spontaneous* eloquence I doubt it. He is *reserved* & so *very cautious*, so *singularly* so for a young man, so afraid of *committing himself* even in common life & conversation with his most intimate friends, that it will throw a *coldness* & want of effect on such speeches of his. Il ne se levera jamais *afin* to carry people's feelings along with him.[2]

That Palmerston did so well, then, in presenting the Estimates was evidently owing to a good deal of laborious preparation. He also had to work hard beforehand, as his surviving lists and tables make clear, to acquire the detailed knowledge with which to answer the probing questions of the House of Commons. While the war continued and patriotism prevailed, the Opposition muted some of its criticism, though even in 1810 they managed to force a reduction in the staff appointments. The following year Palmerston again introduced the Estimates with 'great clearness and precision', and elicited even stronger commendation from the Opposition: 'they never knew the subject better treated, or estimates better framed.' But when the time came in March 1816 to outline the proposals for the first real peace establishment for twenty years, the radicals promised him a very different reception. In the autumn of 1815 he had already told the House of Commons that while the Government was disposed to make substantial economies, he could not say how large these might have to be until it was known what military establishments the other powers proposed to keep up. Although such a standard of comparison was no novelty as far as the Navy was concerned, it was as regards the Army. For the time being the House let the principle go unchallenged but some among them did not fail to note it. So when Palmerston announced the following March that the peace establishment proposed by the Government amounted to 99,000 men and that the 25,000 to be stationed in Great Britain (Ireland was allocated a similar number) exceeded the figure in 1791 by 7,000, there was a great outcry. The battle was sustained during ten nights' debate, and Castlereagh, who had reported at first that Palmerston had spoken 'with much effect and ability', averred that 'the history of Parliament does not furnish an instance of so protracted and determined opposition to the Army estimates'. Brougham in particular harassed the Secretary and taxed the Administration with striking through a standing Army at the liberties of Englishmen and at their constitution. Palmerston retorted that these soldiers were to defend Englishmen, at home and abroad, not to suppress them, and the Estimates were eventually passed by the grudging consent of economizers on all sides of the House.[3]

The Opposition planned to make another assault the following year. Grey, indeed, placed the Estimates at the top of his list. But if the rapidly increasing domestic distress of 1817 strengthened the economizing determinations of those on one side, the accompanying riots and disorders also strengthened the precautious anxieties of those on the other. So when in 1818 Althorp moved for a reduction of 5,000 in order to relieve taxation, Palmerston had little difficulty in fending him off with arguments about the necessity of defending property. 'On the whole', he wrote to his brother, 'the military establishments have passed off very quietly & with little opposition; indeed the House seems tired of the subject.' Still, as things appeared to improve in the country, the Government made plans during the summer for some reduction in military expenditure. But their intention was soon overtaken by the rapid deterioration of the domestic situation into the Cato Street Conspiracy and the Peterloo 'Massacre'. So 1820 found Palmerston, not announcing further reductions but defending the illegal calling out of large numbers of pensioners. Defending, perhaps, is too strong a word. 'The reasons', he told the House, 'were so notorious to every person in the country, that he should consider any attempt on his part to argue the necessity, not only a waste of time in the House, but as trifling with the public understanding.' When the criticism was renewed later in the year as 'a violation of the constitution', he pointed out that it was the sort of 'violation' which had many times occurred in similar crises and of which the House had on this occasion had specific warning, and so by its silence given acquiescence. Nor, he went on, could he accept the charge that it was a step on the road to military despotism. On the contrary, it was rebellion which, if unchecked, would lead to that. So, he concluded in a magnificent convolution of logic, 'the veterans had not been called out unconstitutionally, but to defend from the machinations of traitors those liberties which they had derived from their forefathers, and which, he hoped, they would transmit, unimpaired, to their children'.[4]

By the 1820s Palmerston may have thought his task was easing. Persistent disorder appeared to justify the Government's policy of precaution, if not that of repression, and among his leading critics in the House Sir Samuel Romilly had killed himself, for grief at the death of his wife, and Brougham had preoccupied himself with the affair of the estranged Queen Caroline, for love of money and power no doubt. But Palmerston was not yet to have much relief. Instead he now became the special target of another radical reformer, Joseph Hume. 'Parliament, which was supposed likely to be up early, is now likely to sit some time,' wrote one M.P. in April 1821. 'The fact is that Mr Hume is making himself master of the Army Estimates, and is discussing and dividing on every point . . . Mr Hume is assisted in this by an institution of very late establishment, and one which in general will be beneficial, though not so in the present instance, a Parliamentary Library, in one of the upper rooms, where reports, returns, Acts, and papers of every sort are kept, with a librarian to assist in finding what is wanted.' In spite of this assault, Lady Cowper noted, 'Palmerston has done himself such credit by the talent, discretion, and temper he has displayed during all this time and if Hume has not managed to reduce the estimates, he has at least reduced the Secretary at War, for he has grown as thin again as he was.' But Hume had made so much fuss about the Estimates in 1821 that the following year his objections got little support. Palmerston wrote to his brother: 'He is going down-hill very fast:

indeed, so dull and blunderheaded a fellow, notwithstanding all his perseverance and application, cannot long hold his ground in the House of Commons. It requires some degree of talent, and he does not come up to the mark.'
A similar, though less strongly prejudiced, view was held even among the
Government's opponents. Hobhouse recorded that 'there certainly is a general
feeling of weariness on all sides respecting these details of Hume's & he daily
produces less effect'. But Hobhouse added a warning that 'he may rise again'.
Palmerston would have done well to bear this in mind. Instead it was about
this time that the 'gentlemanlike' quality conceded to him by Lady Minto
began to crumble in the House of Commons and gave to Hume an advantage
he otherwise would not have had. The Secretary at War, Hobhouse had
already noted, 'was flippant in reply'.[5]

No man should be judged too readily on the evidence of his most private
correspondence any more than on that of his public set performances. Each
has its special quality of deception. But there was considerable significance in
the emergence of Palmerston's flippancy into public view. Eventually, of
course, it was considered to be the predominant characteristic of his policies at
home and abroad. To his infuriated critics at the time and since it was all part
of the easy manner that covered with mere technique the absence of principle
and intellectual conviction. It is not surprising, therefore, that earlier writers
have suggested that its striking emergence after Palmerston's first decade in
the War Office was evidence of a growing self-confidence or that more recent
ones have considered it as part of a general ruthlessness and roughness in his
dealings in private and in public. But neither explanation is wholly convincing, though each contains a grain of truth. As will be seen, these were years of
considerable private anxiety for Palmerston, partly on account of his difficult
financial situation and partly because of the trials of his love-life. In short, this
was for him a period of vexation, weariness and worry. Exaggerated and
distorted though it has been, his stiffness at the War Office was perhaps less the
ruthlessness of aristocratic hauteur than the defence mechanism of a
privileged superior. Similarly, his petulant and apparently disdainful treatment of Hume in Parliament was evidence, not of self-confidence, but of strain
and in particular of a temporary inability to cope with all the wearing
preparation of detail required to make a completely effective reply. What
most clearly exposes the origin of his new parliamentary manner and what
completely distinguishes it from that of later years, when it was not so utterly
unsuccessful, was the almost total absence of good humour. Whatever may be
thought of a bluff heartiness in politics and Palmerston's use of it later, his
sneeringly flippant tone in his second decade at the War Office was as a
parliamentary technique patently inferior, and he himself knew it. It gave
unnecessary offence to his opponents and it made even his allies
uncomfortable.[6]

One of the worst examples, also in 1822, was his defence of the Crown's
treatment of General Sir Robert Wilson. Wilson had had an exciting career in

peace as in war. He had served with great distinction in most of the recent European campaigns and then in 1815 had suffered censure by Wellington and imprisonment by the French for getting involved, together with Michael Bruce, in smuggling out of France some Bonapartists condemned for treason during the Hundred Days. He was, in fact, an Opposition man and in 1810-12 especially had supplied his friends with systematic, and perverse, criticism of Wellington's campaigns. In 1818 he had entered Parliament as the representative of the popular constituency of Southwark and made himself a thorn in the flesh of the Government. Finally, in August 1821, when the popular resentment climaxed its association with the cause of Queen Caroline by clashes with the cavalry at her funeral, he intervened to persuade the soldiers to withdraw and soon after was summarily dismissed from the Army. Inevitably Wilson complained and his friends among the Parliamentary Opposition pressed for an explanation in the House. Presented with his customary duty of defending the Army, Palmerston replied in February 1822 that the discipline of the Army and the prerogative of the Crown were involved; Wilson had flouted the one and his supporters were threatening the other. But what gave offence was not so much the substance of his reply – that in any case was not really his invention but Wellington's – but his sneering manner. He omitted any acknowledgement of Wilson's distinguished services and carefully neglected to call him 'gallant'. Even Wilberforce, who did not believe the Crown had acted incorrectly, considered this 'ungenerous'. Others were utterly outraged. Hobhouse commented that Palmerston 'spoke abominably'; Edward Ellice, a Whig, that his reply was 'more miserable than I can describe'. Brougham wrote, evidently this time without much exaggeration: 'Palmerston's total failure no words can describe – and if anything could increase the failure of his case, it would be the vile unfeeling & dull attempts at *sneer* – which were received with *almost equal,* tho' not equally loud, disgust by every part of the House.'[7]

On the whole Palmerston had less trouble with the Estimates in the later 1820s. This was partly, as E. J. Littleton noted, because after Castlereagh's suicide in 1822 the Government's foreign policy under Canning was more popular and the notion of backing it with adequate force more acceptable. But it was also because Palmerston and his colleagues kept a genuinely close eye on expenditure and attempted to anticipate Hume's assaults. In 1827, for example, Palmerston supported plans to reduce the Yeomanry in England from 24,000 to 6,000 and to halt the recruitment of regulars 5,000 short of the establishment in the face of the opposition of Wellington as Commander-in-Chief; and, after Canning's death had suspended both these measures, he preserved the essence of the economies in 1828 by shrewd modifications of detail in the face of Wellington's still more powerful opposition as Prime Minister. So when in 1827-8 Hume made a grand assault upon the Estimates and devoted a whole session of Parliament to laying bare the workings of the War Office, the result was generally reckoned a triumph for the minister. But from another sort of attack Palmerston was never able to protect himself so well.[8]

It was probably General Wilson's persistent attack on flogging that had served to make him as unpopular in the Horse Guards as his support of Queen Caroline made him at court. But in this matter Palmerston also had the unenviable duty of defending in public principles and policies of which in private he might not wholly have approved; and here too his manner in defence markedly deteriorated. He had first been confronted with this question in 1810 after five mutinous militiamen had been awarded five hundred lashes at the hands of German mercenaries. This was too good a mixture of foreign and domestic tyranny to be overlooked by Wiliam Cobbett, the Tory turned radical and sergeant-major turned journalist, and he highlighted the affair in his *Political Register.* As a result Parliament gave military courts the power to award imprisonment, where previously they had no option but to award death or corporal punishment. At the same time Cobbett himself got two years for seditious libel. But the Army did not like the loss of strength nor the Government the expense of money involved in sending men to prison. In any case old practices died hard. So instead of subsiding, criticism of flogging henceforth frequently recurred. Palmerston defended the Army as best he could. When in March 1812 his old enemy Brougham joined the main protagonist, Sir Francis Burdett, in a sustained attack on what they called a sort of 'torture', Palmerston retorted that it was not so degrading as the 'wanton and capricious ill-usage' that he believed obtained in foreign armies, pointing out that a sentence of flogging could only be imposed after formal legal procedures.[9]

It does not appear that Palmerston, even at this stage, thought very deeply about the ghastly situation he defended. 'We had a long debate last night on flogging', he reported to Malmesbury, 'in which I think Burdett was a practical example of the utility of that sort of correction.' Burdett had been imprisoned in the Tower for 'libelling' the House of Commons in 1810; and he was to confirm Palmerston's opinion about the ineffectiveness of plain imprisonment by getting himself put away again in 1820. In 1813 Palmerston rejected protests against floggings, suspended on medical grounds, being completed after however long an interval. Two years later, when he was taxed by one of flogging's most persistent critics, Henry Grey Bennet, with 'indecent haste' in pushing through the Mutiny Bill, he retorted that he would not take lessons on decency from an 'hon. gentleman' who had exhibited such 'specimens' of it as had his critic. But this early and still uncharacteristic example of low abuse was evidently inspired by genuine anger.[10]

In 1812 the Army had agreed to make three hundred the maximum number of lashes that might be inflicted and in 1815, as news of Waterloo was filtering through and Bennet and Burdett attacked again, Palmerston announced that suspended floggings were to be resumed only in the most grave of cases. He still rejected the notion that the British soldier was especially badly treated; if he was punished more it was because he drank and therefore erred more. Above all, he pleaded, this was a matter of military discipline and as such should not be meddled in by Parliament but left to the C.-in-C., who like most of his officers was a merciful man. There may have been something in this (though he apparently overlooked that through a change in the Mutiny Act in 1748 Parliament had gone out of its way to limit and to regulate the Crown's right to inflict punishment under the Articles of War). But it would seem that the campaign was having some effect on Palmerston's individual opinions. After all, he was not merely a member of the generation influenced by Thornton's Clapham Sect and Raikes's Sunday School Movement: through his mother he was related to them both. In 1810 Romilly had noted him among the twenty-two persons in office who had voted against a motion to abolish capital punishment for stealing less than 40/- in a dwelling house. But by the summer of 1812 he was objecting to keeping unnecessarily long in confinement soldiers awaiting trial by court martial; by 1816 he was vigorously supporting in C.-in-C.'s campaign against rogues and vagabonds being sentenced to serve in the Army; and when the soldier's pay-book was introduced in 1815 the penalty for losing it specifically excluded corporal punishment. It was also with his approval that in 1823 the Mutiny Act was again altered, this time to give military courts the power to award hard labour as well as imprisonment. This still further weakened the case for flogging and to anticipate a question from Burdett Palmerston suggested a new limit of two hundred lashes to the punishment that might be awarded by regimental, as distinct from general, courts martial. But this was not accepted, partly perhaps because Palmerston could not resist a note of sarcasm such as by then had become habitual in his communications with Headquarters – he wished 'to submit to the consideration of His Royal Highness whether *200* lashes might not be deemed an adequate punishment for a *small* offence' – but mainly no doubt because it ran directly counter to one of the Army's main defences of flogging, that imprisonment was not a convenient substitute in the field or on colonial service.[11]

So the House of Commons continued to find Palmerston vigorously defending flogging. In 1824 he even argued that the prospective increase in recruiting from urban areas made it more necessary than ever. 'Where large masses of people were collected together in the manufacturing districts,' he said, 'they had not the same simplicity and innocence of manners, which distinguished the agricultural part of the population.' He continued, however, to press for the new limit. Just before the debate on the Mutiny Bill had loomed up, he had tackled the Duke of York's military secretary in person, only to be snubbed the next day. The duke had thought, Palmerston was bluntly told, that the arguments he and the Judge-Advocate-General had produced on the first occasion had been sufficiently convincing. For his part, those 'objections resulted not from any obstinate determination to maintain opinions once formed and expressed, but from conviction of the justice of his view of a question exclusively connected with the *discipline* of the Army, the administration of which belongs so immediately and exclusively to His own Department'. It was not necessary for him to enter into details yet again, but he would reiterate that he objected to *any* change in the present system, which was 'quite good and sufficient towards the double object of maintaining the discipline of the Army and of securing the soldier from the effects of abuses of the power vested in Commanding Officers'. Any further restrictions on the latter's power, he concluded, would be 'pernicious in the greatest degree'.[12]

The duke dealt so severely with Palmerston because he was by this time deep in conflict with him over their respective spheres of authority. But if Palmerston was undiplomatic in his dealings with the duke, it was hardly his fault if he also appeared unconvincing in his public defence of what he disapproved. Symptomatic of his dilemma was the uncharacteristically feeble argument with which he prepared to counter Hume's annual attack again in 1826. Corporal punishment, he was ready to admit, was an evil belonging to 'barbarous ages & ignorant times' that defeated its own object, both as a corrective and a deterrent. On the one hand it hardened the recipient and made him desperate; on the other it aroused the sympathy of the spectator and led him to confound right with wrong. In principle, too, the infliction of bodily pain as a punishment was bad. 'The object of punishment is the mind & not the body . . . to inspire into the mind a controuling motive which shall counterbalance the temptation to a repetition of the crime. But the punishment ought at the same time to soften the mind; now bodily pain irritates & hardens.' So far, so good; the grasp of Utilitarian principles was well worthy of a mind trained in Edinburgh. Yet after all this he could think of nothing but to end up feebly by avowing that the severe discipline required in armies made it impossible to avoid a choice of evils. From the version of his actual speech in *Hansard* it might appear that Palmerston avoided so lame an ending. But even in that discreet record the following speaker is quoted as being convinced by it that Palmerston really agreed in opinion with the attack on flogging, 'though in his situation it might not be prudent to avow it'. It is not surprising, therefore, that by the end of the debate at least one influential senior officer and M.P., Sir Henry Hardinge, thought that the civilian supporters of the Government had put up such a 'lax defence' and that many Army officers had themselves become so persuaded by the radical campaign that it was time to compromise.[13]

What Palmerston proposed immediately after the debate, and with Hardinge's rather lukewarm support, was to introduce something on the lines of the Prussian scheme by which corporal punishment was reserved for a special class of 'degraded' soldiers. The impression that the shame involved in the initial degradation was so great in the Prussian Army as to restrict those in that class to a very small number might have been expected to appeal to the Duke of York's notions of military honour and to meet the case, based on the belief that flogging deterred others but made the recipients incorrigible, for virtual abolition in practice combined with retention in theory. But the scheme was not adopted, perhaps because of the attitude of the Duke of Wellington, who was consulted on this occasion and was to succeed the Duke of York the following year. He was a firm believer in the necessity of corporal punishment in a volunteer army and also in the superiority of British over Prussian discipline.[14]

Palmerston was just as determined as York or Wellington to maintain the Army's national character. A few years before, in defending the Military College against its parliamentary critics, he had declared that 'for his own part, he wished to see the British solider with a British character, with British habits, with a British education, and with as little as possible of any thing foreign'. Nevertheless, he persisted with his proposals about corporal punishment. For some time he had nurtured the idea of recasting the whole of the Mutiny Bill and Articles of War and had even got so far as revising drafts with the War Office Law Clerk. But though the original was somewhat clumsy in its wording, he was not sure that Harrison's 'verbiage' was any better or that it would have been improved by the Judge-Advocate-General either; and the 'antique phraseology' had this personal advantage, that being Dutch William's bill it still commanded 'respect' among a Whiggish Opposition and allowed Palmerston to fend off inconvenient amendments on the grounds that the haste always involved in this annual necessity never allowed time for the careful reconsideration it must deserve. To have gone ahead with his scheme of wholesale remodelling would, moreover, have drawn upon his head the various differences of opinion with the Commanders-in-Chief. So he contented himself with 'mending its details' from time to time, concluding afterwards that he had at least left it better than he had found it. But even on these 'details' Headquarters kept a watchful eye. In March 1827, for example, he suggested that they drop the reference to the punishment for irreverent behaviour in church 'being laid in irons for 12 hours' and substitute 'confinement' in its place. Wellington could think of no serious objection, 'save that it would appear to be made in deference to the morbid sentiment of the times'. But the Judge-Advocate, while conceding that the phrase gave ammunition to the 'anti-punishment gang', wanted to preserve every alternative form of legal punishment available against the day when the abolition of flogging might be carried. So they agreed to the ambiguous compromise of 'corporal punishment', and in spite of his private apprehensions, Palmerston had to continue to defend flogging in the House of Commons right up until his departure from the War Office. Indeed, a few days after his discussion with the Judge-Advocate he was insisting that it would cost far too much in prison-building to abolish it and that it was the foundation of the Army's existence.[15]

The limitation of two hundred lashes suggested by Palmerston in 1823 was not introduced until 1832. The following year, after the then Secretary at War had resigned rather than present another Mutiny Bill that did not abolish the power of regimental courts to award the punishment at all, Palmerston suggested it be done by direct instructions from the C.-in-C. and criticism of flogging in general be fended off by the promise of wholesale investigation and report. But the resistance from the Horse Guards still proved too great and flogging in peacetime remained legal until 1868. One of the main reasons for the delay Burdett himself, perhaps, detected: 'Our flogging & beatings & brutalities civil & military place us on the very lowest grade of the scale of humanity,' he wrote in 1824, '& instead of being the first, as in many respects we undoubtedly are, make us appear the last of the species. I think . . . I will try another motion about military flogging, it is too disgraceful, inhuman and infamous to acquiesce in without protesting.' But, he went on, 'I am fearful the frequent mooting the question without success renders it [flogging] more inveterate, & gives it additional support by every failure.' This certainly seems to have been the effect occasionally on Palmerston who, under the additional strain of private anxiety and overwork, in 1826 and 1827 was attacking Hume with more venom than ever. In December 1826 he sneered at Hume's 'extreme obtuseness of understanding' and the 'impenetrable darkness which dwelt within the interior of his brain'. 'Ld P.'s language was even more insulting than it appears in the reports,' Grey's son wrote, '& his manner was still worse. I thought it very discreditable to him & it gave Hume an advantage over him which he certainly did not possess before, & which might have been turned to great account.' A couple of months later Hume threw all his advantage away by calling into question Palmerston's truthfulness and his character as a gentleman.[16]

One cannot help feeling that both Hume and Palmerston by descending to personalities helped delay the advance of humane relief. For while behind the scenes Palmerston appears to have been gradually persuaded by reason if not entirely moved by sentiment, it was apprehension of attack that usually induced him to suggest modifications in the system of punishments and resentment at its persistence that so often stung him into bitter retort. Private wear and tear would certainly have contributed to both facets of his behaviour. On the other hand, it is only fair to add that he was by no means unendowed with a sort of utilitarian philosophy of humanitarianism. The most obvious example of this was his support over a number of years of Sir William Adams.

Sir William Adams (who later adopted his wife's name of Rawson) was the Prince Regent's oculist and he had been knighted in 1814. But he had aroused a certain amount of professional jealousy, and the Director-General of the Army Medical Department, Sir James Macgrigor, obstructed his attempts to interest the Army in his treatment of trachoma. In December 1814 Adams brought three cases to Palmerston personally to demonstrate the efficacy of his methods and through the Secretary he also enlisted the approval of the Adjutant-General and the Commander-in-Chief. 'I think the country owes it to the Army to use every endeavour to rescue the men from the dreadful calamity of blindness,' Palmerston wrote, '& I am sure that even upon the most illiberal principle it is expedient to prevent so many centres of infection from being turned loose upon the community.' Having argued that it was not intended to set up 'another unnecessary hospital, but a training school for surgeons to undertake this new method of treatment', Palmerston persuaded the Horse Guards to let Adams have a few pensioners at Chelsea as guinea-pigs, and when this proved a general success used new arguments of expediency and economy to win over the Prime Minister. Adams's proposal, he pointed out, was with the aid of two half-pay medical officers to work systematically on the Chelsea cases which were still considered operable and, with the aid of an expected alteration in the law, to retain the men's pensions as a contribution to the expense. Then those who were cured could be discharged from hospital and without the Government having to pay them any further disability pension. As for Adams himself, he would serve without official status or pay but leave it until the Government could assess his efforts by experience and estimate his reward accordingly. With Palmerston's support Adams in 1817 was given the use of part of York Hospital in Chelsea and then of a building specially erected for him in Regent's Park. His enemies still persisted in attacking his efforts and frustrating his reward. When the House of Commons eventually decided to set up a Select Committee, they used it, in the words of one of its members 'to bring Sir W.A. to close quarters whereas without it they could only carry on a paper war'. But Palmerston had personally inspected Adams's patients in company with the Duke of York, and with his warm support Adams carried his cause through the investigations and in July 1821 was finally awarded a gratuity of £4,000.[17]

Palmerston does seem to have been anxious to have justice done generally to civilians performing services for the Army. Early on in office he was urging 'fair', but not full, compensation to innkeepers and for speedier payment to be made to clothiers. In this latter case his motive may really have been to advance his quarrels with the C.-in-C. But, as he himself pointed out, the Secretary at War was the person who stood 'peculiarly between the people and the army, to protect the former from the latter, to prevent their public revenue from being drained by any unauthorized increase of military establishments, and their persons and property from being injured by any possible misconduct of the soldiery; and upon him would Parliament and the country justly fix the responsibility for any neglect of this part of his duty.' In particular he was required by law to remove troops from the vicinity of elections and in the event of his neglecting to do so he was liable not only to the forfeiture of his office but also to disqualification from ever again holding any civil or military position under the Crown. But, to the extent that the awful warnings of the law allowed, Palmerston maintained in general an attitude of cautious impartiality. When, for example, a merchant of Shadwell Street complained in 1818 (as others had before) of the troops marching daily through the narrow streets of Limehouse to the protection of the West India Docks and pushing pedestrians aside and breaking windows on the way, Palmerston adopted as a reply most, but not quite all, the observations of Headquarters. The soldiers had been requested by the merchants themselves; they went by the most convenient route; and if there had been damage then a proper claim for compensation should be made; but he said nothing about the soldiers having as much right to use the streets as any other of His Majesty's subjects. He was also glad to receive suggestions from the Army for doing justice to civilians. When in 1812 a shot fired at an escaping deserter in Liverpool missed and carried off a passing carter, the 'chief support' of aged parents and their numerous other children, the local G.O.C. raised a subscription for the family and recommended too an unsolicited pension. Palmerston readily agreed to the considerable sum of £20 a year being paid for the joint lives of the parents out of the compassionate fund; but he did so in a private letter and insisted that it was not to be regarded as a precedent. He was also quick to acknowledge and support suggestions from civilians that appealed to the sense of economy that had no doubt been cultivated in him at Edinburgh. When, for example, Storekeeper Trotter urged in 1813 a change in the method of procuring military stores he wrote to the Chancellor of the Exchequer: 'Mr Trotter's general principle is that at present by employing many different persons to procure articles of the same description we produce a competition of *buyers*, instead of which if our purchases were confined to one channel, we should have all the advantage resulting from a competition of *sellers*.'[18]

Palmerston was equally quick to take offence at the impertinence of any man whether in or out of office. He had for years disputed the claim of an agent for invalids to handle the pay of the Royal Veteran Battalions; and when in 1813 the agent brought in the help of a Hampshire neighbour of his, the Secretary retorted: 'I have the greatest objection to discuss questions connected with the public business of my office, by the intervention of private individuals.' And in response to their appeal to his recollection of a former conversation he commented: 'I cannot certainly pretend to charge my memory with what passed on that occasion, but can only observe, that every day confirms me in an opinion which a very short experience in official transactions inspired, that the most satisfactory mode of discussing an official question is by letter, by which means the vagueness, ambiguity, & misunderstanding incident to verbal communications are prevented by the precision, & the certainty & facility of reference which recorded correspondence affords.'[19]

Being such a stickler for formality, as these and many other cases showed, meant that although neither radical reformer nor philanthropist, Palmerston was no less anxious to see financial justice done to soldiers too; and in pensions, if not in pay, the Secretary had a good deal of administrative discretion.

Like everything else connected with the early nineteenth-century Army, pensions were distributed in an enormously complicated and arbitrary manner. Until 1806 the claims of both officers and men rested on a muddled variety of Royal Warrants and annual votes of supply. In the case of N.C.O.s and men they also depended to some extent on the caprice of the commanding officer, who might withhold the necessary certificate of good conduct; pensions were only available to them, moreover, if they were disabled by wounds or as some other result of service. But in 1806 Windham had secured an Act which, having introduced the notion of short-service enlistment, gave not only wounded, disabled and infirm but also discharged soldiers a legal right to pensions according to specified periods of service and limited pensioners' liability to be recalled into active service in Invalid or Veteran Companies. After fourteen years' service a foot soldier was entitled to receive a pension of 5d. a day and after twenty-one a shilling. There were somewhat different arrangements for the disabled, whose pensions were calculated according partly to the length of service and partly to the extent of disability. In 1812 Palmerston and the C.-in-C. cooperated to have pensions increased for those whose injuries were so severe as to require constant attendance. The private soldier who had lost more than one limb then received 2/6d. a day. Unfortunately the Commissioners of Chelsea Hospital, who administered both 'in' and 'out' pensions (that is to say, of both residents and non-residents), evidently did not find it easy to work the new system and it was also unpopular with both Government and Army. The Treasury thought it too expensive; the high command too favourable to men who had been discharged as undesirables. The new system therefore came under very considerable parliamentary as well as military pressure.[20]

Palmerston seems to have been far from sympathetic to such criticism of the pension scheme; but he evidently appreciated that it was necessary to give some ground. Encouraged apparently by some sort of conversation with him, the Duke of York outlined early in 1822 a pretty sweeping set of limitations on the men's pension rights. He proposed to abolish the fourteen-year pension; to restore the certification by C.O.s, giving a right of appeal only to the Chelsea Board; to make disability pensions possible only after fourteen years' service; and to enlarge the liability to serve in Veteran Companies. It was probably the last that dampened the Treasury's enthusiasm; for it led the duke to expand at length upon the large and expensive cadre of regular officers who would be needed to run it. But Palmerston contributed a useful degree of opposition. He minuted his protest against the harshness with regard to disability pensions and, when the Government decided only to accept the first of the recommendations, grimly endorsed the scheme for the file: 'Govt do not think it expedient to enter into so large a question, satisfied for present with taking away 14 yrs Pension.' The Chelsea Board's dissatisfaction, however, continued and in 1826 resort was had to a new Act of Parliament for the better regulation of pensions. But this was not intended to overthrow the principle, enshrined in Windham's Act, of a soldier's right to a pension according to length of service or disability; only to remove it on the man's *subsequent* conviction for fraud or felony. Therefore, it did not, as Hardinge for example had hoped, do anything to prevent bad characters taking their discharge in order to enjoy the fruits of an ill-deserving period of service.[21]

The Chelsea Board's disappointment was brought specifically to Palmerston's attention early in January 1827 by complaints about the pension rights of a Sergeant-Major Stride who had been discharged for swindling and theft in Malta and a Private Nugent who had been imprisoned for a year in Poona for attempting to cut the throats of a drummer and a native cook. In neither case had any court martial ordered the forfeiture of pension; but Palmerston's reaction to the avowed wish of the board to exploit whatever discretion the new law had given them is clear and pointed. 'It may be doubted', he minuted, 'whether the court martial which tried Private Richard Nugent awarded a punishment commensurate with his offences.' But even if the court had been too lenient in this case that would be no excuse for giving to Chelsea discretion to decide whether or not a man deserved his pension. '. . . it is undoubtedly right that there should exist somewhere a discretion of this kind, but the regulations of the service have already made provision for it and have vested this authority in a court martial, and it appears to me that a tribunal of officers, acting upon their oath, receiving testimony upon oath, judging the accused by viva voce evidence given in his presence at his regiment & in the midst of his comrades and acting according to the formalities of the law must have far better means of forming an accurate judgment of the conduct of an accused solider than could be come to by any public department in London.' As for Windham's Act and the right to pensions by length of service, 'I have no hesitation in stating that this principle appears to me to be sound & just, & far preferable to the arbitrary system which it superseded.' Perhaps here one may trace the influence, if not of Professor Christian's incompetent Cambridge lectures, then at least of Sulivan's legal experience. In any case Palmerston deserves full credit for his ready grasp and defence of the essential principles of the judicial process. The board did not put up much resistance and on 13 March Palmerston was able to minute on their last feeble explanation: 'This may drop.'[22]

As in other aspects of the ordinary soldiers' welfare, Palmerston's attitude to their pay and pensions was essentially one of paternalism moderated by discretion and tested by efficiency. He resisted, for example, pleas for increased remuneration for regimental quartermasters on the grounds that commanding officers might then be tempted to appoint worn-out N.C.O.s with a view to the rewarding of their favourites rather than to the good of the service. Moreover, although he had opposed the abolition of the short-service pension, once it was decided he himself suggested that they should also abolish the first of the short-service increments of pay. The basic rate of one shilling a day, together with one penny beer money, made the private soldier better off than he had been for a very long time and in his opinion was 'amply sufficient'. So he suggested, and it was agreed, that from 24 January 1823 new recruits (as distinct from those re-enlisting) should not get the former increment of one penny a day after seven years. After fourteen years (seventeen in the cavalry) they would instead get both increments together. The extra two pence, Palmerston argued, would be some compensation for losing their entitlement to a pension at that point, though there was a hidden bonus of retrenchment in that fewer tended to survive to collect an increment after fourteen years than after seven.[23]

Like so many other officers and civilians in positions of authority over the Army, Palmerston simply did not think it wise from any point of view to give soldiers much in the way of cash. Like Wellington, he believed that they would simply drink it away and become useless to themselves and to the state. When he failed to persuade the authorities not to issue to the black troops in the West Indies the rum ration of the white soldiers, he commented bitterly: 'We have at last nearly succeeded thru' the force of institution, regulation and example, in making our black Soldiers almost as drunken and depraved as the Whites, altho' the Negro Tribes, of all the varieties of the human race, savage or civilized, are the least addicted to the vice of drunkenness.' In this instance, he thought, the black soldiers would have been happy with 'a small portion of sugar or syrup instead of rum to mix with water'.[24]

Palmerston often took a more positive line about the soldiers' supposed extravagance. He was generally opposed to lump sum payments or bounties which were liable to be quickly drunk away. 'Property which is acquired by chance or by a blow, like a prize in the lottery or a prize in War, is apt to unhinge the mind, and tempt to irregularities', he argued, 'but property acquired by long continued industry or frugality necessarily, and by the laws of human nature, improves the character of the man who has acquired it.' This remark was provoked in 1825 by differences with the Horse Guards about the desirability of setting up savings banks for soldiers. Palmerston was afterwards reckoned not to have 'pushed' the matter. But since the suggestion had first been put to him in 1816 he had in 1822 established facilities for men serving overseas to send their savings home. He later described his intention as 'to encourage orderly and sober habits in a soldier by giving to him ready and easy means of sending home, without force, any sums which by prudence and frugality he might be able to lay by out of his pay'. He did not think it any business of the Army's what was the purpose of any remittances, whether, for example, for the benefit of his family or the payment of some debt. But he did object to their being the profits from some private trade as 'messmen, sutlers, etc.' and it may have been 'abuses' of this sort that made it impossible for him to argue too much against the Horse Guards. When the proposal was put again to the new C.-in-C. in August 1827, Wellington retorted: 'Has a soldier in the Army more pay than he requires? If he has the soldier's pay ought to be lowered; not to those now in the service, but to others enlisted hereafter. I don't think it desirable to encourage our soldiers to become *over-thrifty*.' Sulivan minuted that the pay was indeed higher than was necessary to the *wants* of the soldier; but went on to point out that this was not necessarily the only criterion. Lukin distinguished between 'overthriftiness which is avarice' and 'a frugal economy'.

Military savings banks were not to be established until as late as 1842. Palmerston's successors evidently found it just as difficult as he had to argue against men who insisted (as in 1825) that a savings account would only make a soldier 'begin to think himself independent of his officers and become insubordinate', or counter their reference to the ready facility of civilian banks by pointing out that 'the lower classes feel confidence in the Savings Banks in their respective neighbourhoods because they are under the superintendence and management of the gentlemen of the district, but that Soldiers would not feel the same confidence in such Banks because they would not have the same sentiment towards the Directors and Managers, and that none but officers of the Army can stand in the same relation to Soldiers in which the gentlemen stand with respect to the lower classes.' [25]

Notions of class, conventional to his time, also dictated a very different attitude on Palmerston's part towards the pay and pensions of officers. Indeed, he specifically acknowledged the desirability of maintaining a standard of living according to rank. [26] But within this limit he did not discriminate in his insistence on justice and equity. Moreover, although much more generous, officers' pensions too were confused in complicated categories and rules. Some were derived from the Royal Bounty, others from parliamentary votes, and still others, for certain dependants, from a compassionate fund drawn from the 'pay' of two fictitious men per company. Since so many commissions were by purchase, they were themselves, subject to certain restrictions as to price and the qualifications of the purchaser, marketable commodities and capable of realizing a tidy sum on which to retire. But in privileged cases, for example as a reward for distinguished service or compensation for wounds, officers might be retired on full pay and a 'reduced commission' of this sort must have been particularly desirable. The principal category, however, was 'half-pay'.

Half-pay was originally less a pension than a retainer and it too had some value in the market. It would be paid only until the reduced officer was re-employed in some capacity or other; hence the prohibition on clerks in the War Office also receiving half-pay. But several modifications of the regulations during the eighteenth century and an Act of 1811 had specifically provided for half-pay to be made also to officers who retired from wounds, ill-health or old age. By 1811, therefore, half-pay had lost much of its original character of a retainer and become a pension. But, as has already been pointed out, Palmerston did his best to preserve as much as possible of the old principle and after the relaxation of the law relating to civilian emoluments, which tended to make half-pay officers less willing to return to active service, he tightened up the regulations in 1824 in order to ensure that they did not voluntarily make themselves less able – in particular enforcing the disqualification of those, other than chaplains, who took Holy Orders. [27]

There was also some provision for officers' widows and families, including even dependent mothers and sisters. This was limited and conditional; but, apart from an orphanage established in 1801 and a system of regimental schools adopted in 1811, there was almost none at all for the families of common soldiers. As Palmerston said when rejecting a complaint about the abandonment of their families by Scottish and Irish pensioners, the Government could not interfere because the soldier's pension was his own and not his family's. He tried to ensure, however, that the Government did not make this situation worse. With his proud patriotism he was not anxious to promote any actual addition to the expenditure on foreign troops; in 1812, for example, he resisted the idea of paying them the same bounty on re-enlistment that was paid to the British. But he disliked the unfairness they suffered through the lack of any provision for paying pensions abroad. As things stood, he pointed out, they had to abandon either their pensions or their families. So, against some resistance, he revitalized old possibilities, arranged new regulations with the Treasury, and even had legislation enacted to permit commutation of both foreign soldiers' pensions and half-pay.[28]

British officers and their families, however, also laboured under an anti-quated and confused system and in their cases too there was a good deal of injustice and abuse. Both faults offended Palmerston, and he did a good deal to try and set things on a more equitable basis. In 1813, for example, he and the Commander-in-Chief submitted a joint memorandum to the Treasury pointing out that the increases in rates of pay to serving officers in 1797 and 1806 had left retirement rates untouched, apparently on the assumption that the increases were temporary and would be cancelled when prices fell. But as they survived into 1813 these discrepancies did not seem to them to be 'reconcilable to any clear & liberal principle'. While too he believed in rewarding rank and merit as much as service, it annoyed him to find senior officers abusing their privileges. In June 1812 a Royal Warrant had laid down rules and a scale of compensation for wounded officers and, in July 1815, another had extended the arrangement in the grateful enthusiasm following Waterloo. They had never intended, however, that someone who had once ruptured a tendon in his leg, but had long since been told it would heal if only he would take off the bandage, should go on receiving an indefinite pension of £300 a year. Palmerston understood that the malingerer bore 'but an indifferent character especially among military men'. But although he bom-barded the Chancellor of the Exchequer with what he admitted was 'rather an alarming mass' of papers, he still found himself bound by previous agreement. The expense of the Waterloo arrangements, however, eventually brought the backing of parliamentary opinion for his views and his successors were able to introduce a regular system of medical re-examination.[29]

The ruptured officer who so offended Palmerston appears to have been a mere lieutenant of marines who had put in other mysterious service in Spain, which somehow or other had gained him special treatment. But it mattered little to Palmerston how powerful a man or how small the sum involved. In the summer of 1825, for example, the new C.-in-C. in India, Lt Gen. Sir Thomas Bradford, decided to leave behind his batman to care for his children and their governess in Uxbridge. He belatedly got the Duke of York's permission to detach the man; but three years later, when he pressed for his batman's arrears of pay, Greenwood & Cox wondered if they really ought to pay it. Palmerston had no doubt whatever: the law required that no man not employed on military duty should receive military pay; the soldier concerned should either be bought out or returned to his regiment. Bradford, however, had already frightened the agents into paying over the £50. 1s. 5d. involved and a battle royal ensued with the Horse Guards backing Bradford and the authority of the now deceased Duke of York, and independent legal opinion reinforcing Palmerston in his duty to uphold the law. Palmerston kept it going bravely till he had left the office; but his successors were weaker than he and decided to forgive the error, even though by that time the soldier had been absent from his regiment no less than five years.[30]

Another case of similar sensitivity which Palmerston tenaciously fought for many years was that of a pluralist staff officer in St Helena. The case of Lt Col. Gideon Gorrequer was complicated and tedious. In brief, after the death of Napoleon in May 1821, the Governor and most of the garrison had left as quickly as they could and Gorrequer, the Governor's A.D.C. and military secretary, had been made acting Deputy Adjutant-General to wind up the establishment and hand the island over to the East India Company. There then began a long dispute over whether he should be paid as acting D.A.G. at the company's rate of 19/- a day or the King's of 38/-, who should pay it, the company or the King, and, indeed, whether as A.D.C. at 19/- a day and military secretary at 38/- he should get anything else at all. Palmerston had no doubt: the man was a pluralist and should repay whatever he had received as D.A.G. He managed to extract £51. 6s. 0d. Gorrequer, however, had persistence and powerful friends. The former Governor wrote constantly to praise his achievements and the Horse Guards to beg that even if it be not strictly regular he should be allowed to keep his extra pay 'in consideration of the zeal with which he had executed certain extraordinary duties'. Palmerston remained adamant: 'If the various staff appointments which were held at the same time by Col. Gorrequer involved the performance of any considerable duties', he minuted, 'it was impossible that those duties could be properly performed by one and the same individual; and if there were no such duties to be performed the appointments ought not to have been kept up merely for the purpose of affording emolument to a given individual.' But such pluralism was technically not against the regulations and the situation was endlessly confused by the overlapping authorities of the Crown and company. The ground was finally swept from beneath Palmerston's feet by the acceptance of financial obligation on the part of the company and their willingness to pay up. So in the end Gorrequer got back his £51. 6s. 0d.; but not until Palmerston had held it up for nearly a decade.[31]

Even where the discretion lay virtually within his own control Palmerston declined to be smug. One would have thought a decade and more of the War Office would have hardened him. He must, for example, have learned something when confronted with the claims of rival 'widows'. The classic case was one that had all the qualities of a tragi-comedy. In April 1817 Mrs Elizabeth Shiel, the widow of a paymaster who had died in the West Indies the previous year, wrote to say that her widow's pension was not enough to support herself and two daughters. Her husband appeared to have given long service; she herself was the granddaughter of the first Earl of Arran; and she had very respectable testimonials. So Palmerston directed that she be given allowances from the Royal Bounty of £14 for each daughter. But the following year there appeared a rival widow of Mr Shiel, née Eleanor Pierce, and a rival mother of the daughters. Palmerston therefore directed: 'There seems to be a mystery about this transaction which requires to be cleared up. Suspend all the allowances till proper certificates of baptism are sent & till it is ascertained to which of the widows they belong.' The first (or, rather, in order of seniority, second) Mrs Shiel then had to explain that hers had been a 'private' (she meant unofficial) marriage and that she had adopted the two girls after they had been deserted, in common with the father, by her predecessor. Palmerston then directed that as she made her case 'in equity though not in law' Elizabeth should have £30 a year for herself and allowances from the compassionate fund for the children but that Eleanor should have nothing. Further confusion of fact and argument then cast doubt again on Elizabeth's story and Palmerston, in some impatience, ordered that since they certainly existed the children might continue to be given allowances but that no pension could be given to either of such doubtful 'widows'. Finally he was convinced that Elizabeth and not Eleanor was the fraud, but regretted that he still could not grant the latter a pension since the principle on which such grants were made was that: 'the widow is by the death of her husband deprived of those means of support which she received during his lifetime. That principle does not apply in any case in which the widow had for many years previous to the death of her husband lived separate from him.' But he ended by directing that she be paid £10 a year from the compassionate fund.[32]

In spite of the experience Palmerston had with Mrs Shiel he continued to be worried, even in 1822, about abuses of the half-pay system, whether by official or private design, damaging the rights of widows. A widow's claim would be affected by the cause of the officer originally going on half-pay and was better if he went on account of ill-health than for his private convenience. He was required to state the reason at the time. But, as Palmerston pointed out, a healthy officer might allege unfitness in order to obtain half-pay and an unfit one disguise it in the hope of being recalled one day. It was agreed therefore to require medical inspections and keep up a record against the day when the minister would have to decide on a pension claim.[33]

Perhaps one must expect Palmerston to have been peculiarly sensitive to the problems of women. Certainly as early as 1812 he had begun to get worried that the amount likely to be made available for officers' widows would not be sufficient. For many years provision had been made in the parliamentary estimates for basic rates of pensions appropriate to the military rank of the deceased officer, namely at £40 for a captain and £60 for a lieutenant colonel. In addition, provision for children at the rate of £16 a year, and even for dependent mothers and sisters, might be made at the Secretary's discretion from his compassionate fund. Anything more had to come from Royal Bounty Warrants. What worried Palmerston was that 'the more extensive & brilliant services' of the Army in recent years would present too many demands upon that source and that in the consequent process of competitive petition injustice would be done to those families who did not have the wit or the well-placed friends to forward their applications. The family of General Le Marchant, who was fatally wounded at Salamanca, received a total of £1,200 p.a.; there was no widow, and the eldest son, although over eighteen, received £300, three younger sons £100 each, and five daughters £120 each. Palmerston's first step was to arrange with the Prime Minister and subsequently with the C.-in-C. that they give preference equally with the dependants of general officers to those of all officers who had died in battle or of wounds. The following year, 1813, he further proposed that in obviously deserving cases they get Parliament to provide double the normal rate of basic pension and so enable them to reserve a larger part of the Royal Bounty for other special cases. In 1823 he also introduced a graduated scale for children and finally in 1824-6 consolidated the complex office rules, clarified some ambiguities, and in many cases improved the scale of pensions and allowances. The warrant of 13 June 1826, for example, laid down revised scales for children according to the father's rank and the circumstances of his death. It also limited the total amount a family might receive, including the widow as well as children. The family of a general officer would ordinarily receive a maximum of £300 a year, or £500 if he had died in battle, other commissioned ranks the appropriate rate of half-pay, or rather more if the father had been killed in battle. Except in the case of bodily or mental infirmity, allowances for sons ceased at eighteen and for daughters at twenty-one or, if earlier, at marriage. But even Palmerston could not steer an entirely safe course between the rival tendencies of parliamentary parsimony and parliamentary indulgence. As early as 1812 he and Perceval had considered limiting a widow's pension according to her circumstances and in February 1818 a House of Commons Finance Committee was led to believe that these pensions were limited to the needy. But when a Royal Warrant was issued that month laying it down that no pension could be granted where the widow had any other Government pension or where her private income exceeded twice her pension, there were immediate protests in the Commons and the warrant had to be withdrawn. So 1827 found Palmerston refusing to take 'private pecuniary' circumstances into account when reviewing the case of Louisa, Countess of Craven and actress-widow of a general officer best known by his appearance among the cocoa-trees on the first page of Harriette Wilson's *Memoirs.* [34]

For all Palmerston's efforts many of the rules and regulations concerning pensions remained extraordinarily complicated. There were particularly complicated rules for widows whose marriages took place after their husbands' retirement. Generally they got full pensions if their husbands had served at least three years on active service; but pensions were not granted to widows whose husbands had died other than on active service within a year of marriage, had lived apart and not supported them, or had been sixty-five or over at the time of marriage. There is a good statement by Palmerston of the principles involved in a particularly complicated case of the claim of the widow of a half-pay officer. Robert Halliday had served some years in the East India Company's Army and in the King's Army but had subsequently sold out, thus forfeiting any future pension claim for himself and his widow. But in 1799 he had bought a reduced full-pay sub-lieutenancy in the defunct Horse Grenadier Guards and enjoyed its income for eighteen years until his death in 1817. To qualify for a pension in the ordinary way Mrs Halliday would have had to have been married before the reduction took place and her husband to have served at least three years on full pay. She had been married six months before the reduction and her husband had served the three years. But, in the one case, her husband had had no connection with the regiment at the time, and, in the other, the full pay was not made in respect of the active service really intended, but not stated, by the regulations. However, some war official argued, the letter of the regulations had been met and, in any case, Halliday must be deemed to have bought all the rights pertaining to the commission. Palmerston would have nothing to do with such sophistry. 'The widow's pension is granted as a bounty of the Crown at its discretion,' he minuted, '& it is in no degree a matter of right on the part of the widow. The grounds on which the Crown make the grant are the services performed or undertaken to be performed by the husband; and I can by no means conceive that a man who never did a single day's duty and who in fact bought a reduced commission as an annuity knowing that no duty whatever was or could be required from him in consequence of it, can have earned for his widow the slightest claim to pension; & it would be a great abuse to grant it in such a case.' On the other hand, a few years after Palmerston had left the War Office a new Chancellor of the Exchequer complained that Palmerston had arranged with his Prime Minister to grant pensions to the widows of officers in the German Legion and not even kept a minute of the conversation. 'We ought', he said, 'to apply every exertion to reduce the pensioners on our Army estimate. The amount paid in pensions is what weighs the country down, and it certainly seems to be carrying the principle of pensions to an inordinate extent to . . .

give them to the widows of officers in a foreign corps, whose services to England, though very important, did not extend over more than a few years.'[35]

This criticism hardly took fair account of the enormous size of the armies needed to fend off the French menace or the immense burden of work that Palmerston and his men assumed. For example, as if all the complications of pay and pensions were not enough, the law and custom of the day between them also kept Palmerston busy with the complaints from the private creditors of individual officers in addition to those from the Army's. Even where no legal responsibility really fell upon the Government, he was concerned at the disrepute sometimes brought upon the service. The common practice of a regimental quartermaster acting privately as 'a sort of general merchant' particularly annoyed him. As a retired N.C.O. the quartermaster was usually 'a merchant without capital and individually without credit; his want of capital compels him to exact unreasonable profits from the men . . . to enable him to bear up against . . . losses . . . , and his individual want of credit makes it often necessary for him to obtain articles from tradesmen by giving . . . a vague notion that he has the security of the public'. On the other hand creditors, as well as deserted wives, certainly did have some claim on the proceeds of the sale of commissions. As always the intermediate status of half-pay officers created particular difficulty.[36]

Since not on active service, half-pay officers were not subject to courts martial but could be removed by the Crown for unbecoming conduct, and this opened the way for many optimistic and inconvenient applications to the War Office from aggrieved creditors. So in June 1823 the Horse Guards forwarded various proposals providing for an effective intervention by the Crown short of the actual dismissal of 'discreditable' half-pay officers. Palmerston, however, replied that it was only natural that people used to employment in the Army and thrown onto what he called the 'scanty' half-pay of ensigns and lieutenants should fall into bad habits. Moreover, having (though he did not say so) some personal experience of pressing tradesmen, he felt that the blame would not all be on one side: 'When, as not infrequently happens, the complaint is by one rogue against another, no harm can result from leaving them to settle their dispute as they can.' Creditors should not be able to rely on the interference of Government departments which were not courts of law and would have only imperfect evidence before them. Those departments should therefore wait until a real court had proved a man to have behaved disgracefully 'as an officer' and then he should simply be removed from the service. Yet it was not easy for Palmerston to keep strictly to his own line, especially where women were concerned. For at pretty well the same time he allowed his office to suspend the pay of a half-pay officer in the West Indies until he made provision of £20 a year for the children he had left with his deserted wife in England; and when that officer went bankrupt a few years later to prohibit the sale of his commission until some new arrangement for them could be made.

Eventually the purchaser himself came to the rescue, which was just as well since by that time both the C.-in-C. and Palmerston had come to appreciate that in their zeal to protect the good name of the Army they had overstepped the bounds of their authority and laid themselves open to an avalanche of new appeals.[37]

Although, then, there were many improvements in the War Office's regulation and administration of pay and pensions, the Secretary's situation left him very exposed to the verdicts of individual supplicants. Naturally these were very mixed. George Jackson, a diplomatic acquaintance of Malmesbury's, several times sought out Palmerston's help for various friends and relations – including one officer whose handling of accounts, in Jackson's own opinion, was lucky not to have got him hanged – and commented always on the minister's invariable kindness and courtesy. Less sympathetic petitioners, however, could record even their successes with scorn. One of Thomas Creevey's stepdaughters, who had been left a lieutenant colonel's widow in 1820, was still having difficulty getting her full pension in 1825. So when Lord Rosslyn, who was a general and 'a really sensible man & quite to be relied upon in counsel', told him Palmerston was 'a very practicall man to deal with personally', Creevey decided to tackle the minister in person at the War Office. But when he got there Palmerston 'hummed & hawed' and then bluffly assured him that he would get an answer 'directly' if only Creevey would let him have a note upon the subject; whereupon the crafty Creevey pulled from his pocket not only a previous letter of his own but Palmerston's acquiescent reply in writing! 'In short,' Creevey spitefully reported to another stepdaughter, 'a fellow more completely roll'd over you never in your life beheld, without a shadow of a case or rule to produce in his behalf, & evidently too happy to be let off so easily.' Creevey could hardly contain his contempt when he left and as he passed among Palmerston's 'understrappers' he reflected, as no doubt had many others with more cause, 'on what a damned thing their labour is & how insufferably hard upon those who suffer injustice from it, merely because they have not the means of facing it'.[38]

Creevey's spite tended to be scattered very indiscriminately, but he seemed to enjoy taking part in the parliamentary assaults on Palmerston and in these he may well have been encouraged by his friend Brougham. Possibly it was this episode, or others like it, which led Palmerston to institute in the War Office the practice of having a basket constantly at hand and by means of which he could have the names of his casual callers, on a given signal, quietly whisked away to the registry and the relevant correspondence promptly returned. Then, it was said, he would interrupt his caller's complaining exposition by saying, 'Dear me! It's very remarkable, but I have your case actually before me now', and send him out satisfied that his case had had his lordship's attention all morning at least. But if this was Palmerston's answer to Creevey's random shafts, it was hardly an effective defence against the more dangerous grudges, indeed the most deadly of any of his aggrieved petitioners', evinced by an obscure lieutenant of infantry.[39]

About 1 p.m. on Wednesday, 8 April 1818, a Lt David Davies called at the War Office asking to see the minister. He was told that Palmerston was out riding, but insisted on waiting in the lobby. Shortly before two Palmerston returned and was going up the first flight of stairs when Davies put a pistol close to his back and fired. Davies made no attempt to escape and was immediately seized by a porter as, 'with an air and a grin of satisfaction upon his countenance', he shouted 'I have killed him'. He had not, however, by any means done so, although it was a very narrow escape. The ball had penetrated both clothes and braces, but what Lady Malmesbury called Palmerston's 'way of springing up stairs' had taken him to the first turn on the staircase just as the shot was fired from below. The ball therefore passed sideways and failing to pierce the flesh lodged instead in the wall. Palmerston was severely bruised and burned close to the backbone and he was heard to groan heavily. He thought himself that he had been seriously wounded, but he continued up the stairs and, after merely telling his secretary he had been shot at, settled down to work. Someone sent for Astley Cooper, the distinguished surgeon who lived near by; but Palmerston kept him waiting too, while he pressed on with urgent business. However, he was eventually persuaded to go home to rest with a cold compress on his back and later that evening the family doctor confirmed that while 'there was not the *least* cause for apprehension', Palmerston ought in view of 'the mental agitation upon so dreadful an occasion' to be 'kept low and not eat meat'. Palmerston allowed himself to be cooped up at home only for a couple of days. On the Saturday he ordered a carriage to take him to the office; and the next day he was walking about out of doors for two or three hours.[40]

Not everyone took the affair so coolly. A desperate Bonapartist had very recently shot at Wellington in Paris, and when they heard of the two attempts some could only contrast the cases and ask, 'Why should a man shoot at Palmerston?' Still, it might possibly have been part of a revolutionary plot. It was, after all, a time of riot and repression in the land; *habeas corpus* had already been suspended and within a couple more years would come the 'Peterloo Massacre' and the Cato Street Conspiracy. Since he was not a member of the Cabinet Palmerston would not have fallen first among the latter's victims; but as a Tory minister, as the link between Army and public, and as a landowner, he was well-known enough to take his turn. During the bread riots of March 1815 several M.P.s were manhandled as they left the Commons and some even had their houses ransacked. No wonder then that Palmerston should have barricaded his doors and windows in Stanhope Street and, as he reported to Peel, have told the servants 'to meet the first discharge of stones with a volley of small shot' so as to 'pepper the faces of the mob without any danger of killing any of them' but as 'an earnest of what a further perseverance in the attack might produce'. In 1819 his friend Lady Cowper had a narrow escape from a stone-throwing Westminister election mob as she returned from a ladies committee at Almack's with her coachman flying her brother's Tory colours, and this must have brought home to him in a very personal way the peculiar tendency of the time to what he called 'brutal outrages'. As a country gentleman, too, he was affected as much as many. When later in the same year the Government's Peterloo critics tried to compensate for Parliament's being in recess by petitioning to hold meetings, Palmerston and Wellington joined with other local landholders to counter the Hampshire applications. The persistence of the riots forced the recall of Parliament and Brougham seized the opportunity to condemn the counter-petitions and to criticize the conduct of Palmerston and Wellington, among others, as improper in Government ministers. But Palmerston thought that this was 'no ordinary moment' in the history of his country and that everything depended 'not merely upon the cold support of the friends of social order, but upon their displaying a zeal and alacrity in some measure corresponding with the activity of those who are endeavouring to overthrow our institutions'. So when in the following year the trial of Queen Caroline backfired upon the Government and roused the Opposition to harass them through the land once more, Palmerston again took the leading role in organizing Hampshire's counter-meetings and loyal addresses. Soon afterwards he was also investigating, on behalf of a dozen neighbours who again included Wellington, the possibility of establishing a 'patriotic' newspaper in Southampton. He contacted Lord Lowther, who had backed a similar enterprise in Kendal, and Dr Stoddart, who was editor of a Government newspaper called the *New Times* and a renegade from the old, and concluded from what they told him that it would require a capital outlay of £3,000. Several projects of this sort, and notably *John Bull*, were put in hand elsewhere. In Southampton there appeared in 1823 a weekly paper of Tory inclinations called the *Hampshire Advertiser*. There is no trace of any payment by Palmerston to its nominal proprietor, a local bookseller called Coupland, but there is an entry under 'miscellaneous' in Palmerston's accounts for 1821 of £200 to a certain 'Saunders'.[41]

It may well have been that Brougham's attack on the Tory counter-petitions had inspired Palmerston with the need for discretion in some things at least. For so cautious was he in the traces he left of his connection with another of Dr Stoddart's enterprises that his enigmatic reference to the 'A.S.S.' has led some to believe that at this impossibly early date he had joined the Anti-Slavery, instead of what he called for brevity's sake the Anti-Sedition, Society. In December 1820 a group of ultra-Tories, who were outraged by the indecent press attacks on the establishment but quite overlooked the example of their own *John Bull*, met to lay the foundations of a society to promote the enforcement of the libel laws. The Constitutional Association for Opposing the Progress of Disloyal and Seditious Principles published its first list of subscribers in May 1821. It included the names of some forty peers and church dignitaries. Unlike Wellington, who put his name down for £25, Palmerston's was not among them. But there were several anonymous or pseudonymous donations, including one from 'P.V.' for £10, which Palmerston's private accounts for 1820 confirm was his. A curious letter of his also survives to show that even at the safe distance of Broadlands he was party to the establishment of the Constitutional Association as early as December 1820. He explained, however, that he was 'quite sensible' of the desirability of such affairs being known to have 'originated with independent men, not connected with office'. It was just as well he had learned to be discreet. The Association had some success at first; but it overreached itself with its indiscriminate prosecutions and in spite of support in Parliament from such as Castlereagh and Wilberforce, Brougham's and Whitbread's attacks on the Bridge Street Gang (as it was dubbed from its headquarters) succeeded in discrediting it by the end of 1821. The *Hampshire Advertiser*, on the other hand, appears to have been an unqualified success, both politically and financially.[42]

It was hardly possible for Palmerston to exercise a similar discretion in his capacity of Secretary at War. When, in the debates on the Army Estimates in March 1818, his old Cambridge opponent, Althorp, proposed a reduction of 5,000 men on the grounds of the supposed evil of deficit spending in a time of general distress, Palmerston rejoined that although he did not believe that a 'numerous population ought to be governed by the edge of the sword', he did feel that 'the experience of the last few years' showed how the people had been 'brought into such a state of fermentation, as to render life and property unsafe, without the protection of a large military force'. He had definite opinions, too, about the sort of men required for keeping internal order, though in this case he evidently saw the Secretary's special role of buffer less as protecting the public from the Army than as protecting the Army from the mob. 'I quite agree', he would write in support of a proposal of 1824 to extend the purchase of commissions to half-pay officers so as to introduce younger officers into the reserve, 'in thinking it expedient, both upon military & constitutional grounds, to give encouragement to the sons of nobility, & gentry, & the possessors of property to enter into the Army. A full & large admixture of such persons raises the tone & character of the profession & binds up the military with the citizen in a community of interest & feeling by which much of the constitutional danger of standing armies is met & obviated; of course there is a limit to this principle and the soldier of fortune ought to have his chance as well as his wealthier brother soldier.' Later, in 1826, he told the House of Commons that the system of purchase was the best means of 'allowing members of high families . . . to get on with greater rapidity than they would by mere seniority' and so keeping the command from falling into the hands of 'unprincipled military adventurers'. This did not mean he was an uncritical supporter of purchase, for as usual he was speaking more for the Army than himself. When putting his views privately before the Cabinet a few months later he admitted that the system would be expensive to dismantle and that it was economical for the state to have superannuated officers bought out of active service, but, his memorandum had begun, 'the principle of making offices of trust under the Crown the subject matter of purchase & sale . . . is in the abstract hardly tenable, & belongs to times & notions long gone by'.[43]

At the other end of the military scale it is interesting to note what he said about territorialization after general service regiments had been abolished in 1816. 'I believe there is a great disinclination on the part of the lower orders to enlist for General Service; they like to know that they are to be in a certain Regiment, connected, perhaps, with their own country, and their own friends, and with officers who have established a connection with that district.' He had, by contrast, a grave mistrust of urban volunteers, having by experience learned to appreciate the wariness of the college heads of his undergraduate days at Cambridge. Too many of the Volunteers were artisans and shop-keepers, who might well decide to go over to the mob; he preferred the country yeomanry and militia, who were officered by country gentlemen like himself and more easily isolated from the townsmen with a view to protecting them from both odium and infection. So as early as 1812 he recommended the Government to disband the Volunteers and strengthen the Yeomanry, and as late as 1820, when the Government decided in preference to expand the regular force in Great Britain and Ireland to nearly sixty thousand men, he vigorously defended their decision against the inevitable attacks of the Op-position. He also had to ask Parliament for a supplementary vote of £70,000 to enable new barracks to be built where the soldiers might be segregated from the local population. The radicals naturally attacked this as a plot to in-timidate free-born Englishmen.[44]

With this sort of reputation being attached to him, perhaps it was not at all unreasonable even in 1818 for some to link the attempt on Palmerston's life with a general conspiracy to assassinate Government ministers. J. C. Hob-house, who had been in the Fusty with Palmerston at Cambridge but was now a better friend of Byron's and a radical M.P. to boot, heard that Castlereagh's brother, Lord Stewart, was talking at Almack's of there being three hundred on the list of intended victims. Hobhouse had very good reason to be alarmed at the rumour since it was he who had the week before enflamed passions on both sides with a scurrilous but anonymous 'open letter', attacking Canning as one of the leaders of popular repression. Hobhouse, however, was very fright-ened by what he had done, especially when Canning challenged his unnamed accuser to a duel. Talk of a revolutionary plot made his situation all the more dangerous and he was evidently very relieved when he heard some general confirmation of his original information that Lt Davies 'had cut off his *penis* in a fit, and then applied as a maimed officer for a pension'. Davies certainly seems to have done something of the sort. At his trial the court was cleared of ladies and medical evidence given of an act of self-mutilation two years earlier that made it all too clear that he was mad. So while Hobhouse sheltered behind his anonymity from Canning's wrath (though he was the next year to be imprisoned in Newgate for a breach of parliamentary privilege), poor Davies was found by his Old Bailey jury to have been 'in a state of derange-ment' at the time of his attempt and so acquitted of the charge but ordered to be detained as a dangerous lunatic during His Majesty's pleasure. The pros-ecution cost Palmerston £58. 19s. 8d.; and Davies would have had no defence counsel if Palmerston had not also sent £20 or £30 to the prison chaplain. Three years later Davies sent a contrite letter from Bedlam asking Palmerston to release him on full pay. Palmerston merely endorsed the note '!!!'[45]

Davies was described at his trial as 'short in stature, of mild manners, and dressed in black'. But he also muttered darkly about his 'secret motives' and it was quite clear that even if he had, in Guedalla's delightful phrase, been 'maddened perhaps by correspondence with the War Department,' he had been unstable for some time. A native of Monmouth and the son of an Army officer (he had a brother in the Navy), David Davies was a former officer of the West Middlesex Militia who in 1814 had offered his services to the regular Army and obtained a lieutenancy in the 62nd Regiment of Foot. He had served for some time in Canada; but soon after returning to England his behaviour had become so strange that in June 1816 he was removed from his regiment and placed on half-pay. It is not clear quite what was the cause of this event. But Palmerston knew enough about it all to reject the stream of petitions and complaints that followed from Davies's pen. Davies spent some time in a military hospital, where he carried out his act of self-mutilation, and was then removed at Palmerston's request and confined by his family in what was called a 'madhouse' in South Wales. When, therefore, he continued to write pressing for an interview, Palmerston firmly and, as he no doubt thought, safely refused this too. But he reckoned without the determination of a madman; for Davies broke free from confinement and made his way to London. There he clashed several times with his landlord over imaginary grievances and had even been charged with 'riotous behaviour and assaults'. But his disturbed condition was so clear that he was allowed to go free. On 16 March he redeemed from pawn a pair of pistols, one of which was later found in his lodgings along with an account of the trial of Perceval's assassin. Even then he might well have made the C.-in-C. rather than the minister his victim, for he first got an interview with the Duke of York. The duke evidently found his conversation very strange, but dealt with him calmly although he pre-sumably did nothing effective either to soothe him or to have him watched. Since matters concerning pensions, which was what Davies's business seemed to be about, were the concern of the Secretary at War rather than the C.-in-C. and the duke had no doubt turned the petitioner in what seemed the right direction, it would perhaps be very unfair to point out that personal and political relations between the duke and Palmerston were on the eve of a rapid deterioration.[46]

There were many reasons why Palmerston might have been regarded with extreme dislike among all ranks in the Army. But the basic difficulty between the Secretary at War and the Commander-in-Chief was undoubtedly the vagueness and uncertainty of the boundaries between their respective spheres of authority. The Commissioners of Military Enquiry could find in 1808 no detailed instructions for the guidance of the Secretary, but they were told by his deputy that he conceived his chief to be 'acting under the immediate authority of the King' and to be governed 'in the discharge of his duty by the existing rules of the Service, as ascertained by law, by His Majesty's Warrant, or by established practice'. But when they came to examine more precisely what this meant, they found that the state of the law was confused and the Royal Warrant, to say the least, ambiguous. The warrant merely required that the Secretary should 'diligently and faithfully execute all things belonging to a Secretary at War, and follow such orders as he shall from time to time receive from His Majesty, or from the General of His Forces, according to the discipline of War'. Thus it seemed to imply that the Secretary, who was supposed to curb the professional extravagance and to restrain the warlike arrogance of the Army, was himself a 'military officer' and therefore the subordinate of the C.-in-C. Unfortunately the Commissioners failed to clear up this dilemma and satisfied themselves with the observation that the Secretary's work was 'grounded, in most instances, on usage'. With sufficient good will between colleagues, these obscurities would no doubt have caused little trouble. But Palmerston, on the one hand, soon proved to be not in the least the 'mere courtier' described by Brougham, and successive C.-in-C.s, on the other, to be much too sensitive to tolerate anything else.[47]

When Palmerston took over the War Office in 1809 the C.-in-C. was not the Duke of York, but General Sir David Dundas, a semi-retired veteran of seventy-four. This was because the duke, the King's second son, had thought it best to resign in March of that year even though his mistress, Mrs Clarke, had not been able to establish her assertions that it was with his knowledge and approval that she had been selling commissions and promotions in the Army. No doubt this would have made any succeeding C.-in-C. sensitive about his situation. But Dundas, 'a tall, spare man, crabbed and austere; dry in his looks and demeanour', was especially so. From relatively humble beginnings, he had risen from 'lieutenant fireworker' to Quartermaster-General, seeing much tough service on the way and, through a passionate interest in drill, earning the nickname of 'Old Pivot'. Major Charles Napier, the future conqueror of Scinde, who was then serving in the Peninsula, believed he would give way before the anger of others because he was 'to be bullied, like all old men'. But

Napier was wrong. In spite of Corunna and in spite of all his angry applications, he did not get promotion from Dundas. Anger, it appeared, worked to arouse the old man's obstinacy rather than to expose his weakness.[48]

Palmerston also found that Dundas did not succumb to bullying. In any case Dundas's personal relations with the fledgeling at the War Office hardly got off to a good start when in November 1809 Palmerston hesitated to sign the warrant that the C.-in-C. required to appoint Lt General Oliver de Lancey to the comfortable sinecure of Commissioner of Chelsea Hospital and then got the Prime Minister to veto the idea. De Lancey had been Barrackmaster-General until 1804, when he was removed for 'culpable carelessness'. He had the habit, among other things, of pocketing one per cent of the expenditure of his department as 'contingencies for additional charge and responsibility for unsettled accounts' and he had appointed barrackmasters where no barracks existed. Naturally Palmerston did not fancy being party to so odious an appointment. Dundas, moreover, was de Lancey's close relative by marriage, and Palmerston may well have been right to attribute to him, as a Scot much like his distant cousin Viscount Melville, who had himself recently been impeached for malversation, 'a strong national propensity to a job'. In any case this minor disagreement can hardly have had a soothing effect on an imminent confrontation over a matter of principle.[49]

The active dispute of principle between the War Office and the Horse Guards did not originate with Palmerston but with Pulteney's limited attempts to follow up the recommendations of 1807-8 by getting the allowances to regimental agents cut by a quarter. Dundas had then objected that in that event the colonels would not be able to find suitable men to accept agencies. He had objected still more to Palmerston's immediate predecessor issuing a circular to the Army which had not first been cleared with the Horse Guards. This action, he had insisted, was a straightforward infringement of the 'rule' that no new regulations concerning the discipline, property or income of the Army should be issued without prior reference to him. Neither the occasion nor the principle of the complaint was in any way trivial. The first involved the efficiency of the system by which the Army was paid; the second the vital constitutional question of the proper distribution of civil and military control over the Army. It is also clear that the confrontation with Dundas antedated Palmerston's arrival in the War Office and was therefore at root not personal at all: it had been Pulteney who had arranged the reduction with the Treasury without either department making any reference to Headquarters, and it had been Granville who had authorized the issuing of the necessary circular without troubling Dundas either. Dundas, moreover, seems to have made little effort to straighten things out in good time. The circular was issued on 24 July and Dundas had sent his protest on 8 August. But although Granville had offered his explanation and invited contradiction very speedily on 14 August, it was not until 3 November that Dundas wrote again. Perhaps for that reason Palmerston also took his time; it was not until the following March that he replied. Of course, as a new man he had a lot to learn, and in any case there was the Treasury to be consulted first. Even so it seems rather a long wait for such an important matter. The result, however, was by no means hostile to the position adopted at the Horse Guards. It was agreed that there should be no reduction of agents' commissions in respect of infantry regiments, where their work was greater, but only for agents of cavalry regiments, where the work had recently been reduced by the transfer of forage to the Commissariat. On the more important matter of principle, however, the Treasury professed no view. Yet Palmerston fully acknowledged the justice of Dundas's observations, even though he insisted at the same time on reiterating the interest of the War Office. 'I am entirely disposed to adopt the course which you have recommended,' he wrote; 'and I make no doubt but that you will see the expediency of giving such directions as may prevent the promulgation from Head-Quarters of any order affecting the Finances of the Army, & more especially sanctioning any new or extraordinary expenditure without the knowledge and concurrence of the Secretary at War.' This all seemed fair enough. But unfortunately there were several other similar disputes already brewing.[30]

Only some of the other disputes were derived directly from the recommendations of 1807-8, but all of them suspiciously concerned circulars or orders issued by the War Office in the same month of July 1810. That this was a coincidence seems too much to believe. Quite possibly Palmerston had for some reason since March decided that there must be a showdown with the Horse Guards. If so, it was probably because of the successful attack upon staff appointments in his otherwise vaunted handling of the Estimates in March. He had tried during the debates to fend off the danger by discreet enquiries at the Horse Guards, but whatever the information he had got, it had not been enough. As a direct result of the unpleasantness in Parliament, therefore, and with a view to eliminating the practice of general officers pocketing the allowances of aides-de-camp who had been provided for but not appointed, the War Office on 21 July sought from the Adjutant-General a list, together with names, of all appointments on the Home Staff. But shortly before that, on 7 July, there had also been a War Office circular to regimental colonels on the knotty matter of bread and forage. This, at least, had been preceded by continuous exchanges between the Deputy Secretary and the Horse Guards; but these had been very confused. To judge from the private correspondence that soon followed between Palmerston and the Prime Minister, the Horse Guards suspected Merry of again making a deliberate attempt 'to exalt the War Office to the degradation of the Comr-in-Chief'. If he was, then he must have calculated, and quite correctly, that he would get stiffer backing from his minister than had been the case with the circular about the reduction of agency fees.[31]

What may probably have encouraged Merry was the groundwork recently laid for yet another quarrel. Although the 1808 report of the Commissioners of

Military Enquiry had brushed aside two decades of mounting criticism of off-reckonings and come down firmly in favour of the colonel as the best man to deal with the soldiers' clothing, steps had been taken to protect the clothiers', as well as the public's, interest. The most important concerned the practice of the colonel 'assigning' his off-reckonings in advance to a third party so that in the event of his quitting his regiment the money was still readily available for its proper purpose. The 1808 report recommended that the fictitious men be abolished and the system of assignments be tightened up. Accordingly an Act of Parliament in 1810 had authorized the War Office to check on outstanding debts before paying up assignments. Consequently, on 26 July, Palmerston informed Headquarters that in future the War Office would pay only the residue of off-reckonings to the colonels themselves and two days later there followed a circular from Merry ordering agents to report on their arrangements with clothiers and warning that in future the War Office would pay assignees only after the clothiers had agreed.[52]

It was the last outrage that on 2 August 1810 brought the first blast from Headquarters, with Dundas raging against an 'innovation' attempted by an Act that was 'novel & extraordinary' and actions by the War Office that were 'so extraordinary and so unintelligible'. The next day there followed an even ruder protest about the circular on bread and forage: 'I wish to ascertain & receive from Your Lordship an explanation.' But it was not until 15 September, after a casual reference in a new communication from the War Office, that there came another about the first offence, the demand for the names of A.D.C.s. In the meantime, and evidently without waiting for an 'explanation' from Palmerston, Dundas had rushed to place his complaints before the Prime Minister, and then, when he realized what had been done about the A.D.C.s, added this to the indictment with which he tackled the P.M. face to face during Palmerston's absence at Broadlands.[33]

Confronted with the task of placating two stubborn personalities, Perceval was not entirely at a loss. With the aid of Dundas's accusing finger he pointed straight to the scapegoat. Palmerston should give Merry 'the most peremptory order' not to make any innovations without previous communication with his chief and Palmerston might find it 'most convenient as well as most proper' then to consult with the Commander-in-Chief. Unfortunately this did not work either. Palmerston was notably loyal to his subordinates and would not have dreamed of abandoning them when he thought them in the right. Nor, rather less wisely, could he ever resist a calculatedly biting retort. 'I regret that the Comr-in-Chief ', his reply began, 'should have given you so much trouble on a subject, on which I can hardly think it could have been necessary to give you any.' As far as the substance of the complaints was concerned, moreover, he was able to point out that in some instances at least Dundas had completely misconceived the situation. The circular respecting bread and forage, far from introducing anything new, merely called for a duplicate return of what had already been fully agreed by the Horse Guards and, what is more, had been requested by the Commissary-in-Chief. On the matter of A.D.C.s Palmerston had still better personal knowledge. The War Office had merely asked, in view of the pressure from Parliament, for names to be added where previously numbers alone had been returned. He was under the impression that he had discussed the matter verbally with the Adjutant-General; in any case this information had been requested and supplied for the previous quarter without extracting any observation let alone a protest from the Horse Guards. All this he had recently explained in a reply from Broadlands sent direct to Dundas. But he was reluctant to show up too clearly Dundas's obvious ignorance of the records of his own office. The fact was that Dundas, 'though at bottom possessed of much good nature, is a little irritable & hasty'. All this being said, the *principle* behind the whole affair was nevertheless of great importance. For his own part he had tried, however imperfectly, to consult with the Horse Guards and in several instances where *they* had invaded the area of *his* authority he had hitherto confined himself to 'private remonstrance'. It certainly seemed now that in the complaints Dundas was making to the Prime Minister he was contriving to subordinate the Secretary at War to the Commander-in-Chief. It had been suggested, for example, that since about the time of Bragge Bathurst's tenure in 1803-4, when the King suffered another bout of madness, the Secretary had been in the habit of receiving the King's pleasure not in person but through the C.-in-C. But, as Palmerston pointed out in a separate memorandum, the assertion and the deduction made in the Horse Guards were quite unjustified:

This is entirely inconsistent with the received opinion and practice of the office; the commands of H.M. on the pecuniary interests of the Army having been always taken exclusively by the Secretary at War & never by the Commander-in-Chief.
That he has *not* a *right* to do so must be distinctly *denied*, that it is highly expedient & necessary for the good of the service and well governing the Army that he should not I am quite ready to admit & in fact no order altering the pecuniary arrangements of the army has been issued from this office without previous communication with the Commander-in-Chief; but no Secretary at War could ever consent to sit as such in the House of Commons & submit to be held responsible for measures . . . over which he does not pretend to have any control.

Such, then, was the importance of the issue of principle now joined that Palmerston felt the Prime Minister ought to consult Yorke about it all.[34]

Within a few weeks Dundas conceded that he had made a mistake over the circulars regarding bread and forage and the A.D.C.s and in response to a specific appeal from Perceval Palmerston agreed to revert to former practice with respect to the assignment of off-reckonings until new and mutually acceptable legislation could be framed. Acknowledging, then, that the practical questions were now resolved, Palmerston was willing to help the Prime Minister out by simply reserving his position over the issue of principle. Dundas, however, was not. He evidently thought the new Secretary at War too arrogant and pretentious; and he owed no political allegiance whatever to Perceval. Perceval's first reply he later described, not inaccurately but with obvious contempt, as 'chiefly recommending mutual concession & conciliation'; his second, to which Palmerston had responded so handsomely, as 'detailed but not satisfactory'. So he continued to press for a definitive settlement of principle and refused to be put off by Perceval's assertion that the question of spheres of authority over the Army was really not his business but the King's. Instead Dundas took this evasion as a hint and grasped the opportunity of what turned out to be the King's final attack of madness to submit the whole matter to the Prince Regent. Dundas wrote to tell Palmerston what he had done on 2 March; but the prince's decision was signed under the date 28 February 1811.[35]

The prince's decision was as explicit and as favourable to his point of view as anything Dundas could have wished. Almost certainly it was a military man who drafted it. The Commissary-in-Chief, Willoughby Gordon, did have something to do with it. For, in addition to quarrelling over bread and forage, he was expecting to succeed Palmerston at the War Office if, as seemed very likely for a while, the prince used his new power as Regent to replace the Whigs in Government. In that event, Gordon had already made clear, he would expect not only to improve the efficiency of the office but also to reverse the Secretary's pretensions 'to convert his powers of *check* and arrangement into powers of direction, controul and management' and to make him once more 'submit to the controul of a Commander-in-Chief'. Gordon's ambitions foundered on the failure of the prince to come to terms with the Opposition. But the prince nevertheless looked forward to the restoration of the Duke of York to the Horse Guards and the reduction of Palmerston to a subordinate role. His formal opinion therefore was still that the duty of the Secretary at War was simply to exert 'a well arranged check upon expenditures of the army' and 'a vigilant control of the financial details'; hence he had no right to issue orders or regulations to the Army without the consent of the C.-in-C.[36]

Dundas's victory was short-lived. Even Perceval could not afford to let it pass. As he soon pointed out, the Regent's decision amounted to a formal expression of displeasure on an existing Act of Parliament and his anticipation of the changes the Prime Minister had promised to a royal command to disobey the law. He had not meant by the diffidence of his earlier communications to free the Regent from his ministerial advisers, and none of them could countersign the order nor the Commander-in-Chief or Secretary at War enter it formally in their records, as the Regent had directed, without being deemed by Parliament to have committed 'a very great breach of its privileges and interference with its authority'. So he saw the prince on 7 March and, having accepted all the blame for misleading the Regent by his previously 'unguarded manner', undertook to consult the warring parties yet again and, if they could not be brought to compromise, to proffer the Government's advice and to receive the Regent's decision in the proper constitutional manner. In the meantime, he suggested, the prince should write to Palmerston and Dundas recalling his recent command.[57]

Dundas evidently thought that he had done enough in spite of Perceval to proceed with what he had already told the Prime Minister was his real purpose, to be able to restore his command to the King 'unimpaired . . . and on the same honourable footing it stood when he was graciously pleased to put it into my hands.' He therefore now offered his resignation to the prince and, after discreet soundings about the likely public reaction, the Duke of York was restored in May.[58]

Palmerston had been too busy with an election campaign in Cambridge in March and a family funeral in Bath in April to return at once even to so important an affair, but when at last he was able to do so he was not in the least deterred by the threat of a royal alliance against his office. Possibly he even calculated on exploiting the early months of the duke's return. Being the least objectionable of the King's sons, the duke was popular with the public as well as with the Army. But even so he could hardly have dared to risk an open confrontation with the civil authority, and perhaps with Parliament, so soon after his recall and with the memory of Mrs Clarke so fresh. And while he waited on the doctor's reports about his father, the Regent too needed all the support in Government and Parliament that he could muster with a view to enlarging the scope and consolidating the power of his new position. It was very probably for these reasons, then, that the Duke of York's reaction was cautious and the Regent's utterly negative when the whole issue was reopened.[59]

Pleading that he had not personally been given an opportunity to submit his case directly, Palmerston sent the Regent about the middle of August a long memorandum in refutation of Dundas's arguments. It was so massive indeed – over 30,000 words – that it must have been an additional reason, if not the sole one, for the Regent passing the whole matter back to the Prime Minister. Not for the first or the last time in his life, Palmerston had rather overdone things and he had accordingly a price to pay. His memorandum was lucid enough but he overloaded it with historical illustrations and tedious repetitions. It was written in his own hand, but the research for it could not have added to his popularity among the overworked clerks of the War Office. It also irritated Perceval, who sarcastically remarked: 'however natural it may have been for Lord Palmerston, for the purpose of repelling the supposition that the modern practice of his Office had been adopted on a spirit of encroachment, to have looked into the ancient history and practice of his Office for a century past, it appears to Mr Perceval that the subject may now be well disembarrassed of that research . . . because it is obvious that the modern practice . . . is very different from the former.' Nor did Palmerston succeed in overwhelming his opponents. The duke put in his own memorandum, and although it pointedly referred to the length of the Secretary's, Palmerston still thought it wise to compose another in reply.

The papers of the duke and Palmerston were both mildly worded and at the end of the year they were still exchanging letters of excessive mutual respect. But the duke's recapitulation of the early stages of the dispute swung Perceval's sympathies back to Palmerston. It was 'most unfair', Perceval recorded on his copy, for the duke to put all the blame on Palmerston. He had been wrong not to consult with the Horse Guards but there was 'no trace' of the 'encroachment' of which he was now accused; rather Dundas, by frustrating the compromise agreed by Palmerston at the end of 1810 and insisting on the reference to the Prince Regent, had exposed that it was the Horse Guards who were determined to get rid of a check upon them. Once again, however, the Prime Minister avoided the fundamental issue and awarded Palmerston the honours only of a rearguard action. Ably supported by the opinions of a Secretary of State for War (Liverpool), a former Secretary at War and current First Lord of the Admiralty (Yorke), and the Lord Chancellor (Eldon), Perceval insisted merely on maintaining the status quo. The issue of principle, he argued, could only be determined by reference to Parliament and the middle of a war was hardly the time for that. Any implication that the Secretary was generally subordinate was therefore ruled out, for the time being at least, as plainly contrary to both established practice and recent legislation in matters of important detail; but the decision about the consent of the Horse Guards being necessary to the issue of any new order or regulation was confirmed. So the two departments must continue with their practical functions as they had for so many years past. It required only mutual forbearance and good will between their respective chiefs. But if they ever should fall out over some proposed new order then they could refer it to the Prime Minister, or the Secretary of State for War, or both of them. Even after this it took so long to find a form of words acceptable to both parties, in particular with regard to the right of access to the Royal Closet, that before a final draft could be submitted to the Regent, time was given for yet another objectionable circular to appear, and it had still not been settled when the Prime Minister was assassinated on 11 May 1812. But even though they had not agreed on every word, Perceval had shortly before his death found the 'substance' of an acceptable version and, affected a little by feelings of guilt perhaps, Palmerston finally arranged the details with the Horse Guards and forwarded an agreed draft for the Regent's signature at the beginning of June.[60]

In spite of the disappointing result of his protest, Palmerston was determined to give as little ground as possible. Even while it was being considered, when one would have thought he would be particularly cautious, there had been another skirmish over the old question of circulars and, only a few days before Perceval's death, a spirited attack on staff officers being paid forage money for horses to which they were entitled but did not actually keep. Perhaps the similarity to the abuse about A.D.C.s was too close and the possibility of a victory over the Horse Guards too tempting for Palmerston to overlook. At any rate he wrote to the Treasury: 'I very much doubt the propriety of continuing the allowances upon the ground which is advanced, namely that if the officers actually kept horses, the expense of their forage would exceed what is now granted as a commuted allowance.'[61]

It is hardly surprising therefore to find rather stiff exchanges passing again between Horse Guards and War Office when the duke protested in 1815 that the Secretary was interfering between the colonels and their agents and Palmerston responded with a rather sarcastic admonition, disguised as an assurance that he would 'at all times be happy to receive any suggestions from your R.H. upon any part of the arrangements of the service within my organization whether they are more or less connected with Dept of the Comm.-in-Chief, because from your R.H.'s extensive & accurate infn upon all subjects connected with the Military establishments of the Country'. In the summer of 1816 there came a protest from the Secretary at War against the omission of any reference to his office in the new form of warrant by which it was proposed to reconstitute the clothing Board of General Officers on a permanent instead of an annual basis.[62]

In the matter of the warrant to revive the clothing board, Palmerston, although objecting 'decidedly', went out of his way to do so privately and to get everything put right without raising an official controversy. Indeed his dealings with the Duke of York seem to have remained quite friendly for some years. The duke had some reputation as the most affable of the royal brothers and Palmerston, for his part, probably made some effort to keep on good terms with him. When, for example, he wished to press on the C.-in-C. the old idea that regimental agents should give sureties like everyone else and so relieve the colonels of a legal responsibility they could rarely fulfil, Palmerston shrewdly argued: 'The Military Service is more productive of honor than of profit.' There was no result, of course; but they did manage to accomplish some good things together. After Waterloo, when Parliament went into raptures over Wellington and made him a grant of £400,000, Palmerston suggested that in addition to the rare campaign medals proposed by the victor they should give other and more material rewards to veterans of the battle. Wounded officers, he proposed, might have their disability allowances raised at each succeeding promotion instead of staying at the rate according to the rank they held at the time of being wounded; and common soldiers might be allowed to count an extra two years' service towards pay and pension, though not towards dis-charge, and henceforth be entered on the regimental pay-roll as 'Waterloo men', so that they might 'constantly keep alive in the minds of the Soldiers of the Army the memory of this unexampled victory'. The idea was immediately approved by the royal duke and with his backing it soon got the consent of the Prime Minister and Prince Regent.[63]

The duke went to stay at Broadlands as late as July 1818 and in the following year he and Palmerston were still dining a good deal together. They must therefore have remained for some time on good personal terms. But the fundamental issue between them as officers of state remained essentially unresolved. So it was probably inevitable that the dispute would one day be revived and revived with very damaging consequences for their personal relations. But who was immediately responsible for that revival is rather difficult to say. Palmerston would later on (in 1826) assert, when referring to the duke's views on the clothing of the Army, that 'not wishing to multiply points of difference, I have always abstained from pressing any alteration in the existing arrangement'. He had even, he said to Sulivan in 1828, declined to raise the very grave constitutional matter of the duke (and his successor, Wellington) formally advising the King about the size of the Army when he ought properly to have confined himself to obeying. But since the duke's advice could not have prevailed without the Secretary's consent and the duke had never disputed the fact, Palmerston had 'never thought it worth while to stir up from the muddy bottom of the official pool a new subject of litigation in addition to the many others which arose of their own accord'.[64]

Sir Herbert Taylor, the duke's military secretary, later said that for years he kept from his master's eyes War Office communications whose tone and substance would have provoked a quarrel. Palmerston certainly had been sniping at the C.-in-C.'s rear from time to time. At the end of 1817, for example, after he and Peel had worked out a number of reductions and economies in Ireland, he commented: 'The Irish Government have behaved very handsomely to us about reductions; for which however the D. of York does not thank them.' And if he did not, in his own word, 'press' the old and thorny question of the colonels and their perquisites from clothing contracts, he certainly raised it from time to time. In 1812, only a year after the duke had returned to the Horse Guards and while the great dispute it had helped to provoke was still in process of examination by the Government and Prince Regent, Perceval had taken it up again. Whether or not Palmerston was behind it then – and it is difficult to believe he was not – he certainly raised it in July 1818 and, in spite of a lengthy rebuttal from the duke, again in May 1820 when a probing question loomed in the House. According to Palmerston's own story, however, it was the duke who about the end of 1818 had made 'a sort of declaration of war' by proposing privately to the Prime Minister to abolish regimental paymasters and to return to the pre-1798 system of having subalterns act directly under the agents. Palmerston acknowledged that the Prime Minister did not appear very impressed with the duke's arguments, but instead of resting content with that he prepared to counter-attack by reviving the suggestion that the rate of agency be reduced. He asked Sulivan secretly to assemble the necessary papers and proposed, if he finally decided to go ahead, to approach the Prime Minister after returning from a trip abroad. He does not in fact seem to have taken up the matter when he returned to London early in November, turning instead in the following spring to another passing oversight of his authority by the Adjutant-General. It was the duke, rather, who first attempted to reopen the major question.[65]

In February 1820 Taylor was persuaded by the new King, his master's elder brother, to accept the representation of Windsor in the House of Commons. If, as was generally believed, this was an attempt by the duke to have his secretary rather than Palmerston speak for the Army in Parliament, it was quickly checked and defeated. Liverpool and Castlereagh, the Leader of the House of Commons, at once sent to Taylor to tell him that he should not interfere in the discussions on the Estimates and that it was the Secretary at War's duty, not his, to defend the Horse Guards. But although the set-battle was avoided, desultory warfare continued and about the same time as the Taylor affair Palmerston provoked another protest from the duke. At the end of February or the beginning of March 1820, the War Office issued a circular to G.O.C.s of districts asking for a return of troops under their command without first clearing it with the Horse Guards. Inevitably on 7 March the duke addressed a note to Palmerston peremptorily demanding an explanation, and, worse, announcing that he had prepared a general order forbidding any response being made to the unauthorized circular. No less inevitably, perhaps, Palmerston took the opportunity to refer the matter to the Prime Minister, Lord Liverpool, and in doing so adopted a most sarcastic manner:

You will see that though in a time of profound peace I am still the Secy *at War*, but I hope you will think that I am acting only upon the strictest principles of self-defence.

I say nothing upon the general tone of the Duke's letter because I presume that Princes of the Blood have certain privileges in those matters; & I know the D. to be so good natured a man, & we are always upon such good terms together in all our personal intercourse that I always impute any roughness of expression in his official letters to the want of epistolatory dexterity on the part of those who frame them for him, rather than any disposition on his part to take an undue advantage of his personal Rank.[66]

It was all very well for Palmerston to sneer at the duke's 'personal rank,' but the Prime Minister could not afford to treat in so cavalier a fashion a prince who, by the death of Princess Charlotte in 1817 and his brother's accession in 1820, had now become the heir presumptive to the throne. While agreeing, therefore, that the duke's order was regrettable, he regretted just as much Palmerston's initial false step. He quite rightly pointed out that the action of the War Office was contrary to the 1812 agreement and that it was also unnecessary to bypass the Horse Guards. The whole quarrel could have been avoided by consultation in advance, and he hoped that it would be settled now by 'personal communication'. In the circumstances Palmerston had no option but to write to the Adjutant-General to explain that the regimental and garrison returns requested were required by the Articles of War, that the District returns had also been made without any difficulty on previous occasions by the G.O.C.s in Scotland, Ireland and the Channel Islands, and that, England having been omitted only by mistake, the new circular was merely a matter of form. With this explanation the duke professed himself 'perfectly satisfied' and Palmerston responded with pleasantries in turn.[67]

Although the Prime Minister expressed the hope to Palmerston that the

Duke of York's letter had put an end to this 'disagreeable business', he must have expected it to be otherwise from the rather petulant letter which Palmerston had sent him on the same day that he made his explanations to the Horse Guards. In spite of what Liverpool had said, wrote Palmerston, he still thought that the Secretary at War was the best judge of what returns he needed and the right man to call for them. Moreover, although he was still on good terms with Torrens (who was now Adjutant-General), the duke himself had taken a different course with this dispute. 'The truth is', he went on, 'that the D. of York always feels that the Secy at War is (as he is constitutionally intended to be) in many respects a check & controul upon the purely mily authorities of the army & he thinks that the service would go on much better if there were no such offr.' Palmerston, indeed, soon made it clear that even though he had lost another battle he was not giving up the war. In September 1820 there was first another minor clash over the court martial of a sergeant who happened also to act as regimental paymaster's clerk. For some reason the C.-in-C., as was his right, had set aside the sentence of loss of rank and pay; but since the clerk had been proved to have taken presents from civilian contractors Palmerston was determined not to let him have any further dealings with regimental pay and proposed to write to the regiment accordingly. Torrens, however, regarded this as an interference with the C.-in-C.'s absolute authority with respect to military discipline and he feared an explosion if the duke found out. It was 'flying in the face of H.R.H.'s decision,' he warned, and urged Palmerston to 'consider the case coolly' while he delayed passing it on to the duke. Although potentially explosive, the issue does seem to have been obscured and smoothed over before the duke's anger had been aroused. But two years later Palmerston repeated his original sin in a way impossible to conceal.[68]

Early in December 1822 Palmerston heard from the Treasury that the Barrack Department was to be transferred from the Q.M.G. to the Ordnance, and since the War Office had no concern with the finances of the latter, he decided to take the opportunity to effect some of the economy so often urged upon him. On 11 January 1823, therefore, he issued a circular to commanders on foreign stations ordering them to dispense with the services of some thirty superfluous clerks. Unfortunately the War Office once again did not bother first to clear the circular with the Horse Guards but casually informed them of what had been done on the same day they issued it. About the same time they also reprimanded a Col. John Ross for submitting his claim for travelling expenses through the medium of the Horse Guards and ordered him not to do it again, and entered into yet another dispute with the C.-in-C. about the appointment of a regimental paymaster. Evidently outraged by Palmerston's repeated disregard for the agreement of 1812, the duke had Taylor draft an order to commanding officers to ignore all War Office instructions not sent to them through the Horse Guards. He suspended the issue of the order pending explanations, but the prohibition on previously approved but directly dispatched communications from the War Office was nonetheless an alarming novelty. So again Palmerston responded by protesting to the Prime Minister, equally resting his case on the orders to defy the War Office rather than upon the original dispute; two days later the duke countered with his own paper, adding still further complaints in what Palmerston called a 'long rigmarole'.[69]

The result of these tedious appeals was much the same as usual though this time Liverpool tried to resolve the dispute even more informally by sending his Paymaster-General, Charles Long, to talk to Palmerston in the House of Commons. Long told Palmerston that 'Liverpool was in a fever & in despair, not knowing what to do, bored with the length of the papers, disliking contact with ye D. & in short labouring under [an attack of] the *weaks*'. So he wanted to urge on Palmerston how difficult it was to deal with princes, that 'though right' Palmerston 'perhaps pushed rightness to extremes', and that it was too much to expect the duke to humiliate himself by cancelling his order. Rather foolishly Palmerston refused to help. He told Long that princes had no 'right to give an affront any more than any other peer of the realm' and that Liverpool 'must make what he can of the matter'. He wrote afterwards to say that if it was too much for the duke formally to withdraw his offensive orders, he, Palmerston, would be satisfied for Liverpool to write to him disapproving them.[70]

This was all pretty high-handed language and unhelpful stuff from a second-rank minister. Long had already set down his disgusted opinion about 'this unpleasant correspondence' and it is perhaps no wonder that two days later Palmerston and the duke each received a copy of a minute from Liverpool condemning them both: the duke should not have issued his offensive order, but Palmerston should not have broken the rule of 1812. Palmerston wrote at once to complain that, having refused to discuss the question of his conduct until the order was withdrawn, he had in effect been condemned unheard. But Liverpool's minute had in fact acknowledged that the War Office instructions would have been perfectly in order if only they had first been cleared with the Horse Guards. So, belatedly taking the hint that the Prime Minister would 'deprecate the continuance of the discussion', Palmerston merely lodged his arguments in Downing Street and pronounced himself satisfied with the repulse of the duke's encroachment on his right to hold direct communications with commanding officers. Apparently the duke was rather less happy with the result; indeed, Palmerston heard that he was 'very angry' with Liverpool's minute. Perhaps that was why Palmerston was able to report ten days later that 'C.-in-C. & Secy at War are going on smoothly' and exchanging 'civil letters'. The duke cancelled his objectionable order to overseas C.O.s and offered to withdraw the similarly offensive instructions that he had sent to Colonel Ross. However, an attempt in April and May to sort out the disagreement of principle between them began unfortunately with a Palmerstonian reiteration of points previously made in passing, and seems to have ended in another aggressive exchange of incompatible memoranda.[71]

Hardly more than a year went by before another Ross found himself in the middle of another row between War Office and Horse Guards. This time it was the Horse Guards who made the first false move and an eagle-eyed War Office that protested. Having only recently come under the protection of the Crown, the Ionian Islands had been provided in 1816 with an over-generous military establishment and so within a few years attracted much economizing attention. But having agreed some reductions with the Colonial Office and communicated the intention to the War Office, the Horse Guards in the spring of 1824 inadvertently overlooked what had been arranged, and compounded the error by neglecting to inform the War Office formally of the appointments to the General Staff of a new Military Governor and a new C.-in-C. (Ross). Evidently the opportunity – or the coincidence – was too good for Palmerston to overlook and instead of approaching the Horse Guards with a friendly enquiry he got Merry to seek an explanation of the Colonial Office. Taylor was absolutely furious; even when he had cooled down he still thought that by concealing the informal communications the War Office had had from the Horse Guards, Merry's 'dry question' was designed to trap the Colonial Office into some statement at variance with the duke's conduct. It was this that made him write to the Colonial Secretary:

. . . I trust I shall stand acquitted of wishing to start difficulties by watching the proceedings at the War Office with so jealous an eye, after what has occasionally been attempted in that quarter. The fact is that I have used my best endeavours to prevent any renewal of difference between the Duke of York and Lord Palmerston and have therefore kept out of his Royal Highness's sight many things which seemed calculated to produce that effect, and have otherwise disposed of them by personal communication with his Lordship, and sometimes by communication with other departments; but, in so doing, I am bound to guard his Royal Highness's authority against encroachment which he would strenuously resist if aware or suspicious of the attempt.[72]

Between them Taylor and the Colonial Secretary patched up a compromise that would silence Palmerston without alerting the duke; and January 1825 could still find the duke enjoying the attractions of Broadlands. But politics as well as personalities were now forcing them far apart. Before the end of the year the Catholic question made the breach more widely known than ever and came very near to making a major explosion in the Government. Probably, too, Palmerston was getting less and less content to bear so unfairly all the sneers and snubs about flogging from Headquarters while suffering so much of the blame in Parliament. So in spite of Taylor's efforts to contrive it otherwise the tranquillity of the Horse Guards continued to be disturbed by professional disputes. In April 1826 Palmerston took advantage of a parliamentary question from Hume to take up once again the old controversy about Army clothing. He still believed, he said, that they ought to abandon the system of off-reckonings and clothe the Army directly as the Ordnance and Marines did their forces. But the duke had 'a very decided opinion the other way'. For years, Palmerston now retorted on his part, he had deliberately refrained from bringing forward a new point of difficulty, but perhaps the Government should now look into it. About the same time, according to Palmerston's later recollection, a new ground of 'squabbling & encroaching' was opened up by the Horse Guards over the dismissal of half-pay officers. No one could challenge the C.-in-C.'s right in this respect, but Palmerston resented the expectation that they would also automatically lose their pay. It was not the C.-in-C. but the Secretary at War who submitted the half-pay lists for the King's approval and he insisted on retaining his formal rights. Once again they patched up their difference of principle with a working arrangement for informal consultation; but each side continued to go out of its way to emphasize its notional independence. Early in 1826, too, an old sore opened up again when Palmerston discovered that a senior officer had been reprimanded for suggesting directly to the War Office improvements in the form of oath extracted from recruits; but he protested so vigorously against the unwarranted strictures on the officer concerned and against what he called the 'uncivil' and 'degrading' implications as regards himself, that he succeeded in getting the reprimand withdrawn.[73]

Obviously things could not have gone on in this way between Palmerston and the royal duke; sooner or later there would have been a major explosion. But towards the end of 1826 the duke fell gravely ill and in the following January he died. By a strange constitutional quirk this brought to Palmerston the powers of both Secretary at War and Commander-in-Chief. So much for the vaunted division of power! But he was only a caretaker; according to his sister, he refused to exercise the patronage of the office and left the command of two regiments vacant for his successor to fill. Apparently he assured the Adjutant-General that he had no wish to disturb the 'routine of military business' and did little more than sign the voluminous papers that Taylor brought before him. Yet only a few days after the duke's funeral he wrote to complain that the Adjutant-General had issued a general order about mourning without first clearing it with him, and though he attributed it to 'inadvertence' and proposed to take no 'further steps' insisted that it was not to be used as a precedent.[74]

On this occasion, for once, the quarrel hardly had much time to simmer, for on 22 January the command was given to the Duke of Wellington. Wellington had no patience with Torrens's fussiness: one of his very first acts was to reduce to still more modest proportions the lengthy panegyric on the Duke of York that the Adjutant-General had composed and Palmerston shortened and approved only the day before. But he was no more likely to suffer any impertinence from Palmerston, whom he knew very well in both London and Hampshire society; and if military success were not a sufficient compensation for his lack of royal birth, he had the advantage over the late duke that he was also a member of the Cabinet. But in April Liverpool's paralytic stroke brought Canning to the premiership and Wellington's loathing for Canning drove the duke out of office altogether.[75]

That Wellington would resign his seat in the Cabinet was not unexpected;

but that he would also resign the command of the Army on the grounds of a supposed insult from Canning created consternation. Worse still, it reawakened the King's ambition to restore the command to the royal family. There had been some talk of this when the Duke of York died; and since the Dukes of Cumberland and Cambridge were both patently unfit the King had proposed to take it on himself with Taylor as his Adjutant-General. On that occasion the scheme had been defeated by the availability of Wellington; but now that this solution had proved abortive, the King revived his monstrous notion. Taylor saw the King several times on 17 and 18 April and reiterated the many difficulties he foresaw. He pointed out that there were already an Adjutant-General and a Q.M.G. at the Horse Guards and that he himself was too junior a Lt General to be raised so high. Why not, he asked, leave them as they were, create a new post to handle the patronage and fill it with a more senior officer such as Sir George Murray? Alternatively, as he heard rumours that Palmerston might be moving to another office, perhaps Murray could succeed him and continue to combine the War Office with the civil functions of the C.-in-C. But the King was determined somehow or other to have Taylor as his personal adviser, if only in the guise of a 'principal aide de camp', and in the end Taylor had to appear to acquiesce.[76]

Taylor, clearly still unhappy with the idea, next day evidently told Palmerston all about it. Some said at the time that Palmerston was frightened by the news. If so, it was with good reason. He immediately rushed around to make his objections in person to the Prime Minister; but was fended off by Huskisson, who told him that Canning already knew all about it but wished to let it 'stand over' for a while. Evidently Canning had no wish to be confronted by another crisis with the King while he was still up to his ears in efforts to form a Government. So Palmerston put his objections on paper and discreetly got out of town. But it seems clear that he had already mapped out in rough the makings of a compromise with Taylor. They utterly agreed that the King could not be his own constitutional adviser; for, as Taylor put it, 'the King can do no wrong' and could not therefore be responsible. Equally, if there were to be a new sort of responsible intermediary, then he could not be a mere 'chief A.D.C.' but must, in Palmerston's opinion, be 'a Privy Counsellor with some definite & recognized official rank; in short, it would in fact be necessary either to employ according to all former usage the Secretary at War, or to create a second Secretary at War.' This was almost precisely how it turned out. Canning seems to have been ready to tackle the matter two days later on 21 April, when he and his Lord Chancellor had several long discussions with Taylor and the King. First he submitted a minute based on Palmerston's letter, which the King was compelled to accept but inclined to meet by suggesting they make the Adjutant-General a responsible adviser. But Canning had another solution in mind. He had already arranged with Palmerston to promote him to the Cabinet at once and to transfer him to a more important office at the end of the session. So he suggested that the King might have the man he wanted and the Government its preferred constitutional forms by having Taylor succeed Palmerston. As it happened, the notion of combining indefinitely the patronage of the Horse Guards with both the office work and the parliamentary duties of the Secretary at War appalled Taylor, and he would not undertake them. So, as he and Palmerston had evidently agreed beforehand, he proposed instead that he should perform the role His Majesty desired but technically as an additional Deputy Secretary of Palmerston's. On 1 May the appointment was formally approved and in the course of the next few days the whole of Taylor's department in the Horse Guards was notionally transferred as a distinct 'Military Branch' to the War Office.[77]

This arrangement was never intended as anything more than a temporary device to fend off the King's inconvenient demands and to keep the way open for Wellington's return. Palmerston and Taylor, as well as Canning and the King himself, were all agreed on that. But when the attempt was made late in May to induce the duke to come back it was a disastrous failure; then, in June, Canning decided he would not promote Palmerston to another place after all. So they all had to think it over again. Taylor was anxious to go in any event: as the King's channel of communication but at the same time as Palmerston's deputy he had 'to convey the King's commands to be executed by his own superior – a situation of extreme anxiety and delicacy,' it was noted, 'and such as very few men could execute at all'. It was no wonder then that Taylor himself should have proposed in June to stay on only until Michaelmas when, perhaps, if something better had still not been arranged, someone more senior might take over in his place. But Taylor had also begun to worry about the effects that a prolonged arrangement of the present kind might have upon the Army, especially if someone other than Palmerston were in charge; less sympathetic observers bluntly said that already the Army was 'going to the devil under Palmerston'. In May, it was true, Secretary at War and Adjutant-General were already clashing, memo. against memo., about their respective responsibilities and roles as advisers to the King. Shortly afterwards Palmerston himself, as well as Taylor and Wellington, avowed that the experience fully confirmed the objections on grounds of principle to the two offices being in the same hands. So in June the Government did turn once more to the idea of making some other senior officer C.-in-C. in all but name. Nothing had been arranged when Canning fell ill and died. But that also smoothed the way at last for Wellington's return.[78]

Wellington's second period as C.-in-C. lasted hardly longer than the first, a mere six months in all; and not long after it was over he and Palmerston were to quarrel irretrievably. Then Hobhouse would say: 'The truth is Palmerston & the Duke of Wellington are not friends & have not been friends since the Duke was made commander-in-chief.' Something seems to have come between them, even during the duke's first and briefest period at the Horse Guards. In the middle of July, as Canning struggled to induce him to return there, Lady Georgiana Bathurst wrote enigmatically: 'To think dear Mr

Arbuthnot we should live to see the Duke of Wellington paying his respects to Ld Palmerston. I think Ld P. if he has any feeling must have been ready to drop when he saw the Duke enter.' When Canning's death opened up the way for Wellington to return, a Johnian and House of Commons acquaintance of Palmerston's suggested to Peel that he would find the War Office 'reduced to its pristine state not so agreeable as it has lately been'. A few days afterwards a leading Canningite reported: 'There is a difficulty . . . about Palmerston who will not continue at the War Office with the D. of W. Commr in chief.' [79]

Palmerston had had time, before the duke returned, to amuse himself a little and military men a lot, by taking the salute from the Coldstream Guards in the full-dress uniform of a colonel of militia. But he seemed as acting C.-in-C. to have kept out of hot water pretty well. When called upon to select an officer for the high command in India he got himself so entangled in the intricacies of Army seniority that he was never able to decide. Lady Cowper, who knew both Palmerston and Wellington very well indeed, claimed that since the Secretary found it too much, even with Taylor as his deputy, to supervise the work of both departments he in fact gave 'away all the things that were before with the Commander-in-Chief '. 'I have swept your table up clear to the day,' Palmerston wrote to Wellington as he surrendered his nominal command; 'and I trust you will find that . . . I have done no mischief.'[80]

Taylor said that Wellington 'seemed much pleased' on his return 'to find that every one of the arrangements he had settled with me, had not been in the smallest degree compromised, but all had gone on exactly the same as if the Duke of York or himself, had remained at the head. I sometimes found this not very easy, especially as every department seemed to rival each other, in cutting at the expense, establishment and distribution of the Army.' But Wellington was not quite so satisfied as he professed. Palmerston had, it was true, been in general careful to consult the duke about proposed reductions, but they differed considerably about them and the signs are that Taylor too was in this respect beginning to think of Palmerston more as a danger than a help. The duke also grumbled about Palmerston having tried to by-pass him over the selection for the Indian command. According to Palmerston's own account the accusation was both unfounded and unfair. On the other hand Palmerston had taken the opportunity to set in train the commissioning of black West Indians for service on the coast of Africa, seeing to it that the first of them, named William Smellie, was provided with the material means of taking up his appointment and commenting to the Treasury in conclusion: 'I trust their Lordships will concur with me in the propriety of an arrangement which while on the one hand it will have the effect of diminishing the afflicting expenditure of human life consequent upon the military occupation of our settlements on the coast of Africa must also tend to raise in their own and in the public estimation that class of men in the West Indies from which these individuals are selected.' On his return Wellington immediately put a stop to what Hardinge called Palmerston's 'radical liberal proceedings' and refused to introduce any more 'officers of colour'. Soon a more familiar sort of warfare seems to have been breaking out again when in January 1828 Palmerston reproved the Adjutant-General for laying down scales of payment and issuing circulars without consulting the War Office. No doubt it was due to 'inadvertence' again, he said, 'but so many instances of similar deviation from the regular distribution of business have at various times occurred in communications from the A.G.'s office' that he thought it best to bring it to the notice of the C.-in-C.[81]

Wellington was reported as saying three years later that Palmerston, while behaving well enough in 'his proper place' at the War Office, showed he never liked him. 'I stood in his way when he attempted and all but succeeded in subordinating the office of Commander-in-Chief to that of Secretary at War, and he never forgave me.' Soon the duke was better placed than ever to prevent it, for Canning's successor, Goderich, was tottering to his fall from the premiership and the lack of any apparent alternative gave Wellington his place early in the New Year. The duke still wanted to hang on to the Horse Guards. Three days after he had kissed hands as Prime Minister he told a meeting of the Cabinet that 'all he was in the world was owing to the Army', that his 'connection with it never could cease be his situation what it might, & that he must always in truth & in fact & morally be the C.-in-C. of the Army of which he was the Senior Officer'. So much did he feel this that if he had a free choice he would rather be C.-in-C. than Prime Minister. But the King had commanded him to form a Government and therefore he could only leave it to his colleagues to decide whether or not he could also continue to command the Army. He then got up and left them to it. Each gave his opinion in the order in which he sat, Peel first and Palmerston last. They were all, of course, agreed: it was quite impossible. But only Palmerston added to the more obvious objections that 'great embarrassment' which would arise, 'if occasion should occur to use military force to preserve public peace, when additional odium would be incurred by its being said that armed force was employed under the very orders of the minister to keep down the discontent occasioned by his own measures'.[82]

So Wellington was obliged to give up the Army to Lord Hill. Perhaps Palmerston breathed a sigh of relief. If so he was very much mistaken; for as Prime Minister Wellington was to prove a very much more dangerous antagonist than any Commander-in-Chief ever was. But the battle with the Horse Guards had been real enough; potentially, at least, it was a vital constitutional issue, and by holding firm Palmerston had played his part in maintaining the supremacy of Parliament. Yet he did not claim that he had ever won the battle; in his opinion the issue was still not decided. Five years later, when the next Government of which he was a member came to reconsider the interrelationship of all the military departments, he summed up his experience in these words:

. . . The present confused and unconstitutional system dates only from the command of the Duke of York. He was a strong man; son of one King & brother of the other; heir presumptive; a political leader; he commanded too in time of war, when all men's minds took a military turn, & were accustomed to defer to military authority; he was always at the head of the army (except during a short interval) and took advantage of every opportunity to push on his encroachments; he had to do with a frequent succession of Secretaries of [*sic*] War, each of whom had to learn his duties & his powers, and many of whom had their pickets driven in, before they had well got into their saddle; some too, like Pulteney & Fitzpatrick, from weakness of character or indolence of habit found it easier to give way, than to battle; Liverpool disliked facing him, as much as a boy fears his schoolmaster; Farnborough [Charles Long] who was Liverpool's great oracle on such matters was a servile toady of the Duke; and thence arose a system which you may be sure was not relaxed by the Duke of Wellington when he succeeded to the office; and thus the Commander in Chief grew to be the head of a great civil as well as military department without any direct contact with Parliament so as to render him practically responsible. There never was so much power wielded with so little parliamentary responsibility as that which since 1795 has been exercised by the Commander in Chief.[83]

V

THE
RULING
PASSION

When the news of Palmerston's appointment to the War Office had broken in October 1809, a young lady of his acquaintance had written: 'That place is now made use of as a sort of seminary for beginners in politics. I suppose we must be glad of it, as it may divert his Lordship from flirting, in the same way as people rejoiced at his predecessor's appointment because it was to cure him of gambling. Nobody knows, however; some latent genius may be discovered by it at last – there's nothing like trying.'[1]

One of Perceval's colleagues, when considering possible Secretaries, had specifically advised that the War Office required a 'great sobriety of conduct', but it no more cured Palmerston of flirting than it did Granville of gambling. Instead Palmerston made it an office of routine, not only because it suited his talents and temperament to do so, but also because he was as much addicted to pleasure as his father. His intellectual and artistic interests lacked the quality of dedicated dilettantism so evident in his father's life. Palmerston's visits to the galleries were, like his reading, dutiful rather than enthusiastic, and his attendance at the opera social rather than devoted. In its general pattern his life in society at large merely followed that of other young men of his kind and period. In addition to the more or less exclusive and respectable men's clubs – Arthur's, White's, the Travellers', the University and eventually the Athenaeum – he was a member of the notorious Watier's and subscribed to the Argyll Rooms as well as the Opera and Drury Lane. But while he dressed and arrayed himself with great care, Palmerston was never quite a dandy, never the true exquisite. The time and effort he put in his youth into dancing and parade, like the rouged cheeks and dyed whiskers of old age, had much too serious a purpose for that. This he summed up in five terse words towards the end of his life. When in January 1863 he heard that his old rival Lansdowne had asked as he lay dying from a fall which had cut his head and knocked out his teeth that he should not be seen in that condition by a handsome American lady in the house, Palmerston noted in his diary: 'ruling passion strong in death'.[2]

Palmerston's attitude to women was formed in the notorious years of later Georgian England. His own parents probably had little direct responsibility for their son's libertine ways. His father, it is true, was a man of the world and distinguished almost solely for his pursuit of pleasure. He had had a number of mistresses, Italian and English, and possibly, though not probably, had also enjoyed the favours of Emma Hamilton. But the spirit of Broadlands in his time was characterized less by the presence of Henry Campbell than by the patent goodness and devotion of Mary Palmerston. Unfortunately, after his parents' early deaths the atmosphere of married life most familiar to the young viscount was not Broadlands but Park Place.[3]

As a dedicated and life-long diplomat the first Earl of Malmesbury had had to spend a good deal of time away from his wife abroad; eventually it became clear that distance and neglect had culminated in indifference and dislike and that he was consoling himself elsewhere. Harriet Malmesbury was commonly called the 'kettle-drum' on account of her 'unceasing *clack*' and loud voice. Her husband was notoriously deaf; but since she hardly ever spoke to him there was more to it than that. 'She is . . . used', remarked an acquaintance, 'to domineer through life [and] delivers opinions without appeal, in the voice of a pea-hen.' She was not the sort of woman, certainly, to let go unrevenged the blows – physical as well as moral – delivered by her husband, and she retaliated by making liaisons of her own. Before Palmerston's parents died, the passage of years had apparently cooled the violent hatred between the Malmesburys; in mutual indifference Malmesbury had accepted his wife's attachments, as no doubt she had accepted his. But there remained, according to the Mintos, a 'rooted, incurable alienation' between them and, although Malmesbury was anxious to protect his girls from scandal, the example and atmosphere of their ménage can hardly have been the best suited to guide young Palmerston through the mild flirtations of his teenage years to the more serious pursuits of early manhood. In all too short a time, indeed, his devoted attendance at balls and dances ceased to be a matter of merely bantering comment from his friends and relations, and like Lady Sarah Spencer they looked forward by 1809 to his settling down at the War Office and in marriage.[4]

In his celebrated exchange of juvenile letters with Francis Hare, the thirteen-year-old Harry had disagreed about women having too many vices for him to contemplate marriage, but nonetheless avowed that he would be 'by no means precipitate about . . . choice'. In her testamentary letter his mother, too, had commended marriage to her son but expressed the hope that in his case it would be 'at no very early age'. In this, as is so well known, Palmerston proved only too obedient. But he had a number of narrow squeaks long before 1839. It is difficult in his teenage years to distinguish in the letters of his own, as much as those of family and friends, what was serious and what was not. All too often the 'young ladies' coupled with him in mutual admiration turn out on closer scrutiny to be either eight or eighty-eight. He was constantly, of course, in the company of Malmesbury's and Minto's daughters and their names were often linked with his in fun. 'My kind love to my daughter in law Catan,' wrote Lady Palmerston in 1802, 'and assure her that Harry is very fond, and very constant, and that he was much charmed with her letter which he means to answer very soon but she knows how much a sportsman's hours are occupied and even Cupid's arrows, I am afraid to say with an Englishman . . . , are superseded by powder & shot . . . he is her devoted slave – after the shooting season.' Harry had captured Catherine Elliot with the present of a pebble heart that spring; but she was only seven to his seventeen. His affection for Minto's eldest daughter, however, may have been more serious.[5]

Anna Maria Elliot was scarcely a year younger than Palmerston, and like him very slow to marry. But theirs would have been an interesting match. According to Walter Scott, who knew her well, she was full of 'wit, good sense, and good-humour'; but, because of her strong powers of observation and still greater ones of expression, was abused by jealous women and silly men as a blue-stocking. Francis Horner (like Macaulay twenty years later) also found her conversation amusing and commented on her good judgement of people, and he was no mean judge himself. Unfortunately neither says much about her appearance, though another casual acquaintance observed in 1829 'the remains of much prettiness'. But while Minto may have been merely joking when he mentioned his hope that Harry would marry her, Ashburton strongly implied that his friend did have a crush on her. Eventually, in 1820, Palmerston made at Broadlands a sort of serious proposal disguised as jest, and received in return a sort of mock refusal that forever separated two childhood friends, who, one suspects, had really wished to marry. In 1832 she married Gen. Sir Rufane Donkin, a veteran of the Peninsular and East Indian Wars and some twelve years older than herself; in 1841 he hanged himself, literally from his deathbed. When Anna Maria died in 1855 Palmerston wrote rather perfunctorily: 'These losses of early ties make us cling closer to those that remain.'[6]

We have equally little knowledge about most of Palmerston's other early offers and adventures. The marriages, to George Villiers (later Earl of Jersey) and to William Lamb (later Viscount Melbourne), of Lady Sarah Fane in 1804 and Lady Caroline Ponsonby in 1805 were noted by his friends and relatives in such a way as strongly to suggest that he had cast an especially admiring eye on both young ladies. Shortly afterwards, in April 1807, Lady Georgiana Morpeth briefly considered him as a suitor for her sister, Harriet ('Hary-O') Cavendish. She did not know him, she said, but had heard 'great praise' of him. Her grandmother, the Dowager Countess Spencer, was also not averse. She too had heard a good deal about him, she replied. 'He is not rich, but I am told his character & his understanding are both excellent.' Palmerston's father had been an old friend of Harriet's mother, (Georgiana) Duchess of Devonshire, and after her death Palmerston still had the entrée to Devonshire House. But there is no evidence that he made any advances there. When Lady Georgiana had married some years earlier he had remarked that he did not think her at all pretty. Her sister was even less handsome. But any Cavendish was a great match. Two and a half years later Hary-O married the handsome, gambling Granville. Early that same year, in January 1809, an attempt was rumoured of a political match between Palmerston and Lady Frances Pratt, the eldest daughter of Earl Camden and the niece of Castlereagh's stepmother; 'a remarkably neat Ministerial Alliance', it seemed to some, though Harriet Cavendish could not resist a little cattiness. 'Lady Camden never opens her mouth', she wrote, 'and Lady Fanny never shuts hers – a happy variety in one family.' Later in 1809 Lady Malmesbury heard another rumour that Palmerston was about to be married; but she named no names. Two years after that, however, she heard yet another and, failing once again to get the name, concluded it must be her informant, Miss Grote. It was probably another joke about an elderly maiden cousin. But Lady Malmesbury had got hold of the wrong end of the stick in any case. It was not Palmerston who was engaged but his sister Lilly at last; Sulivan had been afraid of Lady Malmesbury and he kept the secret from her for a day or two.[7]

Although Debrett seemed very reluctant to correct the gross libel that she was born in 1769, and the child of her father's first marriage, Lilly was really twenty-one when she married. The elder daughter, Frances, did not marry until 1820, when she was nearly thirty-five. Fanny's husband was a captain in the Royal Navy and a relative of the Malmesburys, William Bowles. She died in 1838, a year after her sister, without leaving any children. Her brother, William Temple, never had any either. After qualifying at the bar, he left it for the diplomatic service in 1814 and after that seems to have been only rarely in England. He was often chargé d'affaires while on the legation staff in Stockholm (1814-17), Frankfurt (1817-23), Berlin (1823-28), and St Petersburg (1828-31). He was helped all along by his brother's influence and then in 1833 Palmerston placed him in the plum job of minister in Naples. Curiously, while Naples buzzed with English visitors few seem to have registered more than a perfunctory call and, beyond the fact that he assembled a collection of sculpture to match his father's pictures, almost nothing unofficial is known at all about his life there. One visitor thought that, for all his *bonhomie*, his manner was quite the opposite of his brother's, 'very quiet – almost shy'. Lady Cowper, however, was not very complimentary about his abilities and noted on his return on leave from Germany in 1819 that he had become a drunkard. Twenty years later Holland heard that he had been warned in Naples either to give up his post or the bottle. The warning apparently worked. When he visited England again two years later it was noticed that he had 'quite given up his bad habits'. So for another twenty years he remained in Naples, '*very* dull' but 'amazingly popular', 'plain and sensible in his proceedings' and 'quite capable of *solid* business' from time to time. He returned to England to die in 1856. Even Henry Greville could say no more than that 'he had been minister at Naples for twenty-three years, and was much liked and respected there'. He had never married, though Lady Cowper listed him among the admirers of the mad Lady Westmorland.[8]

Given the attitudes and customs of the times, it must have been rather worrying all around that this generation of Temples, though very loving to each other, were so slow or reluctant to marry. This certainly applied to Palmerston himself. Most, if not all, the rumours about marriage plans seem to have been started by wishful friends and relatives. Yet there he was, tall, dark and handsome, and a real success in life: about five feet ten, with a fresh complexion, dark hair and magnificent blue eyes (though lacking a few teeth from hunting accidents, occasionally inclining to overweight, and with a definitely receding hairline); supposedly a clear £10,000 a year; and a government minister in his twenties! Surely there were plenty of eligible girls who would have been glad to have him? The trouble was, they thought, there were too many, and unable to make his choice Palmerston enjoyed them all. The War Office, it was clear, had by no means cured him of flirting. 'I hope it is not a permanent attachment he has vowed to Lady C–,' wrote one of his acquaintance in December 1812. 'If so she has good reason to fear it may turn out that he meant a temporary one.'[9]

Lady C–, surely, was the daring Countess Cowper. A lively, dark and mischievous-looking beauty, Emily Lamb was truly the child of her mother – which was more than could be said with any certainty about her legal father. A sulk and a soak, the first Lord Melbourne had been raised to the dignity of a viscount only through the wealth inherited from his father and through the unscrupulous ambition of his intimidatingly handsome wife. Many years later the second Viscount Melbourne was heard to say of her: 'A remarkable woman, a devoted mother, an excellent wife – but not chaste, not chaste.' At the time William was supposed to have been looking at her portrait. She was habitually painted wearing a choker round her neck; rumour had it that it was to disguise the marks left by her husband's strangling hands. For Lady Melbourne was commonly supposed to have advised young brides that they owed their husbands but a single male heir.[10]

No one could seriously have believed that Lady Melbourne's husband had fathered any of her children but the first, who died young in 1805. Still, 'he seemed', as some wit observed, 'as fond of them as if they were his own'. They were also an extraordinarily affectionate group. 'Considering,' wrote a friend, 'that those brothers and sisters are in all probability as little related to each other as possible, they are the most attached family I ever saw.' The youngest, George, who was generally considered to be 'merely a good-natured lad' – he was a gifted amateur actor, but according to Byron a poor scribbler of comedies and a not much better minor politician – was believed to be the son of the Prince Regent, whom he much resembled. Certainly the prince was a close friend of Lady Melbourne's and always took a careful interest in her children, more especially in Emily and Frederick. Emily's birth is said to be shrouded in mystery. But Emily and Fred, as well as William, the future Prime Minister, were all thought to be the children of the astonishing Earl of Egremont, whose fortune of £100,000 a year was probably barely enough for the liberality in which he dealt with 'private friends, with artists, and, lastly, with by no means the least costly customers – with [the] mistresses', all of whom he supported in large numbers at Petworth House. The malignants said that he had bought Lady Melbourne from Lord Coleraine for £13,000, with the lady and her husband each taking a commission on the deal.[11]

In later years Emily was to say that 'marriage . . . at best . . . must always be a lottery'. 'I think', she went on, 'for a man's comfort it is almost better to have a bad wife than to have no wife – besides it is always a man's own fault if his wife is *very* bad.' Her husband, Peter Leopold Francis Nassau, had succeeded his brother as the fifth Earl Cowper in 1799 at the tender age of twenty. He was rather reserved – 'not much given to softness', Lady Bessborough remarked – but at the same time apparently well-liked. Sir James Mackintosh called him 'the most agreeable of peers'; his friend Luttrell 'the most open creature in the world', without 'mysterys and reserves'. The Duchess of Devonshire thought he was 'the most amiable [of] creatures' with an 'understanding . . . not only good but cultivated . . . His manners . . . so gentlemanlike & his good nature so evident that I defy him not to be lov'd – as to person, . . . all the young ladies . . . even thinking him handsomer than Ld Granville.' So, the duchess concluded, 'the woman will be happy whose fate depends on C.' But some noted that with all his virtues he did seem rather dull, with 'a slow pronunciation, and a slow gait and pace'. Most of Emily's girlhood friends certainly thought so. Harriet Cavendish claimed on first making his acquaintance to 'dislike him very much, he seems so very heavy and stupid'; and Corisande de Gramont (later Lady Tankerville) called him 'maigre, triste, beau et un peu plus causant'. But it was Augustus Foster, probably, who came nearest to the truth when he said a few years even before Cowper's marriage that 'he, with all his riches, rank, and titles, seems to ennuy in every place he happens to be in'; and some years later Foster's mother made the even more significant observation that as a forfeit at Princess Borghese's *petits jeux* in Rome Cowper was made to 'soupirer pour une dame'. Instead he took to drink and surrounded himself with a circle of wits and dandies in the uncertain hope no doubt of mitigating the utter boredom of his life. From a country-house party Lady Granville once reported to her sister: 'Lord Cowper is aux anges here – he has good shooting, better claret, & a patient audience, with Luttrell to say good things for him.' Occasionally he bestirred himself to make an improvement or two (such as a picture gallery) to his new house at Panshanger, but found it necessary more and more often to take himself off to the Continent in a vain attempt to save his ruined health. So – amiable but slow, rich but bored, handsome and physically attractive, but by women insufficiently attracted – he sank slowly out of sight. Not even politics aroused him much. He had very early on in life been marked out for distinction by the followers of Fox, but somehow he disappointed all their expectations.[12]

To Emily Lord Cowper was an even greater disappointment. 'I think [he] is a charming person,' wrote Lady Charlotte Bury; 'but the world says his wife does not.' They were married in July 1805, when she was eighteen and he was twenty-seven. During the first few weeks of marriage she frequently declared, and with patent sincerity, that she was deliriously happy. Harriet Cavendish, who behind her back was no kinder about Emily than Emily was about her, even wondered if she had not turned 'a little crazy'. She also enjoyed immensely her role as Countess of Panshanger. 'There she is', wrote her sister-in-law and neighbour in Hertfordshire, Lady Caroline Lamb, 'all of a sudden perched up as Queen of the County to whom all the neighbourhood pay their respects, enough wits to pass for clever in a situation to be observed & pretty enough in all conscience to be admired wherever she is.' But with such a lively personality and such a dangerous background as hers, it was no wonder that 'that little devil Emily', as her brother called her, could not make a successful marriage with lethargy and dullness. Sure enough, she was barely pregnant for the first time – 'they really do announce any events of that sort very soon in the Melbourne family', Harriet Cavendish nastily observed; it was to be rather more than nine months after her marriage that her son was born – than she began to wonder if her husband was quite so much in love as she. Apparently he was not around much during the day, and when he was, at a time when he should have been 'all tenderness and attendance, neglected her entirely, hardly answering if she spoke to him and persevering in an invariable sulky silence'. But she comforted herself that it was really being in the country he hated, and insisted that when they were alone together he was very kind and that they played 'about the rooms together'. She admitted to Caroline Lamb that she was 'so extravagantly fond of him that he sometimes appears a little cold to her, but that she supposes all men to be so and does not mind it in the least'. At the end of the year she still seemed 'tolerably contented', believing that in spite of 'the greatest indifference and neglect' he 'really cared for her'. But it was a strange contentment that depended on his returning home drunk enough to talk and at the same time the story was already getting about that she was consoling herself with the admiration of Lord Henry Petty. She denied it, of course, but she was seen wallowing in his admiration. If, however, there was anything in it, it never could have satisfied her; for though Petty never sank into the sort of political obscurity her husband did, he too was a comparative failure and a disappointment to the Whigs; he was lazy and diffident, even as a lover according to Palmerston.[13]

Little wonder then that in 1806-8 there was a note of discontent and inner sadness to Emily's loud behaviour. Even her female friends must have sensed it, since they came to appreciate that for all her biting gossip there was real amiability beneath. Her apparent ill-nature, they concluded, was not 'of the heart but of the tip of the tongue only'. It came from the bad company she kept among her husband's witty friends and was nothing more than habit. To break it, perhaps, Emily herself took to attending the services at St George's, Hanover Square, and talked to Harriet Cavendish of 'nothing but morality, the misery of being with people of bad character etc.' She also put up a brave appearance, maintaining an 'incessant titter' during her husband's long-drawn-out sentences and sometimes even singing through dinner. But it was all a great strain and by 1808, apparently, the gay and warm-hearted Emily had turned into 'Lady C[owper] in a dirty gown and pearls, graceful and cold'. But better times were only just around the corner, brought by her brother William, as careless perhaps of his sister's morals as his wife would say he was of hers.[14]

Palmerston had been acquainted with the Lambs since childhood. Emily had probably danced with him when, with the Cavendish girls and Caroline Ponsonby, she had gone to a children's ball given by the Palmerstons at Sheen in July 1798 to mark the return of the young Temples from Harrow for the holidays. But it was at Brocket and as her brother's guest that Palmerston became her lifelong intimate. How and when Palmerston and William Lamb became friends is much less clear. But Palmerston had visited William and his bride at Brocket as early as August 1805. He was hunting there in November 1808 and again in September the following year. On the second occasion he also went with the party of Lambs and Cowpers to visit the latter's newly rebuilt house nearby at Panshanger, and at the end of 1813 he went again to Brocket to spend Christmas with them all. In the evening they all played what Mrs George Lamb described as 'a most alarming game called Secretaire where every body is obliged to write something – a character of some one'. In her opinion it all led to 'ill-nature', but both the Lambs and Palmerston were pleased enough to preserve several specimens among their papers. But there was evidently more to it all than a harmless holiday game, for a few days later Fred Lamb wrote to his sister: 'there is a tone of happiness and content in yr letter.'[15]

It seems to have been at Brocket that Palmerston and Emily first made love. Twenty years later when Palmerston was staying there again he especially noted: 'Put into Luttrell's room with use of *the* little drawing room.' The Cowpers had lived at Brocket for about two years until the building at Panshanger was ready in September 1809 and it was during that period, Emily recalled in widowhood, she had begun her love affair. Almost forty years later Disraeli vaguely recollected being told it was at the opera they first met and fell instantly in love. The story was supposed to have come from Harriet Cavendish, and certainly hers is the first known pointed mention of seeing Palmerston and Lady Cowper together at a ball in March 1809; little more than a year later the spiteful John Ward was gossiping to the Princess of Wales about them 'as he would of Ld Archibald and Lady Oxford, or any old undoubted intrigue'. Outside of Devonshire and Melbourne Houses, however, there appears to have been little notice taken. Perhaps Palmerston was enormously discreet; more likely he was not yet interesting enough, in politics or in love, for the gossips to make any detailed notes.[16]

Some of Palmerston's own family circle were extraordinarily slow to see how desperately entangled he was with Lady Cowper. It was not until 1816 that even the usually observant Lady Malmesbury noticed it. That was a bad year in which to stay in England. Summer never came and after incessant rain the crops rotted in the fields. There were food riots in many areas and before the year was out a march on London to demand political reform had culminated in the Spa Fields riot. Clearly this was an appropriate time to close up at home and reside abroad, which was the normal recourse for high-spending English aristocrats in need of economy and recuperation. By the autumn, according to one of their number, the Continent was 'absolutely over-run, infested with English, . . . some good, some tolerable, but the greater number of course sad blackguards'. For the Lambs 1816 was a particularly harrowing year – thanks to the two Carolines. Byron, about this time, called them 'a cuckoldy family', and he was in a good position to know. By this time they must have been getting used to bombshells from Caro William, but her attack upon her page in April and the appearance of *Glenarvon* in May were too much; and then in the summer came the shock from Caro George.[17]

Caroline St Jules, as she was named, was one of the two children that the fifth Duke of Devonshire had had by his second duchess before the death of the first. Utterly unlike her sisters-in-law, she seems to have been a quiet and even docile girl – 'a piece of Still life', Emily called her. But after nearly ten years of marriage to Emily's brother George her virtue too gave way. George's red-haired and red-faced appearance belied his character. For him there was a seventh commandment, 'thou shalt not bother'. He patently neglected his wife; she had originally refused to marry him and was miserable when she did. At length, having 'struggled ten years', she gave way to the tempestuous advances of Henry Brougham and went off to meet him in Geneva. But Brougham soon got bored with Switzerland: 'Ennui comes on the third hour, and suicide attacks you before night.' Italy improved his spirits somewhat, but evidently not enough to make him dally long with Caroline. They agreed to separate and early in 1817 he was among the first of the English exiles to leave Rome to return to the excitements of the bar and Parliament. Clearly, having had his way, it did not take him long to come to the same conclusion as a scholarly observer who 'having seen Mr *Anthony* Brougham and Mrs *Cleopatra* Lamb & after looking well at the lady . . . did *not* think the world at all *well* lost'.[18]

It was to break up this affair, as well as to economize, that Emily Cowper went off with her husband to Geneva and Italy. Nonetheless, as even her discreet descendant tells, she 'seems to have enjoyed the idea of the journey, and amused herself to the full while away'. Her mother was worried about her meeting up with Lady Jersey and being led astray. 'I assure you', Emily wrote home, 'she is quite steady & don't lead me into any kind of danger.' But whether or not Sarah was really to blame, Emily was certainly not telling the truth.[19]

1816 was not Palmerston's first visit to the Continent since 1794. Like so many others he had taken advantage of the restoration of peace the previous year to taste the fruits of victory in Paris. As Secretary at War he watched the reviews of the allied armies of occupation and dined with the Tsar, Wellington and Castlereagh. He also began once more a careful journal of his impressions, which was published long after he had intended and then only against the advice of a biographer who thought its patriotic sentiments compromisingly offensive to the French. He kept a similar journal of his trip in 1816, which must have been overlooked rather than suppressed when it came to publication by his executors, since no one could have detected from it that he was really on a ten weeks' hot pursuit of Emily through France and all over northern Italy and Switzerland.[20]

Palmerston had been very harassed and hard-pressed in the spring of 1816 by a particularly vigorous parliamentary assault upon the Army Estimates – during which, incidentally, he clashed most of all with Brougham – and he must have looked forward with especial pleasure to getting away from England and 'damned War Office papers' at the end of August, making his usual meticulous preparations and, so appropriately for that 'most English Minister', beginning his list of 'Things useful for Travelling in France' with 'a portable tea kettle, tea pot, and tea cups'. His sister Fanny and Lady Malmesbury were already in Paris and expected to meet him there, but then they heard that he intended to 'cut' Paris and hurry on instead to Lyons and Geneva. They missed him on the road and then waited for several days in Geneva, where the widowed Lady Minto had a villa nearby, but hearing he had crossed straight into Italy from Lyons they eventually gave him up for lost and returned to England. A few days later Lady Minto ran into him in Geneva, at a reception with Lady Cowper. So that was the reason, it suddenly became clear to Lady Malmesbury, why Palmerston had dashed about so unpredictably. 'I fear it will end ill,' she wrote to her daughter, 'for it *must be very serious* after *this trail.*'[21]

Obviously Palmerston's apparently erratic movements had been dictated by Emily's; and Emily's, he naturally assumed, by the ups and downs of Caro George's affair. So when he heard that Brougham and Caroline had crossed into Italy, so did he. But while he dashed all over northern Italy and found Brougham and Caroline at Milan, the Cowpers and Jerseys had all stayed on in Switzerland. Perhaps they found Geneva less 'boring' than Brougham's affair; perhaps they would not brave the mountain passes then being harassed by a particularly active band of robbers. When he had tracked Emily down at last, Palmerston, loaded perhaps with a Titian and a Veronese – 'quite masterpieces *of course*' – moved northwards by a safer route and the Cowpers and Jerseys eventually crossed only after most of the robbers had been caught. Afterwards Palmerston spent a week touring Switzerland and on the way back through France made a detour to see a review of British cavalry at St Omer. He had only three days with Emily in Geneva, but for Lady Malmesbury the significance was obvious enough. 'This is a [?sad] connexion,' she wrote to her sister-in-law, '& quite *for life* I am convinced.'[22]

Lady Malmesbury was right where John Ward had been wrong. But she could hardly have reckoned on making so accurate a forecast. Palmerston was Emily's lover for almost the last thirty years of Lord Cowper's life and after her brief widowhood from 1837 to 1839 became himself her husband for nearly thirty more. Theirs was by any measure an astonishing romance. It also introduced him to a fantastic world of fashion, intrigue and politics, far different from the bucolic quiet of Broadlands or the Tory dullness of his youth. For Lady Cowper was one of the queens of London society and a leading member of the international set. In this role she passed for a generation between Panshanger, the pavilion at Brighton and Almack's in St James's. In her day admission to Almack's was 'the seventh heaven of the fashionable world'. Of the three hundred officers of the Foot Guards not more than half a dozen were honoured with tickets to that 'exclusive temple'; even the Duke of Wellington was excluded for wearing black trousers. It was a council of eight lady patronesses whose 'smiles or frowns consigned men and women to happiness or despair'. Lady Cowper was the most popular of them, according to Captain Gronow. The others were Lady Castlereagh and Mrs Drummond Burrell (later Lady Willoughby de Eresby) – both 'très grandes dames'; Lady Sefton – 'kind and amiable'; Lady Jersey – a theatrical tragedy queen, who 'whilst attempting the sublime, . . . frequently made herself simply ridiculous, being inconceivably rude, and in her manner often ill-bred'; and the wives of the Austrian and Russian ambassadors, Princess Esterhazy – a 'bon enfant' – and Countess Lieven – 'haughty and exclusive'. They presided over Almack's with a pure female despotism and like all despotisms it was quite capricious. But they smiled upon Palmerston who, while most were still too timid, was to be seen in the course of time 'describing an infinite number of circles' in a daring waltz thigh to thigh with Mme Lieven.[23]

Mme Lieven's was a world of strange intrigue, a tangled mixture of love and politics. Utterly enchanted by her life in English society, she never forgot the interest of Russia. This extended even, or especially, to her love affairs, though her husband often beat her for her pains. But she was not always very lucky with them. Metternich gave her up for a second bride thirty years his junior; Grey presided over the Government that forced her into exile from England. She was not without resource and she cultivated anyone who was, or one day might be, of help – both Castlereagh and Canning, Wellington and Aberdeen, as well as George IV. She was similarly interested in Palmerston as an up and coming man. There is no evidence that they were lovers. She had arrived in

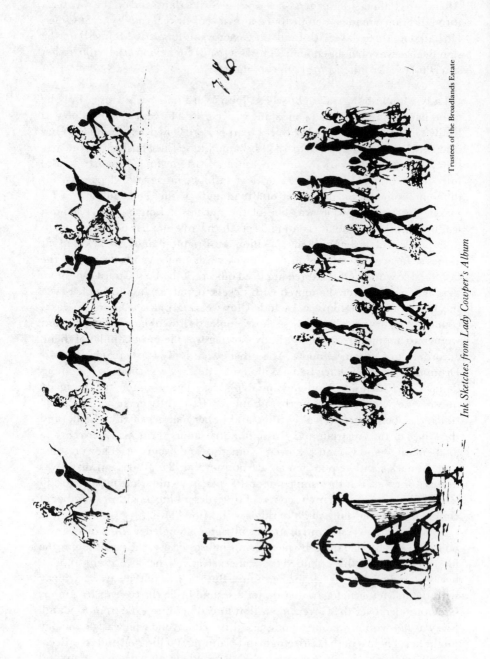

Ink Sketches from Lady Cowper's Album

England with her husband at the end of 1812 and was elected a patroness of Almack's the following year. But the earliest known letter addressed to her by Palmerston dates only from August 1827. Their correspondence after that was fairly full and what survives of it was indeed very intimate in tone. But Mme Lieven made intrigue of everything and the particular reason in this case was that it was sometimes a correspondence *à trois* with Emily.[24]

Emily was Mme Lieven's 'good friend'; Lady Granville, formerly Harriet Cavendish, her 'best friend'. Together with Lady Ossulston, the former Corisande de Gramont of Devonshire House and the future Countess of Tankerville, they formed a quartet of dark intrigue and gay deceit. To serve their needs they employed in correspondence a considerable range of cypher names – 'Henry' for George IV, 'The Corporal' for his brother William, 'Betsy' for Metternich, 'The Child' for Wellington, 'Emilie' for Princess Lieven, and 'Henriette' for Lady Cowper – but occasionally changing them round in order to confuse, and extending the secret to but a very few males. Lady Granville's brother 'Hart', the sixth and bachelor Duke of Devonshire, seems to have been one of them; another was Emily's foul-mouthed but diplomat brother Fred.

Emily's letters to Fred are fascinating, full of gossip from court and country and revealing in their frankness an extraordinarily, almost unnaturally, close relationship between brother and sister.[25] Lady Granville thought them very much alike; 'they are both remarkable for good temper & ill-nature,' she said. Emily seems to have told Fred everything about herself, though sometimes by denying it. She also told him a good deal about everybody else, including her mother's old friend George IV. One long and complicated subject was Fred's desire to marry and his unhappy courtship of Lady Elizabeth Conyngham. Evidently Fred, who had been a notorious rake and figured prominently in the *Memoirs* of Harriette Wilson, was not thought good enough or rich enough for the daughter of George's very good friend, in spite of the mysterious affinity he and his sister had with the King. As Fred was in the foreign service, and for a long period in the embassy at Vienna, Emily's letters went via the Foreign Office in London. But she could not have wished Palmerston any more than Metternich to read them, since she was often quite cool in what she had to say about the 'Viscount' or, when she wished to be particularly critical, 'Mary', which was her nickname for the Foreign Secretary, whether Canning or Palmerston. 'I dare say letters are not read at the office,' she remarked when advising Fred to use the cypher, 'but one cannot be too careful and I always dislike gentlemen meddling with letters.' It is hardly likely, therefore, that she ever gave Palmerston the cypher key; nor does he seem to have had to break the greater part of it. Since it appears in the back of his diary for 1835, and, though incomplete, precisely in the same order as hers, one may suspect that he copied it surreptitiously and in haste one night.[26]

Emily was not only sometimes rather cool about Palmerston behind his back; occasionally she gave people the impression that she was utterly bored with him. Even 'il sposo' Cowper, noticed Mrs Lamb, would scarcely speak to him from time to time. Their friends might charitably conclude it was perhaps to make the lover jealous. But there was a great deal more to it than that.[27]

Contemporary rumour and family legend both conferred upon Lady Cowper the dubious attribute of worldly wisdom. 'Even her faults', they would say, 'came from over-kindness. She was too kind to refuse anybody anything'; and lest their meaning should be overlooked they would add that she had the curious habit of never giving presents. Her descendant Lord David Cecil tells the charming, but utterly improbable, story that at her mother's deathbed in 1818 she was urged to be faithful, not to her husband but to Palmerston. But if something of the kind was ever said it ought to have been by way of reproof rather than approval, for Emily was notoriously unfaithful to husband and lover alike. 'Whatever else may be said of me nobody shall ever doubt my being a good mother and a good daughter,' was her own frank avowal in 1821. Creevey, who was no saint, regarded her as one of 'the most notorious and profligate women in London'. But she had some sense of discrimination; even Lady Granville admitted that her mind was 'perfectly free from general coquetry'. Of Mme Lieven's desperate attempts to fix a further meeting with Metternich in 1823 – she could not leave England unless her husband did, and he could not leave unless King George did; but the King was unwilling to go without Lady Conyngham, and she would not cross the Channel because it made her sea-sick – Emily wrote: 'there is such a combinaison of dates & difficulties that I cannot follow the thread of them & tho' I am vastly edified with the Romance & the constancy necessary for such a sentimental attachment I own that it rather passes my vulgar comprehension.' She scorned love for ambition's sake; it made her 'sick', she said. Certainly she had 'little taste for uncut jewels, but likes those which have taken a high polish from the attrition of society'. So it was the handsomest aristocrats and the most charming dandies of the day who were many of them linked at one time or another with her name. 'Punch' Greville and 'Poodle' Byng were both reputed to have been among her lovers, and both loathed Palmerston. It was said by her family that even at the age of sixty-two she had to ask her grandson: 'Come back with me, Evelyn, to London; Poodle Byng has asked for a seat in my carriage and I don't think Palmerston will like it.' Lady Bessborough teased her own distant lover, the Adonis Granville, about the colour of Emily's daughter's eyes; and a recent writer reports that another child was believed to have been fathered by Pozzo di Borgo, an enemy of Napoleon's in Russian service. This last seems rather unlikely, since while Emily admitted to her brother in 1826 she was enchanted with the Corsican's charm and wit, he was so old and she liked especially men of her own age or even younger. But she had no objection to foreigners.[28]

After her three days with Palmerston in Geneva in October 1816, Emily had gone on with her family and friends to spend several more months in Italy. They visited Milan, Venice, Florence, Rome and Naples, losing on the way a servant from eating oysters out of season. What other adventures Emily experienced are not known. But in one of her letters home she had remarked on leaving the friends she had made in Rome: 'It is quite a meeting of all nations & I shall now only feel sorry to part with people I am now so intimate with & may perhaps never see again.' She was hardly back in England for the summer of 1817 than there appeared in her wake a mysterious 'Count' Giuliano from among them.[29]

That Giuliano had formerly been an A.D.C. to Murat when King of Naples the memoirs of a colleague, Col. Maceroni, make quite clear in an artful footnote about his being 'well-known in England in 1818, especially by the family of Lord Cowper'. Evidently he was Antonio, Marchese di San Giuliano, a member of a cadet line of the Paterno Castello family and an exile from his homeland in the Kingdom of Naples. He was a widower and, supposedly, an orphan too. For shortly after his birth, his father had shot and killed his mother in a fit of jealousy and disappeared from sight. Later it was to be revealed from the stories of an English traveller published about this time that the father had fled to Tripoli, where he had become a Moslem, married the daughter of a bey, and raised another noble family.[30]

Emily described Giuliano to her mother as a 'very civil, well-bred man' and expected her to like him as he was 'so very like an Englishman & certainly the most amiable foreigner' she had met on her travels. To an Irish judge, Jonah Barrington, who met him in Paris during Napoleon's Hundred Days, 'Count Julien' was 'a huge boisterous overbearing fat man, consequential without being dignified, dressy without being neat, and with a showy politeness that wanted even the elements of civility'. But in the mysterious circumstances of their meeting – Guiliano was involved in very complicated and secret negotiations concerning Murat – he had probably neglected his appearance and his diet and Barrington perhaps had mistaken slow-wittedness for guile. For though he was apparently not very bright – 'bother-headed', Mrs Lamb called him – nor, after Murat's death, politically of any importance, he must, in addition to having so romantic a history, have personally been very attractive to have filled subsequently, in Mme Lieven's idle moments, the gap left by the end of an affair she had had with Granville's handsome nephew, Gower. At Whitehall in August 1817, Caro George reported, 'all the same manège is going on as we had at Chatsworth [in October 1815] with Lord Gower – [Count] Lieven frowning et faisant des scènes'. But when Mrs Lamb's half-sister, Georgiana Morpeth, saw them both for herself at Lady Melbourne's the following month she suspected that Giuliano's real object was Emily Cowper. Before the end of the year he was at Panshanger, proving she was right. Even so, Mrs Lamb could hardly believe it was reciprocal. 'I don't think there is much in Juliano's business,' she wrote, 'for Lady M[elbourne] can't disguise how dull she thinks him, and is not fond of him, as she always is of those who admire her daughter. It is more likely that it was only done to make the other jealous.'[31]

If jealousy was Emily's purpose, she certainly succeeded. By some lucky chance, probably their superficial resemblance to mere appointment books, Palmerston's pocket diaries for 1818 and 1819 are among the few to have survived from the first half of his adult life. They show beyond any doubt that Palmerston, far from being easy-going, was driven almost frantic with jealousy. The year 1818 began comfortably enough with visits to Cambridge and Broadlands in January and taking Emily to the opera on his return. But on his first appearance of the season at Almack's on 18 February he clashed with Giuliano and there was a dreadful 'scene'; when he visited Emily three days later it was 'war', he found. Thereafter, and throughout the next two years at least, he recorded in his mixture of English and Italian the campaign's ups and downs. He made it up again at a reception after the weekend – '*pace*' – but could not resist putting his case on paper the following week. In consequence, at Almack's that same evening, it was '*guerra*' once more; and at Lady Cholmondeley's the following night, '*pace*'. For some weeks after that he saw very little of Emily, though when he ran into her at the opera he told her he had 'great hopes'. First Lady Melbourne fell ill and died on 6 April; two days later Lt Davies tried to bring his own life to a finish still more prematurely. Then on 18 May Emily had a miscarriage at Brighton and gave birth to a dead baby boy. Emily returned in June and they had several serious 'discussions' about Giuliano; but these seem to have turned out well, for there were no more rows that year. In the autumn Palmerston made another visit to France, attending some more reviews of the allied armies at Cambray and inspecting the field of Waterloo on the way back. When he returned to London there was another 'discussion' about Giuliano, but all seemed well and in the New Year his romance appeared to flourish more than ever, as he kept assignations with Emily several times a week. Then, like a bolt from the blue, there came an anonymous letter towards the end of April 1819. This time he tried to avoid a new row with Emily; instead he waited a couple of months to confront the man – '*discussio coll' uomo*'. Only after that did he take it up with Emily, and getting from her a suitable bedtime explanation – '*spilgazione*' – allowed himself to be convinced. For a few weeks all was well again; but in the summer came another letter, this time from her neighbours. Emily left town almost at once; but when she got back he harried her from pillar to post – in Kensington Gardens, in her carriage on the way back home from dinner, and at Mr Jenkins's nursery in Regent's Park. Finally, at the opera, it was all '*guerra*' again; and at Melbourne House the next day, when he confronted her with the letter, '*confessiones*'. For the next two months they saw nothing of each other. Emily retreated to Panshanger with the measles and worrying lest she should have another miscarriage; Palmerston diverted himself with killing live birds and other ladies. By the beginning of November they were both back in town and enjoying each other's company again. But 1819 ended with Palmerston still worrying about Giuliano and having further 'long discussions' with Emily on the everlasting subject.[32]

Giuliano probably left England early in the 1820s. He was last noted dining with his small son – who in turn fathered a Foreign Secretary for Italy – at Holland House in July 1822. Four years later he was back in Italy and married for a second time. But Palmerston's relief could not have lasted long, even though there is no diary to record its end.[33]

During 1820 Lady Cowper had been reported rather agitated and unwell, 'deplorably thin', according to Lady Granville, '& combatting her nerves all the time'. When another handsome foreigner therefore came her way in June she would not let him make up to her. It was the bald-headed troubadour, Count Flahault, Napoleon's former aide de camp and reputed son of Talleyrand. He had married Princess Charlotte's friend, Miss Mercer Elphinstone, in 1817; but it was with Emily Lady Granville reckoned he was really in love in 1816. Whatever the truth of that, in the summer of 1820 Emily put it 'quite out of the question'. But by the end of the year she felt 'pretty well' and by February 1821 '*perfectly*' so – her 'nerves' had gone just as they had come. Her friends noticed it too; the hawkeyed Mme Lieven even more. For early in March she was cattily amused to observe the excited interest which her 'young friend' was showing in Lord Clanwilliam, a bachelor a few years her junior, whom Emily admitted she found 'witty and impertinent and . . . very good company'. 'I like the little man very much,' Emily confessed. 'You would not think there was anything wrong in it, if I liked him too much?' 'The young woman is extremely naïve in spite of her intelligence,' said Madame Lieven to Prince Metternich. 'Here is a woman full of wit and insight, letting her head be turned by a pair of black eyes. I left her, and a minute later she was conversing with the eyes in question.' Emily was equally frank, as always, in her letters to her brother Fred, but evidently the affair did not prosper. Greville recorded that Clanwilliam had the reputation of being 'very indifferent to women, and a very good judge of character told me that his object is to amuse himself by playing upon women's feelings, and making them in love with him. His delight is to surmount difficulties, and to succeed in exciting an interest where there is some prejudice against him.' He certainly seems to have attained his object with Lady Cowper; but such a technique could not have kept her long. Eighteen months later she wrote: 'I . . . would at any time do anything to serve him, particularly now when I pity him so much, but I don't know why. I think he always looks upon me as an enemy;' and in the following summer: 'Clan, with all his faults is a nice person. I always feel a great weakness for him tho' I like to plague him a little.' Before long she too could only despise him: 'Clanwilliam has gone to Paris finding he made no sensation here. To be tormented by vanity is like being possessed by a Devil.' So in 1826 and 1827 she was laughing scornfully at his letting the dumpy opera star, Mlle Sontag, make such a fool of him. But by that date Emily too had turned elsewhere.[34]

From her letters to Fred it is clear that Emily got quite a fund of gossip and amusement from the King's affair with Lady Conyngham throughout the

1820s. But from Mme Lieven's to Metternich it is clear that Emily amused herself even more dangerously. 'There is a little affair going on here,' Mme Lieven reported from Brighton. 'The Marchioness's son is to marry an heiress with an income of £40,000. Meanwhile, he is in love with Lady Cowper – she is here with us. She likes the young man; but she is afraid to encourage him, because that would upset the marriage and put her out of favour at court. The young man, too, is anxious not to annoy his mother. So, on both sides, there is a struggle between love and discretion. We have a common drawing-room, which we enter from the wings, for all our rooms open into it. Thus, we have encounters, little *tête-à-têtes*, frights, despairs, a husband, and sometimes interruptions.' She had already told Lady Granville that the young man was 'very much in love' with Emily and that, though he had not two ideas in his head, she was charmed and sat talking with him three hours on end. Lord Francis Conyngham may not have been very bright but at twenty-four he was a strikingly handsome officer in the Guards and he had an interesting cough. Harriette Wilson had been 'much attracted' by his 'beauty'. 'He was perhaps rather cold,' she recalled; 'but amiable and truly unaffected. Such as he was, I remember he interested me very much. I did not fall in love with him, partly because he had the tremendous bad taste not to fall in love with me; but his ill health and his cough induced me to encourage somewhat of the tenderness of a mamma towards him; and I used to dream about his eyes, they were so very blue and beautiful.' Emily saw a good deal of him at court; and her interest was strengthened on Fred's behalf when in December 1823 Francis added the undersecretaryship at the Foreign Office to being Elizabeth Conyngham's brother. But her intrigues for Fred at court were not very successful and at times must have been as dangerous for Francis as they were for Emily herself. At length, if not before, his marriage to Lady Jane Paget in April 1824 probably put an end to their affair. When an Ascot party threw them all together at Windsor with Palmerston in the summer of 1825, Emily wrote to Fred: 'Ld P. and Francis had not spoken for a long while. Jane and I were inseparable.'[35]

Palmerston must not have been on speaking terms with many young men in these exciting decades of his own receding youth – especially if, as was surely the case with such as Lady Granville and Mme Lieven writing back and forth across the Channel, he heard about Emily's continental escapades as well.

John Caradoc or Cradock succeeded his father as second Baron Howden in 1839 and served as minister under Palmerston in Brazil and Spain. He was known as 'Beauty Cradock' in his youth, and as Secretary of the British Embassy in Paris had become famous for his amorous exploits and infuriated Canning by engaging in a duel over the Duchesse d'Esclaux. When he visited England in 1829 Mrs Fitzherbert wrote that 'he was very gay here and had all the ladies at his orders and gave them *little* dinners in his *little* lodgings . . . He went away in time. Had he stayed there certainly would have been some *serious female duels!*'[36]

Emily Cowper herself had fought some such contest when she had visited Paris a few years before and her opponent was no mean contender. Cradock's special friend in Paris was the widow of the victor of Borodino – Gronow's 'lovely Princess Bagration, with her fair hair and delicately-formed figure' who 'never wore anything but white India muslin, clinging to her form and revealing it in all its perfection'. Yet when she encountered Emily in Paris in the winter of 1826 the White Princess found that she was quite outshone. 'Lady Cowper is enchanted with Paris,' reported Lady Granville to her sister, now Countess of Carlisle. '[She] and Cradock have set up a regular flirtation. As he is extremely *empressé*, she can be dignified with perfect impunity, and only looks charmed and thinks Paris the most delightful place she ever was in, and wishes to stay and hopes to come back. Lord [Cowper] seems very easy about it.' The White Princess certainly was not. By turning red at last she even proved she had colour, the tongues reported, and while Major Cradock squired Emily about with 'prodigious self-satisfaction', 'Russia's revenge' was 'to disclaim upon her want of good looks'. Emily, in turn, called the princess 'une grosse chatte blanche', at the same time affecting a charming innocence in herself. 'I never yet saw so gossiping a town as this!!' she wrote to Fred. 'It keeps me in hot water, altho' I am in truth like the Chevalier Bayard sans peur et sans reproche.' [37]

It is doubtful if Emily's brother was deceived or that Emily meant him to be. Certainly no one was in London, any more than in Paris. 'Lady Cowper is amusing herself immensely in Paris,' concluded Madame Lieven. But she hardly knew how much, for in the middle of it all who should turn up in Paris but another young flame of Emily's. The Cowpers had had a bit of a fright in Paris, hearing that Fordwich, their eldest son, was rather ill in Spain. They soon had better news, but the shock had rather unsettled his mother and while she waited for him Emily even began to tire of Cradock. So there she was, sitting with Lady Granville one day early in December, 'languid, listless, her finger in her eye', and thinking it so dull and hot she would really rather go. But when Lady Granville told her no, she had to wait for Robert Grosvenor, Emily 'positively gasped for breath, and turned so pale I thought she would have dropped. . . . From that moment to this Lady C. & Mr G. have been inseparable – they go about together like man & wife . . . and the Major, you ask? Vastly odd isn't it . . . never has appeared since Mr G.'s arrival.'[38]

Christmas 1826 brought Lady Cowper back to Panshanger and Grosvenor to Eaton Hall. 'I am quite stout this year,' Emily was soon to say. 'I believe Paris set me up for ever.' The young man was fourteen years her junior, but he was equally well pleased. 'I passed a *most agreeable* week at Paris,' he said, '& . . . cannot but acknowledge certain regrets that I had not profited by an offer wh. wd have brought me thither a month earlier.' The Honourable Robert Grosvenor was the youngest son of the future Marquess of Westminster and was eventually to be made Baron Ebury. In later life he joined Prince Albert's household and became an ardent Protestant. In his youth the Duke of

Devonshire thought him 'a conceited fellow but goodnatured'; his sister-in-law, 'a most amiable creature and easy friend', full of fun and entertainment. A lady who met him in Malta early in 1830 thought that although tall he was not 'highly favoured by nature'; but he made up for it by art, with a pair of luxuriant moustaches and the manner of one of those 'double refined London dandies'. He was also extremely recherché in his dress, carrying about with him no less than three dozen fancy waistcoats, besides a good stock of plain ones. She also thought his manner extremely affected and his conversation ridiculous. But she detected an element of intelligence as well as much good humour behind it all and could not help liking him a lot. Above all, he was 'totally devoid of that species of finery which displays itself by shewing contempt for others' and to please others there was no trouble too great for him to take. He was not always as successful as he would have liked. He was in Malta on the way from Egypt, he confessed, pining for love of Emily Cowper. His affair with Lady Cowper had probably begun in 1825 when he was only twenty-three or twenty-four and already gaining some reputation for flirting. But the Emily for whom he sighed in 1830 was not the mother but the daughter.[39]

Lady Cowper's elder daughter and namesake, 'Minny', in childhood and adolescence was another spoiled 'devil' like her mother. When she was three Lady Bessborough made a vivid portrait of her in words to match the picture painted about the same time by Lawrence. She was, she said, by far the prettiest and most spoilt child she had ever seen, with dark brown, curling hair and eyebrows, beautiful bright blue eyes – 'brilliant light blue in the middle, with a vein of dark' – rosy cheeks, beautifully formed features, and 'all those graceful round motions so pretty in a child; but, en récompense, she is the naughtiest little thing I ever saw, and rules the house rather unpleasantly.' She was always her mother's favourite; 'droll' and 'amiable' as a child, charming and beautiful in her youth. When Minny was little more than sixteen Fred rather frightened her mother by talking of her coming out and getting married; she did not think her 'stout enough to rake much,' Emily said. Minny came out the following season and before long she was 'the leading favourite of the town', and though, in Creevey's opinion, 'very inferior to her fame for looks, . . . very natural, lively, and . . . good-natured.' All the men were said to be 'more or less in love' with her; among them were a Wortley and a Talbot, Tankerville's heir, Goderich's nephew and Lord John Russell. Eventually in June 1830 she married the handsome but gloomy Lord Ashley and brought a strange new friend into Palmerston's life.[40]

Mrs Arbuthnot marvelled at the future Earl of Shaftesbury, of philanthropic fame and severe morality, marrying into 'one of the most profligate families in the kingdom'. It was, however, a really happy marriage, though by no means unmarked with difficulties and disagreements. It was also not at all an easy courtship, with Minny enticing and rejecting him for a long time and almost to the last flirting with other men. Minny's mother once remarked that she was 'born . . . with far too much heart for her own happiness'; Lady Granville thought she 'loved sport, nothing else'. Perhaps her mother was meant to be among the victims along with all the young men, for Lady Cowper was reckoned to be much more in love with Ashley than her daughter was. Minny's flirtation with Robert Grosvenor was among her first. Harriet Granville could hardly believe it when it came to her ears in September 1827 but by the end of the year he seemed to have 'transferred all his admiration' and become inseparable from Minny. Lady Cowper seemed to take it very coolly. To her brother she merely said that she thought Minny could probably do better than Grosvenor, who was, after all, only a younger son. To the Cavendishes at Chatsworth, however, she said that he was 'of all the men she knows, the one most calculated to make his wife happy'. That left even Lady Granville almost speechless; remembering Paris two years before and hearing that Cradock had just come over, she wondered if perhaps he was to take 'next turn' with Minny. There is no sign that he did; Minny perhaps had never known about him. But Lady Granville was not completely wrong. Grosvenor persisted for about two years and Lady Cowper, as she perceived, remained late in 1828 still 'the most perturbed of hens'. By the end of 1829 Minny was also flirting wildly with Clanwilliam. Lady Granville thought it was 'sport' at first; but decided later they were really in love. Fortunately, after a few disturbing weeks, Clanwilliam left the country and Minny accepted Ashley. But Lady Cowper was certainly very upset while it lasted. Taking revenge perhaps for the scorn he had suffered for the sake of Mlle Sontag, Clanwilliam contrived as late as January 1830 to attend a ball at Hatfield House to which he had not been invited, but to which Minny Cowper had. 'From what I hear of the girl's manner, I am convinced . . . that she is in love with him,' wrote Greville, adding since as usual he knew so much, 'the mother was . . . no doubt on thorns.'[41]

Lady Cowper was not the only one to be worried by Minny's perverse flirtations. Palmerston, too, seemed to Lady Granville to be 'anxious & absorbed'. Probably he had as good reason as the mother. No one ever seems to have doubted that Emily's eldest child, George (Lord Fordwich, later sixth Earl Cowper), was her husband's son. Oddly enough, her youngest son, Charles Spencer, who was born in 1816, also very closely resembled his father. But about the other three children there was no such certainty. Minny was born in November 1810, more than four years after Fordwich and time enough after the beginning of the great affair. She was Palmerston's favourite as well; he brought her back delightful presents from Paris and wrote her charming letters. He also gave her husband a good deal of money, and from the wishes he expressed about the ultimate disposal of his estate and name, it seems very likely that he thought she was his daughter. But no one could be sure. She had his brilliant blue eyes, it was true, but that proved nothing; as

Lady Bessborough pointed out, if only in fun, others had them too. About Emily's next child, on the other hand, few can have had any doubts at all.[42]

William Francis Cowper was born in November 1811, almost exactly a year after Minny; perhaps it was this unaccustomed frequency that had made both Emily and 'il sposo' so irritated with Palmerston only the month before. 'William' was an honoured name among the Temples, and he also looked very much like one. Once, when he was introduced to a visiting ambassador after Palmerston's belated marriage, the poor ignorant foreigner loudly congratulated the father on the resemblance. In other ways he was not so much like Palmerston. He was a happy and rather amorous young man; he became his uncle Melbourne's private secretary and like him rather too fond of Caroline Norton. But he was cruelly struck with domestic tragedy and subsequently became something of a religious fanatic. Once his mother had to rebuke him for frightening the servants; religion, she reminded him, was meant to be 'a comfort and a consolation', not 'made a terror and a torment'. Palmerston often gave quite large sums of money to Lady Cowper, but sometimes earmarked part for William; in 1833 there was £300 for Emily and £400 for William. After the death of his brother in 1856 Palmerston revised his will and, subject only to a life interest for his widow and some legacies to his sister's children, left everything to William Cowper. He also expressed the wish that his heir should take the name and arms of Temple. William served in politics during Palmerston's life and afterwards, and in 1880 was raised to the peerage as Baron Mount-Temple. But although he married twice he left no children and on his death in 1888 Broadlands passed to Minny's second surviving son, her eldest being her husbands's own heir.[43]

Evelyn Ashley, who succeeded Bulwer as biographer, had been Palmerston's private secretary and it was said to have been Palmerston's wish that he should inherit in the event that William Cowper's line should fail. Palmerston was supposed to have said so in a letter that subsequently disappeared. Ashley claimed to have seen it at Brocket, but it evidently gave no explanation, because a few years after he had inherited Broadlands he wrote around among the family to ask if anyone knew why. It was Ashley's son in turn for whom the title of Mount-Temple was revived in 1932 and though there was again no male heir there were two daughters, of whom the elder became mistress of Broadlands and wife of Earl Mountbatten.[44]

Minny and William, whom he came so near acknowledging, were not the only children Lady Cowper was thought to have had by Palmerston. Palmerston himself noted the arrival of a still-born baby boy in May 1818 in such a way as to suggest he thought himself the father: 'premature confinement at 6 this morning at Brighton,' his diary reads. 'Figlio Morto.' Moreover, while none of the surviving replies from the family to Evelyn Ashley quite seemed to answer his question about Broadlands, one of them significantly began: 'Owing to certain circumstances which it is not necessary to enumerate, the Jocelyn family were interested in a more than ordinary way in the matter.'[45]

Emily herself, it is understood, left a clear avowal that her last child, born on 9 February 1820, was also Palmerston's.* No doubt that was why she bore the names of his two sisters, Frances and Elizabeth. Perhaps Palmerston was reassured; but it was the time of the Giuliano affair – hence no doubt Palmerston's great anxiety about it – and Emily loved to tease. 'My little Fanny is beautiful,' she told Fred a few months later. 'I will tell you her likenesses that you may guess at her face. Lord Cowper thinks her like the picture of Lady Lamb at Brocket in the dining room. Caroline W[illia]m says she is like P[rince]ss Esterhazy; Caro G[eorge] says she is like Pamela Fitzgerald. Are not these odd resemblances for a child of mine? her eyes and eye brows are really beautiful & so marked and dark – blue, however.'[46]

Lady Fanny Cowper was in later life a worry to her mother, bullying her and finding it difficult to make a match. She was evidently not a vivacious imp like her elder sister or subtly charming like her mother. She became the young Queen Victoria's friend and bridesmaid. She had some sort of haughty beauty, however, and admirers enough. One of them was Lady Granville's son and heir; he at least thought her more beautiful than her sister. But she refused him and he was left to risk tortures of proximity as Palmerston's Undersecretary. She wanted 'a Hero', her uncle Beauvale reckoned. 'Somebody to look up to and be afraid of, not a smock faced youth. A 2nd Ashley in short.' Eventually she chose a wild and spendthrift youth, the Earl of Roden's heir, Lord Jocelyn. They were married in April 1841 and she bore him four children. Their marriage was not entirely happy, as he would not give up the habits of his bachelor days. He tried his hand at politics and in the 1850s occasionally acted as a contact between Palmerston and the Derbyite Tories. But he continued an active career in the militia and he lost his life when, in the plague of 1854, he insisted on sleeping among his men at the Tower. He died after an illness of a single day in his mother-in-law's house in Piccadilly. After that Fanny became a sort of romantic queen of tragedy, captivating men without being captured by them, sadly outliving all her children, and tyrannizing over her grandchildren. These latter were taught to disapprove of their great-grandmother, Emily Cowper, but even when they became respectively the sixth Earl of Arran and consorts to the eighth Earl of Airlie, the fourth Marquess of Salisbury and the second Viscount Hambleden, they were perhaps still proud to think that Palmerston was probably an ancestor. But Fanny herself resented it. She hardly ever mentions him in her few available letters without some biting remark. 'We are . . . dancing with renewed vigour tonight,' she once wrote from Windsor to her brother William. 'I can't think who with, . . . unless Cupid will condescend. I hear he was made to galoppe the other night. I would have given a good deal to see it.'[47]

*So the late Lady Helen Nutting, a great granddaughter of Fanny Cowper, informed the author. Lady Helen's mother, Mabell, Countess of Airlie, used many of Lady Cowper's papers for her books. In *Lady Palmerston* (i. 46-7) she misdates a letter of Lady Cowper's and consequently the year of Fanny's birth.

'Cupid' was not at all an inappropriate nickname for Palmerston – the press and Lady Jersey were equally proud to claim its invention. Fanny Cowper obviously disliked its every implication. Perhaps she even knew that there were other offspring too. For there is among the Broadlands Papers, endorsed '1840' in a hand that might be hers as much as her mother's, a newspaper clipping beginning 'What has Lord Palmerston *done* with Mrs Murray Mills?'[48]

What Palmerston had done with Mrs Mills was easier to discover than where and when he found her. According to the *Satirist*, which was to expose her in the 1830s, she was the daughter of a publican in Hereford and had made her stage début there in 1811. Shortly afterwards she had moved to London in the guise of Emma Murray and there, according to her own statement, had come into Palmerston's life about 1814. Within a year or two after that he had set her up as an apparently respectable 'widow' in Pall Mall, and shortly afterwards bought her the lease of a house in Piccadilly. The reason for making it a more long-term and stable arrangement was to be found within, a little Henry John. Although no baptism can be traced, Henry John Temple Murray, as he was styled, seems to have been born in January 1816. A few years after that there followed twins (a boy and a girl), another boy and finally in 1829 another girl. Yet none of these others, it seems, was Palmerston's, nor perhaps any but the last really Mrs Murray's. The twins, it was later claimed, were fathered by the last Viscount Clermont and the youngest boy, named Eustace Clare Grenville Murray, by Palmerston's distant relative, the Duke of Buckingham.[49]

After the second Duke of Buckingham succeeded to the title in 1839 he separated from his wife and spent the rest of the family fortune. When he died it was said that 'few men will have passed away less honoured in their life or regretted in their death'. But in earlier days he was 'a gay sinner . . . , and being a very handsome fellow was the chief cock wherever he walked'. Yet, while he may very well have been Grenville Murray's father, he was not, in any case, Mrs Murray's duke. Hers, rather, was the first of that creation – the vain and fat one. He too was very extravagant; in later years Mrs Murray claimed she had lent him back the money he had given her so that he could pay the fees on his dukedom in 1822. Mrs Murray's other kindnesses to him did seem to be carrying family affection rather far, whether she was Grenville Murray's natural mother or merely a well-paid foster parent. But there is no sign that Palmerston bore her any immediate resentment. He went on paying the ground rent on 122 Piccadilly, and only when the stock market was very low did he even contemplate a cut in her allowance of £300 per annum.[50]

Palmerston also helped, with influence, patronage or money, at least some of Mrs Murray's children along in the world. Henry he sent to Sandhurst; Eustace went to Oxford and the Inner Temple, presumably at Buckingham's expense, though for the records of the Inner Temple he named his father as 'Henry John Murray, Captain in the Army, deceased'. His elder brother's

Sandhurst record was rather more discreet: 'Father, Private Gentleman (deceased).' But both boys made false starts and Palmerston eventually placed them in the foreign sevice. He did the same for their brother-in-law, Richard Levinge Swift, who in 1849 had married their younger sister Harriet. Swift was a barrister of the Middle Temple, but he took up various consular apppointments between 1855 and 1871. After a brief period as a clerk in the Audit Office from 1834 to 1838, Henry Murray had an almost equally quiet and undistinguished consular career; he was appointed vice-consul in Tangiers in 1850 and served subsequently as consul in Tenerife, Portland (Maine) and Buenos Aires. In Gibraltar in 1843 he had married Elizabeth Heaphy, the daughter of the Broadlands water-colourist and herself an artist of some distinction. Her husband seems to have published an anonymous article in the *Cornhill Magazine* for May 1866; it was entitled 'A Strange Story', but it reveals virtually nothing about its author. Mrs Murray died in San Remo in December 1882; Murray, who had retired from the service on 1 October 1879, died on 4 January 1894, probably also abroad, and leaving but a single child, Augustus Frederick Temple Murray.[51]

While Henry kept well out of the way and planted his new line of Temples at a safe distance from England, his brother Grenville Murray, on the contrary, exploited his more tenuous connection in characteristically more flamboyant style. His first appointment in July 1851 was as attaché with Lord Westmorland in Vienna. Somehow or other the ambassador soon discovered that Murray was breaking the rules by acting as special correspondent for the *Morning Post*. But the *Post* was Palmerston's organ and Murray may well have been acting with the Foreign Secretary's special permission. Palmerston, it was afterwards said, wanted him to show up the Austrian Prime Minister, with whom he had quarrelled, before the British public. So while Palmerston remained his chief nothing could be done. But the next year, after Palmerston had fallen, Murray was transferred, eventually in a paid capacity to Constantinople. The ambassador there was Stratford Canning, who was not exactly renowned for either modesty or good temper. Before long relations between the two of them were anything but cordial and so Canning banished Murray as vice-consul to Mitylene (Lesbos). From there, under the thin disguise of 'The Roving Englishman', Murray sent a series of articles to Dickens's *Household Words*, mercilessly satirizing the ambassador as 'Sir Hector Stubble'. Yet he still managed to survive.

Some of those who knew him as an experienced journalist rather than a callow diplomat thought Murray was a brilliant writer. He certainly had talent. In addition to his articles he was by this time already author of several books about diplomacy and the foreign service. There was a good deal in them that was shrewd and well-informed, but he could never resist the special pleading of his origins and case. In one of them published in 1855, on *Embassies and Foreign Courts*, he attacked the diplomatic service as the preserve of a few great families. 'Any gentleman with the divine right of a fortunate connexion may prosper prodigiously,' he maintained; 'or a few lucky toadies . . . but the talented are overwhelmed with drudgery and snobbery.' But he also wrote:

> Lastly, in all sincerity let me add, I do not wish to trace one word of factious censure against the present government. For Lord Palmerston especially, I entertain the most loyal respect and the warmest admiration. His colleagues are mostly practical and able men. But who can seriously deny that they are absolutely fettered and shackled by the tyranny and strength of cliques, coteries, and shadows? . . . Let the gentlemen of the press muster manfully and boldly to advocate their own cause, the cause of genius and capacity.

Murray was as indiscreet as he was immodest. It was very probably he who was responsible for the abuse that led to the suppression of the first issue of the *Foreign Office List* for January 1862. At that time more or less a private venture, the *List* had been expanded by popular demand to include biographical details; but these produced loud protests when they appeared. The editor's opinion was that 'the chief objection arose mainly from its being stated that a certain Foreign Office official was *cousin* to a Duke'. By this time Palmerston was Prime Minister and it was probably on that account that the Foreign Secretary, Lord Clarendon, had relented about sacking Murray in 1855. Instead he was sent as consul-general to Odessa, where it was probably hoped to keep him both out of sight and mind. But in Odessa he enjoyed ten years of such discord with his agents at home and English travellers abroad that after Palmerston's death in 1865 there was an avalanche of accusations for him to face. Among those subsequently printed in a fat parliamentary paper were numerous complaints of incompetence, irregularity, corruption, peculation and even an assault upon an 'English lady', who was really, it seems, a prostitute. The commentary of the Registrar-General upon Murray's register of British marriages and births was a particularly nice example of pointed Victorian prose:

> That Miss E. Fletcher on the day following her marriage with R.F. Oakley should produce a child is quite intelligible, and, I fear, by no means unprecedented; but that this child should have been born the next day at such a distance [at Steblow near Kiev] from the place of marriage is strange; but, what is still stranger is that . . . the same mother . . . is recorded, forty-seven days after the birth of Jane Sarah at Steblow, to have produced at Kieff on the 10th October, 1863 another boy . . .
> In this office upwards of 18,000,000 births are recorded . . .; but in all that immense number I do not believe that a similar occurrence as to the birth of twins has been registered . . . I meditate bringing this extraordinary occurrence under notice of the Obstetrical Society . . .

So in spite of the influence he tried to bring to bear upon the Conservative Cabinet of the day, Murray was dismissed in May 1868. Yet his astonishing career was by no means over.

On his dismissal and return to England, the 'Roving Englishman' redoubled his journalistic efforts, and with biting savagery, in the first issues of

Vanity Fair, the *Standard* and *The Queen's Messenger*. One of the first to suffer was the Foreign Secretary with whom he had clashed so recently. Murray baldly referred to him as a thief. Lord Stanley was the son and heir of the Earl of Derby, recently Prime Minister; but he was reputedly a kleptomaniac and could hardly hit back again. Murray, however, was bound to go too far. In June 1869 there appeared an article which the third Baron Carrington took to be a libel on his late father and a few days later he attacked Murray with his stick outside the Conservative Club in London. Murray sued for assault and won; but to do so he committed perjury and on being found out he was forced to flee the country. He never returned to England, settling in Paris, where he assumed the title of Comte Rethel d'Aragon and established a literary manufactory for the supply of the yellow press and the outrage of the aristocracy. He died in 1881, leaving two sons, at least one of whom also made a name as a foreign correspondent.

Some said Grenville Murray made a great deal of money in Paris; others that his brains were mortgaged to his creditors, who made him an allowance out of his vast earnings. A former colleague in diplomacy and journalism, Henry Labouchere, wrote in *Truth* at the time of his death:

When in humour he was a brilliant conversationalist – humorous, caustic, and full of anecdote. In person he was slim, and rather below medium height, with well-cut features, exceedingly bright eyes and with a face that lighted up when he was animated; but few of those who may have seen him in an old felt hat and a still older shooting-jacket, strolling along the boulevards or in the alleys of the Bois de Boulogne, could have imagined that they were in the presence of the ablest journalist of the century.

Thomas Seccombe, by contrast, wrote with superb contempt in the *D.N.B.*: 'He probably did more than any single person to initiate the modern type of journal, which is characterised by a tone of candour with regard to public affairs, but owes its chief attraction to the circulation of private gossip, largely by means of hint and innuendo.'[52]

Palmerston's successors must have cursed him roundly for landing them with Grenville Murray. But what they probably did not know was that he too had long ago been made to suffer for his pleasure. As far as money was concerned Palmerston seems, as was only fair, always to have done well by Mrs Murray. It is not possible to say precisely how much he paid, since his accounts are so detailed and voluminous for this period as by exposing gaps and inconsistencies to underline the folly of assuming that such records ever are complete. All that can be suggested with reasonable assurance is that the lease of 122 Piccadilly cost £348 and that the house was furnished at his expense; the ground rent was £105 p.a., plus rates and other charges, which brought the total to about £140, against the rent of £200, or £232 with other charges, for 12 Pall Mall. The record also shows that he paid Mrs Murray quite large sums of money from time to time, varying in the period 1818 to

1827 between ten guineas and £405 during a single year and averaging £150 per annum. In some years there were also extra payments for Henry's education; but at other times these were probably entered under the general payments to Mrs Murray. It is clear that Palmerston also made her an additional and substantial private allowance. During the 1820s this appears to have been £300 a year; by 1827 it was £200; and in 1828 it was further reduced to £100 and then £50. The first reduction almost certainly had something to do with the difficulties Palmerston got into on account of his stock market ventures. But the others must have been concerned with Mrs Murray's marriage on 7 January 1828 to Edmund Mills.

The estimable and egregious Mr Edmund Mills was the younger son of a Wiltshire family who had made a fortune, so it was later said, in the Indies, East and West. There is every reason to believe that there was some truth in this, but from the grave misfortunes in which Mills was about to be engulfed it seems very likely that he was already in financial trouble. Perhaps therefore his was a marriage arranged by Mrs Murray's grateful but jaded lovers. Palmerston continued, as a wedding gift, to provide 122 Piccadilly at the same expense as before. He withdrew his allowance only in stages, and as well as substantial payments for Henry's education there were further gifts of money to his mother from time to time and amounting in 1828 and 1829 to the same as the average of earlier years. It may also have been by a similar arrangement and on the same occasion that Mills obtained from the Duke of Buckingham a promissory note for £5,000. There was also, as part of what Mrs Mills called her marriage settlement, a small country estate, Binfield Lodge in Berkshire. According to her later account this was Mills's own wedding gift to her; but since it had probably been part of the property inherited by Henry Elliot, one can hardly be blamed for suspecting that Elliot had performed for Palmerston a service peculiarly appropriate to a former private secretary and that this property too had come only second-hand to Mrs Mills.

Whatever the origin of Binfield Lodge, Mrs Mills did not have it long. Soon after their marriage Mills found himself in jail for debt and Binfield Lodge was taken over by his brother as part of the general arrangement by which Mills secured his creditors' consent to his release. Palmerston, too, must have helped out to some extent. He was in any case still responsible for young Henry's education. He paid a final amount for schooling in 1829 of over £90, and when Henry entered Sandhurst that October Palmerston also began payments at the rate of £120 a year for fees and £20 for extras. There seem to have been some occasional cash payments as well; and in the midst of Mrs Mills's troubles he stood as godfather to her daughter, Harriet Frances Victoria, born on 5 May and given the Temple name in addition, but this time in his honour. So Palmerston must have been very relieved when in October the following year there came a letter from Mrs Mills to say that her husband's affairs had lately recovered and even turned out so prosperous that he was able after all to meet her dearest wish to have a real home in the country. They had already found what they wanted, Bulkeley House in Englefield Green, and since it was not for sale they proposed to take a twenty-one-year lease. But, she went on, she was not willing to risk losing it like Binfield Lodge if her husband's affairs were again to take a turn for the worse, and he had very generously agreed to allow the lease to be taken out in Palmerston's name, so that while Mills paid the rent Bulkeley House would nonetheless remain in the face of all misfortune just like 122 Piccadilly, 'as blooming and valuable as ever'. It is impossible to explain why Palmerston should have agreed to this, except to say that wherever women and money were concerned his usual good sense frequently succumbed to generosity, if not to a thoroughly guilty conscience. The inevitable result was that he soon found himself stuck with a twenty-one-year lease he did not want, a rent of £225 a year, and ultimately expenses and dilapidations of another £700 and more.

It had obviously been a trap. The Millses stripped both house and estate of everything they could and paid not a penny of either rates or rent. In April 1831 a distress warrant was issued for the rates and the furniture sold accordingly; Palmerston immediately sent another £100 and in July a further £20. But neither the lover's naïve generosity nor the husband's extravagant deceit could save Mills from being arrested again for debt in December. Mills stayed in jail until February or March 1833 at least, and while he was there Mrs Mills struggled valiantly on through a sea of troubles – young Henry ill at Sandhurst, little Harriet breaking her shoulder, a new baby sister dying of the whooping cough, herself seriously ill with the same complaint and a miscarriage to boot, a bad landlord, worse tenants, unscrupulous agents and relatives, and last but not least her husband's swindling lawyer – all this and much besides filled letter after letter to Palmerston. Mr Mills also wrote, in or out of jail, seconding her efforts though not always quite in tune with them, as when he substituted for whooping cough his wife's bad heart. Mrs Mills even addressed a long memorandum of woe and complaint about lawyers to the Lord High Chancellor, Henry Brougham, stressing as she went along the acquaintance she had enjoyed since 'childhood' with his colleague Lord Palmerston, but professing absolute refusal 'to involve His Lordship's valuable time in an expensive litigation with a man [the lawyer] who appears to have no other object in view, than perhaps to couple his insignificance with His Lordship's name [and] be the medium of subjecting his Lordship to those impertinent observations that are invariably bestowed by the vulgar and inconsiderate upon both the public and private conduct of all official illustrious personages'.

In spite of all this and no doubt other warning evidence Palmerston did not withhold his further help. In October 1832 he paid the landlord of Bulkeley House the whole of the rent outstanding since the Millses moved in, a tidy sum of over £357, and, after a distress warrant had also been laid on the contents of 122 Piccadilly, he arranged for the house to be sub-let and the income assigned to Mrs Mills for the part payment of her husband's debts. Eventually, in May

1835, he even picked up the bailiff's bill. But there was a limit to his patience. When Mrs Mills wrote in June 1833 to complain that the lawyers were taking almost all the income as charges and to ask that it be assigned direct to her, Palmerston ignored her letter, and when she wrote two months later offering, as he was evidently too busy to bother with it, to take the lease of the London house off his hands, he endorsed her letter 'most unreasonable proposal'.

By Mrs Murray Mills's own account the transfer would have enabled her to pay at least part of the rent on Bulkeley House and saved him too, when the lease expired, the expenditure of the £1,000 or so it would have needed to 'beautify' the house before being taken back by the freeholder. And all he had to do to accomplish this was to write on the back of the lease, 'I assign the within term of lease in full to Mrs Emma Murray Mills', and send it off at once. 'God knows', she concluded, 'that my greatest wish and most anxious desire, is to *relieve* you from annoyance, and not be the *cause* of it.' But just to remind him of his obligation she added in a postscript: 'Dear Henry has pass'd through the Book of Euclid since his return [to Sandhurst] with great éclat – he is the only cadet there who has accomplished the task yet this half. He has also made Sir George Scovell [the Lt-Governor] a present of a plan of fortifications that has procured him great praise – he has been twice dining with Sir Edward Paget [the Governor] and 3 times with Sir George – at their own houses since his return to College.' But Palmerston was determined not to be caught again; he had already 'signed too much', he said.

During the whole of 1833, therefore, Palmerston paid no more rent on Bulkeley House and, it would seem, sent no more gifts of cash. Instead, when Mr Mills resumed his correspondence on his wife's behalf and even offered as security for a loan the Duke of Buckingham's promissory note, Palmerston suggested that they sell some more furniture; and when Mills chided him with past promises of jobs in government, Palmerston curtly replied: 'It is not my habit to submit to imposition & I shall not do so in your instance.' He seems to have become still more angry when in the New Year there came a begging letter from young Henry too. It was discreetly signed 'your Godson' and proudly informed Palmerston that the college had agreed to take him for a further year in spite of his now being over age; but it went on to point out that when he was commissioned he would need twice the amount of his pay in private means. Quite what happened then is far from clear. But Palmerston had some sort of 'interview' with his son and also wrote to the mother accusing her of trying a new method of extortion. Henry never returned to Sandhurst; not because Palmerston refused to go on paying – he had continued to pay the fees throughout – but probably because the boy had exhausted his academic credit.

Palmerston also ordered his lawyers to make a full investigation of the situation at both Bulkeley House and 122 Piccadilly. What he discovered must have appalled if not astonished him. For the first time he learned how the house and estate in Englefield Green had been plundered and neglected and that Mrs Mills had borrowed £200 from a man called Sainsbury on the security of her 'interest' in London. Soon afterwards a disinterested bystander wrote to warn him that there was a 'foul conspiracy' afoot between Sainsbury and some unnamed 'spiteful female' (presumably Mrs Mills) for the 'diabolical purpose' of extorting money, and that Palmerston's name had been set down for plucking along with 'several Princes, Dukes, and noblemen besides'. For the next five years or so Palmerston fended Sainsbury off with his lawyers; but it cost him a few pounds at least by way of legal expenses. Nor, even in his most disillusioned state, was there any way in which he could utterly escape his other moral and legal obligations. In the summer of 1834 Emma wrote to say that she had quarrelled with Mills about the rents and that he had left her. So she signed herself simply 'Emma Murray' in recollection of better days, while Palmerston resumed small cash payments from time to time and paid off young Henry's final account at Sandhurst.

By 1835 Edmund Mills was again in jail for debt, this time probably with Palmerston among the plaintiffs. But it was impossible to keep him down. In December 1834 he had been trying to borrow money on the strength of the patronage he claimed he could get through his influence with Palmerston; in August 1835 asking why Palmerston had not secured his release from prison; and in 1836 begging a small loan of £10 and drawing attention to a stream of reports in the *Satirist*. The *Satirist* seems to have been well-informed and what it had to say must have made very unpleasant reading. It mentioned, in addition to Palmerston and Buckingham, others with whom Mrs Murray was supposed to have had affairs, including Glenelg and Leopold as well as the late King George IV. But worst of all was the horrible story that she had abandoned the late Lord Clermont's twins, having first tried unsuccessfully to force the girl into prostitution. The following year, 1837, there came another warning, from someone claiming to be a bill-broker and under the signature 'John Edwards', that Henry Murray had been borrowing money against his mother's drafts and fled his post in the Audit Office to escape payment. Edwards hardly liked to mention such a delicate matter but his lordship ought to order young Murray back to face the music and might even care to have the addresses he enclosed of the creditors concerned. Henry Murray did not hold very long the post that he found in 1834, presumably through Palmerston but possibly with the help also of his mother's landlord (Henry Arbuthnot), who was one of the Commissioners of Audit and naturally shared with Palmerston some interest in the young man's financial stability. But it is not known whether there was any truth in the accusation. Palmerston, who had his lawyers investigate John Edwards first, simply endorsed his letter 'really Mr Mills'.

Edmund Mills died, aged only forty-nine and probably in poverty, in Gravesend on 30 April 1840. It is hardly surprising that when Henry Murray forwarded the news and a deathbed letter commending the family to his lordship's care Palmerston should have endorsed this too, 'Query did he really die?' But he obviously did take care of the family, and not just by finding them jobs. There are no detailed records of his cash payments in this category after 1834, when he paid Emma a total of £50 and Henry a mere £5; but his diary for 1836 records a couple of visits to a certain 'M' in the neighbourhood of Windsor. In addition, when he disposed of the Piccadilly lease in September 1835 he gave Emma the balance and he went on paying the rent on Bulkeley House without getting much of it back by way of sub-letting the farm from time to time. And even if he did manage to dispose of the lease of such a battered property between 1842, when the surviving record of payments for rent runs out, and 1852, when the lease would have expired, he must still have paid something in the region of £1,000 in respect of dilapidations. Moreover, while he remained legally responsible he heard from his solicitors rumours that Emma was still, as late as 1837, trying surreptitiously to raise money on her 'interest' in Bulkeley House, just as she had in the case of 122 Piccadilly. It was also probably at his expense that Mrs Mills eventually established herself at Onslow Cottage, Southampton. But according to her not too unlikely tale, her sons abandoned her; they were both 'scorpions', she said. So poverty presumably eventually forced her to seek economy abroad, though she continued to dun the Buckinghams if not Palmerston to the very last. Her will, which named her cottage in Southampton and with extravagant optimism bequeathed to her daughter the old estate at Binfield, was signed in Brussels in December 1848, and she died in Calais on 3 October 1860, shortly after she had reported the bailiffs knocking at her door, and quite probably in a debtors' jail.[53]

As far as is known there were no other children of Palmerston's. There was a story Poodle Byng told Chichester Fortescue about 'his seeing a man in a theatre in Italy, whose likeness to Lady Jocelyn struck him, and who turned out to be the Duke de Civitella, and the reason of it'. The statement is more ambiguous than Fortescue's editor allows; and it probably confuses Civitella with Castelcicala, whose mother was Giuliano's half-sister. In any case there were plenty of other women in Palmerston's life. For while no one ever quite displaced Lady Cowper, he was about as unfaithful to her as she was to him.[54]

We know a good deal about Palmerston's love-life, for a few years at least, because he left in those innocent-looking diaries of his a detailed score-card of his triumphs and his failures. Emily would not have been pleased, even though she took pride of place. She kept her own album, in her reticule under lock and key; Palmerston had pencilled in it a charming cupid to illustrate a few lines of his father's verse that he had improved. But once at Chatsworth, after one young dandy had been making eyes at her for days on end, she had exclaimed in great impatience that it was 'so stupid of a man to go thro' life with a high flown scrap book of hearts & darts to right and left trying to filer un petit roman with everyone he meets'. She would not have been deceived by Palmerston's mixture of symbols, English *doubles entendres* and shorthand

Italian. His assignations he recorded as 'visits'; his triumphs as '*sera' or 'fine days' and 'fine nights'. He was obviously proud of his appetite and strength; occasionally an emphatic figure '*2*' is entered afterwards. But he also noted systematically the many occasions, morning, noon and night, on which he 'failed'. The record is certainly not complete; apart from the possible references of 1836 there is not a single mention of Emma, not even in 1818. Perhaps there was some sort of class distinction he felt he had to make.[55]

Among Palmerston's papers from the 1820s there survive a semi-literate begging letter from Soho – 'I had just paid a grate bill to my doctor' – and a more elegant production – from 'some procuress' as he endorsed it – inviting him to inspect a 'chef d'oeuvre of the arts'. He gets off with a relatively chaste mention or two in Harriette Wilson's memoirs; but that was probably because he had paid her off. Yet there is probably something rather exaggerated in his popular reputation, like the story Henry Grenfell told years later about 'the two sisters whom he . . . surprised by an ambuscade'. And in that later period, when age, marriage and public favour had made it relatively safe, Palmerston himself, in contrast to his earlier care and discretion, added to the legend. Then, when Minny Shaftesbury remonstrated with the old roué about his 'horribly irreligious' and 'most ungentlemanly' flirtations and suggested they never could succeed with young married women, he replied that while no doubt inconsistent with the teachings of the Church he considered them most gentlemanly and that with him at least they had never failed. Lady Stanley of Alderley claimed he had tried and failed with her. But her story, 'how Pam made love to her, when she first married [in October 1826], in his impudent, brusque way, with a "Ha Ha. I see it all – beautiful woman neglected by her husband – allow me – etc." ', may have had as much spite as truth in it, for by the time she chose to tell it her husband had indeed been neglecting her, and for none other than Lady Jocelyn.[56]

For long periods of his life Palmerston may have distributed a sort of fidelity between Emily and Emma. He records no sexual adventures during that month-long visit to Paris in the autumn of 1818 when his relations with Emily were being badly strained by the Giuliano affair. But her infidelities did occasionally provoke lapses on his part; and resenting her frequent absences as much as he did – he 'dislikes my leaving England so very much that [he] does not willingly facilitate my arrangements in any way', she reported archly to her brother – enforced separations he generally regarded as a licence to experiment. Then, perhaps, few women were safe from his advances, and least of all the wives and daughters of his friends. He undoubtedly sought relief and possibly revenge in that direction when, after their quarrel over Giuliano, Emily went in the latter half of 1819 to mend her health in the country.[57]

Little is known about Palmerston's contemporary at Harrow and St John's, Edward Berens Blackburn, and even less about his wife. He became a rather undistinguished lawyer; his wife, Eliza, however, was the daughter of the John Madocks who had founded Watier's gambling club and later cut his throat,

and the granddaughter of the notorious and beautiful Lady Craven, Princess
Berkeley of Anspach. Mrs Blackburn had already fallen to Palmerston by the
summer of 1819 and she went without her husband to join the usual shooting
party at Broadlands that autumn. Inevitably Palmerston's diary is marked
with almost daily asterisks until her husband came down, and even then he
seems to have managed an appropriately fond farewell of a Sunday morning,
perhaps while her husband was at church. No doubt this sort of thing went on
for some time until 1824 when Blackburn went out, with Palmerston's help, as
Chief Justice to Mauritius. But there poor Blackburn fared still worse. He fell
foul of local politics, his wife was shunned by respectable society when they
heard she had become entangled with his private secretary, and the secretary
finally eloped with his pretty daughter. Not surprisingly, therefore, Blackburn
left Mauritius for good in 1836. But Mrs Blackburn died at St Helena on the
journey home and Blackburn met with further disappointment when he
arrived in England. Since he had made himself very unpopular with the
anti-slavery lobby by his doings on the bench, his friends' attempt to get him a
sinecure on the Privy Council backfired, and was rejected, according to
Greville, as 'one of the grossest and most barefaced jobs ever'. So the Duke of
Northumberland made him commissioner on his estates and Palmerston
placed Eliza's eldest son in the Foreign Office, though only after carefully
ascertaining the young man's age; he was born in 1818. Palmerston's diary for
1818 mentions only 'E' for Emily Cowper.[58]

There are several other suggestive but tantalizing entries in Palmerston's
diaries of his middle years. In that for 1819 there are a couple of entries for 'La
Whaley' and in 1829 three 'Fine Days' with 'La K'. The account for 1829
shows no payment to the latter; but 'Whaley' is credited with no less than
£827 in 1819, as well as a donation of £20 more in 1831. Blackmail may have
been directly involved; years later Mrs Whaley wrote to beg a profitable office
for a 'friend' and on a separate slip of paper mentioned that he would be
prepared to pay £5,000 for it in *cash*. Other names appear in the debit columns
from time to time which he did not bother to enter in his diary, such as £5 or
£20 to a 'Mrs Brown' in the mid 1820s and similar payments to her daughter
'Miss Brown' in the mid 1830s, and each, together with those to Emma
Murray, marked 'AB', 'BC' and so on, obviously with some sort of significance
but in no pattern now discernible. Moreover, if the record of two of his visits to
Paris, in late 1818 and early 1829, remains blank in this respect, the same
cannot be said of another he made at the end of 1829. On this occasion it looks
as though he may have made up either to Mme Flahault or, since she was not
considered good-looking by most, more probably to the former Emily Rum-
bold, who was reputed to have been mistress of the Prince of Prussia and had
acquired riches without satisfaction by being married off to the King of
Prussia's Jewish banker, Baron de Delmar. Then there was Mme Graham, the
Sardinian wife of an attaché in the British Embassy. Ten years later William
Cowper called her 'an odious little maggot', though according to Gronow 'no

one could be in her company long without being inspired with feelings stronger than those of friendship'. But Gronow also insisted that 'not a word was ever said against her honour'. This was not entirely true, for some years later an attempt was made to challenge the legitimacy of her belated son and heir. During that difficult period Lady Palmerston gave her refuge at Broadlands, and in earlier days Palmerston had certainly seen a good deal of her in Paris; but the only traces he left are the charming letters full of gossip that he wrote her in his beautiful French from England. However, he certainly tried with another in Paris. 'Met Mad. Demay at the Petit Trianon,' runs his diary for 27 December 1829. 'Entered porter's lodge. Bother with porter – failed.'[59]

Amidst all this carnage there is no sign of any jealousy on Lady Cowper's part to match that which Palmerston had shown about her affairs. During the 1830s, however, it is very likely that she was rather put out by his behaviour. By the summer of 1833 they seemed at last to have settled down to a permanent, and relatively exclusive, arrangement. Certainly the bracelet which he bought for Emily at Storr and Mortimer's in late September had some special meaning; perhaps it was intended to symbolize at last her firmer bondage to him. It was also by way of a parting gift, for, having on 7 October married off her eldest son and been given the bracelet, she left two days later on an extended trip abroad. But if bondage was intended it was purely a one-way affair, for before the month was out the gossips were making the ears of England and even Europe ring with the news of Palmerston and Emily's old friend and enemy, Lady Jersey.[60]

Lady Jersey and Lady Cowper had for years been joint patronesses of Almacks and queens of London society; but their personalities were too different and their voices too similar – 'Silence' was Lady Jersey's nickname – for them to be firm friends. 'What a contempt I feel for that woman,' wrote Emily; 'an odious little woman.' Yet in spite of growing differences over politics as well they continued to see a good deal of each other. 'The two Countesses are still toiling on with their exhausted friendship,' wrote Greville, 'occasionally relieving themselves by brisk tirades against each other.' Hence it was not so odd that when the Cowpers left for Paris and the Riviera in the autumn of 1833, the Jerseys planned to join them. Lady Jersey was supposed to have been delayed from setting out at once by her husband's gout. So, left in London, she astonished and infuriated everyone by a dazzling flirtation with Palmerston. 'Have you heard the great news of all London – Lady Jersey running after Lord Palmerston?' Madame Lieven asked Earl Grey; 'Lord Palmerston, not a little touched by her enticing ways, paying her visits during his mornings, of two hours' duration, and then little dinners with her, and then going to the theatre together; in short, a perfect family party!' 'Very active and very ridiculous,' Greville noted, 'puts his colleagues in a fury and her in a delight.' Certainly no one could overlook the personal and political spite she had formerly showered upon him. 'May I not derive from it a hope that I, too, may again be taken into favour?' Grey amusedly enquired.[61]

Palmerston himself was certainly flattered and amused by it all; indeed he uncharacteristically neglected the Foreign Office. It was also now suggested that whenever Lady Cowper went abroad he habitually transferred his allegiance to Lady Jersey; and a decade ago she had certainly been insisting that Palmerston was in love with her. But since then, according to Carlisle, she had, rather like her cousin Mrs Arbuthnot, usually 'abused him like a pickpocket'. Caro George did not think it was anything more than a wild flirtation, and if it was, then he was curiously silent about it in that confidential record where pride and jealousy always otherwise triumphed over good taste and discretion.[62]

Lady Jersey had accepted an invitation to Broadlands, and nothing, surely, could be more dangerous than that. One Government colleague (Ellice) suggested that it must all have 'turned her brain' and made the physicians doubt whether hers would 'not shortly be a case, rather for a straitwaistcoat, than one for Broadlands'; another (Holland) that 'political hostility & prudish austerity seem to be alike softened'. But at the last moment her nerve failed or her conscience saved her. When Palmerston went down to Broadlands in November he went alone, and a week after he had returned to town Lady Jersey left for France as unexpectedly as she had stayed behind in the first place. 'She looked pale & care-worn, as if she had made an effort in tearing herself away from England,' wrote Granville when he met her in Paris; 'but why she hastened her departure & left poor Jersey weak & still suffering to follow her by himself to Paris, I could not discover.' What with Ladies Jersey, Sandwich, Lyndhurst and Keith (Flahault's wife) in Paris the British ambassador thought they would be very lucky indeed to survive the winter without some serious escapade. 'I am nearly as hard at work as ever,' wrote Palmerston the day after her departure; 'that is to say I can now almost but not quite get through my public business, leaving everything else to its fate.' Meanwhile, Princess Lieven – that 'Snipe', as Creevey used to call her – had written to Emily: 'Lady Jersey is leaving to-morrow and will be joining you. Her good understanding with Lord Palmerston is causing quite a stir.' But mean and catty though this was, it was by no means an untimely warning, for while Emily was away Palmerston was to find a more desirable, more rewarding, and therefore more dangerous liaison.[63]

By the end of 1833 Palmerston was in his fiftieth year and Emily was not far behind. Laura Maria Petre, on the other hand, was a fresh and beautiful young bride of only twenty-two, married to a most unsatisfactory husband twice her age. Her husband, Robert Edward, was the youngest son of the ninth Baron Petre by his second wife and like her rather gross in shape. He was a well-known figure on the Turf and he entertained a noble sprinkling of fashionable society at Stapleton near Doncaster. But he was both gullible and foolish. Creevey, who labelled him 'dear Eddard' without affection, thought him a good natured fool; Emily Eden 'very rich and very stupid'; Henry Fox 'harmless and very good-natured, but quite a fool and very dirty' – in short an 'animal'. Once he had courted Theresa Villiers and perhaps even Minny Cowper. Fox, who had also trifled with Miss Villiers's affections, suggested that 'his house and station' would 'procure him a wife, when experience has taught him not to seek for one among those whose beauty or whose talents require a better bidder'. But although so gross, Petre was 'as kindhearted, hospitable a man, as ever lived', and in July 1829 he finally secured a desirable Catholic bride in one of Lord Stafford's daughters; even Lady Holland admitted she was 'a very lovely girl'.[64]

Palmerston appears to have known Edward Petre and his family circle for some time. He stayed at Stapleton for the races in 1828 and was planning to do so again in 1830. After Lady Jersey had at last left for France in November 1833 he went down to Broadlands, and the Christmas holidays found the Petres among a whole bevy of diplomats there. By the middle of February the tongues were all wagging again. 'His unpopularity in his own office is quite as great as it is among the Foreign Ministers, and he does nothing,' Greville heard. 'He spends his time in making love to Mrs Petre, whom he takes to the House of Commons to hear speeches which he does not make, and where he exhibits his conquest, and certainly it is the best of his exploits, but what a successor of Canning, whom by the way he affects to imitate.' Before long Palmerston had been dubbed 'the venerable cupid', and when Mrs Petre had to leave him for a while the joke went around that he had engaged himself to Miss Jerningham, one of her sisters. 'Mrs Petre is gone to . . . Scotland,' Lady Holland wrote. 'The world reports that our Secretary is to marry her sister. I conclude if it [is] possible to make a place in the diplomatic department one will be made for her brother . . .' Mrs Petre already had one brother in the diplomatic service and he was not highly regarded by his masters; yet another had been taken on by Palmerston in January 1834; the youngest remained available. Miss Jerningham, apparently, was an unattractive and over-eager female. 'She was at the Russian Embassy yesterday overdressed and bedizened as usual. Madame de Lieven made her a target for her wit, but couldn't quite get out of inviting her. No doubt, in order to avenge this constraint, she said quite loudly that Miss Jerningham reminded her of the usual advertisement in the *Times*: "A housemaid wants a situation in a family where a footman is kept." ' She died a spinster. But there was other sport too for the gossips. 'This day week', old Creevey wrote in May, 'I . . . dine with two as congenial spirits as ever were formed for each other, at Edward Petre's to meet Lord Chancellor Brougham . . . "Ah sure a pair" .'[65]

Shortly after the break-up of his affair with Mrs Lamb Brougham had belatedly got married in 1819. But Mrs Brougham was not, apparently, a very attractive woman, either in personality or, though opinions differed on this, in appearance either. 'I look at her "and am revenged",' rejoiced Lady Cowper. 'They say one Man's Joy is another's pain, but here his Joy was his own pain and our pleasure.' Probably it was a shotgun marriage; certainly it was not a

Fine Day d. 2.

visit d-

Fine Day d - - 5
task leave of
Fine Day 2.   *1/. last 6*

Palmerston's Diary of 7-13 December 1835

Thursday, DECEMBER 10, 1835.

344th day.

d. embarked at 8 for antwerp
visit in morning. dined Bastac;

Friday 11.

345th day.

Saturday 12.

346th day.

Fine Day 2.
dined Sebastiani.

Sunday 13.

347th day.
Third Sunday in Advent.

Fine Day 2.

happy one and perhaps even by the following year they could 'hardly keep up appearances'. Brougham himself had the sort of lively ugliness – 'like a truffle with white tulle', according to Lady Granville – that appealed very strongly to some women. 'Dear me, what a fright,' Emily Cowper once exclaimed. 'Good God, I think him at times quite beautiful.' But whatever his relations with Lady Cowper he was certainly throughout the summer of 1834 fiercely challenging Palmerston for Mrs Petre's favour, accompanying her to a Catholic mass when, as Chancellor of England, he should have been attending divine service at the Temple, giving her 'perpetual junkets & dinners', and rushing through his business in the hope of taking her on a trip up the Rhine.[66]

At first, Lady Grey affirmed, Brougham was, as a lover, 'dead-beat by Palmerston'; later, Lady Holland reported that she 'seems flattered & gives fond smiles & good cheer'. But Brougham may have rather disappointed her by backing out of the junket down the Rhine. Greville said that he discovered 'that he could not leave the country without putting the Great Seal in commission at a cost (to himself) of £1,400. This was a larger price than he was disposed to pay for his amatory trip, so he went off to Brougham instead.' In any event he certainly did not displace Palmerston – not yet at any rate. Many years later, when 'Poodle' Byng was walking with another guest at Broadlands and reminiscing about their host's earlier adventures, 'He talked of a Mrs Petrie, a most attractive woman, always found Pam there; he believes she always kept right; she is now the head of a convent in Belgium.' Edward and Laura Petre had both been born into leading Catholic families and both became celebrated for their patronage, for example of the Catholic Cathedral of Southwark, and after her husband's death in 1848 Laura indeed became a nun, and later sister superior of her convent. But, alas, she had not, as Poodle Byng had put it, 'always kept right'.[67]

Lady Cowper certainly could have had few illusions about it all. She returned to England in the late spring of 1834 to discover also that her friend Princess Lieven had finally exhausted her credit with both Grey and Palmerston. She had encouraged the Tsar not to accept Stratford Canning as the new ambassador in St Petersburg and found herself in turn being recalled forever from London. Emily was rather too sympathetic to her and too critical of Palmerston in that affair; but there was more to her unusually low spirits than that. 'Poor Lady Cowper gets the benefit of all Lord Palmerston's ill-humour, and they say he is very unkind to her,' it was observed in June; and a month later, 'she seemed . . . depressed and preoccupied.' She was not by any means dismissed, however. Rather, when in October Palmerston placed Spencer Cowper in the diplomatic service and made his brother Fordwich the new Undersecretary at the Foreign Office, there was a good deal of muttering about 'petticoat influence . . . in state affairs'. 'We naturally expected Edward Petre . . . but now suppose that he will have something else [as] good, if he can be spared,' wrote 'Poodle' Byng, adding with especial sarcasm, 'perhaps the Russian Embassy.' In 1835 the gossip died down, but Palmerston continued , to divide throughout the year his philandering attendance between the young bride and the middle-aged matron. It culminated in a romping week early in December, at the end of which he made a fond farewell to Laura at five and greeted Emily again at half past six. The Petres were off abroad for economy's sake and after this they were more and more away. Brougham kept up a correspondence. Palmerston left traces of a jealous interest in Laura's comings and goings in his diary for 1836, but there was no more gossip and no further record of love-making.[68]

Laura Petre was probably Palmerston's last great adventure in love, though certainly not his final escapade any more than Francis Conyngham was Emily's. At his age it must have been getting pretty exhausting, even for an athlete like Palmerston. 'The life I lead', he innocently remarked in August 1834, 'is like that of a man who on getting out of bed every morning, should be caught up by the end of one of the arms of a windmill and whirled round and round till he was again deposited at night to rest.'[69]

Palmerston had for years had too little rest, morning, noon *or* night. This was true long before Mrs Petre came upon the scene. All signs are that Emily too lived her life as intensely as was possible for any human being. Neither the dying torments of her mother and the drunken misery of her father, nor the incredible negligence and slow decline of her feeble husband ever crushed her spirits. Instead she plunged herself heart and soul into the affairs equally of a fashionable Almacks and a reprobate court, meddled in and managed the personal and political lives of her three brothers, coped with the errant behaviour of two wilful sisters-in-law, and steered two difficult daughters into unlikely marriages. She enjoyed every minute of it – as much perhaps as her affair with Palmerston, and, probably, her betrayal of him. But what of Palmerston? Alas, an orphan and a bachelor, he had no comfortable family home in London to give him refuge and relief – and Broadlands only put Emily further out of reach.

It was very rarely that Palmerston could enjoy, as in 1829, the luxury of a holiday with Emily, staying together at the Royal Sussex Hotel in Tunbridge Wells and filling his diary with romantic references to walks among the rocks and meetings by night in blissful disregard of the presence of both Princess Lieven and Lord Cowper. Instead for thirty years, almost without a break, there was the terrible burden, first of the dreary War Office and then the arduous Foreign Office. He might very well have constantly annoyed the clerks by leaving them hard at work late in the afternoon, but, after dinner and the requisite appearance for any up and coming young man about town at the opera or a party, there was still for him the business of the House of Commons and the dread he had for so long of having to speak. And when, at twelve or two in the morning, he should have made his weary way home to bed, he had instead to keep his clandestine assignations with Emily – waiting quietly in all weathers to make his way through her garden ('per il giardino') and, if he was lucky, staying in her bed only till four or five in the morning, when he had to drag himself back to his own a short distance away ('Fine night. Restato la sera dalle 12½ fin alle 5'). Considering too that Emily was both busy and unreliable, and Palmerston even more discreet than her husband was complaisant, his life was full of failures and frustrations – all of which he recorded as carefully as his triumphs. 'Failed', he would report, 'through a mutual misunderstanding' ('per spaglio reciprico'); or 'signore in casa'. Lady Cowper certainly made it all the more complicated with her secret cyphers, with the social whirl that led him all over town in search of a rival or an assignation, and with her constant comings and goings between the country and London and between England and the Continent. It may have been exciting; but it was certainly exhausting. It is surely very probable, therefore, that together with the cares and labours of the War Office and Parliament, it contributed a good deal to that frequent irritability of his in office. 'Lord Palmerston', wrote Mrs Arbuthnot in 1827, 'is always quarrelling with every body.' Yet so far as is known he made only one attempt, apart from his half-hearted approach to Anna Maria Elliot, to break free from Emily, and even in that case it is impossible to be sure, since Palmerston did not necessarily associate sexual attraction with marriage.[70]

When, in February 1818, Palmerston's friend, Lord Clive, married Lady Lucy Graham – a woman whom Harriet Granville described as 'one of those girls who look like our ancestors, with an old-fashioned face and a look of cut velvet and parrots on the finger about them' – Palmerston commented: 'She is very sensible & conversible and I think will make Clive a very nice wife. She is not remarkably handsome but has a pleasing countenance & manner & is quite handsome enough for a wife.' But if she was anything like her half-sisters, Lady Jersey, Lady Bessborough and Lady Paget, his own proposal to Lady Georgiana Fane in 1825 could not have been so free from lust. They had been frequently thrown together at dinner parties since August 1818 at the latest. By 1823 they were 'squaddling' [huddling in a squash?] together at the opera and 'shaking a leg' at Vauxhall. In the New Year Lady Granville thought it was 'looking like something' and remarked how sensible it would be of him. By the summer of 1825 Lady Cowper was jealous enough to write: 'Lady Ga Fane hunts Ld P. up & down the rooms & sits like Patience on a monument . . . but I think she will not succeed. If she was handsomer she would have a better chance.' According to Lady Georgiana's cousin Mrs Arbuthnot, who very much approved the match, Palmerston did propose at least twice in 1825. But he was refused both times. Lady Jersey was blamed for going round saying that he was really in love with her and doing everything else she could to break it up. 'I have been very much annoyed lately by the turn my friend Ly G. Fane's flirtation with Ld Palmerston has taken,' Mrs Arbuthnot wrote towards the end of July. 'He appeared to me to be *coming on* again very well; but the other night . . . she thought proper to tell him that she

Left Sandridge at ½ p 1
London. visit at Whitehall morning
to arrange. — just come to Town.
dined Sulivans — Convent Garden
Ld Melbourne & & C.
Fine Night. per il giardino..
delle 2. fine a 5½ della mattina

visit in morning G. St. dined Ld
Malmys.

dined at Ld Melbournes. & & C.
——— & & C. Lamb Montagu
Failed la Notte per sbaglio rui-
-prov waited from 2 to 5 in morning

Palmerston's Diary of 1-3 January 1819

had not changed her mind, that she thought it much better they shd not marry &, having made this strange declaration, she has been miserable about it ever since & certainly likes him very much. There is no accounting for ladies! He has since passed all his time with Lady Cowper.' Emily, on the contrary, complained that, in company with Robert Grosvenor among others, he was constantly hanging about Lady Elizabeth Conyngham.[71]

Palmerston, however disappointed, was probably well rid of Lady Georgiana. In 1825 she was still only in her early twenties, but Peel, who was constantly thrown into her company by Mrs Arbuthnot's intrigues on Palmerston's behalf, had 'long thought [her] the most impertinent and odious woman in England'. Soon after the ruin of her affair with Palmerston she declined into some mysterious and supposedly psychosomatic illness from which many years later she emerged 'half-cracked' to conduct an amorous correspondence with the Duke of Wellington. When he broke with her in 1851 she threatened to sue the eighty-two-year-old veteran for breach of promise. 'He has always had one or more women whom he liked to talk to and go to and be intimate with, and often very odd women too; but the strangest of all his fancies was this tiresome, troublesome, crazy old maid,' was Greville's version. Hers was that it was Wellington who was mad. When she asked Russell if he thought the duke was sane, he replied: 'Never more so, but lately very irritable. You may know the cause.' She died unmarried in 1874, leaving her property to a favourite nephew, Spencer Ponsonby, who had been private secretary to Palmerston.[72]

By this narrow escape Palmerston remained available to marry Emily when her husband set her free. Lord Cowper, as was pointed out over and over again, was quite complaisant about their affair. His health and temperament evidently had a good deal to do with it – though possibly not all. Moreover, as time went on he and Emily, it would appear, came to a little arrangement. 'Dear Lord C[owper]', she wrote to Fred, 'in the most *sheepish* way asked me the other night if I had any objection to L[ad]y Sarah [Bayly] coming to P[anshanger] so I answered in the most frank [and] amiable manner to be sure not, I shall be delighted – oh pray ask her directly . . . so I put him quite at his ease on that score. J'ai voulu lui donné un bon exemple.' He continued to be a nuisance to Palmerston, however, by dragging her off abroad for the sake of his health. They went for the last time in August 1836. She was observed on the way back, eating dinner *en famille* in the annexe of a French hotel: 'the sought for, the adored queen of fashion', 'her slight figure . . . enveloped in shawls, her little head covered with a close bonnet cap'. Her secret, rather pious, observer was 'glad to have seen her thus'. But the sacrifice was all in vain. Cowper survived little more than another six months and died on 21 June 1837. 'At a quarter to nine at night was the last breath of the best of friends and the kindest of husbands,' Emily wrote in her diary. 'The most benevolent and the kindest of men. The most strictly just, and the most considerate of the feelings of others. All his good qualities would fill a page, and his faults were almost none; at least I never knew a mortal in whom was less to blame or more to love and admire and respect.' So the middle-aged lovers of nearly thirty years were free at last to wed. But it was still far from easy. Perhaps, when she was barely out of her weeds, Emily could still not resist a little teasing.[73]

When Francis Conyngham had married Lady Jane Paget in April 1824 'the general feeling' was reported to be one of 'surprise – gladness by a few – doubts of happiness by many – *unqualified* approbation by *none* except those incidentally interested'. Certainly his wife was an odd woman; 'Crazy Jane', Emily called her in her letters to Fred, 'hunting Francis . . . from corner to corner.' Perhaps, then, it is not surprising to find it being said, when he was made Postmaster-General a decade later, that he was 'a young and good-looking man of fashion with many love affairs, who writes and receives more *billets-doux* than serious letters, and is therefore called "the Postmaster of the twopenny post" '. When in 1837 therefore it was rumoured that Jenny had gone mad and been confined, Palmerston again became very worried, for while the accession of Victoria had not yet displaced Francis as court chamberlain, it had through the Queen's attachment to Fanny brought the now widowed Emily back into contact with the court after the brief interval of William's reign.[74]

When the young Queen Victoria sought her innocent pleasure at the Pavilion and Lady Cowper's liver sent her at the same time to take the mineral waters in Brighton, Palmerston evidently reproached Emily with his suspicions and begged her not to go. She immediately sent a whole stream of reassurances, telling him 'that there is not another person in the world of whom I should ever think for one moment in that light, and . . . no other person with whom I could ever have the least prospect of happiness'. So he should cease his 'suspicions' and 'foolish fancies' and come down himself if possible. In the meantime, 'I promise you faithfully that I will receive *no* visits, that I will do nothing that you could find fault with, but don't insist upon my leaving the *only remedy* which I have found to act upon my deranged part.' So far as Lord Conyngham was concerned he would only be there for a few days, she believed, and 'if I was asked to the court, I should undoubtedly send an excuse.' A few days later she reported Conyngham had gone; Palmerston hurried down all the same. But it was to be a far from happy time for him. A fortnight later there came a tear-stained letter from Sulivan to say that his sister Lilly was dead; almost exactly a year after that came the news that Mrs Bowles had also died. There may therefore have been something in the story Disraeli heard about the loss making for some decisive move on Emily's part, though there was certainly not in that about a reconciliation after years of separation. In any case Palmerston still had to wait more than another year before Emily would fill the void at Broadlands.[75]

Although she evidently did enjoy the sport, the delay was not entirely

Emily's fault. Certainly her children and her brothers were far from happy about the marriage. It was because 'Lord Cowper was a man whom people so loved and admired', Melbourne explained to the young Queen Victoria. He could hardly have put it more ingenuously. Fordwich said he would 'rather be hung' than go to the ceremony; William prepared to move out of his mother's house. But it was Fanny who made the most trouble. Everyone knew that she could not bear the thought of Palmerston; and it was undoubtedly very embarrassing that her mother should marry twice before she had done so once. So Emily dragged her about the country houses, trying to make a match; but Fanny refused them all and put her mother in despair. Fred was rather more kind, but in his letters too Emily detected a note of disapproval, and Melbourne warned her that 'it would be a great change for him [Palmerston], accustomed to run about everywhere . . .You mustn't deceive yourself about it; if you do this you must take the consequences.' Naturally enough all this rather made her dither, and that her brothers could bear even less in a woman. Fred therefore advised her 'if she likes it to do it, not to potter about it'. So, a few weeks later, Emily answered: 'The only person I fear now is the Queen, as she may think it foolish in a person of my age marrying.' She need not have worried so much. 'Palmerston', Victoria wrote early in December to her own 'dear Albert', 'is to be married within the next few days to Lady Cowper. . . They are, both of them, above fifty, and I think that they are quite right so to act, because Palmerston, since the death of his sisters, is quite alone in the world, and *Lady C.* is a very clever woman, and *much* attached to him; still I feel sure it will make you smile.'[76]

Emily kept up her modest protestations of doubt to both Palmerston and female friends right up until the last; Fordwich's mother-in-law so lost patience as to advise her 'to take the name and stop one's being told so much about Ld P. & Ldy C.' But, as Fanny said in a very bitter letter to her brother William Cowper, it was all pretence. For, though kept a very close secret, Palmerston had already announced his engagement to his family on 31 October. When it was gazetted at last Fordwich steeled himself to attend the ceremony, Fanny addressed a dutiful letter to Palmerston, and from Paris Princess Lieven conveyed to Emily the rejoicing of her '*sisterly* heart'. On 15 December 1839 Emily wrote in her diary: 'Was alone all day and packing; felt low at former recollections & reading old letters.' The next day she and Palmerston were quietly married at half-past one in St George's, Hanover Square. 'A beautiful day,' she wrote, 'which I accept as a good omen, and I trust the event of the day will contribute to our mutual happiness.'[77]

VI

INTERLUDE I:
SHYCOCK
AND
SPARROW,
1822-8

After their marriage in 1839 Emily and Palmerston enjoyed twenty-five years of unfamiliar married bliss. As Lady Palmerston, Emily also played the acknowledged part of a leading political hostess. It was a new role for her, but by no means a different play. She had always been a political woman and by the 1820s she was meddling in Palmerston's affairs as much as in her brothers'. Between the end of the war in 1815 and the passing of the Reform Bill in 1832, it was said, all the Whig ladies were trying to capture the young men for their side. Until the mid or late twenties there is no real sign that Emily played an important part in Palmerston's political existence. She saved him from social suffocation among the Tories, hardly more. Their mutual acquaintance, the future Lady Byron, described him in 1812 as 'devoid of party spirit, of public spirit, or of spirit of any kind'. But that was obviously as exaggerated a view as Lady Blessington's in 1829:

Lord Palmerston has much more ability than people are disposed to give him credit for. . . . a good man of business, acute in the details, and quick in the comprehension of complicated questions. . . .
Lively, well-bred, and unaffected, Lord Palmerston is a man that is so well acquainted with the routine of official duties, performs them so readily and pleasantly, and is so free from the assumption of self-importance that too frequently appertains to adepts in them, that, whether Whig or Tory government has the ascendant in England, his services will be always considered a desideratum to be secured if possible.[1]

Published with the benefit of hindsight in 1841 and patently designed to flatter, Lady Blessington's opinion is still more implausible than Lady Byron's. But even in that long dull period of his at the War Office he was carving out a role and a reputation on his own behalf. He had not been a great innovator in that office; to it he had brought not genius but dogged perseverance and bureaucratic bustle. On the other hand he had most certainly proved himself a very able administrator. Indeed, if it were not for his

227

domineering tone, one would be inclined to think that he would have made a better civil servant than politician. But if he had one major fault as an administrator, he also possessed one vital asset as a politician – durability.

Palmerston was a member of every administration between 1807 and 1834. Obviously he owed his promotion to the War Office in 1809 to the dearth of talent available to Perceval. Similarly his ascent in 1827-30 to a prominence beyond the measure of his efforts and expectations was owing only a little less clearly to the way fate had picked off his rivals and superiors. If he had been an important or popular member of the Tory Party, the problem would be to explain why he was not promoted earlier. But the fact of the matter is that he was neither. His ability as an administrator was generally acknowledged – at least outside the Horse Guards; but his talents as politician and parliamentarian were not. The essential dilemma, then, is not how he failed to be promoted, but how he managed to survive so long in minor office.

In the eighteenth-century epilogue that stretched over the first two decades of the nineteenth, one must look first to what were called political *connections*. Palmerston, of course, owed his introduction to office in 1807 to Malmesbury, and it was probably also Malmesbury who tried to tie him down still more closely by a marriage alliance with Castlereagh's cousin early in 1809, just as he had endeavoured, equally unsuccessfully, to tie him by office to Canning in August 1807. It was very probably in another attempt to attach Palmerston to Canning that Malmesbury entertained them together at Park Place early in January 1808; for the next month there followed Palmerston's maiden speech in defence of the attack on Copenhagen which Canning had ordered. The blow-up over Walcheren the following year, however, temporarily cut him off from both Canning and Castlereagh. Personally he blamed the commander, Chatham, more than anyone else, but, he wrote, 'if a victim is to be sacrificed to appease the fury of the many headed monster [public opinion], I know no one whose loss would perhaps be less felt than poor Cas, since whatever his talents for business may be, & I confess I rather think highly of them, he is dreadfully unpopular & is somewhat of a millstone about the necks of his friends'. But the breach which then widened between Malmesbury and Canning tended to involve Palmerston as well.[2]

With both Castlereagh and Canning out of office, Palmerston found another leader to admire and one of whom Malmesbury did not entirely approve. Malmesbury's influence with Palmerston was clearly much undermined long before his death in 1820. His patronage was not much in evidence after Portland's retirement and death in October 1809: it was Palmerston himself, not Perceval, who then consulted him about the Exchequer and War Office. Malmesbury seems to have noticed that Palmerston was slipping away from him and falling under Perceval's sway. After their estrangement from Canning, Fitzharris supported Perceval's Government and so did his father; but it was only *faute de mieux*. Both Lady Malmesbury and her sister despised

Perceval as a person. Lady Minto, who regretted in any case that Palmerston should have started out on the '*shabby* side' along with the Tories, in particular complained of his making a 'mere *worm*' like Perceval his 'hero'. But her brother-in-law too thought the Prime Minister a weakling and his Government too 'conceding & complaisant'. Even in Malmesbury's critical opinion, however, Perceval had this great merit, that he was at least fiercely opposed to Catholic Emancipation. But on 11 May 1812 the Prime Minister was assassinated and Malmesbury and his son were soon horrified to find the anti-Catholic character of the Government being undermined by approaches to Lord Wellesley, who had recently resigned the Foreign Office on that issue, and to Canning, whose aggressive posture on it had completed his estrangement from his former friends.[3]

The rump of Perceval's Ministry first tried to prolong its existence by re-admitting Wellesley and Canning under the anti-Catholic Liverpool. Then Prinney, mischievously testing his unaccustomed powers as Regent, attempted to replace it by a pro-Catholic combination of Whigs and Tories. But both attempts broke down, as did other approaches to the Opposition. So on 8 June the prince had no option but to return to Liverpool and Liverpool none but to form an administration on the basis of non-commitment on the Catholic question. Malmesbury and Fitzharris were presumably relieved when the attempt to include Canning broke down towards the end of July on his inability to agree with Castlereagh over the lead in the House of Commons; but they were nonetheless dismayed that the avowedly anti-Catholic character of the Government had been abandoned and disgusted that it should include so many of Sidmouth's friends. They were, moreover, as contemptuous of Liverpool as Prime Minister as they had been of Perceval and bitterly disappointed with the attitude of their erstwhile protégé.

Although the available correspondence between Palmerston and the Harrises is unfortunately incomplete at this crucial point, it is clear that he did not believe the Catholic question ought to stand in the way of re-admitting Wellesley and Canning. Palmerston did not have, he confessed, 'entire confidence' in either of them. 'Lord Wellesley', he wrote, 'has broke the spell which he brought from India, by two years of absolute inefficiency in office; Canning has a long and difficult lee way to make up before he can inspire as much confidence in his character as he extracts from his talents.' On the other hand, 'Liverpool able and useful both in office and in Parliament is hardly of calibre for the head of Government, and Castlereagh is not equal to it'. Indeed, the latter he believed 'could never lead the Commons, he has neither the energy nor the tact'. So, he concluded when he learned of Wellesley's and Canning's initial refusal on 18 May to serve again in a predominantly anti-Catholic Government, 'we *must* have Wellesley [and] Canning if we mean to go on, and surely the Prince will not keep them out from any fears about the Catholic question'.[4]

There is no specific reference to the line Palmerston took about the tortuous negotiations in the two weeks following Perceval's death. But the day after Liverpool was finally commissioned to form a Government Palmerston wrote another letter to Fitzharris, which though not available must surely have expressed approval of the Government, of which he remained a junior member though still outside the Cabinet, being neutral on the Catholic question. For the next day Fitzharris sent him in reply what was evidently intended as a letter of disgust and reproof. Fitzharris got no response to this, which he thought discourteous and indicative, if not of '*dudgeon*', at least of 'apathy' on Palmerston's part. But he was wrong. An aunt who lived in London reported that Palmerston had called on her and, with 'perfect good charity' towards Fitzharris, insisted that if his friend had been 'on the scene of action and heard all that had passed' he too 'would think and act as he does now'. Shortly afterwards, on 22 June, when Canning attempted to strengthen his position by promoting a Catholic motion in the House, Fitzharris reported, 'Palmerston said a few words [to the effect that 'the repeal . . . must in his opinion not be unconditional, but must be guarded by pledges']), and with . . . a great portion of people in office voted with Canning.'[5]

There is little evidence by which to trace Palmerston's conversion from 'Protestant' to 'Catholic' between 1806 and 1812. Probably it was in large part a matter of expediency, rather than of deep-seated religious belief or constitutional theory; and just as 'Simeonite' votes were 'as good as less righteous ones' at Cambridge in 1806, so 'Catholic' colleagues were necessary in Government in 1812. It has also been observed that while his assurances in 1806 about the Test Act had seemed to be 'decided', the criticism he made in his private journal of Grenville's breach with the King in October 1807 was aimed at the circumstances rather than the principle of Catholic relief. Expediency, moreover, was the very word he used when he next spoke openly in support of Catholic Emancipation in March 1813. It was not a matter of 'rights', he said, but of the nation's 'welfare and safety'. He questioned in particular the practical wisdom of excluding from equal opportunities of public service or public honour so large a part of the population and of making enemies by such repression. 'It is in vain to think that by any human pressure, we can stop the spring which gushes from the earth. But it is for us to consider whether we will force it to spend its strength in secret and hidden courses, undermining our fences, and corrupting our soil, or whether we shall, at once, turn the current into the open and spacious channel of honourable and constitutional ambition, converting it into the means of national prosperity and public wealth.'[6]

While there certainly was some sign of Palmerston's developing sense of political survival in all this, there was more to it than that. For the recognition of Canning's necessity to the Administration in 1812 did not require a positive vote in favour of concessions to the Catholics. Such a posture, indeed, directly threatened Palmerston's seat in Parliament and even his place in Government. Rather it marked the ascendancy of Edinburgh's philosophy of common sense over the narrow bigotry of Malmesbury's influence. Very probably Palmerston's first visit to Ireland in the late summer of 1808 had something to do with it. He seems at the time to have left no explicit expression of opinion on the matter, but his practical tolerance and liberal attitude to his tenants' needs then as later suggest that he might well have included in them a measure of Catholic relief.

Another positive factor was no less probably the youthful company Palmerston kept from his earliest days in Westminster. On 10 November 1808 he attended what was possibly the opening dinner party of a newly formed club called the 'Alfred', situated next to the Royal Institution in Albemarle Street. According to his own account, it was a literary club, with an initial limit of two hundred members and a subscription of five guineas a year. There were to be no dice or cards and, instead of large dinner parties, small ones at a charge, including a pint of wine, of seven shillings each. 'The members are many of the most distinguished literary & scientific characters of the day', he reported, '& I think it is likely to turn out a very pleasant thing.' The membership appears to have been political and clerical as well as literary and scientific, and the club was so successful that three years later there were said to be three hundred and fifty-four candidates for six vacancies. Walter Scott and Byron, who had been elected during his absence in Greece, were early members and both were rather sarcastic about it. Scott avowed that it was, like all clubs, 'much haunted with *boars* – tusky monsters, which delight to range where men most do congregate; as they are kept at the spear's point pretty much in private society'. For a while Byron thought it had just about enough 'pleasant' members to balance the bores and to make it, 'upon the whole, a decent resource in a rainy day, in a dearth of parties, or parliament, or in an empty season'. Ten years later, however, he dismissed it as 'the most *recherché* and most tiresome of any'. That famous wit, Lord Alvanley, stood it as long as he could, but 'when the seventeenth bishop was proposed I gave in. I really could not enter the place without being reminded of my catechism.' Palmerston was less fastidious: his accounts show that he remained a member until 1822 or 1823. During that period he also made the club the centre of his literary and political affiliations. [7]

In later years, when the pressures and preoccupations of an almost wholly political existence had finally overpowered the lingering influences of his dilettantish parents, people tended to overlook the fact that in early manhood Palmerston had been accustomed to indulge in all the fashionable literary games. It was about this time, according to his own story, that he joined with Sheridan, Canning and others to form a society projected by Swift for the improvement of the English language. Walter Scott had some reason, presumably, for referring to Palmerston's general reputation as 'a man of letters'. Certainly in 1816 Palmerston was engaged by Emily's brother George to enlist the protection of Peel as Irish Secretary for a reverend Irish playwright (Maturin) against his wrathful archbishop; in 1817-18 he was opposing in the Commons a bill to make copyright libraries pay for the books they received; and when John Wilson Croker was helping to form the Athenaeum in 1823-4 he added Palmerston's name as 'a patron of the arts, and to my knowledge a person of literary powers'. Three years before Croker had consulted Palmerston about some Hampshire personalities named in the papers of Lord Hervey he was editing, and in his letter of thanks had said: 'You are charming and worth all my other helps put together . . . what a pity you do not take to authorship.'[8]

What Croker must have meant was that it was a pity Palmerston did not write more often for publication since Palmerston, Peel and he had for several years past been associated in supplying political squibs and verses to the principal Government newspaper, the *Courier*. Palmerston may have contributed a satirical article to the *Courier* as early as August 1806; several of his efforts were certainly published in it in 1815 and 1816, and these were included in a collected edition compiled by Croker and published by Murray under the title *The New Whig Guide* in 1819. These pieces seem now rather strained and even within a couple of years many of their allusions already needed explanation. Twenty years later Brougham wrote that Palmerston had been one of the best 'squib-mongers' that the Tories had; interestingly enough, Brougham had been Palmerston's principal victim among the members of the Opposition he caricatured. Later Palmerston attacked another old acquaintance when Hobhouse contested Westminster as a radical in 1819 and 1820, and Palmerston took a leading part among the Tories who supported the rival Whig candidate, George Lamb. On the first occasion George Lamb won, but Palmerston's views about Hobhouse could hardly have been soothed in victory after Lady Cowper had narrowly escaped the mob's flying stones.[9]

Palmerston's literary efforts seem to have been inspired by the associations he had formed within the circle of the Alfred. The club was certainly not exclusively Tory; after all, Byron was a member. But it may gradually have become more and more inclined that way, so that by 1820 it was reputed to be the 'asylum of doting Tories and drivelling Quidnuncs'. Croker and Peel were both members and a definite connection between the club and the *Guide* has been made in an unpublished memoir left by another member, Henry Goulburn. Goulburn records that soon after he entered the House of Commons, which was early in 1808, he formed with a small group of other new members of a like age 'a society intimately united in political sentiment & literary tastes', who usually dined together at the Alfred every Wednesday, and someone, possibly Goulburn himself, has entered in the margin at this point the words 'Whig Guide'.[10]

With the exception of three Irishmen – Croker, William Vesey Fitzgerald and Richard Wellesley (the Marquess's eldest illegitimate son) – all of those Goulburn named had been near contemporaries at Harrow or Cambridge. These were in addition to himself, Palmerston, Fred Robinson, Henry Drummond, Robert Pemberton Milnes and Charles Manners-Sutton. 'A short time afterwards', Goulburn adds, they were joined by Peel. Since Peel entered the House of Commons in 1809, before either Drummond or Welles-ley, and Palmerston talked of scarcely knowing Croker in October that same year, it must have been later that this group of ten acquired its distinct form.[11]

Palmerston's Alfred 'set' has been characterized as an earnest, confident and patriotic group of aristocratic or wealthy Tories. But it was probably only as supporters of Perceval's Administration that it took on coherent shape. Seven of them were junior members of his Government – Palmerston called them the 'Sub Cabinet' – and at least two more, probably all three, his active sympathizers. Robert Plumer Ward, who had been Palmerston's colleague at the Admiralty and got on close terms with him, gave a similar character to the company of young Tories with whom he noticed his friend so frequently dined. Their names were not identical with Goulburn's list, but that may not have been anywhere near complete and Plumer Ward certainly described them as 'enthusiastic for such a leader as Perceval'. He also said, however, that they entertained 'a general sentiment against Canning', and this could not be applied without qualification to the Alfred group. Milnes, as well as Fitzhar-ris, had grown cool towards him; but Croker, though never exactly a Can-ningite, was a close friend and, still more important, an equally determined advocate of Catholic Emancipation. On the other hand, Peel (as well as Goulburn) was an opponent of both, and Palmerston seems to have been as close to him as he was to Croker. As Secretary at War, he was necessarily in constant communication with Peel, whether as Undersecretary at the Colon-ial Office, Chief Secretary in Ireland or Home Secretary. But their relations were definitely not, as William Peel's recollection seems to imply, 'almost exclusively political'. For a few years after 1814 they were neighbours in Stanhope Street, where Peel took over a lease from Palmerston while Palm-erston moved further along the street. A year later they were consulting together about how best to repel the mob. Shortly after that, when Peel as well as Palmerston had become a university M.P., they commenced a period of occasional consultation and concert over such matters as the legal rights and powers of Oxford and Cambridge to raise loans for the enlargement of the undergraduate accommodation or to take police action for the control of vagrants and prostitutes. By the mid 1820s too, when Peel was no longer away so much in Ireland, he would also go and shoot at Broadlands.[12]

While, then, Palmerston's votes for Catholic relief in 1812 and 1813 definitely broke his political subservience to Malmesbury, they by no means severed his close connections with the Alfred 'set'. After all, his friends were pretty evenly divided on that question, with Robinson, Croker and Fitzgerald voting with Palmerston, and Drummond, Goulburn and Milnes with Peel. According to Madame Lieven, Palmerston was, when she first arrived in England in September 1812, 'very attached to Tory policy and particularly to Lord Castlereagh'. She knew Palmerston very well and her statements deserve respect. But while Castlereagh also supported Catholic relief there is no real evidence of any political alliance between him and Palmerston. It is surely unlikely that Palmerston would have changed so soon the poor opinion of his talents he had expressed earlier that year. Palmerston was, however, a regular at Lady Castlereagh's dazzling parties, and the princess in recollection may well have been confusing personal with political regard. When Castlereagh died in 1822, Palmerston wrote: 'No one could be a greater loss to his friends for a tender more generous or noble mind never existed,' but added more perfunctorily, 'and by the public his loss will be long & severely felt.' Palmerston's stance in 1812 and 1813 seems rather to have confirmed and strengthened his alignment with what might be called the progressive wing of the Tory Party, who, 'Protestant' or 'Catholic', increasingly in these years pursued commercial and administrative improvement while still combatting parliamentary reform and social disorder. This included Peel, even though he hated the word 'liberal' and belonged by choice with High Tories; as long as the Catholic question was not raised, he was essentially sympathetic. For his part Palmerston worked at the War Office in close cooperation with Peel's reforming zeal, whether in Ireland or at the Home Office. He also welcomed Robinson's promotion to head of the Board of Trade in 1818: 'This is a very good appointment. He has modern & liberal notions about trade & his seat in Cabinet will enable him to give them more weight & effect.' By the mid 1820s he was himself publicly espousing free trade and the gradual abolition of slavery in the colonies.[13]

All this definitely involved Palmerston in that famous process by which the Liverpool Administration was 'liberalized'. He may not by any means have played an important role; but he was an active supporter. It also built a new bridge to Canning, whose lieutenant, Huskisson, found a place in the Government in 1814 and thereafter guided Liverpool along the road to economic reform. Huskisson also improved his personal relations with Palmerston, dropping the severe hostility with which he had greeted the young man's appointment in 1809. Probably this was one of the first political contributions made by Lady Cowper, for Mrs Huskisson was a cousin of her mother's. So, in January 1816, Palmerston and Huskisson were fellow guests of Lady Melbourne's and two years later Palmerston would be found at a dinner of Huskisson's own, among a galaxy of Canningites. Soon after there was another important connection made by the Lambs when William began to move over towards Canning. But the Huskissons were definitely rated as country cousins and neither Fred nor Emily herself, as yet, by any means approved of Canning. In any case, while it all kept him in contact, none of it made a Canningite of Palmerston.[14]

In the course of 1839 an anonymous critic in the *Quarterly Review* sneered at those 'imitators and self-important men', who, as he not implausibly quoted Canning as saying of Palmerston, 'nearly touched the top of mediocrity'. A generation later, when a publisher sent him the draft of a biographical notice to correct, Palmerston struck from it the assertions that it was Canning who had made him 'a politician in reality and depth' and that within a year of Canning's death he 'aimed at acquiring the reputation of being Mr Canning's successor'. The recollection of personal disappointments at Canning's hand may well have made Palmerston gloss over the way in which he had listed himself among the Canningites in 1828-30. But others had similar reservations. Lady Cowper remarked on Canning's death in August 1827 that her friend was 'quite a late convert'. She went on to say that he was by that time 'completely devoted' to Canning; but the jealous Dudley, as John Ward had by then become, was still anxious even a year later to stress that Palmerston's 'connection' was not only 'far more recent' but also 'far less intimate' than his own. Canning's private secretary also asserted as late as December 1830 that Palmerston had never been one of Canning's personal friends. It seems true at least that between Perceval's death in 1812 and Canning's brief premiership in 1827 Palmerston acknowledged no individual at all as his personal leader.[15]

Such independence was dangerous. Acknowledging fealty to none meant that he was constantly in danger of being sacrificed to the needs and ambitions of others. When Liverpool first endeavoured to form a Government in the summer of 1812 he apparently had Castlereagh offer Palmerston the post of Chief Secretary in Ireland. This was, as Palmerston later explained, 'more important, more active, and more likely to lead to distinction' than the War Office. But what he called 'particular circumstances and considerations' led him to decline. What he meant by this is far from clear. Perhaps it had something to do with his domestic comforts; but it might just as easily have been his so far undisclosed views about the Catholic question. Presumably, at this early stage, Liverpool would not have even made the offer had he known of them. In the end it was Peel who accepted the post and made of it an important stepping-stone in his distinguished career. Palmerston would apparently have fared much worse if Canning, rather than Liverpool, had become his Prime Minister in the summer of 1812. For Canning had had Huskisson in mind for Ireland, and even after his vote for the Catholics Palmerston did not figure in his calculations. Instead, he would even have lost the War Office. Nor was he safe after the immediate crisis had passed, but was often in danger of being made the victim of Liverpool's concessions to Canning. In short, his votes for the Catholics in 1812-13, even in an avowedly 'neutral' ministry, alienated his 'Protestant' colleagues without endearing him to the Canningites.[16]

In July 1813 Canning severed his connection with Lord Wellesley and formally disbanded his party. He returned to the Cabinet as President of the

236 · PALMERSTON: THE EARLY YEARS

India Board in June 1816, and though he went out again in January 1821 over Queen Caroline's trial, it remained part of his arrangement with Liverpool that his friends should have honours, places and promotion. In 1814 and 1815 two of them, Huskisson and Boringdon, had been made First Commissioner of Woods and Forests and Earl of Morley respectively. But neither of them was satisfied, and at one time or another it was proposed to pacify each of them at Palmerston's expense. Huskisson presented the first and more serious danger.[17]

It was always a matter of anxiety to Liverpool that if he could not have Canning as a colleague he should not have him as an enemy. The only really safe alternative to Canning's being in the Cabinet, therefore, was to have him accept a post abroad. In 1814-15 he had taken the embassy in Lisbon; in 1821 he agreed to become Governor-General of India. But Liverpool had no sooner overcome the objections the King made about India in 1821 than Huskisson began to demand Canning's old place at the Board of Control. This Liverpool would not grant, since it was already pledged to Charles Wynn, and Wynn had to be taken care of if Liverpool was not to lose the support of the Grenvilles. But he sent an emissary to Huskisson offering to invite the Irish Secretary to make way for him, or '(tho' very reluctantly) to sound Palmerston whether he would retire upon an English peerage; but with a distinct understanding that if he preferred to remain as he is, the choice was to be left to him'. Huskisson contemptuously refused Ireland and continued to insist that if Wynn were appointed to the Board of Control he himself would be forced to resign. He objected in particular to his name being used in any approach to Palmerston and felt that if the Government were going to make 'an arrangement unpleasant to Palmerston' they should do it on their own responsibility. Nor could he see why they should not offer the War Office to Wynn rather than himself. In any event he was 'not prepared to say offhand, whether, under all the circumstances, his [Palmerston's] office could in any case be acceptable' until he had consulted Canning. 'How little do these Cabinet Peers know of the House of Commons', he wrote to Canning, 'if they suppose such an arrangement as this, parting with P. (who is popular) & taking in C.W. would strengthen the Govt.' Huskisson probably meant that Palmerston was less *unpopular* than Wynn. Canning, in any case, was getting a little bored with the dissatisfactions of his old lieutenant. He saw the Prime Minister, but accepted that nothing could be done about Wynn and concluded that for Huskisson to have the War Office appeared a not 'uncreditable solution'.[18]

Palmerston was out of London at the time visiting Fairburn, but at the end of November he received a very cautious letter from Liverpool on the subject. 'I wish you to answer a question quite fairly, explicitly, and without embarrassment,' the Prime Minister began. 'We are as you probably know, in the course of making some new arrangements as to the government. I need not I hope say how sensible I am, as well all my colleagues, of the value of your services. I would not I can assure [you] make the proposition I am about to state, if I thought you would consider it as any disparagement, or that you would have any difficulty in refusing it, if it was not quite agreeable to you.'

With that 'preface', as he put it, Liverpool then asked if it would suit Palmerston's views to be called to the House of Lords, exchanging the War Office for the Woods and Forests but 'with the expectation of being appointed to the Post Office, or to some other more agreeable situation, when the opportunity may offer'.[19]

It is quite possible that Palmerston was not so utterly averse to an English peerage as has usually been supposed. There had been persistent rumours about his seeking one in 1814 and 1815 and, although he took the opportunity of denying them publicly at St John's, Malmesbury seemed to take them seriously and to have feared that a peerage would be the end of him as 'a man of business'. But in 1821, as Palmerston afterwards explained to his brother, a peerage 'though one might have jumped at it if our Party were likely to be turned out for good yet under all circumstances one feels that it is a thing one might at any time have fair pretensions to whenever one wished it'. Moreover, while the offer of a peerage was 'honorable', the office that went with it was lower than the one he held and 'could not have been accepted with credit'. So he was not at all tempted. He was 'very sensible', his reply to Liverpool appropriately began, 'to the obliging manner & flattering terms' of the Prime Minister's communication, but having for twelve years held 'an important, and I can assure you a very laborious office, in point of rank one among the highest of those which are out of the Cabinet, I have discharged its duties faithfully, and I trust not without some credit both to myself & to the government, and taking into view the relative extent of the duties & responsibility of the two offices now proposed to be exchanged I cannot but feel that under all the circumstances the arrangement in question would be liable to misconstruction'.[20]

In spite of Liverpool's cautious compliments and Huskisson's tedious protestations, it is clear that neither the Administration nor the Canningites considered Palmerston indispensable. The suggestion that Castlereagh was behind the proposal that Palmerston be moved was probably correct; the 'Cabinet Peers' named by Huskisson were Liverpool and Londonderry. When Huskisson had his subsequent interview with the Prime Minister he thought 'his manner was cold & ungracious'; but a month later Liverpool wrote to assure him that he had really been 'most anxious' to prevail upon Palmerston, and as a proof mentioned that he had previously obtained the King's authority to offer him a seat in the Lords. Huskisson later admitted that he would have accepted the War Office if the offer had ever actually come; and Binning, another friend of Canning's, commenting already on Palmerston's reputation for 'immovability', wrote around to say how sorry he was that he could not be budged. 'Palmerston is a very shy cock,' he wrote. 'An old pheasant is not more dexterous in eluding dogs, beaters & guns.'[21]

The Canningites continued in their self-seeking schemes and manoeuvres to view Palmerston, if not as easy game, then still as a possible victim. When Castlereagh's suicide in August 1822 plunged the Liverpool Government into a crisis of reorganization by raising once again the question of Canning's return to the Foreign Office and his pretensions to lead the Commons, Palmerston was still not to be counted among Canning's friends. He was realist enough to accept that Canning must have the Foreign Office, but at the same time he hoped and expected that Canning would not in the end insist on having the lead as well. 'Canning Leader of the Commons', he wrote to Sulivan, 'wd be to Liverpool a difft person from Londonderry. The latter was all good faith & honour & disinterestedness; he never was playing a personal & counter game, never tried to make himself any party separate from Liverpool's & the latter might always be sure that whatever Londonderry reported to him was dictated by the clearest discernment and the most scrupulous good faith; this might not always be the case with Canning.' Not only did Palmerston distrust Canning personally; he thought him the less fit for the lead: '. . . fresh as Peel is to the task no man who has seen him do his work can doubt that in discretion, in personal following, in high mindedness he is superior to Canning & though not so eloquent an orator yet speaks quite up to the situation of Leader.'[22]

After Canning had got both the Foreign Office and the leadership of the Commons Palmerston concluded with his customary realism. 'I think that in spite of all the objections which exist against Canning, he will be an important acquisition to the Government,' he wrote to Clive, '& Peel has behaved in this as he is sure to do in every transaction of his life, in the handsomest possible manner.' So Croker was right, when it was suggested that if Peel were given the lead Canning would retaliate by forming a 'Catholic' Opposition, to dismiss the notion of Palmerston leaving his office to join it as 'ridiculous'. Instead, serious consideration was given by Peel's friends to Palmerston's qualifications for promotion to Colonial Secretary and for command of 'the right wing of the army' as Peel's 'lieutenant-general'. For the 'left wing' Robinson was the man in view, and Croker's famous comparison of his and Palmerston's qualifications is well worth quoting as the opinion of a shrewd and well informed colleague:

As none . . . except Robinson, are looked to even to play second fiddle, many persons have turned their thoughts to Palmerston , who they think as powerful in intellect as Robinson, and much more to be relied on in readiness and nerve. I agree in the latter part of this opinion, but not in the former. . . . I think Palmerston's deficiency is exactly that which we are now considering how to supply – that *flow* of ideas and language which can run on for a couple of hours without, on the one hand, committing the Government, or, on the other, lowering by commonplaces or inanities the station of a Cabinet Minister. No Government, I believe, was ever better manned in the subordinate departments than ours. There are, as Lord Londonderry often said to me, in each office, persons able to repel any assailant on the details of the particular office; and of these Palmerston was the very ablest, but is he fit to be a lieutenant-general, and command the right wing of the army?

But there was no real chance of stopping Canning, and so when he got both the lead and the Foreign Office the essence of the talk about Palmerston again concerned his removal rather than promotion. Once more there were rumours about sending him to the Lords, this time in order to make room at the War Office for Lord William Bentinck. Canning, however, was not very pleased with Bentinck at the time and was preoccupied with a complicated scheme to bring back Huskisson into the Cabinet by ousting the Chancellor of the Exchequer rather than the Secretary at War. So Palmerston survived the rearrangement of the Ministry in 1822. He was still by no means safe from the ambitions of Canning's friends:. when Morley pressed again in July 1826, the idea of a peerage and the Post Office was revived. But by that time, at last, it was beginning to dawn on Canning that Palmerston might after all be of real use where he was.[23]

By the mid 1820s the Catholic question was again threatening to break up the careful balance which Liverpool had hitherto preserved so well. The Prime Minister himself was by that time strongly inclined to accept that there must be concessions; but if anything this, and the growing symptoms of trouble in Ireland, only stiffened the resistance of his more reactionary colleagues and, not least, the King. By the middle of 1825, therefore, Liverpool had become convinced that the crisis could not be averted much longer and that the days of his Administration were numbered. There was in particular the imminent prospect of a General Election in which the cry of 'No Popery' was bound to be raised and by its effect on the individual members determine the fate of his 'mixed' Government. Liberal but 'Protestant', the Prime Minister delayed the confrontation as long as he could, and after the dissolution on 2 June 1826 behaved during the elections with scrupulous fairness. Such at any rate is the verdict of history. But very different opinions were held by some of the participants, ranging from Peel on one side to Palmerston on the other.[24]

The General Election of 1826 was one of the most significant experiences of Palmerston's life. For it threatened him at his most sensitive point and from a side he bitterly resented. This was as Member of Parliament for the University of Cambridge. In spite of his two defeats in 1806 and 1807 Palmerston had continued to keep up his interest in the seat. He was safe at Newport, it was true; but only until the next dissolution. In addition to the prestige offered by the university, therefore, he also had the incentive of avoiding the payment of another £4,000 or so after seven years at most. So he maintained his Cambridge committee in being and, with the deliberate intention of keeping his prospective candidacy in view, returned from time to time not only for winter reunions at St John's, 'playing whist and drinking punch with the fellows', but also for Commencement Weeks. 'Our Ball was pretty good,' he reported to his sister in July 1808. 'The display of female beauty was certainly not great; but there were many *masters of arts*.' There was, moreover, very good reason to think that a by-election could not be far away; Grafton, after all, was in his seventies now. Sure enough, on 14 March 1811, the duke's death took Euston to the House of Lords and vacated a seat at Cambridge. Waiting only long enough to carry through the Army Estimates, Palmerston therefore set off 'instantly' for Cambridge.[25]

By 1811 a more unexpected death had also made Lord Henry Petty Marquess of Lansdowne and removed him from the contest at Cambridge. For similar reasons no Yorke threatened Johnian solidarity either. Royston had gone off once too often on one of his trips and had drowned in a shipwreck in 1808; two years later his only brother and successor – incidentally another tutee of Outram's – had also died. But there were willing substitutes for the prize: Edward Law, the heir to the Lord Chief Justice; Charles Manners-Sutton, the son of the Archbishop of Canterbury and a close relative of the Duke of Rutland; and John Henry Smyth, the new Duke of Grafton's nephew. Law, who was a Johnian, had apparently been scouting Cambridge for some time, but Grafton's death came too soon for him; he was still not twenty-one. Sutton also dropped out, possibly because Grafton's death simultaneously vacated the chancellorship of the university: Rutland very much wanted the office and his relative's running against Palmerston would probably have cost him some support. But this coincidental contest also confused the Yorke interest. As First Lord of the Admiralty, Charles Yorke could hardly have disowned his junior colleague; in any case Palmerston had taken the precaution of cornering him a few days before Grafton's death. But for the chancellorship Hardwicke favoured Rutland's rival the Duke of Gloucester, the nephew of the King but a supporter of the Whigs and of the emancipation of slaves. Several of the family's Cambridge connections were therefore puzzled when they heard from Yorke in favour of Palmerston and from Hardwicke in favour of Gloucester. But they guessed correctly that the earl was not committed on the parliamentary vacancy and so voted to fill that as their political inclinations or college loyalties suggested.[26]

Very rich and very well connected, John Henry Smyth had also a very respectable record as a scholar – he had won three Browne's medals – and was supposed to have considerable Etonian and Trinity support as well as his Whig and family connections. But he had no previous experience of public life and there seems to have been little doubt this time that Palmerston would win. During the past four years both his and Malmesbury's confidence had grown immensely as Palmerston rose in the ranks of the Government and Petty had declined and disappeared. This time, too, Palmerston had all the advantages of Treasury support, without the fatal encumbrance of a contesting colleague. Indeed, Palmerston was worried that his supporters might be too complacent. He heard that the Opposition was spreading the tale that he would win so handsomely that a few of his supporters might care to vote for Smyth as a gesture to a friendly figure. So from the Sun Inn in Cambridge he wrote to Sulivan to have a paragraph inserted in the *Courier* to the effect that the contest would be very close. The canvass again lasted about a fortnight, but seems this time to have been pretty dull. Sedgwick reckoned that it

Thomas Heaphy's portraits of the Temple children painted in 1802; *top left,* Henry; *bottom left,* Elizabeth; *top right,* William; *bottom right,* Frances.

Drawn, Etch'd & Pub.ª May. 1809. by Dighton Chaª Cross

A VIEW from Sᵗ IOHN'S COLLEGE CAMBRIDGE.

Opposite page top,
Professor Dugald Stewart

Opposite page bottom,
First Earl of Malmesbury

Left, James Wood (tutor at
St John's, Cambridge),
by Dighton

Below left, Lord Clive,
from the Grillion's Club
series

Right, Marquess of
Lansdowne

Duke of York

Laurence Sulivan (aged sixteen),
by Raeburn

The Horse Guards, Whitehall

Above, Sir David Dundas, by Gillray

Palmerston, by Sir Thomas Lawrence, *c.* 1810-20

Emily Lamb, by Sir Thomas Lawrence, *c.* 1804

Panshanger

Left, Lord Francis Conyngham

Below, Earl of Clanwilliam, miniature by G. Ralph Ward (after Lawrence)

Bottom, Lord Howden (formerly John Cradock), by Aubert, 1860

Above left, Lord Robert
Grosvenor (afterwards
Baron Ebury), from the
Grillion's Club series

Above right, Frederick
'Poodle' Byng, by Alfred
d'Orsay

Charles Greville, by Alfred d'Orsay

aroused little interest outside St John's (where the undergraduates were turned out of their rooms to make way for the non-resident M.A.s); and perhaps it was enlivened only by the contest for Chancellor with Rutland 'parading through the colleges . . . with a tremendous cocked hat'. The poll was held on 28 March, which some of the Opposition thought had been specially selected as the most inconvenient possible for the many lawyers on their side, even allowing for the opportunities of making pairs in London and on circuit. Whatever the reason Palmerston was a comfortable winner by 451 to 345; Smyth got more votes only from Trinity and Christ's.[27]

Such was the supposed loyalty of the university that for some years Palmerston seemed very securely established there. After the dissolutions of September 1812, June 1818 and March 1820 he was on each occasion returned unopposed. In large part this was because Smyth had gained the other seat on Gibbs's appointment to the Bench in 1812; it was thought unwise to flaunt the supposed traditions of the university and, by one side or one college trying to capture both seats, to risk losing the other as well. So only upon the rumours of Palmerston's imminent translation to the House of Lords did would-be successors like Hobhouse or Charles Grant really bestir themselves. Similarly, on Smyth's death in 1822, when there was an unseemly scramble for the succession, Grey's son asserted that still 'the character of the University requires that one of its members should be a Whig'. But the victor was William John Bankes, a Tory and a 'Protestant'. It appeared to Goulburn that what was happening was that the delicate balance of one Tory and one Whig member was being replaced by one 'Protestant' and one 'Catholic'. But so large was Bankes's majority that Colchester reported it to be 'the common talk of London since the election . . . that Lord P[almerston] must look out for some other seat in one of the two Houses of Parliament at the period of the next General Election'. Already, then, some were beginning to think that both seats could be captured for the 'Protestants'.[28]

Palmerston confessed that he was surprised by Bankes's success, and agreed that Protestantism must be 'very rife' at Cambridge. But he professed not to be in the least afraid of a General Election. He simply could not believe that people who had supported him year after year, knowing his views on the Catholic question, would suddenly turn against him. It was also generally agreed that the main strength of the 'Protestants' lay among the non-resident voters and these, though by far the majority, were naturally much more difficult to turn out on polling day. So when he made his usual Christmas visit in 1822 he still concluded: 'Protestantism is abroad certainly, but I am under no apprehensions as to its results; Bankes is here still, feasting with his constituents – my friends however remain apparently unchanged.'[29]

In taking such a calm and sanguine view Palmerston was neither entirely wrong nor utterly rash. James Wood warned him the following year that if he must vote for Catholic Emancipation in the Commons, then he should at least desist from speaking on it. He seems to have heeded the warning; there is no record in *Hansard* of his speaking in the debates of 17 April 1823, 12 May 1824 and 10 May 1825. For the same reason, as he frankly admitted in one case, he also refused to sign petitions on behalf of the Catholic cause; his previous House of Commons vote, he said, was a sufficient record of his view. It was inevitable that he would nevertheless lose the support of people like Milner, who before his death in 1820 had been busy organizing anti-Catholic addresses from the university. Nor was it necessarily disastrous for him that in October 1825 the Whigs 'were, even at Trinity, fast declining into a minority – and the anti-liberals particularly among the juniors getting uppermost'. The Whigs, after all, were still supposed to be his enemies. But what was very damaging indeed was that he should not have the undivided support of his friends in Government.[30]

In spite of what had happened at the by-election of 1822, Palmerston had good reason to expect better treatment than he got in 1825-6. For in September 1825 the Cabinet had agreed to postpone the dissolution until June the following year so as to afford time for the fury among them over the Catholic question to abate. Palmerston was on the way back from Ireland when he heard the news from Peel, 'which rejoiced me greatly by substituting the prospect of killing some partridges for that of canvassing electors'. He did manage to get in two shooting parties, at Broadlands and at Stratfield Saye. But it was nonetheless very annoying for him to discover early in December that two contenders for Cambridge had already opened their canvass and, moreover, that not one but both of them were colleagues of his in Government.[31]

One candidate was Palmerston's old friend Goulburn, now Irish Secretary, and the other Copley, the Attorney-General. Both of them, moreover, were Trinity men like Bankes. Independent observers (like Colchester) suspected that the only explanation must be that Palmerston was to be given a peerage and Bankes to be abandoned by the Government. Bankes, after all, had since his election eloped with Lady Buckinghamshire and, by a quirk of irony on the part of the aggrieved husband, found himself facing as prosecuting counsel on a charge of crim. con. (criminal conversation, i.e. adultery) his former Cambridge antagonist, James Scarlett. Palmerston professed at first to think that after all the comforts of the last decade or so, it was 'rather a bore to have to go through the labour of a canvass so long before the time', but that it had at least come at a time when he had some leisure to attend to it and he would not be sorry to get it out of the way. Evidently it did not really occur to him at first that it was his seat his colleagues were after. Rather he expected to have both 'Catholic' and Whig support entirely to himself, if no Opposition candidate came forward; while Goulburn, Copley and Bankes, being all in competition for the same support in respect of 'college, politics and Protestantism', must in the end agree on only one of them going to a poll.[32]

As it turned out in the course of the canvass Palmerston was justified in his first assumption, but in part perhaps because he was wrong about the second. Such was the fierceness of the 'Protestant' attack upon him that it united the Whigs in his defence. 'Strange things come to pass,' wrote Sedgwick towards the end of December. 'I am now in the Committee room of a Johnian, a Tory, and a King's Minister; and I am going to give him a plumper. My motives are that he is our old Member, and a distinguished Member, and that I hate the other candidates. . . . Bankes is a fool, and was brought in last time by a set of old women . . . Copley is a clever fellow, but is not sincere, at least when I pass him I am sure I smell a rat. Goulburn is the idol of the Saints, a prime favourite of Simeon's, and a subscriber to missionary societies. Moreover he squints.'[33]

For the first time, then, Palmerston found himself favoured by Brougham as well as by Lord John Russell and all of Holland and Devonshire Houses. Nor was he utterly deserted by all his 'Protestant' friends. Shee, of course, promised his allegiance, as well as a couple of other old Johnian fellow-commoners. Peel too, though he did not have a Cambridge vote, very decently divided his sympathy equally among his friends and colleagues, Goulburn and Palmerston. Goulburn was certainly a closer friend than Palmerston, but Peel was inclined to think that Palmerston's years of service put the other members of the Government under some obligation to him; and this feeling became stronger still when he was informed that instead of being 'neutral', as it was supposed to be where the Catholic question was involved, the Treasury was lending its weight against Palmerston. He heard this directly from the Duke of York, who told him shortly before 24 November that Herries, who was now Financial Secretary, had 'pressed [him] to do every thing in his power for the Attorney General'. At first Peel could only express his surprise, but after presumably making some enquiries he tackled the duke again on Christmas Day and subsequently wrote to his secretary to impress upon him that Herries's declaration was 'wholly unauthorized'. 'The Government takes no part,' he wrote, but 'is neutral, all the candidates being friends.' Since the duke's interference was likely to be as dangerous to his friend Goulburn as to Palmerston, Peel could hardly have done less. But as the duke persisted in his course, Peel was said to have tackled him again at a dinner party shortly afterwards: 'P. had the spirit to say that he thought Palmerston ought to be returned, notwithstanding his supporting the Catholics, for that the U. knew that he *would* support them when they elected him before, and had repeatedly elected him with that knowledge, and that he had done nothing to forfeit their good opinion in any other respect. The Duke said with infinite grace and unction, "No! no! I would have *a damned good Protestant!*" '[34]

The duke was an outspoken 'Protestant' and by his speeches in the Lords had done a good deal to provoke the 1825 crisis over Catholic Emancipation. As the close ally of his brother the King and the very special friend of the late Duchess of Rutland, moreover, it was expected that he would exercise a considerable influence at Cambridge. In view of the personal as well as political hostility between them, Palmerston could hardly have been surprised when before the end of the year he heard of the duke's intervention. It happened, in fact, to coincide with one of those periodic passages at arms between Horse Guards and War Office. But what did deeply shock and offend him was the behaviour of the Prime Minister. 'I am inclined to suspect that my friend the D. of York was the prime instigator of the Atty Genl,' he concluded at the end of December, '& if this is so it accounts in some degree for Liverpool's shabbiness though it only makes his conduct the more shabby.'[35]

It was not any unproved partiality on Liverpool's part, but his declaration of neutrality, to which Palmerston objected. Whether or not he knew that Herries had prompted the duke, Palmerston had discovered the Undersecretary at the Foreign Office, Planta, franking Copley's Cambridge letters. Canning had smoothed that affair over, assuring Palmerston that while he had no influence at Cambridge he would, 'on Oxford principles', have been in favour of the sitting member even had he not been Palmerston, and offering compensation by way of an equal number of franks. The offer of franks came too late, but Palmerston seems to have been mollified by it. He was much less pleased, however, with the responses he got when he applied for help from some other senior colleagues. The Prime Minister told him that although his wishes were for the sitting member, he intended to take no part in the contest; the Lord Chancellor that while his personal and his official 'respect' inclined him towards Palmerston, the 'claims' of the others and 'an untimely difference of opinion about the Catholic Question would be puzzling'.[36]

Lady Cowper was worried about the votes of Cambridge curates who had their eyes on the choice preferments in the Chancellor's gift. But Palmerston told Sulivan that he had only written to Eldon, a notorious High Tory, 'as a bit of fun' and that his reply was 'just what I expected & an amusing specimen of his hypocritical humbug'. He seems to have been much more annoyed by the one that he received from the Colonial Secretary. Palmerston ought perhaps to have known better than to write for support to an extreme Protestant like Bathurst, but he somehow found the reply peculiarly offensive. Probably he thought it doubly hypocritical of Bathurst to withhold his support from one colleague on account of an 'intimate official connection' with another, Goulburn, while at the same time assuring Palmerston that 'the University would reflect little credit on themselves, if they were to reject one who has so long served them with general good acceptance, because he has temperately supported a Question which their favourite member, Mr Pitt, originally introduced'. In reply Palmerston was as acid as he alone could be: 'It certainly appears somewhat an unusual case in the reciprocal relation of the members of a political party that an official man should find himself endangered in a seat which he has held for fourteen years, by the undisguised competition of two of his colleagues in office.'[37]

Peel advised Bathurst that Palmerston must have been 'in a pet' to write such a letter; and Bathurst wrote to assure Palmerston that he was not opposed to his re-election but on the contrary felt 'a sentiment of a very different description'. But by now Palmerston was completely convinced that there was 'an underhand Protestant Cabal' against him. That conclusion removed any reluctance he might have had to making a formal connection with the Whigs, such as having them on his committee. It also led him in January 1826 to write an extraordinary letter of protest to the Prime Minister. 'I think I should not be doing justice to myself nor acting candidly towards you,' he began, 'if I were not to state to you frankly and explicitly the extreme embarrassment of the situation in which I am placed by the contest now carrying on for the University of Cambridge; a situation so extraordinary that I can scarcely imagine that any official man could ever before have stood in similar circumstances.' He then proceeded, at some length, carefully to state his objections to what he considered to have been his colleagues' breach of neutrality on the Catholic question, to their being allowed to 'disturb' a sitting member, and to the lack of Government support even after all this. He mentioned 'the most cordial kindness' he had received from Peel and also the Duke of Wellington, but he questioned what was to be the future basis of the Administration and pointed out that he had been forced in self-defence to rely on the Whigs. In view of Liverpool's desperate anxiety for relief from the quarrels between 'Catholics' and 'Protestants', as well as from the burdens of office altogether, there was little that he could say in reply about the Catholic question. But he did imply that he *had* made 'an explicit declaration' that sitting members ought not to be disturbed and that in view of his personal relationship to some of the candidates it was not fair to expect any more of him. This was a reference to his behaviour in 1822 when he had openly supported the unsuccessful candidate, Lord Hervey, who, though a 'Catholic' and a Whig, was nonetheless his nephew. In the 1826 election two of the candidates, Goulburn and Bankes, were also relations. In any case, he observed, 'the elections for the University have always been considered as standing on distinct grounds from any other elections. They are contests for personal distinction.' Palmerston was certainly not satisfied with this, but he was probably too busy fighting for his life at Cambridge to carry on another battle.[38]

Palmerston's friends and relations all thought it was very hard upon him that he should in any case have to begin his canvass six months before the General Election; it had all hung upon him 'like a nightmare', he admitted as the end of the campaign drew near. But the first few weeks seem to have been the worst. In late December and early January his mood swung back and forth almost daily. On 22 December he was already feeling 'much uneasiness'; the next day he wrote that he expected to 'do well'. It was the 'rural reverends' whom he feared most. He remained convinced that he was strong both among the resident voters and with the lawyers in London, but that if the country clergy were now to 'come up in mass against me, their charge will be as formidable as that of the Black Hussars'. A few days later, however, he thought the 'Popery Panic' was dying away and that he was 'going on well but very *piano*'. At the beginning of February some of his closest friends thought him still 'upon very ticklish ground', and indeed the likely loser. But most seem to have thought that he and Copley were the favourites. Palmerston himself certainly thought so. But this made it vitally important to keep in well with the Attorney-General and his supporters. When Sulivan was unwise enough to canvass a vote against him this brought a letter of mild reproof. Palmerston would have liked to send a strong rebuttal but in the circumstances could only pen an anodyne response about Copley being 'a fair and courteous opponent'. Copley, perhaps, accepted the circumlocution at face value, as did his biographer later. Certainly, Palmerston was able to go on counting the number of votes promised to him and the Attorney-General. There was always the danger that Bankes, trailing last, might pull out and turn over all his votes to Goulburn, but a bright young Whig from Trinity, Thomas Macaulay, wrote round anonymously about Goulburn's family estates in the West Indies, and the doubts there were about his views on slavery, and so raised Bankes's hopes at Goulburn's expense.[39]

This was still the situation when Palmerston arrived in Cambridge for the last days of the canvass very early in the morning of Monday, 12 June. He found that Bankes had been writing 'some violent letter' demanding a comparison of strength with Goulburn and that this had been rejected 'of course'. That, Palmerston thought, was all grist to the mill; for there was a feeling in the university that Bankes's behaviour had been 'ungentlemanlike & unfair'. In the meantime Palmerston, in more businesslike a manner, 'stuck up in the old committee room a board with the rates to be paid for horses, places, etc'.[40]

It was still the custom, as it had been when Palmerston first contested the seat in 1806, for the candidates to pay the travelling expenses of their non-resident voters. These do not appear to have been large, when compared with the sums paid in other places, but at the last election – in which Palmerston had played no part – it was reckoned that the candidates had been swindled into paying 'a vast sum'. This probably had something to do with the poll no longer being confined to a single day and an extravagant competition being resorted to in order to bring up voters on the last day. This time, apparently, it threatened to be even worse, as the poll was to extend over three or four days. But Bankes rejected any economical arrangement being made between the committees as a 'trick' that would have reduced the number of the predominantly anti-Catholic country clergy he could hope to bring up to the vote. Subsequently some members of the Senate, including supporters of Palmerston's, insisted on the bribery oath being administered to each voter as he approached the Vice-Chancellor's table. This may or may not have kept the expenses down; Palmerston reckoned the total cost to him this time at a little over £700. But he also reported that it provoked 'the greatest indignation' among the fastidious dons when the poll opened on Tuesday, 13 June; 'at last when dinner had rouzed minds to more than morning calmness', there was 'a scene' and after 'a tumultuous debate' the insulting practice was abandoned.[41]

At the close of the first day's poll, Palmerston lay as expected in second place, but eighty votes behind Copley, only thirty-six ahead of Goulburn and a mere seventeen in front of Bankes. He remained confident, however, that he would win. The next day Sulivan and Shee left the committee in London in the hands of Palmerston's other brother-in-law, Captain Bowles, and his friends, Michael Bruce and Henry Elliot, and brought a number of supporters down to the poll. But during the Wednesday Bankes managed at one time to get ahead of Palmerston by four votes and spoke confidently of beating him 'easily' the next day. Hobhouse, who now found himself in the curious situation of supporting Palmerston on Catholic Emancipation at Cambridge even as he continued to attack him on flogging in the House of Commons, knew better, however, about Bankes. 'He is exactly the same rattling grinning fellow as ever and he talked at the hall table today the same sort of nonsense as he used when a pupil at College.' The fact was that many of Goulburn's supporters, as well as the Whigs, preferred Palmerston to Bankes, and by the close of the poll that night Palmerston was ahead of him by thirty-five. Since Palmerston had been holding his supporters back so that they might make arrangements to split votes with Copley or Goulburn, Wednesday's poll made him 'pretty sure' of victory; and, indeed, when he let his voters loose the following day he ended about ninety-nine ahead of Bankes. Bankes still insisted on extending the poll to a fourth day, but he only worsened his case: the final figures were 772 for Copley, 631 for Palmerston, 508 for Bankes and 437 for Goulburn. 'So much for No Popery,' Hobhouse noted with quiet satisfaction.[42]

'Palmerston's was a glorious victory at Cambridge,' wrote Canning's Political Undersecretary, 'where by the way they characterized their four candidates . . . as Profligacy [Palmerston], Knavery [Copley], Bigotry [Goulburn], & Buffoonery [Bankes].' The 'grand point', as Palmerston rather overoptimistically put it, was that the cry of No Popery had 'everywhere failed; and we may now appeal to the experience of facts to show that there does *not* exist among the people of England that bigoted prejudice on this point which the anti-Catholics accused them of entertaining'. He also reckoned that his own success was personally 'most gratifying, and beyond my expectations'; it made him in particular feel 'pretty secure as to the future'. On the other hand, as he recalled some years later, the Government's behaviour during the election campaign marked in his opinion 'the first decided step towards a breach between me and the Tories, and they were the aggressors'.[43]

It was a bound rather than a step the Tories had made. There was no question of Palmerston concluding with the Bankes family that the Government must have set up Goulburn in order to return Palmerston over the other sitting member. 'Liverpool', Palmerston remained convinced, 'has acted as he always does to a friend in personal questions – shabbily, timidly, and ill.' He had in fact written to the Prime Minister a fortnight before the poll to say that in the event of his being defeated 'it could not be expected that I should continue my connection with a Government under which such a result would have been so brought about'. He wrote before the outcome was known, he explained, in order to give the Prime Minister time in which to make his arrangements and so that he should not 'ascribe to any momentary impulse of disappointment that which in fact has been a determination long since taken'. Liverpool wrote what Palmerston admitted was a 'civil answer', saying that it would be 'painful' for him to enter into such a matter then and begging in the event of Palmerston being defeated to have 'a full communication' with him before he took any 'decisive step'.[44]

Although, as it had after all turned out, Palmerston had kept his seat at Cambridge, it was probably in the aftermath of the election that Peel offered him on Liverpool's behalf the governorship of Madras or Bombay, with the promise of India later. In November the offer of India was renewed directly by the Board of Control. India was a real prize, thought fit in 1822 even as a consolation for Canning, had not Castlereagh's death provided better room at home. But Palmerston replied that he had 'no fancy for such latitudes'. Neither good fortune at the hustings nor dazzling bribes from the Prime Minister could therefore repair the breach with the High Tories. As he said at the time, he felt 'like Caspar in the Fr[e]i[s]chutz Story, quite afraid L[or]d Grey should come with his long arm, & claim him as his own'. However, though very grateful to his Whig supporters at Cambridge, he still looked for colleagues, as he explained to his brother, on the liberal wing of his own party:

I am delighted to see this insurrection of the serfs. As to the commonplace balance between Opposition and Government, the election will have little effect upon it. The Government are as strong as any Government can wish to be, as far as regards those who sit facing them; but in truth the real opposition of the present day sit behind the Treasury Bench; and it is by the stupid old Tory party, who bawl out the memory and praises of Pitt while they are opposing all the measures and principles which he held most important; it is by these that the progress of the Government in every improvement which they are attempting is thwarted and impeded. On the Catholic question; on the principles of commerce; on the corn laws; on the settlement of the currency; on the laws regulating the trade in money; on colonial slavery; on the game laws, which are intimately connected with the moral habits of the people; on all these questions, and everything like them, the Government find support from the Whigs and resistance from their self-denominated friends. However, the young squires are more liberal than the old ones, and we must hope that Heaven will protect us from our friends, as it has done from our enemies. The next session will be interesting.[45]

The session of 1826-7 was to prove more 'interesting' than Palmerston could ever have imagined. Three years earlier he had made his first peacetime speech on foreign affairs in defence of Canning's acquiescence in the French invasion of Spain. It was not undistinguished in either its phrases or its sentiments. So far as useless threats were concerned, he said, 'to have talked of war, and to have meant neutrality, to have threatened an army and to have retreated behind a state paper, to have brandished the sword of defiance in the hour of deliberation and to have ended with a penful of protests on the day of battle, would have been the conduct of a cowardly bully, and would have made us the object of contempt and the laughing-stock of Europe'; and as for delivering 'dissertations on principles' in the form of diplomatic lectures, 'of what use is it to dwell upon abstract principles with those who are accused of measuring right by power and of ruling their conduct by expediency and not by justice?'[46]

An earlier biographer has described this performance as 'rather perfunctory'. But if that were so the same most certainly could not be said of Palmerston's private reaction to the great speech that Canning made on 12 December 1826, when the Foreign Secretary had to explain why after disdaining to intervene in Spain in 1823 he had just ordered British troops to embark for Portugal. In 1823, Canning thundered in reply, 'I called the New World into existence to redress the balance of the Old'; in 1826, 'We go to Portugal . . . to defend and preserve the independence of an Ally. We go to plant the Standard of England on the well-known heights of Lisbon. Where that Standard is planted, foreign dominion shall not come!' This time Palmerston wrote to his brother: 'I confess I heard that speech with peculiar delight; it is most gratifying to hear avowed by the ministers of the country as the guide of their conduct those principles one feels & knows to be true . . . The principles of constitutional freedom are not only the elements of strength to the country which carries them into practice, but the best guarantee of peace to neighbouring nations & it is much for our interest therefore to favour their extension on the Continent.' His preference, then as later, was for the avoidance of 'convulsions' by gradual concessions. 'But the system of Metternich cannot last, and even the empire from which it springs will sooner or later infallibly see it crumble.'[47]

Canning made his great speech of 1826 shortly after returning from an important trip to Paris. Palmerston himself had just returned from another visit to Ireland and here too he registered a small but interesting change of attitude. Ten years earlier he had written to Peel, then Irish Secretary, offering, if it should help in a forthcoming election campaign in County Sligo, to create nearly three hundred voters by granting leases to tenants at will on his estates. Now he wrote to another friend: 'The anti-Catholics are monstrously angry at the successful organization of the 40s voters by the Priests at which I from the bottom of my heart rejoice; it is a great point for us who wish to carry Emancipation, & I hope will sicken landlords of that system of management which they have hitherto pursued, & lead them to try to make their estates produce turnips instead of freeholders by consolidating instead of splitting holdings.' And as for the anti-Catholics among his colleagues, he wrote to William Temple, 'I can forgive old women like the Chancellor, spoonies like Liverpool, ignoramuses like Westmoreland, old stumped-up Tories like Bathurst; but how such a man as Peel, liberal, enlightened, and fresh minded, should find himself running in such a pack is hardly intelligible.' [48]

On 6 March 1827 the Commons again divided after a long debate on the Catholic question and rejected emancipation by a mere four votes. This was a set-back for the 'Catholics', who had passed a similar motion through the Commons two years before, and a harsh corrective to Palmerston's optimistic view of the last elections. But by this time major changes of another kind were already in train, which were drastically to alter the direction of events and with them Palmerston's own fate. The Duke of York had died on 5 January and been replaced at the head of the Army by Wellington. In February Liverpool suffered a paralytic stroke and provoked a long struggle over the succession. At last, on 10 April, Canning replaced him as Prime Minister and four days later, the anti-Catholics including Peel having refused to serve, Palmerston was promised either the Exchequer or the Home Office in the new Cabinet.

Canning's offer was no bolt from the blue. Soon after Palmerston's first speech on foreign affairs Canning was already going out of his way to help Willy Temple up the diplomatic ladder, and Palmerston, who had never got anything for Campbell out of Liverpool, was no doubt duly grateful. By the beginning of 1824 mutual friends were also trying to bring them together socially and by the time of the Cambridge election campaign of 1825-6 Palmerston was clearly on very close terms personally with several Canning-ites; to one of them he pointedly remarked that Liverpool's language to him was, he was 'very sure, not what Canning would use in the same situation'.[49]

Palmerston's success at Cambridge was probably what brought him close at last to Canning, just as it separated him from the High Tories. For the election was hardly over than the news came of the death of Palmerston's old guardian, the Earl of Chichester, and with the vacancy which this created in the Post Office the old scheme to find a place for one of Canning's friends by removing Palmerston from the War Office and to the Lords was revived. Morley, however, was the least able and most disliked of Canning's friends; and neither Canning nor Liverpool was anxious to add to the criticism with which other promotions had recently been greeted. Canning's notion, there-fore, was to obscure Morley's appointment in a general rearrangement. This had the additional advantage, in Canning's view, of providing a means of strengthening the debating power of the front benches in Parliament; and in two out of his three alternative proposals it was Palmerston whom Canning had in mind to do it. One of these proposals was the old idea of giving Palmerston the Post Office with a peerage. But Canning added: 'P. could – & it must be a condition of the peerage that he *should* – give you that effective aid in the H. of Lords, which you have so long wanted.' Better evidence could hardly be provided of how unaware Canning still was of Palmerston's real desires. Liverpool indeed might have been inclined, in view of Palmerston's poor reputation as a speaker, to doubt Canning's sincerity, had it not been for the alternative he proposed – to give the peerage and the Post Office to Robinson and put Palmerston in Robinson's place at the Exchequer. 'I am quite contented with the present position of things on the Treasury Bench in the H. of C.,' Canning said. 'But the removal of Robinson would totally change my position, by totally destroying all balance [on the Catholic question] unless Palmerston were Robinson's successor; – & with an understanding not only that he is to do Robinson's *departmental* business (which he would do of course, & as well, I dare say, as he now does that of the War Office) but that he is to fill, in all respects, Robinson's place. His (Palmerston's) only fault is a habit of non-attendance on ordinary occasions, a fault wholly inconsistent with the *existence* of a Chanr of the Exchequer.'[50]

Canning may not have been quite close enough to Palmerston, even in the summer of 1826, to know his inner thoughts; but at least he had by that time become familiar enough with him to recognize something of his real utility if not his whole potential. Nothing, however, came of any of the schemes, because Canning, when faced with Liverpool's dithering, undertook to bear the responsibility for breaking his promise to Morley. It may nonetheless have been on this occasion that Liverpool sent Charles Long to sound out Palmerston again; a rumour about the Post Office certainly reached Bankes, who at once began a new canvass at Cambridge in the expectation that either of the sitting members might go to the Lords.[51]

That Canning's relations with Palmerston were thought to be changing considerably for the better was probably marked most by his receiving his first ever invitation to Panshanger in September 1826. After all, it was years since Emily's brother had moved over to his side, and hardly less since both the King and Princess Lieven had discovered how attached to him they really were. Even Fred was startled; 'it came very naturally,' Emily assured him, 'not at all impertinent but quite proper and correct.' But that Canning's attitude to Palmerston, though definitely changing, was still very uncertain was illustrated even more clearly when Liverpool quit the stage in the spring of 1827. For a time Palmerston appeared as a key figure in the arrangements by which the 'Protestants' hoped to continue in the Ministry with or without Canning. Croker discussed with Wellington the possibility of giving the Foreign Office either to Robinson or to Palmerston as the nearest means of preserving the status quo under Canning. Palmerston, he thought this time, 'would be a better Secretary of State', but if necessary would probably consent to give way to Robinson's claim of seniority. Sidmouth had a similar notion of one or other of them going to the Lords as Secretary of State under the anti-Catholic Bathurst. But every attempt either to constrain or to avoid Canning failed, and on 10 April he was commissioned to form an Administration of his own.[52]

It could hardly have been a surprise for Palmerston, however, when four days later, on 14 April, he received a request to call on Canning at four or four-thirty that afternoon. The Prime Minister, he was told when he arrived in Downing St, would prefer him to have the Home Office, but if, as the King wished, a 'Protestant' could be induced to take it, then Palmerston should have the Exchequer, in order, as in 1809, to relieve the First Lord of some of his burden in the Commons. It was some little time before Sturges Bourne could be persuaded to take the Home Office, but Palmerston seems to have assumed all the while that he would himself have the Exchequer. Nor was there this time any sign of hesitation on his part. After mastering the intricacies of the War Office he was now convinced, as he said a couple of years later, that there was 'no great mystery in it; nor in any other place'. It was decided, however, that his transfer should not be announced yet but postponed until after the end of the session, so that he should not again be mixed up in a two-seat election campaign at Cambridge. For not only would Palmerston have to seek re-election on taking a new office of profit under the Crown; Goulburn had decided to try again for the other seat now being vacated by Copley's translation to the upper house as Canning's Lord Chancellor. It was quite understandable that Palmerston should wish to avoid anything resembling the trouble and annoyance of the previous year. The delay, moreover, did not affect his entry into the Cabinet – a move, as Sir Charles Webster emphasized, of great importance to an ambitious politician. But it did prove fatal to his expectation of getting the Exchequer.[33]

It is not entirely clear when or why Canning told Palmerston that he had changed his mind about the Exchequer. The occasion was very probably a fifteen minutes' talk to which Palmerston had been summoned before the three o'clock meeting of the Cabinet on 11 June, since the next day he told a colleague that Canning had decided after all to continue as Chancellor while Palmerston would remain Secretary at War for an 'indefinite period'. A possible explanation for the change was that it had something to do with the failure of Canning's attempts to persuade Wellington to return to the Horse Guards. Palmerston later recalled that the matter had been discussed at their meeting and this seems completely borne out by the letter which he sent to Canning a few days later. It would also be consistent with a natural desire not to revive the court's designs on the command of the Army by upsetting the arrangement by which Sir Herbert Taylor had agreed to serve as Palmerston's nominal deputy.[34]

Another possible explanation, favoured by some historians, is that the change was merely one of several made necessary by the belated success of Canning's negotiations with the Lansdowne Whigs. Canning badly needed to strengthen the position of his Government in Parliament, but the divisions among the Whig leaders and the determination of the King to preserve the neutrality of the Government on the Catholic question had constantly frustrated him. By the end of May, however, the King had given up his resistance over the Home Office and agreement had been reached for Lansdowne and some of his friends to join the Ministry. So, just as the exodus of the High Tories had made room for Palmerston's promotion in April, the entry of the Whigs in May filled it up again. But no evidence has been found to establish such a connection. In any case, why should Palmerston have been made the victim rather than Dudley? After all, the original idea was that Dudley should have the Foreign Office only until the way had been cleared for Canning to recover it by the transfer of the Exchequer to Palmerston.[55]

Since Dudley continued to be a reluctant incumbent of the Foreign Office, it would surely be reasonable to suppose that Canning's explanation to Palmerston was the true one: 'it had been strongly pressed upon him by all the financial department that it was extremely important that the First Lord should also be Chancellor of the Exchequer.' Palmerston himself certainly thought so when he wrote about the matter to Sulivan a few weeks later. Given, too, that Canning was breaking his promise to Palmerston, such an explanation would still be compatible with the embarrassment Canning was supposed to have displayed and his relief when Palmerston took it so well. But that there was worse to come soon became apparent at either the same meeting or another shortly after, when Canning offered to make him Governor of Jamaica. Canning's intention, he explained, was to make him a peer and do anything 'practicable' which might be 'agreeable' to him when the appointment of a Commander-in-Chief reduced the duties of the Secretary at War to their former, humbler kind. But Palmerston laughed so much that he thought he had rather disconcerted the Prime Minister; not so much, though, as to deter Canning shortly afterwards from offering India again. This time Palmerston evidently refused more politely, mentioning his previous refusals and pleading, however extraordinary it might seem, the inability of his health to stand the climate.[56]

Mrs Arbuthnot, whose husband had found out about the offer of Jamaica, was certain that Canning was anxious to get rid of Palmerston and give his office to Sir George Murray. Since she had been converted from a devoted supporter to bitter enemy almost overnight by Palmerston's recent consorting with radicals, it is not surprising that she should delight at the prospect of his going. As Palmerston had very recently voted against the majority of his colleagues and in favour of the disfranchisement of a corrupt borough, perhaps he had upset Canning too. But Penryn was not supposed to be a ministerial question and others who voted with him survived unscathed. The fact that Canning was now willing and even anxious to see Palmerston leave the Ministry must therefore mean that the explanations so far suggested are at best incomplete. One other, produced by an earlier biographer and recently repeated, was the revelation of Palmerston's dealings on the stock market.[57]

The assets Palmerston had inherited from his father were by no means inconsiderable.[58] There were fine houses in Hanover Square, Sheen and Broadlands, large estates in Dublin, Sligo, Hampshire and Yorkshire, and a considerable amount of stock. Unfortunately there was not enough stock to cover all the liabilities from outstanding loans and legacies. When in 1811 the executors prepared to wind up their charge on the coming of age of the youngest child, Lilly, it was estimated that there would be a deficiency of about £28,000. The total amount of cash and stock in their hands was valued at £43,000; but, while Campbell's legacy of £10,000 had long ago been paid, there were still outstanding the mortgage of £10,000 on Broadlands, other small debts amounting to £1,200, and legacies of £20,000 to each of the younger children. Fortunately none of the children seems to have had any need of all his capital and so each took rather less than half and left the rest (£10,200 in each case) as a mortgage on Palmerston's Irish estates. This allowed the mortgage on Broadlands and the smaller debts to be paid off, but at the same time encumbered Palmerston with the much larger debt of over £30,000. To service this at 5 per cent cost £1,500.

In addition to all this there was a long list of annuities and voluntary allowances to be provided for. There was a total of about £200 a year, reducing to about £50 by 1830, to old servants in Broadlands and London, including even Ben Mee's former nurse and housekeeper. There was the £200 for the Ravizzottis until the mid 1840s; and another £300 to Mrs Campbell which Palmerston voluntarily transferred after her death to Henry Campbell until he should obtain a living. In June 1813 he bound himself to pay £300 a year to Emma Godfrey and a few years later he was also paying Emma Murray an annual allowance of £300. Finally, on her marriage in August 1820, he made Fanny Bowles an allowance of £500 a year. So by the early 1820s these charges amounted to another £1,800.

Then there were Palmerston's general expenses. In London it took a while to establish a permanent home after Lady Palmerston's death. The house in Hanover Square was expensive to run and unsuitable for the needs of a family of orphans and so it was let. On the other hand, until it was known whether or not William would find a career in London, it was pointless to make any long-term arrangements. So for the first few years Palmerston lived a rather hand to mouth existence, taking bachelor quarters in Dorant's Hotel, in the Albany or with Malmesbury's widowed sister during the working year, but renting a larger house for short periods when his brother and sisters came up for the season. But it was never very easy to find satisfactory family quarters. He would find 'a nice house' in Manchester Square, but reluctantly reject it as 'sadly out of the way'. Another would be too small: 'the want of a fourth bedroom is the universal defect.' So he would have to compromise on a house in Lower Brook St, which, though the furniture was not very new or clean, was very roomy and very well situated for the '*young ladies*'. Another time he would hardly have settled in a friend's house in Lower Grosvenor St than the owner would return from his travels to claim it back. But in May 1811 Palmerston bought a lease on a house (No. 12) in Stanhope St for £1,200; two years later he transferred this lease to his friend and colleague Peel and acquired another,

No. 9, further along the street, for 39½ years from 25 March 1813. The cost of the new lease was £8,000 and he seems to have found it out of capital.[59]

When his father's executors finished their work in November 1811, Palmerston already had stock in his own name to the value of £18,172. Almost certainly this included the proceeds of the sale of the house and estate in Sheen. Temple Grove had been the home of Palmerston's paternal grandmother but after her death in 1789 his father hardly seems to have known what to do with what was really a rather unnecessary staging-post between Hanover Square and Broadlands. According to Minto it was 'a prodigious great magnificent old-fashioned house, with pleasure-grounds consisting of seventy acres – pieces of water, artificial mounts, and so forth'. It would have cost a great deal to repair and modernize. Perhaps that was why it took so long to sell. The second viscount had contemplated disposing of it and in a final, rather pathetic codicil to his will, in which he regretted leaving Harry with so much smaller an income than he had himself enjoyed, 'strongly advised' him to make himself 'rich and easy' by selling all three houses. The executors also recommended that Temple Grove be sold. Castlereagh, who had rented it for some time, moved out at the end of 1805 and the following year a sale was arranged for £6,950. Palmerston was glad enough to avoid the trouble of an auction, though the price was some £3,000 short of valuation. But this sale seems to have fallen through at the last moment and in 1808 Palmerston was delighted to get £12,065.[60]

At the same time as reducing Palmerston's stock and the income from it he had hitherto enjoyed, the purchase of the Stanhope St leases probably increased his annual expenditure quite considerably. In 1818, when the first comprehensive figures become available, he was spending on Stanhope St and Broadlands combined £1,443 for servants, £1,464 on horses and carriages, £1,227 for housekeeping and £1,320 on 'general bills', which included such things as gardeners' wages and internal and external repairs. In addition there was £232 for Emma Murray's rent and taxes and, under the euphemism of 'subscriptions & gifts', substantial additional payments to Mrs Murray (though not her regular allowance) and other women, as well as for Lt Davies's prosecution and defence, amounting to a further £744. Palmerston's personal expenditure, for example on clothes, was included in the total of £691 for 'pocket & travelling'; books and clubs cost a further £176. Finally there was a sum of £200 paid out on the home farm at Broadlands, probably in respect of meat and vegetables supplied to the house. The total was therefore £7,491.

Palmerston eventually worked out his average annual expenditure in 1818-29 as £7,703. This figure is less useful than it might appear to the unwary. After 1818 the remittance to Broadlands Farm disappears and there are changes in Palmerston's system of accounting beyond the apparently arbitrary and inconsistent distribution of certain sorts of payment between 'subscriptions' and 'miscellaneous'. There would also be considerable fluctuations under most heads, for example in an election year or, rather more rarely, when he made an investment out of income. In addition there is the gross distortion caused by the accumulation of tradesmen's bills. Much has been made by both his contemporaries and ours of the way in which Palmerston treated his suppliers; but in itself there was probably nothing unusual about it. Tradesmen to the aristocracy were glad enough on the whole to extend a large amount of credit, and in return expected not to have their accounts too closely scrutinized. But Palmerston was quite often sued for debt (though several of the cases cited relate to the activities of the Murray Millses rather than to anything of his own). Very probably he did not keep to the spirit of the implied bargain. His trainer's son recalled that when once his butcher had cornered him and his bill had been paid and receipted, Palmerston 'drew on a glove, and, taking up the pen which had been used for the purpose, threw it out of the window, in utter contempt for "such a mean action" as a man's asking for his own'.[61]

What no doubt soured Palmerston was the discovery that he was paying usury rather than interest. He suspected that there might be some conspiracy between the tradesmen and his servants. Scattered notes survive showing how he questioned the prices charged in the Stanhope St accounts for tea and washing and asked on one occasion, 'Why has Jackson raised the price of butter since 1822 from 1/6 a lb. to 1/11,' and at the same time directed, 'Townshend Poulterer too dear, to employ somebody else.' At Broadlands things were even worse; at one time or another he discovered that his gardener, his bailiff and even his agent were swindling him. Unravelling their accounts therefore probably had a good deal to do with the fact that by the end of 1823 the total of household bills outstanding had risen to the enormous sum of £6,781 and by the end of 1828 those relating to London alone to over £4,000. But what must have worried Palmerston most of all was that these were piling up during a period when it was in any case becoming increasingly difficult for him to pay his way.

When Palmerston had come of age in 1805 his net income from all sources except stock was reckoned to be £7,902. After the settlement of 1811 it was, with the addition of the income from stock (£1,995) and his War Office salary (£2,480 gross; £2,232 net), £14,356. This included an unusually large figure of £1,260 from the furnished letting of the Hanover Square house. In 1805 it had been only £900; in later years it was usually let unfurnished for £1,000. But it became increasingly difficult to let at all. Eventually, in 1838, Palmerston had to sell it for a good deal less than he had hoped. The figure for his income from stock is also misleading, since his personal holdings of a little more than £18,000 could not then have produced nearly £2,000 a year. It included a small income (£150) from a trust fund of his late grandmother, Mrs Temple, and probably a good deal more from the stock transferred during that year from his father's estate to his brother and sisters. In any case his income from these sources would have been considerably reduced, just as his liabilities were simultaneously increased, by the settlement of the estate and house purchases of 1811-13. But even if his income had been reduced, by parting with virtually all his stock and by the loss of all rent in respect of the London house, to, say, £12,000, this should still have provided a comfortable margin, over the total of average expenditure, annuities and allowances, of about £11,000. He was, after all, only half a libertine. The rumour of 1814 that he had 'lately gravelled himself very much by Gaming' was probably untrue. There is no evidence anywhere that his betting at the table or the track was anything but modest. But Palmerston was as active in his private business as he was in office or in love.[62]

In the first place, Palmerston was not merely a country gentleman; he was essentially an improving landowner. Throughout his unmarried life he was in effect an absentee landlord in all four of his estates. The large acreage in Sligo, the mixture of agricultural, commercial and residential property in Dublin, the farms in Yorkshire and the lands in Hampshire (excluding Broadlands and its park) were all under the supervision of local agents. Sometimes, they would complain, long periods went by without their hearing from the owner. These delays were due, quite paradoxically, to Palmerston's insistence on reserving to himself a close personal oversight of every aspect of life and work on his estates even during those long periods of official business that threatened to overwhelm him. At such times he would leave even quite important matters to accumulate until he was allowed a respite from the affairs of Whitehall. However, at a very early date he also visited each of the estates in turn and laid down a master-plan for their improvement. Since much depended on circumstances outside his immediate control, things did not always work out in detail as he had planned. But what is remarkable is how thoroughly he prepared his plans for a lifetime's work and, still more, how much of them he was able to carry out.

The details of Palmerston's plans deserve a separate chapter. All that needs to be said here is that he conceived a massive programme for improving his estates in Sligo, laid down a long-term plan for enlarging and consolidating the estates scattered around Broadlands and improving the aspect of the house, and more than trebled the value of his Yorkshire property at Fairburn by further purchases of land and the development of a lime-works. Palmerston treated each of his estates largely, but not entirely, as a separate entity and dealt with the agents accordingly. He maintained a separate set of accounts for each and a fifth with Messrs Oddie, Lumley and Forster, who looked after his London affairs and his personal legal business. Mrs Temple's trust was handled by Hankey's but Palmerston's personal bankers were Drummond's, and it was to them that his salary and the net receipts from the various estates were usually remitted. Unfortunately it is impossible to get a complete overall picture of his transactions because the records, though very detailed and extensive, are occasionally obscure, inconsistent in method and patently incomplete. But it is quite clear that the cost of his estate improvements was enormous. The original estate at Fairburn had cost £21,000; by about 1830 Palmerston had spent another £21,000 on additional purchases and a further

£10,000 on improvements. His purchases in Hampshire were still more extensive and, largely because the sellers appreciated how very much he wanted their land, much more expensive. By 1825 he had increased the acreage to over 4,200 but at a cost of nearly £67,000. There seems then to have been a long pause until 1835, when he bought another large farm for £12,000.[63]

His expenditure in Ireland is much more difficult to make out. When he made his first visit in 1808 he decided that there was not much he could do in Dublin, where the most valuable of his properties had been leased by his forebears on ridiculously generous terms. But in Sligo, where he had over 10,000 acres, he conceived a vast plan of improvements which in spite of being almost continuously in process were not finished even by the time of his death in 1865. He proposed to build schools for the education of the peasants and roads for the exchange of sand with bog. In addition he intended to build a 'little manufacturing village' in the centre of the estate and a harbour with a pier projecting into Donegal Bay. He seems to have begun modestly enough; but even during the first decade of progress it must have cost him a few thousand. When he made a series of new visits in the mid 1820s, moreover, he speeded up the work very considerably and contemplated spending at least another £11,000 on the harbour and associated works and a similar sum spread over twenty-two years on improving the boglands.[64]

All this expense Palmerston seems to have met from local resources. He was at first reluctant to raise loans in Ireland, since at 5 instead of 4½ or even 4 per cent they were relatively more expensive, perhaps because the natives were so restless. So the more modest expenditure of the first few years was met out of rent. But from 1826 he obtained grants of £5,000 from the Government and raised a similar sum on mortgage. The whole business seems to have been well planned enough to maintain a very good and generally increasing rate of remittance to London, at least until the troubles of the 1840s. In 1805 the net income from Dublin and Sligo combined was only a little more than £6,100. By 1811 it had recovered to over £8,300. The vast sums expended and the interest which had to be paid out of income in the 1820s seem to have reduced it again to £5-6,000. But by 1830 Palmerston reckoned it could be raised to over £7,000 and by 1840 it had in fact risen to over £11,000. When he last visited his Sligo estate in 1858 he found that the rental for the previous year was, at £7,370, nearly £3,000 more than in 1824 despite the intervening years of deep distress.[65]

The improvements at Fairburn were also very profitable. Palmerston financed the major part of the extensions to the estate out of a loan on the original holding and serviced that loan out of the additional income. In 1805 the net income had been £400; by 1811 it was nearly £850 and by the 1830s over £1,500. But part of this increase was attributable to other improvements and these, costing just over £10,000, seem to have been met by borrowing in two stages, in March 1814 and April 1816, the remainder of Fanny Temple's legacy and setting off the annual charge of about £486, not against the Fairburn income, but against the central account with Drummond's.

The transfer of the charge for Fanny's legacy was probably merely for convenience. But the same could not be said of the charges similarly transferred in respect of Hampshire purchases. To finance some of his early purchases Palmerston cashed the remaining £5,750 of stock; others he bought on mortgages from the previous owners or other local sources. But the charges for these loans absorbed the whole of the profit from the estate and by 1817 would considerably have exceeded it. So in that year Palmerston began to borrow on the market as well as from his family and to charge the interest to his central account. In 1817-18 he borrowed a total of £14,000 from Messrs Wood and Thorold and £13,118 from Messrs Hibbert. Between 1817 and 1823 he borrowed the rest of Willy's legacy and savings, as well as a few hundred from Emma Godfrey and her family. In 1823 he increased his loan from Wood and Thorold by another £10,000; and there was also an occasional overdraft from Drummond's. During this period, moreover, interest rates moved up in England and he often had to pay 5 rather than 4 or 4½ per cent. So when Palmerston came to examine his situation in December 1824 he reckoned that in round figures it looked like this:

Income:	£		Expenditure:		£		
Irish	8,000		Annuities:				
Han. Sq. rent	1,000		voluntary:	Emma Godfrey	300		
Fairburn	1,000			Fanny Bowles	500		
Mrs Temple's				Campbell	300		
Trust	150			Ravizzotti	200		
		10,150		Mrs M.	300		
War Office	2,480					1,600	
			on legacies:	Fanny	500		
				William	500		
				Elizabeth	500		
		2,480				1,500	
Total income		12,630					3,100

Interest on other loans:			
Wood's £24,000 at 4 per cent	960		
Hibbert's £13,000 at 4 per cent	520		
Drummond's overdraft of £2,787 at 5 per cent	139		
William's £9,824 at 5 per cent	491		
Fanny's 16,207 5 per cent consols	486		
		2,596	2,596
Total of fixed payments			5,696

	£
Total income	12,630
Less fixed payments	5,696
Disposable income	6,934
Less estimated expenditure	7,080
Deficit	146

Palmerston thought that he might be able to increase his Irish and York-shire income by £500 each; but in view of the vast improvements contem-plated in Sligo and the almost equally impressive accumulation of household debts of which he was now aware something more far-reaching had to be attempted. He considered selling Fairburn; but it was not like Palmerston to retreat when any alternative offered. That, no doubt, was why he chose instead to plunge into the stock market boom early in the following year.

Palmerston seems to have begun his flutter with the very next remittance of £2,100 from Ireland. Drummond's reported that they had received it at the beginning of February 1825. Palmerston endorsed the statement: Pearl Fishery £700; Pesco-Peruvian £700; Welsh Mines £500; Norfolk Rly £200. Nothing more is found among his papers about the first or the last, nor anything but a further payment of £200 in respect of the Pesco-Peruvian Company. He received an invitation to join the board of the Peruvian com-pany; but he was advised against it. However, he did become a director of the Welsh Iron and Coal Company and regularly paid the calls upon his 100 shares. Later in 1825 he also joined the boards of two other companies launched by the same people. These were the Cornwall and Devon Mining Company and the Welsh Slate, Copper and Lead Mining Company. Palm-erston also became involved in Colonel Trench's Thames Embankment scheme. But in spite of his efforts in private and in public the Government refused to give the financial backing required or Parliament to override the rights of local residents. Whether it cost Palmerston anything more than the £50 he contributed in 1826 towards the provision of technical drawings is unknown. His other investments certainly turned out to be very costly indeed. For he could hardly have chosen a worse moment for his speculations. The boom of 1820-25 had been stimulated by the ready availability of hard cash and the wild optimism about the prospects in the newly liberated colonies of Latin America. Inevitably honest men became entangled with rogues in the scramble for profits and worth-while ventures with wretched frauds in the ensuing collapse.[66]

How much Palmerston lost it is impossible to say; but it was certainly a great deal. In the cases of the Pearl Fishery, the Norfolk Railway and, the extra £200 apart, Pesco-Peruvian, there is no sign that he ever actually paid any further instalments and he may therefore have chosen either to sell his scrip or even to forfeit his deposits. At worst, therefore, he may not have lost more than his initial investment of £1,600 on these. But he behaved very differently with regard to the companies of which he was a director. When the crisis deepened and the companies took legal action to compel their share-holders to pay the full nominal value of their holdings, he could hardly have avoided paying up himself. In addition there are signs that his family was correct in stating that he sometimes cooperated in buying out dissatisfied investors. Considering the vast numbers of shares issued and the size of the losses made, Palmerston's contributions in this way must have been modest.

Probably they were extended only to people who, like his brother and brother-in-law, had joined in on his advice and, unlike them, could not so easily afford to lose. The record shows only that he acquired another twenty-two shares of Welsh Iron in 1827 at the nominal price of £5 a share and forty Welsh Slate at an unknown cost. But to make his holdings fully paid must have cost him very large sums indeed. There are no figures for Welsh Iron in his accounts, probably because the shares were all issued and paid up before he adapted his system of private accounts to include such transactions. But he seems to have paid up the instalments as demanded and so his 100 would have cost him at least £2,500 and his additional twenty-two another £550. It is not known how many shares he had in the Cornwall and Devon Company or whether he felt obliged to buy any others out. Whatever the number he held they cost him a still larger sum. Lady Cowper calculated in the autumn of 1826 that he stood to lose £4,000. His accounts for 1828-33 show only that he paid out rather more than £3,500. But that figure cannot include the deposit and two instalments made in previous years and if, as Lady Cowper's figure suggests, his original holding was eighty shares, then his total loss must have been at least £5,000.[67]

Palmerston's biggest commitment was in Welsh Slate; by the end of 1830 he had paid out for it at least £10,000. Later, with the surrenders and forfeitures made by so many others, Palmerston appears to have been left either the major shareholder or something very close to it; together with his brother's small holding he held almost exactly half the shares. It also turned out to be the one investment of his to make a profit. He had to work hard to get it and to hang on when others wavered; but he never lost interest. He made his first visit to the quarries at Tan y Bwlch, near Portmadoc, on the way back from Ireland in November 1828 and as usual filled several pages of his notebook on massive railway and tunnel projects which, at a cost of £8,000, he reckoned would save £1,500 a year on transport. He also experimented in the 1840s with schemes for the mutual benefit of Sligo and the company, seeking to recruit workmen from his estate for the quarries and to supply slate for the cottages he was building at his port in Donegal Bay. He therefore made the quarries a regular detour en route between Dublin and London. He took Emily along in November 1841 and it was not until October 1865 that old age finally made him send William Cowper in his place; William's report was among the last documents he endorsed. The first dividends paid appear to have been in 1833 and 1834 when he received £560 in each year. But these were a flash in the pan. Soon afterwards further improvements and extensions were undertaken that ate up all the profits for years to come; and as late as 1861 other schemes frightened off even some of those who had held on since the 1820s. Palmerston hung on and eventually he was well repaid. Dividend payments seem to have been resumed in 1847; by 1858 he was receiving an annual return of £7,000 or £8,000 on his original investment and by the 1860s, £9,500. At his death his shares were valued for probate at £44,000.[68]

Although Palmerston's investments may eventually have yielded him a handsome profit, in the short run they had obviously been a near disaster and made him throughout the late 1820s a very worried man.* At the end of February 1826 he sent a letter to his brother bravely putting country before self and patriotism before the price of speculation. 'Our affairs here are rather mending, but slowly,' he wrote; 'I have no doubt however that matters will get right. There has been no interruption of foreign commerce, no loss of national property, no political interference with the channels of trade, no addition to the public burthen. The wealth of the community therefore must be unimpaired, & though individuals are suffering because they have made engagements which when the time comes, they cannot fulfil, still this cannot affect permanently the prosperity of the country.' [69]

Palmerston's papers were soon full of calculations about possible economies, from reducing Mrs Murray's allowance to buying cheaper liveries for the servants. They do not show precisely how he managed, but he raised new loans in Ireland on bonds and mortgages, while to help him meet the payments he granted new leases on his estates, and Fanny Bowles and Henry Campbell voluntarily gave up their allowances. However, the financial significance of his difficulties should not be exaggerated. His Government salary was clearly very helpful and he was therefore glad enough to keep his place as long as he could. But if necessary he could always have rescued himself by selling off one of his estates. His papers show that this is precisely what he had contemplated doing in 1824 when he reviewed various ways of raising the large sum he wanted for his schemes in Sligo. Fairburn had none of

* There is in the Broadlands Papers at Winchester a statement Palmerston compiled of his gross income ('gross', that is, as received at Drummond's and including his W.O. salary), fixed payments (of annuities and central interest payments) and 'disposable' income (i.e. the residue available against general expenditure). Some of the fluctuations from year to year probably reflect haphazard intervals in remittances as well as late payment of interest and non-repeating items. But by adding the figures for his general expenditure in London, they give a good impression of his situation in the 1820s:

	income	fixed payments	disposable	actual expenditure (excluding 'fixed payments')	surplus [or deficit]
1819	14,244	4,614	9,630	9,370	260
1820	8,382	4,806	3,574	8,209	[4,635]
1821	12,539	5,142	7,397	8,011	[614]
1822	9,925	5,672	4,253	6,778	[2,525]
1823	9,106	7,278	1,828	7,511	[6,683]
1824	12,106	4,664	7,341 [sic]	5,403	1,938 +
1825	11,822	6,248	5,573 [sic]	4,963	510 +
1826	8,375	5,442	2,933	7,843	[4,910]
1827	8,885	3,888	4,997	6,846	[1,849]
1828	8,702	5,279	3,423	8,046	[4,623]

+ But the cost of his investments in these years (though not in subsequent ones) is apparently omitted from these figures.

the sentimental attachment that Broadlands or even Sligo had and on his valuation of over £80,000 it would have realized enough to pay off at least the greater part of his debts. It remains of real importance, however, to recognize the coincidence of crises and the accumulation of pressures he must have suffered throughout the late 1820s. It was a period of continuing difficulty with Emily, of blackmailing by Emma, of grave financial trouble and of constant political crisis. That he should have emerged safely from it all, and even as a major political figure at last, was a remarkable proof of his essential vitality and will.

What must have been a particularly worrying feature of Palmerston's financial difficulties was that he could not keep them private. Years after his marriage and his mines had relieved the strain, the notion persisted that he was very hard up. It was the constant need of 'Hush Money', some people would say. It was true there was such a need – probably even as late as his eightieth year of age. But public exposure then, some believed, would have made him more immovable than ever and that had certainly not been the case with his stock-market speculations in the 1820s. That he was involved with fools and swindlers was a matter of public comment before the beginning of 1827. There is no reason to doubt his honesty; rather, when the crash came, he seems to have assumed financial liabilities beyond what the law required. But he had been foolish to speculate so wildly and even more so to associate with the sort of people he did. These circumstances alone would appear to give very strong support to the claim of Princess Lieven (though muddled in chronology) and the more authoritative assertion of Canning's private secretary (though both prejudiced and belated) that it was Palmerston's private speculations which unsuited him for the Exchequer. Canning, as others avowed years later to Prince Albert, very probably did say something of the kind; but it still does not provide a complete explanation of his behaviour, since he had known about the matter for some time before he made his offer. It was in fact to him that Palmerston had written in March 1825 for advice about joining the board of Pesco-Peruvian. Palmerston explained that he would have had no hesitation about doing so as a private individual, but as he was a minister he wished to be guided by the Government. Since about the same time he joined other boards without apparently seeking such advice, one can only suspect that his real motive must have been, as he virtually admitted it was, to extract confidential information from the Foreign Secretary about the Government's policy with regard to the prospective recognition of the revolutionary régime in Peru. That Canning thought so too may perhaps be inferred from the first line of his reply: 'I should incline to – no.' Moreover, if two years later, when he promised Palmerston the Exchequer, Canning was prepared to overlook what at best had been a singularly indiscreet inquiry, he could hardly have ignored the accusations made in the House of Commons less than a week before.[70]

The accusations made about the Cornwall and Devon Company in the House of Commons on 9 April 1827 were far from pleasant hearing for some of the members present, among them both the Chairman, Peter Moore, and the company solicitor, John Wilks, as well as Palmerston. According to a petition presented by some of the shareholders, Wilks had arranged to sell the mining leases to the company at a great profit to himself and before they were legally his; and the directors had subsequently conspired to issue a fraudulent prospectus and to force up the market price of the shares by buying them in at the company's expense. Wilks, in his maiden speech to Parliament, made a long and able defence; Palmerston briefly explained his role and, accusing the petitioners of seeking to avoid their financial obligations, haughtily declared that 'it was a matter of perfect indifference to him' whether the House investigated it or not. When the matter was raised again a month later Brougham, who had been engaged by another M.P. and co-director of Palmerston's, pointed out that it was all *sub judice* and the request for a committee of inquiry was withdrawn. Palmerston merely stated once again that an inquiry was 'a matter of the most perfect indifference' to him. That was pretty cool; by that date the Chairman, Peter Moore, was in gaol and the Secretary, 'Bubble' Wilks, who was connected in the same way with all the other companies of which he was director, he knew was really a crook. As early as September 1825 Palmerston had written to Sulivan, who was also on the board of the Slate Company: 'Your very discreet & mysterious innuendo letter about Slate does not much surprise me. I suppose you had a quarrel between Barrett [the Chairman] & Wilks. The latter I am sure is a bit of a rogue if Nature writes a legible hand; at the same time he is a clever fellow & as long as his interest goes hand in hand with ours will probably do well by us.'[71]

In view of the responsible manner in which he later acted, Palmerston presumably meant only sharp business and not sharp practice by this last remark. But it highlights his naïveté in these affairs and his foolhardiness in consenting to have such associates. Moreover, since Canning's offer came *before* and the withdrawal of it *after* Peter Moore's imprisonment, perhaps he found Palmerston guilty by association. It is still strange that Palmerston left nothing behind to suggest that he too suspected Canning had indeed arrived at that conclusion; but then he had another axe to grind, in that he was the victim of court intrigue.

According to Palmerston's own account, when Canning offered him the consolation of Jamaica he was told that it was at the direct suggestion of the King and that the King had claimed he 'had good reason to know' that this was 'the thing of all others' Palmerston wished to have. Considering how Canning had gone out of his way to conciliate a hostile court through his Foreign Office arrangements when he succeeded Castlereagh in 1822, it is by no means unlikely that in 1827 he would have been prepared if necessary to sacrifice Palmerston to the King. In other words, Palmerston's place may have been needed to instal the Lansdowne Whigs in office, not at their own demand but as a part of the price demanded by the King. The King was believed to dislike Palmerston personally and Sir William Knighton, who was Keeper of the King's Privy Purse – and many other of his most delicate secrets too – to want a more compliant Chancellor.[72]

In spite of Canning's hint about Jamaica Palmerston professed not to have suspected that the court was the real cause of his disappointment until a few weeks later, when history came near to repeating itself. Canning had been a sick man when he undertook at last to form his own Government. At the Duke of York's funeral in January he had lent his hat for old Eldon to stand on and protect his feet from Windsor's icy flagstones. Eldon lived on another ten years, but poor Canning died on 8 August. The rest of the Cabinet were not caught unawares and they had already decided to carry on. As a result the King appointed Lord Goderich, as Fred Robinson had recently become, to fill Canning's place as First Lord of the Treasury and Canning's friend Sturges Bourne those of Chancellor of the Exchequer and Leader of the House of Commons. Beyond this only minor changes were envisaged. But things went wrong right from the start, when Goderich proved utterly incapable of standing up to the King.

It is unnecessary to dwell on the tortuous manoeuvres of the next few weeks. Bourne put the Ministry's survival at risk by refusing to take the Exchequer, and there followed a long-drawn-out battle over the King's attempt to fill it with a Protestant Tory. Quite what the King was up to no one could be sure. He could hardly have been hoping to undermine the Government's 'neutrality' on the Catholic question, since he had already tried that and been forced openly to retreat. Nor does it seem that he really wanted to break up the coalition of Canningites and Lansdowne Whigs and to welcome back the Tory seceders of April. Rather, it appears, such were the confusions and complexities of the negotiations that the issue of principle only developed with the muddle itself, and only then as one of personal pride and power between the King on the one hand and the Whigs on the other, with poor Goderich playing piggy in the middle. It is not clear whether it was George or Goderich who first proposed Herries for the Exchequer while Huskisson took the lead as Colonial Secretary. But there is little doubt that Knighton pressed the notion because Herries was expected to be cooperative about the royal finances. As a Protestant Tory, however, Herries was anathema to the Whigs, and they appeared likely to resign if he were appointed; according to Bathurst, the Whig cleric Sydney Smith said that he was 'praying more earnestly than ever against "All Herries & Schism" '. There were also rumours that by his earlier transactions Herries had placed himself at the mercy of the Rothschilds. It would surely have been rather strange, therefore, if in order to take advantage of the slur, the Whigs had put forward in his place someone tarred with the same brush. For their candidate for the place refused by Bourne was Palmerston.[73]

When the rumour got about, the reactions both in public and in private were very mixed. 'I see the *Times* has become of late adverse to Palmerston,' wrote Peel. 'I know not why. Probably there is no better reason than that he may not have sent the advertisements of his office to it.' The unfriendly Bathurst replied however: 'If Lord Palmerston should be the Chancellor of the Exchequer he will of course insist on his friend Wilks being also in the Treasury.' Grey, who had refused to serve with Canning and was still sulking in the wilderness of opposition, wrote that Palmerston's proposed move was 'rather ridiculous, either as an effective appointment, or as raising their credit'. And Duncannon, Palmerston's campanion at Harrow, wrote to their old 'messmate' Althorp that he would have regretted Lansdowne quitting on account of Herries, whom he considered 'more fit' to be Chancellor than Palmerston. There is in fact no real sign that the Lansdowne Whigs themselves were as a group at all enthusiastic about their choice, though both Holland and Brougham let it be known they thought Palmerston would be 'excellent'. Rather, as even Brougham would stress, it was a matter of resisting the King. The major confrontation came on 17 August when the Privy Council met at Windsor to prorogue Parliament and the King expected to hand the seals to Herries. But Goderich stimulated the King's 'hydrophobia' with floods of tears and eventually it was agreed to postpone the whole thing until Huskisson returned from his convalescent trip abroad. Huskisson arrived back in London at twelve-fifteen on 28 August – only also to refuse the Exchequer. His excuse was the same as everyone else's, ill-health; but his real reason was fear of quarrelling over the royal finances. Resort was therefore had once more to Sturges Bourne, and he, having on 30 August 'yielded in the evening, . . . retracted at night'. Finally, with Canningites and Whigs all trembling for their places, Lansdowne reluctantly consented to be smoothed over in a long interview with the King on 1 September, possibly with the hint that Herries might eventually be replaced by Huskisson.[74]

Made much wiser, perhaps, by his treatment at Canning's hands, Palmerston had behaved with extraordinary patience and good sense throughout. As a member of the Cabinet he was directly involved in some of the discussions about the responses Goderich should make to the King's demands about the Catholic question. But on more personal questions, he kept well out of the way, while rumours flew around that he was destined for the Board of Trade or the leadership of the House of Commons. According to Croker, Goderich was in a dilemma between Peel and Brougham for the lead. These were the two dominating figures to the right and left of the House; neither the Canningite Huskisson nor the Whig Tierney seemed to have the health to match them. Croker thought Palmerston would also have been better than Tierney, but was still of the opinion that he had 'not fluency nor a great knowledge of business'. In any case he 'doubted whether he would or could undertake it'. Palmerston himself had very similar doubts. 'There are very few things indeed in this world which I should so much dislike', he wrote, 'even if I felt that I was fit for it. But in various ways I should be quite unequal to it.' He mentioned in particular that 'of all irksome slaveries' none could be more unwelcome to him than the 'perpetual state of canvass' the lead would require; he also hinted that he felt his debating powers were hardly up to the task.[75]

Although Palmerston presumably made his feelings about the lead well-known to Goderich, he heard nothing about the Exchequer until after his name had actually been proposed to the King on 15 August. His behaviour the following day, when on their way to Canning's funeral Goderich reported to him the reaction this had brought from the King, was still more discreet. He released the Prime Minister from any sense of personal obligation as readily as he had accepted the proposal in the first place. Then, when Sturges Bourne upset the compromise arranged after Huskisson's return, Palmerston wrote to urge upon him that the Exchequer would not be as onerous as he feared and that he owed it to Canning's memory to do anything he could to keep his Government together. So much did Palmerston remain in the background, indeed, that some of his friends concluded that he could not be in Goderich's confidence; his own view was that it all confirmed the wisdom of his having 'studiously avoided' going near the Prime Minister and embarrassing him with 'personal objects'.[76]

Palmerston probably realized that the attentive letters he now received from Brougham identified him as a coming man who no longer needed to press his case. He was certainly amused by Brougham's assurances that through exercising patience now Palmerston's 'power a year hence' would be 'incalculably greater for *every good purpose*', and by his suggestion that Herries be directly asked, 'Have you on your honour ever in your life, since being in a place of trust, directly or indirectly, benefited by stock in any manner of way?' Lansdowne thought that 'no man was fit to sit in a cabinet or even take any office in a Government to whom such a question . . . can be put'. Palmerston, however, wrote that Brougham's was a letter 'which would make even a condemned culprit laugh . . . It is amusing to trace all the different calculations of personal advantage & convenience, and all the individual views which run through his note; it is quite a picture of the man.'[77]

So, while many around him seemed to panic – with Goderich in constant tears, Lansdowne perpetually on the point of breaking up the coalition, and Brougham in anguished fear of still more protracted exile in opposition – Palmerston kept very cool about the whole affair. On the eve of their surrender he calculated that 'even if Herries is forced in the Whigs will remain, for each man appears willing to digest it though each says that all the rest will not'. He also thought it would have been 'very foolish' for the Whigs not to back down if, as he expected would be the case, the King insisted on having his way. It would be unwise for them to resign on personal grounds when they had come in on grounds of public principle, and their going would only throw the Government once more into the arms of 'the prejudiced old Tories from whom it has been as it were by a miracle rescued'. 'There is a fate about the Whigs', he went on, '& therefore I expect them in trying circumstances to do the foolish thing. But if they have common sense they will swallow Herries, Knighton & all & trust to Parliamentary controul to get the Govt out of any difficulties arising from Herries's connection with Knighton, and to time & to the preponderance of liberal views in the Cabinet to neutralize any Tory propensities which he may have.' Herries he thought in any case was being much maligned. 'After all', he had written, 'Herries would really be an excellent man for the office. His knowledge of all the details of the subject would render him most valuable to Goderich . . . He is a very intelligent, clearheaded man, and I believe a man of strict integrity and of honourable feeling. He has not at present perhaps the scope of mind which belongs to a Cabinet situation, but a man's views expand very rapidly with his position, if he has the natural talent to form them.' [78]

Considering how he had been displaced from a higher position after a preparation of almost twenty years, Palmerston was being remarkably generous to Herries. The reason, perhaps, was that his resentment was centered elsewhere. On 3 September he went to Windsor to attend a meeting of the Privy Council and to see Herries sworn in. The next day he reported of the King: 'He sent for me into him to say divers very civil things about the handsome manner in which he thought I had behaved about the Exchequer in not pressing my claim etc etc, all of which was I knew an echo of what Goderich had told him & suggested to him to tell me. I of course was overpowered with a sense of His Majesty's condescending kindness, & only anxious to do anything in my power to be useful to His Majesty & his Govt, & perfectly conscious how much more fit a Chancellor he had got & so we parted *very* great friends.' [79]

Although Palmerston thought that Herries was too 'honourable' to be Knighton's 'creature' and that he had hesitated for discretion's sake as much as for his health, he had no doubt that the Whigs were wrong about it being a political question. The real 'key' to what had happened, he believed, was the court's desire to have a compliant Chancellor dealing with the royal finances. He also began to suspect that it was Knighton who had pressed Canning to retain the Exchequer for himself and to leave much of the detailed work to Herries as Secretary of the Treasury. Certainly there was a revival of the story that Palmerston's 'favourite object' was an English peerage; and once again the source seems to have been the court. Palmerston, however, also believed there was something still more personal behind it this time. 'He certainly dislikes me & would be glad to get rid of me *any*how as the Irish say,' he wrote about the King on 27 August. 'He said to Mad. Lieven the other day "Connaissez vous Palmerston", & then went on, "Il y a quelque chose en lui qui me déplait, il a toujours l'air si fier".' The story has been discounted by English historians as coming from a very doubtful source, but Mme Lieven, while always inclined to exaggerate her own role in things, was very well-informed. Palmerston himself believed her, although 'determined to take no *hints* & to understand nothing short of a positive intimation that my room would be more agreeable than my company'.[80]

Whether or not Palmerston was ever the 'feeble courtier' once derided by Brougham, he never seems to have got on well with George, either as prince or king. On the contrary, he had been in the habit of seeing more of Princess Caroline than was good for his relations with her husband George, playing chess with her at Blackheath and, according to a close observer, paying her 'great court'. One of the Princess's entourage was even supposed to have written:

He is not a man to despise any person or thing by which he can hope to gain power; he has set his heart thereon, and most likely he will succeed in his ambition, like all those who fix their minds steadily to the pursuit of one object; though, excepting a pleasing address, it does not appear to me that he has any great claim to distinction. There is one strange circumstance connected with him, namely, that, though he is suave and pleasant in his manners, he is unpopular. I wonder what is the reason. The Princess is not, I believe, really partial to him, but she is aware that his countenance is of some weight and advantage to her, and she is right to conciliate his favour.

To have noted Palmerston's 'ambition' at such an early date – the letter, though undated, must have been written in 1813 – seems suspiciously premature; perhaps it merely underlines the unreliability of Lady Charlotte Bury as an editor. At that time, rather, Palmerston seems to have been more cautious than ambitious. When the princess sought to succeed her mother as his tenant in Hanover Square until she went abroad in 1814, he refused on the grounds that he could not let it furnished at all or unfurnished for so short a period. In fact, he recorded, he was 'by no means anxious to have the Princess as a tenant'. Similarly, when a few years earlier the notorious Lady Oxford had wanted it, he had 'declined the honour as I thought her Ladyship a better tenant for her visitors than her landlord'. Perhaps it was more dangerous for him when, about the same time as he turned down the princess, he cut out the son of Prinney's favourite at a Windsor ball and danced all night with Princess Charlotte. George, who was always very watchful of his daughter's doings, certainly snubbed them both for it. Quite probably, too, he resented Palmerston's long liaison with Lady Cowper, who was a dear friend at court and whose mother had been dearer still. Instead of this bringing him constantly to court, Palmerston talked as though such invitations were rarely extended. 'I am going down tomorrow for two days to him [at Ascot], a singular and unusual act of graciousness on his part,' Palmerston wrote in 1825, 'I fancy from my having met Lady Elizabeth Conyngham the other day at Mr Hope's and talked to her a good deal by way of something to do.'[81]

It so happened that 1825 was also the year in which his connection was exposed with a certain Catherine Cary. Who Miss Cary really was no one now seems to know. She claimed – as did so many others of her time and circumstance – to be the daughter of a duke in search of her rightful inheritance. More important, she was also the avowedly innocent tool of a conspiracy to plant evidence that the unfortunate Princess Charlotte, who had died in childbed in 1817, had really been poisoned. The story did not become common knowledge until the publication in 1832 of the spurious 'memoirs' of Lady Anne Hamilton. But Catherine Cary had already published her own extravagant and almost incomprehensible tale in 1825 and in it implicated Palmerston. As far as one can make out, she had so anticipated her 'large inheritance' as to land herself in debt and consequently in jail. Palmerston, she claimed, had made her acquaintance through some pension affair of her mother's and in the first instance got her out of jail by offering security for her debts. But subsequently they had quarrelled – because of the jealous accusations of another 'friend', though she naturally insisted her relationship with Palmerston was innocent enough – and she soon found herself back in jail. As it happens, the one aspect of her story that has so far found support is that she was receiving money from Palmerston. His accounts show payments in 1818, 1819, 1820 and 1821 of £66. 17s. 8d., £213, £50 and £127. 1s. 1d., variously to 'Miss C–', 'Cary', and, through a solicitor, 'Yatman, Miss C–'. For her story of the poisoning plot to have any plausibility at all, these must have been the years concerned. They cover, moreover, precisely the period from the suicide of Princess Charlotte's accoucheur to the death of her mother. In any case, if Palmerston was wittingly involved, it might of course have been to quash the scandal.[82]

All in all there is probably little need to look further than the Horse Guards for the source of any personal antagonism between Minister and King. Palmerston's duties as Secretary at War had brought him regularly into contact with George, even before he joined the Cabinet, and on at least one occasion there had been a very unfortunate clash of will and personality. There was some mixup in 1818 over the password to the Tower of London sentries and the Prince had his assistant secretary convey his 'surprise' to Palmerston. The Secretary at War, however, took offence and refused, as one of the 'official advisers of the Crown', to accept such a communication through such a person, even though he acted under the Prince's personal command. He even went so far as to complain to the Prime Minister, stating, as he did so, that he was sure that Liverpool would 'admit that this would be a degradation to which it would be impossible to submit'. Above all, however, there was the running battle with the Horse Guards. George would probably have resisted Palmerston's haughty defence of civilian control over the army even if the C.-in-C. had not been his favourite brother and, after 1818, the heir presumptive to the throne. After the Duke of York's death, moreover, he must have known of Palmerston's opposition to his desire to make himself C.-in-C. and even with the punctilious Taylor as intermediary he seems to have been much annoyed by Palmerston's fussy attention to detail during the interregnum of 1827.[83]

Whatever the reason for the King's hostility, the ministerial crisis seemed by early September 1827 to be safely, if not satisfactorily, passed, and Palmerston was able to get away from London for most of the rest of the year – shooting at Broadlands, sailing at Cowes and inspecting his Irish property. He had not long been back in London, however, when Goderich plunged everything into turmoil once again. Goderich was just about the least fitted man ever for a Prime Minister. He was constantly in a fidget about everything and utterly distracted by the least complaint from his wife; on occasions her petulant demands would bring Cabinet meetings to a halt and her confinement suspend the overall direction of the affairs of State. Palmerston's blunt opinion to Clive was (while wishing her no harm) that she 'really ought either to recover her senses or to die'. But it was her husband who threatened to succumb, mentally if not bodily. In an attempt to counter possible coalitions among the Opposition he sought early in December to strengthen his Government by the admission of Wellesley into the Cabinet and to balance the division of places with the Lansdowne Whigs by admitting Holland too. But the King still refused to accept Holland and an attempt to overawe him with a written protest sadly backfired. 'By the most unaccountable *gaucherie*', Huskisson reported, 'G. tacked to his letter . . . a kind of P.S. stating as an additional reason for acquiring strength, that he (G.) was inadequate to his situation, and adverting to Lady G.'s health as the cause of it.' The King immediately seized the golden opportunity and accepted the postscript as a proffered resignation.[84]

For a short while it seemed as though the King might have overplayed his hand, for between his fear of the extreme Whigs on the one hand and his resentment of the High Tories on the other, he could think of no one to succeed Goderich but Harrowby and Harrowby would not take it on. So after consultations with Huskisson, Lansdowne, Dudley and the Chancellor (Lyndhurst), the King took Goderich back. The relief, however, was brief, for the crisis reduced Huskisson's nerves to the condition of the Prime Minister's and revived Herries's discomfort among such liberal colleagues. Perhaps, as Palmerston afterwards concluded, Herries had originally 'been thrown like a live shell into the Cabinet to explode and blow us all up'. Certainly many of his colleagues thought there was a plot afoot; in any case relations between Herries and Huskisson had clearly become so bad that it was impossible they should go on together. For a while Goderich, among others, dithered and then, as Palmerston complained, instead of explaining to the King that one of the two must clearly go, at an interview on 8 January once again carelessly placed himself at the mercy of the King. Palmerston afterwards put it very neatly: 'Goderich . . . had no advice to give, and did not know what to do. But George knew very well what he had to do: he bid Goderich go home and take care of himself, and keep himself quiet; and he immediately sent for the Duke of Wellington to form a Government.' It was typical of the King that, after nursing his resentment against the duke so long, he should in the end have turned to him for help and that in order to display his power over a patently weak first minister he should have made a reputedly strong one. However, it was no less typical of Wellington and Peel, with whom the duke at once concerted arrangements, that they should take the opportunity to reconstruct the 'great Tory party'. Wellington accepted the King's commission on 9 January; the next day Huskisson told him that he would only join the Government if offers were also made, among others, to Palmerston.[85]

Palmerston's admission to the Wellington Ministry, almost as much as his departure from it less than six months later, marked an important stage in his emergence into the front rank of politics. Although he was a very old acquaintance of Goderich and their infrequent correspondence was always very friendly, Palmerston had not come forward any more prominently in the outgoing Ministry than he had in Canning's. He still had no powerful connections and displayed no overwhelming talents. Thus he was not included, as even Dudley was, in the secret consultations about Goderich's fate in mid-December and, though he denied it, there was a distinct impression about that he rather resented being so ill-informed about the crisis. Nor had Huskisson hitherto regarded him as one of his close associates. They had begun to see rather more of each other socially – Palmerston was at Eartham in October and Huskisson at Broadlands in December – and Huskisson was reputed now to have a real liking for his young colleague. But although he consulted Palmerston when he happened to be at hand, he did not include him among those whose advice he valued personally. Still more significantly perhaps, when it was suggested that Lansdowne might be able to form an administration in Goderich's place, Huskisson's friend and confidant, Granville, wrote to say that he thought Herries would inspire more confidence at the Exchequer and proposed Palmerston merely as one of several possibilities for the Home Office. But things were very different in a Wellington Government. There, as one among a minority of Canningites under an unsympathetic premier, Palmerston was necessary to the nervous Huskisson both as a political ally and as a personal reassurance.[86]

The change in Palmerston's position was very quickly registered in the negotiations for the admission of the Canningites into the Ministry. Huskisson seems to have had conversations with both Wellington and Peel before the duke approached the King for permission to write to the Canningites individually on 12 January. However, when Palmerston went to Apsley House the next morning, a Sunday, he had evidently not had any previous contact with Huskisson. But it was obvious what he should say. He explained to the duke that he would personally feel 'much gratified' to serve under him, but he needed to be reassured about the Catholic question – 'the most important which would probably occur during the rest of my life' – and would not be willing to join with a 'preponderating majority of persons of an opposite creed'. He must know, therefore, of what other persons the Government was to be composed. Since the King had already consented to it, Wellington was able to state that the Government would be neutral like its predecessor; but he simply could not say yet who the others might be. Later that day Palmerston saw Huskisson and discovered that he had been sent for by Wellington because Huskisson had insisted that he could only join the Ministry if Herries were dropped and places in the Cabinet offered to Palmerston, Dudley, Grant and, when his father's death took him to the Lords, William Lamb.[87]

When Palmerston and Dudley compared impressions and calculated their chances the following day, Monday, 14 January, they both felt very optimistic. Goderich, they understood, was unlikely to join, in spite of Huskisson's entreaties. But Palmerston hardly minded now that Goderich's weakness had been so exposed. 'I fight for him manfully to the world at large,' he wrote, 'but in confidence cannot defend him any longer.' It was to others he now looked: 'Dudley's continuance in the Foreign Office . . . would give a security that our foreign relations would be kept up in the same spirit as hitherto while Huskisson's superintendence of our Colonial system and Grant's management of our commercial arrangements would preclude any departure from the much calumniated principles of Free Trade, and then if Peel resumed his domestic reforms in the Home Office, and the Duke were to rule Windsor with proper sternness, I really do not see that any great mischief could arise from giving Melville and Bathurst the few thousand a year each for holding some nominal office.' Eldon was the only one he considered unacceptable as a colleague, for while neither he nor Huskisson felt that they could accept Peel as chief if Wellington preferred to keep the Horse Guards, Peel's inclusion in the Cabinet was a 'great security', as on all but the Catholic question he was '*quite* as *liberal*' as they were themselves. But the principal 'security for the maintenance of those liberal principles' was Huskisson himself. It was Huskisson, however, who hesitated most and once again it was Herries who was the cause.[88]

Huskisson made it clear that he would refuse to serve at all if Herries were kept at the Exchequer, and was not sure that he could even if he were moved to some other place. That there should still be difficulties about getting rid of Herries seemed to Palmerston to provide further evidence of Knighton's evil influence. But they also demonstrated his own rising status with Huskisson when, with Grant and Dudley, he was asked if their leader could serve without compromising his 'personal honour and public character' in a Ministry that included Herries. The 'triumvirate', as Huskisson dubbed them, took their time about making a reply and giving it 'the most anxious consideration & turning the matter in every possible way'. Palmerston himself was inclined to make Herries's total exclusion an 'indispensable condition', but was persuaded that they would not be able to make public their main reason – Huskisson's bad personal relations with him – nor prove their other – that Herries had deliberately set out to bring down the Goderich Government. Huskisson therefore wrote to the duke on 17 January accepting office on condition only that Herries should not have the Exchequer or be allowed to revive their old quarrel.[89]

With this difficulty out of the way at last Wellington submitted his Cabinet list to the King and sent for the negotiators one by one. Palmerston was the first to see him, at 2 p.m. on 18 January. Everything ought to have passed off smoothly, since Palmerston had talked only the day before about relying on the composition of the Government to ensure the continuation of a liberal policy in both foreign and domestic affairs, and now, he discovered, there were to be seven 'Catholics' to six 'Protestants'. But after all that had happened to him before, and with careless people like Huskisson and Goderich around him, it is not perhaps surprising that the passage of another twenty-four hours should only have strengthened his natural caution and suspicion and have led him to demand further and written guarantees about the Catholic question. Not only should the Catholic question be an open one in the Cabinet, but patronage also should be distributed impartially among Protestants and Catholics and neither the Lord Lieutenant nor the Irish Secretary should be a person 'professing decided hostility to the Catholic claims'. He frankly admitted to Wellington that the second of these demands was owing to the treatment he had suffered in the Cambridge election of 1826 and the third to the presence in the Cabinet of Bathurst and Goulburn. The duke had come armed with a memorandum on the general question of 'neutrality', but considering how much he had already conceded it is hardly surprising that he was rather put out by the other demands. 'He seemed to receive these propositions', Palmerston recorded, 'like a person who was more accustomed to prescribe to others than to have conditions suggested to him, but took the line of treating them lightly & laughing them off, saying that the first was asking him if he was honest, the second whether he was a madman.' He had, the duke went on, plenty of experience of Ireland and certainly knew better than to send a firebrand there; rather, he was sure, 'the policy of the Gvt ought to be to keep the Catholic question out of sight by moderation'. This last was not at all what Palmerston wanted: only the day before he had been reckoning on the duke's lack of bigotry leading to an active consideration of the question as soon as time and circumstances permitted. So while he withdrew any demand for written guarantees he nevertheless went away still insisting that there must at least be 'that honourable understanding between man & man which one cd refer to as something definite'.[90]

Although it had been quite clearly understood beforehand that they must all join the Government together or not at all, it was only afterwards Palmerston found that while Grant agreed with him in thinking his propositions if anything 'too little', Huskisson and Dudley thought them 'too much'. The next day he was also disappointed when he approached as a potential ally a new Johnian and 'Catholic' adherent to the Cabinet. Ellenborough, 'too much delighted to have got into the Cabinet to care for anything else' in Palmerston's view, was already displaying that careless arrogance which was shortly to cost him both friends and wife. So Palmerston had to be content with less than he wanted. The 'four', as Wellington came to call them, went again to Apsley House at ten-thirty in the evening of 21 January and came easily to what even Palmerston accepted as 'a perfectly satisfactory under-standing'. The duke 'entirely admitted' that each member of the Cabinet should be free to take the line he wished on the Catholic question, that while not giving any 'pledge' about the future the 'principle of strict neutrality' should include patronage, and that Palmerston's 'propositions' should stand as the record of the views of his friends and as the groundwork of their line on any future Irish appointments. Nothing appears to have been written down about other matters, but in contemporary and later accounts Palmerston also gave the impression that Wellington had promised to adhere to Huskisson's liberal commercial policy and to execute faithfully the international en-gagements Canning had made about Greece. 'The King's treaties must be observed,' he reported the duke as saying; and so there would be 'no change of policy about Greece'. But the phrase about the treaties appears to have been taken, not from anything the duke had said or written to him, but from Dudley's report of his own private interview; and though Huskisson after-wards claimed to have been given a similar promise, it was denied by the duke.[91]

Even if the 'agreements' on policy had been less ambiguously contrived, it would have been rather naïve to think that such unsympathetic spirits could easily work together or that without some Whiggish allies the rump of the Canningites would be strong enough to hold the Government to a liberal policy. Wellington himself talked from the first about being compelled to make a 'hotch-potch Administration'; and few believed that his experiment in reconciliation could possibly succeed. Extreme Tories therefore concluded that his real object in cultivating such a 'Machiavelian parvenu' as Huskisson was to break up a potential Opposition of Whigs and Canningites and to reduce the leading talents among the latter to impotence under his own strong Government. Huskisson, he told the discontented Tories, was 'a good bridge for rats to run over'. Palmerston maintained that he and his friends had taken the course best calculated to ensure that the King's Government was con-ducted on the same principles as before. He certainly thought it a great relief at least to have escaped 'a pig-tail Tory Government'. Most of his friends agreed; but rumour discredited him with being one of those who had per-suaded Huskisson to stay on in office merely so as to keep their jobs. Huskisson's adherence to Wellington was in any case condemned by the Whigs as a cowardly desertion of the coalition with Lansdowne and savagely attacked by Lady Canning as a personal betrayal of her husband. So, with the Whigs driven once more into opposition and the Canningites bitterly divided between Huskisson and Lady Canning, Wellington seemed to be well on the way to success in his supposed ulterior objective of isolating Huskisson and his small group of friends. But in doing this the duke had been forced to recognize the 'four' as a distinct group. They were not yet a party; they were too few and too disorganized for that. But henceforth they have to be distinguished, from the rest of the Government as well as from Canning's other friends, as *Huskissonites*.[92]

All this placed Huskisson in a position of great personal as well as political delicacy in Wellington's Cabinet. When he left it a few months later, it seemed less on account of real political differences than because of a Goderich-like dithering on his own part. But the accusations that had greeted his junction with Wellington had made him peculiarly sensitive to any suggestion that in joining Canning's enemies he was abandoning Canning's principles. Hence, just as for the Canningites Herries had been the 'live shell' in Goderich's Cabinet, for the High Tories Huskisson was the 'dry rot' in Wellington's.[93]

Ellenborough may have been speaking merely with his customary malice when he reported that at the new ministers' first dinner together there was 'no appearance of cordiality or gaiety'. But Emily Cowper also could not see how such a 'monstrous coalition' could last for long. Very soon, while Huskisson's friends were said to be boasting that everything had been conceded to them, Wellington was reported as denying it. A public declaration from Huskisson that the continuation of the Canningite ministers in office was a 'guarantee' that the general principles of policy would remain unchanged was pointedly contradicted by the duke. Shortly afterwards Palmerston joined with Huskisson in publicly differing with the Prime Minister when the question of repealing the Test Act against dissenters came up in Parliament and, as his enemy and the duke's good friend put it, they 'argued for the repeal & voted against it!' This was not so strange as she made it sound. The ancient bar to dissenters holding public office had long been suspended in practice by the passage of an annual Indemnity Act – 'passed yearly', as Lord John Russell put it in his attack, 'to forgive good men for doing good service to their country'. So when the matter had been considered beforehand in Cabinet and Wellington had insisted that they must resist it as a Government, the Huskissonites had retorted that they could do so only on the grounds that it was less urgent than Catholic Emancipation. The duke did not like this; he thought it tended to unite Catholics with dissenters in a single cause. He liked it even less when after the Huskissonites had explained their vote the Government was beaten in the House by a majority of forty-four. The Government wisely bowed to the decision and introduced the repeal themselves. But the whole affair had done no good among them.[94]

There came an even greater row in June when a compromise was patched up over the duty on imported corn, only to have the 'Saintly' Grant resign on the grounds that it was still too high. This was an issue that had strongly divided Canning and the duke before and any compromise was liable to touch again the question of 'betrayal'. It was not unreasonable therefore that Grant, who as President of the Board of Trade would have to present the Government's proposals, should jib at doing so. But after all that had been said by Canning's widow, it would have been intolerable for Huskisson to have been shown up as less devoted to Canning's principles than Grant. Mrs Arbuthnot was delighted at the prospect of a row. It would be 'an excellent riddance', she wrote; 'I only wish Ld Palmerston wd resign with him.' But it was Palmerston who persuaded his old friend to withdraw his resignation. It was done, however, with Cambridge pragmatism rather than Scottish philosophy. They had all come in, he pointed out, on the understanding that they would sink or swim together. If Grant persisted in his resignation, they would be shown up as quite disunited at the same time as they were all forced to follow his example. For while Wellington had really made the greater concession, on such an emotive issue as this Huskisson would not be able to leave the defence of principle to his junior or Palmerston to carry on without Huskisson in a Cabinet dominated by the 'arbitrary party'. Then there would soon be formed a 'purely Tory Government, that would speedily throw over all those measures on which Canning had founded his fame. We should break immediately with Russia, probably also with France, back out of the Greek treaty, and unite ourselves again with Metternich, and adopt the apostolical party in Spain and Portugal.' [95]

What is most interesting about Palmerston's argument to Grant is its preoccupation with Canning's favourite topic of foreign affairs. When he reported to his brother that he had entered Wellington's Cabinet along with Huskisson, he had casually referred to himself as one of the 'Canningites'; but Huskisson and Granville at that same time did not include him in the category of 'Canning's friends' and carefully distinguished him as merely one of the 'Catholics'. To an even closer confidante Palmerston had also remarked about the new Cabinet, 'I think it will do & the Gvt will be strong & liberal', but cynically had added, 'at least if it is not the latter it will soon come to be the former'. This seems to suggest that his gradual emergence as keeper-general of Canning's principles of foreign policy and guardian-in-chief of the Cabinet's liberal conscience was as calculated a move by him as it was a surprise to others. Chance, however, had a good deal to do with it and this was also true of the preparation he had had even before the change of Government. [96]

Six months earlier Palmerston happened to be staying at Eartham when a request arrived from London for new advice from Huskisson about the orders to be sent to the East. During the last year of his life Canning had led England triumphantly out of isolation from a European Concert dominated by Metternich and reconciled English support of the Greeks with the protection of her interests in the Near East by concerting an alignment with Russia and France. His principal object was to restrain Russia by obtaining her consent to act in concert and to fend off an explosive Russo-Turkish war by extracting reasonable concessions from the Turks. Unfortunately the Sultan did not think that it was reasonable to make any concessions to the Greeks, and by both this obstinacy and the employment of the Egyptians in the Morea threatened to make of the allies' cooperation the means by which Russia would be given backing for the more extreme measures Canning had determined to avoid. Where, as Prime Minister, Canning might have succeeded, moreover, Goderich was most unlikely to do so; and in continually dithering and delaying, his Goverment failed in the end either to prevent the destruction of the Turkish and Egyptian fleets at Navarino or to limit its consequences.

All this, however unfortunate, gave Palmerston an important opportunity to develop his ideas on foreign policy. His presence at Eartham led Huskisson to consult him about the instructions to Admiral Codrington and therefore occasioned what seems to have been the very first of a lifelong series of famous memoranda. Unfortunately this paper has disappeared; but it seems to have argued in favour of confining the proposed blockade of Greece to the ships of the belligerents only. Huskisson, however, claimed to have talked Palmerston round, and Palmerston's later attitude was certainly very tough. On Navarino itself he commented in private in that tone of heavy irony of which he was a master. While Goderich and his nervous colleagues trembled at the thought of having to explain the battle to Parliament, Palmerston wrote: 'The mere circumstance of our having made a bonfire of the fleet of our good ally at Navarino is not deemed a reason for assembling Parliament, because this was not a declaration of war but only a slight act of remonstrance struck parenthetically into unbroken friendship; but it was thought possible that the Turk might, upon hearing of this friendly liberty, through his barbarous ignorance of civilized usage, have taken unfounded offence, and, like an ill-bred fellow, have declared war against those allies who, as Codrington says in one of his resolutions, were doing all these things "evidently to the advantage of the Porte itself ".' But the Sultan did take offence and he rejected both allied pressure and Russian threats. Navarino was therefore followed by increasing demands from Britain's allies for further measures against the recalcitrant Turk, from Russia for their consent to her occupation of the Sultan's Danubian Principalities, and from France for the blockade of Constantinople and the supply of loans to the Greek resistance.[97]

Navarino was the greatest possible embarrassment to the Goderich Government, for while they were bound to concert measures with France and Russia, they were no less anxious than before to save the Turks from Britain's allies as well as from themselves. Palmerston believed that they must act to cut the Gordian knot, and on 6 December he sent to the Prime Minister his first Cabinet memorandum on foreign policy. 'Persuasion, reasoning, and threats having failed to sway the Porte, actual coercion must be resorted to,' he argued, 'and it only remains to be considered what shall be the nature and the degree of that coercion and where it can most effectually be applied.' It was no use disguising from themselves or from others that these measures must be either 'actual war or . . . in their nature tantamount to war'; the real question for discussion was how to limit the consequences of that coercion to the pacification of Greece rather than the dismemberment of Turkey by Russia. He was sure that they should not accept the Russian proposition. 'These provinces have long been coveted not only by the Russian Government but by the Russian Nation, [so] it would be more easy to invite the Russian army to enter than to get them out again.' Moreover, since it was 'more consistent with the policy & character of the Turkish Government to be passively recusant than actively resentful', the Russians would in the end be forced to march on Constantinople and so to force the very crisis of the Empire's existence most feared by British interests. For the same reason the first of the French proposals, an allied blockade of Constantinople, would be equally ineffective and equally liable to more dangerous consequences. Nor did he see much point in the alternative French proposal of a loan. For even if Parliament's consent could be obtained and Greek misuse of the money be disregarded, a loan would still not be likely to secure the expulsion of the Turks from the Morea. But there were in Portugal '5,000 men as fine troops as ever took the field'. This was the force that Canning had dispatched a year before to 'plant the standard of England'; and so successful did that intervention appear to have been in bringing Miguel to reason that 'the lapse of a few weeks', Palmerston thought, would probably set the British troops free. They could then be sent to join with others already in Malta and the Ionian Islands with a view to encouraging the Egyptians to leave and if necessary to enforce their departure in concert with the French. 'The advantage of this measure', he concluded, 'would be that it would accomplish the object of the allies without disturbing the Peace of Europe, that it would still keep England in a prominent & advanced position in the confederacy, and that it would bring the matter to an end without our having to wade through the delays & subterfuges of Turkish diplomacy.' But 'nobody else' in Goderich's Cabinet approved it and so British policy drifted virtually out of control.[98]

Wellington's succession to the feeble Goderich did nothing to improve British policy in the Near East; it simply divided the Cabinet by a difference of policy rather than of nerve. 'Huskisson, Dudley, Grant, and I try to keep things together, and have done so,' Palmerston wrote; 'and if Russia and France are *civil* to us, we shall manage it still; but if they send us uncivil papers, we shall not be able to prevent a separation of the alliance.' However, although effective enough under Canning's immediate guidance, the 'fanciful, irresolute, absent' Dudley was hardly competent to cope with Wellington and his Cabinet cronies. Already, indeed, he was showing signs of the mental and physical decay that in all too short a time was to remove him from the world. So chance once more had a good deal to do with Palmerston's coming forward in matters of foreign policy. Hitherto his interest in that subject had been marked by little more than casual comments in private letters, the purchase of Martens's *Recueil de Traités* in 1818, and his 'perfunctory' speech of 1823.[99]

Parliament opened on 29 January 1828 and Palmerston, the only minister in the Commons who did not have to seek re-election, was also the only one present to defend the Royal Address. His sister welcomed the opportunity for him to act as Leader of the House. 'I sincerely wish that he was to remain so for a considerable time & give people an opportunity of judging of his talents,' she wrote, 'for I know the moment Mr Peel etc. take their seats Harry's mouth will be *closed* upon every subject but what relates to the War Office.' Hobhouse, however, noted that he spoke 'miserably'. He was still alone two days later when Hobhouse rose to ask if the Government intended to move a vote of thanks to Codrington for the victory at Navarino. Hobhouse's object was clearly to rebuke the Government for referring to the battle in the King's Speech as an 'untoward event' and to embarrass the Canningites for being party to such an apparent repudiation of Canning's Greek policy. Palmerston extricated himself with some dexterity by interpreting 'untoward' as 'unexpected'. But in spite of the 'security' he thought Dudley's presence in the Cabinet gave for the continuation of Canning's foreign policy, and the assurance he believed Wellington had given about observing 'the King's treaties', Palmerston was not so naïve as to think that difficulties might not arise to upset this 'fragile arrangement', and he was certainly not surprised when at an early meeting of the Cabinet there was a clash over the future extent and nature of Greece. [100]

Palmerston already knew that the Prime Minister intended to propose that 'Greece' be limited to the Morea and a number of islands, and consequently both he and Grant had sought to bolster Dudley in advance with counter-memoranda. Palmerston's paper, dubbed 'excellent' by the Foreign Secretary, argued strongly for a more generous geographical boundary on grounds of both expediency and principle. More extensive limits would be needed to make Greece genuinely self-sufficient for purposes of defence; less would neither pacify the Greeks nor encourage the Russians to subordinate their policy to the objectives of the allies. Finally, while Turkey was concerned to contest the principle of autonomy more than its extent, 'would it not', he concluded, 'be a sort of misnomer to give the appellation of *Greece* to a Territory which should exclude Athens & Thebes, Marathon, Plataea, Salamis & Thermopylae'? It does not seem to have occurred to Palmerston to argue at the meeting of the Cabinet held on 9 March that Greek self-defence would be a barrier to Russia as well as Turkey, and although his hopes of 'liberal support' from Peel turned out to be justified the meeting ended without any real decision. [101]

Relations among the Cabinet took a distinct turn for the worse in March after it was learned officially that Russia intended to declare war on Turkey. This brought Wellington and the Huskissonites closer together in their apprehension of Russia but further apart over how to meet the danger. 'We do not mean to go to war with Turkey; and how, therefore, can we cooperate with Russia if she does go to war?' Palmerston asked. 'We are, however, determined not to throw the treaty overboard on account of this difficulty, but to persevere with France to execute it in our own way.' But what way was that to be? The French were pressing for troops to go out; but Palmerston appreciated that the state of Parliament and public opinion would not now allow it. In fact, the troops were really needed where they were in Portugal, for in the interval since December Miguel had broken all his promises. Yet in spite of Palmerston's objection that to allow the Portuguese constitution to collapse would be to make the British look like 'dupes', Wellington insisted that they must evacuate, leaving only a couple of ships and a battalion of marines to protect British subjects and give refuge to persecuted Constitutionalists, and that the British envoy should 'ask for an interview with Miguel, and expostulate with him in the strongest terms'.[102]

Hitherto Palmerston had relied on Peel, as being 'so right-headed and liberal, and so up to the opinions and feelings of the times, that he smoothes difficulties which might otherwise be insurmountable', and on the argument about the Treaty of London curbing the Russians by cooperation and saving the Turks at the same time as the Greeks. But when the Cabinet meetings recommenced early in April to define the treaty's objectives more clearly, it was still to no avail, though they went over all the old ground about the territorial limits of Greece and the extent of her legal dependence on Turkey. 'As usual, much discussion and entire difference of opinion,' Palmerston noted; 'the Duke, Ellenborough, and Aberdeen being for cutting down the Greeks as much as possible; Huskisson, Dudley, and myself for executing the treaty in the fair spirit of those who made it.' Palmerston himself worked hard and with success on Peel's 'liberal' inclinations, in particular to prevent the Turks being given a veto on the choice of President for Greece. He even wrote to Wellington directly. There is no evidence that he was also party to the underhand manoeuvre contrived within the Foreign Office by which France was encouraged to put pressure on the duke. 'We don't get on about Greece,' wrote the Canningite Undersecretary in the office to the Canningite ambassador in Paris. 'The D. of W. is so obstinate. . . . He cannot bear the idea of the Greeks being independent under *any* circumstances. I suspect that he has but little support in the Cabinet – so that if *France would press* the question of an ultimatum to the Turks . . ., I think the D. must give way. There is one thing to be specially guarded against at this moment – which is anything like a deviation from the Treaty of July. . . . I thought it right knowing this to put you on yr guard in yr interpretations of Dudley's instructions.'[103]

This 'most confidential' letter mentioned only Huskisson and not Palmerston as supplying Dudley's deficiencies in Cabinet. But Palmerston had certainly begun to despair of Wellington's loyalty to the treaty. 'The Duke,' he wrote in April, 'while he professes to maintain it, would execute it in the spirit of one who condemns it.' A month later he wrote to his brother: 'We are not going on as I like.' The initiative so dramatically seized from Metternich in 1826 was being lost again, it seemed to him, in the East as in the West. He suspected even that this was not merely carelessness but collusion. 'The Duke has the strongest dislike to Russia,' he wrote, '– more, I think, from personal feeling than from political. Ellenborough is even more adverse than the Duke: Aberdeen is Austrian, and Bathurst anti-Russian and Austrian; all these would give anything to get out of the Greek treaty, which they hate, and they set about it dextrously. The Duke I believe to be in correspondence with Metternich, and tries to play his game of delay and procrastination.'[104]

This suspicion may have led Palmerston, if not into an actual conspiracy against the Prime Minister's foreign policy, at least into the preparations for one. In his communication to his brother in May he also enclosed an elaborate private code for future use. For a Cabinet minister Palmerston was already going rather far in his letters, even between brothers. Had he been challenged he would no doubt have defended his indiscretions as deliberate but friendly warnings to the Russians that they must try especially hard to reassure an over-suspicious and hostile Wellington. William Temple, as minister *ad interim* in St Petersburg, was ideally suited and obviously intended to pass them on. Wellington had employed similar methods to undermine Canning's foreign policy in Liverpool's Ministry, but if he had had actual proof of them – and being no fool he must have suspected they existed – he would have called them damn near treason. Either, therefore, Palmerston's code was a sensible precaution he had hitherto neglected or he was preparing something still more strong.[105]

No final confrontation came in Cabinet on foreign policy since, Palmerston wrote to his brother, 'the result has not yet been to lead us to *do* anything we disapproved of, but only to make us leave *undone* things we should have wished to have done'. But such tensions and suspicions made constantly for sharp and tiresome clashes in the Cabinet. 'The Cabinet has gone on for some time past as it had done before,' Palmerston noted wearily in his journal towards the end of May, 'differing upon almost every question of any importance that has been brought under consideration:– meeting to debate and dispute, and separating without deciding.' Others felt exactly the same. A generation later Aberdeen still recalled the 'constant disputes' with Palmerston that were 'anything but pleasant'. The Lord Chancellor, a convivial fellow, advised: 'We should have no Cabinets after dinner. We all drink too much wine, and are not civil to each other.' But no one perhaps stirred the pot so much as the Privy Seal, of whom from the earliest days of the Ministry it had been said that he 'already begins to plague his colleagues; having nothing to do at his own Office he is always rummaging in theirs'. Ellenborough was always working on Wellington's vanity and irascibility, especially where the 'four' were concerned. 'The Duke complained to me in the House of the manner in which the *four* hang together,' he wrote in his diary. 'He hoped they would have ceased to do so after the Corn business. He would not be sorry to get rid of Dudley, Grant, and Palmerston.'[106]

Palmerston's behaviour in the confidential discussions of the Cabinet was bad enough; his rarer public interventions in Parliament, in Wellington's view, came near to mutiny. When an attack was made on Canning's memory during a debate about a pension for his family on 14 May, it was Palmerston who leaped to his feet. 'He could not allow that statement to remain uncontradicted,' he said, 'considering, as he did, that the government of this country would be entitled to parliamentary support, in proportion as it adhered to the principles of Mr Canning.' Lady Canning was delighted: Palmerston, she considered, had 'redeemed the want of proper spirit and the coldness of others on the government side' and behaved in sharp contrast to those from whom on personal grounds she might have expected better. Wellington, however, was plainly furious: Huskisson afterwards concluded that this must indeed have been what gave the duke such 'mortal offence' that he decided to put an end to the state of internal warfare. At the time the duke's cronies were also sure that he would act; but, owing perhaps to the unwritten compact of January, they did not expect him to do so until after the end of the session. In the meantime it was rumoured that he had 'determined, when the [Pension] Bill came to the Lords, to state his opinion upon Mr Canning's principles & give Lord Palmerston a good set down'. It did not, however, prove necessary; for within a few days Huskisson, in a passable imitation of Goderich, had given the duke a splendid opportunity of striking even harder and at once.[107]

The cause, or rather the occasion, of the crisis was a difference over the disfranchisement of a couple of corrupt and rotten boroughs and the transfer of their representation to large towns. The Huskissonites were certainly not parliamentary reformers, but their liberal image made them sensitive to extreme cases of corruption. As Palmerston shortly afterwards explained: 'his wish [was] that the franchise should be extended to a great town, not because he was a friend to reform in principle, but because he was its decided enemy. To extend the franchise to large towns, on such occasions as the one in question, was the only mode by which the House could avoid the adoption, at some time or other, of a general plan of reform. . . . When people saw such populous places as Leeds and Manchester unrepresented, whilst a green mound of earth returned two members, it naturally gave rise to complaint.'[108]

There was nothing new in such a view; Palmerston had said much the same to his brother nearly ten years earlier. So when the cases of Penryn and East Retford loomed up he joined with Huskisson and Dudley in favouring the transfer of their representation, while Wellington and Bathurst merely proposed to widen the electorate a little. But neither side really wanted to create a sort of rule that the representation should always be transferred in such cases and they therefore accepted Peel's compromise proposal to transfer Penryn to Manchester but throw open Retford to the electors of the neighbouring hundred. This was the opposite way round to what Huskisson preferred, but as Palmerston supported Peel he reluctantly gave way. Unfortunately they never came to any explicit agreement about what should happen if Parliament were to condemn only one of the boroughs. Huskisson publicly announced that he would give its members to a town; Peel only that he would wait and see. When, therefore, the committee decided that Penryn was not guilty enough to be entirely disfranchised but should be thrown open to the hundred, the Cabinet was plunged once more into disarray. At a meeting on Monday, 19 May Peel indicated that he would keep to his course on Retford and Huskisson protested that this would mean wrecking the compromise by making neither transfer to a town. It was therefore proposed that the question should be made an open one like that of Catholic Emancipation, with each member of the Cabinet being left free in Parliament to take what line he wished. But it is clear even from Palmerston's account that this was never explicitly agreed. It would, in fact, have been difficult to do so, since they had on a previous division in Parliament voted as a Government in favour of Retford constituency being extended into the local hundred. The only agreement come to, therefore, was that they should stick to their original arrangement about Retford in the hope that Parliament would change its mind about Penryn.[109]

Palmerston claimed afterwards to have been very sceptical about their prospects; but Huskisson apparently did go down to the House that night with the intention of voting with Peel. However, during the course of the debate all hope of a change about Penryn was dissipated and Huskisson was taunted with having abandoned his promise about at least one of the transfers being made to a large town. According to Palmerston Huskisson became increasingly uneasy and utterly unable to make up his mind how to vote. 'Stay where you are,' Palmerston advised, and so Huskisson voted against Peel; if Huskisson had had to move, he believed, he would have gone the other way. Grant was absent but Palmerston also voted against Peel, on the grounds that Huskisson's vote 'made the question no longer a Government one'.[110]

Palmerston walked home alone after the debate, hearing no comment from anyone about what had happened; nor, apparently, did he really expect to, since from their silence about the proposal of 'neutrality' the previous afternoon he rather concluded that neither Wellington nor Peel objected, and in any case it did not strike him that Huskisson and he had done 'anything that was a material breach of official allegiance'. On Tuesday he was too busy at home to be disturbed and he did not go down to the War Office until half past three. But at four o'clock he received a note from Huskisson asking him to come over as soon as possible. When he got to Huskisson's, where he found Dudley also, he discovered that after the previous night's debate Huskisson had become so agitated that, without consulting anyone and at two in the morning, he had addressed a letter to the Prime Minister, to the effect that if his vote had made his continuing in office an embarrassment then he wished to relieve the duke of any feelings of personal delicacy and to place himself entirely at the duke's disposal. 'The letter was certainly worded ambiguously & written hastily & might be open to be construed as a simple resignation,' Palmerston noted; 'the Duke chose so to understand it – shewed it to Peel who read it in the same sense & took no time in laying it in that sense before the King & in acquainting Huskisson that he had done so.'[111]

Whatever Huskisson had really meant, he very soon regretted it; and between them his friends tried everything they could to retrieve the situation.

But it was all useless. Dudley had happened to see Huskisson that morning on foreign affairs and Huskisson had then 'incidentally mentioned what had happened the night before, not as a matter of importance, but as one of those little rubs which created difficulties at the moment, but which we should ultimately get over'. So when Dudley saw the duke that day he tried to clear up the misunderstanding; but Wellington would have none of it and subsequently made what Palmerston called the 'dry announcement' that he had sent the resignation in. This seemed to shut the door to further negotiations, but since he too had voted as Huskisson had done it was agreed that Palmerston should also try his hand at explanations.[112]

When Palmerston arrived in Downing St he found not Wellington but Peel, 'evidently hurt and angry, though . . . perfectly kind and conciliatory' to Palmerston. Apparently Wellington had hurriedly left in order to avoid a call from Huskisson. But Palmerston pursued him to the Lords and sent in a note requesting 'a few minutes' conversation'. The duke then came out and, finding no committee room available, they walked up and down the Long Gallery for half an hour together. Palmerston said all he could to discover the extent of the 'misunderstanding' and pointed out that if Huskisson went, then so must he, as he had voted against the Government without even the excuse of being bound by a former pledge. Palmerston claimed to have noted that as he said this the duke 'raised his eyes which had been fixed on the ground as we were walking up and down, and looked sharp and earnestly at me, as if to see whether this was meant as a sort of menace'. But the duke said nothing; afterwards he explained to his Privy Seal that 'he did *not choose to fire great guns at sparrows*'. 'How pleased this expression would make Palmerston,' Ellenborough wrote with his customary malice; thirty years later, when he wished to damage Palmerston's claims as War Minister, he went out of his way to make the story known.[113]

In May 1828 Wellington's pride was more justified and certainly more understandable than Palmerston's. He told Ellenborough that 'he knew the men he had to deal with. The Canningites all entertained an erroneous and exaggerated view of their own consequence, which existed in the minds of none but themselves. They were always endeavouring to lord it. In this case, if he had solicited Huskisson to remain, Huskisson would have been Minister instead of himself.' While, therefore, both Ellenborough and Mrs Arbuthnot believed that the duke had decided to seize the opportunity to rid himself of his awkward colleagues, it is also understandable why Palmerston should have been given the impression that it was all 'a point of etiquette' and that if only Huskisson himself would write again all might yet be saved. So that same Tuesday evening Huskisson composed a new letter of explanation and the next day there followed further communications in writing between him and Wellington.[114]

While Palmerston's diagnosis may have been correct, the cure could not be found as long as Wellington insisted that Huskisson must voluntarily withdraw a resignation which Huskisson on his part refused to acknowledge he had ever actually made. In the meantime, although they absented themselves from the Mansion House dinner, the Huskissonites continued to sit on the Treasury Bench so as to emphasize that they had not resigned, and on Wednesday evening Palmerston went out of his way at Almack's to contradict the report as regards himself. All this created immense confusion out of rumour. But on Thursday, 22 May, there came another letter from Wellington that Palmerston considered 'decisive' in putting an end to all further negotiations; and in the afternoon he went to tell Peel so and to put off the Army Estimates he was due to move on Friday. The only possibility of his staying in, he thought, was that the King might intervene; but he doubted the energy was there for that. Dudley, however, was now very unwilling to give up the office he was at last beginning to enjoy. So the feeble comedy endured a few days more, with Palmerston contriving yet another verbal device for resolving the 'misunderstanding' with honour to both sides and with Dudley insisting that they should not bow down to the duke till Huskisson had seen the King, while the King insisted that he could not see his Colonial Secretary until Huskisson had settled matters with the duke. At length, on Sunday afternoon, they realized that time had finally run out and that the duke must have gone off to Windsor to propose a replacement for Huskisson. In that case, Palmerston declared, there was nothing to be done but send his explicit resignation after Huskisson's ambiguous one.[115]

The Foreign Secretary still clung desperately to office throughout the second weekend of the crisis. 'Dudley', Palmerston wrote, 'stroked his chin, counted the squares of the carpet three times up and three times down, and then went off in the agony of doubt and hesitation.' On Sunday they met again at a friend's and 'after dinner, when the ladies were gone, Dudley came round to me, and told me he was doubtful whether he had done right or not'. Later still he found William Lamb and Dudley again at Huskisson's. 'We all left Huskisson together, and Dudley proposed we should walk up a little way, our cabriolets following. He was in the middle, and said, Well, now we are by ourselves in the street, and nobody but the sentry to hear us, let me know, right and left, what is meant to be done – "in" or "out".' Palmerston replied 'out' and Lamb echoed him, though very regretfully, since he had voted with the Government. But Dudley went on and on about how the King had taken 'a great fancy' to him and how both he and Wellington expected him to stay; he also admitted to some attachment to the duke. Yet he realized how difficult it would be for him, who had so long been attached to Canning, to stay if Palmerston, who was a relatively recent devotee, persisted in his resignation. To settle matters Palmerston wrote out his resignation when he got home and sent it off the next morning. Two days later and much to Wellington's surprise Dudley also resigned, though it was said he had to be taken by the arms, with Lamb on his right and Palmerston on his left, and marched down the Foreign Office steps.[116]

Although Dudley had had to be persuaded out of office by his friends, it was reckoned that Palmerston, like Huskisson, had been 'ejected' by his enemies. There was some truth in this. Before he received Palmerston's letter of resignation Wellington had intended to write and say that after the expiry of Huskisson's time limit he considered also 'Palmerston as gone'; and even after the arrival of Palmerston's letter made this unnecessary he nevertheless revealed in his reply that he had already anticipated its contents in conversation with the King. Palmerston had not in the least disguised that if Huskisson went, then so would he. But it was all rather precipitate on Wellington's part and, like the attempt to keep Dudley, tended to confirm the general impression that it was Huskisson and Palmerston, perhaps even the latter more than the former, of whom the duke wished most to be rid. Lady Cowper knew the duke well and, being 'a Whig only by marriage . . . and a regular courtier at heart', liked him very much; 'there is nothing I would not do to please him,' she said, 'he is such a love.' But her affection for him does not seem to have been such as to arouse the other's jealousy. On her part Mrs Arbuthnot used to think Palmerston 'very gentlemanlike and sensible & [it seemed] very amiable'; in short a 'very delightful person' who she hoped would marry her cousin. But soon she had begun to turn right round against him. In June 1827 she confessed to being 'provoked' by his behaviour; by February 1828 he had become in her opinion 'the shabbiest of all'. What was most responsible for her anger was not any irritations over Army matters – though just before the duke returned to the Horse Guards she too was talking of Palmerston 'always quarrelling with every body' – but that where so short a time before he had been a Tory, to keep his place he now professed to be a Whig. This was a considerable exaggeration; it could also not have been the full explanation for the coolness that so characterized Palmerston's relations with the duke.[117]

It was all very well for Mrs Arbuthnot to cry she could not bear it; the Prime Minister had no other choice when he formed his Government early in 1828. It was Palmerston's attitude to foreign affairs and his pressing it in Cabinet that really drove them to quarrel. Palmerston had realized before he joined Wellington's Cabinet that the duke was 'an apostolical & holy alliance politician'. But he obviously had hoped to counter this by eternal reverence for Canning's 'principles' of foreign affairs and by a firm adherence to the Greek treaty which Canning had manoeuvred Wellington into negotiating for him. It was Palmerston's constant 'pecking' about this that irritated Wellington most and made vanity clash with pride. On the Catholic question, the Test Act and even corrupt boroughs there always seemed room to compromise. But on foreign affairs the deadlock remained unbroken and, as Lady Cowper reported, while the collapse came over East Retford 'they were all pulling different ways before about Russia'.[118]

INTERLUDE II:
JACKDAW AND
PHOENIX,
1828-30

Five months after his resignation Palmerston wrote plaintively to Sulivan: 'I wonder when the widows & soldiers' wives will find out that I am no longer Secy at Wr.' In spite of all the tedious mountain of detail and routine, it is not really any wonder that, after having been so many years in office, his retirement in May 1828 should have left him, as the Duke of Devonshire found, 'very low'. The loss of income from his salary must also have been, as Lady Cowper admitted, rather inconvenient to say the least. But what should be stressed is that neither consideration had made him hesitate, let alone linger as Dudley had tried to do. The question remained, however, what should now be done?[1]

Even assuming that some reconciliation between Huskissonites and anti-Huskissonites was once again conceivable, the reunited Canningites would still not have made a very large group – from twenty-five to thirty in the Commons and a dozen or so in the Lords; 'small' but 'very respectable', Palmerston reckoned. Goderich certainly thought it would be worth-while organizing a distinct faction and immediately on hearing of the exodus wrote first to Huskisson and then to Palmerston to propose a meeting at his house. But that place was 'not relished' according to Palmerston. 'Besides other objections it would have the appearance of putting ourselves under his lead, which, considering what an unfortunate display he made last December as head of a party, it would by no means be expedient for us to do.' So at one o'clock on 2 June Goderich, Palmerston, Grant and Lamb met instead under Huskisson's roof in Downing St.[2]

What was decided at Huskisson's is far from clear. According to what Granville heard, Goderich wanted to go over to systematic opposition; and Huskisson refused. There was plenty to discuss, for the Huskissonites were in a very difficult position. Ejected by Wellington, they were also hated by the Ultra-Tories and distrusted by the Lansdowne Whigs as well as by the friends of Grey and the relatives of Canning. Mrs Arbuthnot was therefore not so very far off the mark when she concluded that they would 'soon be quite forgotten or only remembered to be laughed at'. The worst of their stigmata was the accusation of desertion and inconsistency. This made it more important than ever, both for their personal self-respect and for their political future, to emphasize that their first loyalty was not merely to Canning's memory but more to his 'principles' and to base their public conduct not so much on men as measures. But when they met in Downing St they still could not be sure what Wellington's policies would be. There was some suspicion that their 'ejection' had all been part of an Ultra plot. Palmerston heard that the Duke of Cumberland abused him for being a 'democrat' and for encouraging Huskisson to resign. The plot, he concluded, was to bring back Eldon. It was also noted that the day before the ejected ministers went down to Windsor to deliver up their Seals Wellington attended a Pitt dinner at which Eldon 'begged for "one cheer more" for the toast of Protestant ascendancy'. On the other hand, Peel remained as Wellington's right-hand man and though Protestant too he was nonetheless liberal. Huskisson and Palmerston had both already refused to give one or more of their sympathizers pointed advice not to accept office under Wellington; three others remained in minor offices when the rest resigned. It was also said, though by the biased Bathurst, that they had urged Granville to stay on as ambassador in Paris in order to get them confidential information. Granville did resign, but only very reluctantly since he, like Morley, felt that Huskisson had been hasty and lacked the justification of 'some great difference of principle'.[3]

It would, in view of all this doubt and disagreement, have been both embarrassing and ill-advised for the ex-ministers to have gone directly into systematic opposition before seeing whether or not the duke would grant them retrospective vindication by giving his Ministry a discernible lurch towards the right. So when, on the evening of their conference in Downing St, Huskisson took Canning's old Opposition seat in the Commons and, with Palmerston, Grant and others about him, rose to defend his recent resignation, his speech was probably intended as a sort of probing operation. It seemed, according to one listener, an 'attempt at popularity by accusing standing armies & illiberality, and the Holy Alliance'. It was answered at once, and most effectively, by Peel avowing that the policy of the Government, on foreign and domestic affairs alike, remained unchanged. This would explain why Palmerston, who followed Peel, said more about Huskisson than himself and very little more than that, without Huskisson in the Government, he saw no good guarantee for its liberal principles. After Peel had spoken most of the House had risen to dine and there were few remaining to hear what Palmerston had to say. But he gained more by his speech than Huskisson did by his. Most considered he had spoken 'well' and 'stoutly', whereas Huskisson, according to Lady Grey, was at best 'vindictive'. This seems to show how much Huskisson was disliked and how little people were impressed by Cumberland and his Ultras' view of Palmerston.[4]

As far as the two Canningite speakers in the House of Commons were themselves concerned this effect was quite fortuitous. What the contrast in style must have meant for them was that Peel's speech, coming in between, had put wholly out of the question any attempt at concerted and systematic opposition. The next day Lady Cowper reported to her brother: 'Those who are out of office mean to sit together below the Treasury Bench, & not to join the ranks of the Opposition – dignified & quiet.' She went on, moreover, to suggest that this was what most suited Palmerston personally: 'nobody could feel more anxious to make the thing up, not only because it is very inconvenient to him to lose the salary of his office but because his connections & friends all lye with the Duke's side and because it separates him from the side he likes, to throw him amongst the Whigs with whom he has no interests or friendships.'[5]

Lady Cowper was just as prejudiced as Mrs Arbuthnot but from her side of the affair much the better informed. One suspects that Palmerston perhaps had been teasing the duke's good friend with all those *Whiggish* remarks with which he so annoyed her. On the other hand, he had written to his brother, when the Huskissonites parted company with the Lansdowne Whigs on joining Wellington in January: 'I very sincerely regret their loss, as I like them much better than the Tories, and agree with them much more.' But he had gone on to say, what Bulwer neglected also to underline, that if they had all gone out of office together 'I should certainly not have sat with them in the House of Commons, but should have taken an independent and separate position'. The fact of the matter was that 'Canningism' was no more definite and coherent than any other political creed of the period. It was, as one of Canning's followers had written in August 1827, 'a compound of Whiggism, without the vice of ultra & impracticable principles, with Toryism, divested of its prejudice & prescription . . . of commonsense, of philosophy, in the best sense of the term applied to politics'. So, while by the beginning of 1828 Palmerston definitely regarded himself as an open and unqualified Canningite, neither then nor six months later did he really feel he knew yet quite where that might lead him between the intolerable extremes of the 'stupid old Tories' on the right and the rabid Whigs on the left. In the summer of 1828, therefore, his small group of friends, though relatively disorganized and lacking even an acknowledged leader, remained where he most wished them for the present to be – in a cautious situation of watching and waiting.[6]

This isolated position left the Huskissonites dangerously exposed to piecemeal desertions. But its wisdom was rapidly underlined as the Ultras failed to make any ground in Wellington's Cabinet and as the Government proceeded on a moderate course. In particular, Palmerston observed, it began to take steps that he himself had urged but a little while before, only to be shot down by the duke. Rather inconsistently he was uncertain whether this was due to Peel or Metternich. But while Metternich appeared merely to be bent on leading Europe by whatever means might seem expedient, Palmerston was sure that it was Peel's presence in the Cabinet that would ensure the continuity of policy. 'I do not think that any material change can take place as long as he remains in the government because he himself is perfectly liberal & enlightened on all subjects except the Catholic question on which indeed I suspect he is quite of our opinion but is bound by early pledges. It is not at all impossible that the other members of the govt may be more disposed to be liberal now that they will themselves have the credit of whatever they may do in that line, than they were when they might be supposed to be swayed by their colleagues. This is not unnatural . . . at all events if they do not pursue a liberal course the government cannot possibly stand.'[7]

There was a good deal of truth in Palmerston's speculations. After the passage of the House of Commons resolutions in May in favour of Catholic as well as dissenters' emancipation, both Peel and Wellington had concluded that the emancipation of the former must eventually follow the latter's. Peel thought that he should resign to make way for the measure, but agreed to stay on in view of the departure of the Huskissonites. Then, on 9 June, the duke gave a strong hint in the Lords that he would turn to the Catholic question in the coming session.

Wellington's language and behaviour on the Catholic question were so ambiguous, the real and supposed differences in the Cabinet so considerable, and the prejudices of the King so great that no one could really be sure what would happen. Palmerston certainly thought at first that by his pronouncement in the Lords the duke had 'only meant to palaver the Catholics, & not being quite as skilful in maneuvering words as men, has said a *little* more than he meant'. To him, therefore, the Government remained as he described it to Lady Cowper, 'essentially Tory, with a garnish of Liberals to keep up appearances'. If it turned out that by their retirement, as opposed to their staying in, he and his friends had forced the Government to adopt a more liberal policy, then he would be glad enough about it. 'At all events one thing has been demonstrated,' he wrote, 'and that is that a purely Tory Government cannot face parliament, and that even the Duke and Bathurst are obliged so far to defer to public opinion as to assume the pretence of liberality – whether there will be anything more than pretence we greatly doubt. . . . Time will shew.' A week later he reported to his brother: 'We are going on here quietly, everybody and all parties seem determined to wait and watch and see the result, and whether the declarations which have been made will be kept to. In the meantime there is no opposition, and it is well for the Government there is not, for Peel is the only man in the House of Commons on the Treasury Bench who can make a speech as a minister should do.' So while the Huskissonites were observed to be voting regularly with the Government, Palmerston was privately gloating at the increasing evidence not only of public support for Catholic Emancipation but also of the Government's appreciation of the force of that opinion: 'The tone of public opinion has fairly overpowered them, and, at the moment when they thought everything within their reach, has wrested everything from their grasp.' A fortnight later he came to the conclusion that the Government really had made up its mind to tackle the question.[8]

This in itself would have been welcome to the Huskissonites. Palmerston also expected it would break up the Government even if it did not necessarily drive out Peel. In any case, he thought, the 'Dictator' needed to reshuffle his Administration. 'I have heard', he reported to Sulivan,

that the Duke begins to find that it is not quite so pleasant a thing as he thought it, in the long run, to do everything himself; & that the subserviency of his colleagues does not quite compensate for the helplessness which arises from that want of energy & information by which alone that subserviency & absence of individual opinion can be created; & that he greatly misses the assistance of Huskisson & it is generally thought that before Parliament meets some changes must take place. The Duke brings little to his extensive duties but narrow prejudices & an obstinate will to act upon them, but that forms a slender capital upon which to govern a nation and keep her up to her station among the improving nations of civilized Europe.

In any event he expected an approach would be made before long to the Huskissonites, though he was inclined to think to Huskisson rather than himself, and singly in the hope of detaching him from his friends. He did not expect such a manoeuvre to succeed, and as far as his own return to office was concerned he had 'pretty well made up [his] own mind henceforward to make the Catholic Question a sine qua non'. Nothing could more clearly have demonstrated that even at this late stage Palmerston still considered his political future to be with the Tories rather than the Whigs.[9]

While everything was thus 'at a lull' and his friends were lying on their 'oars & waiting for events', Palmerston decided not to go straight from Broadlands in the early autumn on what was now becoming his annual visit to Ireland, but first to have a look at his estate at Fairburn and on the way take in the St Leger and the country houses of some of his more splendid acquaintances. For the Doncaster races he stayed at Stapleton – 'a house full of people & a very gay assemblage' – and picked up the latest gossip of Rome from its owner Edward Petre, who though a fool himself belonged to a leading family of English Catholics. Then after a short visit to the Marquess of Stafford's at Worksop – 'magnificent but dull' – Fairburn, and the Music Festival in York where he ran into his old friend Cholmeley – 'with a white wand & red ribband officiating as steward, amateur connoisseur & admirateur' – he moved on in turn to the Carlisles at Castle Howard, to Cholmeley's place near by at Brandsby, and to find Lady Cowper in a glittering party at Chatsworth before leaving for Ireland. But among all these Catholics, Whigs and Canningites, no hint of office came his way; only rumours about official messengers flying after Huskisson (who as so often in difficult times was seeking rest abroad) and of offers made to other Opposition men such as Poulett Thomson, Sir James Graham and even Grey. There were also suggestions that Wellington was looking in quite another direction and that the anti-Catholic Westmorland had been offered again his old office of Privy Seal. If that were true, Palmerston concluded, then it would 'clearly indicate the renewed ascendancy of pig tails & simplify matters extremely; it will be a clear proof that the Catholic question is not to be carried this next year'.[10]

In the meantime the excitement in Ireland had been considerably increased by O'Connell's defeat of Vesey Fitzgerald, the ministerial candidate in the Clare election. 'The event was dramatic and somewhat sublime,' Palmerston afterwards noted in his journal. He was not surprised to hear that more troops would be sent out, he told Sulivan, but, he thought, 'the Govt must chuse between the Pen & the Sword; between a Bill of Conciliation & Martial Law'. When he got to Ireland in October he behaved himself with characteristic caution: he declined to attend a dinner of liberals and Catholics in Sligo on the grounds that 'a man who has been in the Cabinet & means to be there again, has no business to go chattering at Tavern Dinners if he can possibly help it, especially in such ticklish times & on such ticklish subjects'. Everything he saw and heard nevertheless convinced him that things were as quiet as the Orange Clubs and the Duke of Cumberland's Brunswick Clubs would let them be; it was the Catholic leaders themselves and not English bayonets who were by their own restraint really 'keeping the King's Peace for the King's Government'. He was also sure that the Catholics would be very 'tractable' if only the Government would show any real intention of offering relief; but they could not be expected to live on hope for ever.[11]

Palmerston's impressions about the Irish, both Protestant and Catholic, were very strongly reinforced by several talks he had with the Lord-Lieutenant, the Marquess of Anglesey, who also astonished him by revealing that he, too, did not know what the duke's intentions were. It was even arranged that when Palmerston got back to England he should communicate to Anglesey whatever he could discover about the Government's policy. 'The Lord-Lieutenant of Ireland begging a private gentleman to let him know, if he could find out, what the Prime Minister meant upon a question deeply affecting the peace and welfare of the country which that Lord-Lieutenant was appointed to govern, and upon which question he was every week stating to the Government the opinions he himself entertained', was, Palmerston truthfully observed in his journal, 'a strange instance of the withholding of that confidence which, for both their sakes, ought to have existed.'[12]

Palmerston kept his word and after his return to London he sent on 18 November a long report which Anglesey acknowledged as one of the best he had had. But this was mainly because of what it had had to say on foreign affairs; on Ireland, Palmerston admitted, his information was scanty and the prospects bleak. A very different impression seems to have prevailed when shortly afterwards, probably early in December, he went with Goderich, Melbourne (Lamb's father had died in July), Grant and another Canningite, Frankland Lewis, to confer with Huskisson at Eartham. Almost nothing is known about the conference. Croker knew a little and it was probably with reference to it that he wrote soon after: 'In politics people begin to talk of the *party* of the three Viscounts. You & I know the three Viscounts; but where their *party* is I cannot guess.' Lady Holland, who was always convinced of both the good and the ill she wished to believe, reported that she had talked to Melbourne on his return from Eartham 'where entre nous he is not likely to get entangled as the liking is quite personal not political, indeed there does not seem much confidence among the few members of that set or party'. Croker also confirmed a report that Planta, who had been patronage secretary to Canning and was now performing the same role for Wellington, had been invited by Huskisson to join his guests. But whereas this 'double-twisted rat', as Lockhart called him, was believed by some to have been negotiating with Huskisson all along on Wellington's behalf, Croker, who may possibly have known better, insisted that there was 'not one word of politics'.[13]

It seems very likely that if nothing positive was said at the Eartham meeting it was only because Huskisson still expected the initiative to come from the duke. But in the Wellington camp they were not yet ready to eat humble pie. They knew all about the Huskissonites' game; and they still relied on Huskisson's bad relations with the Whigs. He had even, it was said, revealed before he had gone abroad that he would be willing to throw over his friends to get back with the duke. Planta may have given some hint about Ireland, however, for Palmerston wrote a few days later that, in spite of his own earlier impressions, with 'the whole of the [Irish] people without any exception . . . now divided into two parties, the agitators & the irritators, the Catholic and the anti-Catholic', it appeared 'quite certain' that the duke now appreciated that he must pass a measure of relief when the new Parliament reassembled. Then Peel would probably retire and in that case the duke, however much he might prefer otherwise, would be forced to call on Huskisson, and since some of the Cabinet would not stay without Peel nor Huskisson consent to serve alone, there would necessarily be a major change of Government. Almost immediately, however, there followed the news of a final disagreement between Anglesey and Wellington and the notice of the Lord-Lieutenant's recall. So when Palmerston sent his next letter to Dublin, just as he was leaving on a New Year trip to Paris, he was rather inclined to expect the worst of Wellington. But that hardly affected his calculation that there would be a major change of Ministry, only that it would be accomplished without the duke rather than with his aid.[14]

A little while before Palmerston left for his holiday in France there was a gathering of Lambs and Cowpers at Windsor, and shortly afterwards what could only be described as a great assembly of Canningites. According to Mrs Arbuthnot 'they passed the whole time plotting against the Govt & settling how their *expected Cabinet* shd be formed'. She did not believe that they had dared to broach it with the King; when Lady Cowper and Princess Lieven had taxed him with dismissing the Huskissonites the previous year, he had become 'excessively angry' and reported them all to Wellington. But behind his back the ladies were soon passing lists around with either Melbourne or Palmerston as Prime Minister at the head. Meanwhile Palmerston was writing to Sulivan of their counterparts in Paris: 'The fine ladies complain that they have lost all their influence in public affairs – when politics were settled in drawing rooms & cabinets, they could do what they liked, but now that ministers must answer to chambers & explain their reasons & conduct to the satisfaction of deputies, the case is wholly altered & ladies become only the ornament of society.' But he was glad enough to carry gifts from Lady Holland to Mme Flahault and learn what he could in the salons of the ladies as well as at Pozzo's dinners. Mme Flahault thought that mixing so much in French society would cure him of his countrymen's conventional distrust of France. It certainly did not; but then nothing he heard in Paris altered his opinion about the Irish question either. 'This system of Government' in Ireland, he wrote to Sulivan, '*will* not & *can* not do; and on this *rock* the Duke's vessel will split.' Yet when he returned for the opening of Parliament in London three weeks later it was with astonishment to hear in the King's Speech that while suppressing the Catholic Association the Government intended also to take up Catholic Emancipation.[15]

Palmerston left London on 7 January 1829 expecting the Government to fall by its opposition to the Catholics; he returned on 3 February to find that it did not break up even by conceding them relief. Patently he had gone over to Paris to prepare for the 'warm work' ahead and for a major offensive in concert with his friends. On the way back he crossed by chance from Calais with Hobhouse and talked politics all the way. 'He is a frondeur now and talked the liberal as well as if he had played that part all his life,' Hobhouse noted. But Palmerston also showed that he had not a notion of what was so soon to come. The Huskissonites in general only got wind of it two or three days beforehand. 'Nothing can equal their mortification,' gloated Mrs Arbuthnot. 'They are all bitter to the greatest degree at finding the ground in a manner cut from under their feet.' The next day, as the King's Speech was read out, 'their squadron looked very silly and fidgety; for the surrender of Peel was the death-blow to their hopes'.[16]

There was still a good deal to fight about in Parliament; and Palmerston put up a very good show. First, there was what he called the Government's 'price', the suppression of the Catholic Association. In his breezy manner he mocked the very idea – 'Put down the Association! They might as well talk of putting down the winds of Heaven, or of chaining the ceaseless tides of the ocean. . . . The Catholic Association was the people of Ireland. Its spirit was caused by the grievance of the nation, and its seat was the bosom of seven millions of its population.' But he was willing to 'make a temporary sacrifice of principle for so material an advantage' and to vote against the association if it would decide others to help remove the Catholic grievance. So the measure was passed and the price demanded paid; a few days later came the news that the association had voluntarily dissolved.[17]

During the debate that followed in March on the second reading of the main relief bill, Palmerston rose again and spoke with more fire than he had ever done before. He warned in particular how dangerously those who opposed the measure risked provoking revolution. It was all very well for 'the gentlemen of England, who live secure under the protecting shadow of the law' and whose harvests had 'never been trodden down by the conflict of hostile feet', to contemplate civil war 'as if it were some holiday pastime, or some sport of children'. But those 'from unfortunate and ill-starred Ireland' had 'seen with their own eyes, and heard with their own ears, the miseries which civil war produces' and 'the barbarity which it engenders'. He recommended impartial Englishmen to go to southern Ireland 'to see what a fierce and unsocial spirit bad laws engender; and how impossible it is to degrade a people, without at the same time demoralizing them too'; and if that failed to convince them then they should also go to the north to see 'how noble and generous natures may be corrupted by the possession of undue and inordinate ascendancy'. He conceded that in the event of civil war 'the crimsoned banner of England would soon wave in undisputed supremacy', but it would be 'over the smoking ashes of their towns, and the bloodstained solitude of their fields. . . . England herself never would permit . . . such a conquest; England would reject, with disgust, laurels that were dyed in fraternal blood.'[18]

Mrs Arbuthnot returned to town the day after Palmerston had spoken and heard that the Catholic Emancipation Bill had passed after two full days of 'dull debate'. But other amateurs and experts on every side buzzed with excitement and astonishment at Palmerston's effort. Greville heard everywhere that it was 'brilliant'; Althorp called it 'first-rate'; Grey's son 'excellent'; and even Ellenborough said he spoke 'admirably'. 'It is impossible to describe the credit Palmerston's speech has universally obtained,' went the report among the Hampshire neighbours. 'Everybody was dazzled by it. Sturges Bourne said . . . that he thought eloquence in the House of Commons had expired with Canning, but that it had actually and positively revived in Palmerston. He always, when in office, spoke well and sensibly, but this burst was in the highest style of oratory and argument; . . . I did not think he possessed powers of such a superior cast.' It was, agreed the old Opposition leader George Tierney, 'an imitation of Canning, and not a bad one'.[19]

As *tours de force* Palmerston's speeches were indeed impressive efforts; but so far as disturbing the Government was concerned they were quite irrelevant. Their purpose, indeed, was to support the Ministry's own bill against its many opponents among the Tories. With their help the bill went very safely through the Commons; but other parts of the Government's arrangements for Ireland found the Canningites themselves awkwardly divided. The day after his great speech upon emancipation, Palmerston spoke vigorously once more, this time against the Government's determination to restrict the county franchise in Ireland. He condemned it as too high a price to pay, saying that the notion that it was part of a package deal, which must be accepted *in toto*, was contrary to the Commons' duty to deliberate. But similar proposals had always been part of Canning's programme to make the emancipation of Irish Catholics acceptable in England, and the vote that evening found his followers as divided as his enemies had been the previous day. Huskisson spoke against the bill but abstained on the vote; the Grants and others voted for it.[20]

Two months later the East Retford question came up again, and the Government won through even more decisively. Sensing that the Government would be presented with an embarrassingly large majority, some of the Huskissonites had attempted to bargain for postponement. No doubt this reflected their anxiety not to have their weakness shown up and the impression confirmed that the concessions to the Catholics had wrecked their prospects for ever. So evident was their dismay, indeed, that Ellenborough surmised the real object of their advances was to frustrate some 'mischievous designs' of Palmerston with which the majority disagreed. It was true that Palmerston was determined to press on with opposition and that he had a second line of attack in mind. But when it came, in the form of another surprising speech on 1 June, it was not on any question of parliamentary reform, but against the Government's policy on foreign affairs.[21]

Palmerston had been preparing such an attack just as long and just as thoroughly as that he had made so impressively on the Government's Irish policy. There can be little doubt that Princess Lieven was at him all the time about Greece; Lady Cowper certainly was over Portugal, on her brother Fred's behalf. 'There is F. Lamb who is gone into opposition,' Dudley used to say of his ambassador at Lisbon, 'and writes short pamphlets against the govt which he is pleased to transmit to me under the whimsical title of "Despatches".' He continued, after his recall, to complain very loudly that all his work there was wasted. But the trouble with both Greek and Portuguese affairs was, all along, that the Government's policy was difficult to attack. In Greece they had proceeded in the second half of 1828, when Palmerston was out of office, to do what they had refused in the first, when he was in their Cabinet – to escort French troops to clear the Turks from the Morea and to recognize its independence. In Portugal, where Miguel completed his usurpation of both throne and constitution, Palmerston confessed that it was difficult to see what Wellington could have done since 'to have interfered by force to dictate to the Portuguese a particular form of Govt would have been at variance with all our principles'. But he thoroughly distrusted and despised both the Government's motives and their manner. 'We certainly are going rapidly downwards in the public estimation of Europe,' he asserted in a letter to Sulivan, '& shall continue to do so, as long as we have the leaden weight of Tory narrowmindedness hanging about our necks.' As far as Greece was concerned he reported to Anglesey that Wellington was still merely following the lead of Metternich, urging peace upon Russia in order to deny her a substantial victory and holding language to Turkey 'of remonstrance mixed with friendly assurances, the latter of which are more calculated to encourage her to hold out, than the former are likely to induce her to come to terms'. The result, if this dithering continued, would be to spread the war to the westward and to imperil the Rhine frontier by bringing in France with Austria against Russia backed by Prussia. In Portugal, too, he thought the Government might at least have avoided what he described to his brother as those 'little things' like Aberdeen's speeches, which created the impression that England was the tyrant's friend.[22]

So Palmerston continued through 1828-9 to consider and confer on foreign affairs. He had got at Lady Granville as soon as her husband was recalled from Paris in July 1828. But he did not by any means confine his consultations to his own friends and countrymen. In London he discussed with the Russian and French ambassadors the threat of slavery that still hung over Egypt's Grecian captives, and where his erstwhile colleagues had treated their condition, Bathurst 'as a good joke, Aberdeen as the exercise of a just right, & Ellenborough as a laudable action', from Lieven he got real interest and from Polignac positive indications of action. In Paris, where he had told his brother some time before that he contemplated another visit 'to get acquainted with some people there whose names one hears much & often', he met Sébastiani and Talleyrand in the New Year and held several conversations about Russia's position and policy with her ambassador there, Pozzo di Borgo. When he got back to London he kept up a correspondence with Mme Flahault and, through her and her friends in the Chamber of Deputies, put pressure on the French Government to accommodate their policy in both Portugal and Greece to his own views. He soon armed himself, too, with secret information about Portugal from Fred Lamb and made his final preparations amid all the consternation over Ireland. 'We must have a turn out upon foreign politics before the session is over,' he wrote at the end of March 1829. 'Portuguese matters cannot be allowed to pass unnoticed; the conduct of the Government has been too bad upon that subject.' They very nearly did escape, however.[23]

The peg, on which it was clear the attack on the Government's foreign policy would hang, was a motion laid by an old Whig, Sir James Mackintosh. This was originally due to be heard towards the end of February; but the Whigs were afraid that what with support from both Canningites and embittered Tories, it might bring the Government down too soon and so imperil the still uncompleted Catholic Bill. In consequence it was put off until after Easter and then, Palmerston feared, the members might be too bent on their holidays to care. When Palmerston rose at last, on 1 June, it was indeed very late at night and before an almost empty House. But the word of his triumph again made the excited round of friend and foe. Huskisson let it be known that he too considered there had been nothing like it since Canning, and even those who would not go so far felt that it was even better than Palmerston's last, 'a very effective & useful speech'. Its topics, too, they all agreed were 'well selected & well put'.[24]

Palmerston's stirring passages were not concerned solely with Portugal; towards the end he attacked the Government's persistent efforts to restrict the boundaries of independent Greece in tones that rang with emotion and with words lifted straight from his memorandum of February 1828:

There are two great parties in Europe; one which endeavours to bear sway by the force of public opinion; another which endeavours to bear sway by the force of physical control; and the judgment almost unanimous of Europe, assigns the latter as the present connexion of England.

The principle on which the system of this party is founded is, in my view, fundamentally erroneous. There is in nature no moving power but mind, all else is passive and inert; in human affairs this power is opinion; in political affairs it is public opinion; and he who can grasp this power, with it will subdue the fleshly arm of physical strength ... those statesmen who know how to avail themselves of the passions, and the interest, and the opinions of mankind, are able to gain an ascendancy, and to exercise a sway over human affairs, far out of all proportion greater than belong to the power and resources of the state over which they preside; while those, on the other hand, who seek to check improvement, to cherish abuses, to crush opinions, and to prohibit the human race from thinking, whatever may be the apparent power which they wield, will find their weapon snap short in their hand ...

But most of what he had to say referred in detail to Portugal. He castigated the Wellington Government for giving, in the name of neutrality, solace and support to Miguel – 'this destroyer of constitutional freedom, this breaker of solemn oaths, this faithless usurper, this enslaver of his country, this trampler upon public law, this violator of private rights, this attempter of the life of helpless and defenceless woman' – and accused them of submitting to usage from him such as, 'coming from another quarter, would have roused them, like a lion from his slumber'. He also discovered an idea of lasting importance to his own handling of foreign affairs, how to resolve the difficulty he had earlier outlined to his brother about interfering in Portugal's internal affairs:

If by interference is meant interference by force of arms, such interference the government are right in saying, general principles and our own practice forebade us to exert. But if by interference is meant intermeddling, and intermeddling in every way, and to every extent, short of actual military force; then I must affirm, that there is nothing in such interference, which the laws of nations may not in certain cases permit ...

... any bystander is at liberty to interfere, to prevent a breach of the law ... so also, and upon the same principle, may any nation interpose to prevent a flagrant violation, of the laws of the community of nations.[25]

By the summer of 1829 Palmerston had gained a lot from experience; he had learned as much from others; now he needed new opportunities to practise what he preached. Some set down a good deal to the influence of Princess Lieven. Greville thought his success showed how much he owed to the accident of Canning's death. For twenty years Palmerston had been in an office of 'dry and dull detail, and he [had] never travelled out of it'. Probably, Greville thought, he had been too much in awe of Canning. But latterly he had gained confidence from higher situations and opportunities from the removal of greater men. So now he had 'launched forth, and with astonishing success'. Granville had said that he had always thought Palmerston capable of more than he did, but that Canning would never believe it. However, after his two recent speeches on Ireland and Portugal many others were at last convinced. Both were polished up for printing and the copies distributed widely. What must have pleased him most, surely, was the report he had from Mme

Flahault of the reactions in Paris of Talleyrand and others: 'c'est vraiment le discours d'un homme d'état. Votre Ld Palmerston est un jeune homme qui ira loins, qui se fait pour être premier ministre – le seul qui pourra remplacer Canning.' In London they also expected that offers and opportunities must soon come his way. Some, on the Tory side, thought that the Huskissonites would unite with the 'low' Whigs, with Lansdowne leading in the Lords and Palmerston in the Commons, and open their ranks to the 'discontented' of all parties.[26]

For his part, Palmerston had been very concerned at all the 'coquetting' going on between the Whigs and the Government while they worked together to carry the Catholic Bill through Parliament; and it was in part at least to disturb these good relations that he had pressed his attack on foreign policy on 1 June. There was subsequently, as Sulivan casually mentioned, some sort of approach made on behalf of the Lansdowne Whigs by his old Edinburgh friend, now second Earl of Minto. But nothing came of it, perhaps because Palmerston, although liking to think himself an independent, was not prepared to snatch from the unacceptable Huskisson the lead he was offered in the House of Commons. By now he too had come back to the notion of an alliance with the Low Whigs, but also to the view that the best Government would be one made out of a union between Huskisson and Lansdowne – 'in short, the Government of Goderich, with a better head and some changes, omitting Herries and some subordinates'. All this, however, he admitted was 'moonshine'. For he did not expect his speech to bring Wellington's Government tumbling down; the duke, he was sure, would in foreign as in domestic policy keep well afloat by trimming his sails to the wind of public sentiment. Lady Grey, however, had already warned her husband that there was a plot afoot between Palmerston and his associates to exclude him once again from power by a junction with Lansdowne. Consequently the symptoms of an alignment on the 'Left' were not entirely discouraging from the Government's point of view. They thought it would prevent the reunion of the High Whigs with the radical 'Mountain', encourage Grey to throw in his lot with Wellington, and in this way make unnecessary any great concessions to the extreme Tories. But the main tactic of the Government was, from the three groups of Huskissonites, High Whigs and secessionist Tories, to seduce 'not a *batch* of any one of them', but 'out of each, such *individuals* as are open to kind embraces, and so decimate each'. They had therefore already approached Grey, and when the King still demurred they had taken Lord Rosslyn as his substitute. It was also expected that now Palmerston had proved his worth as an individual, in Westminster as well as in Whitehall, Peel would prevail upon the duke to make an approach in that direction too. But the next move that way came from quite another place.[27]

After spending much of the last decade in virtual exile on the Continent, the unpopular Duke of Cumberland returned to England in 1828 and 1829 to take up the standard of Protestant ascendancy from his brother York's dead hand and to support Wellington in the fight he was expected to make. But when he discovered that the Prime Minister's policy was survival by concession he became the acknowledged leader of the resisting and secessionist Tories. He and his friends, Eldon & Co., looked everywhere they could for some means of resisting further concessions on such matters as parliamentary reform, and so great was their hatred of Wellington as the traitor to the cause that they toyed with the notion of joining even with Canningites to bring him down. Mme Lieven, and through her Lady Cowper, may have played an important part in the ensuing intrigue. The princess had long since despaired of working her peculiar spell on Wellington, and even Emily, in spite of lingering affection for him, condemned his behaviour as every day more 'childish' ('The Child' was the cypher name she gave him). Greville detected that 'the Princess and the other foolish woman' had become the focus of intrigue and the medium of communication between Cumberland and the Huskissonites as early as the beginning of March. Presumably there was something in this, because by June Palmerston was reporting impressions of it to his brother. Lady Cowper probably overstepped the mark in defending Cumberland against the accusations of attempted rape made by the Chancellor's wife; her brother, Melbourne, certainly thought the Lieven had been meddling too much in England's domestic affairs. In addition there was so much doubt and so little cohesion among the Ultras that it was not until October that any actual approach appears to have been made and then, apparently, only to Palmerston and mainly with the intention of detaching him from Huskisson.[28]

That autumn Palmerston intended to make another trip to Ireland, via Liverpool, and on the way to pay some country-house visits to his friends. He expected in particular to be at Littleton's in Staffordshire about 29 September. He did not turn up at Teddesley, however, until almost a week later. His host thought he had been thrown over 'for some fair lady in the South'. But Palmerston seems rather to have been delayed by the information that a certain Cornish baronet wished to have some confidential conversation with him.[29]

Although very young, Sir Richard Vyvyan was one of the leading Ultras in the Commons and during 1829 he had become involved with Cumberland, Eldon and the Duke of Newcastle in the scheme to displace Wellington by a junction with some of the Canningites and even an ambitious Whig or two. Apparently they had thought of approaching Huskisson, but had concluded he was too unpopular with the country gentry and turned instead to Palmerston as one they thought less committed to free trade.

Vyvyan was not so implausible an agent as the distance from Cornwall to Hampshire suggests. Palmerston afterwards explained that he had had frequent communications with him on both foreign and domestic affairs while he was in the Cabinet and that in order to dissuade him from putting down a hostile motion in the Commons he had with Dudley's consent read to him such a mass of Foreign Office papers on the war then going on between Russia and Persia as to bring him right over to the Canningites' way of thinking on foreign policy. In 1829, however, Vyvyan still thought he must act with considerable precaution. 'I mean to try to get Palmerston,' he wrote on 7 September, 'but I shall be very careful how I do it.' He proposed at first to go and stay with a neighbour of Palmerston's he knew, and his prospective host, Sir William Heathcote, called at Broadlands to say that Vyvyan would very much like to meet Palmerston when he came to stay.

No contact had actually been made when Palmerston decided to leave for London. However, when he went to dine at the Travellers' on 3 October whom should he see but Vyvyan in an otherwise empty room, and so he went over and joined him. 'We discussed all sorts of topics,' Palmerston reported 'in *strict* confidence' that evening to Lady Cowper, 'and among others, the government, its merits, and its chances of holding out, and so forth. The result of a very long talk downstairs and upstairs, piano and forte, was, that it seems the Tories imagine that they may possibly wheel out the Duke [of Wellington] in the next fortnight or three weeks, and that they are planning administrations with all possible diligence and ingenuity.' What they had in mind, he found, was a mixed administration under Lord Mansfield and with people like Eldon and Newcastle on the one hand and Stanley and Brougham on the other. They still thought there might be a possibility of including Huskisson as Chancellor of the Exchequer; but in view of his unpopularity they would propose the leadership of the House of Commons, as well as the Colonial Office, for Palmerston, who had given no inconvenient pledge in public about either finance or free trade. Vyvyan's colleagues wished to know, therefore, whether Palmerston would be willing to serve if necessary without Huskisson and whether they might submit his name to the King. In all this – and the conversation went on some time – Palmerston claimed to have played the part 'chiefly . . . of listener, or suggester of general remarks for the purpose of leading on the conversation'. But he did make a number of significant responses and remarks. He said that he did not see himself as 'tied to any man, although attached to certain opinions'. So far as Huskisson was concerned he explained that they had simply happened to find themselves acting and a-greeing together. Each was perfectly free, he again underlined, to accept office without the other. 'I consider myself as being free if I chose,' he said, 'because we never have met or consulted or acted in concert as a party, & have upon no one occasion voted as a body; we sit together, but upon almost every question last session voted different ways.'

On the specific questions of free trade policy and paper currency he agreed that he had had no occasion in public so far to explain his detailed views; but he did have 'pretty strong opinions' about them and in general they were those with which Huskisson's name was so often associated and for which he had been so unjustly censured. This was not any mere convenient afterthought. He had made a definite if general declaration in favour of free trade in the House of Commons in March 1826 and he had several times expressed his detailed views on the inflationary evils of paper currency in letters to his friends and relatives. These views were directly opposed to those of the landowners who formed the backbone of the Ultras, and however rare and muted his public expressions might have been, he would not, he explained, like to join an administration which contemplated measures at variance with them. Moreover, while he could have 'no personal objection' to joining the Tories, seeing that he had spent his entire official life among them, he could only say to Vyvyan now what he had said to Wellington in January 1828: 'First tell me who are your men, and what are to be your measures and then I shall be able to say whether it would suit me to become your colleague.'

Vyvyan went away perhaps encouraged but still very cautious: 'I have nothing however but a conversation without the presence of a third person which will authorize me to affirm that he would be with us, and if such an intention on his part were made public or reached his ears through any other channel he might easily discern it and declare that I had either misunderstood or misrepresented him. I am particularly anxious that the fact of his being so well inclined towards the Tory party should be kept perfectly secret.' He was right to be so careful. There probably was something in the notion that Palmerston was by no means averse to tempting offers from almost any direction; but hardly from this one. His reaction to the rumours he heard about the project in June had been that it was 'a thing impossible for many reasons'; now the idea of a Cabinet including such a motley crew as Eldon, Brougham and himself seemed merely 'comical'. 'Upon what would all these people agree, I wonder, except to come in?' In lighter vein he wrote again a few days later: 'what a notion that a man should leave a set of clever gentlemenlike men with whom he finds himself acting, in order to join the noodles of Boodles, and become leader of the lame and the blind.' He thought the approach had been a serious one and he agreed to give Vyvyan his address in Ireland. But while he also thought it very likely an attempt would be made to disturb the Duke of Wellington, he expected this particular plan to 'end in smoke'. For he was sure the duke must have got wind of it and that it was not unlikely he would 'anticipate his enemies, and try to get into his Govt some of the people whom they are reckoning upon for theirs'.[30]

The secret of Vyvyan's approach to Palmerston seems, on the contrary, to have been kept very well. The first mention of it to be found among the Whigs was when Grey's son Howick asked Ladies Granville and Cowper about it in March the following year; and, strange to say, they managed to convince him there had been no such 'projected junction'. But as far as the duke's general tactics were concerned Palmerston was right nonetheless. Early that same October 1829 Wellington made an approach to the Whigs; and towards the end of the month a mutual friend brought him and Huskisson together at a country house in the hope of contriving a political reunion. But Wellington refused to take the Whigs *en bloc,* or to exchange with Huskisson anything more than 'common civilities'.[31]

So generally distrusted was Huskisson that the rumour even that he and
Wellington had met did his reputation no good. He must have been acting, it
was said, 'on the well-founded supposition that he has no character to lose'. In
view, too, of the offers of the lead Palmerston had now had from two different
sets of Wellington's opponents, Sulivan also urged his friend to shake off his
association with Huskisson. Personally he thought that there was no good
reason now why Palmerston should not return to a liberalized Government
led by Wellington; or, if this were not acceptable, throw Huskisson overboard
and gather about himself a party of disorganized Whigs and 'dumb' Tories.
'But you must take a *bold* line if you mean at last to raise yourself above the
rivalry of inferior men and above the influence of Royal dislike.' An amendment to the King's Speech regarding the Russian war, he thought, would give
him occasion enough in the New Year for 'a very brilliant attack'.[32]

Palmerston's interest in foreign affairs was still very strong. With the help of
Princess Lieven, no doubt, he had already discovered the secret of Russia's
recently revised policy in the Near East, that in view of the threats and dangers
from the other powers which Turkey's collapse would bring and the objections
they would make to Russia's occupation of the Straits, she thought having a
weak Turkey was 'the next best thing to having no neighbour at all'. 'I
confess', he went on, 'I should not be sorry some day or other to see the Turk
kicked out of Europe, & compelled to go and sit cross-legged, smoke his pipe,
chew his opium, & cut off heads on the Asiatic side of the Bosphorus; we want
civilization, activity, trade, & business in Europe, & your Mustaphas have no
idea of any traffic beyond rhubarb, figs & red slippers; what energy can be
expected from a nation who have no heels to their shoes and pass their whole
lives slip shod?'*

Palmerston was also in complete agreement with Sulivan that the King's

---

*Both Fay (*Huskisson,* pp. 95-6) and Aspinall (*Brougham,* pp. 286-7) printed extracts from the
Hatherton Papers from this letter of Palmerston's to Littleton, dated 16 September 1829. But Fay
omitted to mention that the word 'sorry' in the first line quoted here had been carefully changed
at a much later date, though in Palmerston's hand, to 'surprised', and Aspinall printed the word
'surprised' without mentioning that it had originally read 'sorry'. But the circumstances in which
this significant change was made, at a Woburn house party in December 1856, are related in
Littleton's unpublished diary. 'There was nothing very extraordinary', runs the entry for 7
December, 'in this wish [to see the Turk 'kicked out of Europe'], nor at all inconsistent in his recent
policy. Who would not gladly see an enlightened and *independent* Greek Government supply the
place of the Turkish in their European provinces? Yet who would consent that the Russians
should supply that place? The knowing however how likely it is that my papers may soon fall into
other hands, & under the inspection of Palmerston's enemies, I insisted on Palmerston's altering
the word "sorry" into "surprised". I had great fun with Palmerston about it. He was astonished at
the sight of his letter. I begged Lady Palmerston to watch his face while I read it. With his usual
readiness he gave a loud laugh at the discovery – & justified his expressions as I have done in this
entry. But Lady Palmerston observed that they might give occasion to party misrepresentation
hereafter – & I declaring my intention to restore him the entire letter (which I wished to keep) if he
did not alter the expression, he took his pen, & made the safe correction I have mentioned.' One
can only wonder why, if he thought his papers at risk, Littleton revealed in his diary what he
concealed in his correspondence.

Speech would be the best occasion for a general attack on the Government. So in December he went on another round of conversations with diplomats and politicians in Paris, where he also joined a newly established Anglo-French club to provide him with a future *pied à terre* and attended for his further education lectures by Charles Dupin on the State of Industry and Wealth, by Villemain on the Progress of Modern Languages, and by Guizot on the Progress of Civilization in Europe. Since these lectures were given two or three times a week and, being gratis, were attended by several hundred people, he thought that they 'must have a great effect in enlightening the public mind'; and, he noted with as much surprise as approval, the professors were 'entirely liberal in their doctrines, though paid for their efforts by the Government'.[33]

In Paris the word went around among the Ultras that Palmerston and his English friends were setting up a committee of management for 'the propagation of liberalism all over the world'. This was a 'slander' and even the leaders of the Ultras admitted it. But in Paris Palmerston did meet Minto, who continued there to press upon his old friend the necessity of restoring in England 'habits of confidence and good will amongst persons of liberal opinions by as much intercourse and concert as was practicable amongst the leaders, and by engaging their followers in the support of common principles & a common cause'. Otherwise, he suggested, 'the fragments of a variety of angry but disunited parties' might 'by raising occasional questions' present the duke with a majority against him from time to time, but could never 'improvise a new government of sufficient strength to stand against the united ultras of England'. So far as concerned Palmerston's personal opinions and powers of leadership, Minto seemed very pleased with what he heard. 'He goes home I think', he reported to Lansdowne, 'quite resolved to take up his own position as a rallying ground for liberal opinions; and however inferior in talent & intrigue to Canning, he has the honesty and righteadedness which the other wanted and the advantage of being quite free on many subjects where Canning was inconveniently committed, or under the influence of inveterate prejudice. Indeed in the course of much conversation with Palmerston I always found him ready to go quite as far as I should have done, even in those questions where we were most likely to differ.' On the necessity of concerted opposition Palmerston's views seemed not quite so satisfactory, since he saw less difficulty 'in conjuring up a strong liberal government at a moment's notice, but he is young in opposition. I think he feels his own value and that you will see him next session take his own line as a leader. His language to me is that there are in fact but two great parties: those who hold liberal opinions and are friendly to improvement; and those whose prejudices are opposed to all innovation. This is an answer to your question . . .'[34]

Although no mention was made in Minto's letters of Huskisson by name he evidently meant to imply that Palmerston was throwing off his shackles and his past and would soon coalesce with Lansdowne and his kind. But between Ireland and Paris Palmerston had had in late November an important conference on tactics with the Lamb brothers at Brocket. There, indeed, they had resolved 'to take a bold and decided line' on the very first day of the session. Melbourne in particular was 'in a state of great pugnaciousness', prepared 'for fighting everybody and everything'. On domestic affairs they were in complete agreement that 'the only salvation of the country is to be found in a metallic currency . . . and that the advantages of free trade are too demonstrable . . . to allow any man who sets up for a statesman to argue against that system'. The Lambs, however, were not quite so sure as Palmerston that they would get enough support for an attack on the Government's foreign policy, since the Whigs wanted to expel the Turks from Europe while the Tories wanted them helped to stay. But Palmerston pointed out the peculiar merit of the Canningite line on Greece in this respect, that the present Government could be blamed by both sides for not having acted vigorously upon Russia's declaration of war to enforce a satisfactory settlement in accordance with the Treaty of London and to seize for England both the leadership of Europe and the protection of Greece as well as Turkey. He also supplied the Lambs with a set of the Greek papers which had been confidentially printed for the original Wellington Cabinet, and encouraged Melbourne to prepare by his attack to take the lead of the Opposition in the House of Lords.

No other prominent liberal peer, Palmerston pointed out, would be a match for the duke. Lansdowne had lost ground during both his short periods in office; Grey had 'bolted out of the course and never can win the race'; Holland was 'getting old and infirm'; Goderich had 'been tried and can never lead again'. Melbourne, on the other hand, had 'peculiar advantages, from his personal character and the course he has hitherto pursued in politics; though a liberal he is a great favourite with the Tories; the Whigs of course consider him as a kinsman; and he is personally liked by the King. He is therefore well with all parties; and his style and manner of speaking particularly hit the fancy and taste of parliament.'

There was not the least intention on Palmerston's part of breaking with Huskisson. Rather, while Palmerston was away in Paris, Melbourne was to talk everything over with him. With the Whigs, on the other hand, there was to be no preliminary concert. On this Palmerston and Melbourne were completely agreed, that there was to be no pledge that they would not take office without the Whigs and that it was better to keep themselves free. 'I know no good in people pledging and binding themselves in any way beyond what is absolutely necessary,' Palmerston wrote; 'and it is frequently, and in many unforeseen, and not to be foreseen occasions, a great advantage to find oneself free and unshackled. People with whom you link yourself may often act in such a way as to make you wish you had not bound yourself to them, although they mean well, and may give you no just reason for parting company; besides, which is the most important, persons with whom you are so deeply pledged acquire a right to be consulted as to your course, and have some voice in deciding your conduct.' [35]

On the opening of Parliament on 4 February 1830, Huskisson and his associates turned out 'in battle-array in their old places below the gangway' and with High Tories and Low Whigs voted for an amendment to the King's Speech complaining about the widespread distress in the country. The next day Palmerston and Grant made what Hobhouse called 'furious speeches' on foreign policy. On 16 February Palmerston spoke again on Greece and once more on the theme of England being responsible for her having such narrow boundaries. But what was really interesting about it was that it marked the beginning of a personal as well as a political breach between him and Peel. They had parted company officially two years before with strong and evidently sincere expressions on each side of personal regard. This time, too, they ended with professions of friendship and no division in the House. But their friendship had really cooled for ever. For Peel accused Palmerston of betraying Cabinet secrets and, in an obvious reference to his contacts with the Russian ambassador and his wife, asked 'whom did he represent'? Palmerston replied indignantly that he represented his own opinions.[36]

There was something more material in Peel's attack than Palmerston's constant contact with Prince Lieven and his wife; Palmerston was too well trained a Canningite to become Russia's tool. But he had shown confidential Cabinet papers to the Lambs in November and shortly afterwards there had appeared two anonymous pieces on foreign affairs, strongly attacking the Government's record and full of confidential information. One of these, on Portugal, was a pamphlet by Fred Lamb, which even in the opinion of Greville, who helped him with it, was not very well done. By taking even Canning to task it offended his widow and led her to make a brilliant riposte. But the other, an article on Greece, was considered by Greville 'remarkably able' and by Grey 'very clever'. It was not by Palmerston or by anyone known to be connected with him. But it did follow much the same line that he had outlined at Brocket and it was full of information that could only have come from a mixture of highly placed British, French and Russian sources. So it is not surprising that while Lady Cowper strenuously denied it, Wellington and his friends should have been convinced that Palmerston was the author. When, shortly afterwards, Prince Leopold was making difficulties about the scheme to place him on the throne of Greece, they concluded from reports of Palmerston's movements to and from the Russian embassy that he was behind that too, and when Leopold finally declined the throne that Palmerston even drafted his refusal.[37]

Melbourne, in the meantime, was not doing very well in the Lords. On 13 February he supported Holland in an attack on Greek policy; but Wellington easily outmanoeuvred them by picking on the weak parts of their speeches and leaving the rest alone. On 19 February Melbourne brought on his own motion on Portugal, but he handled it still worse: 'case very negligently got up, weakly stated, confused, and indiscreet', Greville remarked. 'He did not speak like a man that has much in him.' Unfortunately, too, he followed his brother's argument so closely that he went further than Palmerston had intended, and gave such offence that he brought both Goderich and Lansdowne to speak for the Government.[38]

As if to make up for Melbourne's failure in the House of Lords Palmerston made another of his imitations of Canning in the Commons when he rose to put a motion about Portugal on 10 March. It was again a carefully prepared set-piece: his sisters went up into the ventilator to hear it and Princess Lieven thought that by its strong attraction it 'somewhat spoilt' her ball. It provoked another clash with Peel; they were going to be frequent from now on. It was also full once more of fine phrases and high ideals. By an irony of fate he talked, as well as Cobden ever would, of there being no great mystery in foreign affairs and no particular difficulty in any man grappling with them. 'The days are gone by, when diplomacy was an occult science,' he said. 'Plain dealing, sincerity, and a regard to justice, are the most successful policy' in 'the intercourse of nations' as well as in 'that of individuals'. So men talked again about it being 'excellent' and 'admirable'. However, while it all seemed splendid enough, it was a considerable strain on Palmerston to have turned himself from the nervous and diffident speaker of his War Office days into the leading orator among the Opposition. 'Palmerston looks pale and jaded, and five years older since last summer, from his parliamentary anxieties and displays,' reported an acquaintance from Hampshire. Worse still, he did not seem to be achieving quite the desired effect. 'Palmerston makes good speeches – but the People want bread and don't care about Portugal,' Jekyll wrote. 'Huskisson got damaged and Althorp deserted the debate tho' now named as the Leader of a large opposition party.' [39]

Jekyll was right about Palmerston's emphasis on foreign policy not concentrating the Opposition sufficiently behind him. It was true that at Holland House the subject was enormously appealing. For though essentially a disappointment, Holland was not for nothing Fox's heir; and he continued throughout his life his uncle's traditional interest in foreign affairs and his belief in their importance for Britain's domestic liberty. In January 1829, when Whigs and Huskissonites alike were preparing their assaults on Wellington, Holland had written to Althorp: 'I hope . . . the attack will not be confined to Ireland and Catholics, but that some of you will condescend to cast away a thought on foreign politics.' But Althorp's views remained unchanged: 'I cannot feel any interest in foreign affairs', he wrote to Brougham, 'while Ireland is at stake.' How gratified must Holland have been, then, when Palmerston shortly afterwards took up the cause of continental liberty and enlightened foreign policy.[40]

The Hollands and Cowpers had long been friends; there is also a mysterious reference to Palmerston consulting one of the Hollands' political friends as early as 1818. They were told then that though 'clever and agreeable' he was not honest about being a 'serious liberal', and his name does not appear among the dinner guests at Holland House until 16 October 1827.

Thereafter it appears very frequently indeed. It was foreign affairs, more even than Lady Cowper, which gave him entrée. Soon Holland House too was on his route between London and Paris. In January 1829 he was carrying small gifts from Lady Holland to Mme Flahault and bringing back in turn 'dispassionate' accounts of the Restoration Monarchy's plunge towards reaction.[41]

By February 1830 Holland had become convinced by Palmerston's letters and speeches that he was a man of real political consequence. In a letter to Grey he described him as Peel's 'most formidable or at least most avowed adversary' and looked forward to the restoration of 'the old approved system of two parties in the H. of Commons, each under a man of honour & character who owes his character to parliamentary talent & consideration in society.' For his part Palmerston remained extremely cautious, warning Lady Cowper in November 1829 not to go gossiping at Holland House about the plans he had made with her brothers for the coming session. But word got about in spite of him, and rumours followed on all sides that he and Melbourne intended to abandon Huskisson and by their own parliamentary efforts invite offers from anyone in or out of office. There are signs that early in January 1830 Lansdowne was trying to follow up Minto's Paris conversation with Melbourne in London, and at the end of the same month John Russell also suggested that, while it might not yet be time to make any formal junction, they might arrange to act in 'concert & mutual good will'. Yet nothing appears to have come of any of this. In part, perhaps, this was because the Huskissonites would not repudiate Huskisson himself. But it was mainly because no common denominator could be found among the Opposition.[42]

As far as foreign policy was concerned, some saw well enough that the coincidence of Foxite enthusiasm and Canningite dexterity was merely superficial: 'I have no patience with Huskissonian patriotism,' confided Hobhouse to his journal. Most of the Whigs at that time, moreover, were more interested in domestic affairs. On parliamentary reform both they and the Huskissonites were divided among themselves. But while many of the Whigs leaned more and more towards a general scheme of moderate reform, most of the Huskissonites continued to act on the piecemeal principle enunciated by Palmerston two years before, voting with the Whigs to transfer seats from corrupt boroughs to great towns but sternly opposing general reform. The question of economic distress, on the other hand, did appear to inspire a common interest against the Government among Whigs, Huskissonites and to some extent even Ultras, and it was on this issue that a group of Whig M.P.s managed during March to organize themselves under Althorp.[43]

As well as being few – there were only about fifty – Althorp's group lacked the front-bench talent and experience of office the Huskissonites could supply. But they were too uncertain of themselves and too internally divided to propose any formal union yet. Above all the Opposition lacked a leader. The only possible candidate was Grey. But he was still hiding in Northumberland, nursing his resentment against the Lansdowne Whigs and, like the Huskissonites, looking both ways at once. So things drifted through the spring, with groups and individuals carrying on a mixed and desultory warfare amongst themselves as much as against the Government. 'Parties are . . . in a very disjointed state,' Palmerston reported to Minto; 'Althorp and what are called the Charlies* are anxious to keep in the present Government on condition that they are allowed to be vice-roys over them, & as far as beer and leather are concerned they certainly have attained their object; and if they would press the Duke hard upon anything else he would give way in the same manner.' Nothing, he thought, could be 'weaker & less creditable' than the Treasury Bench; but that weakness was the Government's strength. For Wellington was smoothing over all difficulties by 'timely concession'. From his side Ellenborough found the behaviour of the Opposition equally weak and complaisant: 'in short, everybody seems to be of opinion that the worst thing that could be done would be to turn out the Government.' Then, early in April, everything was changed by the news that the King was fatally ill and that within six months of his death Wellington would be forced to hold a General Election.[44]

Although no one could be certain what changes a new King and a new Parliament would bring, they were bound to be considerable and, in all probability, decisive. It was natural, therefore, while everyone waited two impatient months for George to die, that tentative feelers should be exchanged among the various parties. Late in April Princess Lieven brought a message from Grey to Palmerston; early in May Littleton approached Grey's son at the Travellers on behalf of 'Huskisson and his friends'; and before the end of June Wellesley took a message from Huskisson to Grey. Nothing is known about the first, neither its character nor even who had taken the initiative. But the second was an offer to support Wellington's Government if Grey replaced Aberdeen at the Foreign Office; and the third to serve under Grey in 'systematic opposition'.[45]

Little more, it would seem, can be discovered now about the details of these exchanges, probably because Grey had come down to London in April and conducted them by word of mouth. It must, in any case, have been a matter of some embarrassment as well as delicacy since he, like almost everyone else, had made no secret two years before of his views about the supposedly shabby and shuffling character of 'that rogue Huskisson'. When he had heard of Althorp's timid organization of the 'Charlies' in March, he had approved their decision not to commit themselves to any union in advance largely because of his low opinion of Huskisson's character and his 'fear of him in the government'. But he had gone on to say that he thought even that objection might be lessened by the inclusion of the people with whom he was associated, and, moreover, that he did not see how in the present state of the House of

---

*So called, as the party who was to watch and wait, after the nickname of the city watchmen, and not to be confused with those of an opposite political persuasion who almost exactly a year later began what was to become the Carlton Club in a house in Charles St, and so were for a while also called the 'Charlies'.

Commons any administration could conduct its business there without the assistance of Huskisson and some of his friends. But he hoped this could be accomplished by taking only some of them into office, in particular Palmerston and the Grants, and leaving Huskisson to support them from the back benches. 'At all events', he would 'strongly recommend' that the lead in the Commons should go neither to Huskisson nor to Brougham; rather he would adopt Holland's recommendation. 'Peel & Palmerston', he concluded, 'seem to me, at present, the persons best qualified for that situation, on opposite sides, if they cannot be brought together.' Howick, already showing something of the awkwardness that was to be such a nuisance to Palmerston more than a decade and a half ahead, was inclined to argue even with this. Charles Grant, he reckoned, was the best speaker in the House of Commons and, though perhaps too indolent, a thoroughly honest man besides; but Palmerston he classed with Huskisson as bad characters who 'once in power would be too willing to retain it by a ready compliance with all the wishes & caprices of the King'. He admitted that 'in talents & in knowledge of the true interests of the country' he thought them superior to Wellington and Peel; but the only way of keeping them under control was for his father to be Prime Minister.[46]

When the actual exchanges had got under way in May, Grey did tell his son that it was 'clear' the ensuing Government would have to include both his friends and Huskisson's, and Palmerston was said to have attended at least one of the meetings held by the Whigs at Lansdowne House. But the personal objection to Huskisson was thought to have prevented any definite agreement. When Wellesley called on Grey shortly before the end of June to give him not a message but a hint that Huskisson would be prepared to serve under him, Grey certainly refused to commit himself. 'He did not think an open & avowed union at this moment advisable,' he told his son he had replied, 'but that they ought severally to continue as heretofore vigilantly to watch the measures of the administration & that if these were such as to require it a more intimate connection might hereafter be formed, that he had no indisposition towards Huskisson & his friends but that on the contrary he was quite ready to act with them when the occasion should offer. With this answer he has since heard that H. is perfectly satisfied.' Soon after that, on 26 June, the King died at last and four days later Grey stated in the House of Lords that the Government had shown themselves 'incompetent to manage the business of the country'. In view of the earlier exchanges with Huskisson's emissaries, and in particular that with Littleton, it would seem clear that this was, as he claimed, an ultimatum to the duke to make an offer of Cabinet rearrangement or suffer the consequences of 'systematic opposition'. Wellington, however, decided that the price was too high and took it as a declaration of war. He and Peel decided, therefore, to look elsewhere for the support they so badly needed.[47]

The duke had long been expected to make a move of this kind. But it was talent he wanted, even more than numbers; and the trouble was, as Brougham neatly put it, that 'the Ultras have no *pieces* – the Huskissons no *pawns*'. An even greater obstacle to his choosing among the Huskissonites was his pride; while on their part the 'ejection' of 1828 counselled caution to each and every one. When, early in the year, the rumour had got about that Ellenborough was to be removed and Palmerston to have his place at the Board of Control, Palmerston had written to Sulivan: 'How can your friend . . . be such a ninny as to fancy that the Duke would ask me, or that I should accept.' About the beginning of July, after Grey's ultimatum had made him think very hard about his prospects, the duke was still saying that he did not believe he 'could or ought to sit in a Cabinet again as the First Lord of the Treasury with Mr Huskisson, Lord Palmerston, or Mr Charles Grant'. But within a few days either way of this – probably at the end of June rather than the beginning of July – an approach was being made on his behalf and in that direction.[48]

Wellington's approach to the Huskissonites in the summer of 1830 was made in a very cautious manner and in the first place to Melbourne. Fred Lamb was laid up in Melbourne House with a broken leg and one day when he was being visited by a mutual friend of his and Wellington's, Lady Burghersh, she told him that the duke had asked her to say that he would be glad if Melbourne would rejoin his Administration. Apparently, in a patent attempt to salve his pride and separate Melbourne from his friends, the duke professed to think that the real reason why Melbourne had resigned his Irish secretaryship was the 'scrape' he had got into with another man's wife in Dublin. But guilty though he undoubtedly was with Lady Branden, Melbourne would have none of it. He had resigned, he said, because of the way the duke had treated Huskisson; and as far as coming back was concerned he replied to the duke – in writing, 'to prevent mistake' – that he could not do so singly. Wellington was supposed to have observed when he received this answer that he had no objection to Palmerston coming in as well but that he could not 'well propose to Huskisson' and therefore wished to have forty-eight hours to consider. In the meantime, however, Melbourne consulted with his friends, Huskisson, Palmerston and Grant, and found that they viewed their 'ejection' as being caused by political as well as personal differences in the Cabinet.

On 2 July, or thereabouts, Huskisson took Palmerston aside and told him that while he had come to the conclusion that, in view of past events, he would 'lose character by . . . joining the Duke's Govt constituted as it then was & had therefore made up his mind not to accept an offer if made', the same objections did not apply to Palmerston, Grant and Melbourne, and that he would support a Government to which they belonged. For his part, Palmerston then explained that he had come to precisely the same conclusion about his own position. He was 'decidedly' averse to returning to the 'irksome' situation of 1828; indeed, he reckoned it would be even worse in 1830, since he believed the duke's power to have considerably increased and the chances of making their opinions prevail to have proportionately diminished. He was also concerned about what the world would think. Seeing that there was nothing to justify their now approving a 'policy & system' which they had been loudest in condemning during the last two years, would it not be said: 'These gentlemen were turned out unceremoniously in 1828, from that time to this they have lain like ejected dogs at the door growling & snarling at those who expelled them but the moment the door is opened they march in again wagging their tails & take their places good humouredly by the fire.' The possession of office might be very desirable 'because it may give a man some little consequence & credit & may enable him to bring into practice principles which he believes to be just'. But taking it in these circumstances would be to betray those principles and to earn contempt from the public and bitter resentment in Parliament. For himself, therefore, unless the duke would undertake 'a general or larger reconstruction of his administration', he would not accept 'the very best offer' even if the duke were willing to treat with them as a party. So lest Wellington should otherwise conclude that he had been led on into a trap Melbourne sent word, before the duke's forty-eight hours were up, that 'no adequate Govt cd be made without comprizing not only Huskisson but also Ld Grey'.[49]

Wellington had no intention of surrendering in such a manner; afterwards he disavowed the approach altogether. But Melbourne's reply did not entirely put an end to thoughts about recruiting from the Huskissonites. For word came soon after that both Palmerston and Grant were really quite willing to come over and that Huskisson would in that case support the Government even while himself remaining out of office. That either Palmerston or Grant had so changed his mind is very unlikely. For during the week following the approach to Melbourne they had heard from what Palmerston called 'an unquestionable authority' – it was Princess Lieven – that only ten days before Wellington had authorized a similar one to Grey. There appears to be no trace of such an offer in Grey's papers, and probably the princess had heard of it from the other side. But the Huskissonites felt so indignant about it that they took care that Grey should also hear about the one made to them, either from the princess or from Holland House. The new story about Palmerston and Grant was probably due, therefore, to some misunderstanding about their real attitude. It came from an old Canningite, Lord Wharncliffe, via his son Stuart-Wortley, who had accepted junior office in February, and was almost certainly based on what Littleton had told him about the views held by Huskisson prior to the conversation with Palmerston on 2 July. But it was given circumstantial credence by the simultaneous information that, at a meeting of the 'Charlies' at Althorp's house on 4 July, it had been decided to harry the Government in future on the lines recently announced by Grey, but still not to make any formal concert with the Huskissonites.[50]

In Wellington's camp all was still uncertain. The duke frequently lost his temper when Peel and others pressed him about their weakness in the Commons and it is impossible now to make out quite what he meant from day to day. He would not hear of Grant, but seemed to indicate that he would be willing to entertain an approach from Palmerston, though not to make a new one from himself. His friends had better consult Peel, he said. But Peel again revealed how much his attitude had hardened against Palmerston during the last few weeks. He was supposed to be desperately anxious for help in the House of Commons; yet according to Mrs Arbuthnot, who admittedly damned him almost as much as she did Palmerston, he said that Palmerston would be 'too discreditable and unsafe, that he wd not come alone & wd be paralysed in speaking by fear of attacks from those he quitted'. Possibly they compromised by deciding to wait until after the elections; Palmerston was returned unopposed.[51]

Although Palmerston got off very lightly at Cambridge – the election began at 10 o'clock on a Saturday morning and was all over by half-past – the Government generally pursued the Huskissonites with relentless opposition in the elections of July and August 1830. The Government's strenuous efforts were not, however, very successful; there were a few defeats but no decisive change in the numerical balance of power. Considering the advantages of influence that Government possessed, this was in itself a serious moral setback. All parties, moreover, were startled by a great outburst of agitation about the electoral system, including wholesale revolts against vested interests and individual declarations (including one from Grant's brother) in favour of parliamentary reform. Then, before the elections were over, but too late to affect them very much, came the news of the revolution in France. Palmerston greeted it in terms of rapture, and composed on the occasion what is probably his most quoted private letter:

We shall drink the cause of Liberalism all over the world. Let Spain & Austria look to themselves; this reaction cannot end where it began, & Spain & Italy & Portugal & parts of Germany will sooner or later be affected. This event is decisive of the ascendancy of Liberal Principles throughout Europe; the evil spirit has been put down and will be trodden underfoot. The reign of Metternich is over & the days of the Duke's policy might be measured by algebra, if not by arithmetic.[52]

Palmerston's predictions were over-optimistic, but they were obviously sincere. He had, as he claimed, diagnosed the rot in France on his last visit to Paris. Nor was he, unlike Wellington, at all astonished by the ease with which the mob had defied the Army or by 'what could be effected by an unorganized multitude, where every individual is animated by an enthusiastic intensity of will'. He was also impressed by the contrast with 1789. 'Now no violence seems to have been committed, beyond what was absolutely necessary for the security of the Constitution. Is not this the most triumphant demonstration of the advantages arising from free discussion, from the liberty of the Press, from the diffusion of knowledge, and from familiarizing even the lowest classes with the daily examination of political questions?' But what was most important at this stage was that he also considered that it dramatically underlined the plentiful warnings in the recent elections that in England too men were no longer prepared to tolerate the present situation: 'nobody stands out as Champions of the Government, because no man can say what is the present meaning of the word Government translated into political principles; it can only be rendered by the paraphrase of vacillation in public measures, & jobbing in patronage.'[53]

There is nothing now to show how far Palmerston had moved along the path of parliamentary reform; certainly it was nothing like so far as some. Probably, since for all his talk about principles he was essentially a pragmatist, he was not yet sure how far it was necessary to go. But there can be no doubt that, although unscathed himself at Cambridge, he too, like the Huskissonites in general (as well as increasing numbers of Whigs), was reacting to the duke's resistance and tempted by the prospects of power. The long summer recess, however, gave plenty of time not only for reflection and manoeuvre, but also for rumour and mischance. While the Huskissonites seemed to be waiting quietly for an approach, the Whigs were still divided about whether to make one. In August Lord Sefton sent around asserting a junction had been made, and then tried to arrange it afterwards. But all that anyone achieved was an assurance from Huskisson that only on the basis of 'entire reconstruction' could there be any treating with Wellington. Grey and his son-in-law, Durham, both accepted that 'no efficient government' could be formed that did not include Huskisson, Palmerston and Grant, but wanted to delay active discussions until almost the last moment, until the week before the opening of Parliament in fact, for fear that too early and too open a junction would alienate the disgruntled Ultras, who equally distrusted Huskisson. Brougham, on the other hand, seems by this time to have wanted an early junction for fear of losing the Huskissonites to Wellington.[54]

There were several rumours in the summer that Huskisson had agreed terms with Wellington and that Palmerston was on offer even if Melbourne was not. Palmerston denied it, but there was a timely leakage of Lady Burghersh's doings to give it substance. Prince Leopold thought that Wellington's tactics were to divide by rumour and recruit piecemeal; so he urged a close understanding without delay. Althorp was also worried, not least because the admission of the Huskissonites to the Administration would have undermined the Opposition's agreed line of attack, that the Government was 'inefficient'. But he too did not believe the reports and Durham correctly divined that the papers were dating the Burghersh affair much too recently. He and Grey, therefore, still preferred to wait and even to forego any previous junction at all; rather they would have it develop naturally once Parliament had reassembled. They did not by any means preclude the notion of 'previous communication', but there was to be no 'direct treating' before a 'concert' had been established *de facto* by a period of active opposition. However, while the

Whigs all dithered, there were plots afoot on the other side to bring Huskisson and Wellington together again.[55]

There were, early in September 1830, quite a few people who looked with peculiar interest to the gathering of politicians that would assemble in the vicinity of Liverpool for the opening of the railway to Manchester. Not least among them was Lady Cowper. From her correspondence with Brougham it would even appear that the idea of his seizing the occasion to launch a major attack on Wellington came through her, though it may not have been of her own invention. Brougham was in written communication with Huskisson at the same time and hoped to 'sign a treaty' with him at Liverpool. Melbourne was unable to attend because of a minor operation; and Palmerston had no intention of abandoning Cowes and Broadlands, though he intended afterwards to meet up with Huskisson and Grant when he went to Edward Petre's for the Doncaster races. Very probably he expected to meet Brougham there too. He was certainly party to the plot. The main idea, apparently, was that Brougham would publicly attack the duke for his supposed part in the events leading up to the revolution in Paris. Fred Lamb went off to Paris to gather 'evidence' and Lady Cowper urged Brougham to get some there as well; typically he proposed to speak first and go later. She also took the opportunity, when Brougham heard of a speech of Grant's in defence of his *past* service with Wellington and interpreted it as a hint of *future* cooperation, to assure him that the revelation of the earlier failure of Lady Burghersh's approach really proved that the Huskissonites were not to be caught and ought to inspire the Whigs with full confidence in them. But Lady Cowper had been as well trained by Princess Lieven to look both ways at once as Brougham was by nature. The next day Arbuthnot heard from Greville that she had just told him the Huskissonites were 'quite ready to join the Government, but they should expect to be taken largely'. Two days later Littleton also wrote to Wharncliffe suggesting that although he had not discussed it with Huskisson, who had been with him on his way north a few days before, a reconciliation with Wellington would still be no more difficult than it might have been in July if only 'concessions were made on certain points'.[56]

All these plots were checked and all these speculations made suddenly out of date when on 15 September Huskisson failed to get out of the way in time and was fatally injured by Stephenson's *Rocket*. He was a notoriously clumsy man and not too well at the time, but he may have been put into an unusual agitation, if not by the handshake that Wellington had given him a little while before, perhaps by the letter to Wharncliffe that Littleton had just shown him. There was no doubt that his death entirely altered the party situation. 'What luck the D. of W. has! ' wrote Durham to Grey. 'His most formidable opponent in the Commons removed! ' It was also appreciated that it might have destroyed whatever cohesion Huskisson's party had, and by removing too the personal objections to their leader in the most effective manner set his followers free to join either the Opposition or the Government. So while

Brougham professed to think that they were 'now worth but little to anybody' as a party, he nonetheless wrote around to urge that 'clever and good men' like Palmerston and Grant be saved from all temptation by offering them a speedy junction with the Whigs. Their 'late conduct', he said, had been 'perfect – above all praise for sense as well as honour', and their rejection of the approach to Melbourne gave them 'large claims' upon the Whigs. Huskisson's death, moreover, would also remove the objections of the Ultras and of the Whigs' own 'old stager' (he meant Grey presumably).[37]

Brougham also heard about the 'evil things' Lady Cowper was supposed to have been saying to Greville. 'All I know is she is the last person I could have suspected of such a perfidy & therefore I don't believe it,' he wrote. 'But if they do join by all the Gods & Godesses & by the river Stix let them look sharp. They are ruined if they do. . . . if it prove true Palm. will return to insignificance with a ruined character & no real good will ensue to the Dictator. I shall deeply regret it on account of a man whom I really like . . .' It made him all the more anxious for the junction, however; perhaps, if the story was true, that had been its purpose. So he asked a young friend in London, who had been attending a good deal at both Holland House and Panshanger in recent months, to contact Lady Cowper with a view to making the union which, he said, though plainly he was lying, both Althorp and Grey now wanted as much as he did.[38]

Agar Ellis – afterwards the Lord Dover whom Greville called 'a sort of Jackal' of Brougham's – had in fact already acted. Taking the lead from earlier letters of Brougham's and hearing that the Hollands were going to stay at Panshanger, he had written to Lady Holland to propose that she and her husband take occasion to broach the subject. 'Lady Cowper has more power with that party than any body', he had written, '& you have Melbourne there also under your hand.' Ellis therefore decided to await the Hollands' return to town before taking any further action. The result of this was that no direct proposal was made to the Huskissonites. For though Holland had also had a letter from Grey hinting that he should ask them directly whether or not they would entertain an offer from the duke, he was not told to make any offer on behalf of the Whigs.[39]

There was almost frantic movement back and forth to Panshanger in the middle of September. It had probably been intended to have a conference; instead there was an inquest. Princess Lieven was there, inevitably it always seems, to hear of poor Huskisson's death; so was the convalescent Melbourne. On 20 September Palmerston also turned up, having cancelled his visit to Doncaster although both Durham and Brougham were there. Two days later Holland showed him Ellis's letter. What must his face have shown when he read the comment about Lady Cowper? Holland took Melbourne and then Palmerston aside to ask them Grey's questions. According to Holland's report each said 'substantially' the same thing: that Huskisson's death had made them even more averse to joining Wellington, since they would be more than ever 'at his mercy' as a minority in the Cabinet; that they would not join with him therefore unless it was in sufficient numbers and in a Ministry so remodelled as to give them 'equality', and not even then unless they were 'headed or connected' with someone strong enough to stand up to the duke. As far as a junction with the Whigs was concerned, they said that there was neither public principle nor personal feeling to stand in the way. They hinted they would prefer Grey as chief, but seemed to have no objection to any other peer and scarcely any commoner save Althorp, whose judgement they doubted, and Brougham, whose 'designs' they suspected and whose jealous temper they thought inconvenient to party cooperation.[60]

With this account Palmerston's letters and another brief reference he made shortly afterwards pretty well agree. He told Grant, who was not at Panshanger, that he could see no possibility of joining the duke unless foreign affairs, finance and commerce were all taken out of his control and the three of them (Melbourne, Grant and he) backed by other accessions to the Cabinet. Such concessions hardly seemed conceivable; and yet, so fond was the duke of 'his favourite Pastime Govt' that he might give up everything else. 'He wd rather march manacled at the head of the regiment than not march with it at all.' Palmerston also added a decided indisposition to respond to Brougham's approach: 'it seems to me that it is our business to maintain the dignified & imposing attitude of independence which we have hitherto prescribed, & that however we may admire the faculties of Brougham & court his cooperation whenever we agree with him it wd do us no good to merge ourselves among the followers of his erratic standard.'[61]

Ellis, therefore, did not have entirely the wrong impression from the report at Holland House that 'the Huskisson Party are like to join us Whigs, & not to throw themselves into the jaws of Wellington'. Brougham understood Palmerston to have agreed that they should all meet and, in what he took to be the actual words used, 'take council together' just before Parliament met in October; shortly afterwards Grey, who suspected Brougham's approach had been an attempt to seize the lead of the Opposition for himself, concluded that he could rest secure for a while without making any compromising alliance. However, on the same day that Ellis called at Holland House, Palmerston told Littleton that what he had written to Wharncliffe about giving a hint to the duke was 'perfectly unobjectionable'.[62]

There was nothing intentionally deceitful about Palmerston's behaviour towards the Whigs. In the first place he had probably not had any idea beforehand that Littleton was going to make such a move. Palmerston, it was true, had met with Huskisson at Sturges Bourne's a week or so before Huskisson left for the north. Nothing is known about what they may have decided, but Huskisson shortly before was writing to Granville that he did not expect the duke to agree to an 'entire reconstruction of the Cabinet' and his friends were described immediately after as 'all ripe for mischief & full of fight'. Nor had Littleton discussed his project with Huskisson at Teddesley, but only on the day of the accident itself. In addition his first report of it to Palmerston was not written until 20 September. Whatever one may think of Lady Cowper's reputed behaviour and the reassurances she sent when tackled about it by Brougham, the disavowals of any offers from the Government that went from Panshanger on 19 September to Grey via Princess Lieven, and to Brougham direct from Melbourne, were, as far as the Littleton affair was concerned, not only strictly accurate but also unpretending. In the second place, although Palmerston had arranged for Littleton's letter to be forwarded to Panshanger, there was nothing in his handling of it that was at odds either with the substance or the spirit of what he had said to Holland. He did not tell either Littleton or Holland that the Huskissonites would refuse all offers from Wellington; only that he did not expect any to be made that they ever could accept. There was also the important consideration that he ought not to do anything to alienate Canningites like Littleton or Wharncliffe, who obviously preferred a reconciliation with Wellington. By Planta's account the Huskissonites numbered only eleven in the new House of Commons. Finally, what probably made Littleton's letter '*perfectly*' unobjectionable was that he had also suggested that even an unacceptable response 'would at least be useful as a confession of weakness' on Wellington's part.[63]

Littleton had had time before Huskisson's fatal collision with the *Rocket* only to get his verbal acquiescence, and Wharncliffe a mere quarter of an hour in which to open the subject with Arbuthnot. But this, together no doubt with the report of Lady Cowper's indiscretions, was enough to set something in motion – at least, that is, once Huskisson himself was dead. That event, Arbuthnot wrote to Peel, 'has made a most important change, & has removed great difficulties'. The personal objections that the duke and many other Tories had felt no longer stood in the way; and just as did Brougham on the other side, they too felt they must act quickly to forestall the junction of Low Whigs and Ultra Tories with Huskissonites. It was Palmerston they had first in mind. He seemed the natural leader of the rump; Leopold's offer to negotiate with him on behalf of the Whigs was not taken up, but it was to him the prince addressed a letter of condolence and Littleton took this as an acknowledgement that Palmerston was now the chief. After Huskisson's death Wellington went to stay a few days with Peel near Tamworth and there, on 22 or 23 September and in company with Aberdeen, Goulburn, Arbuthnot and their Chief Whip, Billy Holmes, he decided to offer Palmerston Murray's place at the Colonial Office. The duke was warned that Palmerston was unlikely to come in alone but the whole subject plainly irritated him and he insisted on confining things to the single offer first. Mrs Arbuthnot was also there and it was she who suggested the following day that, since Lord Clive was a great friend of Palmerston's and was supposed to have reported Palmerston's anxiety to come back, they employ him as negotiator. It did not really matter that he was 'deaf as a post and not very bright', she said, because he would never have to explain it all to Parliament.[64]

Considering that it was all supposed to be so urgent, it was perhaps the duke's petulant reluctance that made him wait until 30 September before writing a letter to Clive, and as Clive by then was in Wales he did not get it until late the next day. Clive concluded that he was supposed to see Palmerston in person, but since he did not know where he was – in London, Broadlands or Ireland – he had to make enquiries first. He had the wit to write ahead, quoting the duke at length, but even this did not reach Palmerston at Broadlands until the morning of 4 October. Palmerston responded at once, with sentiments that matched the hypocrisy of the duke's and in substance just as brief. To Wellington's profession of feelings that had never been 'otherwise than friendly' and were always 'unattended by anything like personal or political hostility', he replied that on his part he had never altered his 'feeling of individual regard' for the duke and that he had 'during many years of private intercourse invariably experienced so much personal kindness from him, that I could hardly conceive any degree of political hostility ... which on my part could be converted into personal hostility'. To the talk about 'high office' for himself he answered that, while he certainly had 'no disinclination' to contribute what 'little assistance' he might have to the public service, yet from a 'variety of circumstances' which were so obvious that he need not elaborate them he was obliged to say that he 'could not singly, join His Majesty's Government, constituted as it now is'. Since, however, he was coming up to London the next day, he offered to see Clive in Stanhope St and Clive called at noon two days later.

While on his way to Stanhope Street, Clive had stopped first at Apsley House and shown Palmerston's letter to the duke. 'This is an answer & apparently a positive one,' Wellington remarked. 'He won't come in singly but who are his friends? ' When Clive speculated that Grant was his closest political associate, Wellington had replied: 'Well it is not so easy to make room for a number of persons, it is easier to form a Cabinet than to break one up.' Palmerston must have smiled wryly at this in recollection of May 1828; and he had no intention of making things easy for the duke. He added Melbourne to Grant and then said, in effect, that he did not wish it to be understood that if an offer to all three were made it would necessarily be accepted. So far, he had been asked only one question and had answered for himself alone: beyond that he 'wished to follow the true grammatical rule of not giving a second answer till a second question was put'. He made it clear, moreover, that he did not expect any further enquiries. When Clive returned to dine with him that evening he brought none; the duke had merely repeated his previous observations and thanked him for his services.* Clive did suggest, however, that it was the Colonial Office the duke intended for Palmerston.[65]

*Lyndhurst told Princess Lieven that Palmerston had also had an interview with Wellington and discussed parliamentary reform; Eldon repeated a similar story (*Lieven-Palmerston*, pp. 19-20; *Eldon*, iii. 117-18). But the story is false in both respects. In a letter written some years later (Lorne, p. 64) Palmerston mentioned meeting the duke, the next day he thought, after his talk with Clive. But he must have been confusing the occasion with the meeting he had after returning from Paris. His near contemporary memo. makes it quite clear there was no meeting with the duke before then.

In the course of the next few days Palmerston heard the same thing from several other sources, and notably from Princess Lieven. 'Amuse yourself, because you will not be able to do so for long,' she had told him at the beginning of September. Then, on the day that he received Clive's first letter, she had written again to say that she had learned, 'd'une manière très intime', that some proposition had been put to him and urged him, not merely out of personal friendship but for Europe's sake, not to lose a moment in responding. But when Palmerston replied she found, and perhaps not to her surprise, that she knew more about the plan than he did. In a strange letter, which was addressed half to Lady Cowper and half to Palmerston and which she vainly begged should be burned – 'There is nothing more compromising than the job I do' – she revealed that her confidential source was the Chancellor, and that from him she understood Cabinet places would be offered to the Huskissonian triumvirate of Palmerston, Melbourne and Grant, and in addition to Goderich; Grey, however, was to be offered Ireland. She admitted that this was a strange notion but made it plain that she hoped it would succeed for Europe's sake – she meant Russia's of course. This was probably why she told Grey rather less about it; her principal objective was to see Wellington retained as Prime Minister and Ireland would not be enough to revive Grey's interest in that particular notion. She suggested to Palmerston, however, that the whole thing was such an 'odd idea' as to indicate that the duke would be prepared to offer even more; but hardly had she written that than there came Palmerston's note saying he would stipulate for at least three Whigs.[66]

As Palmerston explained when he saw Clive again on the following Sunday, 10 October, and revealed to him the approach that had been made to Melbourne earlier that summer, Huskisson's death had not lowered but raised their price. He did not specify any number but mentioned Grey, Lansdowne, Holland and Carlisle (the last an old friend of Canning) as names from which 'a selection' might be made. According to his much later account Clive then protested that this would amount to a surrender on Wellington's part and mentioned Goderich's name instead. Palmerston of course replied that he could not consider Goderich as a substitute for Grey and Lansdowne. To Littleton he wrote that the original offer for him to come in singly was like 'asking me whether I was disposed to jump off Westminster Bridge' and that while Goderich was 'an excellent fellow, . . . an able head of a department, and . . . a most agreeable colleague', he was hardly a plausible guarantee that there would be no repetition of May 1828.[67]

In the 'Autobiographical Sketch' Palmerston wrote about a decade later he also claimed that 'to cut the matter short, and to avoid further communications' he then set off 'immediately' for Paris. There may have been some truth in this. Although he considered Ireland out of the question that year, he had been hoping all along to get to France as usual and, like so many others no doubt, in particular to gather new ammunition against the duke's foreign policy. But right up until at least 2 October he intended to defer it until after

the opening of Parliament. However, by 5 October, the day after he received
the first intimation of Wellington's approach, it was known that he was about
to leave for Paris. But Palmerston did not set off for France 'immediately' after
his Sunday morning conference with Clive. Instead he went to Broadlands,
and he offered while he was there to see Clive again on the Tuesday and even
gave him detailed information about his intended port of embarkation
specifically so that the duke could recall him if he wished. Moreover, as Clive
pointed out to the duke, Paris was not all that far off and a journey there did
not consume so much time as one back and forth to Scotland.[68]

No word came to keep Palmerston from Paris. So from his base in the Hôtel
de la Tamise in the Rue de Rivoli he paid his customary respects to the ladies,
Mme Flahault and Mme Graham, added an introduction to Lafayette to his
list of noble statesmen, and dispatched to his family and friends the usual wise
remarks upon the politics of France. But while he was away the duke's
approaches to the Ultra Tories got tangled up in terms, and it was decided to
make another attempt on Palmerston. Either Wellington's vanity had made
him extraordinarily obtuse or Peel's desperate prospects in the Commons had
made them clutch at the feeblest straws. For after all that had passed it really
was rather strange that they should still be reckoning on a mere three isolated
places for the Huskissonites and planning to substitute for Grant a former
Huskissonite, Wilmot Horton, who had abandoned them that same year and
had not even been included among their list of 'friends' at Huskisson's funeral.
Some of this may have been Clive's fault. It was all very well to discount his
having to make explanations to Parliament; but what about his report to
Wellington? Clive did not, as it happened, visit Palmerston at Broadlands; he
was too anxious to get back to Wales. For the same reason he appears not
to have seen Wellington again after the final Sunday morning talk with
Palmerston. Palmerston had, according to his memorandum, intended his
views about the necessity of a larger reconstruction of the Ministry and the
inclusion of several Whigs to be brought thus indirectly to the knowledge of
the duke. Even Clive, deaf and dim though he may have been, seems to have
appreciated this. But he resorted to a method too subtle to succeed. Design-
edly or not, on the Sunday or Monday morning before he left London, he saw
not Wellington but Planta, and with him cooked up a memorandum which,
after elaborating how inadequate the Ministry was to face the coming session
of Parliament, suggested the addition to the Cabinet not only of the triumvirate but also of either Grey or Lansdowne and Carlisle. There was no mention
of Holland or that at least two or possibly all three Whigs might be required;
otherwise it was not at all a bad version of Palmerston's wishes. But it had two
fatal flaws. The first was that Clive chose to make it so indirect a hint as to
convey not the least idea that a word of it had passed from Palmerston's lips.
The second was that Planta ratted on him, taking his own name from a paper
they had composed together and passing it on to Wellington and Peel as

though it was merely Clive's. Their masters both considered it, Planta none-
the less reported, 'a powerful & useful paper' and he expected it to induce
them to review their position 'more maturely than they have ever yet done'.[69]

It is not very likely that Wellington and Peel paid even a moment's attention to notions coming, as they understood it, from a single and so uninspired
a source. They may even have believed it when they put the word around that
they knew Palmerston himself really wished to join them. After all, Princess
Lieven hoped he would; possibly Lady Cowper too; perhaps even Palmerston
did at heart. He may have kept out of sight for a bit when he got back from
Paris. Parliament was due to assemble on 26 October and there is no reason to
think that he changed his plan of returning that evening or early the following
day; but Princess Lieven was under the impression that he did not return until
29 October and even Lady Holland could get no more than a 'glimpse' of him
that day.[70]

Palmerston was not slow to respond, in any event, when on 30 October he
received a note from Wellington asking him to call; he was at Apsley House by
11 a.m. Their interview, however, was very brief; about six minutes as he
recalled it. The duke offered to try and find unspecified places for Palmerston,
Melbourne and Grant, once he knew they were willing; Palmerston replied
that there would have to be a much larger reconstruction than that and
without mentioning any names hinted at a substantially Whig administration
under the duke and Peel. It was hardly a promising confrontation; according
to Princess Lieven the duke even expressed surprise at the suggestion of the
Whigs, saying that it was all new and unexpected. Immediately afterwards
Wellington reported it to Peel and they agreed that 'such notions put the
matter quite out of the question' and to fight on as they were.[71]

Mrs Arbuthnot, who never forgave 'his shabbiness in professing himself a
Whig just at the moment [in the summer of 1827] he thought it politic to do
so', commented: 'Ld P. did not say one syllable upon *policy* or *principles*; it
turned entirely upon *places*.' This may seem rather unfair; after all, the men
were supposed, not merely to provide safety in numbers, but also to act as
guardians of principle and advocates of policy. But Melbourne had made a
similar point, though in a very different tone, when he gave a qualified
approval to Palmerston's initial response to Clive's original approach. He had
agreed that it was necessary to have both Grey and Lansdowne in with them;
but it was also essential that they should be told a great deal more about
Wellington's policy and ideas. 'We might do ourselves credit and the country
service but a Cabinet formed upon a principle of balance and difference and
commenced in distrust and hostility can never be of much use to the public
nor, to the members of it, any other than a source of annoyance and disquiet.'
On 31 October Grant, who had rushed down from Scotland, also wrote to say
that he had serious doubts and wanted to talk before any final reply was made
to the duke; Palmerston replied on 1 November that he would not commit
anybody without full communication first.[72]

Before the end of October the opening of the new Parliament and the imminence of the debate on the King's Speech had also stirred the Whigs into action. Grey had come down belatedly to London and at a meeting of Whig M.P.s at Althorp's on Sunday, 31 October, it had been determined to harry the Government to its fall and that the party's programme should be retrenchment and reform. That evening a dinner party of Whigs decided that it would be 'highly expedient' to ascertain how far 'the Palmerston folks' were prepared to go in the matter of parliamentary reform.[73]

The emissary the Whigs chose was Sir James Graham. How and when he had become intimate with Palmerston is unknown; but he had throughout 1830 been urging a closer concert with the Huskissonites than most of the Whigs were prepared to envisage. This may even have been one of the reasons, in addition to disapproval of the limited nature of their programme, why he deliberately abstained from attending the original meeting that Althorp had held on 3 March. He had attended on 4 July, when they had determined on 'systematic opposition', but had pointedly dissociated himself from the decision not to seek a coalition with the Huskissonites, and confessed that he had already been in touch with Huskisson, since he was convinced that no Ministry could be formed without him, Palmerston and the two Grants; and at the beginning of September he had reported to Brougham that he believed the Huskissonites were anxious to make comon cause with the Whigs in an entire reconstruction of the Government. Quite possibly it was Palmerston who encouraged Graham and Huskisson in the eager exchanges about cooperation that passed between them during August. For he had already opened a friendly correspondence direct with Graham himself and exchanged enthusiastic greetings on the July Revolution in France. They may even have been thinking of a joint onslaught on the Game Laws. For about this time Palmerston was preparing lengthy drafts and memoranda for such an attack – one of them included the statement in reference to the ancient restrictions on the right to take game: 'Qualification Laws belong to the age of privileges. This is the age of rights' – and Graham was listing it among the objectives he outlined to Brougham as the basis for a coalition.[74]

It is not known how soon it was after the Whig dinner of 31 October that Graham communicated anew with Palmerston. Brougham had said he wanted an answer in time for a second meeting the Whigs were to have the following Sunday evening, when they hoped to settle what sort of parliamentary reform to press for. But there was more urgency about it than this seems to imply. Most were agreed that an early declaration of war based on reform was necessary; Brougham, Althorp and John Russell were even competing for the honour of making it. Nothing very specific could be said, however, until it was known how large – or small – an area of agreement there was among the Opposition. Brougham expected the Huskissonites to make difficulties about household suffrage in particular and Graham, who would have known even more about their views, replied that 'much discussion, negotiation, and arrangement will be required . . . before we can bring Palmerston's friends into line'. Graham was evidently worried, on the one hand, that they would find Brougham's ideas too radical; their 'common object', he reminded Brougham, was to 'reform to the extent necessary for preserving our institutions, not to change for the purpose of subverting'. Perhaps, on the other hand, he was not so confident that an arrangement between Palmerston and Wellington would prove impossible in the end, nor so unwilling as he seemed to be a party to it.[75]

Early in October Holland had refused to believe in the rumours of Government overtures to Palmerston but had forecast nonetheless that 'an extension of representation to the populous towns, & an open trade to India & China will . . . form part of the ministerial measures this year. We shall perhaps hear that poor Huskisson was in truth the great obstacle to these concessions as Canning had been to the Catholic Emancipation & that none but persons who had signalized themselves in resisting them, could or ought to be the instruments of carrying them.' When it was discovered that the duke had made new approaches to Palmerston – Lady Holland had 'screwed' the fact out of him, Palmerston explained on the eve of his departure for Paris – it was widely suspected that these must be a prelude to the concession of a modest measure of parliamentary reform.[76]

At least one of the Huskissonites evidently thought that an agreement on reform was possible, and concluded that it might provide the opportunity for one last attempt at a reconciliation with the duke. This was Littleton, of course. He had run into Arbuthnot in the street on Monday, 1 November, and arranged to meet at the other's house before dinner the same evening. What he then said was that if in addition to concessions which he believed would not create any difficulty – on the China trade, the Civil List, reductions of pluralities in the Civil Service, and the arrangements for the regency in case the King should die before the young Victoria came of age – the duke would only agree to give members to three large towns now and promise transfers from boroughs found corrupt hereafter, he was sure that Palmerston, the Grants, Graham and Stanley (the future Earl of Derby) would 'immediately' join him. Arbuthnot promised to pass this on, but Littleton at once returned to say that when Palmerston had told the duke at their interview two days before that he required a more extensive reorganization of the Ministry, it was not at all Brougham and the Whigs he had had in mind, but Graham and Stanley. Graham himself had told him so, and Stanley too that very morning.[77]

Littleton's story is very strange; it probably reveals more about him than about anyone else. In a letter he wrote to Brougham early in September Graham had referred to rumours of the Huskissonites' negotiations with Wellington and asked: 'Is it possible that they can have committed such an act of political suicide?' Presumably it was Littleton's story that made Arbuthnot complain a little later that Graham was 'not an honest man'. When Littleton heard in 1856 that the late Duke of Wellington's papers were being arranged for publication, he showed considerable anxiety lest Arbuthnot's record of their conversation should be found among them. The prospect of having Brougham in power, however, frightened even more sensible men almost out of their wits, and Littleton, perhaps, may have easily interpreted an attempt to reassure him with mollifying words as a scheme to cultivate the duke. He also seems to have misunderstood Palmerston, though he admitted he had no authority at all from him to make such an initiative as he had to Arbuthnot.[78]

Even up to this point, the beginning of November 1830, there was still no clear idea where Palmerston really stood on parliamentary reform. In his response to the scheme Littleton had been hatching with Wharncliffe just before Huskisson's death, he had mentioned the wisdom of granting representation to large towns and speculated too that Wellington might concede it to save his place. He had not said it, however, as though he thought it might form the basis of a future compromise; but neither had he made any attempt to correct Littleton's impression that their little group should also remain independent of the Whigs. 'Incorporation', Littleton argued, would weaken Palmerston's position and strengthen the Government by depriving independent members of a nucleus around which to gather; he even advocated some occasional votes against the Whigs as a deliberate demonstration of their independence. As a comment on Palmerston's general tendency to extract the maximum personal advantage from his stiuation, this was probably not so far wrong. But it made the common error of underestimating Palmerston's commitment to policies and principles. Very probably too Palmerston's views on parliamentary reform moved forward in company with so many others, especially if, as is quite possible, he took any notice of the advice he had received from Anglesey, to the effect that it would be best to adopt 'so ample a reform, as shd put the noses of the hacknied reformers out of joint for many a day'. In any case, before Littleton could be disillusioned by Palmerston, he was disillusioned by the duke.[79]

Concerned lest all the unfounded rumours that he was going to make concessions to enlist new supporters should alienate the ones he already possessed, Wellington announced in the Lords on 2 November his belief in the perfection of the existing constitution and his perpetual resistance to measures of reform. Two nights later Littleton approached Arbuthnot in the Commons and asked if he had anything to say. 'Nothing,' Arbuthnot replied, and Littleton could only observe that he had 'expected it would be so, as the door was now shut against junction'. There were some on the other side who were even slower than he to realize it. A few days later Croker, who but a very short while before had been reassuring Peel that Palmerston and Grant were 'really nothing but froth', asked Palmerston to reconsider his reply to the duke. 'After talking some time', Palmerston recalled, 'he said, "Well, I will bring the matter to a point. Are you resolved, or are you not, to vote for Parliamentary

Reform?" I said, "I am." "Well, then," said he, "there is no use in talking to you any more on this subject. You and I, I am grieved to see, shall never again sit on the same bench together." ' In fact Palmerston's eleven had already met in Stanhope Street on 6 November to consider their reply to Graham and had agreed to vote for Brougham's motion provided it were 'vaguely worded'. No one was sure what this meant, beyond the enfranchisement of the larger towns, and Howick doubted if it went so far as the majority of the Whigs wished. But according to Palmerston the resolve to support a suitable motion was 'quite determined' on his part, the Grants' and even Littleton's. Patience had been rewarded at last.[80]

Soon the patience of twenty years was to be rewarded in still more striking fashion. Wellington's bombshell had demolished the last chance of any reconciliation with the Huskissonites and it had blown Palmerston decisively in the direction of the Whigs. On the evening of the meeting in Stanhope St Agar Ellis entertained Lady Holland, the Lievens, the Cowpers, Palmerston and John Russell. 'Had a long & very satisfactory political conversation with Palmerston after dinner,' he wrote. Two nights later at another dinner party it was noted that there was 'a great deal of talking' between Palmerston and Russell. On 13 November Ellis called on Palmerston to tell him that the Whigs had just agreed on a reform motion as vague as any he could have wished, and aimed, as Brougham had already told the Commons it would be, not at 'revolution, but restoration'.[81]

Invitations had already gone out from Littleton for another meeting in Stanhope St late on Sunday afternoon. This time Goderich also came. But Dudley refused; he had supported the duke's Government pretty consistently since his reluctant resignation and he would not desert it now even though he thought that a grave tactical error had been made in not conceding the transfer of representation from corrupt boroughs. It is not clear what the others had to say. It was hardly necessary for them to have discussed, as Littleton suggested was intended, the details of what kind of reform they could accept. Palmerston's report to Ellis simply said: 'We have just had a meeting of a select few to consider the proposed resolution and we are all prepared to support it.'[82]

Brougham never got the chance to move his resolution. The Stanhope St eleven had told Graham after their first meeting that 'they were prepared to go all lengths, so far as respected turning out the Government'. On the evening of 12 November Palmerston had personally promised Ellis to try and get the Ultras to join them in supporting the vague motion he was assured was likely to come. But the embittered Ultras were not all agreed that they could go so far in their vendetta against the duke. They decided first therefore to give their support to another Whig motion on the Civil List. The Commons debated it on 15 November, the day before Brougham's was due, and with Whigs, radicals, Ultras and Huskissonites voting against them, the Government were defeated by 233 to 204. Wellington resigned the next morning and in the afternoon Grey was summoned to St James's. 'As soon as Lord Grey was commmissioned by the King to form an adminstration', Palmerston concluded the 'Autobiography' in which he explained for Lady Cowper's benefit how he came to be where he was in November 1830, 'he wrote to me to offer me to form a part of it.'[83]

The impression conveyed by Palmerston's terse account was not entirely incorrect. Grey saw the King between three and four in the afternoon of Tuesday, 16 November and Palmerston the same evening. It was inevitable, in the coalition of Whigs, Huskissonites and Ultras Grey was forming, that Palmerston and his friends would be accorded special importance on account of their greater experience in office and the debating power they were supposed to have in the Commons. They ended up with India and all three secretaryships of State. But it was by no means certain from the beginning what position Palmerston would have. When Grey asked Palmerston to call on him between nine and eleven on that Tuesday evening it was to the leader of the Huskissonites he wished to talk. Holland had recommended Palmerston in that capacity earlier that day; and Grey had already sent off his invitation on the same assumption. After an interview of what Durham called 'considerable duration', Palmerston left having undertaken to consult with Melbourne and Grant, and possibly (though it may not have been until another meeting the next day) also to use his influence with some of the Ultras. The only record that appears to have been left by Grey stated: 'I have had a very satisfactory conversation with Ld Palmerston, & tho' no particular arrangements are yet made, I have the pleasure of adding that I have every reason to expect that he & his friends will form a part of the new Government.'[84]

Something must surely have been said about the likely distribution of offices. Palmerston almost certainly went to Grey thinking that he would be offered the Exchequer and the lead in the House of Commons, and he left Littleton the next day with the impression that this had been Grey's first intention. Littleton was an unreliable reporter, but it was as the future Leader that Grey had talked of Palmerston earlier that year and it was not any more improbable that this should have been his first idea in November than that he should have offered Brougham a second-rate post earlier that day. Others, like James Abercromby, saw that a House of Commons with Brougham as Attorney-General and Palmerston as Leader simply would 'not do'. Rather, to curb the dangerous Brougham, the Whigs insisted on having Althorp as Leader and Althorp would not serve at all, either as Chancellor of the Exchequer and Leader or as anything else, if Brougham remained in the Commons.[85]

Palmerston afterwards claimed to have suggested the device of tempting Brougham with the Great Seal and so removing him to the Lords; and Caro

George, who knew them both so well, believed this was indeed the case. If so, for Palmerston to have set Brougham on the course that destroyed his public reputation and wrecked his political career forever was a very high price to exact for the slights of 1806-9. But by the time the difficulty about Brougham was resolved Althorp had already been given the lead and Palmerston a different destination. So whatever Grey might have had in mind at first, the prospect that he seems definitely to have held out to Palmerston at their second meeting on Wednesday morning, if not on the evening before, was the Home Office. In any case Grey certainly did not have Palmerston in mind as his first choice for Foreign Secretary.[86]

According to his son-in-law, Durham, Grey would have preferred to take the Foreign Office, his old one under Fox, for himself. But he knew that as Prime Minister he would have to take the Treasury. He may therefore have offered the Foreign Office to Holland early on the first day of his negotiations; and if so Holland refused on account of his perennial attacks of gout. He certainly offered it to Lansdowne when he called on him that evening about the same time as did Palmerston. Lansdowne, who had had enough of office even after a very brief experience, took twenty-four hours to make up his mind. He saw Grey again on Wednesday and presumably reiterated his doubts; for by that evening Palmerston knew that if Lansdowne refused it the Foreign Office was to be his. On Thursday morning Lansdowne finally wrote to tell Grey that he had made up his mind and Palmerston wrote to his sister: 'The Whigs wish Althorp to lead as likely to keep their Party from straying. Perhaps this may be well; as I have the Foreign Office I do not care.' Clearly he had expected the lead and would have been upset had he not been offered compensation.[87]

Professor Webster may have been correct in suggesting that even after his House of Commons triumphs in 1829-30 Palmerston was still very apprehensive of speaking in public. That is no reason for believing he did not expect to have the lead. For what Palmerston disliked still more than being asked to speak was to be refused what he thought his due. He never speculated what had put the idea of the Foreign Office into Grey's head, although the only person who seems to have suggested it hitherto was the utterly insignificant Shee. Few others have resisted doing so. Webster suggested that both Holland and Lansdowne had recommended it. Holland might easily have done so, considering how much he and Palmerston seemed to agree on the subject of foreign policy. By this time, too, Holland House seems to have been deeply involved in the schemes that had sent Palmerston, as well as Brougham and Russell, on the mission to gather evidence of the abortive conspiracy supposedly concocted between Metternich and Wellington against the chartered liberties of France. Both Hollands commended Palmerston to their son in Paris. 'He has improved in publick speeches & risen in publick estimation since you left England,' wrote Lord Holland. 'Among many merits he has that, a rare one in our politicans, of being earnestly & honestly interested in foreign questions & understanding them.' 'You will meet Ld Palmerston & upon acquaintance will like him much,' added Lady Holland; 'his [?finical] manner & sly laugh is against him. [But] it is impossible for any man to have conducted himself more uprightly & honourably than he has done.' It was, however, as a prospective Leader of the Commons that Holland had always commended Palmerston to Grey; and when he first heard that Lansdowne had turned down the Foreign Office, he urged Grey to go on pressing him and made no mention of any alternative. But by then Grey had already given up on Lansdowne and turned instead to Palmerston. As Lansdowne had suggested this in his letter that morning the credit has been more plausibly given to him. But it is clear from the tone of his letter that the idea was a novel one to him; and Palmerston, after all, heard of the possibility from Grey the night before. Perhaps, then, there was something in the claim made by Princess Lieven in her so-called diary and subsequently dismissed by virtually every historian.[88]

According to Princess Lieven's account, it was she who turned her lover against Lansdowne and persuaded him instead that Palmerston was the man. Grey, she said, went to her every day while the arrangements were being made, not only to report developments but also to seek advice. Initially she had refused to compromise herself by offering any opinion about the Foreign Office even though she had serious doubts about his first choice. But first Lady Cowper and then Palmerston himself had come begging her to press his claims, and finally, for friendship's sake, she had promised to do so. When she named him, Grey 'recoiled and hestitated much'; he hardly knew Palmerston and doubted if he deserved his good reputation among foreign diplomats. So the matter hung fire for two more days. In the meantime Palmerston left her no peace, galloping daily after her as she passed between her houses in Richmond and in town. Still, her desire to help him really was as great as his 'obsession was keen'. So she kept up her pressure on Grey. Finally the Prime Minister came, 'with a mixture of joy and hesitation', to say that the Foreign Office was Palmerston's.[89]

Princess Lieven's account was written years after the event and is patently exaggerated and inaccurate. It is very unlikely that Palmerston ever begged political favours from anyone, not even from ladies. Her claim that this was the second occasion on which she had saved the Foreign Office from Lansdowne is also utterly without support, though there is no doubt she believed it at the time as well as later. She must surely have played some sort of part, and as she had been plotting in every camp, she had to exercise some degree of caution. She may very well have been genuinely annoyed with Palmerston for ruining the last chance of keeping Wellington as Prime Minister, since she was apprehensive of Grey's 'liberal' views. But she could never have resisted the temptation, or as she saw it the political compulsion, to follow up her years of careful cultivation. She had coached Palmerston for the part as assiduously as anyone, and not realizing that he was more Canningite than 'Russian', she now pronounced his appointment to be 'perfect in every way'. It is, rather, the effectiveness of her intervention that one must doubt. Quite probably Grey still did have doubts about Palmerston's ability. But once the three elder statesmen among the Whigs had each in turn disqualified themselves, Palmerston was the obvious candidate, easily marked out as such by his speeches and activities more than by Princess Lieven's lavish praises. In short, Palmerston's name could never have been so startling a suggestion as the lady's account maintained. Grey's vanity may, as Greville said, have 'all his life made him the fool of women'; but he was not as great a fool as that.[90]

VIII

'LIBERALISM ALL OVER THE WORLD', 1830-34

Palmerston received the Seals of the Foreign Office on 22 November 1830. The following evening he went off to Cambridge to see through the formality of his re-election. He did not return to town until the 26th and so, like Grey who was ill, missed the 'great dinner' with which Agar Ellis greeted the new Government on 24 November. But the following week he dined with Prince Esterhazy at the Austrian Embassy in order to meet the new French ambassador, Talleyrand. 'There was a grand ceremony', Littleton reported, 'about making the new Secretary for foreign affairs walk out first.' Finally, Esterhazy and Talleyrand each took him by the arm and they all walked out together. Before long, however, the ambassadors were to complain, and Palmerston to plead, that he hardly had time or energy for social niceties. In August 1834, shortly before the end of his first spell at the Foreign Office, he explained to one of his own neglected diplomats: 'The life I lead is like that of a man who on getting out of bed every morning, should be caught up by the end of one of the arms of a windmill and whirled round and round till he was again deposited at night to rest.' [1]

Few Foreign Secretaries can have been plunged with so little previous experience into such a storm of foreign complications as was Palmerston in the winter of 1830-31. There were not only the Miguelite usurpation in Portugal and the still unsettled question of Greece, but also the spreading consequences of the revolution that he had welcomed so enthusiastically in France the previous summer. To Palmerston's own surprise, perhaps, the Wellington Government had steered England and Europe clear of any immediate confrontation with the parvenu régime of Louis Philippe. But there were complications enough arising from the contagious spirit of revolution. In August the Belgians had risen against the union with Holland which the victorious allies had imposed upon them in 1814-15; and within a few days of Palmerston's arrival at the Foreign Office the Poles were to turn on their Russian masters in Warsaw, while in the New Year revolutions would also convulse much of Germany and large parts of Italy.

It was the Belgian question, however, which almost completely preoccupied the opening years of Palmerston's career as Foreign Secretary. This was hardly surprising, since it concerned what few on any side of politics would have denied was England's most vital interest abroad, the keeping of the Scheldt Estuary – and hence the control of a large part of western Europe's foreign trade and of the principal bases for the invasion of England – out of the hands of any great power. At the same time it was one of the most difficult, complicated and prolonged disputes with which he ever had to grapple, for the Dutch and Belgians were insanely obstinate and the powers full of dangerous intrigue and disagreement. Long before it was over one British diplomat, who believed he had little reason to admire his chief, avowed that it was 'the most difficult negotiation ever known in our history'. Yet inexperienced though he was in the practice of foreign policy, and inclined at first to be in too much of a hurry, Palmerston did great work in battling with a mountain of detail and against a sea of troubles. Even Brougham acknowledged that this was so. But in the first heady weeks of office, the Chancellor may have been overflowing with good will to those who could repay him with additional patronage. More convincing were the early plaudits of Palmerston's foreign colleagues. Talleyrand, the acknowledged master of diplomacy, wrote that he was one of the most able if not the ablest man of affairs that he had ever encountered. 'In a year's time', wrote one Austrian representative, 'he would be the best informed minister in the whole of Europe.' What most impressed them all was Palmerston's handling of the conference on the Belgian question.[2]

The conference of ambassadors had been summoned in response to an appeal from the King of the Netherlands for the powers' aid against his Belgian subjects, and Palmerston was very fortunate when he arrived at the Foreign Office to find it sitting in London, far away from the skilful manipulation of Metternich and right under his own thumb as Chairman. But he was still marvellously quick and adroit in learning how to master and exploit it. Meeting several times a week for long periods on end during the first two years of the crisis and then lingering in suspense for nearly a decade until the Treaty of April 1839, the conference exhausted the patience of his Cabinet colleagues and strained the diplomatic composure of his ambassadorial associates. Yet as Chairman, and the only representative to remain unassisted and, with the exceptions of his brief periods out of office, unchanged, Palmerston was by far the hardest worked of all of them. The formal sessions would take up half the day and much of the evening as well; the more crucial meetings would go on to two or three in the morning for several days on end. And then he would have to sit down to write his summary reports to the Prime Minister and several diplomats as well. 'It is *very* late at night,' he wrote to Fred Lamb at a particularly anxious stage of the matter, '& after a very long conference I have had to write to all our ministers about this Belgian affair, & therefore I have neither time nor wakefulness enough to answer your letters.'

Then he proceeded to add another thirteen sides of lucid and colourful comment on Metternich and Europe in general. There was also a great deal of work to be done behind the scenes, mastering a mass of technical detail (without much help it would appear even from the Foreign Office) and tackling the representatives individually on many a tricky question. As host he wined and dined the delegates with zest, but he complained how little he saw of Broadlands and Lady Cowper how much it disrupted her social life. 'Leopold was here last week & Lord Grey,' she reported from Panshanger in January 1831, 'but the Ambassadors & Secretary for foreign affairs made our party so political that there was no going into any room without disturbing a conference. . . . Our friends will I hope do themselves great credit & save the country if it is to be saved, but their society is certainly the worse for their exertions.'[3]

After a year of it Palmerston too began to lose his patience. 'The Conference is tired of conferring and the mediators can mediate no longer,' he wrote in irritation to Brussels; 'all things have their end and the patience of the five Powers has reached its limits.' But the Belgian question really provided just the sort of work, coping with masses of detail and drafting endless papers, at which Palmerston excelled; it was for this that in a mixture of contempt and admiration he gained his first nickname in the Foreign Office of 'Protocol Palmerston'. Of course he made mistakes, especially in the early days when his anxiety to reach a settlement led him to gloss over the complexities of apportioning both territory and debt among Dutch and Belgians. But he learned from his mistakes and by much hard work and sheer persistence kept the conference going. In this way he helped maintain at least the outward semblance of the powers' unity; and this was more important than it seemed. For what essentially he did was to use the conference as a method of containment, bringing the combined pressure of the powers to bear against intransigents among either Dutch or Belgians and against intriguers among the powers themselves, and so far as possible ensuring that in the event of failure Britain would not have to stand alone in defence of her vital interests. Thus within the first few weeks he had joined with Talleyrand to persuade the conference to agree on 20 December to independence for Belgium and with the others to force Talleyrand to accept on 20 January 1831 a self-denying ordinance and repudiate compensation for France.[4]

It was a considerable step forward to have got the legitimist powers, two of whose rulers were closely related to the embittered King of Holland and all of whom were in dread of the success of revolution, to agree to the independence of Belgium. Palmerston was duly, and genuinely, grateful to them. But in view of their universal apprehension that France might otherwise exploit the Polish distraction and the Belgian revolution, they were ready enough to seize the opportunity of saving Belgium from France by granting her independence, provided that some gesture were made to the sensibility of the Dutch King and the legitimacy of the Vienna Settlement. It was, however, Palmerston who, in an early example of diplomatic draftmanship, invented on the day before the meeting of 20 December 1830 the expression 'future independence'. By implying due process and satisfactory assurances all round this bridged the negotiating gap between France's insistence on immediate independence *de facto* and the allies' regard for international order *de jure*. Palmerston therefore had some personal reason to boast in his report to Grey: 'It is a great step gained to have got Russia and Austria to admit the necessity of early independence.'[5]

Since it was England who had taken the leading part in pressing the original Netherlands Union, some of Palmerston's critics felt that his real object in promoting Belgian independence a mere fifteen years later must have been to destroy Holland as a commercial rival. There was really no inconsistency that needed to be explained away. Britain's overriding objective remained in 1830 essentially what it had been in 1814, the security of the Channel. Union with Holland had patently failed to provide a safe solution; hence an independent Belgium was the obvious alternative. But it had to be real independence, buttressed by a sound economy, a stable constitution, a dynasty committed to no other power and effective boundaries; and while the behaviour of Holland and her Eastern supporters presented very irritating obstacles from time to time the most serious danger came from the very country against whom the original Netherlands Union, and the construction of a line of barrier fortresses on its south-western frontier, had been designed – from France.[6]

Both Palmerston and Grey had been suspicious from the beginning that France might be harbouring some notion of profiting from the Belgian affair, since Talleyrand seemed to them during the first few meetings of the conference to be putting unnecessary difficulties in the way of an armistice; and before long the air was thick with talk of annexation and partition, or at least of a dynastic alliance between Belgium and France making mockery of the independence Talleyrand had been foremost in demanding. As France was the principal 'victim' of the Vienna Settlement, and of the Netherlands Union in particular, the new and insecurely established Orléans Monarchy believed that it had to placate public opinion with some material gain, but was quite unable to decide what it should or could be. The French Foreign Minister, Sébastiani, wanted something grand, Talleyrand a more modest acquisition, while the ambassador's reputed son and certain rival, Flahault, came over to England to propose an arrangement which he apparently arrived too late even to reveal. Grey was inclined to conclude that Louis Philippe might be more honest than his agents; Palmerston that the French were full of dangerous schemes. But they were neither of them at all sympathetic to any need of the Orléans Monarchy to curry public favour in the Belgian question and were utterly agreed that nothing could be conceded in a matter involving

England's most vital strategic interest. So when, on 2 or 3 January 1831, Talleyrand for the first time openly raised the French desire for territorial compensation, Palmerston stood absolutely firm, warning the ambassador that to press such a proposal would 'make it impossible for us to continue on good terms'. There remained, however, the question of finding a satisfactory sovereign for Belgium.[7]

There were plenty of names being bandied about for King of the Belgians, chief among them being the Duc de Nemours and the Duc de Leuchtenberg. But Nemours, being Louis Philippe's second son, was unacceptable to the powers and especially to Britain, and Leuchtenberg, being an adopted Bonaparte, was anathema to the Orléans family. A number of alternative candidates were therefore put forward, the leading two among them being Prince Leopold of Saxe-Coburg and Prince William of Orange. The idea of making Leopold a sort of Anglo-French candidate by marrying the widowed son-in-law of George IV to a daughter of Louis Philippe seems to have been initiated in London by Talleyrand and agreed shortly afterwards between Grey and Leopold, though for the time being it was not pressed, probably because neither the Russian Emperor nor the French King was personally very keen on him. The attraction of the Prince of Orange was that he was acceptable to the Eastern courts – and to the English King – as a concession to the King of Holland's pride and their own legitimist sensibilities, and he was expected to make himself welcome to the Belgians by bringing with him the best possible frontiers. But neither prince would have made a French puppet. So when Palmerston directly proposed the union of Belgium and Luxembourg under William, Talleyrand talked about this presenting a threat at the weakest point on France's frontiers and suggested that Luxembourg should go to her instead; when they reverted to discussing Leopold without Luxembourg, he talked of France getting the more modest acquisition of Philippeville and Marienburg; and in between Palmerston heard the still more alarming story that Talleyrand had been secretly attempting to arrange a deal with Prussia by which the Rhenish provinces would be transferred to France, Prussia compensated with Saxony and the Saxon King placed on the throne of Belgium.[8]

Palmerston and Grey were both very much alarmed by all this. The Prime Minister feared that things were leading 'too probably to war', and characteristically sent word to Lord Holland, presumably in the expectation that his emotional and indiscreet colleague would rush with useful warnings to his friend the French ambassador. No less characteristically Palmerston wrote to his ambassador in Paris, Granville, that he should 'hint' to the French Government 'upon any fitting occasion' that while England was anxious to be on friendly terms she had 'a deep interest' in France keeping to her existing borders and that good relations depended on her not opening 'a new chapter of encroachment or conquest'. There followed Palmerston's second great success in the Belgian conference on 20 January. For two days beforehand, Palmerston reported, Talleyrand 'fought like a dragon' to get something for France, but Palmerston led a still more determined resistance, and finally, between nine and ten at night, 'brought him to terms by the same means by which juries become unanimous – by starving'.[9]

Both Palmerston and Talleyrand afterwards claimed credit for inventing the device by which France was induced to sign with the rest a self-denying ordinance about territory, influence or advantage. But it seems clear that at the time neither of them at all appreciated the importance the neutralization of Belgium would one day assume, thinking of it more as a concession to French self-respect than as a guarantee of international peace. Moreover, it was almost at once obscured by the consequences of the rare but vital error Palmerston made at the conference the following week. In his haste to settle things he even, for once, glossed over details about the division of debt and domain between Belgium and Holland and on 27 January concluded in conference so-called *bases de séparation*, which were much too favourable to Holland. He was not entirely surprised that the Belgians should oppose them, any more than that the Dutch should accept; but he was disgusted and outraged to find the French Government supporting the Belgians and reviving schemes of dynastic aggrandizement and symbolic compensation. Hardly had Talleyrand signed the protocols of 20 and 27 January, indeed, than Palmerston heard that the French were secretly encouraging the Belgians to choose Nemours for King; and 1 February found Talleyrand trying to revive the question of Philippeville and Marienburg and arguing that the 'spontaneous' election of Nemours was not ruled out by self-denying ordinances.[10]

Once again Palmerston resorted to strong language, and brought the unity of the conference to bear against the apparent aggressor. Nemours as King would be 'tantamount to the union of Belgium with France', he told Talleyrand, and the duke's acceptance if elected would in his 'personal opinion . . . produce a general war'. Then he went into the conference and easily obtained a new protocol confirming that princes of the ruling houses of the powers were in all circumstances to be excluded from the throne of Belgium. Although he retreated a little, Talleyrand dared not go so far as this and his Government in Paris both rejected the new protocol and, to improve upon the popularity of the House of Orléans in Brussels, repudiated the *bases* of 27 January. Palmerston at once went to the Cabinet and got full approval to renew his threats through his ambassador in Paris. 'We are reluctant even to think of war,' he wrote on 2 February, 'but . . . we could not submit to the placing of the Duc de Nemours on the throne of Belgium without danger to the safety and a sacrifice of the honour of the country. . . . we require that Belgium should be really and not nominally independent.' Two days later, when Granville saw Sébastiani at one o'clock, he found the French Foreign Minister 'warm, warlike, and mounted on his highest horse'; but at half-past five Sébastiani came again to announce the news of Nemours's election, 'and in a much subdued, but most friendly tone' that it had been refused by the King of the French.[11]

After the showdown at the beginning of February 1831 the temper of Anglo-French relations ostensibly improved. On the French side, where a good deal of the trouble earlier had been due to personal rivalry and divided counsels, the left wing was checked and Sébastiani put under control by the appointment of the conciliatory Casimir Périer as Prime Minister. On the British side there followed in April an agreement with the other members of the old anti-French Quadruple Alliance to demolish some of the barrier fortresses as a gesture. But there were many lingering traces of France's cupidity, and however relieved his Government might be, Palmerston personally reserved his judgement and kept a watchful eye upon the French. Their assurances of friendship and peace might indeed be 'incessant and uniform', he wrote in the middle of February; but they persisted with their 'endless intrigues and plots', 'actively preparing for war when nobody threatens them, and . . . every day betray an unceasing disposition to pick a quarrel'. 'I wish the French Government would make up their minds to act with good faith about Belgium, and we should settle the matter in three weeks,' he wrote at the beginning of March; 'but the men in power cannot make up their minds to be honest with stoutness, or to play the rogue with boldness.' After all, he pointed out to his colleague Holland, while Casimir Périer's appointment was to be welcomed, Sébastiani nevertheless remained. So, he complained, the French were still 'scrambling and intriguing for such pitiful objects' as a ruined castle. But Paris must 'understand that France cannot have Belgium without a war with the four powers. Whether she could have it by a war . . . is another matter.' England, however, would on principle stand firm to deny her even 'a cabbage garden or a vineyard'.[12]

It was this 'principle' of resistance to encroachment by France that led Palmerston to be very stiff about the fortresses, even though he had been aware from the beginning that Belgium could not afford to keep them all in a state of defence and that many of them would therefore fall in the event of war immediately into the hands of their powerful neighbour. So even after the French had publicly reaffirmed their commitment to the January protocols he insisted that France should not be party to the fortress convention or be consulted subsequently about the particular forts to be dismantled. Generally, then, Palmerston refused to believe that Casimir Périer's appointment, though an improvement, marked in French or justified in English policy any fundamental change with regard to Belgium. 'France has not of late shown a *less* steady determination to get hold of Belgium whenever she can,' he impressed on Grey on 17 April, 'nor has the conduct of the French Government been calculated to inspire *more* confidence in her regard for her engagements; and whatever reliance we may have upon the integrity & good faith of

Casimir Périer, the personal character of one single man who might cease a fortnight hence to have any influence over the councils of his country could hardly justify us in giving to comparatively permanent arrangements, a character which it would not upon other grounds be expedient to assign to them.' Palmerston was more prescient than he knew; the following year cholera forever silenced Casimir Périer's conciliatory voice, though fortunately not until after the climax of Palmerston's suspicions had been reached and safely passed.[13]

With France chastened if not entirely checked by the Nemours affairs and the Eastern powers still curbed by the addition of the disturbances in Germany and Italy to the Polish problem, Palmerston might have expected to settle the Belgian question in the spring or early summer of 1831. But the crisis was prolonged and the field for suspicion fertilized again by the behaviour of the small states of Belgium and Holland. The immediate problem was still to find a King for the Belgians. With every other choice ruled out, both the English and, after a little more pressure, the French naturally reverted to Leopold married to the French King's daughter – 'a good *Belgian king*', Palmerston forecast; 'no more English than French.' But Leopold, having once burned his fingers over the Greek throne, had no intention of endorsing an unpopular settlement in Belgium. It was not therefore until the middle of the summer that, with concessions on the part of both the conference and the Belgians, the powers modified the *bases de séparation* by the Eighteen Articles of 26 June and Leopold agreed to assume the throne on 26 July. Once again Palmerston played the leading role in a masterly and audacious handling of the conference. He frightened Leopold (and Grey as well!) by warning that if his obstinacy should provoke another war with Holland the Eastern powers would be bound to come to Holland's aid and, after all the past negotiations and cooperation, that England would be bound in honour to join them; and he frightened the Eastern powers into modifying the *bases* in Leopold's favour by invoking the awful prospect of an English 'conjunction with France'. But hardly had the compromise been made than on 2 August the Dutch King denounced it and marched his troops into Belgium. Leopold at once appealed to both England and France. Within two hours of receiving this news on 3 August the Cabinet, at Palmerston's request, ordered a British squadron to assemble in the North Sea Downs. But while the English moved 'quietly' and with some uncertainty, the French Army crossed the frontier and marched to the defence of Brussels.[14]

Since the French move was undertaken without any previous concert with England or the conference, there was a good deal of resentment in London and not a little apprehension that once they had possession of any part of Belgium it would be difficult to get the French Army out again. Palmerston was of course more suspicious than anyone; but having been warned that it would be impossible for the Navy to do anything effectively to hamper the

French advance, he recognized that England had been presented with a *fait accompli*. Rather, therefore, than 'remonstrate & pick a quarrel', he thought the 'wiser course' was through the conference 'to try to obtain a hold over the future proceedings of the French troops'. Evidently this was no easy task. 'I found a great disposition in Bulow & Matuscevitz', he reported of the Prussian and Russian representatives when the conference met to consider the news of the Dutch invasion, 'to take the part of the King of Holland, & to find every fault possible with Leopold; Esterhazy & Wessenberg [the Austrian representatives] were impartial, & Talleyrand supported me feebly now & then, but said little.' But by the evening of Saturday, 6 August, he had persuaded the conference to bring the French under control by 'legitimizing' their action retrospectively as that of the conference itself and by extracting from Talleyrand a verbal undertaking that the French Army would be withdrawn as soon as the Dutch returned across the border.[15]

That evening Palmerston told the Commons that 'peace was by no means hopeless', and the House, according to Hobhouse, was 'astonished'. But the Cabinet was by no means satisfied when it met later still that night. Since the Government, and Palmerston in particular, was under considerable attack for allowing France to move at all and Brougham, for example, inclined to dismiss 'those endless conferences' as 'mere cloaks for chicane', some members very much resented that, as an act of equity, Palmerston should have consented to place the English squadron also at the disposal of the conference. So 'the misfortune of the night', reported one minister to Grey, 'was that [in the Prime Minister's absence in attendance on the King], every member of the cabinet – old & young – able & decrepit – thought himself at liberty to discuss the whole state of Europe. The consequence was that nothing was done & everything adjourned.' But although he too disliked the restriction on the British squadron, Grey was soon converted and, with but a minor qualification, pronounced the protocol 'perfect'. Palmerston's principal objective, however, had been to keep the conference together and in the event of further trouble with France to ensure that England did not stand alone; and in this he was completely vindicated when it was learned a few days later that although the Dutch had retired the French had not, but were talking of doing so only when 'peace' was formally concluded. Immediately afterwards Palmerston also learned that Talleyrand had begun again to talk, as Palmerston had all along warned both Dutch and Belgians he would, about his 'old and favourite project' of partition with Prussia. Faced already with accusations in Parliament and the press that he had been negligent, Palmerston countered in the Commons with unusual effect and in cross-Channel warnings with characteristic vigour. In five days' time, he wrote to Granville, he would be required to give 'a categorical answer, Yes or No, to the question, Do the French troops evacuate Belgium or not?' It was 'a question of war or peace', he said. Three days later, seeing 'the sky begin to darken' and fearing that 'the storm will soon break', he wrote again to say that he expected to be at war in ten days. In any event, 'one thing is certain – the French must go out of

Belgium or we have a general war, and war in a given number of days'. The next day he received private assurances from Paris that the French Army would evacuate but linking that prospect to further arrangements about the barrier fortresses. Palmerston firmly repulsed what he called dictation 'at the point of the bayonet'; in any case to make France party to the selection of the forts to be razed would be like consulting 'the housebreaker which of the bars & bolts of your doors & windows you might most safely dispense with'. 'I have seldom seen a stronger feeling', he said, 'than that of the Cabinet about this question of the fortresses.' [16]

There undoubtedly was a strong feeling in the Cabinet; but it was far from being quite as Palmerston described. Some, like Althorp, thought that his threats were more likely to provoke war than to induce the French to give way, and that it would be better to surrender Belgium than to fight. Others, like Lord Holland, had always hankered after a close understanding with France and were willing to give up a good deal for it. 'Those damned Belgians are the origin of all mischief,' Holland wrote. 'I heartily wish they had been well dismembered & partitioned between France, Holland, Prussia & England 16 years ago – & when the time comes as it inevitably will, if I am alive I shall rejoice at it.' He constantly wrote around, not only to Palmerston himself but also to Grey and to Granville, to preach goodwill and softness to France. Granville, too, already had serious reservations about Palmerston's impatience with Sébastiani's little 'tricks' and his tendency to get England into quarrels over every 'trivial offence'. But for all his Devonshire and Holland House connections Granville was a loyal Canningite and he ably executed his chief's instructions. From Paris, however, the Flahaults wrote and travelled constantly to remind the Whigs of Palmerston's Tory origins and Russian affiliations. But their talk of Viscount Castlereagh and Princess Lieven was countered by powerful support for Palmerston in England. Not least there was the King, who made no secret of his hatred of France and gave Palmerston his very special approval. Still more important was the attitude of the Prime Minister. [17]

For Count Flahault to complain to Grey about Russian petticoat influence was marvellously unwise. There was in any case very little trace in Grey of the Whigs' addiction to France, and probably more than anyone else in the Cabinet he was in sympathy with Palmerston's foreign policies. But as Palmerston's dogmatic statements and belligerent assaults persisted in the face of so many French retreats, Holland's doubts about the wisdom of his policies and Granville's disquiet about his tactics rekindled and Grey's mood too began to change. On 13 August Grey was agreeing that French evacuation 'must be insisted upon . . . & peremptorily if any hesitation should appear'; and on 17 August he was still reported as talking of 'holding very strong language' to France. But he took the talk about partition schemes far less seriously than Palmerston. By 19 August he was 'spoiling' Palmerston's dispatches and withholding any time limit or other ultimatum about evacuation, by 28 August reproving Palmerston for quarrelling over matters of 'form', and by 2 September confessing to 'the belief that, do what we may to ensure its independence Belgium must, for some time at least, be looked upon as strongly connected in interest with France'. Talleyrand must soon have guessed that Palmerston was deceiving himself about the Cabinet's strength of feeling, for when on 22 August Palmerston told him it was 'impossible' for the fortress question to be settled before the French evacuation, Talleyrand specifically asked that the Cabinet be consulted again. The reply that emerged after the next day's Cabinet, that they agreed France could not be a party to the discussion of the fortresses, Palmerston represented as complete support for the position he had all along maintained. But the fact of the matter was that they had agreed to reopen the question with England's old allies and commissioned him to commence discussions with them when France formally promised to evacuate but before she had actually done so. By 27 August Palmerston even had to tell Talleyrand that there would be no objection to a small French force staying on.[18]

It was symptomatic of Palmerston's awareness that the Cabinet's determination was cracking and its support for his policies weakening that he began to look to the conference to put more effective pressure not only on France but also on his own Government. By 25 August he was, in his letters to Granville, already shifting the burden of objection to French participation in the negotiations about the fortresses from England to 'the other Powers, . . . and especially Prussia'. At the beginning of September he professed in his letters to Grey to 'concur' in the Prime Minister's opinion that England could hardly insist on French evacuation until Leopold also did, and when the Eastern powers' representatives pressed him at the conference to agree upon an ultimatum he replied that he 'did not like to concur in so decisive a measure' without consulting the Cabinet. But at the same time he wrote to Grey to 'confess' that it seemed to him there was 'a great deal of force in their observations', especially in view of the impression of resolution the Government had already sought to give in Parliament, and therefore to request that the Cabinet again be summoned. Palmerston seems to have expected support for a tough line from Graham and Stanley (who had joined the Cabinet as Chief Secretary for Ireland in June), but whether or not he got it when they met on Sunday, 4 September, the Cabinet evidently endorsed Grey's distrust of the Eastern courts and instructed Palmerston to limit his pressure on France to verbal and not formal demands. Palmerston had a rather difficult time at the conference the next day, especially with his Prussian colleagues, but after 'much battling' he finally persuaded them to give up the idea of a protocol. The following week came news that the French would complete their evacuation by the end of the month. Palmerston had been proved wrong and Grey was 'radiant'.[19]

From this point a significant change became evident in Palmerston's policy. Before the end of September 1831 he was complaining of the support the

Eastern courts were giving the Dutch King's resistance to a final settlement with Belgium, and threatening them with an Anglo-French understanding. These 'hints' served, and on 14 October, after working 'like dray horses' on a new compromise, the conference was persuaded to adopt Twenty-Four Articles in place of the Eighteen. Then, when Leopold reluctantly accepted the Articles but the Dutch King rejected them, Palmerston further persuaded the conference to sign an actual treaty on 15 November guaranteeing the new settlement would be upheld. 'Conferences and elephants', he wrote, 'have the same period of gestation, twelve months with a fortnight occasionally over their time.' But, he went on, 'in sagacity [also] the resemblance holds good'.[20]

In the autumn of 1831 Palmerston once again congratulated himself on keeping the conference together, in much the same way as he had on getting the declaration about 'future independence' almost a year before: 'It is an immense thing done to have got Austria, Russia and Prussia to sign a formal treaty of friendship and guarantee with Leopold. Belgium is thus placed out of all danger and the sulky silence of the Dutch King becomes at once a matter of little or no importance to anybody but himself.' But he neglected to mention here a secret undertaking he made simultaneously to the Russians, that England would continue after the separation of Belgium from Holland to pay the share of the interest on an old Russian debt to the Dutch, which she had assumed in 1814 in return for Russia's consent to the union of the Netherlands. More important, he grossly underestimated the ability of the Dutch King to delay matters and the unwillingness of the Eastern powers to bring pressure to bear upon him. Their attitude to the conference, he eventually discovered, was '*restons unis*, while I say *marchons ensemble*'. It was months before the powers could be brought to ratify the treaty of 15 November and years before the Dutch King would finally submit. Emily Eden thought she knew why the King was slower even than his friends. 'I am proud of my skill in discovering', she wrote after a visit to Holland in 1833, 'that King William is not so sulky at being deprived of Belgium as at having been left with Holland.' The awkward possibility of coercion was therefore constantly in prospect.[21]

Palmerston had begun to suggest naval preparations against the Dutch as early as 24 and 25 October 1831. But at that early date he still hoped that any resort to coercion would be made under the aegis of the conference. That this was best was underlined by another unpleasant quarrel with France about the fortresses in December. To avoid France's continual complaints, the four powers decided to dispose of the problem by a secret treaty with Belgium and to reveal the treaty to France only as a *fait accompli* after ratification. But when he submitted it to the Cabinet Palmerston omitted to give a special warning not to let Talleyrand know, 'forgetting at the moment', he afterwards explained, 'that he is every evening at Holland's elbow'. Holland at once revealed it to the French ambassador and a major row ensued. Holland defended himself by blaming it all on personal pique. Having, in the autumn improvement, coupled 'the manly & straightforward conduct of Talleyrand' with 'the temper, judgment and assiduity of Palmerston', he now grumbled in the winter discontent about Talleyrand on one side and Palmerston on the other choosing 'to exalt a mere blue bean in a blue bladder, worthless but capable of making a great lather, into an affair of importance'. That 'lather', he was soon however to discover, was increasingly liable to divide Palmerston from his Eastern allies and consequently to revive the Anglo-French entente so dear to Holland's heart. When Holland came grumbling to the Foreign Secretary in December about the revival of the Holy Alliance, Palmerston growled again to him about 'all those faculties of intrigue of which Talleyrand, Sébastiani and Louis Philippe are such unrivalled possessors'. But in January Palmerston was pointing out emphatically to Grey that the violence of the French demands 'increases or diminishes according as his [Talleyrand's] reports indicate concession or firmness in the Four Powers'. Consequently, as the Eastern powers continued to prevaricate, Palmerston's resentment shifted significantly from France to them.[22]

Almost certainly Palmerston had designed the secret treaty about the fortresses to please German as much as British opinion, since they also figured large in Prussia's tradition of national self-defence. But as the ratifications of the treaty of 15 November still did not arrive he grew increasingly impatient that effective pressure on the Dutch never would emerge. In February 1832 he was again complaining of Russian influence and talking of Anglo-French cooperation as an alternative to the concert of the five powers. In March he was still hesitating to make a decisive break with the conference. 'We were not pretending, at present at least, to march forward with France to the exclusion of the Three,' he explained, 'but we only refused to move a step with anybody till we know whether we are to go on, Two or Five.' Then, after hearing what had seemed good news from Vienna, he exploded when he learned at the beginning of April that Austria's ratification depended on Prussia's and Prussia's presumably on Russia's. 'Metternich & Ancillon are really too bad,' he wrote of the Austrian and Prussian ministers; 'but they have no right to make April Fools of us, & play off the tricks & juggles with which they have lately been amusing themselves at our expense.' If they did not immediately exchange ratifications, he went on,

there is an end of the Conference, and of the Alliance; and England, France, & Belgium must then take the matter in hand, & settle it their own way. If we could quite trust France, or had an army of our own to send into Belgium, that Triple League would *now* not be the worst way of settling the matter, & the Three Powers who have ratified might shew the Three who have not, that by keeping aloof, they only deprive the King whom they want to protect of patrons in the executing body. But even distrustful of France, & without disposable troops, we might by a blockade of the Dutch ports bring Holland to reason.[23]

The week after Palmerston wrote this the ratifications arrived, soon enough to prevent the break-up of the conference but hedged about with qualifications enough to frustrate decisive action yet again. At Palmerston's urging contingent plans were therefore made during the summer for an eventual Anglo-French blockade of the Dutch coast. But even now he was reluctant to move abruptly, since while the conference remained in being he had some hope of acting under its apparent authority or at least with its tacit consent, and even as his patience was running out he was always seeing 'a bit of blue sky'. [24]

There was also a less welcome reason for yet further delay in the usual unfortunate discovery that the latest compromise proposals, the treaty of 15 November, were also deficient in their details. This time, therefore, Palmerston dedicated himself with enormous patience and industry to resolving the detailed problems of trade and communications and, though it too had subsequently to be modified, produced in September a masterly and comprehensive plan. Called Palmerston's 'Theme', apparently in derision though he did come to employ the term himself,[25] this was eventually approved by the conference as a basis for negotiation and, after the usual pressure had been variously brought to bear in Brussels and omitted in The Hague, accepted by the Belgians and rejected by the Dutch. Yet even though the conference had again proved nothing but wind, there was another long delay while the English Cabinet screwed up courage and unity enough to impose the 'Theme' by force. It was Grey, harried by domestic care, who now voiced loud distrust of the French and Palmerston who found the Francophobia of the King the greater nuisance. In the discussions about naval cooperation during the summer it had been Grey who moaned about Britain being isolated with nothing but a treacherous France for company, and Palmerston who was impressing upon him that to desert Belgium would surely consolidate French influence in Brussels at England's expense, and that England ought to sail 'a straight course':

It may be true [Palmerston conceded in a letter of 24 July] that England & France will have to execute the Treaty alone, but it is perfectly certain that England & France alone *can* do so if they chuse to set about it . . . It is true that it would be very convenient to us to get rid of this question anyhow for the moment . . . No great operation can be accomplished without difficulties but sometimes difficulties are in reality and in the long run increased by declining to face them, and I am disposed to think that this is one of the occasions in which that position holds good. All Europe have their eyes fixed upon us watching to see whether we shall carry our point, or give way to the Three Courts, and upon the issue must the future position & influence of England in Europe very much depend.[26]

In one respect at least Palmerston was soon proved right. One reason for his pressing for naval cooperation in June 1832 was to avoid the delicate question of a French army again entering Belgium. But by the autumn, when it looked as though the Dutch and Belgians might come independently to blows again, the season was well past its best for naval action; it would have been unlikely, in any case, to dislodge the Dutch garrison that the armistice of 1830 had left undisturbed in the citadel of Antwerp. So in September, when it was thought a new Dutch invasion would provoke the advance of the French Army upon the citadel, Palmerston suggested that this might now be the 'best solution' and attempted to counter the King's alarms by proposing a token British occupation of Ostend. But the disagreement persisted. The King considered land operations in concert with France both dangerous and distasteful. The token force that England could spare would not act as a restraint but only as an excuse for France to extend her operations wherever she wished; and the very idea of British troops marching in concert with those of 'Revolutionary France' struck him with horror. The Cabinet, too, remained divided. Brougham and Althorp wanted to leave it all to the French; Melbourne and Graham disagreed, though the latter, as First Lord of the Admiralty, did not think the Ostend scheme either practicable or desirable. Lord Holland, complaining now more of Grey's inaction than Palmerston's prejudice, wanted 'vigorous measures'; so, too, did Russell. But during the long parliamentary recess Grey lingered on at his home in Northumberland and a firm lead from France also seemed ruled out by the prolonged ministerial hiatus following Casimir Périer's death in May. So in an attempt to break the deadlock at the end of September Palmerston turned once again to the conference for 'something decisive'.[27]

What Palmerston proposed to the London conference was, in effect, a pecuniary fine on Holland of a million florins for every week her troops remained in Antwerp. The idea had originally been suggested by Metternich in an attempt to preserve the unity of the powers and Palmerston thought he had obtained the consent of all their representatives. Even that troublesome 'little Polish renegade', as Palmerston would call Matuscevitz in 1833, would be powerless this time to upset things. A genuine devotee of English country pursuits, Matuscevitz had nevertheless exploited them often enough to make diplomatic absences and dramatic reappearances. But this time he was hoisted with his own petard. 'Matuscevitz has been shot in the thigh at Heaton & cannot come south yet awhile,' Palmerston reported with satisfaction to Lady Cowper; 'some Lancashire squire, or perhaps a Belgian in disguise, was the shooter.' At the last moment, however, the Russian made an unexpected appearance and his Austrian and Prussian colleagues 'changed round like the wind'. Palmerston was furious; but it proved a blessing in disguise. For he produced intercepted dispatches to demonstrate that Matuscevitz had been working hard behind the scenes to thwart England's policy. Palmerston was therefore able to work up both King and Prime Minister to fever pitch. 'That little villain,' wrote Grey. 'I never read anything more disgusting than his letter, every line of which is marked with the characters of fraud and falsehood.' Better still, by laying it on, as he admitted, 'rather thick', Palmerston brought even King Billy to agree that some sort of coercion was now inevitable. So by 6 October Palmerston was pretty confident. Matuscevitz's scheme, he wrote to Fred Lamb, had been to drive England and France into such independent and ill-concerted action as would be bound to make them quarrel; but he had 'overshot his mark' and brought the conference virtually to an end.[28]

By early October 1832, therefore, it remained only for England and France to agree on doing something effective on their own. A 'mere blockade', it was thought would no longer be enough, because of the encouragement given to Holland by the behaviour of the Russians and others behind the scenes. So Palmerston proposed a joint naval blockade of the coast and an attack by the French Army on the Dutch garrison in Antwerp, and both Grey, who had remained so long in the country, and Durham, who had been on a special mission to St Petersburg and stayed with Leopold on the way back, returned to London to bring their views to bear. Durham afterwards claimed to have found the Cabinet irresolute and weak and left it united and determined. But the English ministers had already been much encouraged by the news of the formation of the Soult Administration in France, and Althorp, even, was relieved to hear that the action proposed for England would add nothing to the estimates. So the plan adopted by the Cabinet on 11 and 12 October was precisely Palmerston's own, though Durham's support must have helped, especially in obtaining a reaffirmation of the Cabinet's decisions in the face of threats from Prussia and renewed objections by the King.[29]

The onset of the elections in Britain and a determination to limit military operations (and the possibility of French opportunism) by a convention delayed matters briefly, but the convention was signed on 22 October, the French entered Antwerp on 19 November and the Dutch garrison surrendered on 22 December. The King of Holland continued to prevaricate and the Russians brought the conference to a halt by withdrawing on 28 October. But the Dutch troops went out of Antwerp and so, much to Britain's pleasure and relief, did the French. Moreover, the naval embargo was kept up and the suspension of the conference also backfired. The Russians professed that their withdrawal was 'temporary', but the conference did not formally meet again until 1838. 'As to conferences,' Palmerston wrote, 'we are sick of them and we have made a vow against any more Protocols.' But amid a growing euphoria of *entente cordiale* he could afford to allow the Russians 'private conversations', and seeing that he had most of the cards in his hands these led to their bringing pressure on the Dutch King. Palmerston conceded that it was Russia's pleas rather than England's complaints that led to the replacement of the unpopular Dutch emissary to the conference by a man whom he found he liked. Dedel, he reported with approval to his brother, was an Etonian and, better still, a Johnian; it was like dealing with 'a gentleman', he said later, 'instead of an . . . Old Bailey Attorney like Zuylen'. But by a stranger twist it was the wily Matuscevitz who designed the convention to which Dedel eventually agreed on 21 May 1833. Technically it was only a provisional agreement pending a definitive treaty, and the Dutch continued for another

five years to make endless difficulties. But by securing free navigation of the
Scheldt and an armistice which left Belgium in temporary possession of the
lion's share of disputed territory, it transferred the material disadvantages of
delaying a final settlement from the Belgians to the Dutch; and Palmerston
had already come to the conclusion in November 1832 that the real explanation of Dutch behaviour was that it was for them all 'a question of business
and balances'. So while it was not until March 1838 that the Dutch King
accepted the Twenty-Four Articles and not until April 1839 that the matter
was finally settled by international treaty, the convention of May 1833 was the
crucial triumph for Palmerston. It completed the process by which the hands
of the Eastern powers were morally tied and, as he claimed in 1834, relieved
Belgium and the Western powers of all anxiety about further delay.[30]

Palmerston has been much praised for the tenacity and skill with which he
manoeuvred in his first testing campaign in foreign affairs. Sir Charles
Webster's verdict is unchallengable: 'His energy, patience and resource were
inexhaustible and he used every art of diplomacy – persuasion, intimidation,
exhaustion of an opponent, appeal to personal interests, recourse to higher
authority.' For there can be no doubt that in spite of some important mistakes
his disposition of diplomacy and threats was masterly and his manipulation
both of the conference and of its subsequent suspension wonderfully successful. Even the statesmen with whom he battled admitted that. But what is still
more remarkable, yet easily glossed over, is the transformation which overtook
his attitude towards France during the course of the Belgian crisis.

During Palmerston's first hectic twelve months or so in the Foreign Office
his policy had been rather disappointing for the Foxite Whigs led by Lansdowne and Holland. They believed that by joining the coalition against
France in 1793 England had tied herself to a reactionary conspiracy; that
whatever the misdeeds of the Napoleonic Empire, the settlement of 1814-15
had enslaved the peoples of France and Europe; but that in 1830 the dawn of
liberty had risen again. They had never trusted Canning and Palmerston also
had clung too long to the Tories. But in fighting his battle at Cambridge in
1826 Palmerston had severed himself from the 'pig-tails' and in greeting the
July Revolution so enthusiastically he had brought to their logical climax at
last his loud trumpetings about what Canning would eventually have done
with regard to Portugal and Greece. So the belated junction under Grey of the
followers of Fox and Canning had seemed to make a marriage of conviction as
well as of convenience. The Whigs had proclaimed 'their principle', wrote
Lord John Russell many years later, 'in the toast, "the cause of civil and
religious liberty all over the world". Lord Palmerston, in joining the Whigs,
thoroughly adopted this sentiment.' So Palmerston's Foxite colleagues had
expected him to lead England into a coalition of parliamentary monarchies
with France and against the Holy Alliance of reactionary despotisms led by
Russia.[31]

As the Foreign Minister of an essentially maritime power, Palmerston could certainly appreciate the importance of having continental assistance and the desirability in the pursuit of the balance of power of having European cooperation. He was also able, in a way Canning never managed – or intended in view of his dislike of them as the instruments of reaction and repression – to turn international conferences like that on Belgium to very good account. But he was never so naïve as to accept that an alliance or special understanding, even with a parliamentary monarchy in France, was synonymous with the maintenance of British interests. On the contrary, he was very much inclined to think that a France of any sort was England's natural and permanent enemy. 'The policy of France', he professed to fear after only a few weeks' experience of the July Monarchy's opportunist intrigues in the Belgian crisis, 'is like an infection clinging to the walls of the dwelling, and breaking out in every successive occupant who comes within their influence.' His attitude, moreover, was always highly coloured. He undoubtedly enjoyed French culture and Parisian society more than most, yet even as he travelled through France he recorded in his journal in 1815: '. . . if you kick a Frenchman he is civil but if you are civil he kicks you, & the more I see of the nation the more I am satisfied that this is their character. They are insolent to the yielding, & yielding to the insolent'; and in 1818: 'a Frenchman, generally speaking, *can not* tell the truth on any subject which concerns his personal or national vanity.' As late as 1870 his official biographer could still wince at the indelicacy, though others were inclined to think it natural enough in a man who had spent most of his preceding thirty years in an atmosphere of wartime patriotism and hate. But too often, and throughout his later life, that national cocksureness of his gave rise to expressions highly offensive to opinion across the Channel and shocking even to his friends. He evidently gloried in his power of diatribe and denigration; even those who disapproved were sometimes compelled to admire. Once, Gladstone recalled 'with much relish . . . , a Frenchman, thinking to be highly complimentary, said to Palmerston, "If I were not a Frenchman, I should wish to be an Englishman," to which "Pam" coolly replied, "If I were not an Englishman, I should wish to be an Englishman." '[32]

While there was a substantial quantity of national pride and prejudice in Palmerston's Francophobia there was also genuine political principle and realistic strategy. With or without official backing, one thing that Flahault certainly proposed on more than one occasion in London was a secret Anglo-French alliance, 'founded', as he said, 'on the principle of non-intervention and for the maintenance of peace'. Adopted by the July Monarchy as being simultaneously a repudiation of aggressive intentions on the part of France and a declaration of principle against reactionary interference on the part of the Holy Alliance, the idea of a 'non-interventionist' alliance was very much in line with the notions of the Foxite Whigs; and even as an expression it was calculated to have a particular appeal to the followers of Canning. Palmerston disliked the word 'non-intervention' for simply being French. But he would not have been any more responsive in 1831 had Flahault written 'non-interference'. He assured Flahault that if France were 'unjustly attacked, England would beyond a doubt be found on her side'. But, as he later explained to Granville, so far was he from believing in the threatening disposition the French professed to see in the Eastern powers that 'the English Government could almost take upon itself to be answerable . . . for the sincerity and good faith of the pacific declarations of the other Powers'. To Flahault he stated categorically that 'on the contrary, if danger exists, it is more likely to come *from* than *against* France'. When he first came to the Foreign Office in the autumn of 1830, he wrote in another letter, he was in common with the rest of his colleagues most anxious 'to be well with France', feeling 'strongly how much a cordial good understanding and close friendship between England and France must contribute to secure the peace of the world and to confirm the liberties and promote the happiness of nations'. But such goodwill had been undermined by the constant appearance since of ill-faith on the part of the French, and 'the spirit of aggression and the ardent thirst for aggrandizement which was betrayed, instead of being concealed by the underhand intrigues and double diplomacy which was intended to veil them, proved to us that those who thus had been courting our alliance only meant to make us the instrument of their own ambition'. All this, however, was meant for French consumption and instruction. To Lord Holland he unfolded with less bombast and more simplicity the conviction, to which he was to adhere for the rest of his life, that 'the great security of Europe against the inveterately encroaching spirit of France' resided in the Treaty of Vienna, 'however objectionable in some of the details of its arrangements', and 'the best security for peace in the cordial good understanding of the other four powers, in the unfitness of the French army as yet to take the field against Europe, and in the dread which the French feel of a maritime contest with England'.[33]

In view of these opinions it is tempting to suggest that Palmerston began to change tack in September 1831 merely because he found himself in a minority in Cabinet. After all, he continued to evince occasional suspicions of France's Belgian policy and to grumble from time to time about Talleyrand's 'favourite object' of partition. There was a strong personal element in these suspicions; all were agreed on that. 'I think with you', wrote Granville to Holland, 'that Palmerston's Foreign Politicks are essentially good & liberal, but he is constantly apprehensive, not of being duped, but of being thought to be duped by Talleyrand & the French Government.' Talleyrand was too clever by half and his personal rivalry with Palmerston was to have unfortunate results, for Talleyrand even more than for Palmerston. Lady Cowper, still better informed than Granville, also believed that like Princess Lieven the viscount mixed too much personal feeling with his politics.[34]

Palmerston's principal objective remained the preservation of England's vital interests and on the mainland of Europe the maintenance of the balance of power in particular. He had not discarded his opposition to the Metternich System: 'The policy of Austria', he told Grey in January 1831, 'is still widely different from our own.' But during his first year in the F.O. the real and immediate threat to the peace of Europe, it seemed to him, came mainly from France. He continued, moreover, to watch pretty closely such moves as the French expedition against Algiers, especially as the suspicion grew that, once established in North Africa, the French would not go out. He regretted he could not publicly underline how much Aberdeen was to blame for not securing a binding undertaking from France not to make her occupation permanent. 'What do you think of the Algiers Papers laid before the House of Lords?' he asked Fred Lamb in May 1833.

> If we had had nothing to do but to make a case against our predecessors, we could easily have done so, by shewing how loudly they insisted upon having more distinct explanations in writing, and how they submitted to the refusal of the French Govt to give such explanations. But that would weaken our case against France, whenever we take the question up for discussion with the French Govt. I suspect that they would not be sorry for a fair excuse for abandoning so expensive and unprofitable a possession, and that they may end by doing so of their own accord.[33]

When in 1840 the French advance threatened to spread to Morocco he displayed still more anxiety about British interests. But by that time the *entente cordiale* with France was utterly in ruins. In the interval he had been concentrating his attention on the Eastern powers. For by the winter of 1831-2 he was well on the way to thinking that, for the time being at least, the greater threat was coming from them. Hence his response also changed, and not only in Belgium but in the Mediterranean and central Europe as well. He was assisted, of course, by the defeat of the restless 'parti de mouvement' in Paris and the moderation of France's Belgian policy. But hardly less important in redrawing the lines of battle was that just as domestic politics in France helped to bring the French Government closer in foreign policy to England and gave plausibility to the *entente cordiale*, so in England they tended to separate the other powers from her and to initiate a bitter conflict of principle. And for Palmerston individually the connexion he made between foreign and domestic affairs accentuated his differences with the Eastern powers and reconciled him more willingly to what his colleagues wished for, both in the Government's relations with the French abroad and in its concessions to the English at home.

Palmerston had been complaining as early as December 1831 of the way in which the Dutch were supplying the Tory Opposition with ammunition enough to assail the Government's foreign policy in Parliament and in the press. But it was not until March 1832 that he began to make a direct link between the crisis over the Reform Bill and the difficulties the three Eastern courts were making about the Belgian question. They would be much better disposed, he concluded, when the bill was passed and their hope of a change of Government bringing a change of policy dashed. When news came the following month that Metternich had made an April Fool of him with false promises of ratifying the Belgian treaty, he became convinced the link with England's domestic crisis was still more intimate. 'The fact is,' he wrote, 'it is all a miserable intrigue between the D. of Wellington & Metternich, & the D. of Cumberland & the Prussian Princes.' It was the King who was the main hope of the Tories – foreign or domestic; and before long he was indeed threatening to behave as awkwardly over foreign affairs as over the Reform Bill, calling for papers and insisting that no instructions went out without his written approval. The intriguers' main hope, of course, was to work up the King's fear and hatred of France; and Palmerston had given them plenty of ammunition by talking publicly in the House of Commons in March of 'a firm and strict alliance' with France being the best way of defending England's interests. 'My way of counteracting these plans', Palmerston reported in May, 'is, to point out to him every instance which occurs, & fortunately they are not scanty, of bad faith, or secret views, or double policy on the part of the three powers; & thus to set suspicion to work against suspicion.' It seems to have worked, at least so far as foreign policy was concerned; shortly afterwards the King gave Palmerston the G.C.B. in special approbation, Lady Cowper was assured, of his conduct of foreign affairs. But at the same time it moved Palmerston inevitably into a position of ideological confrontation with the Eastern courts. 'I have long had an instinctive contempt of these arbitrary Cabinets,' he wrote to Fred Lamb at the same time as he complained of being made an April Fool, 'but it is only of late that I have learnt how just this sentiment has been.' It was no coincidence, then, that the spring and summer of 1832 saw the confrontation between England and France on the one hand, and Austria, Prussia and Russia on the other, spread from the Belgian question to the affairs of central and eastern Europe.[36]

The process of extension, in the confrontation between East and West, seems to have begun with Poland. The Polish insurrection against Nicholas of Russia aroused a good deal of sympathy in Britain, where Nicholas was regarded simply as a tyrant, but no support from the Government, who knew that Poland was too far away to be helped. The revolt, the ministers therefore felt, was brave but futile. To Palmerston, during his early period of Francophobia, it was still worse; for it diverted Russia in the East when at any moment she might be needed to help check French aggression in the West. He had little difficulty in holding the Cabinet to this line, since the right of Russia to resist revolution was unchallengeable and the support for Poland disorganized. So when Talleyrand and Flahault came pleading for joint mediation in Poland and Lord Holland for mutual conciliation in Belgium to permit it, they were all easily put off. 'Can we take the Insurgents under our protection,'

Grey asked, 'for such would be the fact, without incurring the imputation of holding out encouragement to revolt, wherever it might take place, & setting a precedent of interference between the sovereign & the subject which might not improbably (in Ireland for instance) become inconvenient to ourselves. . . . We must be careful also not to engage in measures, which might separate us from the other Continental Powers, & leave us exposed to great difficulties.' To Holland Palmerston replied with his defence of the Vienna Settlement, including the disposition of Poland, 'as the great security of Europe against the inveterately encroaching spirit of France'.[37]

It was not that either Grey or Palmerston lacked sympathy for Poland. When Palmerston heard of the setbacks suffered by the Russian forces in the spring of 1831 he wrote that the Poles 'seem to be making a gallant fight, and if one did not want the Russians to keep Soult [the French Minister of War] in order one should wish them heartily success'. But he still did not believe they could win and the pressure he put on Austria and Prussia not to come to Russia's aid was designed to fend off a reaction from France that would be bound to plunge the whole of Europe into war. As far as Russia was concerned he confined his interventions to mild and mostly informal pleas. He told Princess Lieven in London that he hoped the Tsar would make concessions and he kept a Tory ambassador in St Petersburg in the hope that Lord Heytesbury's good relations with Nicholas would make that advice the more acceptable. There was on 1 July a curious report that Palmerston had told Matuscevitz that both Poland and Lithuania were 'lost' for Russia. But this probably had something to do with reports of new Russian reverses and with Palmerston's irritation about a dispute concerning Polish refugees in Austria. It seems to have caused widespread disquiet in the East, but it was really much less significant than the fact that throughout July Palmerston was still firmly fending off pressure from France for intervention. Talleyrand had even gone so far as to suggest that squadrons should be sent to the Baltic and Black Seas, and in general he was so pressing and his proposal so extreme that it had to be considered by the Cabinet at length. Seeing that Russia had so recently condescended to accept the Eighteen Articles, Palmerston had no doubt what the reply should be. 'Russia has behaved well and handsomely through the whole of the transactions of the last eight months, and it would be rather an ungracious thing to turn upon her the very instant we have obtained even half a settlement of the Belgian affair,' he wrote to Granville. 'There is no pretence for interfering in any way than by a simple offer of mediation because it is a clear case of civil war . . . in which the usual observances of modern times would forbid at least friendly powers from intermeddling by force.' And as far as 'a simple offer of mediation' was concerned, this should be put off until the autumn, when the course of events would show more clearly whether or not Russia was likely to accept it. Evidently no one in the Cabinet seriously demurred, though Holland as usual wanted to soften the blow to France. Similarly, towards the end of August, when the Polish patriot Prince Czartoryski sent a letter as President of the Polish Diet asking the King to receive a delegation, Palmerston was quite certain that the King could not even receive a letter from the head of a Government which was not recognized by England but 'came in existence through revolt against an allied sovereign', and among the other members of the Cabinet only Carlisle, Grant and Lansdowne wished the letter to be accepted and only Holland the delegation to be received.[38]

For a long time, then, the Russians had little reason to complain about the British Government or Palmerston over the Polish affair. Princess Lieven, who in November 1830 had naturally dubbed the appointment she claimed as her own achievement 'perfect in every way', continued through much of 1831 to boast of her good relations with the Foreign Secretary. When news finally came in September that Warsaw had fallen and the emphasis of Palmerston's pleas changed from conciliation to clemency, she still wrote that England was 'Russian' in spite of all principles and speeches. But during November she heard that Palmerston was preparing a rather stronger appeal and before the end of the month she had decided that he was 'detestable' after all. What offended her, as she knew it would her master, was the British claim that the Poles had been guaranteed a constitution by the Treaty of Vienna and that as a signatory power Britain had herself a right to remind Russia of it. Since the capture of Warsaw had undoubtedly relieved Russia from a grave preoccupation and Palmerston did soon after profess to think that he detected the beginnings of a new obstructiveness in Russia's Belgian policy, it may be he felt inclined to retaliate. But he had always been careful to reserve England's international rights in the Polish affair. As long ago as January he had told Granville, who would have preferred intervention in cooperation with France, that both in legality and in interest England must take her stand upon the Treaty of Vienna. But if in the spring that meant non-interference in Russia's attempt to preserve her rule in Poland, in the autumn it meant interference to preserve the rights of the Poles under that treaty. When he had composed a plea for good behaviour in March, he had done it, as he admitted, for the record; and it was parliamentary and public opinion he had undoubtedly had in mind. But when he had drafted the note rejecting armed mediation with France in July, he had gone out of his way not to base it solely on Russia's loyalty to England hitherto, but to leave it open to interfere later on other grounds. Moreover, when he suggested the November appeal – in the name of 'humanity and policy' – he was probably influenced less by the Belgian question, about which he had just obtained a promising new treaty, than by misleading impressions gained from Polish exiles about the effect it might have in St Petersburg. When the Cabinet came to consider it, some, like Lansdowne, were inclined not to go ahead on the grounds that England's right to interfere was doubtful; others, including Grey, because 'however much . . . we may be in the right, it is seriously to be considered whether we should take any measure which we have no means that I can see of enforcing'. But

Palmerston pointed out that when France had gone ahead alone with her offer of mediation, she had not beeen met as was predicted with anger or insults from Russia, and that, from all he heard, the Tsar was really quite willing to concede everything that England might ask. In any case, as Palmerston virtually admitted, the important thing was to get something on the record against the day when they would have to defend themselves in Parliament. So satisfied with Grey's ruthless excision from the offer of all and everything he thought might be offensive to the Tsar, and distracted by a more difficult decision to make about Portugal, the Cabinet gave way.[39]

The advice had little or no effect in Russia, save to mark the progress of deterioration in her relations with England. In the New Year there followed a minor but unpleasant incident in London. Among the Polish refugees flocking into London was Czartoryski, and Grey, thinking to do him a harmless act of kindness, invited him to dinner upon an evening on which it happened, 'by accident' according to Palmerston, he had also invited his Foreign Secretary. Grey had known the Polish exile in much happier days and he was therefore astonished when he heard that Prince Lieven had called on Palmerston to protest at his receiving 'a State criminal' and very much annoyed when the princess followed this up with a personal letter to himself. Palmerston characteristically replied by dining two days running at Holland House so as to be sure of meeting the Pole once at least. So in a new atmosphere of distrust and dislike, Prime Minister and Foreign Secretary both tended more and more to see secret objectives and intrigue in every Russian move on Belgium. 'These d . . . d Russians are doing all they can to throw the whole Belgian affair into confusion,' wrote Grey at the beginning of January. This was rather unfair, as the Russians seem genuinely to have wished the matter settled. But they were not prepared to go as far or as fast against the Dutch as England, and even though his suspicions may have begun a little prematurely Palmerston certainly had reason to complain when he found the Russians were delaying their ratification of the November treaty guaranteeing a favourable settlement to Leopold. By early March, as the Russians still delayed and in doing so encouraged the Dutch King to persist in his resistance and Austria and Prussia to follow in their train, Palmerston opened a long letter of complaint to Fred Lamb: 'I begin to think that the *franc et loyal* Nicholas deals not in double but in treble and quadruple diplomacy.' About the same time came news of the Tsar's formal abolition of the Polish constitution and Palmerston responded with more allusions to the obligations of the Treaty of Vienna. But as he told Czartoryski there was nothing effective that England could do. 'We cannot send an army to Poland, and the burning of the Russian fleet would be about as effectual as the burning of Moscow.' And as the King told Palmerston, when the Tsar replied that the Poles had forfeited their rights by rebellion he certainly had a point.[40]

However futile it may have been from the point of view of Poland, it was nonetheless necessary for the British Government to go on making the right noises in public. After keeping pretty quiet throughout 1831 the House of Commons made something of a fuss just before the Easter recess of 1832. It demonstrated, Palmerston said, that the Government had not 'outstripped' public opinion on Poland. 'Men of all parties, Whigs, Conservatives, & Tories, persons of the most moderate & respectable characters ... had all been loud in condemning the conduct of Russia, & ... the only contest had been as to who should convey their censure in the strongest language.' But he had in fact tried to put off the debate, and he was saved from having to say anything compromising one way or the other by being called away from the House to attend an important conference on Belgium. In June he was again given friendly warning of a motion on Poland, which he succeeded this time in changing from a demand for interference to one for papers! So when the debate came on during the evening of 28 June and unpleasant criticism began to be made about Russia, Palmerston rose in order to cut it short with a few anodyne remarks about his confidence in Russia's good behaviour and a promise of papers to come. But he was followed by speaker after speaker – 'the riff raff' and 'the blackguards' using 'blackguard expressions', according to Lady Cowper – calling Nicholas a 'miscreant barbarian' and 'a monster in human form', and by his further silence Palmerston, too, earned nothing but abuse from either side. The radicals called him 'a Russian tool'; Princess Lieven wrote to Grey to complain of Palmerston's 'forgetfulness' and to give him 'a bit of my mind'. When Lady Cowper tried to explain (as Palmerston at least also tried to do during the debate) that having spoken once Palmerston was not able by the rules to speak again, Princess Lieven's husband retorted that he and all the other ministers ought to have walked out one by one. 'But', Palmerston let Fred Lamb know, 'the misfortune was that nobody could deny the truth of the allegations.' Grey made what amends he could in the Lords a few days later; but he made it pretty clear to Palmerston that he thought more could have been done from the Government benches in the Commons.[41]

What bothered the Prime Minister about the personal attacks on the Tsar, more than Princess Lieven's angry letters or King Billy's grumpy protests, was the reception he expected they would earn in St Petersburg for the newly announced ambassador extraordinary. Heytesbury had been anxious to retire from his embassy for some time, and mounting criticism of retaining the Tories in the diplomatic service had made the matter rather urgent by the time the second Polish debate came on. Unfortunately it was not at all easy to find a successor. Bagot, who was one of the senior Canningites in the service, refused, and none of the senior Whigs seemed any good. The elderly Foxite Sir Robert Adair, who had become as much a nuisance to his patrons as he was to Palmerston, was written off in Emily's phrase as 'an old idiot', and the amorous Lord Ponsonby, who had made rather a mess of things in Brussels when they were looking for a King, was written down as 'incapable'. Stratford Canning was the obvious man. But though George Canning's cousin and a very experienced diplomat, he had a reputation for bad temper and, by putting it around that in 1825 he had insulted Nicholas when Grand Duke, Princess Lieven made Grey and Palmerston think again. What the Russians really wanted, Emily reckoned, was Lord 'Gower or Wm Temple or some soft serviteur'. She therefore thought it was a wonderfully amusing 'jump out of the frying pan into the fire' when the irascible and radical Lord Durham was named.[42]

Grey may have named his son-in-law in order to give him some hope of distraction from grief at the death of a daughter. But Durham was an uncomfortable colleague (as well as a difficult husband) and for that reason too Grey would be well rid of him if only for a while. This was certainly what Palmerston thought about the benefit to himself. 'It would be better for a permanency', wrote Emily to her brother, 'but any departure is good. There is no knowing whether he may not take a fancy to stay, and once out of his place [there] is always a good chance of his not getting back again.' As well as being critical and restive Durham was also believed to have his eye on the Foreign Office itself. In any case Palmerston probably regarded it as a good joke to answer criticism of his Tory appointments with the man who was suspected of having inspired it, and a still better one to send on a mission of goodwill to the proud and autocratic Tsar the Cabinet's most vain and radical member. Having had to secure Durham's consent by flattery, moreover, he may well have got some pleasure in return by keeping the ambassador waiting for his instructions in London while he went off himself to Cambridge on an ostentatiously snail-paced canvass. Durham was furious, as he also was about King Billy's honest doubts. But while Grey converted the King, Princess Lieven also reassured the Tsar. In a remarkably astute assessment, she outlined how to make him 'ours, both by conviction and inclination'. She was absolutely right, and as his mission drew to a close in September she summed it up for Wellington: 'Nous avons noyé Lord Durham dans les politesses; et lui, ne nous a pas fait la plus petite question incommode; et voilà son *importante* mission terminée. . . . C'est une drôle de promenade!' But the joke was double-sided. For Palmerston was not in the least deceived and hardly discommoded by Durham's praises of the Tsar and reports of Russian goodwill; and the mollifying explanations and assurances Durham gave about British policy were almost exactly in line with the instructions Palmerston had himself drawn up, a catalogue of harmless pleasantries.[43]

In their different way Durham's communications performed the same useful purpose in private in St Petersburg as did some of Palmerston's public speeches in London. Several times during 1832 Palmerston had to rise in Parliament in order to defend the Government's actions over the Russo-Dutch loan, in January to fend off a motion of censure before the disclosure of his secret agreement with Lieven, and in July, while Durham was away, to get the agreement itself approved. The Law Officers had reported that they thought England was still bound to make the payments, and armed with this opinion

Palmerston had, in order as he said to please the Russians, persuaded the Cabinet in November 1831 that England was 'justly and honorably bound' to continue them. In honour, perhaps, England was bound to take on the obligation; but from a technical point of view it was all overlaid with doubts and as an arguably new commitment of public money ought first to have been approved by Parliament. This in itself would have been enough to offend some of the 'economists' and to present the Opposition with a golden opportunity. With the Government caught completely off its guard, it looked for some time during six hours of debate on 26 January as if they might well be beaten, and in that case, Althorp insisted, he would resign. Since everyone knew that the Government would then collapse, Althorp was begged to move the adjournment and so gain time to hold a party meeting and bring the dissidents to heel. But he was adamant, even though first Brougham and then Grey sent down urgent appeals from the Lords where another great battle was going on over the Belgian question in general. It would be 'disgraceful', Althorp claimed, to seek safety by such a means. But whether he approved or not the Chief Whip made sure the radicals knew of his threatened resignation and this no doubt had a good effect. But it was not to Althorp, who made no secret of his wish to retire from politics, that Grey and others afterwards attributed their survival. 'At half past three o'clock in the morning', Littleton recorded, 'Lord Palmerston rose to make a gallant rallying speech amidst loud cheers. He ventured on the bold insinuaton that the separation between the two countries was not yet complete, inasmuch as the King of Holland had not yet ratified the Treaty, and this [by resting the payments on the legal fiction that the old agreement still held good in Russia's view] induced ten or twelve members to change their intention of voting against us – and gave us a bare majority. A bold stroke on the part of his Lordship, considering the King's Speech at the opening of the Session had proclaimed the complete separation.' Palmerston was driven to such boldness by the failure of the Law Officers; they had left the Government utterly unprepared and their own contributions at the beginning of the debate 'displayed', according to Greville, 'an ignorance and stupidity which was quite ludicrous'. But there was another aspect of the debate in which the curious circumstances of the loan drove him to what might well have been an even bolder step. For, against the background of mounting public concern over the Tsar's treatment of the Polish rebels, it was a very unfortunate fact that the loan itself should have had its origin in the Polish partition. 'And so it came to pass', as Herries's biographer summed up this marvellous opportunity to attack his old enemy, 'that the British nation, taking upon itself the liquidation of debts for funds employed in the extinction of the Polish nationality, became an accessory after the fact to that political crime.' Yet to smooth the way through the Commons Palmerston was obliged to risk the outrage of the radicals and to make complimentary noises and unusual excuses about Russia's conduct. January had found him referring back to Russia's 'gratuitous generosity' in 1815; July and August, when no one could any longer equivocate about the Low Countries being legally separated and the debate on the new agreement came on, found him defending her against accusations of breaking the provisions of the Treaty of Vienna on the simple grounds that 'the Poles, not the Russians, were the aggressors, for they commenced the contest'. Fortunately for Palmerston and the Government, perhaps, his own inconsistency was no greater than that of the Opposition and his embarrassments no more obvious than those of the radicals. As Hume pretty well admitted in July, they 'would' in Hobhouse's words 'vote black white, rather than assist the Tories in turning out the Ministers'.[44]

Palmerston's behaviour with regard to the Dutch loan and Durham's behaviour in St Petersburg both made a very good impression on the Tsar. But if Durham's absence from London could be turned to good account, the same could not so easily be expected of his return. At the suggestion of the Russians he briefly entertained the idea of returning via Berlin and Vienna. Fred Lamb, who could hardly be pleased about the implications for his own position, wrote warningly from Vienna: 'It is evident that Durham's mission has been a mere party of pleasure, meant for nothing else and which has done nothing – but if he comes here and goes from hence through all the German Courts to Paris, may it not be inconvenient to you to sit in a Cabinet with a man arriving with all the Sovereigns of Europe in his pocket?' In her disenchantment with her old protégé and her over-confidence in Durham, Princess Lieven seems to have had some such hope as this. 'He and Palmerston detest one another,' she wrote to St Petersburg. 'Thus, we can have recourse to Durham in every case in which Palmerston's actions do not suit us and he will always be on our side when it is a question of condemning the other's conduct.' Palmerston, she went on, was a 'bon enfant' and her relations with him had been very close. 'But the inconvenience of his Liberal principles and obstinate character are very great and we would see him go without regret. If Grey is as Liberal and vain, he is flexible and his opinion can be easily changed. Palmerston is a mule.' No one knows whether she ever actually proposed to Grey that he make Durham Foreign Secretary, and so, as Granville later believed, provoked Palmerston when he found out to a declaration of war against her. But this time she had in any case quite miscalculated and weakened no one but herself and Durham.[45]

As a rival to Palmerston Durham's force was already nearly spent and as the dupe of Russia nothing like so gullible when well away from St Petersburg. 'These journies [*sic*] will certainly give him for some time after his return, a troublesome importance,' Palmerston admitted when discussing them with Fred Lamb in September 1832; 'but I am not afraid of him, he has no influence in the Cabinet except upon Grey, being by all the rest most especially disliked . . . & I believe they all dislike his journies & mission much more than I do, unless they should give him a turn for foreign service. But I am strong enough with Grey & my other colleagues not to fear Durham, and . . .

on any point on which his travelled opinions might fall short of mine, I should be at no loss for support in the Cabinet, and when I might want to temper the ardour of some of my colleagues, he might be used to advantage. Durham is a clever man, but very different from Wellington; he must get rid of his inordinate vanity, and his childish pettishness before he can gain much ascendancy over his equals.' As it happened Palmerston had no great difficulty in deflecting Durham from his grand tour; the patent insincerity of the ambassador's compliment-seeking protestations about the personal inconvenience of such diversions was more than matched by Palmerston's reply. 'Durham in the meantime had written', Palmerston reported, 'to say that he should naturally pass through Berlin, but that he wished *not* to go so far round as Vienna, at *this season of the year*, unless it was *absolutely necessary*. You may suppose that I have not gratified him by saying that his presence at Vienna *was* absolutely necessary.' Immediately on his arrival back in London he behaved, moreover, exactly as predicted and aided rather than upset Palmerston's Belgian policy. And much more impressive than the loud and lengthy claim to all the credit that he left *after* the October Cabinet meetings on the extent of Anglo-French sanctions against Holland was the brief request to see him that Palmerston sent immediately *before*.[46]

Far from serving Princess Lieven's purposes Durham's return immediately revived the vexed question of finding a regular ambassador to Russia and thereby eventually wrecked her life in London. For by the rules of diplomacy, if a British ambassador acceptable to Russia could not be found, then his counterpart in London would also have to leave. When St Petersburg told her in the spring of 1831 to do everything she could to counter Stratford Canning's appointment she had replied that she did not wish to get too mixed up with Palmerston for fear of making a jealous man of Grey. But it was on Palmerston she concentrated, and although Grey knew of the proposal he knew nothing of Russia's objections until after Durham's return. The princess had taken the trouble to enlist Durham in the campaign against the appointment as soon as she heard of his special mission, but in the meantime Grey became as worked up as Palmerston about Russian policy over Belgium and just as anxious for a strong man in St Petersburg. 'We must now hold very firm language there,' he told Palmerston in late September, 'and the sooner Stratford Canning can go the better.' So hardly had Durham returned than he found that Palmerston had sought and obtained the King's approval for the appointment. The princess at once tackled Emily about sending her brother Fred instead, and Durham rushed round to his father-in-law to warn him that Russia objected to Canning. 'Do you know the cause of this opposition?' Grey asked Palmerston, adding, however, that he did 'not feel at all inclined to give way'. Nor did Palmerston. He had already (in June) put it into Lady Cowper's head that the supposed insult to a Grand Duke was 'a story got up to avoid a person whom they could not manage'; and by the end of October he must have become quite certain that it was all as much political as personal. However, he had previously gone out of his way to accommodate an old friend, if in a teasing manner, by responding literally to the Russian request for 'anybody but Canning' and seizing upon the suggestion of that 'radical' Durham. So while Durham's mission was only a temporary relief and Palmerston always denied Princess Lieven's assertion that he had promised never to mention Canning again, perhaps he would have done something more for her if in the meantime he had not heard that she was intriguing with Durham to oust him and had now gone behind his back to Grey. He therefore wrote at once to St Petersburg that they should be made to 'understand very civilly that the King of England is the best judge of whom it may be for the good of his service to employ . . . and that we cannot allow any foreign authority to dictate to us on such matters or to *taboo* our best men *merely because* they are so'. 'Canning', he added, moreover, 'was a member of the small political party to which I belonged while out of office and was the instrument in placing me in the office which I now hold.' To Grey he explained that the only complaint that Lieven could now come up with when pressed was that 'Canning's manners are thought to be angulaires, & that he is a hard negotiator. To this I reply, that his angles must have been a good deal worn off by jostling in the world for six years since Nesselrode saw him, & that when they negotiated last, it was upon two points . . . upon which England & Russia materially differed. But in private at least Canning is mild in his manners & he may not be the worse for our purpose for being a little hard in negotiation.'[47]

The basis for Canning's reputation for bad temper was, it was true, not always easily apparent. A very unsympathetic observer confessed after a dinner party in 1834 that so witty and courteous had he been that, were it not for 'a certain contraction of the lips' and 'the oppressed air of his wife, one could hardly understand the bad accounts of him which one hears almost everywhere'. But it is impossible to believe that in 1832 Palmerston really believed that Canning's manner had mellowed much or at all since the mid 1820s, when he was supposed to have offended at St Petersburg and upset his masters in London. 'I wish heaven had gifted him with a larger share of the first of diplomatic virtues – patience,' Dudley had then complained, adding a little later: 'I wish he would turn member of parliament altogether, & give up diplomacy. He is a man of worth & talents – but his perverse & ungovernable temper makes it a very unpleasant task to deal with him.' The famous story that Canning lost his temper waiting in Palmerston's ante-chamber and took it out on a mild-mannered foreign ambassador came from Princess Lieven's own biased tongue in 1833. But it was probably true, and in 1842 Palmerston himself admitted that Canning 'is certainly clever and active, but he wants temper, judgement and decision (and being well supplied with vanity he has been much duped . . .)'. Palmerston's opinion had clearly worsened in the intervening decade but there can be no doubt that Canning's temper had not improved and that in 1832 Palmerston already knew it. But the Russians had made a false step in making their objection so personal.[48]

Canning could never remember any meeting with Nicholas in 1825, and the

Russians eventually had to withdraw the story. Nevertheless there does seem to have been something personal in their objections. Perhaps it was the suspicion that Canning had somehow been mixed up with either the Decembrist or the Polish rebels. The suggestion alone would have been enough to poison Nicholas's mind; but it was far too nebulous ever to be hinted in London. Probably Lady Cowper was right in thinking that it was simply that once committed both parties were too stubborn to give way. Certainly this was the view she always held, even though uncertain who was more at fault, Palmerston or Mme Lieven. But most historians have favoured the view that Palmerston himself put forward when he first explained the situation to Grey. Having added that Canning would have good grounds for resentment if after doing so well at Constantinople he appeared to be passed over, he concluded: 'The fact is that Canning's knowledge of Greek & Turkish affairs renders him peculiarly fit for this post at the present moment, though the reasons which may make him useful to us, may perhaps also make him the less agreeable to Nesselrode. Canning is sharp, active, & conversant with his business.' So he had already had the appointment gazetted on 30 October. The princess went again to her lover, complaining 'loudly' of Palmerston's broken promises; 'I never saw her so montée,' Grey reported. This time Palmerston sent her a sharp retort direct and wrote to Grey that: 'When Mad. de Lieven says that I gave her or Lieven an assurance that Stratford Canning should not be appointed to Petersburgh, she exercises largely the privilege which belongs to her, in her double capacity of a lady and a diplomatist, namely the privilege of fibbing.' To both of them, moreover, he made it clear he thought it was a political matter at root. 'I quite understand', he wrote to Mme Lieven, 'that it is the condition of more important matters that disposes you to pick a quarrel with me.' To Grey he elaborated: 'The Holy Alliance really want to ride us rather too hard; but the Russian branch of it, is so angry with us at present, for what we are doing about Belgium, that they are glad to fasten upon any collateral topic, and to vent upon it, the wrath which belongs chiefly to more important matters.'[49]

As Canning was not due to take up his post until the spring of 1833 there was an uneasy lull in London while the latest word was awaited from St Petersburg, and, at Grey's suggestion, the *bête noire* himself was sent off on a special mission to Madrid. In the meantime Princess Lieven maintained a cold but dignified silence. 'The political clouds of which you spoke to me, My Lord,' she had answered Palmerston's rebuke, 'are nothing to do with me. I am not seeking a quarrel; you are. . . . [But] I know that it is perfectly useless for me to debate with you. So please look upon this matter as quite at an end between us.' There followed, as Lady Cowper saw, an uneasy calm between them. Emily did her best to smooth matters over, inviting them still to meet at Panshanger and encouraging 'the Viscount' to please her friend with the appointment of a consul in Riga. But she realized they were both too stubborn to retreat over the main issue. 'Emilie', her cypher letters reiterated, 'is a dear good soul, but very like a Spoilt Child, cannot bear contradiction and has not temper to stand things turning out differently from her wishes'; 'Mary got piqued and angry and thwarted and then bad became worse.' Lady Cowper's only hope was for her brother to exchange appointments with Canning. She had mentioned the possibility to Fred as long ago as June and both she and Mme Lieven did so again after the row had broken in October. This was done in the first place without a word to Palmerston, and though it seems unlikely that he could have remained in ignorance of it, there is no reference to the notion in his letters. In any case, Fred himself soon killed it; later he was supposed to have said he actually mentioned it to Metternich, who told him Canning was the one ambassador whom Austria never would accept. So matters were no better when towards the end of January 1833 the news arrived from St Petersburg that in no circumstances would the Emperor receive Stratford Canning. This broke the princess's silence and forced her to write to Palmerston a curious letter in which she passed gradually from a cool report and reasoned argument before a Secretary of State to an anguished appeal for the compassion of an old friend. She frankly admitted that it was the threat to her life in London she dreaded most. 'All my dignity deserts me when I think of it,' she said. It would be humiliating too after such an appeal if she were to be proved wrong; but she could not believe that the blow would come from 'the man whom I regard as the best of my friends'.[50]

No reply of Palmerston's has ever been found to Princess Lieven's anguished letter; but it does not appear that he was utterly unresponsive. Lady Cowper no doubt worked upon him. Quite possibly she had had something to do with the princess's appeal in the first place; it was, after all, written from Panshanger. The following month Emily wrote to her brother Fred: 'Mary has been wrongheaded & absurd through the whole thing, and tho' she will not allow herself to be in the wrong now I don't think she has any wish to drive things to extremity.' Had Palmerston known that the princess had but a few weeks before been bluntly urging St Petersburg to refuse Canning 'and teach these islanders manners', he might not have bent at all. But he offered to the Russians to make Canning's stay among them a brief and token affair and at Grey's suggestion he tried to get Canning to accept Madrid as a permanent appointment. However, after some hesitation, Nesselrode refused and Canning would not voluntarily withdraw without some special mark of favour that the Prime Minister was unable or unwilling to give. Yet somehow or other Mme Lieven got the impression from Grey that a different ambassador would eventually be found, while he understood from her that the Russians would be content with a chargé d'affaires indefinitely. So throughout 1833 the princess lingered on, in 'agonies of doubt' as Greville put it. But the Tsar's patience at last ran out and in May 1834 her husband was recalled.[51]

Mme Lieven left amid a show of mixed regret and relief. The King told Palmerston that the news of her recall gave him 'sincere pleasure', and in *The*

Times there was a vulgar and brutal attack upon her. The princess was deeply hurt, though with a brave attempt at humour she wondered if she had refused once too often a ticket of entry to Almack's. In any case she deserved and was given a leavetaking by her friends well worthy of a Queen of Fashion. The Duchess-Countess of Sutherland gathered two dozen female friends in London society to present her with a bracelet and there were numerous farewell dinners and parties. Palmerston, it was said, was scrupulously shut out from all of them, even Grey's. However, while others made some bad *faux pas* – Lady Cowper told the princess that it was because her husband was such an effective ambassador that England would 'profit' by his going, and the Spanish ambassador, as a young beauty glided by, squeezed Mme Lieven's hand reassuringly and told her he liked 'les femmes un peu passées' – the villain of the piece behaved for his part with perfect good taste and in a manner fitting for 'the best of friends'. He professed to believe what was in all probability partly true, that the recall in the end had as much to do with the Lievens' enemies in St Petersburg as with those in London, and, seizing upon the fact that the ostensible reason for it was the prince's appointment as governor of the Emperor's children, put it about that it was all 'merely' a matter of 'a domestic arrangement or intrigue' at St Petersburg or a wish of Orlov's to have the London Embassy; and the last 'melancholy dinner' was at Palmerston's own house.[52]

Palmerston must certainly have had more than a minor twinge of regret at the leaving of an old friend, even if she was not a discarded mistress. 'I am sorry on every account public and private,' he told Granville. But her long decline had been marked by attacks and intrigues against him more certain than any suspicions that may still survive about his own conduct in this sad affair. 'She has done much mischief here by meddling and intriguing,' he told his brother; 'a busy woman must do harm because she cannot do good.' Yet there would have been no personal quarrel but for the political contest between them. For she never had been and never would be able to separate politics from friendship or even love. In what must often have seemed a bewildering and even unnatural sequence she had tried to cast her spell over Castlereagh and Canning, Wellington and Grey. And whatever personal pleasure she may have had from it all, she never lost sight of the main objective – to tie England and Russia more closely together. Although the extent of her role in leading and pushing Palmerston out of his relative political obscurity in 1827-30 remains unclear – and certainly it was less than she claimed – there can be no doubt that she believed he owed her a great deal. What she was demanding when he became Foreign Secretary was that he should pay his debt, in political terms as well as in personal friendship. In spite of the extraordinary mixture of personal and political intrigue into which her hopes and disappointments led her, her behaviour was not entirely unattractive. Even Emily, who ten years before had been so full of scorn about love for ambition's sake and mocked at Mme Lieven's desperate pursuit of Metternich, saw something sympathetic in the Canning business. 'Emilie', she told Fred, 'lets her friendship predominate over political feelings & this I like her for.' Palmerston, however, had been 'provoked with her interference', and when 'her temper had got the better of her, and she had thought to carry it with a high hand having been used to have her own way, . . . he had thought both *She* and her *Court* wanted to be taken down a peg'. A less friendly witness concluded: 'Palmerston has got rid of her because he is afraid of her, & he is right but that does not diminish our loss.'[53]

Whatever the effect personalities may have had on the Lieven-Palmerston affair, the price the princess asked for friendship was to Palmerston politically too high. It was subservience, he had come to believe, not friendship that Russia demanded of England; that much the Belgian and Polish questions had now made clear. Instead, by her behaviour, Russia had driven France and England together willy nilly. Consequently by the spring of 1832, Palmerston believed, Russia's principal objective had become to separate them again. To this end the Russians looked far beyond the Low Countries. Palmerston suspected that they might even be responsible for spreading the rumours of French designs on Minorca which so alarmed the King. But it was in Italy and Germany that the Russians' best hopes lay.[54]

During that first suspicious year of Palmerston's at the Foreign Office, the various attempts made to alert him to the danger of French aggression in Italy were by no means unsuccessful. When Piedmont complained at the end of 1830 of French encouragement to the plots of Italian refugees Palmerston told Granville to make representations in Paris, and when revolution actually broke out a few months later he seems to have been prepared to give Piedmont a guarantee against a French invasion. It is more than unlikely that the Cabinet would have been prepared to go so far; but they were all very worried in London that England's Mediterranean interests would compel her intervention between France and Austria in the peninsula. When revolution broke out in Parma and Modena, and Austria marched in to restore her client rulers, even the French could not object in view of the special interest that Austria was recognized as having there. But entering the Papal States and threatening to extend Austria's moral and material influence still further in Italy was a very different matter. Palmerston was inclined to blame both sides, Austria for taking action likely to provoke war and France for over-reacting. He had tried to fend off revolution and the consequent interventions by urging reform upon both the King of Piedmont and the Pope. But while he professed his desire to see the peninsula freed from both powers, he preferred Austrian to French predominance there. 'I am sorry for the determination of Austria about Italy,' he wrote to Granville when he heard her troops were about to move; 'it is wrong and foolish; and brings on at once a general war, which one had hoped might have been avoided. The inevitable consequence will be, the expulsion of the Austrians from Italy; and for that, one shall not be sorry, provided the French are not established there, in their stead.' Even the detested Metternich recognized where England's preference lay and he asked accordingly for the strengthening of her naval force in the Mediterranean. But Palmerston had no wish to depart from strict neutrality. 'It will be impossible for England to take part with Austria in a war entered into for the purpose of putting down freedom and maintaining despotism; neither can we side with France in a contest the result of which may be to extend her territories; we shall therefore keep out of the contest as long as we can.'[55]

Palmerston took a similar line in 1832 when new disturbances led Austrian troops again into the Papal States and an even more vigorous reaction by France sent her forces to make a counter-occupation of Ancona from the sea. He told Granville that he was a 'good deal annoyed' by France's precipitate actions and Lamb that he did not trust her enough to enter into any long-term undertakings. But in this matter too there was a perceptible change in his attitude since last year. He had already suggested to Grey that he presumed there was 'no particular objection' to the French expedition, and he subsequently sent very friendly communications to Paris, accepting all the French assurances of good faith. To Vienna, on the other hand, he sent frequent warnings about the miscalculations he accused Metternich of making. He was particularly annoyed at the failure of the attempts to make the Pope secularize and reform his administration, and was certain Metternich was the cause. 'It may not be amiss', he wrote to Lamb,

to let Metternich understand that we are aware of his maneuvres [sic], and that we know that he is trying to give the Ancona affair an importance which he does not really attach to it, merely for the purpose of converting it into a pretext for not carrying into execution the necessary reforms in the Papal States. But he should be told or let to perceive that although we should be perfectly ready to take up the cudgels for him against the French if there was the least appearance of any views of aggrandisement or aggression on their part in Italy, yet we are not such children as to be led on into a foolish discussion about nothing at all . . . The short argument seems to be that unless reforms are made, Austrian interference will be perpetually required to preserve order, but that other Powers in Europe cannot be expected to look on quietly, at repeated Austrian interference; and thence will arise imminent danger of war. War so excited must be necessarily a war of principles & opinions, and that cannot be for the interest of Austria whose maxim is quieta non movere. In such a war too, she must not expect to have England on her side.[56]

Palmerston also took the trouble to emphasize to the Russians that their hopes of the Anglo-French cooperation over Belgium capsizing in Italy were utterly unfounded. 'Ancona has no doubt excited hopes of rupture and war,' he wrote, 'but those hopes have burst like bubbles and the only effect of the episode will be to shew Austria how inconveniently a union between England and France may bear upon Austrian objects and interests.' On the contrary, he told Lamb, he expected that the symptoms of Anglo-French accord in Italy would make Metternich more accommodating over Belgium. But the Austrian ratification of the Belgian treaty soon proved a 'fraud'; and Palmerston did not easily forgive Metternich for making an 'April Fool' of him. So their relations in the Italian question deteriorated still more rapidly. From time to time Palmerston accused the Austrians of seeking to expand their rule in Italy; while Metternich accused the British of being more subversive in Italy than the French.[37]

It was about this time, it seems, that Palmerston earned for England the credit of the moral leadership of the Italian movement. But it was earned only by the accidental publication of his views on Austria's encouragement of papal misgovernment, and there was no intention as yet of going any further. Palmerston had, in particular, no illusions about the prospects of Italian unification. 'The Giovine Italia men are enthusiasts,' he wrote in 1834; 'I had a long talk with one of them some time ago, and tried to demonstrate the folly of thinking that Italy or any considerable part of it could be united into one state, unless previously crushed into a single mass by the pressure of foreign conquest. But my friend was too rooted in his opinion to be shaken by my arguments.' For his part, however, Palmerston was too rooted in his opinion about the risk it would entail to the balance of power in Europe to welcome any sort of upheaval in Italy. So as he watched with disapproval Austria's continued domination and complained from time to time of Italy's 'miserable' or 'dreadful' state, he sought to combat it only rather feebly, with the futile advice to such rulers as the Pope and the King of Naples to strengthen their independence by moderate reform.[38]

What Palmerston had to say about Germany was similarly ineffectual in improving the lot of its inhabitants, but even more effective in promoting differences with Austria and extending them to Prussia. For his part, Metternich had been growing ever more alarmed at the progress of the liberal movement in south-western Germany and Switzerland. Constitutions had been granted in Hesse, Baden, Bavaria and Württemberg, and in Switzerland the liberals had given refuge to revolutionary plotters from elsewhere in central Europe. While Palmerston remained more apprehensive of France than of any other power and Metternich kept his fears within bounds, the two did not seriously clash. As late as the end of February 1832 Palmerston was still using the growing signs of trouble in Germany only to warn Metternich how much he needed to avoid quarrelling with France. 'If Austria is determined,' he wrote, 'to undertake a crusade against popular feeling & popular institutions in Germany, she will do well to get rid of the Belgian Question forthwith, or she will find that she has more upon her hands than all the means of herself and her allies will enable her to deal with. She may possibly think that Belgium unsettled, may afford occupation to France, & leave Austria more at liberty in Italy and in the [German] Confederation; but surely this would be a fatal miscalculation; till Belgium is settled, France cannot & will not disarm.' But following hard upon Metternich's supposed interference with the Parliamentary Reform Bill and the April Fools affair over Belgium came the German liberals' festival at Hambach in May, after which Metternich replied to their toasts to Lafayette and German unity by getting the German Diet to adopt his famous Six Articles of repression.[59]

Palmerston claimed that Hambach was largely due to Austrian *agents provocateurs*, just as Metternich's meddling in the affairs of Switzerland and the assembly of Austrian troops on her frontier were likely to 'goad them into some absurdity'. In any case it was too good an opportunity to miss for making a retort to the meddling he detected in England's domestic affairs. 'I am afraid Metternich is going to play the Devil in Germany with his Six Resolutions,' he wrote to Lamb at the end of June, 'but this system cannot last, and must break down under him, and whenever it does there will be a crash. . . . *Divide et impera* should be the maxim of Govts in these times. Separate by reasonable concessions the moderate from the exaggerated, content the former by fair concessions and get them to assist in resisting the insatiable demands of the latter. This is the only way to govern nowadays . . .'[60]

Palmerston, as will be seen, could hardly have described more aptly his own attitude to the Reform Bill in England. The connection was further strengthened when Hanover voted in the Diet for the Six Resolutions and King William answered his English minister's protest by reaffirming his approval of what his Hanoverian minister had done. This made Palmerston look rather foolish, and so, when the French shortly afterwards suggested that England and France make a joint protest about 'the system which Metternich is pursuing in Germany', Palmerston was far from unwilling. 'If we could hit upon a good ground upon which to rest it,' he suggested to Grey, 'perhaps the effect might be useful.' Lord Holland, inevitably, was all for it and the 'grounds' were easy to find since the German constitution was part of the Treaty of Vienna and Palmerston could claim that the Diet had violated it. But in the anti-climax following the crisis over the Reform Bill there were few meetings of the Cabinet in the summer of 1832 and not much enthusiasm for foreign any more than home affairs. 'Goderich is nervous', Holland reported to Carlisle, ' & truth to say we are none much prepared . . . to enter into foreign affairs generally.' Grey, too, was nervous. He did not object, he told Palmerston on 21 July, to 'a friendly and confidential exposition of our fears', but he opposed acting in concert with France and doubted the expediency . . . , and perhaps the right' of interfering in an internal matter on which the German sovereigns and more particularly the King of Hanover were agreed. Ten days later his doubts had not diminished and he confessed to having amended Palmerston's draft dispatch with 'a good deal of freedom' so as to avoid such detailed 'speculations or discussions' as might provoke difficulties, especially with the King. Even so, when Palmerston's draft was read to the Cabinet on 1 August it still seemed to Holland 'like all from Palmerston's pen, clear, judicious, and forcible'. Moreover, when a motion was made about the Six Articles in the House of Commons the following day, Palmerston accepted the opportunity, however cautiously, to declare his liberal position much more unequivocally in public than he had since entering Grey's Government. He stated his opinion that the intentions of the Diet had been misrepresented and exaggerated and that the 'King of Hanover' was fully alive to his responsibilities as a constitutional monarch. But by adverting to what he professed to think was not the case he also conveyed some pretty blunt warnings. 'I am prepared to admit,' he said, 'that the independence of constitutional States, whether they are powerful, like France or the United States, or of less relative political importance, such as the minor States of Germany, never can be a matter of indifference to the British Parliament, or, I should hope, to the British public. Constitutional States I consider to be the natural Allies of this country.' Moreover, he went on, if the Six Articles were fully implemented, 'it would, perhaps, give rise to a war, not merely between the States of Germany, but a war of opinion, which would spread its influence beyond the country whence it had its source; in which case this country would not only be entitled, but called on, to take such steps as circumstances might require . . . '. For, 'as long as our commerce is of importance to us – as long as Continental armies are in existence – as long as it is possible that a power in one quarter may become dangerous to a power in another – so long must England look with interest on the transactions of the Continent, and so long is it proper for this country, in the maintenance of its own independence, not to shut its eyes to anything that threatens the independence, of Germany'. Finally he reminded his audience that the Government's pledge on taking office was for Peace, Retrenchment and Reform. 'There was nothing about non-interference. He should not talk of non-intervention, for it was not an English word. . . . Now, he thought, the principle for this Government to proceed upon was that of non-interference by force of arms in the affairs of any other country; but he did not think that we should be precluded, where it was expedient for us to do so, from interfering by friendly counsel and advice.'[61]

There were apparently only eleven members present when Palmerston made his speech and he could have had the House counted out instead. So he had evidently gone out of his way to declare his position in public. He followed it up the next day with a characteristically bombastic private letter to Lamb. He confessed that he thought 'war on the Rhine need not necessarily disturb the Peace on the Thames' – nor the House of Commons consider

its fate in any way bound up with that of the Bavarian or Wurtemberg Assemblies. But nevertheless these things are alarming and even if there should be no immediate outbreak, the seeds of great mischief are sown. Metternich is again bringing into activity his never dying hatred of free institutions. His arrangements have been well laid, and his means well prepared, and he may have a temporary and limited success; but a permanent triumph, the nature of man and things forbids, and whenever the reaction comes, it will be proportionally more violent in consequence of his momentary advantages. It may be practicable to destroy free institutions in an insulated country like Poland, crushed in the grasp of a colossal enemy and surrounded by pretended neutrals . . . but to wrest free institutions from ten or twelve millions of Germans, swarming with professors and newspaper editors, and in actual contact with France is a quixotic enterprize. . . . It is strange that Metternich cannot be content with despotic authority over thirty millions of well behaved Austrians, that he should not be satisfied with measuring the columns of their newspapers, prohibiting any books that anybody would wish to read and ruling as Lord Paramount of Passports, but why on Earth must he set all the rest of the world by the ears, to gratify his priggish vanity? [62]

Metternich's agents, as Palmerston well knew, often intercepted such letters and by one means or another this one was probably intended more to wound the Austrian Chancellor than to instruct the British ambassador. But the encouragement given to the liberals by Palmerston's speech certainly worried Metternich, who complained that 200,000 copies had been ordered for circulation in Germany. The King, of Hanover and of England, was also very annoyed. The following day he sent what Holland called 'a plaguey cross letter' relating to 'German politicks & Palmerston's views of them which he bitterly disapproved of, inveighing against revolution, innovation & the press'. And how, the King had asked, could he do anything as King of England which was not consistent with what he had done as King of Hanover? The question, as Grey and Palmerston agreed, was an important one and in the Prime Minister's opinion required in reply an equivalent 'manifesto' such as he averred Palmerston was best equipped to draft. Palmerston for his part had no doubt that 'if the politics of the two countries are to be thus bound together, England being the most powerful and important is entitled to lead Hanover, and not Hanover to lead England; [and] that if the English Government is to be tied by that which the Hanoverian has done, they ought to be previously consulted'. But it took all Palmerston's skill to draft an answer tactful enough to be submitted to the King, yet firm enough to carry the point. He succeeded admirably, by emphasizing that it was 'better that the British Cabinet should be taxed with entertaining groundless or premature apprehensions than that it should be accused of blind indifference to events which might place the peace of Europe in jeopardy' and by cleverly arguing that its peaceful interference was truly 'conservative', since it sought to prevent an attack upon existing institutions by arbitrary power. [63]

Charles Grant may not have been so pleased. He had wanted 'to make some kind of stand against the despotic system', and he must have meant something rather strong, since he wrote of the sort of pacific and moral influence exercised in Canning's day no longer serving against the 'violence' of the 'revived Holy Alliance'. But Grant was too ill to attend the Cabinet that considered Palmerston's draft on Sunday, 5 August, and the eleven who were there agreed unanimously that it was, in Holland's words, 'a long & spirited answer [to the King] gently & civilly reminding him of the nature of their constitution & of his title to the crown'. 'I shall be curious', Holland mused, 'to observe whether the invitations to Palmerston to Windsor and St James's, which have been somewhat more frequent than those to most of his Colleagues, since his and the Duke of Richmond's unwillingness to make peers [to pass the Reform Bill through the Lords], become more rare after the receipt of this letter.' As it happened the King took it very well, replying at great length but with many compliments to Palmerston and however reluctantly acquiescing in the dispatch.[64]

There was then another month's delay while Grey waited for the situation to clarify and made further alterations designed to minimize the risk. 'The chief object', he frankly admitted to Palmerston, 'has been not to commit ourselves by too confident a prediction of consequences, and . . . to add a hint . . . that they must be prepared to act without our assistance, if they get into a war.' The dispatch went off at last, on 7 September, not to Munich, as had originally been intended, but to Vienna and Berlin, where Palmerston's old friend Gilbert Elliot, now Earl of Minto, had just been appointed Britain's representative. Palmerston believed that what he thought was a 'lull' in German affairs was 'just the moment for such a step'. But, as Webster comments, 'no document could have been worse received'. Metternich assumed it was meant for public consumption and prepared a skilful counter-manifesto. In fact neither was published, though both circulated unofficially. But in Berlin they refused to receive Palmerston's dispatch at all.[65]

Prussia's rejection was a serious blow for Palmerston. It had always seemed to him that Austria was utterly committed to a policy of fierce repression in Germany at least as much as anywhere else, but he always professed – for example in June 1833 – to have hopes of Prussia, as Protestant and progressive like England. He had no sympathy for Prussia's territorial ambitions in Luxembourg or anywhere else. Rather, he lumped together Prussia's attempted 'nibblings' in the Belgian affair with those of France: 'if once these great Powers begin to taste blood,' he wrote to Granville in August 1831, 'they will never be satisfied with one bite, but will speedily devour their victim.' Nor did he like Prussia's exclusive commercial policy, and so he worked actively to limit the expansion of the *Zollverein* by concluding most-favoured-nation treaties with the minor German states, his most notable success being one with Frankfurt in May 1832. But he had pinned his greatest hopes on some day convincing the Prussians that they had no interest in supporting Russia against the Poles or Austria against the French. However Ancillon, the Prussian Foreign Minister, merely dithered and delayed. Lord Holland called him 'a doctrinaire and a coxcomb'; Palmerston said he was 'such a weathercock that one cannot rely upon him for a fortnight together'.[66]

When Palmerston heard that his German dispatch had been rejected by the Prussians, he suspected it was all another Tory plot. They were 'in constant communication with their friends at Berlin,' he complained, 'but that is only a reason the more for resenting the affront & requiring satisfaction'. Indeed it turned out to be a very useful way of working up the King's resentment against the Eastern courts and undermining his opposition to cooperation with France against the Dutch. 'He . . . ordered me', Palmerston smugly reported to Vienna, 'to make immediate enquiries as to the period within which a powerful fleet of 10 or 12 additional sail of the line could be got ready, convinced that such insolence on the part of Prussia, & such double-dealing on the part of all three [over the Belgian question] could only proceed from a deliberate determination to pick a quarrel with England & France & however unwilling he might feel to find himself fighting side by side with Revolutionary France he would never submit to insult or duplicity.' Palmerston, of course, did not really expect war; rather, he suggested shortly after, Prussia and Austria might come to appreciate how much easier it would be to check French revolution and aggression by joining with England to control her policy by means of cooperation rather than confrontation in Belgium.[67]

By the end of 1832 the row with Prussia over the dispatch was patched up, thanks in large part, as even Palmerston admitted, to Metternich's genius for diplomatic compromise: Ancillon agreed to accept the dispatch and Palmerston not to insist on a reply. 'I never saw a more laughable wry face,' reported Minto when he had handed it to Ancillon. Apparently the Prussian minister had been forced to give way by his masters in Berlin, and so in the New Year Palmerston resumed his attempt to woo Prussia away from Austria. When revolutionary plots in Germany culminated in a crazy attempt to seize Frankfurt early in April 1833 and provoked the further strengthening of the Metternich System, Palmerston's public and official response was more restrained than it had been the previous year. But his correspondence with Lamb contained a bitter and vigorous assault and though marked 'private' was probably again intended for Metternich to read as well. He opened, on 6 April and in spite of being very unwell, with a characteristic piece well worthy of a pupil of Dugald Stewart, for its art if not its sincerity:

. . . *all* countries, not Germany only, are, and always have been in a state of transition and it is the character and purpose of human nature that all societies should be constantly altering. Were this not so we might still have [been] painted blue like the Britons. The province of a wise Govt is to keep pace with the improved notions of the people; not to insist upon knowing better than those they govern, what those they govern wish; neither to chain down society to a point, nor to hurry it along too fast, to be ever and anon modifying institutions to suit them to altered habits, and new wants. Thus to render safe and tranquil those changes which if made violently might be dangerous – to lead & direct, and not to hold back till a superior force drags them along.

But Metternich was unwilling and unable to follow such a wise course.

He thinks it more agreeable and less troublesome to govern Austria as it is, than to found his fame upon renovating her strength, and developing her resources; his personal habits, the cast of his character, his want of proficiency in those acquirements and in that general knowledge which qualify a man for being the regenerator of a great empire, all unfit him for so arduous, and with all deference to him be it said, so noble a task. But he has sagacity enough to perceive that no impassable barriers can be erected to shut out ideas; and consequently that if constitutional improvements take place in neighbouring countries, a wish to enjoy the same advantages will soon spread through the Austrian dominions. Therefore, in order to save himself from trouble at home, he takes infinite trouble abroad, and strives to perpetuate and even to increase every existing abuse and political evil in every other country in Europe.

But such a system was bound to alienate even moderate men and so was doomed to failure. 'Coercion and compression may be carried so far, as to unite the feelings of all against its authors.'[68]

Palmerston more than once suggested, to both Austria and Prussia, that the occupation of Frankfurt could only be counter-productive. But for the time being he did not make any actual protest against it, though the French had already done so and pressed him to follow suit. Instead he concentrated on trying to separate Austria from Prussia. At Vienna he hoped that the *Zollverein* at least would serve that purpose. 'Can or will Austria do nothing about the commercial question?' he asked. 'And is she prepared to submit to the encroachments of Prussia? That is a nail to drive.' But he really had more hopes of Prussia, 'certainly the power on the Continent whose real interests must coincide the oftenest with ours'. In Prussia's case he placed his hope on her traditional fear of Russia. Only that power, he warned Berlin, could gain from a policy of repression. 'Whatever happens she must gain. If arbitrary principles gain the ascendancy that will suit her creed, & will be convenient for Poland. If disturbances ensue, Austria & Prussia will be occupied, and that is no harm for her.' But it was still not too late for Prussia to change course. 'What a commanding position Prussia might take in Europe,' he went on, 'if her Govt would place itself at the head of the juste milieu in Germany, protect the smaller states instead of helping to oppress them, encourage sober improvement and the redress of real grievances and set her face against violent innovation and abrupt changes in existing institutions! She might rally round her all that is enlightened and intelligent in Germany and exercise a political influence not to be measured by returns of rank and file under arms; this would be the real conservative system, but alas!' His pessimism was fully justified, though his efforts were not entirely without success and several times the Prussians showed signs of hesitation and temptation. After a series of meetings in Münchengrätz and Berlin in September and October 1833, the King of Prussia finally succumbed to Metternich and joined the other Eastern monarchs in a reaffirmation of the old commitment to mutual aid against revolution.[69]

There was little that the Eastern bloc could do by 1833-4 to upset the Anglo-French solution of the Belgian question; indeed, by that time they had themselves become increasingly impatient of the Dutch King's obstinacy. In Switzerland too the cooperation between France and England served to moderate the renewed attempts by Metternich to bully the Swiss about foreign refugees and revolutions. But in Germany Palmerston's defeat was pretty well complete. On the one hand he had not been able to check the progress of Prussia's *Zollverein*; nor, on the other, Austria's repressive grip. It was in the free city of Frankfurt that his failure was most obviously marked, in both respects. When the Diet sent in their troops in May 1834, he finally protested that it was all contrary to the Treaty of Vienna. But like his protests over Poland this too was for the record, and lest he be attacked in the House of Commons. In Germany it was completely without effect upon her oppressors, and while he could reasonably claim that an ineffective protest was better than tacit acquiescence, he suffered a definite rebuff, which was made still worse when before the end of the year he was compelled to release Frankfurt from her commercial treaty with England.[70]

Although the Anglo-French entente was of some real effect in the West, Palmerston was worried that the new solidarity of the reactionary powers extended beyond central European affairs to those of the Near East. Metternich had told Lamb that the meetings of the three Eastern monarchs in the autumn of 1833 merely registered an 'épanchement d'amitié'. But Palmerston suspected that something more concrete had been accomplished, and he was right. The agreement about intervention was only one of the secret arrangements made in Münchengrätz. The other, concerning the Turkish Empire, was if anything an even greater setback for Palmerston. Ostensibly – if one can use such a word about a secret treaty – it agreed to maintain the Sultan's dynasty against usurpers and to that extent fitted in well with the other agreements against revolutions. But what was possibly sinister about it was that it also provided, in the case of the Sultan's fall, for common action to preserve individual interests and the balance of power, in such a manner as to suggest that it was partition the signatories really had in mind.[71]

When Palmerston entered the Foreign Office in November 1830 his view of Near Eastern affairs was still the Canningite one he had earlier expressed with regard to Greece. So it probably gave him considerable satisfaction the following month to press in European councils for more extensive frontiers for Greece. Getting better frontiers and even a satisfactory ruler for the new kingdom, however, proved more difficult than he had imagined: it took eighteen months of negotiation, the guarantee of a loan for Greece and a great deal of pressure in Constantinople. Even then the result was a grave disappointment. For Prince Otto of Bavaria, to whom Palmerston eventually agreed since he was both acceptable to Russia and yet appeared to offer some prospect of granting a liberal constitution to Greece, brought nothing but chaos and misrule. Palmerston certainly took it personally, for it was precisely what he had worked hard to avoid. 'It would not be fitting', he had sternly objected in March 1832, 'that the Allies should have taken so much trouble merely to substitute in Greece one tyranny for another.' But he was not concerned merely with an affront to his private feelings or public reputation. For, in addition to outraging British public opinion, 'a despotic Government too would be as little likely to be lasting as it would be creditable'. Subsequently he elaborated: Greece had no chance of real independence except by the establishment of a constitutional form of government as much as by the acquisition of solid frontiers; for Otto could only maintain his autocracy against the wishes of his new subjects by turning for help to either Russia or Austria and so becoming the puppet of one or the other.[72]

Palmerston's experience in the Greek question had a good deal to do with the development of his attitude towards the Turkish Empire as a whole. In June 1831 he still held what he thought was a good Canningite view of the Eastern question, that the Turkish Empire was 'falling rapidly to pieces',[73] and that successor states like Greece, with strong frontiers and good government, would much better serve Britain's interests in protecting the route to India and in preserving the balance of power in Europe. But to get the Sultan to cooperate in granting better frontiers to Greece, Stratford Canning, who had been specially sent to Constantinople for that purpose, had been obliged to leave the impression that the British would help defend the rest of the Empire, and as disillusionment with Greece intensified Palmerston gradually came to the conclusion that the preservation of the Empire might after all be the only practical solution.

The preservation of the Empire was at once both an external and an internal problem: how to defend it against external attack and from internal decay. Stratford Canning therefore soon recognized that it was essential for the Empire to be reformed. But he was not optimistic that the Sultan could carry out such reform,[74] and so the vital question in the 1830s was whether or not Mehemet Ali should be allowed to do it in his stead. Nominally the Sultan's lieutenant in Egypt, this Albanian adventurer had built up an army and a navy to rival his master's, and introduced such Western, and particularly French, methods as apparently to promise a better basis of reform and of strength than did the Sultan's decaying administration. Gradually he had extended his rule, ostensibly as the Sultan's vassal, south and eastwards into the Sudan and the Arabian peninsula, and his aid in the Greek War of Independence had brought him Crete as well. But he had been promised even more, only to have both the promise and his fleet shattered at Navarino. So he turned for compensation to Asia Minor and, after months of bickering and intrigue, in November 1831 had provoked a clash with the Pasha of Acre with a view to seizing Syria also from his master.

Preoccupied as he was with the Belgian affair, Palmerston was unwilling at first to get involved in the Egyptian question. It has been suggested that the return of Stratford Canning to England on 17 September and his interview with Palmerston the following day may have been decisive in making up the mind of the Foreign Secretary. But if Canning had really had a decisive

influence, it must have been before his return to England and owing rather to
the stream of letters and dispatches he had sent from Constantinople. For it
was earlier in September, when a British agent brought a plea for help from
Mehemet, that Palmerston had expressed a definite opinion about Britain's
interests:

It may be well to keep friends with Mehemet, especially if he should succeed
[Palmerston wrote to the Prime Minister two weeks before Stratford
Canning's arrival], but the Sultan is surely of the two, the most important ally
for us to uphold. If Mehemet is beat the Sultan reenters into possession, and
there is no harm done for us; but if the Sultan is beat his empire may tumble to
pieces, and the way in which the fragments may be disposed of may essentially
affect the balance of power in Europe; Russia would profit by the scramble, to
a degree which might be highly inconvenient to her neighbours. It is true that
if we repel Mehemet's advances & the French receive them, and he should
hold his ground, French influence will gain strength in Egypt, but after all
perhaps that would not do us any great harm till we went to war with France,
and then our naval superiority would bring us back the friendship of
Mehemet who would not like to have his navy sent to an English port. If both
parties were to ask our mediation there could be no harm in giving it; but
probably the Sultan will ask us for military assistance to crush Mehemet,
while Mehemet requests our interference to persuade the Sultan to give him
Syria. Under all the circumstances perhaps I had better plead the dispersed
state of the cabinet as a reason for futher delay.[75]

Palmerston's considered preference, then, was for the Sultan, in spite of the
advantage this might give to France in Egypt. In view of the line he was to take
a few years later about France this may seem remarkably sanguine, but what
it really underlined was the effect upon him of Russia's subsequent intervention. For the time being there seemed no good reason to Palmerston for
anything but delay. Hence during 1832 he had combined private and non-
committal advice to Stratford Canning to convey to the Sultan the
Government's 'general wishes to maintain and uphold him as an ancient ally
and old friend and as an important element in the balance of power in Europe'
with 'vague and general assurances of goodwill' sent to Mehemet Ali. The
Sultan, however, followed up these 'hints' by sending a special mission to
London to seek the loan of some warships in return for expenses and commercial concessions.[76]

Palmerston seems to have got on quite well with the Sultan's special emissary, a Fanariot Greek called John Mavrojeni serving as Turkish chargé in
Vienna, who, he said, was 'a respectable man, talks French well, & looks like a
half shaved old clothesman', and he told Granville in Paris quite plainly that
he wanted to help. But the reply Mavrojeni got on 5 December has usually
been thought to be a substantial refusal: it deferred the matter of ships and
tendered for the present only good offices, coupling with the offer verbal
advice about the absolute necessity of Turkish reform. In April 1833 Palmerston would recall having proposed to the Cabinet 'last autumn [*sic*], that we
should take our line in favor of the Sultan, & make a decisive communication

to that effect to Mehemet Ali', perhaps in concert with the other powers, but that 'the morbid sensitivity of some' had prevented any 'timely steps'. But it was only later that he realized delay had really meant refusal. At the time it was intended only to postpone a decision until the December General Elections were safely passed and the Cabinet could give more thought to the whole Egyptian problem. There was a reply at all only because Mavrojeni had pressed for one, and so, Palmerston explained to Grey, he had 'tried to put a few unmeaning phrases together', while Grey in turn had toned them down still further lest they be taken as holding out 'too much expectation'. In the meantime Grey asked Stratford Canning, who was between special missions to Constantinople and Madrid, to put his views on paper as a basis for discussion by the Cabinet or by those among them most actively interested in foreign affairs.[77]

Canning's memorandum of 19 December 1832 was written in haste and completed only after he had left for Paris en route to Madrid. Though long-winded its main arguments and recommendations were clear enough. It stressed that Mehemet Ali's victory or even a protracted war would dangerously weaken the Sultan's ability to resist Russian encroachment, while Britain's naval interference to stop the war would increase her influence with the Sultan, particularly with a view to encouraging reform. The elections and then no doubt Christmas and New Year festivities seem to have delayed further consideration, although the Sultan sent a more senior emissary, Namick Pasha, to hurry things along and both France and Russia proposed schemes of interference by the powers. Lord Holland scribbled anti-Turkish and pro-French remarks all over Canning's memorandum and towards the end of January followed them up with a paper of his own. Grey, apparently, tended to agree with Holland. He had long been inclined to consider the dissolution of the Turkish Empire inevitable and therefore to favour Mehemet Ali extending his power under British influence. But pessimist that he was, he had nonetheless agreed with Palmerston about the desirability of delay. However, at the same time as he received Holland's memorandum, on the evening of 24 January, there arrived also the news that the Sultan's Army had been decisively defeated by the Egyptians at Konieh and that if England did not act he was likely to accept an offer of naval and military assistance from Russia. Holland was not particularly alarmed. That Russia would profit from the decline of Turkey was, he felt, inevitable. There was no question, he said, of guaranteeing the Porte 'against external much less internal destruction. It is jumping into a sinking boat.' But he would nonetheless seize the opportunity to promote cooperation with France. Althorp was even less alarmed at the prospect of armed Russian interference: 'it concerns Austria much more than it does us & it very probably will induce Austria to be a little more jealous of Russia than she has been for some time past which will be a very good thing.' The Chancellor admitted, however, that some of his colleagues were very much alarmed. Among them were both Foreign Secretary and Prime Minister.[78]

Palmerston had already begun to suspect that Russia was up to something and he had warned how dangerous her interference would be and how little could be expected of Metternich. 'Can there be', he had pondered early in December 1832, 'a sort of incipient understanding between Russia and Austria by which encroachments of the one in Italy are to be supported on condition that the other should be allowed to advance a little towards the Black Sea?' What Russia was up to he admitted shortly afterwards he could not quite make out; but 'in this absence of grounds for judgment', he went on, 'one must go by the general rules and believe that where Russian agents are employed there must be intrigue on foot'. He was confident in particular that Russia intended to gain from the situation in the Near East, whether from the Sultan or from the Pasha. During one of the debates on the Russo-Dutch loan in August 1832, when a speaker charged Russia with 'pursuing a continued system of aggression' towards Persia and Turkey, Palmerston had actually replied that in neither case had Russia been 'in the slightest degree the aggressor'. But during the latter half of 1832 the Foreign Secretary was bombarded with a series of reports and information suggesting that he really must take a much more serious view of Russian activities in central Asia and these led him towards the end of the year to seek expert advice about the implications of Mehemet Ali's activities for the security of India. The reply he received in January 1833 gave much added weight to his opposition to the Pasha's success. The expansion of Mehemet Ali's dominion to Syria and Bagdad, he was told, would quite possibly lead to a joint partition of Persia with Russia and the establishment of a vigorous Moslem state in the vicinity of the Persian Gulf. In that event there would be two dangerous neighbours established on the Indian frontier. Alternatively Russia might align with the Sultan to defend him against the Pasha in the hope, Palmerston suspected, of being rewarded by the Sultan with Trebizond on the Black Sea or Mitylene (Lesbos) in the Aegean. In any case he did not trust Metternich's repeated assurances of Nicholas's good faith or accept that Austria would actually fight if Russia limited her gains to central Asia or even the Aegean archipelago. Nor was he any happier about the French proposals for mediation. From his conversation with Talleyrand, he concluded that the French were far from unsympathetic to the Pasha and would make of mediation 'a virtual though partial dismemberment of Turkey'. They would assign Syria to the Egyptians and so make them masters of Bagdad and the Persian Gulf.[79]

Faced with so much expert evidence, Grey too became alarmed. He no more believed in a Russian attack on India than did Holland, he said, but Russia's influence in Greece and Turkey, combined with a naval base in the Mediterranean, made 'the danger of her power in that quarter of the world . . . neither remote nor chimerical'. But how could it best be counteracted? Austria was useless, since Metternich was so blinded to her real interests by his preoccupation with suppressing revolution; cooperation with France, whatever she intended, he professed to think ruled out by King William's hatred and suspicion; and it was doubtful if either Parliament or people would support a war for the sake of such a 'remote and problematical interest'. Yet when the Cabinet met, on 27 January 1833, they decided to refuse the Sultan's renewed request for aid, 'in the first instance' at least, and to offer him instead England's 'good offices in conjunction with France'. They agreed nine battleships should be got ready so as to strengthen the Navy in the eastern Mediterranean as soon as the situation in Belgium and Portugal permitted; but in the meantime authorized only that a new representative should go out to Egypt in an eighteen-gun warship to put pressure on Mehemet to come to terms.[80]

Quite what Palmerston personally had wanted is unclear, though shortly afterwards he said it was for England to have 'taken a more prominent part'. Whether he meant a large and immediate strengthening of the Mediterranean squadron or even acceding to the Sultan's request, he certainly thought it best to offer England's aid or mediation separately from either Austria or France. But Holland, he said, was 'bitten' by a French doctor of Mehemet's, Althorp and Brougham were afraid of war, and the rest of making applications to Parliament for naval increases. 'We have some of us', Palmerston confessed with wry good humour to Granville, 'made flaming speeches against the Turk when the Greek question was before Parliament.' The crucial objection, as his Tory critics were soon suggesting, was that his Belgian and Portuguese policies had committed too much of the Royal Navy to the Scheldt and the Tagus to leave force enough for England to act independently and decisively in the East. A fresh application might therefore have had to be made to Parliament for naval appropriations and there was Althorp as usual to oppose it. So, Palmerston added a few years later, Grey, though in agreement with him, was 'weak and gave way'. Still he hoped that England would do 'tolerably well'. But he had been misled into optimism by reports that French interference had brought Mehemet to terms and so removed any need on the Sultan's part for Russian aid. For the news was false, and by early April 1833 Russian troops had actually landed on the shore of the Bosphorus.[81]

By April 1833, then, developments in the Near East had reached what Palmerston considered a potentially disastrous situation. Yet he was in a double dilemma. On the one side British interests were being threatened simultaneously by the Egyptians in Asia Minor and the Russians in the Bosphorus; on the other he was hampered in taking more vigorous counter-measures both by a timorous Cabinet and by his own suspicions of the partners available for great-power intervention. For some time therefore he could only feel his way cautiously and with hesitation. He seems to have persuaded Grey that the situation now required, and the earlier Cabinet deliberations allowed, the execution of further naval measures. So on 3 April the Admiralty was instructed to reinforce the Mediterranean squadron with two battleships and to send out contingent orders for diplomatic pressure against Mehemet Ali to be backed up if necessary by a blockade of Alexandria. When Althorp found out he inevitably protested that such measures were neither necessary nor agreed; but Grey felt the situation was too dangerous to give way and a month later, when circumstances permitted, further reinforcements went out so that a small British squadron might cruise off the Dardanelles. But neither admiral nor ambassador was at this stage given discretion to act without instructions from home. Instead Palmerston concentrated on containing the crisis by cooperation amongst the great powers and on the Canningite principle recently underlined in the Belgian affair of defending national interests by international concert. The difficulty here was that he distrusted the French and Austrians hardly less than the Russians. The French, he suspected, were tempted to back Mehemet Ali and at the very least favoured the Pasha's having Syria, which, Palmerston thought, would set a very dangerous example to the rest of the Empire and in particular open the way for that Russo-Egyptian partition of the Euphrates valley and the consequent threat to India about which he had been warned. So Palmerston, perhaps even more than some of his colleagues, was unwilling to join with France alone in anything more than simultaneous action. With the Austrians, on the other hand, he felt England had an obvious mutual interest both in Egypt and in the Balkans. The diplomatic pressure each brought to bear on Mehemet conspicuously reflected it. But there was no corresponding action at Constantinople, largely, he suspected, because Metternich was either the unwitting dupe or the secret partner of the Russians. For that reason alone he would have resisted Metternich's attempt to coordinate international action from Vienna. There were also reasons of a different kind, both personal and political. 'This proposal', he wrote to Grey, 'is probably only a little venting of Metternich's vanity, and a proof of his impatience at having been so long what he calls "Spectateur Responsable" instead of immediate Director of European Affairs; but I do not think it would suit *us* to be parties to Metternich Protocols, issuing from a Vienna Conference. The *pure* principles of absolutism which would mark the acts & language of such a conclave would not do here; and our ambassador however he might soften phrases, and mitigate doctrines would of course not be allowed to draw up documents, and could not entirely change their character.' On the other hand he could not but be impressed with the fact that differences of opinion among his Cabinet colleagues would make it impossible to tackle the grave dangers he believed were confronting British interests save by reviving the concert among the powers. But he had learned his Belgian lesson well. So in 1833 there began that famous contest between Palmerston and Metternich to make London or Vienna the centre for a concert.[82]

Palmerston's first move, in response to the proposals with which he had been bombarded by Paris and Vienna, seems to have been made from his sick-bed. Just after the decision to send out contingent orders to the squadron in the eastern Mediterranean, Palmerston was suddenly struck down with what was generally understood to be a particularly virulent form of influenza. But this was only put about – among both family and friends – in order to avoid alarm; according to his doctor's recollection it was really the Asiatic cholera that had first reached England some eighteen months before. For a short time it totally incapacitated Palmerston and, though he soon became 'quite impatient' to resume work, greatly weakened him and for about ten days confined him to his house in Stanhope St. For his part, Grey, under pressure on the one side from Brougham and Althorp and on the other from Talleyrand and Princess Lieven and contemplating defeat in the House of Commons, was full of gloom. He doubted after all, he said, that they had been right to back the Sultan even to the extent they had. 'The truth is that the fate of the Turkish Empire has long been sealed. It was sinking from internal decay, and the Greek affair, which led to the war with Russia, has produced the present crisis in the dangers of which we might have involved ourselves more deeply but could not have prevented them by an earlier interference.' On the other hand, while he did not blind himself to the consequences of the Russian protectorate, he did not see how England could spare the forces necessary to counteract it. But he had already evaded Talleyrand by sending him to Palmerston's sick-bed and he ought not to have been surprised that the result was a plan combining Talleyrand's and Palmerston's favourite notions – a convention providing for great-power interference but containing a self-denying ordinance and centred on London.[83]

Metternich dithered so long about subordinating Austria to England's lead, that Palmerston grew more and more to suspect, as he told Lamb in May, that he was 'far advanced in a secret understanding with Russia for a partition of Turkey in certain contingent cases – a regular Polandising of Turkey'. He had therefore looked upon the proposal of a self-denying ordinance as a test of Metternich's good intentions as much as a check to Nicholas's aggressions. By refusing to follow London's lead Metternich, in Palmerston's view, had clearly failed the test. So in June he brushed aside the Austrian Chancellor's pleas and the English ambassador's explanations of real goodwill:

> We wish to see a strong and independent state in the countries which constitute the Turkish Empire; Austria wishes to see a weak one and a dependant. We prefer the Sultan as its chief, if the Sultan be sovereign of an empire and not vassal of Russia. Austria would rather he were vassal of Russia than able to act upon a policy of his own, and Metternich declares . . . that sooner than see Mehemet Ali at Constantinople he would join with Russia in partitioning Turkey! Why, does not this pithy declaration let us into the secret of his thoughts, and does it not show that he has already come to an understanding with Russia as to the principle of an eventual partition of Turkey? Not indeed that there is a convention with a head and tail and numbered articles signed upon this matter, but that the sympathy of kindred spirits and the confidence of congenial principles have clearly led the two Courts to, a tacit perhaps, but very decided understanding.

Palmerston was undoubtedly wrong about Metternich's wishes and intentions for the Turkish Empire. His ambassador in Vienna was much nearer to the truth when he remarked: 'When I ask what has prevented him and you from perfectly understanding each other throughout this question, I can find no other answer than in his determination to treat it in Vienna and yours to treat it in London.' Indeed, by their rivalry Palmerston and Metternich each contributed to the accomplishment of what they both most feared – the establishment of Russian influence and power at Constantinople.[84]

Although they could not possibly hope to be anything like so effective as Russia's warlike preparations or France's persistent influence, Austrian and English pressure on Sultan and Pasha had some useful effect. Early in May the Porte found a face-saving formula by which to surrender both Syria and Adana to Mehemet and the immediate cause of the crisis receded – at least for the time being. Palmerston professed to be ready to make the best of a botched-up job. After all, it was far more important to get the Russians away from Constantinople and the Straits than to deprive Mehemet Ali of control of the passes into Asia Minor and the approaches to the Persian Gulf. To his relief the Russians left the Bosphorus on 10 July. But they did so only after securing from the Sultan the Treaty of Unkiar Skelessi two days earlier. Thanks to his new ambassador at Constantinople – the supposedly 'incapable' Ponsonby – and to England's friends in the Porte, Palmerston was sent the text of both the treaty and its famous secret article almost immediately afterwards. He soon came to appreciate that it made no legal difference to the existing international status of the Straits, since in effect it merely confirmed their closure to the warships of all nations including Russia's. To that extent it emphasized the continuing defensive preoccupation of Russia at the Straits, that is her fear of being attacked through them rather than her hope of using them to attack others. But Palmerston also appreciated that the treaty was nonetheless highly objectionable, since it consolidated Russian influence at Constantinople and in effect made the Russian ambassador 'chief Cabinet Minister of the Sultan'.[85]

Palmerston's first reaction to the news about the treaty was to urge the Turks not to ratify and the Admiralty to send out more warships as 'a powerful instrument of negotiation'. But the state of the Portuguese question made it impossible to spare any more ships for the time being, and in any case Britain's policy in the East had so far been too hesitant and her intervention too limited and too late for the Sultan to put much reliance on it now. Palmerston also had difficulty in getting his colleagues to agree to a protest being made in St Petersburg as well as in Constantinople. Grey thought that it would be 'a gratuitous act, the only effect of which would be to bring us into an angry discussion, which will come soon enough if circumstances require it, but which we had better avoid while we can, in the hope that we may eventually be able to avoid it altogether'. Palmerston retorted by muttering about Mme Lieven's influence, which only upset the Prime Minister, and about the likely reactions of their bellicose King, which worked much better. The result of his protest appeared even less satisfactory in St Petersburg than in Constantinople, for the Russian reply was tantamount to a snub, although the Tsar's genuine anxiety not to quarrel eventually led to conciliatory gestures and before the end of the year even to explanations. But it was on material precautions that Palmerston really wished to rely. For a while the preoccupation with Portugal continued to hold up any significant measures, but by the beginning of October he had got Grey and Graham, the First Lord of the Admiralty, to agree that some more ships should go out to the Near East. For the time being Grey would not authorize contingent instructions for the fleet to move up the Dardanelles; such an operation, he thought, was too difficult and too dangerous. So at his suggestion it was arranged for the fleet to be stationed throughout the winter at Malta, where it could more easily be dispatched to either east or west as necessary. But Palmerston employed the interval in making active preparations, both diplomatic and military, in case the worst should happen in the spring. He successfully underpinned the neutrality of Sweden so as to counter any move Russia might make in the Baltic, and in the New Year he obtained permission to give the ambassador in Constantinople instructions to call up the fleet against a Russian attack, provided that the Sultan asked for it and the Admiralty agreed that it was safe.[86]

What had begun as a device for putting pressure on the Sultan ended up, then, as a gesture of support for him. This, surely, was what Palmerston had always preferred. It is true that he had toyed with the idea of reversing his Egyptian policy and turning to Mehemet instead of the Sultan in order to build up a new barrier against the Russians. Indeed, it was more than the notion of 'a fleeting moment'. Rather, between May and October 1833, when the Sultan seemed destined to become the puppet of Russia, he had continually referred to it. Holland naturally did the same, and Grey also tended to revert to his original point of view. But for Palmerston, when used in his letters to ambassadors in Constantinople or Vienna, it was an obvious threat with which to belabour both Turkish Sultan and Austrian Chancellor. Really, he admitted, he had no faith in Mehemet Ali's word or character; he was sceptical about the claims made on behalf of his enlightened administration or his economic prospects. 'Under Mehemet Ali and his Egyptian system of peasant-squeezing', places such as Crete would 'always be in a state either of revolt or suffering', he warned Grey in 1834. He also doubted the competence of the Pasha's heir. Above all, Mehemet Ali was a usurper and lacked the inherent advantage of a legitimate line. If the worst came to the worst and the Sultan fell, either to Russia or to revolution, England could then turn to Mehemet as an alternative. But in the meantime her proper policy, and the purpose of her fleet, was to fend off a new clash between Sultan and vassal and gain time for the Empire to acquire strength by improvement and reform.[87]

How much faith Palmerston had in Turkey's recovery it is difficult to say. 'We must all of us try to bolster up the Sultan & by good propping he may keep his legs for many a good year to come,' he would write to his brother. But his easy recantation of earlier doubts and the jaunty confidence with which he wrote hardly seemed convincing. Even less so was his faith in the effective restraint of Mehemet Ali by the Concert of Europe. 'He has found out the real sentiments of the Great Powers,' he wrote to Ponsonby in July 1833, 'and he must have discovered that he owed his success to their want of concert, not to any difference of opinion among them; and that a second time they would be ready almost as soon as he. As long as England and France pull together, they can prevent Mehemet from molesting the Sultan.' But Palmerston really could not put any such reliance on the cooperation of the powers. For his King's distrust of France made open cooperation very difficult and his own distrust of Austria ruled her out as well.[88]

It is only fair to state that Palmerston misjudged Metternich's complicity as much as he exaggerated the evil of Nicholas's immediate intent. Neither of them was actively aiming at anything but the preservation of the Sultan's sovereignty over the Straits. But just as Palmerston recognized the unaccept-able implications of the Treaty of Unkiar Skelessi, so too he did those of the still more secret convention of Münchengrätz. Palmerston had been wrong when in June 1833 he had talked of tacit agreements between Austria and Russia for the partition of Turkey. But Metternich made his suspicion come true when he signed with Nicholas (and later also with William of Prussia) the Münchengrätz Convention in September 1833. For while that convention avowedly sought to maintain the integrity of the Sultan's dynasty, as an integral part of the European conservative system, it said nothing about his territorial integrity (save against Mehemet Ali taking over his possessions in Europe) and by a secret article promised mutual consultation in the event of the Sultan's collapse. So while Palmerston knew nothing of the actual details of the treaty, he was not really so very far wrong when he surmised that it was an agreement for partition. It was, as he said, a plan to take Turkey rather 'by sap than by storm'. But Metternich was an unwilling partner to such an agreement. He assured Palmerston over and over again through Lamb how much he appreciated Austria's and Britain's common interest in upholding the Sultan. He even professed his willingness, as suspicion smouldered on into 1834, to submerge the objectionable bilateral arrangements – Unkiar Skelessi and Münchengrätz – in a new five-power treaty. But Palmerston had already brushed the idea aside when proposed by France in October 1833 and again in March 1834. It was too late, he said; now England must rely on her own naval power and if necessary in the last resort make Mehemet Ali himself her ally against Russia. In any case, he added, and probably with rather more justification when one recalls the views of such colleagues as Holland and Althorp, the Cabinet would never agree to such a guarantee. So Metternich delayed his own proposal until Melbourne had succeeded Grey as Prime Minister and there seemed a better chance of Lamb's views prevailing over the Foreign Secretary's. But the device was as transparent as Metternich's attributing to the Tsar the insistence that the 'centre' of such international cooperation should be Vienna rather than London. Palmerston, with an air of amused contempt, dismissed the project as of no practical value.[89]

Fred Lamb, and others too, could not understand why Palmerston was so obstinate and wrote constantly to Melbourne to set him right. He had begun writing behind Palmerston's back as soon as he had heard his brother was likely to succeed as Prime Minister. Metternich's proposal, he had written in July, was 'a perfect Godsend' and neither Ponsonby's bellicosity at Constantinople nor Palmerston's obstinacy in London should be allowed to stand in the way. 'Ponsonby', he went on, 'is a mere dreamer, taking the phantoms of his imagination for realities – but a most dangerous talker doing all he can to convert them into truths.' Palmerston he attacked more obliquely in a later letter: 'If the humiliation of Russia is the object sought and preferred to the strengthening of the Turkish Empire, it is a personal not a statesmanlike object and will produce mischief to them who pursue it.' Metternich's proposal, on the other hand, was designed to submerge Russia's Near Eastern policy in the general will and 'contained one simple idea – Concert – and an offer if you adopted that idea to give you further explanations'.[90]

Responding to advice in letters that began, 'Read this when you are alone – and let *nobody* know that I have written it', or 'Secret. There are things I can not say even to Palmerston but which you ought to know', was by no means easy, especially for someone of Melbourne's easy-going temperament. But the new Prime Minister must have intervened to some effect, for while Palmerston described Metternich's reliance on Russia's good faith as 'absurd and childish' and his approach to London as 'vague and unsatisfactory', he nevertheless admitted to Lamb on 23 August 1834 that it offered 'an opening of which we are bound to take advantage at least to ask him what he means and what are his notions upon the general subject and this I mean to do'. Yet much to Lamb's annoyance it was another month before Palmerston even submitted a draft reply to Melbourne and then it was one that in the Prime Minister's opinion seemed designed to discourage Metternich from persisting in his initiative. 'It is exactly as if you wrote,' Melbourne went on, ' "For God's sake make no proposition to us; our opinions & feelings upon this subject are so completely adverse & opposite, that we never can agree upon any part of it." '[91]

Since Melbourne confessed that it was 'only lately' that he had taken much interest in the matter and Palmerston must have known very well who had stimulated that interest, the Foreign Secretary took great pains to educate his new Prime Minister. The matter was a good deal 'more puzzling' than Melbourne supposed, he said.

The despatch of July is truly a specimen of Metternich's mind, policy, & style of writing. He begins by a couple of pages of unmeaning jargon which are more like a disputation or a review than a despatch. He then in page 4 lays down as an undeniable fact that Russia is now for maintaining the Turkish

Empire, an assertion which we utterly disbelieve & deny, & he launches into an attack upon the policy of England & France about Greece; and then he says pray let us have no recriminations and no polemical discussions. In page 6 he insinuates that England & France are not as sincere as Austria & *Russia* in their wish to maintain Turkey independent; and in page 7 he repeats what he had said in a former despatch still more broadly, namely that, if we want a complete security against the ambitious projects of Russia against Turkey we may find it in 'the moral guarantee of Austria'. What the precise meaning of a moral guarantee is, I am sure I do not know; but I presume it means nothing more than Metternich's simple assertion that he is convinced of the disinterestedness of Russia. I should like to hear any man get up & repeat such a statement as this in the House of Commons as a motive for conduct on the part of the English Government.

. . . Strictly speaking, the despatch contains no proposal; intimates no intention of making any; and does not ask us to make any; but if we are to take up what is implied, but not expressed, we must find his proposals in his statement of the views & sentiments of Austria; and then the basis on which he proposes to negotiate seems to be, complete confidence in, and *cooperation* with Russia; guarantee of the authority of the Sultan against internal as well as external attack; and necessarily, as a consequence, a systematic interference in the internal affairs of Turkey. Now to none of these principles of action could we, I apprehend, agree. If the proposal made to us was, that Austria, France, England & Russia, should mutually engage in no case to appropriate to themselves any part of the Turkish Empire, to such an agreement *we* could have no objection but how it would . . . be taken by Nicholas . . . I know not. But to enter into an engagement which should bind us to cooperate with Russia in the affairs of Turkey, upon Russian & Austrian principles, would surely be very embarrassing.

We know that our interests & views differ diametrically from those of Russia; to go into conference with a previous consciousness of entire disagreement, could hardly lead to any good; and as to controuling Russia I believe we can do that more effectually by keeping our hands free.

So, Palmerston concluded, it would be quite impossible in any reply to overlook points of difference and disagreement and thus invite negotiation to open on an entirely false basis. If, however, Melbourne thought his own draft 'too discouraging', perhaps the best course would be simply to say that *England* had nothing to suggest but was perfectly prepared to hear whatever *Austria* might care to propose. This was actually the alternative Melbourne preferred and a dispatch went out accordingly to Vienna on 9 October. Palmerston did not expect any good to come of it: 'Metternich', he bluntly told Lamb, 'on Turkish affairs seems evidently to be the mouthpiece of Russia, and it is not likely that any proposal of Russia should lead to good result.' Metternich put his faith again in Melbourne and urged Lamb to return to England to give greater force to his advice, but it was too late; by the time Lamb arrived in London Melbourne's Government had fallen.[92]

Metternich always claimed that Palmerston had wrecked the Concert of Europe and driven Austria into the arms of Russia by spurning his approaches. There was some truth in this, but not so much as in the inexorable pressure of Metternich's own determination to secure Austrian interests through a conservative alliance among the Eastern powers. A concert centred on Vienna was objectionable to Palmerston not merely on the personal grounds that it would be led by Metternich but also on the political grounds that it would perform an essentially reactionary role in European affairs. It was in this sense that Unkiar Skelessi was linked with Münchengrätz and the Eastern question with the Belgian, Polish, German, Swiss and Italian questions. In the course of 1832 Palmerston had several times warned Metternich, in private and in public, that his policies in the Netherlands and in central Europe would necessarily force closer together the constitutional states of the West. But for all his talk of a 'natural alliance' with France and other constitutional states it was only after Unkiar Skelessi and Münchengrätz that Palmerston began seriously to work for one. The foundations for it, however, he discovered not in the East but in the West. 'Things look well in the Peninsula', he wrote to Ponsonby in November 1833, 'and if the two little queens succeed, which I have no doubt they will, we shall make up a powerful western alliance to counterbalance the Holy Alliance of the East. England, France, Spain and Portugal will be a good counterpoise morally and physically against Russia, Austria and Prussia.'[93]

Portugal was as emotional a word as Greece for Palmerston the Canningite, and in the not very long run it was to provide just as disappointing an experience. Since Wellington's abrupt withdrawal of British troops had opened the way for Miguel, there was little that Palmerston could do for Portugal when he first came into the Foreign Office. But though nothing to compare with the expanded frontiers of Greece, it must have given him some satisfaction at once to order the British packet agent to stop publishing lists of letters arriving from England, 'thus pointing out to the persecution of the Portuguese government all those persons in Lisbon who hold correspondence with the Portuguese emigrants in England'. Direct intervention against Miguel would have been popular in England, where he was stigmatized with considerable justification as a usurping tyrant, destroyer of the Portuguese constitution and persecutor of the English. But the fact remained that Miguel appeared to have the tacit support of the mass of the Portuguese people and Britain had no sufficient justification for interference. Donna Maria's supporters, however, had set up a Government in Terceira and Palmerston well knew that they were planning with the aid of her father, the Emperor of Brazil, to launch an invasion of Portugal at the earliest opportunity. He and Grey agreed in January 1831 that they could not give any open support in advance; but it was clear that they hoped the invasion would succeed. 'We have not yet recognized Don Miguel,' Mrs Arbuthnot observed, 'and Ld Palmerston is said to protest he never will.' In the meantime Palmerston limited his active interference to the protection of British citizens and property.[94]

Intoxicated a little perhaps by his success in standing up to France in Belgium, Palmerston urged Grey in April 1831 to have a couple of battleships sent to Lisbon with a forty-eight-hour ultimatum for Miguel. 'I fear', he said, 'that if we do not do something vigorous, we shall soon get into a scrape.' Grey's fear was quite the reverse: 'Seamen are apt to be a little too prompt on such occasions,' he replied. But the Cabinet evidently backed Palmerston and Miguel was forced to come to terms over British rights and property. This was what Palmerston had expected, but he frankly admitted to Granville that he would have been 'glad if our necessary vindication of our honour and our rights were to bring about the dethronement of Miguel'. When, later in the summer, after being ousted by revolution from Brazil, Pedro came over to England with his daughter, ostensibly for William's coronation but really to raise support for Maria's cause in Portugal, Palmerston almost certainly would have wished to help. But it was difficult enough to get the King even to receive the two exiles; and the Cabinet, for their part, chose 'to know nothing' of Dom Pedro's plans. However, Pedro made no secret of his determination to use every effort to restore Maria to the Portuguese throne and he subsequently crossed the Channel in the hope of a better reception in France.[95]

Pedro was by no means disappointed by the French and this worried the English very much; naturally enough, so soon after the Belgian crisis, they conjured up the dreadful thought of a marriage between Maria and Nemours. To keep Pedro and his daughter out of the hands of both Metternich and Louis Philippe had indeed been Palmerston's conclusive argument in persuading Grey and Lansdowne to support their visiting England in the first place. Now, after they had had a better reception in France, Lord Holland seized the opportunity to recommend cooperation with France and the joint recognition of either Pedro or his daughter in order to counter the support which Spain was giving to the rule of Miguel:

By such a measure we rescue Portugal over from Spain & keep her still in connection with us. A contrary course leads to one of two events equally injurious to us, namely a union of Spain & Portugal (the real object of Ultra policy) or the establishment of a national & separate government under the protection of France & utterly independent of English connections. Pedro very handsomely gives us the choice, . . . & I cannot but think we are fools if we do not accept it.[96]

Holland touched here upon a very sore point, though rather too soon. Encouraged by England's example, though certainly not by Palmerston's advice, the French had also sent a squadron to the Tagus to seek redress for grievances against Miguel. Palmerston fully admitted that the French were within their rights. 'Indeed', he wrote to Grey in June, 'when we have just been appealing to our treaties with lighted matches in our hands, we could hardly turn round upon Portugal and deny their force.' But he was very apprehensive about the French move. He had told Grey in May that though Miguel was clearly in the wrong, if the French were to attack Portuguese territory, 'we should probably not consider the character of Dom Miguel & the nature of our relations with him, so much as the natural & permanent interests which connect us with Portugal'. Neither he nor Grey was very happy even when the French confined their measures to the capture of Portuguese ships; and it was to get the French away as soon as possible that he constantly urged the Portuguese to come to terms. At the same time the French expedition also confronted Palmerston with a new decision about giving aid to Donna Maria. For the French had seized some Portuguese ships in the Tagus and in August put it squarely to the British that perhaps they should be handed over to Pedro. Palmerston was strongly tempted. 'Really', he wrote to Granville, 'when one reads what is going on in Portugal one feels tempted to throw the principle of non-interference overboard.' So while officially commending non-interference, he privately suggested the ships be sold to Pedro at a nominal price. Pedro did not get the ships; but his envoy in London, Palmella, obtained something of far greater value, Palmerston's more open support.[97]

Count Palmella was an old inhabitant of London and Paris and was much liked by Palmerston. What he provided for Palmerston was what the Foreign Secretary thought was at last a clinching argument for intervention – that without it there would be civil war in Portugal, which would spread over into Spain (where trouble was also clearly brewing over a question of royal succession) and then embroil France and England in their centuries-old Iberian rivalry. Spain herself had only recently underlined that this was not mere speculation by seeking to purchase support for Miguel and, as she thought, peace for herself at home. She had secretly offered a base in Port Mahon to England, while France, her minister said, had sought one from her on the Atlantic coast. But what made Palmerston more receptive still was that he had just passed the climax of his anti-French phase and was seeking opportunities to demonstrate to the Eastern courts that the new-found solidarity of France and England over Belgium was no mere passing or limited thing. The change in Palmerston's attitude to Portugal was one of degree rather than kind, but it closely followed the more radical change he exhibited during the course of September 1831 with regard to France and Belgium. When Palmella presented him with his detailed arguments and proposals on the morning of 20 September, Palmerston passed them on to Grey without comment of any kind. Ten days later, in the same letter in which he first reported to Grey that he had been threatening the Eastern courts with 'the hint that France & England might come to an understanding' over Belgium, he commented on Portugal: 'One knows well enough what one wishes; but it is too important a step to take without full consideration.' And towards the end of October, after he had seen Palmella again, Palmerston admitted to Graham that he had found 'much force in his reasoning' and to Grey that 'the more one looks at this complicated and difficult question, the less one can see any way out of it except by the success of Donna Maria'. Accordingly he drafted on 1

November a long memorandum on the whole affair and sent it to Grey three days later.[98]

Palmerston began his memorandum:

The affairs of Portugal seem fast approaching to a crisis in which it will scarcely be possible for England to avoid taking some decisive step in favor of one or the other of the parties who are contending for dominion in that country. If things are allowed to take their own course, there will probably be civil war in Portugal; an interference of Spain or France, or both, in the contest; danger to the tranquillity of the Peninsula; and possibly also to the peace of Europe, unless at last England interposes to settle the matter. The real question therefore rather seems to be at what time & under what circumstances England shall interfere than whether she shall interfere or not.

He then went on to suggest how England could publicly justify her interference, and what shape it should take. He began with a hostile review of Miguel's career and conduct from which he deduced that notwithstanding any appearance to the contrary there must be considerable opposition among the Portuguese people. 'Can a Government really be founded on the affections of the People, which pursues such a system of boundless violence & oppression?' he asked. 'If such measures of severity are required for the security of the Government, that very fact proves, that there must be a large & powerful party, which cannot be reconciled with the present order of things; if on the contrary these extensive persecutions are not called for by any real necessity, to what a degree must they not alienate the people from the Government.' In any case Miguel's rejection by the people of the Azores demonstrated that 'the contest . . . is no longer between a queen de jure and a king de facto, since the queen de jure is now actual sovereign of no unimportant portion of the dominions of the Crown of Portugal'. Also, Pedro could argue that Miguel by his conduct had broken faith and released Pedro from the engagements by which he had abdicated his throne. In either event it was not rebellion but civil war which was threatened by the expedition preparing in the Azores. It was inconceivable that England should prevent that attack by intervening against the constitutional party 'which has clung to English connection and never yet abandoned the hope of English support'.

On the other hand, the success of the expedition would lead to the intervention of Spain and Spanish intervention to that of France. The question therefore seemed to reduce itself to this:

Will England connive at the excitement of civil war in Portugal, while she has the means of preventing that evil; and will England prevent that civil war by immediately recognizing Dom Miguel, & by thus crushing at once, all the hopes of that party which looks to English connection; or will England exert her influence to bring about, in conjunction with France, & if possible Spain, an arrangement between the competitors for the throne of Portugal, which should lead to the retirement of Dom Miguel, & the establishment of Donna Maria, without a military contest.

It was surely not impossible, Palmerston suggested, that Spain might agree, for what she feared above all were the spread of civil war from Portugal and the example of free institutions being established across the frontier. But could she not be persuaded to avert the first danger, not by the recognition but by the abdication of Miguel? And while 'it would be impossible for England & France to be parties to an arrangement which would absolutely & entirely abolish the Portuguese Constitution', the promise of some revision might be secured from Pedro since it could 'not be denied that some considerable modifications of that constitution would fit it better for the existing condition of Portugal, and render it more palatable to a large portion of the people'. So, he thought, 'the first thing to be done would be, to come to a full understanding on the subject with France, so as to be sure that her action would keep even pace with, and not diverge from that of England'. It would also be more likely to induce Spain to agree, and the other, reactionary powers not to interfere. Finally, he asked, if all this were not agreed:

Is the matter then to be allowed to take its own course, and in an affair in which English interests are so much concerned, and in which it is probable that ultimate interference may become inevitable? Is the English Govt for the present to remain passive spectator of the contest, with the certainty that if Dom Pedro fails they will be accused by his partisans of having connived at, and abandoned him; and that if he succeeds an opportunity will have been lost of directing the course of events so as to make the change as harmless as possible, and of strengthening and confirming the influence of England in Portugal?[99]

Palmerston's long and skilful paper was based very substantially on what Palmella had put to him and Grey, but it proved much more effective than anything the Portuguese had done in bringing the Prime Minister round. Torn between sympathy and discretion, Grey had found it impossible, he had admitted in September 1831, to take 'a decided measure to overthrow a Government established de facto, and which is submitted to by the people'. He remained of the same opinion right up to the end of October in spite of all Palmella's entreaties. He was also made very uneasy by the way in which the Government was slipping into covert support for Pedro's expedition. Ships were being prepared for it in English as well as in French ports, and since this was plainly illegal the ships could have been seized at once by the customs on a word from Government. At Palmerston's urgent request, Grey agreed to delay any such instruction. But he was very unhappy about it. 'It is certainly not a policy which I like,' he wrote to the Foreign Secretary, 'to give encouragement in secret, to what we do not openly support. . . . I feel that in all this we are getting into a rather awkward position; but the alternative, in taking direct measures, is very disagreeable.' A few days later orders were given for the ships to be seized. But by that time Grey had received Palmerston's paper and had been given by it arguments with which to reconcile his wishes with his conscience. It was an 'excellent paper', he said, and he wanted it copied and circulated among the Cabinet.[100]

Among the Cabinet ministers Lansdowne seemed already to be moving in the same direction even before he had seen Palmerston's paper. 'To raise the standard of civil war by foreign influence in Portugal, without a reasonable certainty of an immediate as well as successful result would', he thought, 'be equally impolitick & unjust.' But if France and Spain would only agree to it, the scheme suggested would 'cut off all hope from ultras on the one hand & liberaux on the other'. Even Russell, according to Palmerston, supported the notion of Pedro's suspending the constitution indefinitely 'under the plea of the disturbed condition of the country'. Graham too was worried lest by her inactivity England should allow France to intervene and then find herself faced with the alternative of opposing French influence to the advantage of Miguel or acquiescing in it to the disadvantage of England's influence with Pedro and Maria. Holland, of course, was delighted with the change that Palmerston had wrought in Grey. He was greatly excited by the thought of active cooperation with France, especially in a part of the world where he had personally felt torn between admiration and abomination of Napoleon. He had recently been in indirect touch with the French, who wished the British Government to know that while they preferred open concert with England to clandestine communication with Pedro, they would in any event soon be forced to intervene. A few days later, at the end of the first week in November, Talleyrand came and said much the same directly to Palmerston. But to their dismay the stalwarts soon discovered that the majority of the Cabinet were utterly opposed. They 'are afraid of taking up Pedro', Palmerston reported to Lady Cowper; 'they think it too strong an act of interference; & doubt our right, & are in short very mealy mouthed.' Palmerston waited a few days so that Holland could come up from Brighton and add his weight to the minority. But it was no use. When they met on 17 November the Cabinet decided to do nothing, at least for the time being.[101]

According to Holland, Palmella was 'heartbroken' at the decision – 'or rather no decision', as he put it. But Palmerston took it very coolly, largely, as he said, because his colleagues' hands would eventually be forced by events. 'Perhaps on the whole this [doing nothing] is the safest course,' he admitted to Lady Cowper. 'The other would have been the most able & most according to the grand scale of policy, and my own conviction is that we should have got Miguel out as easily as a rabbit was ever drawn out of his hole by a ferret; however the matter will take its own turn and by the spring we shall probably see Pedro & Maria at Lisbon.' It is not surprising, perhaps, that Palmerston's notion of letting the matter 'take its own turn' was, with Grey's approval, to encourage it a little by pressing Palmella's scheme upon other powers and removing every obstacle he could to Pedro's expedition. But it is very puzzling indeed that Grey, in view of his earlier attitude, and the majority of the Cabinet, in view of the decision that they had forced on 17 November, should have winked at the aid covertly given to Pedro's expedition. Yet a convenient loophole was found for releasing Pedro's ships from the clutches of the customs, and consequently, by one means or another, ships, arms and volunteers

– including a British naval captain, Sartorius, to take command of his fleet – went pouring out to Pedro; and secret service money went to support a few Portuguese exiles as it had some Poles before. When Peel chastised Palmerston about it all in the Commons, the Foreign Secretary merely denied all official knowledge and repudiated the notion of interfering with 'the property and pursuits of individuals'. At the same time, Palmerston did all he could to bully or cajole the Spanish into strict neutrality.[102]

As the spring approached and the time for Pedro's expected expedition got nearer, Palmerston also pressed his colleagues to agree to a British naval force being sent out to counter any moves Spain might make in favour of Miguel. As an elementary precaution two battleships had been left at Lisbon after the successful vindication of British honour and property the previous summer. Now, Palmerston understood, the Admiralty had two or three more they thought they could spare, and these, together with as many marines as could be carried on them, might go out under the pretence of protecting British lives and property. There was conveniently at hand a complaint from an Irish Trappist monk that he had recently been expelled by Miguel, and if either Spain or Portugal gave them any more excuse the ships could actually intervene to settle matters. The reinforcements were made ready and orders prepared, but still Grey would not give the word, perhaps because he wanted first to see how the Government would fare when their 'neutrality' hitherto pursued in Portugal was attacked in the Commons. But the Government survived the debate of 26 March 1832 very well and in the meantime Palmerston had discovered, with the help of the Admiralty, that if the squadron were not to be reinforced it ought to be withdrawn altogether, as it would be too small to be of any use. Faced with the alternative of making what would be a very unpopular move, Grey, as Palmerston wished and expected, chose reinforcement.[103]

Palmerston anticipated that Spain would be deterred by Britain's naval action and that as soon as Pedro landed Miguel's supporters would melt away. But Pedro's fleet amused itself first with besieging Madeira and with chasing prizes and when his force was eventually landed at Oporto in July 1832 it allowed itself to be bottled up by Miguel's. Palmerston had intended, and the Admiralty's orders stipulated, that the moment a single Spanish soldier crossed the Pyrenees the fleet should actively assist Dom Pedro. But while the Spaniards assisted Miguel only with money and advice, the warnings of the Law Officers and the caution of the Royal Navy prevented effective British aid being extended to Pedro. Grey soon became despondent and even the optimistic Palmerston could only agree with him. Palmella came over to ask for 'a general, money, & recognition'; Holland wanted something effective done; and from successive representatives in Portugal there came also vociferous appeals. But Palmerston felt that unless as many as ten or fifteen thousand men were sent they would really be risking failure and that if such a force as that were sent the Government would be flying in the face of everything they had said in parliamentary debates and diplomatic dispatches.

If we had taken Pedro up at the Azores and landed him at Lisbon [he lamented], all Portugal would probably have submitted & we should have been sanctioned by the voice of the Portugueze nation. But now that Pedro has landed & made his appeal & hitherto without effect, to help him to *conquer* the Portugueze as it would be represented would be quite against all our principles. Pedro must do the thing himself, or give it up.[104]

At first, then, the ministers were inclined to send Palmella back, as Lady Cowper put it, with nothing but 'good wishes'. But an outbreak of cholera soon dispersed all of them save Melbourne, who had the gout, and Palmerston, who was too busy. Opinion was shocked at this behaviour at such a critical time, which left Palmerston virtually alone to deal with what seemed to be a rapidly deteriorating situation. When the news arrived that Pedro had been badly defeated Palmerston was ready to press for an armistice and to order the British squadron to cover the evacuation of Pedro's forces to the Azores. This turned out to be unnecessary, since Miguel neglected to follow up his victory and Palmerston found by intercepting Pedro's letters to Palmella that he had been deliberately exaggerating his plight. But the comparative failure of the expedition had underlined the need for more troops and better commanders, and far from changing his mind Palmerston confirmed that he was prepared to consent to a French general being appointed if a willing Englishman could not be found, and he actually persuaded the French to find for Pedro the money which he knew the English Parliament would never provide. In contrast to the view he was inclined to take only a year before, he was far less worried, he said in September 1832, about the consequences of French interference than by the prospects of Pedro's defeat.[105]

In spite of all these efforts, the stalemate in Portugal continued. Grey was naturally despondent. Even Palmerston began to despair. 'I wish we could find any way to help Pedro, but how can we acknowledge Maria now not having done so sooner?' he asked Lord Holland in November 1832. 'If Pedro would get to Lisbon that would be quite another thing. Can you strike out anything that we could do? I confess I can not.' Some were quite sure that they would have to recognize Miguel. This was what the minister in Madrid had all along been urging, and Palmerston evidently feared that Grey was beginning to think him right. Fortunately one of Pedro's English volunteers returned in the nick of time to tell him that all was not yet lost. Col. Hodges turned out later to be in his own way just as opinionated and unreliable as the British minister in Madrid. But for the moment it suited Palmerston to follow everything he said. Hodges had returned to England, Palmerston reported him as saying, because he did not like the company of his fellow countrymen in Portugal, deserters and N.C.O.s masquerading as captains, and blackmailers and bankrupts, like Harriette Wilson's 'husband' and Sir John Milley Doyle, as commanders. But he insisted that Pedro's situation was hardly any worse than hitherto; that there was no immediate danger of catastrophe; that 'a very trifling aid' would give him the upper hand; but that without it he would have to capitulate in a couple of months.

Considering that Miguel's Government [Palmerston concluded his report of this conference to Grey] is the sublimated essence of tyrannical absolutism, that his triumph . . . would be the doom of immense numbers, that to assist in bringing about that triumph would be the act for which your administration would find it the most difficult to give a satisfactory account, & that it would be a practical abandonment of the cause of just & civilized government, nothing probably would induce you to take steps pointing to such a result, except dire necessity, and the absolute impossibility of finding any other practicable course.

Fortunately the reports sent home by Addington, the British minister in Madrid, did, without him realizing it, suggest another course – namely to renew pressure on Spain and to do it by replacing him temporarily with Stratford Canning.[106]

It was evidently as clear to Palmerston as to any of his colleagues that some additional 'trifling aid' was not really going to turn the tide in Portugal. Rather, if English volunteers and French money were to achieve success for Pedro, Spanish support must be withdrawn from Miguel. That prospect no longer seemed so hopeless in consequence of a turn in the fortunes of Spain's own war of succession between the 'Apostolicals', who supported King Ferdinand's brother Carlos, and the 'Christinos', who supported Queen Christina's daughter Isabella. For as the ultra-Catholic and reactionary party, the Apostolicals favoured Miguel in Portugal, and the Christinos, bidding by contrast for relatively liberal support, favoured Maria. When, therefore, the news arrived in London at the beginning of October 1832 that Ferdinand had dismissed his old Ministry and recalled the ambassador in London, Zea Bermudez, to form a new one, and, more or less simultaneously, it was secretly intimated from Lisbon that a significant part of Miguel's supporters would be willing to throw him over, Palmerston conceived the notion of a new diplomatic initiative. The idea was to acknowledge that Pedro had failed to gain the support of the Portuguese people and to offer Maria, without the burden of either her father or a constitutional charter, to supposedly moderate opinion in both Portugal and Spain; and given all the circumstances, of the Apostolicals' support hitherto for Miguel and the Christinos' need of support against Carlos, it was expected that joint Anglo-Spanish mediation to achieve all this in Portugal would be secured by sending out a special mission to Madrid, offering the prospect of English support for Isabella in return for Spanish recognition of Maria.

It is doubtful that Palmerston really thought the scheme had much chance of success. He was worried that the continuing misfortunes of Pedro's forces would rally Miguel's disloyal supporters, and he had wanted to accompany the special mission to Madrid by another to Lisbon designed to arrange an armistice. Otherwise, he feared, if Pedro were defeated and Spain refused to recognize Maria, the only basis on which Canning could agree on mediation with Zea would be that of securing the orderly withdrawal of both Pedro and Maria and of recognizing Miguel. But too many of the Cabinet were hostile and persuaded Grey that it was inconsistent and dishonourable for England to negotiate in Portugal between Miguel and Pedro and in Spain for the disposal of both. This did not stop Palmerston and Grey, however, persisting with secret negotiations to induce some of Miguel's supporters to go over to Maria, or their speeding Canning on his mission. Canning's mission would at the very least provide a convenient device for giving ostensible, if temporary, employment to a high ranking diplomat whom the Tsar's pride had made redundant but whose own vanity and Palmerston's obstinacy made it impossible to retire. He might even secure Spain's agreement to the deal. In any event time would be gained and the necessity, as some were inclined to see it, of recognizing Miguel indefinitely postponed.[107]

Much against Palmerston's desire, Grey tried to gain Austria's support for Canning's mission and, much less to Palmerston's surprise, completely failed. More disappointing was the lukewarm response Canning got on his way through Paris. The French were doubtful about Maria's prospects and even more so about Christina's. All that they would give, therefore, was limited support in Madrid for Canning's search for an armistice, and they refused to be associated with his reliance on the Christinos. The mission was in any case doomed to failure since the Spanish Prime Minister was essentially an absolutist and had no intention of stimulating strife in Spain by supporting Maria's cause in Portugal. The British representative in Lisbon had predicted that Canning would treat the Spanish Government 'like soft wax and . . . mould it to his pleasure'. Palmerston thought that Zea, though bigoted if not bribed in favour of Miguel, was a 'timid' man whom Canning would have no difficulty in cowing by his hectoring manner if he failed to outmanoeuvre him by his diplomatic skill. But Zea stood his ground and forced Canning to look back to London for better weapons. At the ambassador's urgent pleading Palmerston sought and gained permission to offer what was virtually a promise of recognition for Isabella's right of succession in the hope that this would provoke a final confrontation between the Prime Minister and the Queen and end in the fall of Zea. But the strategem failed. Before the end of March 1833 Zea had succeeded in obtaining the dismissal of his more liberal colleagues and at the beginning of May Canning finally admitted defeat.[108]

Canning's failure plunged Palmerston into black despair; but only for the moment and largely, perhaps, because of the weakening effects of the cholera. A week later, though still damning Zea as 'bound to Miguel as Faust to Mephistopheles' and, rather contradictorily, with 'the passion of a mother for her deformed child', Palmerston nevertheless professed to think that the contest in Portugal was 'anybody's race yet' and that the setback in Madrid, 'by proving that nothing is to be expected from diplomacy, and that the bayonet and not the pen must determine the issue', would stir Pedro into action. What he looked forward to was 'a vigorous and daring effort' upon Lisbon. Before long, however, it looked as if any such move would be anticipated by more vigorous counter-measures on Miguel's behalf, since for him, too, ships and men were also being hired and French and British commanders found. Seeing that all this was done in league with Spanish Carlists, French legitimists and English Tories, Lord Holland was the first to press for intervention by the Government, though he inadvertently missed a crucial Cabinet. 'I think we are now for the second or rather third time', he wrote, though too late, 'losing our opportunity of restoring Portugal to her natural station & connection with us from overscrupulousness & somewhat pusillanimous conduct. The consequences will I think be that in the event of *Pedro's success* Portugal will be a French rather than English dependency, . . . & in the other event of *Miguel's triumph* the whole Peninsula will be ultra & hostile to us & we shall be laughed at.' Grey, rather, was inclined to scoff at him. All that he would do was finally to reveal to Palmella, who for months had been begging constantly for money if not men, that he thought the best solution would be for Pedro as well as Miguel to go. But in June Palmerston too stepped up the pressure against England's being so 'squeamishly neutral'.[109]

Stunned first by a Government defeat over Portugal in the Lords and encouraged afterwards by an enthusiastic reversal of that vote in the Commons, Palmerston began again to press for naval reinforcements to protect English commerce from ill-treatment and, if necessary, to answer Carlist aid for Miguel. Then, in the middle of July 1833, news arrived which promised at last to transform the situation; Sir Charles Napier, under the guise of 'Admiral Carlos de Ponza', had replaced the ineffectual Sartorius and with a handful of converted merchantmen routed Miguel's fleet off Cape St Vincent. 'Carlos de Ponza forever!' Palmerston exclaimed to Lamb; 'Was there ever a more gallant exploit in the annals of seamanship?' Holland wanted Canning's mission revived at once; Palmerston waited until the news arrived that Pedro had entered Lisbon and then, on 2 August, proposed that the Cabinet should recognize Maria and prepare to resist any opposition from Spain by sending out reinforcements to the Tagus and lifting all legal restrictions on British volunteers. In this, apparently, he had the entire support of both Graham and Russell, as well as Holland, but not of Grey. The trouble was that Grey had no faith in Pedro, yet Napier's victory was bound for the time being to strengthen Pedro's determination to stay on as Regent. So the Cabinet decided on 3 August not to send any reinforcements immediately to Portugal but to have them in readiness at Gibraltar (for either Lisbon or Constantinople) and to send to Lisbon and Madrid merely contingent instructions for the recognition of Maria and the revival of the mediation proposal. Palmerston regretted his colleagues' timidity about reinforcements, but appreciated, more readily than Holland, the difficulty about Pedro.[110]

As it happened, the Spanish King expired the day after the arrival in Madrid of the new British minister, George Villiers, later Earl of Clarendon, and having, as soon as the British Cabinet could be assembled to agree, recognized the succession of Queen Isabella under her mother's regency, Villiers revived the proposal of cooperation in Portugal. Meanwhile the British representative in Lisbon, Lord William Russell, overwhelmed with hatred for Miguel, exercised his discretion to recognize Maria. But Grey soon proved the better judge when Pedro by his misbehaviour proceeded to alienate his supporters and give new heart to his enemies. Grey hoped that the military misfortunes provoked by all this would lead to Pedro retiring from the regency; instead they threatened to bring down Maria as well. So, unable to discover a clear way ahead, the British Government dithered for nearly six whole months. They tried to find a better substitute for Pedro by settling on a suitable husband for Maria; but each candidate only opened up old sores of suspicion between England and France.[111]

Grey wanted to avoid any 'measures of an indirect, doubtful, and under-hand character'; but another 4,000 muskets and 2,500 volunteers went out to Pedro before the middle of October. The muskets were sold, as an ostensibly commercial arrangement; the volunteers were described as 'Belgians' and Palmerston claimed to have been entirely innocent of their going, though all but 400 were natives of the British Isles. In fact he knew all about them and their origins. He was also well aware of a proposal brought via a merchant house in London to buy off with £40,000 Miguel's French commander, who was then marching on Lisbon. According to Wellington General Bourmont was 'a good soldier, a clever man, and brave, but a most venal rascal'. Palmerston did not recommend the scheme since, as he said, anyone who was willing to be bought out of his first engagement might just as easily break his second. On the other hand, Wellington and Grey both commended it and Bourmont did quit Miguel's service, though only after his attack on Lisbon had failed. 'Maria's cause has won the day', wrote Palmerston, 'though the race is not quite over.' But hardly had he said so than there came the news that Carlos had raised the standard of revolt in Spain. Grey was worried that civil war in Spain would inevitably drag in France and he wanted Palmerston, as the Cabinet of 3 August had authorized, to concert policy with the French with a view to discouraging them from taking any step that might provoke a quarrel with Britain and, possibly, a war with the reactionary powers. Palmerston, pooh-poohing any fear of France, wanted to leave the Spanish contestants to fight it out alone and to take advantage of their quarrel to enlist the Christinos openly against Miguel.[112]

Whatever differences there might still have been between them over tactics, it was clear that by the autumn of 1833 Grey was rapidly moving into line with Palmerston about the necessity of more active intervention in the Peninsula. 'Nobody adheres more scrupulously than I do to the principle of not interfering,' he had written early in September. 'But this like every other principle must have its practical limits, & the continuance of a bloody contest, absolutely destructive of Portugal, & dangerous to every power connected with that Country, may at last both on the score of humanity & policy compel us to interfere.' A week later he considered it 'impossible' to look on much longer as 'passive spectators'; and before the end of the month he was asking Palmerston to consult with others about possible operations. But there was considerable doubt how far to go. Holland was all for urging on the Queen of Spain – or rather her mother as Regent – that she should announce her intention of liberalizing her country's institutions and, without going so far as to repeat the radical 'follies' of 1812 and 1823, unite opinion against the common enemy of reaction throughout the Peninsula. Palmerston had some sympathy with this: he had already decided that Don Carlos's revolt would only lead to his defeat and therefore to the 'constitutionalizing' of Spain. But he was discreet enough not to trumpet it so much, especially in King William's hearing. Moreover, since Don Carlos's 'legitimist' connections had cooled the ardour of Louis Philippe to help him, there were advantages for England, Palmerston saw, in limiting her interference in Spain to merely moral support for Isabella, and by winking at Spain's pursuit of Carlist forces operating from Portuguese territory, gaining both her acknowledgement and her active support of Maria.[113]

Grey, too, was tired of devious schemes; he wanted the affair finally settled, if only because of the dangers looming up in other places like Constantinople. In any case, the presence of Carlist troops on Portuguese soil justified English intervention even more than Spain's by virtue of the Anglo-Portuguese treaty. It appears to have been the Prime Minister, therefore, who just before Christmas 1833 initiated active discussion of military intervention by Spain and England in concert. Palmerston, however, soon took it up with enthusiasm: 'our course is clear, if our nerves are good.' Spain and England would jointly offer to 'squash' Miguel and to support Pedro if only he would replace his ministers with moderates, summon the Cortes and grant a general amnesty; if he refused they would still intervene, but to get rid of him as well. But there must be nothing half-hearted about it: England must send at least five or six thousand men along with Spain's ten. Encouraged by the support received not only from some of the Cabinet (from Graham and John Russell as well as Holland) but also from Windsor, arrangements were even made to assemble a suitable force in southern Ireland – the King thought Catholic regiments peculiarly suitable for the purpose – and a new minister, Lord Howard de Walden, was especially selected for the diplomatic part of the scheme. But there was never any question of evading a full discussion by the Cabinet as soon as one could be arranged after the holidays. The arrival in London of a new emissary from Pedro promising to meet virtually all England's conditions only made it look all the more desirable.[114]

Palmerston saw the Portuguese envoy on 8 January 1834, the day after a meeting of such members of the Cabinet as were available had agreed that matters could not be allowed 'to go on in their present course without the greatest danger' and authorized Grey and Palmerston to draw up a detailed plan of interference. They could hardly have done more since Brougham, Lansdowne, Melbourne and Carlisle were all absent, and so another meeting was arranged for 13 January. At that meeting Grey discovered that Althorp, Stanley, Richmond and Melbourne were 'decidedly against' any British expedition. Grey had known beforehand that Althorp would be opposed. He had warned the Chancellor how his thoughts were turning as long ago as the end of September and had received a pretty blunt reply: 'With respect to Portugal, I thought things appeared to be going on very well, and to call as little for our interference now as at any previous period of the contest.' And early in the New Year the Chief Whip, Edward Ellice, had warned Grey that such an expedition would not be popular in the country. But having gone so far in concerting measures, Grey was evidently rather taken aback by what some saw as 'a *great* split' developing in the Cabinet on 13 January, and so he deferred any decision until they could consider a formal written proposal of his at a meeting the following day at five. All the ministers were present at their second meeting, save Brougham, who was detained by legal business, and Carlisle, who was often absent from Cabinets. But Brougham sent word of his strong support by letter and Grey and Palmerston of course had Graham, Holland and Russell firmly on their side. Goderich was also in favour of the expedition and so, at first, was Lansdowne. But when the dissentients declared their strong opposition – 'scruples founded on the principle of non interference and yet more strongly [in Althorp's case] misgivings that Parliament would not sanction a war or vote the necessary supplies', according to Holland's account – Grey was apparently ineffectual in reply and this increased the 'timidity' of others, including Grant and Lansdowne. This still left the interventionists in the majority but the Cabinet split right down the middle, Whigs and Canningites alike; and if, as they threatened, the dissentients were to resign, they would leave Palmerston and Graham in a sad minority in the House of Commons. Grey therefore insisted that if the Cabinet were not unanimous, the expedition would have to be given up; and that if the expedition were given up, he would have to resign.[115]

Grey had always been worried that the death of Althorp's father would before very long fatally weaken the front bench in the Commons, and on other grounds as well he had frequently threatened to give up. It was, in fact, a mere four months or so since he had last spoken of his resignation as an imminent probability. But his colleagues had talked him out of it then, and they evidently reckoned to do so again in the Portuguese crisis of 1834. So Grey was persuaded to suspend his resignation until after they had met for dinner at Althorp's house following the Cabinet meeting of 14 January. This time Brougham did manage to attend though Carlisle was still absent and possibly, for part of the time at least, Grant was as well. However, food and drink failed to resolve their differences and Grey finally left telling his colleagues that he would be taking his resignation to the King the following day. After he had gone, Brougham urged upon his colleagues that the dissolution of the Government would put both the monarchy and the country in danger and insisted with what Holland called 'his usual vehemence and exaggeration' that the Portuguese question really was not worth the risk. Eventually they all signed an appeal to Grey to suspend any action on his decision. Grey again agreed and postponed his trip to Brighton, where the King was in residence, for another twenty-four hours, but evidently without much enthusiasm. He did not see, he told Brougham, why an alternative Government should not be formed without him. But this the others would not even consider – or so Brougham said. Rather they felt they had to find some basis on which Grey himself would continue. Holland, at first, was all for accepting the dissentients' resignations. Melbourne and Stanley, he thought, might be prevailed upon to stay and in that case Althorp's loss, though 'almost an irreparable calamity', would not make the continuation of the Ministry utterly impracticable. But he soon came round to thinking that some sort of compromise would have to be the answer; and shortly after noon on 15 January he thought he might have found one. What this turned out to be was really the abandonment of any expedition and mere words of sympathy for Maria and of hostility to Miguel in the following week's Address by the King to Parliament.

Whether Palmerston also thought that Grey could have dispensed with the dissentients in the Cabinet is not known. But he wrote to the King's private secretary to say that he agreed he could not in present circumstances go on without Grey and that interference in Portugal was not worth the crisis a Tory administration would produce in England's affairs. However, Ellice at the time and Grey's son some years later both blamed Palmerston for having pushed the Prime Minister into his unhappy position over Portugal in the first place. But both were enemies of Palmerston's, and Howick, at least, ought to have recalled that, while his father waited passively in Downing Street on 15 January, he, Howick, had pressed on Palmerston a compromise that would give merely British encouragement to Maria but get Spain to declare war on Miguel, and that he had found the Foreign Secretary by no means opposed to it. Moreover, while it was true that Palmerston had advocated direct intervention much earlier and more consistently than Grey, in the three months or so preceding the Cabinet crisis it had been Grey who had been warmer for it, and Palmerston who at one time had suggested to him instead almost precisely the 'compromise' subsequently proposed by Howick.

When Holland went at about one o'clock on 15 January 1834 to persuade Grey of the merits of the so-called compromise, he found the Prime Minister utterly preoccupied with a deputation of religious dissenters. But later that day first Palmerston and then Brougham cornered Grey and secured his apparently reluctant consent to pursue the suggested course. It was Palmerston, however, who more or less alone took on the task of tackling Althorp. At first Althorp seems to have been very willing, but since, as he later wrote to Palmerston, he was 'only too well aware' how much he was influenced by the desire to relieve Grey's anxiety, he insisted before he finally gave way on consulting his four supporters, and to every compromise proposal they at least found 'serious objections'. So Althorp overcame his 'weakness' and on the evening of the 15th wrote to tell Palmerston that he could not make any compromise proposal to the Prime Minister. The next day he reported to his father that the affair had taken place 'without any or at least with very little angry feeling'. What he may have meant by his belated reservation, if the story that circulated in the London clubs had any foundation, was that after getting Althorp's letter Palmerston had cornered him in his house and passed much of the night in such angry altercation that the noise if not the actual words could be heard outside the room. Neither of them, apparently, got to bed at all that night and early the following morning began to knock up their colleagues. But it was all to no avail and at nine Grey set off from Downing Street to see the King at last. Where the Cabinet had failed, however, the King – with a little help from Ellice – more easily succeeded. At his first audience on the 16th Grey was unmoved, but H.M. called in Edward Ellice, who said he had been summoned 'unexpectedly', and with talk of 'the possibility of convulsion & revolution' if the Government should fall, together they persuaded Grey to give way over Portugal and yet again to carry on his Government. The gloomy Grey did not neglect, however, to emphasize very strongly to them both that he had 'acted for the first time in his life contrary to what he considered right, & . . . consented to remain in office knowing himself to be unable to regulate his foreign policy according to his own views of what was safe and expedient'.[116]

'Non-intervention is of course the result, & I am disposed to think the right one,' Ellice reported rather smugly to Durham. But he reckoned without the tortuousness of Iberian politics and the resilience of Palmerston's policies. For hardly had the crisis been resolved in favour of the faint-hearted than the news came from Spain of Zea's fall. The King expressed his 'earnest hope' that Villiers had not been responsible, especially not in league with his French colleague. Villiers had certainly proposed to help the plot along but Palmerston had taken care to send him an official though utterly anodyne rebuke. The result in any case was favourable to Palmerston's policy. Spanish incursions in pursuit of Carlists in Portugal were stepped up and at the end of March a new Spanish envoy came to Palmerston proposing an Anglo-Spanish treaty that would both guarantee to Portugal that Spain's interference against Carlos would not take an unacceptable turn and give some reassurance to Spain that she would not have to face the hostility of the Holy Alliance alone. Almost before the Spanish and Portuguese representatives could think twice about it, Palmerston had converted this proposal into a scheme for a tripartite treaty to include Portugal, and had extracted from the same old Cabinet approval for a scheme of interference which appeared to their satisfaction both more limited and more safe than the previous one. He stressed to Grey that by limiting Britain's liability to naval assistance, which in any case was 'merely put in to save appearances', the proposal got rid of the difficulty of approaching Parliament for money. But what may have persuaded the Cabinet was the fright Palmerston probably gave them by pointing out that England's existing treaty obligations were probably more onerous than those he now proposed. For if Spanish troops invaded and Portugal called on her old ally to oppose them England would have no choice by her ancient treaty but to send troops, and for a much less desirable purpose. So with Grey's approval Palmerston drew up a new convention on 11 April and in the course of the next two days obtained the consent of the Cabinet and the King. 'I carried it through the Cabinet by a *coup de main,*' he boasted to his brother, 'taking them by surprise, and not leaving them time to make objections.' But when he showed it to Talleyrand he found to his surprise that the old fox was full of objections.[117]

What Talleyrand particularly disliked was France being invited to accede almost as an afterthought to a convention already drafted and dotted. In fact this was deliberate on Palmerston's part, both to overcome the reluctance of the King and to be certain of a wording that would prevent French interference across the Pyrenees except with England's consent. Talleyrand countered, first with a series of alterations that would have made fundamental changes and then by proposing instead an actual treaty of alliance between England and France. This was something he had been pressing ever since he had returned from a prolonged absence in Paris in December 1833. What he had in mind was some sort of mutual protection against the threat of war with the Eastern powers. At first he offered as bait a special guarantee of the Ottoman Empire. But not even Grey or Holland had shown much enthusiasm, let alone Palmerston, who made a classic (if not entirely accurate) response:

As long as the interests and sympathies of the two nations are united, as they now are [Palmerston wrote], an alliance does exist, cemented by motives as strong as the articles of the treaty. . . . We have no objection to treaties for specific and definite and immediate objects, but we do not much fancy treaties which are formed in contemplation of indefinite and indistinctly foreseen cases. We like to be free to judge of each occasion as it arises, and with all its concomitant circumstances and not to be bound by engagements contracted in ignorance of the particular character of the events to which they are to apply.

To Holland, Grey put it more bluntly. There was no need that he could see to accede to Talleyrand's wish to give public expression to what he called the 'union' of England and France. If France were in good faith, then her *actions* would demonstrate it well enough. In any case King William's attitude would be a great obstacle.[118]

The utility of an alliance for propaganda purposes had by no means escaped Palmerston's alertness and attention. For he had long since observed that what he called Metternich's 'monomania about revolutions', and with it the unholy alignment of the three Eastern powers, extended also to Spain and Portugal. When Austria, Prussia and Russia joined in the summer of 1832 to put pressure on England to allow Spain to intervene in Portugal on Miguel's behalf, Palmerston had observed that their action amounted to the 'revival of the Holy Alliance', and he had already let it be known in Berlin that 'the days of the Holy Alliance are gone by never to return and that such propositions do not belong to the present time'. Later, in December 1832, he heard that the Russians had been pressing Spain to put an army on the Pyrenees in case war broke out between France and the Eastern powers; so after the change of régime in Madrid had upset the joint efforts he knew the Russians were making abroad and the Tories at home to frustrate Stratford Canning's mission, he rejoiced that it would free 100,000 Frenchmen for the Rhine. As early as April 1832, when he had warned the Austrians that a Spanish intervention against Miguel would mean a British intervention on behalf of Pedro and their minister in London had replied that it was French meddling they feared, not British, Palmerston had responded:

I begged him to look at the present state of public feeling, for it is more than opinion, in Bavaria, in Baden, in Hesse, and in many other parts of Germany & then tell me what would be the consequence of a war waged and begun against France, by what would be called the arbitrary governments of Europe, in order to prevent France from interfering to assist the Constitutional party in Portugal . . . Austria would in that case deliberately and of her own malice prepense, be beginning a war of principle in Europe, and I should like to see the man, who would venture to predict how it would end, and who would be the greatest sufferers by it.

He did not then say specifically that England would be found with France, but when to the differences over the eastern question were added those about Belgium, Germany and the Iberian Peninsula, the point finally became explicit; and after the meetings in Münchengrätz and Berlin he warned, 'if the Three Powers choose to make one unity, they must not be surprised if the other Two make a second unity'. It was therefore but a short step he took less than two months later:

The moment it was decided in Spain to oust Carlos and uphold Isabella, it was necessarily decided to pursue a more liberal system of policy than that of Ferdinand. An estrangement from the Holy Alliance and an approximation to England and France must follow such a change of system; and we shall ultimately have England, France, Spain, and Portugal united in a liberal alliance in the West, and by their moral power keeping in check the unholy allies in the East, and preserving the peace of the world.[119]

So when Palmerston boasted, in reporting his triumph to his brother, that the April 1834 convention was 'a capital hit, and all my own doing', he was not too far from the truth. He had, as he said, been contemplating 'a powerful counterpoise to the Holy Alliance' ever since the death of the King of Spain, but not until the last approach from Madrid had he seen how to give it 'a substantive and practical form'. He was more realistic than Talleyrand in appreciating that it was the material objective of intervention in Portugal that gave the alliance its necessary basis of solidarity. It was because this would be lacking that he turned down the ambassador's proposal to extend the alliance to Belgium, Switzerland and Naples. The time for such action in Belgium was past and in Switzerland it was difficult to see where British sea power could be brought to bear. But it is only fair to add that not long before Palmerston had himself included Belgium in his own list and talked even of his hopes for Greece. In Naples, where he had placed his brother, he also worked constantly against the Metternich System, encouraging liberal measures in both government and trade and, indeed, thinking that there might well be some sense in pursuing Talleyrand's suggestion in this case. But he did not achieve much material success and when he thought he was on the eve of detaching her, along with Sardinia, from Metternich's system, he found that they were both secretly helping Carlos.[120]

All in all it was not surprising that in order to meet Talleyrand's objections to the original convention Palmerston should have agreed to make France a full contracting instead of an acceding partner in the Quadruple Alliance, and then have gained the King's consent by emphasizing that the alterations were merely 'slight changes of form', all underlining France's subservience to England. For some time, too, Grey had been indicating to the King that he had got it all the wrong way round. 'I had once thought', he had confessed to Palmerston in October 1833, 'of writing fully to convince him that a war of principle on the continent is much more likely to arise from the conduct of the Three Powers than from that of France; & to warn him that if such a war should be decided, it would be impossible for this administration to advise him, as he has more than once stated would in such a case become necessary, to take part against France; & that he may be assured the Country would not bear it.' When Wellington heard what Palmerston and Grey had done he claimed that 'there never was a more fatal treaty for England'. It could have only one object, he said, 'to have a treaty of any sort with France – and to get rid of the ancient alliance of England with the Northern powers'. Princess Lieven was shrewder, observing that its terms were 'so delightfully vague that its actual execution may give rise to a thousand causes of misunderstanding between the two Powers. . . . Politically it is impossible for France and England not to quarrel over the question of preponderance in the Peninsula.' But this was mainly a long-term forecast, though there were some disappointments even in the short run. In May 1834 the Spanish forces decisively defeated Miguel and both he and Carlos surrendered. But while Miguel passed into oblivion, over-optimism and negligence (including some on Palmerston's part) allowed Carlos in July to escape and rouse again rebellion in Spain. Additional articles were hurriedly contrived for the Quadruple Alliance to deal effectively with him and as a gesture a few British warships were dispatched to the northern and eastern coasts of Spain in order to help the French in stopping his supplies. But this assistance was not very effective: the Navy was unenthusiastic and the Law Officers hampered all the efforts the seamen were prepared to make. So while the war in Portugal seemed over and Pedro's departure assured, civil war in Spain dragged on. Still, if Palmerston exaggerated in calling his alliance 'a powerful counterpoise', he had considerable justification in emphasizing its 'moral effect'. For it gave new heart to desponding liberals in central Europe and was, as he said, a warning that 'if the three Northern Powers should be disposed to be frisky we shall be four to three at all events'.[121]

The Quadruple Alliance, then, was a fitting climax, in Palmerston's view, to the transformation of France from enemy to ally. But it also pretty well marked the end of his first period at the Foreign Office. For hardly had it been concluded than the Whig Ministry was plunged into a series of political crises that led in July 1834 to the resignation of Grey and then, in November, to the dismissal of his successor Melbourne. 'We are all out,' wrote Palmerston to his brother on 16 November; 'turned out neck and crop: Wellington is Prime Minister, and we give up the seals, etc, to-morrow at St James's at two.' 'Tell

The British Library of Political and Economic Science

'Receiving the Fatal News!' by HB (John Doyle), December 1834

this immediately to Metternich,' he added in a postscript to Vienna. 'It will gladden his heart and be the most agreeable thing he has ever heard from me.'[122]

Others also felt that even if it was not all the result of a plot, the changeover was made with most unseemly haste. Palmerston stayed up literally all Sunday night arranging his papers in the F.O. He was glad it had not all happened six months before, 'as several questions have since then been placed in a much better condition. Portugal is settled; Spain is safe; Belgium cannot be ruined . . .' But, he went on, 'I wish we had gone on six or eight months longer; and then really I should not have been sorry to have had some good long holidays, after four years or more, as it then would have been, of more intense and uninterrupted labour than almost any man ever went through before'. He also did not forget the clerks whose labours had assisted his own. He addressed a letter to his Undersecretary, asking him to communicate to them his 'sense of the indefatigable zeal and unwearied cheerfulness with which they have, during the last four years, gone through the unusual labour and submitted to the excessive confinement arising out of the extraordinary pressure of public business'. But according to one old stager in the office – who was probably right – this acknowledgement 'rather affronted than pleased them. They think it ridiculous after his constant harshness & the total absence of laudatory words during the whole time, that he should wind up & smooth them down by telling them they were good boys.' When they heard the following January that he had lost his parliamentary seat they would have liked, they said, to illuminate the Foreign Office, just like their counterparts at the War Office a mere six years before.[123]

IX

THE
FOREIGN OFFICE

The Foreign Office which Palmerston entered for the first time as chief on 22 November 1830 was a shambles of two former private houses and their annexes in Downing Street. One of the houses happened to contain a grand salon, which served (until 1856) better than anything in No. 10 for Cabinet meetings. But for the actual purposes of the office the arrangements were all very inconvenient. The Secretary of State himself apparently had to pass through two other offices in order to reach the Cabinet room; the 'library' was scattered all over the place; and the printers' machines and fount placed in the attics threatened to crush the 'rickety old shored-up buildings' beneath them. It is not surprising, therefore, to find Palmerston urging within a very few years the construction of a more imposing and efficient set of buildings and while still a bachelor in 1836 pointing in particular to the need for special facilities to dine at one go forty or fifty guests. Possibly he hoped to take advantage of a fire that broke out in the reference room during the Christmas holidays at the beginning of that year. Foreign Office legend, which afterwards muddled the date of the incident, recollects that while some elusive clerk shouted mockingly after Palmerston, in reference to the interminable records of the Belgian conference, 'for God's sake take care of the protocols', the Foreign Secretary had gone straight to the attic floor to convey a gentle warning about the fire to the old German translator still working there. Apart from setting the date of the fire aright, a contemporary report by one of the senior clerks mentions only that 'our chief acted as a chief should do'. Although a House of Commons select committee was appointed to investigate Palmerston's recommendations in 1839, it was not until 1861 that the old buildings were pulled down and it was July 1868 before the new ones in Whitehall were ready for occupation. By that time Palmerston was dead. But as Prime Minister he had nonetheless set his mark upon them, rejecting Sir Gilbert Scott's ornate Gothic design in favour of an Italianate façade; Scott, it was said, saved his Gothic plans for St Pancras station instead.[1]

In spite of the unsatisfactory buildings, Palmerston was not faced in 1830, as he was in the War Office twenty years before, with a mountain of arrears and an urgent need of wholesale reorganization and reform. The F.O., too, had its odd traditions, very eccentric hours and a deeply entrenched system of patronage and perquisites. Yet it was generally regarded, evidently with much justification, as an efficient department. That this was so owed something to the piecemeal improvements effected by Canning and still more, apparently, to his other, less tangible methods of encouraging effort and efficiency. The F.O., moreover, was in size much smaller and in scope much simpler than the War Office. There was an army of consuls and diplomats abroad who sent in a flood of reports as numerous perhaps as paymasters' returns. But to deal with these there was in 1830 a staff of only about thirty in contrast to the one hundred and more Palmerston had left behind him in the War Office two years before. Immediately beneath him in the F.O., however, Palmerston had not one but two Undersecretaries.[2]

The existence of two Undersecretaries derived from the fact that the modern F.O. had been formed towards the end of the eighteenth century by the partial amalgamation of two offices of State, and the differentiation between their origins, functions and prospects was still in process of evolution. The Undersecretaries were of equal rank in the office and, small perquisites apart, enjoyed the same salary on a scale of £2,000–£2,500 per annum. They were also both political appointments made personally by the minister, but by 1830, while one continued to be known as the 'political' Undersecretary and came and went with the minister, the other had stayed on and was already in process of becoming the 'permanent' Undersecretary. Throughout the whole of Palmerston's first and second periods at the F.O., in 1830–34 and 1835–41, this, the senior, Undersecretary was John Backhouse.[3]

Canning had brought Backhouse from an office stool into Government service in 1816 and had made him Foreign Undersecretary in 1827. Backhouse was evidently an able and industrious man, but dogged by ill-health. Already in the mid 1830s he was often forced to take long periods of leave, and was even contemplating an early retirement. In September 1835 Melbourne told Palmerston that if the post were to become vacant then his own secretary, Tom Young, would like to have it. This was rather an extraordinary suggestion, since Young had been exposed about a year before as being behind an unpleasant press attack on Althorp and Brougham. Quite possibly Melbourne was under some sort of pressure; Brougham said Young was not only his master's pimp but his blackmailer as well. It is clear from what Melbourne wrote, however, that he did not really support Young's appointment, though he expressed himself very discreetly; perhaps, therefore, he had reason to think that Palmerston was implicated in some of Young's press manipulations. In any case Backhouse held on. But his health did not improve. A newcomer to the office in March 1840 said he liked him 'very much', but found him 'nervous & fidgety'. Backhouse welcomed Aberdeen's return in 1841 with both 'delight and Gratitude'. A year later he nevertheless resigned, broken down apparently both in body and in mind, and died shortly after in 1845.[4]

It was unfortunate that Backhouse went when he did, since it opened up the way for Aberdeen to make a Tory appointment. The man he chose, Henry Unwin Addington, was a nephew of Sidmouth's and a plain reactionary. Worse still, he was a man whom Palmerston had forced to retire from the diplomatic service more than a decade earlier as being too stupid and too ill-willed. It was probably also Addington who was responsible for getting Aberdeen into something of a mess over the Oregon negotiations with the United States. In the office he was for some reason nicknamed 'Pumpy', but he does not seem to have been popular and in 1848 he got into an awful row with the Chief Clerk Lenox Conyngham, who was possibly still more detested in the office. Palmerston, who disliked them both, supported the Permanent Undersecretary in the contest for seniority, but he must have been very glad when in 1854 Addington at last surrendered his place to a strong partisan of his own, Edmund Hammond.[5]

During Palmerston's lifetime the role of the other, 'political' or 'governmental', Undersecretary gradually evolved into that of 'parliamentary' Undersecretary. This was because most nineteenth-century Foreign Secretaries were English peers with seats in the House of Lords, and needed well-informed, responsible spokesmen to deputize for them in the Commons. As M.P.s neither Canning nor Palmerston had had much need of these; Canning had even checked the practice of the Undersecretaries being M.P.s at all, and made them look for prospects of promotion to the diplomatic service rather than to politics. But the appointment was still very much a personal one and this was why Palmerston was able to offer it in the first instance in 1830 to Lady Cowper's son-in-law, even though Ashley was a Tory M.P. Although the office was not then considered to be one of profit under the Crown, Ashley would presumably have had at once to give up his seat and, perhaps, substitute a diplomatic career for his philanthropic future. For the first reason, if not the second, he declined the honour, though his voluminous diaries continued to the last to underline how strong his interest was in foreign affairs. So, after a delay of two or three days and a petulant enquiry from a 'certain Galway baronet', Palmerston offered the post instead to Shee.[6]

Although Shee was another old friend and Palmerston had glowingly defended his work as Agent-General for Militia, it is pretty clear that he never enjoyed the same degree of personal intimacy or official confidence as Sulivan. In the first place his pretensions were greater than his station or his competence justified, and they occasionally irritated even his old friend. 'Don't be a goose,' wrote Palmerston when Shee complained of being overlooked at the formation of Grey's Administration, 'but come to Town forthwith.' Among diplomats and politicians Shee soon acquired the reputation of being Palmerston's *âme intime* at the F.O. Probably Shee did take on some of the dirtier jobs and certainly he had the special, and distinctly unsavoury, role of press manager. In the second place a couple of unfortunate marriages contrasted ill with Sulivan's wise choice of Lilly Temple. His poor first wife, who bored and distracted him with her inconvenient illnesses, died in October

1832. Subject to epileptic fits, she fell out of a boat while fishing and was drowned. 'The manner of the thing was shocking,' Palmerston wrote, 'but the thing itself is no loss to him.' Shee accepted all the more readily the promotion to Berlin which Palmerston offered him in 1834. But the appointment shocked people in and out of the service and was cancelled by Wellington during his brief tenure of the Foreign Office in 1834-5. Since the duke's intervention was perfectly proper, Palmerston was rather annoyed by Shee's complaints of ill treatment and still more so by the attempt he made to claim the 'outfit' expenses for both posts when Palmerston's return to office secured for him the legation in Stuttgart instead. In Stuttgart Shee once more tried to assume a rather special role among the German states and meddled this time with the foreign press. Palmerston does not seem by any means to have discouraged him, though he authorized the buying of occasional articles rather than of whole newspapers. But in October 1844 Shee was recalled from Württemberg and never returned to the service. He had finally wrecked his chances, apparently, by marrying his mistress. It was the Tories again who sacked him, and Shee thought Palmerston ought to offer him a new job on his return to the F.O. in 1846. But Palmerston agreed completely with what Aberdeen had done. Respectable English and foreign visitors might call with their wives and daughters on a minister who kept his mistress upstairs and out of sight, but not, Palmerston admonished, on one who produced her belatedly as his wife. What hypocrisy, perhaps, and certainly what a change since Naples in the days of Lady Hamilton and Palmerston's parents.[7]

In 1834 Palmerston had offered Shee's place in the F.O. to Lady Cowper's eldest son, Fordwich. The prospect caused some surprise: Fordwich suffered from ill health like his father and had also a considerable reputation as gambler, libertine and idler. But he held the post only a few days until Melbourne's Government collapsed and he did not return with Palmerston in 1835. Instead the place went on Fred Lamb's recommendation to an old aide of his in Vienna who was a close connection of Holland's and a brother-in-law of Lansdowne's, William Fox-Strangways, afterwards fourth Earl of Ilchester.[8]

Strangways's was an odd recommendation and a strange appointment, for someone had already given Lady Cowper to understand that he was 'certainly a very dense fellow'. Others merely thought him 'a curious specimen', good-natured, but more interested in gardening than politics. But with both the Hollands and the Lansdownes always pestering him on Strangways's behalf Palmerston probably buried his doubts. Unfortunately these soon proved only too well-founded, for Strangways was neither particularly industrious nor completely reliable. Worse still, he did not get on with his chief, in part perhaps because he tried to assume more authority than Shee had had. Before long Palmerston was finding fault with his Undersecretary over inaccurate estimates and snapping at him 'for not looking sharper after the matter'. Once he even chastised him for sending papers after him into the country by special messenger, when the mail coach would have done, and 'that at a time when constituents & races, and ordinaries and balls overfill every minute of the day & when I could not have read or written a line if you had sent me twenty messengers'. After four years Palmerston decided he had had just about enough. 'Strangeways[*sic*]', he wrote to Fred Lamb in August 1839, ' is utterly incompetent to do anything, but make foolish suggestions about insignificant trifles. . . . he has not force of mind to dive to the bottom of anything. I must get rid of him & put him to some small mission. He is worse than useless to me.' Strangways, everybody heard, was equally unhappy. So when a vacancy loomed up in Frankfurt towards the end of the year Palmerston jumped at the chance it gave him. Strangways refused the offer, grumbling to everyone that it was not good enough and making Palmerston doubt that he really wanted to leave the F.O. at all. For several months he dithered and delayed, but Palmerston had already offered the undersecretaryship to his successor, and finally, after three months' battle, Strangways gave way.[9]

The new Undersecretary at the F.O. in March 1840 was Granville's son, Lord Leveson, who having made a promising beginning in the Commons a few years before now gave up his seat to take his new appointment. The appointment was almost certainly made to please his father, for relations between Palmerston and Granville had about this time begun to be a little strained owing to differences over the Mehemet Ali question. But Leveson was not a success. About a year earlier Granville had expressed considerable doubt about taking up another offer because, he said, it was important for his son to have a place where the necessity of hard work would overcome his 'idle habits'. Leveson's parents also feared that he might find it rather awkward to be working with Fanny Cowper's stepfather. Instead it was his engagement very soon afterwards to another girl that strained relations between them. Palmerston, it was said, did not think he had any business getting married so soon after entering upon so arduous an office and he scolded the young man for his irregular attendance. Very probably Palmerston was recalling the difficulties Canning had had with Fitzharris; but possibly it was because the bride was a foreigner – she was Acton's mother – that he so disapproved. Very soon Leveson's letters to his parents showed a distinct shift of sympathy from his chief towards the harassed and complaining clerks.[10]

When Palmerston returned to the F.O. in 1846, Leveson did not go with him, though his translation in the meantime to the Lords might have made him more useful than before. Instead Palmerston chose Edward Stanley (later Lord Stanley of Alderley). Quite why or how this came about is unknown. Although a *bon viveur* Stanley was notorious for his bad temper; he was nicknamed Ben on account of it, after Sir Benjamin Backbite. When he took over the Post Office some years later he was described by one of the clerks there as 'cross-grained and tyrannical, . . . stingy to the letter-carriers and messengers, . . . [and] insolent and overbearing to his subordinates'. Perhaps in the F.O. he made a useful foil to his chief's mellowing personality. Certainly they seem to have got on well enough, which is all the more remarkable in view of their former behaviour. For Stanley had been plotting to exile Palmerston to the Lords in 1836, more than a year after most others had given up all hope; and Palmerston knew that in 1840 Stanley had been helping Russell to counter his Eastern policy in the press. But by 1846 all this was in the past. Palmerston did not seem to mind that Stanley had once been Durham's secretary, nor Stanley that Palmerston had once approached his bride. Durham after all was dead, and Stanley was too full of admiration perhaps for Fanny Jocelyn.[11]

Beneath the Undersecretaries the business of the F.O. was divided among an administrative department and six other 'divisions'. The first was headed by the Chief Clerk (Thomas Bidwell in 1830), who supervised domestic affairs and office discipline and kept the accounts of both the office and the diplomatic service. He was in short what Bidwell's successor would have liked to have been specifically acknowledged, a sort of *chef du bureau*. None of the four senior clerks beneath him did any political business either. One, Frederick ('Poodle') Byng, the third in seniority in 1830, assisted the Chief Clerk in examining the accounts of foreign missions. Another, Henry Rolleston, then fourth in seniority, looked after treaties and Royal Letters. The first senior clerk (Thomas Bidwell's cousin, John) looked after the Consular Department founded by Canning in 1825, and the second senior clerk (James Bandinel) directed the Slave-trade Department. The other four divisions were political ones, and were contrived in 1831 by splitting each of the Undersecretaries' departments into two.[12]

In 1830 the Undersecretaries were still notionally equal in status and in pay. But Canning had long since restricted the disbursement of secret service money to Backhouse and, following a House of Commons select committee recommendation about 'parliamentary under-secretaries', the Treasury ordered that the salary of his colleague should be reduced to £1,500 from 5 April 1831. Palmerston tried again, as he had in the War Office before, to help his friend Shee, arguing in particular that he was after all not an M.P. But he failed and henceforth he too felt compelled to consider Shee the 'junior under-secretary'. The two Undersecretaries continued, however, to divide the affairs of the world between them, as in the eighteenth-century system of completely separate departments of State, with each supervising the work of two 'political' divisions. The distribution of work betweeen them was far from equal. Already the 'permanent' Undersecretary's two divisions customarily included three out of four of the most important countries – France, Russia and (from 1831) Turkey – and this inequity was further reflected in the amount of paper work handled by their respective divisions. Conscientious and dedicated though he was, Backhouse frequently complained of the unfair burden placed upon him and, as the business of the office increased, proposed in 1838 a fairer redistribution of the world with Fox-Strangways. In the long run the unequal burden further consolidated the nascent primacy of the permanent official; but it was not until 1848 that the Permanent Under-secretary was formally recognized as the head of the office, over the Chief Clerk.[13]

Although the system possibly worked well enough, the labour was so un-evenly distributed that from the beginning it was offensive to Palmerston's tidy mind. He particularly objected to the fact that the Chief Clerk and the four senior (or first-class) clerks should have virtually no political work, while the two Undersecretaries had to supervise four political divisions and a staff of about a dozen third- and fourth-class (junior and assistant junior) clerks, with the help of only three out of the seven second-class clerks. In February 1831 he changed the office title of the second-class clerks in charge of the political divisions from the misleading 'private secretaries' to that of 'clerks assistant' to the Undersecretaries; then, at Backhouse's request, he added a fourth to their number in April 1836 so that each division should have one. He also indicated how strongly he felt that such positions should be filled by senior clerks and called for a thorough-going review of the work the senior clerks did at present.[14]

The Chief Clerk's duties, Palmerston had already discovered, were very slight, and those of the superintendent of the Treaty Department a positive sinecure. He had found it far from easy, however, to make the senior clerks take on any share of political work. Rolleston had sent him a heart-rending account of how for month after month and from five or six in the morning till late at night he had dedicated himself to the treaties of peace – nearly twenty years before! Palmerston could not have been impressed; but, as at the W.O., he thought it best to proceed by the process of natural attrition. When Rolleston died in 1834 Palmerston tried to make his successor, George Lenox Conyngham, add the affairs of China to his care of treaties. After his death in 1866 Lenox Conyngham would be remembered in the office as a dedicated and hard-working man. But he had lost a leg in youth and was made bad-tempered by the pain he suffered, especially in wet weather. He certainly protested in 1834 at being expected to take on political work, and while Wellington took over the F.O. for a brief period in 1834-5 the change was not enforced upon him. But soon after Palmerston's return, it was; and by 1840 Lenox Conyngham's China and Bandinel's slave-trade business had vaguely been placed under Leveson's general supervision. So Lenox Conyngham's grumbles continued. The China business might not have been heavy at first, he said, but it had soon become so. It included important private correspond-ence with the British agent in Canton, which was unusual at such an early date. Lenox Conyngham was right, moreover, to detect in Palmerston's orders an important precedent. For his chief was well aware that both Thomas Bidwell and Fred Byng were near retiring age, and Palmerston planned to take advantage of their going to undertake a complete rearrange-ment of their work.[15]

Palmerston uncovered his plan to the office on 12 March 1839, a couple of months before Byng's retirement. Its crucial feature was the abolition of the chief clerkship when Bidwell also went. Obviously the intention was to redress the balance at the top in favour of political business. But he was probably very much surprised when his plan was met with almost universal horror; Palmerston's 'Papier Monstre', they called it in the office. The two Under-secretaries, though troubled in the past by Bidwell's inefficiency, nevertheless blanched at the extra responsibility the abolition of his post would throw on them; Lenox Conyngham, with his eye clearly upon the succession, vigorously protested; and, with the exception of the raw recruits, the whole of the office signed a remonstrance against proposals they saw would make their bad promotion prospects even worse. There followed a war of memoranda and counter-memoranda, until a hard bargain was struck. Palmerston agreed to retain the chief clerkship, to accelerate promotion and to compensate those who could not be promoted; and Lenox Conyngham and others evidently agreed in return not to oppose the Foreign Secretary's filling vacancies among the senior clerks with heads of political divisions. So when Byng retired Palmerston was able to give his duties to Bidwell and his senior clerkship to one of the clerks assistant; and when Bidwell was finally pushed out, a year or so over his time in 1841, Lenox Conyngham, as the new Chief Clerk, retained his treaty business while giving up his political work and his senior clerkship to another of the clerks assistant.[16]

In the meantime the Treasury nearly upset Palmerston's side of the bargain by making difficulties about the additional expense involved. They accepted Palmerston's request for a net increase of two in the F.O. establishment, but they did not like it that the compromise proposals they were sent in July 1839 should have envisaged a significant improvement in the ratio of senior to junior posts, and new special allowances for those who did not benefit as a result, without such compensating attractions as the abolition of the chief clerkship. False hopes were raised in August 1839 when it was heard in the office that the Chancellor of the Exchequer was to be sweetened by having a son appointed to their number. The Hon. Charles Spring Rice did enter the F.O. – he had a very good hand – and eventually he became Assistant Undersecretary and father of a famous ambassador. But Lord Monteagle gave up the Exchequer that same month and his successor, Francis Baring, began all the Treasury objections anew. Not until March 1840 was Baring's consent 'reluctantly' conceded and not until August 1841 was the new establishment formally approved.[17]

The clerks had sometimes suspected that Palmerston was ratting on them. But in the end he not only got the new salaries backdated, but also had the net increase of two made in the number of senior rather than second- or third-class clerks, and so was able to complete the promotion to that rank of all the former clerks assistant. Not everyone was pleased. Two second-class clerks, who had seen themselves passed over in favour of clerks assistant, protested that Palmerston had violated the established principle of promotion by seniority. Palmerston had no patience with that principle. It was, he had written only a short time before, 'the prescriptive right of idleness and dullness to succeed hackney coachlike from bottom to top of an office by dint of more living'. So he announced in reply that 'in promoting from one class to another my rule has been and will be to select the individuals whom I may think the best qualified without reference to seniority'. In practice this 'rule' was applied rigidly only to the more senior posts, and in the junior ranks promotion went by seniority as long as there was ability enough to warrant it. But after so many promotions in 1839-41 there seems little doubt that future prospects dimmed. Nor were the numbers in the new establishment enough. 'It will', one anxious junior had said of the 1839 proposal, 'raise the establishment to the number Canning said was absolutely essential & the work is now doubled.' There was a further increase before 1849, but Palmerston continued to create more work than clerks to handle it. If efficiency and morale were high and could in part be said to be 'owing to a due proportion having long existed between the work to be done and the number of those who are to do it', it had also, a F.O. retort to the Treasury insisted in 1850, to 'be attributed in no small degree to the intelligence and right feeling of the heads of department'. Both these latter, Undersecretaries as well as the minister himself, it appeared, still spent much of the day working at home. Subsequently an avalanche of business during the Crimean War forced a substantial increase in the number of clerks. [18]

Palmerston's very limited F.O. reforms were designed to tidy up and not at all to increase the scope of real responsibility enjoyed by even its most senior staff. He knew that in Paris and Vienna very much more was done for the ministers. But that, he thought, was dangerous, as he once explained to Granville:

I infer from all these quarrels in which France is embroiled with foreign states that her relations with other Powers are left to the conduct of the clerks of departments instead of being really managed by the responsible Ministers. Your clerk of a department is always for some measure of great vigour without much consideration of its expediency or justice. He is pleased at the notion of producing an effect, and, if a principal signs and does all that is thus proposed to him, he is sure to get into difficulties.

The superintendents of the Consular and Slave-trade Departments (which his 1841 'reforms' also separated) did enjoy a considerable degree of independence, largely because of the technical nature of their work and the length of time each had held his post. But so disappointing did John Bidwell's successors turn out to be that the Consular Department also lost its relative independence in 1854. An appointee of Palmerston's, Francis Cavendish, was given *carte blanche* to clear it out in 1858 and after eighteen months was transferred to the Slave-trade Department, which he considered was 'the least interesting of any'. [19]

It was not until the 1860s, long after Palmerston had gone, that even the Permanent Undersecretary was able to assume the role of political adviser, while his colleague declined in importance as merely a parliamentary spokesman. Before that, and under Palmerston in particular perhaps, the Undersecretaries were both little more than intermediaries. When illness confined him to his bed in Stanhope Street in April 1833, and reduced him to dictating brief outlines of dispatches to Shee, his doctor asked him why on earth he did not leave more of the work to his Undersecretaries. 'When I communicate to them my ideas,' Palmerston was supposed to have replied, 'I leave them to embody them in suitable phrases. They are both clever, sharp enough, and with much command of their pen; but what they tell and write, however instructed, is not what I should have said or written.' Fox-Strangways's main fault, Palmerston complained in August 1839, was that he had been quite unable to act even on outline instructions. Leveson had described his own position in 1840 as that of a 'sandwich'. He also recalled that Palmerston almost never spoke to him about any of the subjects with which he dealt. This does not appear to have been literally true, though apparently it was very nearly so when he first entered the office. Perhaps more out of nervousness than daring, he went into Palmerston's room to ask a question soon after entering the F.O. in March 1840. Palmerston was evidently surprised but 'very civil' about it, and soon Leveson was habitually doing so. This, Backhouse told him, was what they used to do in Canning's day. But since then, apparently, they had been summoned or sought advice only by communications on paper. According to Leveson Palmerston must have recognized how much trouble the change would save him; perhaps Leveson's hand, which was notoriously illegible in later years, was already too bad for him to tolerate.[20]

As far as the Undersecretaries' duties were concerned, then, Palmerston did little or nothing more than to impose regulation and system on what had previously been practised. By a regulation of 1829 royal messengers were obliged to deliver dispatches direct into the hands of an Undersecretary in or out of office hours; during Palmerston's time it was still the practice to require one or other Undersecretary to be always on duty and, when there was a Sunday Cabinet, to have in addition a few clerks as well. 'Backhouse and Strangways', wrote Palmerston, 'are very much like the two figures in the Weather House and rusticate and labour alternately.' Backhouse, it would also appear, habitually took the morning shift, being in the office long before the rest came along at noon and being relieved by Shee, and presumably later by Strangways, at four in the afternoon. It is not clear, however, that the duty Undersecretary was always required actually to be in the office itself; an F.O. minute of July or August 1834 suggests that he had only to be 'in town', and the diary of a junior clerk appears to indicate that in 1837 it was already from among the junior clerks that a resident duty officer was found. By 1841, certainly, there were two clerks – and by 1861 four clerks – always in residence to receive dispatches coming in out of hours and, after docketing them with the date of receipt, to forward them to the Undersecretary's London home. The Undersecretary then passed the dispatches on to the Foreign Secretary, who would minute them with his instructions and return them to the office for registration and action. The only material difference during office hours was that the dispatch would be registered first and the whole process, subject only to the minister's whereabouts, handled internally.[21]

With few exceptions (principally, apart from Lenox Conyngham's Chinese letters, in the making of straightforward summaries and abstracts) the task of even the most senior clerks, where political business was concerned, was merely to compose replies based on the Foreign Secretary's outlines and usually to make fair copies of what he had written out in full. In 1854 Addington told a Treasury Committee, who wished to introduce an inferior class of copying clerk, that it was impracticable in the F.O. to distinguish between 'intellectual' and 'mechanical' work. In any case the work was too confidential to be entrusted to any but 'gentlemen', and gentlemen would have to be paid appropriately. Moreover, another F.O. paper had earlier observed, the variety of papers to be copied 'so well excited' the interest of the clerks that it could not properly be classed with 'ordinary copying'; it tended, 'in truth, rather to expand than to contract the intellect'. More convincing, surely, was what one of those clerks had scratched with a diamond on the window pane of the old F.O.:

> *Je suis copiste*
> *Affreux métier!*
> *Joyeux ou triste*
> *Toujours copier!*

Even the Undersecretaries did little more than to check the style and content of what the clerks had written. They even passed incoming domestic letters unopened to their chief. Foreign ones they did open, apparently to help to keep themselves informed; Backhouse once asked to have 'a selection of any dispatches of special interest' sent to him when he was away ill. But it is difficult to understand why he should have bothered, since 'Lord Palmerston', Shee explained in 1832, 'never consults an Under Secretary. He merely sends out questions to be answered or papers to be copied when he is here in the evenings.'[22]

The 'unsocial hours' the clerks were called upon to work do seem to have had something to do with their well-known resentment against Palmerston. Twice in 1832 some of them protested about the late hours they were forced to keep. On the first occasion they were provoked by their Minister's simultaneously cutting down their perquisites and he acknowledged there was justice in their protest by granting special compensation. A few months later there followed another protest, this time from an anonymous but 'well-meaning friend', complaining that they were being kept from their dinners at home and so forced to yet further expense in eating out. Palmerston certainly did not introduce these unpopular hours at the F.O. When he assumed office he was informed that the clerks worked at home in the mornings, to the detriment of their health and of their 'domestick economy and comfort', but were required to attend at the office by noon and stay on as late as seven or eight, sometimes even till nine or ten. But Palmerston's constant need of reassuring preparation, combined with his irregular private life, probably made the clerks' resort to overtime both more frequent and more uncertain.[23]

Since Palmerston's policy was also so controversial, among colleagues as well as in Parliament, the clerks were often kept busy searching records for precedents with which he could fend off attacks. 'F.O. at 11', recorded an embittered junior clerk on 5 April 1834, 'for damned papers on Spanish & Portuguese affairs for dispute in House of Lords.' Once when Brougham, having been ejected from the Cabinet, gave warning of an attack on the Government's slave-trade policy in February 1838, this same junior clerk – he was Walter Scott's younger son Charles – recorded how returning home at midnight from a Sunday evening chop he found an urgent summons to the F.O. written a mere three hours before. He ignored it and went to bed. But even though others had been hard at work while he slept that night, he found when he turned up at the office the following morning that there was still a great deal to do in order to arm Melbourne in the Lords to Palmerston's satisfaction. The librarian, Hertslet, also recalled that when the famous attack on Palmerston's Greek policy came on in 1850 they all had to search through some two or three thousand volumes of manuscripts.[24]

The ups and downs of politics and foreign affairs as well as interference by bad weather with cross-channel mails inevitably made routine impossible to attain. 'Hard' and 'busy' days at the office chequered the brief and bitter entries in young Scott's diaries. 'Sadly bothered at F.O.,' he would write; or 'fagged away at F.O. till completely knocked up'. Once, on 30 April 1837, he recorded: 'Worked for F.O. at home from 10 to 5.' At other times there was very little to do indeed. Scattered among Scott's 'hard' and 'busy' days are similar numbers of 'idle' ones with 'nothing to do'. But it is equally evident that it was the late and uncertain hours kept by his chief and the insistence on someone always being in attendance that upset the clerks most. Once, when Palmerston called unexpectedly with Emily and found the head of one department absent, she had gently to remind him that some people went to church on Sundays. However, during the very busy periods of the Greek and Belgian conferences, many of the clerks, and also the librarian and the sub-librarian, were often kept at hand even on a Sunday. The preparation of papers for Cabinet or Commons similarly played havoc with their lives. 'Went to F.O. about ¼p. 4,' wrote Scott on Christmas Day 1838, 'but everyone had left.' The following day, however, he was 'hard at work at F.O. preparing Persian Papers for printing for the Cabinet'. Two days later he and another clerk were still going at it and even on the Sunday they were in the F.O. from two until four. Even so the Persian papers were not all arranged in time to avoid a severe embarrassment in Parliament.[25]

The clerks, as Scott's diary makes very clear, often made up for their evening and weekend hours by coming very late to the office next day – sometimes not until four – and occasionally, when Palmerston was out of town, by staying away altogether. It was also easy enough for them to slip away in mid afternoon to gobble a chop nearby. But the situation obviously deteriorated. In April 1831 one senior clerk had written: 'Palmerston is much liked in the office – tho' he has killed off some of the young ones by hard work.' Ten years later Palmerston's triumphs had made him 'the dominating star', but he was by no means worshipped in the office. 'Bright' he was, Charles Scott admitted to Maria Edgeworth; indeed 'the cleverest of them all as to absolute ability but insufferably unfeeling and disliked by all under him – each under unbearable discord crying out against him as loud as they dare and cursing deep.' Within a couple of years of entering office, it seems, Palmerston had begun to stay away in the early afternoon in order to get his work done in peace and quiet at home. But his turning up later at the office kept both clerks and messengers waiting on him more often than they liked, especially when he broke off to visit the House of Commons and by coming back again kept some of them around well into the night. A man about town like Poodle Byng must then have deeply resented the disruption in his social life, even if, as one of his juniors records, he retired on full pension in 1839 after forty years of 'far niente'. Scott, the disappointed son of a famous father, also bitterly complained of the casual way 'My Lord' would arrive around five or six, just as everyone else was preparing to leave, and keep them waiting more and more often till eight or nine at night. Things seem to have become worse in this respect after Palmerston's return to office in 1835. The autumn of that year was a particularly bad time. 'Ld P. continues his bad habits,' Scott recorded on 26 October, '& did not make his appearance at the F.O. till after 6 so nearly 8 before I cd get away.' But there was worse to come: before the end of 1840, when the Eastern crisis pressed, Scott sometimes found himself not leaving until around midnight. On one occasion, it was afterwards remembered by others against Palmerston, he kept them copying dispatches almost all night while he was at the opera. On another, in October 1838, Scott recorded, 'Messenger for St Petersburg. Ld P. sent out his long notes of 17 sheets *of course late.*'[26]

Scott evidently thought that such behaviour would rarely have been necessary but for the selfishness of his chief. 'He is so reckless of the feelings and time of his Clerks and *Messengers*', he told Maria Edgeworth,

that he will send for a messenger say go to Constantinople immediately and bid the clerks get ready dispatches and take a pen to make out the minute for their orders for Despatches But keeping them all – pens up – mouths open ears cocked waiting – he will lay down his pen and turn to the box of arrears of letters and set about looking them over and minuting for them – regardless of both Clerks in the office and messenger in the antechamber cooling or kicking his poor heels – and when at length reminded of Messenger in waiting "Oh too late for today. Let him be here tomorrow" – and tomorrow tomorrow – and tomorrow – fresh kicking heels – if not cooling temper the Messenger is doomed to endure and this sometimes for 10 days consecutively.[27]

Gradually increasing resort to the telegraph would cut down the number of King's Messengers, but in 1830 there were no less than eighteen of these very expensive individuals in the service of the F.O. Yet Palmerston would still find it necessary to order extra efforts, occasionally, as he was entitled to do, calling on the home messengers to go on foreign service and keeping the foreign messengers waiting hours and even days without any consideration for their time or the nation's purse. It does not seem to have been by any means a rare practice for Foreign Secretaries to order messengers to hire small boats to take them across the Channel. On one occasion Palmerston did so because a dinner engagement with the Lievens made him too late with his Vienna letters for them to catch the regular packet. Until someone pointed out that their companions might be of actual help, he thought of forbidding messengers to economize by carrying passengers in their carriages and he condemned as not 'secure' the resort to private travellers, which had been made during his brief absence from the office in 1834-5, in place of the very expensive special courier between London and St Petersburg. One senior clerk told Granville that £11,000 had been spent in a single year on special arrangements to overtake the mail with the private letters Palmerston had failed to write in time. And Scott, when noting on 4 May 1840 that £64,000 for F.O. postage and £7,000 for messengers had been additionally voted in Parliament that day, suggested that these amounts had been deliberately left out of the previous F.O. estimates in order to make things look better than they were.[28]

Palmerston's prodigality did not pass unnoticed outside the F.O. When, in attempting to cross the Channel in February 1832, young Gladstone found the Ostend packet detained three hours in Dover for the results of Palmerston's Belgian diplomacy, he tersely entered in his diary: 'a strong proof of his incompetency to conduct the affairs of the country, that he should have kept us waiting thus long.' Palmerston had another view, as he told Granville when he heard in November that same year that the French wished to introduce into a new postal convention an undertaking not to delay mails and packets:

This may sound very easy or even very pretty on paper, but I cd not possibly have carried on my business during the last two years under such an engagement as that. I am perpetually obliged to detain both mails & packets from the physical impossibility of getting my dispatches closed in time for the usual period of departure, and the greatest public inconvenience wd very often have arisen from my being obliged to keep till the next post day, the communics wh. wd have been too late for the mail or packet.

In short they might as well ask me to regulate by Treaty the hours of attendance of my clerks or the time a King's Messenger may take to drive down to Windsor.[29]

It was another kind of disregard for others that probably upset the clerks the most. For the Foreign Office drew most of its recruits from the younger sons of

the aristocracy, often university men, and whether they were in the legitimate
line of descent or not they seem to have found more irksome than the hours or
even the drudgery of copying the manner their chief adopted towards them.
They had not liked, for example, being summoned to the Secretary by a bell
and had been grateful to Canning for abolishing the practice. They must also
have been irritated in a very similar way by some of those famous office
memoranda of Palmerston's. Occasionally they exuded what seems to have
been good humour. As the lower age of entry into the office was sixteen or
seventeen, though most entered a year or two later, a room was set aside in the
attics as the 'nursery', where young men could amuse themselves with the
piano, foils or boxing gloves with which they stocked it. Once, as young men
will, they fell to flashing mirrors into the faces of the pretty dressmakers across
the way, and when the other residents complained, Palmerston checked his
fledgelings with a kindly enquiry as to the identity of the 'unmannerly youths
who have been casting Reflections on young ladies opposite'. His absolute ban
on smoking was certainly more seriously meant, and probably much more
irritating; but his attitude was quite conventional – it was one of the few
things he shared with Addington, who also tried to ban smoking in the nursery
– and quite often circumvented by a visit to the rooms of one of the resident
clerks. More resented were Palmerston's strictures, to clerks and diplomats
alike, on the use of bad ink, bad paper and a bad hand. Some of them are
always worth repeating.[30]

In minute after minute throughout the rest of his life Palmerston objected
to handwriting which could only be compared to 'Iron Railings leaning out of
the perpendicular' and letters sloping backwards 'like the raking masts of an
American schooner'. One writer was told that he 'should form his letters by
connecting his slanting down strokes by visible lines at top or bottom according to the letters which he intends his parallel lines to represent'; another that
reading his hand was 'like running Penknives into one's Eyes'. When in
September 1835 a consul in Venezuela was promoted, Palmerston wrote:
'Request him to have his despatches written in a larger hand now that he is
chargé d'affaires.' High and low, ambassadors and consuls, all received
rebuke. 'These Consuls are too bad,' he wrote in 1851; 'there is hardly one of
them that writes a decent hand and with readable Ink. . . . if they do not write
larger and more legibly, and with black Ink, I shall be obliged to send all their
despatches back to them to be written over again; and if they do not pay more
attention to their Instructions, other persons will be found who will do so. . . .
Life is not long enough to decipher their scribbling.' When the attachés in
Vienna put him 'out of all patience by the paleness' of their ink, he told them
he had put them at the bottom of the lists for promotion and warned them
that if they did not mend their ways they too would get the sack. And on a
number of despatches from the minister in Mexico he wrote in 1837: 'Send Mr
Pakenham back one of these invisible ink dispatches & say that I hope I shall
not again have to observe upon such a neglect of standing instructions.' Ten

The greater Portion
of the Foreign Office
Hands are Excellent
and admired by all
but there are some
few on the Establish
ment who might
improve their Hand
writing if they would
take more Pains
to form their letters
distinctly

℘ 20/11–48

Foreign Office Minute on Handwriting by Palmerston, 1848

years later he was having to say much the same to the ambassador in Madrid. It was not only his own convenience he had in mind; it was very important, he said, that the ink used in the office and abroad should last. In January 1833 he had a circular sent round to all ministers and consuls 'requiring them to be more careful to use good ink in their communications to this office; the paleness of the writing makes their dispatches frequently inconvenient to read, & renders them less durable as Public Records.'[31]

Palmerston paid no less attention to style and punctuation. 'Write private to Mr Wilson and Mr Hamilton', he directed, 'to say that . . . all dispatches . . . should comprize the matter which they contain within the smallest compass consistent with perspicuity. I should wish that after they have written their dispatches and before they have them copied out for signature they would run them over and strike out all words which may not be necessary for fully conveying their meaning.' When the two offenders still persisted he minuted for the one:

Mr Belford Wilson seems to think that Secretaries of State have nothing else to do but to read his despatches, admire his long sentences, his multitude of words, and his never-ending remarks. It is highly desirable that he should be more pithy and concise.

and for the other:

If Mr Hamilton would let his substantives and adjectives go single instead of always sending them forth by Twos and Threes at a time, his dispatches would be clearer and easier to read.

Naturally Palmerston's office clerks came in also for their share of criticism. On a badly worded draft he wrote:

The construction of sentences is stiff, strained, and roundabout; words are used in meanings which they are not accustomed to bear, and relatives and antecedents are so mixed up as to leave the meaning of sentences often obscure. Sentences should be constructed to begin with the nominative, to go on with the verb, and to end with the accusative, and the mind of the person who reads should follow the sentence without effort. Life is not long enough to correct them and put them into plain English, planting Sugar Canes would not be more laborious.

He had a particular dislike of gallicisms. He had one diplomatist rebuked for using 'adhesion' when he meant 'adherence'; another for making a 'reclamation,' when he intended a 'complaint'. He objected even to the use of the conventional phrase '*corps diplomatique*', insisting rather on 'diplomatic body'. His strictures on the use of 'intervention' instead of 'interference' are famous. In one of the first examination papers designed for entrance to the Foreign Office or diplomatic service in 1856 one question, as a preliminary to asking the candidates to distinguish in diplomatic usage between moral force and naval force, simply asked the difference between 'non-interference' and 'non-intervention'.[32]

Palmerston more than once avowed that the F.O. was 'not a spelling school'. He grew weary, he claimed, of correcting punctuation:

Write to the Stationery Office for a sufficient supply of Full Stops, Semi-colons, and Commas; but more especially Semi-colons, for the use of the copying clerks of the office; I furnish these things out of my own private stores when I have time to look over despatches for signature, but I am not always sufficiently at leisure to supply deficiencies.

Perhaps Foreign Office English was none the worse for a shortage of Palmerston's all purpose semi-colons. But since the clerks were, after all, copyists by trade, there was in general considerable justification in his attempts to raise their standards. For the same reason they ought also to have been grateful that someone with a history of headaches and eye trouble should have so reproved the diplomats and attachés who sent in so many thousands of reports they might one day have to copy. It was rather unreasonable of him, however, to demand of others as good a hand as his. And if a rich vein of humour sometimes softened the reproof – once when a waggish clerk presented him with but three lines to a page, Palmerston minuted upon it: 'The Writer of this Paper would write an excellent hand if he wrote a little larger' – a sarcastic tone too often intruded and in that lucid style of his made even greater the hurt. Leveson said that what he found most embarrassing was having to correct the English of some of the most senior and able clerks:

J. Bandinell for instance, who I believe knows as much about his department, the Slave Trade, as anyone can know on such a subject, expresses himself very awkwardly. It is disagreeable for me to correct, as if he was a schoolboy, all his sentences . . . and yet, if I do not do this, Palmerston sends it back, slashed about with very cutting observations.

On one occasion Bandinel was so disturbed by Palmerston's comments on his draft that he ordered it 'to be kept *for the hereafter*'. Flippancy cannot possibly have soothed hurt feelings either, especially with someone like Lenox Conyngham with his bad leg and bad temper. When Backhouse once protested how 'grievously disturbed' Conyngham was by a minute implying that he had, when a second-class clerk, been guilty of 'wilful neglect' where there was only unconscious omission, Palmerston merely responded: 'I am very glad the mistake did not occur . . . and, as it did not occur, of course, my remarks fall to the ground.'[33]

Palmerston, it seems, was not unaware of those who served him well, 'but', Holland observed, 'he often speaks more warmly in commendation of, than to, the person commended'. Moreover, while numbers in the F.O. were held down by economy and reduced by illness, its work expanded enormously during Palmerston's first period there. He required, as 'a standing and invariable rule of the office', that any communication it received should be duly acknowledged, if only to fend off accusations of neglect. 'When Parties who apply are allowed to remain for many weeks without any reply', he wrote, 'they naturally go about saying how idle and inattentive the Foreign Office is – not knowing the cause which has delayed the final answer, and the office thus gets a character the very reverse of what it deserves.' On a later occasion he revealed more plainly that it was himself he wished to protect by giving extra labour to the clerks: 'It is very disagreeable for me to be blamed individually in the House of Commons for omissions which arise from inattention on the part of the clerks in the office to the elementary routine of business.' At the same time the number of incoming dispatches doubled and the instructions sent out increased from under 3,500 in 1829 to nearly 9,000 in 1840. Much of this was due to the ever expanding interests of England, but much also personally to Palmerston's own vigour and activity. As Backhouse pointed out, Palmerston's particular desire to see all his agents kept properly informed had caused a rise in the number of circulars sent out by his department alone from 200 in 1829 to over 700 in 1831 and over 1,500 in 1832. When someone queried in 1835 whether or not a particular dispatch was to be copied for the embassy in Paris, Palmerston replied: 'Everything should go to Lord Granville unless I give a special direction to the contrary.' Years later it was still the same, and people wondered how the ambassador could possibly read it all. Palmerston no doubt assumed that everyone, especially in Paris, would be as assiduous as himself. And all this, in turn, multiplied the work of copying involved, for example, in the circulation to the Cabinet both of dispatches and of the daily bulletins Palmerston devised for those who were out of town. Even Backhouse, who usually made up the bulletins with the help of his two senior assistants, complained: '. . . the effect of this augmentation of labour and confinement having impaired the health of many of the clerks has reduced almost continually the number of those in attendance so that even for a double amount of work there has been fewer hands . . . I venture to entreat your Lordship if my services have any title to your consideration (I would also say in *mercy* to me) take this matter into your favourable consideration at the earliest convenient time.'[34]

During the brief interlude of Peel's first administration of 1834-5, advantage seems to have been taken of Palmerston's absence to wait until the original dispatches had been returned by the King before making copies for the Cabinet, or even for the Prime Minister. It took some weeks after his return for Palmerston to discover what he called this 'idle innovation'. When he did, he indignantly ordered the immediate reversion to the former practice of having copies made for the Prime Minister as soon as he had himself returned the dispatches and before they went off to the King. 'It is preposterous', he wrote 'that the First Lord of the Treasury should be kept in ignorance of dispatches till they have gone down to Windsor and come back again. If Lord Melbourne happens to be a few miles out of town himself this may keep him three or four days in arrear.' He was also very careful to keep the office up to the mark with the bulletins. When some of his colleagues complained that they had not been getting any, Backhouse explained that Palmerston often kept the dispatches till so late at night that there really was neither time nor assistance to tackle the bulletins as well as the copies. All he could suggest was that the work might be done in future before the dispatches were sent on to Palmerston, and he volunteered, poor man, to devote part of his mornings to any that came in early in the day. Preferring not to wait upon the convenience of others, Palmerston acknowledged that there had been a very great increase in the labour of the office and agreed that the bulletins could if necessary wait a day. But the complaints persisted and in the face of all excuses Palmerston insisted that it was up to the office to devise a system for knowing which Cabinet minister out of town required them, and that a daily bulletin of news should always be sent, even if it was merely to say 'there is no news' today. The practice was later discontinued, perhaps because of the greater resort to printing copies of dispatches for circulation. If so it merely transferred the burden from the clerks above to the printer below. 'The printer thinks', Backhouse once reported about a Cabinet memorandum of Palmerston's, 'that by working day and night and all Sunday he may be able to supply the copies on Monday afternoon.'[35]

It was probably a reflection of the amount as well as the nature of F.O. work that Palmerston enjoyed there the services, not only of two Undersecretaries, but of two private ones as well, though one, by then usually considered the junior, was called a précis-writer. The private secretary proper copied much of the private and confidential correspondence of a semi-official kind (though Palmerston's was so extensive that the regular clerks were sometimes also employed upon it), and the précis-writer made abstracts and copies of the outgoing official correspondence for his chief's private use. Each position was worth £300 a year, and neither had to be recruited from among the clerks, though the précis-writer usually was.[36]

Palmerston's first private secretary was Colonel John Walpole, a younger brother of the Earl of Orford and a veteran of the Peninsular War. He was three years younger than Palmerston and like him a bachelor. The war had left him with a crippled left arm and in 1830 he was M.P. for the family seat in King's Lynn. But he had become security for a brother officer and been left with the liability for a considerable sum when his friend fled the country. Palmerston, as 'an old friend', asked Grey to find him one of 'the inferior situations about the Ordnance or the Court'. But Grey, too, was indebted to Lord Orford for his proxy in the Lords and so when the earl said it was diplomatic service his brother wanted the Prime Minister passed him back to Palmerston. Walpole seems soon to have been performing very confidential services for his chief. In Palmerston's accounts for 1831 there appears one of those teasing entries: 'A. B. Walpole £100.' But he was obviously not a success in the F.O. and their 'friendship' was sorely tried. It was barely 1831 before Palmerston was complaining that he could not send Grey an important letter because Walpole had gone off with the keys. By the middle of 1832 at the latest, Palmerston was looking for an opportunity of removing him and glad that his increased financial troubles required him to be some distance from his creditors. In June he thought Walpole would take the Consulate-General in Guatemala; in September it was Chile instead. 'He grumbles at going to either,' Palmerston wrote, 'as if it was a favour he was doing me, instead of its being salvation for him. I believe he fancies himself fit to be Minister Plenipotentiary or an ambassador at St Petersburg. There is nothing so tiresome as people being dissatisfied when you go out of your way to do everything you can for them.' Walpole was still 'lingering' almost a year later in spite of Palmerston's attempts to hurry him off. But in May 1833 Palmerston had officially replaced him as his private secretary by his nephew Stephen.[37]

Having followed his father and his uncle to St John's, Stephen Henry Sulivan left after two years without taking his degree. When discussing whether he should go up in October 1830 as Fellow Commoner or Pensioner Palmerston had given the opinion that the advantage of the former would be for his nephew to be thrown into 'better society', while its disadvantage in encouraging expensive habits to the neglect of study would not apply in this particular case. But by laying so much stress on risks that he insisted did not arise he was perhaps implying with due politeness that both father and uncle knew very well they did. In any event Stephen went as Pensioner and not Fellow Commoner to St John's and though he subsequently acquired a so-called scholarship he was not very good at mathematics, and his father decided he might just as well not complete his academic career but begin in his chosen profession as soon as was allowed. Stephen was therefore withdrawn from college after only two years and appointed by Palmerston as F.O. clerk in 1832 and as his précis-writer a few months later.[38]

Rather incongruously for a Secretary of Legation of long standing, William Temple had acted a précis-writer hitherto while waiting for an appointment as minister, and whenever a move was rumoured for him the place had been eagerly sought for other youngsters. Lady Holland had thought of it for her son in June 1831 and Lady Cowper for Fordwich the following summer. But when Temple at last got his post abroad, the précis-writership went to Stephen Sulivan, and when Sulivan was promoted private secretary it was offered first to one of Grey's younger sons and went eventually to John Ponsonby, the son of Palmerston's old friend, Duncannon. This all made another old Whig, Lord Sefton, look very grim, seeing that his own son, who was already a clerk in the office, had been passed over. But Palmerston liked to use the post to bring in new blood; in any case Francis Molyneux's handwriting provoked him 'beyond expression'.[39]

Stephen Sulivan seems to have been successful enough in the F.O.; it is doubtful otherwise if even avuncular affection would have kept him in the post of private secretary for the rest of Palmerston's first period in the office. For what it is worth Palmerston told his brother William in June 1833 that Stephen 'does his duty extremely well, and shows much industry and intelligence', and in October the same year that he 'makes a capital private secretary, and improves daily'. And just before he went out of office in November 1834 Palmerston took the trouble to find his nephew a paid attachéship abroad. Two years later Stephen was promoted Secretary of Legation. But he soon proved a failure as a diplomat. There may have been nothing particularly significant in the rather rapid moves he made from capital to capital during the 1830s. But his health was never very good, and when his younger brother went out to Munich to bring him home after a particularly dangerous attack in 1842, that sensitive young cleric found to his horror that his much respected elder brother had formed a shocking liaison with an Italian lady. All three, it seems, returned to England, in some expectation that it was for Stephen to die. But while Harry relapsed from the shock into a prolonged attack of madness Stephen miraculously recovered and in a rashness of generosity married the lady in recognition of her loyalty in such trying circumstances. With great hypocrisy Palmerston warned Stephen that he was putting his diplomatic career in jeopardy; after only a few years Stephen wrote to admit that he had made a dreadful mistake and, having separated from his wife and acquired a new mistress, to beg for another post as far away as possible. This time Palmerston promoted him Consul-General and chargé d'affaires – in Santiago de Chile. As an earnest of reform, perhaps, Sulivan took with him his wife rather than his mistress. But en route Mrs Sulivan quarrelled over some hotel rooms with the wife of a travelling U.S. consul and after joining in the verbal warfare her husband was publicly thrashed by the consul, who happened to be a 'Southern' man. A passing English traveller commented: 'He is certainly an uncommon ass and most unfit for his appointment.' He did not keep it long. In Santiago he made a new liaison and had another sort of duel. So in 1853 he was transferred to Lima, where the Foreign Secretary, Lord Clarendon, had to rebuke him for being 'too violent & too bullying'. He was assassinated there in August 1857 in circumstances in which politics and passion seemed only too mixed up.[40]

With Sulivan's successors in the F.O., Palmerston also had rather varied fortune. Just before he left office in November 1834 he had made a clerk of another of Lady Cowper's sons, and when he returned in April 1835 he made him his private secretary. The appointment of Spencer Cowper, as clearly one of Earl Cowper's sons as Fordwich was, must have made less noise than William Cowper's would have done, though it still annoyed Lady Jersey. She may have had an eye on the vacancy in the F.O. for a son of her own. If so, Palmerston had a lucky escape. For Francis Villiers seems to have been a ne'er-do-well, who, after a brief sojourn in the Commons in the 1850s, was said to have forged bills for £20,000 and fled the country. Spencer Cowper, on the other hand, was generally considered to be about the cleverest of Lady Cowper's sons, and as good tempered but gayer than his father. Even Lady Holland thought him 'a delightful companion, very merry and sharp as a needle'. But he was inclined to be extravagant and rather too fond of

Crockford's. This may have been the reason why it was decided to send him abroad at the end of 1839, though he considered it 'lucky' he was going because he, too, was upset by his mother's second marriage. He was made Secretary of Legation in Florence; but he soon came back after an old crony of his father's had left him in 1843 both Sandringham and money enough to live on handsomely ever after.[41]

Cowper's successor as private secretary, in January 1840, was the Earl of Suffolk's youngest son, James Kenneth Howard, whom Palmerston had made his précis-writer at Holland's request in 1835. Howard's place as précis-writer was filled up for six months until June 1840 by Edward Pleydell-Bouverie, the Earl of Radnor's second son and another of Fanny Cowper's rejected suitors, and then, for the rest of Palmerston's second term at the F.O., by his friend Minto's second son, Henry Elliot. When Palmerston returned in 1846-1851, first Viscount Anson (afterwards Earl of Lichfield) and then, when Anson turned M.P., Stanley of Alderley's eldest son and heir served him as précis-writers. But his private secretary throughout – and afterwards for Granville and Clarendon too – was a man whom Palmerston had brought into the Foreign Office at the age of sixteen in 1840 and who seemed in every respect the fittest of any for the place. A fine cricketer and, like so many in the F.O., an accomplished actor, Spencer Ponsonby was much liked and admired and lived to a great old age. He happened to be Duncannon's sixth son; but he was also Georgiana Fane's favourite nephew and heir.[42]

Whatever the quality of the personal assistants Palmerston had in the office, he still reckoned on having to read most of the incoming political correspondence and on drafting or at least outlining all the replies and memoranda himself. The greatest burden, nervous as well as physical and mental, must therefore have fallen on the minister himself. Even the clerks who hated him acknowledged that. As Greville dutifully noted:

I was surprised to hear them (Mellish particularly, who can judge both from capacity and opportunity) give ample testimony to his abilities. They said that he wrote admirably, and could express himself perfectly in French, very sufficiently in Italian, and understood German; that his diligence and attention were unwearied – he read everything and wrote an immense quantity.

Poodle Byng also admitted that Palmerston drove himself as hard as any of them. 'Palmerston never can last at the rate he is now going,' he wrote in January 1832. '2 o'clock is supposed to be early getting away from the office – sometimes 5 in the morning. He deserves that his labours should be crowned with success.'[43]

It was to be expected that, having no previous experience of the office, Palmerston should in his first month or two have felt 'like a man who has plumped into a mill-race, scarcely able by all his kicking and plunging to keep his head above water'. But even after he had settled into a routine he did not find that things improved. During his first few years it was Palmerston's custom when in town – and he was there almost all the time – to keep himself available to visitors in Stanhope Street or, after his marriage, in Carlton House Terrace at noon and at the Foreign Office from 2 until 4 or 5 p.m., when he expected to get away for a meal before going to the House of Commons. He hoped always to be able to keep up with paper work between visits. But he soon discovered that it was impossible to cope, even in the holidays. 'There are always people enough in London', he once wrote to Lady Cowper, 'to employ a Secretary of State from 12 to 7 every day in talking, and despatches come from foreign parts in September as well as in any other month.' So finding that once he had gone to the office he was 'lost for the day', whenever he had a particularly important piece of writing to do he stayed at home, sometimes for two or three days on end. But this meant breaking appointments and adding to his reputation for lack of punctuality and courtesy.[44]

In later years, certainly in 1838-40 and again in 1851, Palmerston made himself much less easily available at the F.O., and as far as afternoon Cabinets and Windsor visits allowed made 5 p.m. his regular hour for visitors there, though even then he often had to go off to the Commons before he had seen them all. But he could not do this during his first two years or so because of the almost ceaseless burden in the evenings of the conferences on Greece and more especially Belgium. 'I have been labouring like a dray horse or a methodist preacher about Belgium,' he complained to Grey in June 1831, '& did not leave Talleyrand's (where we assembled last night) till two this morning.' One conference lasted eleven and a quarter hours and finished at four in the morning; it left old Talleyrand, Greville heard, 'half-dead'. But though a much younger man, Palmerston had many other duties to burden him. Once in November 1831, when in a single day he had to combine the conclusion of a treaty about Belgium with a Cabinet on Portugal and an important private interview on the Reform Bill, he worked from 11 a.m. right through, with only a single break of an hour for dinner, until 3 a.m. the following day. On the last day of the same year he wrote to Lady Cowper:

> We did a great deal of business here in town yesterday and I hope with future good results. My day was not an idle one; for having left the office at only 3 in the morning the night before, I had before the cabinet at 1, to write an important despatch to Vienna, to hear Czartorisky's account of the whole Polish war, and to discuss with Ompteda [the Hanoverain minister] all the squabbles of the German Diet. At our cabinet my despatches to Berlin & Vienna were approved & amended. I then had to see Van de Weyer, Lieven, Bulow, Esterhazy & Wessenberg, upon various different subjects, and afterwards to send off messengers with various different messages & private letters to Vienna, Berlin, Paris & Brussels. However I contrived to get it all done by about 2 this morning; and now for my consolation I have staring me in the face 13 boxes full of papers, which are all to be read and which have come to me since yesterday morning.

This may have been an exceptional day with which to round off his first full year in office. But there were many others nearly like it. The Belgian conferences in particular continued to be both tedious and frustrating, time and

time again keeping him so late that he had to attend to correspondence well
into the early hours. 'It is now one o'clock in the morning,' he would begin a
letter to Fred Lamb; and once he even closed another, of three sides, 'Come
there goes five o'clock in the morning and I think that is late enough so I shall
send off my messengers & go home to bed'. To Emily he remarked over and
over again in the autumn of 1832, when his problems were crowding in upon
him, that he was being 'really worked to death'.[45]

Palmerston maintained a large private correspondence of a semi-official
kind, especially with his three or four ambassadors, but with many heads of
legation as well. Much of it was copied for his records and survives still among
the Broadlands Papers; but some, perhaps a sizeable portion, he considered
too confidential even for a private secretary[46] and, though one suspects he was
too careful not to have kept some sort of record for himself, can be found now
only among the papers of his correspondents. In any event, men like Fred
Lamb in Vienna, Granville in Paris, Ponsonby in Constantinople and Villiers
in Madrid, as well as William Temple in Naples, might usually expect to have
such private letters, some of them several sheets long, as often as once or twice
a week. So too would others in times of crisis.

There was also for Palmerston the burden of correspondence with his Prime
Ministers. That with Grey was the more onerous. Melbourne did concern
himself with Palmerston's policy and still more with its manner, but it was
Grey with whom Palmerston had more discussions of drafts and to him more
conference meetings to report. Nor was all this made any lighter by Grey's
frequent absence out of town. 'With Lord Grey at Sheen and the King at
Brighton', Palmerston wrote, 'it is rather a slow process to write a dispatch
upon any important subject.' When the Prime Minister went home to
Howick, as he often did for long periods, it was far worse. Palmerston by
contrast rarely got away to Broadlands. During the cholera epidemics of 1831
and 1832 he was almost the only minister to stay regularly in London. In
August 1832, after Parliament had been prorogued, Grey went off to Howick
for six or seven weeks, leaving among the members of his Cabinet the three
Secretaries of State alone in London. Grey had had a particularly harrowing
session in Parliament; but so too had his colleagues. Indeed, Palmerston told
Fred Lamb, after nearly two whole years in office, he had not managed to
spend seven consecutive days in the country. People, it was said, were everywhere astonished at Grey's behaviour. He was away even longer the following
year. So it may seem very unfair that his colleagues at home and diplomats
abroad should this time have complained more of Palmerston's neglect than
Grey's.[47]

Palmerston's neglect of foreign business towards the end of 1833 was naturally blamed on his fling with Lady Jersey. Granville may have exaggerated
the delay of letters and instructions he suffered. But there was certainly
something to complain of. In February 1834 Villiers, the minister in Madrid,

joined his voice to the chorus of complaints, and well-informed rumour added Mrs Petre to the list of Palmerston's distractions. Yet while Palmerston may sometimes have reacted overmuch from the great burden of his work, his lapses were not necessarily entirely his fault nor always without design. The absence of instructions to Paris and Madrid in 1833-4 was probably occasioned by an unexpected delay in the assembly of a Cabinet to approve them, and then, when it had assembled, by the still more unexpected crisis it provoked. When everything had quietened down again and the pressure upon him had been relieved a little, Palmerston was claiming, in April 1834, that he was never more than a day behind in answering letters and dispatches, and 'seldom so much as that'. The further delays that Villiers complained of in October 1835 were also probably due to Palmerston's unwillingness to rebuke him until it was quite certain the Cabinet would tolerate no other answer to that minister's rashness in diplomacy. He held up a similar reproof for his ambassador in Constantinople the following summer in the hope that the delay would enable the diplomatist to justify his rashness by success. The delays that Granville complained of in December 1838 were, on the other hand, plainly the result of Palmerston's grief and near collapse following the death of his elder sister.[48]

Perhaps it is no wonder then that, with all the burden of work and Lady Jersey's teasing and Mrs Mills's blackmail, as well as Lady Cowper's and Mrs Petre's coming and goings, Palmerston should have continued at the F.O., as at the W. O. before, to treat with very little patience human frailty and to condemn as slovenly incompetence or wilful neglect what were merely clerkly peccadillos. Even marriage hardly softened him before the first long holiday of 1841-6. 'The clerks detest him,' Leveson still found early in 1840, 'and have an absurd sort of fancy that he takes pleasure in bullying them.' It surely all reflected, rather, his taking too much upon himself. Once, when Queen Victoria asked him about some reference to 'bureaucratic' influence in Prussia, he explained why the word was so unfamiliar to her: 'In England the Ministers who are at the head of the several departments of the State, are liable any day and every day to defend themselves in Parliament; in order to do this, they must be minutely acquainted with all the details of the business of their offices, and the only way of being constantly armed with such information is to conduct and direct those details themselves.' Yet he ought to have been able to delegate better than he did. He even insisted on checking all the drafts the senior clerks concocted from his memoranda lest some carelessness of his or theirs should misrepresent his real intention. But fear of failure and dread of ridicule still dogged him even as he triumphed on the European stage. So he drove himself and others to check and double-check, and the combination of interminable drudgery and unceasing apprehension inevitably made him irritable and impatient. The fact of the matter, then, is that he dreaded the public responsibility for Foreign Office errors and he resented, even while he insisted on it, that so much work should fall upon himself.[49]

A similar burden had contributed to the premature death of Castlereagh, if not of Canning, and perhaps to Dudley's as well. Palmerston, fortunately, had tremendous energy and enjoyed great good health. His temperament, too, saved him a good deal of wear and tear in grand matters of State, if not in the smaller details of F.O. business. Lady Cowper remarked that 'a person of a less sanguine disposition than his would have been quite worn out long ago' by the Belgian affair. When Benjamin Haydon called to arrange a sitting, he was 'amazingly impressed by his good humoured elegance'. (He also thought, incidentally, that Palmerston's head 'looked weak', though 'his nose is small, forehead fine, & he is handsome'.) Later they had 'delightful conversations' and Haydon came away thinking he was 'a fine, a delightful fellow', 'quite natural' and with 'no affectation', even avoiding French expressions in his speech. Yet people who knew him better and saw him more often, and when he was less on his guard perhaps, often commented on Palmerston's haggard and harassed appearance; and he himself complained several times not only of his 'old friend' the gout, but also of persistent boils.[50]

One doctor who called to treat Palmerston at the F.O. discovered him tucked away in a tiny room at the rear of the building overlooking the park. A large room, Palmerston explained, prevented him 'reflecting', and since he needed no amanuensis he found his 'little snuggery' quite sufficient. Ordinarily no visitors were admitted; indeed there was hardly room for any. There was a small settee in one corner and a single chair by its side, so that two people could sit comfortably. But Palmerston himself worked standing up at a high desk (just as he did at Broadlands). On Easter Sunday 1840 he stood so at his desk in Carlton Terrace for about seven hours, going over a report with its author line by line. In later years he explained to another doctor that the burden of his work had led him into the habit of writing standing up, so that if, as was often the case, he fell asleep the fall would wake him up! The one doctor advised him to get more air, the other more rest. Palmerston himself attached more importance to exercise.[51]

'Every other abstinence', Palmerston once explained, 'will not make up for abstinence from exercise.' In the late 1830s he seems habitually to have made a horse-ride of his daily trip to the F.O. and, when his move to Carlton Terrace in 1840 made the distance too short for that, to have taken off half an hour each day between eleven and one for a ride in Hyde Park. Yet in the early days of Greek and Belgian conferences, he seems not to have been able to follow the advice he regularly gave to Sulivan. After he had fallen victim to cholera in April 1833 he regularly took his doctor's advice to go riding in the park every morning before breakfast. But it must have been merely a temporary relief. When in the brief interval out of office in 1834-5 the elections took him for a while to Broadlands he galloped about everywhere. 'I have lately enjoyed the luxury of bodily fatigue from exercise out of doors,' he wrote, 'to which I had been a stranger for four years.' But for most of his first decade at the F.O. Palmerston frequently complained that its business rarely allowed him to get out of town, except for a few days at Broadlands in the autumn or at Christmas.[52]

At Broadlands too Palmerston was pursued by red boxes, and if he had a little time to spare estate business would pretty well consume it. After his marriage he went there more often. Before the end of 1839 the railway to Basingstoke had reduced the journey to one of five and a half hours, and by the following spring its extension to Winchester to four and a half: by 1850 the completion of the line to Romsey provided two good trains from London at 1 and 5 p.m., each taking a little over two hours. But the railway also brought Broadlands within easy reach of both invited and uninvited guests. The growing crisis in the East made him invite two ambassadors down even for his honeymoon in 1839; and a year later the unsnubbable agent from Texas would also rush down uninvited. In 1850 the visitor to Broadlands would find Palmerston taking a hard ride of ten or twenty miles every afternoon at four. But he was still being pursued there by F.O. business: after dinner he would leave the ladies for an hour to read dispatches, and then, after coming back for tea at eleven, go away again and work in his study quite often well into the night. Before his marriage he also paid fairly frequent visits to Panshanger. These certainly provided a change; but they can hardly have been a rest. His turns at Windsor, rather, in those days gave him almost, if not quite, as much relief as they did his F.O. clerks. 'I am leading a wholesome life here,' he wrote from Windsor in September 1838. 'I go to bed by 12, am up soon after 7, on the Thames rowing between 8 & 9 & come here to breakfast at 10. We then ride out with the Queen from 4 to 6, & the morning is devoted to business.' Quite often he would swim in the river instead of rowing before breakfast. 'He came from this latter performance this morning,' reported a lady-in-waiting in 1841, 'as fresh as a – no I beg a rose's pardon! – but as an old river-god, to his customary hearty meal.'[53]

Palmerston's relations with William IV were infinitely better than they had been with George. Palmerston treated him with care and courtesy, since he was a man of fixed opinions as well as of limited ability. He was also on very good terms with the King's private secretary, Sir Herbert Taylor. Palmerston's flirtations with France and with German liberalism worried William a good deal; but Palmerston was usually able to work effectively on his patriotic fervour and sense of national dignity to win him sufficiently around. Indeed, William usually excepted Palmerston, alone or in company with one other such as Melbourne, from the many disagreements and discontents he expressed so often about his Whig ministers. He even singled Palmerston out for the unusual favour of receiving the G.C.B. in June 1832, a very short while after the Foreign Secretary had spoken so enthusiastically in Parliament about the alliance with France and his sympathy for German constitutionalists.[54]

Palmerston's dealings with William were strictly businesslike. With the young Victoria, on the other hand, his horse rides and the special attention he generally paid her caused only little less remark than Melbourne's. 'It is not quite seemly in a maiden Queen,' Peel wrote. 'She may not know their characters – but they must know their own.' Haydon prayed for her protection 'from the poison of Melbourne & Palmerston – too dangerous, too fascinating for her purity or her principles'. From others the thought of the Maiden Queen's closest associates being the 'two greatest *Roués* of the Age' provoked some very suggestive cartoons. One by 'HB' (John Doyle), showing Palmerston playing the Queen at chess, with Melbourne looking over her shoulder, was bluntly headed, 'The Queen in Danger'. Lord Munster thought that neither of them would dare to whisper 'soft nonsense' but only 'soft Politics' into her ear. But Palmerston was certainly careful to treat her as a woman as much as a monarch during her first years on the throne. Before and after her ascent she had found him most amiable and agreeable. Soon he was not only helping to teach her chess but amusing her still more by arguing violently about it with others.[55]

Palmerston was also very condescending but charming with the Queen when it came to business. By established constitutional practice all important draft instructions were submitted for the royal approval, though Palmerston

A GAME AT CHESS (again)
THE QUEEN IN DANGER!
"A Change came o'er the Spirit of my dream"

'The Queen in Danger!' by HB (John Doyle), October 1837

had already got into the habit with William of having them copied and sent on their way in urgent cases before the word could come back from Windsor. If it turned out to be unfavourable, then a substitute could always be made out and a correction sent afterwards by flying messenger. All incoming dispatches of any importance were also sent to Windsor, immediately after being seen by Palmerston. In William's time this occasionally included some that it was not considered wise to circulate even to the Cabinet. But it is not clear what were the criteria of 'importance' or who interpreted it when, as must often have been the case, Palmerston gave no *ad hoc* instructions. From the very first he testified to the young Queen's good sense and natural understanding. But she still found it all rather hard going, and much appreciated Palmerston's coming to her to explain things verbally. Once, when having dealt with Spain he followed with an analysis of the Belgian question from the union of the Netherlands to 1838, she wrote: 'I must say, intricate and difficult as the subject is, Lord Palmerston explained it in such a very clear, plain and agreeable manner, as to put me quite *au fait* of the whole thing. The explanation took an hour.' On another occasion in August 1837 she added that as she had so many foreign dispatches to read he should send her no more until she had done with what she had. A month later he directed that the F.O. send only 'the most interesting dispatches' to Windsor and Lenox Conyngham amended it to '*interesting* and *romantic*'. The following summer Palmerston directed: 'The less you send the Queen this next week . . . the better, as her time will be much occupied by Ascot.' Eventually he went too far. 'Send the Queen private letters & all the foreign despatches of any importance & keep her well informed upon foreign affairs,' Melbourne told him in November 1838. 'She rather complains that when I am not there, she hears nothing.' It was probably because she was so lonely and missed Palmerston's talks only a little less than Melbourne's that she so complained; while Palmerston on his part evidently began to find her demands upon his time, including even the late afternoon rides, rather a distraction than a relief from business.[36]

Early in 1840 the void that Disraeli was to fill during Queen Victoria's widowhood was temporarily filled up by marriage. Palmerston now took on Prince Albert at four-handed chess. But his place as the Queen's mentor in foreign affairs was gradually taken over unofficially by Albert and soon a new interest and a new touchiness became evident in her dealings with Palmerston. An unsuccessful assault he was supposed to have made before her marriage upon one of her ladies-in-waiting who had moved into a room at Windsor, where he was usually more than welcome, was carefully kept from the Queen and, for the time being, from her husband too. But the Queen soon began to notice some of Palmerston's other little tricks, having been enlightened no doubt (as Melbourne hinted) by Albert and perhaps by Fanny Cowper too. 'The Queen fears', she wrote in May 1841, 'there must be some mistake about sending the despatches, as she has not received one box for the last five days.' When they came in all at once, as often was the case, she pointed out, she had no time to read them. More ominously still she went on: 'She has also perceived once or twice that they have sent to her drafts to approve when the originals have already been sent away, which of course renders her doing so useless.' With great condescension she ended by suggesting that these 'mistakes' were no doubt due to 'the quantity of business . . . to be transacted', and with equal aplomb Palmerston blamed it all on the clerks' neglect during the absence of both Undersecretaries, and promised he would 'pointedly repeat' his orders that dispatches should 'never' be sent out till the drafts had been approved and returned. He had in fact laid it down before only as 'a general rule' and, as Backhouse pointed out, had several times himself given orders to ignore it in specific cases. Whether or not he now kept his promise to be inflexible in future, their relations avoided breaking point for the time being, even under the strain of the second Egyptian crisis. When Melbourne's Government fell in August 1841 Victoria wrote: 'The Queen seizes this opportunity to express to Lord Palmerston her sincere regret at losing his valuable services, and her wishes for his and Lady Palmerston's welfare and happiness.'[37]

The Clerks in the F.O. might not have minded taking all the blame if, like their predecessors in the old W.O., they had not also suffered at Palmerston's hands the effects of deliberate economy. Palmerston was by no means indifferent to anyone's need of material well-being. But it was very difficult to ensure when there was such great pressure on him to reduce the expenses of his office. For expenditure on foreign relations was coming more and more under parliamentary as well as Treasury scrutiny and the Government of which Palmerston was a member was pledged to retrenchment as well as to peace and reform. So although the office was really a very cheap one, he had had at the beginning to promise the Prime Minister that he would indeed make cuts.[38]

Major economies were all the more difficult to accomplish since Aberdeen had already made a considerable reduction in expenditure and Palmerston was in the process of making a great expansion of the work of the department. In 1827 and 1828 total expenditure under all heads had been reckoned at about £475,000; in 1829 and 1830 it had been reduced to £450,000. Yet for 1830-31 Palmerston was able to report that he had added savings of almost £38,000 to those already made by Aberdeen and, in spite of his continued vigour and activity, nearly another £24,000 the following year. In fact in the second year the cost of the diplomatic service had increased a little and the net saving overall was more than accounted for by a drastic cut-back in the payments made to consuls. In the F.O itself only small savings were made, though Palmerston himself was a major victim of economy and as unwilling a one as any. For he began, in common with the other Secretaries of State, with a reduction in his salary from £6,000 to £5,000 a year. Since his personal finances were still under very considerable pressure, this evidently hurt. Having already had deducted fees for the bureaucrats of £246 1s. 0d. and £27 11s.

6d. from his first, short, quarterly payment of £775 17s. 0d., he enjoyed only one further payment at the full rate of £1,500. The next was only £1,250 and when he entered it in his private account book on 15 July 1831 he noted in the margin: 'F.O. salary reduced 1000 a yr by Recommendation of Hs. of Cmns Committee on pub. offrs' salaries.'[59]

Palmerston could not, as has been seen, save the Political Undersecretary suffering a reduction. But he did so far as possible ensure that others in the office did not also suffer financially. When Canning had made Backhouse Undersecretary at £2,000 a year in 1827 he had intended that after five years he should receive one increment of £500. No doubt it was the increased discrepancy this would produce that led Backhouse, with extraordinary generosity, to offer when Shee's salary was under attack to give up part of his own remuneration to his colleague. It was just as well Palmerston refused to permit such prodigality. For when Backhouse's five years were up the Treasury insisted on applying to him the regulations introduced in 1831, by which the salaries of the Undersecretaries were fixed, without increments, at £1,500 and £2,000 respectively. Backhouse, who apparently had no private means, naturally protested. 'Men should not be weighed down', he wrote, 'by sickening cares attendant upon a struggle to maintain with insufficient means appearances proper to their station.' Palmerston seems to have fought bravely for him and eventually in 1838 secured a special increment of £500 backdated to October 1837. Nor was he so unsympathetic to the position of his junior clerks as some of them often felt. 'Devil damn the Gov.', Scott exclaimed in April 1838, 'that do not pay their servants their due, but expect them to appear as Gents.' This was rather unfair. For Scott probably owed the disappointment of his expectations more to his father's financial troubles than to the meanness of the Government.[60]

In 1835, after only seven years in the office and thanks, probably, to powerful outside support, Scott was somewhere near the top of the scale of the six third-class clerks. This was £150, rising by increments of £10 to £300 a year. Below that the salaries of the six assistant junior (fourth-class) clerks were set at £100, rising by increments of £10 to £150 a year. The seven second-class clerks above Scott began at £350 a year, rising by increments of £15 to £545 (though those in charge of the political divisions received an additional responsibility allowance). The four senior clerks received £600 or £700 a year, rising by annual increments of £20 to £800 or £900; the Chief Clerk received £1,000 p.a., rising by £50 a year to £1,250. According to a statement attached to the reforms of 1841, no one was promoted to senior clerk who was not fit for the job, and the senior clerks alone at that date received any significant improvement in their scales of payment, their maximum being raised by £100 to £1,000. But the salaries below these were not exactly on the poverty line, even for 'gents'. Moreover, when the third-class clerks pointed out to Palmerston in 1839 that his prospective rearrangement of the office would not leave room for all of them, he increased the number of the class above to take care of as many as he could. He did not move as fast as they would have liked, probably out of a quite justifiable apprehension that the Treasury would make difficulties. But when he finally got permission he had their promotion backdated, and for those he could not promote he secured 'compensation' to protect their now off-scale salaries.[61]

There were several devices by which members of the F.O. might augment their salaries, similar in some cases to those lingering eighteenth-century practices in the old W.O. Some of the clerks, for example, continued to act as private agents for diplomats abroad and to receive in return a commission on salaries not exceeding 1 per cent. By the middle of the century, it was said, a total of over £3,500 was shared out in this manner. Palmerston did not touch the agency system, probably because it was considered beneficial to the service and cost the public nothing. After his death public criticism mounted, aided in particular by the attacks made by Grenville Murray on his own former agent in the service, John Bidwell jr, and in 1870 the practice was finally abolished, though only after the provision of substantial compensation. On the other hand Palmerston, so he had told Backhouse in 1835, had 'an unsurmountable objection to special allowances . . . It is a bad principle to overburthen one person & then to increase the charge on the public as a counterbalance for the increased burthen thrown on a particular individual. This is a false doctrine of equilibrium.' So he reverted to the practice of employing supernumerary clerks in preference to special payments for over-time, and at the time of his 1841 reforms promised the Treasury to eliminate other special allowances as and when he could. Generally speaking he adopted the same approach as in the W.O., forcing pampered clerks to give up en-trenched positions on promotion and extending special allowances only until the retirement of the individuals concerned. He must have made some notable progress; when the Crimean War brought a great increase of work Clarendon obtained a grant of some £2,000 of compensation for the clerks' extra work, pending the expansion of the department.[62]

There seems to have been no need for a major onslaught on the F.O., largely because, with one or two exceptions, such old-fashioned practices were much less in evidence there than in the W.O. The Fee Fund of the F.O. had long since been devoted almost entirely to contingencies. 'Chancery Presents', gifts of money from foreign Governments on the ratification of treaties, were abolished in 1831 and the annual compensation provided by the Treasury used by them to justify their reduction in the salaries of the Undersecretaries (it was a double share of this, £500, not part of his salary as Webster says, that Backhouse offered to concede to Shee before he discovered that his own increment was also to be withheld). But the Chief Clerk continued to receive about £30 or £40 a year from consuls on appointment and the office-keepers were paid substantial sums by the publishers of the *London Gazette* in lieu of a fixed number of free copies. At Christmas the office-keepers also sent one of their number to collect gratuities at the houses of foreign ambassadors; even the Undersecretaries, it appears, were not above accepting Christmas boxes. Palmerston is supposed to have been 'perfectly astonished' when he discovered what the office-keepers were doing in 1834, but still to have done nothing about it. Possibly he recognized that if he struck at the practice further compensation would have to be paid out of public funds. When the Treasury investigated the situation late in 1836 and it was brought to Palmerston's notice that his own porter in Stanhope Street was doing much the same, he ordered him at once 'to cease such brigandage'. At the same time, on the recommendation of the Treasury, he ordered the office employees to stop it too. Thereafter small sums were paid by way of compensation to the individuals concerned, amounting in 1839 to a total of £72. At the same date almost £830 was still being paid by way of compensation for 'loss of Treaty Presents' to the clerks and Undersecretaries.[63]

Later on Palmerston also cut down the free distribution of F.O. publications to private individuals, including Lady Holland. He even for a moment in February 1832 seriously considered stopping the abuse of diplomatic bags by ordering that they be opened at the post office and postage charged 'on all letters & parcels addressed to private individuals which may be found therein'. When, nearly two years afterwards, he asked the next messenger for Calais to bring back '8 pieces of stuff for gowns, belonging to Lady Cowper', he added that he would pay the charges. He kept a close watch on the office contingency fund, and personally checked the accounts for fuel. One of the first things he did was to see, in Webster's words, that it 'no longer rained snuff boxes' on visiting dignitaries in London. For he had hardly been in office for a month than he found himself obliged 'to hand over to a brace of German gentlemen, who had come over to congratulate the present King upon his accession, two splendid boxes, for each of which we are to pay £400; and which made up the complement of eight or ten, which had been allotted by Aberdeen'. So he called for a memorandum from the F.O. showing how much had been spent on 'diplomatic presents' during the previous nine years and giving the reasons for them. What he found seemed ripe for cutting down. 'I confess', he wrote to Grey, 'that the impression on my mind is, that these presents might one and all be discontinued; at least it seems to me much easier to find reasons for abolishing them, than for maintaining their continuance, in debate in the House of Commons.' Presents on particular occasions to 'chiefs barbaric, from whom commercial or political advantages are thus to be purchased', he admitted might be justified by circumstances. But he did not see how routine courtesies to other states could justify an average of £5,600 per annum. He questioned in particular why every change of ambassador at Constantinople should cost nearly £4,000 in presents. 'We have hitherto treated the Sultan as a Barbarian, too ignorant to form any estimate of our power, except by reckoning up the pistols & watches which our ambassador might spread out before him. But Mahmoud having now voted himself a

442 · PALMERSTON: THE EARLY YEARS

civilized sovereign, might we not in this respect, at least, take him at his word, and expect him to be satisfied, if we treat him henceforward, no worse than we do his great instructor in civilization, the Emperor Nicholas.' Moreover, when the cost of giving presents to special missions of congratulation to William on his coronation was added up, it was reckoned to be no less than £6,225. Consequently very considerable reductions were made in this sort of expenditure and British ambassadors abroad subsequently found it difficult to obtain funds not only for such occasions but even for secret service.[64]

It may seem surprising that Palmerston of all people was willing to reduce the amount of secret service money. He valued very highly the interception of foreign and diplomatic correspondence and he took no part in the suppression in 1844 of the Secret Office and Deciphering Branch of the Post Office. That decision followed the exposure in Parliament that Mazzini's letters were being intercepted at the request of the Austrian Government. Palmerston, who had carefully absented himself from the debate, claimed in private that he had never issued any warrant at the request of foreign ministers but had rather opened all of their own letters. It was also he who as Prime Minister ordered that £600 be handed over to some desperate revolutionaries in Naples for the purchase of a vessel with which to rescue a couple of unfortunate prisoners of Ferdinand's. The ship was so purchased, but it was lost at sea and the prisoners had after all to wait for their release on Ferdinand's mercy. When Villiers was in Spain in earlier days he used to spend about £600 a year of secret service money, of which £70 was devoted to the relief of distressed British subjects and the rest to paying correspondents in various parts of Spain and buying other information wherever he could get it. This Palmerston considered money 'well spent', and when the minister suggested that he might obtain a commercial treaty if he were provided with 'a great *lump* of money' for bribes, Palmerston authorized him 'to go to any reasonable extent of outlay for that purpose'. But in general Palmerston seems to have had a pretty healthy scepticism about such expenditure. 'It is not unlikely', he wrote to Aberdeen's Undersecretary in 1841 when explaining why he had turned down some apparently tempting 'offer' from Paris, 'that a Frenchman who was to begin by betraying his own government and national interests to us, might end by betraying us, and our interests to his own government.' When in 1837 Clarendon proposed to take up an offer from someone called Buschenthal to buy off a number of Carlists for between £3,500 and £4,000, Palmerston replied: 'I think it a dangerous course, our means are too scanty – you can never be sure that you have got Punch even when you have bought him, and uno avulso non deficit alter [and where one man is bought off, another will take his place]; and if once a bridge of gold is thrown over the Gulph, no man will pass it by any other road.' Clarendon's private secretary, who had been pretty nearly a journalist, did have dealings with Buschenthal, but Palmerston concluded in 1839 that he was indeed 'a double dyed servant doing a little business occasionally for both parties'.[65]

Palmerston was not much more indulgent with long-standing arrangements with so-called secret agents. For years secret information had been supplied from Paris by a certain Lewis Goldsmith. Goldsmith was a British subject but formerly a Jacobin. In 1803 he had been employed by Talleyrand for a few months as editor of a revolutionary journal in Paris. He was subsequently, in 1809, landed by accident in England instead of America and having been twice bound over he commenced in 1811 a patriotic British newspaper later called the *British Monitor*. He was paid £1,200 a year to attack the French in it. He also received £800 a year from the F.O. for intelligence from France, where his wife had continued to reside. In 1824 he decided he would rather give up newspaper work for some safer job and, like Harriette Wilson, threatened if he did not get one to write his memoirs. In the end Canning agreed to let him earn his £800 a year henceforth with his wife in Paris, and the following year the *Monitor* expired. But Goldsmith's reports were still coming in to the F.O. and, presumably, he was still receiving his £800 a year when Palmerston became Foreign Secretary in 1830, though, because of his special connection with Canning, he dealt with Backhouse rather than Shee. However, Palmerston soon grew disillusioned about them. 'I really think Goldsmith's Bulletins ought to be discontinued,' he wrote in January 1833. 'They are worse than trash; let Ld Granville tell him we will have none of them.' Backhouse agreed that they 'abounded of late in stupid twaddle' and were 'stuffed with worthless reports' which anyone might have picked up any day in the streets of Paris. Goldsmith also wrote, he said, as though he were really an agent and propagandist for the Tories. Even while Goldsmith had been in England it had several times been suggested that he was a double agent; and it seems very likely that after his return there in 1809 he was also in the pay of the Bourbons, if not the Bonapartes. Very probably Palmerston also had some suspicion that Goldsmith was working for *The Times;* Goldsmith had in fact been their Paris correspondent since 1831, and in spite of Palmerston's objections continued in that role until his death in 1846. Nor did he hesitate to press the Treasury for unpaid expenses or Palmerston to make his son-in-law attaché at Frankfurt. Another child of Goldsmith's, his daughter Georgiana, was already well provided for; attracted once again by a dark complexion, though her father it seems was not a Jew, the aged Lord Lyndhurst had taken her as his second wife in 1837, a few years after the death of his first.[66]

Palmerston was also very sceptical about spending too much money in that cesspit of corruption, Constantinople. One of his last instructions to Ponsonby was to order him not to scruple to draw £1,000 of secret service money if that would secure permission to build a Protestant church in Jerusalem. But that was done under strong pressure from Ashley and with a desire to mark with special credit his own departure from the F.O. In general he knew that he could never compete with the vast sums of money spent by the Russians. Nor would it necessarily have been very useful. After he had refused £1,000 for one Grand Vizier, the Russians came up with a snuff-box worth £1,500; and that particular Turkish minister was reckoned even by his enemies to be politically incorruptible. The most useful of British serviteurs, who supplied among other scoops almost immediate details of the Treaty of Unkiar Skelessi, received by contrast only relatively small sums, as an earnest of goodwill apparently. The Sultan had to be content with gifts of horses and a carriage, weapons and scientific instruments; his ambassadors with such manufactures as sporting guns and pistols. Similar gifts, to the Imam of Muscat in 1838, had to be provided out of secret service funds. Palmerston realized that England would have to follow the United States' example and if her agents were not to be allowed to give presents to forbid them also to accept them. Accordingly in January 1831 orders went out that presents on the ratification of treaties should no longer be given or accepted. Hence the compensation to the clerks concerned of nearly £830 a year. Hitherto their average annual income from presents appears to have been nearer £2,900. But for the diamond snuff-boxes which the Secretary of State himself had habitually received on such occasions, Palmerston himself appears to have received no compensation whatever.[67]

In Webster's view 'the spectacle of the richest country in the world saving a few pounds by petty meanness at the expense of its representation abroad is not a pleasant one'. But it ought to be remembered that Palmerston had plenty of experience from the W.O. of what such practices might lead to. In any case, he made some compensation, partially at his own expense, in giving lavish entertainments. Before his marriage he was limited by lack of time and social resources. Yet even in those days he occasionally invited ambassadors to Broadlands and gave not infrequent dinners at the Foreign Office or Stanhope Street. Theoretically the Secretary of State had an official residence in Downing Street; but none had lived there since Canning and by Palmerston's time the rooms were all needed for the conduct of ordinary business. Palmerston was not convinced that an official residence was really necessary (and he resented the fact that his salary had been reduced partly on the theoretical assumption that he had possession of one), but he did want better provision made for the great dinners he was obliged to give on royal birthdays and on the arrival of foreign princes. Then, he said in 1836, the number of guests was nearer fifty than forty and, since very few private houses in London could cope, provision ought to be made in any reconstruction of the office for a suitable dining-room, reception-room and kitchen. Nothing was done in his time and he continued to have to make do with existing resources and to pay for any extra expense involved substantially out of his own pocket. He was able to give dinners for up to sixteen or eighteen people at Stanhope St; and, after his marriage in 1839, for as many as thirty-six 'without difficulty' in the house he rented in Carlton Terrace. But until 1840 the bigger ones for up to forty people he held in the F.O. itself. There were usually only one or two of these a year, on the King's and the Queen's birthdays; but sometimes also for the royal visits by people like Dom Pedro in 1831 and the Duke of Orléans in

1833. For these he had to hire at his own expense both plate and cooks. The first usually cost him about £50. The second he would borrow from his grander friends. He paid Lord Tankerville's cook nearly £50 for three dinners in 1832 and Lord Cowper's over £100 for all those provided between October 1833 and April 1834. For his first birthday dinner, at a cost of £150, he hired Talleyrand's famous chef, Louis, then considered the best in Europe.[68]

Under pressure from his colleagues Palmerston also cut still further into a diplomatic establishment already 'pruned', he said, 'with an unsparing hand' by Aberdeen. He tightened up the scales for both salaries and pensions and from 1832 a fixed sum of £180,000 was provided annually for them. Out of this total the sum of £140,000 for salaries and allowances remained ostensibly the same as in Aberdeen's last year. But that sum included provision for new missions in Belgium and South America and the charges for paid attachés which had previously been made separately, these extra expenses being absorbed by the reduction to missions of the embassies in Lisbon and The Hague. Palmerston still had trouble in getting his colleagues to agree, being pressed, as he later recalled, 'to leave some courts without any mission at all . . . and at others to have only a chargé d'affaires, with a few hundreds a year to walk the streets on foot, and to live at a *caffè*'. But they eventually consented, as did the House of Commons Committee on Civil Affairs after he had personally appeared before them, to go 'through the whole of that estimate, count by count, and item by item, explaining all the changes and reductions I had proposed, with my reasons for making them, and for not making more'. The result, he pointed out, was that the service was left so short of funds – he had, for example only £5,900 for all the South American missions together – that to make it stretch he had to rely on savings from the occasional unpaid leaves of absence taken by ministers abroad. However, as long as he kept within the grand total of £180,000 he was able in practice to arrange things virtually without outside interference, and it is worth noting that the system he invented lasted until 1869, when the cost of the service was transferred to the ordinary budget and salaries and pensions henceforth voted annually by Parliament.[69]

Although lack of funds might have severely restricted the amount of patronage available to Palmerston in the F.O., the turnover of staff, owing perhaps to the hard work he demanded, was large enough to put at his disposal a fair number of places. Soon after he entered the F.O. his old friend Michael Bruce accepted a valuable six months' appointment as a claims commissioner in London and just before he left it the son of War Office Rich was found a place in the Librarian's Department at the F.O. In March 1836 the death of the F.O. housekeeper also allowed him to give her place to the recently widowed wife of his gardener at Broadlands. His rearrangements in the diplomatic service and the office in the previous October enabled him to find a clerkship for Augustus Leopold Coles, the son of his 'right-hand man' in his new constituency in Tiverton. In 1841 Coles was joined by the son or nephew of the Mayor of Tiverton, John Boger Hole. Other appointments he made to clerkships included, in 1834 and 1841, a nephew of Huskisson's and others, with names suggestive of the past such as Browne and Dowling, in the Slave-trade Department. Then there was young John Edward Blackburn, about whose age he enquired so carefully before appointing him as an assistant junior clerk in November 1834.[70]

Whether these were good appointments or not is very difficult to say. Huskisson died in 1849. Blackburn was considered a wit and was popular enough in the office, but he was often absent from it on sick leave and he retired on a pension after only seventeen years' service. Young Rich was even less successful in the F.O. than his father in the W.O.; Aberdeen dismissed him in April 1845. Neither Browne nor Dowling fared much better. Browne's sister and both his and Dowling's mother had figured in the dunning correspondence and debit columns of Palmerston's private accounts. For good measure Browne also gloried in the names of John Henry Temple and impressed Backhouse with his easy confidence. But he proved so troublesome and inattentive that Wellington dismissed him shortly before leaving office in April 1835, and though reinstated by Palmerston in 1837-40 he resigned when he sensed his patron might not survive in office much longer. He was, too, a chronic debtor all the while, and Palmerston tried unsuccessfully to find him alternative employment out of the way abroad, in a merchant's house in Dunkirk in 1835 and in the vice-consulate in Cette in 1841. Daniel Morton Dowling he succeeded in placing at the F.O. shortly before leaving it himself in 1841. But soon Dowling too was in financial difficulties and unable to come to the office as his creditors were 'watching in the street' for him. He continued for a while to draw his pay but shortly, like Browne, disappeared from view. Only the men from Tiverton made much progress in the office, both of them becoming senior clerks, the one taking charge of the Consular Department and the other of the East European. But Coles was given the Consular Department only because it was so unpopular with better men, while he was notoriously incompetent.[71]

Nepotism was no stranger to the F.O. Both the printers and the binders were virtually family concerns. More than one Rolleston, Staveley and Hammond turned up in the nineteenth-century F.O., and numerous Bidwells and Hertslets. Palmerston made the Undersecretary's son, George Canning Backhouse, a clerk in 1838; like Sulivan he was murdered while on foreign service in the 1850s. Aberdeen, it was said, made a special point of favouring the families of his clerks. There were also the recipients of royal favour. The fateful appointment of David Urquhart was owing to some connection he had with the King's private secretary, Sir Herbert Taylor; and in 1830 there were already in the F.O. at least two other clerks with origins close to the court, Richard Mellish and Adolphus Kent Oom. Mellish, who had been a gentleman usher to Queen Adelaide and was said to be a distant relative of hers, became head of the German Department and is still recalled as one of the mere three who were supposed to be able to understand the Schleswig-Holstein question. Oom, whose grandparents had both been in the service of Queen Charlotte and who was himself godson to the Duke of Cambridge and for good measure stepson of Joseph Planta of the Foreign Office, is remembered only as an amateur theatrical and a very popular man.[72]

Not all the royal place men were so popular or so successful. Edward Scheener was denounced by a fellow clerk (Lenox Conyngham) in 1826 as 'a scoundrel and a disgrace to the character of a gentleman' and, when he refused to fight, as a 'coward' as well. He also plagued his masters with unreasonable demands and was twice suspended from duty. Finally, in 1830, he was compulsorily retired. He appealed to the next Foreign Secretary, but after reading the voluminous papers concerned Palmerston in June 1831 upheld the decision of his predecessor. Such treatment seems to have been very uncommon, although Palmerston himself had occasion to dismiss two more, Frederick Dudley Ryder and Charles Parnther. Neither had been appointed by him, but both were the sons of old friends. Parnther was reinstated on appeal, though he had been accused of mishandling agency fees where Ryder had been guilty merely of 'neglect of duty'. But as for Scheener, Canning had bluntly told one royal duke that he would rather copy all the F.O. dispatches himself than have back in the office 'an individual so wrong-headed, of a nature so suspicious, and of a temper so ungovernable'. Scheener, so he claimed with plausibility, was the natural son of the Duke of Kent and so nephew to King William IV and half-brother to Queen Victoria.[73]

The knowledge of Scheener's origins may have confirmed Palmerston's prejudices against having foreigners in the office. He appears to have had little hesitation about appointing Drummond Wolff in October 1846; after all, if his father, though famous for his journey to Bokhara, was a converted German Jew, his mother was the daughter of an English earl and his godfather a very wealthy banker. Drummond Wolff recalled that on first being interviewed by Palmerston:

He asked me several questions about my education, and on hearing the number of different places to which I had been, he made a remark which was perfectly true – that I had picked up what I could where I could, instead of going through a settled course of education. He desired me, however, to write him a letter giving him my history, and to allow him to see my handwriting.

There was, when Palmerston first entered the F.O., already there a young man called Kuper, who though possibly born in England was 'by descent and blood' a foreigner. But he had been appointed only as a favour to the court (where his father was chaplain to Queen Adelaide) and on condition that he should never seek promotion or even consider himself really in the diplomatic service. When Queen Victoria early in 1841 sought on her mother's behalf to have Kuper made Secretary of Legation, Palmerston politely pointed out:

It is for many reasons desirable that all your Majesty's diplomatic agents should be entirely and unquestionably British subjects, both by birth and by blood. For first of all there are so many reputable subjects of your Majesty and many of them persons of good family, who are always candidates for every appointment which may anywhere fall vacant, that it would tend to give well-founded dissatisfaction if foreigners were on those occasions to be preferred; and then, in the next place, no diplomatic agent who is not purely and entirely British can represent with full advantage and the necessary weight British interests in foreign countries.

Kuper never rose above paid attaché, though he acted as chargé d'affaires in Frankfurt on more than one occasion and eventually transferred into the consular service. To the Queen's Mistress of the Robes Palmerston carried the point still further. When in 1840 the Duchess of Sutherland sought a clerkship for the sixteen-year-old William White, Palmerston replied: '. . . it is of great importance that persons appointed to that office should in all respects be purely & entirely English, & should have no foreign connections; now Mr White, though I believe a British subject, has been brought up abroad, & is entirely foreign in his appearance and language, & very much in his connections . . .' White's father did have some mysterious connection with the Polish patriot Czartoryski and was even rumoured to be an illegitimate connection of his. For a brief time the father had been vice-consul in Memel and after being removed at Prussia's request, no doubt as a friendly gesture to Russia, was made a consul in Granville in Normandy. The son did eventually enter the diplomatic service in 1880 and later became a distinguished ambassador in Constantinople; but only by a lucky transfer from the consular service, which he had entered, also by a back door it would seem, in 1857.[74]

Both William White and his father, Arthur, were probably employed in between and in addition to regular consular duties as British intelligence agents. They were by no means the only ones. Arthur White's predecessor in Memel, Frederick Chatfield, wrote unsolicited intelligence reports from sick leaves in Aix in 1830 and was rewarded with a new consulate in Warsaw. Since there was not enough commercial work in Poland to justify his post, he managed to annoy both the Russian and the British F.O.s by his meddling in politics, and was soon recalled. But he was sent on another, and authorized, intelligence mission to the Belgian frontier and was again rewarded with a consular appointment, this time in Central America, which Chatfield calculated – quite correctly – would soon make a diplomat of him and – incorrectly – would give him the opportunity for developing a grand scheme for the expansion of British dominion. Chatfield was a former lieutenant of cavalry with a mere three or four years of service, but vanity enough to think it qualified him for greater things. Palmerston seems to have been irritated by his impertinence but attracted by his enthusiasm and nerve. But neither the man nor his story was untypical of the consular service.[75]

In 1825 Canning had established a small Consular Department in the F.O. and, by prohibiting its agents from engaging in trade or taking any but carefully regulated fees, made them the paid servants of the State. But the department in the F.O. was grossly understaffed and the scale of remuneration for the consuls utterly chaotic. Palmerston did not do much about the Consular Department. Deceived perhaps by John Bidwell's comparative efficiency, he left it still with a staff of only four in 1851, although the paper work it handled was then more than half that of all the political divisions put together. The consuls' salaries, however, he radically revised. Canning had attempted to arrange them according to the rigours of the posts and the expense of living at them. But, however justified in part, the variations were too great and the total cost too large. Since a major attack had already been launched upon his predecessor in 1830, by Hume among others, Palmerston in 1831 undertook a complete overhaul of the system with a view to making a major economy. He reduced the number of consulates and abolished all the Consulates-General save those, in South America for example, where the principal business was commercial rather than political, and so might be conducted by a Consul-General also acting as chargé d'affaires. But this did not satisfy the critics, and after another attack in the Commons in July 1831, he reviewed the salaries of the remaining consuls one by one and reduced the overall expenditure by nearly another third. Then, in order to distract the remaining critics, he coopted them onto a commission of enquiry in July 1835.[76]

There is no doubt that in Palmerston's reconstruction of the consular service, efficiency was sacrificed to economy. Granville loudly complained that the loss of the Consul-General in Paris would only make more work for him; the consuls themselves that they could not live on their new salaries and, since the surviving Consulates-General, being to some extent political, became virtually the preserve of the diplomatic service, that they also had little prospect of promotion. One of Palmerston's perhaps unintended victims in 1832 was the tragic figure of Beau Brummell, eking out his days of exile in poverty in Caen. Eventually Palmerston made him a small compensation of £200 from public funds. He also removed Canning's bar on consuls trading (except in such places as Havana where, he said, all trade 'resolves itself ultimately into slave trade') and where both duties and remuneration were slight resorted to honorary consuls and even foreigners.[77]

Despite the many complaints, some of the larger consulates, such as those in Mediterranean and North American seaports, were well worth having, and the consular service as a whole provided Palmerston with his most useful area of patronage, particularly as he always maintained that it required no particular training or education. Nor was he hampered in the appointment of vice-consul, consul or even Consul-General by any rules or precedents regarding transfer or promotion. It was 'entirely at the discretion of the Secretary of State', he told a select committee in 1847, 'to appoint whom he pleases to any vacancy which may happen, whether that person has or has not been in the line before'. The consequence was, according to *The Times*, that the Secretary of State was 'perpetually assailed by all the influential relations of

half the blockheads in the kingdom'. However mixed or unfortunate the
consequences may have been, the system – or rather the lack of system –
allowed Palmerston to go on appointing to the consular service a strange
variety of more or less seedy characters to be rewarded, bought off or merely
exiled. For though there were some plum jobs among them, most consular
posts were not regarded as providing much more than a supplement to private
or other income. Thus fleeing bankrupts and literary dilettantes continued to
swell the ranks of the service.[78]

The worst of Palmerston's recruits, it was said, was a 'very bad character'
named Jacob James Hart, who was reckoned to have paid money to some of
the Foreign Secretary's constituents in Tiverton for his appointment as consul
in Leipzig in 1836. Palmerston was almost inundated with requests from the
West Country and if he wished to keep his seat he had no choice but to meet at
least a number of them. But Hart seems to have had no connection with
Tiverton and to have owed his appointment to the radical Joseph Parkes,
probably in return for what Parkes had done for Palmerston in the press.
Rumour had it that Hart, having prospered in trade, was both an habitué and
part-owner of gaming tables in London and Paris. In Paris, it was also said, he
had even been discharged by his French teacher as incapable of learning the
language. He was also accused of being scandalously in debt. His own story
was that there was only one case of the latter sort, arising out of 'a foolish
fondness for a lady' and blown up out of all proportion by a man he had
disappointed in a vice-consulate, and who had hence become his enemy. This
seems to have convinced the Foreign Secretary, but Palmerston's own enemies
naturally made all they could of it. Howick reckoned it proved the minister's
own unfitness for the F.O. and 'Ben' Stanley plotted to use it to winkle him out
of office. Both Hart and Palmerston survived – until 1841, that is, when
Backhouse went out of his way to reveal the scandal to Aberdeen and to get
Hart removed as soon as possible after the departure of his patron. Backhouse,
like others before him, made much of there being no business at Leipzig for
Hart to do. But Hart had made reports that were possibly of some use for
commercial purposes, and Aberdeen himself had shortly afterwards to appoint a successor to watch the progress of the *Zollverein*.[79]

Others who found places in the consular service in Palmerston's time
included T.C. Grattan and Charles Macfarlane, both of whom at one time or
another wrote for *The Times*. Grattan was saved from a debtor's prison and
rewarded for favours to Leopold of Belgium with the consulate in Boston. He
made a bad job of it (and eventually handed it over to his son), though not so
bad, surely, as his colleague William Peter, who had been saved from ruin also
by being given Philadelphia. Both of them, moreover, continued to devote
their energies mostly to paid writing. In addition William Perry, the eldest son
of the former proprietor and editor of the *Morning Chronicle*, and numerous
Crowes who were connections of a leader-writer for that paper, also found
consular posts abroad.[80]

The Crowes had a direct connection with Palmerston through the press, but they and most of the others owed at least as much to the support of people like Holland. Holland, indeed, was very pressing. He even obtained a place in Naples for a certain John Goodwin, whom the Foreign Secretary afterwards concluded was 'quite unfit'. But Palmerston hesitated to move Goodwin further away than Palermo, since he suspected that Goodwin was Holland's natural son. Palmerston also looked after his own relatives and connections. Grenville Murray's disastrous descent from the diplomatic corps, through journalism, into the consular service has already been mentioned. So too has the fact that, in contrast to Grenville Murray's noisy contributions in the press and conspicuous failures in the consular service, his brother Henry wrote very little and performed his official duties with quiet efficiency. In 1839 the ruined Godschall Johnson obtained from Palmerston the consulate in Antwerp. He also had at least six sons for whom to badger his distant cousin. For one of them he sought promotion in the Navy; for another in the colonies. Still another, disappointed in various vice-consulates, was consoled with the position of Queen's Messenger, also in 1839; his son, or perhaps a much younger brother, joined him in turn in 1863.[81]

The elder of the Johnson messengers seems to have been quite a character. A 'great big fellow' and one of the very few in mid century to wear his official uniform, he 'would stride down Dover pier arrayed in a flowing cloak, with his silver greyhound badge round his neck, and a string of porters following, clearing his way with "Room for Her Majesty's despatches!" '. Apparently his 'braggadocio manner carried him far'; but he was often in a scrape both at home and abroad. On one occasion in 1850 he had an altercation with an official in Russia and was forbidden to re-enter the country; being very like the Emperor Nicholas in appearance, apparently, he was unable to do so without detection. But he continued in the service until his retirement in 1876; his son or brother retired in 1887.[82]

Appointments as Queen's Messenger were highly prized. They carried only a relatively small salary of £60 a year but a mileage allowance brought their net remuneration to about £1,000 or £1,200 per annum in the late 1830s, and it was still reckoned to be as much as £800 in the late 1850s. Probably it was at its largest in Palmerston's heyday, since he used the messengers so often. Interestingly enough he also sought to maintain their social status, resisting the resort to a 'lower class of officer' made by other Secretaries of State, and formally announcing in 1839 that vacancies among the Foreign Service messengers would in future be filled by 'gentlemen'. Granville wondered if it would any longer be possible for the ambassador to ask messengers to carry with them as 'companions' between Paris and London such people as the son of Lady Holland's cook or for the messenger to require 100 francs a time for doing so. Soon afterwards Palmerston also ordered that mention be made on his travel documents of a messenger's military rank. Of the next two 'gentlemen' appointed one was 'Captain' Cecil Godschall Johnson; his rank was derived from service with the British Auxiliary Legion under the Queen of Spain. The messengers were still considered a distinct peg below the F.O. clerks and diplomats; but not as low as the consuls, where the Murrays had to find their refuges, though in Grenville Murray's case, it must be admitted, this was only after he had been ruined by his indiscreet beginnings as an attaché.[83]

Illegitimate sons could also find a start in the diplomatic service. It was Palmerston who opened a distinguished career for the Earl of Scarbrough's son, John Savile Lumley. But in his attitude to the diplomatic service, as distinct from the consular, Palmerston certainly recognized the need for a degree of professionalism. One interesting evidence of this was his experiment with the training of interpreters for the Levant. Habitually, the embassy in Constantinople had employed local interpreters or dragomen. But these were considered venal and untrustworthy. Accordingly in 1841 Palmerston invited the Vice-Chancellors of Oxford and Cambridge each to nominate a student of his university for training as interpreter attachés in Constantinople. Two went out the next year and Aberdeen followed Palmerston's example with two more in 1845. But the scheme failed because the candidates were not content to stay on as junior interpreters in Constantinople and wanted to take their chances of promotion in the service at large. The ambassador seemed to think that this was inevitable, since young men who had been picked out for 'the independence of their characters' were unlikely from their origins and education to assume the 'submissive and patient demeanour' expected of interpreters in the East or to submit to 'the attendance and drudgery' involved. Palmerston, however, put it differently, confessing in a minute of 1848:

I made a mistake in asking the Vice-Chancellors of Oxford or Cambridge to select and recommend students. I ought to have known that the learned bodies would be sure to make a job of such an invitation, and to pick out young men by favour and not for merit, and so it has happened, at least in the case of my own University of Cambridge. Any other young men wanted from England should be got from the London University, where there would be a better chance of a bona fide choice.

As far as is known Palmerston never had occasion to act on his own suggestion, though he contemplated doing so for the consular, as well as the diplomatic, service in the Levant. However, when Clarendon in 1854 sent five interpreters to China, he took one each from King's and University Colleges in London and from the three colleges of Queen's University in Ireland. Shortly afterwards he took six more from King's, and when Russell opened up recruitment to limited competition he nevertheless reserved six places for that college out of consideration for its having sent the F.O. in the past 'some very good men'.[84]

Palmerston also had rather mixed views about the introduction of competitive entrance examinations into the service. It was he who as Prime Minister in 1855 promised, when questioned in the Commons by J. A. Wise – 'an ill-named man', Palmerston said, who had once been an unsuccessful candidate for the service – that examinations would be introduced and approached his Foreign Secretary, whom he knew to be hostile, saying they were now 'the order of the day'. Some time later he explained to Croker, whose grandson had just failed to get into the Treasury, that while examinations were but crude instruments for measuring 'relative ability and attainments', they at least ensured a minimum standard. But when he saw the sort of papers set by the Civil Service Commissioners Palmerston exploded at what he called their 'absurd pedantry'. So far as concerned an examination for F.O. clerks, his view was probably much the same as Hammond's: he wanted not scholars but affable, industrious and trustworthy copyists. For the diplomatic service, however, he thought the candidates ought to offer either German or Italian as well as French. He even proposed that geometry be included as an ideal training for the sort of 'argument to conclusions' needed in diplomacy. 'Nothing strengthens the reasoning faculty more than Geometry,' he wrote in an uncanny echo of the first Lord Malmesbury. But in the end he told his Foreign Secretary to 'do as he liked'.[85]

The first F.O. examination in 1856 turned out to be almost a farce – except in so far as the candidates' handwriting was concerned. The exam for the diplomatic service was somewhat more searching and, in the opinion even of one of its harsher critics, at least kept out the 'notoriously incompetent'. But the examinations were not made competitive until 1883. This meant that while the Secretary of State's office patronage was carefully preserved by his adhering to a system of nominating the candidates himself, so too was his exposure to outside pressure. When in August 1831 the King was considering opening up the junior classes of the Bath to civilians Palmerston objected on the grounds that it was likely to lead to abuse. 'Diplomatic services are something known and tangible, & can be measured by years and publick events,' he advised the Prime Minister, '& no great abuse is likely to be practised in rewarding such by the Bath. But other civil services are so much more vague and indefinite in their nature, & are so much more mixed up with the struggle of home politicks.' From the very beginning, however, he was under considerable pressure to refill diplomatic places with friends and relations of the Whig magnates.[86]

After so many years in the political wilderness the Whigs were eager in 1830 to distribute the spoils of office even among the fledgeling and the incompetent. The various connections of dukes seem to have been a particularly heavy burden for Palmerston to bear. There was, for example, the Secretary of Legation in Paris. When Granville returned there as ambassador in 1830 he already knew from previous experience that Hamilton Charles James Hamilton was 'extremely inefficient' and he asked Palmerston to relieve him of his presence at the earliest opportunity. According to Lady Granville, Hamilton, 'as he grows older and less sanguine about his own affairs, is left

with the outward man entirely unstuffed, not one idea or *quantité* of understanding, that can make him of the slightest use or relief in any one branch of
Diplomacy'. Her opinion did not improve, although she became, apparently,
a very close friend to his wife: 'The place of Secretary of Legation is filled, but
not occupied,' she wrote in April 1831. 'Mr Hamilton, harmless, inoffensive
man, can neither comprehend nor reply to even a question about etiquette or
the news of the day. "What sort of weather is it to-day, Mr H.?" "God bless my
soul, it never occurred to me to make an observation. It seems to me, I may err,
I would not pronounce rashly, but I'll step out and make a point of ascertaining it"; a nervous, bilious, conscientious, *pauvre sire.*' Such, then, was the
second man in England's most important embassy. In time Granville hardly
dared to leave the embassy at all; for the French complained that Hamilton
was too much of a 'nonentity' for them to deal with as chargé d'affaires.[87]

Palmerston in London could not say that Hamilton had shown himself such
a 'goose' as everybody claimed. But he had to admit that the Secretary had not
been severely tested in office and that on his own private visits in earlier years
to Paris he had written him down as 'conceited, consequential & empty'.
However, he could not deal with him in too cavalier a fashion since, as well as
being the second most senior man in his rank, he was a cousin of the Duke of
Hamilton and set down in his entail. In May 1832 Palmerston took advantage
of the first vacancy that arose to offer Hamilton Buenos Aires and to move
Arthur Aston, the very successful chargé in Rio, to Paris as Secretary of
Legation. Aston's appointment was as much a success as Palmerston could
have wished. But instead of thanking the Foreign Secretary for the promotion
which his predecessors had long denied him, Hamilton hesitated between
accepting exile and resigning his post, and sent his cousin the duke to badger
Palmerston. Palmerston had already been criticized in the newspapers for
promoting Hamilton at all, and he told the duke quite frankly that Hamilton
was lucky to get his promotion and insisted, as if he knew from personal experience, that 'it was a mistake to suppose Buenos Ayres a bad climate, for . . .
on the contrary it was rather a good one'. In any case, 'though it might not be
so agreeable a residence as Paris, people who are in a profession, must of course
take their turn of duty, & the rough with the smooth'. This was certainly what
he had always told his brother William. The duke seemed to take it very well,
and it was rather unfair, if understandable from other experience, for Palmerston to add when reporting to Grey: 'these grandees are very difficult
gentlemen to satisfy, but I do not see what we can do at present for Hamilton
Hamilton, Esq.'[88]

Palmerston certainly had no intention whatever of promoting Hamilton
over the head of Francis Forbes, who 'though not very brilliant', was the most
senior Secretary of Legation and had served nearly two years longer in that
rank than Hamilton. Moreover, Palmerston thought Forbes 'a very good little
fellow', if 'by no means a wise one', and though 'not the sort of person whom
one should chuse, for his own qualifications, to make a minister of ', he was the

son of the Earl of Granard. So Forbes got Dresden, a pleasant post where he represented England, according to a contemporary, 'petitement et sottement' for more than the next quarter of a century. Finally, in December 1858, a few months before his retirement, he was sent on a special mission to the Emperor of Brazil. Hamilton had to make do with South America all along. Once there he irritated Palmerston by the prolixity of his dispatches and by falling into an unseemly quarrel with his colleague across the Andes. Having, moreover, delayed taking up his new post for two years in the first place on grounds of ill health, he stayed there only eighteen months before transferring to Rio. Eighteen months after that he was taking sick leave again, and after he had passed a whole year in England Palmerston ordered that he be told it was 'impossible to allow diplomatic appointments to be converted into sinecures and to be performed by deputy'. If his health was too bad for him to return to Brazil, then he should take a pension. But in no case would Palmerston extend his leave beyond the end of August 1840. In July of that year Palmerston ordered Hamilton back to his post 'forthwith', but by delaying his departure from packet to packet on the pretence of waiting for a warship – to which form of conveyance his diplomatic rank entitled him – Hamilton still managed to spin out his leave till the summer of the following year. He finally set out in the summer of 1841 and stayed all of five years at his post before returning once again on sick leave in August 1846. This time he did not go back to Brazil and he died ten years later at the ripe old age of seventy-seven.[89]

Secretary of Legation or Embassy was the highest rank in the junior branches of the service and the next step to becoming minister or ambassador. Palmerston was not by any means sure that the incumbents all deserved their rank. 'Many Secys of Legation', he wrote in October 1832, 'think that their special duty is to do nothing but the regulation of the Service is that they are to be the principal assistants of their chief.' Lord William Russell once suggested that as heads of missions never got on with their Secretaries it would be better to abolish Secretaries altogether and send them F.O. clerks instead. His brother John also thought that a man would be a far better Secretary of Legation if he were to start in that capacity from a desk in Downing Street rather than after 'lounging some years in Paris & Vienna'. But senior men, with diplomatic experience, were needed to act as chargés d'affaires when their chiefs fell ill or went on leave and until the prejudice against integrating F.O. clerks with the diplomatic service was overcome there could hardly be a regular system of exchange.[90]

Palmerston said in 1834 that he was averse to making clerkships stepping-stones to headships of missions or even secretaryships of legation. Probably he needed some system of defence against all the pressures put upon him. But having mortally offended Sefton by making his son serve, however briefly, as attaché, and having warned the Cowpers about his rule, Palmerston made Spencer Cowper a Secretary of Legation immediately on his leaving the F.O.

Nevertheless Secretaries of Legation were usually recruited from the attachés
who did their duties abroad. These duties were not very taxing. When in 1837
Charles Murray wanted to be Secretary of Legation in America, where he had
fallen in love, but doubted if he had a chance since he had no previous
experience, the outgoing ambassador, like him a Fellow of All Souls, reassured
him: 'the art in being a good *attaché* consists in diligence and discretion, in
learning to cipher and decipher, and in writing a good hand.' Murray did not
get the post from Palmerston, though he was a younger son of the Earl of
Dunmore and nephew by morganatic marriage to the Duke of Sussex. Instead
he got a court appointment from Melbourne. But when he did begin his
distinguished if hectic career in the foreign service, in 1845, it was straight
away as Secretary of Legation in Naples, and less than a year later he was
appointed Consul-General in Egypt. Less favoured or fortunate individuals,
seeking a career, usually had to serve for many years as attachés, first in an
unpaid capacity.[91]

Unpaid attachés were so loosely attached to the service and so apt to come
home on indefinite leave from places they did not like, that no one knew at any
one moment how many of them should properly be considered still to belong
to the service. Palmerston was a firm believer in his diplomats taking reasonable amounts of leave in England.

It would [he said in 1837] be very unjust towards persons employed abroad in
diplomatic situations, particularly in despotic countries, when they perform
their duties zealously and faithfully, to refuse them permission to come home,
and refresh themselves by reviving their English feelings, and witnessing more
closely the operation of those constitutional doctrines in which they have been
brought up. Indeed, I attach so much imortance to this point, that if an English minister did not make an application of this nature, after a lapse of five or
six years, I should feel disposed to order him home.

But there were limits, and with junior attachés in particular Palmerston tried
to establish a rule that they could go on leave only with the permission of their
chiefs. It is doubtful if he made much of an impression on this branch of the
service. Too many of them were what someone called 'mere saunterers'. When
two attachés on French leave from St Petersburg were ordered back to their
posts, both resigned, leaving the minister with only one assistant. After all, as
one of their colleagues later wrote: 'The British tax-payer could owe them no
grudge: they were unpaid. Society could expect nothing of them but amusement and a disposition to enjoy themselves; and they had no responsibilities,
unless it was that of not misleading the chief by wrong deciphering or an
incorrect translation.' So they remained, in Palmerston's view, 'encumbering
idlers in time present, and troublesome and hopeless suitors in time future'.[92]

It was easier to impose some semblance of discipline on paid attachés, who
by 1846 were receiving salaries of between £200 and £400 a year. There was no
actual regulation that they should undergo a few months' probation in the
F.O. until 1853 and there was no entrance examination until 1856. But in
1833 Palmerston was already going out of his way to ensure that a candidate

for Vienna could read not only German but also German script, and by the beginning of 1838 care was also being taken that men did not go out as attachés until they had passed muster during a short period in the F.O. Since 1825, moreover, no attaché could officially be nominated by anyone but the Secretary of State. When Francis Cavendish sought to become attaché in Vienna in 1846, the newly appointed ambassador, Ponsonby, bluntly told him that such appointments rested not with him but Palmerston, and it was Palmerston who gave it to him. However, this merely exposed the Foreign Secretary to constant pressure from personal and political friends who could afford to pay for the prestige and protection that nomination as attachés would give to their connections and dependants. Moreover, while additional and unpaid attachés might appear to be no burden on the State, neither they nor their paid colleagues were always popular with their seniors. As Palmerston explained to a Cabinet colleague in October 1835:

The number of attachés cannot be increased arbitrarily; a certain number are wanted at the greater and at some of the smaller missions to assist the ministers to get through their work; but when the minister has as many as he wants, or does not want any at all, it is a great infliction to send him a young gentleman to educate and look after; and it would be the harder to entail these burdens upon our ministers now, because their salaries have been much reduced, & an attaché is always a charge upon the minister to whom he is sent.[93]

Sometimes ministers felt willing or obliged to make attachés almost members of their families. They must in any case have often wined and dined them. In Paris, where there were sometimes as many as five, Lady Granville had them all to dinner at the embassy on the dispatch days for England, which were twice a week, on Mondays and Fridays. In Vienna, wrote Lamb, three attachés were as much as the place could bear; 'more would be like keeping a pension for grown-up pupi[l]s.' William Russell, too, protested against having any more. 'When they are so numerous the Chancery becomes a sort of Coffee House where the despatches are read and criticised like newspapers. Besides some are the lovers of women, some drink, some gossip from vanity, and between their vices and their follies everything transpires.' Grey, too, believed that the life of an attaché was one of 'complete idleness, and exposed to every specimen of temptation'. His youngest son had expressed a strong desire for a career in diplomacy, and Grey was worried both about the expense and about his son's tendency to idleness. So in September 1835 he favoured a clerkship in the F.O. as a compromise. With this his adviser Holland was in complete agreement. 'A clerkship in the F.O. is a good mezzo termino,' he wrote, 'for it ensures work & confinement & at the worst some emolument.' Interestingly enough, in view of all the clerks' complaints, Howick on the other hand thought that his brother was at sixteen much too young either for the diplomatic service or for 'the lounging & gossiping life of a clerk in the Foreign Office'. In the end it was decided to make the poor young man spend a few years first at a German university.[94]

The Greys were strongly of the opinion that diplomacy was a poor profession, most unlikely to lead to either monetary reward or political distinction. Palmerston, for his part, was also very much aware that the needs of the service required careful and constant attention to justice as well as efficiency in the lower ranks, where the maintenance of good morale demanded a career open to talents and experience. 'With respect to my children abroad,' he wrote to the Duke of Devonshire, employing, almost immediately on entering the office, what was already or was soon to become the traditional metaphor of its inmates, 'there is always as you may easily conceive, a difficulty in adopting a new one into the family, since those who have passed regularly through the nursery expect to succeed to the best appointments.' To the Prime Minister Palmerston explained in more detail the following year:

. . . I should feel very great pleasure in being able to attend to Mr Howard's wishes in favour of his son, consistently with a just regard to the fair claims & pretensions of other persons in the same career; but I fear it would not be possible to do what he now wishes without affording to a large number of those who are senior to his son, well founded grounds of complaint.
The three junior classes in diplomatic gradation, are secretaries of legation, paid attachés, and unpaid attachés; and the natural course of the service is, that persons should rise from the last of these classes, to the first mentioned, through the second.
A vacancy has occurred in the Secretaries of Legation by the resignation of Mr Tierney, and Mr Howard wishes his son to be appointed to it; But there are 12 paid attachés, who would all, coeteris paribus, have claims to that vacancy in preference to any unpaid attaché; and there are 26 unpaid attachés who have all served longer than Mr Hy Howard, many of them indeed more than twice as long.
I have a very good opinion of Mr Hy Howard, who is highly spoken of by Lord Erskine, . . . but I am afraid that it would not be possible just at present to give him the promotion which he wishes for.[95]

Henry Francis Howard, though connected to almost all the magnates, nevertheless had to wait another fifteen years for his promotion and afterwards enjoyed only a very modest career in the service. Others were even less lucky and blamed Palmerston forever after. George Stapleton had been an unpaid attaché only since April 1830, rather later than Henry Howard. His father was one of three illegitimate sons of the Earl of Morley and as 'a very old friend' Morley 'attacked' Palmerston 'often and vigorously' about his grandson. But Palmerston refused to do such injustice to all the others ahead of him, and Stapleton soon passed out of the service and into obscurity. His uncle, who had been George Canning's private secretary and after his master's early death assumed his public defence, in subsequent years went much out of his way to deny Palmerston's supposed claims to be his master's natural heir.[96]

By October 1835, it seems, Palmerston reckoned he had cut down the number of unpaid attachés by half. But some of the remainder had still been waiting six to eight years for a paid position, and even as late as 1861 there was a wide discrepancy in the periods which even those who had managed to become ministers had previously served in their apprenticeships as attachés. William Temple had gone from unpaid attaché to Secretary of Legation in but a single year (1814); under Palmerston promotion prospects in the lower ranks became steadily worse. But his own 'jobs' were probably fairly few and far between. The appointment of W.D. Christie as Secretary of Legation in 1851 after only three years as agent and Consul-General with the Mosquito Indians, and his promotion to Rio in 1859, were matters of some remark. Brougham's stepdaughter, Lady Malet, said that he was 'clever & learned' but 'as mad as Bedlam, vulgar, & mental & quarrelling with all classes & people'. She was by no means an unbiased witness. Her husband, Sir Alexander Malet, was a rival in the service and Brougham had not been particularly successful in badgering Palmerston on his son-in-law's behalf. He had plotted, when Shee left the F.O. in 1834, to see Malet made Palmerston's précis-writer. Rather more than a year later Palmerston made Malet Secretary of Legation in The Hague, where he stayed about nine years, and 'Brougham's petticoat', as Lady Malet was called in the F.O., was credited with retailing all the gossip of London. Malet finally got promotion when Shee was ousted from Württemberg and was afterwards moved to Frankfurt. But while Brougham's cronies looked forward to Palmerston's displacement in 1851 making further opportunities, Malet never rose any higher. On the other hand, Christie's may have been almost as dirty a job as Lady Malet thought. When he exchanged his parliamentary seat for a diplomatic post in 1847 it does seem likely that it was to get out of some financial scrape. But he afterwards acknowledged that he had no serious claim on Palmerston, either personal or political. It was Minto, whose private secretary he had been at the Admiralty, for whom Palmerston was doing the favour.[97]

In general, indeed, Palmerston probably did as much as he could to resist inconvenient and unjustifiable demands for appointments and promotions. This was true even where the Prime Minister himself was personally concerned. Palmerston did consult Grey not only about all his senior appointments but about many of those at the very lowest levels too. However, when Grey sought even a small move upwards among the unpaid attachés for a young relative of his own, Palmerston explained at length that, though he had heard 'a very good account' of Charles des Voeux, there were others ahead of him in the queue. When the Prime Minister also passed on, for a second time, a request for diplomatic employment for a son-in-law of the Duke of Grafton, Joseph St John, with the comment that he was personally obliged to the duke, he was also firmly though politely refused. Palmerston had already been approached directly by the duke and had demurred, in spite of the fact that he also was obliged to him for help in Cambridge. Subsequently he explained to Grey:

I should be very glad to oblige the Duke of Grafton if an opportunity of so doing can be found, but it is very difficult to introduce new persons into the inferior situations; there are plenty of eligible candidates among those who have been serving for years, & there seems no particular reason for inserting a stranger over their heads, and I can have no protection against the younger sons & cousins of half England, except the observance of some rules on this subject.[98]

It was much more difficult to call upon 'rules' to protect the plum positions at or near the top of the service: by custom and tradition special missions and even regular residencies often went to distinguished politicians and wealthy aristocrats. At first Grey refused to give way to what he called 'the pretensions of the Tory-phobia'. Lord Heytesbury was persuaded to stay in St Petersburg, since the Tsar liked him, and the undistinguished Chad was kept on in Berlin for eighteen months, since he had only just been appointed; Sidmouth's nephew, Henry Unwin Addington, even survived in Madrid for almost another three years in spite of his evident stupidity. In Vienna and Paris, however, more or less immediate changes were considered necessary, in the first case because the Tory incumbent wished to go and in the second because his post was needed for Granville. Granville's return to Paris was hardly questioned, since he was not only a leading Canningite and a friend of Palmerston's but also a man of proven and superior fitness for the post. Although by the 1830s he was getting old and gouty his steadiness in Paris and his good private relations with Palmerston served very well until overstrained by the Anglo-French crisis of 1839-40.[99]

In Vienna Palmerston's Whig colleagues wished to see appointed an even older friend of theirs, Sir Robert Adair. Adair was Charles James Fox's last surviving friend and an experienced diplomat. But among the Canningites he was best remembered as a victim of their wit, 'a dull fool' and a 'silly coxcomb'. Palmerston probably recalled how inconvenient, too, some of his love affairs had been. For the mistress Adair had eventually married was generally believed to have been a French spy and that belief had already seriously damaged his credit, even among the Whigs. It said very little for his discretion as a diplomat, moreover, that he should eventually have replaced her with another of the same sort. He certainly believed that Palmerston was loath to keep him informed. In any event, it said equally as little for his personal and political judgement that he should eventually have advised his Government that to settle Belgium and save Turkey they should accede to the Convention of Münchengrätz. Grey had mentioned Adair for Vienna when he had first invited Palmerston to join his administration, but Palmerston had from the beginning displayed a distinct lack of enthusiasm. He gently indicated to Grey that he considered Adair too old and infirm for such an arduous post. Later he told Lady Cowper that Adair was fit only for 'a hospital'; aware perhaps that he had once made a fool of himself in his advances to her mother, Emily had already concluded for herself that he was simply 'an old idiot'. So Palmerston refused to give way and Grey could only acknowledge the absolute right of the Foreign Secretary to control the patronage of his own office. But while Grey too soon got bored with Adair's continual complaints and 'habitual gloom', he regretted for his peace of mind that he had not made Adair's appointment to Vienna a stipulation of Palmerston's having the Foreign Office in the first place, and he continued to press his colleague to find him something better. So Palmerston sought to placate the Whigs by offering Adair his old place in Constantinople, and when that was indignantly refused elevated Brussels to the status of a special mission for him. In Brussels, according to his successor, Adair, being 'accustomed to the old routine of affairs, imagined almost everything too insignificant for the handling of so great a man as a British ambassador'. He boasted, it was understood, that he did not read 'the trumpery Belgian papers, and he was equally proud that, with the exception of a few Orangists, he did not mix with the trumpery Belgian people. Thus, except at critical moments, when he showed his former energy & ability, his time was passed in a state of besotted irritation, carrying on warlike correspondence with quarrelsome English gentlemen, and amatory correspondence with accommodating French & Belgian ladies.' Consequently, in 1835-6, Palmerston created another special mission for him in Berlin as a short 'bridge' to a comfortable retirement.[100]

In the crucial embassy in Vienna Palmerston insisted on having Emily's brother Fred. The appointment, made in May 1831, was a good one, since Lamb (who had been knighted in 1827, and was to be created Baron Beauvale in 1839 and to succeed his brother as third and last Viscount Melbourne in 1848) was already recognized as one of the most able among the career diplomats. But he was a hard-headed reactionary who did not mince words in his letters any more than in his speech. His voluminous private letters to his chief amounted to a searching and powerful critique, which Palmerston probably appreciated even though they cost him an equal effort in riposte and sometimes sounded too much like what he called 'Metternichs'. Palmerston does not seem to have taken amiss, either, the very critical letters that Fred sent to his brother, even though they armed Melbourne, as Grey's successor in 1834 and 1835, with very powerful ammunition against the Foreign Secretary. There is no doubt that Fred Lamb disapproved both of Palmerston's policy and of his attachment to his sister; that Palmerston, rather uncharacteristically, failed to react with any ill feeling was probably due to a well justified sense of caution and discretion where Emily's devotion to her favourite brother was concerned. 'The Sister would not hesitate between the Lover and the Brother,' wrote Greville, 'and any injury to the latter would recoil upon the head of the former.' For Palmerston, therefore, Lamb's position in Vienna was 'sacred ground', no matter how 'be-Metternich'd' he was. Emily, on the other hand, pressed her brother constantly to return to England, since Palmerston so resented her own absences abroad. But, rather prolonged leaves of absence apart, he stayed until shortly after Palmerston's own departure from office in 1841. It was his pension, perhaps, that kept him so long abroad. 'The foolish women', he wrote to his brother about their nearest and dearest, 'persecute me because I do not choose to sacrifice the reward of years of labour.'[101]

Diplomatic pensions were a very difficult problem. 'You should contrive to lay by something every year,' Palmerston warned his brother when he heard he was living 'very hospitably' in Naples,

for pensions are precarious things, & always liable to cutting down. Though the diplomatic ones, having been placed on the Consolidated Fund are safer than the rest; but new regulations may be made, increasing periods of service, & diminishing rates of pension. Not that anything of the kind is in contemplation at present. But satisfy yourself by inspection of accounts that you are receiving yearly more than you spend.

But though safe for the present, one unfortunate consequence of its being in the Consolidated Fund was that the total of £180,000 did not necessarily provide money enough for all who might qualify for pensions by the rules of the service, even though those rules did not count service as attachés. In fact the total of pensions already exceeded the amount laid down by Act of Parliament in 1832 and until it was reduced to the permitted level Palmerston was further required to limit new ones to a total of £2,000 in any one year.[102]

Since it was only fair to give incumbents the chance to build up sufficient service, the lack of ready funds for pensions was occasionally a useful argument for fending off the appointment of an unwelcome outsider or for protecting the position of a valued ally in diplomacy – for example, when the critics of Palmerston's Eastern policy in 1840 sought to get rid of his vigorous ambassador in Constantinople. But too often the result rather was that either the efficiency of the service was damaged by retaining the old or incompetent or the grievances of those who could not be found employment or a pension were compounded. One whom Palmerston in consequence found it difficult to get rid of was Sir Robert Gordon. According to Melbourne Gordon was 'a man of integrity, but . . . tiresome, long and pompous'. His sister Emily, however, liked him 'very much' and tried to destroy what she called Palmerston's prejudice against him. It was true that Palmerston had some; after all, Gordon was Aberdeen's younger brother and if Emily found him attractive so much the less would Palmerston. He certainly made unnecessarily nasty comments about Gordon. When ill health or the destruction of the embassy by fire forced Gordon to abandon Constantinople without leave in September 1831, Palmerston reported to Grey that he had 'bolted'. He refused to consider Gordon for St Petersburg the following year, and insisted afterwards that he could find him neither post nor pension though he was qualified by service for the latter at least. The death of another pensioner soon made room for him, after all, to receive part of what was due, and the rest was made up from the Civil List. But not until his brother returned to the F.O. did Gordon find employment again, as Lamb's successor in Vienna. Another old Harrovian who lost employment with Palmerston and regained it only with

Aberdeen was Lord Burghersh, later Earl of Westmorland. As Burghersh was both an ally and a relative of Wellington's, it is doubtful if there was much left of the old school friendship between him and Palmerston. In addition the diplomat's running correspondence with Palmerston and Shee shows that he bore a special grudge against them for denying him a pension; by March 1832 he was complaining that he had lost £10,000 by their refusal.[103]

What Burghersh had wanted was something good in Italy, preferably to return to Naples. When Malmesbury succeeded to the F.O. in 1852, Palmerston, besides damning several ministers whose hands were quite illegible, said that when diplomats came to him seeking appointments Malmesbury would soon be struck with a very curious circumstance, namely that 'no climate agrees with an English diplomatist excepting that of Paris, Florence, or Naples'. With a warm and healthy climate and a sympathetic atmosphere of cultivated taste alloyed with many English visitors and residents, Italian posts, and that at Naples in particular, were the plums among the second class. Another old acquaintance who was soon pestering Palmerston for one of them was Viscount Normanby. Normanby, subsequently the first marquess of that name, was the eldest son of Palmerston's old chief at the Admiralty, the Earl of Mulgrave. He was said to be a vain and self-important man, always on the look-out for his own promotion. He had no sooner heard of Palmerston's accession to the F.O., therefore, than he had written to the Duke of Devonshire: 'Palmerston is a very old friend of mine from whom no former political differences ever estranged me.' Yet it was perhaps an augury of the strange behaviour he would one day display towards his 'old friend' that after Palmerston had responded with regret that he could not yet make use of his 'knowledge of Italian politics & his talents & attainments', Mulgrave (as he had by then become) should at the next supposed opportunity have thought of uniting in himself three or four missions in northern Italy and so have written accordingly direct to Grey: 'Before I left Italy my wishes on the subject of an appointment there were mentioned not by myself to Palmerston and the answer was kind and favourable expressing a desire to attend to them whenever an opportunity occurred. But I communicate direct with you because I *should* on public – as I *would* on *private* grounds – much rather owe such a thing to you than to one to whom I never was politically or personally attached.'[104]

Mulgrave did not get anything in Italy or in the diplomatic service elsewhere; instead he took the Government of Jamaica in 1832. Grey in fact had someone else in mind for Naples and Palmerston eventually had to appoint him. This was Lady Grey's brother Lord Ponsonby. He was not one of the Ponsonbys Palmerston had known at Harrow, but a cousin of theirs and a handsome, dangerous man, who had serious love affairs with Harriette Wilson and Princess Lieven as well as Lady Conyngham. It was said – with truth – that Canning had placated George IV by appointing Ponsonby far away to South America. Ponsonby had managed to escape from there even before George's death, but he was very hard up and Grey naturally wished to obtain for him a lucrative post nearer at hand. For about six months, from December 1830 to June 1831, he had acted in Brussels as joint representative of the London conference. But he had often embarrassed Palmerston by exceeding or ignoring the letter of his instructions and finally, on 6 June, had had to be recalled. Grey could not deny that the recall was necessary, but he did not want his brother-in-law banished once again to South America, and Ponsonby's fate evidently caused some real strain in his relations with Palmerston; inside information at the F.O. even insisted it contributed to talk of resignation.[105]

Evidently Palmerston was not anxious to fulfil the sort of half promise he had made to give Ponsonby the impending vacancy in Naples; and though he soon gave way the appointment was not gazetted, for some reason, until 1832. In the meantime Grey suggested him as a substitute for Stratford Canning in St Petersburg and as his successor in Constantinople. Presumably it was Palmerston from whom Lady Cowper got the idea that Ponsonby was 'incapable' of filling the embassy in St Petersburg satisfactorily; but the Foreign Secretary jumped at the suggestion of Constantinople. The discrepancy is curious. Perhaps it was Ponsonby's liaison with Princess Lieven that disqualified him for St Petersburg. For it was also vital to have an effective representative in Constantinople in order to rebuild the influence Great Britain had lost through her failure to help the Sultan against Mehemet Ali. Ponsonby got off to a bad start by dallying too long in Italy before going on to Turkey; and he was strongly criticized for it both at the time and since. But it was Palmerston who insisted he must first perform a token visit to his previous post in Naples, and unfavourable winds that finally delayed his leaving it.[106]

Ponsonby was also accused of indolence in Constantinople. It was true he disliked routine, but he tackled his principal task with characteristic vigour. Probably he was the right man at the right time. He often strayed again from the strict letter of his instructions, but he did a great deal to re-establish Britain's influence. He was therefore an excellent instrument for the prosecution of Palmerston's policy. Palmerston not only acknowledged it; he also defended Ponsonby vigorously against the attacks of his critics both in the service and in the Cabinet. Fred Lamb, Melbourne and Russell all at one time or another sought to oust him, and Palmerston saved his ambassador again and again. Not until 1849 did he finally quarrel with him. Quite what it was all about remains a partial mystery. Ostensibly it concerned the strongly anti-Austrian line Palmerston had recently been taking, and the indiscreet manner in which Ponsonby had tried to counter it. But so waspish were Palmerston's reproofs and so unmeasured Ponsonby's retorts, that probably there was also something very personal involved.[107]

In the end, then, Ponsonby gave Palmerston more trouble in the diplomatic service than Grey's other close relation by marriage, Durham. On the whole Palmerston preferred having Durham in St Petersburg than intriguing

Lady Jersey

Princess Lieven

Laura Petre

Palmerston, 1838

Lady Cowper, by Hoppner-Jackson, *c.* 1820

Minny Cowper

Fanny Cowper

William Cowper, photographed by
Heath and Beau

No. 9 Stanhope Street (now Stanhope Gate),
photographed in 1946 before alterations

Wellington ejecting Huskisson from the Cabinet, caricature by Heath, 20 May 1828

Above, a detail of
'The House of Commons
in 1833', by Sir George
Hayter

The study of Palmerston
made by Sir George Hayter for
the preceding picture

The old Foreign Office (left), Downing Street, 1827

Stephen Henry Sulivan,
by John Lucas

Sir George Shee

Lord Brougham, by John Doyle

Earl of Durham

Earl of Clarendon

Edward Ellice, by HB (John Doyle)

against him nearer home. But a man of Durham's restless temperament and insatiable ambition was unlikely to remain contented anywhere for long and the prospect that loomed up in the summer of 1834 of having him in the still more sensitive post in Paris, as will be seen, appalled Palmerston. So, probably, did the suggestion of Vienna shortly after. Palmerston was therefore delighted and relieved when Melbourne managed to persuade both Durham and the King that the radical earl should return to Russia in 1835. This second mission was still more successful than the first in smoothing matters between the rivals, and after Durham left Russia in 1837 another satisfyingly distant appointment was eventually found in Canada.

With Stratford Canning still ruled out, the difficulty of finding a suitable successor for St Petersburg returned with Durham's departure in 1837. It may therefore have given Palmerston, as Webster suggests, wry satisfaction to send George Canning's daughter where the Tsar had refused his cousin. Melbourne, however, had strong objections to both the Clanricardes. When the suggestion was first mooted, he told Russell that he would not give way to Clanricarde's 'blackguard insolence' in trying to force an appointment out of the Government by turning all his influence against them both in England and in Ireland. He also thought neither the husband nor the wife likely to please the Tsar, who 'lays great stress upon moral character & very much dislikes & discountenances vice & immorality. He particularly dislikes intriguing, intermeddling women'. Clanricarde bore a reputation as a womanizer even worse than Palmerston's; there was also still upon him the taint of 'that gambling transaction' that had brought his father-in-law hurrying back from important business in Paris to save him from disgrace as an accused cheat in 1826. Lady Clanricarde was a beautiful but imperious woman who pursued her late father's supposed enemies and betrayers with still more 'political virulence' than her mother had. She continued to condemn Palmerston long after Lady Canning had professed to have forgiven him for joining Wellington's Government. So, at any rate, Mme Flahault took pains to report of her sayings in Paris. Lady Clanricarde was completely in the hands of Mme de Dino, she wrote, extremely ill disposed towards Melbourne's Government, and spreading 'idle stories' about Palmerston with a view to doing as much mischief as possible. Yet it was probably Palmerston who suggested Clanricarde for Russia in 1837, as he certainly did in 1838. Melbourne was as much against it as ever. 'There is Clanricarde himself,' he wrote, 'a little insipid in character, of diplomatic abilities unknown, of discretion doubtful, & then there is Lady Clanricarde, a clever lively woman thinking & talking of nothing but politics, a decided enemy.' But Palmerston professed to think that the Clanricardes' bitterness was more personal than political and directed more at Melbourne than himself; and tacitly recalling Durham and Grey to mind suggested they would be better out of the way in Russia. Indeed, Clanricarde might even be useful there; he might not have been tried in diplomacy but he was 'a clever and active-minded man', who from his connection with Canning

– he had briefly been his Undersecretary as well as son-in-law – would be more familiar with foreign affairs than anyone else outside the diplomatic line. Failing him there was among the senior professionals only the harmless but pedestrian Vaughan; and outside it 'to send some foolish peer who has never been in public life, has never thought about foreign affairs, and has even the alphabet of his business to learn, is not only throwing away the money he would cost, but exposing the public interest to the chances of suffering seriously'. Clanricarde got the job and proved a competent ambassador.[108]

Like Grey, Holland had several relatives whom he wished to place or promote in the foreign service; and with none of them could Palmerston entirely feel content, not with another cousin or a son, let alone with Fox-Strangways and John Goodwin. In November 1832 the minister in Washington, Charles Richard Vaughan, wanted to quit his post while he could still 'leave off [a] winner'. Since no room could be found for him on the pension list and Palmerston thought him 'a steady sensible man, though not very showy' he was considered for The Hague. For some reason the appointment was never made; nor, though he was several times suggested, did he go out as substitute to Constantinople or St Petersburg. Instead he had to be content with a knighthood in 1833 and a pension in 1836. Meanwhile the legation in The Hague remained in the hands of a mere Secretary and, moreover, a man whom both Palmerston and Grey seem to have agreed was 'a great fool'. But George Jerningham also happened to be Laura Petre's brother and, in any case, Palmerston judged that in view of the persistently bad state of their relations the Dutch deserved no better. On the other hand Vaughan's politics were said to be adverse to the Whig Government, and Palmerston thought he would be less harmful in America than in Europe. Besides, he agreed, Vaughan's acquaintance with American affairs and men would make him more useful across the Atlantic than elsewhere.[109]

Vaughan's remaining so long in the United States probably had something to do with the unpopularity of Washington, which was unfinished and unhealthy and considered both an expensive and a vulgar place to live. In 1832 two people in the service had wanted it, Sir Edward Disbrowe, who was a relation of Lord Ailsa, and Henry Stephen Fox, who was another cousin of Lord Holland's. Palmerston had 'no great opinion' of Disbrowe's talents and no personal knowledge of Fox at all. So he wondered if they should not look outside the service for 'a good man'. But everyone kept telling him that Fox was 'a very clever man' and Palmerston agreed that 'his name & connexions' well fitted him for the post. In particular Fox's appointment would have had the merit of pleasing a Cabinet colleague and keeping an improvident relation safely out of Europe. 'In Europe', Palmerston observed, 'his name has been a little too much associated with the gambling table, and it would be for his own advantage to give him opportunities of establishing his professional reputation as a diplomatist in a responsible situation elsewhere.' It was for that reason he had been moved to South America by Canning in the first place.

Palmerston had mixed feelings about Fox's performance in Rio. 'But', he admitted to Holland, 'he is an able man and if he will only go on [at] a steady pace constantly, instead of standing still for a year, and galloping for a week, he will do credit to himself, and his name.' So when ill health finally forced Vaughan to leave Washington in 1835, Fox was appointed to succeed him.[110]

Palmerston had originally intended to replace Vaughan in Washington with Disbrowe, but he had been found a post in the meantime in Sweden. It is doubtful however if Fox's appointment can be considered a success, though, like Vaughan, he stayed in Washington for nearly a decade. Vaughan, who does not seem to have been a jealous man, reported in 1837 that his 'successor shuts himself up, shows no disposition to mix with the Americans, or do anything but save money'. A few years later Brougham put it more bluntly: 'H. Fox in Republican America rises at 6 p.m., games all night – sees no one, [and] pays no debts but game debts.' When Aberdeen, on succeeding Palmerston as Foreign Secretary late in 1841, decided he must make a special effort to repair the damage he believed Palmerston had done to relations with America as well as Europe, he deliberately by-passed Fox by appointing a special envoy and three years later formally replaced him. Fox himself claimed to think it was his name alone his new masters had against him. Perhaps it was; but his record does not impress. However, the move to America certainly succeeded in keeping him out of Europe; he stayed on in Washington and died there three years later.[111]

It was, of course, still more difficult for Palmerston to please his colleagues when their offspring and connections were in direct competition for jobs. Holland also had a son who was soon placed in the diplomatic service, Henry Edward Fox, later fourth and last Baron Holland. But so had James Abercromby, who having risen in the private service of the Duke of Devonshire became a busy fellow among the Whig M.P.s, entering the Cabinet as Master of the Mint in 1834 and becoming Speaker in 1835. Abercromby's son Ralph had already shown how eaten up with ambition he was, and his father buttonholed Palmerston on his behalf as soon as he entered office. When Abercromby became a Cabinet colleague he was still more pressing. Palmerston did very well by him, making his son Secretary of Legation in Berlin in July 1831. He did even better by Holland, raising his son to a similar post in Turin the following July, after only a year in the service, and promoting him to Vienna a mere three years later. In the meantime Ralph Abercromby's relatives and friends became anxious that he should move from Berlin, on account of his health, they said, but really because of a most 'unfortunate connection' he had made there. When in 1835 the opportunity came of his having either Paris or Florence, they rather feared that Fox would win whichever prize became available, seeing how he had been favoured in spite of being very much Abercromby's junior. Palmerston, in fact, had hoped to satisfy them both and when all chance of that evaporated he persuaded Holland House of Abercromby's stronger claims to be minister in Florence.[112]

Fox accepted his disappointment with apparent good grace but real resentment. So unimpressed had he been, apparently, with his already rapid promotion that his father had to write to explain how Palmerston made it a rule if possible that everyone should 'go through the intermediate offices'. From Vienna he was soon continually complaining, after his ambassador Fred Lamb returned to England on long leave, that he was being left too long where his wife's health was suffering and almost simultaneously that he should have to give up his leading role whenever his chief returned. When it was found that Abercromby's old flame, or possibly a new one, had followed him to Florence his family again thought how desirable a move would be; yet when the rumour got around how inconvenient it was for a minister to have his mistress in residence, they also feared it might have been put about with the aim of replacing Abercromby's woman by Fox's wife. It was all denied, of course, but there was probably something in it. Not long after, Fox said he was willing to accept demotion to Constantinople rather than stay in Vienna, but Constantinople had already been promised elsewhere. Fox also took unofficial leave so often that Palmerston warned that awkward questions might soon be asked in Parliament. He was in any case, as he showed in a letter to Lamb, losing patience with his protégé:

Hy Fox begs not to be sent back again to Vienna; he says the climate disagrees with Ly Augusta, & that as to himself he succeeded there so well, & left it [last] with such flying colours that it would be hazardous to go back as he would not improve his popularity, & might diminish it! Pretty well this! is it not?[113]

At length, in April 1838, Palmerston did move Fox to Frankfurt, but evidently it still did not satisfy. Melbourne, who was being harassed as Prime Minister just as Palmerston was as Foreign Secretary, was equally tired of both young men. 'It is not worth while bothering about Abercromby & Henry Fox,' he warned off Edward Ellice. 'They are neither of them fit for their situations. They have not [fitness?] for any other. Let them rest.' But Abercromby's marriage to Minto's eldest daughter late in 1838 gave him the wish, and Palmerston the interest, to change places at last with Fox. Fox played out his second-rate career in Italy till 1846. In 1840 Palmerston contrived to have Abercromby join him there – but not without another clash with Holland House. For Palmerston had intended to use Abercromby's vacant place to ease Fox-Strangways out of the F.O., and, when both insisted on having Turin, he found himself in what Greville called 'a prodigious imbroglio' between not only Devonshire and Holland but Lansdowne and Minto too. In the end, according to Ellice, Palmerston washed his hands of the matter and turned it over to Fred Lamb for decision. Strangways was the loser.[114]

Another colleague's close relation, who gave Palmerston a good deal of trouble, was John Russell's elder brother William. During the four years of Miguel's usurpation in Portugal, the unofficial care of British interests in Lisbon was left in the hands of a series of acting Consuls-General. But when in the summer of 1832 Pedro's landing brought matters to a head the situation was thought promising enough to warrant something better, and so John Russell suggested his brother. William, he admitted, had only a minimum of diplomatic experience but his previous military service made him especially suited to the task ahead. In Lisbon, however, Lord William Russell and his wife soon got emotionally involved, and not always on the right or even the same side. Weighed down by the 'terrible burthen' of his mother-in-law's constant attendance on her daughter, embarrassed by the undisguised Tory sentiments of his wife, and pulled in all directions by his own humanitarian sympathies, William Russell could not help quarrelling even with his English colleagues in Portugal, both diplomats and naval men. He soon fell out with the Consul-General, Richard Belgrave Hoppner, the painter's son, reporting him to his brother John as a 'sanguinaire sans-culotte' and to his chief as 'sour, suspicious, malignant, vain, irritable, envious, heartless & false'.[115]

Hoppner was an over-zealous supporter of Pedro, while Russell was as critical of Pedro as of Miguel. This was not too far from the line eventually adopted by Palmerston, but unfortunately the rash and unsophisticated Russell was led by his disgust into a trap set by the Spanish Apostolicals. Russell's hope, presumably, was that the Spanish would bring about an acceptable compromise in Portugal and this was indeed something like the plan adopted by his Government after the change of régime in Spain. But Russell was premature in his policy and Zea's ambassador in Lisbon was merely playing with him. Palmerston could see it even at a distance. 'Do not place too much confidence in Cordova,' he warned, 'it is evident he is a mere tool of Zea's.' Then, in August 1833, after Lisbon had fallen to Pedro, Hoppner sent home to Palmerston some captured Miguelista papers, which not only demonstrated how Cordova had made a fool of Russell but suggested to some that he had even made a conquest of his wife.[116]

Hoppner's malicious interference did him no good. Grey had already decided he was 'doing all the mischief' he could in Lisbon and the recognition of Maria was used as an excuse to recall him. Palmerston, for his part, had decided that Russell too was quite unfit for such a difficult post. When Russell wrote back to complain so bitterly about Hoppner, Palmerston gently pointed out: 'You exhaust upon Hoppner all the epithets which the language affords, but you do him great injustice; . . . those which describe a little irritability of temper & sensitiveness of character are alone deserved. . . . Cordova was charged to set you and Hoppner by the ears, & he seems to have succeeded pretty well.'[117]

Russell soon realized that his behaviour and his reports were considered indiscreet and he toyed with the idea of seeking his recall. But he was evidently both sorry and surprised to hear that Palmerston had promised Lisbon elsewhere and intended him for Stuttgart. It was proposed, he concluded, to put him 'on the shelf'. In the end he took Stuttgart only because everyone so pressed him. He was bitterly unhappy there, but determined not to ask any relief from Palmerston, as he explained to his brother John in April 1835: .

Whatever you do let me beg of you not to ask Palmerston for anything for me neither directly, nor indirectly, don't even name me to him – he has his own coop of favorites to which I don't aspire to belong – nor have I nous enough to comprehend his policy, nor have I activity enough to meddle as much as he likes – so as a favor I entreat of you, not even to name me to him. I don't want money, I don't want diplomatic rank nor diplomatic honors, & am very well here untill my services are necessary elsewhere. Then employ me where & how you please.

Two months later Palmerston offered him Brussels and, when he declined, anything he pleased. He chose Berlin. But William Russell blamed his wife for his unhappiness even more than Palmerston, and during the summer had fallen wildly in love with another woman. Probably she was the widowed daughter of a well-known banker from Karlsruhe. To his brother, and to others, her faith made the scandal all the worse. He has 'suddenly & unaccountably become entangled with a Jewess', wrote John Russell to Palmerston, 'a woman of very bad character, very greedy, very intriguing & very mischievous'. So Palmerston willingly recalled him on leave. In December that same year he took up his new post in Berlin, where he passed the next six years of boring routine, though earning there some posthumous and perhaps undeserved notoriety by his report on the 'very second rate nature' of the abilities of Captain Helmut von Moltke. 'There is positively nothing to do here,' he wrote to his brother. 'I am always at Potsdam shooting wild ducks.' According to others he was more busily employed than he would admit, and carried rather further afield. 'Lord William extends the area of his amusements more and more,' wrote the French minister, 'he is now divided between three ladies, one of whom attracts him with some frequency to Mecklenburg.' When Palmerston left office in 1841 Aberdeen immediately recalled Russell from Berlin with suitable 'expressions of regret and personal kindness'. Palmerston knew well enough how to exploit his opportunities. 'Went to Broadlands,' William Russell recorded on 16 December that year. 'I like Palmerston much, he is very agreeable and has always been very civil to me, ay, more, kind. He says Aberdeen has behaved most indecorously to me.'[118]

The diplomatic career of Palmerston's own brother was also not entirely untroubled, though the mystery of William Temple's bachelor existence remains undiscovered. Presumably Palmerston kept him in the surprisingly humble place of précis-writer in 1831 until he could find a good opportunity to promote him. The first place he seems to have thought of for that purpose was that of a discredited Tory. For the reports of Algernon Percy on Swiss affairs were so reactionary that Grey was led to write in October 1831 that he 'did not think there existed in the shape of a man such a fool'. In the spring the Prime Minister insisted that Percy would have to go, and Palmerston did not disagree. A few months after he was recalled, Percy, who had been made a thorough Frenchman by sharing twenty-one years' internment in wartime with his father and consequently always felt uncomfortable in England, called

on Palmerston to have it out and both lost their tempers. Immediately afterwards Percy collapsed and died. It was not apoplexy but the cholera to which
Palmerston only seemed immune. In the meantime, when Swiss affairs in his
opinion required 'an active and intelligent minister', Palmerston had thought
of sending his brother. But unexplained 'personal reasons' made him think
again, as did the apprehension of it being thought 'a job' to benefit his brother.
So he sent instead the retiring Consul-General in Paris, David Morier, and
would have made available to Percy, if he had needed it, the pension Morier
would otherwise have had. A few months later Palmerston was thinking of
sending his brother to The Hague, but in view of the continuing bad relations
with the Dutch at length decided that 'the brother of the Secy of State for
Foreign Affairs might not perhaps be the most agreeable minister' for them.
He had thought, therefore, of sending William to Dresden, knowing it to be 'a
pleasant place', but when Ponsonby's move to Constantinople opened up the
way he seized at once the Naples plum.[119]

Leaves of absence apart, William Temple remained minister in Naples until
his death in 1856. He was also made K.C.B. in 1851. But neither fact is any
indication that he was a good diplomat. Palmerston certainly tried to make
him a better one. He had always exhorted his brother to improve his grasp of
languages and in 1832 was still hoping he would be able to master both Italian
and German. From his private letters, indeed, one can get a good idea of what
Palmerston ideally wanted from his representatives abroad, in addition to
their following specific instructions. In May 1834 he wrote to William:

> I wish you could contrive to put something more in your despatches than
> the movements of the royal family. Tell us now and then what the Neapolitan
> Government think or mean to do about the affairs of the world – Spain,
> Greece, Italy, Morocco; what is the internal state of the country, as to com-
> merce, finance, army, etc. We hear of a war between Naples and Morocco: is it
> true, and what is it about?[120]

William Temple probably benefited from all his brother's advice, a drunkard and a 'soft serviteur' or not. Palmerston certainly said he had. He also
seems to have been a very popular man among his small group of English
friends, including some at least of his staff. But this did not stop Palmerston's
enemies at home reaching out to hurt him through his brother. Palmerston
had probably never been happy about having had to remove Hoppner from
Lisbon and it was as some kind of compensation that he made Hoppner's
brother-in-law, Captain Thomas Gallwey, consul in Naples. But Gallwey
nonetheless stabbed Palmerston in the back by sending home, for the use of his
chief's enemies among the radicals, what really do seem to have been spiteful
reports about the supposed neglect of British commercial interests in Naples.
A still more serious attack was mounted at the height of the 1840 Egyptian
crisis, after a prolonged visit to Naples by the Joint Secretary of the Board of
Trade, John MacGregor. MacGregor was supposed to arrange a revision of
the Anglo-Neapolitan tariff and had specifically been ordered by Palmerston

not to concern himself with a new commercial treaty then under contemplation. But with all the arrogance of his radical species, MacGregor had gone ahead regardless and presented Palmerston with the heads of an agreement, signed page by page by the Neapolitan Foreign Minister and himself. Although the draft was defective as well as unauthorized, Palmerston nevertheless used it as the basis of new instructions to his brother. But Temple, too, was ordered not to open negotiations until the settlement of other more serious disputes, and while the F.O. waited MacGregor leaked misinformation to the press and Opposition, and so Palmerston and his brother found themselves being bitterly attacked both in *The Times* and in the House of Lords. Naturally Urquhart jumped in head first with a pamphlet accusing them both of treason. MacGregor, however, had lied as well as leaked, as the succeeding Conservative Undersecretary at the F.O. eventually acknowledged.[121]

The appointments of Granville and William Temple were not the only ones Palmerston made at a senior level from among his own political and personal connections. As time went by and senior posts inevitably fell vacant, he tended to fill them more readily than in the past from outside the service. He was well aware that before the end of 1835 he had by this means 'very much' reduced the promotion prospects among the lower ranks; but this was probably because of his growing distrust of the Tories and of the criticism he had suffered in the Whig press for retaining them in the early years. It was also partly because he had come to the conclusion that there was a dearth of talent among the professionals. In the summer of 1832, for example, he was glad enough to receive an offer of resignation from Chad when even that stubborn Tory fell out at last with the tortuous Prussian minister. As well as being a Tory, he was at best a mediocre diplomat – 'he was no great thing', Lady Cowper heard – and he had been distinctly unenthusiastic about carrying out his instructions on behalf of the Poles. According to Lady Cowper, Palmerston complained that as far as his post in Berlin was concerned, 'people in the line are so stupid & such inferior people that he could not find one he wished to promote, or thought worthy of it'. So he approached his old friend Gilbert Elliot, Earl of Minto since 1814. Lady Cowper assured her brother that Minto was 'a very sensible moderate man'; the Austrian chargé denounced him as a radical. Minto apparently needed the job since he had a large family to support, and considering the difficult circumstances in Berlin he was certainly a real success. 'Minto's letters', Grey commented, 'are like everything he writes, clear, sensible, & marking in every instance the utmost candour, & the highest sense of honour.' But Minto found himself involved in one or two unpleasant incidents and, like Chad and others before him, soon lost his liking for Berlin. When Lady Minto fell dangerously ill the following spring, only Palmerston's urgent pleas persuaded him to pass one more winter there; in the summer of 1834, however, he insisted on coming home. The following May he offered as a joke to go to St Petersburg and Palmerston, not misunderstanding, tried to interest him seriously in the idea. But Minto was to be summoned to the Admiralty instead and undertook only one more special mission for Palmerston, to Switzerland and Italy in 1847-8.[122]

Palmerston achieved a somewhat more lasting and notable success with the change he made in Madrid. Sensing his new master's dissatisfaction, Addington soon came to the conclusion that 'his very name was against him'. But Addington was not merely a High Tory; he was also very stupid, as even Greville acknowledged. He persisted in a line of policy often quite contrary to that which Palmerston wished him to follow. The last straw was a dispatch which Palmerston called 'an asinine production' and which, Grey felt, so misconceived and misrepresented his instructions as to prove him utterly unfit. The object of that dispatch, they both agreed, could only have been to leave on record in the archives 'a manifesto' against his own Government. It was clear therefore that Addington would have to go. There was some hope that Stratford Canning might be persuaded to take over in Madrid on a permanent basis, but it was not agreeable to him. In any case, his special mission, as has been seen, was far from being a success. Consequently Madrid went to another.[123]

Palmerston cannot quite be said, by his next choice for Madrid, to have launched George Villiers, later fourth Earl of Clarendon, on his distinguished diplomatic career, for Villiers had been an attaché in St Petersburg some ten years before. But poverty had compelled him then to abandon diplomacy for a commissionership of Customs. On the formation of Grey's Ministry he was immediately chosen to conduct some fiscal negotiations in Paris and the following year to join with Dr John Bowring to carry on an investigation there into commercial relations with France. Villiers was a Johnian and nephew of Palmerston's friend Lord Morley. Whether Palmerston was responsible for either of these appointments is not known, though Althorp certainly consulted him about the second. However, Villiers's sudden selection as minister to Madrid in July 1833 was attributed by his family to Palmerston, and this seems to have been true.[124]

In Madrid, as in Paris before, Villiers proved himself an extremely vigorous and enterprising negotiator. If anything he was too vigorous even for Palmerston, who had to reprove him for secretly negotiating tariff advantages behind the back of Britain's allies, and often suspected he meddled too much in Spanish politics. For his part Villiers complained about 'the old women of Downing Street' and the neglect of his dispatches in 'that Temple of Procrastination', the Foreign Office. In his letters he pointed to 'the mediocrity of those at home – their incapacity or unwillingness to look a difficulty in the face or deal greatly with a great question' and his continual lack of 'an instruction or a single crumb of support'. 'If all the rest of our foreign policy is managed like the Spanish branch,' he concluded, 'why – it must be a great satisfaction to our enemies!' Villiers, on the other hand, was generally considered, though a charming conversationalist, a quite unscrupulous intriguer. But Palmerston certainly appreciated his good qualities and saw him as an obvious candidate for political preferment when he succeeded his uncle as Earl of Clarendon in 1838. In 1839 Clarendon was recalled to be made Lord Privy Seal. In the Cabinet, too, he was by no means subservient to Palmerston; he made an outspoken challenge to Palmerston's Near Eastern policy in 1840 and was suspected for it of plotting to succeed him. But Palmerston's respect eventually recovered from that crisis of confidence and he kept him on as Foreign Secretary after he had himself become Prime Minister in January 1855.[125]

A very different, but in its way also very successful, appointment to the diplomatic service was that of Henry Lytton Bulwer. A Harrow and Cambridge man, though of a later generation than Palmerston, Bulwer had been a radical member of Parliament since 1830 and a close associate of Durham. He was also a writer like his more famous younger brother, later Lord Lytton. So when Granville heard that Palmerston had appoined Bulwer as unpaid attaché in Paris in November 1832, he wrote back in some alarm: 'may there not be some inconvenience in Mr Bulwer (an author as well as an orator) having the privilege of coming over from London to Paris when it suits his fancy, to rummage the Archives of the Embassy and then return to his Parliamentary duties as soon as he has gratified his curiosity?'[126]

Bulwer's was indeed a strange appointment and many commented in similar manner on it and his later moves. It was said in the F.O. that he wrote leading articles for the *Morning Chronicle* about twice a week and was also a close associate of Albany Fonblanque, editor of the *Examiner*. In fact Bulwer was not entirely new to diplomacy, having served as attaché in 1827-30 successively in Berlin, Vienna and The Hague. He did not stay long in Paris either; according to Palmerston he resigned his attachéship because he found it incompatible with his position as an independent Member of Parliament. However, he consistently supported the Government, and Melbourne in return pressed him constantly on Palmerston's attention.[127]

When, towards the end of 1835, Bulwer expressed a wish to resign his seat and return to diplomacy, it was Melbourne who suggested he be sent as chargé to Brussels, and Palmerston willingly agreed. There were the usual murmurs in high places and so Melbourne asked Palmerston to delay while they reconsidered, but Bulwer had already received the King's approval and announced his impending resignation in public. A few weeks later, after Leopold had questioned whether Bulwer was not rather a 'Jacobin', Palmerston suggested he might be transferred to Cracow, where an enterprising English appointment was thought to be needed in view of the suspicion that the Eastern powers were about to move against that free city. Melbourne claimed he knew Bulwer to be politically sound – 'not . . . a Jacobin at all, but a very high aristocrat & a very sharp fellow' – and admitted he was also anxious to advance his career. In any case, he went on, if Bulwer's name was so controversial it would make 'rather more row than necessary' in Cracow. Consequently Bulwer did get his appointment to Brussels and before very long had certainly established himself as one of Palmerston's favourites. When Ponsonby quarrelled with his Secretary of Legation in 1837, Palmerston promised the position to Bulwer and he kept his promise over Fred Lamb's protests that Bulwer was too radical.[128]

In Constantinople Bulwer got on surprisingly well with Ponsonby and, though he did afterwards claim too much credit for the policy behind it, concluded with quiet efficiency the negotiation of an important commercial treaty with Turkey. At the same time he conducted with Palmerston a private correspondence highly critical of his chief and confirmed Fred Lamb's opinion that he could not be trusted. Lamb therefore redoubled his pressure on Melbourne to secure the recall of both Ponsonby and Bulwer. On the other hand, Granville must in the meantime have completely changed his mind about Bulwer. For when Arthur Aston was given a well deserved promotion into Clarendon's place in Madrid in 1839, Granville asked for Bulwer to succeed him. Brougham, who was well hated by Fonblanque and attacked in his columns even more vigorously than in *The Times,* was astonished. 'Palm. appoints L. Bulwer, libeller of Louis Philippe & publisher of private household matters of Ld Granville's family, *Secry of Embassy* over all men's heads! Why? Because he negotiated the purchase of the *Examiner* Paper & is a *penny-a-line* Gentleman.' Granville had complained about the articles in the press; but if the ambassador thought Bulwer was their author he had evidently been forgiven. When Bulwer returned to Paris, Lady Granville wrote: 'Henry Bulwer is arrived and is extremely agreeable and efficient, and will, I think, be a great addition in society and a very useful one in business.'[129]

Palmerston probably knew more about press intrigues than most, and Bulwer does not seem to have ever suffered by it. From Paris he was moved as minister to Madrid (1844-8), Washington (1849-51) and Florence (1852-5), and finally as ambassador to Constantinople (1858-65). Yet he was always a very controversial figure. He was expelled by the Spaniards from Madrid for being more Palmerstonian than even Palmerston could decently defend. 'Thrown away on the stupid Americans', according to Emily, he proceeded in Washington to tackle with characteristic vigour a problem that had bedevilled transatlantic relations for years and to conclude in a matter of weeks a treaty which, by glossing over the difficulties and adding differences of interpretation to differences of interest, succeeded in making matters worse thereafter. Finally in Constantinople he so wallowed in its corruption as to propel his more sensitive successor into a reaction of purity that weakened British influence there for ever. Emily thought him a fascinating person. But nobody trusted him. Melbourne wrote to the Queen, when proposing he accompany the Governor-General to Canada in 1841: 'He is clever, keen, active; somewhat bitter and caustic, and rather suspicious. A man of more straightforward character would have done better . . .' Queen Victoria had a real 'antipathy' for him; Clarendon thought she would not have tolerated his going as minister to Berlin in 1856, after her daughter had become engaged to the Crown Prince of Prussia. John Russell refused to see him made a peer while he remained Prime Minister. And in the end Palmerston too concluded he was 'a great intriguer'. Yet it was not too surprising that Palmerston's heirs should have selected Bulwer to be his official biographer – and even less that he should have carried out his task in the manner that he did.[130]

Palmerston always had a great weakness for journalists. He was also a great favourite with them. One, James Grant, who in earlier years and under cover of a pseudonym had been nothing like so kind, said he was their very special favourite. It was, in his opinion, easy to see why. For Palmerston treated them for fully half a century not only with studied geniality but also with real consideration. He would supply them with rich political anecdote from his plentiful personal store and go out of his way, by amending his timetable or (as must then have been unusual) by providing notes in advance, to ensure that their reports of his speeches would go to press in time.[131]

Although, as his concern with the *Hampshire Advertiser* in 1823 shows really well enough, Palmerston's special interest in newspapers reached back to an early date, it is very doubtful if he adopted his genial manner with either journalists or editors quite so soon as Grant would later claim. His breezy manner about personal attacks in the press also belongs to a much later date. Twice in the summer of 1834 he contemplated legal action when Tory newspapers tried to cry down the Quadruple Alliance and revived the stock-jobbing accusations of 1827. Neither came to court, as the *Standard* agreed to print an apology when it realized that it had named the wrong mining scandal and the *Morning Post*, Palmerston's lawyer advised, left its hints too vague to warrant any legal action. However, when the Tory *Albion and Star* on 8 June 1835 charged Palmerston with exploiting his official position to speculate in foreign stock, he sued the editor and won a published retraction. He also more than once wanted to take action against *The Times*, in November 1837 when it printed accusations about the way he had obtained a parliamentary seat in Tiverton and in September 1839 when it suggested he had used secret service money to undermine the loyalty of a Carlist general in Spain. His lawyers again advised against it, as they did also with respect to Urquhart's activities in 1839-40. Outwardly Palmerston accepted these opinions with great good humour: public men could not pre-empt the law courts all the time, he told Brougham, and in any case an action would only have given Urquhart the sales publicity he wanted.[132]

Palmerston was probably the most publicity conscious of all British Foreign Secretaries. Even before he entered the F.O. he reckoned on spending some £30 a year on newspapers. He regularly took a Sunday and a morning paper (the *Chronicle*) and two copies of an evening one (the *Courier*) as well, one of these being sent on as a gift to Cambridge, probably for St John's. After he had become Foreign Secretary this expenditure seems to have gone up to £50 a year and perhaps even more; in 1834 he paid £100 to his old newsagent in addition to other payments to booksellers, stationers and circulating libraries for such items as the *Mirror of Parliament* and no less than £24.15s.0d. in one go for Maclean's caricatures. He was also a great producer of material. When he made one of his important speeches he did not neglect to see that it was printed and personally distributed copies at home and abroad. Once, when he sent several copies of a speech in May 1841 to the Texan agent in London, he was promised: 'I will make the most of them and such is the fecundity of our press that 50 copies will be printed in America for *one* in the United Kingdom.'[133]

Palmerston also resorted more than had any of his predecessors to the official means at his disposal. It was he who began in 1831 the practice of putting Hertslet's printed collections of *State Papers* on public sale. 'If I find that I do not lose by the sale', he wrote, 'I shall think the advantage of diffusing information a gain and shall have all the former volumes successively re-printed for general sale.' He had in general, too, a genuine concern for the historical record beyond the requirement that it should be legible. 'My view of the records of the Foreign Office', he wrote to Russell in 1849, 'is that they should contain as full a record as possible of all that passes and of the real motives and grounds of events.' This did not mean that they should be exposed too early to the historian, let alone the public eye. His principal purpose in producing the reams of dispatches published in the so-called Blue Books produced for Parliament was clearly propagandist.[134]

The overall supervision of the production of parliamentary papers Palmerston shared with the Prime Minister – or to be strictly accurate with Grey, though possibly not with Melbourne – and where appropriate, as in the case of central Asian affairs, with other heads of department in the F.O. He usually left the initial selection of papers to his juniors, but he was careful to go through their work both in draft and in proof; occasionally he sat up all night to do so. Palmerston certainly did much of his 'editorial' work very skilfully. It was already the established convention that the words of a dispatch should not be altered; but equally that nothing should be included that might be offensive to individuals and especially to princes.[135] Sometimes these omissions though innocently intended, backfired. The most notorious case is that of the so-called 'garbled' Blue Books of 1839, in which the Government attempted to justify as necessary to the defence of India its resort to military intervention in Afghanistan. In this case it was the Cabinet who decided on what 'principles' the selection should be made, though Palmerston still had to stay up till five one morning in February to supervise the task, and to make the selection, so he said, as complete as those principles allowed. There appears, unfortunately, to be no record of what the Cabinet had intended, but there was an evident attempt by omission to protect the reputation of both the Russian Emperor and the local British agent, which led to an explicit accusation of 'pure trickery' by that agent himself. Hobhouse, as President of the Board of Control, got more of the blame than Palmerston, though according to what he wrote in his journal the omissions were those proposed by Palmerston. When they heard that the Blue Books were going to be attacked, Palmerston told him that 'he knew of no instance in which the reports of confidential agents were given to Parliament exactly as written' and that 'he was fully prepared to defend the course' they had taken. But after the Afghan War had turned from triumph to disaster and Palmerston had tried to put the blame on their successors, the accusation was frequently revived against both of them, right down to the time Palmerston had become Prime Minister and, by historians, down almost to the present.[136]

Sir Charles Webster was of the opinion that the central Asian Blue Books were not particularly distorted and that opinion has recently been vindicated with complete authority. But this is not to deny that these, like other Blue Books, were compiled in order to make a case. The Peel Government, who really knew that Palmerston's central Asian policy had been essentially a continuation of their own, resisted criticism of the Afghan Blue Books avowedly on the now familiar grounds that over-eager retrospective searches by one Government into the records of its predecessor's policies could only be 'a check upon the future usefulness of public servants'. But when Grey had been helping Palmerston in 1832 to prepare papers for the Lords on the subject of England's allowing the French to undertake unfettered their expedition against Algiers, he had proposed they should go through the drafts together especially 'to put in what Aberdeen will leave out'. The famous 'Levant Papers', in which Palmerston sought to justify at great length his policy in the second Mehemet Ali crisis of 1839-40, are really another case in point. According to a not very sympathetic historian they gave all 'the great essential facts'. But if they gave the facts about the final stages of Palmerston's quarrel with France, it was only because he had a good case; in other places the picture was completely distorted.[137]

Whether Palmerston, in general, was more or less scrupulous than other Foreign Secretaries it will probably never be possible to say. That his use of publicity was very effective, on the other hand, is beyond any doubt at all. However, publicity had its price. Fred Lamb pointed out that such 'full publications' might make others less willing to hold confidential communications. 'I published nothing unadvisedly on the Syrian Question,' Palmerston breezily replied; 'for I shewed before hand to Brunnow, to Schleinitz or Bulow, and to Neumann all that related to their respective Governments: at least all the papers & despatches communicated by those Govts; and I omitted everything which they struck out. The feeling about publicity is very difft in London from what it is at Vienna, and even an Austrian gets stronger nerves on that subject by living in our atmosphere.' Still Metternich, it appears, did occasionally withhold further confidences in writing on the grounds that Fred Lamb had indicated. The fear of dispatches afterwards being published also led to the increase in Palmerston's own private correspondence with diplomats abroad. Moreover, publicity for short-term ends could in the long run become counter-productive. Although much fairer than their critics thought, the Afghan Blue Books played down Russia's threat in central Asia because in 1839 Palmerston was already seeking her cooperation against France in the Near East. But this followed a sustained and successful campaign by Palmerston to expose Russia as the great threat to British interests both in Europe and in the East. Hence the explanation of a megalomaniac like Urquhart that his former patron and chief must have been bribed.[138]

According to Gladstone the English people simply would not read Blue Books. But those papers provided the raw material not only for debates in Parliament but also for innumerable pamphlets and books. The indefatigable and fanatical Urquhart made great use of both. He had begun with Palmerston's encouragement and many others received it as well. As far as is known Palmerston personally made very little in the way of a direct contribution himself. At Grey's invitation he had a major hand in *The Reformed Ministry and the Reformed Parliament,* a pamphlet in defence of the Government's first session, which appeared in September 1833. The Prime Minister dubbed it 'excellent' and it certainly had a considerable success. Sefton volunteered the services of his son to furnish the part on foreign affairs. But Le Marchant, Brougham's secretary and the director of the enterprise, simply stated that Palmerston 'wrote the foreign policy'; in view of the Foreign Secretary's opinion of his hand, Francis Molyneux would probably never have been allowed to present him even with a draft.[139]

Whether Palmerston took part in any similar efforts subsequently is not known. There appeared in the autumn of 1837 a pamphlet widely publicized as coming from the Government but which Melbourne disavowed. It was written by a man called Squire, a foreign editor of the *Morning Chronicle* and, according to Melbourne, 'rather a favourite' of Palmerston's. When Palmerston brought to the Prime Minister's attention what Squire proposed to write, Melbourne objected to its being avowedly connected with the Government, especially as he thought its tone and argument 'timid, retracting, [and] apologetic'. Palmerston was therefore supposed to have warned Squire not to connect the Government with what he wrote, but later, Melbourne understood, there was some 'misunderstanding'. On the other hand, in 1839 Melbourne commended the editor of the *Edinburgh Review* to Palmerston as a reliable man who wanted to establish connections with the Government on all matters foreign and domestic, and later that same year Palmerston was approached via another of his colleagues for 'advice and help' in the production of an article that Monteagle was preparing for the *Review.* An article in the *Review* on the crisis with France over Mehemet Ali in 1840 was, according to Macaulay, written by Henry Bulwer from the Paris Embassy but revised by Palmerston in London (as well as by Macaulay himself). Subsequently

Macaulay recommended Palmerston to the editor as a regular reviewer; 'he writes excellently,' he said. Palmerston was evidently quite flattered by such a commendation from such a source; but though he took his time in considering the invitation that subsequently came his way, he eventually decided that even though by then in opposition he was much too busy still. He was, however, also confidentially credited with a still larger share, with Bulwer, in the authorship of an article about the 'Spanish Marriages' in the *Edinburgh Review* for April 1847. He was certainly the author of a collection of newspaper articles attacking Aberdeen's American policy, and particularly the Webster-Ashburton Treaty of 1842. This collection, however, was only a small sample of his writings for the newspaper press.[140]

In August 1831 Palmerston replied to a taunt of Croker's in the Commons by saying: 'I for one do not write in the newspapers.' Sir Charles Webster allowed the assertion to pass, with the observation that the transcripts of articles for the press preserved among the Broadlands Papers date only from the end of 1832. But Croker knew it for a lie, though he was hardly in a position to refute it by referring in the House to the pieces they had written together for the *Courier* and the *New Whig Guide*.[141]

Since the days of the *New Whig Guide* Palmerston had changed his political affiliations. This meant that the success of the *Hampshire Advertiser* he helped set up in 1823 had subsequently become a personal and political embarrassment. So when he failed to get re-elected as M.P. for South Hampshire in January 1835 the idea was put to him that he might care to subscribe to a new 'liberal' paper to be run by a former parliamentary reporter on the London *Morning Chronicle*. After the *Hampshire Independent* had been successfully established it was rumoured Palmerston had contributed no less than £1,000. Palmerston's own endorsement on the original invitation merely said: 'agreed provided I have no connection with the paper as proprietor, & my £50 is taken as a gift.' But this is not conclusive. Subsequent correspondence between Palmerston and his Romsey agent, Holmes, suggests that the £50 may have been only a beginning. Apparently the *Morning Chronicle* man, John Wheeler, was notoriously a 'creature of impulse', with many 'generous qualities' according to a friend and colleague, but simply bad-tempered according to Holmes. In any case he soon fell out with his principal backer or associate, a man called Drew. 'They are both in my opinion equally vain & vulgar,' Holmes reported, suggesting that if Wheeler were to ask for further aid to compensate for Drew's withdrawal, Palmerston might better 'pause a little'. 'Your Lordship's note on this subject is destroyed,' he went on. 'No one knows that it was ever written.' With or without any further help from Palmerston, Wheeler succeeded in establishing his paper and, according to his friend, in raising it to 'a very respectable position', though he was beset with constant libel suits. One of his successors as editor, Thomas L. Behan, was rewarded by Palmerston when Prime Minister with the still very valuable sinecure of the editorship of the *London Gazette*.[142]

Quite when and how Palmerston contrived to weave a new connection with the 'liberal' press in London is much more difficult to say. Calculating on an appropriate reward, the *Courier* changed its allegiance when Grey's Government was formed and earned from Cobbett the description of 'heirloom of every minister'. Palmerston seems to have given the *Courier* some sort of privileged communication with the F.O. But by January 1832 he had already severed contact, because, he said, he had found that Talleyrand was 'tampering' with it. Perhaps, too, he was unhappy that it should have been so much in Brougham's hands. Between them Brougham, Ellice and Durham also, for a time, exercised a considerable influence on *The Times* and the *Morning Chronicle* among other leading journals. Probably at Brougham's request Palmerston cooperated to a considerable extent with these and other so-called 'ministerial' journals. But he was far from happy about *The Times*. That newspaper's attempts to encourage the more radical reform of Parliament – in line with Durham's views – simply outraged him, and the way it responded to the divisions within the Cabinet and to the impulses of its own demagogic ambitions meant that it was never a whole-hearted supporter of the Government's policy. The days indeed were gone when a Government could have any major English paper in its pocket. When Princess Lieven complained about the attacks made in the *Courier* upon the Polish policy of her country and her Emperor, Grey explained very clearly to her why there was no such thing as a Government paper: 'We might purchase a paper that is not read, which would do us no good till it got into circulation; and then it would do just like the others. The truth is, that the profits of a paper extensively taken in are so great, that they are quite beyond any temptation that could be held out to them.'[143]

French and other continental papers were more easily persuaded or controlled. Shee was providing articles for the *Allgemeine Zeitung* in December 1836 and when Palmerston wanted some more in March 1840, with a view to 'keeping Germany right', Shee seems to have had no difficulty in placing them as well. Palmerston drafted them himself – stressing that Mehemet Ali's claims to be the 'promoter of civilization' were false, his territorial ambitions dangerous to the existence of the Turkish Empire, and France's policy by contrast with Russia's fatal to European peace – and Shee, who was in Stuttgart at the time, expanded them for the press. But even with foreign journals Palmerston seems to have been by no means spendthrift. He occasionally spent small sums of money on lesser journals in minor places, where a little went a long way. But he never seems to have thought it worth-while actually to put a paper in his pocket. When a certain Dr Weil, who claimed a connection with the *Courier Allemand*, came to him in the summer of 1841 seeking money for a new periodical to advocate 'constitutional principles' in opposition to the 'Russian' press in Germany, Palmerston refused. Shee might if he wished supply information, though even that had better be avoided since Weil was already in communication with the *Chronicle*. As for money, there was simply none to spare; in any case it would never have given Palmerston control and if it were discovered would have harmed England's relations with Austria and Prussia and upset any chance of an alignment with them in the east. So, he hoped, any money had better come from Louis Philippe. In France, it has been suggested, Palmerston spent no money at all on the newspapers. But if this was true in his first two periods in the F.O., he was not so fastidious in the third. For the story told by the 'Chevalier' Wikoff seems, in all essentials, true.[144]

A United States citizen who had travelled back and forth across the Atlantic, become for a time manager and companion to the dancer Fanny Elssler and written up an interview with the Prisoner of Ham (Louis Napoleon), Henry Wikoff was approached, in the street apparently, by Richard Edwardes, the acting British Secretary of Legation in Paris, in August 1850, and shortly afterwards he was given a letter of introduction to Palmerston in London. The Foreign Secretary must have been expecting him, since he at once invited this obscure and not very savoury individual to visit him at Broadlands. Shortly afterwards he had Addington engage his services for one year, in the first instance at a rate of £500 per annum.

Quite what Wikoff was supposed to do never became clear. Addington later stated that it was to propagandize in the French and American press 'the liberal, and especially the pacific character' of Britain's policy. Since Wikoff had had some, though not particularly successful, journalistic experience in America, and had written some interesting pieces in the Paris press shortly before Edwardes approached him, this was probably true. But when Wikoff got back to Paris he noted that he was expected not to make contact with the ambassador, the Marquess of Normanby, and concluded that he was intended to exploit his old acquaintanceship and make contact instead with Louis Napoleon behind the ambassador's back. Since Palmerston was at odds with Normanby over the attitude to be adopted towards the French President but hampered by the ambassador's powerful connections at the English court, there may have been something in this. If so, there seem to have been some early second thoughts and Wikoff was left without any real instructions at all. However, being an enterprising man, he wrote articles for the French newspapers, which may well have done Anglo-French relations some good, and others for the American press, which represented Palmerston as saying that England had abandoned her old antagonism to the United States.

Unfortunately Wikoff frankly revealed that Palmerston had said the improvement in Anglo-American relations was being forced upon England by the attitude of her transatlantic merchants, and this indiscretion was probably what determined the F.O. to terminate Wikoff's engagement. Edwardes hinted to him he should resign; Palmerston kept him waiting for hours at both the F.O. and his house in London, and in the end did not see him at all, though he agreed in November 1851 to extend Wikoff's salary for another six months in lieu of notice.

In the meantime Wikoff, despairing of official remuneration much longer, resumed contact with a young English heiress and, having followed her to

Genoa and tried to force her into marriage by abduction, found himself in February 1852 sentenced to eighteen months' imprisonment. Since the British consul in Genoa disavowed him, Wikoff saw in him his enemy and, behind the consul, Palmerston. His attitude consequently changed peremptorily from something like that of a spy to something more like that of a blackmailer. In February 1855 he published *My Courtship and Its Consequences; And Revelations from the Foreign Office.* But while this dealt pretty fully with the sordid affair in Genoa it did not reveal very much about the F.O., probably in the hope they would yet be frightened into paying him off. Then, following a categorical repulse from Palmerston, who had since become Prime Minister, there appeared his explicit and final revelations in 1857 and 1858, entitled, the first for the American public, *The Adventures of a Roving Diplomatist,* and the second, for the British, *A New Yorker in the Foreign Office and His Adventures in Paris.*[145]

Whatever the extent of Palmerston's dabblings with the foreign press, he undoubtedly made more consistent efforts to keep in well with English newspapers. Support for his policies at home and abuse for Foreign Ministers abroad were secured in these cases less with money than with a supply of Government advertisements and advance information. But, as Palmerston himself pointed out to Lady Cowper, the return was strictly limited:

The fact is that the only influence which my office possesses over the Courier or any other paper is *positive* not *negative.* I could get him [the editor] to insert any article I wished to-day but I have no means or power of preventing him from inserting any other of quite a different kind to-morrow. I can impel but I cannot control. The only communication that takes place is that every now and then when we have any particular piece of news, it is given to the editor and he thereby gets a start of his competitors, and on the condition of receiving these occasional intimations he gives his support to the Government. But no editor would bring his daily articles to a public office to be looked over before they are printed and no public officer who had any sense in his brains would undertake the responsibilities of such inspections . . . Though they look to Government for news, they look to their readers for money, and they never can resist flying out upon popular topics when they think that by a flourish they shall gain a little éclat among Club and Coffee House politicians and have their paper talked of for four and twenty hours.

This was evidently written for Princess Lieven's benefit. For Metternich's, Palmerston frequently expounded to Emily's brother Fred what was meant by the 'freedom of the press' in England. Once, when Metternich complained of some leak of official information in December 1832, he wrote:

I can quite understand that in a country like Austria and Prussia where the Press is under strict restraint and nothing appears in the newspapers without permission, such a publication as this must appear to be a breach of confidence by the Government, and that it must be supposed that the Government furnished the communication. I suppose it would be hopeless to attempt to explain to an Austrian minister that what is called a Government paper in England is one which abuses the Government only twice a week instead of six times like the rest, and which employs the other four days in defending its friends in office against all attacks but its own . . .

A year later he was still persisting with his lessons. 'Try to persuade them at Vienna', he wrote in January 1834, 'that a government paper in England is not a paper written under the controul of office, but one which is written in support of the government and that we have no power of *preventing* articles from appearing which we should not have approved of.' At the same time Palmerston could display as sure an understanding as Grey of the true policy and interest of the English press at this time. 'In fact', he went on, 'if any paper was to put itself into such complete trammels under the government it would soon lose its circulation in consequence of its tameness, and we should have no means of repaying it for its loss.'[146]

What Palmerston said of the press in general was true in particular of *The Times* and its view of Palmerston's foreign policy. Its relations with him were not too bad at first but by 1831 it was already printing articles written by a man who was actually in the pay of the Opposition and by early 1834 a wide breach had opened up between the paper and Palmerston. In public its columns attacked his 'Tory' appointments; in private its editor pressed for his replacement by Durham. The quarrel seems largely to have been personal. Apparently the editor, Barnes, thought he was not receiving good enough treatment from the F.O. It was not the first time he had complained of Government neglect: he had done so in August 1831 when he said he was not getting a 'full share of patronage in advertisements, etc'. Holland suspected he had also been provoked by the astounding and insulting rebuff Palmerston had just made to Croker about the press. Early in 1833 Barnes had also accused Granville of not taking any notice of his Paris correspondent. And in January the following year he had written: 'Lord Palmerston ought certainly to communicate any important intelligence, but he does not. Occasionally that very good-natured but useless person Sir George Shee sends a paragraph – but generally long after we have had the news from some other quarter. Lord Palmerston should give positive directions on the subject to some person whom he can trust and who has ability to understand what is told him.'[147]

The particular reason for Barnes's quarrel with Palmerston seems to have been the behaviour of the legation in Lisbon. According to Barnes the minister there hampered the transmission home of news from English merchants in Portugal and failed to give special consideration to the needs of *The Times* correspondent, O'Brien. O'Brien, according to the minister, was an 'unscrupulous liar', and he was attacked in articles in the *Globe* which Barnes several times attributed to Shee. When he received no satisfaction about Lisbon, Barnes opened up a broadside in an article of 25 June 1834 on what he called the Foreign Secretary's 'unprincipled shuffling'. 'What an offensive union is that of a dull understanding and an unfeeling heart,' he went on. 'Add to this, the self-satisfied airs of a flippant dandy, and you have the most nauseous specimen of humanity – a sort of compound which justifies Swift in the disgusting exhibition of the Yahoos.'[148]

Barnes's treatment of Palmerston was especially unkind. But, aided by the quarrelsome intrigues of Brougham and Durham, the affair had already widened into a general 'war' between the Government and *The Times*. The Whigs had therefore decided to secure a safer instrument by sponsoring the purchase of the ailing *Morning Chronicle* by John Easthope, a stockbroker and M.P. In addition, Brougham, who knew as much as any man about intrigue among the press but was as unreliable a witness as he was a colleague, may have been right about Bulwer's connection with the *Examiner*. After Melbourne's succession to the premiership its editor Fonblanque certainly became much less severe a critic of the Whig Government.[149]

Palmerston made use of both the *Examiner* and the *Chronicle*, but of the second in particular. Joseph Parkes, who had been recruited from the radicals as a party manager by the Whigs and concerned himself a good deal with the press, introduced Easthope to him in June 1834 and by November that year Palmerston was already telling his brother to take the *Chronicle* rather than *The Times* because it was 'a much better paper'. After 1835, at the latest, Palmerston had got into the habit of meeting Easthope or his editors. No letters survive from John Black, the first of these editors, with whom Palmerston was said not to get on too well. Evidently Palmerston continued to work through Parkes for some purposes at least: in one letter of May 1839 he pressed him to have some insertions made in the *Chronicle* in answer to *The Times* and made himself 'answerable' for whatever was the cost. There is also a note from Easthope during the great Eastern crisis of October 1840, announcing his editor's intention of calling so that he could 'observe the right line'. Perhaps this was the occasion when Black irritated Palmerston by 'launching out into half an hour's dissertation on the ethnological peculiarities of the yellow-haired races of Finland' instead of sticking to foreign affairs. The next morning, however, there appeared in the *Chronicle* an article that to Greville had 'every appearance of being written by Palmerston himself . . ., most violent, declamatory, and insulting to France'. There also survives a substantial correspondence both with Easthope and with Andrew Doyle, who was Easthope's son-in-law and who, after running the paper's foreign department, succeeded Black as editor in 1843.[150]

The foreign department of the *Morning Chronicle* had been specifically established when the paper passed under Whig control early in June 1834, because the 'opening political prospects of the west of Europe' were, according to Joseph Parkes, 'a subject every daily morning newspaper must make a distinct feature of if it is to live with its contemporaries'. The first foreign editor was Michael Joseph Quin, a writer on travel and politics and until then the paper's Paris correspondent. Quin was expected by Palmerston's enemies among the more radical Whigs to criticize him savagely. Instead he began with what Parkes called 'Irish blarney' about the Foreign Secretary and 'ill-judged & vulgar abuse' of *The Times*. Palmerston already had some sort of connection with Quin. Indeed, it was sufficiently direct for Quin to have gained the impression that he had been commissioned to write what Palmerston described as a 'Report on the Currency Question'. The report, presumably, was designed to guide Palmerston in his attitude to the renewal of the Bank of England's exclusive charter in 1833. Quin threatened to go to law if he were not paid and Palmerston paid up £117. 10s. 0d. from his own purse rather than add to it any lawyer's bill. As a result, perhaps, Quin continued his close connection with the F.O. In July 1834 he went off abroad, and with letters of introduction from Palmerston, to arrange 'an extensive system of foreign correspondence'. Palmerston was still ordering the F.O. to send him information in February 1836. But for some reason, probably to make room for his boss's son-in-law, Quin left the *Chronicle* later that year. He sought a vice-consulate from Palmerston, but, remembering perhaps that he had already been paid so much, the Foreign Secretary bluntly refused. Quin became the editor of the *Dublin Review* instead; probably he was also the 'Dr Q—' who continued to bombard the Foreign Secretary with claims against a foreign Government until, having installed himself one day in the F.O. to insist upon a satisfactory answer, the threat of a policeman both saw him off the premises and silenced him forever. Quin died, in France, in 1843.[151]

Palmerston continued his close contact with the *Chronicle* after Quin's departure. Easthope, in his first letter to the Foreign Secretary on 7 June 1834, had proposed to consult him about the selection of his correspondents in Paris and Brussels; he was doing so again at the beginning of 1837 about changes in Lisbon and Madrid. Palmerston also instructed his missions abroad to give the *Chronicle* as much or even more information than *The Times* and he tried to help it compete with that paper in the rapid transmission of foreign news. All this continued in spite of complaints that Easthope's correspondents in Paris and Madrid also acted as his stock jobbers and were, what was possibly worse, 'vaguely radical'. Easthope himself consulted Palmerston about the state of Anglo-French relations with a view, as he freely confessed, to the protection of his investments and in February 1845 even made a direct offer to Palmerston of a secret share in his railway speculations in France. Palmerston, however, had no intention, even with the use of a nominee, of playing into his enemies' hands and making himself again an easy target.[152]

Palmerston was instrumental in securing Easthope his baronetcy in 1841 and Doyle his appointment to a Poor Law inspectorate when the *Chronicle* fell upon hard times in January 1848. He also had few scruples about getting consulates for newspaper men and their sons. In addition to what he did for Perry and Grattan, he secured a consulate in Greece for the youngest son of E.E. Crowe, who became the *Chronicle*'s Paris correspondent in 1834 and its leader writer on foreign politics in London in 1843. Another son, Joseph Archer Crowe, supported Palmerston in a variety of journals and subsequently secured employment on foreign service from John Russell, who was Palmerston's Foreign Secretary at the time, and later was made Consul-General in Leipzig. The famous Eyre Crowe, Permanent Undersecretary in the time of Edward Grey, was Joseph's son.[153]

In the diplomatic service, on the other hand, one cannot find many professional journalists. If one discounts Bulwer, there seems apart from Grenville Murray only to be Villiers's secretary in Spain, Henry Southern. According to Webster Southern was 'energetic, skilful and not too scrupulous', and maintained 'extensive connections with men of all kinds'. Palmerston must have known and approved. For he sanctioned Southern's acting subsequently as chargé d'affaires in Madrid when his chief left in 1839 and his transfer as Secretary of Legation to Lisbon later the same year. When Queen Victoria objected to his behaviour being 'ultra Progresista', Palmerston also struck a bargain with her by which Southern went out as minister plenipotentiary to the Argentine. In the Foreign Office he appears to have introduced no journalists at all. Probably he shared Canning's view that it was better not to have anyone there who, whether innocent or not, would be bound to be accused of leaking information. In any case Palmerston wanted to keep all that to himself.[154]

In September 1840, when the controversy within the Cabinet about Palmerston's policy was raging at its highest, it was believed at Holland House that 'all the articles on the Eastern question published in the *Morning Chronicle,* the *Globe, Examiner* & *Observer* are either written or corrected by Palmerston himself'. The reference to the *Examiner* was a wild exaggeration. But Ellice asserted that he knew the *Observer* was being paid out of secret service funds, and Palmerston was certainly in touch with its editor and giving him directions. There were many others in the Cabinet who were worried, particularly about the partisan attacks they supposed Palmerston was inspiring in the *Chronicle*. On one occasion in 1839, when Russell was being violently attacked in its columns for not being radical enough, he appealed to Palmerston to punish the paper by depriving it of F.O. information. The very next morning Palmerston was continuing his stream of advice to Doyle as though nothing had been said. On his part Easthope did not hesitate to communicate to Palmerston confidential correspondence that identified some of his enemies among the Whigs.[155]

For the period before Palmerston went out of office in 1841, only one short draft of an article for the *Chronicle* survives in the Broadlands Papers – on Naples in 1840 – though there are several other notes of suggestions and information supplied. Palmerston also made vigorous use of the paper when in opposition. It was there that he first published his series of articles attacking the Ashburton Treaty, and by the autumn of 1842, it was said, the Whigs were calling him 'Viscount Chronicle'. In November the following year he even sent to Doyle a copy of a confidential print concerning his recent Chinese policy. Palmerston had told Melbourne, indeed, that it was even more important to have a paper on one's side when out of office than in, and it was in order to get a hold on the *Chronicle* that he had advised the baronetcy for Easthope shortly before going out of office. When he returned to office in 1846 the exchange of F.O. leaks for partisan support and the complaints of his colleagues revived. When the *Chronicle* got into serious financial difficulty in

1847, Palmerston seems to have hoped to save the paper, but in February the following year it was sold to the Tories.[156]

Once the *Chronicle* had been lost Palmerston's correspondence with both Doyle and Easthope virtually ceased. But he continued to command special support from the elder Crowe, who in 1845 had gone over to the newly established *Daily News* and in 1849-51 became its editor. The *News* also shared some of its foreign services with the *Morning Herald*, which after its purchase by Edward Baldwin in 1843 had become a strong supporter of Palmerston's views on continental affairs. Apparently they did not take the *Herald* at Broadlands, but when Ashley showed Lady Palmerston a copy in 1849 she was so pleased with it and thought that morning papers had so much more effect than evening ones that she wished her husband would give it F.O. patronage and information. But both papers soon deteriorated and the *Herald* passed back again into the Conservative camp. Neither, in any case, ever came anywhere near filling the gap left by the loss of the *Chronicle*. Palmerston, in fact, had looked higher. For a day or two after the *Chronicle* made its first appearance on 21 February 1848 as an Opposition paper, Andrew Doyle approached the editor of *The Times* on Palmerston's behalf, offering both information and regular communication if he would enter into an alliance with the F.O. There had been a partial reconciliation, engineered by Clarendon, and a resumption of F.O. communications with the paper the previous summer. But it had proved too fragile and the new approach also failed, as did an interview with Palmerston shortly afterwards. It was not long, however, before the Foreign Secretary managed to find another journal.[157]

Nearly ten years earlier, in the summer of 1840, a young man called Peter Borthwick had sought an interview with Palmerston and subsequently wrote to say that while he was opposed to most of the Government's policies he was an admirer of Palmerston personally. Borthwick had been a supporter of the Carlists in Spain and a member of the Young England Party; but he had been seriously embarrassed by an election suit a couple of years before. Whether any financial arrangement was made is simply not known; possibly not, since Borthwick entered Parliament again in 1841 and that year also visited Jamaica. But about this time he discovered an interest in journalism and was certainly receiving information from Palmerston by 1849. The following year he became editor of the *Morning Post*. The *Post* had been a strong protectionist paper and, as for foreign policy, Easthope had even suggested in August 1840 that it was subsidized by Mehemet Ali. Perhaps, in the turmoil of party politics following the repeal of the Corn Laws, and still more after Russell's dismissal of Palmerston in 1851, Borthwick and his backers shared the common hope that Palmerston might one day himself change sides. But it is noteworthy that the former owner and editor, C.E. Michele, became consul in St Petersburg after selling out in 1849. It is also worth mentioning that Borthwick had tried and failed to secure a diplomatic position from Aberdeen in 1843 and that in 1851-2 his son may have been frustrated in a like ambition only by Palmerston's dismissal. In the meantime, too, Grenville Murray had set out into the world of diplomacy and journalism by becoming in 1851 both attaché in Vienna and correspondent for the *Post*. Certainly by that date Palmerston was very thick with Borthwick; under his editorship, and from 1852 under that of his son Algernon (later Lord Glenesk), who had been a correspondent in Paris and confidant of Louis Napoleon, the *Post* became Palmerston's principal support among the press. At his instigation it mounted a vigorous attack on Austria in 1849-50 and followed him again in the crisis that led to the Crimean War. By the end of that war, according to Greville, it had become, so far as Palmerston was concerned, the successor to the *Morning Chronicle* and he was placing articles in it 'full of arrogance and jactance'.[158]

The tie between Palmerston and the Borthwicks remained apparently unbroken until his death in 1865, even though the *Post* was reckoned on account of it to have lost a considerable number of its Tory readers. In the meantime a significant change had also overtaken Palmerston's relations with *The Times*. During the second Mehemet Ali crisis of 1840, Barnes's francophobia, and perhaps a hope of detaching Palmerston from the Whigs, had restrained even his lust for revenge, and his successor in 1841, John Thadeus Delane, though unwilling to bind himself to anyone, had always been more sympathetic to Palmerston. From one at least of his correspondents Palmerston, indeed, had received much more than sympathy. Possibly Andrew O'Reilly, *The Times* correspondent in France, owed him a favour or two. Palmerston had given official assistance to his cause in 1841 when he needed hard evidence to back up in court an accusation he had made about organized swindling, and during the row with France over the Spanish marriages affair Bulwer had supplied him with much confidential information. For his part O'Reilly had a source in the French F.O. and in 1847 and 1848 he was passing on secret intelligence to Palmerston. According to Clarendon, with whom O'Reilly also communicated, his information was 'sometimes true & sometimes absurd'. Palmerston, however, had no doubt whatever that he had been supplied with convincing and complete proof that Louis Philippe was conspiring with the English court to turn him out of office. O'Reilly, however, did not represent a real liaison with *The Times* itself. At the end of 1848 he was dismissed from the paper, expressly for financial extravagance, and Palmerston sought to rescue him by asking Clarendon to give him first a consular appointment and then secret service work. Not until 1853, after first taking up the cudgels with the *Post* over the new crisis emerging in the Near East, did Delane quarrel with Aberdeen and declare openly for Palmerston. Subsequently, and throughout Palmerston's Ministries in 1855-65, *The Times* was generally his supporter.[159]

The rapprochement with Delane resolved in a most satisfactory manner Palmerston's relations with the press when Prime Minister. During his periods at the F.O. there had also been one single paper with which he had managed to maintain a personal connection throughout. The *Globe* was by no means his exclusive literary property. During the reforming Ministries of the thirties, Althorp and, still more, John Russell had very sympathetic contacts with it and the *Globe* continued in the forties to reflect the internal divisions among the Whigs, printing, for example, anti-Palmerstonian articles written under the signature 'Pacificus' by Durham's crony, Charles Buller. Earlier, in 1834 or 1835, the *Globe*'s assistant editor, Gorton, had committed suicide after being compelled to incriminate Melbourne's private secretary in one intra-Cabinet intrigue. There is no correspondence in the Broadlands Papers with the *Globe*'s editors and proprietors of the 1830s, Torrens and Coulson, but there is none surviving there either with John Blackett who as a contributor and probable joint proprietor was certainly in frequent communication with Palmerston in 1851-2. According to Barnes Gorton had 'some connexion' with the F.O. in 1834 and Palmerston stated that he had established a communication with the *Globe* in the *Courier*'s place some time before January 1832.[160]

The *Globe* had certainly become Palmerston's special vehicle before the end of 1832. One important reason for this, in addition to his dissatisfaction with the *Courier*, was surely that it was much less under Brougham's control than any other of the ministerial papers. Another perhaps was that as an evening paper it could be used to make immediate retorts to anything hostile in the morning press. It was probably the very special favour shown to the *Globe* of having pretty regular articles from the pen of the Foreign Secretary himself that most upset *The Times*. Certainly Barnes complained more than once about 'the gross personal attacks in the *Globe* sanctioned by Lord Palmerston and written indeed by Sir George Shee under his direction'. 'The *Globe* of yesterday', wrote Parkes in December 1833, 'had a most miserable reply to me – which I have no doubt was Shee's article. You know the wheels within wheels. The *Globe* is his tool.' Very probably Shee did write some of the articles in the *Globe*. According to Grey in 1834 the paper's very 'stupidity' was 'a presumptive evidence of his writing in it'. Two years later, however, another hostile critic noticed that the *Globe* more consistently admired Palmerston's foreign policy than did any other paper and suggested that 'a certain air of faded dandyism distinguishes some of the articles on foreign affairs, much resembling the self-satisfied simper of the noble Secretary himself'. When Russell as Prime Minister chided Palmerston, and not for the first time, on some anti-Russian articles in the *Globe* in May 1850, Palmerston replied: 'I do not write the *Globe,* nor indeed do I always read it. I see the People who write the Foreign articles, when they come to ask to be kept right as to Facts & Events, & that is very seldom, scarcely once in 3 weeks or a month; but they take their own time [line?] & write their own articles.' There are 124 articles surviving in the Broadlands Papers for the period 1832-51 – all written in Palmerston's hand and destined for the *Globe*.[161]

While Palmerston, unlike some of his colleagues, was notably disinclined to make a war of personalities among the English, many of the press attacks on foreign diplomats and statesmen in the 1830s were attributed to him. Granville made a point of bringing to his notice the pain caused to Louis Philippe by articles in the *Morning Chronicle* and Lamb protested vigorously at those attacking Metternich in the *Globe*. Metternich and his henchman Baron Neumann both claimed to have detected Palmerston's handiwork. They may or may not always have been right. 'You will have seen very violent language in the "Times" against France,' Palmerston wrote to Granville in August 1831. 'We cannot help it. The "Times" breaks loose every now and then, and goes its own way.' But he had to admit that its 'tone' on this occasion might have been useful in showing the French that the English Government would be supported in the line it was taking at the time over Belgium. It may well have been the same with the attacks on Metternich in the autumn of 1833, which seem to have been ordered by Grey. Some of these attacks Palmerston conceded were counter-productive: 'the very coarseness and virulence of the attack', he wrote of one that appeared in *The Times* in December 1832, 'defeated its own purpose by necessarily disgusting many who read it.' An extract from the *Globe* that Fred Lamb sent him in complaint and Palmerston insisted was 'pure Torrens', he admitted shortly afterwards was also no more useful to England's policy than it was complimentary to Metternich personally. 'But I will instil all moderation,' he promised, 'if I can for the future.'[162]

Very probably, then, Palmerston was not responsible for what he too called the 'blackguard attack' on Talleyrand that appeared in *The Times* early in January 1832. It is doubtful, however, if he could have sustained the claim for long. For by 1835, according to Greville, all the foreign ministers in London detested him. Perhaps Palmerston took more than his share of the blame. Lamb concluded from what Palmerston told him that Grey was more personally ingratiating with foreign ministers than one would have thought from the contributions he made in Cabinet to policy making; 'it gives him', Lamb wrote back to Palmerston, 'all that is grace and favour and leaves you all that is harshness and insistence.' But for Palmerston to have become so unpopular so soon with the ambassadors in London he must have been singularly blunt and hectoring in his dealings with them. Certainly he seemed to find it difficult to preserve good personal relations with almost any of them (save Talleyrand's successor) when he was at odds with their countries politically. Thus the Spanish ambassador, Zea Bermudez, 'that good and worthy bore' in February 1831, became by the end of 1832 a sinister and intriguing fellow, and even the popular Falck suffered from Palmerston's political ill-humour.[163]

Falck had been Netherlands ambassador in London for several years and he and his wife were valued members of high society. But the Belgian business put them in a very difficult position, though according to Littleton it gave Talleyrand a good opportunity to make one of his famous jokes. When Madame Falck, who was very fat, alarmed her fellow guests by launching into a waltz at a ball of Princess Lieven's, Talleyrand easily explained: 'C'est pour intimider quelques Belges.' Palmerston's decision to reduce The Hague to a legation made Falck's remaining as an ambassador in London technically impossible, and Princess Lieven and Lady Holland, who believed that privately Falck differed with his masters over Belgium, urgently pressed both Palmerston and Grey to change their minds. But Palmerston, who suspected Falck of supplying ammunition to the Tory Opposition, was adamant. 'Falck is an agreeable and intelligent man,' he wrote to Grey, but he had little influence on his King and provided no grounds for a reciprocal post at The Hague. To Lady Cowper he commented still more bluntly: 'Now really, if one is to fight a gross job through the House of Commons, at least let it be for an Englishman & a friend, & not for a gouty old Dutchman for whom one cares not a farthing.' So Falck had to quit his post in May 1832.[164]

After Falck's departure Palmerston still had to deal in the Belgian conference with his aide Zuylen van Nyevelt, whom he utterly detested; but things much improved in 1833 when Dedel, a Johnian and a gentleman, replaced Zuylen in the conference. Palmerston worked even better, of course, with the first Belgian minister in London, Sylvain Van de Weyer, though on their first meeting Van de Weyer commented that he preferred Grey to Palmerston. More surprising at first sight was that Palmerston should have got on so well with the Austrian ambassador Prince Paul Esterhazy. But the Esterhazys had been in London since 1815 and were fully-fledged members of the fast and fashionable set. Princess Esterhazy, like Madame Lieven a patroness of Almack's, was accused of leading young ladies astray; her husband was sent by his Emperor the Order of the Golden Fleece in the hope that the overwhelming honour of it would shock him into a more orderly way of life. Esterhazy, moreover, was more than the half the time away from London and therefore left much of the work, both as chargé d'affaires and in the Belgian conference, to his Secretary of Embassy, Baron Neumann.[165]

Neumann was not only a great admirer of Metternich but possibly his half-brother. There was, therefore, very naturally a good deal of apprehension – and not only on Palmerston's part – when in February 1832 Metternich threatened both to make Neumann Austria's first representative at the Belgian conference, in place of Esterhazy, and to recall her second, Baron Wessenberg. Wessenberg had worked hard from his side to bring about a settlement, but he was very tactless in communications with Vienna and according to Palmerston Metternich hated him. Palmerston may well have prevented his recall; but although he tried he could not stop Wessenberg being joined by Neumann. Palmerston had known Neumann too for many years; the baron was also a long-standing member of the fashionable set in London and had some reputation as a ladies' man. But unlike his chief he was by no means popular with everyone. Lady Cowper had long since set him down as pompous; Palmerston came habitually to call him 'Pomposo' and occasionally 'Baron Cocksure'.[166]

After Neumann's appointment to the conference, their mutual dislike measured more accurately than any barometer the deterioration in Anglo-Austrian relations. At first Palmerston, while anticipating some trouble from him, expected the conference soon to 'tame him & make him docile'. A month later he still hoped to 'neutralize' him; 'as he is nearly as vain as Metternich,' Palmerston remarked, 'a little attention and complimenting will go a great way with him.' But by August 1832 Palmerston had become convinced that Neumann was too much under the influence of the Tory Opposition to report anything fairly to Vienna, and by the following February that he had 'contributed greatly' to the irritation between their two Governments. Palmerston then burst out:

He has lived, God knows how long here, in a subordinate and irresponsible capacity; and has therefore been accustomed to give vent to his personal feelings to a degree which responsibility, as Head of a Mission, would have prevented; . . . his friends are in factious opposition, and those whom he bitterly dislikes are in power. . . . With many good and estimable qualities, Neumann has not the talent of making himself generally agreeable, and his personal unpopularity makes him experience a degree of coldness from those who do not know him intimately, which he very naturally ascribes to political bitterness; and he attributes to enmity to Austria, that which in truth is merely an indication that the Chargé d'affaires is considered to be a bore.[167]

That Palmerston most resented Neumann talking as bluntly to him as Palmerston was accustomed to talking to others became very clear when Neumann began lecturing him in March 1833 on Switzerland and Palmerston complained:

As to Swiss affairs Neumann's ill-judged importunity . . . has exceeded the limits of diplomatic privilege. He has persecuted me day and night with the paper of Prince Metternich's in his hand and as if I had nothing to do but sit down and write what the sapient Neumann chooses to dictate. . . . on one occasion he broke in upon me at half-past ten at night to insist upon my writing . . . as he wished me to do so by a messenger who was putting on his cloak and lighting his cigar with his post-chaise at the door.

So that summer Palmerston pressed over and over again for Neumann's removal and before the end of the year had succeeded in his object. Metternich thought of sending Prince Felix Schwarzenberg to be chargé d'affaires. But Palmerston preferred not to have him; Schwarzenberg was, he thought, 'a silly & conceited fellow'. He therefore simply reminded Metternich through Lamb that on Schwarzenberg's last visit to London he had been named as co-respondent in Ellenborough's notorious divorce case. In Neumann's absence the counsellor of the embassy, Hummelauer, took over when Esterhazy was away and with him Palmerston got on quite well. Yet at the end of 1839 Metternich chose to send Neumann back to London in order to concert with Palmerston their policy in the revived Eastern crisis. Fred Lamb thought at once that he detected the return of Palmerston's bad temper with Austria. But by great good fortune Metternich had chosen his moment well. For Neumann arrived in England two days after Palmerston's marriage and in a new mood of bonhomie Palmerston invited him down at once to Broadlands.[168]

Neumann's good reception at Broadlands obviously owed most to Palmerston's need in 1839-40 of a concert with the Eastern powers. Neumann's fellow guest, Count Brunnow, received similar treatment. Until then Russian representatives in London had not fared well at all. Palmerston's quarrel with the Lievens had also embraced their successor, Pozzo di Borgo, whom Palmerston treated with studied disrespect when he came over to England in 1835. Even the Tsar's confidential adviser, the huge and popular Count Alexis Orlov, who made special visits to London in 1832, 1837 and 1839, was treated with considerable caution. 'As he tells everybody he speaks to,' Palmerston wrote to Lamb, 'that he is franc et loyal, & no diplomatist, & unable to say anything but what he thinks, one is bound to believe everything he says.' With the Prussian ambassador, Count Bulow, Palmerston got on personally so much better that when he found Bulow avoiding him he concluded it must be out of political circumspection. 'Bulow has kept quite aloof from me for a very long time,' he wrote to Minto in May 1834; 'he is afraid of being thought on intimate terms with me, for fear that the Lieven should write to complain of him to his court for being so, & should get him recalled. I leave him to himself, because I wish to keep him here.' The following year Bulow told Greville that he was on such bad terms with Palmerston that it was impossible for him to stay in London. Bulow in fact stayed on until ill health drove him home in the summer of 1841. But Palmerston was certainly correct in thinking that Princess Lieven was trying to set all the ambassadors against him. Given the condition of England's relations with the Eastern powers in the early 1830s it is no wonder that she should have had so much success; what is surprising in this context is that Talleyrand too should have joined the conspiracy.[169]

In Palmerston's first days at the F.O., nothing could have exceeded, it seemed, the flattering consideration with which he treated the French ambassador. For in spite of his years – Talleyrand was seventy-six when he came to London – the old prince still had the power to fascinate. 'His long powdered hair hanging down over his shoulders, his cadaverous complexion and his deformed foot give him a most extraordinary effect,' wrote Lady Georgiana Ellis after meeting him for the first time in September 1830. 'There is something very clever in the expression of his countenance . . . His having been so great an actor in all these transactions gives a great interest to all he says, in spite of one's disapprobation of the manner in which he was so often concerned in many of them.' Palmerston, however, was not the man to be intimidated, least of all by reputation; soon, his portrait-painter noticed, he was talking in idle conversation of ' "Old Talley", as if he was a match for

'The Lame Leading the Blind' [Talleyrand and Palmerston] by HB (John Doyle), January 1832

him'. Curiously he and Talleyrand seem to have got on well enough personally while relations between France and England were most at risk politically.
In part, probably, this was because Talleyrand was at odds with his chief in
Paris, Sébastiani, and looked to Palmerston for support. But Palmerston often
suspected that Talleyrand harboured schemes of partitioning Belgium and
blamed him accordingly both for the trouble over the barrier fortresses and for
not helping enough to persuade the other powers to agree upon a settlement.
He also wondered if Talleyrand was not trying to keep the Belgian affair open
in order to impress upon England her need of French assistance and so
prevent, for example, any awkward interference in what France was doing in
North Africa. Holland believed that Palmerston for his part was a little too
susceptible, 'either directly or indirectly through other female friends', to
suggestions from Mme Lieven, who naturally wanted to embroil England
with France. There was some truth in this. But so was there in Palmerston's
suspicions that the ambassador sometimes manoeuvred in diplomacy to make
profits on the stock-market. Palmerston also sensed that Talleyrand's lack of
cooperation was often due to 'personal pique' and 'wounded vanity'.[170]

It upset Talleyrand that both the English and the French Foreign Ministers
preferred to work through Granville in Paris and it outraged his vanity that he
should be kept waiting for an interview in Palmerston's anteroom. Clarendon
told Greville that Palmerston made everyone take his turn, regardless of rank.
Probably the Foreign Secretary could not have kept to a system any other
way, and even Greville recognized it as 'a merit'. An American visitor was told
that Palmerston always placed upon his desk the cards of those he intended to
see and removed them only after he had seen them. Diplomats may have had
precedence over others, though since Palmerston had no wish at all to receive
this particular American it is impossible to be sure.[171]

Ellice afterwards spread the story that Palmerston deliberately kept Talleyrand waiting and that on one occasion Grey went over to sit with the
ambassador so as to soften the offence. According to Palmerston, on the other
hand, Talleyrand on his part always showed a complete lack of regard for the
Foreign Secretary's time:

I have never kept him when I could help it. I am not master of my time and he
forgets that he has but one business to do and that I have many . . . other
diplomats who want me come and pop into my room at Stan. Street at 12 and
come in and go out in a short time; he does not weigh anchor till after one or
near two; and what he likes to do is come and establish himself in the armchair
at the office about four, just as I want to go away to eat something before I go
down to the He of Commons. This I always try to fight off; for his visit never
lasts less than an hour including getting up and sitting down and that throws
us out as to everything to be done afterwards.

But being kept waiting for any reason was not much appreciated by self-
important diplomats, by Talleyrand any more than by Stratford Canning.
Worse still were the occasions when Palmerston neglected to keep his ap-

pointments at all. This no doubt was also due to pressure of business, but unkind people, in the office as well as out of it, said it was merely Palmerston's 'pleasure or caprice'.[172]

Talleyrand spent much of 1832 and 1833 on leave in Paris. When he returned in December 1833 it was in the hope of recovering the initiative in foreign affairs by turning the Anglo-French entente into a formal treaty of alliance. It was, he thought, to be the closing triumph of his career. He soon dropped the idea when he saw how little enthusiasm there was in London for it. But he was bitterly disappointed and resentful, especially towards Palmerston. These feelings strengthened when in the following spring he caught Palmerston assigning to France a secondary role in the Quadruple Alliance. Shortly afterwards, in August 1834, he left London, vowing never to return. No one knew whether to believe him. Palmerston himself was puzzled, as unaware as ever how easily he had given offence. 'But for a couple of months before he went away', Palmerston had noticed, 'he was finding fault with everything I did and complaining of me to all my friends who were likely to repeat to me what he said; just like a man who is trying to pick a quarrel and cannot exactly find a good ground to put it upon.'[173]

From Paris it soon became apparent that Talleyrand was advocating a new concert with the Eastern powers. In part this had a good deal to do with his disappointment about the Anglo-French entente; it also reflected genuine disagreement with Palmerston's approach to the Mehemet Ali question. But many of the English spectators, including Holland and Granville as well as Palmerston himself, recognized that it was as much personal as political. One main objective was evidently to demonstrate to England that her relations with other powers would be the better for a change of Foreign Secretary. Talleyrand was by no means alone in this. By this time, as Lord William Russell put it, Palmerston gave 'them all the stomach-ache'. Palmerston concluded that Madame Lieven and Talleyrand's niece and companion Madame Dino had worked upon him. He was certainly right, though it was not entirely clear what it was that Palmerston had done to drive the Dino into an open alliance with the Lieven, whom she hitherto had hated. No doubt it was something personal, probably his off-hand manner. 'At the big Diplomatic dinner for the [King's] birthday', wrote Madame Dino in May 1834, 'Lord Palmerston . . . sat between the Princesse de Lieven and myself. He was chilly on the right and breezy on the left, and obviously ill at ease, though his embarrassment was not at all increased by the fact that he was not in his drawing-room ready to receive the ladies as they arrived, but came in afterwards without making the slightest excuse.' Soon afterwards she was urging on Talleyrand not to return to London as much on account of the 'frivolous, presumptuous, arrogant Minister, who pays you none of the respect due to your age and position', as of the 'current of Revolution' she saw sweeping through England after the passage of the Reform Bill. Madame Lieven, on the other hand, had obvious reasons for spreading the tale that, having got rid of her, Palmerston was now 'moving heaven & earth' to get rid of Talleyrand. Metternich, too, joined in the plot. When he heard that Melbourne had succeeded Grey as Prime Minister he ordered the Austrian chargé d'affaires in London to have as little as possible to do with Palmerston and urged Fred Lamb to return to London so as to work upon his brother.[174]

By the time Lamb arrived in England the Whig Government had fallen and Palmerston with it. It was only a short interlude; in the following spring the Whigs were recalled to power and Palmerston to the F.O. He had shown his usual self-confidence in the face of Metternich's plot. 'I have no doubt whatever', he had written in October, 'that . . . the Holy Alliance Govts have entered into a solemn league and covenant to demolish the Secy of State for foreign affairs; but I will back him against them all and wager odds that he makes his stand good against the whole gang.' Yet it was in fact a very near thing. When Bulow, on behalf of the Eastern courts, went pleading to the Whig elder statesmen, Lansdowne and Grey, he was given a severe rebuke; Palmerston's policy, he was told, was the policy of all the Cabinet. But this simply was not true, and when Fred Lamb set to work upon his brother he soon found that he had allies enough in the former Cabinet to bring him within a whisker of ousting Palmerston.[175]

CABINET
AND
COMMONS

Although, under Grey, Palmerston's position had not been as safe as he probably thought, he had in general got on rather well with the Prime Minister. 'No two men I believe', wrote Palmerston in 1833, 'ever went on better together in office, and very few half as well.' There were occasional breezes, especially when Grey wanted too much done for one of his friends or relations. But while Palmerston could be adamant where he thought something important was at stake – such as Lamb's appointment to Vienna in preference to Adair's – it was perfectly true, as the Grey papers underline, that he went out of his way to consult the Prime Minister about his diplomatic appointments, both high and low. With Palmerston's policy in general there was also probably nobody in the Cabinet as much in agreement as Grey; Wessenberg at first called Palmerston 'only the organ of Grey'. Nonetheless the degree of tutelage which the Prime Minister exercised over his Foreign Secretary has been grossly exaggerated, not least by Grey's family and Palmerston's opponents.[1]

In contrast to Palmerston, Grey had had no experience of office since 1807 and as Prime Minister he was too busy with domestic affairs to take the lead in foreign policy. The foreign ministers in London complained a good deal about his superficial grasp of foreign politics and his lack of energetic control over Government departments. He had good instincts – he warned Palmerston about the unsatisfactory contriving of the Belgian *bases de séparation* – and he occasionally altered Palmerston's dispatches, usually to cut out any unnecessary detail or to soften some over-strong expression. During the first few months in particular Palmerston also undoubtedly found it very useful to maintain a close communication and almost daily correspondence with him. But to the extent that there was anything in it beyond customary practice and collective responsibility, he probably kept in such close touch with his Prime Minister in order to secure an effective defence in the House of Lords and a powerful ally in a coalition Cabinet dominated by Whigs.[2]

The British Prime Minister, by constitutional convention, had a special duty of watching over foreign policy and of ensuring that the decisions of the Cabinet were carried out. But the special confidence Palmerston shared with Grey was extended among the Cabinet to Lansdowne and to Holland. To these two (and subsequently also to Hobhouse after he had become President of the India Board) dispatches continued to be specially circulated as a matter of routine after the practice had been abandoned for all the others except the Prime Minister. Lansdowne, though he shared with Grey and Holland the eminence of seniority among the older Whigs, was rather diffident, or frankly indolent according to his harsher critics, and he was by no means constant in his attention. But observers in society noted soon after the formation of the Government 'great whisperings' between Palmerston and Holland and remarked 'how thick' the Foreign Secretary was both with Holland and with Grey. Sir Charles Webster rather dismisses Holland's influence in foreign affairs, and it is true that his ideas were somewhat superficial and, in his last few years, perhaps even silly. Yet he and his formidable wife entertained a lot at Holland House and carried on extensive correspondence with important individuals at home and abroad. He was also an elder statesman among the Whigs and the family custodian of a proud tradition in foreign policy that he resented seeing thwarted. The 'dangerous Netherlands', the clever Talleyrand called him. So Palmerston had to be doubly careful with him, especially where relations with France were concerned. On the other hand, the emergence of an ostensible *entente cordiale* in 1832 strengthened his position with Holland without weakening that with Grey, and he sometimes found the Foxite connection and the hospitality of Holland House even very useful. Still, Holland's Cabinet leaks – and even more his wife's – were always a considerable nuisance.[3]

During his first period at the F.O. Palmerston seems to have had no intention of concealing information from the Cabinet. 'You may think it absurd to write long despatches & give details,' he once admonished Lamb, 'but pray continue the practice; remember that people in the Cabinet cannot know what you do or say unless you please to tell them; and as it will always be for your advantage that what you say & do should be known to the Cabinet, I hope you will not be afraid of being thought lengthy.' Although, therefore, Palmerston formed with Grey, Lansdowne and Holland a sort of inner Cabinet on foreign affairs, he did not by any means exclude the rest of his colleagues. They too had a right to see diplomatic correspondence. In 1831, according to Francis Molyneux, when one of the Undersecretaries received a dispatch he put it in a box to circulate among them. Some time later Palmerston, in place of general circulation, had dispatches put in a box in the Cabinet room at the F.O., where any member might inspect them. For those who were out of town, he initiated (or reintroduced, since something of the sort seems to have existed in Canning's time) a daily bulletin or abstract of incoming dispatches.* Some time after October 1840 this practice ceased,

---

*Presumably the bulletins were afterwards recovered and destroyed, for Webster states (i.40 n.3) that he never came across one. In the Goodwood Papers there is a whole packet of them (item 652) retained by the Duke of Richmond and belonging to the year 1832. They are variously endorsed 'precis', 'bulletin' or 'abstract' and consist of very brief summaries. (See also Middleton, p. 54 n.70.)

possibly because greater resort to the printing press could serve all these and other purposes at once. When important questions were to be decided by Cabinet, Palmerston of course made special arrangements for copies of memoranda and dispatches, and even draft instructions, to be submitted to them.[4]

In spite of Palmerston's care and effort for them – at least in the first few years; there were more complaints about him during Melbourne's Administration – most of his Cabinet colleagues outside the inner circle took but a slight and intermittent interest in foreign policy. Even the Canningites were not very strongly behind him. Melbourne was much preoccupied with domestic disturbances, and Goderich as feeble and annoying as ever. Among the other senior Canningites Carlisle seems to have been rather inactive and aloof, and Grant very unpopular with both King and colleagues. Grant occasionally fired off one of his memoranda on foreign affairs in Palmerston's direction and as President of the Board of Control he must have often worked together with the Foreign Secretary. But Grant was reckoned to be as indolent in his office and inattentive to the Commons as he was emphatic with his unsympathetic opinions in Cabinet, and Palmerston worked much more closely with Graham, who though not a Canningite by origin was, as First Lord of the Admiralty, perhaps Palmerston's closest collaborator in a foreign policy that was so dependent on ships and marines in the Scheldt, the Tagus and the Mediterranean.[5]

Palmerston's recollection of Graham, after he had left the Government, was far from complimentary. He liked him personally, he told Hobhouse, but in their dealings at the Admiralty had found him 'timid & vacillating & afraid of responsibility'. What he was probably recalling was that while Graham had been most cooperative when the Admiralty had the ships, he was no more anxious than Althorp to approach Parliament for money when they did not. Behind Palmerston's back, in correspondence with Richmond for example, Graham had been by no means uncritical of his foreign policy. But to his face Graham's praise of Palmerston was the most extravagant and extraordinary of them all. 'You are the most amiable of colleagues', he wrote in December 1832, 'on account of the good humour with which you tolerate the utmost freedom of discussion on every plan and on every paper which you propose.'[6]

Eventually, in 1833, the Canningites completely split over the Portuguese question. But it is doubtful if they had ever formed an effective group in either the Cabinet or the Commons. Palmerston occasionally tried to organize their back-benchers in advance for parliamentary debates on foreign affairs, but the tools usually broke in his hands. Littleton was plainly too nervous and Gally Knight, who was more a friend of Stratford Canning's, was by no means uncritical of Palmerston's policy, over Poland in particular. The front-benchers, too, were a very disappointing lot in the Commons. Grant often did not bother to attend and when he did usually seemed to doze; Graham, when trying to fill his place, was not very effective. Unfortunately, with very few exceptions, Palmerston's own interventions in debate, whether on foreign or domestic affairs, were also disappointing.[7]

In view of the slowness with which Palmerston's 1829 successes at House of Commons oratory had come, it is hardly surprising that there was considerable disagreement about his talents in this direction at the formation of Grey's Government in November 1830. Joseph Jekyll predicted that he would have to 'speechify' for Althorp, who was himself no great dab. Croker, too, talked of Palmerston being 'prompter to the puppet' and avowed that the Government in the Commons would have 'talkers' enough. He did not expect them to do it very well. Palmerston and Grant, he had written to Peel, were 'nothing but froth'. When Althorp was absent from the House Palmerston was expected to deputize for him, but he spoke, it seems, as little as he could. Before the end of 1830 even, some of those who had wanted him as leader when the coalition was formed began to change their minds.[8]

Both Brougham and Grey sent Palmerston vociferous congratulations when he dealt so ruthlessly with Croker and the press in Parliament in August 1831. Everyone agreed that he had also made a very effective intervention in the debate on the Russo-Dutch loan in January 1832; most thought that it had even saved the Government. But Hobhouse, who had probably missed the first, believed this to be the '*only* good speech' Palmerston had made since becoming Foreign Secretary. On the same subject in July and August 1832 his interventions were 'weak' or 'tiresome', and overall, Greville concluded at the end of Palmerston's first spell in the Foreign Office, 'he cut a very poor figure in Parliament all the time he was in office, and considering his post a very contemptible figure'.[9]

When Parliament was prorogued in the summer of 1832 Lady Cowper admitted to her brother Frederick that no one was more relieved than Palmerston. The fact of the matter was, as a hostile critic noted, that Palmerston too was irregular in attendance and disinclined to be stirred up by anything but 'a regular attack' either upon himself or upon the conduct of his department. Occasionally he would put up a creditable performance, but, in spite of having a clear and strong, if rather harsh, voice, he would too often stammer and stutter 'to a very unpleasant extent' and make 'altogether an indifferent exhibition'. So, as even friendly witnesses would recall, his speaking was 'laborious', the continued working of his hands betraying that it was all a 'perpetual effort'. Soon he was falling back again into what Ellenborough called his old 'lackadaisical manner' and time and time again, Hobhouse recorded, was laying himself open to Peel's taunts of political trimming and personal inconsistency. 'The truth is', Dover understood from Brougham, 'that Palmerston, Graham, & Grant have all failed lamentably in speaking and in courage.'[10]

So Palmerston was, apparently, an easy target for the less steady of his Cabinet colleagues. Althorp and Brougham both gave him some trouble.

Althorp continued, almost as if still in opposition, to contest every penny spent on defence or foreign policy, and since Grey thought his popularity in the Commons and the party made him indispensable, his activity was often also very awkward. Brougham's opinions and alignments were, on the other hand, so mercurial that they made him much less dangerous than he thought. John Russell was hardly more reliable, especially where foreign policy was concerned. Sometimes he was more urgent for action, even in Portugal, than either Palmerston or Grey; at others he would carp and criticize. Russell's elder brothers too were often at him. William Russell's campaign of vituperation against Palmerston did not begin until after his removal from Lisbon. But Tavistock, the heir to the dukedom of Bedford, always resented, more perhaps than his brother did, that Palmerston's appointment to the F.O. had prevented little Johnny becoming Holland's Undersecretary there. Afterwards, he hardly ever missed an opportunity to censure and complain, especially in correspondence with his joint custodian of the Whig tradition at Holland House.

The constant criticism from Woburn Abbey had until 1839 comparatively little effect at Holland House except, through Holland's communications with Granville, to put the Canningites on guard. For while Palmerston seemed to be improving England's relations with France and until the second Mehemet Ali crisis of 1839-40 brought a major change in that respect, Holland firmly supported Palmerston at the F.O. In the meantime the real danger came instead from another and more radical wing of the Whig party, led by Grey's son-in-law Durham and by his brother-in-law Ellice. For these two Palmerston was doubly an anathema. As the leader of the Canningites he obstructed their plans to radicalize the Government; and as Foreign Secretary he stood in the way of an obvious promotion for Durham. There is no doubt they plotted against him. Both encouraged the press to attack his policy, and time and time again, when some Cabinet crisis loomed, the rumour took off that Palmerston was to be ejected from the F.O. and Durham given his place. That rumour seems to have surfaced first as early as June 1831. It was occasioned, according to Creevey's information, by the quarrels Palmerston was supposed to have had, on the one hand with Grey about Ponsonby and on the other with Brougham about some outspoken comment of the Chancellor's concerning foreign affairs. But what in all probability really lay behind it was the growing dissatisfaction of Durham and the radicals, not so much with Palmerston's foreign policy as with the difficulties he was making over the Reform Bill.[11]

Although Palmerston was to clash with his Whig colleagues over parliamentary reform, the doubts that had existed about the Canningites' commitment to it at the formation of Grey's Ministry were not really justified. In the first place his own view of the matter was essentially consistent. In 1828 he professed to be in favour of limited reform in order to preserve the essence of the existing order of things; in 1830 he recognized that if revolution was to be averted and property preserved a great deal more would have to be done. In the second place, this was not really so different from the way the Whigs looked at things. Thus Grey and Palmerston were at bottom agreed that the objective was to preserve aristocratic predominance and that to do so required the extension of the franchise to the middle classes. Where they differed was in their rough calculations about how far it was necessary to go. Neither of them had any wish for the sort of battle that would drive things to extremes or any intention of allowing the floodgates to open; whatever was done would be both moderate and 'final'. Grey would go 'far enough to satisfy Althorp', forecast Croker, 'and not so far as to frighten Palmerston'. But Palmerston thought the best chance of securing the passage of a bill was to make it moderate, and Grey that it must go far enough to put Parliament under pressure. In practice this meant that while Palmerston wanted to ensure that the middle-classes' power would be strictly limited by the workings of the bill, Grey was prepared to risk a good deal more and to rely in the end on their traditional deference to aristocracy.[12]

These differences took some time to appear. The first draft of a bill, prepared by a sub-committee of the Cabinet under Durham, certainly exceeded the limits Palmerston desired. For it proposed to take away both M.P.s from those constituencies of less than 2,000 inhabitants (Schedule A) and one from those with under 4,000 (Schedule B), to redistribute about three-fifths of the 167 seats to be abolished partly among new one- and two-member town constituencies (Schedules D and C), and partly among the counties, to adopt a uniform franchise of £20 rental in the towns, and to introduce the secret ballot. It was rumoured among the Opposition as early as December 1830 that Palmerston seemed 'embarrassed'. Yet historians have noted that, with the exception of substituting a £10 franchise for the secret ballot, these recommendations were endorsed by the Cabinet with very little opposition, and they have overlooked the fact that initially Palmerston even appeared to welcome the substance, if not the prospects, of Durham's draft:

I like the working of the plan much, that is viewing it as a measure to be octroyé by ordonnance from a liberal autocratic authority but I own I feel some apprehension as to our success in carrying it through Parliament; & the more so when I consider that besides all the phalanx naturally opposed to reform there will be the members of all the boroughs which are to be lopped & topped who of course will oppose us tooth & nail, – however we shall see . . .

The last few words are very revealing when examined in the light of what Grey concluded had subsequently happened to make Palmerston so hostile – that he had been worked upon by others.[13]

The committee on the bill, consisting in addition to Durham of Althorp, Graham and Russell, had worked in great secrecy and sprung their recommendations, even on most of their colleagues, as a great surprise. Durham shortly afterwards gave Littleton the impression that Palmerston and Grant were also members of the committee, which they certainly were not, and that they had met 'regularly' at his house to discuss the principles of the bill, which seems very unlikely. Probably Durham was exaggerating grossly in order to reassure a troubled Canningite slowly turning Whig. Palmerston's first and rather casual welcome may therefore have been due, partly to his early preoccupations in the Foreign Office and partly, perhaps, to a desire to appear well with the son-in-law of the Prime Minister while privately relying on Parliament to throw out the bits he did not like. His public defence of the bill in the Commons, when he was attacked by Peel for inconsistency, seemed to many unconvincing and insincere. Typically he reacted to these public attacks with fervour and with confidence in his private letters. 'Reform is thriving, inconceivably popular in the country, and likely to be carried in the House,' he wrote to Granville, 'and, whatever the Tories may say, will not be Revolution, but the reverse.'[14]

It was just as typical of Palmerston that the first real note of disquiet he is known to have expressed should have been inspired, not by any democratic tendencies he detected in the bill, but by the claims put forward to their existence made by some of his colleagues. 'He is much dissatisfied,' reported his colleague Stanley towards the end of February, 'and complains of the impression created throughout the country by the newspapers supposed to be the organs of the Government, and really the organs of some members of it, that we are identifying ourselves with the Radicals, and breaking down all our established institutions.' He claimed not long afterwards to have told the Prime Minister before the bill was introduced on 1 March that he could not bind himself 'to stand and fall' by the bill as it stood in all its details. But his recollection was not always accurate and from the surprise and hurt he caused and the tone in which he expressed himself it seems much more likely that the first reasoned objections he made to Grey followed again from an external nudge, this time in the form of a personal approach from his old friend Clive.[15]

Clive came to Palmerston early in April 1831 to say that, dreading the violence of conflict that would ensue if the Commons threw out the bill and the Government either resigned or resorted to a General Election, he and others who were opposed to reform would consider supporting a more moderate measure. What they had in mind, Clive indicated, was the raising of the £10 franchise and the maintenance of the existing total of seats so as to reduce the number of places to be disfranchised, and, while extending the representation of the great towns, not to give seats in the metropolis itself to 'the poorest and worst parts of its suburbs', who would return 'persons undesirable as members of the House'.[16]

Palmerston replied to Clive that there was no question of the Government abandoning the 'principles' of the bill. But he was personally of opinion that both the figure of 2,000 inhabitants and that of £10 were negotiable. Furthermore, in reporting all this to Grey, he 'confessed' that he would 'view with great satisfaction' some such modifications as these and that if the Government decided against them and so were defeated, as he expected they would be, he would 'find himself in an embarrassing situation' whether the Government resigned or called a General Election. 'Notwithstanding all the applause which has been bestowed upon the Bill', he went on, 'we must not disguise from ourselves, that there is a vast mass of intelligence, of property, of liberality and even of Whiggism, by which its provisions are looked upon, with some uneasiness as too sweeping and too extensive.' He suggested, therefore, that the £10 qualification should be raised and the existing number of members be retained by leaving the towns in Schedule B with both their members and by giving more seats to the largest counties.[17]

Stiffened by Durham, who recognized that Clive's modifications, in addition to attacking his cherished £10 franchise, would undermine the principle of abolishing *all* rotten boroughs, and who accused Palmerston of being prepared to give way on everything, the Prime Minister refused to budge. 'I confess', Grey wrote in answer to Palmerston's letter, 'it has given me some pain, as you must be aware, after having twice declared it in the House of Lords, that I am left without the possibility of compromise or retreat.' However, he went on to ask for half an hour's conversation in which they could discuss possible 'alterations or corrections' which did not conflict with the principles of the bill. There is, unfortunately, no record of such a conversation. But one thing at least is clear, that the incident established Palmerston as a leading voice for compromise and the main channel of communication in future attempts to bargain with the Tories. In the meantime personal experience further convinced him of the necessity of moderation.[18]

The Reform Bill had passed through its first reading in the Commons at the beginning of March without a division; but that had been owing to the tactical decisions made in advance by the Opposition, and its second reading on 22 March had been passed by a majority of only one. Then on 19 April an amendment was carried by eight votes against the Government and, after another defeat on the evening of 21 April, Grey, with the King's reluctant consent, decided on a dissolution. The King went down to the Lords to announce the dissolution in person on the afternoon of 22 April; the next day Palmerston's election committee was already at work; and the day after that Palmerston was himself in Cambridge canvassing.[19]

A Cambridge by-election in 1829 had given Palmerston a new colleague in the person of William Cavendish, Devonshire's heir-presumptive. Palmerston had rejoiced then, thinking that by restoring the traditional balance of one Whig and one, albeit Huskissonite, Tory, there would be less chance of a contest at the next General Election. In this the election of the following year proved him justified. But it had aleady occurred to others that his changing role in Westminster might make the university think it had two *Whigs* in place of two Tories, and having actually joined Grey's Government Palmerston realized, as he told Lansdowne, that he 'could not go gayly and carelessly to a Dissolution'.[20]

When Palmerston arrived in Cambridge in April 1831 things seemed even worse than they had in 1826. 'Shocked earlier by his Catholic opinions,' as Guedalla put it, the university 'was frankly scared by the graver heresy of Reform.' Trinity once again, seemed 'zealous & cordial'. But St John's was getting 'blacker & blacker'. Some of his old supporters, he heard, intended to plump for Cavendish; others were going to vote for his opponents, Goulburn and William Peel, who was the Opposition leader's brother and both old Harrovian and Johnian. Even Wood, Palmerston suspected, would keep away rather than vote, and his place on Palmerston's committee was taken by another Johnian, J.S. Henslow, the Professor of Botany and Darwin's teacher. While his old secretary, Elliot, looked after the business details in London, Palmerston stayed on a couple of days in Cambridge, and his obvious reservations about the bill – in his election circular he went out of his way to spell out his commitment to 'the fundamental Principles of the Constitution' – may have done some good: on 24 April he had reported he would be in a minority among the resident votes, and the next day that he believed he would get the majority after all. But there were only 180 resident voters out of a total of between 1,800 and 2,000. His committee, he reported, were inclined to 'talk big & confidently, & say to each other who's afraid'; personally he hoped to succeed by making great efforts but he admitted the danger was 'very considerable'.[21]

Having made 'great efforts' – even to the extent of summoning an attaché in the Paris embassy to come over for the poll – Palmerston felt by the time it came to return to Cambridge on the evening of 1 May that the result of his canvass was 'on the whole encouraging'. But it was 'not sufficiently decisive' to make him confident of success. What worried him most were the plumpers promised to Cavendish; these left him with only 500 firm promises to Goulburn's boasted 600. Though far from happy in the company their protégé kept, Cavendish's committee subsequently persuaded most of his supporters to split their votes with Palmerston. But at the end of the first day's poll on 3 May this left Palmerston at the bottom with 250 votes and Cavendish with only one above him, against Peel's 321 and Goulburn's 323. Palmerston admitted that he would have been 'better pleased' to have found himself only twenty or thirty behind instead of seventy. However, several people whom he had not expected had turned up to vote for him, while the enemy had made great efforts to get their supporters up that day. So, ever the optimist in such situations, he professed the situation to be 'by no means' hopeless and looked rather to the following day to decide. But the next day saw the clergy 'pouring in from the fens', and at the end of it Palmerston found himself still bottom of the poll, thirteen votes behind Cavendish and nearly two hundred behind Peel and Goulburn. He knew that he and his Whig colleague were both 'decidedly beat'. They insisted on keeping the poll open another day and a half for latecomers and when it closed at noon on 6 May the total of voters was, at 1,450,157 more than ever before. But to Palmerston it seemed that 'all the anti-Reformers in England are concentrated in Cambridge; there is no end of them here'. So, at the end of it all, he found himself where he had begun twenty-five years before, at the bottom with 610 votes to Cavendish's 630, Peel's 804, and Goulburn's 805.[22]

While Palmerston was being defeated in Cambridge, reform was sweeping the country so as to convert the majority for the Government Bill from one to 136. According to Mrs Arbuthnot the Government newspapers had been whipping the people into 'a perfect state of madness'. 'At Cambridge', she went on, 'the Ld Chancellor promised livings to those who voted for their candidates, & perpetual war against those who did not.' Hobhouse, finding himself again in a position to support his old debating pal, had travelled down to Cambridge in a barouche full of voters and journalists, all excited by 'the triumphant news . . . thronging in from the all parts of the country', and doomed to disappointment in the Senate House. Both sides believed that Palmerston, as a member of the reforming Cabinet, had 'pulled Cavendish down'.[23]

There is no doubt that Palmerston thought that the Cabinet had pulled him down with Cavendish and, as even Lady Holland noticed, was 'deeply vexed' by it. 'We have done all that could be effected in the time,' he told Grey, '& have got votes from Scotland, Ireland and Paris. But the fears of the clergy that Reform will endanger tithes, and the objections felt even by reformers to the £10 franchise have been too much for us.' This was on 4 May. He had told his chief the same thing and at some length in his letter of 25 April. The 'great danger', he had then observed, was not simply the 'activity of our adversaries', but also 'the comparative coolness of our friends', and he was speaking not merely of those who made up their committees but 'generally of the friends of Government & Reform'. They did not really understand why there had had to be a General Election at all, seeing that Lord John Russell had publicly stated that the Government would not 'resist to extremity' every modification and specifically that it would acquiesce in maintaining the present number of M.P.s. But since their opinion had been asked they were bound to give it even if it meant voting against the Government. 'I am constantly told by men, who have been reformers all their lives, that it goes much beyond what necessity required, or prudence would have counselled.' The bill was 'too sweeping' and the disfranchisement 'carried much too far'; the number of seats and the balance of distribution among the three kingdoms ought not to have been altered; and the £10 qualification was too low, bordering in the large towns on 'universal suffrage'. 'I am bound to say to you', he went on, 'that I really doubt whether there are *six* men in university who do not feel strong objections to our Bill upon these grounds. These objections are felt by staunch & tried Whigs, and reformers of long standing; by men, not cloistered monks, but persons mixing in the world both in town & country, and likely to be expositors of the opinions of a class of men, among the public, whose opinions, though not loudly expressed in newspapers & at county meetings, is [sic] nevertheless a large ingredient in the formation of public opinion.'[24]

After the election was over Palmerston also wrote to Holland House, where he had little hope of changing anyone's opinion, and to Bowood, where his chances were much better. He tried to impress upon the first that there were many laymen among the M.A.s who had deserted him on account of the radical nature of the bill, but Holland dismissed his defeat as 'a monument to the wisdom of the Church'. Lansdowne, however, wholeheartedly agreed with his old Cambridge rival. Palmerston had evidently sent him some possible modifications on the lines of those he had outlined to Grey after the meeting with Clive in April. But while 'very glad to agree' Lansdowne did not expect they could prevail over Althorp's and Brougham's determination to curry favour with the large towns. When *The Times*, working as Palmerston knew hand in glove with Brougham, threatened the Lords if they should throw out the bill, Palmerston appealed to Grey: 'is it not possible either to keep this foul mouthed paper in some controul, or else to disavow it?' For the object of the paper, like that of some of the Government's supporters, seemed to be 'to drive & goad us on, without giving us time to breathe or look back', and it did more than anything else to 'inspire me with unpleasant misgivings that we are hurrying on too fast'.[25]

Palmerston got Littleton to supply him with ammunition against too low a franchise and Lady Cowper also went around – to Brougham, to Russell and to Durham himself – protesting loudly against the bill. But Grey brushed Littleton's advice aside and Lady Cowper only succeeded in annoying him with her 'hollow friendship'. 'Palmerston on the one side worked upon through Lady Cowper by Fredk Lamb', the Prime Minister complained, 'with Lansdowne to aid him, & both leaning too much, without considering consequences, to restrict the popular effect of the measure, & Lambton's [i.e. Durham's] impracticability on the other, almost distract me.' Warned no doubt by Princess Lieven, Emily wrote at once a careful explanation to Grey, ending with the assurance that having 'always been a very good & true Whig' she would continue to support the Government. But the rumour persisted that she was about to leave the party, and Prince Leopold continued to debate with Littleton whether she was 'the more influential politician' or was 'only playing Ld Palmerston's game'. For, as Princess Lieven recognized, Palmerston's position in the Cabinet was now doubly weakened by the result of the elections.[26]

Palmerston was the *only* member of the Cabinet to have lost his seat in an otherwise triumphant election and he was dependent on the Treasury for another. Grey had taken the precaution of asking the Chief Whip, Edward Ellice, to reserve one for him as soon as he heard in April how bleak Palmerston thought his prospects were in Cambridge. The one they had in mind was Bletchingley, one of whose sitting members, Charles Tennyson, afterwards Tennyson d'Eyncourt, was Clerk of the Ordnance. Brougham wanted it for another Canningite aspirant for office. 'Why can't Palmerston take Liverpool where he could walk over the course?' he asked. A seat at either Liverpool or Nottinghamshire was bound to become vacant, since each had elected the same man, and Palmerston did actively consider them both. But election campaigns in Liverpool were very expensive affairs – the by-election of 1830 had cost its contestants nearly £100,000 – and he feared that the sitting ultra-Tory had been defeated in 1831 only by a 'manoeuvre' and that he would put up a very fierce and expensive fight in any new election. In the end he and his colleague both found seats in Bletchingley. Palmerston was very relieved. His failure in Cambridge had already cost him about £1,650; and £800 for Bletchingley was cheap indeed, so much so that he ought to have suspected there was a misunderstanding somewhere. In any case, while he waited for it, Mme Lieven said, Palmerston was 'forced to bend, to give way, and to obey'.[27]

Durham told his father-in-law that Lansdowne and Palmerston 'are not & never were sincere friends of the measure – & it would be madness to lose the confidence of the country & the majority of the House of Commons . . . in order to remove their scruples'. So when the Cabinet came on 29 May and again on 8 June to discuss modifications to the bill Grey's 'expressions were so strong that they silenced Palmerston'. Lansdowne ratted by agreeing it was too late to make a change, and Palmerston was left in isolated opposition when the others all agreed that to attempt to conciliate the Lords would only alienate the Commons. So as the bill passed through its committee stages in the Commons during July, August and early September, Palmerston could make only impotent and token protests. 'The discussions on Schedule B', he wrote to Grey in July, 'are painful to those, who think the disfranchisement of the places uncalled for, and unnecessary for the fair execution of any of the main principles of our measure, and whose judgement is convinced by the arguments in debate that many of the places do not fully fall within the scope of our own rule.' And in September, as *The Times* sought to intimidate the Opposition:

Pray look at the leading article in the Times today and see printed in capital letters, a direct incitement to the army to a general mutiny, if we should be turned out. Surely such support as this is more hurtful to a government than any attacks, because those who know the intercourse which exists between the adherents of the Govt & the editors of this paper, will have no means of discriminating from which source such abominable suggestions proceed; are there no means of keeping the zeal of our friends within the ample bounds of legal & constitutional order?[28]

Still Palmerston put a brave face on it all. He told Granville that reform was 'going on well, but slowly'. He also rather slyly drew the Prime Minister's attention to his not having been asked to the Mansion House dinner, at which Johnny Russell was to be honoured for his part in promoting the bill, and secured a last-minute invitation. 'The Kingdom of honest politicians is certainly not of this world,' Hobhouse observed. But Palmerston was nevertheless widely reported as being 'very much dissatisfied' with his situation, and not only about reform but also about his colleagues' interference in the Foreign

Office. Brougham had made some insulting observations on a diplomatic dispatch that went the rounds of the Cabinet; and Grey too was resented for defending the gaffe that Ponsonby had made in Brussels. Soon the rumour was flying about that Palmerston was likely to lose his office to Durham. However, Palmerston survived, and to fight another day.[29]

Although the General Election had secured the Reform Bill's passage through the Commons there remained a majority of opposition to it in the Lords. The Cabinet neither wished nor expected to have to create the large number of peers it would have required to secure a majority. Rather, they hoped that the feeling in the country would cow the Lords and that all they needed was a nudge in the right direction. When the election of the Scottish representative peers turned out badly, five new United Kingdom baronies were created in June. Palmerston, whom Grey had gone out of his way to consult, commented in reply: 'Your five new peers . . . are excellent men & well chosen, and it is quite natural that on your accession to power you should recommend such personal & political friends to royal favour; one should be sorry however if the public were to look upon these promotions as a preliminary to a coup d'état . . . upon the House of Peers.' He must have been rather more concerned when another sixteen, the largest number for which precedent could be found, were put in the King's coronation list the following month. But he admitted that an increase of strength was necessary and was subsequently reassured to think with his colleagues that these few would be enough. Then at 6 a.m. on 8 October the Lords threw out the bill on its second reading by 199 to 158. Palmerston was evidently not displeased. 'I did not expect so large a majority against us,' he wrote to Lady Cowper, 'but at least it has one good effect, it puts out of the question any idea of making a batch of peers to carry the bill.' Since the King also made his opposition to such an idea unmistakably clear, even those who had previously entertained it had quickly to agree. They came just as quickly to the conclusion that they ought not to resign but seek to resolve the crisis for which they shared a good deal of the responsibility. It was clear that this meant submitting a new bill. But whether or not it should be pretty well the same bill provoked a sharp difference of opinion. That Palmerston was at the bottom of it is well known; on closer examination Grey's role also appears rather less straightforward than has usually been assumed.[30]

The Cabinet met on Saturday, 8 October, and postponed any definite decision about what they should do until after the feeling of the Commons had been tested by a motion planned for Monday evening. Althorp, it was intended, would then make a statement about the conditions on which the Government would continue. Palmerston evidently said enough to make Althorp aware that he was concerned about the precise wording of the statement and Holland recorded that Palmerston, Lansdowne and the Duke of Richmond (the coalition's recruit from the old Tories) had made 'some faint distinctions' about the principles of the bill. All the rest were firmly for the bill to its 'full extent', and in the circumstances it was thought only 'fair' to warn the King. So after the meeting Grey wrote to Windsor that he contemplated carrying on only if the King supported the Government in a measure of reform 'not less efficient' than the defeated bill. Quite possibly someone at court reported this to Palmerston and Palmerston in turn concluded Grey had gone further than the Cabinet had specifically agreed. That Grey was aware of this, moreover, would seem to be confirmed by his having made his statement to the King a personal one, not on behalf of the Cabinet.[31]

In spite of the characterization Holland later gave it there was therefore really nothing 'strange' about the letter Palmerston addressed to Grey on 9 October protesting against the pledge to reintroduce the old bill, which he now assumed Althorp was to make the following evening. He had, 'on principle', he said, 'a great dislike to prospective pledges' because they fettered one's judgement in future contingencies when circumstances might have changed in ways that could not have been foreseen. But he had a particular objection to the pledge he understood Althorp intended to make, because it would imply his own unqualified commitment to a bill he did not entirely like. Moreover, with the passage of a bill by the creation of peers ruled out, the only alternative was to do it by persuasion. As he understood it, the Lords had thrown the bill out not because the majority disapproved of it root and branch, but because it was too extensive – 'because, in short, it tended to give too great and sudden an increase of power to the democratical influence'. This was his own opinion and, he believed, that of 'the great bulk of the gentry' and even 'in some degree' of the majority of the bill's supporters in the Commons. What alterations might be necessary to reach a compromise could only be decided 'upon very mature deliberation'; but in the meantime it was only fair for him to make it clear that he could not be a party to a pledge never to propose anything less than the present bill.[32]

Palmerston's letter gave him, Grey confessed the following day, 'great uneasiness'. The Cabinet had already discussed the proposed statement and, he thought, it had been clearly understood that without something of the sort the Government could not honourably continue in office; for they were, he insisted, 'unequivocally pledged' to bring forward a measure which, though possibly different in its details was 'equally efficient'. By equally efficient, he explained, he meant the disfranchisement of nomination boroughs, the transfer of their members to counties and large towns, and such alterations in the voting qualifications as would 'ensure a fair representation of the people in Parliament'. But having said all that, he went on to outline a form of words he thought would satisfy both Palmerston and Althorp:

that the Administration, if it continues, does so with the hope of being able to bring forward with better success an efficient plan of Reform, which may satisfy the just expectations of the public [and] that this will be carefully reconsidered after all the lights which the late discussions have thrown upon the measure.[33]

This wording, as Palmerston at once acknowledged, was precisely what he wanted; by omitting the expression '*as efficient* or *as extensive* as the late measure' it left the question of 'reconsideration' wide open. It also left it open to Althorp, when addressing the House, to state on his own behalf that he would not continue in office another hour unless he felt 'a reasonable hope that a measure as efficient' as the old might be secured, a personal plea from Stanley alone dissuading him from restoring also the expression 'as extensive'. But it had occurred to others that this also left it open to Palmerston to make a personal statement to the House about his own position. So the next morning the faint-hearted Lansdowne went rushing round to find him, and, when he failed to do so, Melbourne sent Palmerston a written appeal in the evening not to say anything that would provoke others to state a contrary position and, by starting 'a general convulsion', wreck the chances of future agreement. Perhaps this convinced Palmerston, for Althorp was the only one to rise from the Government benches that evening.[34]

Before writing to Palmerston on 10 October Grey had checked with Althorp both in writing and in person that he had never intended to commit Palmerston individually by what he had to say in Parliament. He had also specifically warned Palmerston that Althorp intended to say 'for himself individually' that he could not be 'a party to anything less efficient in principle and in substance' than the former bill; and he had suggested that Palmerston meet with Althorp beforehand in order 'to obviate anything that might appear to engage you personally for more than you are prepared to consent to'. Perhaps Althorp was no more able to find Palmerston that day than Lansdowne; perhaps they met and disagreed. For the words afterwards used by Althorp when explaining to the House what he meant by 'as efficient' were much less accommodating than those Grey had used to Palmerston.[35]

As well as remaining silent in the House, Palmerston also acquiesced in Cabinet the following day in a minute for the King, stating that they had unanimously agreed his support for a new bill of 'equal efficacy' would be the essential condition of their continuing in office. Holland thought Palmerston must have been 'reconciled' by his colleagues; Palmerston, rather, considered he had been muzzled. For later that day he sent to Grey a fiercely worded letter of complaint. He could not quit the subject, he wrote, without again registering his protest against individual members of the Cabinet making pledges on controversial subjects in Parliament that tended to inhibit future argument and 'to substitute in the deliberations of the cabinet dictation for discussion'. It was a practice, he concluded, 'which is in my opinion incompatible with the understanding upon which alone, any public man ought to continue to be one of the responsible advisers of the Crown'.[36]

Grey assumed that the accusation of 'dictatorship' was aimed at him personally when, after what he claimed was an 'accidental' oversight, he replied to Palmerston on 14 October. But the wording of the Cabinet minute, when contrasted with his earlier letter to Palmerston, makes it all very strange indeed that his reply this time was concerned, not with any decision in Cabinet, but with his right as an individual to make his own continuation in office dependent on the same conditions as had Althorp. For what Palmerston was really getting at was, as everyone then believed, that Althorp's resignation would have been followed by Grey's and Grey's by the collapse of the Government. Hence the importance of finding an acceptable form of words about a new bill. But there was a grave discrepancy between the bargain Grey had seemed to be making with Palmerston on 10 October and the form of words adopted by the Cabinet the following day.[37]

Why Palmerston, having passed on the first day from loud complaint to sulky silence in the Commons, should return on the second from reluctant acquiescence to loud complaint in the Cabinet is also very difficult to understand. Perhaps, just as Melbourne had got at him before the Commons meeting on the tenth, Lady Cowper had got at him after the Cabinet on the eleventh. Perhaps, rather, it was because Palmerston sensed he stood little chance of making much impression on Grey with Holland and Althorp at his elbow in Cabinet, and more by writing the sort of pointed letter at which he was so skilled. For Grey's reply, though equally indignant, left him a distinct opening by stating that there was 'no bar to any alteration in the measure of reform which would not diminish its efficiency' and by asking 'what indeed can be more general than a pledge to a measure of equal efficiency?' In any case Palmerston was not slow to take advantage of it.

Durham, who had been sent a copy of Palmerston's protest, warned his father-in-law that it showed Palmerston's 'cloven foot'. He was really 'a thorough anti-reformer', he said, and was seeking as restricted a franchise 'as will make those large towns as little representative of the people as the boroughs he has destroyed'. There was a hard core of truth in this. But as far as Grey was concerned his differences with Palmerston lay as much in tactics as in substance. Grey believed that the conciliatory expressions made in debate by some of the peers indicated that they would ultimately surrender rather than risk a showdown; Palmerston believed that they were genuine offers of compromise which, if refused, would provoke the very showdown both he and Grey abhorred. There was something in both points of view; but Palmerston had more determination to press his than Grey, and he accordingly opened up communications with the leading Opposition 'waverers', as they were called, Harrowby and Wharncliffe.[38]

It is known that the waverers themselves made two separate approaches during October, first through Carlisle and then through Stanley. But Wharncliffe afterwards told Greville it had all begun with a conversation Palmerston had had with his son in London, and subsequently, while Stanley worked on Althorp, it was Palmerston who worked on Grey. At first things seemed to go well, and the word went about that Grey had said the bill must be 'improved' to tempt the moderates. Stanley persuaded Althorp to reopen the whole question and Grey gave his blessing to Stanley's calling on Har-rowby en route to his post in Ireland. So when Wharncliffe came to London early in November with a paper on the sort of concessions required – prin-cipally the virtual abandonment of Schedule B and the raising of the £10 franchise – Palmerston had no difficulty in arranging for him to discuss them 'quietly' with Grey at Sheen. The discussion, which took place on 16 November, was long but conducted in 'a very fair and amicable spirit' and afterwards Grey submitted a record of it to Palmerston for Wharncliffe's amendment and approval and for the information of the Cabinet. Nothing was settled, but on his part Wharncliffe agreed in principle to accept Schedule A, the enfranchisement of large towns and even something near the £10 qualification, while Grey seemed willing to curtail Schedule B and to preserve the existing number of members.[39]

Immediately after the first meeting Grey had reported to Lansdowne that things looked 'upon the whole satisfactory'. After the second they began to go badly wrong. Palmerston had come to the conclusion that he could reckon on the support of Stanley, Graham, Carlisle, Holland and even Russell, as well as Lansdowne, Melbourne and Richmond. But he had always recognized that it would take time to bring the 'democrats' in the Cabinet, like the 'waverers' on the Opposition side, to what he called a 'reasonable' point of view. It was Althorp who worried Palmerston most; for if, as he suspected would be the case, Althorp was 'impracticable' and refused all modifications, then, he feared, Grey would not venture to part company with him. It was of crucial importance, therefore, to postpone the recall of Parliament as long as possible so that the new bill would not have to be presented until a reaction in the country had had time to work its moderating influence.[40]

There probably was some such reaction as Palmerston wanted; but there was also such an outbreak of verbal warfare in the press and such riotous disorder in the country as strongly to suggest the wisdom of recalling Par-liament soon both to pacify and to repress. At a meeting on 15 November only Carlisle, Brougham and possibly Althorp had been unreservedly in favour of a recall before Christmas and Grey himself 'decidedly' against. But they deferred a decision until 19 November, the last possible moment, and then, after a meeting of five long hours, divided eight to three against Grey, Rich-mond and Palmerston. Palmerston was shocked and annoyed to find himself in such a small minority; according to Holland so much so that he protested only 'faintly'. But all these discussions and dissensions coincided precisely with the most pressing phases of the Belgian question and consequently he did not organize his forces as well as he might have done. In particular, while he took the trouble to send around copies of his October exchanges with Grey, he neglected to keep everyone equally up to date about the negotiations with the waverers.[41]

Richmond, apparently, first learned about the negotiations from Greville, and neither he nor Melbourne had yet seen the minute of Grey's conversation with Wharncliffe, which could not, as Greville understood it was, have so far been approved by the Cabinet; Grey did not send Richmond a copy until the day after the Cabinet meeting. This probably did not matter as much as Palmerston maintained; but Melbourne, he still thought, had proved the weakest reed. This was a role usually played by Lansdowne, who stayed away, as he often did, at Bowood; while assuring Richmond that he would have voted with the minority had he been present, he had given Grey in writing his advance acquiescence in whatever the majority might decide about the recall of Parliament. The four absentees therefore might have divided equally, and so too, Palmerston implied, would the strongest voices among those present, had not Melbourne, who in spite of his personal preferences had previously admitted that it was 'a very dangerous way of dealing with a nation to attempt to retract that which you have once offered to concede' and was now as Home Secretary more harassed than anyone by the riots, 'turned the scale in favour of meeting in a fortnight'. Seeing that Russell was determined to present his bill, all cut and dried, a week after that, Palmerston did not believe it was possible in the time to conclude an arrangement with the waverers on the other side. 'I fear it is hopeless,' he chided Melbourne; 'and we shall meet Parliament with a Bill not to *our* liking, and without having secured the support of a majority in the House of Peers.'[42]

Palmerston was right about there being no chance of an agreement with the waverers after the decision of 19 November, though he continued to act as intermediary between the Government and Opposition and to urge concessions in the bill. A few days after the Cabinet's decision Palmerston saw Wharncliffe by arrangement and assured him that Grey had commissioned him to say that Parliament was being recalled, not with a view to breaking off negotiations, but in order to gather support for keeping order in the country. Consequently Wharncliffe drew up a memorandum of the points on which the waverers would insist and Grey arranged with Palmerston and Lansdowne that the Cabinet should meet to consider it on the following Friday and Saturday. The idea was that they should settle as many points as possible at the first meeting and then go on the next day to deal with the more difficult problems. Grey was absent from the first meeting, and while he was away Brougham led a fierce resistance to any changes being made at all. But when Grey joined them the following day it was to support a 'compromise' that Palmerston found even worse than the original scheme.[43]

Palmerston was pleased to see the lower classes altogether excluded from the electorate in the large towns by the £10 franchise being defined in such a way that it covered less than 10 per cent of the population, and he must have been further mollified by seeing the urban electorate diluted by the extension of the town boundaries into their rural surroundings. He must also have welcomed the decision to concede the Opposition's demand that the number of seats in the Commons be kept to its original 627. But he particularly disliked the way in which it was proposed to distribute the extra twenty-three that were still required after various other minor modifications. He was glad enough that eleven of them would be found by reducing the number of constituencies who were to lose one member under Schedule B. But along with Richmond and Melbourne (and to a lesser extent Lansdowne and Goderich) he strongly objected to the representation of the manufacturing towns being increased by a fifth through the transfer of ten large towns from the single-member Schedule D to the two-member Schedule C. This, he wrote to Melbourne, could 'hardly be a *bridge*' to the waverers. What he would have preferred, he said, was to have limited their number to six and to have given the rest to large counties. 'To the reformers we could say that we give the balance in favor of large & popular constituencies,' he wrote to Richmond. 'To the antireformers we could shew that we give the majority to the conservative & agricultural interests.' In Grey's opinion giving two seats to all ten towns was the necessary 'equivalent' of reducing the amount of disfranchisement and so, when Wharncliffe told him on 29 November he too disliked the so-called 'compromise', and Palmerston and Melbourne came the following day to insist they would rather have the old bill, the Prime Minister decided that the Cabinet would indeed have to 'reconsider' the position again. Presumably that was why he had his secretary send 'without an instant's delay' for Richmond, who had gone off on a minor mission for him to the country, and Richmond no doubt confirmed the opinion he had recently given to Stanley that he too would prefer the old bill.[44]

No sooner had Grey begun to report all this to the King than there came a note from Wharncliffe that he considered there was no longer any basis for continuing negotiations, and when the Cabinet met for dinner on the evening of 30 November there was evidently no 'reconsideration' after all. Lansdowne was absent again, but this time Stanley had returned to rejoin Melbourne, Palmerston and Richmond. Yet the only objection to the 'compromise' came from Durham who, deranged perhaps by the death of his son, had just returned from the Continent to condemn all his father-in-law's 'concessions'. Perhaps their embarrassment at the violence of his outburst helped to silence the 'moderates'; probably Wharncliffe's note had shattered all their hopes. So the majority of the Cabinet could rest on Grey's compromise. They knew from the recent negotiations what concessions would probably be needed to ensure a majority in the Lords and they had incorporated the bare minimum of them in the new draft. Hence there was no need to risk the odium of their more radical supporters by making a bargain with the enemy.[45]

Palmerston seized every passing prospect that his colleagues might be proved wrong to revive his alternative proposals; and the King tried to revive negotiations with the waverers by sending Chandos to him, so that a new meeting was arranged on 10 December between Grey, Althorp and Brougham on the one side and Chandos, Wharncliffe and Harrowby on the other. But Brougham came only when the meeting was nearly over, Grey's manner was 'haughty & cold', and Althorp 'sat saying nothing, with his hands in his pockets'. So while the arrangement of the final details kept Russell busy till the last moment, the plan he at last unfolded before the Commons on the afternoon of 12 December contained no more concessions to Palmerston's point of view. Among the ministers only Althorp spoke in addition to Russell, and of the Canningites Robert Grant sat in the gallery and his brother Charles never came at all; 'Palmerston came in late, and seemed to go asleep.'[46]

When she heard of Palmerston's last-minute attempt to arrange a compromise through Chandos, Mrs Arbuthnot concluded that the Palmerston 'faction, true to their usual dirt, are now backing out & pretend to be afraid; they no doubt think the ship is sinking &, like true rats, are running away'. Palmerston, however, did not run away, even through the waverers soon came to tell him that the concessions in the new bill were not enough to make them vote in its support. Instead he clung to the hope that new opportunities would be found in the committee stages of the bill to make it acceptable to the Lords. This, in fact, was what his colleagues had indicated at the end of November when they rejected his pressure for more concessions in advance. At the time he had scorned the notion; a few days after the introduction of the revised bill, however, he wrote to remind Russell about it.[47]

If the Prime Minister had originally had any intention of making concessions in committee by the end of December he had abandoned it altogether. He had already made as many concessions as his position could bear, and as his gamble had not succeeded the only recourse now was to secure a majority in the Lords by creating new peers or to resign. The ground upon which Palmerston fought his rearguard action therefore changed again. He had never made any secret of his opposition to creating a large number of peers; the twenty-five which would be necessary to carry the bill, he had told Littleton in November, he considered to be 'an evil to be avoided at almost any hazard'. Instead, he thought it was 'not improbable' that Grey might wish to honour five or six old Whig pledges. But by the New Year Grey was coming round to the view already put forward by Brougham, that they might have to create twelve at once, as an earnest of their determination to create more should the Opposition force the necessity upon them. The Prime Minister appreciated that Richmond and Palmerston were very much opposed and that their resignations would probably be 'fatal' to the continuation of the administration. But there seemed no alternative now and so, when the Cabinet met, Grey supported the idea of asking the King for some token creations at once and the promise of a large number whenever they became necessary.[48]

Goderich, Graham and Brougham (who was ill) were the only absentees from the Cabinet of 2 January and the meeting was 'very long, but more amicable' than Stanley, for example, had expected. But with five 'moderates' lining up against seven 'ultras' and all on the brink of a precipice the atmosphere was very gloomy: 'Lord Grey very desponding, Palmerston bored,

Melbourne more hesitating than I ever saw him, Grant balancing which was the greatest danger till he came to no conclusion at all. The rest much as usual.' As far as Stanley could recall, however, Palmerston was alone in protesting against the pledge of a 'large batch' in the future, and Durham, on the other hand, received little or no support for the immediate creation of forty or fifty peers. In these circumstances Brougham's proposal, though with a smaller number of immediate creations, emerged as an acceptable compromise.[49]

The King disliked the idea of token creations and his reluctant promise of a 'sufficient number' if they became necessary in the future was hedged about with conditions and made under the impression on both sides that it would amount to only a few more than twenty-one. Still, according to Lady Cowper, both Melbourne and Palmerston 'detested' and 'abhorred' what had been decided though they were uncertain whether or not to resign. But the Opposition waverers urged them to stay and fight the ultras and gave Palmerston a new role as go-between when, in their anxiety to avoid the Government resorting to new peers, they offered to support the bill's second reading in the Lords if the Government showed itself disposed to make concessions during the committee stages. Palmerston very probably was, as John Russell said, as lukewarm as ever about reform. But he was now satisfied that the £10 franchise in the towns was not as dangerous as he had originally thought and there can hardly be any doubt that his overriding objective in these revived negotiations was to avoid a constitutional crisis.[50]

Palmerston soon discovered that the principal concessions the waverers had in mind were an urban franchise based on rates rather than rent, a prohibition on urban freeholders who did not qualify by residence to vote in the towns voting instead in the elections for the surrounding counties, and a reduction in the number of the new London constituencies. No actual agreement was reached. A meeting arranged on 16 February between Grey and the leading waverers, Harrowby and Wharncliffe, left everything, as Greville heard, 'dans le vague'. But 'a disposition to mutual confidence was evinced', and on 20 February Palmerston reported to Fred Lamb that 'Grey is becoming much more reasonable about modifications'. As far as he could see none of those suggested conflicted with the fundamental principles of the bill and the only question remaining was how large the Government's majority would be on its second reading in the Lords. His confidence seemed justified. For among the Cabinet he was helped, on the one side, by the realization that the threat of peermaking was alienating some of the bill's supporters, and, on the other, by the King's refusal to give a blank cheque with regard to numbers. So Grey fended off the impatient peermakers and during the debate on the second reading conceded on 11 April that neither the actual number of boroughs in Schedule A nor the £10 franchise would be defended as an unalterable principle in the committee stages. As a result the second reading was passed with a majority of nine.[51]

Palmerston urged Lamb to report the second reading abroad as 'the Waterloo of parties in England, and as deciding the continuance of the present
ministry in office'. But he was a little disappointed in the size of the majority;
he had expected ten at least, and he was not entirely confident that his
colleagues would feel it was enough to dispense with creating new peers. No
one suggested it when the Cabinet met the following day, and he was relieved
at that. It was important, however, to guard against the possibility by maintaining the supposed concert with the waverers. Grey evidently thought so too,
and at his suggestion Palmerston arranged another meeting between Grey
and Brougham on the one side and Wharncliffe on the other. It took place on
28 April and, since it was held in Palmerston's own house, this time he was also
present. Once again nothing was actually settled, Wharncliffe specifically
insisting that it was to be exploratory or 'preliminary'. But the others were left
with the distinct impression that all would be well and Palmerston did not
even think it necessary to come up from Broadlands for the Cabinet meeting
at which it was to be discussed, though he did send a careful letter reiterating
his arguments for closing with the waverers.[32]

No further meeting with the waverers took place. Instead Wharncliffe
found that he could not sway enough of his party, who in an effort to keep
together had decided to have Lyndhurst lay down a motion to postpone the
disfranchising clauses of the bill until after the enfranchising ones had passed.
They knew Grey could not accept this, since saving the unity of the Opposition in this way would break that of his own party, and they therefore
forebade Wharncliffe to have any further contact with the Prime Minister
before the vote. Instead of a concert being reached, therefore, the offensive
motion was introduced in the Lords on 7 May and passed against the
Government with the support of Wharncliffe and the waverers.[33]

This turn of events completely upset all of Palmerston's hopes and calculations. Worse still, it left him utterly disgusted with the waverers, since at
the meeting of 28 April Wharncliffe had given him the distinct impression
that he would not support such a motion. Hitherto Palmerston had been
among the strongest opponents of peermaking. At a Cabinet meeting on 31
March he had even tried, though in vain, to persuade Grey that they should
avoid an immediate creation and go on seeking a compromise with the
waverers even in the event that the bill were defeated on its second reading. At
another a few days later, when they discussed more fully how far to press the
King for a definite pledge as to the number of new peers such a defeat would
require, Palmerston, though 'as usual civil, courteous, and fair' – he even
helped improve the wording of the Cabinet minute – distinctly 'marked his
disagreement'. Indeed he showed himself so anxious for a compromise and so
unwilling to tie the King down that the others wondered, on the one hand,
how he could with honour to himself go on with his present colleagues and, on
the other, how he could envisage cooperation in any future compromise
administration with such people as Wellington, with whom he had 'always

been on bad terms', and Peel, whom he did 'not like'. However, after Lyndhurst's motion, he was so angry and dismayed at the Opposition's behaviour that when the Cabinet met at eleven on the morning after, he argued as strongly as anyone against an immediate resignation such as Melbourne preferred. Instead it was he who actually proposed that they should first ask the King for an unequivocal pledge to create forty or fifty peers. If the defeat had occurred, he said in excusing his actions to Fred Lamb, over the sort of modification recently discussed then he would have stuck to his former view. But the successful amendment was

either nothing but a mere preference of arrangement, or it was an opinion against disfranchisement. If it was the former, the making it a pitched battle, & defeat of the Govt, was intended for the purpose of compelling the Govt to resign. If the latter, it attacked a fundamental principle of the bill. In either case we have no longer any power over our own measures in the Lords, & must either strengthen ourselves or retire.

In the end the Cabinet decided to leave it to the King to choose which it should be.[34]

Grey and Brougham went down to Windsor on the afternoon of the Cabinet and the reply came early the following morning accepting their resignations. At a *levée* that afternoon the King unsuccessfully pressed Brougham and Richmond to stay on in a new administration committed to 'extensive' reform, and the rumour went around that he had spoken similarly to Palmerston. In his report to Lamb Palmerston, though he mentioned the approach to Brougham, said only that to himself the King was 'pointedly kind & civil'. But Palmerston was among those who urged that a new administration – even one that included Wellington – be given a chance to pass a reform bill before being turned out. Since his defeat at Cambridge he was probably one of those who wished to avoid having another General Election in the atmosphere of incipient violence produced by the failure of the bill. But he told Graham he was 'delighted' with the Whigs' decision because 'it is infinitely wise, because it is perfectly honest, and will place our conduct and motives in a most honourable contrast with those of our opponents. The idea of standing over the new Ministry with the rod of adjournment in one hand and the physic-boat full of Reform in the other, and compelling them to swallow the dose properly is excellent.' However, he wrote to Grey, the notion of a Tory administration without either Wellington or Peel at its head but with the Speaker, Manners-Sutton, as 'the Addington of the day' was an arrangement that he was sure 'never would do'. Even so he was surprised by the virulence of the attack which the prospective ministers faced when they met the House of Commons on the evening of 14 May. 'The debate of last night', he reported to Lamb, 'was the most remarkable expression of public opinion, upon the political conduct of public men, which I ever remember to have witnessed.' It was enough at any rate to deter the Opposition from their attempt to form a Government.[35]

On 15 May the King turned again to Grey to resume his office but with a view to agreeing on a modified bill. This condition, as Grey at once pointed out and even Palmerston would presumably have acknowledged, was now utterly out of the question; rather it was only a question whether or not it would be necessary to make peers. The Cabinet met several times to discuss it all, and this time at the meeting on 18 May both Palmerston and Lansdowne pressed for an immediate creation of ten or fifteen peers 'as a demonstration', though in the end it was again decided to insist only on an undertaking to create them if necessary. There was then a short delay while, at the King's request, the Cabinet waited for an open declaration from the Tories that they would not force the Government to such a resort, but when this was not forthcoming Grey finally extracted from the King a firm and unequivocal promise.[56]

Rather than risk wholesale peermaking, most of the Reform Bill's opponents in the Lords subsequently withdrew until the bill had passed into law during the first week in June. Palmerston, too, was virtually silent on the matter, in private as well as in public. According to Lady Cowper both he ('Mary') and Melbourne ('Bob') were 'much grieved at it [the crisis provoked by Lyndhurst's motion] and this little episode has made it much more awkward than ever to alter the odious bill. They are both frightened at the public determination shown but at the same time feel spiteful with the Tories for having tried to play this trick and made them less able to assist themselves.' 'Many of our friends are very unhappy about it,' she added a few days later, 'particularly Bob but he drowns his cares in wine.'[57]

Palmerston certainly very much regretted what had happened. 'It is in vain to disguise from oneself ', he wrote to Lamb on 18 May, 'that the events of the last ten days have struck a harder blow at royal and aristocratical power in this country than anything since the days of Charles the First, saving the expulsion of James 2nd.' But where, a mere six months before, he had been urging military preparations in order that rioting radicals might be 'driven like chaff before the wind', he now admitted that he found 'the excitement of spirit . . . universal & alarming'. So, like the conservative he really was, he accepted the inevitable; and, like the liberal he thought he was, advocated concession to avert what would surely be worse. He summed up the position of the 'Reform' Government in a letter to Minto in June 1833:

We have lost a little of our extreme popularity by our Irish Coercion Bill, by our resistance to change of the Corn Laws, by our promptitude in putting down riots & radicals and by the various other proofs we have given that we are conservatives in the true meaning of the word. But though all this may have stripped us of our mob popularity, it has only seated us more firmly in the good opinion of the respectable part of the community, and more especially in the confidence of the House of Commons.[58]

At the same time Palmerston did not disguise from himself that in the country at large the Government had weakened its position without much strengthening that of the Opposition. The Tories could frustrate the Government by their power in the Lords, but they could not replace it on account of their weakness in the Commons. An appeal to the country would only make things worse, for then, he wrote to Lamb, 'all the tail of the Whigs, who are kept in decent order now by their leaders in office, would if a change took place immediately join the Radicals'. So in the face of adverse votes in the Lords he would urge neither resignations nor elections. 'I confess', he wrote to Grey after a setback in the Lords to the Poor Law Amendment Act,

I look with very great alarm to the attempt to form a Tory Govt, because it must lead to a rapid advance of the Democratic Principle and like John Russell I am against a Revolution once a year. The continuance of *your* administration is the only barrier that stays the flood.[39]

These were views and arguments to which Palmerston continually reverted in the 1830s. 'We are getting a stronger hold every day on the country at large', he wrote in March 1834, 'by shewing that we are ready to reform everything, but wish to overthrow nothing.' Four months later, after the Whig Government had survived the succession of Melbourne to Grey, he was again expressing his great relief at having avoided an appeal to the country following the successive defeats of Whig and Tory Governments. 'The majority would have come back from the hustings,' he wrote, 'the one pledged deeper than the other & there is no limit to the extravagances which they would have bound themselves to accomplish. Such a H. of Cmns would have scorned the men & the measures with which the present is content; nothing would have satisfied them but Durham & Hume, triennial parliaments & a voluntary church.'[60]

Some would say – and, looking at the way he clung so to office in a Government that went further than he often wished, no doubt did say at the time – that Palmerston displayed all the determination of the political trimmer. After the passage of the Reform Bill Lady Cowper admitted that he was glad to have kept his place. But that his attitude was determined by more than mere instincts of self-preservation seems easily demonstrated by the way in which it was also reflected in his foreign policy. As has already been explained, the change in his Belgian policy from an anti-French line to something approaching a genuine *entente cordiale* was a perfectly comprehensible attempt to maintain the essential objectives of vital interest. However, just as the moderation in the domestic politics of France made that change possible, so the simultaneous domestic developments in England made Palmerston more enthusiastic about it than calculated national interest would have required. The connection worked both ways, each with a good Canningite precedent or pedigree. First Palmerston, among many others, detected an international intrigue against the Government such as Canning had faced after Castlereagh's suicide had disappointed the Holy Alliance. Secondly he reaffirmed and extended the Canningite principle of wise concession in good time; and just as he claimed that Canning would have come, as he himself had done, to recognize the necessity of parliamentary reform in England, so he condemned his erstwhile colleagues on the Continent and at home alike as blind reactionaries.[61]

There was obviously also an intimate connection between Palmerston's attitude towards the Reform Bill and the radicals' wish to oust him from office. But their plot had no chance of success while the reformers needed Grey and while Grey in turn needed – or thought he needed – Palmerston and the Canningites. Consequently it was no coincidence either that their outcry against Palmerston should have revived as soon as the bill was safely passed, even though Palmerston had finally swallowed it whole. This time the theme of the criticism in the press was Palmerston's 'Tory appointments'. Brougham subsequently insisted that these attacks were not merely instigated but actually written by Durham. Whether this was so or not Palmerston had no hesitation in attributing them to the disappointment felt by Durham and Ellice at not getting diplomatic situations for relatives. There was probably some truth in this. Durham's vanity and bad temper were notorious and no one could escape them. 'Not one of my requests has been attended to', he had stormed at his father-in-law the previous August, 'by the two of my colleagues to whom I have addressed them, viz. yourself & Lord Palmerston.' So both Grey and Palmerston had cause to be relieved when Durham accepted the special mission to St Petersburg in June 1832 – as fitting a retort to the criticism of Palmerston's 'Tory' apointments as to the Russians' objections to Stratford Canning.[62]

Palmerston probably hoped, like Emily, that Durham would not come back. But return he did, a couple of months later, and having reconciled himself to Nicholas in mutual flattery – having been 'thoroughly bamboozled', Palmerston bluntly said – he formed his alliance with Princess Lieven to harass Palmerston over the Stratford Canning affair. Both of them overplayed their hands. The princess virtually forced her own recall; Durham made himself less tolerable than ever in Cabinet. 'Since his return', wrote Palmerston, 'he has been sullen, silent, & sulky. He sits in cabinet like the statue of a presiding deity, not condescending to take part in the discussions of mortal men. He is dying for an active office, mine, Grant's, Goderich's, anybody's, and he plagues Grey to death, and somewhat offends him.' Late in October 1832 Palmerston casually asked Grey if he thought Durham might still be interested – as had been suggested earlier – in succeeding Ponsonby in Naples. This, it seems, no longer suited. But, Palmerston reckoned, if the Cabinet were now to be re-elected by secret ballot among themselves, every one of them would blackball Durham. In particular there was, he went on in his letter to Lamb, 'another young gentleman by name Edward Stanley, who is fully as anxious for a remove, & more likely to obtain it'.[63]

The Hon. E.G. Stanley (later fourteenth Earl of Derby, and not to be confused with E.J. Stanley, later Lord Stanley of Alderley) entered the Cabinet as Irish Secretary in June 1831 at the same time as Lord John Russell. Stanley had already something of the reputation that gained him the nickname of the 'Rupert of Debate'; Russell was raised to the Cabinet in recognition of his role in planning and promoting the Reform Bill. At the time Palmerston welcomed both as 'most useful acquisitions'. Stanley's must have been particularly pleasing to him, for Stanley had been among those the previous year who had pressed Palmerston on Grey as Leader of the House. Evidently Palmerston already saw in him another personal ally, though from the opposite wing of the Whig party to Graham. Stanley indeed proved as 'lukewarm' as Palmerston on the Reform Bill, though he buried his resentment too in the interest of aristocratic survival. But trouble was soon brewing between the two new members of the Cabinet over other matters. For having helped in opposition to secure so much for Ireland, most of the Whigs in Government were unwilling to do much more. Faced with local disturbances in Ireland, they too resorted to coercion and confronted with a tithe war merely tinkered with the problem of the established church in Ireland.[64]

At first Palmerston seemed satisfied with what was done for Ireland. 'The harvest has been abundant, cholera is rapidly abating, the weather has been for this season miraculous and the revenue is increasing at a great rate,' he wrote jauntily to Lamb in September 1832 when looking forward to the first elections under the new Reform Act. 'The cravens are quite in the dumps for want of their proper food, especially as Ireland is getting quieter ...' When the first reformed Parliament proceeded in March 1833 to pass the Irish Coercion Bill by thumping majorities he even employed the opportunity to lecture Metternich on the virtue of reform over repression:

It is putting a reformed House of Commons to a hard trial [he wrote to Lamb] when you call upon them as their first act, to pass the most severe & arbitrary measure that ever was made law; and to pass it without enquiry or secret committee, & simply upon general notoriety, and upon the statements made by ministers in their speeches; and yet this bill the reformed House are passing by majorities far greater than in close borough times ever voted for any similar measure. So much for the prediction that Reform was Revolution. On the other hand what are the fruits of Metternich's policy? What is the state of Italy? Worse & worse every month ...

More soberly Palmerston wrote to his brother: 'It is a real *tour de force*, but then it is to be followed by remedial measures, and there is the difference between us and Metternich or the Pope; we coerce as they do, but then we redress grievances as they do not.' There followed in August the tentative reduction of the Irish church establishment. Palmerston had reported it to Lamb to be 'as unobjectionable as possible' and he doubted that the Opposition would take 'so desperate a plunge' as to quarrel with it. But some members of the Cabinet, particularly Althorp, Durham and Russell, wanted to tackle Protestant ascendancy more effectively. In October 1832 Russell had even threatened to resign if it were not done; in March 1833 Durham actually did so. 'His loss is a great gain,' Palmerston wrote to his brother.[65]

Although Durham pleaded ill health rather than Ireland as the reason for his resignation, Stanley had gone to Grey in December 1832 demanding his own promotion and Durham's removal. Althorp, echoing Palmerston's opinion about Durham's universal unpopularity, and Brougham, uttering some unconvincing threat, both let Grey know that they agreed with Stanley, and Grey had promised to make some changes whenever he could. Durham's going voluntarily in March provided only a partial solution, for his place as Privy Seal suited neither Stanley's position nor his talents. So another victim was needed and this was intended to be Goderich, who had not put up a very impressive performance in the Colonial Office and was thought incapable of seeing through the difficult matter of slave emancipation. But Goderich, if incompetent, was obstinate. In October 1832 he had refused to move to the Post Office; in March 1833 to the Admiralty; and in between Melbourne had declined to make way for him at the Home Office by going to Ireland as Lord Lieutenant. When Grey suggested to him that he should succeed Durham as Privy Seal, he again demurred. When Grey found that Stanley, too, was adamant, he feared the Government would have to break up. Palmerston and Melbourne also, Arbuthnot heard, had declared they would resign if Goderich did. If so, then they must still have thought themselves a triumvirate of Canningite Secretaries of State, considering how little they thought of Goderich personally. But there is no evidence to support the rumour, though Palmerston had tried to avoid the problem by suggesting Stanley be given the new office that would have been created by the scheme then under consideration to separate military affairs from Goderich's care of the colonies.[66]

Grey did send Palmerston to plead with Goderich, and more than once. On the second occasion, during the evening of 26 March, Palmerston was to point out to him 'the consequence of his refusing to take the Privy Seal'. By this Grey meant the break-up of the Government. Whether Palmerston offered Goderich some inducement to accept the change is not known; he reported to Grey simply that he had made him understand that the Prime Minister considered the arrangement necessary and recommended that Grey now tell him bluntly there was no alternative. But Goderich did not give way until after what Grey called 'a painful scene' on the morning of the twenty-seventh and a promise that he would be given both a better office and the Garter, with a step up in the peerage whenever a vacancy occurred.[67]

Goderich became Earl of Ripon in April 1833; but he never lived to receive the Garter. Stanley got free of his Irish responsibilities, but continued in the Cabinet to frustrate effective church reform. He was succeeded as Chief Secretary first, and briefly, by Hobhouse and then in May 1833 by another old friend of Palmerston's, Littleton. According to Greville's editor, Littleton's appointment was made at Russell's suggestion, but Palmerston must surely have had something to do with it. Littleton could probably have had a job at the formation of the Government, but he had expressed a preference to be Speaker whenever the chair became vacant and gained a promise of support from Palmerston and a somewhat less positive response from Grey. Littleton always knew that the Whigs would have candidates of their own, and rather relied on Palmerston being 'proud of shewing the World a proof of his influence in the Government'. When it came to the point, in June 1831 and again in January 1833, the Cabinet had decided to avoid the issue by supporting the re-election of the sitting Speaker. The Irish Secretaryship was therefore by way of being compensation for Littleton, and Palmerston must surely have been party to it. In any case he must soon have regretted the move.[68]

Greville was pretty near the truth when he said that Littleton's only qualification was his wealth. He certainly could not have coped with the differences between Stanley and Russell, even if he had been admitted to the Cabinet with them. As it happened, the Irish tithe bill he presented to the Government in February 1834 reflected Stanley's views and Russell was forced to give way rather than break up the Government. But when the bill came up for second reading in the Commons and Russell found himself taunted with having given way in Cabinet, he forcefully reiterated in public on 6 May his personal commitment to the appropriation of the surplus revenue of the Irish church. Immediately afterwards Stanley handed Graham a note beginning, 'John Russell has upset the Coach. We cannot go on after his declaration . . .' Brougham naturally thought he could set matters right. But when the Cabinet assembled the following evening and several members urged Russell to retreat, Althorp disagreed and Russell refused. Brougham expressed his great disgust and, according to William Russell, Palmerston urged that John Russell be dismissed at once. There appears to be no corroboration for this, though Palmerston did feel that Russell had behaved 'like a goose'.[69]

Very probably Palmerston was among those who urged Russell to give ground. But once that had failed he certainly switched over to putting pressure on the other side. Grey had been threatening for a long time to throw off the weary burden of his office. In August or September 1833, after a particularly harrowing session in Parliament and in Cabinet, he had explained to each of his colleagues separately that he must resign and when they protested agreed to wait only until they reassembled in the winter. They had again persuaded him during the Portuguese crisis of January 1834 but he had then or subsequently warned them that there would have to be a reconstruction of the Government during the coming summer recess. Brougham was already preparing to resist a wholesale reconstruction when the new crisis broke and Palmerston immediately joined him in the attempt to keep a Whig Government in office.

I entirely agree in the view which the Chancellor takes of the present state of parties & principles in this country [he wrote in a memorandum for his colleagues on 9 May]. A Tory Government could not stand; a Radical Government thank Heaven is impossible; a mixed Government consisting of men who have carried Parliamentary Reform, and of men who have violently & even desperately opposed it, would, *as yet*, be ruinous to the public characters of those who might compose it; unless the amalgamation were the forced result of some great necessity, obvious to all mankind, & beyond the possibility of dispute.

The late struggle [over reform] is too recent; the heats which it engendered are still too fresh in the recollection of all; the extreme differences of political principle which it disclosed are still too applicable to questions yet unsolved, to allow of such a government being formed at present with advantage to the Country or with credit to the individuals who might compose it.

But if an administration composed of the same kind of materials as those of the existing one appears to be the only government consistent with the public interest in the present state of the Country, surely it is for the public benefit no less than for the personal credit of all who compose this Govt, that no separation should take place as long as it can possibly be avoided. Principles, no man of course would sacrifice; but those who stand out upon abstract principle should well consider whether the necessity of the particular occasion calls for, or even admits, the rigid & extreme application of their abstract principles.[70]

Not everyone was in agreement with Brougham and Palmerston. Lansdowne admitted he was not so 'sanguine'; Althorp was supposed to be delighted at the prospect of leaving office. Palmerston persisted, however, in trying to persuade Stanley and his friends that the occasion of such a future reconstruction of the Ministry would be the 'natural time' for them to make their point and one that would not leave them 'exposed to misrepresentation'. Any chance of his succeeding was ruined by a private member, Plumer Ward's son Henry, laying down a motion in the Commons designed to force the issue. If the Government determined to oppose it, they would alienate Althorp and Russell; if they supported it, Stanley and Graham. At a Cabinet meeting on Sunday, 25 May, Brougham seems to have suggested as a compromise the appointment of a commission of enquiry. But one side, if not the other, objected that this would not really solve anything since the Government would be bound to follow very largely the commission's advice and so offend one or the other of them. What followed is not entirely clear. It seems very likely that after the majority had decided in favour of the commission and Stanley, Graham, Richmond and Ripon had declared that in that case they would resign, someone – quite possibly Palmerston – suggested that both moves be suspended until they had tried instead to move the previous question when the debate forced by Ward took place on Tuesday, two days later.[71]

When some of the Cabinet assembled for a *levée* at St James's earlier on Tuesday, several of them seemed to have decided, from a bewildering variety of motives, to force the issue prematurely. Brougham urged upon the King that Stanley and Co. should be got rid of at once; Holland and the Chief Whip, Ellice, supported him by saying that only in this way could an angry and unpleasant debate be avoided; Lansdowne and Palmerston objected strongly to such a change of course, arguing once again that Ward's motion could easily be put off; Grey was merely 'hurried and agitated'. As soon as he could the Prime Minister rushed away, apparently by the back stairs, leaving the King 'much perplexed', Lansdowne and Palmerston in argument with Holland and Ellice, and Stanley and Graham with the impression that it would be best if they both resigned at once. So after Grey had left, Stanley, Graham, Richmond and Ripon offered their resignations to the King and, although Holland and Ellice failed to persuade Lansdowne and Palmerston that this was the right course, the King insisted on accepting. Afterwards, when the Cabinet reassembled at Grey's, there was another row, with Lansdowne threatening to resign if Ward's motion was not met with the previous question and Althorp to do the same if it was. Eventually Althorp was persuaded to compromise by seeking an adjournment instead and Lansdowne was mollified with a Cabinet post for his friend Lord Auckland.[72]

Although he too seems to have been very angry with what had happened at the palace, Palmerston afterwards made much less fuss than Lansdowne. This was partly a matter of temperament; Palmerston was always easily reconciled to the inevitable. It was also because he was much more anxious for the Government to survive and relieved to find himself still a member of it. Probably the King had assured him that the resignations had only been accepted on the express condition that Grey remained Prime Minister. Palmerston regretted the loss of his old colleagues; three of them – Stanley, Graham and Ripon – were men whom he counted among his most intimate political friends. But on the whole he was pleased enough with their replacements: the new Government, he said, was 'conservative, but reforming'. What he meant was that while they had been forced to swallow Ellice's promotion to the Cabinet, Durham had not got back in. Upon his resignation in 1833 Durham had gained at last what he had sought so long and so bitterly from Grey – his step up in the peerage to an earldom. But his ambition to displace the Foreign Secretary, if not the Prime Minister, had not ceased. Thus when Hobhouse had resigned the Irish Secretaryship in the previous May, the story went round that Palmerston was going to India and that Durham was to be brought back into the Cabinet as his successor. The following August Ellice wrote to Durham about how to form a more radical Government when Grey finally carried out his threat of resignation, and he condemned Palmerston to the same sort of exile. Ellice also left it on record that he had been pressing Grey to resign in the autumn of 1833 so as 'to force the remodelling of a new cabinet'.[73]

There was, then, plenty of justification for the common suspicion that Durham and Ellice were perpetually intriguing to force a Cabinet crisis. As it happened Ellice did not think that the Portuguese affair in January 1834 was well suited to his purpose. But no sooner had Russell 'upset the coach' in May that year than the editor of The Times wrote to Brougham's secretary to suggest that Durham would make 'a good exchange' for either him or Palmerston, and after Palmerston had made a 'woful exhibition' of himself in Parliament the following week – attempting a new line in a speech on Portugal, that of humour – the word quickly went about that he 'was out and Durham in his place'.[74]

For his part Palmerston was quite convinced that Grey's indiscreet talk about resigning 'was dexterously made use of' in the Cabinet quarrels over Ireland. Members were told, he wrote to Lamb, that it would be better to force a crisis before Grey's intended resignation than to go to the country after a series of House of Commons' divisions on the Irish coercion bill, which would inevitably undermine their popularity with some large part of their constituents. So, he reckoned, even if Russell had not been got at to 'upset the coach', after he had spoken up in the Commons 'Durham and Co. immediately put their wedge into this crack' and got Ward to put his motion on the Irish church. Then, Palmerston thought, Ellice must have calculated that when Stanley and his friends had gone, Grey would have either to send for Durham's aid or, since a Tory administration was believed to be impossible, to give way to a radical Government formed by Durham and Brougham. But the second scheme was defeated by Grey's decision to carry on and the first by the opposition of his colleagues.[75]

Once again, according to Brougham, the Cabinet were unanimous. Durham and Grey were 'so invariably disputing that no one could live in a Cabinet with them', he had told his private secretary, adding, rather disingenuously, that he would not on the other hand object to having Durham as a colleague if Grey went out. Even if Brougham could have sunk so low, at least three or four of the others – Lansdowne, Grant and possibly Melbourne as well as Palmerston – never could have served with Durham.[76]

Grey's own scheme was to get Durham out of the way on another diplomatic mission, this time to Paris, and to recruit Granville for Graham's empty place at the Admiralty. The idea had probably been planted in Grey's head by Ellice, who had suggested it to Durham in August 1833, obviously as a device for undermining Palmerston at the F.O. So when Grey mentioned it during one of his wife's Saturday parties, Palmerston protested vigorously. He said that what he needed at the 'pivot' of his foreign policy was a man he could trust and a friend in whom he could have confidence, whereas Durham was his enemy.[77]

How Grey could have believed it when he replied that Palmerston was mistaken about Durham is almost beyond comprehension; even his son Howick marvelled at the idea of Durham and Palmerston ever again working in harness together. Palmerston returned the next day to press his objections only to find that Durham did not like the idea either. Having insisted on it over Palmerston's initial objections, Grey apparently did not feel he could press it when his son-in-law also demurred. Durham was said to be 'furious' that such an offer had ever been made to him, even though it was supposed to have been hinted that it would be but a step to the F.O. itself. Durham's own notion, almost certainly, would have been for Palmerston to go to Paris and himself to the F.O. at once. Either scheme, however, would probably have been doomed to failure, in any case, by Granville's unwillingness to take on a Cabinet post; even the F.O. apparently would not have tempted him. Rather he loyally insisted that Palmerston was essential where he was. But while the failure of this scheme led to Grey's placating Lansdowne by bringing Auckland to the Admiralty, he continued to insist that it was 'indispensable' for him to have in the Cabinet Spring Rice as Colonial Secretary and Ellice in his existing situation. Brougham objected to Ellice almost as much as he did to Auckland. Auckland, he said, was 'a wet blanket' and Ellice a mere 'stock jobber'. But Lansdowne insisted on the one and Grey upon the other.[78]

Palmerston thought the new members of the Administration a great check to the radicals' hopes. With one exception they were all 'good appointments; . . . steady, and able [and] all in the Conservative (not Tory) line'. Ellice, he confessed, was not an improvement, but even he, Palmerston hoped, would perhaps be 'less mischievous' in the Cabinet than out of it: he would have a greater interest in preserving the Government and they a better opportunity to keep an eye upon him. There was some truth in this. In less than a month Durham had quarrelled with Ellice over their dealings with the press. At the same time Ellice was still spreading the story that Palmerston was not destined to stay very long in the F.O. after the resignation of his friends and before the end of June he had already made it up with Durham. Ellice and his friend Joseph Parkes continued therefore to serve Durham's interest by attacking Palmerston in the press, and if it is still possible to think that Durham had once been only the tool of the radicals and the Russians, this time his knowing complicity is beyond doubt. For his correspondence with Parkes makes it quite clear that in June 1834 he was in contest with Palmerston for control of the *Morning Chronicle*'s line on foreign policy. At his request, Parkes sent for Dr Quin and 'explained to him that the *M.C.* had distinctly opposed itself to Lord Palmerston's Tory system of diplomacy, and that the *Chronicle* must not on any consideration – or for any *scraps of news* – be *used* by the Foreign Office. . . . I further told him that it would be grossly inconsistent to pursue an opposite course as the *M.C.* had in fact been *the* paper to *steam* Lord P. for his misdoings.'[79]

As has been seen, Palmerston won the battle for the *Morning Chronicle*, and the danger from Durham receded, almost never to revive. In October Durham made a violent speech in Glasgow, openly advocating the secret ballot and other 'radical' measures. This, Palmerston told his brother, 'I think excellent because he throws off the mask and declares for all sorts of things which disqualify him from being Minister until a revolution which I trust is by no means likely to happen'. Palmerston also thought that the reconstituted Government was 'quite safe for some time to come' from other attacks as well. He did not believe that a man of Stanley's talents would be for long content to take a back seat and expected that he would therefore gradually 'slide into more active opposition'. But it would not be creditable for the seceders to join too promptly with Peel, and the Tories in any case would not be strong enough to trouble the Government for at least a year.[80]

Hardly had Palmerston written this, on 6 July, than the Cabinet was suddenly plunged into yet another turmoil by the Irish question. It was Littleton who was largely responsible. More frightened of O'Connell than even of his colleagues, he had given the demagogue the impression that the Government would drop some of the more objectionable clauses when the Coercion Bill came up for renewal. When the misunderstanding became public in the House of Commons debates, Althorp decided it would be dishonourable to continue with the bill at all and, as Grey disagreed, he sent in his resignation on 8 July. 'Althorp has resigned,' wrote Grey at once to Palmerston, '& you will not be surprised to hear that I must take the same step – the Govt, therefore, is at an end.'[81]

Grey had always maintained that he could not continue without Althorp's assistance in the Commons, though he had rather expected to lose it by Earl Spencer's death translating Althorp to the Lords. His notion had that happened was for Althorp to become Prime Minister while he smoothed over the transition by staying on for a time as Privy Seal. With Althorp gone altogether, this was quite out of the question. That evening Grey communicated the resignations to his colleagues in the Cabinet and handed Melbourne a summons to aid the King in the formation of a new Ministry. Melbourne was the popular choice for premier: according to Durham he was the only one of whom no one would be jealous. But it was a new coalition the King had in mind, with Melbourne going cap in hand to Wellington and Peel.[82]

The King's notion horrified Palmerston, who wrote to Brougham:

As to an attempt to unite Parties, who up even to yesterday afternoon, had been in direct collision not only on principles, but on practical measures, my opinion is that this would be the way to destroy in public estimation two great parties, or at least the leading men of those parties; and out of their discredited remnants to make a compound which would speedily crumble under the pressure of the third [i.e. radical] party.

To Melbourne his language was much more discreet, probably so that his memorandum could be shown to the King. A coalition of Wellington, Peel, Stanley and some of Grey's Cabinet would be 'an excellent arrangement', he said. But he did not mince words about its meagre chances of success or the boost its failure would give to the radicals. On the other hand a Wellington and Peel Government, he thought, would also be 'attended with fatal consequences'. It could not survive the hostility of the present House of Commons and new elections would lead only to greater excitement and such clashes between a reforming Commons and a resisting Lords as he did not like to anticipate. Nor was it possible for Stanley and Co. to rejoin their former friends or coalesce with the Tories: the separation from the one was too recent and the junction with the other too soon for either to be creditable. What then remained? Shee had just written to him as though it might have passed through Palmerston's mind that he himself could attempt to form a Government, but he could not have succeeded, Shee had said, with both Left and Right against him. So the only possible solution, Palmerston concluded, was the return of Grey and Althorp. He admitted that Althorp and his sympathizers would not come back unless the objectionable clauses in the Coercion Bill were dropped. But as no Government could be found to carry those clauses, they might as well be abandoned.[83]

It would appear that Grey was approached with a view to his serving as Privy Seal under Althorp, but that this time he refused the notion with 'disdain', presumably because he was too angry about what had happened. In any case the proposal was utterly wrecked by Althorp's refusal to become Prime Minister. But with some difficulty Althorp was persuaded to retain his old office under Melbourne by being assured that the clauses in the Coercion Bill would be dropped and by being told that otherwise no Government could be formed. So at the beginning of August Palmerston could write to his brother: 'Melbourne pleases the House of Lords, & is more personally and politically popular in that House than Ld Grey was, while in the House of Commons we have liberality enough on the Treasury Bench to satisfy any but Radicals.' Nor, indeed, did he see how any other Government could be found 'for a long time to come'.[84]

At the beginning of November 1834 Palmerston still felt very confident. 'All the empire is quiet; and even Ireland tranquil,' he wrote. 'Melbourne goes on very well, and the Government is, I think, likely to stand.' He was far too optimistic. He ought to have remembered, as Grey had always done, that Althorp was not a permanent fixture. On 10 November Lord Spencer died and Althorp moved with as much relief as grief into the House of Lords. Two days later Melbourne went to remind the King that his Government had been formed initially on the basis of Althorp's role in the Exchequer and in the Commons, and to ask if he should attempt to 'make fresh arrangements' or give up the task to someone else.[85]

In fact Melbourne and his colleagues had already agreed that Russell should succeed as Leader. But for some reason – probably because he considered him damn near a revolutionary – the King never could 'bear' John Russell. Once, during September 1832, after Russell had referred in a speech to his constituents to the abuse of local influence by Tory landlords being the only thing that could convert him to the idea of secret ballot, the King had complained to Palmerston at Windsor, 'Well so Lord John Russell has got into another scrape.' Palmerston had smoothed things over very well by explaining that Russell had only meant to emphasize how far he was as yet from supporting the ballot. But the doubts persisted, and were shared by Melbourne too. 'Johnny can be quiet about nothing and will give us a great deal of trouble,' he complained in August 1834. 'He is in my opinion . . . worse than Durham.'[86]

When a little more than three months later Brougham suggested Russell should succeed as Leader in the Commons, with Grey's son Howick as Chancellor of the Exchequer, and Melbourne consulted his colleagues, their doubts concerned Howick rather than Russell. Palmerston, Abercromby and Rice all declared they were not interested in either the Exchequer or the lead, though Palmerston offered, in spite of the 'inconvenience' it would add to his conduct of foreign affairs, to take on the lead if that was what the Government wanted. When Spencer had been thought to be about to die some three years earlier, the choice was then said to have been between Russell and Stanley, though some were supposed to prefer Palmerston to either.[87]

Palmerston's reputation as a speaker was perhaps no worse than Althorp's, but he was much busier in office and less popular in the House. 'The duties of Palmerston's office', Holland wrote, 'would hardly leave him leisure, if there were not in truth other & weightier objections which he has too much sense not to feel & too much tact to force others to express. He is not popular with the bulk of our Hse of Commons supporters & has not, as Stanley *perhaps* has, great promptitude & talent in debate.' It is equally doubtful that Melbourne really had Palmerston in mind as a possibility in 1834. When he discussed with the King the alternatives to Russell, only Abercromby, Rice and Hobhouse appear to have been mentioned. Nevertheless, when Russell heard how strongly Palmerston urged his having the lead, it pleased the little man 'exceedingly' and Holland hoped it would 'soften the opprobrious and unjust epithets which he is too much disposed to lavish on Palmerston's measures and manners'. But the King did not change his mind; rather his opposition was strengthened by the fear that Russell might make an alliance with O'Connell against the church. So he told Melbourne he was going to send for Wellington and on 15 November the duke accepted all the seals of office pending Peel's return from abroad.[88]

The Tory interlude did not last long. New elections failed to gain a majority for Peel and after a series of defeats in the Commons he resigned on 8 April 1835. The King therefore had no choice but to turn once again to the Whigs and, though he tried to avoid him, eventually to Melbourne. But the King was probably no more hurt and surprised by his humiliation than Palmerston was when he found that his old friend was by no means sure he wanted him back in the F.O. And what made Palmerston peculiarly vulnerable was that in the recent elections he, alone of all the former Cabinet, had also been rejected by his constituents.

A completely 'rotten' borough, Bletchingley lost both its members by the Reform Act of 1832. This turned out to be no great loss for Palmerston, since he had found Bletchingley to be much less of a bargain than he thought. Ellice and Duncannon had arranged the whole thing for him and Palmerston had paid £800 to Ellice in October 1831. This was less than the going rate per annum and Palmerston must have known it. But he professed both anger and surprise when Ellice wrote in March the following year to ask for another

£800. He had not been given even a hint, Palmerston said, that he was expected to pay anything more. He also suspected that he was being made to pay for some new arrangement between Government and borough monger. Otherwise it was a rather remarkable coincidence that Tennyson, who had given up his seat to Palmerston in 1831, had just been persuaded to surrender also his Clerkship of Ordnance to another favourite of Government. At first Ellice denied there was any connection; then he confessed that he had hoped Tennyson would consider a privy councillorship sufficient compensation for giving up his office. Finally Palmerston told Ellice bluntly that Tennyson had admitted to him face to face some time ago how he had obtained his clerkship in the first instance and to a Cabinet colleague only recently how he had been persuaded to surrender it.[89]

Macaulay thought Ellice 'the greatest liar and jobber' he had ever known. Palmerston perhaps would have been asked for rather less if he had agreed at this time to make Ellice's eldest son an attaché in Vienna. But Fred Lamb had no more liking for Ellice's 'Cub' than for the old 'Bear' himself. 'Two such damned fellows I never saw,' he wrote to Palmerston. 'Pray let nothing induce you to put the Cub upon me – I certainly could not stand him.' Ellice senior, he wrote, was but a 'scheming ragamuffin', plotting to redistribute the embassies among his near connexions and, he suspected, leaking Cabinet secrets to *The Times*. And to cap it all, when the Ellices passed through Vienna in the autumn of 1832, they 'amused' his attachés with plans for sweeping away the diplomatic establishment altogether. So Durham instead took the young man with him to St Petersburg, as was the undisputed right of an ambassador on special mission. In any case Palmerston adamantly refused to pay what was asked for Bletchingley and in May he compromised with Ellice on a second and final payment of £500 to cover the period until the first General Election due under the new Reform Act.[90]

Palmerston had talked immediately after his defeat in Cambridge of returning there as soon as the electors had recovered their senses, and an endorsement he wrote on an approach from Cambridge Town showed that this was still his plan in June 1832. That was why he went off to Cambridge for the Commencement on 2 July, even though he was needed in London to sort out Durham's instructions for St Petersburg. Unless he turned up, he was warned, he would be considered to have abandoned all hope of standing again for the university. But if he made an appearance then he had some chance, not of being elected by the Liberal vote alone but of splitting his opponents'. For, according to the Master of Corpus, some of his former supporters at St John's were 'beginning to see that the *really* Conservative party is Ld Grey's administration'. So Palmerston tested the ground at Cambridge and wrote to James Wood to suggest that by opposing the Reform candidates in 1831 the church had dangerously separated itself from the nation and ought now to change its tactics. But Wood told him that 'no candidate who is not a Conservative can have a chance of success', and by the middle of August Palmerston had given up all hope of the university.[91]

Fortunately Palmerston had already had several other approaches, from South Hampshire, Lambeth, Tower Hamlets and Falmouth and Penryn. In South Hampshire he probably doubted his chances; even in the old days before the Reform Act he had, as he told Sulivan in 1820, reckoned 'the honor of representing a County . . . one which . . . one rather covets for one's friend than for oneself'. In Lambeth and, presumably, Tower Hamlets he was offered election free of all expenses; but they were two of the new metropolitan boroughs he distrusted and had large electorates to be canvassed; Tower Hamlets, with nearly 10,000 voters, was one of the four largest among the English boroughs. So it was Falmouth and Penryn with a mere 900 he favoured, and while he canvassed Cambridge he sent off his brother, on leave from Naples, to do the same in the West Country.[92]

William reported that although more than two-thirds of the vote at Falmouth would be his, Palmerston could rely on hardly more than a fifth of those at Penryn and this would leave him a long way short of certain victory. It also meant that the election would be very expensive, Reform Act or no. For the old borough of Penryn had been notoriously corrupt, and the addition of Falmouth to it by the act had merely enlarged the area of corruption. 'They want [£]5 a piece for their votes,' reported Lady Cowper; 'so much for bribery being put down by the Bill.' So while keeping Falmouth and Penryn on ice, Palmerston decided after all to have his prospects at Lambeth investigated more closely. Apparently the reports he received were by no means unpromising. 'Lambeth', Lady Cowper gathered, 'seems to lean upon this principle that the moderate part of the constituency would like him, the Tories would prefer him to a radical & the radicals have got no votes as they have omitted to pay their rates.' Palmerston therefore let go the opportunity in Tower Hamlets and turned down new offers, from Southwark for example, on the grounds that he was already 'pledged'. But he was evidently not much happier with Lambeth than he was with Falmouth and Penryn, because being so busy at the F.O. he was determined to waste as little time as money on a canvass, and insisted on standing there only if entirely uncontested.[93]

Early in September 1832 Palmerston was again pressed both by the local reformers and by his colleagues to stand jointly with Sir George Staunton for the new constituency of South Hampshire. Again he replied that he was already pledged, but his 'pledges', it would seem, were still contingent upon a final assessment of his chances. Russell urged him to accept the Hampshire offer. Graham frankly warned him off both Falmouth and the metropolis. He ought not to dirty his hands with Falmouth and Penryn, who only looked to Palmerston, he said, in the hope of his persuading the Government to restore the packet line out of which they had previously made such iniquitous profits. Nor, he went on, would a metropolitan borough suit Palmerston since what he called the borough-mongering 'tradesmen' would be sure to outbid him in purchasing votes from 'the great unwashed'. In South Hampshire, on the other hand, it seemed that many of the 'gentry' wanted him; his Tory neighbour Sloane Stanley actually wrote to suggest Palmerston stand with the 'Conservative' candidate John Fleming, who was 'going well' against Staunton. Graham did not think Palmerston should have anything to do with that, for while it might be Palmerston and Fleming the 'gentry' wanted it was Palmerston and Staunton the reformers wanted. So, Graham suggested, Palmerston should send a 'Zuylen' answer to Sloane Stanley and test the chances of the reformers by a trial canvass and their goodwill by a strict limitation on expenses. Palmerston accepted Graham's advice and wrote accordingly to Southampton, tentatively setting his personal contribution at £500.[94]

It was not easy to calculate the chances of success in what seemed likely to be a three-man bid for a constituency with only two seats. Two members of the reform committee, Nightingale (Florence's father) and Bonham Carter, wrote to him on 3 October that after a three-day canvass they already had a thousand promises. Palmerston still did not think these were enough, but Nightingale pointed out that it was difficult to get firm promises when Palmerston would neither canvass nor stand firmly forward. Before the end of the month, moreover, the reformers reckoned they could deliver nearly 1,500 out of 3,200 electors. Since, by the beginning of November, his supporters could assure him only 1,700 out of 4,900 votes in Lambeth, South Hampshire seemed to Palmerston to offer the best prospect of success even if it would be a 'hardish' contest. He waited another week and kept on ice another offer, of Windsor, while the whole constituency was canvassed, and then when he heard that it was most unlikely there would be another Conservative candidate joining Fleming and that he would not have to pay more than £1,000, or possibly not even half of that, he formally accepted South Hampshire on 10 November. He claimed shortly afterwards, in a letter to Fred Lamb, that he would have been 'assured' of election in both Falmouth and Lambeth. So possibly he had more confidence in the assurances of the Hampshire reforming gentry about the limitation on expense than in anyone else's promises. In any case, once he had openly declared, his canvass gained still more rapid ground. By 26 November the canvass of the final list of 3,114 voters put him in first place with 1,612 firm promises. 'This last return', he wrote to Sulivan two days later, 'is equivalent to 4 by honors & the odd trick.'[95]

Although Palmerston had insisted he could not spare the time to canvass in person, he had to be present for the nomination on Saturday, 15 December, for the poll on the following Tuesday and Wednesday, and for the declaration at 11 a.m. on Thursday. He resented the time these cost him away from London and according to Grey they did interfere with F.O. business. By his own account Palmerston arrived in Southampton at 2 a.m. on 15 December and 'took the field at nine amidst a drenching rain, which however did not thin numbers nor damp ardour'. The nominations were made an hour later from an open balcony and as each stepped forward he took his turn for a drenching and a speech. Palmerston reported to Grey that they all got 'as good a hearing as I suppose is to be expected on such occasions'. But according to newspaper accounts he was 'assailed with such vehement hisses and groans' that he could not get a hearing at all until his opponent intervened and got silence enough for Palmerston to make what he himself called 'a quiet un-provoking speech'. He had to make six more market-place speeches as he rode from polling station to polling station. But nowhere, he reported, was he asked to make a pledge of any sort or pressed to state any opinion more definitely than he wished. 'I was told at Fareham that a word or two about the Corn Laws would be acceptable, and some Quakers at Ringwood hinted that they should wish me to say something about Colonial slavery,' he reported to Grey at the close of the poll; 'but everywhere the people were perfectly willing to take the past as an earnest of the future, and instead of asking me to thank them for voting for me they everywhere thanked me for enabling them to keep out a Tory candidate.' When the result was declared the next morning he found that his hopes were pretty well fulfilled. The poll gave him forty-two votes fewer than he had been promised, but with 1,625 he was still at the head, almost 100 more than Staunton and 450 more than Fleming.[96]

'Palmerston is much tickled, as he ought to be, by his election,' wrote Holland. 'A little relish for popularity will do him no harm.' Lady Dover thought he was perhaps a little too elevated, which was not like him, she admitted. There was no doubt he was absolutely delighted with his triumph. He even consented to stay over in Hampshire for a celebration dinner and ball, lavished a gift of £100 upon the Southampton poor in lieu of letting them chair him through the town, and made what the Opposition called some 'swaggering speeches'. He claimed the result, then, as a triumph for the Reform Act and for himself. The Tories had been proved wrong when they forecast the bill would ensure the election of 'riff-raff'. Instead, while he did have the votes of many of the gentry, few of them but his personal friends had made an active canvass and the men who had brought him in were the 'wealthy farmers, men engaged in business, chiefly above the class of shop-keepers, and two or three attorneys who gave their services gratuitously'. And as regards himself personally, the attempt to damn his foreign policy by raising the cry of 'Dutch War' had failed miserably and backfired upon the Duke of Wellington, whose political representative Mr Fleming was.[97]

There was no doubt the Tories had overplayed their hand in Hampshire in 1832. Having been refused an arrangement with Palmerston, William Sloane Stanley gave Fleming his plumper. But he and his kind made themselves not only last but, many thought, ridiculous by their fervour.

I condole with William [wrote Jekyll to Lady Gertrude] on the oaths and guineas he squandered to save his property from revolution, by supporting the talent of Fleming, and unfortunately giving victory to such villains, rascals, scoundrels, burkers, vampires, cheats, and swindlers as neighbours Palmer-ston and his gang. As he has had a long experience of managing lunacy, Brougham thinks the Hampshire Tories might be confided to his care in Chancery.

Instead, when the opportunity came only two years later, the Tories chose to give Fleming a fellow Conservative, and a stronger one, to counter Palmerston's claims.[98]

Although Palmerston did not think much of the Peel Government's chances, like everyone else he was pretty uncertain whether or not they would risk a dissolution. But if they did, he was sure they would not improve their position in Parliament. In the middle of November 1834 he thought he might look forward to some hunting at Broadlands and even three weeks in Paris. In any event he considered himself 'pretty safe' in Hampshire. Towards the end of the month, when an election seemed rather more likely, he was if anything still more confident. 'I have excellent accounts from Hampshire,' he told Lady Holland; 'a large committee formed, an immediate canvass resolved upon; and very favourable reports received from all the Districts.' This time, he knew, he could not excuse himself from canvassing but would have 'to take the field, and commence itinerant spouter at inn meetings of freeholders, and to ride about the country canvassing'. But he dallied still in London, until suddenly, on the night of 2 December, he rushed off to Hampshire after hearing that Fleming had been joined against him by Henry Compton. Fleming, so Palmerston told Mrs Sulivan, was not only very unpopular personally but also 'a bad canvasser, stiff and unconciliatory'. Compton was another local landowner and, as Palmerston seems to have told Lady Holland, a 'formidable' opponent, being 'no high flying Tory, but very good and personally extremely popular'. Within a few days, therefore, Palmerston was 'hard at work canvassing from nine in the morning till night', and hoping the dissolution would be announced soon so that he did not have to go on thus till Christmas.[99]

Parliament was not dissolved until 30 December 1834 and so Palmerston found himself, well into the New Year, still in Hampshire and still 'working like a horse, up every day by candlelight, & toiling till late at night, driving, riding, walking, talking, shouting'. He found it quite a task, canvassing some 3,000 electors scattered all over the countryside. 'Yesterday', he wrote to his sister from Broadlands on 28 December, 'I started from hence on horseback for Southampton at a qtr before nine; sailed across to Hythe; canvassed there; returned to Southampton; canvassed there till six; & rode back to dinner here.' He finished his preliminary canvass on 8 January and then rushed back to London on the ninth for 'visits' to Laura Petre on each of the following three days. Having said farewell to her at 3 p.m. on the afternoon of the twelfth, he was in Southampton by 3 a.m. the following day and making his contribution to the nomination speeches that lasted from 11 a.m. to 4.30 that same afternoon. Then, after a good night's sleep at Broadlands, he spent the next three days riding about the country on a final round of canvassing.[100]

The campaign, Palmerston reported to his brother, was 'a wholesome life and an excellent change' from his last four years of confinement, and this time the weather was also very good, raining on only one day during the whole of the canvass. He was also still 'quite sure' of his re-election. 'The Tories have set every engine to work,' he wrote; 'The influence of Govt, landlords, magistrates & parsons, intimidation of all kinds, & a suitable mixture of lies. But it will all prove fruitless at least as far as I am concerned.' However, when the poll came on at last, on 17 and 18 January 1835, he found himself trailing in third place at the end of the first day and still there at the end of the second, with hardly more than 1,500 votes. He was just ahead of Staunton but nearly 200 behind Compton and 250 behind the 'unpopular' Fleming.[101]

All Palmerston's enemies rejoiced at his defeat. 'A great man greatly fallen,' exclaimed Princess Lieven. By his friends it was by no means unexpected; only Palmerston himself, it seems, felt confident almost to the very last. Since he was no longer the Government candidate he had always recognized that he could not expect so large a majority as in 1832. This time, for example, he knew he could not rely on patronage in the Portsmouth dockyards. But, in spite of the accusations his opponents had made against him in 1832, there were only 125 votes in the dockyards and even without them the agricultural interest would still have carried Palmerston to victory then. So, he had told Melbourne, 'the dockyard did me no great good last time, & therefore will do me no great harm this time'. He was therefore confident until almost the last moment of the 1835 campaign and when he was beaten he admitted to his sister that he 'never was more annoyed & disappointed' in his life. Naturally Palmerston blamed his supporters for not having begun their exertions early enough and his opponents for resorting to 'dishonourable means'. The Whigs had been negligent to the point of stupidity about keeping up the register of voters; this was 'the root of the evil', he told John Russell. The Tories, moreover, had been careful not only to register new voters but also to use threats and influence to make men break their promises to Palmerston. His opponents had broken precedent by establishing a committee in the dockyard itself and at a time of low prices for corn, Fleming had made abatements of rents to farmers who had voted for him at the last election and squeezed those who had voted against him. The lesson, according to Palmerston, was not lost. Fleming was also a great proprietor of tithes in Romsey parish and had consequently had all the clergy with him as well as most of the gentry. So, Palmerston had said as he watched the fight in progress, it would have been almost enough to make him a convert to secret ballot had he not felt that that would be rendered ineffectual by people being 'bullied for their promise, as they are now bullied for their vote'.[103]

After the heat of battle had passed, Palmerston still felt that he had been beaten by the influence 'landlords and tithe lords' exercised upon distressed farmers. 'The squire & the parson never had such a pull before,' he thought. But cooler reflection made him conclude that his Tory friends had only done their duty according to their opinions, though mutual accusations continued to be bandied about regarding undue influence in the dockyards. In 1832, when similar charges had been made by Fleming, Palmerston, hearing that his opponent was afterwards to leave the country, had gone out of his way to ask that they should meet in order to shake hands first. He was less charitable after his defeat in 1835. He could not forgive Sloane Stanley, he said, for having made an offensive attack upon his personal character on nomination day. He told him so to his face and refused an offer of amends. Sloane Stanley's only excuse, he told Sulivan, was that he was 'a regular ass'. More serious was the strain the defeat put on Palmerston's political alliance with Staunton. Palmerston came away from Hampshire declaring that with a little more care he would be able to put 'several hundred good votes' on his register before the following July. Staunton equally felt he had been pulled down by Palmerston's unpopularity and wrote immediately afterwards to say that there could not again be any 'coalition' between them.[104]

Whatever hopes there might be of South Hampshire in the future, Palmerston had in the meantime to look about for another seat in 1835. Finding one was not all that easy; he still had not done so by March, though his solicitors had been in touch since January with a certain Joseph Croucher who said he could produce one for £3,500. By April some promising negotiations must have been begun, since he turned down an approach from North Essex. Probably he was already treating through the medium of Joseph Parkes with James Kennedy, one of the members for Tiverton. Kennedy, who was a barrister 'of great eloquence but scanty means', had won the hearts of the reformed electorate of Tiverton and gained its second seat by a large majority in the General Election of December 1832. But he was a failure in the Commons and had rather a hard time afterwards proving either his legal or his personal qualifications as M.P. So in the General Election of 1835 he had only just scraped through. A short time later the electors received a letter from him saying that 'from considerations affecting his health, profession and other circumstances, he gave up the seat for which he had not received any profit, or place, or promise of either'. The truth was that in 1834 he had failed to sell his seat only because he kept on raising his price and that in 1835 Palmerston had paid him £2,000 to vacate it.[105]

Although the payment to Kennedy was supposed to have been on the 'distinct understanding' they were quits, Palmerston seems to have been seeking a colonial appointment for him too, and though disappointed in 1835 Kennedy did obtain from Palmerston a valuable post in Havana in 1837. Later, in 1852, his son was made a clerk in the F.O.; but Charles Malcolm Kennedy at least had a Cambridge double first behind him and a distinguished career ahead, becoming in 1872 the first chief of the Commercial Department in the office. Palmerston's incidental expenses in Tiverton in 1835 accounted for another £300 beyond what he had paid to Kennedy. In the previous November he had casually remarked in a letter to his brother that 'elections nowadays are cheap amusements compared with what they used to be, one or two thousand cover all expenses'. Perhaps so; but Reform Act or no, he had had a pretty expensive time of it since the advent of the Whigs. Cambridge in 1831 had cost him about £1,650, and Bletchingley another £1,300. Success in South Hampshire in 1832 had been bought with an outlay of only £1,100; and failure in 1835 at little more than £1,390. This last, he said, was 'cheap enough in a county contest'. But it left out of account the expenses of his abortive canvasses in Falmouth and Lambeth, which altogether cost him nearly another £700. This made up a hefty sum at a time when he had lost his F.O. salary and was still burdened with Mrs Murray Mills and others. He had borrowed another £2,000 on a long-term loan from William in October 1830, and, briefly, another £1,200 for Cambridge in 1831-2 and £1,000 again for Tiverton in 1835. But the last, at least, was money well spent.[106]

Palmerston's election in Tiverton on 1 June 1835 was a pretty quiet affair. His dress seems to have been by far the loudest thing about it – white hat, white trousers and blue frock coat with gilt buttons. Nonetheless his personal appearance, though 'conspicuous', made 'a most favourable impression'. It also intimidated the opposition. The Tories, he reported, had applied to eight different people, but none would stand since the electors – a mere 220, all 'perfectly independent, all liberal' – were so clearly determined to have him. He made a single address, on all the achievements of the 'Reform Government', at the Three Tuns on 29 May; and his chairing on 1 June was 'a procession like a triumph'. Immediately afterwards he rushed away, pleading pressure of public business. 'They were delighted to have me', he told his brother, 'for as you well know, in this country even the veriest Radicals love rank & station, & had ten times rather be represented by a gentleman than by a person of their own class.' And they had told him, he added, that 'I shall be able to keep my seat as long as I like'. Indeed he was, as he said, 'singularly fortunate in lighting upon Tiverton'. It served him for the rest of his life.[107]

While Palmerston waited for a parliamentary seat – and still more eagerly, for the fall of Peel's Government – he professed not to be unduly worried. After all, he said, if his return were deferred until after the formation of a new Whig Government, it would save him the trouble of a double election. But all the time, whether in or out of office, an avalanche of opposition among the Whigs was threatening to engulf him. It had in fact begun to gather strength in the summer of 1834, when the rumour spread that an attempt was being made yet again to interest him in India. Bentinck, the first Governor-General under the new India Act, was in bad health and anxious to retire. It is not possible to make out who first suggested Palmerston. It does not appear to have been Melbourne; his initial reaction on hearing in the middle of September definite news of Bentinck's intention to resign was to approach Auckland. About the same time Brougham named Palmerston among others to the Prime Minister and a few days later made him his number one choice: '*Pam*'s your man – & Granville for the F.O.'[108]

Brougham also recommended replacing Granville in Paris by Lamb and Lamb in Vienna by Durham. Whether or not Durham would have been satisfied with Vienna, the idea of banishing Palmerston to India was already known in the Durham camp by the beginning of September. There, however, it was said that the Directors had refused to consider either him or Grant. That this was so seems to have some foundation. It was also stated that Palmerston had nonetheless been approached but refused the opportunity. Melbourne had answered Brougham on 22 September: 'Palmerston would not take India – who in his senses would leave being Secretary of State here to be Governor General, unless absolutely compelled by necessity.' Within a few days the word was going around that Palmerston had indeed refused to go. But Melbourne's words did not really imply that he had actually been approached. Grey evidently did not think he had, and there is no mention at all of India in Palmerston's correspondence at this time. However, since no announcement was made for some time, the rumour about Palmerston persisted both in the F.O. and out of it. [109]

One reason for the persistence of the rumour that Palmerston was going was that his new appointments and arrangements in the F.O. in the autumn seemed to indicate some preparation for departure even before the crisis produced by Spencer's death. Shee's nomination to Berlin in particular had caused a great commotion when the news spread in October 1834. 'Tout le monde sera surpris,' said Talleyrand, 'y compris Sir George Shee.' But while Frenchmen professed to be amused, Englishmen were really shocked. Everyone looked upon it as a 'job'. Grey considered that however desirable it was to get Shee out of the F.O. the appointment was nonetheless 'abominable' and bound to bring 'discredit' to the Government. Ellice condemned it as 'indecent'; Brougham as 'very, very, very bad' – but he consoled himself with the hope that it might open up the way to the précis-writership for his stepdaughter's husband, Malet. Melbourne, who was simultaneously preparing to get rid of his equally unsavoury secretary, Tom Young, by making him Receiver-General in the Post Office, evidently told Brougham he was unreasonable to complain of Shee's promotion after seeking so long to get him out of the F.O. But Grey suspected Melbourne was being so compliant in order to make room for his sister's eldest son, Fordwich. In Paris Mme Dino offered the explanation that 'it is by what they demand that men preserve their influence over women, while it is by what they concede that women preserve their influence over men'. [110]

Holland, who also considered Shee's 'a good riddance but a bad appointment', recognized that an international conspiracy was on foot against Palmerston. What he wrote to Granville subsequently showed how far his attitudes to Palmerston and Talleyrand had changed round:

There is both *intra muros & extra*, a great and unmerited run at Palmerston. The Holy Alliance who wish through him to ruin our Ministry, some individuals piqued or disappointed in personal objects, the resentment & manoeuvres of Durham & such party as he has & in some measure we must acknowledge his ungracious exercise of his patronage, all combine to render the attack however unjust, very formidable. It would really be the grossest folly as well as impropriety for my friend Talleyrand or any of the French agents, either from levity or accident to lend their assistance to such a plot. Whatever may be the merits or demerits of our Cabinet or individuals in it, there can be no arrangement more favourable to the great object of establishing & cementing a firm alliance between the Constitutional Governments of Europe with England & France at its head, than that which keeps you at Paris & Palmerston at Foreign Affairs.[111]

Granville wholeheartedly agreed with Holland. 'Nothing can exceed the activity & perseverance of the agents in this intrigue,' he replied; 'these agents engage indiscriminately male & female recruits in England & on the continent . . . Talleyrand . . . chuckles at the notion of no ambassador being sent to England as long as Palmerston remains at the F. Office.' Chuckling or sulking there is no doubt that Talleyrand, like Princess Lieven before him, grossly overplayed his hand. Whether an unwilling or merely an unwitting candidate for the F.O., Granville asked Holland to warn Melbourne that 'the removal of Palmerston, be his successor who he may, will be regarded as a triumph effected by Metternich over the system of union with France, & alliance with the constitutional states of Europe'. Refusing to return from Paris also weakened Talleyrand's position by making him look more petty and personal than Palmerston. Mme Flahault probably thought it opened up great prospects for her husband and though she was greatly deceived, for all sides in London dreaded that possibility, all the gossip and intrigue she fostered must further have damaged Talleyrand. When he failed to return on Wellington's succession to the F.O., Greville heard the unlikely tale that it was because Mme Dino had very carelessly as well as inconveniently become pregnant.[112]

Although Talleyrand's schemes had failed, there can be no doubt that Palmerston had made himself very vulnerable. It was worrying to his colleagues that a Foreign Secretary should have made himself so unpopular with all the foreign ministers. Esterhazy too, it was rumoured, would not be coming back; and Shee's appointment, Brougham pointed out, had merely got Palmerston out of the frying-pan into the fire. Morley, though influenced more perhaps by past disappointments than present disapproval, reported to Granville in November that Palmerston was 'at the lowest state of degradation both in the House & in Europe'. More ominous was the growing opposition from Woburn. In October John Russell had bitterly contrasted Shee's appointment to Berlin with the posting William Russell had been given to Stuttgart: 'Nothing but a renegade Tory can expect success in diplomacy,' he wrote. His eldest brother too had long since written off Palmerston and the Canningites as bought too dearly with their three secretaryships of State. So at any rate Arbuthnot reported Tavistock as saying, and the Duke of Bedford's later correspondence certainly registered a growing antagonism to Palmerston. 'This administration', he told Lady Holland when first he heard about Shee, 'can in my opinion never go on, unless they get rid of Palmerston.'[113]

The Duke of Bedford kept up his bombardment upon Holland House throughout October and November, saying that it was the first he had heard of Palmerston being an enemy to the Holy Alliance. 'The only person I have heard speak well of him', he wrote to Holland on 13 November, 'is a *holy alliance* man (Aberdeen) who is indignant at the Court of Directors thinking him an *unfit* person to go to India.' And when the Government fell, he rejoiced that it had been saved from internal decay arising out of 'intrigues, and squabbles, and jealousies', and looked forward to the party taking the field once more, 'formed of Whig & Liberal principles', its 'character . . . neither dishonoured nor disgraced', and, finally, having got rid of 'a few black sheep such as Palmerston'.[114]

Warned from abroad by both Minto and Granville, Palmerston was by no means unaware that a run was being made against him. He had no doubt at all what Talleyrand was up to. But at home he attributed it all to Durham and his friends. When Brougham and Durham, having quarrelled, pursued each other with speeches, Durham had surprised some, like Holland, by keeping silent on matters of foreign policy, and Brougham disgusted others, like Grey, by attacking Palmerston in private while harassing Durham in public. But when Palmerston heard that Durham had returned to London, he wrote to warn Melbourne: 'You ought to be looking after your stray sheep. That wolf Durham is prowling about the fold.' Ellice, too, he thought was up to his usual dirty work. 'He *can not* act openly and honestly by anybody,' Palmerston wrote to his brother early in March. 'Me he has long disliked. Heaven knows why; unless it be that he believes me an honest man.' It was William's place in Naples Palmerston thought was in danger, but two weeks later Ellice wrote to Melbourne suggesting that if he were called upon to form a new administration he should not only remove Grant from the India Board but transfer Palmerston from the Foreign to the Colonial Office.[115]

Ellice admitted in his letter to Melbourne that he was touching upon 'a tender point'. About the same time, in March or April 1835, the ambassadors of the three Eastern courts appealed to both Grey and Lansdowne against Palmerston's return. This, as Metternich instantly recognized, was a completely false step, and the ambassadors were made to feel that their interference was unwelcome. Their clumsiness may also have made Fred Lamb a less enthusiastic member of their plot. He had come home on leave to persuade his brother of the importance of improving Anglo-Austrian relations and, finding his Government overthrown, had worked hard to ensure that Palmerston should not return to the F.O. But he recognized that Palmerston had to be in any new Whig Cabinet, though only, perhaps, in order to defeat Brougham's scheme of placing Granville in the F.O.; according to Mme Dino Lamb detested Granville. Perhaps the Colonial Office scheme was really his; he was certainly talking about it before Ellice's letter to Melbourne. But as soon as the foreign ambassadors had made their false step, Lamb asked that they reassure Metternich that it would not, after all, be disastrous if Palmerston were to return to the F.O. 'My mission here', he was quoted as saying, 'was to improve him not to change him.'[116]

Palmerston, too, knew that he must 'improve'. It was not his foreign policy, but his parliamentary performance he had in mind. For shortly after the fall of Melbourne's Government he had written to his brother: 'Really and truly, for my own comfort and enjoyment, I should not at all dislike a year's respite from the confinement of office. It would not be a bad thing for me either, in a political point of view, to take a turn at House of Commons work as a regular employment.' This was before his defeat in Hampshire. A few days after it, he later told his brother, some members of his party had suggested he go to the Lords. Holland thought his refusal was due to wounded pride at his election defeat and 'in his circumstances, singularly injudicious'. But Palmerston had seen at once that 'their object was to shelf me and get rid of me'. The Upper House had its attractions for a man in a laborious office and would have saved, he knew, all those election expenses. But the Commons, he said, was 'the place where a man *out* of office can make himself of consequence'. Hence, in February 1835, he was thinking rather that Peel might reward Fleming with a peerage and so create a new vacancy for himself in Hampshire. However, after Peel had resigned on 8 April, the Lords may not have seemed so unattractive to him, since on 11 April he attached his name to a petition which would have given the F.O. to Grey and to himself, presumably, the 'laborious office' of the colonies.[117]

The approach to Grey was an attempt to resolve a confusion of difficulties felt on many sides to stand in the way of re-forming a Whig Government in April 1835. The King, who resented the collapse of his scheme to build up a Tory administration, had no wish to come to terms again with Melbourne; Melbourne, for his part, was worried almost to distraction about the King, Ireland and the internal controversies concerning both Brougham and Palmerston. The solution was to appeal to Grey to take the Treasury and, when he refused, then the F.O. under Melbourne instead. Palmerston not only signed the request to Grey; he even said that this was the solution he preferred. He seems therefore to have been so anxious for Melbourne to succeed that he was willing to accept the Colonial Office and, as a letter written very shortly afterwards to his brother strongly suggests, even a peerage. Quite possibly he did not really believe Grey would ever accept, and calculated that instead of sending himself to the Colonial Office Grey's reply would quickly reinstate him in the F.O. If this was so, then he still had a bitter blow to suffer at Melbourne's hands.[118]

When he had heard of Palmerston's defeat in Hampshire Melbourne had expressed genuine regret and the hope of soon seeing it reversed. But while he may never have mastered the minutiae of foreign policy or been so constantly on the alert as Grey, Melbourne had already learned he must intervene to curb his Foreign Secretary from time to time. In September 1834 he too had become worried about Palmerston's relations with foreign powers and their ambassadors and in October the same year had warned him that he sometimes expressed himself too harshly. So on the evening of 10 April 1835, according to what Ellice told Grey, Melbourne was definitely thinking of offering the F.O. to Russell and the C.O. 'probably' to Palmerston. But he may have felt so uncomfortable, squeezed as he was between his sister Emily and his brother Fred, that when the King commissioned him the following day to form an administration, he jumped instead at the idea of a written appeal to Grey.[119]

The letter of appeal to Grey was composed at Lansdowne House on the morning of 11 April; but the scheme that lay behind it had been concocted elsewhere and some time before. Greville knew about Russell's destination the same day; but rumours about it had reached Paris more than a week before. The notion of appointing Grey to the F.O. instead of either Palmerston or Russell seems to have been suggested by Charles Wood, another son-in-law of Grey's, as early as 8 April, when Grey first indicated that he would be very unwilling to return to the Treasury. But though Howick also supported it and Lansdowne said he 'approved of it very much', Lady Grey did not, and in spite of the pressure of his King and colleagues Grey on 12 April categorically refused both Treasury and F.O.[120]

The day before Grey's refusal, John Russell, having married in the morning, had waited till two for a word from Melbourne before setting off on his honeymoon, uncertain whether he was to go to the F.O. or not. Then, on the twelfth, Melbourne recalled him 'immediately' from Woburn. 'The questions of Brougham and Palmerston are of the utmost importance,' Melbourne wrote. 'Pray do not delay.' The following evening Melbourne came to grips with the more obvious of his problems. More than six weeks before he had made it clear to Brougham how much he held against him. Now, on the evening of 13 April, he went to the Chancellor's house and after a stormy session of three hours bluntly told him he must give up the Great Seal. Elated perhaps by his firmness and success with Brougham, Melbourne then summoned Palmerston.[121]

The meeting Melbourne had with Palmerston at 2 p.m. on 14 April 1835, though probably a much shorter affair than that with Brougham, was just as sharp but by no means as conclusive. Palmerston's diary breaks off at this point for five months. But he had already heard the rumour about Russell replacing him and told Lady Granville he simply could not believe it. Melbourne seems to have tried to be as diplomatic as possible. 'All I said', he repeated afterwards, 'was that it appeared to me and to others that it would be of service to the Government, if you could reconcile it to your feelings to accept another office of equal rank and almost of equal importance.' He evidently meant either the Colonial or Home Office, probably with a peerage. But instead of a quiet compliance there followed 'a full and plain conversation', in which Melbourne told Palmerston there were 'many objections' felt 'in various quarters' to his returning to the F.O. and that it would also be 'more advantageous' to relations with other powers if Palmerston took a different office, and Palmerston retorted, 'distinctly, unequivocally, unalterably', that if he could not return to the F.O. then he would rather not have any office at all.[122]

Palmerston's short retort seems to have unnerved Melbourne more than any bluster of Brougham's had done and he wrote at once to Grey, purportedly to seek his advice but plainly to pass the buck. Inevitably Grey refused it; but he did not omit to refer to 'the objection . . . so generally felt' to Palmerston and to suggest that he ought therefore to give way. Palmerston, to whom Melbourne passed on Grey's letter, was evidently both surprised and hurt by it. Yet for some time past there had been an air of resentment about Grey, owing it would seem to some imagined slight on Palmerston's part.[123]

After his departure from Downing Street, Grey had behaved as though he had been pushed out rather than had fled. His criticism of his former colleagues and successors led Melbourne to write to Palmerston: 'He never was contented for a moment with his own Government & cannot therefore reasonably be expected to be so with that of anyone else.' He seemed especially resentful of Palmerston. When Grey left Downing Street in July 1834 there had been an exchange of compliments, but warmer perhaps on Palmerston's part than Grey's. Probably Grey had neither forgotten nor forgiven the trouble Palmerston had made over the Reform Bill. For some reason Grey also turned down an offer from Palmerston of the précis-writership for one of his sons in 1833 after having earlier expressed the wish for him to have it. Two years later, when he was thinking about placing his youngest son in the F.O., he was very reluctant to approach Palmerston. 'I do not think I have met with the attention from him which I had a right to expect,' he explained to Holland in 1835, 'and he has an ungracious manner of answering some applications, which I am not in a humour to bear.' Thanks to Holland's intervention Palmerston offered a supernumerary place in the F.O., saying that he liked young Grey. But it was not until Aberdeen's return that it was taken up.[124]

Grey had in fact begun to complain that Palmerston was telling him nothing of foreign affairs as soon as he had left office. When he said so to Princess Lieven it may have been a convenient way of fending her off. But there was a genuine air of personal pique about it and he had in fact made much the same complaint to Melbourne before he had been a month out of Downing Street. 'Neither Palmerston nor Talleyrand have said a word to me as to what is intended about Spain,' he had responded to a request for advice in July 1834; 'I can give no opinion.' Someone probably gave Palmerston a hint about it, for early in December he sent to Grey a long report of his doings in South Hampshire and his analysis of future politics. Grey replied with an equally long response from the north, but, as he admitted, left himself neither time nor space for foreign affairs. He would only say that he concurred 'generally' in what Palmerston had said on that subject and that he had done right to check Mehemet Ali. 'I hope', he concluded however, 'that the *suaviter in modo* was observed as much as possible.'[125]

If hint there had been to Palmerston about conciliating Grey in December 1834, it had probably come from Holland House, where a copy of Grey's July letter to Melbourne was sent. There seems to be no truth whatever in the story that at this time Holland was as anxious as Grey to see Palmerston out of the F.O. Probably it derived from a simple confusion of Holland with Howick. Holland's political journal is silent on the matter, breaking off its account of the April crisis abruptly with the round robin to Grey. But later that month Holland wrote to his son that Melbourne's new administration was nearly settled with 'Palmerston, I presume & hope, at F.O. again'. Palmerston was also told, in his interview with Melbourne on 14 April, that the King completely disassociated himself from the general opposition to his return and with one or two exceptions 'entirely approved' of his official conduct. If that was a hint as well, Palmerston seized it at once. It must, in any case, have strengthened his resolve to gamble on the F.O. or nothing. So late in the evening that same day he reaffirmed his attitude in writing and, referring to the comment Grey had made, embarked upon a vigorous defence of his policy. 'It is always disagreeable to speak of oneself,' he wrote, 'but upon this occasion I must be permitted to say, that I consider myself to have conducted our foreign relations with great success.'[126]

If Palmerston was gambling, then, it was probably with loaded dice. Grey and Ellice both sensed that Melbourne would give way. Wood pressed Ellice to work on Melbourne and Ellice himself still hoped the F.O. would go to Russell. But it was known at Holland House on 14 April that Russell would probably have the Home Office, and the following morning Melbourne wrote an anguished letter to Palmerston that ended: 'I trust, that I am not to consider your communication of last night as going to this extent, that you would now decline the Foreign Seals if they were offered to you.' That same day, the fifteenth, Howick laid out the list of the proposed Government in his diary and at the F.O. placed Palmerston, 'having carried his point'. Palmerston was not yet told. On the sixteenth he had still heard nothing more from Melbourne; but, as he told his brother-in-law, he had good reason to believe that the F.O. was his once more. It was on others Melbourne waited now. The new Cabinet was completed on the eighteenth and Palmerston received the seals the same day. Three days later he reported to his brother: 'Here I am again at my old work. . . . I shall remain in the House of Commons,' he added, 'Grant goes to the Lords.'[127]

XI

WARS
AND
REPRISALS,
1835-41

'Lord Palmerston's return to office', wrote Princess Lieven in April 1835, 'will certainly give an unpleasant shock of surprise to the whole of Europe. Everybody thought he had made himself sufficiently unpopular in political circles for foreign Governments to be spared the infliction of having again to do business with him.' But having had a fright, Palmerston seems to have been so relieved to find himself back at the F.O. that he may even have made a serious effort to meet his critics half-way at least. Even in the F.O., Grey heard, everything now was '*couleur de rose*'. Palmerston's subordinates were supposed to be 'delighted with the kindness of their chief ' and the foreign ministers too were praising his 'manner of doing business'. Lieven's successor, Pozzo, was said to be 'highly satisfied'; and Talleyrand's successor, General Sébastiani, though given indigestion by English society, was to be constantly gratified by Palmerston's 'little attentions'.[1]

Among the English ministers, too, there seemed to be a new spirit of cooperation and unity. In the Cabinet, Holland recorded, there was a greater disposition than in any other he could recall to treat appointments as general rather than departmental matters; and Palmerston 'very wisely' evinced a particular desire to consult his colleagues about a new ambassador for St Petersburg. With their help Durham was persuaded to take the mission again in June 1835. Palmerston told him that they had had it in mind ever since the beginning of the Ministry and had delayed approaching him only until they were sure that Russia would make no difficulties about it. Holland hoped that when Durham heard how Palmerston had 'corrected the habits which rendered him unpopular' he would on his part 'find some pretext for overcoming his *invincible* repugnance to serving under him'. Durham was evidently very flattered and when Melbourne heard he had accepted, he congratulated Palmerston on pulling off a 'capital thing'. The whole plan nearly came unstuck when the King blew up, partly because he had not been consulted in advance and partly because he considered Durham still as Russia's dupe. According to Holland he got so angry at one point that he showed a distinct inclination to dismiss his Foreign Secretary. However, after Melbourne had worked upon him and insisted on taking as much of the blame as he could, the King settled for an expression of his 'high displeasure and extreme disapprobation'. He also graciously condescended to allow Durham to proceed. Ellice, who was not in Melbourne's new Administration, went with Durham as far as Constantinople and though this had its distinct disadvantages it nonetheless made life much easier at home.[2]

Externally the Cabinet seemed to be faced with the implacable hostility of both King and Lords and since it also had an uncertain grip upon its majority in the Commons few thought it could possibly last for long. Yet it survived, with only a brief interruption, for more than six years. Palmerston's good new resolutions, however, lasted hardly for a month. For as early as the middle of May 1835 Holland was hearing new tales about 'those little blemishes in Palmerston's ministerial character', how he had been keeping English diplomats waiting hours at the F.O. and then leaving without seeing them at all. By the following February, after Palmerston had held up an official dinner for an hour and kept both friends and foreign diplomats 'dancing in attendance', Holland concluded that all Palmerston's old habits in office had returned, and with them their inevitable consequences.[3]

In fact Palmerston had been made late for his dinner by constant interruptions at the F.O. and had broken off his work to dress only at 7 p.m. But he had unquestionably fallen once more into his inconsiderate habits and his cavalier treatment of others. No doubt it was because he found the burden of work upon him to be at least as great as ever, 'having every day', he reminded the unfortunate Shee as early as May 1835, 'to endeavour to cram six hours' business into four hours' time'. It was surely also the result of the very rapid recovery his spirits had made from the shock of April 1835. Unlike others, Palmerston had from the first believed the Government would last. If the Lords threw out their two principal measures – on Irish tithes and municipal reform – then he expected that an appeal to the country would strengthen the Whigs and weaken the Tories. He must also have sensed that his position in the Cabinet was much stronger than before. Brougham, as well as Durham and Ellice, was now gone from the Cabinet, and though it harboured another awkward relative of Grey's in Howick at the War Office, there was powerful support for Palmerston where he wanted it most, in Hobhouse, who took charge of India when Grant, now made Lord Glenelg, moved to the Colonial Office, and in Minto, who took over the Admiralty when Auckland left for India in September. His relations too with Holland seemed more satisfactory than ever. But in foreign policy the comparative unity of the Cabinet depended on the Anglo-French entente and the entente in turn on opposition to the Eastern powers.[4]

There can be no doubt that relations with France had suffered sadly from the quarrel between Palmerston and Talleyrand and that they promised to recover when a new ambassador was at last appointed in London. But the weakness of the entente was more deeply rooted than in personal pique. The entente had arisen in the first place, Fred Lamb was constantly assured by Emily, only because the other powers had forced it on England by refusing to act with her against Holland. Palmerston himself even claimed in May 1833 to be 'the member of the Cabinet who would perhaps be the most easily persuaded to forget the past, and hope for better things for the future'. All this, of course, was written for Lamb's reassurance and Metternich's instruction. There was a good deal of truth in it nonetheless, and a good many reminders too of the underlying jealousies in Anglo-French relations. There was still, for example, the nagging complaint about commercial relations.[5]

Palmerston did not believe in tariff wars: they did more harm than good, he said. If another state kept out Britain's manufactures by tariff barriers, then the most effective retort, if only he had his way, would be for Britain to lower hers and by a flood of imports create such an imbalance of trade by smuggling as to force the enemy to terms. But he did not deny that bad commercial relations damaged political sympathy. He frequently warned both Spain and Portugal quite 'unequivocally' of this. 'It is only by extensive Commercial Intercourse', he said, 'that a Community of Interests can be permanently established between the People of different Countries.' He was also very well aware of the damage done to trade by internal or international war. In the New World Palmerston several times offered his mediation to France, most successfully in her dispute with the United States in 1835-6. The idea of the American mediation was suggested by Fred Lamb, but Palmerston took it up with vigour and carried it through to a triumphant conclusion. It was also in negotiations for commercial reciprocity with France that Villiers had made a reputation for himself in the early 1830s; but only by way of contrast to the aggressive dexterity of his co-negotiator, John Bowring, who was disliked and distrusted by French and British alike. In terms of actual achievement there was very little to show, either from this attempt or, with the notable exceptions in Vienna and Constantinople in 1838, from the many others subsequently made in France and elsewhere in Europe.[6]

Bowring, or others just as rash and radical, figured in most of these negotiations – the 'commercial knight-errant', Melbourne called him. Palmerston, too, had been opposed at first to Bowring's employment abroad and between 1831 and 1834 he seems to have been as affronted as anyone by Bowring's indiscreet behaviour. But Bowring's survival and his failure in France were a symptom and a consequence of bad relations rather than their cause. By 1836 Palmerston was already defending Bowring's reports as 'able documents' providing 'much valuable information' and the man himself as 'a very good-humoured, lively, agreeable, well-informed man', and though 'a complete Republican in his opinions', one who 'would put up the guillotine in a manner as gentle and kind-hearted as that in which Izaak Walton would handle the frog he was to impale'. By 1839 Bowring's aggressive tactics were, in

Palmerston's view, the most likely to succeed with France. It was the French Government, Palmerston concluded, who were to blame for the lack of progress in commercial negotiations; and when agreement was nearly reached in 1840, it was the general state of relations that wrecked it. Palmerston had hoped that success would make the entente popular with the radicals in Parliament and the manufacturing classes in the country; instead failure led him to conclude that the French must be as jealous of England's commercial prosperity as they were of her political power.[7]

It was in Spain that the political strain on Anglo-French relations first began to reappear. There, after the escape of Don Carlos, the standard of revolt had been raised again and by the summer of 1835 the position of the Queen Regent and the Constitutionalists had become so desperate that both England and France found themselves presented with a plea for help, in the spirit if not the strict letter of the Quadruple Alliance. The request presented many difficulties, since for their different reasons neither the French nor the English King wished to grant it. Louis Philippe was determined not to help the Christinos and so, knowing that William would never agree, made his intervention dependent on a British guarantee against the Eastern powers. With the help of the French Prime Minister, de Broglie, Palmerston devised a compromise scheme to ensure the sort of limited assistance he believed was all that was really necessary in Spain and the most that King William could be persuaded to accept. He had no wish to see the sort of intervention by France that would establish her predominance any more than Louis Philippe wished to see a similar success for England. So picking up a hint from the French ambassador, Palmerston suggested instead that France lend her Foreign Legion to Spain while another 'auxiliary legion' was raised in England and Belgium. Shortly afterwards it was also agreed that units of the French and British fleets should operate off the northern coast of Spain, though not jointly on account of William's francophobia.[8]

This limited intervention was a device, not only for reducing Anglo-French suspicion, but also for soothing the sensibilities of the ultra-liberals in Spain, who, Villiers had warned, might triumph over the Queen Regent even if the Carlists did not. But in both respects the intervention failed. The British auxiliary legion was about twice as large as the French, but its commander, de Lacy Evans, proved unequal to the task. The legion enjoyed only very mixed fortunes and was never able to exert a decisive influence. So the Spaniards became more unwilling, as well as perhaps unable, to give it its pay. Disgusted and disheartened it had eventually to be disbanded in 1837-8. In the meantime financial aid poured in for the Carlists from the East and, rather as Villiers had predicted, the liberals rebelled in August 1836 and imposed the Constitution of 1812 upon Christina.[9]

King William strongly objected that by consenting to suspend the ban on foreign enlistment he had never intended to aid rebels against the Queen of

Spain; Palmerston professed to believe that 'our principle is to let other nations decide what their own form of government shall be'. In any case, events in Spain made Palmerston anxious for more effective intervention, even for the entry of French troops. But his colleagues were very reluctant and his 'allies' very uncooperative. In December 1835 the Cabinet frustrated, as provocative to France, a scheme of Villiers's to induce the Cortes to consent to a reciprocity treaty in return for a loan and to persuade Parliament to consent to a loan in return for reciprocity; and having ordered the two schemes to be separated, they refused in March 1836 to permit a Government guarantee for a private loan.[10]

Melbourne told a Cabinet colleague that he was so worried about Palmerston's 'meddling' in Spain that he could not sleep; and Hobhouse also noted that Palmerston 'showed symptoms of that indomitable perseverance' that had carried him triumphant through so many earlier difficulties. However, when Palmerston did manage to persuade the Cabinet as an alternative to send out more marines (Howick alone stood firmly against it), Louis Philippe again refused to order his troops across the frontier. Palmerston knew that the French King had no wish to encourage extreme liberals in France by helping their cause in Spain. He suspected, on the contrary, that Louis Philippe wanted to prolong the contest so that eventually he would be in a better position both to make a decisive intervention that would consolidate French influence and to arrange a compromise settlement that would facilitate an Austro-French reconciliation. Palmerston was not surprised about the French refusal because the previous month the King had removed de Broglie, 'the honestest man in France', and had put 'in his place – Thiers!' De Broglie's fall, Holland heard, was considered part of the plot Talleyrand and Lieven had been conducting on both sides of the Channel. Thiers, as it happened, came near to accomplishing a more effective intervention by France, but Louis Philippe found him out and drove him from office in the autumn. His successor was the most hostile to England of all the possible choices, Count Molé – he was 'Russian', Palmerston heard.[11]

This was certainly an exaggeration, but Molé did cut off what little aid France was then giving to the Queen of Spain. At the end of 1836 he even let Palmerston know that France was determined to oppose England's attempts to negotiate more liberal commercial relations with Spain and, indeed, with any country save Portugal. England never did get her commercial treaty with Spain; nor Spain the loan she wanted. The war dragged on for years and inevitably Palmerston, and English opinion in general, grew tired of the Spaniards. There were continual quarrels and even threats of force about the rights of British merchants and creditors and about the pay of British volunteers; and in March 1838 it was decided not to extend the suspension of the Foreign Enlistment Act beyond the summer.[12]

In spite of all these difficulties Palmerston kept his head. As far as the claims were concerned, he told Melbourne in July 1838, it was 'quite true that the

Spaniards are tricky fellows; but so are all people who are driven hard to pay what they have not got'. As for war and revolution, his maxim always was that 'Peninsular affairs are so bad that they cannot become worse, and must therefore become better'. In fact the tide had turned against Carlos when he failed to take Madrid in the summer of 1837 and within the next two years he was expelled from Spain and a moderate constitutional régime established in Madrid. The 'peace' was a very unstable one: before long internal dissensions were to upset almost everything and the question of a husband for the young Queen would revive the Anglo-French contest for influence in still more angry terms. But in the short term Palmerston's gamble had come off. Following a rout of the auxiliary legion and an attack by the Tories, Palmerston had made one of those rare fighting speeches of his after a three nights' debate on Spain on 19 April 1837:

It is there [he said] and upon that contracted scene that is to be decided by issue of battle that great contest between opposing and conflicting principles of government – arbitrary government on the one hand and constitutional government on the other – which is going on all over Europe.[13]

Palmerston took Molé at his word about France's opposition to his commercial negotiations, though he recognized that the struggle between England and France was essentially political. In spite of Molé's reservation, this was true of Portugal as well; so much so indeed that, in contrast to their behaviour in Spain, the French were believed to be siding with the radicals in order to secure a Government more sympathetic to France. On the other hand, when the moderates tried and failed to rescue the Queen from the extremists in the summer of 1836, many observers, including some in the Cabinet, suspected Palmerston was behind it and either condemned or teased him accordingly. There seems to have been no foundation for the suspicion; Palmerston and his agents had rested their hopes upon quite a different counter-revolutionary stroke. But Palmerston was convinced, as he told the First Lord of the Admiralty, that hostility to England was 'a species of agitation kept up for party purposes in Portugal'. So it would cease with the domestic struggle that caused it, and England could be confident of ultimate success without recourse to actual intervention. 'Lay on your oars', he told his restless minister in Lisbon, 'and wait till the [Portuguese] Government comes round to you.' Palmerston was much too optimistic about the Portuguese, who continued to obstruct his campaign against the slave trade as well as to pile up large financial claims against themselves. So he began to consider stronger measures, including, at Hobhouse's request, the seizure of Goa. But he may only have done so to humour his staunchest colleague, and when Russell and Melbourne objected that the occupation of Goa would make England's anti-slave-trade policy look nothing but disguised aggression, he did not press it.[14]

In Greece Palmerston was much less circumspect and, partly for that reason, even less successful in combating foreign influence. Being too free with his advice and increasingly angry that no liberal constitution emerged, he really helped to undermine British influence with King Otto to the benefit of Russia and Austria. Here, too, he found that the French, being more unscrupulous or perhaps more sensible, gave him little or no support but competed for ascendancy in Athens. 'France plays a miserable part in this as well as in most other European affairs,' he wrote to Shee. 'It is very extraordinary that there should always be such a want of dignity, honesty, and good faith in French policy.' When prospects at last improved in 1840-41 it was too late: England was embroiled with France in the Near East and had no intention of helping Greece in her claims against Turkey.[15]

It was a similar story of Anglo-French friction and suspicion almost everywhere else in the world. Whether England wanted any more colonies or not she was determined France should have as few as possible. Palmerston suspected Louis Philippe of wanting to establish a connection with Ranjit Singh in the Punjab, and cast an equally unfavourable eye upon his interest in the Philippines (while refusing all temptation to establish England there). He continued, in particular, to watch the French very closely in North Africa. When, after a successful French expedition against Constantine, Sébastiani assured him in October 1837 they would soon evacuate the city, Palmerston was rightly very sceptical. 'If they do', he wrote to Lamb, 'one does not exactly see the use of throwing away so many lives and so much money as the expedition will cost, for no permanent object.' As the French continued to suffer great misfortunes, he decided on more mature reflection that they would probably decide to abandon the interior and hold on to the city and immediate surroundings of Algiers. But that was precisely what was most objectionable. In January 1838 he wrote:

Colonization in a desert country, or in one very thinly peopled by wandering and barbarous tribes may be an easy thing and implies appropriation of waste; but colonization in a country like Algiers already for many centuries occupied by a nation which was highly civilized, and is still not to be called barbarous, is synonymous with rapine, robbery, [and] expulsion and these things may be submitted to for the moment, but are not acquiesced in permanently.[16]

These colonial adventures, Palmerston believed, would prove a grave embarrassment to France whenever trouble arose in Europe. But England would not in any case repeat the mistake Wellington's Government had made and allow France to turn next to Tunis. So when the French suggested in September 1837 that they join together to help Portugal defend Ceuta against a supposed threat from Tunis, Palmerston concluded it was a trap to associate England with French expansion. In fact Louis Philippe was hoping to reassure the English his intentions were not aggressive. Even the Algerian affair, inherited from his predecessor, was kept going as an expensive attempt to satisfy 'La Gloire' without upsetting the powers; it was 'our opera box', he said. But he could not soothe Palmerston's suspicions that France was aiming to weaken England in the Mediterranean and to cut her off from the interior trade of Africa, particularly when there were rumours too about Morocco and Port Mahon. So in 1838, without any consultation even with Melbourne, Palmerston sent an English officer to reorganize the Bey of Tunis's army and two years later was stopped from aiding Abd-el-Kader's rebellion against the French only by the intervention of his colleagues.[17]

A similar apprehension lay behind Palmerston's attitude towards French policy in Latin America, notably her coercion of Mexico in 1837-9 and Buenos Aires in 1838-40. Whatever Molé might have said or his local agents hoped, there was no appreciable danger or any real intention of France challenging England's commercial supremacy in Latin America. Nor did Palmerston contest the right of France to use force where her subjects suffered so much abuse. England, after all, had similar grievances and also used or contemplated using force in order to redress them. But the past had taught Whitehall the need to make her actions both short and sharp, and not to get involved in chimerical political adventures. 'The situation of affairs changes so frequently and so rapidly in these South American states', Palmerston wrote in 1835 or 1836, 'that the safest course for English authorities to pursue seems to be to abstain rigidly from all interference in the internal dissensions of these republics.' He doubted that the French had learned such wisdom and feared that their methods would backfire and their forces get dragged further and further into the mire. At the very least British trade would then suffer more serious inconvenience from blockade; at the worst the French might develop political ambitions. Molé, Palmerston was inclined to think, had always harboured them. He feared that the French had their eye on San Juan d'Ulloa, 'the Maritime Key of Mexico', and when Molé confined himself to merely verbal assurances Palmerston told Melbourne that these were 'shuffling and unsatisfactory' and that he was determined not to repeat in Mexico Aberdeen's mistake over Algiers.[18]

If Palmerston had had his way in September 1838 orders would have been sent out to the British naval commander in the Caribbean that would have led to an immediate confrontation. But Melbourne was worried at the risk of war involved. 'The French, individually & collectively,' he replied, 'are quick & irritable & appear to me often to act from immediate temper without much calculation of consequences.' So the Prime Minister countered successfully with a compromise proposal that gave the Navy a watching brief and British diplomacy the task of finding a solution. Melbourne's scheme succeeded in bringing France and Mexico to terms in 1839, thanks largely to the ill-fortunes of the French coercion, but partly also to Palmerston's agreeing to play down Britain's role though he was much attacked in Parliament and in the press for what they called his weakness.[19]

In the affairs of Buenos Aires, where British trade was admittedly much less disturbed by French blockading operations, Palmerston was also very moderate. But while, unlike Aberdeen a few years later, he was careful not to let England be dragged into the affair, he noted a French tendency to get involved in Latin American domestic politics and suspected they might be planning to set up a client state. So when the French refused what he thought were reasonable terms and in March 1839 redoubled their naval efforts, he sent the French ambassador in London an eighty-one page denunciation of French duplicity and intrigue and a week later expanded it into one hundred and thirty-four pages for his master in Paris.[20]

Although the French naval reinforcements continued on their way to Buenos Aires, Palmerston's intervention did have a notable effect and, in general, things seemed to improve after May 1839, when a combination of Left and Right ousted Molé and brought back Marshal Soult as French Prime Minister. 'Soult is a jewel,' Palmerston explained, though no doubt adding mentally, as he literally did on another occasion, 'for a Frenchman, I mean.' Soult was not to last for long. He was in any case already too late; by the end of 1836 the entente seemed to both sides to be in ruins.[21]

In September 1836, when Melbourne had urged the Foreign Secretary to restrain the attacks of the English press on Louis Philippe lest the French King be driven into the arms of the Holy Alliance, Palmerston had replied that on the contrary the attacks might do him good. Early in 1837 the French annoyed Palmerston by omitting in the Address from the Throne any reference to his successful mediation in their quarrel with the United States. Palmerston retaliated by dropping from the King's Speech any reference to the French. 'We can say nothing in their praise,' he explained to Granville, 'and therefore silence is the most complimentary thing we can bestow upon them.'[22]

Palmerston had already admitted in the summer of 1836 that he only wanted French help in Spain when England's efforts seemed to fail; by September 1837 he had decided it would be too risky to have it at all. As far as the Quadruple Alliance was concerned its only merit, apart from its foreign and domestic value as propaganda, was as a restraint upon France. For he had already decided that Louis Philippe was 'as ambitious as Louis XIV'. 'But we are married to him, & therefore must not abuse him more than may conduce to his amendment,' he wrote to Fred Lamb. 'The great interests of the two countries are so alike in many points, that the range of his divergence from us is limited – and we are sure to have him again for certain purposes of common policy.' Holland believed, indeed, that Palmerston had checked the newspapers a little. So a façade of entente was kept up, more by others than Palmerston perhaps, but even he recognized that it was better so. 'It may perhaps tell best for Spain alone that we should not be seen to be taken in by the French,' he wrote to his ambassador in Madrid in November 1837; 'but with reference to Europe at large it is better that the Holy Allies should see that France & England can ever differ without quarrelling.' Above all, he thought, the appearance of concert was especially needed to counter Russia in the East, where by 1837-8 the attention of both Palmerston and public was rapidly being drawn away from Spain.[23]

In the heady days of triumph following immediately upon the signature of the Quadruple Alliance in the spring of 1834 Palmerston had written to Lamb:

The Peninsula thus set at rest, and the affairs of Belgium being in a condition in which they may remain for an indefinite period, our attention must be steadily directed to restrain the encroachments of Russia, whose greedy and indefatigable ambition of conquest is the great danger with which Europe at present is threatened.

Russia remained his preoccupation, even though events in the Iberian peninsula turned out so much more complicated than he had hoped. For there was not only Russia's encouragement of repression in Europe and her entrenched position in Turkey still to be checked and undermined; there was also her pressure on the nearer approaches and frontiers of India to be resisted. 'It seems pretty clear', he would say in a famous letter of February 1840, 'that, sooner or later, the Cossack and the Sepoy, the man from the Baltic and he from the British Islands will meet in the centre of Asia.'[24]

There was nothing new about British apprehension of Russia's advance into central Asia. But Russia had made great gains with her military victories over Persia in 1828 and over Turkey in 1829 and these had led the Wellington Government of that time to initiate a policy of British counter-penetration from India. Anxious at first to get on well with Russia and, still more, to concentrate his Government's attention on French 'encroachments', Palmerston had begun by playing down the Russian problem. 'Whether Russia possesses a degree or two of latitude more or less in the Caucasus', he had written to Holland House in May 1831, 'cannot be of the same importance.' As late as 1834 he was still resisting suggestions from Ponsonby that Britain should help the Circassians against Russia on the Black Sea coast and trying to avoid a confrontation with her even in Persia. But after Unkiar Skelessi and Münchengrätz he grew more and more suspicious. 'These Russians!' his reports had led the Prime Minister to exclaim by 1834. 'Wherever we move we find them like the Ghost in Hamlet, following & annoying us.' So Palmerston put himself constantly on the alert. In 1835 he made new diplomatic arrangements in Persia so that a closer watch might be kept upon the Russians; and when the Persians were nonetheless encouraged in 1837 to try again to seize Herat from Afghanistan and the Afghans to seek compensation in the Punjab, he backed the Government of India's counter-expedition to Kandahar.[25]

The First Afghan War (1839-42) led ultimately to military disaster. For this Palmerston's enthusiasm must bear some responsibility, though he had originally intended to make Afghanistan an ally, not a conquest. If, however, he underestimated the military difficulties, he was certainly not alone; and in its immediate political objectives, which were more properly his sphere, the expedition had a very real success, since for the time being at least Russian policy was severely checked. For this achievement Palmerston owed a good deal to the support in Cabinet of Hobhouse and Minto. Melbourne, too, had finally agreed with Palmerston's view that 'Affghanistan must be ours or Russia's'. But the Prime Minister and the majority of the Cabinet had only gradually been brought to this conclusion; and while Palmerston had certainly used to this end both cajolery and argument, he had also brought to bear pressure of opinion.[26]

Quite how deeply Palmerston was involved in the campaign of public vilification of Russia that characterized the English press in the mid 1830s will surely never be known. It would certainly be a gross exaggeration to say that he directed and controlled it. Much, after all, followed from the earlier activities of Polish propagandists, and these had begun uncomfortably early. British sympathy for the Poles was sharply revived when the Tsar declared publicly in November 1835 that Poland's national independence was finally at an end. Palmerston wanted to make a vigorous riposte, on the basis of the Vienna Treaty, but Melbourne intervened against it. Something had to be said, however, when the debate on the Address came on early in February 1836, especially as Palmerston was given the task of spinning it out until enough members could be assembled to avert a defeat on Irish affairs.[27]

Palmerston was, as the Russian ambassador acknowledged, extraordinarily dextrous in avoiding anything polemical in the debates of February 1836. But such dexterity became virtually impossible when towards the end of the same month the three Eastern powers exercised their right of 'protection' to intervene in the independent republic of Cracow on the pretext of putting down disorder. This, Palmerston believed, really could not be overlooked, for England was party to the treaty by which the republic had been established in 1815. When Melbourne again suggested caution, he agreed to reduce the status of his protest from a note to a dispatch. But a protest he insisted there must be, and a strong one at that. For Parliament would eventually insist on something and he did not want to find himself again in the position Grey had placed him in 1831-2, when, having softened his dispatches on Poland, the Prime Minister then refused to produce them in Parliament on the grounds that they had not said enough.

I confess [he wrote to Melbourne] I do not quite agree . . . that it is undignified to remonstrate & protest in cases in which you are not prepared to follow up your protest by war; it seems to me on the contrary, that it is much more undignified to be afraid of speaking out, and of expressing one's opinion of an act of injustice, merely lest we should give offence to those by whom such acts may be committed; and as to practice & precedent, nothing I apprehend is more common in diplomacy than the making of such protests. Neither does it seem that it can justly be said that such protests are useless; the very anxiety which the aggressive parties invariably manifest to prevent such protests from being made, seems to prove the contrary. Public opinion has great power, even in despotic states, and well-founded censure does more or less restrain the will even of autocrats. With regard to the policy of speaking out, on such occasions, I confess it appears to me that it never can be impolitic for a government to speak the truth, and to proclaim that which is just. Silence never gains one anything from one's adversaries, & loses one the confidence of one's friends. By saying nothing on these occasions we should indeed encourage the three powers to repeat acts of the same kind, but we should never get them to be a whit more inclined to help us in the Peninsula or other quarters. The power of England is a moral power quite as much as a military one.[28]

The Cracow affair turned out to be much more unpleasant than Palmerston had intended, when the Prussian Ancillon again refused to accept his dispatch and all three Eastern powers rejected his accompanying proposal to appoint a consul in the city. This threatened to upset the posture he had designed for himself in Parliament and forced him to retreat over the appointment of a consul. But what may have been almost as disappointing to him was that Metternich behaved better in this affair than Ancillon, and Nicholas better than either of them. For by this time, certainly, he was committed to a great publicity campaign against Russia.[29]

'Russia has advanced specially because nobody observed, watched and understood what she was doing,' Palmerston had written to Melbourne in October 1835 when answering the pleas of Ellice and Durham for circumspection in his dealings with her. 'Expose her plans, and you half defeat them. Raise public opinion against her and you double her difficulties. . . . Depend upon it, that is the best way to save you from the necessity of making war against her.' The 'exposure' of Russia had been given a considerable boost after the return to England in 1834-5 of a number of minor but very active and enterprising individual agents from the Near and Middle East. Notable among them were James Baillie Fraser, John McNeill and David Urquhart. They were a motley crew: McNeill was a surgeon in the service of the East India Company; Fraser and Urquhart both had naval experience; all three were experienced travellers in the East. McNeill had been some years with the British mission in Teheran and had become convinced that his chief there was quite incapable of restoring British influence in the face of Russian intrigue. Fraser, who had been sent on a special mission to gather information in Persia, evidently agreed with him, and so did Ponsonby, with whom he specially made contact.[30]

Ponsonby also greatly encouraged Urquhart's rash activities. Urquhart's mother was a friend of Sir Herbert Taylor and through him had obtained the patronage of both King and Foreign Secretary. In 1833-4 he had been sent by Palmerston to collect information on the economic situation in central Europe and the Near East, and in the course of a visit to the Circassians had conceived the idea of supporting their resistance to the Russians. While Ponsonby certainly sympathized with Urquhart's notions, Palmerston had become alarmed and recalled him. But once back in London, Urquhart, McNeill and Fraser put their heads together and produced a stream of articles and pamphlets, all designed to highlight the danger from Russia in the East. Much, if not all of this, had the backing of Taylor and the King, who brought in to help yet another protégé of theirs, the Queen's private secretary James Hudson. Palmerston also encouraged them, though he had serious reservations about the methods and language used. He objected, in the case of McNeill's 1836 pamphlet on the *Progress and Present Position of Russia in the East*, that it was so extreme that its publication would undermine the position he had designed for the author as the next minister in Teheran. The new map that McNeill had produced to underline Russia's encroachment he thought would be damning enough. But Palmerston seems to have been satisfied by the pamphlet appearing anonymously.[31]

Urquhart's activities were much more difficult to control. The first that Palmerston knew of the extremely anti-Russian *Portfolio* was when Van de Weyer handed him the first issue late in 1835. It was true that it contained material Palmerston had planned to publish and that Urquhart had had discussions about it within the F.O. But the *Portfolio* also contained much that was critical of British policy and of Palmerston's colleagues, and was most certainly not authorized. Palmerston at first took it all remarkably coolly; so much so indeed as to bring upon himself apparently quite unwarranted suspicions of complicity.

I am amused at what you said of Urquhart & Ponsonby [he wrote to Melbourne]; they may both have their faults & weaknesses but such are the tools with which those who have to govern mankind must work. We cannot expect to find perfection; and if men whom we employ are eager in the cause in which they have to act, & zealous to accomplish our purposes, and are with that quicksighted & active, they make not bad tools. . . . The great enemy of England is Russia – not from personal feeling but from her having views & objects quite incompatible with our interests & safety; and the main object of our foreign policy must be for years to counteract her; but this cannot be done unless we employ agents who meet the unsleeping activity of hers, with something like equivalent zeal.[32]

Palmerston persisted in the intention he had formed of sending Urquhart as Secretary of Embassy to Constantinople. This may have been suggested by Windsor; but Urquhart had the merits of knowing some Turkish, when the dragomen had proved so treacherous, and something about commerce, when a commercial treaty with the Sultan was in mind. There was also some incidental merit, it was thought, in getting him away from London, where his pamphlet had upset personally so many diplomats and politicians, including even a member of the Cabinet, Poulett Thomson. Even Melbourne took this line. 'I doubt whether he will do you more harm here or there,' he wrote in February 1836, 'but I rather think the former.' But following a Cabinet meeting early in March he wrote after all to suggest Urquhart be sent somewhere else.[33]

The Cabinet meeting of 5 March 1836 had been confronted with reports of Ponsonby's aggressive behaviour in Constantinople, and the thought of having two such rash and dangerous individuals as Ponsonby and Urquhart simultaneously dealing with the Turks genuinely alarmed Melbourne. Lady

Cowper suspected that Ellice had also been at work, and she was absolutely right. 'I have made an insurrection of the *whole Cabinet*,' he boasted to Durham. He had remonstrated with Melbourne more than once, and threatened to ask an awkward question in the Commons. Holland, and probably Hobhouse and Russell too, also let Palmerston know they were against Urquhart's going. Poulett Thomson even threatened to resign. He had been personally insulted by Urquhart, though Lady Cowper thought that Ellice had put him up to complaining, and she particularly regretted it as Palmerston and Thomson got on so well in office.[34]

Palmerston held firm in the face of all of them. Not to send Urquhart, he told Melbourne, would be truckling to Russia and offensive to the English King, who had suggested him. Besides, Urquhart's 'consequence' lay in England as a writer, not in Constantinople where he would be a mere subordinate. 'Pozzo & Poulett Thomson should remember that it is better for them that Urquhart should be smoking hookas at Constantinople than publishing dispatches . . . in England.' So Urquhart was sent off – though only after a very long delay during which, one must say, he gave Palmerston both further cause and surely opportunity enough to get out of the whole affair. But go Urquhart did, and before long he was as much at odds with Ponsonby as both of them were with Russia.[35]

Superficially the influence Russia had established in Constantinople in 1833-4 was consolidated and extended in 1834-6, notably by making an easy bargain with Turkey for the payment of the war indemnity outstanding since 1829 and evacuating in return the territory in Silistria that had been held as security. But Palmerston intended to put up a very strong contest through Ponsonby and Urquhart. Using such passionate characters, however, turned out to have its disadvantages. Ponsonby was so hostile to the Russians that he often tended to discredit his own side, and so abrupt with the Turks that he sometimes threatened to antagonize them personally. Palmerston was by no means uncritical of Ponsonby, but he thought his faults were on the right side and loyally stood by him. When Ponsonby had intervened too roughly with the Turks in the summer of 1836, peremptorily demanding the dismissal of a minister who had trampled on the rights of a British journalist called Churchill – in order to curry favour with the Russians, Ponsonby thought – it was several months before Palmerston let him know he had gone too far. But the Foreign Secretary had really wished to uphold his ambassador and even to move him up a step or two in the peerage. It was rather the Cabinet who had decided otherwise, and the delay that followed in conveying their view was not negligence on Palmerston's part but, as he hinted, a deliberate attempt to give Ponsonby time to succeed in his course before new orders could check him. When the Cabinet met to decide between the 'difficult' course of upholding Ponsonby and the 'dishonourable' one of abandoning him, Palmerston presented them with the news that the offending Turkish minister had already been dismissed.[36]

Ponsonby's behaviour over the Churchill affair may have encouraged Urquhart, if any encouragement were needed, to behave more rashly and aggressively than ever. Almost at once he began to negotiate a commercial treaty with the Turks behind Ponsonby's back and in conflict with his own instructions. Before long they were hardly on speaking terms and Ponsonby, who wished to come home on leave, dreaded leaving Urquhart behind as chargé d'affaires. When Palmerston heard how bad things were between them, he planned to give Vaughan the rank and title he had so far unluckily missed by sending him out as a temporary ambassador. But Vaughan never got beyond Malta because in the meantime one of Urquhart's plots had blown up in his face. This concerned the seizure by the Russians of the *Vixen*, a British vessel they believed to have been communicating with the Circassians. The Russians, claiming sovereignty over the Circassians, dubbed them rebels. But Palmerston could not acknowledge that; to have done so would have damaged him too much among the Russophobes he had stirred up at home. He may even have considered at one time giving material aid to the Circassians, but if so he had decided against it as ineffective and impracticable. After the arrest of the *Vixen*, however, it soon transpired that while Palmerston and probably Ponsonby too were both innocent of any deliberate involvement, Urquhart was neither innocent nor repentant. He had himself visited Circassia and subsequently encouraged the *Vixen*'s owners with a view, it would appear, to promoting an Anglo-Russian incident. All he succeeded in doing was to place Palmerston in an awkward position in England and his own career as a diplomat in serious peril. Eventually, with Russia's aid, Palmerston extricated himself by acknowledging the Russians' right to seize the *Vixen* on grounds that involved no recognition of her sovereignty. Urquhart, who had so exposed his master to public criticism, was recalled and dismissed. He forgave neither the Russians nor Palmerston, and when his chance came, as it did in 1840, to connect them in a secret alliance against both him and England, he did not hesitate to seize it.[37]

Urquhart, clearly, was a paranoic; Bulwer, his successor in Constantinople, suffered merely from delusions of grandeur. At the time and afterwards Bulwer claimed all the credit for bringing to a successful conclusion the negotiation of the commercial treaty with Turkey and complained that his efforts were not appreciated. Probably he was responsible only for details and Ponsonby for the overall design. In any case the treaty was a considerable success. Designed to replace Russia's exports to England by Turkey's and so to weaken Russia at the same time as strengthening Turkey, it also expanded British trade in the Levant and, more important, weakened Mehemet Ali's resources by rendering illegal his system of monopolies. On the other hand, the general intention of strengthening Turkey internally hardly made much progress. Palmerston had only the most limited of expectations and concentrated on improving the army, the navy and finance. But even in these respects Ponsonby's success was severely checked both by Russian counter-action and by his own Government's refusal as yet to help the Sultan destroy Mehemet Ali. Here again differences between Palmerston and Ponsonby were merely ones of emphasis, though they were none the less important. Palmerston concentrated on the need for postponing the showdown with Egypt until the Turks were really ready; Ponsonby on looking forward to it.[38]

Until Turkey's strength and England's influence with her were sufficient to cope with a new challenge in the East, Palmerston was anxious to safeguard the situation in the meantime by some sort of concert among the powers. Eventually he developed the idea of destroying Russia's special influence in Constantinople by 'merging' the Treaty of Unkiar Skelessi into a new European arrangement. But it took him some time to discover this course and even when he had he found Metternich still too much under Russia's influence to risk it. His first proposal, made early in December 1835, followed alarming reports of the state of Russia's naval armament in the Baltic. Reckoning no doubt that Durham would again send back a stream of advice about Russia's real goodwill and evident good intentions, Palmerston had sent with him in the first place both naval and military experts to make independent investigations and reports. Consequently he was able to inform Melbourne that Russia had kept up, even in peacetime, a force of twenty sail in the Baltic, and Melbourne agreed that it would be necessary to approach Parliament for a larger naval vote.[39]

When the Cabinet met on 2 December 1835 to discuss the proposed approach to Parliament, Palmerston also suggested that he should ask France if she were willing to join with England in an overture to Austria and Turkey for a ten-year guarantee of the independence and integrity of the Ottoman Empire. All the members of the Cabinet were present, save Lansdowne and Duncannon, but the discussion seems to have been surprisingly brief and only Howick demurred, saying that the alliance 'must lead to war'. So after the assent of the King had been secured on the fourth, Palmerston communicated his scheme to the French ambassador on the morning of the fifth. Sébastiani, according to Palmerston, was absolutely delighted and promised to write at once to Louis Philippe and de Broglie. 'There shall be but three in the secret,' he promised, 'the King, the Duc de Broglie & I. There shall be no fourth. Ah ma foi! We must not tell Thiers.' The secret was closely guarded; Fred Lamb later assured Palmerston he would not find anything out about it in France even if he had Thiers's chambers searched, and even Professor Webster could find nothing in the Quai d'Orsay. But it was soon apparent that the three parties were not equally enthusiastic. Louis Philippe, already leaning heavily towards reconciliaton with Austria, was more interested in the notion, attributed by Palmerston to Metternich, of arranging a general treaty guaranteeing the status quo all over Europe. However, the initial response seemed to be encouraging, especially from Palmerston's point of view. For de Broglie replied suggesting that England and France should first conclude an agreement and then submit it to Turkey and the other powers. Otherwise, he said, if Austria were approached in the first instance, Metternich would communicate the proposal to Russia and the Russians would intrigue in Constantinople and Vienna to frustrate it. At the same time he suggested that just in case the Sultan should still refuse what ostensibly depended on his full participation, England and France should add to their convention a very secret article making the guarantee nonetheless binding on them both.[40]

The suggestion of an additional secret article was hardly likely to be accepted by the Cabinet and indeed at their meeting on 23 December 1835 they unanimously rejected it, 'at least unless greatly modified', according to Howick. On the proposal concerning Austria there was a very long discussion. Palmerston had neither wanted nor expected this, since he shared de Broglie's suspicion of Metternich, and at the meeting on the second the Cabinet had agreed with him that Austria would only try to bring Russia into the alliance and so turn it into a plan for general 'interference'. Now Palmerston found the Cabinet divided half and half, with Minto, Russell and (as it was the more restricted plan) Howick joining Palmerston in favour, and Hobhouse, Glenelg and Spring Rice joining Melbourne against. The King was strongly on Palmerston's side and for once with France, but it was plainly impossible on such an important matter and in such a divided Cabinet to go against the Prime Minister. So Melbourne, as Howick put it, was given 'a casting vote' and it was settled that Palmerston should tell Sébastiani that they could agree to draft a treaty but not to sign it until after Austria had been approached.[41]

The implication of the Cabinet's decision was that if Austria refused England would also give up the whole idea of a treaty of guarantee. Yet Palmerston refused to accept defeat and it was probably on account of this that a new complaint against him appeared among some of his colleagues. When Grey chided his eldest son with neglect of foreign affairs, Howick excused himself on the grounds that his name was last on the circulation list for dispatches, that by the time he saw them they were already out of date and that outgoing instructions were 'very seldom' circulated at all. Another, more senior, minister complained that he and his colleagues hardly ever saw Palmerston and when they did 'conversed chiefly upon indifferent matters'.[42]

For six weeks, as he frankly admitted to Granville, Palmerston 'abstained' from making any overtures to Austria and tried everything he could to make Melbourne change his mind. He warned the Prime Minister that the de Broglie Government might fall at any moment and that a conference would only drag out time and split the powers point by point. On the other hand, a speedy agreement with France on the simple lines of the drafts and redrafts with which he tempted Melbourne would tie de Broglie's successor, and though Austria might ostensibly reject it, it would secretly be welcomed even by her, and would give England the advantage over Russia in the East. Simultaneously there appeared the revelations in the *Portfolio*, but these had a rather adverse effect on Melbourne, though he admitted he had known for some time that they were on the way. 'There appears to me already to be rather more indignation in the public mind against Russia, than will permit us to act reasonably,' he wrote to Lady Holland.[43]

Melbourne acknowledged to Palmerston that the *Portfolio*'s revelations were of 'great importance', but insisted that 'the principal reason, which makes me timid & unwilling to proceed, is a feeling that the matter has not been sufficiently considered & is not clearly understood, & I have a great dread of treaties made in the dark'. Melbourne had little help from his brother; for once Fred Lamb was on Palmerston's side. So Melbourne wrote desperately to Grey, purporting to recall that his predecessor had always been against arrangements with foreign powers. Grey's advice was even more negative than Melbourne could have wished. He agreed with Durham that Russia was in no condition yet to pursue any grandiose objective and that England's intention to resist if and when the time did come was already sufficiently clear. This drew a furious reaction from Palmerston, who still resented how in 1832-3 he had been stopped from giving the Sultan aid enough to prevent his turning to Russia. Melbourne in turn pointed out to Grey that he did not seem to have considered one of Palmerston's principal points, that the treaty would fend off the prospect of a revived connection between France and Russia.[44]

The Prime Minister, then, was not quite so 'inexorable' as Palmerston claimed. There was more justification in his fear that Melbourne's doubts had spread to others. Ellice, who was plotting across the Channel with Talleyrand and Mme Lieven to turn out both de Broglie and Palmerston and to replace Lamb with Durham in Vienna, probably had little effect in London save to confuse. 'I do not exactly make out Ellice's French politics', wrote Holland to Granville, 'but I think there is still a great sediment of hostility to Palmerston in his mind.' So he let Ellice know quite clearly that he was a great believer in the Anglo-French alliance and that there could be no better Foreign Secretary than Palmerston 'for our purposes of peace & liberal system'. But before the end of January Holland too let Melbourne know that he was worried by the growth of anti-Russian propaganda and that he wished to suggest a plan of his own for a treaty designed to deter Russia by its existence but not to fetter England by its provisions.[45]

Holland's 'plan' was quite incomprehensible and Melbourne suspected it would embroil England even deeper in the East. 'The Black Sea & the Caucasus & these great Asiatic empires inflame imaginations wonderfully,' he commented to Palmerston. On the other hand, both Melbourne and Russell were seriously worried by reports coming from Berlin that Ancillon was claiming to have detected in Palmerston's manoeuvres a plan to detach Austria from Russia, and was complaining that, on the contrary, they would only drive the Eastern powers closer together and, with the Cracow affair, divide Europe into armed camps. Palmerston was plainly upset by the doubts that these reports aroused among his colleagues, especially as Russell had backed him hitherto. He told Russell that he was so annoyed with the way things had gone that he hesitated to approach the Cabinet again until he could see a clearer course ahead. To Melbourne he emphasized that if Europe was divided into two camps their separation was 'not one of words, but of things; not the effect of caprice or of will, but produced by the force of occurrences. The three and the two think differently, and therefore they act differently.' Far from inventing that division, England had saved Europe from war by standing firm by France. If, however, she now went cap in hand to Metternich over the Eastern question and accepted his preference for a general conference, her agents would be smothered in 'a labyrinth of negotiations', as would have happened in the Belgian affair had the conference not been held in London, where England possessed the advantage of superior weight. So England and France would be faced with having to give way or to make matters worse by breaking up the conference. Far better, then, for them to take their ground boldly in the first place and plan, as he had originally proposed, to make Metternich 'edge away' in their direction.[46]

Palmerston's argument did not prevail among his colleagues. Melbourne pointed out that the change of Government and the fall of de Broglie in France had radically altered the situation. Russell wrote to say that if an initiative was so important, then it had better be tried in Vienna now that Paris was ruled out:

I mean we ought to make Austria as much our friend as we can; otherwise we are running the risk of a war, without the chance of finding an ally. If F. Lamb were to go to Vienna, with general instructions to be friendly & open with Metternich, some good might come of it, & we should not be thought such bugbears as I am afraid we are now.

After some delay on account of illness, Lamb went off to Vienna in May 1836, though armed with instructions to concert with France as well as Austria. As Palmerston had expected, he got nothing but words. So for a couple of years Palmerston concentrated on Spain, leaving matters to rumble uneasily in the East. But he continued to watch Russia's activities very closely in central Asia, and, while he watched, worked with Ponsonby to rebuild British influence in Constantinople and relied on the naval increases voted in March 1836 to keep Mehemet Ali quiet.[47]

The next crisis over Mehemet Ali came sooner than Palmerston had hoped: Turkey was not ready nor the Anglo-French entente repaired. But he still distrusted Austria even more than France, and so when the news came towards the end of May 1838 that Mehemet Ali was planning to declare his independence, Palmerston revived the 1835 scheme of offering an Anglo-French alliance to the Porte or, if that failed, an English alliance alone. 'If England allows and acquiesces in the assertion of independence by Mehemet Ali, she seals the doom of Turkey, and hands over the Dardanelles to Russia,' he wrote to Melbourne; 'it is not too late even now to act . . . but we must act promptly and vigorously – naval aid is all we need afford . . . and if we should thus restore to Turkey Syria & Egypt, we shall have given great additional stability to the Balance of Power in Europe.'[48]

Palmerston knew it would be difficult to get what he wanted. 'There are very few public men in England', he warned Granville, 'who follow up foreign affairs sufficiently to foresee the consequences of events which have not happened.' This was a conscious reference to Melbourne, who had already told him he did not trust France and did not like to bind England in advance. Sure enough, when the Cabinet discussed the situation on 6 June, only Hobhouse supported Palmerston's desire for immediate measures. After deliberating 'for some time' they agreed that if Mehemet Ali persisted the fleet should go out to blockade him in Alexandria and menace him in the Red Sea. Once again, however, it was thought best not to act alone but to 'proceed in concurrence with all the great powers'.[49]

Palmerston did not give up hope. He discussed repeatedly with Hobhouse how they might do 'something to repair the crime committed by allowing Russia & Turkey to conclude the treaty of Unkiar Skelessi'; enlisted the support of both Minto and Lansdowne by devising a secret article to bind the untrustworthy French; tempted Melbourne and anticipated Disraeli by promising 'Peace with Honour'; and asked Granville to sound out the French regardless. But whatever success Palmerston had in London was at once upset in Paris. For this time the French were not prepared even to pretend an interest.[50]

In view of the attitude of the Cabinets in London and Paris Palmerston had no alternative but to take up the idea of a concert of the five powers, which only a short while before he had brushed aside as 'a tedious matter to arrange'. At least there were some encouraging signs, in a revival of the Belgian conference after the King of Holland's virtual surrender in the spring and in Metternich's apparent willingness to join in some sort of cooperation based even on London. So Palmerston worked hard during July and August 1838 at what he had spurned as coming from Metternich in 1834 – a concert and a treaty among all the powers. He did not succeed, because Mehemet Ali was sufficiently impressed with the enormity of his plans to decide upon retreat, and in that case neither France, nor Austria, nor Russia saw any need of a formal compact. Louis Philippe did not want to be seen, either by the Egyptians or by the French, to be too unpleasant to the Pasha; Metternich did not want to offend Nicholas or to give Palmerston too solid a ground in London; and the Russians had no desire unnecessarily to surrender their advantage in Constantinople. But Palmerston had come to two important conclusions: that there was no prospect of being able to detach Austria from the Münchengrätz alignment by the threat of an Anglo-French concert in the East and that the best chance of dislodging the Russians from Constantinople lay in compelling them to submerge the Treaty of Unkiar Skelessi in a general compact among the powers. After all, he knew, the Egyptian crisis was by no means solved and when it exploded again the danger from Russia would be as real as ever.[51]

While Palmerston tried to hold the threads of their foreign policy together, it seemed very doubtful that the Government would survive. There had been a very dangerous moment in the summer of 1836 when Melbourne looked like suffering disgrace over the Caroline Norton trial. For the plaintiff, when got at, as it was assumed, by the Opposition, refused to make a deal. Even that, however, Palmerston may have turned to some small advantage personally. With Fred Lamb out of the country and Melbourne laid up in bed Palmerston played a larger role in trying to avert disaster than perhaps he might otherwise have done. Actual negotiations with the husband were left to the lawyers and to Edward Ellice. Even so Palmerston did not miss his opportunity to give Melbourne much advice and his brother Fred regular reports, and at the same time to score off an old enemy. 'Ellis [sic] has been active & busy, and I hope sincere,' he wrote to Lamb; 'but one never knows what secret views or oblique purposes he may be actuated by.' A week later Ellice was reported as 'very lukewarm, and much disposed to do . . . as little as possible'; and a few days after that as having 'bolted' abroad, ostensibly to see to his affairs in Canada but 'evidently', Palmerston said, 'to avoid being made a witness; and either finding he could do nothing, or thinking it better on the whole to attempt nothing'. Luckily the case against Melbourne failed, with or without Ellice's help. But the condition of the Government continued to be very unsafe.[52]

Although, with the Canningites no longer in existence as a group, Melbourne's second Cabinet was peculiarly Whig, it depended in the Commons on the support of both radicals and Irish and expected to placate them with municipal reform in England and appropriation of surplus church revenues in Ireland. Unfortunately the Lords kept on butchering or rejecting their legislation and throughout 1835-7 crisis followed rapidly on crisis. The climax came in the spring of 1837 when another confrontation over Irish legislation coincided with the news of Evans's defeat in Spain. Spencer Cowper was found arranging his chief's papers in the F.O. and clerks like Charles Scott looked forward with grim pleasure to his going. But the Government survived its crucial vote on Ireland and Palmerston made his brilliant speech on Spain.[53]

The behaviour of the Lords did not in fact worry Palmerston too much. If they kept on as they were doing, rejecting even the best of legislation, he thought they would only strengthen the Government. For they would make it all the more difficult for the Opposition to form an alternative administration in the face of outraged radicals and Irish and ensure a Whig triumph in any General Election in the face of offended public opinion. He professed to regret the damage all this would do to aristocratic influence. But to underline the threat he himself gave a vote to the radical candidate in a by-election at

Westminster in May 1837. His action shocked many who observed it; it was, he said, only a gesture. Leader's radical opinions were merely 'harmless doctrines' because they never would be accepted; on the contrary, the defeat he eventually suffered in the election proved 'how right we were in our anticipation of the effect of the Reform Bill. We always said it would satisfy the great bulk of the Reformers, and would separate reasonable men from exaggerated doctrines.'[54]

So Palmerston looked with equal equanimity at the prospects of a General Election. He certainly preferred it to Russell's favourite alternative, though he was nothing like so opposed as he had formerly been to the creation of a large batch of peers. Melbourne did not much like either possibility. He was uncertain of public support in an election, and the King was bound to be uncooperative whatever course he took. But the King's death on 20 June 1837 finally removed every doubt by bringing on the General Election, as constitutional practice then required, and the following month Palmerston was once more in Tiverton.[55]

Palmerston had not been neglecting his constituents since his election in 1835. He had dealt with their complaints about tithes and quarter sessions, franked their letters, and selected for the F.O. from among them. He had also spent a week in Tiverton early in November 1835, probably to make up for his sudden recall to London after his initial election. He calculated on not having to do so again for quite a while, though he was eventually to discover that he was expected every year to act as steward at their races. But much to his annoyance he was summoned in April 1836 by rumours that a local Tory squire was already beginning a canvass. Probably it was the embattled state of Parliament and some rumour of a General Election that caused it. It cost Palmerston a week he could ill afford to spare – 'working like a twopenny postman from morning till night, & reading like a newspaper writer from night till morning'. But he 'brought back a healthy face' and made, he thought, everything safe.[56]

Whether Palmerston was really safe at Tiverton only the election of July 1837 could prove. According to some of his supporters the refusal of a quarter sessions court put the matter very much in doubt. The Opposition, Palmerston afterwards reported, also employed both bribery and intimidation 'to an immense extent'; the innkeepers all deserted to the other side when they heard he was going to give a hundred guineas to the poor instead of public dinners; he was heckled constantly about the Poor Law and his love life; and State business again recalled him prematurely, this time in the middle of his canvass. In his absence the Whigs heckled his opponent about a distant relative of his they had discovered in the workhouse, and whenever the Tory tried to make a rally they unloaded barrels of cider in the fields near by to deprive him of an audience. 'All the people', Palmerston concluded when reporting to his brother, were on his side, 'men, women, & children.' He did not, however, come top of the poll. His Whig colleague did, by a very long way. But then John Heathcoat was the proprietor of the local lace-factory and won every election there between 1832 and 1852. However, their lone opponent was much further still behind, and so Palmerston was safely re-elected.[57]

Throughout the country generally the Whigs were not so fortunate; rather they lost ground. The losses were not enough to displace Melbourne's Government, especially with the favour he enjoyed from the Queen. But they were enough to underline the importance of strengthening the Government's base, especially among the radicals. Russell had already suggested they ought perhaps to readmit Durham, who had recently returned from Russia, and at once the rumour had gone around that Palmerston was to make room for him by taking the Privy Seal and an English peerage. After the poor election results Russell several times returned to the need for taking Durham in, but Melbourne was adamant against it. The Prime Minister did not want to make the Government more radical. Durham, moreover, was 'dishonest and un-principled'. Any Cabinet that included him was bound to break up; but if 'met finally' outside of it, he would prove to be 'nothing'. Besides, though they did not mention Palmerston in their correspondence, it would have been a pity to remove him when he got on so well with the Queen, and, after the death in November of his younger sister, Mrs Sulivan, too cruel a blow to add.[58]

If a sacrifice were needed from among Melbourne's Cabinet there were better ones at hand than Palmerston. Thomson, at the Board of Trade, was in Melbourne's view 'a man of little use & much unpopularity, . . . troublesome, always dissatisfied, inefficient in parliament'. 'If he were to choose to go', the Prime Minister concluded, 'I should have no objection.' Then there was Spring Rice at the Exchequer, 'cautious from timidity' according to Hob-house, and in the view of some on the fringe of the Cabinet 'false, palavering, and evil'. But the universal favourite for a shift was the Colonial Secretary, Glenelg. An amiable man, with considerable ability and powers of speechify-ing, he was still too sparing of both. Hobhouse did not think him lazy, merely too slow and scrupulous. Characteristically, Melbourne thought he had been the best Colonial Secretary they had had for some time, for, he explained to Hobhouse, 'he did less than anyone else'. When the news reached England in December that rebellion had broken out in Canada, Russell and Howick both urged that something must be done to strengthen the Colonial Office. The simplest solution, they each suggested, would be for Russell to exchange his office with Glenelg. Melbourne again refused. Instead he sought to reassure them that the Canadians would be fairly but deliberately dealt with by persuading Durham to go out as their first Governor-General. This seemed to have the usual merit of getting Durham out of the way, but whatever he may have done for Canada his departure merely postponed the rifts within the Cabinet.[59]

By his free-handed acts in Canada Durham got the Government in London into trouble again and again in 1838. He outraged moral opinion by his choice of personal staff and constitutional delicacy by his proclamations, and when the Government tried to bring him back to some sense of order he angrily resigned. All this very naturally led Russell in October 1838 to revive the call for the strengthening of the authority of the Colonial Office by Glenelg's removal. Once again it was by exchanging offices he hoped to do it, though this time not on the basis of equality. Instead, he thought that the ill health of the Comptroller-General of the Exchequer would soon provide a comfortable and lifelong alternative for Glenelg and that then they would bring Carlisle's son, Morpeth, into the Cabinet. But Morpeth, who was Irish Secretary, could hardly be promoted over the head of his Lord Lieutenant, the vain and ambitious Normanby, who wanted to leave Ireland in any case. Normanby's solution was for himself to have the Home Office and Russell either Glenelg's or Palmerston's place. But Russell told Melbourne that he had 'not the smallest wish to deprive Palmerston of an office he fills so well, & likes so much'. Indeed, if Glenelg were to go, Russell thought Palmerston could look after both offices until some permanent solution could be worked out.[60]

For a while domestic tragedy intervened with both Russell and Palmerston. At the beginning of November 1838 Russell's first wife died and at the end Palmerston's elder sister. Both took their losses very hard. As everyone acknowledged, Palmerston was extremely affectionate to his family and, as he himself told Shee, losing Fanny so soon after Lilly made it all the harder: 'It is as if half myself had ceased to exist; it is the cutting off of all the dearest & tenderest recollections of one's past life & earliest years. I trust, however, . . . that these misfortunes may tend to improve the temper of my mind, & lead my thoughts & feelings more towards things of a more lasting nature than the joys & the sorrows of this life.' It was an unusual sentiment for Palmerston; but patently sincere. He tried to keep up with his work, but for once at least found it too difficult a task. His colleagues noticed his absence from Cabinets and soon he was compelled to seek a few weeks' rest at Broadlands among what he called the remnants of his family, the Sulivans and Bowles. Palmerston's double loss seems to have inspired some equally unusual sympathy in Melbourne and, far from making Palmerston a victim of any Cabinet reshuffle, he contemplated giving him first refusal of the lead if Russell insisted on giving it up. 'He would do it well', he told Holland, 'with John's assistance upon internal affairs.'[61]

Palmerston had certainly been making a better impression in Commons debates in recent years. Of one on Spain in February 1836 Howick wrote, 'Palmerston and Hobhouse both spoke very ill.' But Holland said Palmerston's recent speeches had all done him 'great credit', and of another on Spain in April 1837 even Bedford and Byng agreed with him that it had been 'triumphant'. In December 1837 Hobhouse was even saying that 'Palmerston spoke well, as he always does', and at worst in June 1838 that since he had the gout he had not spoken 'so well as usual'. Due allowance must be made for the need of Palmerston's friends and colleagues to see him doing well. Yet in August 1839 even Howick talked of his having made 'a most excellent speech' on the slave trade and in April 1840 'much to my surprise . . . a most admirable' one on China.[62]

Clearly there had been a considerable improvement in Palmerston's speech-ifying, though one due more to the confidence gained from growing familiar-ity with his subject than to anything more radical. The essential weakness of his style remained – a monotonous tone and a hesitating manner. However, Leveson noted with uncharacteristic shrewdness about the China speech, 'Lord Palmerston spoke admirably as indeed I think he always does on a great occasion.' Great political issues and crises, as opposed to personal attacks, tended always to bring out the best in Palmerston. So Melbourne's suggestion in December 1838 of giving him the lead that he had avoided offering directly in November 1834 was not really surprising. It was also true that the loss of his wife did make Russell think of giving something up rather than taking on more.[63]

In the New Year both bereaved ministers recovered something of their spirits. 'I was near 3 weeks at Broadlands, and took a course of hunting & shooting medicinally, and with perfect success,' wrote Palmerston; '& have returned to town in very good health.' Russell, for his part, returned with still more determination to the problem of the Colonial Office. Howick, however, struck first, declaring his intention to resign when the Cabinet endorsed a policy for Jamaica which Glenelg proposed and he deplored. Curiously, in view of the poor relations between them, Palmerston went first to remonstrate with Howick and presumably failed. He was followed by Russell, who per-suaded Howick to stay, but made Melbourne choose between Glenelg or himself. Faced with such a threat, the choice Melbourne made was inevitable. The story went around the F.O. that it was Glenelg's old colleague Palmerston who told him he was to go; 'et tu Brute,' Scott muttered in his diary.[64]

Palmerston, in fact, would much rather the stiff and bad-tempered Howick had gone than either Russell or Glenelg. When Howick had made trouble over Glenelg's instructions to Durham the previous February, it was Palmerston in particular he remembered as having been 'excessively angry' with him. Much more recently Howick had opened up a bitter quarrel with Spring Rice over their respective spheres of departmental authority and as an old Secretary at War Palmerston had been called upon to mediate between them. By contrast, Palmerston and Glenelg were old comrades in arms and Palmerston had defended Glenelg with spirit in the Commons when his colleague was attacked on Canadian affairs in March 1838; and he had gone to Glenelg the following February not to betray him but to smooth things over. It was Melbourne who, quite properly as Prime Minister, had told Glenelg on 5 February he must go; but he had made an utter mess of it, letting something slip about more 'energy and activity being wanted at the Colonial Office', and neglecting to make it clear that Glenelg could have the Privy Seal instead. So Glenelg resigned and Palmerston went to see him later that day only to try and set things right. But if he managed to soothe Glenelg's feelings, he could not make him change his mind. Glenelg therefore went out of office in February 1839 and Normanby came in in his place.[65]

The replacement of Glenelg by Normanby was by no means the end of the Government's difficulties. Harried in the Lords about Ireland and in the Commons about Jamaica, more and more members of the Cabinet turned their thoughts to resignation. Palmerston, as usual, was all for pushing on. When the Cabinet met on 22 March 1839 to consider an adverse vote on Ireland in the Lords, the two new members, Normanby and Morpeth, were the most determined on resignation, Poulett Thomson and Palmerston the most 'vehemently against it'. It was decided to carry on and to seek a vote in the Commons in answer to the Lords. After it was successfully carried Palmerston wrote to Lamb (who had just been raised to the peerage as Baron Beauvale while Ponsonby became a viscount): 'we have weathered our late storm, and shall probably have comparatively speaking smooth water for the rest of the Session; at all events I do not think there is any danger of our foundering yet awhile.' It was an extraordinarily smug assertion – and quite unjustified. A fortnight later Peel's attack on the Jamaica Bill reached its climax and the Government scraped through in the early hours of 7 May by a mere five votes, eleven of those they ordinarily relied on voting against them. When the Cabinet met at noon the same day, Palmerston again 'rather wished to wait'. But only Hobhouse and Spring Rice, 'a little', supported him; the rest were all for resignation and in the end they decided so unanimously.[66]

As Hobhouse and Palmerston walked away together from the Commons on the evening after the Government's resignation on 7 May, they agreed that it had been brought about more by internal than external causes – by 'jealousies, discontents, weariness in one leader, laziness in another'. Hobhouse asked Palmerston if he intended to go ahead with an F.O. dinner he had arranged next day for the Tsarevitch. 'What! lose my place, and my dinner too?' Palmerston responded. So he had his dinner; nor did he expect to lose his place for long. Melbourne had been turned out, he concluded, 'by a Radical manoeuvre rather than by Tory force'. Peel would hold an election and perhaps gain a little by it. But then he would have even more trouble with his diehards than Melbourne with his radicals. At best, by pursuing a moderate course, he might hang on with Whig support. 'However all this is too remote a speculation,' Palmerston admitted to Lamb on 8 May; 'sufficient for the week are the events thereof.' He was wrong about that: within two days the Queen's refusal to change her household ladies had forced Peel to give up his task and left Melbourne's Government in.[67]

Peel's behaviour was a 'most miraculous blunder', Palmerston thought, and he was one of the strongest in the Cabinet for backing the Queen's decision. He was far from sure that they would be able to stay in for very long; people were inclined to think they would have to make still more concessions to the radicals in order to survive. In fact they were to have two more years of life. They were very different ones than heretofore, and their beginnings no more auspicious for Palmerston than for any other of his colleagues. After a long review of the state of the country and the Government's prospects, Greville had written in March:

Palmerston, the most enigmatical of Ministers, who is detested by the *Corps Diplomatique*, abhorred in his own office, unpopular in the H. of Commons, liked by nobody, abused by everybody, still reigns in his little kingdom of the Foreign Office, and is impervious to any sense of shame from the obloquy that has been cast upon him, and apparently not troubling himself about the affairs of the Government generally, which he leaves it to others to defend and uphold as they best may.

In mid 1839 there were many who agreed with Greville's opinions, exaggerated by spite and jealousy though they were. By 1841 they would not have changed their minds very much – except to admit that Palmerston's handling of the new Mehemet Ali crisis had brought him nonetheless a tremendous personal triumph.[68]

Palmerston always realized that the final crisis in the Near East might come from either Pasha or Sultan. With Mehemet Ali he was determined to be tough. When it was decided in December 1838 to check the Egyptians' advance into Arabia by occupying Aden, Palmerston had written to Hobhouse: 'Make no ceremonies with Mahomet Ali, nor be under any apprehension about offending him. Mahomet Ali would not dare move his little finger in hostility to England.' He also continued to suspect a secret alliance between Pasha and Tsar for the partition of the Turkish Empire. It was a strange idea. But, as Palmerston had pointed out in 1836, it hardly mattered if it were literally true or not: Egypt's expansion and Russia's counter-action in Constantinople would produce the same result. Nor, while his agents fell one by one under the Pasha's spell, did Palmerston change his mind about him. 'For my own part', Palmerston wrote in June 1839, 'I hate Mehemet Ali, whom I consider as nothing but an ignorant barbarian, who by cunning and boldness and mother-wit, has been successful in rebellion; . . . I look upon his boasted civilization of Egypt as the arrantest humbug; and I believe that he is as great a tyrant and oppressor as ever made a people wretched.' By contrast, Palmerston could see no reason why the Sultan's empire should not in turn 'become again a respectable Power'. He did not expect dramatic results. But to talk about its 'being a dead body or a sapless trunk, and so forth', he believed, was 'pure and unadulterated nonsense'. However, improvement would take a good deal of time, and though he could not deny the Sultan's right to punish his rebellious Pasha, he would rather he did not do so yet. He was prepared, if pressed, to conclude a defensive treaty and in March 1839 was able to say that the Cabinet would agree to it. But that was no longer enough for the Sultan. Towards the end of April he launched his army into Syria; six weeks later it was routed by the Egyptians and his fleet went over to Mehemet.[69]

Palmerston's first thought, as soon as he heard of the reopening of hostilities, was to take steps to prevent Russia exploiting the situation in Constantinople; he even contemplated ordering the Navy to move into the Dardanelles in case the Sultan should invoke the Treaty of Unkiar Skelessi. But he did not propose to revive the notion of an Anglo-French guarantee even though the objectionable Molé had just been displaced. Possibly this was because the Cabinet had upset that plan so many times before. In any case it was soon to seem unnecessary, as Soult proved himself a 'jewel' by quickly agreeing to naval cooperation with England and by putting pressure on the Egyptians to keep their armies in check. At the same time Metternich displayed unusual enterprise and energy in organizing a diplomatic effort to contain the Near Eastern crisis and to prevent a breach between Russia and the Western powers. Palmerston was delighted to see him so active. 'He deserves the highest praise,' he wrote to Beauvale. 'His line is bold and statesmanlike, and cannot fail to be successful.' It must have been obvious to Palmerston that Metternich had it also in mind to make himself indispensable and Vienna the centre of things. But with disaster after disaster befalling the Sultan, Palmerston preferred action to disagreement and recognized that Vienna was better placed by geography to concert it; Beauvale, he hoped, would have skill and influence enough to keep Metternich on the right lines.[70]

When, in response to Metternich's initiative, the ambassadors of the five powers drew up a joint note to the Porte on 27 July 1839 claiming that the settlement of the crisis belonged to the European concert, it really looked as though Metternich's promise of managing Russia while Palmerston managed France was really going to work. But while Metternich wanted merely to smooth over the immediate crisis, Palmerston was determined upon a final and permanent settlement and this, he had already decided, must be achieved by the withdrawal of the Egyptians from Syria. Mehemet Ali's family might be conceded the hereditary possession of Egypt but only by their giving up Syria would the threat to Constantinople be removed and the Sultan relieved of all necessity for invoking his treaty with Russia.[71]

Palmerston had outlined his objectives at the first Cabinet on 15 June, saying that he thought France, in spite of her sympathy for Mehemet Ali, would be brought to agree out of fear of Russia exploiting the crisis. For some time he continued to think it would work out that way, since the French and all the other powers more or less indicated that they agreed the Sultan should have Syria back. When, in the middle of July, the French proposed a five-power guarantee of Turkey's 'independence and integrity', he was again absolutely delighted with Soult, 'a capital fellow', so much better than that 'tricky, narrow minded, slippery, unstatesmanlike pedant', Molé. So at the beginning of August he still thought them all in agreement enough for either Metternich or himself to press on with Soult's proposal and so 'neutralize' the Treaty of Unkiar Skelessi and make it 'sink into nothing'. But beyond attempting to bring about an immediate cessation of hostilities, the powers were much less in concert than he thought.[72]

Granville and Holland both tried to impress upon Palmerston that the French in particular were far from committed to his point of view. After all, the Egyptians had neither begun this new war nor been defeated in it and French opinion would not tolerate their being treated like defeated aggressors. France had already noted with disapproval that to bring hostilities to an end the British squadron had been empowered to act more aggressively against the Egyptians than the Turks. Nor, since even the Turks did not insist upon it, did she see why Mehemet should be deprived of Syria in his lifetime; even when he died, she thought, it might be divided among his sons. In any event the French could not possibly lend themselves to using force, whether to take back Syria or the Turkish fleet, either now or in the future.[73]

Palmerston, and surely he was right, felt very strongly that if the powers did not act immediately about Syria they never would. As for dividing Syria among the Pasha's sons, that would be the surest way of accelerating the final break-up of the Sultan's empire. So before the end of August he had come to the conclusion that he must press on with his plans, with or without French cooperation. His main reliance was on Metternich and Austria, and on 25 August he instructed Beauvale to say, officially if necessary, that Austria and England should act together to force the Pasha to give up at once both Syria and the Sultan's fleet. 'We wish to act with the Four,' he explained in an accompanying private letter, 'but will act with Three or with Two.' He still believed Louis Philippe and Soult would give way, he said, but if Austria and England did not act quickly the 'Gallo-Egyptian interest' in France would grow in strength and force their Government to side openly with the Egyptians and so threaten the break-up of the Turkish Empire.[74]

Before the end of August 1839, then, Palmerston had taken a decisive step towards settling the Near Eastern crisis in defiance of France. But he had not yet found the partner he knew he had to have. For Metternich had already got cold feet. His anxiety all along had been less to contrive a final solution of the Egyptian problem than to rebuild the ascendancy of Vienna by damping matters down. It was vital to him, therefore, to keep well with Russia while drawing England closer; and to his horror he had found that the Tsar considered his Vienna concert to be aimed against Russia and a betrayal of the neo-Holy Alliance. Metternich, consequently, beat a rapid retreat to his family estates and left to others the task of settling the crisis and rebuilding Austro-Russian friendship.[75]

Things seemed to be going as badly for Palmerston as for Metternich. The alignments with both France and Austria had failed him. Nor would the

Cabinet allow him to act alone. When Hobhouse had proposed at the meeting on 15 June that England should immediately seize the Egyptian fleet, 'this suggestion was denounced as an Indian mode of warfare'; when at that of 27 July he hinted they ought to send a force of 10,000 men to seize the Pashalik of Baghdad, 'Melbourne looked up with a significant smile'. After the breach with France had become clear they were even less keen on direct action. When Palmerston tried to get them to face up to the situation at a meeting on 17 September, they would agree only to one thing, that if France would not cooperate then there was to be no question of recovering the Turkish fleet by force. And as far as the possession of Syria was concerned they were no doubt inclined to agree with Russell that England must concede it to Mehemet Ali and his heirs as well. The important thing, Russell felt, was to prevent France going even further in support of the Egyptians. 'In fact', he concluded, 'no power but Russia can keep Mehemet Ali out of Syria, & she would only do it at the price of Turkish independence.' But this was precisely where he was wrong.[76]

There had long been differences of opinion in Russia between the protagonists of forward and defensive policies in the East. In the view of the Russian Chancellor, Nesselrode, the real merit of Unkiar Skelessi was the protection it gave Russia in the Black Sea, not the opportunity in the Mediterranean. He had also been trying to impose the same view in Persia and central Asia, where the deception or indiscipline of local agents had brought Russia on to a collision course with England. The aggressive Russian agents who had so annoyed the British in Persia had already been recalled, and a definite decision made not to encourage opposition to the British in Afghanistan. But Nesselrode had not been able to do more than limit the objectives of Russia's expedition against Khiva or persuade Palmerston to come to an explicit understanding on having buffer states between India and Russia. So an alarming degree of distrust and danger remained in central Asia. At the same time England, France and even Austria seemed to be moving into an alignment over the Eastern crisis that was more anti-Russian than anything else; and while their fleets had been given contingent orders to pass through the Straits, Palmerston had time and time again told the Russians that they would never again be allowed to do the same. Yet Russia feared the first more than she wanted the second. So, Nesselrode suggested to the Tsar in August 1839, why not break up the hostile alignment by offering to England to give up Unkiar Skelessi and to replace it with the more general European agreement he claimed he wanted? In that event they would both secure their vital *defensive* interest, the closure of the Straits. Since he was so angry with Metternich, the Tsar rejected the Austrian proposal for a conference in Vienna and quickly agreed to Nesselrode's idea of an approach to London; and when he heard that France and England were quarrelling it seemed all the more desirable, as a means of keeping them apart. So in the middle of

September Baron Brunnow arrived in London to offer assurances about Khiva and a deal over the Straits.[77]

The Russian approach may have rescued Palmerston from a deteriorating position, but he already knew that Russia was a possible alternative to either France or Austria. 'I find Russia is courting us,' he had ended his letter to Beauvale on 25 August. 'The Emperor has sent the Queen a great malachite vase from the Hermitage, which I am told is the most magnificent thing of the kind that exists.' When he knew that a special mission was also on its way, his first thought seems to have been that it would revive Metternich and frighten France. He did go out of his way to let the French know that 'instead of wanting their aid to keep Russia in check, we shall probably have the aid of Russia to do without them'. But he was well aware that Russia was seeking to separate England from France, and his own objective, he explained to Beauvale, was still to bring them back together. This objective, however, soon took second place after Brunnow's arrival.[78]

Immediately after his arrival in England on 15 September Brunnow went to pay his master's respects to the Queen at Windsor. Palmerston and Melbourne also happened to be at the Castle but each saw Brunnow separately, on 19 and 20 September, and did not have a chance to talk together until after Brunnow had left on the morning of the twentieth. So, luckily, Palmerston provided Melbourne with a couple of letters and a memorandum of how things were going. It is not clear that he had had any serious discussions with Brunnow when he sent his first letter and memorandum of proposals, dated 19 September. But he intended to propose, when he and Brunnow met that afternoon, a specific plan of coercion should Mehemet Ali refuse to accept Egypt alone. It envisaged naval measures in the first instance, but if necessary the landing of troops in Egypt and, in order to prevent Ibrahim's army marching upon Constantinople, even Russians in Asia Minor. And, Palmerston believed, they should go ahead with the plan even if France refused, though like the Egyptians he expected her to knuckle under at the threat itself. When he met Brunnow later that afternoon things seemed to go as well as he could possibly have wished. The Tsar proposed, he learned, that the other three (or four) powers should operate in the Mediterranean, while his forces acted exclusively in the Straits; he would object, Brunnow insisted, even to a token British force there. But he would act in the name of the concert and to underline it he was perfectly willing to make an agreement for the future closure of both Straits (the Bosphorus and the Dardanelles) and to agree not to renew the Treaty of Unkiar Skelessi when it expired.[79]

Palmerston was absolutely delighted with his discussions. That he was no longer so alarmed about prospective Russian operations in the Straits was probably in part because he thought they would never turn out to be necessary. In any case the burial of Unkiar Skelessi in a European Straits convention was worth the risk. He knew that the closing of the Straits would be to England's advantage, since when the Sultan was at peace it would prevent

Russia reaching into the Mediterranean, but when he was at war with Russia it would not stop him calling for Britain's naval aid and letting it pass into the Black Sea. All that was needed to round off the settlement, Palmerston therefore thought, was a ten-year agreement between the powers to maintain the independence and integrity of the Turkish Empire; and within the next few days, apparently, he got the impression from Brunnow that this too would be conceded.[80]

Palmerston was wrong about the Russians making any further concessions. In any case he had a heavy task ahead of him to persuade his colleagues. For it remained to overcome both the russophobia he had done so much to stimulate in recent years and the francophilia many of his colleagues still retained. Melbourne had told him at once that the plan he had put to Brunnow was 'of vast importance & very difficult'. Palmerston was well aware of this. Even while he was at Windsor he had received a letter from Morpeth, who was at Chatsworth with his uncle Granville, that positively exuded fear of a breach with France; and the previous week Russell had warned him how vital it would be to have Austria so materially committed as to guard against a Russian betrayal in the Near East. So immediately after quitting Windsor Palmerston took care to communicate with both the Austrian and French ambassadors. Esterhazy, he later said, was 'perfect' throughout; but Sébastiani 'seemed little pleased' and reverted to the plan of giving the Pasha part of Syria.[81]

It was always clear that no final decision could be made about the Russian approach without full consultation with the other ministers. When the news arrived a few days after Brunnow's initial conversations that force was also likely to be required to compel a due respect for British subjects and British trade in China, Melbourne decided to summon as many of the Cabinet as he could to Windsor. It was decided to have it at Windsor because there was going to be a Privy Council on the morning of 30 September to swear in a new Secretary at War. Howick's vanity and bad temper had finally got the better of him when he found that Melbourne intended to strengthen the Colonial Office, not by putting him in place of Normanby (who had proved no better than Glenelg), but by an exchange of offices with Russell. He had therefore finally resigned and been replaced by Macaulay. Macaulay was sworn in in the morning; immediately after lunch the Cabinet met in Melbourne's room.[82]

There were eight members present at the crucial Cabinet meeting of 30 September 1839 – Hobhouse, Russell, Cottenham (the Lord Chancellor), Baring and Labouchere (who in August had replaced respectively Spring Rice at the Exchequer and Poulett Thomson at the Board of Trade), and of course Macaulay, Palmerston and Melbourne. Duncannon (Privy Seal), Lansdowne, Normanby, Minto and Morpeth were the absentees. But at least Minto, like Morpeth, had already made his views known in writing: unlike Morpeth, he was in favour of the agreement but did not approve of leaving the Russians in 'sole charge of Constantinople'. The last remaining member, Holland, did not write since he intended being at the Cabinet, but the night before there was a fire at Lilford, where he was staying with his son-in-law, and though the session was a long one, he arrived half an hour too late. When Holland afterwards complained that Palmerston had got England into a dreadful tangle with France, Melbourne several times told him that things might have been very different if he had arrived in time.[83]

Melbourne may have exaggerated Holland's weight, but he was right about the importance of the meeting which has usually been both misunderstood and misrepresented. Palmerston began by proposing, not his own plan of 19 September, but Brunnow's. He explained how Austria and Prussia both seemed ready to accept, and how France did not. He particularly stressed Russia's friendly behaviour – her readiness 'virtually to do away with the treaty of Unkiar Skelessi' and, what seems to have been due to a partial misunderstanding on his part, to agree to the idea of a ten-year treaty of guarantee. On the other hand, he emphasized France's 'exceedingly jealous' attitude towards English policy. The discussion was very long – it went on till nearly six so that China had to be left over for a further meeting the next day – and it ended by deciding that Palmerston should ask Brunnow for a modification of Russia's plan so as to permit a 'small' British and French squadron to act in the Dardanelles if Russia entered the Bosphorus. This was the 'token' concession Palmerston had initially sought himself, though one he had called 'childish' when Sébastiani also asked for it. Otherwise, the Cabinet agreed, the plan proposed by Russia should be adopted by all the five powers in order, according to Hobhouse's record, 'in some way or other [to] dispossess Meh. Ali of Syria & secure Egypt to him and his family'. So it is very misleading to say that the Cabinet 'unanimously rejected' Palmerston's plan.[84]

Melbourne, and the Lord Chancellor, had begun by wishing to leave the Pasha with Syria as well as Egypt. Labouchere had said little and Baring nothing. But Macaulay 'talked a good deal & rather anti-Russian' – as he was to talk anti-Chinese the following day; so much so, indeed, that, Labouchere whispered to Hobhouse, 'if he was always so powerful in talking, no business would be done'. More effectively perhaps, Palmerston, Russell and Hobhouse strongly urged the necessity of dispossessing the Pasha of Syria; Hobhouse, who also reported assurances from Brunnow about Persia, even urged an English attack on Alexandria, though he was supported in this only by Palmerston himself. In the end Melbourne came round to saying that Mehemet Ali would have to be expelled from Syria, if necessary without the cooperation of France. To that extent, then, the Cabinet of 30 September had reached a vital turning point, as both Melbourne and Palmerston afterwards acknowledged. But as usual no explicit decision was made on what several members considered a contingent, and undesirable, possibility. What was explicit was the decision to attempt to tie up Austria by getting her forces also involved and to enlist France in the Russian project by returning to the idea of what Brunnow had called 'a naval pic-nic' in the Straits.[85]

Although the Cabinet of 30 September 1839 was really vital, it was not in itself decisive. Instead there followed a nine-month delay while Palmerston tried to get Russia and France to agree to the revised plan and Austria to blow more hot than cold. As far as Russia was concerned, the initial delay seems to have been due to a misunderstanding. Brunnow told Palmerston he had no authority to agree to the 'naval pic-nic' and returned to his post in Stuttgart; and while Palmerston waited to hear something from St Petersburg, Nicholas waited to hear something from London. At length, it became clear what had gone wrong. Palmerston wrote the necessary dispatch to Russia; the Tsar consented to the picnic; and in December Brunnow returned to England to arrange the necessary convention.[86]

Two days before Brunnow landed in England again, Emily had at last married Palmerston. They had kept their plans extraordinarily quiet. To her friends Emily kept hinting at her doubts long after she must have promised to make herself his officially; while with his friends Palmerston was so silent and secretive as to offend Sulivan and to forget whether or not he had told Shee. In the F.O. the rumour only reached them late in November. On the day itself Mrs Backhouse wrote to her daughter: 'Lord Palmerston is married *today*; he wrote to papa last night, past 11 o'clock to desire him to send the boxes after him. These were the words of his note "I go to Broadlands tomorrow after my marriage, and intend staying about ten days". That was all he said about it.' Others, naturally, said a good deal more. Graham, rather wickedly, wrote: 'How strange will be Palmerston's Honey-Moon! There will be nothing new about it except the marriage vow which they both know does not bind them.' Holland, a more kindly man, looked forward to marriage 'softening' Palmerston and by bringing a hostess to the F.O. making him more accessible to diplomats and travellers, especially those who might correct his views on Egypt.[87]

Palmerston was certainly made more accessible, even on his honeymoon. But it was not any admirer of Mehemet Ali's he allowed to break in upon them at Broadlands and to pre-empt the first Christmas of his married life, but Brunnow and Neumann. Brunnow had hoped to concert with Esterhazy and bring him back to London with him, but as usual the Austrian ambassador was too busy with his private affairs and Metternich sent Neumann instead. This time there were no complaints from Palmerston, who always knew better than to make a fuss when things were going his way. At Broadlands, between 23 and 26 December, the three of them patched up an agreement on the East. It was full of holes: the Russians said nothing about a guarantee for Turkey; they seemed to think that the Sultan should agree to close the Straits in both peace and war; and they insisted that any agreement about the Straits was dependent on one about joint coercion and vice versa. All this was to give Palmerston considerable trouble, not least because it gave Metternich plenty of opportunity to revive his doubts. But Palmerston's difficulties with Austria and Russia were far less than those with France.[88]

Palmerston made concession after concession to persuade the French to join the Anglo-Russian project. But it was all to no avail. When he told them the modification about the Straits had been made in deference to France, they told him plainly that they would not consent to coercion at all, and when he offered a life tenure for Mehemet of a token part of Syria they rejected it with contempt. When they heard of the Tsar's consent to the naval picnic, they professed to be delighted at Russia's 'surrender'; but when in January 1840 Palmerston formally proposed the plan, it was again immediately rejected. Palmerston tried to draw further concessions, to have, not token English and French forces in the Straits, but ones that were equal to the Russian, and to begin with a rather more limited coercion against Mehemet Ali. These too made no impression. Nor did the replacement of Sébastiani in London by Guizot. Guizot was delayed in Paris until the end of February by the political crisis that brought down Soult, and when Princess Lieven followed him to London in June she certainly did not help. Just before she arrived Brunnow handed Lady Palmerston a list of Russians to whom he wished her, as the Foreign Secretary's wife, to be civil and obliging, and added afterwards: 'there is another, Mme de Lieven, too, but I am not anxious that you should put yourself much out of the way for her.' Fanny Jocelyn burst into a loud roar of laughter, much to the consternation of the ambassador, who could not quite make out why. Thiers, as Soult's successor, claimed it was his wish to preserve the *entente cordiale*. So when he asked for the return of Napoleon's body from St Helena, Palmerston readily agreed. 'This will amuse the public mind for six months to come and make those full grown children think less of other things,' he wrote. But when he offered to let Mehemet Ali have much more of Syria for his lifetime, Thiers at length refused that too. Privately Thiers believed there would have to be a compromise in the end and that Mehemet Ali must understand that France would not sacrifice her alliance with England for any 'unreasonable pretensions' of his. He was gambling on delaying things long enough to get as much as possible for the Pasha, and on France's friends in the English Cabinet overruling Palmerston.[89]

Palmerston was all along aware that it was in London that the French hoped his policy would be overcome. Personally he no longer cared whether France went with the rest of the powers or not, though he expected her to follow in the end where the others led. The difficulty was to persuade his colleagues, who valued so the Anglo-French entente and doubted that France would ever consent to coercion, that England must go ahead without her in the first place. He seems to have tried to force the issue early on by sending to Granville on 29 October 1839 – without any consultation even with Melbourne – a dispatch which summarized French policy in very offensive terms and ordered him to communicate it to the French Government! No doubt Palmerston expected the French to respond in a way that would make further negotiations impossible and force his colleagues, whether they liked it or not, to face up to the fact. But thanks to Granville his attempt completely misfired. Influenced as he naturally was by what he had heard in Paris, Granville did not believe that either the Pasha or the French would give way to Palmerston's demands, and the result, he feared, would be rupture and even war. So strongly did he feel this that he neglected to communicate Palmerston's dispatch to the French Government and wrote back to London begging him to send him out a more gently worded version. Just in case of difficulty he also went behind Palmerston's back. While on leave at Chatsworth a short time before he had already worked hard to sway his nephew Morpeth, even though he knew Palmerston would regard it as a betrayal and had refused to say anything about it on paper. But he did not have the same hesitation about writing to Holland. His anguished letters continued after he had returned to Paris, and when he received Palmerston's dispatch of 29 October he immediately reported it to Holland House.[90]

Like Howick, Holland had also noticed some time earlier that Palmerston was no longer so scrupulous in keeping his colleagues informed. In February 1837 he had noted that Palmerston was showing him communications to the French only after they had already been sent. More recently, he knew, many incoming reports were not being circulated early enough, or even at all. In October Holland also adverted to a lack of Cabinet meetings and to Palmerston's neglect in making contacts of any kind with his colleagues. Later, when Melbourne chided him for having missed the Windsor Cabinet, he recorded in his journal that the Prime Minister had always misled him about that Cabinet by saying that 'nothing was definitively settled . . ., that . . . there would [be] no embarrassment and above all no necessity of coercion or war whatever . . . [and] that by temporizing and leaving things to chance, we should very possibly hear no more of it'. Armed as he was by Granville's warnings, Holland did, as he recalled, press his doubts 'repeatedly' on Palmerston and 'usque ad nauseam' on Melbourne. But Palmerston, while always sending 'civil, long, elaborate' answers by return, nonetheless insisted that he would ultimately achieve a complete success both in persuading France and in coercing the Pasha, and Melbourne, while very much sharing Holland's opinions, bade him be quiet.[91]

Melbourne's advice was futile, though Holland used it as an excuse for the failure of his efforts. These Webster wrote off as merely foolish. It was true that Palmerston, while sending long and civil replies, filed Holland's epistles with curt and crude endorsements. They were 'twaddling' and 'wrongheaded', he noted. He also sent back to Holland some caricatures of the Pasha's 'ugly face', to frighten him, Holland suggested, out of his wits. But by being so well informed – he even found out that the admiral in the eastern Mediterranean

believed Mehemet Ali should be supported as the only man capable of
defending Constantinople against the Russians – Holland put up a resistance
to Palmerston that was more than merely irritating. He certainly succeeded in
countering Palmerston's offensive dispatch of 29 October, by revealing its
existence very cautiously to Melbourne and getting him to soften it still more
than Granville had done.[92]

   Though an obstinate man himself, Palmerston was never slow to recognize
when he had been outmanoeuvred. Before long, and in spite of Holland's and
Granville's caution, he would realize how he had been thwarted. In any case
he had to put a brave face upon it. So while pointing to the Sultan's recent
announcement of a programme of reform as confirmation of Turkey's imminent regeneration and France's naval movements as proof of her ill will, he
nonetheless impressed Granville with his new-found 'candour & sense' and
persuaded Holland at least that he was bent on reconciliation after all. To his
more sympathetic correspondents, like Beauvale, Palmerston made it clear
that he still relied on the negotiations with Brunnow to bring matters to a
conclusion, with or without France. There was also the news of a rising in
Algeria to keep the French 'quiet'. Later he seriously suggested that Britain
give covert support to Abd-el-Kader. But the simultaneous news of Russia's
march on Khiva, he realized, would hardly help his powers of persuasion in
London, and Holland's intervention had ensured that he must continue with
conciliatory gestures to France, if only in the hope that she would reject them
and so demonstrate the futility of seeking her cooperation. In any case there
was still a great deal to do to bring the Cabinet round to his point of view.[93]

   It did not help Palmerston's efforts to resolve the Eastern crisis that it
coincided with an avalanche of other foreign troubles – not only with France
in Africa and Latin America and, just as a definite if temporary triumph was
being achieved in Afghanistan, with Russia's advance on Khiva, but also with
China, Naples, Portugal and the United States. With the United States
Palmerston did not really expect things to get too bad. He was still basking in
the self-satisfaction of his Franco-American mediation. It was true that the
Texan revolt in 1836 and the Canadian rebellion in 1837 had aroused American expansionists and revived old differences on the frontiers. But Palmerston
was impressed with the moderation of President van Buren and personally
uninterested in adventurous schemes to contest American power. All this
would eventually change. But for the time being he was moderation itself.
When internal sectional differences in the United States led to the rejection of
Texan annexation, he was not really tempted by talk either side of the
Atlantic of fostering Texan independence as an entrepôt for British power and
trade. He knew that the United States must have Texas whenever they
wished; his main concern was to reconcile Mexico to her loss, thus ensuring
that another war did not cost her another defeat and the loss of yet more land.

He was also very sanguine about the long-standing boundary dispute between New Brunswick and Maine. He had been perfectly willing to accept arbitration, and no less so to forego it when the United States Government objected to the award made by the King of the Netherlands in 1831. Even when the other troubles on the frontier threatened to inflame it, his policy was merely to postpone the matter by arranging joint surveys and commissions of enquiry until American feelings were quietened down and British distractions had passed away.[94]

In China trouble had been brewing ever since the East India Company's monopoly of trade there had been abolished. For the protection of British traders then passed into the hands of British officials, whose status as the representatives of a notionally equal power the Chinese refused to accept. The assertion of Chinese superiority was itself unacceptable in turn to Britain and it became still more so when the Chinese authorities tried to suppress an opium trade they had so long connived at by methods which appeared illegal where Western observers considered Chinese law did not apply and arbitrary even where it did.

At first Palmerston seems to have tried to be scrupulously correct with Chinese officials and British traders alike. In 1836 he ordered his agent, Captain Charles Elliot, a cousin of Minto's, 'to avoid giving just cause of offence to the Chinese authorities' but at the same time to be 'very careful not to assume a greater degree of authority over British subjects . . . than that which you in reality possess'. So while he insisted on Elliot maintaining his dignity as representative of the Crown he also insisted on British subjects obeying Chinese laws. In both he was entirely unsuccessful and matters came to a head in 1838-9 when the Chinese authorities in Canton forced the British traders to surrender opium that was technically outside their territorial waters and British ships forcibly resisted their attempt to seize an accused sailor who was also outside their jurisdiction.[95]

Palmerston was afterwards blamed for having allowed matters to drift towards a direct clash and having let the British Government be manoeuvred into protecting an immoral trade. There was something in both accusations. But it had been impossible to tie down too tightly a responsible official operating in doubly difficult circumstances and thousands of miles away. It was also very difficult to tell when he had overstepped the bounds of prudence and discretion. But everyone in the Cabinet agreed that the limits of tolerance had been passed when they heard that the Chinese had obtained the merchants' opium from Elliot by force. A military response was therefore never in doubt. The only serious questions they had to consider were whether to fulfil Elliot's promise of British Government compensation to the merchants for voluntarily acceding to his 'agreement' with the Chinese and what should be the extent and objectives of the military expedition. Palmerston had no doubt that, however ill advised, Elliot's promise to the merchants must be met and that the Chinese in turn should compensate the British Government. He was also determined that Britain's commercial and political relations should be put on an acceptable basis once and for all and to ensure it by occupying a suitable island off the coast. He had little difficulty in getting his way – except from Elliot, who again tried to settle for less than his orders envisaged and was accordingly replaced. Hence the origins of the first Chinese War; 'Opium War' was a characterization Palmerston skilfully, though never quite conclusively, repudiated in debate both before and after the event.

The crucial decision to endorse hostilities against China was taken at the extended Windsor Cabinet on 1 October 1839. 'Before we separated', Hobhouse recorded, 'I whispered to Macaulay that the charges made against us of idleness could hardly be sustained; for at the first Cabinet which he had attended we had resolved upon a war with the master of Syria and Egypt, backed by France, and also on a war with the master of one third of the human race.' Though he did not think they had decided quite so much, Macaulay laughed at this. There was still more laughter when the Cabinet met on 11 April the following year for one of their debates on whether or not the time had come to press on in the Near East without waiting any longer for France. The discussion went on so long that even Hobhouse took up his hat to walk away. But Russell stopped him, saying, 'Stay, and you will hear of more wars & reprisals.' Sure enough, Palmerston then announced that he was about to send a 'strong letter' to Lisbon demanding the immediate payment of outstanding debts with interest due to British subjects and threatening 'strong measures' if this were not complied with.[96]

What Palmerston did not say, presumably, was that he had already sent a strong demand, threatening to seize the Portuguese colonies, and that this had been done in spite of serious doubts in the Treasury about the validity of the claims themselves. 'I am much strengthened in this impression', the Chancellor had written in October, 'from your not having sent us the opinion of the Queen's Advocate whom you usually consult in such matters.' It was Melbourne who insisted, after Palmerston's first threat was held up by the minister in Lisbon, on submitting the matter to the Cabinet. But when it came to the point all he said was that he deprecated going to war for money or commercial advantages but supposed they had no choice. 'I told you so,' Russell said to Hobhouse, when the matter was brought up. And no sooner had the matter been agreed than they were invited to consider sending a squadron to Naples, who by granting a monopoly to exploit sulphur mines in Sicily had apparently offended a most-favoured-nation treaty with England. 'You see how it is,' Russell said to Hobhouse. This time Palmerston too joined in the laughter.[97]

It was not as bad as it seemed. Palmerston's brother had been assured on the high authority of the Neapolitan Foreign Minister that, with a little encouragement, his master was sure to relent. But it was a quiet retreat King Ferdinand had wanted, having been bullied enough, in his opinion, by Palmerston over his refusal to permit a Protestant chapel in Naples and his treatment of his younger and rakish brother, Capua, who had been foolish enough to marry a commoner and a British subject. So pushed beyond his very limited endurance, Ferdinand exiled his Foreign Minister and defied the British Navy to do its worst. Palmerston saw very well the need of protecting both his brother William and himself from accusations of neglecting British interests. No doubt he also enjoyed the favour of liberal opinion by provoking an unpopular King. Some of his dispatches, Melbourne objected, read like recommendations for both a free Parliament and a free press. But before the British fleet had even begun to make reprisals Palmerston already knew the French had offered their mediation. It provided an opportunity for both sides to climb down with dignity. It was also a way for Palmerston to conciliate France without risking very much, since he knew that the Orléans had no wish to favour the French Bourbons, who happened to be the principal beneficiaries of the Sicilian monopoly.[98]

Hobhouse had left the Cabinet early on 11 April 1840, saying as he went 'it was really time to go – as I was certain that some of us would get hanged if we went on making war with one nation after another'. There was no war with either Portugal or Naples. The Portuguese claims were compromised in May and the sulphur monopoly rescinded soon after. But the Mehemet Ali question was certainly no joke, even within the walls of the Cabinet. Indeed, the argument there continued as bitterly as ever, throughout the whole of the first half of 1840, between those who wanted to pursue coercion at the price of the Anglo-French entente and those who wished to preserve the entente at the price of the Anglo-Russian rapprochement. Sébastiani and Guizot had all the help of Holland House; Palmerston that of Brunnow and Neumann. But it was a very unequal battle; for Neumann's connections were all with the Opposition. By the New Year it had become more unequal still with Clarendon's arrival in England to take Duncannon's place as Privy Seal (though Duncannon stayed in the Cabinet).[99]

After all his years of struggle and intrigue in Spain, Clarendon was by no means a friend of Louis Philippe's. But he was one of those who thought the Pasha of Egypt a better prospect than the Sultan, and on his way back from Madrid he had stopped in Paris to be further instructed by Granville and disarmed by Louis Philippe. There was a danger too, he told Greville, of 'Palmertson's getting too closely connected with Russia, while keeping France in check'. Before the end of January 1840 he was in communication with Holland and by March with Ellice.[100]

According to Lady Clarendon, her husband and Ellice had been brought only casually into contact over the Eastern question. The occasion of their correspondence in March was a long letter from Ellice's friend, George Dawson Damer, expounding Mehemet Ali's virtues. Holland sent long extracts of it, purportedly from 'An English Traveller', to Palmerston for circulation; and

Palmerston, to kill the idea, at once riddled it with contempt. It was also at this time that Palmerston pointed out to Holland that the issue had already been settled in principle at the Windsor Cabinet. But he evidently guessed that Clarendon had also had a copy of the traveller's letter and so sent him a copy of his retort as well. This led to a long exposition of his views from Clarendon, but also to a denial of any conspiracy with Ellice to displace Palmerston at the F.O. 'I saw in the *Morning Post* some time ago', Clarendon wrote, 'that my name was coupled with that of Ellice as being engaged in some intrigue against you; and although I know myself to be as incapable of an intrigue as of picking a pocket, yet others might not, and I was extremely annoyed by the slander.' In fact it was Ellice who had drawn his attention to the *Post*, only the week before. Ellice had also thought it worth-while to send him Damer's letter; and whether Clarendon was aiming at the F.O. or not, he was certainly encouraging Holland to complain of Palmerston to Melbourne, and Lady Clarendon was noting with satisfaction that 'the public' had for some time been pointing out her husband 'as the man for managing Foreign Affairs'.[101]

Clarendon had a considerable reputation as an unscrupulous adventurer and a regular intriguer. Young Leveson thought he stooped lower than his chief and dealt with 'adventurers and claimants' whom even Palmerston would scorn. Fred Lamb had long ago reported him to Melbourne as 'the only man of any cleverness' in the diplomatic line but 'of the dishonest and fanciful school . . . fitter for mischief than good'. Few did not believe he was plotting against the Foreign Secretary. Palmerston himself knew well enough from his old protégé's Spanish correspondence that he was as capable of intrigue as anyone ever could be. Perhaps he had even scented a plot early in the New Year. In the F.O. they had noticed before the end of January that 'some crisis' appeared to be hanging over him – 'at least', wrote Backhouse's son, 'I can in no other way account for that extraordinary degree of absorption & abstraction which engrosses him at present, and makes it next to impossible to get his attention to any ordinary business.'[102]

By March 1840 Palmerston was also preparing a counter-stroke to the intrigue against him. To make sure that Thiers's new Government was under no illusions and that Granville and his correspondents in England should have no false hopes, Palmerston warned his ambassador that while the French might 'talk big' they could not afford to make war. Granville also thought he recognized as one by his master a leader in the *Chronicle* that 'blasted' all his hopes. It seems really to have been written by Doyle; but it had Palmerston's entire approval. It was also at this time that Palmerston wrote to Shee to have some articles against Mehemet placed in the German press. Perhaps he had something too to do with the accusations in the *Post*. Holland and Granville certainly thought he suspected them all of plotting against him.[103]

At a Cabinet on 23 May Palmerston disposed of any doubt there might have been by making a formal complaint that some of his colleagues had talked to Ellice in such a way as to suggest that apart from Russell the Foreign Secretary 'stood alone' on the Eastern question. He added that Thomas Waghorn, a somewhat fanatical conveyor of mails across Egypt and therefore one of the Pasha's lobbyists, had also stated that no less than five members of the Cabinet had 'confessed' to him their dissent from Palmerston's policies. In the Cabinet Clarendon spoke up first. He had, he admitted, spoken to Waghorn, but not about his differences with Palmerston. Lansdowne, Hobhouse and either Labouchere or Macaulay said much the same. Holland said he had declined to meet Waghorn but confessed to having seen several other notorious 'Egyptians'. He also admitted, as Clarendon may not have done, that he had spoken to Ellice as well. Ellice, he said, no longer accused Palmerston as he used to do. But he agreed with him about Egypt. On the other hand Hobhouse, who had also spoken with Ellice, insisted he did not agree. What is more, he had added, he 'did not attach the least weight to any assertion made by Ellice. Ld M[elbourne] said the same & added that he had seen denials of facts in Ellice's handwriting which contained proof positive that the facts were true – his looseness & involuntary perversions made him utterly unsafe, yet he was a very good fellow & a great friend of the government.'[104]

Lady Palmerston also thought that Ellice was a 'very good fellow', though utterly unreliable and unscrupulous and, as she said when she heard he was getting married again in 1843, 'too great a fidget to make a comfortable husband'. Her brother too was playing a very curious game. Palmerston had told Hobhouse in November 1839 that 'Melbourne was a very odd fellow about some things & from a wish to avoid anything like exaggeration or importance fell into the contrary extreme of indifference & not attaching due weight to important events'. There was something in that; he was rather diffident by nature and the way his wife had hurt him, it was thought, had taught him not to show much feeling about anything in life. While he kept on telling Holland that there would in the end be no coercion, he also let Palmerston go on thinking there would. He said it was a deliberate plan, that Palmerston must be given time 'to retrace his steps and . . . that urging him strongly to change his course would make him persist in it more obstinately'. Yet at about the same time he told Palmerston that he had 'no doubt' that a 'large majority' of the Cabinet would go with him. They would 'do it with fear,' he went on, 'reluctantly & upon the ground that they are bound by what has already taken place'. But Clarendon, he thought, had grown more 'reasonable' and Holland 'much softened & anxious to keep things together'. He ended in June 1840 by saying of Holland to Palmerston pretty well what he had been saying of Palmerston to Holland: 'He now talks of a pretext or of something which will show if this measure leads to war, that he was against it.' Then, when in the following month Palmerston proposed to take him at his word, Melbourne turned right about. 'The more I think of the matter', he wrote, 'the more I am convinced that you will not be able to persuade a majority of the Cabinet to concur.'[105]

Melbourne's warning was occasioned by a proposal of Palmerston's to bring matters to a head by a final offer to France. Hitherto, perhaps, Palmerston had not been in any great hurry, though there was always the danger that Nicholas would lose his patience and Metternich his nerve. But in June 1840 there came news that Syria had risen in revolt against the Egyptians and that Ponsonby had final proof of France trying behind the backs of the other powers to induce the Turks to make a deal with Egypt. These, Palmerston thought, must finally convince his colleagues that Mehemet was a tyrant and Louis Philippe a rogue. At Austria's insistence further concessions were made to France, offering still more of Syria to Mehemet for his lifetime. But misled perhaps by Princess Lieven into thinking they still had time to manoeuvre, the French refused and to his satisfaction Palmerston found that Metternich as well as Nicholas now agreed that the other four powers must go ahead, if necessary without France.[106]

When at Palmerston's insistence the Cabinet met on 4, not 5, July 1840 – Saturday was Melbourne's usual day for Cabinets – it still proved impossible to come to an immediate decision. After first reviewing the state of the Neapolitan sulphur question – in which, incidentally, France's latest contribution he also showed up as 'very shabby' – Palmerston stated that the Egyptian question had 'arrived at a point which required immediate decisions'. France had 'positively refused' to cooperate in coercing the Pasha; Russia, Austria and Prussia were all willing to join with England, and without France, in compelling him to accept the hereditary possession of Egypt and Syria for his life. The question therefore was whether England should take the same line as France and leave the Sultan to be assisted by Russia, fight it out with the Pasha, or make a treaty with the other three powers guaranteeing Turkish integrity, but leaving the exact mode of doing so to 'future arrangements'. This last was Palmerston's choice.

In the ensuing discussions Baring, Labouchere and Macaulay (surprisingly) took no decided part. But inevitably Clarendon and Holland – who thought he had better information of Austria's intention to give only moral, not material assistance – 'protested against interference without France'. Russell and Minto, on the other hand, supported Palmerston, as did Hobhouse 'strongly'. Morpeth (and possibly Russell) suggested he would have been against coercion had he not felt the powers were all committed by their collective note of July 1839. Melbourne said he saw no harm in a treaty of guarantee, except that then there came the question, what did 'integrity' mean? Lansdowne, who said he had no objection to the treaty, otherwise said very little but felt they ought first to know rather more about the means of coercion anticipated. Consequently Palmerston read a memorandum detailing the measures the Russians had proposed. What exactly these were is not clear, but Holland immediately 'declared very strongly that nothing should induce him to be a party to such measures'. When therefore Normanby intervened to say that such an important matter ought not to be settled at once – after eight or nine months of argument – Melbourne seized upon the suggestion of delay and Palmerston reluctantly consented.[107]

As he left the meeting of 4 July Palmerston begged his colleagues 'that nothing might be said out of the Cabinet on the subject, as intriguers were at work in every direction'. That same evening, at an 'assembly' of Lady Palmerston's, the Prussian ambassador came up to Hobhouse and said: 'You have done a very bad thing today.' Perhaps it was this that determined Palmerston to force the issue more decisively and more quickly than he seems at first to have intended. Immediately after the Cabinet Melbourne had left it to him to arrange another meeting with Russell and they had settled on the afternoon of Wednesday the eighth. Palmerston had added in a postscript, however:

I look upon the question for decision to be, whether England is to remain a Substantive Power, or is to declare herself a dependency of France. In the event of the latter decision you had better abolish the office of Secy of State for Foreign Affairs and have in London an Under-Secy for the English Department deputed from the Foreign Office at Paris.

The following day, perhaps after hearing that Granville had arrived from Paris to confer at Holland House, he sent to Melbourne complaining of his colleagues revealing Cabinet disagreements and handing in his resignation. He had thought over the matter very carefully, he said, and had come to the conclusion that he could not consent again, as he had in 1833 and 1835, to be overruled on such a vital matter. It would make England 'subservient to the views of France for the accomplishment of purposes injurious to British interests'. The immediate result, when Russia went ahead alone, would be the Treaty of Unkiar Skelessi 'renewed under some still more objectionable form'; the ultimate result 'the practical division of the Turkish empire into two separate and independent states, whereof one will be the dependency of France, and the other a satellite of Russia'.[108]

Melbourne was evidently as much puzzled as concerned by Palmerston's resignation. He replied the following day that he did not think the majority of the Cabinet was so decisively against him as Palmerston implied and wondered why he could not wait till after they had had another meeting, especially as a simultaneous domestic crisis might by then have removed the problem anyhow by breaking up the Government. He added in a postscript that he would 'of course not mention the matter at present'. In fact, as soon as he had had a reply from Palmerston later that day, agreeing to wait till after the next meeting, Melbourne contacted both Clarendon and Holland, and probably Lansdowne and Russell as well. Russell, who had also consulted

Clarendon, made a last attempt to reconcile differing views by suggesting they make a four-power convention, not about coercion but about 'fair terms' for the Pasha.[109]

Nothing came of Russell's suggestion, though Melbourne commended it to Palmerston. This was probably because Palmerston already knew that both Clarendon and Holland were in retreat and had offered their resignations in place of his own. Holland offered to declare his 'age and infirmities' as the reason, lest the Government otherwise break up. But this was not good enough for Melbourne, who also sharply rebuked Clarendon for threatening a course that while giving way to Palmerston would simultaneously weaken his hand. So on the morning of 8 July Melbourne and Holland arranged between them that the dissentients' view might be recorded in a separate minute and then they crossed over the road together from No. 10 to the meeting of the Cabinet at 2 p.m.[110]

In presenting his case to the Cabinet of 8 July Palmerston, as Holland admitted, was 'very calm' throughout, but dwelt a good deal on the way the Syrian revolt had rendered the matter urgent and exhibited a 'sanguine assurance' of success if only England acted quickly. In the ensuing discussion many of the members kept entirely silent, but the meeting nonetheless went on till about 6 p.m. Holland and Clarendon naturally spoke most against a course they said would wreck the alliance with France, and two or three others, especially Morpeth, also expressed some hesitation about it. But Morpeth again emphasized that he considered England bound by her earlier decisions and Hobhouse and Minto, as usual, strongly supported Palmerston, while Melbourne and Russell (with reservations) both declared in his favour. There was no vote but, very unusually, Russell drew up a memorandum designed to serve as an authority for Palmerston to tell Brunnow that they were willing to go ahead without France, and Holland read a rough note which he afterwards circulated, reserving his final opinion until Palmerston had put his detailed proposals in writing. At the Cabinet on 11 July Palmerston still had only a rough draft of his proposed convention at hand. But he had already used the authority given him to begin negotiations on the ninth and these led to the signature of two conventions on the fifteenth. So at the next Cabinet on the eighteenth he presented his minute and Holland and Clarendon their joint protest. No one said anything about the protest except Hobhouse, who asked what was to be done with it. Lansdowne suggested it be left with Melbourne and, after they had been backdated, both papers were subsequently submitted to the Queen as minutes of the Cabinet of 8 July.[111]

The conventions of 15 July 1840 covered both the objectives and the means of the powers' intervention. They provided that Mehemet Ali was to be offered the hereditary possession of Egypt and the Pashalik of Acre for life. If he did not accept in ten days the offer of Acre was to be withdrawn and if not in a further ten days the hereditary possession of Egypt as well. Palmerston had moved with great speed. He also seemed rather elated. 'Lord P. continues very busy and over worked,' wrote his wife, 'but his health stands it – and the interest of his department is so great it carries him through.' At Holland House they even for a moment thought that, having won his point, he was prepared to be more friendly to the French. At the Cabinet on 11 July he had told Holland he had no objections to communicating the convention to Guizot, though only after it was signed and asking for his plain 'concurrence'.[112]

The French, and their English sympathizers, afterwards rested much of their resentment on Palmerston's failure to consult them beforehand. But as Palmerston then pointed out, while the Russians would have refused to go ahead if France had been at once brought in, the French had always insisted that they could not consent to what the others were in process of agreeing. He also maintained that while Guizot may not have had the precise details, he knew well enough what was going on. If he had been misled into false optimism, it was by Princess Lieven, who was only too glad to see the Anglo-French entente being wrecked. She was said afterwards to have assured the French ambassador, on the basis of information from Bulow, that there were no negotiations in train or that they would be upset by lack of instructions

The British Library of Political and Economic Science

'A Joculator! Or Teacher of Wonderful Animals' by HB (John Doyle), November 1840

from Berlin. But Palmerston had also got the representatives of the other powers to agree that action in the Near East could begin before the conventions were even ratified and sent off orders to the fleet the morning after they were signed. Whatever else he may have suspected, Guizot was badly upset by this. 'Guizot and Madame de Lieven have looked as cross as the devil for the last few days,' Palmerston wrote. Ten days later, when Palmerston asked him very insensitively to sign an anti-slave-trade treaty he had been working for for years, Thiers paid him back by saying the time was inappropriate.[113]

Although there were a good many bitter outbreaks from France and even active preparations for war, Thiers was gambling on a compromise and Palmerston was determined to call his bluff. Relying on an extravagant idea of Mehemet Ali's power of defence and delay, and on a rather less exaggerated notion of the doubts of the allies and of the English Cabinet, Thiers offered mediation to the Pasha in the hope of securing better terms for him and of recovering a little self-esteem for France. But having seized the initiative, Palmerston was determined to carry things through to a rapid conclusion. He remained remarkably cool and confident throughout. The Anglo-French alliance was dead, he knew, but the bluster in Paris was nothing but 'vanity' and the sabre-rattling there merely 'temporary swagger'. Louis Philippe openly admitted it, and secret intelligence confirmed it. If the allies held firm, French and Egyptians both would have to knuckle under. Unfortunately others, in Austria and Prussia as well as in England, were not so sure; and there was always the danger that public opinion might drive the French Government further than they wished. So in a dangerous inflationary spiral, fears about France stimulated doubts among Palmerston's colleagues about the wisdom of his policy and the increasing signs of doubt in England encouraged further resistance and bluff in France.[114]

During the first week of August 1840 Palmerston drafted a dispatch for Granville in which he forcefully justified his policy. When his colleagues saw it they all expressed their horror. 'Minutes of Timid Cabinet Ministers,' Palmerston endorsed their views a few years later. Holland wrote something incomprehensible about the draft; Russell objected to its 'tone'; and Morpeth suggested that it would be better to say nothing at all than to offer the French such 'irritating expressions'. Of the others, Cottenham, Duncannon, even Macaulay, all agreed with Morpeth. Clarendon and Normanby rather presumed Palmerston had already sent it off. He had not, however, and so it was withdrawn – but only for the moment, since he probably felt confident that things would work out pretty well as he wished when the Cabinet dispersed after the prorogation on 11 August. The Queen, worked on by her husband and her uncle, was apprehensive of trouble with France, but said she 'yielded to the majority of her Cabinet'. Melbourne was showing some uneasiness; but there was nothing new in that. Just before the Cabinet dispersed the Prime Minister received a letter from Spencer, who had taken time off from his cows to warn that there were 'not ten men' among the liberal party outside the

Cabinet who would support a war with France for the sake of the barbarian Turks and in alliance with Russia. But Palmerston easily brushed this aside, recalling his old colleague's fatuous behaviour in Grey's Cabinet and suggesting it was Ellice who had put him up to writing such a letter.[115]

Spencer was easily satisfied – though only for the moment – by the news of Palmerston's last and conciliatory speeches in Parliament. They encouraged Holland House and Clarendon as well. But Ellice, who had indeed been stirring up Spencer, was also agitating others, in particular John Russell. It was naturally not his first attempt. In March Russell had repulsed him by saying that England must support Turkey if the Pasha remained recalcitrant and in July the Colonial Secretary had been Palmerston's most important supporter. But Russell had always emphasized the desirability of conciliating France, his willingness to do so by leaving the Egyptians with Syria, and the importance of Austria's active cooperation. On all three counts his support for Palmerston was fragile. It was not made any firmer by the office he now held. For as Colonial Secretary Russell was worried about Canada and much more frightened than Palmerston that the United States might really go to war. He tended throughout to think that the F.O. was dragging its feet over the Maine boundary question; eventually he came to the conclusion that Palmerston was definitely playing it down in order to concentrate on Egypt, while he, Russell, wished to smooth over the Mehemet Ali question in order to concentrate on Maine.[116]

Ellice had been shrewd enough to mention the boundary question in his letter of March; whether he did so in August is not known. The second letter was in any case not enough to stop Russell leaving London, for having lost his first wife he had fallen in love with Minto's daughter and was anxious to go in her family's carriage when they left for the north on 13 August. But perhaps Ellice's letter preyed upon his mind; when they reached Naworth, Carlisle's place in Cumberland, he lingered there and even thought of returning to London, instead of going on to Minto, if matters did not improve. 'While there is any danger,' he explained to Minto, 'I think we are bound to be making every effort for peace on the one hand & for war on the other.'[117]

What Russell had in mind was some sort of conciliatory gesture to France combined with major naval reinforcements in the Mediterranean. Melbourne was puzzled by his behaviour, since he had hitherto understood Russell to be one of Palmerston's strongest supporters over the Eastern question. The Prime Minister nevertheless believed that there was much to be said in favour of his proposals. They were in fact very similar to what Wellington was advocating: Graham, who may have first suggested them, was in communication at this time with both Peel and Russell about the crisis. In any case the proposals very much appealed to Melbourne as a way of reconciling Opposition views, on both the Tory and Whig front benches, to Palmerston's policy. It also seemed a very favourable moment, with Leopold on a visit to Windsor and Guizot returned there after a quick consultation in Paris. Even Palmerston, Melbourne thought, was 'not averse'. But Guizot was still bent on getting Syria for

Mehemet's lifetime and when Palmerston discovered this he soon reverted to his tough line, if he had ever dreamed of relenting. Melbourne obviously must have been put right about it too. When Russell wrote again the Prime Minister replied that he did not think Palmerston would concur, though he did pass it on with an avowed approval. A few days later (31 August) Palmerston finally addressed a dispatch to Paris that put the French firmly in their place; Melbourne called it 'a capital paper'.[118]

Clarendon thought Melbourne really agreed with Palmerston's critics, but was afraid to tell him so. Russell, who knew much less about human frailty in anybody but himself, had simply taken him at his word. In mid August Russell had been told there was no need for him to come south until Guizot's new instructions were known; at the end of the month that he need not do so until some definite news had been received from the Levant. The first advice led him to go on to Minto after all; the second to stay a few more days, even though he read there another despondent letter of Spencer's which caused him to revive his proposals for conciliating France. But since he expected decisive news very shortly, he decided he could not be away much longer and at 7 a.m. on 3 September he set out for the south, leaving behind in writing at Minto the marriage proposal he had not ventured to make in person. The following evening he was at Windsor with Melbourne and Palmerston.[119]

What the three ministers said among themselves is unknown, though Russell had written to Palmerston shortly beforehand giving further details of his plan. All that one can be sure of is that Russell must have been in high dudgeon, while Palmerston was in great spirits. Russell received at Windsor a refusal from Lady Fanny Elliot, and Palmerston had just come back from seeing his horse Iliona win everything in Tiverton. Nor was Palmerston anything but pleased to hear that Mehemet Ali had rejected the allies' terms: it would leave them free to turn the Pasha out, he said. Palmerston got into a little trouble with Emily, who did not like being on her own at Broadlands, but he returned to her on 7 September, as soon as the Queen and F.O. business would let him, and stayed there for another week shooting partridges, concerting with Neumann, and waiting calmly for all the old 'twaddles', as he usually called any doubting admirals or diplomats, to bring Mehemet Ali to his knees. In the meantime, Russell, having dined at Holland House with Clarendon and Guizot two days before, on 10 September, sent Melbourne yet another plan of action and conciliation, this time saying that if it were not adopted he would not feel justified in taking a share of responsibility any longer. Then, on 15 September, having taken advice at Woburn, he explicitly threatened resignation.[120]

Russell went so far as to threaten resignation partly because he had concluded in the interval that Palmerston was interfering in military matters that were properly his own province as Colonial Secretary. He was also annoyed that Palmerston had not answered his latest conciliation proposals, though Melbourne had sent them on immediately to Broadlands with his commendation. Possibly, since they included a scheme to by-pass Ponsonby, Palmerston considered them impertinent. Emily became so alarmed that she urged Beauvale to come home to put more pressure on his brother and wondered at the same time if her husband should not 'give in a little'. Palmerston, however, had also not bothered to come up for a meeting of the Privy Council on the eleventh. Emily was his unnamed excuse. But he must have known the Cabinet members of the council would take the opportunity of discussing the crisis. Plainly he was in a rather cocky humour. On the other hand Russell also left for Woburn, though he must have known Palmerston would come up on the sixteenth for the ratification of his convention.[121]

Palmerston continued with Russell, both at a distance and via Melbourne, a contest of words very similar to the 'boxing match' he still kept up with Holland House. Palmerston had the best of both, reminding Melbourne that the Cabinet ought to give a fair chance to a policy they had long ago authorized and certainly not, like Holland, go gossiping all over the place against it. Finally, in a memorandum of 19 September – which, he said, he was 'perfectly ashamed of not having sooner sent' but had been too 'hunted by people & hailed upon' by dispatches to do so – he demolished Russell's proposals one by one. They were all based on a presumption of failure and no failures had yet been signalled or reported. Poor Melbourne hardly knew what to do. He begged Russell not to break up the Government by being 'precipitate'; Palmerston not to do so by failing to bring matters to a 'speedy termination'. He told Palmerston that the talking at Holland House was 'incredible' and that his arguments against Russell were 'quite conclusive'. But, he added, 'you calculate a little too much upon nations and individuals following reason'. So, when Russell persisted and asked for a Cabinet, Melbourne said he was quite right and summoned one for the twenty-eighth.[122]

While they waited for the Cabinet to assemble, ostensibly to decide whether or not to recall Parliament with a view to the possibility of war with France, Russell and his sympathizers made preparations for a showdown. Spencer encouraged him by saying that he was quite sure the majority of the Cabinet were for peace and that if Palmerston resigned the Ministry could survive it. Shortly afterwards Hume wrote to show he had radical support as well. Russell was still more encouraged by hearing that the French had been pressing a compromise on Mehemet Ali, which, Thiers had said, would restore the *entente cordiale* if all the powers accepted it, but commit France to the support of the Pasha if only Mehemet did. This, Russell pointed out to Melbourne, meant that if England rejected the compromise she would no longer be opposed openly to Egypt alone but to France as well. When Melbourne tried to point out that Ponsonby would probably make sure the compromise was not accepted in Constantinople, Russell merely retorted that that was precisely the reason why Ponsonby should be removed. Otherwise, as he had pointed out in an earlier letter, what with Palmerston also dragging his feet over the Maine boundary question, they would soon at be at war with both the U.S. and France.[123]

As soon as Charles Greville heard from Woburn via the Duke of Bedford that Russell was 'disposed to make a stand', he determined to do what he could to help. He had already intervened earlier that summer to counter Palmerston in the press. Aberdeen, who approved of Palmerston's line in the East, had persuaded Barnes, the editor of *The Times*, to be 'passive' at least. Greville nonetheless managed eventually to get Barnes to accept a series of very critical articles written by a junior colleague of his at the Privy Council Office, Henry Reeve. But at the end of August Reeve had to go abroad and soon Palmerston had re-established what seemed to be a virtual monopoly in the press. Greville was pressed to take Reeve's place, but though he did make better contact with Guizot through Madame Lieven he was reluctant to get too directly involved with the newspapers. On the other hand he had no such compunction about strengthening what he called 'the peace party' by acting as intermediary between Woburn Abbey and the French embassy, and, having extracted from Guizot an undertaking that the French would contemplate using force against Mehemet Ali if he rejected their new terms, Greville even proposed it be kept from Palmerston lest he defeat it in advance by attaching impossible conditions. Even to his diary Greville made excuses that do not quite ring true. Clearly, he was attracted as much by the prospect of getting rid of Palmerston as of preserving peace.[124]

Whether Clarendon and Holland – who were willing parties to much of what Greville was doing – approved of this particular scheme is not known. But Russell, who refused to talk directly with Guizot for fear of giving Palmerston 'umbrage', even though he soon dropped all pretence of dealing with Greville only through his brother, to his credit refused to allow it. Instead, by Greville's own account, Russell concerted with Clarendon (and probably Holland) to give Palmerston the chance to adopt the French proposal but, if he would not do so, to propose it themselves in Cabinet and resign if it was still rejected. Russell told Melbourne quite frankly that he intended to resign if he were overruled. Then, he went on, if Palmerston succeeded without war he would have secured a real triumph; but if war threatened, Russell would prefer to be free to oppose Palmerston's policy in Parliament.[125]

The next day, Sunday, 27 September, Guizot told Palmerston of the offer he had been authorized to make; but Palmerston was not prepared to entertain it. It is not clear from Greville's confused chronology quite when Palmerston saw the French ambassador that day. But he had already made up his mind about this latest 'offer' from France. He had written back to Paris five days before that Thiers's proposal, which had so attracted Russell, was merely 'absurd'. Previously France had talked about letting the Egyptians have Syria for Mehemet Ali's life; now they were talking of it for Ibrahim's, which was something more, not less. 'Really,' he said, 'Thiers must think us most wonderful simpletons to be thus bamboozled.' Lady Palmerston, too, had already spoken to Greville with such bitterness and contempt about this proposition as to make it quite clear to him as well what her husband's view would be. All that Palmerston said to Guizot when the French ambassador at last communicated the French proposal to him, was that the powers would have no difficulty in carrying out their present plans, and that France might join them or not as she pleased.[126]

On Sunday, 27 September, therefore, everything seemed set for the showdown in Cabinet the following day. But before the Cabinet met Russell was already being forced into a retreat. Early on Sunday he received from Melbourne a letter opposing his arguments against Ponsonby and forwarding a communication from the Queen. There was nothing new about the Ponsonby business; 'but for God's sake', went the Queen's letter, 'do not bring on a crisis'. The language was so like Melbourne's own that earlier historians automatically assumed it was his letter. In one sense it quite probably was. According to Greville the Queen was all the time 'in a great state of nervousness and alarm . . . terrified at Palmerston's audacity, amazed at his confidence, and trembling lest her Uncle [Leopold] should be exposed to . . . a war between his niece and his Father-in-law'. So, Greville understood, the Prime Minister was so plagued by 'pressure from without, and doubt and hesitation within' as to be robbed of both 'appetite and sleep'. Greville also accused him of hurrying back to Windsor after every crisis when he might have stayed in London to smooth things over. 'So melancholy a picture of indecision, weakness, and pusillanimity as his conduct has exhibited, I never heard of,' Greville wrote. Instead Melbourne really used the Queen's 'delicate state' (she was pregnant for the first time) in order to bring pressure to bear upon both Palmerston and Russell. He had already warned Palmerston, not only that Russell was growing 'very uneasy' about France and 'a good deal annoyed' about Palmerston's cavalier treatment of his proposals and complaints, but that the Queen too was pressing for a conciliatory gesture for France. What she dreaded most was the fall of the Government, and it was Russell's talk of resignation that threatened to present her with the detested Peel in her beloved Melbourne's place.[127]

Melbourne must also have appreciated that Russell's agitated apprehensions were more easily worked upon than Palmerston's jaunty confidence. At first Russell rejected the Queen's appeal about resignation as he did Melbourne's argument about Ponsonby. He was sorry for the Queen's 'painful situation', he wrote on 27 September, but Spencer had told him that the only way of maintaining the Ministry was by maintaining peace. He agreed to see Palmerston at two that afternoon and Melbourne at three. Melbourne also arranged to see Palmerston at four-thirty or five. But no progress was made, apparently because Russell still thought Palmerston would be the one to give way. The interview between Palmerston and Russell, Greville heard, was 'amicable enough in tone, but unsatisfactory in result – no change'. So, after Melbourne had seen them both, he reported to the Queen that he did not see 'much approach towards an agreement in opinion'. The following morning Melbourne wrote to Russell to say that he had forgotten to tell him at their interview that the Queen had 'charged' him with asking her Colonial Secretary not to take or pledge himself to 'any decisive step' without first seeing her. Probably Melbourne had not forgotten at all, for by delaying matters he ensured that Russell would not have time to see the Queen before the Cabinet and therefore not be able to take any irretrievable stance when they all met that afternoon.[128]

Since Russell had no real option but to agree to the Queen's request, the Cabinet of 28 September was long – from three till ten past seven – but inconclusive. All the members were there save Lansdowne, Duncannon, Morpeth and Hobhouse, but the only first-hand accounts of the meeting are the rather perfunctory reports from Melbourne to the Queen and from Palmerston to Hobhouse. Neither even mentioned – and Greville never did discover – that when it began each member found upon the table before him an apparently official letter marked 'Private and Immediate' and placed there unwittingly by the F.O. doorkeeper. These were all copies of a letter Urquhart had addressed to Melbourne in August accusing Palmerston of high treason.[129]

After such a beginning it seems quite probable that, instead of the two protagonists stating their views, as Melbourne reported, 'very calmly & temperately', it was, as Hobhouse recorded being told by Labouchere, a 'stormy' meeting. This makes Greville's tale, which he stated he had heard from Clarendon, of how Melbourne fell asleep all the more unlikely. There was probably more truth in his impression of Melbourne attempting to 'shuffle off the discussion' and Russell to bring it to the point. The two accounts naturally differ, with Labouchere characterizing Palmerston as behaving 'with admirable coolness' while Russell's proposals were 'intemperate and ill-advised', and Clarendon talking of Palmerston's 'violent philippic against France' but Russell's 'admirable, though very artful speech'. According to Clarendon, Melbourne, Cottenham and Baring took no part in the ensuing discussion, Minto supported Palmerston, Macaulay 'talked blusteringly about France' and Labouchere was 'first one way and then the other'. According to Labouchere, Melbourne, Minto, Cottenham and 'the majority' declared in favour of standing by the convention of 15 July. Palmerston's account confirmed what Labouchere had told Hobhouse and added that Normanby had not come down positively on Russell's side nor Baring, out of a Chancellor of the Exchequer's natural desire to avoid war, any more so on Palmerston's. Whatever the truth the result was the same – that it would be disrespectful to Lansdowne to come to any decision in his absence and so, having agreed only to delay the recall of Parliament till 5 November at the earliest, the Cabinet was adjourned until Thursday, 1 October. Labouchere attributed this to Palmerston's contrivance; but it was the Queen who had for the moment won, though Lansdowne carried the blame.[130]

That evening, after the Cabinet was over, they were all due to dine with the Palmerstons, 'and a queer dinner it must have been', wrote Greville. It can hardly have been anything but uncomfortable, considering how many plots were thought to be in train. Russell had continually complained in Cabinet about the newspapers supporting Palmerston; Palmerston, on his part, afterwards complained to Russell that the affair of Urquhart's letter seemed to show how Cabinet secrets got out. Like her husband, Lady Palmerston considered the proposal Russell had made in Cabinet quite 'absurd' and the trouble it provoked a 'very anxious worrying affair'. Clarendon also had the impression that the Palmerstons' suspicion about his F.O. ambitions had been revived. Emily certainly knew he was a member of what she called the Holland House 'cabal' and, as she later told Morpeth, blamed Clarendon for it more than Holland, who, she said, at least meant well. So she must have found her situation as hostess rather difficult. Yet Clarendon thought her dinner 'went off well enough'. He had a long talk with his hostess and thought he had made some impression. But when several of them dined the following day at Holland House she showed quite plainly that she was furious.[131]

Russell, Lady Palmerston said, had no business differing with her husband about the execution of the July convention after having contributed so decisively to getting it adopted in the first place. There was also what she herself described as 'rather a warm discussion' about the Hollands' conduct. 'I was angry', Emily admitted in her diary, '& thought it a good measure to show it.' For the Palmerstons had heard again from Paris about the hopes there of a cabal against Palmerston among his colleagues and they complained bitterly to Holland about the French knowing before the Foreign Secretary himself that he was to be attacked in Cabinet. So Palmerston, too, had a rather uncomfortable discussion with Holland. He had a more friendly one with Clarendon but would not budge from his position. Morpeth, who had reluctantly come up at Russell's urging, could not understand why there should be any question of changing course and considered it 'an extraordinary whisk round'. Even Clarendon and Greville thought Russell had been inconsistent and that Palmerston to that extent had some cause for complaint against him. But Lansdowne was also on his way, and he was as solidly with Russell as his character allowed. On 25 September he had written to Melbourne echoing Russell's original emphasis on cooperation with Austria as a necessary check upon Russia; on 29 September, as he paused at Birmingham on his way southward for the adjourned Cabinet meeting, he wrote that he was now inclined to support Russell's new proposals.[132]

Melbourne sent Palmerston a copy of Lansdowne's second letter on 30 September. Up till then Palmerston had shown little sign of budging. At an interview the previous day he did leave Normanby with the impression that he was willing to revert to the compromise of allowing Mehemet Ali to keep Acre. Normanby had proposed this at the indecisive Cabinet on 28 September and Melbourne had subsequently commissioned him to take it up individually with Palmerston and then Russell. He was an unlikely mediator and he probably overestimated his success. Rather he may have helped alert Palmerston to the dangers to his policy.[133]

Palmerston still had the best of the press; and some thought he was gaining ground among the back-benchers as well. But he knew he was growing more isolated in Cabinet; and he wrote at once to Hobhouse urging him to come up for the adjourned Cabinet, since he was apprehensive of Russell being supported, not only by Holland and Clarendon, but also by Baring, Labouchere and Normanby. The letter Melbourne sent him from Lansdowne therefore merely confirmed his fears. More significant was the memorandum of Prince Albert's that Melbourne enclosed along with it. This concerned an old suggestion of Metternich's to Leopold that France should be invited to declare her adherence to the 'principle' of the July convention and her willingness to join in other, undefined steps if the measures of coercion she disapproved of should turn out a failure. This did not appeal to Palmerston, since it envisaged the collapse of his current policy and offered prospects both to his doubting colleagues and to the French of making new complications. But he was not insensitive to Windsor's power. He had already agreed at Melbourne's request to 'soften down' an earlier retort to Leopold's interjections.[134]

When Melbourne subsequently passed on part of the Queen's agitated reaction to the news she had been given of his failure to reconcile the differences in Cabinet, Palmerston agreed to try Metternich's plan. The Queen's letter, apparently, made some reference to personal quarrels among her ministers endangering peace and then went on to point out that, if the present attempts at coercing the Pasha should fail, it would be less humiliating to England to have made a conciliatory approach in advance and, if they succeeded, less humiliating to France to have accepted it. Melbourne omitted the personal references from the extract he sent to Palmerston, while sending the whole letter to Russell. Russell was rather piqued that he should have been treated with less discretion than Palmerston and bluntly told Melbourne that the Prime Minister was responsible for having 'spoilt' his Foreign Secretary by a lack of 'control or contradiction'. But Melbourne's tactics paid off. Russell at once agreed to the proposed plan. Palmerston does not seem to have done so until after Melbourne had sent him Prince Albert's additional memorandum; probably he gave way only at an interview with Melbourne shortly before the Cabinet met.[135]

When the adjourned Cabinet met on the afternoon of Thursday, 1 October, everyone was there except Duncannon, and he had sent Melbourne his proxy. The meeting began, as had been agreed beforehand, with Melbourne taking the initiative in proposing Metternich's scheme, though in a quiet, earnest and perhaps rather nervous manner. Palmerston then pulled the details out of his pocket, 'all cut and dry', as Greville put it, and read them very quietly. There was a good deal of talk, though no symptoms of anger as far as Hobhouse could see. Russell was good-humoured and even cheerful. Only Holland and Clarendon objected, on the grounds that it was not much of a concession to France. Lansdowne said very little but both he and Cottenham highly approved. Hobhouse talked a good deal, but according to Greville nobody listened. When he asked what had happened to justify such a departure from the July convention, most of those who had been present at Monday's meeting answered him only with smiles. Palmerston turned to say that he entirely agreed, but that 'to fall in a little with the views of others' he had consented to a course which he did not think would do much harm, 'nor any good'. Clarendon reported to Greville, however, that the others considered this was 'a prodigious concession and change from his former tone'. It was then agreed that Palmerston should see the allies' ambassadors early the following day with a view to a concerted approach to France. They were not certain whether Palmerston should say anything to Guizot about it if Brunnow insisted, as Palmerston predicted he would, on consulting St Petersburg first. So they finally decided that if Brunnow agreed, Palmerston could communicate a note direct to Guizot or through Granville to Thiers; but that if Brunnow wanted to consult his Government they would all have to meet again to decide what, if anything, might be said to France.[136]

According to Greville's undoubtedly exaggerated version, Melbourne had begun the Cabinet very nervously and ended it 'swaggering like any Bobadil, and talking about "fellows being frightened at their own shadows", and a deal of bravery when he began to breathe freely from the danger'. But the following day there appeared in the *Morning Chronicle* another anti-gallican article and Bulow as well as Brunnow told Palmerston he wished to refer back to his Government. Russell at once told Melbourne he considered the object of the article was to drive him out of office; Clarendon concluded that Palmerston had never had the least intention of taking too seriously his concession to the Cabinet. There was more truth on Clarendon's side than Russell's. But Palmerston had never made any secret of his lack of expectation or enthusiasm. Clarendon ought also to have been more careful about throwing stones. He insisted afterwards that Palmerston had promised the Cabinet Brunnow would not make any trouble. But if Hobhouse's account is to be believed – and the fact that the Cabinet had so carefully considered what to do if Brunnow referred back to St Petersburg rather bears out his account – Palmerston had stated quite clearly his belief that that would be the Russian's initial response. It appears to have been Clarendon, on the other hand, who commissioned Greville to tell Guizot an offer was coming, in spite of the Cabinet's deferring any decision on that until after they had seen Brunnow's reaction. And the article Palmerston inspired in the *Chronicle* was a retort to a pro-French one Greville had placed in *The Times* a few days before.[137]

Considering these circumstances the Cabinet was in a surprisingly good humour when it reconvened at 5 p.m. on Friday, 2 October, to consider Brunnow's reply. Holland greeted Hobhouse in a rather 'dry' manner when they met shortly beforehand at Brooks's, though he made a 'waggish' comment or two during the Cabinet itself. Clarendon never appeared at all, having missed his train from Watford. Labouchere, as well as Duncannon, was also absent; and Macaulay went away early. Russell, however, had greeted Hobhouse very cheerfully at Brooks's, while Hobhouse's own interventions in the Cabinet discussions were so ignored by the Foreign Secretary that he concluded Palmerston and Russell must again have made a pact beforehand. In this he was probably right. Palmerston made the best he could of some new reports of French misdeeds in Spain and restated his opposition to communcating anything about the new proposal to Guizot before the Tsar had been consulted. But he had been rather put out by the news that the Sultan had deposed Mehemet Ali for not accepting the powers' terms and that Metternich had condemned this as a 'serious mistake'. As Palmerston must have expected, Ponsonby was given all the blame. So this time Palmerston quite definitely indicated his willingness to let Mehemet Ali hold on to Acre. Hobhouse, too, was shaken by Metternich's attitude. Nonetheless he objected when it was proposed by Melbourne, as a sort of compromise, that instead of telling Guizot anything Palmerston should authorize Granville to 'hint' to Thiers that some proposition would probably be made. But no one else objected, and Palmerston ignored him.[138]

By the Holland House account Palmerston was supposed to send his 'hint' to Granville that very evening, though the Cabinet broke up late at 7.45 p.m. But Palmerston wrote nothing about it to Paris, either officially or privately, until 6 October. He was obviously delaying again in the hope that events would overtake it. It was a tactic his colleagues found quite infuriating since it was not easy to discover and defeat. According to Holland House, Melbourne had also had to work upon Palmerston to produce pertinent dispatches from Vienna at Friday's meeting of the Cabinet. On the following Saturday morning several of the ministers assembled at Claremont for a Privy Council to extend the prorogation of Parliament, and afterwards a sort of Cabinet meeting was held in Melbourne's room. It is not clear precisely what it was about; probably Russell insisted on it in view of further damning information from Constantinople about Ponsonby's conduct. The result therefore appears to have been that Palmerston agreed to inform Granville that the deposition of the Pasha was not to be taken too seriously. In fact he had already done so, but he repeated it after the Claremont meeting. Yet still he did not say anything to the French about Metternich's scheme.[139]

When Guizot called on Palmerston the following day, Sunday, 4 October, and reported news that the allied squadron, having resorted to coercion in view of Mehemet Ali's rejection of their terms, had bombarded Beirut and landed Turkish troops near by, he was absolutely delighted. 'Napier for ever!' he wrote the next day to Granville. 'Pray try to persuade the King and Thiers that they have lost the game, and that it would be unwise now to make a brawl about it.' The English members of the cabal also seemed to realize it. Clarendon could not help admiring Palmerston's calm and courageous defiance of his colleagues. At Holland House he seemed to them so 'cock-a-hoop' that they thought he must have made a compact with the Tories. Russell was at his wits' end. Palmerston had put his 'extinguisher', as Greville described it, too many times upon all his schemes, and being unwilling for the moment to stand up to Palmerston any more he was even anxious to resolve matters quickly by ordering an early attack on Acre. This could have done nothing to dispel the Palmerstons' anger at Russell's inconsistency and their conviction that he was the 'weakest' man in the Cabinet and worked on by two of the 'greatest fools' outside it – Bedford and Spencer.[140]

Palmerston was not utterly reckless. When both Melbourne and the Queen pressed him about the hint he was supposed to have told Granville to give in Paris he finally sent the necessary order on 6 October. But he sent it off, as the Queen complained to Melbourne, without letting her see it first, and when finally she did see it, 'too late to alter or soften an expression', she and Melbourne agreed that it was indeed 'a great deal too short and dry'. They would probably have been still more disappointed had they known that in an accompanying private letter Palmerston had told Granville to be careful not to make any commitment on England's part to Metternich's scheme and very much alarmed had they known of another letter two days later that made the 'hint' sound more like a threat. Palmerston, however, felt very confident. All his private information, he told Melbourne, indicated peace in Paris. The King 'decidedly' wanted it; Thiers *said* he did. The French Finance Minister was complaining of the extravagance of the military preparations; and the Ministers of both War and Marine were drawing attention to the deficiencies of stores and equipment. In short, then, 'the French cabinet is still more divided than other cabinets we know of '. So that evening he set off happily for Panshanger, where Emily had been awaiting him for some days with much impatience.[141]

As it happened, Palmerston's cavalier instructions about Metternich's scheme, as Melbourne had realized by the time he heard of them, hardly seemed to matter, since they were immediately overtaken by another fit of energy on Russell's part. Russell seems to have been stung into action by learning that Granville had been left so long without instructions and by the accounts of that ambassador's genuine apprehensions of war. So on the morning of 8 October Clarendon found him again preparing for a 'flare up' and later that same day Russell sent the Prime Minister yet another demand for a Cabinet to consider new proposals. What he had in mind was to ask the French directly what terms would satisfy them and then to have these terms pressed on Constantinople by someone other than Ponsonby. The Queen, getting very near her time, was furious with Russell for upsetting things again. So was Melbourne, who was ill in bed with lumbago. It was too late, he told Russell. He was also sure that Palmerston would never accept since Russell's proposal was virtually submitting to French arbitration. But he pleaded Windsor to both – again handing to Russell a letter from the Queen which he only mentioned to Palmerston – agreeing to a Cabinet, and begging Palmerston to think of some 'mode of reconciling matters'.[142]

Before the Cabinet met on Saturday, 10 October, Palmerston and Russell exchanged civil letters of disagreement. Palmerston sent what he thought was still more evidence that France did not really mean to theaten war; Russell considered it simply proved what a good moment it would be to make a new approach. From what Russell said to Clarendon, however, he clearly contemplated that the Cabinet discussions might lead to the break-up of the Government. In that case, he said, as the Queen objected to Peel, he would advise her to send for Grey, Spencer or Lansdowne. From what Palmerston wrote to Melbourne when he returned from Panshanger for the Cabinet to find the Prime Minister's appeal awaiting him, a final clash seemed inevitable. No man could wish to create differences less than he did, Palmerston wrote half an hour before the Cabinet was due to begin at three; it was others who were trying to change a policy they had agreed to long ago. For himself, he was more convinced than ever that the Cabinet's original decision was the right one. 'But', he went on,

how can any man conduct advantageously the business of such a department as mine, in which his power of negotiation depends essentially on the weight attached by foreign powers, & their agents here, to what he says, if every ten days some of his colleagues try to force his hand & to drive him out of his course, and if the foreign Government with which he is dealing, is to be regularly informed beforehand of what is going to be proposed. This is the sure way to paralyse not the man who is thus attacked but the government whose organ he is, and to bring the country into discredit and disaster.

What probably had annoyed Palmerston most was that on returning to London he should have found a letter from Guizot asking to see him before the Cabinet that day. Since Russell had not let him know at Panshanger precisely what the Cabinet was for, Palmerston must have concluded that Guizot knew more than he did and suspected the plotters were again at work to hinder him. But this time Guizot's visit had precisely the opposite effect: it halted Russell's move instead.[143]

Guizot wanted to call because he had just received two important communications from Thiers. One, dated 3 October, was a belated response to a great exposition of his policy that had been sent by Palmerston to Paris on 31 August and had subsequently found its way into the newspapers. The French reply was intended to be moderate in tone, though it chided Palmerston by recalling his earlier proposals for Anglo-French cooperation in the East at the same time as trumpeting the *entente cordiale*. But it was so clumsily concocted that Guizot held it back a few days in order to correct its errors. He therefore armed Palmerston before the Cabinet only with the second letter, dated 8

October, which though much graver in tone was in substance also very moderate. It merely stated that France would regard the deposition of Mehemet Ali as a threat to the balance of power.[144]

Palmerston said little or nothing to Guizot about Thiers's second letter, but took it straight to the Cabinet and read it aloud. At the Cabinet he must have said much more. Unfortunately even the first-hand accounts are far from detailed or explicit. 'You know', Labouchere wrote to one of the few absentees, 'how confused an impression Cabinet meetings leave upon the mind.' Most of the reports, moreover, came from Palmerston's opponents. He was, they said, disposed to haggle and humiliate. Very probably he wanted any reply to stick firmly to the allies' present course, leaving France bluntly to take it or leave it. According to Greville's usual highly coloured accounts, while Melbourne, 'sprawling on the sofa', hardly said a word, Palmerston showed his 'same overweening confidence' and determination to gloss over whatever did not suit his views. But he was completely isolated in the Cabinet. Hobhouse had returned to his family in the country; and even Macaulay was impressed with the moderation of the French note. After all, as Clarendon pointed out and the note itself acknowledged, France's implied *casus belli* was something the English had already virtually disavowed, the deposition of the Pasha; and what clinched the argument against Palmerston was that Melbourne saw in Thiers's note a way of heading off the crisis forced by Russell. The result, therefore, was a compromise between the policies advocated respectively by Palmerston and Russell. Palmerston was to tell Guizot that he was going to draft an 'amicable' response and he was also to submit it to the Cabinet for their approval. On the other hand it would take the form of an assurance that the four powers would use their good offices in Constantinople to persuade the Sultan to rescind the Pasha's deposition and it would therefore have to be agreed beforehand with the ambassadors of Russia, Prussia and Austria. Beyond that Palmerston was left with complete discretion to get the best settlement he could, save that if France insisted on the Pasha's having part of southern Syria as well as Egypt he was not to break with her over that, since it was after all what the July convention had originally envisaged.[145]

The Cabinet cabal seemed to have secured an important and very unusual check on Palmerston by requiring to see his draft reply to France. Holland regarded it with 'unfeigned delight'. On the other hand, as Clarendon said, they feared he would still pursue a final settlement 'in a spirit of huckstering & bargain rather than of friendship & generosity'. They were wrong on both counts. Guizot's pleas, Palmerston wrote some time later, were 'humbugging'; the Cabinet's policy a plan for entering into negotiation with France, 'that is, that we should yield to French threats and intrigues, which I was fully resolved never should be done by *me*'. He wrote this as an endorsement on a note from Melbourne reminding him how anxious the Cabinet had been for immediate action on their decisions. Melbourne's note was written two days after the Cabinet; Palmerston in fact had returned to Panshanger as soon as the

Cabinet had ended, although he was supposed to have communicated some assurance to Guizot and consulted with the other ambassadors 'immediately'.[146]

Presumably Palmerston was, as Holland House suspected from his insistence on a joint response by all four powers, trying once again to delay things until military operations in the East had strengthened his hand. Melbourne believed he really was hanging on in the hope of seeing Mehemet Ali out of Egypt as well as Syria. Stuffed as usual by Clarendon with all the Cabinet's secrets, Greville had immediately taken it on himself to tell Guizot to expect a conciliatory call from Palmerston and to warn him that if Palmerston instead 'evinced any disposition to haggle' Guizot should not be deceived into thinking that this had been the Cabinet's intention. Greville had even deferred a trip to the Newmarket races so that he could report back to the cabal how faithfully Palmerston had carried out his colleagues' wishes as far as Guizot was concerned. He need not have bothered. On Sunday and Monday, 11 and 12 October, the complaints came pouring in that Palmerston had seen neither Guizot nor the other ambassadors.[147]

Guizot urged Melbourne to put pressure on his Foreign Secretary; Melbourne, though still unwell, did so. At last on Monday afternoon Palmerston came up to town and met the Eastern ambassadors at three. But Brunnow again made 'difficulties', and so when Palmerston at last saw Guizot that evening he apparently felt unable to say anything about the proposed reply to France. Guizot, however, now communicated Thiers's other dispatch, which was fortunate since, through a chain of errors between Thiers, Reeve and Greville, it appeared in *The Times* the following morning. 'What a way of doing business,' reported Emily smugly to her brother. Palmerston saw Melbourne later that evening and agreed to make another attack on Brunnow the following day at noon. But it was no more successful than the first and immediately afterwards the Palmerstons left, as they had promised Melbourne they would, for a few days' visit to Windsor.[148]

While Melbourne remained ill in bed, Russell also went down to Windsor to explain to the Queen that his attitude on the Eastern question was not really so inconsistent as she thought. On Wednesday, 14 October, the Queen had long talks with both Russell and Palmerston and that evening Palmerston went to Guizot with a proposal he had worked out with Russell. Since this was, as far as Guizot was concerned, the first response to the previous Saturday's Cabinet, observers naturally concluded the Queen had managed by knocking their heads together to instil some sense in both of them at last. Even Lady Palmerston's language, they heard at Holland House, had grown more pacific. But if the Queen's anxieties were crucial, they had acted beforehand through Melbourne. For Palmerston and Russell had already arranged a compromise before setting out for Windsor. Probably Thiers's second letter had had something to do with it. For Palmerston would certainly have wished to answer some of Thiers's points. Guizot put it rather oddly later. 'Lord

Palmerston has a theological mind,' he said; 'he will let no objection pass without an answer.' This was misunderstanding both the man and his method: Palmerston's wars of words were for the edification of public opinion, not scholars or mandarins.[149]

At a meeting which Melbourne knew of and probably arranged, Russell and Palmerston agreed that the Foreign Secretary should prepare an instruction to Ponsonby to work in Constantinople for the rescinding of Mehemet Ali's deposition; and that a copy of it should be communicated to the French Government by Granville. It was hoped, of course, that the allies would send similar instructions, but it was much less offensive to go ahead alone with these, if it turned out to be necessary, than with any new approach to France. It also offered Russell an indirect means of giving assurances to France, while allowing Palmerston to make a separate retort to Thiers's published letter. The Queen, however, did make one important contribution when Palmerston returned to Windsor on Thursday, 15 October. She made him 'promise' to add to the covering letter by which he sent a copy of Ponsonby's instructions to Granville that 'it would be a source of great satisfaction to England, if this would be the cause of bringing back France to that alliance (with the other Four Powers) from which we had seen her depart with so much regret'.[150]

When the Cabinet assembled, as Russell insisted it should, on the afternoon of Thursday, 15 October, it was accordingly all very good-humoured. Melbourne felt well enough to attend and though Holland did not, Russell reported to him that there were now better hopes of peace. Lansdowne, who had come up early to press Palmerston beforehand, probably said little or nothing at the meeting. But Normanby spoke up 'decidedly' for peace, while Minto this time said little in support of Palmerston and Baring 'for the first time' also made a remark in favour of a pacific policy. Palmerston, taking his cue, they thought, from Windsor, 'acted his part on this occasion, with self command and apparent good humour'. He read out his draft to Ponsonby, which had already been approved by Russell even though it contained no rebuke for the ambassador. It was probably sent off the next day; and a copy followed shortly after to Paris. 'Thus', wrote Lansdowne, as the Cabinet dispersed again about the country, 'a door at least is opened & a pause secured which may be turned to account.'[151]

It was probably because he thought that Windsor had got as much as could be reasonably expected from Palmerston that Melbourne now decided to warn the French it was time they ceased sabre-rattling so much. When Leopold persisted with his pleas for Louis Philippe and his criticism of Palmerston – Palmerston 'likes to put his foot on their necks', he had written to the Queen at the beginning of the month – Melbourne sent an angry reply on 20 October, saying that if France persisted with her armaments he would recall Parliament and ask for counter-measures. He seems to have sent this without consulting anyone and to have mentioned it in the first place only to Russell. Shortly afterwards, when Beauvale warned how extensive had been the international intrigue, with Leopold working on Windsor and Windsor on Melbourne so as to isolate Palmerston and have Clarendon replace him, Melbourne reckoned it was his letter that had broken up the conspiracy. When Thiers had proposed to open the forthcoming debate in the French Chamber with a warlike speech, Louis Philippe had refused permission and Thiers had resigned. Although it would appear that Louis Philippe had long ago decided that Thiers would have to go in any case, Melbourne either thought or professed to think that his warning had been responsible. He consequently wrote to Palmerston on 25 October telling him about his correspondence with Leopold and urging, in view of the state of French opinion, that a new gesture from England would help Thiers's successor in a policy of reconciliation and possibly save Louis Philippe from revolution.[132]

Guizot, who had been recalled to become Foreign Secretary in the new French Ministry and was 'in great spirits' at the prospect, also hinted he would like a gesture of good will when he called to say farewell to Palmerston. Granville and Madame Lieven wrote as well from Paris. 'M. Guizot begs me to remind you', the Princess wrote to Emily, 'that today he is in the position of going half way but that you must help him by making your husband go the other half towards him.' Lansdowne, Russell and Clarendon all wrote to Melbourne from their country retreats to the same effect. But not Holland. He had died on 22 October, raving, it was said, about France and Syria. Some were unkind enough to say that he had been killed by the 'accursed' July convention and by his fear of war with France. Palmerston always insisted that Holland had never mixed personal with public feelings and that he had remained cordial towards him to the last. Emily's account was not so confident; and the final blow may well have been a letter Holland had received a day or two before his death from Melbourne, telling him that Metternich had given Beauvale irrefutable evidence that Palmerston was right in attributing Cabinet leaks to talk at Holland House. Reeve thought that Holland's death would render Clarendon's position in the Cabinet too isolated for him to stay on. In fact it raised him temporarily to the Duchy of Lancaster, but as he admitted it also made Palmerston 'master of the ground'.[133]

Melbourne probably thought it was a good joke to promote Clarendon, even temporarily, where Palmerston had very pointedly asked for a man who would be both discreet and sympathetic to his policy. Clarendon in turn had a good point when he said, about a gesture to Guizot, that the successes the allies were achieving in Syria allowed England to afford it and Thiers's deposition allowed Palmerston to concede it. But Melbourne did not send Palmerston Clarendon's letter to follow up his correspondence with Leopold, only Lansdowne's and Russell's. Palmerston did not need to say anything new about Russell's; Lansdowne's merely showed how much he had fallen under

French influence; Leopold's that all the French armaments had been 'a mere trick'. He also had objections, both in practice and in principle, to making any concessions. It was now clear, he told Melbourne, that if they held firm they would recover the whole of Syria for the Sultan, and seeing that England would have done it with little help from anyone but the Turks this would for years to come give England 'great additional weight' in European councils. To Granville he wrote that the ambassador would have to make it clear in Paris that it would be 'quite impossible' for England to 'make to the entreaties of the King those concessions' which had already been refused to 'the threats of Thiers'. It was not a matter of spite or ill will towards any individual. It was a matter of European interest. Besides, French public opinion would always believe that any concessions were made to their threats rather than to the King's entreaties. So while conciliation by words was perfectly proper, conciliation by concession was out of the question. Nothing was more unsound than the notion that there was anything to be gained by appeasing those who sought to intimidate. He did not think that there would be war at present, because England was backed by all the rest of Europe and even France was 'not mad enough to break her head against such a coalition'. However, he went on:

I have for some time seen a spirit of bitter hostility towards England growing up among Frenchmen of all classes and of all parties; and sooner or later this must lead to conflict . . . All Frenchmen want to encroach and extend their territorial possessions at the expense of other nations . . . I do not blame the French for disliking us. Their vanity prompts them to be the first nation in the world; and yet at every turn they find that we outstrip them in everything. It is a misfortune to Europe that the national character of a great and powerful people, placed in the centre of Europe, and capable of doing their neighbours much harm should be such as it is. [154]

Melbourne found it very difficult to answer Palmerston's objections to concession, but there was also Russell, ever on the alert for some complaint to make. Minto found him on 31 October, Palmerston heard, expressing general dissatisfaction but unable to make any specific complaint. But by rummaging among the F.O. boxes that same day Russell soon found not one but two. First he discovered that Palmerston had recently turned down a suggestion of Metternich's to hold a conference in Wiesbaden; then that Ponsonby had been allowed to order the extension of operations against Mehemet Ali in Egypt. He was perfectly well aware, he wrote to Melbourne, that Palmerston considered frequent meetings of the Cabinet liable to give 'an appearance of uncertainty' to his policy and so do 'harm abroad'. But he had never expected such 'great questions' as these to be decided without his being consulted. So finding that his opinions were of so little weight, whether he carried the Cabinet with him or not, he could see no other course but to resign. 'Indeed', he concluded, 'it is much better that Palmerston should lead in the House of Commons than that I should degrade myself by pretending to an influence which I do not possess.' [155]

At Melbourne's desperate request Palmerston saw Russell on the afternoon of 1 November. When they began Russell, according to Palmerston's report, was 'very cross and somewhat sour', but by admitting his error about the conference and humbly begging Russell's pardon Palmerston made him more 'relaxed & softened'. In particular, Palmerston had noticed, Russell talked about proroguing Parliament in a manner hardly consistent with a man who was about to resign. So, it seemed, that 'little cloud' had blown over. But they still had to be careful, since someone was obviously at work again to 'pique him'.[156]

Palmerston was quite right. Clarendon had been working 'like a horse' at Windsor to get Melbourne moving; Bedford was again spreading the word from Woburn that a break-up was coming in the Government; and while Clarendon leaked what was going on to Greville, Bedford told it to Ellice. Ellice, Palmerston was sure, was 'as hard at work as ever', and writing every day to stir people up against him in both London and Paris. Urquhart and Attwood were also in Paris, conspiring with Thiers, and it seems to have been about this time that Palmerston seriously considered suing them for libel when they returned. According to Neumann, Urquhart was also responsible for several leaks of F.O. information made during this same period to the Tory *Morning Herald*. Palmerston thought Clarendon was behind them. He probably also remembered that it was Clarendon who had pressed him in the spring to let the Board of Trade send the statistician G.R. Porter to Paris to try his hand at commercial negotiations. Palmerston was now secretly informed that Porter was organizing commercial opinion against him at home and abroad and got him peremptorily recalled.[157]

Palmerston also discovered that Russell had tried to influence both the *Globe* and the *Chronicle*. Thanks apparently to 'Ben' Stanley's influence or connections, Russell had managed to place an article in the *Globe* on 7 October advocating conciliation of France. In Greville's opinion it was very moderate and by no means personally offensive to Palmerston, but the next day the editor was summoned to the F.O. and hauled over the coals by Palmerston. The following week Russell retaliated upon the proprietor of the *Chronicle* by telling him that his paper's tone was equally distasteful both to Melbourne and to himself. When Palmerston complained of his interfering with his favourite newspaperman and defended what he himself had done with what must have seemed barefaced lies, Russell denounced them both to Melbourne. Melbourne merely replied that, as far as the newspaper press was concerned, he had 'long since given it up in despair'.[158]

Palmerston concluded that Ben Stanley was second only to Ellice in the cabal against him. A short time before Ashley had also warned him that Punch Greville was at its centre. It could hardly have been a well kept secret. But Palmerston reported Greville to the Prime Minister and after a particularly objectionable article in *The Times* Lady Palmerston charged her old friend to his face. Greville denied it, of course, both to her and to his journal;

but a month before he had boasted plainly enough to Reeve that he had been supplying Barnes with articles almost every day for more than a week. He thought he had convinced Emily; but as Leveson knew, he was still 'in great disgrace' in Carlton Terrace. He had certainly been at work again to force a new concession out of Palmerston – say a part of Syria or Crete for the Pasha's possession and France's *amour propre*. So had the radicals, in the belief that the recall of Parliament could not be delayed much longer. Hume was planning to mount an attack in the Commons and asking Brougham to lead it in the Lords. Of more immediate importance was the Cabinet. Reeve was confident that he could rely on Lansdowne, Baring and Labouchere, as well as on Clarendon and Russell. Leopold also joined in again and Bulow, the Prussian ambassador, more or less concerted their moves after returning from leave in Berlin, where he had been rebuked for his earlier errors of cooperation with Palmerston. Metternich, they naturally assumed, would follow the line of least resistance, but the two principals, Russell and Guizot, turned out to be the weak links in the chain.[159]

Pressed by both Melbourne and the Queen to stay and fight Palmerston from within, Russell modified his position from holding out a definite threat of resignation to maintaining a refusal to attend Cabinet meetings until the question of Ponsonby's recall was decided. Pressed by Palmerston to give Ponsonby the little time the ambassador needed to earn a pension, Russell agreed first to circumvent him by a special mission of concilation, but then decided that things were moving to such a speedy conclusion in Syria as to make even that unnecessary. Greville tried, through Clarendon, to get Russell to make his retreat conditional on a gesture being made in the direction of Guizot, but when the Cabinet met on 7 November to consider the recall of Parliament, it was without any positive stipulation on Russell's part. Palmerston's position in fact was gaining strength almost daily. Hobhouse, who had obviously been irritated on earlier occasions by Palmerston asking him to leave his family only to find in Cabinet that everything had been compromised beforehand, this time refused to come up. This left Palmerston very nearly isolated and therefore forced to make some gesture towards the French. It hardly mattered in view of the way the military situation was moving. There was no point in offering to let Mehemet Ali keep what might in the meanwhile have been taken from him by force, Palmerston was able to argue. So it was merely agreed that Guizot should be asked to state what terms France would consider satisfactory, though for the same reason there could be no undertaking in advance to meet them.[160]

The cabal was gambling on the advent of winter bringing the military operations in the East to a halt and a response from Guizot bringing diplomatic matters to a conclusion, specifically by agreeing that the Egyptians should have a piece of southern Syria. But the following day, 8 November, brought news of the Egyptians' decisive defeat near Beirut and the day after that of Guizot's failure to state any specific terms. Palmerston, as even Greville acknowledged, had conveyed the Cabinet's request to have these terms 'very faithfully'. But the warning about giving no promise to accept them had ensured that Guizot would offer none, since in the face of an angry and expectant French opinion he could not afford to risk another rebuff. Thanks to Palmerston's 'theological' bent he had already had to suffer – and publicly since Palmerston always believed in giving tit for tat and had had it published as well – a skilful reply of Palmerston's to Thiers's dispatch of 3 October. So in the absence of a French response to what they had previously achieved, the cabal's new scheme collapsed in frustration and confusion. The Cabinet met very late on 12 November to consider what to do, but broke up without coming to any conclusion. The following day, after a meeting of what was probably a sort of inner Cabinet, an instruction was given to the Admiralty to authorize the squadron commander off the coast of Syria to offer Mehemet Ali the hereditary possession of Egypt.[161]

The Admiralty's orders went out on 14 November. For some reason they omitted any reference to 'hereditary' possession. This was, as Russell told Melbourne when he belatedly discovered it, 'rather singular'. Perhaps it was an accidental error of the Admiralty's; in the F.O. Leveson knew it was meant to be included. Perhaps Palmerston had given a hint to Minto, seeing that he had just heard how news of military success had sent a rush of blood to Metternich's head and made him once more fierce against the Pasha. Russell again began to complain that he was no better informed about F.O. business than were newspaper editors and that he had no means of knowing if the Cabinet's decisions had ever been carried out. Afterwards Palmerston had the audacity to say to Melbourne that the Admiralty's instructions were 'not essentially different' from what had been settled by the Cabinet. But by that time everything was moving implacably in Palmerston's direction. Reports of the debates that had just begun in the French Chamber gave credit to all that he had ever claimed against the French. They openly admitted that Thiers had relied on Holland's help and the divisions in the British Cabinet, and revealed that his Government had harboured schemes for building up Mehemet Ali's empire as a second-class maritime power by which to counter Britain's naval strength in the Mediterranean. 'I really think', wrote Clarendon shortly afterwards, 'you must have had Thiers in your pay during the last 3 weeks, for even in every lie he has told he seemed to have no other object but to make out a good case for you.' Lansdowne said much the same.[162]

On 21 November the young Queen gave birth to her first child. Victoria Adelaide Mary Louisa the Princess Royal was named; 'Turco Egypto', her mother had thought she might have had to call the child. The event allowed Russell to think of the Queen soon being ready to open Parliament again, and so of the need to call a Cabinet to decide upon the date. The morning before it met news trickled in that Acre's vaunted fortress had fallen to a short bombardment by the Navy and that the Egyptians' final evacuation of all of Syria would necessarily follow. When the Cabinet met on Wednesday, 25 November, everyone was there save Minto and Morpeth. But they merely approved a treaty Palmerston had arranged with the Texans to exchange recognition of their temporary independence for abolition of the slave trade. Nothing was said about Mehemet Ali or France, though afterwards Clarendon congratulated Palmerston on his successes.[163]

As confirmation of the news about Acre poured in, other members of the cabal followed with acknowledgements of Palmerston's success, and not only to his face. Like Clarendon, Ben Stanley talked of Palmerston having had the 'luck of the devil'; more shrewdly, Reeve wondered if it were not 'superior knowledge' rather than 'superior luck'. The Foreign Secretary's assessment of the naval situation in the Near East had been, like that of France's mood and policy, 'a calculated gamble'. The Royal Navy was generally thought to be weaker in the Mediterranean than the French, and the Egyptians' power and Acre's defences stronger than they really were. Had Palmerston been obliged to seek more ships from the Cabinet and Parliament, the likelihood is that his policy would have been rejected, just as it was in 1832-3. Similarly, Melbourne subsequently admitted to the Queen that if Palmerston 'had not had as devoted an assistant as the *Morning Chronicle*, he would hardly have been able to maintain his course or carry through his measures'. Even the grudging Greville admitted that Palmerston's firmness of method had carried him successfully through a policy he nonetheless despised. He also acknowledged that 'Palmerston had taken his success without any appearance of triumph or a desire to boast over those who doubted or opposed him'.[164]

It was probably Palmerston's generosity towards Russell that Greville had in mind. Russell had written to Palmerston on 2 December to say, not only that his colleague's policy had been 'eminently successful', but also that it had proved after all to have been the least dangerous course of any. Palmerston had replied that he owed it all to Russell's initial support of the July convention. This was not quite so generous as it seemed, since it was by implication a criticism of Russell's wavering since. But the more important question now was whether Palmerston was going to be sincerely generous to France. The English press moved almost universally to Palmerston's side. Aberdeen was no doubt responsible for *The Times* moving into line again; but even the *Herald* came over. They were all adamant in condemnation of France, who continued her warlike preparations, though only for the purpose of domestic propaganda. For the same reason Guizot continued to demand or beg a favour from Palmerston. But Palmerston was determined that the successes brought by English policy and English forces should be consolidated.[165]

When good news flowed in on 8 December, from Afghanistan and China as well as Egypt, Palmerston wrote:

This day has brought us a flight of good news: Mehemet's submission, Dost Mohammed's defeat, and the occupation of Chusan. The first settles the

Turco-Egyptian question. The great point now will be to decide on what yet remains to be arranged, in such a way that Mehemet shall be really and *bona fide* a subject of the Sultan, and not a protected dependent [*sic*] and tool of France.

Palmerston's plan was not to deprive Mehemet of hereditary rule in Egypt, which he acknowledged had now been promised by England, but to make him as practically as possible subservient to the Sultan. On the other hand, Palmerston had no wish to tie England too closely to Russia or to exclude France permanently from the Concert of Europe. So the following day there appeared in the *Chronicle* a distinctly positive declaration to that effect.[166]

Not long afterwards Palmerston politely but firmly rejected an offer from the Tsar to make the breach with France and the cooperation with Russia permanent by some sort of engagement, formal or otherwise. Palmerston wrapped up his reply in conventional verbiage about England's traditional and constitutional objections to making alliances for hypothetical purposes. But the wisdom of his refusal was no less clear, or the implied retort to critics like Urquhart or Ellice any less well-founded. Similarly he turned down Austria's proposals to rebuild a self-denying concert centred on Vienna. Metternich denounced him for it in language as violent as any Palmerston had ever used about the Austrian Chancellor. But Palmerston's was a natural response, in view of the shortcomings of the Metternich System and its failure in the Near East.[167]

Palmerston also rejected a secret proposal of Metternich's to conciliate France by a formal recognition of her conquests in Algeria. He was tempted, rather, to help the resistance to the French then being made by the Emir Abd-el-Kader. But he recognized that the Emir could not hold out forever and that the outside help he was already getting, from Morocco in particular, was liable to give France an excuse to extend her operations and her ambitions. So lest England be dragged into the fight, he agreed with Russell and Melbourne to urge discretion on the Moroccans, but at the same time not to make any such recognition of the French position in Algeria as would strengthen the legal basis of their complaints against their neighbours in that part of the world. That France would eventually conquer the whole of Algeria he clearly foresaw as an important legacy of Aberdeen's neglect. But England could never permit the French to gain Tunis and Tangiers and so cut off British trade and communication with the interior. This had already been made clear; but perhaps, he added archly, England might now remind the French 'that the Balance of Power requires that they should not do so, much more than the said Balance requires that Mehemet should continue in Egypt'. The difficulty remained, however, how to cut the ground from under France's feet in Egypt while restoring her position in the concert, for Guizot naturally refused to agree that France be formal party to the first. Palmerston had no wish that France should be so; it would only give her further opportunities for meddling. Instead he outlined at the end of November what was in a large measure to be the eventual solution, a Turco-Egyptian settlement without French participation, followed by a Straits Convention and treaty of guarantee for Turkey among the five powers, including France.[168]

Working out a final solution of the Mehemet Ali question took a very long time. It took three months to agree that the concert would have to be rebuilt on a simple Straits Convention, since no general guarantee that France could sign would ever be acceptable to Russia; and another three before the separate Turco-Egyptian settlement could therefore be arranged. Some thought that Palmerston was dragging his feet again, but the difficulties were more in Constantinople than in London. Acting, though he could not have known it, more in line with the Cabinet's wishes than the Admiralty's instructions, Admiral Napier had concluded an armistice with Mehemet in November based on hereditary rule. Palmerston was perfectly prepared to accept it since, as he wrote to Melbourne, it was not a concession made unwillingly to France but a settlement imposed on Mehemet by force. But in Constantinople Ponsonby was furious, and the Sultan rejected Napier's armistice and imposed very stringent restrictions upon the offer of hereditary rule. Quite probably Ponsonby was influenced by Palmerston's undisguised emphasis in private letters upon the desirability of making the Pasha truly subservient. Beauvale, who was well aware of what was going on in Constantinople and alarmed at returning symptoms of what Greville called Palmerston's 'flippancy' in dealing with Austria, again bombarded Melbourne with secret denunciations and advice. Ponsonby was frustrating a settlement out of personal pique, he said, and 'that iron-headed' Palmerston endangering the concert against France (of which he of course approved) by his 'policy of expediency'.

You may wish to know how Palmerston and Ponsonby understand each other so well. It is this – Palmerston sends him his instructions with which you are acquainted, adding to them as he does to me, a long private letter in which he acknowledges the error that has been made in offering hereditary succession to Mehemet Ali, expressing a doubt whether the Porte can ever be called upon to grant it, and a hope that events may have taken place in the mean time . . . which leading to the overthrow of Mehemet, may make it unnecessary to do what has been offered him. I put the private letter in my pocket & abide by my instructions. Ponsonby on the contrary crumples up his instructions and takes the apparently mere gossiping letter for his guidance.

So he urged Ponsonby's recall and stated that he felt it important enough to warrant a change of administration if that was the only way of doing it.[169]

Melbourne told Palmerston that both he and the Queen believed Ponsonby had indeed been intriguing in Constantinople and ignoring instructions when it suited him. Even Emily agreed her husband trusted him too much. Palmerston again stood by his ambassador; in the end he even asked Melbourne to raise him to an earldom. But he was well aware that public interest in the Eastern question was declining and that his hopes of strengthening Turkey were fading as the Sultan dismissed his supposedly reforming advisers. Finally he ordered Ponsonby to bring the Sultan to terms, and after this was done France joined the other powers in signing the Straits Convention of 13 July 1841. France was brought back into the Concert of Europe and the Treaty of Unkiar Skelessi had been submerged at last in a general European arrangement. 'Palmerston is gone to town this morning to sign the treaty,' Melbourne reported to Russell, 'so that now France may re-enter into the great European family – There has been something ridiculous in this from the beginning.'[170]

XII

PROSPECT
AND
RETROSPECT

'Ridiculous' was a strange word to use about Palmerston's policy in the Mehemet Ali question. But in characteristic fashion Melbourne was expressing a doubt held by most men even while they acknowledged Palmerston's triumph. Palmerston himself had no such doubt. Hardly anyone quarrelled with his conviction that an independent empire in the Near East was vital to the balance of power in Europe and to the protection of British India and of British routes to the East. But had he, to borrow a later phrase, backed the wrong horse? Certainly, by 1841, he had pretty well reverted to the scepticism about the reform of the Turkish Empire that he had still been expressing in 1831.

Palmerston had never had any really extravagant hopes of Turkish Reform in any case. His emphasis had all along been upon those limited measures by which Turkish defence might be strengthened and European hostility softened. On the one hand he expressed an anxiety not to undermine the Sultan's authority (as had been done in Egypt); on the other to demolish the fallacies of those who 'from mistaking a metaphor for an argument' and by comparing 'a community to a man's body and to an old tree' forecast the inevitable collapse of the Turkish Empire. What, in any case, was the alternative? Not Mehemet Ali, in Palmerston's view. 'There never was such a fabric of humbug and delusion as this power of Mehemet Ali,' he once wrote to Beauvale. This view must have been based more on instinct than, as Reeve suspected, on superior information, since most reports went quite against it. Subsequent events were to prove him right, as subsequent opinions have no less justified his rejection of Mehemet Ali's pretensions to moral, as well as material, power. To have gone over to the support of the Pasha would therefore have been much more risky and doubtful than Palmerston's critics thought.[1]

If there were to be successor states to the Ottoman Empire – and almost certainly Palmerston believed that one day there would have to be – then they should be civilized, constitutional ones such as he had hoped would be made of Greece. To that extent he would have agreed with Gladstone about the breasts of free men making better barriers against foreign aggression. It was a

621

firm general belief of his that men were necessarily better off under constitutional régimes. He wrote to Beauvale in 1841:

You say that a constitution is but a means to an end and the end is good government; but the experience of mankind shews that this is the only road by which the goal can be reached and that it is impossible without a constitution fully to develop the natural resources of a country and to ensure for the nation security for life, liberty and property. I hold that there is no instance in past or present times under a despotic government where these objects have been attained.[2]

There was no question of imposing such régimes on others. Nor did Palmerston think the British model everywhere the most appropriate, acknowledging, as he had in 1832, that they 'must vary according to the social habits & existing institutions of each nation'. He would answer his critics in 1848:

I hold that the real policy of England – apart from questions which involve her own particular interests, political or commercial – is to be the champion of justice and right; pursuing that course with moderation and prudence, not becoming the Quixote of the world, but giving the weight of her moral sanction and support wherever she thinks that justice is, and wherever she thinks that wrong has been done.

But there were to be no crusades. Palmerston was an optimist, not an enthusiast; a pragmatist, not a moralist. He began his political life with a fair-sized store of wisdom, but it was wisdom learned by rote, not by the mind or heart.[3]

Palmerston subsequently added to his store of wisdom, but it was by personal experience and not by the instruction of others. This was essentially the case with his famous dedication to the elimination of the slave trade. It was neither a crusade nor the cover for a grand design of empire. He certainly pursued foreign governments relentlessly. He secured new anti-slave-trade conventions from France in 1831 and 1833, from Spain in 1835, and to deal with Portuguese evasion of her treaty obligations an act of Parliament in 1839 that enabled him to treat their slavers also as if they were British criminals. He made an anti-slave-trade treaty a condition for recognizing Texas, and though American suspicions and American interests combined to prevent an effective treaty with the United States, he even managed to extract from time to time a degree of cooperation from them. Finally, in the summer of 1841, he was on the point of arranging a comprehensive treaty among the five European powers when his tactless treatment of France upset it.

The setback to the five-power treaty was a deliberate tit for tat by Guizot. If anything could have made Palmerston embark upon an actual crusade against the slave trade it was something personal like that. Later, perhaps, he did adopt the notion as part of his personal mythology. Beforehand, his treaty-making efforts had probably begun as part of the Grey Administration's commitment to retrenchment and in an attempt to reduce the amount of naval force Britain was obliged to maintain off the coast of Africa on account of France's non-cooperation. If there was any passion in his policy, it was probably more against Frenchmen and, still more, Portuguese than for the slaves. As far as slavery itself was concerned he gave no sign of having reconsidered his commitment to gradual abolition. He had voted against immediate abolition before coming to power in 1830, and when challenged during his South Hampshire election campaign in December 1832 he replied that it was as necessary to do justice to the owners as to the slaves and that 'although there must be much abuse where arbitrary power is vest yet the planters do not always eat the young negroes or salt the old ones for winter provision, but that the infants & the infirm & the aged are supported by the master and that to emancipate 800,000 negroes by the stroke of a wand, without many accompanying provisions would be to deprive all but the able bodied of their present means of existence'.[4]

Palmerston had also gone along with the rest of the Government in relieving the West Indian plantation owners by a temporary system of enforced apprenticeship for freed slaves and defended himself for doing so by arguing again in Tiverton about the obligations the Government owed to those owners. On the other hand his public condemnation of the slave trade was by no means cautious. No doubt he remembered that it was accusations of lukewarmness on this issue that had cost him crucial support in Cambridge in his first effort to enter Parliament. To attack the foreign slave trade was also universally popular in England and the criticisms of the expense involved easier to bear in Palmerston's opinion than accusations of neglect. As he told Lady Cowper, it pleased both the abolitionists, who demanded a world-wide effort, and the West Indian interests, who wanted their slave-based competitors undermined in some compensation for the sacrifices that had been forced upon them.[5]

All this did not mean that Palmerston was insincere about the anti-slavery campaign; for him, as for the Whig Administration in general, it was a happy coincidence of humanitarianism and expediency. For the same reasons Palmerston was not slow to seize upon Buxton's 'remedy' of attacking the trade at its roots in Africa by supplanting the economy that supported it with England's commercial penetration. But he was well aware of its practical limitations. He realized that it was impractical to dream of a ring of sovereign British entrepôts around the whole of Africa or of Moslem rulers being willing to help eradicate the system on which their power and authority depended. In the one case only very special acquisitions, such as the cession of Fernando Po as a naval base for action against the slave trade in return for the cancellation of Spanish debts, could be considered; in the other, some compensation would have to be offered, such as protection for the Imam of Muscat and Zanzibar against his enemies. Palmerston was also very sceptical about African emigration schemes displacing the slave trade. Reviewing in August 1839 the long history of dissatisfaction with Portugal's 'cooperation' in the suppression of the slave trade, he wrote of her demand that slaves should be returned to her jurisdiction after being liberated by the Royal Navy: 'The Portuguese wanted

... that negroes so captured, & nominally emancipated should be hired out as apprentices to the highest bidder, that is to say in other words should be sold by auction as slaves.'[6]

Where the Portuguese were concerned, in Europe or Brazil, Palmerston was never mealy-mouthed; he was to say the same of French schemes many years later. It is not known what he thought about the resort to 'voluntary' emigration from Sierra Leone made in 1840 by a Government of which he was a member. Probably, believing as he did that there was all the difference in the world between Englishmen and Portuguese or French, he relied on the apparently stringent regulations to correct abuse. But there is no reason to expect of Palmerston, before he had this popular reputation attached to his name, any greater sensitivity about the slave trade than might be found among his colleagues. He was merely one member, and by coalition moreover, of a Government several of whose other members were more committed by their previous record. It was inevitable in such a Government that the Foreign Secretary, whoever he might have been, should have contacted Talleyrand as soon as possible with a view to securing a more effective anti-slave-trade treaty from France. Palmerston's special contribution was persistence, expanding the resources of suppression in the F.O. and badgering the Admiralty and C.O., as well as foreign Governments, to do the same.[7]

It is equally unreasonable to suspect Palmerston or his Government of harbouring some grand design of empire, either commercial or political, behind the cover of an anti-slave-trade policy. This is not to deny that there were assumed to be potentially large concomitant benefits to England. With the notable exception of the defence of the Indian frontier and the route to the East, Palmerston's policy was centred in Europe. Anyone who doubts that – and is persuaded otherwise by his assiduous attention to all the details of F.O. business and by his constant alertness to French intrigue all over the world – should be compelled to weigh against such records the overwhelming mass of European papers and correspondence. The principal duty of a British Foreign Secretary was to see to the maintenance of the balance of power in Europe, as the essential prerequisite for the security of the United Kingdom. It was in Europe, too, that would be found the diplomats whose social and political status dictated that Palmerston maintain a regular correspondence with them. For there alone were the courts cherished by a class-conscious diplomatic service. It is all the more remarkable, therefore, that he paid as much attention as he did to mundane extra-European affairs.

Palmerston was not an undiscriminating annexationist. He shared the view conventional to his time that colonies were more trouble than they were worth. 'The value of such appendages,' he wrote in 1837, 'is in general opinion much over rated.' This did not mean that he was willing to let the Old Empire go where it might damage England's prestige and add power to her enemies. But he was aware of the dangers of holding on too long where a peaceful transition via self-government to independence offered a solution. 'Palmerston started the question wh. I had been afraid to suggest,' Howick recorded of one of the cabinets on Canada in 1836, 'of whether we had any interest in governing the N. American colonies in a manner distasteful to themselves, & expressed the opin[io]n which I was glad to find generally acquiesced in that our great object ought to be to prevent a contest which wd bring disgrace & defeat upon us & not to dream of keeping up the connect[io]n for ever.'[8]

Acquiring new colonies was also in Palmerston's view generally both unnecessary and unwise. 'If once we get back into Java', he mused when contemplating coercion of the Dutch in 1833, 'I do not think that we should go out again in a hurry for . . . it is the only colony we want in addition to those we have.' Subsequently he did advocate or accomplish other acquisitions – Aden, Goa, Hong Kong, Fernando Po – but these were really very few and for specific purposes, above all for the sake of security. They were, to that extent, defensive, though this may not in some views make them any more defensible. Nor, while remaining ever on the alert, was he unreasonably jealous of what other powers were doing, as he told Minto when considering the question of China in September 1837:

We certainly have no right to meddle with what the Americans do, so long as they do not interfere with our possessions; and as to the idea that we are to prevent any & every other nation in the world from having settlements to the East of the Cape, it is founded in a jealousy which is in a great degree mistaken, and in an assumption of a political power which we do not possess. Unless we are prepared to go to war with all the maritime powers in the world in order to maintain a monopoly which would probably be useless to us, we must make up our minds to see American & French settlements in the Eastern seas. But after all, the more civilization & commerce are extended among savage races, the better for all civilized & trading nations.[9]

Palmerston accepted most of the precepts of the free trade school in which he had been trained at Edinburgh, though in practice he favoured a policy of gradually freer trade. His role in the expansion of trade is nonetheless controversial. There is no doubt about his interest in it. He told the Commons in 1834 that to accuse a Foreign Secretary of indifference to commerce was to accuse him of a lack of common sense, and in 1839 that no other Government had paid so much attention to it. 'It is the business of the Government', he wrote in 1841, 'to open and to secure the roads for the merchant.' The military expeditions to Afghanistan and China, the surveys of Abyssinia and Arabia, all in the not-too-distant future would bring 'a most important extension' to commerce and, what was in a political point of view just as important, the great expansion in the mercantile marine whose sailors were so vital to England's power. So, the suggestion has been made, Palmerston was pursuing what has been called the 'informal empire' of trade, finance, influence, threats and gunboats. But it has been seriously questioned that he was willing to go so *far.* All the examples cited were undertaken for other motives, though Palmerston was not slow to point to incidental material compensation and advantages. It was Aberdeen who drifted into coercion of Buenos Aires in 1844 and Palmerston who condemned it as a blunder. Such aggressiveness he preferred to leave to private individuals and companies; and they were warned over and over again that the protection Government could give them was severely limited. For his foreign policy was essentially non-interventionist. 'Gunboat diplomacy' was reserved for the redress of wrongs to life and liberty. Example and persuasion were the instruments by which commercial treaties were to be secured.[10]

The object of Palmerston's commercial treaties was free trade for all, not for the exclusive advantage of Great Britain. What became known as the 'Open Door' in China was also sought in Latin America and in Africa. 'Being convinced that commerce is the best pioneer for civilization, and being satisfied that there is room enough ... for ... all the civilized nations of the rest of the world', Palmerston wrote in 1850, Britain 'would see with pleasure every advance of commerce in Africa, provided that such commerce was not founded on monopoly and was not conducted upon an exclusive system.' It was where other European nations threatened to establish monopolies that Palmerston was prone to abandon 'non-intervention'. It was this – as well as the implications for the strategic command of the Mediterranean – that made him so anxious about the French expansion beyond Algeria, to the extent that he contemplated encouraging Abd-el-Kader's resistance. But with his colleagues restraining him in some of his more exuberantly anti-French moments, he continued, in the face of increasing opposition from other European powers, to preserve his simple faith in the material and moral merits of free trade, 'leading civilisation with one hand, and peace with the other,' he said in 1842, 'to render mankind happier, wiser, better'.[11]

It was a similar axiom of simple faith for Palmerston to propose that constitutional states were England's natural allies. There is no reason to doubt his sincerity. At various times he explained earnestly enough that constitutional monarchies were both more stable and more peaceful. 'As to Constitutional states,' he wrote to Fred Lamb in August 1832, 'it is not as it seems to me a piece of mere pedantry to think well of them, for surely they are less likely to go to war than despotic governments because money will not be voted lightly.' But it has to be recalled that he said what he did about England's natural allies during the brief honeymoon of the *entente cordiale* with the Bourgeois Monarchy of France. After it had ended, Melbourne confided to Greville how much he agreed that Palmerston would one day join the Tories at home. Aberdeen, on the other hand, approved Palmerston's Mehemet Ali policy because he thought it would free England from her Jacobin entente and lead her back into the conservative camp abroad. They were both wrong; Palmerston's views on foreign policy would have kept him apart from the Tories even if nothing else had done. Palmerston himself blamed Louis Philippe for destroying the entente.[12]

When one remembers how Palmerston had come in the first place to adopt the French entente and when one makes proper allowance for the bombast of his style in letters and in speech, it is clear that for him alliances were really a matter of expediency rather than principle. Spain and Egypt reminded him that England's interest was not necessarily identical with France's; on the contrary they were traditionally and actually in constant conflict. Louis Philippe had merely demonstrated that allies were fickle friends, and vital interests of enduring importance. Hence he rediscovered and strengthened the Canningite principle, which he expressed so well in March 1848 when defending his record in the Commons against Urquhart and his gang: 'I say that it is a narrow policy to suppose that this country or that is to be marked out as the eternal ally or the perpetual enemy of England. We have no eternal allies, and we have no perpetual enemies. Our interests are eternal and perpetual, and those interests it is our duty to follow.' Nor was this any belated discovery of Palmerston's. He had spelled it all out in a private letter to Lamb ten years earlier:

... my doctrine is that we should reckon *upon ourselves*; and act upon principles of our own; use other governments as we can, when we want them and find them willing to serve us; but never place ourselves in the wake of any of them; lead when and where we can, but follow, never. The system of England ought to be to maintain the liberties and independence of all other nations; out of the conflicting interests of other countries to secure her own independence; to throw her moral weight into the scale of any people who are spontaneously striving for freedom, by which I mean rational govt, and to extend as far and as fast as possible civilization all over the world. I am sure this is our interest; I am certain it must redound to our honor; I am convinced we have within ourselves the strength to pursue this course, if we have only the will to do so; and in yr humble servant that will is strong and persevering.[13]

It was therefore not really fair to criticize Palmerston for inconsistency. He may have allowed himself to exaggerate, as he often did in words, and to spout language that was conventional to an age of warring ideas. But he never really lost sight of the main objectives of vital interest and he adjusted his alignments accordingly. In this respect his policies in the Belgian and Egyptian questions were essentially the same: he used the Eastern powers against France and France against the Eastern powers as he needed. It was his manner and his method that could more reasonably be questioned. In the letters to Fred Lamb that he hoped the Austrian Chancellor would intercept and read, Palmerston loved to write of 'Metternich's System of universally meddling and bullying'. By contrast, the kindly Holland thought, Palmerston's faults were little ones of manner. 'I should a little doubt', he once wrote about a missive of Palmerston's to France, 'the prudence or policy of proving yourself so clearly & so *forcibly* in the right.' However, if Palmerston's external behaviour was sometimes or even increasingly unwise, the principles he professed and proclaimed remained well-based and true. On one occasion he advised a diplomat in South America intent on proclaiming in advance a triumph of foreign influence:

628 · PALMERSTON: THE EARLY YEARS

the first place as a general rule it never answers for one government to

> In the first place as a general rule it never answers for one government to boast of its influence over another because boasts of this kind are very likely to destroy the influence to which they relate.
>
> In the second place it is still less expedient to make such a boast with respect to the announcement of an intention, because the pride & vanity of the government which has announced this intention must naturally be wounded by the boast made by the agent of another government & means and pretexts may be sought for and found to avoid execution of the announced intention; and thus the government by whose agent such premature boasts have been made not only fails in accomplishing its purpose, but becomes exposed to humiliation.

He was probably not a conscious hypocrite – not yet at any rate.[14]

While Palmerston had an educated grasp of the principles involved in seeking long-term objectives and an instinctive gift for the tactics to gain immediate objectives, he had only a hazy view of the middle ground of international politics. It has already been pointed out that in cultivating russophobia in England he made matters more difficult for himself when he wished to align with Russia afterwards against Mehemet Ali. Hence perhaps there was a need to make his opposition to France all the more vociferous. But it would be wrong to suggest that Palmerston really ever led any movement of opinion. It was because he so patently lacked qualities of moral leadership that in later years people like Gladstone were appalled to have him as Prime Minister. Rather he went with the tide of public opinion. In personal appearance and private manner he may have been one of the last survivors of the eighteenth century and well near a regency dandy – Disraeli's 'Lord Fanny of diplomacy . . . cajoling France with an airy compliment, and menacing Russia with a perfumed cane'. But as Webster has pointed out, he was 'in his attitude to Liberalism, to nationality and to economics' one of the first Victorians – a man whom Tenniel made a plausible subject for caricature by drawing him chewing on a straw, as he surely never did in real life.[15]

Believing in improvement through prosperity, the removal of abuses, and fundamental change only where it seemed necessary to avert revolution, Palmerston considered himself a moderate. Conservative by nature and by outlook, he had nearly been made a lifelong Tory by a generation of war and revolution. He was saved from it partly by his liberal education and perhaps by his maternal inheritance as well. They gave him what a Tiverton observer remembered as 'a happy knack of referring to the Tory party as if their opinions and his were wide as the poles asunder'. When he joined with the Whigs in 1830 many of the Tories expected soon to have him back with them. Personal experience also had a great deal to do with stopping that.[16]

The election campaign in Cambridge in 1826 drove Palmerston away from the reactionaries; the campaign in 1831 might have driven him back again had he not detected among them those who conspired against his foreign policy. This was not the behaviour of a mere office-seeker. It was true that once committed he liked to keep his place, even while he complained so much about the work. He also needed the money – but never as much as in the late 1820s, when he allowed himself to be ousted, although by sucking up to Wellington he could surely have held on. Thereafter, although never flush with money until Emily inherited it from her brothers and his slate mines began to pay, he could always have managed. Quite possibly being out of office in 1841-6 made him better able to face the losses he must have suffered in Ireland in the years immediately after.

Palmerston patently lacked political passion or real ambition. What then kept him going? Obstinacy, many would have said. But this too was a consequence not a cause. The truth probably was that he was impelled by a need to do, not what he thought was right, but what he thought was expected of him, eventually by public opinion but first by his family and guardians and then by his friends, especially the women among them. The ladies of his most intimate acquaintance, whether Whig or Russian, *happened* to be very political. It was their influence, one suspects, that drove him in the late 1820s nearest to the brink of audacity. The accidents that disposed of the Canningite leaders he seems to have regarded as presenting less an opportunity than a duty. He never made any unequivocal claim to be Canning's heir; in dealing with Grey in November 1830 he behaved more like a broker than a leader. The most revealing political confession of his life was when he told Malmesbury that he had rejected Perceval's offer of the Exchequer in 1809 for fear of aiming too high.

Once Palmerston had been pushed forward, the fear of failure made him work too hard for his own comfort, or that of his assistants, and pride made him prickly about anything he thought a challenge to his authority. After 1839 an unaccustomed domesticity soothed his temper and made him far less irritable. By the middle of the century he was to gain a reputation for personal affability remarkable even among politicians. But there persisted in him a definite quality of ruthlessness. It reflected in part the addition of a certain degree of confidence to his pride. He never became a consistently impressive public speaker, though he continued to make brave attempts when his political existence was threatened, and he learned eventually how to carry with him the humour of the hustings and the Commons. His experience in Cabinet after Canning's death made him much less frightened of his ministerial colleagues. With Grey he was circumspect without being subservient, and when they differed feathers were inclined to be ruffled. With Melbourne he did not quarrel. Melbourne tried to stand up to him only once (in 1835), and was then faced down. It was probably unfortunate for Palmerston's development that the easy-going Melbourne was ever his Prime Minister. For in 1835-41 he learned how far he might go in getting his own way.

In September 1840 Melbourne warned Palmerston about his Egyptian policy that 'never, I will answer for it was a great measure undertaken upon a basis of support so slender and so uncertain'. Palmerston's case, by contrast, was that 'a few plotters' had woven around the Cabinet 'a web of delusion'. When he failed to dispel it by argument he gambled on events doing so. It was a brave if doubtful tactic. But it was not so difficult as it might have been in other Cabinets. From the various diaries still extant it would seem that the meetings of Melbourne's Cabinet were more like seminars than executive sessions. Opinions were aired and policies discussed; but rarely were definite decisions come to, at least in foreign affairs. Nor, in Melbourne's Government, does there appear to have been an effective inner Cabinet such as Grey had had. Holland and Clarendon were unable to get a grip on Melbourne. Russell came nearer, but in the end also proved unequal to the task. So while Melbourne certainly did interfere in foreign affairs, Palmerston had a considerable advantage of diligence and character over him and useful allies, where foreign policy was concerned, in Minto and Hobhouse.[17]

After the fall of Beirut and Acre and Thiers's inept performance in the French Chamber, pretty well all his critics admitted Palmerston had been right, even if lucky too. But, though stifled for a while, there was a great lingering doubt in Cabinet about his methods and his manner towards France. Mme Lieven wrote to Emily on the first anniversary of the four-power convention of 1840 that 'this 15 July has made enough noise in the world, really more noise than harm, but plenty of bad blood'. Leopold put his finger on a future source of trouble with Windsor when he dubbed Palmerston in a letter to his niece '*rex* and autocrat'. Clarendon predicted a store of future French revenge. He was by no means the only one who thought Palmerston had persisted much too long and quite unnecessarily in denying to Guizot the honourable retreat he more reasonably refused to Thiers.[18]

Palmerston was convinced that to appease French opinion would be to encourage its bellicosity in the future. He did not believe there was any immediate danger of war with France about the Egyptian question; and his information and his judgement in that respect proved better than that of his critics. But he disapproved in principle of appeasement and so disillusioned was he with the Bourgeois Monarchy that he professed to think war was, on some future occasion, quite inevitable. 'If we carry our point which I am now convinced we shall,' he wrote to Beauvale, 'we shall read France quietly a lesson that will be useful to her for three or four years to come. I cannot hope that anything short of a good physical thrashing will make an impression much longer than that.' However, for the time being, it was only necessary to ensure that France was readmitted to the concert on England's terms, not hers; otherwise, Palmerston recognized, she might exploit any apparent concessions with a view to dividing the other powers from England. When he was sure his colleagues would no longer challenge him in this, he even went out of his way to avoid anything like brag. In January 1841 Emily, reporting to him how even the *Examiner* was coming round, wrote what 'a great pleasure' it was 'to see all our enemies floundering in the mud'. But Palmerston readily agreed to say nothing of France in the Queen's Speech in Parliament and with the rest of the 'opposition' – on both sides of the House – supporting what he had done, the debate that followed on Syria was in Hobhouse's view 'far from lively'. Hobhouse thought Palmerston was tired and his statements 'rather flat'; but even Greville acknowledged they were free from 'anything like triumph or exultation' and that Palmerston had finally justified his success by moderation.[19]

Overall in 1830-41 Palmerston proved himself a masterly Foreign Secretary. His pragmatic grasp of Britain's material interests and his realistic and flexible approach to the balance of power set him above Castlereagh; his manipulation of conference diplomacy and his tactical skill in ensuring that Britain was never isolated were superior even to Canning's. His successes were substantial and undoubted. Nor was he lacking in vision. One cannot but agree with the Foxites that in Palmerston's policies vital qualities were lacking, both of the mind and heart. But by contrast with him they were naïve romantics and their criticism was for the moment stilled. Russell made a sort of truce with Palmerston on a visit to Broadlands just after Christmas 1840. Grey and Howick sullenly accepted the 'fait accompli'. In September 1841 even Spencer felt compelled to write to him: 'When a man finds he has made a mistake in criticizing the conduct of another he can do no less than avow it. If the person he has criticized is his friend the reason for his doing this is so much the stronger. I therefore desire no thanks for saying I was wrong & you right about the Syrian business.' The Queen had already asked Palmerston to Windsor to sit for a German artist, and the city of Liverpool – the constituency of Canning and Huskisson – that he should honour them by seeking election as one of their members in the General Election of that summer.[20]

Palmerston played some part in bringing on the elections of June 1841, but not as big a one as the depression in world trade. That depression ensured that the Chancellor of the Exchequer would have to do something dramatic to make up for the deficits which had overcome the budgets of 1838, 1839 and 1840. Baring therefore proposed in his 1841 budget that the duties on foreign sugar and timber should be drastically reduced in order to stimulate demand and relieve domestic distress and to these Russell had subsequently added the duty on imported corn. Corn, of course, was a great emotive and political issue. But sugar was hardly less so. The Government, indeed, was accused by abolitionists and planters alike of planning to give an advantage to foreign sugar already subsidized by slavery. During the course of the debate Russell made a brilliant speech, pointing out that there was no such simple distinction between the sources of supplies or any moral consistency in the present position. What was the morality, he asked, in putting 'free' sugar into 'slave' coffee? Palmerston rose towards the end of the debate on 18 May 1841 to make a speech on similar lines, repeating virtually all the points that Russell had made initially but emphasizing too that charity should begin at home with the English working classes and pointing to the Government's record of anti-slave-trade activity and treaty making. He pointed out that foreign sugar was after all still not going to be admitted on equal terms and in any case he professed to be committed to the belief that 'free' sugar was always cheaper. By demonstrating England's sincerity in that belief with the new budget and subsequently proving it as a fact the Government would be making a better contribution to the elimination of the slave trade and slavery than its critics. He also took the opportunity to repeat once more his faith in freer trade. 'The question is, whether the great springs of our national industry shall be relieved from ... artificial obstructions ... The question is between free trade ... and monopoly ... The question is between reason and prejudice; between the interests of the many, and the profits of the few.'[21]

According to Russell, Palmerston spoke 'exceedingly well' and when Russell decided to publish his own speech Palmerston determined to do so with his as well. Hobhouse considered it had been an effort of 'great spirit and intelligence' on Palmerston's part to have kept the debate alive for nearly two more hours. But to do so – evidently in the hope of driving away as many waverers as possible – Palmerston was very long-winded and repeated much that Russell had already said. Greville thought that it was 'a speech of smart, daring, dashing commonplaces, not bad, but', as an answer to Peel's, 'very inferior'. Peel, indeed, had spoken more brilliantly on the other side than anyone and enough abolitionists among the Government's usual supporters voted with him to ensure a crushing defeat for the Ministry by 317 to 281.[22]

At five the following day, 19 May, the Cabinet met to decide what to do. They had known for some time that they could not go on as they were, but had been uncertain how they ought to leave. Russell wanted to ensure that any succeeding Tory administration was also compelled to face up to the great issue of the Corn Laws; Melbourne was personally against tackling them at all. They were also divided over whether to resign or to dissolve. 'The Cabinet are much divided in opinion,' Emily wrote, 'and Wm, always feeling as he does when two lines are open to him, rather desirous to take the one of least responsiblity.' So pleading the 'awkward' position the Queen would be placed in by any other course, Melbourne was all for plodding on. Russell too was often undecided. But Palmerston had no doubts. No Government, he had long ago decided, could go on with the present House of Commons, and so the Whigs ought to keep whatever advantage an election might give the sitting Government rather than surrender meekly to the Tories. Perhaps, he added as optimistically as ever, they might not even lose. He had continued to urge this point of view even as the crisis deepened, during the early part of May. He thought the 'anti-slavery cry' had failed and that that about the Poor Law would do the same; and in the Tory camp, he claimed, he saw also a prevailing atmosphere of gloom. The adverse vote of 18 May must have disappointed him in the Commons, but he still had faith in the country. In any case it made a decision unavoidable at last. When Melbourne went to report to the Queen the following day he was surprised to find she too wanted a dissolution, hoping her favourite would regain his majority by it. So after Palmerston had made 'a short but decided speech' in the Cabinet and the majority had given him their support, Melbourne at last gave way. On 4 June Peel carried a vote of no confidence against the Government by 312 to 311 and three days later Russell announced the forthcoming dissolution.[23]

Palmerston hurried off as soon as he could from London on 16 June and by covering the last forty miles with relays of carriage horses reached Tiverton between nine-thirty and ten at night after a journey of nearly twelve hours. Emily went with him again (as she had for the races the previous year) and they stayed again at the Three Tuns. It was 'a poking little inn', she reported. That, no doubt, was why in later years Palmerston had his own four-poster installed and did perhaps convert it thereby into what tradition says was a 'supremely comfortable hotel'. Soon after his death it was renamed The Palmerston, though oddly enough only after changing from the headquarters of the Liberals to those of the Conservatives.[24]

Apparently Palmerston went off very hurriedly to the elections in 1841 because he needed to see whether an offer from Liverpool that he had turned down in January might after all have to be seriously reconsidered. For this time, he had heard, the Tories intended to put up a more dangerous candidate against him in Tiverton. According to Emily's account he was greeted on arrival with 'such crowds and cheers' that they had difficulty in getting through the town. Palmerston, too, was reporting confidence enough the following day to spurn Liverpool, though offering to let his name go forward simultaneously both there and in Tiverton if that would help keep out another Conservative. For a first day's canvass of the town had convinced him there was no danger about the Corn Laws. The Government's proposals, he reported to Melbourne, were popular among the townsfolk and would not hurt him much among the farmers either. He therefore ended his canvass with a speech claiming his constituents' support both 'upon the principle of being an enemy to the system of [political] monopoly' and on the ground of supporting 'the principle of extending freedom in our commercial relations', and returned to London for the prorogation of Parliament.[25]

According to Emily, Palmerston had met with hardly a single refusal in the town and had expected to be nearly as successful among the neighbouring farms. But by other accounts he was again given a rough time of it over the Poor Law. He had not himself originally been in favour of taking the system of relief out of the hands of the local gentry. But his colleagues had soon convinced him in Cabinet that the magistrates had not managed things at all well, and in 1834 he too had voted to put it into the hands of a central commission. Whether this necessarily implied a preference for cold-hearted bureaucracy over enlightened humanity will probably never be decided.

'But', Palmerston advised one of his leading but worried supporters at Tiverton in January 1841, 'I am deeply impressed with a rooted conviction that it has been one of the most advantageous and important reforms of our domestic system which have been effected even in these reforming times.'[26]

The local butcher, William Rowcliffe, who was an active Chartist and a future parliamentary rival to Palmerston in Tiverton, heckled Palmerston constantly about the 'Poor Law Bastilles' and asked how Palmerston would like to be separated in one from his wife. The Conservative candidate, for his part, made great play with the fact that when the Poor Law Amendment Bill was before Parliament he had voted against it. But Palmerston merely laughed at Rowcliffe and Emily soon discovered that Charles Ross, though a Conservative Whip, was a 'poor candidate'. Her one fear was that he might turn to bribery as a last resort, and that would be a great pity as the constituency was 'at present particularly pure and good – and such honest open-hearted people, I am quite fond of them.' 'They all laugh at Chas Ross,' she added the following day, 'and I should think he would hardly come to the Poll.' She was quite right, and all that Ross's appearance cost her were her blue ribbons and blue silks – about half her wardrobe, it was reckoned – since blue was Ross's colour. For the day after she and Palmerston had returned to London, the chairman of their committee (Charles Warren) had heard from his opposite number that the canvass Ross had made did not appear to him to justify his standing. So when the Parlmerstons returned for nomination day on 28 June, it was also for the liberal candidates to be returned unopposed. 'Nomination, speech & triumphant return,' Emily wrote in her diary, 'chairing, rejoicings & even gratifying expressions of regard from the whole town, as the few discontented Tories went off to Exeter.' Palmerston took the time to make a stout attack on France's military policy in Algeria – purporting to contrast her army's savage treatment of the local inhabitants with England's 'scrupulous' behaviour in India – and they both got up at five the following morning so as to be at Broadlands as quickly as they could.[27]

Emily, who was rather pleased at having got Fanny's marriage to Jocelyn settled at last in March and professed to be equally so at her brother Fred's belated marriage to an Austrian countess half his age, had expected Palmerston to be 'quite safe in office' for the year. 'Foreign Affairs', she wrote, 'have placed us on a pinacle [sic] of Glory.' But Palmerston's Tiverton triumph was less typical of the Government's common experience in the elections than was his coming last in Liverpool. For the Government suffered a complete defeat and faced the prospect of a majority against them of perhaps seventy-seven. The Queen displayed her great annoyance with her subjects' behaviour in the elections by pointed visits in July, along with Melbourne and the Palmerstons, to Woburn, Panshanger and Brocket. At Panshanger Emily had to give way to her daughter-in-law, but at Brocket she acted hostess for her brother, making his house 'so smart with red cloth and carpets, and ornaments and flowers'. However, there was nothing to choose between the two of them when it came to lack of punctuality, making the Queen wait both at Panshanger and at Brocket for her dinners and her drives till anyone else would have been furious, as one of her ladies said. Palmerston's bad habits were very catching.[28]

The Queen's visits were considered a great success; but, as Mme Lieven took care to point out from Paris, such demonstrations of partiality could only damage her standing with an electorate who had chosen differently. In any case there was no escaping defeat. The new Parliament assembled on 24 August; the Government was soon defeated in both Houses; and at last on 30 August Melbourne resigned. This final act of the Government's decline and fall was delayed by Russell's refusal to forfeit a second honeymoon; his persistence had at last been rewarded by Fanny Elliot's hand. Palmerston employed the interval so busily in 'wiping off old scores' that according to his wife he had 'hardly time to eat or sleep'. He cleared up all the arrears of work and did what he could for his friends and protégés in and out of the F.O. There was no opportunity to promote his nephew, but he had already secured a comfortable convalescence for Stephen by a temporary appointment in Naples. Five new young men also got paid attachéships and Easthope his baronetcy.[29]

Melbourne disliked endowing all that had figured in the *Chronicle* with an appearance of his personal approval. But Palmerston pointed out that they would need a morning paper even more in opposition than in power and that, in competition with the inducements of official information and advertisements that the Government could offer, it would cost them a great deal of money to buy one. Easthope's admission now to what he called 'the small aristocracy' was a bargain at the price. Moreover, if he were given his baronetcy, his views would probably be moderated; otherwise, they would become more and more radical. It was lucky, he concluded, 'that the proprietor of a great paper should happen to be a man not unfit to be made, and desirous of being made [a baronet]. The men most difficult to manage, are those who want nothing or those who are unfit for anything.' In the end, since Russell did not object to seeing his attacker honoured, Melbourne reconciled himself to it by dwelling on other recipients who in his opinion were still worse.[30]

In *The Times* and in the F.O. they thought Palmerston's new attachés quite unnecessary – 'all foul jobbing at the public expense', Mellish said. There were a Howard, an Elliot and a Duff provided for, together with a son of Augustus Foster's to compensate for the father's having to make way for Abercromby. The fifth, whom Mellish did not name, was Charles Scott, rewarded at last after half a decade of complaints, only to die almost as soon as he arrived at his post in Teheran. Still, he left many sympathizers behind him and Greville naturally noted how detested Palmerston still was in the F.O. 'They say he is "a Bully, a blackguard and a Coward"; still, they do justice to his ability and to his indefatigable industry.'[31]

After ten years of such labour, the Palmerstons both felt that the Foreign Secretary needed a rest. According to his old friend Littleton, made Baron Hatherton in 1835, the diplomatic corps in London were 'indecently anxious' for it. So were they too in Paris, according to Mme Lieven, and she wrote especially to say so. But, as Emily retorted, it seemed a good moment for Palmerston to go, at the pinnacle of his fame. 'He will have successfully carried through four big problems – Portugal, Spain, Belgium and the East, apart from several others which are being tackled now, China, America, and the recognition of Texas, etc. Englishmen of all parties are at last giving him his due, which is delightful for me, who have seen him so long the butt of slander and malice.' Her husband, however, had a nagging fear that his successors might reap some of the credit from unfinished business. He was anxious that the Indian Government should complete their successes in central Asia by occupying Herat and worried that the news of it would not arrive in time to crown his triumph; he was not to know that the Peel Government was about to reap instead a harvest of disaster at Kabul. In China, on the other hand, the Tories did receive the credit, if that was what it was, for finishing what Palmerston had been forced to leave with them.[32]

Whatever his original moderation might have been, once committed Palmerston was all for taking a firm line in China. To this there had been no real opposition in Cabinet, but his agents let him down by settling for much less than he had ordered. He wanted to disavow Elliot and repudiate his settlement; Melbourne agreed to recall Elliot but, of course, wanted to settle for what he had obtained. The Cabinet, according to Hobhouse, did not seem very determined; this time even Russell dozed. In the end they compromised by giving discretion to the Government of India, who were in a better position to know what might be gained. So a new campaign ensued, which brought matters to a conclusion only after Palmerston had resigned.[33]

In the case of the American trouble it was Palmerston himself, in Russell's view, who risked endowing his successors with a triumph, if not a war. The troubles and tensions on the North American frontier had led inexorably to international incidents and, for his supposed involvement in the burning of the *Caroline*, an American vessel supplying the Canadian rebels, to the arrest of a British subject, Alexander McLeod, on capital charges of arson and murder. On 6 February 1841 the Cabinet had decided unanimously that, since McLeod had only been carrying out his orders, his trial in New York State was quite illegal and that if he were executed their minister in Washington should be withdrawn at once. Palmerston made no bones about it: 'McLeod's execution', he wrote, 'would produce war, war immediate and frightful in its character, because it would be a war of retaliation and vengeance.' And, as for Washington's plea that they could not interfere with the judicial processes of the Sovereign State of New York, then their sincerity in that could easily be tested by declaring war in the first instance only on that state. But Palmerston said this only in a private way and clearly believed there would be no war, despite categorical statements made in public and in Congress by supporters of the incoming American Government. 'When a man connected with a government . . . holds such language in Parliament, it seems clear to me that it is for the purpose of holding high a principle which he thinks will not be carried into practice.' He also knew that McLeod had an alibi and, if justice meant anything in Albany, was most unlikely ever to be convicted. Palmerston was right, but he was never proved so until McLeod himself arrived, alive and free in Liverpool, after the change of Government in England. So Aberdeen again acquired the credit and built upon it, as Russell had warned he would, by settling the disputed Maine boundary as well.[34]

Aberdeen was expected also to repair the *entente cordiale*, but not, it was important to emphasize, by any breach with the conservative alliance. Guizot, whom he considered to be his friend, went out of his way to help him to an excellent start by refusing to conclude with Palmerston the five-power Convention for the better suppression of the slave trade. As it turned out French opinion decided later that Guizot should not be allowed to conclude it with Aberdeen either. Palmerston was not in August 1841 to know that this would be the case. 'It is very shabby of Guizot', he wrote, 'to sign with Aberdeen a treaty which I have been hammering at these four years.' But this time, certainly, Palmerston had no one to blame but himself. For what had stung Guizot into acting so was the speech Palmerston had made in Tiverton in criticism of the French in Algeria.[35]

It is difficult to decide what had possessed Palmerston to make his Tiverton speech. It was not, as has been suggested, made merely in the heat of an election or designed to distract attention from the attacks made upon him on account of his domestic record, for he had already known for a week or more that his re-election was safe, and he repeated what he had said after he was elected in the columns of the *Globe*. Nor was it, as has also been suggested of his approach to Thiers on the slave trade the previous year, made in a moment of unusual carelessness and insensitivity. For it was very carefully planned. He had gone out of his way to ensure that it was given the widest possible publicity. He had made special arrangements for the representatives of the London press to hear him speak and he had confined what he had to say to twenty minutes' duration so that they could convey it back to the capital by the last train that day. He explained his choice of place – he felt the hustings appropriate for a subject in which the Government had no standing to make comments either in parliamentary statements or in diplomatic notes. But he never explained his choice of subject. Perhaps the sentiment he expressed really was sincere; more probably it was another warning to the French about England's material interests. Wherever they had clashed he had tried to check them; Egypt and North Africa, he was warning them again, were not to be their freehold. Yet what was hardly less significant was that the cold-hearted bureaucrat, as Ridley has shrewdly noted, was becoming a national demagogue.[36]

It was not to be long before Aberdeen was finding for himself that Anglo-French conflict was not merely personal to Palmerston and also that Anglo-American relations were less easily soothed than he had thought. Palmerston believed that Aberdeen was far less competent than he. He was quite sincere in this and far from wrong. But there was also something very personal about Palmerston's resentment. He was plainly furious to have had so much credit taken from him by what he considered a sequence of accidents, and it was largely for this reason that he devoted a surprising amount of time and energy, in defiance too of many in his own party, to condemning in press and Parliament the Anglo-American settlement made by Aberdeen in 1842. What made it particularly galling for Palmerston was that his successor and beneficiary should be his old rival. He would much rather it had been Stanley, he confided to Hobhouse. Still, there was some consolation, Palmerston told his brother, in thinking how surprised Aberdeen would be to find the turnover of dispatches doubled since 1828-9 and how much harder than before Aberdeen would therefore have to work. As for himself and his colleagues, he wrote to Shee, 'a couple of years out of office . . . will do us all good in every way, both as to health and as to public favour. Ten years is a long innings to hold; and in order to know our value, the country must have a taste of our opponents.' He lingered in London a little longer than his colleagues, so as to cast a disapproving glance upon Peel's new Government. But Broadlands, Ireland and the Continent beckoned and in the autumn of 1841 he went off, Emily wrote, to 'enjoy his freedom like a boy escaped from school'.[37]

'The Last Rose of Summer' by HB (John Doyle), October 1842

NOTES

CHAPTER I: ORIGINS AND EDUCATION (*pages 1-47*)

1. *Palmerston*, i. 5 (cf. Ashley, i. 4); Cokayne's *Complete Peerage*, x. 295; *Grote*, pp. 1-2, 6, 10; Connell, pp. 23, 108, 138-9, 143, 383.

2. Elliot to Lady Elliot, 8 Jan. 1788, 14 April 1792, M.P.; *Glenbervie*, ii. 93; Connell, p. 156; Guedalla, pp. 27, 463; Lady Palmerston to Elliot, 20 Oct. 1785, M.P. (*Minto*, i. 98).

3. Connell, pp. 90-91, 154, 160, 165, 169, 175, 195, 206, 213, 285, 311, 312, 315; Walter Sichel, *Sheridan from New and Original Material; including a Manuscript Diary by Georgiana Duchess of Devonshire* (1909), i. 455; Elliot to Lady Elliot, 24 Dec. 1785 (*Minto*, i. 98), 3 May 1787, M.P.; *Memoirs of William Hickey* (1913-25), ed. Alfred Spencer, iii. 275-6, iv. 66-8, 85-93, 98-105, 147-52, 493.

4. *Minto*, i. 106-7, iii. 13; Elliot to Lady Elliot, 8 Jan. 1788, M.P.

5. Lady Palmerston to third Viscount Palmerston, 23 April 1802, B.P.W.; *Minto*, iii. 350; *Scott's Journal*, i. 61-2, ii. 10; Lady Holland's journal, 1 Nov. 1797, H.H.P. (*Lady Holland's Journal*, i. 161-2).

6. Connell, p. 459; *Minto*, iii. 379-80; Florence MacCunn, *Sir Walter Scott's Friends* (1910), p. 361; *Mrs Arbuthnot*, i. 419; Elliot to Lady Elliot, 22 May 1787, 14 Ap. 1, 27 Dec. 1788, 5 July 1798, M.P.; Alfred Cobban, *Ambassadors and Secret Agents. The Diplomacy of the First Earl of Malmesbury at The Hague* (1954).

7. *Minto*, i. 167, iii. 7; Connell, pp. 169, 176, 206, 215-60, 285.

8. Connell, pp. 211, 228-9, 321; printed handbill advertising the school for young ladies the Ravizzottis afterwards opened in London, B.P.W.; Lady Palmerston to Minto, 3 June 1800, M.P.; preface to Gaetano Ravizzotti, *A New Italian Grammar* (1797); Gaetano Ravizzotti, junior, to third Viscount Palmerston, 1 Mar. 1848, B.P.W.; Ashley, i. 4; *Minto*, ii. 253 n. 1; Harry Temple to Lady Palmerston, 25 Jan., 28 Feb., 4 May 1795, [? 25] Feb. 1802, B.P.W.; *Palmerston*, i. 8.

9. Thornton, pp. 195-7, 202; *Harrow Register*, p. 157.

10. Third Viscount Palmerston to W. Temple, 25 Dec. 1804, B.P.W.; Thornton, pp. 184 n., 196; Connell, pp. 322-4.

11. Connell, pp. 323-5, 420, 421; Mrs Bromley to Lady Palmerston, 4 Feb. 1796, 25 Oct. 1797, B.P.W.; Lady Palmerston to Palmerston, 11 Sept. 1788, 3 Dec. 1790, B.P.W.; *Palmerston*, i. x-xi; Bell, i. 5; Thornton, pp. 147, 153, 173-4, 319; MS 'Harrow Bill' for July 1799, enclosed in Baron Platt to third Viscount Palmerston, 5 July 1853, B.P.W.; Lady Palmerston to Minto, 23 Dec. 1799, M.P.; Harry Temple to Lady Palmerston, 20, 21 June, 17 [Sept.] 1795, [25 April], 29 May 1796, 10 Feb., 8 July, 14, 24 Oct., 21 Nov. 1798, 31 May, 29 June 1800, B.P.W. (Lorne, pp. 2-3).

12. B.P.W. no. 391; Thornton, pp. 178, 362; Lady Palmerston to Minto, 6 May, 3 June 1800, M.P.; Harry Temple to Palmerston, 13 June, 28 Nov. 1800, B.P.W.; Ashley, i. 9.

13. Ashley, ii. 408; 'On Public and Private Education. Jan. 1801', B.P.W.; third Viscount Palmerston to W. Temple, 10 Dec. 1845-26 Jan. 1846, B.P.

14. Palmerston to Prof. Dugald Stewart, 13 June, B.P.W. (Ashley, i. 9, and, al-

though misdated, Connell, pp. 425-6); Lady Palmerston to Minto, 24 June 1800, M.P.; Connell, pp. 424, 434, 461; Malmesbury to third Viscount Palmerston, 9 June 1802, B.P.W.

15. Thornton, pp. 196-7, 434-5; Palmerston to Lady Palmerston, 12 Dec. 1790, Harry Temple to Palmerston, 23 Oct. 1799, Dr Bromley to Palmerston, 15 Oct. 1795, Lady Palmerston to Harry Temple, 1 Feb. 1797, and Harry Temple to Lady Palmerston, 24 Oct. 1798, 1 Dec. 1799, B.P.W.; *Palmerston*, i. 8.

16. Harry Temple to F. Temple, 5 July 1799, B.P.W.; *Minto*, iii. 117-18; Lady Palmerston to Minto, 25 July 1800, M.P.

17. *Mackintosh*, i. 29; Connell, pp. 430-31; Lady Holland, *A Memoir of the Reverend Sydney Smith* (1855), i. 98; Laurance James Saunders, *Scottish Democracy 1815-1840* (1950), pp. 329, 361; *Farington*, i. 332.

18. Connell, pp. 427-31; Harry Temple to F. Temple, 20 Sept., and to E. Temple, 16 Oct. 1800, B.P.W.

19. Harry Temple to E. Temple, 16 Oct., 15 Nov. 1800, B.P.W.; *Sulivan*, pp. 44-5.

20. *Lady Holland's Journal*, ii. 23; *Cockburn*, p. 20; Lady Palmerston to Minto, 24 June, M.P.; Connell, p. 426; Harry Temple to E. Temple, 16 Oct. 1800, B.P.W.; Lady Minto to Minto, 17 Oct., 11, 24 Nov. 1801, M.P.; *Minto*, iii. 231-2, 234-5.

21. Connell, pp. 431-5, 438, 440; Harry Temple to Palmerston, 10 Dec. 1800, 3 Feb., 28 Mar. 1801, to Lady Palmerston, 23 June, 16 Dec. 1802, to E. Temple, 15 Nov. 1800, 7 Dec. 1801, 17 Jan., 6 April 1802, and to F. Temple, 28 Feb., 9 May 1803, B.P.W.; Lady Palmerston to Palmerston, 29 Nov. 1800, B.P.W.; 'Journal of a Tour from Edinburgh to St Andrews, etc.', 11 May-27 June 1803, and a separate sketch book of 1805, B.P.W. 1945, 1946; *Farington*, i. 327; *Sulivan*, p. 30; Lady Cowper's commonplace book, B.P.W.

22. Connell, pp. 438, 444; Harry Temple to Palmerston, 8 Dec. 1800, 3 Feb. 1801 (Connell, p. 441), 22 Mar., 6 Nov. 1801, to Lady Palmerston, 20 Dec. 1801, 23 June, 17 July 1802, 16, 23, 28 Nov. 1804, to E. Temple, 15 Nov. 1800, 13 Nov., 7 Dec. 1801, 1 Mar. 1802, and to F. Temple, 22 Jan. 1801, B.P.W.; *Minto*, iii. 230-35; Lady Minto to Minto, 10 April 1802, M.P.; *Palmerston*, i. 5-8; *The Letters of Sydney Smith* (Oxford, 1953), ed. Nowell C. Smith, i. 67 n. 2; Augustus Hare, *Memorials of a Quiet Life* (1877), i. 97-8, 144; *Gronow*, ii. 98; *Dudley to Llandaff*, p. 198.

23. Palmerston to Lady Palmerston, 2 Dec. 1800, Harry Temple to Palmerston, 28 Nov., 10 Dec. 1800, 3 Feb. 1801, to Lady Palmerston, 20 Dec. 1801, to E. Temple, 15 Nov. 1800, 28 Mar., 14 April 1801, and to F. Temple, 26 Nov. 1800, B.P.W.

24. Webster, i. 7 n. 1 (cf. *Greville*, iii. 157); Harry Temple to E. Temple, 28 Mar., 13 June 1801, 16 Nov. 1802, to Palmerston, 22 Mar. 1801 (Connell, p. 441), 8 Feb. 1802, to Lady Palmerston, 28 Mar. 1801, 23 June, 11 Nov. 1802, and to F. Temple, 21 Feb. 1807, B.P.W.; Lady Palmerston to Harry Temple, 2 April, Stewart to Palmerston, 10 May 1801, and [Emma Godfrey] to W. Temple, 26 [April 1806], B.P.W.; third Viscount Palmerston to W. Temple, 3 April 1818, 26 Aug. 1828, B.P.; *Sulivan*, pp. 165-6; third Viscount Palmerston's diary, 18-21 July 1829, B.P.; third Viscount Palmerston's 'Analysis of Expenditure since 1818', B.P.W.

25. Harry Temple to Palmerston, 18 April, Stewart to Palmerston, 10 May, and Harry Temple to F. Temple, 13 June 1801, B.P.W.

26. Mrs Stewart quoted in Lady Palmerston to Harry Temple, 3 Dec. 1800, B.P.W.; Connell, pp. 441, 456; Lady Minto to Minto, 29 May 1802, M.P.; *Minto*, iii. 234-5.

27. Lady Palmerston to Palmerston, 4 Dec. 1800, Harry Temple to Palmerston, 3 Feb., 6 Nov. 1801, 8 Feb. 1802 (Connell, p. 456), to Lady Palmerston, 20 Nov. 1801, 23 June 1802, and to E. Temple, 13 Nov., 7 Dec. 1801, 6 April 1802, and Stewart to Palmerston, 10 May 1801, B.P.W.; Connell, pp. 433-4, 454; F. Horner to L. Horner, 23 Nov. 1803, Horner Papers.

28. Connell, p.457; *Minto*, iii. 247; Minto to Lady Minto, 20 April 1802, M.P.

29. Connell, pp. 160, 349, 378-91; *Grote*, p. 10; Mary, Lady Palmerston's journal, 'Sat. 20' [Aug. 1803], B.P.W.

30. Connell, pp. 379-85; 'Abstract of the Will and Codicil of the late Viscount Palmerston', 21 July 1792, 'Allowances made by the executors of my father's will to my mother for the maintenance of the children', 18 May 1802, and 'State and Estimate of the late Lord Palmerston's Personal Estate now remaining to be applied and of the Debts and Legacies unpaid', B.P.W.; Minto to Lady Minto, 17, 23, 27 April 1802, M.P.

31. Harry Temple to E. Temple, 28 Sept. 1800, and to Lady Palmerston, 15 May 1801, B.P.W.; Lady Palmerston to Minto, 2, 22 June 1801, copy of Harry Temple to Henry Campbell, April 1802, and Minto to Lady Minto, 23 April 1802, 25 Jan. 1803, M.P.; *Alumni Oxon.* ('Henry Campbell'); *New Letters of Robert Southey* (1965), ed. Kenneth Curry, i. 47, 51.

32. Palmerston's account book, P.P. 48584; Lady Palmerston to Palmerston, 23 April 1802, B.P.W.

33. Palmerston to F. Temple, 9 Jan. 1802, Campbell to Palmerston, 9 Nov. 1801, 18 June 1827, 31 Jan. 1828, 12 Dec. 1839, Mrs Campbell to Palmerston, 31 Jan., 31 July 1845, William Rose to Palmerston, 14 Feb. 1846, and Philip Rose to Palmerston, 6 Sept. 1848, B.P.W.; Malmesbury to Lady Malmesbury, 21 Sept. 1802, Malmesbury Papers; Palmerston to Peel, 27 June 1813, Peel Papers; Palmerston to Liverpool, 27 Dec. 1815, Liverpool Papers, Perkins Library, and 8 July 1825, L.P.; Palmerston to W. Temple, 14 Feb. 1846, B.P.; Campbell's will, P.R.O., PROB 11/2032, Mar. 176.

34. Connell, pp. 330-32, 402-3, 447-8, 451-3; Palmerston to Malmesbury, [18 Jan. 1802], Malmesbury (Aspinall) Papers; Palmerston to Pelham, 1 July 1802, and Malmesbury to Pelham, 4 July 1804, Chichester Papers.

35. Minto to Lady Minto, 25 April, and Lady Minto to Minto, 29 May, M.P.; *Minto*, iii. 251; Palmerston to Malmesbury, 2 June, Malmesbury (Aspinall) Papers; Palmerston to E. Temple, 15 June, and to Lady Palmerston, 19 June 1802, B.P.W.

36. Minto to Lady Minto, 24 April 1802, M.P.; Connell, pp. 458-9.

37. Palmerston to Pelham, 1 July, Chichester Papers; Palmerston to Malmesbury, 24 July, 14 Nov., Malmesbury (Aspinall) Papers; Lady Minto to Minto, [23 April], M.P.; Malmesbury to Palmerston, 23 Nov. 1802, B.P.W. (Connell, p. 461); Palmerston to F. Temple, 28 Feb. 1803, B.P.W.

38. *Cockburn*, pp. 20-23.

39. *Horner*, i. 101, 130-31, 156; *Dudley to Llandaff*, pp. 214-15, 221; *Cockburn*, pp. 22, 23.

40. Harry Temple to Lady Palmerston, 8 Dec. 1800, B.P.W.; Lady Minto to Minto, 13 Nov. 1801, M.P.; Connell, p. 461.

41. *Cockburn*, pp. 68-9; Harry Temple to Lady Palmerston, 8 Dec. 1800, 28 Mar. 1801, to Palmerston, 10 Dec. 1800, 22 Mar. 1801, to F. Temple, 22 Jan., 1 Mar., to E. Temple, 28 Mar. 1801, and Lady Palmerston to Harry Temple, 15-16 Dec. 1800, B.P.W.; *Sulivan*, p. 11 n. 43; *Minto*, iii. 220.

42. Palmerston to Lady Palmerston, 17 Jan., 9 Feb., 16 Mar., 6 April, 21 May, and to F. Temple, 2 Feb., 18 June, 2 July, Lady Palmerston to Palmerston, 2 Feb., and Bromley to Palmerston, 16 April 1803, B.P.W.; *Minto*, iii. 293; 'Journal of a Tour from Edinburgh to St Andrews etc.', 11 May-27 June 1803, B.P.W.; Winstanley, p. 187; Palmerston to Malmesbury, 2 June 1802, Malmesbury (Aspinall) Papers.

43. Palmerston to Lady Palmerston, 26 Oct., and Bromley to Palmerston, 11 May, B.P.W.; Lady Palmerston to Minto, 23 June 1803, M.P.; Mary Frances Outram, *Margaret Outram 1778-1863. Mother of the Bayard of India* (1932), p. 111; Thomas Baker, *History of the College of St John the Evangelist, Cambridge* (Cambridge, 1869), ed. John E. B. Mayor, ii. 1094-1104; Gunning, i. 83.

44. Palmerston to F. Temple, 11 Nov., to Lady Palmerston, 26 Oct., 2 Nov. 1803, and to E. Temple, 11 Feb. 1804, B.P.W.

45. Miscellaneous college bills in B.P.W. no. 393; Palmerston to Lady Palmerston, 26 Oct. 1803, B.P.W.; *The Cambridge University Calendar for the Year 1804*, p. 189.

46. Palmerston to Lady Palmerston, 26 Oct., 15 Nov. 1803, and to Ravizzotti, 13 Oct. 1804, B.P.W.; W. Temple to Malmesbury, 11 Dec. 1806, Malmesbury (Aspinall) Papers.

47. Malmesbury to Palmerston, 6 Dec. 1803, B.P.W.; Connell, p. 461.

48. Winstanley, pp. 49-51; *Pryme*, p. 92; Robert Southey, *Letters from England* (1951), ed. Jack Simmons, p. 180; *Sedgwick*, i. 82-3; *Campbell*, i. 170.

49. Winstanley, pp. 199, 317, 325; Lady Palmerston to Palmerston, 2 Feb., and Palmerston to Lady Palmerston, 26 Oct. 1803, B.P.W.; *Palmerston*, i. 367.

50. Palmerston to Lady Palmerston, 26 Oct., 15 Nov. 1803, 23, 28 Nov., 16, 17, 19/20 Dec. 1804, Outram to Palmerston, 8 June, and Lady Palmerston to Palmerston, 13 Dec. 1804, B.P.W.; Palmerston to Malmesbury, 29 Nov. 1803, Malmesbury (Aspinall) Papers; *Palmerston*, i. 368; *Sulivan*, p. 36; St John's College, Cambridge, Papers.

51. Palmerston to Lady Palmerston, 26 Oct., 2, 15 Nov. 1803, 2 Mar., and to F. Temple, 3 May 1804, B.P.W.; *Palmerston's Opinions*, p. 264; *Notes, by Sir Robert Heron, Baronet* (1851), pp. 290-91; Palmerston to Malmesbury, 29 Nov. 1803, Malmesbury (Aspinall) Papers; *Sulivan*, p. 47; Gunning, i. 190-200.

52. Minto to Lady Minto, 3 April 1804, M.P.; *Glenbervie*, ii. 93.

53. Minto to Lady Minto, 10 Mar., 15, 21, 22, 26, 28 May, 13, 26 June, 2 Dec. 1804, M.P.; *Minto*, iii. 347, 350-51; Malmesbury to Pelham, 4 July 1804, Chichester Papers; *Sulivan*, pp. 29, 30-31, 36-7; Malmesbury to Mrs Gertrude Robinson, 13 Dec. 1804, Malmesbury Papers; Palmerston to W. Temple, 21, 30 Jan. 1805, B.P.W.

54. Minto to Lady Minto, 5 May, 26 June 1804, 18 Feb. 1805, and Lady Palmerston to Minto, 22 June 1801, M.P.; Lady Palmerston to Palmerston, 23 April 1802, 16 May 1804, Ravizzotti to Palmerston, 20 July, Palmerston to Ravizzotti, 13 Oct., Palmerston to Malmesbury, [?13] Dec., Malmesbury to Palmerston, 14 Dec., Palmerston to Pelham, n.d., Pelham to Palmerston, 23 Dec. 1804, Mrs Sulivan to W. Temple, 4 Feb. 1828, Palmerston to F. Temple, 23 April 1805, Gaetano Ravizzotti, junior, to Palmerston, 28 Feb. 1840, 11 April 1846, 1 Mar. 1848, and Palmerston's Accounts, B.P.W.; F. Temple to Palmerston, 11 Dec. 1803, 10 Mar., 27 May 1805, S.P.; Palmerston to W. Temple, 5 Dec. 1817, B.P.

55. Palmerston to F. Temple, 10 June, and to E. Temple, 4 July, B.P.W.; *Sulivan*, pp. 41-4; Kielder Castle Game Book, 2-18 Sept. 1805, Alnwick Castle Papers (I am grateful to the Duke of Northumberland for permission to use these papers).

56. Palmerston to F. Temple, 7 Nov., B.P.W.; *Palmerston*, i. 368; Palmerston to Malmesbury, 19 Nov. 1805, Malmesbury (Aspinall) Papers.

57. Brougham to [W. Wilberforce], 17 July 1804, Chatham Papers, P.R.O. 30/8/116 (*Brougham*, i. 309-13); Palmerston to F. Temple, 11 Nov., 7 Dec. 1803, Palmerston to W. Temple, 25 Dec. 1804, Malmesbury to Palmerston, 6 Dec. 1803, Palmerston to Lady Palmerston, 26 Oct., 2, 23 Nov. 1803, B.P.W.; [William Otter], *Life and Remains of the Rev. Edward Daniel Clarke* (1824), p. 543; Cooper, iv. 478-9; Gunning, ii. 187-9; *Pryme*, pp. 57-8; Ridley, p. 495.

58. Teignmouth, i. 38-9; Mrs Stewart to Palmerston, 3 Jan., and W. Temple to Lady Palmerston, 26 Mar. 1804, B.P.W.; *Sedgwick*, i. 78; Palmerston to F. Temple, 10 Nov. 1804, and to Lady Palmerston, 15 Nov. 1803, B.P.W.; *Sulivan*, p. 40; Guedalla, p. 46.

59. *Sulivan*, pp. 9-11, 40-41, 45-7; Palmerston to F. Temple, 24 Feb. 1804, B.P.W.; Hobhouse's journal, 26 Jan. 1832, 29 May 1847; *Stratford Canning*, i. 28; *Palmerston*, ii. 298-9.

60. *Sulivan*, pp. 12, 177.

61. *Sulivan*, p. 12; Lady Palmerston to Palmerston, 23 April 1802, and 'Things

Bought April 1824', B.P.W.; Palmerston to W. Temple, 5 Dec. 1817, B.P.; *Palmerston*, i. 367; 3 *Hansard*, cxxxvii. 243-8; Bell, ii. 286-8.

62. Journal of Countess of Malmesbury, Mar. 1810, Lowry Cole Papers 37; *Cockburn*, p. 21.

63. Mrs Stewart to Palmerston, 24 April, 1 May, 28 July, Maria Stewart to Palmerston, 23 June 1828, Mrs Bowles to Palmerston, 2 Oct. 1836, and Lady Donkin to Palmerston, 26 Aug. 1846, B.P.W.; *Cockburn*, pp. 200-201; Minto to Lansdowne, 25 Dec. 1824, Bowood Papers.

64. 3 *Hansard*, lxxx. 407 (9 May 1845); Palmerston to Malmesbury, 10 Dec. 1805, Malmesbury (Aspinall) Papers; Palmerston to Liverpool, 15 Nov. 1820, 24 June 1819, 28 June 1820, L.P.; Palmerston to Peel, 18 April 1826, Peel Papers.

65. Bruce, i. and ii. *passim*; Palmerston's diary, 15 Aug. 1818, and Palmerston to W. Temple, 4, 21 Aug. 1818, B.P.; Mrs Sulivan to W. Temple, 16 June 1826, B.P.W.

66. Ashburton to Palmerston, 10 Nov. 1803, B.P.W.; *Mrs Arbuthnot*, ii. 389; Frances, Baroness Bunsen, *A Memoir of Baron Bunsen* (1868), ii. 152.

CHAPTER II: INTO PARLIAMENT, 1806-7 (pages 48-79)

1. Mary, Lady Palmerston, to Palmerston, 23 April 1802, and Malmesbury to Palmerston, 6 Dec. 1803, B.P.W.; Connell, p. 459.

2. Connell, pp. 423, 452-3; *Minto*, iii. 380; *Sulivan*, pp. 32, 38, 41.

3. *Malmesbury Memoirs*, i. 6; Palmerston to Malmesbury, 13 Oct., Malmesbury (Aspinall) Papers; Malmesbury to Palmerston, 15 Oct. 1805, B.P.W.; Oldfield, iii. 551.

4. *Palmerston*, i. 367-8.

5. *Colchester*, ii. 28; Malmesbury to Louisa Harris, 23 Jan., Malmesbury Papers; *Sulivan*, pp. 49-50; Palmerston to F. Temple, 23, 24 Jan., B.P.W.; *Palmerston*, i. 14-17; Allen's journal, 22 Jan.; *P.O.W.*, v. 311-12; Horner to Stewart, 23 Jan., Horner Papers (*Horner*, i. 353-5); Gunning, ii. 215-25; *G.L.G.*, ii. 164; Sulivan to Palmerston, [Jan. 1806], B.P.

6. Malmesbury to Palmerston, [late Jan.], 28, 29 Jan., 2 Feb., B.P.W.; *Malmesbury Diaries*, iv. 358; *Perceval*, p. 106 n. 4; Horner to Stewart, 23 Jan. 1806, Horner Papers; *Creevey Papers*, i. 76; *Sulivan*, p. 51; cf. Ridley, p. 20.

7. Roberts, p. 330; Horner to Stewart, 23 Jan. 1806, Horner Papers.

8. *Glenbervie*, i. 45; *Rose*, ii. 262-4; Wood to Hardwicke, 10 Jan. 1802, Outram to Hardwicke, 10 Dec. 1805, Yorke to Hardwicke, 23 Jan., Yorke to Marsh, 24, 26 Jan., and Millers to Yorke, 28 Jan. 1806, Hardwicke Papers.

9. Yorke to Marsh, 24, 26 Jan., and Marsh to Yorke, 28 Jan., Hardwicke Papers; Oldfield, iii. 118-19, 125; Sulivan to Palmerston, 24 Jan., B.P.; *Alumni Cantab.* ('Mortlock'); Rutland to Lady Malmesbury, 25 Jan. 1806, B.P.W.; *Sulivan*, pp. 50-51.

10. *Palmerston*, i. 14-17; Althorp to Lady Spencer, 31 Jan., A.P.; Malmesbury to Palmerston, 29 Jan., B.P.W.; Yorke to Hardwicke, 29 Jan., 2, 5 Feb. 1806, Hardwicke Papers; *Sulivan*, p. 53.

11. *Sulivan*, pp. 50, 53; *Creevey Papers*, i. 76; *P.O.W.*, v. 312 n. 1.

12. *Sulivan*, pp. 49, 50, 52-3; Horner to Stewart, 23 Jan., Horner Papers (*Horner*, i. 353-5); W. Temple to Palmerston, 29 Jan., B.P.W.; Sulivan to Palmerston, 24, 28 Jan., [29-30 Jan.], B.P.; Whishaw to Holland, 24 Jan. 1806, H.H.P.

13. *Palmerston*, i. 368; *Malmesbury Diaries*, iv. 358; *G.L.G.*, ii. 173; *Althorp*, p. 88; Malmesbury to Palmerston, [late Jan. 1806], B.P.W.

14. Horner to Stewart, 23 Jan. (*Horner*, i. 353-5), and to Murray, 7 Feb., Horner Papers; Sulivan to Palmerston, 28 Jan., [29-30 Jan.], B.P.; Althorp to Spencer, 25, 27 Jan., 2 Feb., A.P.; *Sulivan*, p. 52; Whishaw to Holland, 24 Jan. 1806, H.H.P.; *Dudley to Ivy*, p. 35; *Lady Holland's Journal*, ii. 100; *P.O.W.*, v. 311 n. 2.

15. *Althorp*, pp. 72-8, 83-6; Petty to Lady Holland, 26 Jan., H.H.P.; *Sulivan*, pp.

50-51; *Palmerston*, i. 14-16; *Creevey Papers*, i. 76; Petty to Creevey, 30 Jan., Creevey Papers; Petty to Althorp, 28 Jan., and Althorp to Spencer, 25, 27, 30 Jan., A.P.; Malmesbury to Palmerston, 29 Jan. 1806, B.P.W.

16. *Sulivan*, pp. 49-50, 54, 55; *Palmerston*, i. 14-17; Hardwicke to Yorke, 28 Jan., Hardwicke Papers; Malmesbury to Palmerston, 24 Jan., B.P.W.; Petty to Creevey, [25 Jan.], Creevey Papers; Horner to Stewart, 23 Jan. 1806, Horner Papers.

17. *Creevey Papers*, i. 76; Sulivan to Palmerston, 24 Jan., B.P.; *Sulivan*, pp. 51-2; Malmesbury to Palmerston, 29 Jan., and Frances and Elizabeth Temple to Palmerston, 26 Jan. 1806, B.P.W.

18. *Sulivan*, p. 51; *Wilberforce*, iii. 254-7; Petty to Creevey, [25 Jan.], 1 Feb., Creevey Papers; *Wilberforce Correspondence*, ii. 64-7; Roger Anstey, 'A Re-interpretation of the Abolition of the British Slave Trade, 1806-1807', *E.H.R.*, lxxxvii (1972), p. 321; Horner to Stewart, 23 Jan. 1806, Horner Papers; Lorne, p. 9.

19. Horner to Murray, 16 Mar. 1805, 6 Feb. 1806, Horner Papers; *Sulivan*, p. 66; 'Epigrams at Brocket Hall, Dec. 1813', B.P.W.; Connell, p. 213; *Wilberforce*, iii. 256-7.

20. *Wilberforce*, iii. 256-7; W. Temple to Palmerston, 15 Feb., and to E. Temple, 16 Feb. 1806, B.P.W.; *Palmerston*, i. 16; *Sulivan*, pp. 52-5.

21. *Sulivan*, pp. 53 n. 3, 54, 55; Petty to Creevey, 30, 31 Jan., 1 Feb., [2 or 3 Feb.] 1806, Creevey Papers.

22. *Pryme*, p. 79; Malmesbury to Palmerston, 2, 3 Feb., B.P.W.; *Wilberforce Correspondence*, ii. 68 (amplified, through the kindness of the late Professor Roger Anstey, from the Wrangham Papers); Milner to Palmerston, 9.30 [a.m., 7 Feb.], B.P./ SLT1; Horner to Stewart, 8 Feb. 1806, Horner Papers.

23. *Palmerston*, i. x, 16, 368; Lady Amherst to Lady Malmesbury, 9 Feb., Malmesbury to Palmerston, 24, 29 Jan., 2, 8 Feb., B.P.W.; *Minto*, iii. 380; *Althorp*, p. 87; Petty to Creevey, [2 or 3 Feb.], Creevey Papers; Sulivan to Palmerston, [? 29-30 Jan.], B.P.; election expenses, Cambridge, 1806, B.P.W.; *Sulivan*, pp. 50-51, 55.

24. *Sulivan*, p. 56.

25. *Althorp*, p. 88; Sulivan to Palmerston, 28 Feb., S.P.; *Sulivan*, pp. 56, 59; [Emma Godfrey] to W. Temple, 26 [April], W. Temple to E. Temple, 16 Feb., 26 Mar., 14 June, Palmerston to F. Temple, 'Tues. Feb. 1806', and Blackburn to Palmerston, 13 Mar., B.P.W.; Minto to Lady Minto, 6 Mar., 6 June 1806, M.P.; *Minto*, iii. 390; *An Englishman at Home and Abroad 1792-1828 with Some Recollections of Napoleon: Being Extracts from the Diaries of J.B. Scott of Bungay, Suffolk* (1930), ed. Ethel Mann, p. 29.

26. 'Journal Historical and Political commenced June 1806', B.P.W. (*Palmerston*, i. 24-77); Palmerston to Shee, 17 July 1806, B.P.; *Sulivan*, p. 59.

27. *Sulivan*, pp. 57-66; Shee to Palmerston, 1 Aug., and Sulivan to Palmerston, 11 Aug., B.P.; Palmerston to Malmesbury, 17 Sept., 1 Oct. 1806, Malmesbury (Aspinall) Papers.

28. Albery, pp. 142-93; Edward and Annie G. Porritt, *The Unreformed House of Commons* (Cambridge, 1909), i. 357-8; *Sulivan*, pp. 63, 68 n. 1; Malmesbury to Palmerston, 25 Sept., B.P.W.; Palmerston to Malmesbury, 1 Oct., and Malmesbury to Fitzharris, 5 Oct. 1806, 8 Jan. 1807, Malmesbury (Aspinall) Papers.

29. *Sulivan*, pp. 67-8; Malmesbury to Fitzharris, 'Fri. noon' [17], 19 Oct., Palmerston to Malmesbury, 'Fri.' [17], 18, 23 Oct., and W. Temple to Malmesbury, 11 Dec. 1806, Malmesbury (Aspinall) Papers.

30. *Sulivan*, pp. 68 n. 1, 71 n. 2; Palmerston to Malmesbury, 1, 31 Oct. 1806, Malmesbury (Aspinall) Papers.

31. *P.O.W.*, v. 429-32; *Sulivan*, p. 66; *Palmerston*, i. 37-40.

32. *Sulivan*, pp. 68-70; Palmerston to Malmesbury, 26 Oct., 'Wed.' [29 Oct.], Malmesbury (Aspinall) Papers; Palmerston to Hardwicke, 'Saturday' [?25 Oct.], and Euston to Yorke, 27 Oct. 1806, Hardwicke Papers.

33. Malmesbury to Palmerston, 28 Oct. 1806, B.P.W.; Albery, pp. 192-8.

34. Albery, pp. 131, 197-200; Fitzharris to Malmesbury, 4 Nov. 1806 (2 letters), Malmesbury (Aspinall) Papers.

35. Fitzharris to Malmesbury, 4, 6 Nov., and Malmesbury to Fitzharris, 5, [*c.* 11], 17 Nov., Malmesbury (Aspinall) Papers; *Farington*, iv. 107-8; Albery, p. 229; Malmesbury to Palmerston, 13 Nov. 1806, B.P.W.

36. *Sulivan*, pp. 70-71; Palmerston to F. Temple, 6 Nov. 1806, B.P.W.

37. Palmerston to Malmesbury, 16 Nov., 4 Dec. 1806, and Malmesbury to Fitzharris, 1, 8, 9, 11 Jan. 1807, Malmesbury (Aspinall) Papers; *Sulivan*, pp. 75, 77; Malmesbury to Palmerston, 11, 28 Dec. 1806, 20 Jan. 1807, B.P.W.; Albery, pp. 230-32.

38. *Palmerston*, i. 369; Albery, pp. 232-9, 251; Palmerston to Malmesbury, 21 Jan. 1807, Malmesbury (Aspinall) Papers.

39. Malmesbury to Palmerston, 20 Jan., B.P.W.; Palmerston to Malmesbury, 21 Jan., 26 Feb. 1807, Malmesbury (Aspinall) Papers.

40. A.M.W. Stirling, *Coke of Norfolk and his Friends* (1908), i. 221, ii. 59-63; Richard Mackenzie Bacon, *A Memoir of the Life of Edward, Third Baron Suffield* (privately printed, Norwich, 1838), pp. 27-32, 45, confuses the General Elections of 1806 and 1807 and like most published works muddles many of the details; I am indebted to Mr Rowland Thorne of the History of Parliament Trust for help in clarifying the election and its aftermath; Palmerston to F. Temple, 'Sat.' [28 Feb. 1807], B.P.W.

41. Palmerston to Malmesbury, 26 Feb., Malmesbury (Aspinall) Papers; Palmerston to F. Temple, 'Sat.' [28 Feb. 1807], B.P.W.

42. Malmesbury to Palmerston, 5 Mar., and Palmerston to F. Temple, 'Sat.' [28 Feb.], B.P.W.; Palmerston to Malmesbury, 'Monday night' [2 Mar. 1807], Malmesbury (Aspinall) Papers.

43. Palmerston to Malmesbury, 5 Mar., Malmesbury (Aspinall) Papers; *House of Commons Journal*, lxiii. 36 (1 Jan.), 197-8 (3 Mar.), 229 (11 Mar. 1807).

44. *The Journal and Correspondence of William, Lord Auckland* (1861-2), ed. [George Hogge], iv. 293; *Perceval*, p. 74; *Malmesbury Diaries*, iv. 389.

45. *Sulivan*, pp. 79-84; Sulivan to Palmerston, [?27 April], S.P.; *Malmesbury Diaries*, iv. 393; Palmerston to F. Temple, 26 April, and W. Temple to E. Temple, 'Wednesday' [29 April 1807], B.P.W.

46. *Sulivan*, pp. 79-80; Henry Roscoe, *The Life of William Roscoe* (1833), i. 403; *Sedgwick*, ii. 87; endorsement on Palmerston to Percy, 30 Oct. 1806, B.P.W.; Lord Grenville to Hardwicke, 'Monday' [27 April], and Prof. Sir Busick Harwood to Hardwicke, 4 May, Hardwicke Papers; Malmesbury to Palmerston, 27 April 1807, B.P.W.

47. Malmesbury to Palmerston, 4 May 1807, B.P.W.; *Sulivan*, pp. 80, 81-2.

48. *Malmesbury Diaries*, iv. 390; *Sulivan*, p. 79; 'Lord Chief Justice Gibbs', Henry, Lord Brougham, *Historical Sketches of Statesmen who Flourished in the Time of George III* (1855), i. 215-24; *Campbell*, i. 219; *D.N.B.* ('Gibbs'); *Perceval*, pp. 82, 135-6, 252; Sulivan to Palmerston, [27 April], S.P.; Malmesbury to Palmerston, 29 April, and W. Temple to E. Temple, 'Wednesday' [29 April] 1807, B.P.W.

49. *Palmerston*, i. 19; Lady Malmesbury's journal, 12 May, Lowry Cole Papers 37; Malmesbury to Palmerston, 2 May 1807, B.P.W.

50. *Sulivan*, pp. 80-81, 83-4; Malmesbury to Palmerston, 1, 2 May 1807, B.P.W.; *Sedgwick*, ii. 87.

51. *Palmerston*, i. 20; *Sulivan*, p. 85; Petty to Lady Holland, 'Friday night' [8 May 1807], H.H.P.; *Pryme*, p. 79.

52. *Palmerston*, i. 22, 369-70; *Sulivan*, pp. 85-6.

53. *Sulivan*, pp. 85-6; Petty to Lady Holland, 3 May 1807, H.H.P.

54. Malmesbury to Palmerston, 2, 4, 9 May [1807, though the last is endorsed '1806'], B.P.W.

55. Oldfield, iii. 555-7; Connell, pp. 207-8; *Palmerston*, i. 370; Malmesbury to Palmerston, 4, 9 May [1807], B.P.W.

CHAPTER III: ADMIRALTY AND WAR OFFICE, 1807-28 (*pages 80-132*)

1. Mulgrave to Malmesbury, 1 April, B.P.; *Palmerston*, i. 369; *Croker Papers*, i. 18; Lady Malmesbury to Minto, 10 April 1807, M.P.; Lorne, pp. 43-4.

2. Sulivan to Palmerston, 4 Nov. 1807, S.P.; *Sulivan*, pp. 99-100, 106-7; Malmesbury to Palmerston, 16 Dec., and W. Temple to E. Temple, 23 July 1808, B.P.W.

3. Sulivan to Palmerston, 9 Aug. 1808, and Malmesbury to Palmerston, 9 Jan., 21 Mar., 7 July, B.P.; W. Temple to E. Temple, 22 May, B.P.W.; *Sulivan*, pp. 89, 92, 98, 106, 126; Palmerston to Malmesbury, 6 July 1809, Malmesbury (Aspinall) Papers.

4. *Palmerston*, i. 371; *George III*, v. 423 n. 5; *Sulivan*, p. 99; Palmerston to Malmesbury, 18 Feb. [1809], Malmesbury (Aspinall) Papers.

5. *Palmerston*, i. 80-82, 371; W. Temple to F. Temple, 5 Feb. 1808, B.P.W.; 1 *Hansard*, x. 300-301; B.P./SP/A1.

6. *George III*, v. 15; W. Temple to F. Temple, 5 Feb. 1808, B.P.W.; *Palmerston*, i. 81-2, 371.

7. *Palmerston*, i. 83; *Lady Holland's Journal*, ii. 240; Gilbert Elliot to Minto, 8 Feb. 1807 [*sic*, but really 1808], and Lady Malmesbury to Minto, 10 April 1808, M.P.; W. Temple to F. Temple, 5 Feb. 1808, and to Palmerston, 19 April 1807, B.P.W.; Mulgrave to Palmerston, 4 Feb. 1808, B.P./SP/A1; *Sulivan*, p. 99.

8. *Sulivan*, pp. 86-98.

9. Canning to Mrs Canning, 26 Mar., 6 Aug., C.P. 22; *Perceval*, pp. 91-2; *Malmesbury Memoirs*, i. 1-2; Malmesbury to Portland, [12] July, and Fitzharris to Malmesbury, 13 July 1807, Malmesbury (Aspinall) Papers.

10. *Perceval*, p. 266; *Malmesbury Letters*, ii. 13-20; Malmesbury to Portland, [12] July, and Palmerston to Malmesbury, 8 Aug., Malmesbury (Aspinall) Papers; Malmesbury to Palmerston, 7 Aug. 1807, B.P.W.

11. Malmesbury to Palmerston, 7, 9, 13 Aug., B.P.W.; *Canning and Friends*, i. 242-3; Palmerston to Malmesbury, 14 Aug., Malmesbury (Aspinall) Papers; *George III*, iv. 589 n. 1; Canning to Mrs Canning, 26 Mar., 6 Aug. 1807, C.P. 22.

12. *Malmesbury Letters*, ii. 181-6; *Rose*, ii. 355-6; Palmerston to R. Plumer Ward, 2, 11 Oct. 1809, B.P.

13. *Palmerston*, i. 90-95; Palmerston to W. Temple, 16 Oct. 1809, B.P.

14. *Palmerston*, i. 90-91.

15. *Perceval*, p. 361; *Palmerston*, i. 90-95; Palmerston to Plumer Ward, 2 Oct., B.P.; *Colchester*, ii. 179-80, 185, 193, 215-16; *Rose*, ii. 402-3, 409; Yorke to Hardwicke, 4 Oct. 1809, Hardwicke Papers.

16. *Palmerston*, i. 90-95.

17. *Palmerston*, i. 92.

18. *Palmerston*, i. 90-95, 371; Yorke to Hardwicke, 4 Oct., Hardwicke Papers; *Colchester*, ii. 218; *Perceval*, pp. 262, 268; Grey to Tierney, 21 Oct., Tierney Papers, Hampshire Record Office; *George III*, v. 418 n. 1; Palmerston to F. Temple, [22 Oct. 1809], B.P.W.

19. *Palmerston*, i. 96-7, 100; *Ward*, i. 249-50; W. Temple to Palmerston, 17 Oct. 1809, B.P./GMC2.

20. *Perceval*, pp. 257-61, 362; *Palmerston*, i. 97-103; T. Wemyss Reid, *The Life, Letters, and Friendships of Richard Monckton Milnes, First Lord Houghton* (1890), i. 13; Palmerston to F. Temple, 23 Oct., B.P.W.; Malmesbury to Palmerston, 18 Oct., and Perceval to Palmerston, 23 Oct. 1809, B.P./GMC4, 11.

21. Perceval to Palmerston, 26 Oct., B.P./GMC13; *Palmerston*, i. 101-4; *Perceval*, p. 363; *George III*, v. 417-18.

22. *Ward*, i. 250; *Perceval*, pp. 129, 269; Ellenborough to Sidmouth, 1 Nov., Sidmouth Papers 1809 OZ (pkt 54); Canning to Mrs Canning, 23 Oct., C.P. 23; *Herries*, i. 13; Brougham to John Allen, [19 Oct.], H.H.P.; *Dudley to Ivy*, p. 82; Malmesbury to Palmerston, 30 Oct. 1809, B.P.

23. *Rose*, ii. 429; Granville to Palmerston, 26 Oct. 1809, B.P./GMC15; *Palmerston*, i. 104.

24. Clode, ii. 181, 205-6, 768; *Perceval*, p. 329.

25. Clode, i. 195-205, ii. 688-9.

26. Clode, ii. 182-93.

27. Clode, i. 134-40, ii. 688.

28. Clode, i. 106-7.

29. Clode, i. 105-6, ii. 27-30; Dupin, i. 206; W.O. 43/179; 'Sixth Report of the Commissioners of Military Enquiry', *BPP*, 1808, v. 323-5.

30. *BPP*, 1808, v. 367-76, 381-2; W.O. 43/280.

31. Palmerston to Treasury, 19 June 1815, W.O. 4/427; *BPP*, 1808, v. 372; W.O. 43/296; Clode, ii. 211-13; *Perceval*, pp. 329-30.

32. Clode, ii. 299-303; *BPP*, 1808, v. 304-88; Palmerston to Treasury, 7 Jan. 1812, W.O. 4/441; W.O. circulars 181, 10 July 1813, 150, 26 December 1813, W.O. 4/464, 329, 19 June 1816, W.O. 4/466; W.O. 43/566; *BPP*, 1850 (662), x. 851-6.

33. *Palmerston*, i. 107-8.

34. *BPP*, 1837, xxxiv, Pt I, p. 177; Malmesbury to Palmerston, [13 Nov. 1809], B.P.; W.O. to Treasury, 17 Oct. 1807, W.O. 4/422; *BPP*, 1808, v. 276-643 (especially 280-82, 294-5, 401-2); Clode, ii. 254 n. 3 (W.O. 43/508), 688-9; *BPP*, 1809, v. 3-5, 53; *P.O.W.*, viii. 53-9, 63-4, 73; *Ward*, i. 427, 430.

35. *BPP*, 1808, v. 306-8; *BPP*, 1809, v. 1-24.

36. *BPP*, 1808, v. 278, 282-93, 418-19.

37. *BPP*, 1808, v. 291-4, 498-9; Pulteney to Treasury, 5 May 1809, W.O. 4/423.

38. *BPP*, 1808, v. 283-5, 296-7, 304, 311, 410-13, 503; Palmerston to Lushington, 26 Nov. 1821, P.P.; *Sulivan*, p. 20 n. 66; *BPP*, 1809, v. 1-24, 123-268.

39. Dupin, i. 29-30; *BPP*, 1808, v. 284-5, 308-11, 320, 348-52, 383-8.

40. *BPP*, 1808, v. 323-8.

41. *BPP*, 1808, v. 286-8, 290, 299, 354-5.

42. *BPP*, 1810, xiv. 18-19; *Palmerston*, i. 108; W. Temple to F. Temple, 8 Nov., B.P.W.; Treasury to W.O., 7, 25 Mar., 29 April, and W.O. to Treasury, 9 Mar., 13 April, 24 May 1809, W.O. 4/429.

43. Treasury to W.O., 20 July, and W.O. to Treasury, 28 July 1809, W.O. 4/429.

44. Palmerston to F. Temple, 9 Nov., B.P.W.; Treasury to W.O., 23 Nov. 1809, W.O. 4/429.

45. W.O. to Treasury, 30 Nov. 1809, 21 Feb., and Treasury to W.O., 16, 19 Feb., W.O. 4/429; W.O. to Treasury, 13 Mar. 1810, W.O. 4/376.

46. W.O. to Treasury, 25 May, 13 July, 10, 27 Aug. 1810, W.O. 4/424; W.O. 43/438 (Moore's retirement).

47. Palmerston to superintendents, 7 Dec., note by Moore on superintendents to Palmerston, 18 Dec., and Granville to Treasury, 12 Oct. 1809, W.O. 4/429.

48. Palmerston to superintendents, 20 Dec., W.O. 4/429; Dundas to Palmerston, 3 Nov. 1809, and Palmerston to Dundas, 6 Mar., B.P.; W.O. to Treasury, 31 Aug. 1810, W.O. 4/424.

49. W.O. to Treasury, 1 Mar. 1811, W.O. 4/425, 1 June 1810, W.O. 4/437; Palmerston to Commissary-in-Chief, 14 June 1810, P.P.; *Sulivan*, pp. 121-2; Charles Long to Perceval and Perceval to Herries, 3 Nov. 1811, Herries Papers.

50. P.P. 48417, ff. 9-20, and W.O. 4/437, 440, 441, 443, for correspondence between the War Office, the Horse Guards, the Treasury and the Commissary-in-Chief.

51. *Perceval*, pp. 325-6; S.G.P. Ward, *Wellington's Headquarters. A Study of the Admin-*

istrative Problems in the Peninsula 1809-1814 (1957), p. 60; Roberts, p. 159; War Office circulars nos. 272 of 12 May, 301 of 3 Nov. 1815, W.O. 4/465; Taylor (H.G.) to Merry (W.O.), 23 July 1822, and internal W.O. minutes, W.O. 43/179.

52. Palmerston to Commissary-General of Musters, 18, 25, 30 Jan., 21, 22 Feb. 1811, W.O. 4/431, 26 Sept. 1812, W.O. 4/434; *BPP*, 1810-11, iii. 1018; Palmerston to Treasury, 7 Jan. 1812, W.O. 4/441.

53. *BPP*, 1810-11, iii. 1018; Sulivan's 'Account of his Public Service', 17 Jan. 1851, S.P.; Palmerston to Dods and to Sulivan, 28 Jan. 1811, W.O. 4/431; *Sulivan*, p. 122, S.P.

54. Palmerston to Treasury, 6 June, W.O. 4/439, and to superintendents, 6 June 1811, P.P.; Palmerston to Treasury, 20 Mar. 1812, W.O. 4/425; W.O. to Treasury, 24 May, 28 July, and Treasury to W.O., 23 Nov. 1809, W.O. 4/429; Palmerston to superintendents, 9 Sept. 1813, P.P.; *BPP*, 1837, xxxiv, Pt I, p. 177, and Sulivan's 'Account', 17 Jan. 1851, S.P.

55. *BPP*, 1837, xxxiv, Pt I, pp. 177-8; W.O. to Treasury, 8 Dec. 1814, 28 Feb. 1815, W.O. 4/427; *BPP*, 1817, iv. 61, 66; W.O. to Treasury, 31 Mar. 1828, W.O. 4/724; *Sulivan*, p. 175; Palmerston to F. J. Robinson, 11 June 1826, R.P.; W.O. 43/564; W.O. to Woods and Forests, 13 Mar. 1830, W.O. 4/724; Sulivan's 'Account', 17 Jan. 1851, S.P.

56. Palmerston to Harrison, 23 Sept. 1813, W.O. 4/426.

57. *BPP*, 1817, iv. 61-6; 'Statement . . . in the spring of 1817, showing . . . the higher salaries in the War Office . . . ' and 'Comparison of the Expense of the War Office and Pay Office for 1818', P.P. 48418; Palmerston to Treasury, 3 Dec. 1817, P.P., 22 Jan. 1818, W.O. 43/933; *BPP*, 1818, iii. 99-103, 118; W.O. to Treasury, 31 Mar. 1820, W.O. 4/724; 2 *Hansard*, vi. 895-915, 920-23, 1178-86, 1215-28 (especially 1218-19); Lushington to Palmerston, 13 Aug. 1821, W.O. 43/148; Palmerston to Lushington, 26 Nov. 1821, P.P.; Palmerston to Robinson, 11 June 1826, R.P.

58. Palmerston to Lushington, 26 Nov. 1821, P.P.

59. Lushington to Palmerston, 30 Jan. 1822, W.O. 43/147; 'peace' establishment as agreed by Treasury at the beginning of W.O. 4/724; Palmerston to Treasury, 31 Jan. 1825, 30 Aug. 1826, W.O. 4/724; Palmerston to F.J. Robinson, private, 11 June, R.P.; Palmerston to W. Temple, 10 Aug., B.P.; Treasury to W.O., 16 Sept. 1826, W.O. 43/564.

60. W.O. to Treasury, 31 Mar. 1828, W.O. 4/724; Palmerston's office memo., 12 Sept. 1822, W.O. 4/724 (cf. Ridley, p. 56); Palmerston to Treasury, 3 Dec. 1817, P.P.; Palmerston to Lushington, 26 Nov. 1821, P.P.; Lushington to Palmerston, 30 Jan. 1822, W.O. 43/147; Palmerston to F.J. Robinson, private, 11 June 1826, R.P.; W.O. to Treasury, 30 Aug. 1826, W.O. 4/724.

61. F. Temple to Palmerston, [Oct. 1809], B.P.W.; *Mrs Arbuthnot*, ii. 190; *Palmerston*, i. 108; *Jackson*, i. 90.

62. Palmerston to the Horse Guards, 1 May 1825, W.O. 43/322.

63. W.O. 43/160 (surgeon-major's widow); Palmerston to William Beresford, 27 Nov. 1852, Beresford Papers, Perkins Library, Duke University; Palmerston to Treasury, 21 Jan. 1811, W.O. 4/425; Clode, i. 227, 255-6; W.O. 43/184 (Irish medical officers), 200 (militia pay and allowances).

64. W.O. 43/136; [E. Temple] to Palmerston, 6 Feb. 1804, S.P., 2 Feb. 1806, B.P.W.; undated minute on draft reply to letter from C.-in-C. of 14 Sept. 1825, W.O. 43/286.

65. Palmerston's minute of 18 Mar. 1827, W.O. 43/256; W.O. 43/239; W.O. 43/205 (unnecessary warrants), 174 (widows' certificates), 130 (Audit Office's interference).

66. Palmerston memos, P.P. and Bell, i. 33; Gash, *Secretary Peel*, pp. 116-17.

67. Palmerston to superintendents, 2 Nov. 1810, W.O. 4/431; Palmerston's office

memo., 25 Nov. 1820, W.O. 4/724; W.O. 43/576 (venison and inkstand); Bell, i. 33; Merry to J. Lukin, 2 June 1812, W.O. 4/434.

68. *Perceval*, p. 328 n. 1; Palmerston to Treasury, 10 April, 21 May 1811, W.O. 4/425; *The Life and Correspondence of M.G. Lewis* (1839), ii. 98-106; Palmerston's diary, 19 Dec. 1819, B.P.; Mark Boyd, *Reminiscences of Fifty Years* (1871), pp. 43-4.

69. Clode, ii. 110-11; Palmerston to Liverpool, 15 May 1818, L.P.; W.O. 43/136.

70. Palmerston to W. Temple, 5 Dec. 1817, B.P.; W.O. to Treasury, 28 Jan. 1811, W.O. 4/425.

71. Palmerston to Torrens, 27 July 1816, 28 Mar. 1817, P.P., and W.O. to Treasury, 11 Feb. 1815, W.O. 4/427 (Holland case).

72. W.O. to Treasury, 28 July, 18 Dec., and Treasury to W.O., 23 Nov., 20 Dec. 1809, W.O. 4/429; Palmerston to Robinson, 11 June 1826, R.P.; *BPP*, 1808, v. 282, 289, 404; *BPP*, 1817, iv. 61; *The Diary of the Rt Hon. William Windham 1784 to 1810* (1866), ed. Mrs Henry Baring, p. 387; Granville to Treasury, 10 Oct. 1809, W.O. 4/429; Dupin, i. 174 (cf. Ridley, p. 56).

73. *Sulivan*, pp. 136-8, 208; Palmerston's 'Journal of Tour in France, Italy & Swizzerland in 1816', vol. ii, f.1, B.P.W.; *BPP*, 1837, xxxiv, Pt I, pp. 177-9; Palmerston to W. Temple, 5 Dec. 1817, B.P.

74. *Farington*, i. 199, ii. 81; Palmerston to Treasury, 3 Dec. 1817, P.P.; *Sulivan*, p. 168; Palmerston to Canning, 26 July 1827, C.P. 74; Taylor to Melbourne, 12 Nov. 1835, enclosing Mrs Lukin's memorial, RA, M.P.; Palmerston to Treasury, 30 May 1828, W.O. 4/724.

75. Palmerston to F. Temple, 23 Nov. 1809, 17 Jan. 1811, B.P.W.; Godschall Johnson to Althorp, 7 June 1828, A.P.

76. *The Diary of Sir John Moore* (1904), ed. Major General Sir J.F. Maurice, ii. 232; W.O. to Treasury, 31 Mar. 1828, W.O. 4/724; Mrs Sulivan to W. Temple, 16 June 1826, and Palmerston accounts for 23 April, 4 Aug. 1831, B.P.W.; W.O. 43/148; *Farington*, iii. 8, 253; *Authentic and Interesting Memoirs of Mrs Clarke* (Chapple, 1809), pp. 94, 106, 108-9; *D.N.B.* ('Glasse').

77. *Sulivan*, pp. 17, 93, 110; *Palmerston*, i. 120-21; Longlands to Yorke, 6 Sept., 25 Oct., and Yorke to Longlands, 7 Sept., 5 Nov. 1810, Hardwicke Papers; *The Marlay Letters 1778-1820* (1937), ed. R. Warwick Bond, p. 163; Michael MacDonagh, *The Viceroy's Post-Bag. Correspondence Hitherto Unpublished of the Earl of Hardwicke First Lord Lieutenant of Ireland after the Union* (1904), pp. 49, 203-6.

78. *BPP*, 1808, v. 352-4; Palmerston to Hiley Addington, 15 May 1815, P.P., to C.-in-C., 22 July 1815, W.O. 4/420, and to Liverpool, 17 Dec. 1816, 9 Jan. 1817, P.P.

79. Lady Malmesbury to Palmerston, 3, 11 Nov. 1809, B.P.; *Sulivan*, pp. 113-15; *BPP*, 1808, v. 596, and 1809, v. 51; W.O. to Treasury, 5 May 1809, W.O. 4/423.

80. Sulivan's 'Account', 17 Jan. 1851, S.P.

81. W.O. to Treasury, 15 Mar. 1815, W.O. 4/427, and 25 Jan. 1832, W.O. 4/724; Palmerston to Commissioners of Public Audit, 26 Feb. 1811, W.O. 4/439.

82. *Sulivan*, pp. 21-2; Lady Minto to Minto, 28 Nov. 1811, 30 Mar. 1812, M.P.

83. Sulivan to Palmerston, 13 Nov. 1837, B.P.; *Sulivan*, pp. 22-7.

84. *Sulivan*, pp. 21, 57, 122, 123, 136-8; E. Temple to Palmerston, 2 Feb. 1806, B.P.W.

85. Correspondence between Palmerston, the Foveaux and the Treasury, Nov.-Dec. 1821, P.P. 48419.

86. Palmerston to Lushington, 26 Nov. 1821, P.P.; Palmerston to Robinson, 11 June, R.P.; Palmerston's memo., 20 Sept., W.O. 43/564; list of promotions and appointments, 25 Sept. 1826, W.O. 7/724.

87. ['C. Pritchard'] to ? Sinclair, 17 Feb., and 'C. Pritchard' to [? Althorp], 20 Mar. 1832, Broughton Papers.

88. *Sulivan*, pp. 206, 250-51, 253.

89. *Sulivan*, pp. 19, 255, 278-81; Capt. Owen Wheeler, *The War Office Past and Present* (1914), p. 120; Hardinge to [? Treasury], 16 July 1830, W.O. 4/724.

CHAPTER IV: THE ARMY AND THE NATION (*pages 133-80*)

1. 1 *Hansard*, xv. 661; *Palmerston*, i. 115-16; *George III*, v. 527; George Rose to Malmesbury, 3 Mar. 1810, Malmesbury (Aspinall) Papers.

2. Malmesbury to Palmerston, 4 Mar., B.P.; Lady Minto to Minto, 18 Mar., M.P. (*Minto*, iv. 331); Lady Malmesbury's journal, Mar. 1810, Lowry Cole Papers 37.

3. Ridley, pp. 41, 55-6; *George III*, v. 545; *P.O.W.*, vii. 262; *Ward*, i. 404; T. Grenville to Holland, 6 Sept. 1815, H.H.P.; 1 *Hansard*, xxxiii. 76-117; *George IV*, ii. 155, 156; *Palmerston*, i. 134-5.

4. Grey to Holland, 8 Dec. 1816, H.H.P.; Palmerston to W. Temple, 13 Mar., 21 Aug. 1818, B.P.; 2 *Hansard*, i. 825, 1078-82.

5. *Colchester*, iii. 219; Lever, p. 79; Ashley, i. 88; Hobhouse's journal, 12, 22 Mar. 1822.

6. Cf. *Palmerston*, i. 145-6, and Ridley, p. 61.

7. Roberts, pp. 150-51; *W.N.D.*, i. 180-81; *Wilberforce*, v. 120; Hobhouse's journal, 13 Feb.; Ellice to Grey, 'Thursday' [14 Feb.], G.P.; Brougham to ?, 'Thursday' [14 Feb. 1822], Brougham Papers.

8. Littleton to Granville, 7 Mar. 1825, Gran. Papers 6/3 no. 93; *Melbourne Papers*, pp. 109-10; *Goderich*, p. 174; Palmerston to Peel, 14 Feb. 1828, Peel Papers; Ashley, i. 140; Sulivan's 'Account of his Public Service', 17 Jan. 1851, S.P.

9. Clode, i. 155; 1 *Hansard*, xxi. 1204-9 (6 Mar.), 1269-92 (13 Mar. 1812).

10. Palmerston to Malmesbury, 14 Mar. 1812, Malmesbury (Aspinall) Papers; 1 *Hansard*, xxvii. 215-17 (29 Nov. 1813), xxix. 1243 (3 Mar. 1815).

11. Clode, i. 148, 155; 1 *Hansard*, xxxi. 936-7 (21 June 1815); Ridley, pp. 57, 78-9; *Memoirs of the Life of Sir Samuel Romilly, Written by Himself; With a Selection from his Correspondence*, edited by his sons (1840), ii. 323; Palmerston to Calvert (Adjutant-General), 10 June 1812, and to Sidmouth (Home Secretary), 8 Feb. 1816, P.P.; circular no. 289, 31 Aug. 1815, W.O. 4/465; Palmerston's minute, 11 Mar. 1823, W.O. 43/199; *W.N.D.*, iii. 198-201.

12. 2 *Hansard*, x. 933 (11 Mar.); Taylor to Palmerston, 4 Mar. 1824, copy in Hope of Luffness Papers M.

13. 'Mem. for Speech on Corporal Punishment. Hume's motion in Comm. on Mutiny Bill', Mar. 1826, B.P./SP/A5; 2 *Hansard*, xiv. 1303-4 (10 Mar. 1826); *W.N.D.*, iii. 198.

14. Palmerston's endorsement on Taylor to Palmerston, 13 Mar. 1826, B.P./WO33; *W.N.D.*, iii. 198-201, 276-80; Taylor to Peel, 6 April 1826, Peel Papers; Sir Herbert Maxwell, *The Life of Wellington. The Restoration of the Martial Power of Great Britain* (1900), ii. 129-33.

15. 2 *Hansard*, i. 454 (16 May 1820), xvi. 679 (26 Feb. 1827), 1136-40 (12 Mar. 1827); *Sulivan*, pp. 221-3, 230.

16. *Broughton*, iv. 208-9, 295-7; Palmerston to Grey, 3 April 1833, and Howick to Grey, 9 Dec. [1826], G.P.; Clode, i. 155; Burdett to Hobhouse, 1 May 1824, Broughton Papers; 2 *Hansard*, xvi. 328 (11 Dec. 1826), 469-71 (14 Feb. 1827).

17. Palmerston to the Adjutant-General, 14 Dec. 1814, to Torrens, 20 July 1815, and to Liverpool, 21 June 1817, P.P.; George White to Palmerston, 9 June 1821, B.P./WO10 no. 2; Palmerston's diary, 8 July 1819, B.P.; Ridley, p. 60; *D.N.B.* ('Rawson'); 1 *Hansard*, xl. 315-30 (11 May 1819); 2 *Hansard*, i. 838 (2 June 1820), ii. 321-2 (10 July 1820); *Journals of the House of Commons*, Sess. 1821, lxxvi. 1233-4.

18. Palmerston to ?, 29 Mar. 1813, P.P.; *Palmerston*, i. 412; Clode, i. 201, 555-6; minutes on Jonathan Williams to Palmerston, 19 Mar. 1818, W.O. 43/119, and on

Major General A. Dixon to Torrens, 25 May 1812, W.O. 43/381; Palmerston to Vansittart, 19 Aug. 1813, P.P.

19. Palmerston to Brooksbank, 2 Mar. 1813, P.P.

20. Clode, i. 366-84, ii. 281-2, 287; Palmerston to C.-in-C., 23 April, 6 July 1812, W.O. 4/416.

21. Duke of York to Palmerston, 28 Jan. 1822, B.P./WO11; Clode, i. 367-8, ii. 281-2.

22. W.O. 43/239 (Stride and Nugent cases).

23. W.O. 43/286; Palmerston to Taylor, 21 April 1822, P.P.; W.O. 43/189.

24. Ridley, pp. 58-9.

25. Palmerston to Taylor, 31 Mar., 7 April, and Taylor to Palmerston, 4 April 1825, P.P.; W.O. 43/317; Clode, ii. 437.

26. Palmerston's memo., 3 July 1815, P.P.

27. W.O. 43/225.

28. Palmerston to Lord Beresford, 13 June 1823, P.P.; Ridley, p. 60; Clode, ii. 283; Palmerston to Long (P.M.G.), 27 Dec. 1811, P.P.; Palmerston to Harrison (Treasury), 20 Aug. 1812, 14 May 1813, W.O. 4/426; W.O. 43/430.

29. W.O. memo., 18 Dec. 1813, P.P.; Clode, i. 378; Palmerston to Robinson, 8 Nov., and Robinson to Palmerston, 25 Nov. 1824, R.P.

30. W.O. 43/432.

31. W.O. 43/273.

32. W.O. 43/889.

33. W.O. 43/175.

34. Palmerston to Liverpool, 14 Oct. 1812, Palmerston to Torrens, 13 Nov. 1812, 5 April 1813, and Torrens to Palmerston, 19 Nov. 1812, P.P.; *BPP*, 1818, iii. 116; Palmerston to Liverpool, 23 April 1818, L.P.; 1 *Hansard*, xxxviii. 376-95; Clode, i. 381; Palmerston's minute, 4 Feb. 1826 [but really 1827], W.O. 43/235 (see also Clode, i. 366-84, *BPP*, 1828, v. 523-6, and W.O. 43/123).

35. W.O. 43/123 (widows' pensions), 376 (Halliday case); Althorp to Grey, 31 Dec. 1831, A.P.

36. W.O. 43/286.

37. Clode, ii. 79, 102; Palmerston to Taylor, 7 June 1823, P.P.; W.O. 43/391.

38. *Jackson*, i. 439, ii. 11-12; Creevey to Elizabeth Ord, 12 Mar. 1825, Creevey Papers.

39. Walpole, ii. 448 n. 1.

40. *The Times*, 9, 10 April, 9 May; *Sulivan*, pp. 138-9; *Malmesbury Letters*, ii. 523-4; Palmerston to W. Temple, 9, 10 April, B.P.; Lady Malmesbury's journal, Lowry Cole Papers 41; Palmerston's diary, 8, 11, 12 April 1818, B.P.

41. *Canning and Friends*, ii. 77; *Peel*, i. 168-9; Ashley, i. 87; Malmesbury to Lady Lowry Cole, 7 Oct. 1819, Lowry Cole Papers; papers on Hampshire counter-petition, Address, and a weekly newspaper, Oct. 1819, Dec. 1820, Jan., April 1821, and Palmerston's Analyses of Expenditure, 1820 and 1821, B.P.W.; 1 *Hansard*, xli. 676 (2 Dec. 1819), 2 *Hansard*, v. 890-93, 1046-53, 1486 (23, 30 May, 3 July 1821); *Malmesbury Letters*, ii. 531; J.E. Cookson, *Lord Liverpool's Administration. The Crucial Years 1815-1822* (1975), pp. 278-82; Grant, pp. 235-6.

42. Walpole, ii. 18-21; Aspinall, *Press*, pp. 64-5; *Annual Register*, 1821, pp. [60-63], 205-9; Palmerston to ?, 13 Dec. 1820, B.P./SLT2 (cf. Ridley, p. 79); William H. Wickwar, *The Struggle for the Freedom of the Press 1819-1832* (1928), pp. 181-204.

43. 1 *Hansard*, xxxvii. 869 (6 Mar. 1818), 2 *Hansard*, xvi. 191-3 (30 Nov. 1826); Palmerston to Taylor, 28 Oct. 1824, P.P.; Palmerston's memo. for the Cabinet, 1 June 1827, B.P./WO52.

44. Clode, ii. 22; Ridley, pp. 66-7; Palmerston to R. Wharton (Secretary of the Treasury), 8 Nov. 1812, P.P.; 2 *Hansard*, i. 1078-82 (14 June), ii. 357 (11 July 1820).

45. Hobhouse's journal, 8, 9 April 1818; Michael Joyce, *My Friend H: John Cam*

Hobhouse Baron Broughton of Broughton de Gyfford (1948), pp. 123, 358; J.J. Wilson to Palmerston, 8 May, S.P.; *The Times*, 9, 10 April, 9 May; Palmerston's diary, 7, 8 May, and Palmerston to W. Temple, 26 May 1818, B.P.; Palmerston's Analysis of Expenditure for 1818, B.P.W.; Davies to Palmerston, 14 July 1821, B.P.

46. Guedalla, p. 96; *The Times*, 9, 10 April, 9 May 1818; Lady Malmesbury's journal, Feb.-July 1818, Lowry Cole Papers 41; *The Diary of Frances Lady Shelley 1818-1873*, ed. Richard Edgcumbe (1912-13), ii. 5-6; *Malmesbury Letters*, ii. 523-4; Palmerston to W. Temple, 9, 10 April 1818, B.P.

47. *BPP*, 1808, v. 277-80.

48. Lt Gen. Sir Henry Bunbury, *Narratives of Some Passages in the Great War with France, from 1799 to 1810* (1854), p. 46; Lt Gen. Sir W. Napier, *The Life and Opinions of General Sir Charles James Napier* (1857), i. 134.

49. *Palmerston*, i. 109-10; Clode, ii. 240-53.

50. Granville to C.-in-C., 14 Aug. 1809, W.O. 4/413; Dundas to Palmerston, 3 Nov. 1809, B.P.; Palmerston to Dundas, 6 Mar. 1810, W.O. 4/437.

51. *George III*, v. 545; Palmerston to Torrens, 12 Mar., and Merry to Adjutant-General, 'Immediate', 21 July, W.O. 4/437; Superintendents of Military Accounts' circular, 7 July, and Perceval to Palmerston, 28 Sept. 1810, P.P.

52. *BPP*, 1808, v. 366-88; Palmerston to C.-in-C., 26 July, and Merry to Army Agents, 28 July 1810, P.P.

53. Dundas to Palmerston, 2, 3 Aug., 15 Sept., Dundas to Perceval, 29 Aug., 20 Sept., Perceval to Palmerston, 28 Sept. 1810, P.P.

54. Palmerston to Perceval, 30 Sept., P.P.; Palmerston memo. on Dundas's protests of 2 Aug. 1810, L.P. 38245 and B.P., G.C./DU14.

55. Correspondence between Palmerston, Dundas and Perceval, Oct. 1810-Jan. 1811, P.P. 48417 and L.P. 38245.

56. *P.O.W.*, vii. 47, 186-8; Bell, i. 36.

57. *P.O.W.*, vii. 259-61, 267-8.

58. Dundas to Perceval, 11 Jan. 1811, P.P.; *Perceval*, p. 423.

59. *P.O.W.*, vii. 285, 328.

60. Palmerston's memo. to the Prince Regent, 16 Aug., with appendix, table and observations by Perceval, Eldon, Liverpool and Yorke, Dec., P.P. (*Palmerston*, i. 384-417, and Clode, ii. 689-722); Perceval's draft of his observations, [19 Dec.], H.P. 38361; memos by the Duke of York, 23 Sept., and Palmerston, 23 Nov., P.P.; [Perceval's ?] pencil notes on the Duke of York's memo. of 23 Sept. 1811, L.P. 38361; Palmerston to Perceval, 7 Jan., 18 April, and Duke of York to Perceval, 15 Jan., L.P.; Palmerston to Torrens, 27 Mar., enclosing circular of Feb., and Torrens's reply, 4 May 1812, P.P.; Clode, ii. 722-3.

61. Palmerston to Torrens, 27 Mar., and Torrens to Palmerston, 4 May, P.P.; Merry to Torrens, 9 Mar., W.O. 4/415; Palmerston to Harrison, 4 May 1812, W.O. 4/425.

62. Palmerston to C.-in-C., 22 July 1815, W.O. 4/420, and Palmerston to Calvert (Adjutant-General), 27 June 1816, P.P.

63. Palmerston to C.-in-C., 28 Nov. 1813, P.P.; W.O. memo., 3 July, Torrens to Palmerston, 5 July, Liverpool to Palmerston, 10 July, and W.O. memo., 12 July 1815, P.P.; W.O. circular no. 207 of 31 July 1815, W.O. 4/465; Ridley, p. 53.

64. Palmerston's diary, 20-22 July 1818, 25 Mar., 1 April, 12 June 1819, B.P.; Palmerston to W. Temple, 4 Aug. 1818, B.P.; Palmerston to Robinson, 11 April 1826, R.P.; *Sulivan*, pp. 220-21.

65. *Bathurst*, p. 566; Palmerston to Peel, 19 Dec. [1817], Peel Papers; Duke of York to Palmerston, 15 May 1820, B.P.; *Sulivan*, pp. 139, 140; Palmerston to Torrens, 14 April 1819, P.P.

66. *BPP*, 1837, xxxiv, Pt I, pp. 43-4; Duke of York to Palmerston, 7 Mar., and Palmerston to Liverpool, 11 Mar. 1820, B.P.

67. Liverpool to Palmerston, 13 Mar., Palmerston to Torrens, 14 Mar., Duke of York to Palmerston, 16 Mar., and Palmerston to Duke of York, 17 Mar. 1820, B.P.

68. Liverpool to Palmerston, 18 Mar., Palmerston to Liverpool, 14 Mar., Torrens to Palmerston, 9, 17 Sept., and Palmerston to Torrens, 20 Sept. 1820, B.P.

69. Harrison to Palmerston, 5 Dec. 1822, Palmerston to O.C.s Overseas, 11 Jan., Merry to Taylor, 4, 11 Jan. 1823, Taylor to Merry, 31 Dec. 1822, 16, 20 Jan., Palmerston to Taylor, 25 Jan., Taylor to O.C.s Overseas and to Col. Ross, 20 Jan., Palmerston to Liverpool, 6, 10 Feb., and Duke of York to Liverpool, 8 Feb. 1823, L.P.; *Sulivan*, p. 156.

70. *Sulivan*, pp. 156-7.

71. Memos by Long, 12 Feb., and by Palmerston, 17 Feb. 1823, L.P.; *Sulivan*, pp. 157-9.

72. *Bathurst*, p. 566.

73. The *Courier*, 17 Jan. 1825; Palmerston to Robinson, 11 April 1826, R.P.; *Sulivan*, pp. 188-9; Torrens to Palmerston, 22 Jan., and Palmerston to Torrens, 23 Jan. 1826, together with an undated memo., P.P. 48420.

74. Mrs Sulivan to W. Temple, 12 Jan., B.P.W.; Palmerston to Torrens, 9 Jan., and Torrens to Palmerston, 12 Jan. 1827, W.O. 43/270. (W.O. 43/938 contains a memo. of 16 Sept. 1853 summarizing the *modus vivendi* arranged between Palmerston and Torrens in Jan. 1827.)

75. Palmerston to Torrens, 21 Jan. 1827, W.O. 43/938; B.P./WO38; *W.N.D.*, iii. 564-6.

76. *Hobhouse*, pp. 129-30; *W.N.D.*, iii. 531-6, 645-9.

77. *Hobhouse*, p. 132; Palmerston to Canning, 19 April, C.P. 74; Taylor to Palmerston, 'private & confidential', 22 April, B.P.; *W.N.D.*, iii. 507; Palmerston's order, 1 May, and Palmerston to Treasury, 10 May 1827, W.O. 4/724.

78. *Palmerston*, i. 187, 191; Taylor to Palmerston, 22 April 1827, B.P.; *Hobhouse*, p. 139; *George IV*, iii. 253-4; *W.N.D.*, iv. 29, 222-8; *Creevey Papers*, ii. 123; Clode, ii. 269-71, 739-45; B.P./WO48-51.

79. Hobhouse's journal, 23 May 1828; Aspinall, *Canning's Ministry*, p. 265; Sir Alexander Cray Grant to Peel, [18 Aug.], Peel Papers; Seaford to Granville, 21 Aug. 1827, Gran. Papers 9/5 no. 52.

80. *W.N.D.*, iv. 82-3, 91, 132; Palmerston to Huskisson, 10 Oct., H.P.; Aspinall, *Canning's Ministry*, p. 217; Palmerston to Wellington, 25 Aug. 1827, B.P./WO56.

81. Taylor to Gen. Sir Alexander Hope, 7 Sept. 1827, Hope of Luffness Papers M; *W.N.D.*, iv. 64, 70, 106-18, 397-9; Palmerston's minute of 11 Feb. 1828 about commissioning of black West Indian, W.O. 43/299; Hardinge to Londonderry, 15 Oct. 1827, Londonderry Papers; Palmerston's minute of 23 Jan. 1828, W.O. 43/318.

82. Gleig, p. 41; Palmerston's memo. of 24 Jan. 1828, B.P./CAB/A1.

83. Palmerston to Althorp, [?13] Feb. 1833, E.P.

CHAPTER V: THE RULING PASSION (*pages 181-226*)

1. *Lyttelton*, p. 85.

2. *George III*, v. 416 n. 1; entry at end of Palmerston's diary for 1863, B.P.

3. Connell, pp. 20, 250-56, 334-40.

4. *Letters of Lady Louisa Stuart to Miss Louisa Clinton* (Edinburgh, 1901), ed. James A. Home, pp. 189-90, 195; Elliot to Lady Elliot, 22 May 1787, 12 Feb. 1789, 5 July 1798, M.P.

5. *Palmerston*, i. 5-8; Mary, Lady Palmerston to Palmerston, 23 April, B.P.W.; Lady Minto to Minto, 10 April, and Lady Palmerston to Minto, 9 Sept. 1802, M.P.

6. *Scott's Journal*, i. 238; Horner to Lord Webb Seymour, 27 Sept. 1812, Horner Papers (cf. *Macaulay Letters*, ii. 153); Emily Henderson, *Recollections of the Public Career*

and Private Life of the Late John Adolphus (1871), p. 141; *Minto*, iii. 118; Ashburton to Palmerston, 10 Nov. 1803, 29 Aug. 1804, and Anna Maria Elliot to Palmerston, 26 July 1823, B.P.W.; *Neumann*, ii. 167; *Sulivan*, p. 309.

7. Minto to Lady Minto, 25 June 1803, M.P.; W. Temple to Palmerston, 19 May 1805, B.P.W.; Lady Georgiana Morpeth to Georgiana, Lady Spencer, 'Fri. 17 April', and Lady Spencer to Lady Georgiana Morpeth, 17-19 April 1807, C.H.P. 1/98; Duchess of Devonshire to Palmerston, endorsed June (but really May) 1802, B.P.W.; *Hary-O*, p. 13; Palmerston to F. Temple, 28 Dec. 1820, B.P.W.; *Correspondence of Charlotte Grenville, Lady Williams Wynn and Her Three Sons* (1920), ed. Rachel Leighton, p. 132; *Hary-O*, p. 305; Lady Malmesbury to Palmerston, 13 Sept., B.P., and to Lady Minto, 15 Sept. 1811, M.P.

8. Drummond Wolff, i. 190; Lady Cowper to Fred Lamb, 'Sat. 25 Oct.' [1817], Panshanger Papers 17, 3 April [1819], Lever, pp. 17-18, and 25 Dec. 1819, B.P.W.; H. Fox to Holland, 1 June 1838, and Lady Holland to H. Fox, [*c.* 3 Feb.], 14 Feb. 1840, H.H.P.; *H. Greville*, ii. 380.

9. *Dudley to Ivy*, p. 185.

10. Lever, pp. 62-3; *Melbourne*, i. 214-15; Airlie, p. 2.

11. *Glenbervie*, ii. 23, 83; *Eden*, p. 167; *Minto*, iii. 361; *Melbourne*, i. 33, 39; *Creevey Papers*, ii. 164.

12. Lady Cowper to Fred Lamb, 12 Feb. 1821, B.P.W.; *G.L.G.*, ii. 169; *Mackintosh*, ii. 333; Airlie, pp. 81-2; *Broughton*, iii. 107; *Hary-O*, pp. 56, 113; *The Two Duchesses. Georgiana Duchess of Devonshire. Elizabeth Duchess of Devonshire* (1898), ed. Vere Foster, pp. 174, 424; Lady Granville to Lady Georgiana Morpeth, 10 [Nov. 1815], C.H.P. 1/151-8.

13. *Bury*, ii. 193; Airlie, pp. 84, 182; *Lady Palmerston*, i. 15; *Hary-O*, pp. 118, 138-9, 151, 160, 173; Lady Caroline Lamb to Lady Georgiana Morpeth, [summer 1805], C.H.P. 1/120; Caroline St Jules to Lady Georgiana Morpeth, 'Wednesday 9' [Oct. 1805], C.H.P. 1/121; *Sulivan*, p. 101.

14. *Hary-O*, pp. 160, 162, 281; Lady Caroline Lamb to Lady Georgiana Morpeth, 14, 26 Nov. 1806, 26 Nov. 1807, C.H.P. 1/120; Caroline St Jules to Lady Georgiana Morpeth, 'Sat. 15' [Aug. 1807], C.H.P. 1/120; *Lady Morgan's Memoirs: Autobiography, Diaries and Correspondence* (1862), ii. 199.

15. *Minto*, iii. 13; Palmerston to E. Temple, 10 Aug. 1805, W. Temple to F. Temple, 21 Nov. 1808, and Palmerston to F. Temple, 5, 14 Sept. 1809, B.P.W.; *Lady Bessborough and Her Family Circle* (1940), ed. the Earl of Bessborough, p. 191; *Sulivan*, p. 109; Mrs Lamb's diary, 23 Dec. 1813, Dormer Papers; Panshanger Papers 17 and 'Epigrams at Brocket Hall by me', Dec. 1813, B.P.W.; Airlie, p. 177.

16. Palmerston's diary, 23 Nov. 1829, B.P.; Lady Palmerston's diary, 13-15 June 1866; *Disraeli*, p. 123; *Hary-O*, p. 307; Lady Granville to Lady Georgiana Morpeth, 'Fri. 24' [Aug. 1810], C.H.P. 1/151-8.

17. *Canning and Friends*, ii. 36; *Lady Palmerston*, i. 54.

18. *Broughton*, i. 194; Ziegler, p. 79; Airlie, p. 187; *Creevey Papers*, i. 258; Mrs Lamb to Lady Georgiana Morpeth, 14 Jan. [1817], C.H.P. 1/120; *Stafford*, p. 128; Lady Holland to Grey, quoting the classical scholar, Peter Elmsley, 28 Dec. 1816, G.P.

19. *Lady Palmerston*, i. 20; Airlie, p. 191; Lady Cowper to Lady Melbourne, 1816-1817, Lamb Papers.

20. *Selections from Private Journals of Tours in France in 1815 and 1818* (1871), and 'Journal of Tour in France, Italy & Swizzerland in 1816', B.P.W.

21. *Palmerston*, i. 133-4; 'Things useful for Travelling in France', B.P.W.; Lady Malmesbury to the Dowager Countess of Minto, 27 June, 31 Aug., 16 Sept., M.P.; *Sulivan*, pp. 132-6; F. Temple to Palmerston, 13 Sept., B.P.W.; *Stafford*, p. 113; Lady Malmesbury to Lady Frances Lowry Cole, 1 Sept., 12 Oct. 1816, Lowry Cole Papers 107 (Palmerston's name has been cut out from the Lowry Cole Papers, but the circumstantial evidence of identification is overwhelming).

22. *Sulivan*, pp. 135-6; Lady Malmesbury to Mrs Robinson, 20 Oct. 1816, Lowry Cole Papers 4.

23. *Gronow*, i. 31-3.

24. H. Montgomery Hyde, *Princess Lieven* (1938), pp. 68, 74; Palmerston to Princess Lieven, [17 Aug. 1827], Lieven Papers. Commenting on the twenty or so surviving letters from Palmerston in the Broadlands and Lieven Papers during the two years after 1828, Webster, i. 16 n. 2, says 'their tone is intimate'. Ridley, pp. 43, 179, makes much of this comment, but it is in fact very ambiguous. The most striking element in that intimacy is political. For Mme Lieven to Lady Cowper *and* Palmerston, see 7 Oct. [1830], B.P., G.C./LI32.

25. Much of this correspondence has disappeared or been destroyed. However, an occasional cypher word in the Chatsworth Papers shows that the Duke of Devonshire was privy to at least part of his sister's game with Princess Lieven, and Mme Lieven seems to use the same code in some of her letters to Lady Cowper as the latter does in hers to Fred Lamb (e.g. 13 June 1826, B.P., G.C./LI43). A substantial part of the latter correspondence has been published by Lady Airlie (in *Whig Society* and *Lady Palmerston and Her Times*) and still more by Tresham Lever. But neither comes to grips with the substantial portions using cypher names and the dating in both cases is often very unreliable. The original letters are now scattered. A few have been left by chance in the Panshanger Papers (Box 17); a more substantial portion was placed by Lady Airlie in the B.L. and at her insistence has until very recently remained inaccessible. A large part, badly muddled and very difficult to put together, is in B.P.W. Lady Cowper's holograph key is in B.P./MIS/C24 and Palmerston's copy is at the back of his diary for 1835 in B.P. Neither is complete and other cypher names have been identified from the context. But great caution still needs to be exercised. In addition to Lady Cowper applying personal names to office holders rather than individuals so that, for example, 'Mary' may be either Canning or Palmerston according to date, she seems deliberately to confuse by using both cypher and *en clair* names for the same person in a single sentence and not infrequently she also forgets to make the sex consistent with the code.

26. Lady Granville to Lady Georgiana Morpeth, 24 Aug. 1818, C.H.P. 1/151-8; Lady Cowper to Fred Lamb, 20 Mar. 1821, B.P.W.

27. Mrs Lamb to Lady Georgiana Morpeth, 'Wednesday 30' [?Oct. 1811], C.H.P. 1/125.

28. Airlie, p. 195; *Melbourne*, i. 214; *Fortescue*, p. 165; Lady Cowper to Fred Lamb, 20 Mar. [1821], 24 Oct. 1826, B.P.W., 30 May, 15 July [1823], Panshanger Papers 17; *Creevey Papers*, ii. 199; Lady Granville to Lady Georgiana Morpeth, 'Wednesday' [30 Aug. 1820], C.H.P. 1/151-8; *Arbuthnot*, p. 119; *A Selection from the Correspondence of Abraham Hayward* (1886), ed. Henry E. Carlisle, ii. 111-12; *Lady Palmerston*, ii. 121; *G.L.G.*, ii. 494; Ridley, p. 43.

29. *Stafford*, p. 123; Lady Cowper to Lady Melbourne, 11 Feb. 1817, Lamb Papers.

30. *Memoirs of the Life and Adventures of Colonel Maceroni* (1838), i. 478, ii. 202-3, 257-8; Francesco Paterno Castello di Carcaci, *I Paterno di Sicilia* (Catania, 1936), pp. 327, 339-41; Sir James Rennell Rodd, *Social and Diplomatic Memories (Third Series) 1902-1919* (1925), pp. 119-20.

31. Lady Cowper to Lady Melbourne, 9 Jan., 20 May, Lamb Papers; Sir Jonah Barrington, *Personal Sketches of His Own Times* (1869), ii. 97-8; *Fox*, p. 203; *Blessington*, i. 113; Mrs Lamb to Lady Georgiana Morpeth, 9 Aug., 1 Oct., 'Tuesday' [late 1817], C.H.P. 1/125; Lady Georgiana Morpeth to Devonshire, 13 Sept. [1817], Chat. Papers.

32. Palmerston's diaries, especially entries for 18, 21, 23 Feb., 4, 6 Mar., 1 April, 18 May, 19, 23 June, 13 Oct.-10 Nov., 3 Dec. 1818, 29 April, 20 June, 1, 17, 29, 31 July, 7, 8 Aug., 13-25 Sept., 10, 24, 27 Oct., 15 Nov., 15 Dec. 1819, B.P.; Palmerston to W. Temple, 26 May 1818, B.P.; Lady Morley to Mrs George Villiers, 3 June [1818], Morley Papers; Lady Granville to Lady Georgiana Morpeth, [20 Sept.], and Mrs

Lamb to Lady Georgiana Morpeth, 30 Sept. 1819, C.H.P. 1/151-8, 125.

33. *Fox*, p. 136.

34. Lady Granville to Lady Georgiana Morpeth, 'Monday' [5 Feb. 1816], 'Wednesday' [30 Aug. 1820], [1, 2 Feb. 1821], C.H.P. 1/151-8; *Lieven-Metternich*, p. 126; Lady Cowper to Fred Lamb, 28 Dec. [1820], 1 Feb. [1821], Lever, pp. 66, 67, 6, 20 Mar. [1821], B.P.W., 10 Sept. 1822, *Lady Palmerston*, i. 103, 8 July 1823, Panshanger Papers, 14 July, 8 Aug. 1826, 7 June, B.P.W., 27 July 1827, *Lady Palmerston*, i. 137; *Greville*, i. 101-2.

35. *Lieven-Metternich*, p. 149; *Mrs Arbuthnot*, i. 147-8; Lady Granville to Lady Georgiana Morpeth, 30 Dec. 1821, C.H.P. 1/151-8; *Harriette Wilson*, ii. 669; Lady Cowper to Fred Lamb, 7 June 1825, B.P.W.

36. *Some Official Correspondence of George Canning* (1887), ed. Edward J. Stapleton, i. 332-3; *Stafford*, p. 201; *Mrs Fitzherbert*, p. 216.

37. *Gronow*, i. 300; Lady Granville to Lady Carlisle, 30 Sept. (*Lady Granville*, i. 395), 9 Oct., C.H.P. 1/151-8; Mme de Coigny to Lady Jersey, n.d., Jersey Papers 669, Middlesex Record Office; Lady Cowper to Fred Lamb, 11-13 Nov. 1826, B.P.W.

38. *Lieven-Grey*, i. 29; Lever, p. 153; Lady Granville to Lady Carlisle, 'Monday' [?4 Dec. 1826], C.H.P. 1/151-8.

39. Lady Cowper to Fred Lamb, 27 Mar. 1827, B.P.W.; Grosvenor to Devonshire, 'Sunday 31' [Dec. 1826], and Devonshire's diary, 12-24 Sept. 1826, Chat. Papers; Gervas Huxley, *Lady Elizabeth and the Grosvenors: Life in a Whig Family, 1822-1839* (1965), pp. 17-18; Mrs Seymour Bathurst's journal, 3, 19 Feb. 1830, Bathurst Papers 57/80; *Mrs Arbuthnot*, i. 384.

40. *G.L.G.*, ii. 494-5; Airlie, pp. 192-3; Lever, p. 15; *Lady Palmerston*, i. 135, 148; *Creevey Papers*, ii. 198; *Lady Granville*, ii. 42; *Lady Holland's Letters*, p. 70; Prest, p. 71.

41. *Mrs Arbuthnot*, ii. 306; Battiscombe, pp. 59-61; *Lady Palmerston*, i. 86; *Lady Granville*, ii. 42, 47; Lady Granville to Lady Carlisle, 16 [Sept.], 'Monday' [17 Oct.], n.d., 'Fri.' [?Dec. 1827], 'Thursday' [?9 Oct.], 'Monday' [?13 Oct. 1828], 'Tuesday', [?Jan. 1830], C.H.P. 1/159, 160; Lady Cowper to Fred Lamb, 14 Aug. 1828, B.P.W.; Greville to Granville, 2 Jan. 1830, Gran. Papers 6/7 no. 69.

42. Lady Granville to Lady Carlisle, 'Thursday' [?9 Oct. 1828], 'Fri.' [13 Dec. 1833], C.H.P. 1/160, 163; *Lady Holland's Letters*, pp. 210-11; Battiscombe, pp. 53, 281; Lady Cowper to Palmerston, 3 Jan. 1830, B.P.W.; *G.L.G.*, ii. 494.

43. Mrs Lamb to Lady Georgiana Morpeth, 'Wednesday 30' [?Oct. 1811], C.H.P. 1/125; *My Recollections* (1909), by the Countess of Cardigan and Lancastre, pp. 152-3; Battiscombe, pp. 177-8; Lady Cowper to William Cowper, *c*. 1860, B.P.W.; Palmerston's 'Analyses of Expenditure', 1818-30, 'Paid & Received', 1829-34, and his wills dated 19 Aug. 1856, 1 Dec. 1857, 22 Nov. 1864, B.P.W.

44. Ashley to Messrs Manisty, 11 April 1892, B.P.W.

45. Palmerston's diary, 18 May 1818, B.P.; Arran to Ashley, 13 April 1892, B.P.W.

46. *Lady Palmerston*, i. 69.

47. *Lady Palmerston*, ii. 35; *Thatched with Gold. The Memoirs of Mabell Countess of Airlie* (1962), ed. Jennifer Ellis, pp. 13-17; Mrs Lamb to Lady Carlisle, [1840], C.H.P. 1/125; Lady Fanny Cowper to W. Cowper, [2 Nov. 1839], B.P.W.

48. Bedford to Lady Holland, 23 April [1837], H.H.P.; newspaper clipping, 1840, B.P.W.

49. *Satirist, passim*; Mrs Murray Mills to Palmerston, 3 June 1834, and Palmerston's accounts, B.P.W.

50. *H. Greville*, iii. 395; *Hanover*, p. 168; correspondence of Mrs Murray Mills, Richard Levinge Swift and Eustace Murray with the Dukes of Buckingham, Buckingham Papers, Huntington Library.

51. *F.O. List*, 1895, and Mrs Elizabeth Murray's will, Somerset House Probate Records, 1906.

52. Jones, pp. 97-8; Hertslet, pp. 207-13, 248; *BPP*, 1868-9, lxiv. [4163], 'Papers Relative to the Complaints made against Mr Grenville-Murray as Her Majesty's Consul-General at Odessa; and to his dismissal from Her Majesty's Service. 1858-69', p. 226; Mrs Murray Mills's will, Somerset House Probate Records, 1861; Fox Bourne, ii. 301-4; Algar Labouchere Thorold, *The Life of Henry Labouchere* (1913), pp. 61-3; *Truth*, 29 Dec. 1881; *D.N.B.* ('Grenville Murray').

53. Correspondence of Mr and Mrs Murray Mills, Henry Murray, John Charles Wilson Price, Sainsbury, 'John Edwards' and Lumley with Palmerston, 1830-42, B.P.W.; Palmerston's accounts in P.P. 48584 and in B.P.W.; Mrs Murray Mills to Brougham, Feb. 1833, Brougham Papers; Palmerston's diary, 6, 19 Sept. 1836, B.P.; Mills to Palmerston, 13 Nov. 1836, B.P.; The *Satirist* for November 1836; *The Register Book of Marriages belonging to the Parish of St George Hanover Square in the County of Middlesex* (1897), ed. George J. Armytage, iv. 85; register of admissions to the Royal Military Academy, Sandhurst; records of deaths, General Register Office, London; *G.M.*, 1840, Pt I, 667; correspondence of Mrs Murray Mills, Richard Levinge Swift and Eustace Grenville Murray with the Dukes of Buckingham, Buckingham Papers, Huntington Library.

54. *Fortescue*, pp. 135-6.

55. *Eden*, p. 6; Lady Cowper to Mrs Lamb, 7 Feb. 1815, Dormer Papers; Palmerston's diaries, especially 24, 25 July 1818, 26 Feb., 13 Sept. 1819, B.P.

56. Caroline H. Graham to Palmerston, 22 Oct. 1822, and Mrs Webster to Palmerston, 15 Jan. [1826], B.P.W.; *Fortescue*, pp. 59, 162; T.H.S. Escott, *Great Victorians. Memories and Personalities* (New York, 1916), p. 194; *The Ladies of Alderley* (1938), ed. Nancy Mitford, pp. 163, 167, and *The Stanleys of Alderley* (1939), ed. Nancy Mitford, pp. 50, 55.

57. Lady Cowper to Fred Lamb, 18-20 May 1832, B.P.W.

58. *Raikes*, iii. 85-8; Palmerston's diary, 16 Aug., 13 Sept.-15 Oct. 1819, B.P.; *Sulivan*, pp. 160, 258, 264; P.J. Barnwell, *Visits and Despatches (Mauritius, 1598-1948)* (Port Louis, 1948), pp. 241-3, 247; Palmerston to W. Temple, 1 June 1836, B.P.; *Greville*, iii. 75.

59. Palmerston's diary, 24, 27 Oct. 1819, 28 May, 11, 13 Sept., 27 Dec. 1829, B.P.; Mrs Catherine Whaley to Palmerston, 'Wednesday Morning', [23 Aug. 1831], B.P/PAT/W28; Palmerston's 'Analyses of Expenditure', 1818-30, and 'Paid & Received', 1829-34, B.P.W.; Mrs Warrenne Blake, *An Irish Beauty of the Regency* (1911), p. 240; *Fox*, pp. 284-5; William Cowper's diary, 29 Sept. 1839, B.P.W.; *Gronow*, ii. 79; Mme Pauline Graham to Brougham, 16 Sept. 1851, Brougham Papers; Palmerston's letters to Mme Graham, *passim*, Graham of Drynie Papers, B.L.

60. Palmerston's diary, 27 Sept., 7-10 Oct., B.P.; Palmerston's 'Paid & Received', 30 Sept. 1833, B.P.W.

61. Lady Cowper to Fred Lamb, 8 June 1821, B.P.W.; Lever, p. 118; Greville to Granville, 2 Jan. 1830, Gran. Papers 6/7 no. 69; *Lieven-Grey*, ii. 473, 484, 486; *Greville*, ii. 422.

62. Granville to Holland, 20 Dec., H.H.P.; *Creevey Papers*, ii. 268; *Mrs Arbuthnot*, i. 406, 424; Carlisle to Lady Holland, 20 Nov., H.H.P.; Mrs Lamb to Lady Carlisle, 28 Nov., C.H.P. 1/127; Palmerston's diary, Oct.-Nov. 1833, B.P.

63. Ellice to Durham, 'Sat.' [16 Nov.], Lambton Papers; Holland to Granville, 19 Nov., Gran. Papers 409; Granville to Holland, 25 Nov., H.H.P.; Palmerston to Clive, 21 Nov. 1833, Powis Papers; *Lieven-Palmerston*, p. 50.

64. *Creevey Papers*, ii. 130-31; *Eden*, p. 28; *Fox*, pp. 147, 178; Lord William Pitt Lennox, *Fifty Years' Biographical Reminiscences* (1863), ii. 145; Lady Holland to H. Fox, 14 July 1829, H.H.P.

65. *Sulivan*, pp. 213-14; Palmerston to Clanricarde, 13 Sept. 1830, Clanricarde Papers 68; Palmerston's diary, 13 Dec. 1833, B.P.; Petre to Richmond, 'Saturday' [21

Dec. 1833], Goodwood Papers; *Greville*, iii. 11-12; Lady Holland to H. Fox, 4 Mar. [1834], H.H.P.; *Dino*, i. 34; Creevey to Miss Ord, 18 May 1834, Creevey Papers.

66. *Lady Palmerston*, i. 53; Lady Cowper to Fred Lamb, 'Sat. 29th' [?1820], B.P.W.; *Lady Granville*, i. 169, 201; *Creevey Papers*, ii. 107, 287-8; Frances Hawes, *Henry Brougham* (1957), pp. 89-90; Lady Granville to Lady Georgiana Morpeth, 'Sunday' [?28 Oct. 1815], C.H.P. 1/151-8; Holland to Granville, 5 July 1834, Gran. Papers 9/4 no. 69; *Dino*, i. 126.

67. *Creevey Papers*, ii. 276; Lady Holland to H. Fox, 29 July 1834, H.H.P. (*Lady Holland's Letters*, p. 152); *Greville*, iii. 71-2.

68. *Dino*, i. 94, 135; Bedford to Lady Holland, 15 Oct., H.H.P.; Byng to Granville, 21 Oct., 27 Nov. 1834, Gran. Papers 7/13 nos. 33, 39; Palmerston's diary for 1835, especially 6-10 Dec., B.P.

69. Webster, i. 58.

70. Palmerston's diary, 28 July 1818, 1, 3 Jan., 7 Nov. 1819, 22-27 July 1829, B.P.; *Mrs Arbuthnot*, ii. 135.

71. *Lady Granville*, i. 134; Palmerston to W. Temple, 26 May 1818, B.P.; Dover's diary, 24 Aug. 1818, 25 July, 28 Aug. 1820; Lady Granville to Lady Georgiana Morpeth, 'Wednesday', 'Tuesday Morning' [1823], 'Sat.' [31 Jan. 1824], C.H.P. 1/151-8; *Mrs Arbuthnot*, i. 409, 419, 424; Lady Cowper to Fred Lamb, 7 July, B.P.W., 17 July 1825, Lamb Papers.

72. *The Private Letters of Sir Robert Peel* (1920), ed. George Peel, p. 87; *Mrs Arbuthnot*, ii. 35, 51, 71; *Greville*, vi. 297-8; Lyndhurst to Brougham, 1 Dec. [1851], Brougham Papers.

73. Lady Cowper to Fred Lamb, [?1825], B.P.W.; Edward Heneage Dering, *Memoirs of Georgiana, Lady Chatterton* (1901), pp. 41-2 (cf. Lady Palmerston's diary, 2 Aug.-1 Nov. 1836); *Lady Palmerston*, i. 193.

74. Howard de Walden to Granville, 5 April, Gran. Papers 6/7 no. 51; Lady Cowper to Fred Lamb, 7 July 1824, B.P.W.; *Dino*, i. 92; *Disraeli-Londonderry*, p. 6.

75. Lever, pp. 212-13 (where the extracts printed from the letters in B.P.W. omit the references to Palmerston's apprehensions about Conyngham and are described simply as Emily's responses to his pressing her to marry him); Sulivan to Palmerston, 13 Nov. 1837, B.P.; *Disraeli*, pp. 123-4.

76. *Q.V.G.*, ii. 260, 275, 296; Mrs Lamb to Lady Carlisle, 26 Nov. [1839], C.H.P. 1/129; *Lady Palmerston*, ii. 31-41; *Q.V.L.*, I, i. 255.

77. Devonshire to Lady Carlisle, 22 Dec., C.H.P. 1/111; Mrs Lamb to Lady Carlisle, 14 Nov., 'Sunday' [?17 Nov.], 'Friday' [?22 Nov.], 'Tuesday' [?3Dec.], C.H.P. 1/129; Lady Fanny Cowper to W. Cowper, 'Wed.' [13 Nov. 1839], B.P.W.; *Lieven-Palmerston*, p. 177.

CHAPTER VI: INTERLUDE I: SHYCOCK AND SPARROW, 1822-8 (*pages 227-87*)

1. Ethel Colburn Mayne, *The Life and Letters of Anne Isabella, Lady Noel Byron* (1929), p. 45; Lady Blessington, *The Idler in France* (1841), ii. 127-8.

2. Frances Temple's diary, 8-11 Jan. 1808, B.P.W.; *Sulivan*, p. 112.

3. Lady Malmesbury to Palmerston, 3 Nov. 1809, B.P.; Lady Minto to Minto, 18 Mar., M.P.; Malmesbury to Palmerston, 28 July 1810, B.P.

4. Palmerston to Malmesbury, 18 May 1812, Malmesbury (Aspinall) Papers.

5. Fitzharris to Malmesbury, 10 (forwarding a rough sketch of his reply to Palmerston's of 9 June), 16, 23 June 1812, and Mrs Robinson to Fitzharris, n.d., Malmesbury (Aspinall) Papers; 1 *Hansard*, xxiii. 707.

6. *Palmerston*, i. 62-76 (cf. Bell, i. 21); 1 *Hansard*, xxiv. 971-6.

7. Palmerston to F. Temple, 11 Nov. 1808, B.P.W.; Thomas Moore, *The Life, Letters and Journals of Lord Byron* (1860), pp. 147, 303, 578; Lewis Melville, *The Beaux of the Regency* (1908), i. 225.

8. Ridley, pp. 45-6; R.H. Cholmondeley, *The Heber Letters* (1950), pp. 242-3; *Croker Papers*, i. 256; Croker to Palmerston, 10 Jan. 1821, Croker Papers, Clements Library.

9. Aspinall, *Press*, p. 244 n. 3; Palmerston's drafts of published and unpublished satirical articles, B.P./PRE/B; Ashley, i. 87.

10. *Dudley to Llandaff*, p. 251; unfinished autobiography of Henry Goulburn, Goulburn Papers.

11. *Goderich*, p. 30; *Sulivan*, p. 10; Palmerston to Plumer Ward, 11 Oct. 1809, B.P.

12. *Goderich*, pp. 30-31; *Sulivan*, p. 124; *Ward*, i. 341, 351, 368, 385, 429-30; *Peel*, i. 30-31, 168-9; Gash, *Secretary Peel*, pp. 80, 269, 392; Palmerston to Peel, 23 Dec. 1813, 6 Feb., 26 Mar., 5 April, 20 June 1814, March and May-June 1825, Peel Papers.

13. *Goderich*, p. 33; *Lieven Diary*, p. 163; *Sulivan*, p. 152; Palmerston to W. Temple, 29 Jan. 1818, B.P.; 2 *Hansard*, xiv. 918-19, 1088.

14. *Brougham*, ii. 308-9; Palmerston's diary, 15 Mar. 1818, B.P.; *Lady Palmerston*, i. 68.

15. *Quarterly Review*, lxiv (1839), p. 84; Bell, i. 59; Lever, p. 173; *Dudley to Ivy*, p. 339; Aspinall, 'Canningite Party', p. 215.

16. *Palmerston*, i. 371-2; *Colchester*, ii. 398; Aspinall, 'Canningite Party', p. 190 n. 1.

17. Aspinall, 'Canningite Party', pp. 193-6, 198-9.

18. Huskisson to Canning, 21 Nov., and Canning to Huskisson, 23 Nov. 1821, H.P.; *Mrs Arbuthnot*, i. 126-7.

19. Liverpool to Palmerston, 29 Nov. 1821, B.P.

20. *Broughton*, i. 149; Hobhouse's journal, 6 July 1814, 16 Feb. 1815; Malmesbury to Fitzharris, 4 Feb. 1815, Malmesbury (Aspinall) Papers; Palmerston to W. Temple, 5 Dec. 1821, B.P.; Palmerston to Liverpool, 30 Nov. 1821, L.P.

21. Webster, i. 10; Huskisson to Canning, 4 Dec., [Christmas], Binning to Huskisson, 11 Dec. 1821, and Liverpool to Huskisson, 8 Jan. 1822, H.P.

22. *Lady Palmerston*, i. 100; *Sulivan*, pp. 152-3.

23. Palmerston to Clive, 13 Sept., Powis Papers; Croker to Peel, 18 Aug., Peel Papers; *Croker Papers*, i. 230-31; George Dawson to Peel, 18 Sept. [1822], Peel Papers; Aspinall, 'Canningite Party', p. 209; W.R. Brock, pp. 162-3.

24. W.R. Brock, p. 273.

25. Palmerston to F. Temple, 8 July 1808, B.P.W.; Palmerston to Malmesbury, 6 July 1809, Malmesbury (Aspinall) Papers; *Palmerston*, i. 111-12, 114; *Ward*, i. 404.

26. George Eden to Auckland, [Mar.], Auckland Papers; *Palmerston*, i. 114; Palmerston to Yorke, 6 Mar., and letters to Hardwicke from Henry Pepys, 18, 22 Mar., Thomas Sheepshanks, 20, 23 Mar., and Dr S. Weston, 21, 23 Mar. 1811, Hardwicke Papers.

27. *Pryme*, p. 100; *Sedgwick*, ii. 108-9; Pepys to Hardwicke, 18 Mar. 1811, Hardwicke Papers; *Ward*, i. 404; *Sulivan*, pp. 120-21; F. Horner to H. Hallam, 21 Mar. 1811, Horner Papers; Cooper, iv. 495.

28. Lansdowne to Tavistock, 19 June, G.A. Browne to Hobhouse, 25 June, and Lord John Townshend to Hobhouse, 10 July 1814, Broughton Papers; *Broughton*, i. 154, 157; Howick to Grey, [23 Oct.], G.P.; Goulburn to Peel, 7 Nov., Peel Papers; Colchester to Yorke, 30 Nov. 1822, Hardwicke Papers.

29. *Sulivan*, pp. 153-5.

30. Wood to Palmerston, 6 Feb. 1823, L.P.; Palmerston to Downshire, 5 June 1825, B.P.; *Sedgwick*, ii. 117-19, 126-7; Hobhouse's journal, 2 Oct. 1825.

31. W.R. Brock, pp. 270-71; Palmerston to Peel, 30 Sept. 1825, Peel Papers; *Mrs Arbuthnot*, i. 419.

32. Colchester to Sidmouth, 5 Jan. 1826, Sidmouth Papers; *Clarendon*, i. 37; *Palmerston*, i. 161, 166.

33. *Sedgwick*, i. 268.

34. Palmerston to Devonshire, 19, 21 Dec. 1825, Chat. Papers; Russell to Lady Holland, 16 Jan., H.H.P.; Palmerston to Brougham, 3 June 1826, Brougham Papers; *The 'Pope' of Holland House. Selections from the Correspondence of John Whishaw and his Friends*

1813-1840 (1906), ed. Lady Seymour, p. 253; *Sulivan*, p. 179; Peel to the Dean of York, 23 Dec., to Goulburn, 24 Nov., 28 Dec., and to Taylor, 28, 30 Dec. 1825, Peel Papers; Peel to Palmerston, 15 Jan. 1826, B.P.W.; *Canning and Friends*, ii. 328-9.

35. *Sulivan*, pp. 178-9.

36. *Sulivan*, pp. 177-8; Palmerston to Canning, 22 Dec., C.P. 74; Canning and Planta to Palmerston, 21 Dec., Palmerston to Eldon, 26 Dec. 1825, and Eldon to Palmerston, n.d., B.P.

37. Lady Cowper to F. Lamb, 2 Feb., Lamb Papers; *Sulivan*, pp. 177-8; Bathurst to Palmerston, 10 Jan. 1826, B.P.W.; *Bathurst*, p. 598.

38. Peel to Bathurst, n.d., Bathurst Papers; *Bathurst*, pp. 598-9; *E.H.D.*, xi. 105-8; *Sulivan*, pp. 178-80.

39. Mrs Bowles to W. Temple, 26 Jan. 1826, B.P.W.; *Palmerston*, i. 166; *Sulivan*, pp. 177, 179, 180; Palmerston to W. Temple, 23 Dec. 1825, B.P.; Aspinall, *Brougham*, p. 137; Lever, p. 146; F. Byng to Granville, 27 Jan., Gran. Papers 7/12 no. 26; Copley to Palmerston, 26 Jan., and Palmerston to Copley, 29 Jan., B.P.W.; *Lyndhurst*, p. 207; [Macaulay] to President of Queens' College, Cambridge, 26 Feb. 1826, and Macaulay to Goulburn, 2 June 1831, Goulburn Papers.

40. *Sulivan*, pp. 181-2.

41. *Sulivan*, pp. 182-3; *John Bull*, 30 April, 28 May 1826.

42. *Sulivan*, pp. 180, 182-3; Hobhouse's journal, 4, 14 Mar., 14, 16, 17 June 1826; *Palmerston*, i. 168.

43. C. A. Ellis to Devonshire, 20 June 1826, Chat. Papers; *Palmerston*, i. 168-71, 374.

44. *Colchester*, iii. 442; *Palmerston*, i. 167, 169; Palmerston to Liverpool, 31 May, and Liverpool to Palmerston, 1 June 1826, B.P.W.

45. *Palmerston*, i. 171-2, 372; Lorne, p. 43; *Lady Palmerston*, i. 132.

46. 2 *Hansard*, viii. 1452-9 (4 April 1823).

47. Bell, i. 52; Palmerston to W. Temple, 25 Dec. 1826, B.P.

48. *E.H.D.*, xi. 310; Palmerston to Littleton, 7 Oct. 1826, Hath. Papers; *Palmerston*, i. 178-9.

49. Canning to Palmerston, 15 July 1823, B.P.; Palmerston to Canning, 1 Jan. 1824, C.P. 74; Palmerston to Littleton, 9 Jan. 1826, Hath. Papers.

50. Liverpool to Canning, 10 July, and Canning to Liverpool, 10, 11 July 1826, C.P. 72; W.R. Brock, pp. 274-5.

51. *Mrs Arbuthnot*, ii. 38-9; *Palmerston*, i. 372; Gunning to Palmerston, 23 May 1827, B.P.W.

52. Lady Cowper to Fred Lamb, 18, 24 Sept. 1826, B.P.W.; *Croker Papers*, i. 363-5; Sidmouth to Bragge, 4 Mar. 1827, Sidmouth Papers.

53. *Sulivan*, p. 187; *Palmerston*, i. 188-9, 374-5; Lorne, pp. 40-43; *Broughton*, iii. 300; Webster, i. 13.

54. Canning to Palmerston, 10 June, and Palmerston to Canning, 14 June 1827, C.P. 74; *George IV*, iii. 253-4; *Palmerston*, i. 376.

55. *Canning*, p. 442 n. 2, and *Lieven Diary*, p. 164 n. 1.

56. *Palmerston*, i. 375-6; *Sulivan*, p. 194; Lorne, p. 42; *Mrs Arbuthnot*, ii. 129.

57. *Mrs Arbuthnot*, ii. 125, 128-9; Aspinall, *Canning's Ministry*, p. 233; Hobhouse's journal, 7 June 1827; Bell, i. 56-7; Ridley, p. 89.

58. The financial and estate records of the third Viscount Palmerston are detailed and voluminous, but the first in particular are very uneven and incomplete. Details of the second Viscount's financial affairs at the time of his death may be found principally in the following papers in B.P.W.: 'Abstract of the Will and Codicil of the late Viscount Palmerston'; 'State and Estimate of the late Lord Palmerston's Personal Estate now remaining to be applied and of the Debts and Legacies unpaid', 5 Jan. 1811; and 'State of Residue of the late Lord Palmerston's Personal Estate and of the proposed Applicn thereof', Nov. 1811. There are also in the same deposit some

important papers concerned with his widow's estate: Lady Palmerston to third Viscount Palmerston, 23 April 1802, and 'Monies paid on account of the executorship of Lady Mary, Viscountess Palmerston, decd'.

Palmerston's account book with his London solicitors and agents, Messrs Oddie, Forster & Lumley, survives for the period 1806-42 in P.P. 48584 (P.P. 48585 is a duplicate). But it covers only one aspect of Palmerston's affairs. Only incidental mentions in other papers have been found concerning his accounts with Drummond's and Hankey's; and the accounts relating to the individual estates are broken up and incomplete. Nonetheless there is a large amount of material available. P.P. 48586 is an account book for Broadlands covering 1834-8; and there are similar items and much other relevant material among the voluminous estate papers in B.P.W.

By far the most important are the miscellaneous accounts and financial papers in B.P.W. Most of these concern the period up to June 1830, but that fortunately is the most interesting and important period. There are various notes and memoranda in Palmerston's own hand, a few of them concerning his affairs in 1805, 1811 and 1812, but mostly his difficulties in the 1820s. There is a particularly useful comparative table for his expenditure over the years 1818-29, and for the same period, with the addition of the single year, 1834, there are detailed 'Analyses of Expenditure', and for 1831-4 daily entries of income and expenditure. These last two series give a good picture of Palmerston's overall financial position. But they are full of traps. Palmerston was not always accurate in his arithmetic and transcription or consistent in his methods. Above all, it is important to allow for deliberate omissions, such as the payments for annuities and interest during some periods and all those not met from his central account at Drummond's. Income is even more arbitrarily handled; for the most part it does not appear at all.

Unless otherwise stated, the information in the following pages is drawn from these sources.

59. Palmerston to F. Temple, 2 Jan., 24 Feb., 12 Mar. 1808, B.P.W.; *Palmerston*, i. 83; *Sulivan*, p. 100; Palmerston to E. Temple, 29 Jan., S.P.; Lady Malmesbury to Palmerston, Feb. 1811, B.P.; Palmerston to Peel, 23 Dec. 1813, Peel Papers; Lumley to Palmerston, 27 Oct. 1840, 13 June, 19 July 1842, B.P.W.; Gash, *Secretary Peel*, p. 116.

60. *Minto*, i. 311; Minto to Lady Minto, 23 April 1802, M.P.; Malmesbury to Palmerston, 21 Nov. 1805, Peter Coxe to Palmerston, 7 Jan. 1806, Palmerston to F. Temple, 'Tues. Feb. 1806', 23 July 1808, B.P.W.; *Sulivan*, p. 58.

61. Ridley, pp. 61-2; *William Day's Reminiscences of the Turf* (1886), p. 217.

62. Lumley to Palmerston, 13 Feb., 13, 19 May, 6 July 1837, 26 April 1838, B.P.W.; Bruce, ii. 271.

63. Estate papers in B.P.W., especially 'Calculation of capital laid out in purchases of land & income arising therefrom', [*c.* 1818-19], and 'Lands added to my original estate 1863'.

64. Palmerston to F. Temple, 31 Aug. 1808, James Walker to Palmerston, 30 Oct. 1815, Palmerston to Alexander Nimmo, 1 Aug. 1825, B.P.W.; *Palmerston*, i. 85-7, 158-9; Palmerston to W. Temple, 28 Nov. 1817, B.P.; Palmerston's pocket-book memoranda, '1824 Irish Memoranda', 'Ireland 1827-8', 'Abstract of Sligo Accounts for the year ending July 1826' [subsequently extended to 1852], 'Abstract of expenses incurred in Ahamlish in 1825-26-27', 4 Nov. 1827, and 'Instructions for Lynch 18 Nov. 1829', B.P.W.; 'Ireland 1826', B.P./D25.

65. *Ibid.* and Palmerston to Lady Palmerston, 14-15 Aug. 1858, B.P.W.

66. Drummond's to Palmerston, 2 Feb., B.P.W.; Palmerston to W. Temple, 22 April, B.P.; Palmerston to Canning, 15 Mar., and Canning to Palmerston, 16 Mar. 1825, C.P. 74; Dover's diary, 17 July 1824; Palmerston to Peel, 29 Dec. 1824, 5 Feb. 1825, Peel Papers; Palmerston to Agar Ellis, 19 Nov. 1825, Chat. Papers; Palmerston's 'Analysis of Expenditure' for 1826, B.P.W.

67. Palmerston to W. Temple, 22 April, B.P., 2 June 1825, B.P.W.; *Palmerston*, i. 157, 162; *Sulivan*, pp. 173, 175; Lady Cowper to Fred Lamb, 18 Sept. 1826, B.P.W.
68. Memoranda in B.P.W., especially 'Slate Quarries 1828 Nov.' in Palmerston's pocket memo. book, 'Ireland 1827-8', Kincaid to Palmerston, 15 Nov. 1845, Secretary of Welsh Slate Company to Palmerston, 28 Mar. 1846, Palmerston to Lady Palmerston, 5, 6, 7, 8 Aug. 1858, 22 Nov. 1864, and William Cowper's report, 4 Oct. 1865, B.P.W.; Palmerston's diary, Oct.-Dec. 1841, and Palmerston to W. Temple, 19 June 1855, B.P.; *Palmerston*, iii. 178.
69. Palmerston to W. Temple, 28 Feb. 1826, B.P.
70. *Disraeli*, p. 142; *John Bull*, 30 July, 3 Sept. 1826; *Lieven Diary*, p. 164; Guedalla, p. 470 (though the Stapleton memo. cited cannot now be found among his papers in Leeds); Prince Albert's memo. of conversation with Wellington, 21 Jan. 1852, RA, A80/131; Palmerston to Canning, 15 Mar., and Canning to Palmerston, 16 Mar. 1825, C.P. 74.
71. 2 *Hansard*, xvii. 299-343 (9 April), 845-53 (15 May 1827); W.J.F. Powlett (later third Duke of Cleveland) to Brougham, 2 Feb. 1827, Brougham Papers; *Sulivan*, p. 175. See also Henry English, *A Complete View of the Joint Stock Companies, formed during the years 1824 and 1825* (1827), *A General Guide to the Companies formed for working Foreign Mines* (1825), and *A Compendium of Useful Information relating to the Companies formed for working British Mines* (1826).
72. *Palmerston*, i. 376; *Lorne*, pp. 42-3.
73. *Goderich*, pp. 152-67, and Aspinall, 'Goderich Ministry', pp. 533-59. *Palmerston*, i. 377-8, is not entirely accurate and is refuted at length by *Herries*, i. 153-236: he was not 'immediately' requested by Goderich to take the Exchequer; he did tell his family about the offer; and the council he describes at Windsor took place on 17, not 12 Aug. (see also *Sulivan*, pp. 190-200). Bathurst to Hay, 2 Sept. 1827, Bathurst Papers.
74. *Bathurst*, p. 644; Bathurst to Peel, 23 Aug., Peel Papers; Grey to Creevey, 23 Aug., Creevey Papers; Aspinall, 'Goderich Ministry', pp. 541, 546; Holland to Lansdowne, 22 Aug., Bowood Papers; Aspinall, *Brougham*, p. 158; Devonshire to Lady Granville, 26-28 Aug. 1827, Chat. Papers.
75. *Sulivan*, p. 191; Hardinge to Peel, 11 Aug., Peel Papers; *Croker Papers*, i. 384-90; Croker to Lowther, 11 Aug. 1827, Croker Papers, Clements Library; *Palmerston*, i. 194-6.
76. *Palmerston*, i. 196-7, 377-8; Palmerston to Sturges Bourne, 30 Aug., B.P./GMC17; *Sulivan*, p. 195.
77. *Sulivan*, pp. 198-9; Lansdowne to Devonshire, [28 Aug. 1827], Chat. Papers.
78. *Sulivan*, pp. 194, 196, 199; *Palmerston*, i. 197-200.
79. *Sulivan*, p. 200.
80. *Sulivan*, pp. 194, 198; Lord St Helens to Sir Henry Fitzherbert, 6 Sept. 1827, Fitzherbert Papers; *Lorne*, p. 43; *Webster*, i. 12 n. 1.
81. *Bury*, i. 107, ii. 345; Palmerston's endorsements on letter from Lady Charlotte Campbell, 1 June 1813, Palmerston to F. Temple, 27 Feb. 1810, and Palmerston to W. Temple, 2 June 1825, B.P.W.; *Letters of the Princess Charlotte 1811-1817* (1949), ed. A. Aspinall, p. 62.
82. *Memoirs of Miss C.E. Cary* (3 vols., 1825).
83. *George IV*, ii. 256-7; Aspinall, *Canning's Ministry*, p. 263.
84. *Sulivan*, pp. 201-2; Palmerston to Clive, 19 Dec., Powis Papers; Huskisson to Granville, 'Most Secret', 11 Dec. 1827, Gran. Papers 9/9 (3) no. 28; *Goderich*, pp. 188-92.
85. *Goderich*, pp. 193-4; *Palmerston*, i. 378-9; Hardinge to Londonderry, 25 Jan. [1828], Londonderry Papers; Aspinall, 'Last of the Canningites', p. 641.
86. *Goderich*, p. 193; Goderich to Palmerston, 17 Dec., and Palmerston to Goderich, 18 Dec., B.P.; Lady Granville to Lady Carlisle, [Aug.], C.H.P. 1/159; Huskisson to Dudley, [9 Oct.], Huskisson to Goderich, 26 Dec. [but marked 'not sent'], and Gran-

ville to Huskisson, 21 Dec., H.P.; Huskisson to Granville, 'Private and Secret', 28 Dec. 1827, Gran. Papers 9/9 (3) no. 31.

87. *W.N.D.*, iv. 187-99; Palmerston's memo., 13 Jan., B.P./GMC18; Palmerston to Lady Cowper, 'Sunday' [13], 14 Jan. 1828, B.P.W.

88. Palmerston to Lady Cowper, 14 Jan., B.P.W., and to Clive, 15 Jan. 1828, Powis Papers.

89. *Huskisson Papers*, pp. 281-3; Palmerston to Lady Cowper, 17 Jan. 1828, B.P./GMC30.

90. Palmerston to Huskisson, 18 Jan., H.P. (the enclosed 'propositions' are printed in *Huskisson Papers*, pp. 283-4); *W.N.D.*, iv. 194; Palmerston's memo., 18 Jan., B.P./GMC25; Palmerston to Lady Cowper, 18 Jan. 1828, B.P./GMC31 (Lorne, pp. 46-7).

91. Palmerston's memo., 19 Jan., B.P./GMC25; Palmerston to Lady Cowper, 19 Jan., B.P.W., 21 Jan., B.P./GMC32; *Palmerston*, i. 219, 380; *Arbuthnot*, p. 99; Devonshire to Lady Granville, 11 Feb. 1828, Chat. Papers; Lorne, p. 63.

92. *Broughton*, iii. 239; *Arbuthnot*, p. 98; *Lady Holland's Letters*, p. 74 n. 2; *Palmerston*, i. 218; Hobhouse's journal, 24 Jan. 1828.

93. *Arbuthnot*, p. 98.

94. *Ellenborough Diary*, i. 2-3; Lady Cowper to Brougham, 'Monday' [21 Jan. 1828], Brougham Papers; *Creevey Papers*, ii. 144-5; *Greville*, i. 205; *Mrs Arbuthnot*, ii. 166; *Sulivan*, p. 207.

95. *Mrs Arbuthnot*, ii. 171; *Palmerston*, i. 239-46.

96. *Palmerston*, i. 220; Granville to Huskisson, 21 Jan., and Huskisson to Fitzgerald, 22 Jan., H.P. (cf. Aspinall, 'Last of the Canningites', p. 642 n. 1); Palmerston to Lady Cowper, 21 Jan. 1828, B.P./GMC32.

97. Huskisson to Dudley and Granville, 9 Oct. 1827, H.P. (cf. *Goderich*, pp. 178-9); *Melbourne Papers*, p. 108.

98. Palmerston to Goderich, 6 Dec. 1827, B.P./MM/GR2; *Palmerston*, i. 227; Palmerston to Lady Cowper, 25 July, B.P.W.; Palmerston to W. Temple, 26 Aug. 1828, B.P.

99. *Palmerston*, i. 227; *Colchester*, iii. 534; Palmerston to W. Temple, 19 June 1818, B.P.

100. Mrs Sulivan to W. Temple, 4 Feb., B.P.W.; 2 *Hansard*, xviii. 64, 76 (29, 31 Jan.); Hobhouse's journal, 29 Jan. 1828 (*Broughton*, iii. 238, has softened 'miserably' to 'not well').

101. Palmerston's 'Remarks on the proposal to confine within the limits of the Morea the continental portion of the Grecian province to be established under the Treaty of London', 15 Feb., B.P./MM/GR4; Dudley to Palmerston, 17 Feb. 1828, B.P.; *Ellenborough Diary*, i. 49-50; *Palmerston*, i. 229-31.

102. *Palmerston*, i. 223-8, 236-9; *Ellenborough Diary*, i. 63.

103. *Palmerston*, i. 223, 246-50; *W.N.D.*, iv. 339-40; Peel to Palmerston, 8 April, B.P.; Howard de Walden to Granville, 'Most Confidential', 6 April [1828], Gran. Papers 14/5 no. 87.

104. *Palmerston*, i. 225-6, 246.

105. Palmerston to W. Temple, 8 May 1828, B.P.

106. Ashley, i. 146; *Palmerston*, i. 250; Bell, i. 65; *Ellenborough Diary*, i. 76, 98; *Howard Sisters*, p. 108.

107. *Ellenborough Diary*, i. 106-7, 109; 2 *Hansard*, xix. 722 (14 May 1828); Aspinall, 'Last of the Canningites', p. 645 n. 5; *Huskisson*, p. 93; *Mrs Arbuthnot*, ii. 187.

108. 2 *Hansard*, xix. 1538 (27 June 1828).

109. Palmerston to W. Temple, 12 Mar. 1819, B.P.; *Palmerston*, i. 234-5, 253-6.

110. *Palmerston*, i. 256-8; *Broughton*, v. 203-4; Palmerston to W. Temple, 22 May, B.P.; Morley to Granville, 27 May 1828, Gran. Papers 9/2 no. 44.

111. *Palmerston*, i. 255, 258, 422; Palmerston to W. Temple, 22 May 1828, B.P.

112. *Palmerston*, i. 259-60.

113. *Palmerston*, i. 260-65; *W.N.D.*, iv. 453-5; Palmerston to W. Temple, 22 May 1828, B.P.; *Ellenborough Diary*, i. 115-16 (cf. 3 *Hansard*, cxxxviii. 468 (14 May 1855)).

114. *Ellenborough Diary*, i. 115; *Mrs Arbuthnot*, ii. 188; *Palmerston*, i. 266-7, 423-6.

115. *Croker Papers*, i. 423; *Palmerston*, i. 266-8; *Ellenborough Diary*, i. 112; Palmerston to W. Temple, 22 May, B.P.; Palmerston to Huskisson, 23 May 1828, H.P.; *W.N.D.*, iv. 458-65.

116. *Palmerston*, i. 272-4; *W.N.D.*, iv. 465-72; Ziegler, p. 98.

117. *Broughton*, iii. 271; *Bathurst*, p. 653; Palmerston to Wellington, 25 May, and Wellington to Palmerston, 26 May, B.P.; *Ellenborough Diary*, i. 103-4, 113; Littleton to Mrs Littleton, 25 May 1828, Hath. Papers; *Eden*, p. 107; Lever, p. 138; *Mrs Arbuthnot*, i. 419, 424, ii. 125, 129, 135, 162.

118. *Mrs Arbuthnot*, ii. 159; Gleig, p. 41; *Sulivan*, p. 196; Lady Cowper to Fred Lamb, 21 May [1828], Panshanger Papers.

CHAPTER VII: INTERLUDE II: JACKDAW AND PHOENIX, 1828-30 (*pages 288-331*)

1. *Sulivan*, p. 221; Devonshire to Lady Granville, 27 May, Chat. Papers; *Dudley to Ivy*, p. 339; Lady Cowper to Fred Lamb, 3 June [1828], Panshanger Papers.

2. *Palmerston*, i. 276-9; *Goderich*, pp. 210-11; Goderich to Palmerston, 30 May, B.P.; Huskisson to Goderich, 2 June 1828, H.P.

3. Wilmot Horton to Granville, 21 Oct. 1830, Gran. Papers 6 no. 70; *Mrs Arbuthnot*, ii. 195; *Palmerston*, i. 277-8; Palmerston to W. Temple, 8 June, B.P. (Lorne, pp. 47-9, and Ashley, i. 163-4); Horace Twiss to Huskisson and Palmerston to Huskisson, 29 May, H.P.; Huskisson to Palmerston, 29 May, B.P./GMC29; *Ellenborough Diary*, i. 136; Granville to Morley, 12 June 1828, Gran. Papers 396.

4. 2 *Hansard*, xix. 917-80 (2 June); Hobhouse's journal, 2 June (*Broughton*, iii. 275-7); Lady Grey to Grey, 'Tuesday' [3 June] 1828, G.P.

5. Lady Cowper to Fred Lamb, 3 June [1828], Panshanger Papers.

6. *Palmerston*, i. 220; Wilmot Horton to Granville, 26 Aug. 1827, Gran. Papers 9/6 no. 54; Aspinall, 'Last of the Canningites', pp. 659-60.

7. *Palmerston*, i. 282-3; Palmerston to W. Temple, 8 June 1828, B.P. (Lorne, pp. 47-8).

8. *Sulivan*, p. 207; Palmerston to Lady Cowper, 19 June, B.P.W.; Ashley, i. 164; Hobhouse's journal, 20 June 1828.

9. *Sulivan*, pp. 212, 213, 215.

10. Palmerston to W. Temple, 26 Aug. 1828, B.P.; *Sulivan*, pp. 213-17.

11. *Palmerston*, i. 306; *Sulivan*, pp. 217-21.

12. *Palmerston*, i. 308-10; *Sulivan*, p. 219.

13. Palmerston to Anglesey, 18 Nov., and Anglesey to Palmerston, 19 Dec., B.P.; Croker to Hertford, 8, 9 Dec., Croker Papers, Clements Library; Lady Holland to [?Morpeth], 'Tuesday' [?9 Dec.], C.H.P. 2/11; *The Private Letter-Books of Sir Walter Scott* (1930), ed. Wilfrid Partington, p. 157.

14. *Arbuthnot*, p. 110; Palmerston to W. Temple, 9 Dec. 1828, and to Anglesey, 6 Jan. 1829, B.P.

15. *Mrs Arbuthnot*, ii. 193, 195, 235, 339; *Sulivan*, pp. 226, 227; Mme Flahault to Lady Holland, 12 Jan., 3 Feb. [1829], H.H.P.

16. *Palmerston*, i. 323-4; Hobhouse's journal, 2 Feb. 1829 (*Broughton*, iii. 300); *Mrs Arbuthnot*, ii. 237; *Broughton*, iii. 302.

17. 2 *Hansard*, xx. 235 (10 Feb. 1829).

18. 2 *Hansard*, xx. 1237-53 (18 Mar. 1829).

19. *Mrs Arbuthnot*, ii. 255; *Greville*, i. 274; Althorp to Brougham, 19 Mar. 1829, A.P.; Bell, i. 80; *Ellenborough Diary*, i. 399; *Jekyll*, p. 196.

20. 2 *Hansard*, xx. 1352-6 (19 Mar. 1829).

21. *Ellenborough Diary*, ii. 27.

22. Lady Cowper to Fred Lamb, 2 July, B.P.W.; Dudley to Granville, 28 May, Gran. Papers 14/4 no. 82; Lady Carlisle to Carlisle, 'Thursday' [18 Dec.], C.H.P. 2/13; *Palmerston*, i. 287-90, 299-304; Palmerston to W. Temple, 8 June, 26 Aug., B.P.; Palmerston to Lady Cowper, 25 July, B.P.W.; *Sulivan*, p. 213; Palmerston to Anglesey, 18 Nov. 1828, B.P.

23. Lady Granville to Devonshire, 23 July, Chat. Papers, and Palmerston to Lady Cowper, 25 July, B.P.W.; *Sulivan*, p. 213; *Palmerston*, i. 290-95, 305-6, 313, 316-20, 329, 334; Palmerston to W. Temple, 27 June 1828, B.P.; Countess Flahault to Palmerston, [9 April], B.P.; Fred Lamb, 'Secret', to Palmerston, Feb. 1829, B.P.

24. Althorp to Brougham, 14, 18 Mar., A.P.; Palmerston to W. Temple, 6 May, B.P.; Abercromby to Brougham, [?2 June], Brougham Papers; Howick's diary, 2 June 1829; *Greville*, i. 296.

25. 2 *Hansard*, xxi. 1643-70 (1 June 1829).

26. Abercromby to Brougham, [? June], Brougham Papers; *Greville*, i. 296; *Palmerston*, i. 333-4; Mme Flahault to Palmerston, 28 June [1829], B.P.; *Arbuthnot*, p. 116.

27. *Palmerston*, i. 328-9, 334, 336; Sulivan to Palmerston, 11 Oct. 1829, B.P.; Bell, i. 76; Arbuthnot to Peel, 15 April, Peel Papers; *Eldon*, iii. 93; Abercromby to Brougham, [21 June 1829], Brougham Papers.

28. G.M. Willis, *Ernest Augustus Duke of Cumberland and King of Hanover* (1954), pp. 169-95; *Greville*, i. 262, 311-12; *Palmerston*, i. 335-6; 'Vyvyan', pp. 142-7.

29. Palmerston to Littleton, 16 Sept. 1829, Hath. Papers; *Sulivan*, p. 231; *Huskisson*, p. 168.

30. *Palmerston*, i. 336; Sir Hughe Knatchbull-Hugessen, *Kentish Family* (1960), pp. 178-80; 'Vyvyan', pp. 148-9; Palmerston to Lady Cowper, 3, 10 Oct., B.P.W.; *Sulivan*, pp. 231-6; and, for Palmerston's earlier views on free trade, etc., Palmerston to Clive, 19 Dec. 1827, Powis Papers, Ashley, i. 165-6, and Palmerston to W. Temple, 6 May 1829, B.P.

31. Howick's diary, 7 Mar. 1830; Aspinall, *Brougham*, pp. 170-71; Hyde Villiers to Stapleton, 22 Oct. 1829, Stap. Papers 51; *Greville*, i. 324-5; *Mrs Arbuthnot*, ii. 312.

32. Hyde Villiers to Stapleton, 22 Oct. 1829, Stap. Papers 51; Sulivan to Palmerston, 11 Oct. 1829, B.P.

33. *Palmerston*, i. 347-59; *Lady Palmerston*, i. 162-71.

34. Minto (Paris) to Lansdowne, 16 Dec. 1829, 6 Jan. 1830, Bowood Papers.

35. Palmerston to Lady Cowper, 25 Nov. 1829, B.P.W.

36. Hobhouse's journal, 4, 5, 16 Feb. 1830 (*Broughton*, iv. 7-8); *Palmerston*, i. 261, 269.

37. Temperley (*Canning*, p. 516) asserts (without any explanation, but probably following *Lieven-Grey*, i. 464-5, a source which he usually distrusts) that *Observations on the Papers lately submitted to Parliament upon the Subject of the Affairs of Portugal* (1830) is not by Fred Lamb; but *Greville*, i. 343, 374, plainly shows that it is. The authorship of 'The Greek Revolution and European Diplomacy', *Foreign Quarterly Review*, v (Nov. 1829), pp. 271-317, was attributed inevitably to Brougham and to various Canningites by, for example, *Greville*, i. 343-4, *Lieven-Grey*, i. 397, Russell to Lady Holland, [?Dec.], and Lady Holland to H. Fox, 30 Dec. 1829, H.H.P., and *Mrs Arbuthnot*, ii. 323; but none of them named James Murray, the foreign editor of *The Times* who apparently was the real author (*Wellesley Index*); *Times History*, i. 419-20; *Mrs Arbuthnot*, ii. 339; *Ellenborough Diary*, ii. 253.

38. *Greville*, i. 374, 375.

39. 2 *Hansard*, xxiii. 76-103; *Lieven-Grey*, i. 466; Howick's diary, 10 Mar.; Dover's diary, 10 Mar.; Hobhouse's journal, 10 Mar.; *Howard Sisters*, pp. 125-6; Jekyll to Lady Gertrude Sloane Stanley, 29, 15 Mar. 1830, Sloane Papers, Hampshire Record Office (*Jekyll*, pp. 229, 118, wrongly places the latter as a postscript to another letter of 7 Oct. 1821).

40. Aspinall, *Brougham*, p. 169; Althorp to Brougham, 14 Feb. 1829, A.P.

41. Bedford to Lady Holland, 10 Sept. 1818, Holland House Dinner Book, Mme Flahault to Lady Holland, 12 Jan., 3 Feb. [1829], H.H.P.

42. Holland to Grey, 22 Feb. [1830], H.H.P.; Palmerston to Lady Cowper, 25 Nov. 1829, B.P.W.; Ellice to Grey, 18, 22 Jan. 1830, G.P.; *Lieven-Grey*, i. 416, 421; *Blessington*, ii. 310-11; Lansdowne to Melbourne, 12 Jan., B.P.; Russell to Brougham, 30 Jan. 1830, Brougham Papers.

43. Hobhouse's journal, 5 Feb. 1830; M. Brock, pp. 74-6.

44. Mitchell, pp. 226-8; M. Brock, p. 67; Palmerston to Minto, 23 Mar. 1830, M.P.; *Ellenborough Diary*, ii. 214-15.

45. Princess Lieven to Palmerston, 24 April 1830, B.P. (asking simply for an appointment, but endorsed by Palmerston: 'Wanting to see me about proposed cooperation between us & Ld Grey'); Mitchell, pp. 230-31; *Grey*, p. 218.

46. *Creevey Papers*, ii. 145; Grey to Howick, 9 Mar., and Howick to Grey, 11 Mar. 1830, G.P.

47. Howick's diary, 13 May, 27 June 1830; *Ellenborough Diary*, ii. 262; *Mrs Arbuthnot*, ii. 360, 361; *Lieven-Grey*, ii. 12; M. Brock, pp. 72-3.

48. Brougham to Durham, 'Monday' [28 Dec. 1829], Lambton Papers; Ellice to Grey, 1 Feb. 1830, G.P.; *Sulivan*, p. 239; *W.N.D.*, vii. 108.

49. *Palmerston*, i. 381; Palmerston's 'Memo. of the Duke of Wellington's proposal to Ld Melbourne at the end of June 1830', B.P./GMC33; *The Correspondence of Priscilla, Countess of Westmorland* (1909), p. 32.

50. *Greville*, ii. 91; Palmerston's memo., B.P./GMC33; *Lieven-Grey*, ii. 27; M. Brock, p. 73; Arbuthnot to Peel, 8 July, Peel Papers (cf. Littleton to Wharncliffe, 12 Sept. 1830, Hath. Papers).

51. Arbuthnot to Peel, 8 July 1830, Peel Papers; *Ellenborough Diary*, ii. 306, 312, 316; *Mrs Arbuthnot*, ii. 372-3.

52. *Lady Palmerston*, i. 172-4; M. Brock, pp. 86-7, 103; N. Gash, 'English Reform and French Revolution in the General Election of 1830', in *Essays Presented to Sir Lewis Namier* (1956), ed. Richard Pares and A.J.P. Taylor, pp. 287-8.

53. *Palmerston*, i. 350-51, 357; *Graham*, i. 85; Webster, i. 80-81.

54. *Greville*, ii. 32-3; Sefton to Brougham, 27 Aug., Brougham Papers; Mitchell, p. 239; Durham to Grey, 'Sunday' [29 Aug.], G.P.; *Brougham*, iii. 45; Brougham to Durham, [Aug. 1830], Brougham Papers.

55. *Greville*, ii. 39; *Howard Sisters*, p. 138; *Ellenborough Diary*, ii. 359; Leopold to Durham, 3 Sept., and Durham to Leopold, 6 Sept., Lambton Papers; Althorp to Brougham, 5 Sept., and Durham to Brougham, 7 Sept. 1830, Brougham Papers.

56. Brougham to Lady Cowper, 3 Sept., B.P.; Lady Cowper to Palmerston, 'Sunday-Monday' [12-13 Sept.], B.P.W.; Palmerston to Clanricarde, 13 Sept., Clanricarde Papers 68; *Greville*, ii. 47; *Brougham*, iii. 66; Lady Cowper to Brougham, 'Thursday' [9 Sept.], Brougham Papers; Arbuthnot to Peel, 10 Sept., Peel Papers; Littleton to Wharncliffe, 12 Sept. 1830, Hath. Papers.

57. Durham to Grey, 17 Sept., G.P.; *Greville*, ii. 46-7, 332; Brougham to Morpeth, 'Thursday Mg' [16 Sept. 1830], C.H.P. 2/14; *Graham*, i. 88; Aspinall, *Brougham*, p. 181.

58. Brougham to Devonshire, 'Tues.' [21 Sept. 1830], Chat. Papers (Aspinall, *Brougham*, p. 182).

59. Ellis to Lady Holland, 20 Sept., H.H.P.; Dover's diary, 23 Sept. (cf. Mitchell, p. 240, who is unaware of Ellis's role); Grey to Holland, 19 Sept. 1830, G.P.

60. *Lieven-Grey*, ii. 90-91; Durham to Grey, 26 Sept., G.P.; Holland to Grey, 25 Sept. 1830, H.H.P.; Mitchell, pp. 239-40.

61. Palmerston to Grant (extract), 25 Sept., and Palmerston's 'Proposal made to me by the Duke of Wellington to join his Govt', Oct. 1830, B.P./GMC35, 38.

62. Dover's diary, 25 Sept.; Brougham to Devonshire, 'Thurs.' [30 Sept.], Chat. Papers; Durham to Grey, 4 Oct., G.P.; M. Brock, p. 107; Palmerston to Littleton, 25 Sept. 1830, Hath. Papers.

63. Huskisson to Granville, 25 Aug., Gran. Papers 9/3; *Sulivan*, p. 241; Anglesey to Wharncliffe, 12 Sept., Hath. Papers; Littleton to Palmerston, 20 Sept., B.P./GMC34; Brougham to Devonshire, 'Thurs.' [30 Sept.], 'Fri.' [1 Oct.], Chat. Papers; *Brougham*, iii. 66-7; *Lieven-Grey*, ii. 90-91, 94; Planta's list, 21 Sept., Peel Papers; Palmerston to Littleton, 18, 25 Sept. 1830, Hath. Papers (Aspinall, *Brougham*, pp. 180-81).

64. Littleton to Palmerston, 20 Sept., B.P./GMC34; Arbuthnot to Peel, 17 Sept., Peel Papers; *Ellenborough Diary*, ii. 362-3; *Arbuthnot*, p. 131; Leopold to Durham, 25 Sept. 1830, Lambton Papers; Webster, i. 19 n. 1; *Mrs Arbuthnot*, ii. 387-9.

65. *W.N.D.*, vii. 281; Clive to Wellington, 11 p.m., 1 Oct., Powis Papers; Clive to Palmerston, 1 Oct., B.P./GMC36; Palmerston to Clive, 4 Oct. (two letters), Powis Papers (B.P./GMC37 and *W.N.D.*, vii. 328); Palmerston's 'Proposal made to me by the Duke of Wellington to join his Govt', Oct. 1830, B.P./GMC38; *Palmerston*, i. 381-2.

66. Princess Lieven to Palmerston, 2 Sept., 4, [6-] 7 Oct., B.P. (but cf. *Greville*, ii. 90); *Lieven-Grey*, ii. 105; Princess Lieven to Nesselrode, 20 Sept. 1830, Lieven Papers; *Lieven-Benckendorff*, p. 256.

67. Palmerston's memo., Oct. 1830, B.P./GMC38; Aspinall, *Brougham*, pp. 182-3; *Palmerston*, i. 382.

68. Palmerston to Clanricarde, 13 Sept., Clanricarde Papers 68; Palmerston to Mme Graham, 2 Oct., Graham of Drynie Papers, B.L.; Mrs George Lamb's diary, 5 Oct., Dormer Papers; Palmerston's memo., B.P./GMC38; Clive to Wellington, 10 Oct. 1830, Powis Papers; *Sulivan*, pp. 241-2.

69. Palmerston to Holland, 12 Oct., H.H.P.; *Sulivan*, pp. 242-7; *Mrs Arbuthnot*, ii. 393; Wilmot Horton to Granville, 21 Oct., Gran. Papers 6/70; Clive to Wellington, 10 Oct., memo. of [?10] Oct., and Planta to Clive, 21 Oct. 1830, Powis Papers.

70. *Mrs Arbuthnot*, ii. 390; Lady Holland to Carlisle, 'Saturday' [23 Oct.], C.H.P. 1/139; *Sulivan*, p. 247; Lady Holland to Henry Fox, 29 [Oct. 1830], H.H.P.

71. *Lieven-Benckendorff*, p. 262; Wellington to Palmerston, 30 Oct. 1830, and Palmerston's record of his interview, B.P./GMC41, 42; *Mrs Arbuthnot*, ii. 395; *Palmerston*, i. 382-3.

72. *Mrs Arbuthnot*, ii. 390, 396; Ziegler, p. 117; Grant to Palmerston, 31 Oct., and Palmerston's reply, 1 Nov. 1830, B.P./GMC43.

73. Mitchell, pp. 236-7, 242-3; M. Brock, pp. 115-16; New, *Brougham*, p. 413.

74. Graham to Morpeth, [*post* 6 Mar. 1830], C.H.P. 2/12 (cf. M. Brock, p. 67); Hobhouse's journal, 4 July; Mitchell, p. 218 n. 5; Graham to Brougham, 1 Sept., [late Sept. or early Oct. 1830], Brougham Papers; Ward, *Graham*, pp. 89-90; Palmerston's drafts and memos on the Game Laws in B.P.W. and B.P./SP/A26; *Graham*, i. 84-5.

75. *Graham*, i. 96-7.

76. Holland to Carlisle, 8 Oct., C.H.P. 1/139; Palmerston to Holland, 12 Oct. 1830, H.H.P.; M. Brock, p. 108.

77. *Peel*, ii. 163-6; Littleton to R. Wellesley, 20 Dec. 1830, Hath. Papers; *Mrs Arbuthnot*, ii. 398.

78. Graham to Brougham, [7 Sept. 1830], Brougham Papers; Aspinall, *Three Diaries*, p. 23; Hatherton's diary, 22 Sept. 1856, Hath Papers.

79. Aspinall, *Brougham*, p. 181; Littleton to Palmerston, 2 Oct., and Anglesey to Palmerston, 2 Oct. 1830, B.P.

80. M. Brock, pp. 114-18; *Peel*, ii. 167; *Croker Papers*, ii. 74; *Palmerston*, i. 383; *Broughton*, iv. 60; Ziegler, p. 118.

81. Dover's diary, 6, 13 Nov. 1830; *Howard Sisters*, p. 157.

82. Goderich to Littleton, 12 Nov., and Dudley to Littleton, 'Sunday' [14 Nov.], Hath. Papers; Palmerston to Agar Ellis, 'Sunday' [14 Nov. 1830], St John's College, Cambridge, Papers.

83. *Broughton*, iv. 60; M. Brock, p. 128; Palmerston's 'Autobiographical Sketch', B.P.W. (cf. *Palmerston*, i. 383).

84. *Brougham*, iii. 48-9; Holland to Grey, 16 Nov., G.P.; *Grey*, p. 241 n. 1; Grey to

Palmerston, 16 Nov., B.P.; Leonard Cooper, *Radical Jack. The Life of John George Lambton First Earl of Durham* (1959), p. 99; Aspinall, *Three Diaries*, p. xxviii n. 2; Grey to Devonshire, 17 Nov. 1830, Chat. Papers.

85. Aspinall, 'Last of the Canningites', p. 663 n. 2; Aspinall, *Three Diaries*, p. x; Abercromby to James Brougham, [endorsed 18/19 Nov. 1830, but probably earlier], Brougham Papers.

86. New, *Brougham*, p. 415; Mrs Lamb's diary, 19 Nov. 1830, Dormer Papers; Allen's diary, 7 May 1831, H.H.P.

87. *Durham*, i. 216; Augustus Clifford's diary, 16 Nov., Dormer Papers; Palmerston to Littleton, 'Wedy night' [17 Nov. 1830], Hath. Papers; *Grey*, pp. 378-9; *Sulivan*, pp. 247-8.

88. Webster, i. 21; Shee to Palmerston, 16 Jan. 1828, B.P.; Bullen, p. 3; Holland and Lady Holland to H. Fox, 12 Oct., H.H.P.; Holland to Grey, 'Thursday 4 o'clock' [18 Nov. 1830], G.P.; *Grey*, pp. 378-9.

89. *Lieven Diary*, pp. 165-7.

90. *Lieven-Benckendorff*, pp. 275-6; *Mrs Arbuthnot*, ii. 399-400; *Greville*, ii. 85.

CHAPTER VIII: 'LIBERALISM ALL OVER THE WORLD', 1830-34 *(pages 332-407)*

1. Palmerston to Littleton, 23 Nov., Hath. Papers; Dover's diary, 24 Nov.; Littleton to R. Wellesley, 5 Dec. 1830, Hath. Papers; Webster, i. 58.

2. Webster, i. 33 n. 1, 102, 115; Brougham to Spencer, 22 Jan. 1831, A.P.

3. Palmerston to Lady Cowper, 15, 16 Nov. 1831 (Lorne, p. 67); Palmerston to Lamb, 21 Sept. 1832, RA, M.P.; Webster, i. 108, 109, 156; Lady Cowper to Devonshire, 'Sat.' [8 Jan. 1831], Chat. Papers.

4. Webster, i. 108, ii. 801-2; Hertslet, p. 60.

5. Palmerston to Grey, 19 Dec. 1830, G.P.; Betley, pp. 69-70.

6. Donald Southgate, *'The Most English Minister . . . ' The Policies and Politics of Palmerston* (1966), p. 32; 3 Hansard, xi. 912-13 (26 Mar. 1832).

7. Palmerston to Grey, 'Friday' [10 Dec.], G.P., and Grey to Palmerston, 10 Dec. 1830, B.P.; Webster, i. 121, 128; Palmerston to Granville, 21 Jan. 1831, Gran. Papers; Betley, p. 80; *Palmerston*, ii. 27-9, 75.

8. Webster, i. 123; *Palmerston*, ii. 27-9.

9. Grey to Holland, 6 Jan. 1831, H.H.P.; Bourne, p. 218; *Palmerston*, ii. 30-31.

10. Webster, i. 125-6; Bell, i. 123.

11. Palmerston to Grey, 1 Feb. 1831, B.P. (Webster, ii. 816-17); *Palmerston*, ii. 36-8.

12. *Palmerston*, ii. 41, 45, 48-9, 51-3, 60; Palmerston to Holland, 9 April 1831, H.H.P.

13. Palmerston to Grey, 6, 11 Jan., 17 April 1831, G.P.; *Palmerston*, ii. 45, 64, 70-73.

14. *Palmerston*, ii. 62; Webster, i. 134-8; Palmerston to Grey, 13 June, [?21 June], 3 Aug., G.P.; Grey to Palmerston, 3 Aug. 1831, B.P.; Bell, i. 131.

15. Palmerston to Grey, 4 Aug., 'Sat. Evng' [6 Aug. 1831], G.P.

16. Hobhouse's journal, 6 Aug.; *Brougham*, iii. 124; Durham to Grey, '½ past 12' [6 Aug.], G.P.; Grey to Palmerston, 7, 8 Aug., B.P.; Palmerston to Grey, 'Saty night' [25 June], [11 Aug. 1831], G.P.; Webster, i. 135-6, 139; *Palmerston*, ii. 102, 105, 106-8, 111-13; Bourne, pp. 219-20; Bell, i. 133.

17. Althorp to Brougham, 'private & confidential', 'Wednesday' [17 Aug.], A.P.; Holland to Grey, 7 April, G.P.; Granville to Holland, 21 Feb., H.H.P.; Mme Flahault to Lady Holland, 17 Jan., 22 July 1831, H.H.P.

18. Flahault to Grey, 17 Jan., and Grey to Flahault, 20 Jan., G.P.; Holland to Palmerston, [6 Aug.], B.P.; Granville to Holland, 27 Aug., 2 Sept., H.H.P.; Grey to Palmerston, 13, 28 Aug., 2 Sept., B.P.; Althorp to Brougham, 'private and confidential', 'Wednesday' [17 Aug.], A.P.; Webster, i. 34 n. 1, 139; Palmerston to Grey, 22, 27 Aug. 1831, G.P.; *Palmerston*, ii. 114-16, 120.

19. *Palmerston*, ii. 119; Palmerston to Grey, 2, 3, 5 Sept. 1831, G.P.; *Dino*, i. 4.

20. Palmerston to Grey, 28, 29 Sept. 1831, G.P.; Bell, i. 135; Webster, i. 111.

21. Webster, i. 145, 150-51; Palmerston to Lady Cowper, 3 Oct. 1832, B.P.W.; *Clarendon*, i. 79.

22. Palmerston to Grey, 24, 25 Oct. 1831, 20 Jan. 1832, G.P.; Webster, i. 146, ii. 818; Holland to Brougham, 27 Oct., 24, 27 Dec., Brougham Papers; Palmerston to Holland, 22 Dec. 1831, H.H.P.

23. Palmerston to Lamb, 19 Feb., 16 Mar., 10 April 1832, RA, M.P.; Webster, i. 151.

24. Palmerston to Grey, 5, 7, 8 June and 1, 3, 24, 26 July, G.P.; Webster, i. 164; Palmerston to Lamb, 30 June 1832, B.P.

25. Webster, i. 156, is in error when he states that Palmerston never used the word; cf. Palmerston to Grey, 10 Nov. 1832, G.P.

26. Webster, i. 164; Grey to Palmerston, 24 July, B.P.; Palmerston to Grey, 24, 29 July 1832, G.P.

27. Palmerston to Grey, 21 June, 17 Sept., G.P.; William IV to Palmerston, 18 Sept., B.P.; Webster, i. 167-8; Melbourne to Lansdowne, 28 Sept., RA, M.P.; Graham to Palmerston, 28 Sept., B.P.; *Graham*, i. 156-7; Holland to Granville, 2 Oct., Gran. Papers; Russell to Palmerston, 23 Sept., B.P.; Palmerston to Lamb, 28 Sept. 1832, B.P.

28. Webster, i. 168-9; Palmerston to Lamb, 2 May 1833, B.P.; *H.H.D.*, p. 204; Palmerston to Lady Cowper, 27 Sept., B.P.W.; Palmerston to Grey, 27, 28 Sept., 2 Oct., G.P.; Palmerston to Lamb, 6 Oct. 1832, RA, M.P.

29. Webster, i. 169-72; Bartlett, p. 87.

30. Webster, i. 171-5; correspondence between Grey, Taylor and the King, 13-19 Oct., RA, G.P. 1996-2015; Palmerston to Grey, 18 Nov. 1832, G.P.; *Palmerston*, ii. 147, 164-5, 166; Palmerston to Lamb, 13 Nov. 1832, RA, M.P., and 30 May 1833, B.P.; Palmerston to Minto, 31 Jan. 1834, M.P.

31. Webster, i. 109, 149 n. 1; *Russell E.C.*, i. 317.

32. *Palmerston*, ii. 36; Palmerston's unpublished journals of travel in France and undated letters from Bulwer and Abraham Hayward to William Cowper, *c.* 1870, B.P.W.; *The Personal Papers of Lord Rendel Containing his Unpublished Conversations with Mr Gladstone* (1931), p. 60.

33. Webster, i. 128 n. 1; *Palmerston*, ii. 38-9, 56-7, 82-3; Palmerston to Holland, 9 April 1831, H.H.P. (Bullen, p. 5).

34. Webster, i. 172; Holland to Granville, 19 Jan., Gran. Papers 409; Granville to Holland, 23 Jan., H.H.P.; Lady Cowper to F. Lamb, 20 Aug. 1832, B.P.W.

35. Palmerston to Grey, 16 Jan. 1831, G.P.; Grey to Palmerston, 21 Feb. 1832, 8 Sept., 16 Dec. 1833, B.P. (Webster, i. 827); Palmerston to Lamb, 21 May 1833, B.P.

36. Aspinall, *Three Diaries*, pp. 171-2; Palmerston to Lamb, 7 Mar., 10 April, 7-9 May, RA, M.P.; Webster, i. 215 n. 1; Palmerston to Grey, 17 April, G.P.; Holland to Carlisle, 20 April, C.H.P. 1/139; 3 *Hansard*, xi. 882 (26 Mar.); Lady Cowper to Lamb, 5 June 1832, B.P.W.

37. Grey to Palmerston, [?Dec. 1830], B.P., G.C./GR 1947; Palmerston to Holland, 9 April 1831, H.H.P.

38. Palmerston to Holland, 20 Mar., H.H.P.; Webster, i. 68, 184-8; Palmerston to Grey, 6 Jan., G.P.; Betley, pp. 169, 171-2, 188, 216-17; Bell, i. 169; Palmerston to Granville, 12 July 1831, Gran. Papers 404.

39. *Lieven-Benckendorff*, p. 276; Webster, i. 184, 186-7, 189, ii. 825; Palmerston to Grey, 18 Mar., 21 July, 28, 29 Sept., 6, 7 Nov., G.P.; Bell, i. 167, 169; Lansdowne to Palmerston, 13 Nov. 1831, B.P.

40. Palmerston to Grey, 2 Jan., G.P.; Grey to Holland, 4 Jan., H.H.P.; *Lady Holland's Letters*, p. 127; *Lieven-Grey*, ii. 311-22; Webster, i. 190-91; *Brougham*, iii. 165; Palmerston to Lamb, 7 Mar., B.P.; *Palmerston*, ii. 127-8; Taylor to Palmerston, 22/23 April 1832, B.P.

41. Palmerston to Grey, 23 April, 1 June, G.P.; Palmerston to Lamb, 15, 19 April,

30 June, B.P.; 3 *Hansard*, xii. 653, xiii. 1115-52; Lady Cowper to Lamb, 2 July, B.P.W.; Webster, i. 191; *Lieven-Grey*, ii. 359-61; *Lieven-Benckendorff*, p. 329; Grey to Palmerston, 29 June 1832, B.P.

42. Grey to Palmerston, 29 June, B.P.; Grey to Holland, 29 June, H.H.P.; Lady Cowper to Lamb, 2 July [1832], B.P.W.

43. Webster, i. 191-5; Aspinall, *Three Diaries*, p. 277; Lady Cowper to Lamb, 22 June, B.P.W.; *Durham*, i. 300-303; Palmerston to Durham, 1 July, and Grey to Durham, 1, 2 July, Lambton Papers; Durham to Grey, 'Monday' [2 July], G.P.; Palmerston to Lamb, 14 July 1832, RA, M.P.; *Lieven-Benckendorff*, p. 328; *W.N.D.*, viii. 403.

44. Palmerston to Grey, 9 Nov., G.P., and to Lady Cowper, 15 Nov. 1831, B.P.W.; Webster, i. 150-51; *Herries*, ii. 131-58; 3 *Hansard*, ix. 963-8, xiv. 1215; Aspinall, *Three Diaries*, pp. 184-6, 196-8; Althorp to Spencer, 27 Jan. 1832, A.P.; *Greville*, ii. 243-4; *Broughton*, iv. 248-9.

45. Webster, i. 151, 195, 197; Granville to Holland, 7 July 1837, Holland Papers, Perkins Library, Duke University.

46. Palmerston to Lamb, 21 Sept., RA, M.P.; Palmerston to Durham, [11 Oct. 1832], Lambton Papers.

47. Grey to Holland, 12 June, H.H.P.; Webster, i. 192, 321-3; Lady Cowper to Lamb, 14 June, 27 Oct., 6 Dec., B.P.W.; Walker, p. 59; Lever, p. 196; Bell, i. 175-6; *Greville*, ii. 358; Palmerston to Grey, 1 Nov. 1832, G.P.

48. *Dino*, i. 38; Dudley to Granville, 2 Nov. 1827, n.d., Gran. Papers 14/4 nos. 33, 86; *Greville*, ii. 423; Palmerston to Russell, 14 Nov. 1842, Russell Papers 4c.

49. Littleton's diary, 19 July 1834, Hath. Papers; *Stratford Canning*, ii. 18-19; Walker, pp. 62-4; Lady Cowper to Lamb, 27 Oct., 1 Nov., 19 Nov., 6 Dec. 1832, 14 Jan., 26 Feb. 1833, B.P.W.; *Greville*, ii. 358; Palmerston to Grey, 1, 4 Nov., G.P.; Grey to Palmerston, 2 Dec. [really 2 Nov.], Webster, i. 325; author's translation of Palmerston, in French, to Mme Lieven, 4 Nov. 1832, Lieven Papers.

50. Palmerston to Holland, 26 Nov. 1832, H.H.P.; Mme Lieven to Palmerston, 5 Nov. 1832, 26 Jan. 1833, and Lieven to Palmerston, 16 Nov. 1832, B.P. (all translated); Lady Cowper to Lamb, 27 Oct., 1, 19, 26 Nov., 6 Dec. 1832, 14 Jan. 1833, B.P.W.; Lever, pp. 196, 202; *Dino*, i. 210; see also Webster, i. 323-6.

51. Lady Cowper to Lamb, 26 Feb. 1833, B.P.W.; Webster, i. 324-8; Grey to Holland, 'Thursday Evng' [22 May 1834], H.H.P.; *Greville*, ii. 353.

52. *Dino*, i. 62, 70, 81, 94, 145; Webster, i. 330-32; *Stafford*, p. 187; *Greville*, iii. 50; Holland to Grey, 22 May, G.P.; Holland to Granville, 'Friday' [24 May], Gran. Papers 9/4 no. 64; Palmerston to Lamb, 30 May 1834, RA, M.P.

53. Webster, i. 331; Lady Cowper to Lamb, 20 Aug. 1832, B.P.W.; *Greville*, ii. 358; *William Russell*, p. 313.

54. Palmerston to Grey, [16 or 17 April 1832], G.P.

55. Webster, i. 201-3, 206-7; Bell, i. 161-2; Palmerston to Granville, 11 Mar. 1831, Gran. Papers 404 (*Palmerston*, ii. 50-51).

56. Webster, i. 211; Palmerston to Lamb, 15 April, RA, M.P.; Palmerston to Grey, 20 Feb. 1832, G.P.

57. Webster, i. 210, 211, 213, 218; Palmerston to Lamb, 13 Mar. 1832, B.P.

58. Webster, i. 218, 219; Palmerston to Lamb, 14 Nov. 1833, 26 Feb. 1834, B.P.; *Palmerston*, ii. 154, 183; Palmerston to Temple, 6-7 Oct. 1833, B.P. (*Palmerston*, ii. 167, 172).

59. Palmerston to Lamb, 26 Feb. 1832, B.P.

60. Palmerston to Lamb, 30 June, Webster, i. 226, and 3 Aug. 1832, B.P.

61. Webster, i. 229, ii. 828-9; Palmerston to Grey, 19 July, and Holland to Grey, 30 July, G.P.; Holland to Carlisle, 30 July 1832, C.H.P. 2/13; *H.H.D.*, p. 200; 3 *Hansard*, xiv. 1045-9, 1066-9.

62. Webster, i. 230 n. 1; Palmerston to Lamb, 3 Aug. 1832, B.P. (Webster, i. 227).

63. Webster, i. 230-32, ii. 819, 829-30; Holland to Carlisle, 6 Aug. 1832, C.H.P. 2/13.

64. Grant to Palmerston, 5 Aug. 1832, B.P.; *H.H.D.*, p. 202.

65. Webster, i. 233-4, ii. 831; Palmerston to Grey, 7 Sept. 1832, G.P.

66. Palmerston to Minto, 5 Oct. 1832, 25 June 1833, M.P.; *Palmerston*, ii. 122; Bell, i. 152-3; *Brougham*, iii. 450.

67. Palmerston to Minto, 26 Oct., M.P.; Palmerston to Lamb, 6, 27 Oct. 1832, RA, M.P.

68. Palmerston to Minto, 20 Nov., 7 Dec. 1832, M.P.; Webster, i. 233, 357; Palmerston to Lamb, 6 April, 18 June 1833, B.P. (Webster, i. 357-8).

69. Palmerston to Lamb, 18 June, and to Minto, 18 June (Webster, i. 356-7), 25 June 1833, B.P.

70. Palmerston to Grey, 11, 14 May 1834, G.P.; Webster, i. 367-8; Bell, i. 159; Brown, pp. 102-3.

71. Webster, i. 309-10.

72. Webster, i. 261-71; Bell, i. 114-15.

73. Webster, i. 82.

74. Webster, i. 264-5.

75. Webster, i. 279; Vereté, p. 148; Palmerston to Grey, 6 Sept. 1832, G.P.

76. Palmerston to Grey, 5 Nov. 1832, G.P.; Webster, i. 279-80.

77. Palmerston to Grey, 5 Nov., 2 Dec. 1832, 22 April 1833, G.P.; Webster, i. 281-3; Palmerston to Mandeville, no. 8, 5 Dec. 1832, F.O. 78/212; Grey to Palmerston, 3 Dec. 1832, B.P.

78. C.W. Crawley, *The Question of Greek Independence, 1821-1833* (Cambridge, 1930), pp. 213-14, 237-45; Vereté, p. 151; Grey to Palmerston, 15 June, 8 Sept. 1832, B.P.; Grey to Holland, 25 Jan., H.H.P., and Holland to Grey, 25 Jan., G.P.; Althorp to Spencer, 25 Jan. 1833, A.P.

79. Palmerston to Granville, 4 Dec. 1832, 29 Jan. 1833, B.P.; Bell, i. 181; 3 *Hansard*, xiv. 1215; Vereté, pp. 148-9; Palmerston to Grey, 28 Jan. 1833, G.P.

80. Grey to Holland, 25 Jan., H.H.P.; Grey to the King, 28 Jan., enclosing Cabinet minute of 27 Jan., RA, G.P.; Grey to Palmerston, 28, 29 Jan., B.P.; Palmerston to Grey, 29 Jan., G.P.; Palmerston to Granville, 29 Jan. 1833, B.P.; Webster, i. 283-8.

81. Palmerston to Temple, 21 Mar., B.P. (*Palmerston*, ii. 144-5); Palmerston to Grey, 29 Jan., G.P.; Palmerston to Granville, 29 Jan. 1833, B.P.; Webster, i. 283-4.

82. Temperley, p. 63; Althorp to Grey, 7 April, and Grey to Althorp, 8 April 1833, A.P.; Webster, i. 302; Palmerston to Granville, 29 Jan., and to Ponsonby, 17 Feb. 1832, B.P.; Palmerston to Grey, 18 April 1833, G.P.

83. *Palmerston*, ii. 150-51; *Dr Granville*, ii. 261-6; Webster, i. 294-5, ii. 832; Grey to Palmerston, 10 April 1833, G.P.

84. Palmerston to Lamb, 2 May, 10 June 1833, B.P.; Webster, i. 300.

85. Webster, i. 305; Palmerston to Lamb, 21, 30 May 1833, B.P.

86. Palmerston to Graham, 2 Aug., Graham Papers; Grey to Palmerston, 4, 7, 9, 10 Oct., B.P.; Webster, i. 315-19, 333, ii. 819, 836-8; Grey to Graham, 4 Oct. 1833, G.P.; Bourne, pp. 221-3.

87. Webster, i. 307; Palmerston to Lamb, 21 May, 30 May, 10 June, 17 Oct., B.P.; Bourne, pp. 221-3; Holland to Palmerston, 21 May, and Grey to Palmerston, 26 Sept. 1833, B.P.; Palmerston to Grey, 26 Jan. 1834, G.P.; Palmerston to Lamb and to Ponsonby, 1 July 1833, B.P.

88. Palmerston to Temple, 7 May, and to Ponsonby, 8 July 1833, B.P.

89. Webster, i. 309-14, 343-6; *Palmerston*, ii. 179; Palmerston to Lamb, 17 Oct. 1833, 8 Mar. 1834, B.P.

90. Lamb to Melbourne, 19 July, 14 Sept. 1834, RA, M.P.

91. Lamb to Melbourne, 11 Sept., 1 Nov., RA, M.P.; Palmerston to Lamb, 23 Aug.,

B.P.; Melbourne to Palmerston, 29 Sept. 1834, B.P.

92. Palmerston to Melbourne, 30 Sept., RA, M.P.; Melbourne to Palmerston, 3 Oct., B.P.; Webster, i. 345-6; Palmerston to Lamb, 16 Oct. 1834, RA, M.P.

93. Palmerston to Lamb, 30 June, B.P.; 3 *Hansard*, xi. 882 (26 Mar.), xiv. 1045-9 (2 Aug. 1832); Palmerston to Ponsonby, 4 Nov. 1833, B.P.

94. Bell, i. 141; Palmerston to Grey, 10 Jan., G.P.; Grey to Palmerston, 10, 11 Jan. 1831, B.P.; *Mrs Arbuthnot*, ii. 411-12.

95. Palmerston to Grey and Grey to Palmerston, 12 April 1831, B.P.; *Palmerston*, ii. 73, 94; Webster, i. 242.

96. Palmerston to Grey, 14 June, G.P.; Grey to Palmerston, 14 June, 25 Aug., B.P.; Holland to Grey, 1 Aug. 1831, G.P.

97. Palmerston to Grey, 6 May, 14 June, G.P.; *Palmerston*, ii. 85-7, 89, 92, 93, 120; Grey to Palmerston, 18 July, B.P.; Webster, i. 241-2 (see also Palmerston to Grey, 26 Aug. 1831, G.P.).

98. Grey to Palmerston, 27 May, B.P.; Palmerston to Grey, 16 June, 20, 29 Sept., 29 Oct., G.P.; Palmerston to Graham, 27 Oct. 1831, Graham Papers 138.

99. 'Memorandum on the Affairs of Portugal, Foreign Office, 1 Nov. 1831', forwarded by Palmerston to Grey, 3 Nov. 1831, G.P.

100. Webster, ii. 825; Melbourne to Grey, 28 Oct., 6 Nov., G.P.; Grey to Palmerston, 29 Oct. (though headed 'Nov.'), 30 Oct., 6 Nov. 1831, B.P.

101. Lansdowne to Palmerston, 13 Nov., B.P.; Palmerston to Grey, 7 Nov., G.P.; Graham to Holland, 14 Nov., H.H.P.; Holland to Grey, 1, 2, 8 Nov., G.P.; Palmerston to Lady Cowper, 15, 17 Nov. 1831, B.P.W.

102. Holland to Grey, 18 Nov., G.P.; Palmerston to Lady Cowper, 15, 17 Nov., B.P.W.; Webster, i. 244-6; Palmerston to Grey, 8, 11, 14, 22 Dec. 1831, G.P.; Palmerston to Lamb, 26 Feb. 1832, B.P.; Graham to Althorp, 1 Jan. 1832, A.P.; Grey to Palmerston, 25 Dec. 1831, B.P.; 3 *Hansard*, xi. 917 (26 Mar. 1832).

103. Palmerston to Grey, 9, 20, 21 Mar., 8 April 1832, G.P.

104. Palmerston to Lamb, 10 April, 25 May, 14 July, RA, M.P.; Bullen, 'Portuguese Question', p. 5; Webster, i. 248-9, ii. 829; Palmerston to Holland, 7 Aug., H.H.P.; Palmerston to Grey, [8 or 9 Aug.], 9 Aug., G.P.; Palmerston's memo. of 6 Aug. 1832, F.O. 96/17.

105. Lever, pp. 198-9; Webster, i. 41, 249; Palmerston to Grey, 22, 23, 25, 27, 29 Aug., 5 Sept. 1832, G.P.

106. Grey to Palmerston, 15 Nov., B.P.; Palmerston to Holland, 21 Nov., H.H.P.; Webster, i. 69, ii. 577-8; Palmerston to Grey, 23 Nov. 1832, G.P.

107. Palmerston to Holland, 25, 26 Nov., H.H.P.; Palmerston to Grey, 27 Nov., 1, 2, 8, 20, 25 Dec., G.P.; Grey to Palmerston, 27 Nov., 1, 3 Dec. 1832, B.P.

108. Webster, i. 252-3; Bullen, 'Portuguese Question', pp. 9-21; Palmerston to Grey, 20 Dec. 1832, G.P.

109. *Palmerston*, ii. 153; Holland and Grey to Palmerston, 21 May, B.P.; Palmerston to Grey, 13 June 1833, G.P.

110. Palmerston to Grey, 13, 16, 30 June, 4 July, 2, 4 Aug., G.P.; Palmerston to Lamb, 16 July, RA, M.P.; Holland to Grey, 16 July, G.P.; *H.H.D.*, p. 237; Grey to Holland, 12 Aug., H.H.P.; Palmerston to Lamb, 2 Aug. 1833, B.P.

111. *Palmerston*, ii. 168; Grey to Palmerston, 22 Aug., B.P.; Grey to Durham, 22 Nov. 1833, Lambton Papers; Webster, i. 378-9.

112. Webster, i. 370 n. 2, ii. 832-5; Palmerston to Grey, 19, 21, 25 Sept., G.P.; Grey to Palmerston, 14, 26 Sept., 2 Nov. 1833, B.P.; William Bollaert, *History of the Wars of Succession of Portugal, from 1826 to 1840* (n.d.), p. 367; *Palmerston*, ii. 168-9; *Brougham*, iii. 316; Palmerston to Minto, 8 Oct., M.P.; Palmerston to Holland, 9 Oct. 1833, H.H.P.

113. Grey to Palmerston, 8, 14 Sept., B.P. (Webster, i. 377); Webster, i. 335-6; Holland to Palmerston, 18 Oct., B.P.; *Palmerston*, ii. 168; Palmerston to Grey, 21 Oct., 21 Dec. 1833, G.P.

114. Grey to Palmerston, 20, 31 Dec., B.P.; Palmerston to Holland, 26 Dec., H.H.P.; Palmerston to Grey, 28 Dec., G.P.; Palmerston to Graham, 30 Dec. 1833, Graham Papers 138; Palmerston to the King, 8 Jan. 1834, B.P.; Webster, i. 387-8.

115. Grey to Taylor, 6, 8, 13, 14, 15 Jan., and to the King, 15 Jan., RA, G.P.; Howick's diary, 14 Jan. 1834; *Brougham*, iii. 325; Grey to Althorp, 29 Sept., and Althorp to Grey, 3 Oct. 1833, A.P.; Aspinall, *Three Diaries*, p. 376; Grey's 'Minute proposed to the Cabinet by me, 14 Jan. 1833' [*sic*], G.P.; Brougham to Grey, 'Monday' [13 Jan.], Brougham Papers; Holland to Grey, 14 Jan. 1834, G.P.; *H.H.D.*, pp. 247-9.

116. *H.H.D.*, pp. 247-9; Holland to Grey, 14 Jan. (two letters), G.P.; Howick's diary, 15-16 Jan.; Lansdowne to Grey, 'Wed. Morng' [15 Jan.], G.P.; *Brougham*, iii. 329-34; Holland to Brougham, '20 minutes past one' [15 Jan.], 15 Jan., Brougham Papers; Palmerston to Taylor, 15 Jan., B.P.; *W.P.C.*, i. 417, 426, 428; Bell, i. 146; Althorp to Palmerston, 'Wednesday Night' [15 Jan.], B.P.; Althorp to Spencer, 16 Jan., A.P.; Ellice memo. on Lady Grey to Ellice, 'Friday' [17 Jan.], E.P.; Ellice to Durham, 'Monday 20 Jan.' [1834 and not 1835 as endorsed], Lambton Papers; Webster, i. 388-9. (In the second-hand accounts the roles taken variously by Grant and Graham and Richmond and Ripon are often confused; so are the accounts in *Lieven-Benckendorff*, pp. 364-7, and Aspinall, *Three Diaries*, p. 377.)

117. Ellice to Durham, 'Monday 20 Jan.', Lambton Papers; Palmerston to Grey, 29 Mar. 1834, G.P.; *Palmerston*, ii. 180-81; Webster, i. 393, ii. 805-6.

118. Webster, i. 386, 394 (cf. Christopher Howard, *Britain and the Casus Belli 1822-1902* (1974), pp. 7-28, 53); Grey to Holland, 8 April 1834, H.H.P.

119. Webster, i. 246-7, 375-6; Palmerston to Grey, 26 Dec. 1832, G.P.; Bell, i. 178; Palmerston to Lamb, 11 April 1832, 10 Dec. 1833, RA, M.P.; Palmerston to Minto, 3 Sept., M.P.; Palmerston to Villiers, 27 Oct. 1833, B.P.

120. *Palmerston*, ii. 169, 181, 186; Webster, i. 398-400.

121. Webster, i. 395-406, ii. 807-8; Grey to Palmerston, 25 Oct. 1833, B.P.; Carola Oman, *The Gascoyne Heiress. The Life and Diaries of Frances Mary Gascoyne-Cecil 1802-39* (1968), pp. 126-7; *Lieven-Benckendorff*, pp. 372-3.

122. *Palmerston*, ii. 207; Webster, i. 410.

123. *Creevey Papers*, ii. 299; Lady Holland to H. Fox, 21 Nov., H.H.P.; *Palmerston*, ii. 211; Hertslet, p. 64; F. Byng to Granville, 21 Nov. 1834, Gran. Papers 7/13; *Greville*, iii. 145.

1. Hertslet, pp. 14-23, 27-8, 33-5, 45; Webster, *Diplomacy*, p. 196; F. Byng to Granville, 22 Jan. 1836, Gran. Papers 7/13 no. 60; Jones, p. 145 n. 1.

2. Tilley and Gaselee, p. 46; *Edgeworth*, p. 578.

3. Jones-Parry, p. 314.

4. Webster, *Diplomacy*, p. 190; Hertslet, pp. 127-8; Middleton, 'Backhouse', pp. 31-2, 43-4; Melbourne to Palmerston, 20 Sept. 1835, B.P.; Aspinall, *Press*, pp. 244-5; Ziegler, p. 138; Leveson to Granville, 10 Mar. 1840, Gran. Papers 6/4 no. 88; *Sulivan*, p. 281.

5. Frederick Merk, *The Oregon Question. Essays in Anglo-American Diplomacy and Politics* (Cambridge, Mass., 1967), pp. 199-204; *The Cambridge History of British Foreign Policy* (Cambridge, 1923), ed. A.W. Ward and G.P. Gooch, iii. 585; West, i. 25; Tilley and Gaselee, pp. 69-70; Cromwell, 'P.U.S.', *passim*.

6. Bindoff, *passim*; Jones-Parry, pp. 308-20; Middleton, 'Backhouse', *passim*; Battiscombe, p. 62; Shee to Palmerston, 20 Nov., and Palmerston to Shee, 23 Nov. 1830, Shee Papers.

7. Palmerston to Shee, 23 Nov. 1830, 4, 19 Dec. 1835, Shee to Palmerston, 17 Nov., and Palmerston to Shee, 18 Nov. 1846, Shee Papers; Webster, i. 65; *Sulivan*, pp. 259, 287; Palmerston to Temple, 26-28 Nov. 1841, 15 Nov. 1845, B.P.

8. Lady Carlisle to Morpeth, [18 Sept. 1833], C.H.P. 2/15; Lady Holland to H. Fox,

[15 Nov. 1839], H.H.P.; Lady Palmerston to Melbourne, 5, 6 Sept. 1841, RA, M.P.

9. Webster, i. 65; Lady Cowper to Lamb, 12 Aug. [1832], B.P.W.; *Eden*, p. 53; Ilchester, p. 207; Lansdowne to Palmerston, [? Aug. 1832], B.P.; Tilley and Gaselee, p. 59; Middleton, p. 119; Palmerston to Beauvale, 12 Aug., and Melbourne to Russell, 19, 21 Dec. 1839, RA, M.P.; Melbourne to Palmerston, 17 Feb., enclosing Lady Lansdowne to Russell and Russell to Melbourne of 16 Feb., B.P.; Leveson to Granville, 24 Jan., 6 Feb. 1840, Gran. Papers 6/4; *Greville*, iv. 247-8.

10. Granville to Holland, 1 Mar. 1839, H.H.P.; Webster, i. 65; *Granville*, i. 28-31.

11. *Edmund Yates: His Recollections and Experiences* (1884), i. 104; *Durham*, ii. 67; *Fortescue*, p. 162; Howick's diary, 18 May 1836.

12. Tilley and Gaselee, pp. 52-3; Cromwell, 'P.U.S.', p. 100; Jones, pp. 13-18; Platt, p. 58; *Foreign Office Records*, p. 13.

13. Jones-Parry, pp. 312 n. 3, 315, 318; Cromwell, 'P.U.S.', pp. 102, 113; Middleton, 'Backhouse', pp. 34, 42-3.

14. Jones, pp. 15-16; *Foreign Office Records*, p. 8.

15. Tilley and Gaselee, pp. 51, 63-5; Cromwell, 'P.U.S.', pp. 101-2; Hertslet, pp. 142-4; *Cavendish*, pp. 235-6; W.C. Costin, *Great Britain and China 1833-1860* (Oxford, 1937), p. 31; Leveson to Granville, 3 April 1840, Gran. Papers; Middleton, 'F.O.', p. 375.

16. Charles Scott's diary, 1839-40; Middleton, pp. 190-92, 204; Middleton, 'F.O.', pp. 375-6; *Foreign Office Records*, p. 18; Tilley and Gaselee, pp. 58-9; Cromwell, 'P.U.S.', pp. 100, 102.

17. Middleton, pp. 204-6; Charles Scott's diary, 1839-40.

18. Charles Scott's diary, 1839-40; Middleton, p. 207; Jones, pp. 24-40, 151; Tilley and Gaselee, pp. 60-69; *Foreign Office Records*, p. 7; Drummond Wolff, i. 47, 49, 208; *Cavendish*, p. 297.

19. Webster, i. 57; Jones, p. 17; A. Iliasu, 'The Role of the Free Trade Treaties in British Foreign Policy, 1859-1871' (unpublished University of London Ph.D., 1965), p. 269; *Cavendish*, p. 343.

20. Middleton, 'Backhouse', p. 34; *Dr Granville*, ii. 265-6; Palmerston to Beauvale, 12 Aug. 1839, RA, M.P.; Leveson to Granville, 6 Feb., 13, 23 Mar. 1840, Gran. Papers; *Q.V.L.*, I, ii. 423-4; Hertslet, p. 98.

21. Wheeler-Holohan, p. 82; Webster, *Diplomacy*, pp. 189-90; Middleton, 'Backhouse', pp. 38-9; Backhouse's minutes, 16 July, 4 Aug. 1834, F.O. 96/17; Charles Scott's diary, 1837; Jones, pp. 20-21, 150; Drummond Wolff, i. 49.

22. Jones, pp. 24-5, 151-2; Redesdale, i. 108; Webster, *Diplomacy*, p. 190 n. 29; Tilley and Gaselee, p. 3.

23. Middleton, 'F.O.', p. 372, and 'Backhouse', pp. 37-8; B.P./FO/A10; Tilley and Gaselee, pp. 53-4; Jones, pp. 149-50.

24. Charles Scott's diary, 1834, 1838; Melbourne to Palmerston, 13 Feb. 1838, B.P.; Hertslet, p. 72.

25. Charles Scott's diary, 1838-9; Hertslet, p. 61; Alder, p. 234.

26. Byng to Granville, 26 April 1831, Gran. Papers 7/12; *Edgeworth*, p. 578; Hertslet, pp. 23-4; Charles Scott's diary, *passim* (but cf. *Canning*, p. 263); Drummond Wolff, i. 48.

27. *Edgeworth*, p. 579.

28. Wheeler-Holohan, pp. 60-68, 71; Hertslet, p. 159; Palmerston's minute, 14 Nov. [? Oct.] 1833, F.O. 96/17; Webster, *Diplomacy*, p. 193; *Greville*, iv. 418; Charles Scott's diary, 4 May 1840.

29. *The Gladstone Diaries* (Oxford, 1968), ed. M.R.D. Foot, i. 407; Palmerston to Granville, 13 Nov. 1832, B.P.

30. *Canning*, pp. 260-61; Jones, p. 149; Hertslet, pp. 23-5; Drummond Wolff, i. 67; *Cavendish*, pp. 160-61, 180.

31. Hertslet, pp. 78-81; Palmerston's minutes, 13 Jan. 1833, 9 Sept. 1835, 26 Nov. 1837, F.O. 96/17, 18, 19; *Palmerston*, v. 305.

32. Palmerston's minute, 3 July 1835, F.O. 96/18 (Webster, *Diplomacy*, p. 193); *Palmerston*, v. 305; Hertslet, pp. 81-2; Webster, *Diplomacy*, p. 193; Palmerston's minutes, 23 May 1831, 22 June 1834, F.O. 96/17, 20; Specimen F.O. exam. paper, Nov. 1856, F.O. 519/269.

33. *Palmerston*, v. 305; Hertslet, pp. 78, 81, 142-4; *Granville*, i. 29; Middleton, p. 201; Webster, *Diplomacy*, p. 191.

34. Holland to H. Fox, 22 Nov. 1831, H.H.P.; Webster, *Diplomacy*, pp. 185, 192, 193; Palmerston's minute, 13 Nov. 1835, F.O. 96/18; Redesdale, i. 151-2; Webster, i. 64.

35. Webster, *Diplomacy*, pp. 183-7; Middleton, 'F.O.', p. 374.

36. Charles Scott's diary, 10 May 1836; Jones, p. 15; Bindoff, pp. 152-3.

37. Palmerston to Grey, 19 Nov. 1830, 10 Jan. 1831, G.P.; Grey to Palmerston, 25 Nov. 1830, B.P.; West, i. 277-8; Palmerston's 'Analysis of Expenditure', 23 Aug. 1831, B.P.W.; Lady Cowper to Lamb, 14 June, and Palmerston to Lady Cowper, 18-19 Sept. 1832, B.P.W.; *Palmerston*, ii. 164.

38. *Sulivan*, pp. 246, 250.

39. Melbourne to Palmerston, 3 June 1831, B.P.; Lady Cowper to Lamb, 14 June 1832, B.P.W.; Palmerston to Grey, 22 April 1833, G.P.; *Palmerston*, ii. 160-61.

40. *Palmerston*, ii. 164, 173, 211; *Sulivan*, pp. 22-6.

41. F. Byng to Granville, 27 Nov. 1834, Gran. Papers 7/13 no. 39; William Cowper's diary, 11 April 1855, B.P.W.; *Q.V.G.*, ii. 79; Lady Holland to H. Fox, 8, 15, 28 Nov. [1839], H.H.P.; Mrs G. Lamb to Lady Carlisle, 26 Nov. [1839], C.H.P. 1/129; *Lady Holland's Letters*, pp. 210-11, 215.

42. *Lady Holland's Letters*, p. 156; *Foreign Office Records*, p. 151; Lady Palmerston to Lady Holland, 'Thursday' [? 1842], H.H.P.; Sir Henry Elliot, *Some Revolutions and Other Diplomatic Experiences* (1922), edited by his daughter, p. 4; *Ponsonby Family*, pp. 159-63.

43. *Greville*, iii. 157; F. Byng to Granville, 6 Jan. 1832, Gran. Papers 7/13 no. 1.

44. *Palmerston*, i. 365, ii. 151; Palmerston to Grey, 29 Mar. 1832, G.P.; Webster, i. 409; Palmerston to Clive, 25 Sept. 1833, Powis Papers; Palmerston to Lady Cowper, 18 Sept. 1832, B.P.W.; Webster, *Diplomacy*, p. 191; Leveson to Granville, 13 Mar. 1840, Gran. Papers 6/4.

45. *Granville*, i. 29; Palmerston's minutes, 23 Dec. 1838, 30 Jan. 1839, F.O. 96/19, 20 (Webster, *Diplomacy*, p. 191 n. 32); letters from Gen. Hamilton, 1840-41, B.P.; Wikoff, pp. 195, 198, 200; Palmerston to Grey, 'Thursday' [23 June 1831], G.P.; *Greville*, ii. 233; Palmerston to Lady Cowper, 15 Nov., 31 Dec. 1831 (Lorne, pp. 69-70), 27 Sept., 5 Oct. 1832, B.P.W.; Palmerston to Lamb, 11 April, 27 Oct. 1832, RA, M.P.

46. Palmerston to Lamb, 7-9 May 1832, RA, M.P.

47. Webster, i. 32 n. 1, 41; Palmerston to Lamb, 28 Aug., 28 Sept. 1832, B.P.; Lever, p. 199.

48. *Creevey Papers*, ii. 268-9; Granville to Holland, 20 Dec. 1833, 21 Dec. 1838, H.H.P.; Webster, i. 385, 434, ii. 533-5; *Greville*, iii. 9-12, 21; *Palmerston*, ii. 185; *Clarendon*, i. 101.

49. *Granville*, i. 29; *Q.V.L.*, I, i. 136; Webster, *Diplomacy*, p. 187.

50. Lever, p. 200; *Haydon*, iii. 650, iv. 131-2; F. Byng to Granville, 25 Aug. 1835, Gran. Papers 7/13 no. 50; Mrs Sulivan to Temple, 28 Mar. 1836, B.P.W.; *Q.V.L.*, I, i. 86; *Lady Holland's Letters*, p. 170; Palmerston to Temple, 9 Feb. 1841, B.P.

51. *Dr Granville*, ii. 367-8; G.W. Featherstonhaugh to Sir John Harvey, Harvey Papers, Public Archives of Canada, MG24, A17, vol. 6; *Memoirs and Letters of Sir James Paget* (1901), ed. Stephen Paget, pp. 401-2.

52. *Palmerston*, iii. 34, v. 300; Mrs Bowles to Temple, 21 May 1833, B.P.W.; *Sulivan*, p. 259.

53. Palmerston to Temple, 6 Sept. 1839, B.P.; Wikoff, pp. 79, 86-90; Hamilton to Palmerston, 1 Jan. 1841, B.P.; Palmerston to Shee, 14 Sept. 1838, Shee Papers; Byng to Granville, 26 Sept. 1837, Gran. Papers 7/13 no. 96; *Lyttelton*, p. 311.

54. Devonshire to Brougham, 21 Jan. [1831], Brougham Papers; Aspinall, *Three*

Diaries, p. 42; *Melbourne Papers*, p. 278; Lady Carlisle to Lady Granville, 'Friday' [? 1835], Gran. Papers 17/5 no. 15.

55. *Arbuthnot*, p. 210; *Haydon*, iv. 448; *Mrs Fitzherbert*, p. 326; Cecil Woodham-Smith, *Queen Victoria. Her Life and Times* (1972), i. 149-50, 154; *Q.V.L.*, I, i. 80.

56. Webster, *Diplomacy*, pp. 183, 187-9; Palmerston's minute, 21 Nov. 1836, F.O. 96/18; *Creevey Papers*, ii. 324; Connell, *Regina v. Palmerston*, pp. 9, 16; Melbourne to Palmerston, 22 Nov. 1838, B.P.; Palmerston to Temple, 24 Sept. 1839, B.P.

57. *Broughton*, v. 100; Roger Fulford, *The Prince Consort* (1966), p. 61; Melbourne to Palmerston, 14 Dec. 1840, B.P.; Connell, *Regina v. Palmerston*, pp. 21-31; memoranda by Backhouse and Palmerston, Nov.-Dec. 1840, B.P./ FO/B35.

58. Webster, i. 45, 72; Palmerston to Grey, 27 Nov. 1831, G.P.

59. Comparative statement of F.O. expenditure for the years 1830 to 1832, B.P./ FO/A9; Palmerston's minute, 5 Aug. 1833, F.O. 96/17; Palmerston's 'Analysis of Expenditure' for 1831, B.P.W.

60. Jones-Parry, p. 318 n. 5; Backhouse's memo., 23 July 1831, B.P., G.C./BA1 (Webster, i. 65 n. 1); Tilley and Gaselee, p. 60; Charles Scott's diary, 20 April 1838.

61. *Scott's Journal*, ii. 364; *Foreign Office Records*, p. 8; scale of salaries for 1835 attached to Scott Papers, NLS 1554 f. 209; Tilley and Gaselee, pp. 54, 61; Charles Scott's diary, 4 April, 18 July 1839, 13, 27 Mar. 1840.

62. Tilley and Gaselee, pp. 61-2, 209-13; Middleton, p. 188; *Cavendish*, p. 297.

63. Hertslet, pp. 167-76; Webster, i. 72 n. 2; B.P./ FO/B3.

64. Palmerston to Lady Holland, 31 July 1831, H.H.P.; Palmerston's minute, 29 Feb. 1832, F.O. 96/17; Webster, *Diplomacy*, pp. 191-2; Tilley and Gaselee, pp. 56-7; Webster, i. 72; Palmerston to Grey, 20 Dec. 1830, 16 July 1831, G.P.

65. Kenneth Ellis, *The Post Office in the Eighteenth Century. A Study in Administrative History* (1958), pp. 139-42; Hobhouse's journal, 24 June 1844; Gavin B. Henderson, 'Lord Palmerston and the Secret Service Fund', *E.H.R.*, liii (1938), pp. 485-7; Villiers to Palmerston, 10 Mar., and Palmerston to Villiers, 19 Mar. 1838, B.P.; Palmerston to Viscount Canning, 1 Oct. 1841, Harewood Papers N; Villiers to Palmerston, 28 Jan., and Palmerston to Villiers, 30 Jan. 1837, B.P. (cf. Webster, ii. 853-4); Palmerston's minute, 27 Aug. 1839, F.O. 96/20.

66. Aspinall, *Press*, pp. 91-3, 166-7, 173; *Times History*, i. 490-91; Webster, *Diplomacy*, p. 190 n. 29; Backhouse to Granville, 18 Jan. 1833, enclosing Palmerston's minute of 3 Jan., Gran. Papers 14/3 no. 44; Holland to W. Cowper, 8 Aug. [1837], B.P.W.

67. Webster, i. 266-7, 304, ii. 528-9, 764-5; Palmerston to Melbourne, 1 Nov. 1838, RA, M.P.; Palmerston to Grey, 20 Dec. 1830, G.P.; Hertslet, pp. 175-6; Jones-Parry, p. 317 n. 2; Tilley and Gaselee, p. 49; B.P./ FO/D1-7.

68. Webster, i. 72, 75, 101; *Lady Holland's Letters*, p. 164; Palmerston's minute, 25 May 1836, F.O. 96/18 (Webster, *Diplomacy*, p. 196); Palmerston to Temple, 11 Feb. 1840, B.P.; Lady Palmerston to Lady Holland, [*passim* 1843], H.H.P.; Dover's diary, 11 July 1831; *Dino*, i. 67; Palmerston's accounts, 1831-4, B.P.W.

69. Palmerston to Grey, 27 Nov. 1831, G.P.; Backhouse's minute of revised scheme of salaries, 27 Aug. 1831, F.O. 96/17; Tilley and Gaselee, pp. 253-8; Bindoff, p. 148.

70. Bruce, i. 322-3; Palmerston to Temple, 1 Oct. 1835, B.P.; Mrs Sulivan to Temple, 28 Mar. 1836, B.P.W.; *Foreign Office Records*, pp. 152, 153.

71. Drummond Wolff, i. 63; Middleton, pp. 16, 268, 275; Jones, pp. 85-6.

72. Hertslet, pp. 36, 46, 93, 128; Drummond Wolff, i. 51-5; *Cavendish*, p. 123; *Court and Private Life in the Times of Queen Charlotte: Being the Journals of Mrs Papendiek* (1887), ed. Mrs Vernon Delves Broughton, ii. 301-2; West, i. 25.

73. *Canning*, pp. 262-3; Tilley and Gaselee, pp. 43-5; Jones, p. 182; Middleton, 'F.O.', p. 370.

74. Drummond Wolff, i. 46; Connell, *Regina v. Palmerston*, pp. 29-30; Palmerston to Lady Sutherland, 19 June 1840, B.P.W.; Irena M. Roseveare, 'The Making of a Diplomat', *Slavonic and East European Review*, xli (1962-3), pp. 484-93.

75. Mario Rodríguez, *A Palmerstonian Diplomat in Central America. Frederick Chatfield, Esq.* (Tucson, Arizona, 1964).

76. Platt, pp. 14-15, 37, 58; Kenin, pp. 294-300.

77. Kenin, p. 301; Webster, i. 72 n. 1; Platt, pp. 37, 38, 53; Captain Jesse, *The Life of Beau Brummell* (1927), ii. 77-9, 198; Palmerston to J. Russell, 6 July 1840, B.P.

78. Platt, pp. 23, 37-44, 49, 53.

79. Cyrus Redding, *Fifty Years' Recollections* (1858), ii. 26-8; Hart to Palmerston, 1 April, B.P./PAT/H16; Howick's diary, 18, 19 May 1836; Brown, p. 98; Hart to [? Parkes], B.P., G.C./HA296; Middleton, 'Backhouse', p. 44; 'Report from the Select Committee appointed to enquire into the Consular Service and Consular Appointments', *BPP*, 1857-8, viii (482), pp. 329, 331.

80. Kenin, pp. 309-14.

81. Holland to Palmerston, 15 Feb., 4 Aug. 1832, B.P.; Palmerston to Temple, 6-7 Oct. 1833, 21 April 1834, B.P.; Kenin, p. 348; B.P./PAT/J10-19.

82. *Bligh*, p. 95; Sir James Rennell Rodd, *Social and Diplomatic Memories 1884-1893* (1922), p. 42; Wheeler-Holohan, pp. 86-7, 99, 232-3; Hertslet, pp. 161-3.

83. Wheeler-Holohan, pp. 72-80; *Bligh*, p. 95; Granville to Holland, 26 July 1839, H.H.P.

84. S.T. Bindoff, 'Lord Palmerston and the Universities', *Bulletin of the Institute of Historical Research*, xii (1934-5), pp. 39-43; Platt, pp. 164-5.

85. Jones, pp. 41-3, 194 n. 1; *Dod*, i. 415; *Croker Papers*, iii. 364-5; Ashley, ii. 469; Tilley and Gaselee, p. 98.

86. Tilley and Gaselee, pp. 72-6, 257; Palmerston to Grey, 27 Aug. 1831, G.P.

87. *Lady Granville*, ii. 74-5, 99, 117, 328; Palmerston to Grey, 21 Nov. 1832, G.P.

88. Palmerston to Grey, 26 May, 16 July, 21 Nov. 1832, G.P.; *Palmerston*, i. 204, 209.

89. Palmerston to Grey, 16 July, 1 Nov. 1832, G.P.; *William Russell*, p. 386; Webster, *Diplomacy*, p. 193; Palmerston's minutes, 4 Dec. 1838, F.O. 96/19, 12 May 1840, 9 May 1841, F.O. 96/20.

90. Palmerston to Adair, 2 Oct. 1832, Lambton Papers; Webster, i. 70; *William Russell*, p. 472; Tilley and Gaselee, pp. 90-91.

91. Holland to Grey, 16 Sept. 1835, H.H.P.; *Murray*, pp. 144, 210.

92. *Palmerston's Opinions*, p. 356; Webster, *Diplomacy*, p. 194; Bindoff, pp. 148-9; Backhouse's minute, [? Feb. 1834], F.O. 96/17; Hubert E.H. Jerningham, *Reminiscences of an Attaché* (1886), p. 37; Middleton, 'Backhouse', p. 40.

93. Bindoff, pp. 147, 148, 150; Webster, *Diplomacy*, p. 195; Jones, p. 27; Middleton, 'F.O.', p. 369; Middleton, 'Backhouse', pp. 41-2; *Cavendish*, pp. 120, 122, 123; *Bligh*, pp. 80-81; Palmerston's minute, 2 Oct. 1838, F.O. 96/19; Palmerston to Hobhouse, 24 Oct. 1835, B.P.

94. Tilley and Gaselee, pp. 257-8; *Lady Granville*, ii. 74; *Memoirs of Sir Richard Blount* (1902), ed. Stuart J. Reid, p. 32; Webster, i. 70; Grey to Holland, 13 Sept. 1835, 24 Jan. 1836, and Holland to Grey, 16 Sept. 1835, H.H.P.; Howick to Grey, 15 Jan. 1836, G.P.

95. Palmerston to Hobhouse, 24 Oct. 1835, B.P.; Palmerston to Devonshire, 13 Dec. 1830, Chat. Papers; Palmerston to Grey, 10 July 1831, G.P.

96. Boringdon to Morpeth, 12 May 1804, C.H.P. 2/154; Palmerston to Grey, 23 Oct. 1832, G.P.

97. Palmerston to Hobhouse, 24 Oct. 1835, B.P.; Tilley and Gaselee, pp. 255-6; Bindoff, pp. 151-2; Lady Malet to Brougham, 25 Jan. [1862], Brougham Papers; Brougham to Melbourne, [? Oct. 1834], RA, M.P.2/4; Lord Stanley of Alderley's diary, 4 May 1847, Cheshire County Record Office; Alfred Montgomery to Brougham, 22 Dec. 1851, Brougham Papers; *Dod*, i. 76; Christie to Palmerston, 29 Dec. 1851, B.P./GMC72.

98. Grey to Palmerston, 12 Nov., B.P., and Palmerston to Grey, 16 July, 12 Nov. 1832, G.P.

99. Webster, i. 67-9.

100. George Thomas, Earl of Albemarle, *Fifty Years of My Life* (1877), pp. 8-15; *Canning and Friends*, i. 142-3; *Croker Papers*, i. 293-4; Dorothy Margaret Stuart, *Dearest Bess. The Life and Times of Lady Elizabeth Foster, afterwards Duchess of Devonshire* (1955), pp. 135-6; Holland to Palmerston, 4 Aug. 1832, B.P.; Adair to Holland, 31 Dec. 1833, 10 Jan. 1834, 27 Jan. 1836, H.H.P.; Grey to Holland, 14, 19 Jan. 1831, G.P.; Palmerston to Grey, 16 Jan. 1831, G.P.; Lady Cowper to Lamb, 2 July, 27 Oct. [1832], B.P.W.; *G.L.G.*, i. 356; Webster, i. 67; Grey to Palmerston, 17 Jan. 1831, 27 Feb. 1832, B.P.; Bulwer to Durham, 2 Mar. 1836, Lambton Papers.

101. *Greville*, ii. 399; Lamb to Melbourne, 19 July 1834, RA, M.P.

102. Palmerston to Temple, 21 April 1834, B.P.; Tilley and Gaselee, pp. 253, 255-6; Palmerston to Grey, 19 Jan. 1833, G.P.

103. *Lady Holland's Letters*, p. 123; Prest, p. 169; *Q.V.L.*, I, i. 451; Lady Cowper to Lamb, 31 May 1832, B.P.W.; Palmerston to Grey, 29 Sept. 1831, 1 Nov. 1832, 18 Jan., 17 July 1833, G.P.; Lady Palmerston to Lady Holland, [?Dec. 1841], H.H.P.; Webster, i. 322; Westmorland Papers (Northampton County Record Office), 7, xi; Grey to Palmerston, 14 June 1831, B.P.

104. *Malmesbury*, i. 318; Normanby to Devonshire, 29 Nov., and Palmerston to Devonshire, 13 Dec. 1830, Chat. Papers; Mulgrave to Grey, 22 Oct. 1831, G.P.

105. *Ponsonby Family*, p. 80; *Greville*, ii. 158, 177-8; Betley, pp. 146-7; Grey to Palmerston, 14 June, B.P.; Creevey to Miss Ord, 13, 15 June 1831, Creevey Papers (*Creevey*, pp. 345-6).

106. Grey to Palmerston, 14 June 1831, B.P.; Lady Cowper to Lamb, 2 July, B.P.W.; Palmerston to Grey, 9 Aug. 1832, G.P.; *Greville*, ii. 258; Webster, i. 289, 301.

107. Webster, i. 258, 301-3, ii. 530-35, 756-7; *Russell*, ii. 53; *Disraeli-Londonderry*, p. 148.

108. Melbourne to Russell, 8 Aug. 1837, B.P.; *Macaulay's Letters*, ii. 66-7; Mme Flahault to Palmerston, 25 May 1835, B.P. Melbourne to Palmerston, 13 Feb. 1838, B.P. (Webster, ii. 562); Palmerston to Melbourne, 13 Feb. 1838, RA, M.P.

109. Palmerston to Grey, 4 Nov. 1832, G.P.; Grey to Palmerston, 2, 18 Nov., B.P.; Palmerston to Lamb, 18 June 1833, B.P.

110. Keppel, p. 316 (but wrongly applying the remark to Holland's son); Palmerston to Grey, 19 Jan. 1833, G.P.

111. *Murray*, p. 146; Brougham to Croker, [Nov. 1843], Brougham Papers, Clements Library.

112. *Lady Granville*, i. 398-400; Devonshire's diary, 24 Oct. 1830, Chat. Papers; Lansdowne to Minto, 4 Jan. 1833, M.P.; J. Abercromby to Melbourne, 9 Oct. 1835, RA, M.P.; Palmerston to Holland, 25 Oct., and to Fox, 27 Oct., 26 Nov. 1835, H.H.P.

113. Holland to Fox, 2 June 1835, H.H.P.; Strangways to Lamb, 10 May [1836], RA, M.P.; Palmerston to Lamb, 18 July 1836, 11 May 1837, RA, M.P.; George Edgcumbe to Palmerston, 17 Nov. 1836, B.P.; Palmerston to Lady Holland, 25 Jan., 'Wed. Evng' [25 Jan.], 27 Jan. 1837, H.H.P.

114. Keppel, pp. 318, 321, 324; Melbourne to Ellice, 22 Aug., E.P.; Palmerston to Lady Holland, 29 Nov. 1838, H.H.P.; *Greville*, iv. 247-8, 418; Ellice to Mrs Damer, 29 Feb. 1840, E.P.

115. Graham to Holland, 22 April 1832, H.H.P.; Webster, i. 138 n. 3; *William Russell*, pp. 262, 265, 266, 278; *Russell E.C.*, ii. 39.

116. *William Russell*, pp. 247-8, 271, 273-4, 276-7.

117. Grey to Holland, 12, 30 Aug. 1833, H.H.P.; *William Russell*, pp. 278, 280; Webster, i. 385.

118. *William Russell*, pp. 256-9, 281-2, 285, 289-91, 327-8, 332-6, 348, 376, 454; J. Russell to Palmerston, 1 Nov. 1835, B.P. (Webster, i. 68 n. 1); Webster, ii. 546-7; *Greville*, iv. 434.

119. Webster, i. 227, ii. 828; Palmerston to Grey, 26, 27 May, 1 Nov., G.P.; Mrs

Charles Bagot, *Links with the Past* (1901), pp. 28-9; Palmerston to Lady Cowper, 18-19 Sept. 1832, B.P.W.

120. Palmerston to Temple, 8 April 1832, B.P.; *Palmerston*, ii. 187.

121. Palmerston to Temple, 1 Aug. 1834, 10 Mar. 1835, 14 April 1838, B.P.; Drummond Wolff, i. 190; McGregor's memo., 25 Mar., RA, M.P. 12/31; Palmerston to Melbourne, 4 May, B.P.; Palmerston's memo., 26 May, RA, M.P. 12/43; Palmerston's minutes, 22 Aug. 1840, 29 Jan. 1840 [*sic*: 1841], F.O. 96/20; Palmerston to Labouchere, 2 Sept. 1840, Labouchere Papers, Perkins Library, Duke University; Richard Shannon, 'David Urquhart and the Foreign Affairs Committees', in *Pressure from Without in Early Victorian England* (1974), ed. Patricia Hollis, p. 245; Viscount Canning's memo. on the McGregor affairs, n.d., Harewood Papers M; Brown, pp. 123-4.

122. Lady Cowper to Lamb, 12 Aug., B.P.W.; Palmerston to Lamb, 28 Aug. 1832, B.P.; Webster, i. 68, 185, 223, 233, 353-4, 362 n. 1; *Palmerston*, ii. 156, 173; Grey to Palmerston, 31 Aug., B.P.; Palmerston to Minto, 30 Sept., 29 Oct. 1833, 4 May 1835, M.P.

123. Webster, i. 69; *Greville*, ii. 399; Palmerston to Grey, 6 Oct., G.P.; Grey to Palmerston, 9 Oct. 1833, B.P.

124. *Clarendon*, i. 28, 47, 61-3; Mrs George Villiers to Lady Morley, 18 July 1833, Morley Papers.

125. *Clarendon*, i. 92, 98, 101, 105-6.

126. Webster, i. 70 n. 1.

127. Byng to Granville, 11 Dec., Gran. Papers 7/13; Palmerston to Shee, 17 Dec. 1835, Shee Papers.

128. Melbourne to Palmerston, 26 Oct., 24 Nov. 1835, 26 Feb. 1836, B.P.; Palmerston to Lamb, 11 May 1837, RA, M.P.

129. Webster, i. 52, ii. 537 n. 1, 548-55; Lamb to Melbourne, 19 Sept. 1838, RA, M.P.; Granville to Holland, May-July 1839, H.H.P.; Brougham to Croker, [June 1839], Croker Papers, Clements Library, f. 170; *Lady Granville*, ii. 293: *Lady Holland's Letters*, p. 177.

130. Lever, p. 307; *Q.V.L.*, I, i. 419; Clarendon to Palmerston, 5 Sept. 1856, B.P.; Palmerston to Russell, 10 May 1865, Russell Papers 23.

131. Grant, ii. 205-8.

132. Clippings from the *Standard*, 22 May, and *Morning Post*, 20 June 1834, and accompanying correspondence, B.P.W.; correspondence with Oddie, Forster and Lumley, June-Nov. 1835, B.P.W.; *Palmerston*, iv. 367-8; opinion of William Mackworth Praed, 22 Nov. 1837, and correspondence with Lumley, Oct.-Nov. 1839, B.P.W.; Webster, *Diplomacy*, p. 223; Palmerston to Brougham, 26 Aug. 1839, Brougham Papers.

133. Palmerston's 'Analysis of Expenditure from 1818 Downwards' [1818-1834], 'Actual Expenditure 1827. Paid & Unpaid', and 'Calculation of Average Annual Expenditure. June 1830', B.P.W.; *Sulivan*, p. 117; Hamilton to Palmerston, 26 May 1841, B.P.

134. Palmerston to Lady Holland, 31 July 1831, H.H.P.; Palmerston to Russell, 29 June 1849, Russell Papers.

135. Webster, i. 61; Palmerston's minutes, 11 June 1837, F.O. 96/17, 30 June, 3, 5 July 1839, F.O. 96/20; Palmerston to Melbourne, 19 Feb. 1839, RA, M.P.

136. Palmerston to Melbourne, 19 Feb. 1839, RA, M.P.; Hobhouse's journal, 29 May 1842.

137. Webster, ii. 744 n. 1; Alder, pp. 229-59; Grey's minute, 26 April 1832, F.O. 96/17; *A Century of Diplomatic Blue Books 1814-1914* (1938), ed. Harold Temperley and Lillian M. Penson, p. 82; Webster, i. 62 n. 1.

138. Webster, i. 62-3; Palmerston to Beauvale, 15 Sept. 1841, RA, M.P.

139. 3 *Hansard*, cxliii. 146; Aspinall, *Press*, pp. 158-60; Aspinall, *Three Diaries*, pp.

369-70; Grey to Palmerston, 13 Aug. 1833, B.P.; *Brougham*, iii. 306.

140. Melbourne to Russell, 15 Sept. 1837, B.P.; Melbourne to Palmerston, 28 April, and Monteagle to Palmerston, 25 Oct. 1839, B.P. (cf. 'Foreign Policy of the Government', *Edinburgh Review*, lxxi (July 1840), pp. 545-93); 'France and the East', *Edinburgh Review*, lxxii (Jan. 1841), pp. 529-56; *Macaulay's Letters*, iii. 349, 358-60, 363-4; *Selections from the Correspondence of the Late Macvey Napier* (1879), edited by his son Macvey Napier, pp. 398, 401-2, 537-8 (cf. *Edinburgh Review*, lxxxv (April 1847), pp. 538-9); *Wellesley Index; Lord Palmerston on the Treaty of Washington* [1842] (cf. B.P./PRE/B17-22).

141. Webster, i. 52 n. 1.

142. William Lankester to Palmerston, 3 Feb. (with Palmerston's endorsement of 4 Feb.), and Holmes to Palmerston, 25 Oct. 1835, B.P.W.; Grant, iii. 236-8.

143. Aspinall, *Press*, pp. 236, 238 n. 6, 241-2; Webster, i. 51, 54; Webster, *Diplomacy*, p. 195; *Lieven-Grey*, ii. 183.

144. B.P./MM/GE5; Palmerston to Shee, 12, 26 Mar. 1840, B.P. (cf. B.P./MM/TU21); Palmerston to Shee, 9 Aug., 14 Sept. 1838, Shee Papers; Webster, i. 53.

145. Duncan Crow, *Henry Wikoff. The American Chevalier* (1963). Wikoff's story is substantially borne out by the few mentions of him in Lady Palmerston's diary (3 Sept., 15 Oct. 1850; Palmerston's diary for 1850 is lacking). See also Edwardes to Palmerston, 16 Sept. 1850, and Wikoff to Palmerston, 10 July 1852, B.P.

146. Palmerston to Lady Cowper, 21 Sept. 1831, Lieven Papers 47355 (Webster, i. 47-8); Palmerston to Lamb, 5 Dec. 1832, 5 Jan. 1834, RA, M.P. (Connell, *Regina v. Palmerston*, pp. 51-2).

147. Webster, i. 51; Aspinall, *Press*, pp. 250-51, 253, 255, 429; Holland to Fox, 17 Aug. 1831, H.H.P.

148. Webster, i. 51; Aspinall, *Press*, pp. 191-2, 253-4, 258; *Times History*, i. 308.

149. Aspinall, *Press*, p. 257; Fox Bourne, ii. 124-5.

150. Parkes to Palmerston, 7 June, B.P./PRE/A2; Palmerston to Temple, 28 Nov. 1834, B.P. (Webster, i. 52); Webster, i. 51; Palmerston to Parkes, 27 May 1839, Parkes Papers; *D.N.B.* ('John Black'); Easthope to Palmerston, 1 Oct. 1840, B.P.; *Greville*, iv. 305; correspondence between Palmerston, Easthope and Doyle in the Easthope Papers and B.P.

151. Fox Bourne, ii. 91-3; Parkes to Durham, 26 June 1834, Lambton Papers; Crowe, p. 4; *D.N.B.* ('Quin'); Palmerston's minute, 22 Feb., F.O. 96/17, and entry under 28 Feb. 1834 in Palmerston's 'Analyses of Expenditure', B.P.W. (cf. B.P./CAB/A16, 17); Palmerston to Temple, 21 July 1834, B.P.; Palmerston's minute, 14 Feb. 1836, F.O. 96/18; B.P./PAT/Q9-11; Hertslet, p. 187 (cf. Crowe, p. 4).

152. Webster, i. 52-3; Villiers to Palmerston, 5 Aug. 1834, B.P. (Webster, i. 52); Easthope to Palmerston, 31 Aug. 1840, 18 Feb. 1845, B.P.

153. Bullen, p. 29 n. 17; Palmerston to Easthope, 23 Jan. 1848, Easthope Papers; Grant, i. 310; Crowe, pp. 4-6, 13-14, 34-5, 91, 373-5, 433; Fox Bourne, ii. 91.

154. Webster, i. 424; Connell, *Regina v. Palmerston*, pp. 47-58; *The Autobiography of William Jerdan* (1852-3), iv. 161.

155. Allen's journal, 21 Sept. 1840; *Melbourne Papers*, p. 472; Webster, i. 47 n. 1; *Russell L.C.*, i. 18, 26; *Times History*, ii. 556-7; Aspinall, *Press*, p. 241; Russell to Palmerston, 11 April, and Palmerston to Doyle, 12 April 1839, B.P.; Easthope to Palmerston, 1 Aug. 1840, B.P.

156. B.P./PRE/B12, 13, 15, 16; Bullen, pp. 29, 33 n. 38; Palmerston to Doyle, 3 Nov. 1843, B.P.; Howick's diary, 12, 13 Feb., 2 Mar. 1847; Fox Bourne, ii. 152-3; Bell, ii. 33.

157. Crowe, pp. 54, 64, 96-7; Lady Palmerston to Palmerston, [19 April 1849], B.P.W.; Fox Bourne, ii. 143-4, 224-6; *Times History*, ii. 238-9, 558-9.

158. P. Borthwick to Palmerston, 27 Aug. 1840, B.P.; *Glenesk*, pp. 39-41, 43, 49, 56,

73, 126-9; Easthope to Palmerston, 1 Aug. 1840, B.P.; *D.N.B.* ('Grenville Murray'); Grenville Murray to Borthwick, 31 Dec. 1851, B.P./GMC108; Drummond Wolff, i. 42-3; Kingsley Martin, *The Triumph of Lord Palmerston. A Study of Public Opinion before the Crimean War* (1963), p. 89; *Greville*, vii. 175.

159. *Glenesk*, pp. 126, 192-3; *Times History*, i. 378-83, 416-17, ii. 138-9, 559, 566-7; Webster, i. 53 n. 1; O'Reilly to Palmerston, 30 Sept. 1847, B.P.; Clarendon to Palmerston, 6 Jan., 27 Feb. 1849, B.P.; Kingsley Martin, pp. 93, 111-14, 168-9; Temperley, pp. 373-4; Arthur Irwin Dasent, *John Thadeus Delane* (1908), ii. 151; Fox Bourne, ii. 244.

160. Aspinall, *Press*, pp. 244-7, 256, 316; *Times History*, ii. 155; Bullen p. 33 n. 40; Blackett of Wylam Papers, Northumberland Record Office; Webster, i. 54.

161. Webster, i. 50, 52; *Times History*, i. 301, 460, ii. 560; Parkes to Littleton, 7 Dec. 1833, Hath. Papers; Aspinall, *Press*, pp. 243-4, 255; Grant, ii. 72-3; B.P./PRE/B23-147 (cf. Webster, i. 50 n. 1).

162. Webster, i. 52, 53; *Palmerston*, ii. 123; *Brougham*, iii. 312; Palmerston to Lamb, 5 Dec. 1832, 5 Jan. 1834, RA, M.P.

163. Webster, i. 34, 54; *Greville*, iii. 157.

164. Webster, i. 74, 110-11; Littleton's diary, 11 April 1832, Hath. Papers; *Lady Holland's Letters*, pp. 124-5; Aspinall, *Three Diaries*, p. 171; Palmerston to Grey, 27 Nov., G.P.; Palmerston to Lady Cowper, 15 Nov. 1831, B.P.W.

165. Webster, i. 73, 111, 175; Hobhouse's journal, 16 Jan. 1831; *Neumann*, i. 207-8, 233.

166. Webster, i. 73, 74, 110-11; *Neumann*, i. xvi-xvii, ii. 134-5; *Hanover*, pp. 60-61; *Greville*, i. 110; Lever, p. 14; Palmerston to Lamb, 19 Feb. 1832, 14 Sept. 1833, RA, M.P.

167. Palmerston to Lamb, 6 Feb., 3 Aug. 1832, 8 Feb. 1833, RA, M.P.; Palmerston to Grey, 23 Mar. 1832, G.P.

168. Palmerston to Lamb, 15 Mar., 10 June 1833, 24 June, 16 Oct. 1834, RA, M.P.; Webster, i. 73; *Neumann*, ii. 134-5.

169. Webster, i. 58-9, 73, 75, 110; Palmerston to Lamb, 10 April 1832, RA, M.P.; Palmerston to Minto, 6 May 1834, B.P.; *Greville*, iii. 158.

170. Carlisle to Lady Holland, 16 Jan. 1831, H.H.P.; *Howard Sisters*, pp. 145-6; *Haydon*, iv. 452; Webster, i. 101-2, 128, 131-2, 142-3, 147 n. 1, 155, 172; Palmerston to Grey, 24 Dec. 1831, 22 April 1833, G.P.; Holland to Granville, 17 April 1831, Gran. Papers 9/4.

171. Webster, i. 165, 353, 407, 408; *Greville*, ii. 406; Wikoff, pp. 196-7.

172. Col. Grey's memo. of conversation with Ellice, 2 Jan. 1852, RA, A80/101; Webster, i. 409; *Greville*, iii. 157.

173. Webster, i. 395, 408; *Dino*, i. 162.

174. Webster, i. 290-92, 398, 407-9; *H.H.D.*, p. 272; *William Russell*, pp. 328, 351; Granville to Brougham, 7 Nov., Brougham Papers; *Dino*, i. 67, 159; Bedford to Lady Holland, 21 Aug. [1834], H.H.P.

175. Webster, i. 409, 417-18.

CHAPTER X: CABINET AND COMMONS (*pages 499-549*)

1. Webster, i. 32-3, 66-7; *Creevey Papers*, ii. 286; *H. Greville*, ii. 158; *Russell*, i. 363.

2. Webster, i. 32-4, 112.

3. Webster, i. 37, 40; Lady Carlisle to Morpeth, 'Thursday', 'Tues. eveng' [Jan. 1831], C.H.P. 2/14; *Dino*, i. 38.

4. Palmerston to Lamb, 30 May 1834, RA, M.P.; *Creevey*, p. 345; Webster, *Diplomacy*, pp. 184-7; Lansdowne to Palmerston, 13 Oct. 1840, B.P. (referring to a bulletin).

5. Holland to Granville, 24 Feb. 1831, Gran. Papers 9/4; Littleton's diary, 7 July 1832, Hath. Papers.

6. Hobhouse's journal, 14 Aug. 1841; Bartlett, pp. 91-2; Graham to Richmond, 6, 25 Sept. 1832, Goodwood Papers; Webster, i. 31.

7. Palmerston to Littleton, 1, 2 Feb., 13 Mar. 1832, 10 May 1833, Littleton to Palmerston, [2 Feb. 1832], and Littleton's diary, 2, 3, 5 Feb. 1832, Hath. Papers; Gally Knight to Fitzherbert, 9 Dec. 1830, Fitzherbert Papers; Hobhouse's journal, 20 Mar. 1831.

8. *Jekyll*, p. 256; *Croker Papers*, ii. 80; Croker to Peel, 30 Nov., and to Hertford, 21 Dec. 1830, Croker Papers, Clements Library; Aspinall, *Three Diaries*, pp. 2 n. 6, 36.

9. Grey to Palmerston and Brougham to Palmerston, [13 Aug. 1831], B.P.; Althorp to Spencer, 27 Jan., A.P.; *Greville*, ii. 243-4, iii. 157; Aspinall, *Three Diaries*, pp. 185-6, 197; Hobhouse's journal, 26 Jan., 12, 20 July 1832.

10. Lady Cowper to Lamb, 12 Aug. [1832], B.P.W.; [James Grant], *Random Recollections of the House of Commons* (1837), p. 226; Hobhouse's journal, 8, 18 Feb., 3, 24 Mar. 1831 (*Broughton*, iv. 90, 97); Teignmouth, ii. 214; Dover's diary, 25 Mar. 1831.

11. Creevey to Miss Ord, 15 June, Creevey Papers (*Creevey*, pp. 345-6); *Lieven-Benckendorff*, p. 305; Littleton's diary, 30 June 1831, Hath. Papers.

12. *Croker Papers*, ii. 104; M. Brock, pp. 144-6; Milton-Smith, pp. 64, 67.

13. Aspinall, *Three Diaries*, p. 38; *Grey*, pp. 274-5; Palmerston to Durham, 'Sunday night' [27 Feb. 1831], Lambton Papers (cf. Durham to Palmerston, 28 Feb., B.P.); Milton-Smith, p. 67.

14. Littleton's diary, 29 June 1831, Hath. Papers; *Graham*, i. 105; *Broughton*, iv. 90; *Campbell*, i. 506; Aspinall, *Three Diaries*, p. 63; *Palmerston*, ii. 48.

15. *Graham*, i. 104; Guedalla, p. 159.

16. Palmerston to Grey, 8 April 1831, G.P.

17. Palmerston to Grey, 8 April 1831, G.P.

18. Durham to Grey, 'Sat. night' [10 April], G.P.; Grey to Palmerston, 10 April 1831, B.P.

19. Hobhouse's journal, 23 April 1831; *Sulivan*, p. 248.

20. *Palmerston*, i. 339; *Arbuthnot*, p. 116; Guedalla, p. 159.

21. Guedalla, p. 160; Palmerston's accounts for 1831, B.P.W.; *Sulivan*, pp. 248-9; Palmerston to Grey, 25 April 1831, G.P.

22. Byng to Granville, 29 April, Gran. Papers 7/12; Palmerston to Grey, 1, 2 May, 'Tuesday 7 o'clock' [3 May], 4, 5 May, G.P.; Lady Carlisle to Morpeth, 4 May [1831], C.H.P. 2/14; Cooper, iv. 570; *Sedgwick*, i. 376.

23. *Mrs Arbuthnot*, ii. 419; Hobhouse's journal, 4, 5 May (*Broughton*, iv. 111); Hardinge to Londonderry, 4 May, Londonderry Papers; Lady Blanche Cavendish to Lady Carlisle, 'Wed.' [27 April] 1831, Chat. Papers.

24. Lady Holland to Granville, 'Fri.' [May], Gran. Papers 9/4 no. 35; Palmerston to Grey, 25 April, 4 May 1831, G.P.

25. Palmerston to Lady Holland, 'Sunday' [8 May], H.H.P.; Holland to Granville, 'Fri.' [May], Gran. Papers 9/4 no. 28; Lansdowne to Palmerston, 'Monday Morning' [?May], B.P., G.C./LA40 (cf. B.P./CAB/B5, 7); Palmerston to Grey, 14 May [1831], G.P.

26. Aspinall, *Three Diaries*, p. 98; *Lieven-Grey*, ii. 218, 220-22; Grey to Holland, 28 May, G.P.; Lady Cowper to Grey, 'Sat.' [?7 May], G.P.; Littleton's diary, 28 June 1831, Hath. Papers.

27. *Lieven-Benckendorff*, p. 305; Grey to Palmerston, 25 April, B.P.; Grey to Ellice (copy), [?25 April], and Brougham to Ellice (copy), [?May], E.P.; M. Brock, p. 149; Palmerston to Littleton, 14 May, Hath. Papers; Palmerston's accounts for 1831, B.P.W.

28. Durham to Grey, 'Friday night' [3 June], G.P.; *Grey*, p. 302; Palmerston to Grey, 30 July, 12 Sept. 1831, G.P.

29. *Palmerston*, ii. 91; Palmerston to Grey, 'Monday' [5 July], G.P.; Hobhouse's journal, 9 July (cf. *Macaulay's Letters*, ii. 91); *Arbuthnot*, p. 141; Creevey to Miss Ord, 15 June, Creevey Papers (*Creevey*, pp. 345-6); *Lieven-Benckendorff*, p. 305; *Mrs Arbuthnot*, ii. 425-6; Littleton's diary, 30 June, Hath. Papers; Lady Keith to Lady Holland, 1 July [1831], H.H.P.

30. Palmerston to Grey, 15 June, G.P.; Littleton's diary, 20 July, Hath. Papers; *Palmerston*, ii. 120; Palmerston to Lady Cowper, 8 Oct. 1831, B.P.W.; M. Brock, p. 244.

31. *H.H.D.*, p. 65; *William-Grey*, i. 364-6; Milton-Smith, p. 69; Althorp to Grey, 9 Oct. 1831, A.P.

32. *H.H.D.*, p. 66; Palmerston to Grey, 9 Oct. 1831, G.P.

33. Grey to Palmerston, 10 Oct. 1831, B.P. (*William-Grey*, i. 375-8).

34. Palmerston to Grey, 10 Oct., G.P.; 3 *Hansard*, viii. 460; Stanley to Palmerston, 28 Oct., B.P.; Melbourne to Palmerston, [endorsed 'evening, 10 Oct. 1831'], B.P. (Ziegler, p. 147); M. Brock, p. 244.

35. Althorp to Grey, 9 Oct., A.P.; Grey to Palmerston, 10 Oct. 1831, G.P.; 3 *Hansard*, viii. 461.

36. *William-Grey*, i. 373, 377-8; *H.H.D.*, p. 66; Palmerston to Grey, 11 Oct. 1831, G.P.

37. Grey to Palmerston, 14 Oct. 1831, G.P.

38. *Durham*, i. 269, and New, *Durham*, p. 153; Grey to Palmerston, 10 Oct., B.P.; Palmerston to Grey, 10 Oct. 1831, G.P.

39. Milton-Smith, p. 70; M. Brock, pp. 246-7; Butler, pp. 301, 319; *Greville*, ii. 214-16; Aspinall, *Three Diaries*, p. 181; Palmerston to Grey, 18 Nov., G.P.; Grey to Palmerston, 18 Nov. 1831, B.P.

40. Grey to Lansdowne, 14 Nov., Bowood Papers; Milton-Smith, p. 70; Palmerston to Lady Cowper, 15 Nov. 1831, B.P.W.

41. M. Brock, pp. 247-58; Palmerston to Lady Cowper, 16 Nov., B.P.W. (Lorne, pp. 67-8); *H.H.D.*, pp. 81-2; Palmerston to Richmond, 8 Nov. 1831, B.P.

42. Lansdowne to Richmond and Grey to Richmond, 20 Nov. 1831, Goodwood Papers; *Melbourne Papers*, pp. 135, 140-42; M. Brock, pp. 259-60.

43. Palmerston to Grey, 20 Nov., G.P.; Lansdowne to Richmond, [24 Nov.] 1831, Goodwood Papers; *W.N.D.*, viii. 74; M. Brock, pp. 260-61; *H.H.D.*, p. 84.

44. Palmerston to Melbourne, 27 Nov., RA, M.P.; Palmerston to Richmond, 27, 29 Nov., Goodwood Papers; Palmerston to [Lady Cowper], 28, 29 Nov., B.P.W.; *H.H.D.*, pp. 85-6; Palmerston to Grey, 29 Nov., G.P.; Wood to Richmond, 29 Nov., and Richmond to Stanley, 24 Nov. 1831, Goodwood Papers.

45. *H.H.D.*, pp. 87-9.

46. *W.N.D.*, viii. 124-5; M. Brock, pp. 265-6; Aspinall, *Three Diaries*, pp. 162-3; Palmerston to Melbourne, 7 Dec. 1831, RA, M.P.; *William-Grey*, i. 451-7; B.P./CAB/B 6; *Croker Papers*, ii. 141.

47. *Mrs Arbuthnot*, ii. 437; Palmerston to Lady Cowper, 28 Nov. 1831, B.P.W.; *Russell E.C.*, ii. 27-8.

48. Aspinall, *Three Diaries*, p. 155; *Grey*, p. 331.

49. *Graham*, i. 134-5; M. Brock, pp. 168-70.

50. *Greville*, ii. 233-6; M. Brock, p. 271; Aspinall, *Three Diaries*, p. 205.

51. *Greville*, ii. 258-9, 261; Palmerston to F. Lamb, 20 Feb., 7, 16, 30 Mar., RA, M.P.; Palmerston to Grey, 23 Feb. 1832, G.P.; M. Brock, pp. 277-81; *Broughton*, iv. 197-8.

52. Palmerston to F. Lamb, 14-15 April, 7-9 May, RA, M.P.; *Brougham*, iii. 181-3; *Greville*, ii. 290; Grey to Palmerston, 21 April, B.P.; Palmerston to Grey, 25, 27 April, 1 May, G.P.; Palmerston to Holland, 28 April 1832, H.H.P.

53. M. Brock, pp. 283-90.

54. Aspinall, *Three Diaries*, p. 242; *Greville*, ii. 293-5; *H.H.D.*, pp. 165, 167-8; Palmerston to Lamb, 7-9 May 1832, RA, M.P.

55. M. Brock, p. 292; *H.H.D.*, pp. 177-8; Palmerston to Lamb, 7-9, 15 May, RA, M.P.; *Graham*, i. 143; Palmerston to Grey, 'Sunday half past Ten' [14 May 1832], G.P.

56. *H.H.D.*, pp. 180-84; M. Brock, pp. 301-5.

57. Lady Cowper to Lamb, 16-18, 31 May 1832, B.P.W. (Lever, p. 192).

58. Palmerston to Lamb, 18 May 1832, RA, M.P.; Palmerston to Lady Cowper, 4 Nov. 1831, B.P.W. (cf. Bell, i. 107); Palmerston to Minto, 7 June 1833, M.P.

59. Palmerston to Lamb, 10 June, RA, M.P.; Palmerston to Grey, 26 July 1833, G.P.

60. Palmerston to Lamb, 8 Mar., RA, M.P.; Palmerston to Temple, 15 July 1834, B.P.

61. Lady Cowper to Lamb, 16-18 May 1832, B.P.W.

62. Aspinall, *Three Diaries*, p. 275; Lever, p. 194; Brougham to Melbourne, 2 Sept. 1835, B.P., G.C./BR75b; Durham to Grey, 'Confidential. Thurs. night' [25 Aug. 1831], G.P.

63. Lady Cowper to Lamb, 2 July, B.P.W.; Webster, i. 194; Palmerston to Lamb, 27 Oct., RA, M.P.; Palmerston to Grey, 25 Oct., G.P.; Grey to Palmerston, 26 Oct. 1832, B.P.

64. Palmerston to Grey, 15 June 1831, G.P.

65. Palmerston to Durham, 21 Sept., Lambton Papers; Palmerston to Lamb, 28 Sept. 1832, 17 Mar., 18 June, RA, M.P.; Palmerston to Temple, 21 Mar. 1833 (*Palmerston*, ii. 147-8).

66. Althorp to Brougham and Grey, 4, 5, 7 Dec. 1832, A.P.; *Brougham*, iii. 256-7; Grey to Holland, 25 Mar., G.P.; Holland to Carlisle, 28 Mar. [two letters], C.H.P. 1/139; *Goderich*, p. 228; Ziegler, p. 153; Howick's diary, 25 Mar.; *Broughton*, iv. 295; *Arbuthnot*, p. 168; Palmerston to Grey, 22 Mar. 1833, G.P.

67. Grey to Holland, 25, 27 Mar., G.P.; Howick's diary, 25-26 Mar.; Palmerston to Grey, 26 Mar. 1833, G.P.; *Goderich*, p. 229.

68. *Greville*, ii. 332, 372; Aspinall, *Three Diaries*, pp. x-xi; Littleton to Mrs Littleton, 12 Dec. 1831, and Althorp to Littleton, 31 Dec. 1832, Hath. Papers.

69. *Greville*, ii. 372; Prest, p. 64; *Graham*, i. 187; Aspinall, *Three Diaries*, p. 379; Russell, *Recollections*, p. 121; *Russell*, i. 200 n. 1; Palmerston to Temple, 27 June 1834, B.P.

70. Grey to Durham, 8 Sept. 1833, Lambton Papers; *Graham*, i. 189; *Brougham*, iii. 357-64; Palmerston's memo., 9 May 1834, Brougham Papers.

71. Lansdowne to Brougham, 'Friday' [9 May], Brougham Papers; Arbuthnot to Peel, 26 May 1834, Peel Papers; *Graham*, i. 189; Aspinall, *Three Diaries*, pp. 378-9; Russell, *Recollections*, pp. 122-3; *Sulivan*, p. 256.

72. *Graham*, i. 190-92; Aspinall, *Three Diaries*, pp. 379-80.

73. Palmerston to Temple and to Minto, 27 May 1834, B.P.; *Greville*, iii. 43; *Sulivan*, p. 256; H. Fox to Lady Holland, 18 May 1833, H.H.P.; Ellice to Durham, 'Monday' [26 Aug. 1833], Lambton Papers; memo. on Lady Grey to Ellice, 'Friday' [17 Jan. 1834], E.P.

74. Granville to Holland, 26 May, H.H.P.; Aspinall, *Press*, p. 255; *Greville*, iii. 34.

75. Palmerston to Lamb, 30 May, RA, M.P.; Palmerston to Temple, 27 June 1834 (*Palmerston*, ii. 195-7).

76. Aspinall, *Three Diaries*, p. 380; Palmerston to Lamb, 30 May 1834, RA, M.P.; *H.H.D.*, p. 254.

77. *Palmerston*, ii. 195-6; Ellice to Durham, 'Monday' [26 Aug. 1833], Lambton Papers.

78. Howick's diary, 30 May; Grey to Brougham, 28 May, Brougham Papers; *Palmerston*, ii. 196; Althorp to Ellice, 29 May, E.P.; *Broughton*, iv. 350; Granville to Holland, 30 May, 6 June 1834, H.H.P.; *Brougham*, iii. 372.

79. Palmerston to Lamb, 30 May, RA, M.P.; *Broughton*, iv. 350; Parkes to Durham, 26 June 1834, Lambton Papers.

80. Webster, i. 402; *Palmerston*, ii. 194; Palmerston to Lamb, 6 July, RA, M.P.

81. Grey to Palmerston, 8 July 1834, B.P.

82. Grey to Durham, 8 Sept. 1833, Lambton Papers; Grey to Palmerston and Palmerston to Minto, 8 July 1834, B.P.; *Palmerston*, ii. 203 n.

83. Palmerston to Brougham, 10 July 1834, Brougham Papers; Palmerston to Melbourne, 12 July, RA, M.P. (cf. Shee to Palmerston, 9 July 1834, B.P.).

84. *Dino*, i. 139 (cf. Holland to Carlisle, [July], C.H.P. 1/139); Palmerston to Temple, 1 Aug. 1834, B.P.

85. *Palmerston*, ii. 206; Melbourne to Palmerston, 13 Nov. 1834, with enclosures, B.P.

86. *Greville*, ii. 87; Palmerston to Grey, 19 Sept., and Melbourne to Grey, 20 Sept., G.P.; Russell to Palmerston, 23 Sept. 1832, B.P.; Ziegler, p. 129.

87. *H.H.D.*, pp. 269-71; *Palmerston*, ii. 208; Lady Carlisle to Lady Granville, 22 July, Chat. Papers; Holland to Granville, 19 July [1831], Gran. Papers 9/4 no. 37.

88. *H.H.D.*, pp. 270-72; Baron E. von Stockmar, *Memoirs of Baron Stockmar* (1872), ed. F. Max Muller, i. 330; Prest, p. 69.

89. Palmerston-Ellice correspondence of 6, 12 Mar. 1832, B.P.; Palmerston's accounts for 1831 and 1832, B.P.W.

90. *Macaulay's Letters*, ii. 262; Palmerston to Lamb, 7 Mar., and Lamb to Palmerston, 16 Oct., 24 Nov., RA, M.P.; Palmerston to Durham, 1 July 1832, Lambton Papers.

91. Palmerston to Lady Holland, [8 May 1831], H.H.P.; Gunning to Palmerston, 11 June, and Dr Lamb to Palmerston, 26 June, B.P.W.; Palmerston to Grey, 1 July, G.P.; Palmerston to Wood, 5 July, B.P.; Wood to Palmerston, 10 July, B.P.W.; Lady Cowper to Lamb, 2 July (Lever, p. 206), 12, 27 Aug. [1832], B.P.W.

92. Lady Cowper to Lamb, 21 June, B.P.W.; Melbourne to Palmerston, 22 June 1832, B.P.; *Sulivan*, p. 148.

93. Temple to Palmerston, June-July, and letters and other papers relating to Lambeth, Aug. 1832, B.P.W.; *Althorp*, pp. 442-3; Gash, *Politics*, pp. 75, 123-4, 449.

94. Papers concerning Lambeth and S. Hants elections, Sept.-Nov. 1832, B.P.W.; Russell to Palmerston, 13 Sept. 1832, B.P.

95. *Sulivan*, pp. 252-4; Palmerston to Lamb, 4 Jan. 1832 [*sic*: 1833], RA, M.P.

96. Palmerston to Lamb, 13 Dec., RA, M.P.; Palmerston to Grey, 15 Dec., 6 p.m. 19 Dec., G.P.; Grey to Holland, 20 Dec. 1832, H.H.P.; Staunton's diary, 1831-7, and accompanying press clippings, Staunton Papers; Hampshire elections file, B.P.W.

97. Holland to Granville, 25 Dec., Gran. Papers 409; *Howard Sisters*, p. 258; Palmerston to Grey, 20 Dec., G.P.; Palmerston to Taylor, 23 Dec., B.P.W.; Palmerston's accounts for 24 Dec. 1832, B.P.W.; *W.P.C.*, i. 52.

98. Sloane Stanley to Palmerston, 18 Nov. 1832, B.P.W.; *Jekyll*, p. 310.

99. Palmerston to Temple, 16 Nov., B.P. (*Palmerston*, ii. 207-11); Palmerston to Lady Holland, 25 Nov., 7 Dec., H.H.P.; *Palmerston*, ii. 213; *Sulivan*, p. 259.

100. Palmerston to Temple, 9 Jan., and Palmerston's diary, 8-17 Jan. 1835, B.P.; *Sulivan*, p. 259.

101. Palmerston to Temple, 9 Jan. 1835, B.P.

102. *Lieven-Grey*, iii. 84 (see also *Creevey*, p. 403, *Greville*, iii. 145, and *The Letter-Bag of Lady Elizabeth Spencer-Stanhope* (1913), ed. A.M.W. Stirling, ii. 156); Holland to Grey, 'Sat.' [17 Jan. 1835], G.P.; *Sulivan*, pp. 260-61; Palmerston to Melbourne, 2 Dec. 1834, RA, M.P.; Palmerston to Lady Holland, 7 Dec., H.H.P.; Palmerston to Mrs Huskisson, 19 Dec. 1834, H.P.

103. *Sulivan*, pp. 259-62.

104. *Sulivan*, pp. 261-2; *Russell E.C.*, ii. 71-2; S. Hants election papers, B.P.W.; Staunton's diary, 1831-7, Staunton Papers; Palmerston to Fleming, 28 Dec. 1833 [*sic*: 1832], B.P.W.; Staunton to Palmerston, 9 Feb. 1835, Staunton Papers.

105. *Palmerston*, iii. 3-4; Joseph Croucher to Palmerston, 24 Jan. 1835, and Oddie, Forster and Lumley to Palmerston, 'Tues.' [April 1835, and not 1836 as endorsed],

B.P.W.; Palmerston to Palmer, 15 April, B.P.W.; Palmerston to Parkes, 13 April 1835, Parkes Papers; Snell, pp. 12, 31, 32-3, 36; *Campbell*, ii. 44; Webster, i. 417 n. 2.

106. Webster, i. 417 n. 2; Hobhouse's journal, 17 April 1835 (cf. *Campbell*, ii. 44); *The Times*, 20 Nov. 1837; Jones, pp. 88, 175; Lumley to Palmerston, '6 o'clock. Fri. afternoon' [22 May 1835], B.P.W.; Palmerston to Temple, 16 Nov. 1834, B.P.; election papers, Staunton to Palmerston, 21 Feb. 1835, and Palmerston's accounts, 1830-34, B.P.W.

107. Snell, p. 71; Tiverton election papers, 29 May, 3 June, B.P.W.; Palmerston to Temple, 2 June 1835, B.P.; Webster, i. 417 n. 2.

108. *Palmerston*, iii. 3-4; Melbourne to Auckland, 17 Sept., Auckland Papers; Brougham to Melbourne, [?16 or 17 Sept.], 'Sat.' [?20 Sept. 1834], RA, M.P. 1/116, 122.

109. E.J. Stanley to Durham, 9 Sept., Lambton Papers; Edward Thompson, *The Life of Charles, Lord Metcalfe* (1937), pp. 314-15 (see also Ellice to Grey, 12 Oct., G.P.); Melbourne to Brougham, 22 Sept., Brougham Papers; *Dino*, i. 177; Grey to Ellice, 15 Oct., E.P.; Byng to Granville, 7 Nov., Gran. Papers 7/13; Poulett Thomson to Ellice, 16 Oct., E.P.; Howick's diary, 13 Oct. 1834.

110. Howick's diary, 13 Oct.; *H. Greville*, i. 23; Lady Clanricarde to Granville, 19 Oct., Gran. Papers 6/7; Grey to Holland, 14 Oct., and Ellice to Grey, 12 Oct., G.P.; Brougham to Melbourne, [Oct.], RA, M.P. 2/4, 6; Holland to Carlisle, 10 Oct., C.H.P. 1/139; Grey to Ellice, 15 Oct. 1834, E.P.; *Dino*, i. 81.

111. Holland to Granville, 3, 21 Oct. 1834, Gran. Papers 9/4.

112. Granville to Holland, 24 Oct. 1834, H.H.P.; Webster, i. 408; *Greville*, ii. 149.

113. *Greville*, iii. 86; Webster, i. 345; Lady Clanricarde to Granville, 19 Oct., Gran. Papers 6/7; Brougham to Melbourne, [Oct.], RA, M.P. 2/6; Morley to Granville, 20 Nov., Gran. Papers 9/2; Russell to Holland, 11 Oct. [1834], H.H.P.; Arbuthnot to Peel, 18 Mar. 1833, Peel Papers; Bedford to Lady Holland, 15, 27 Oct. [1834], H.H.P.

114. Bedford to Holland, 13 Nov., and to Lady Holland, 18 Nov. 1834, H.H.P.

115. Webster, i. 407, 418 n. 2; Palmerston to Lady Holland, 9, 11, 25 Nov., H.H.P.; Holland to Granville, 4 Nov., Gran. Papers 9/4; Grey to Holland, 25 Oct. 1834, H.H.P.; Ziegler, p. 189; Ellice to Melbourne, 'private & confidential', 26 Mar. [1835], RA, M.P.

116. Webster, i. 417-18; *Dino*, i. 209-10.

117. *Palmerston*, ii. 213-14; Holland to Lansdowne, 23 Jan., Bowood Papers; Webster, i. 421 n. 1; Palmerston to Staunton, 10 Feb., Staunton Papers; Palmerston's diary, 11 April 1835, B.P.

118. *Palmerston*, iii. 6; Webster, i. 419.

119. Melbourne to Holland, 21 Jan., H.H.P.; Webster, 36-7, 345; *Greville*, iii. 86; Howick's diary, 10 April 1835.

120. *Greville*, iii. 196; *Raikes*, ii. 75-6; Howick's diary, 8-12 April 1835.

121. *Greville*, iii. 196; *Russell*, i. 232; Aspinall, *Brougham*, pp. 214-17; *Melbourne Papers*, p. 268.

122. *Lady Granville*, ii. 186; Webster, i. 420, ii. 841; Hobhouse's journal, 17 April 1835; *Melbourne Papers*, p. 268; *Greville*, iv. 286.

123. Webster, i. 420.

124. *Creevey Papers*, ii. 296; Melbourne to Palmerston, 28 Aug. 1834, B.P.; Webster, i. 401-2; Palmerston to Grey, 22 April 1833, G.P.; Grey to Holland, 22 Sept. 1835, 24 Jan. 1836, and Holland to Grey, 15 Oct. 1835, H.H.P.

125. *Lieven-Grey*, iii. 5, 8; Grey to Melbourne, 29 July, G.P.; Grey to Palmerston, 9 Dec. 1834, B.P.

126. Bell, i. 203; *H.H.D.*, p. 287; Holland to H. Fox, 17 April 1835, H.H.P.; Webster, i. 420, ii. 840.

127. Howick's diary, 14, 15 April; Ellice to Durham, 'Tues. 14 April', Lambton

Papers; Prest, p. 92; Allen's journal, 15 April 1835; Webster, ii. 841; *Sulivan*, p. 263; *Melbourne Papers*, p. 277; *Palmerston*, iii. 5-6.

CHAPTER XI: WARS AND REPRISALS, 1835-41 *(pages 550-620)*

1. *Lieven-Grey*, iii. 108-9, 119; *Dino*, i. 258.

2. *H.H.D.*, pp. 292, 293, 298, 313-14; Palmerston to Durham, 24 June 1835, Lambton Papers; Melbourne to Palmerston, 26 June 1835, B.P.; Webster, ii. 560; *Melbourne Papers*, pp. 333-4.

3. *Lieven-Grey*, iii. 111; *H.H.D.*, p. 298; Holland to Granville, 26 Feb. [1836], Gran. Papers 409.

4. Hobhouse's journal, 1 Feb.; Palmerston to Temple, 2 Feb. 1836, B.P.; Palmerston to Shee, 9 May 1835, Shee Papers; *Palmerston*, iii. 5-6.

5. Lever, p. 202; Palmerston to Lamb, 17 May 1833, B.P.

6. Palmerston to Holland, 17 May 1837, H.H.P.; Ridley, pp. 185-6; Lamb to Melbourne, 'Wednesday' [1834], RA, M.P.; C.K. Webster, 'British Mediation between France and the United States in 1834-6', *E.H.R.*, xlii (1927), pp. 58-78.

7. Melbourne to Palmerston, 5 Nov. 1835, B.P.; Durham to Grey, 21 Nov. 1831, G.P.; Villiers to Auckland, 1 May 1834, Auckland Papers; *Palmerston*, iii. 18; Bell, i. 195-6; Webster, i. 490; Brown, pp. 118-27; Bullen, p. 14.

8. Palmerston to Melbourne, 31 May 1835, RA, M.P.; *H.H.D.*, p. 313; Webster, i. 427-30.

9. Webster, i. 427-9; *H.H.D.*, p. 307.

10. *Melbourne Papers*, pp. 351-2; Palmerston to Holland, 24 Aug. 1836, H.H.P.; Webster, i. 434, 437-9; Hobhouse's journal, 7, 15 Dec. 1835.

11. Hobhouse's journal, 9, 12 Mar. (*Broughton*, v. 50-51); Palmerston to Villiers, 10, 14 Mar., 20 June, 14 July, B.P.; Howick's diary, 12 Mar.; Webster, i. 438, 440, 445; *H.H.D.*, p. 338; Palmerston to Melbourne, 27 Aug. 1836, RA, M.P.

12. Webster, i. 445-7.

13. Palmerston to Melbourne, 27 July 1838, RA, M.P.; *Palmerston*, iii. 21; Webster, i. 450 n. 1.

14. Webster, i. 448, 485-7, 490-93; *Lieven-Grey*, iii. 217; *Dino*, ii. 76-7; Howick's diary, 14 Nov., and Howick to Grey, 19 Nov. 1836, G.P.; Palmerston to Minto, 9 Oct. 1837, M.P.

15. Palmerston to Shee, 10 April 1837, Shee Papers.

16. Palmerston to Hobhouse, 2 Nov. 1835, B.P.; Ridley, p. 203; Webster, i. 446, 460; Palmerston to Lamb, 9 Oct. 1837, 1 Jan. 1838, B.P.

17. Palmerston to Minto, 9, 28 Sept., M.P.; J.P.T. Bury, *France, 1814-1940* (1964), p. 59; Palmerston to Melbourne, 17 Oct. 1837, RA, M.P.

18. G.F. Hickson, 'Palmerston and the Clayton-Bulwer Treaty', *Cambridge Historical Journal*, iii (1929-31), p. 295 n. 1; Palmerston to Melbourne, 7 Sept. 1838, B.P.

19. Melbourne to Palmerston, 18 Sept. 1838, 11 April 1839, and Palmerston to Doyle, 9, 12 April 1839, B.P.; Morgan, pp. 100-117.

20. Morgan, pp. 135-65; Ferns, p. 245.

21. Morgan, p. 166; Ferns, p. 245; *Palmerston*, ii. 295; Palmerston to Beauvale, 20 June 1839, B.P.; Webster, i. 449.

22. Melbourne to Palmerston, 12, 16 Sept., B.P.; Webster, i. 452; *Palmerston*, ii. 243.

23. Palmerston to Lamb, 14 June, 11 Nov. 1836, RA, M.P.; Palmerston to Villiers, 23 Sept., 30 Nov., B.P.; Palmerston to Minto, 20 Oct. 1837, M.P.; *Palmerston*, iii. 19; *H.H.D.*, p. 352.

24. Palmerston to Lamb, 6 May 1834, B.P.; Guedalla, p. 225.

25. Bullen, pp. 6-7; Grey to Palmerston, 2 Jan. 1834, B.P.

26. Palmerston to Beauvale, 13 July 1839, B.P.; J.A. Norris, *The First Afghan War*

1838-1842 (Cambridge, 1967), p. 214.

27. Webster, ii. 567-81; Hobhouse's journal, 4-5 Feb.; Holland to Granville, 'Fri. 6' [?p.m., 5 Feb.], Gran. Papers 409; Palmerston to H. Fox, 6 Feb. 1836, B.P.

28. Palmerston to Melbourne, 10 April 1836, RA, M.P.

29. Webster, ii. 568-70; Bell, i. 267-70.

30. Webster, ii. 563.

31. Palmerston to Auckland, 17 Aug. 1833, Auckland Papers; Webster, *Diplomacy*, pp. 199-202; *Memoir of the Right Hon. Sir John McNeill, G.C.B. and of his second wife Elizabeth Wilson* (1910), by their granddaughter, pp. 169-70, 176-8, 180, 182-3; Palmerston to McNeill, 21 Feb. 1836, B.P. (cf. Webster, ii. 742 n. 1).

32. Webster, *Diplomacy*, pp. 206-7; Palmerston to Melbourne, 24 Sept. 1835, RA, M.P.

33. Webster, *Diplomacy*, p. 208; Howick to Grey, 9 Feb. 1836, G.P.

34. Howick's diary, 5 Mar.; Lady Cowper to Lady Holland, [?15 Mar.], H.H.P.; Ellice to Durham, 21 Mar., Lambton Papers; Hobhouse's journal, 20 Mar.; Russell to Melbourne, 21 Mar., Melbourne to Palmerston, 21 Mar., and Melbourne to Russell, 22 Mar.1836, B.P.

35. Palmerston to Melbourne, 13 Mar. 1836, RA, M.P.; Webster, *Diplomacy*, pp. 208-12.

36. Webster, ii. 533-5; Hobhouse's journal, 9 July 1836.

37. Webster, *Diplomacy*, pp. 212-22; Webster, ii. 570-75.

38. Webster, ii. 537, 548, 598-9.

39. Melbourne to Palmerston, 27 Nov. 1835, B.P.

40. Howick's diary, 2, 23 Dec.; Hobhouse's journal, 2, 4, 5 Dec. 1835 (cf. Webster, ii. 583-4, where, owing to errors in Palmerston's retrospective survey of 9 Feb. 1836, the opening moves are dated a few days too soon).

41. Howick's diary, 23 Dec. 1835; Palmerston to Granville, 9 Feb., B.P.; Palmerston to Lamb, 17 May 1836, RA, M.P.

42. Howick to Grey, 15 Jan. 1836, G.P.; *The Diary and Correspondence of Henry Wellesley First Lord Cowley 1790-1846* (n.d.), ed. F.A. Wellesley, p. 203.

43. Palmerston to Granville, 9 Feb., B.P. (Webster, ii. 586); Palmerston to Melbourne, 7 Jan., RA, M.P.; Melbourne to Palmerston, 7 Jan. 1836, B.P.; Melbourne to Lady Holland, 31 Dec. 1835, H.H.P.

44. Melbourne to Palmerston, 24 Dec. 1835, B.P.; Melbourne to Grey, 5, 7, 19 Jan., G.P.; Grey to Melbourne, 8 Jan., B.P. (cf. Grey to Durham, 15 Jan., Lambton Papers); Palmerston to Melbourne, 12 Jan. 1836, RA, M.P.

45. Holland to Granville, 8, 25 Jan., Gran. Papers 409; Holland to Ellice, 5 Jan., E.P.; Ellice to Durham, 21 Mar., Lambton Papers (*Durham*, ii. 111); Holland's 'Precautions against Russian Encroachment on Turkey', 21 Jan. 1836, B.P.

46. Melbourne to Palmerston, 23 Jan., B.P. (Webster, ii. 586); Palmerston to Russell, 7 Mar. 1836, B.P.; *Melbourne Papers*, pp. 337-40.

47. Webster, ii. 587, 852; Russell to Melbourne, 21 Mar., B.P.; *Palmerston*, iii. 9; Palmerston to Holland, 10 Feb. 1836, H.H.P.

48. Palmerston to Melbourne, 4 June 1838, RA, M.P.

49. *Palmerston*, ii. 266; Webster, ii. 855; Hobhouse's journal, 6 June 1838.

50. Hobhouse's journal, 6 June; Minto to Palmerston, 16 June, B.P.; Lansdowne to Palmerston, 'Monday Morning' [18 June], B.P., G.C./LA49; Palmerston to Melbourne, 13 June 1838, B.P.; Bourne, pp. 229-31; Bullen, p. 18.

51. *Palmerston*, ii. 268; Webster, ii. 594.

52. Palmerston to Lamb, 10, 17, 24 May 1836, RA, M.P.

53. Charles Scott's diary, 23 Mar.; Leveson to Granville, 10 April 1837, Gran. Papers 6/4.

54. *Palmerston*, iii. 5-6, 8-9, 13-14, 16-18; Palmerston to Lamb, 14 June 1836, 10 April

1837, RA, M.P.; *Lieven-Grey*, iii. 236-7; Palmerston to Shee, 11 May 1837, Shee Papers.

55. Melbourne to Palmerston, 9 Jan., B.P.; Palmerston to Shee, 10 Oct. 1837, Shee Papers.

56. Palmerston's correspondence with the Mayor of Tiverton, Francis Hole, and with his election agent, George Coles, 1836-41, B.P.W.; Palmerston's diary, 6-10 Nov. 1835, 7-12 April 1836, B.P.; Holland to H. Fox, 22 Aug. 1837, H.H.P.; Palmerston to Shee, 18 April 1836, Shee Papers.

57. W. Chapple to Palmerston, 6 May 1836, B.P.W.; Palmerston to Temple, 4 Aug. 1837, B.P.; Snell, pp. 55-6; Ridley, p. 277; Palmerston to Durham, 12 July, Lambton Papers; G. Coles to Palmerston, [July 1837], B.P.W.; Gash, *Politics*, p. 197.

58. Byng to Granville, 26, 30 June, Gran. Papers 7/13; Melbourne to Russell, 7 July, 7 Sept. 1837, B.P. (Prest, pp. 117, 119-20).

59. Melbourne to Palmerston, 7 Sept. 1837, B.P.; *Broughton*, v. 104, 176; *Creevey*, p. 437; Hobhouse's journal, 16 Feb. 1836; Russell to Melbourne, 26 Dec., and Howick to Melbourne, 27 Dec. 1837, RA, M.P.; Prest, pp. 129-30.

60. Prest, pp. 135, 139; Russell to Melbourne, 18 Oct. 1838, B.P. (*Russell*, i. 308).

61. Lady Holland to H. Fox, 30 Nov., H.H.P.; Palmerston to Shee, 12 Dec., Shee Papers; Mrs Lamb to Lady Carlisle, 2 Dec., C.H.P. 1/129; Holland to Granville, 7 Dec., Gran. Papers 9/4; *Q.V.L.*, I, i. 180; Melbourne to Holland, 12 Dec. 1838, H.H.P.

62. Howick's diary, 26 Feb. 1836, 8 Aug. 1839, 17 April 1840; Holland to Granville, 26 Feb. [1836], Gran. Papers 409; Holland to H. Fox, 21 April, H.H.P.; Byng to Granville, 21 April, Gran. Papers 7/13; Bedford to Lady Holland, 23 April, H.H.P.; Hobhouse's journal, 14 Dec. 1837 (*Broughton*, v. 114), 21 June 1838.

63. Leveson to Granville, 10 April 1840, Gran. Papers 6/4.

64. Palmerston to Shee, 20 Jan. 1839, Shee Papers; Howick's diary, 2 Feb.; Charles Scott's diary, 9 Feb. 1839.

65. Hobhouse's journal, 6 Mar. 1838, 5, 19 Feb. (*Broughton*, v. 175); Howick's diary, 10 Feb.; Rice to Melbourne, 26 Jan., and Howick to Melbourne, 27 Jan., RA, M.P.; Palmerston to Melbourne, 5 Feb. 1839, RA, M.P.

66. Howick's diary, 22 Mar., 7 May; Palmerston to Beauvale, 22 April 1839, RA, M.P.

67. *Broughton*, v. 188-9; Palmerston to Beauvale, 8 May 1839, RA, M.P.

68. Palmerston to Beauvale, 14 May, RA, M.P.; Hobhouse's journal, 11 May 1839; *Greville*, iv. 138.

69. J.B. Kelly, *Britain and the Persian Gulf 1795-1880* (Oxford, 1968), p. 302; Webster, ii. 597, 607, 614-15; Palmerston to Holland, 10 Feb. 1836, B.P.; Temperley, p. 89; *Palmerston*, ii. 298-9.

70. Marlowe, pp. 287-9; Palmerston to Beauvale, 13 July 1839, B.P.

71. Hobhouse's journal, 27 July 1839.

72. Hobhouse's journal, 15 June; Webster, ii. 638; Palmerston to Beauvale, 1 Aug. 1839, B.P.

73. Granville to Holland, 2 Aug., H.H.P.; Holland to Palmerston, 8 Sept. 1839, B.P.; Webster, ii. 638-9; Marlowe, p. 239.

74. Marlowe, pp. 245-7; Webster, ii. 637-8, 641; Palmerston to Beauvale, 25 Aug. 1839, B.P.

75. Webster, ii. 641-3.

76. Hobhouse's journal, 15 June, 27 July, 17 Sept.; Russell to Palmerston, 27 July 1839, B.P.

77. Harold N. Ingle, *Nesselrode and the Russian Rapprochement with Britain, 1836-1844* (1976), pp. 77-92, 108-9, 114-15.

78. Palmerston to Beauvale, 25 Aug., 14 Sept., B.P.; *Russell E.C.*, ii. 265.

79. *Q.V.G.*, ii. 251-2; Palmerston to Morpeth, 20 Sept., C.H.P. 1/30; Palmerston to Melbourne, 19, 20 Sept., RA, M.P.; Palmerston's 'Scheme to compel Mehemet Ali to

evacuate Syria', 19 Sept. 1839, B.P./MM/TU16 (cf. Webster, ii. 651, where the account is a little garbled for lack of Palmerston's letters to Melbourne).

80. Palmerston to Melbourne, 20 Sept., RA, M.P.; Palmerston to Morpeth, 20 Sept., C.H.P. 1/30; Hobhouse's journal, 30 Sept. 1839; Webster, ii. 652.

81. Melbourne to Palmerston, [end. 19 Sept.], B.P.; Morpeth to Palmerston, 18 Sept., B.P.; Russell to Palmerston, 11 Sept. 1839, B.P./MEL/RU99; Webster, ii. 650; *Palmerston*, ii. 299-303.

82. Melbourne to Minto, 26 Sept. 1839, M.P.

83. Minto to Palmerston, 28 Sept., B.P., and to Melbourne, 28 Sept. 1839, RA, M.P.; *H.H.D.*, p. 411; Keppel, pp. 329-30.

84. Hobhouse's journal, 30 Sept. 1839; Webster, ii. 651; *Palmerston*, ii. 301.

85. Hobhouse's journal, 30 Sept., 1 Oct. 1839 (*Broughton*, v. 227-9); Palmerston to Holland, 11 Mar. 1840, B.P.; Palmerston to Morpeth, 5 Oct. 1839, C.H.P. 1/30.

86. Palmerston to Morpeth, 5 Oct., C.H.P. 1/30; Hobhouse's journal, 2, 28 Oct., 3 Nov. 1839; Webster, ii. 658-9.

87. Lady Cowper to Mrs Huskisson, 6, 7 Nov., H.P.; Palmerston to Shee, 14 Dec., Shee Papers; *Sulivan*, p. 270; Charles Scott's diary, 26 Nov.; Mrs Backhouse to Jane Backhouse, 16 Dec., Backhouse Papers; Graham to F.H. Bonham, 29 Nov., Peel Papers (I am grateful to Dr John Prest for this reference); Holland to Granville, 5, 13 Dec. 1839, Gran. Papers 409.

88. Webster, ii. 660-63.

89. Webster, ii. 653, 660, 666-7, 683, 688; Marlowe, pp. 254-7; Leveson to Granville, 26 May 1840, Gran. Papers 6/4.

90. Carlisle to Morpeth, 28 Sept., C.H.P. 1/33; Granville to Holland, 2, 21 Oct., 1 Nov., H.H.P.

91. Holland to Granville, 25, 29 Oct. 1839, Gran. Papers 409; *H.H.D.*, p. 411.

92. Palmerston's endorsements on B.P., G.C./HO133-5, 137-8; Holland to Palmerston, 15, 17 Oct., B.P.; Holland to Melbourne, 'confidential', 5 Nov., Panshanger Papers; Granville to Holland, 8, 15 Nov., H.H.P.; Melbourne to Palmerston, 16 Nov. 1839, B.P.

93. Holland to Granville, 19, 22, 29 Nov., Gran. Papers 409; *Palmerston*, ii. 305-7; Palmerston to Beauvale, 7, 14 Dec. 1839, RA, M.P.; Palmerston to Melbourne, 2 Jan. 1840, B.P.

94. Palmerston to Lady Cowper, 4 Nov. 1831, B.P.W.; Palmerston to Russell, 20 Oct. 1839, Russell Papers 3D, and 2 June 1840, B.P.; *Palmerston*, iii. 37-8; *Melbourne Papers*, pp. 458-9.

95. Ridley, p. 251.

96. Hobhouse's journal, 1 Oct. 1839 (*Broughton*, v. 228), 11 April 1840.

97. Ridley, pp. 194-5; Baring to Palmerston, 30 Oct. 1839, RA, M.P. 1/39; Palmerston to Melbourne, 2 April, RA, M.P.; Melbourne to Palmerston, 3 April, B.P.; Hobhouse's journal, 11 April 1840.

98. Harold Acton, *The Last Bourbons of Naples (1825-1861)* (1961), pp. 112-26; Melbourne to Palmerston, 4, 8 Feb., B.P.; Palmerston to Melbourne, 7 Feb., RA, M.P.; Hobhouse's journal, 14 April 1840; Ridley, p. 230.

99. Hobhouse's journal, 11 April 1840.

100. Granville to Holland, 20 Dec. 1839, H.H.P.; *Greville*, iv. 223.

101. Clarendon to Holland, 30 Jan., 5 Mar., H.H.P.; Ellice to G. Dawson Damer, 3 Mar., E.P.; Holland to Palmerston, 4, 11 Mar., and Palmerston to Holland, 8, 11 Mar., B.P.; *Clarendon*, i. 184-93; Clarendon to Ellice, 5, 7 Mar. 1840, E.P.

102. Leveson to Granville, 8, 11, 18 Dec. 1840, Gran. Papers (*Granville*, i. 30); Lamb to Melbourne, 25 June 1838, RA, M.P.; *Arbuthnot*, p. 225; John Backhouse, jr to his sister, 22 Jan. 1840, Backhouse Papers.

103. *Palmerston*, ii. 309; Granville to Holland, 9 Mar., and Allen's journal, 5 Mar.,

H.H.P.; Palmerston's minute, 17 Mar., B.P., G.C./DO28; Palmerston to Shee, 12 Mar., B.P.; Granville to Holland, 16 Mar., H.H.P.; Leveson to Granville, 17 Mar. 1840, Gran. Papers 6/4.

104. Hobhouse's journal, 23 May (cf. Allen's journal, 25 May 1840).

105. Lady Palmerston to Lady Holland, [Oct. 1843], H.H.P.; Hobhouse's journal, 3 Nov. 1839; Allen's journal, 10, 25 May, 6, 8, 19 June; Melbourne to Palmerston, 7 June 1840, B.P.; Webster, ii. 857.

106. Webster, ii. 684-9.

107. Hobhouse's and Allen's journals, 4 July 1840 (cf. Webster, ii. 689, where the Cabinet is wrongly dated and subsequent events therefore a little garbled).

108. Hobhouse's journal, 4 July; *Russell L.C.*, i. 6; Allen's journal, 6 July 1840; *Palmerston*, ii. 356-61.

109. Webster, ii. 690, 857-8; *Palmerston*, ii. 361-3; Lansdowne to Melbourne, 'Wednesday Morning' [?8 July 1840], Panshanger Papers; Russell to Melbourne, 8 July, B.P.

110. *H.H.D.*, pp. 417-18.

111. *H.H.D.*, pp. 418-20; Allen's and Hobhouse's journals, 8, 11, 18 July; Holland's 'protest', 8 July, B.P.; Russell's minute, 8 July 1840, B.P./CAB/A44.

112. Webster, ii. 690; Lever, p. 229; Allen's journal, 11, 18 July; Hobhouse's journal, 11 July 1840.

113. Allen's journal, 9 July 1841; *Palmerston*, iii. 426-33; Webster, ii. 688, 692-5; *Dino*, ii. 262; Hobhouse's journal, 18 July 1840; Johnson, p. 286.

114. Webster, ii. 695, 702-3, 705, 709; *Palmerston*, iii. 44; Palmerston to Melbourne, 28 July 1840, RA, M.P.

115. B.P./CAB/A48-51 (Aug.); Allen's journal, 28 July, 7 Aug.; Melbourne to Palmerston and Palmerston to Melbourne, 8 Aug. 1840, B.P.

116. Spencer to Ellice, 13 Aug., and Clarendon to Ellice, 8 Aug. 1840, E.P.; Russell to Melbourne, 10, 18, 19 Oct. 1839, 22 Jan., B.P.; Russell to Ellice, 16 Mar., and Ellice to Russell, 17 Mar. 1840, E.P.

117. *Russell*, i. 347; *Lady Russell*, p. 35; Melbourne to Palmerston, 12 Aug., B.P.; Russell to Minto, 17 Aug., M.P.; Allen's journal, 20 Aug. 1840.

118. Webster, ii. 858-9, 700-701; Melbourne to Holland, 30 Aug., H.H.P.; Graham to Peel, 3, 24 Aug. 1840, Peel Papers; *Melbourne Papers*, pp. 460-68.

119. Allen's journal, 31 Aug.; Melbourne to Russell, 19, 27 Aug., 1 Sept., RA, M.P. (*Melbourne Papers*, pp. 460-62); Russell to Melbourne, 28 Aug., B.P., and to Holland, 31 Aug. 1840, H.H.P.; *Russell*, i. 347-8; *Lady Russell*, pp. 35-6.

120. Russell to Palmerston, 30 Aug., B.P.; *Lady Russell*, p. 36; Lady Palmerston's diary, 26-28 Aug., 7-12 Sept.; Palmerston to Labouchere, 2 Sept., Labouchere Papers; Palmerston to Lady Palmerston, 5 Sept. 1840, B.P.W.; *Russell*, i. 348-9.

121. Webster, ii. 711-12; Melbourne to Palmerston, 10 Sept., B.P.; Russell to Holland, 15 Sept., H.H.P.; Palmerston to Melbourne, 9 Sept., RA, M.P.; Lever, p. 234; Allen's journal, 10 Sept. 1840; *Greville*, iv. 284.

122. Webster, ii 712 n. 1; *Melbourne Papers*, pp. 474-5, 477-8; Palmerston to Melbourne, 22 Sept. (enclosing memo. of 19 Sept.), B.P.; Melbourne to Palmerston, 14, 17 Sept. 1840 (cf. Webster, ii. 712, 713); *Russell*, i. 349-50.

123. *Russell*, i. 350-51; *Palmerston*, ii. 324-5; Russell to Melbourne, 20, 26, 27 Sept. 1840, Russell Papers 3D (*Russell*, i. 351-2); *Melbourne Papers*, p. 480.

124. *Greville*, iv. 276-7, 281-2, 285, 289-96; *Times History*, i. 379-82; *Reeve*, i. 120-21; Allen to Ellice, 14 Sept. [1840], E.P.

125. *Greville*, iv. 293-6; *Russell*, i. 351.

126. *Greville*, iv. 293-4, 298-9; *Palmerston*, ii. 329-30.

127. *Q.V.L.*, I, i. 290; *Greville*, iv. 290-92, 298, 301-2; Melbourne to Palmerston, 16, 19, 20 Sept. 1840, B.P.

128. Russell to Melbourne, 27 Sept., and Melbourne to Russell, 27, 28 Sept. 1840, B.P.; *Greville,* iv. 298; *Melbourne Papers,* p. 482; *Russell,* i. 352-3.

129. Melbourne to the Queen, 28 Sept. 1840, RA; Webster, *Diplomacy,* pp. 223-4; Palmerston to Hobhouse, 29 Sept. 1840, Broughton Papers.

130. *Greville,* iv. 298-301; Allen's journal, 28 Sept.; Palmerston to Hobhouse, 29 Sept., Broughton Papers; Hobhouse's journal, 1 Oct.; Allen to Ellice, 29 Sept. 1840, E.P.

131. *Greville,* iv. 302; Webster, *Diplomacy,* p. 224; Lady Palmerston's diary, 28 Sept.; *Clarendon,* i. 210; Lady Palmerston to Morpeth, 'Monday' [5 Oct.], C.H.P. 2/40 (cf. Lever, p. 235); Clarendon to Holland, 29 Sept. 1840, H.H.P.

132. Lady Palmerston's diary, 29 Sept.; Allen's journal, 29 Sept.; Russell to Morpeth, 24 Sept., C.H.P. 1/31; *Greville,* iv. 286, 291; Lansdowne to Melbourne, [25 Sept.], Panshanger Papers 17, and [29 Sept.], enclosed in Melbourne to Palmerston, 30 Sept. 1840 (Webster, ii. 718 n. 2).

133. Allen's journal, 28 Sept.; Normanby to Melbourne, 29, 30 Sept., RA, M.P.; *Q.V.L.,* I, i. 292.

134. E.J. Stanley to Ellice, 18 Sept., E.P.; Allen's journal, 18, 23 Sept.; Palmerston to Hobhouse, 29 Sept., Broughton Papers; Palmerston to Melbourne, 27 Sept. 1840, RA, M.P.

135. Webster, ii. 859-60; *Melbourne Papers,* pp. 482-3; *Russell,* i. 354; Prest, p. 168; Ziegler, pp. 318-19; *Greville,* iv. 302.

136. Duncannon to Melbourne, 21 Sept., RA, M.P.; *Greville,* iv. 303-5; Hobhouse's journal, 1 Oct. 1840; *Q.V.L.,* I, i. 292.

137. *Greville,* iv. 304-5; Palmerston to Melbourne, 2 Oct., RA, M.P.; *Russell,* i. 354; Clarendon to Holland, 4 Oct. 1840, H.H.P.

138. Hobhouse's and Allen's journals, 2 Oct. 1840; *Q.V.L.,* I, i. 293.

139. *Greville,* iv. 306, 312-13; Palmerston to Granville, no. 272 of 2 Oct. and no. 275 of 5 Oct., F.O. 5/600B.

140. Guizot, pp. 362-8; *Palmerston,* ii. 333-4; *Clarendon,* i. 211-12; Allen's journal, 5 Oct.; *Greville-Reeve,* pp. 39, 40, 42; *Arbuthnot,* p. 222; *Greville,* iv. 308; Russell to Palmerston, 4 Oct. 1840, B.P.

141. Melbourne to Palmerston and Palmerston to Granville, 6 Oct., B.P.; the Queen to Melbourne, 8 Oct., RA, C3/72; *Q.V.L.,* I, i. 296, 298; Palmerston to Granville, no. 280 of 6 Oct., F.O. 5/600B; *Palmerston,* ii. 339-40; Palmerston to Melbourne, 8 Oct., RA, M.P.; Lady Palmerston to Morpeth, [5 Oct. 1840], C.H.P. 2/40.

142. *Greville,* iv. 311-12, 315-16; *Clarendon,* i. 212; *Russell,* i. 354-6; *Q.V.L.,* I, i. 297-8; Webster, ii. 860; Allen's journal, 9 Oct.; Russell to Melbourne, 10 Oct. 1840, B.P.

143. *Russell,* i. 356-7; Russell to Melbourne, 9 Oct., Russell Papers, Perkins Library, Duke University; *Clarendon,* i. 212; Palmerston to Melbourne, 10 Oct. 1840, RA, M.P.

144. Webster, ii. 721; Guizot, pp. 371-2; Lansdowne to Carlisle, 16 Oct. [1840], C.H.P. 1/26.

145. Allen's journal, 10 Oct.; Clarendon to Morpeth, 12 Oct., and Labouchere to Morpeth, 14 Oct., C.H.P. 2/40; *Q.V.L.,* I, i. 299; *Greville,* iv. 314-15; Webster, ii. 860-61; Allen to Ellice, 14 Oct. [incorrectly endorsed 26 Sept. 1840], E.P.

146. *Melbourne Papers,* p. 483; Clarendon to Morpeth, 12 Oct., C.H.P. 2/40; Webster, ii. 860-61; Allen to Ellice, 14 Oct., E.P.; Normanby to Melbourne, 'Sunday night' [11 Oct. 1840], RA, M.P. 10/125.

147. Allen's journal, 10 Oct. 1840; *Q.V.L.,* I, i. 303; *Greville,* iv. 316-17; *Russell,* i. 357-8.

148. Webster, ii. 860-61; *Q.V.L.,* I, i. 302-5; Melbourne to Russell, 12, 13 Oct., RA, M.P.; Lever, pp. 234-6; Guizot, p. 370; Allen's journal, 12 Oct.; Melbourne to Palmerston, 13 Oct., B.P.; Clarendon to Morpeth, 16 Oct. 1840, C.H.P. 1/27.

149. *Q.V.L.*, I, i. 302-6; Melbourne to Russell, 13 Oct., RA, M.P.; Clarendon to Morpeth, 16 Oct., C.H.P. 1/27; Allen's journal, 18 Oct.; *Greville*, iv. 318; Melbourne to Palmerston, 13 Oct. 1840, B.P.; *Dino*, ii. 295-6.

150. *Q.V.L.*, I, i. 305-6.

151. Lansdowne to Palmerston, 'Thurs. mg' [15 Oct.], B.P.; Lansdowne to Carlisle and Clarendon to Morpeth, 16 Oct., C.H.P. 1/26, 27; Allen's journal, 16 Oct. 1840; *Greville*, iv. 318-19.

152. Webster, ii. 722-3; Beauvale to Lady Palmerston, 30 Nov. 1840, Lamb Papers; Lever, pp. 244-7; Johnson, p. 285; *Q.V.L.*, I, i. 294-6, 307-9; *Melbourne Papers*, p. 487 (the date of Melbourne's missing letter to Leopold is given in Leopold's reply enclosed in B.P., G.C./ME542).

153. Palmerston to Melbourne, 25 Oct., RA, M.P.; *Greville-Reeve*, pp. 37-8, 42; Mme Lieven to Lady Palmerston, 30 Oct., B.P.; Lansdowne to Melbourne, 25 Oct., Panshanger Papers; *Russell L.C.*, i. 29; Clarendon to Melbourne, 27 Oct. 1840, RA, M.P.; *Greville*, iv. 321, 324; *Reeve*, i. 133; Lever, pp. 237-8; Ilchester, pp. 281-3.

154. Palmerston to Melbourne, 25 Oct. 1840, RA, M.P.; Webster, ii. 848-9; *Melbourne Papers*, pp. 487-90; Bourne, pp. 250-52.

155. *Melbourne Papers*, pp. 485-6; Melbourne to Palmerston, 26 Oct., B.P.; Palmerston to Melbourne, 1 Nov. 1840, RA, M.P. 13/8, 9; *Russell*, i. 359-60.

156. Prest, pp. 168-9.

157. *Greville*, iv. 321-2; *Reeve*, i. 133; Webster, ii. 727-8; Bedford to Ellice, 5 Nov., E.P.; Palmerston to Granville, 20 Oct., B.P.; Melbourne to Palmerston, [Nov.], B.P., G.C./ME448; Neumann to Metternich, 16 Oct., V. St A.; Lansdowne to Palmerston, 13, 19 Nov., B.P.; Hobhouse's journal, 28 Nov.; Allen's journal, 20 Nov.; Palmerston to Lansdowne, 18 Nov., Bowood Papers; Clarendon to Palmerston, 12 April, and Fearon to Palmerston, 20 Oct. 1840, B.P.

158. Allen's journal, 7 Oct.; *Greville*, iv. 313-14, 320-21; Russell to Easthope, 13 Oct. 1840, Easthope Papers; *Melbourne Papers*, p. 486.

159. Hobhouse's journal, 28 Nov.; Ashley to Palmerston, 3, 6 Oct., B.P.; Hardinge to Londonderry, 8 Oct., Londonderry Papers; Palmerston to Melbourne, 8 Oct., RA, M.P.; *Greville-Reeve*, p. 12; Leveson to Granville, 20 Nov., Gran. Papers 6/4; Hume to Brougham, 9 Nov. 1840, Brougham Papers; Webster, ii. 727-8.

160. *Melbourne Papers*, pp. 491-2; *Greville*, iv. 323-7, 330; *Russell*, i. 360-62; Hobhouse to Palmerston, 6 Nov., B.P.; Hobhouse's journal, 6 Nov. 1840.

161. *Greville*, iv. 330-31, 333-4; Webster, ii. 727-9; Johnson, p. 284; Leveson to Granville, 13 Nov. 1840, Gran. Papers 6/4.

162. Webster, ii. 729-33; Melbourne to Palmerston, 28 Nov., B.P.; Leveson to Granville, 13 Nov., Gran. Papers 6/4; *Russell*, i. 363; Palmerston to Melbourne, 27, 29 Nov. 1840, RA, M.P.; *Palmerston*, ii. 350-51; Lever, pp. 241-2.

163. *Q.V.L.*, I, i. 306; Melbourne to Palmerston, 23 Nov., B.P.; Hobhouse's journal, 25, 28 Nov. 1840.

164. Stanley to Carlisle, [Nov. 1840], C.H.P. 1/30; *Greville-Reeve*, p. 48; Bartlett, p. 147; *Q.V.L.*, I, i. 471; *Greville*, iv. 334-5.

165. Russell to Palmerston, 2 Dec. 1840, B.P.; *Russell*, i. 362.

166. *Palmerston*, ii. 367; Palmerston to Melbourne, 29 Nov. 1840, RA, M.P.

167. Webster, *Diplomacy*, p. 179.

168. Russell to Palmerston, 9 Nov., 2, 19 Dec., Palmerston to Russell, 10 Nov., and Melbourne to Palmerston, 25, 29 Dec., B.P.; Palmerston to Melbourne, 23 Dec., RA, M.P.; Webster, ii. 736-7; Palmerston to Beauvale, 29 Nov. 1840, B.P.; *Palmerston*, ii. 363-6.

169. Palmerston to Melbourne, 14 Dec. 1840, RA, M.P.; Beauvale to Melbourne, 17 Jan., 5 Feb., 19, 21, 26 Mar., 5 May 1841, RA, M.P.; *Greville*, iv. 366-8, 372.

170. Melbourne to Palmerston, 26 Mar., 9, 15 April, B.P.; Lady Palmerston to Beauvale, 26 Jan., B.P.W.; Melbourne to Russell, 13 July 1841, RA, M.P.

CHAPTER XII: PROSPECT AND RETROSPECT (*pages 621-38*)

1. F.S. Rodkey, 'Lord Palmerston's Policy for the Rejuvenation of Turkey, 1839-1841', *Trans. of the Royal Hist. Soc.*, 4th ser., xii (1929), p. 171; Palmerston to Beauvale, 4 Aug. 1840, B.P.

2. Webster, ii. 787.

3. Palmerston to Lamb, 7 May 1832, RA, M.P.; 3 *Hansard*, xcvii. 122 (1 Mar. 1848).

4. Ward, *Graham*, p. 124; Ridley, pp. 184-5; Palmerston to Sir Herbert Taylor, 23 Dec. 1832, B.P.W. (see also Palmerston to Grey, 19 Dec., G.P., and to Dr Robert Lindoe, 28 Nov., B.P.W.).

5. Ridley, pp. 184-5; Bartlett, pp. 116-17; Lorne, p. 69.

6. Palmerston to Melbourne, 4, 19 Sept. 1838, RA, M.P.; Robinson and Gallagher, pp. 43-4; Kenneth O. Diké, *Trade and Politics in the Niger Delta, 1830-1885* (Oxford, 1956), pp. 57-9; Howard Temperley, *British Antislavery 1833-1870* (1972), pp. 45-6; Palmerston's memo. on the 'Portuguese Slave Trade Bill', Aug. 1839, RA, M.P. 12/4.

7. Johnson U.J. Asiegbu, *Slavery and the Politics of Liberation 1787-1861* (1969), pp. 43-5, 59; Grey to Holland, 23 Dec. 1830, H.H.P.

8. Brison D. Gooch, 'Belgium and the Prospective Sale of Cuba in 1837', *Hispanic American Historical Review*, xxxix (1959), p. 421; *Palmerston*, iv. 266; Howick's diary, 21 April 1836.

9. Palmerston to Lamb, 17 Mar. 1833, B.P.; Palmerston to Minto, 13 Sept. 1837, M.P.

10. D.C.M. Platt, *Finance, Trade and Politics in British Foreign Policy 1815-1914* (Oxford, 1968), pp. xiv, 35-7, 322-3; Webster, ii. 750-51; Robinson and Gallagher, pp. 4-5.

11. Robinson and Gallagher, p. 35; 3 *Hansard*, lx. 619 (16 Feb. 1842).

12. Palmerston to Lamb, 28 Aug. 1832, B.P.; *Greville*, iv. 344; Aberdeen to Peel, 15 Jan. 1841, Peel Papers.

13. 3 *Hansard*, xcvii. 122 (1 Mar. 1848); Palmerston to Lamb, 21 Mar. 1838, B.P.

14. Palmerston to Lamb, 28 Aug. 1832, B.P.; Holland to Palmerston, 14 Feb. 1837, B.P.; Palmerston's minute, 16 Aug. 1840, F.O. 96/20.

15. *Whigs and Whiggism. Political Writings by Benjamin Disraeli* (1913), ed. William Hutcheon, p. 284; Webster, ii. 793.

16. Snell, p. 71; Aspinall, *Three Diaries*, p. 23; *Arbuthnot*, p. 134; *Croker Papers*, ii. 99.

17. Webster, ii. 712; *Russell*, i. 356.

18. Princess Lieven to Lady Palmerston, 14-15 July 1841, B.P.; *Q.V.L.*, I, i. 315; Clarendon to Morpeth, 30 Nov. 1840, C.H.P. 1/27.

19. *Palmerston*, ii. 74-5; Palmerston to Beauvale, 27 Oct. 1840, B.P.; *Lady Palmerston*, ii. 58; *Q.V.L.*, I, i. 323; *Broughton*, vi. 3; Hobhouse's journal, 26 Jan. 1841; *Greville*, iv. 350-52.

20. *Russell*, i. 364; *Greville*, iv. 339, 342, 344; Grey to Howick, 31 Jan., and Howick to Grey, 2 Feb., G.P.; Spencer to Palmerston, 10 Sept., B.P.; Guedalla, p. 238; Birch to Melbourne, 14 June 1841, RA, M.P.

21. 3 *Hansard*, lviii. 641-63.

22. *Russell*, i. 374; Palmerston to Temple, 25 May 1841, B.P.; *Broughton*, vi. 25; *Greville*, iv. 380.

23. *Palmerston*, iii. 46-7; *Greville*, iv. 373-4; *Broughton*, vi. 19-20, 22-3, 27; *Q.V.L.*, I, i. 340-41, 346-7, 353-4; Lever, pp. 251-3; *Melbourne Papers*, pp. 419-20; Lorne, pp. 78-9; Prest, pp. 172-7.

24. Lady Palmerston's diary, 16 June; Lady Palmerston to Lady Holland, 17-18 June 1841, H.H.P.; Snell, p. 101.

25. Francis Hole to Palmerston, 25 May, 14 June, B.P.W.; Lady Palmerston to Lady Holland, 17-18 June, H.H.P.; Palmerston to Melbourne, 17 June 1841, RA, M.P.; Ashley, i. 410-11.

26. Lady Palmerston to Lady Holland, 17-18 June, H.H.P.; Palmerston to G. Coles, 20 Jan., and to William Hole, 11 Jan. 1841, B.P.W.

27. Lady Palmerston to Lady Holland, 17-18 June, H.H.P.; H.S. Hodges to Charles Warren and Francis Hole to Palmerston, 22 June, B.P.W.; Lady Palmerston's diary, 21-29 June 1841 (*Lady Palmerston*, ii. 61); Ridley, pp. 279-82; Snell, pp. 68-70.

28. Lever, pp. 251, 253-5; *Lieven-Palmerston*, pp. 205-7.

29. Princess Lieven to Lady Palmerston, 14-15 July, B.P.; Prest, p. 164; Lever, p. 254; Palmerston to Temple, 17 Aug. 1841, B.P.

30. Russell to Melbourne, 24 July, Russell Papers, Clements Library, Ann Arbor; Melbourne to Russell, 20 July, and Palmerston to Melbourne, 16 Aug., RA, M.P.; Melbourne to Palmerston, 19 Aug. 1841, B.P.; Ziegler, p. 305.

31. *Greville*, iv. 418; J.G. Lockhart, *Life of Sir Walter Scott* (1888), ii. 801.

32. Hatherton to Granville, 28 May, Gran. Papers 6/3; Princess Lieven to Lady Palmerston, 14-15 July, B.P.; *Lieven-Palmerston*, pp. 212-13, 215-16; Hobhouse's journal, 14 Aug. 1841.

33. *Melbourne Papers*, pp. 493-4; Hobhouse's journal, 30 Jan., 21 April, 1 May 1841 (*Broughton*, vi. 13-14).

34. Russell to Palmerston, 7 June, B.P.; Hobhouse's journal, 6 Feb. 1841; *Palmerston*, iii. 46-50; Lever, p. 248.

35. *Palmerston*, ii. 375.

36. Webster, ii. 775-6; Ridley, pp. 280-81; Bullen, p. 23 n. 88; Johnson, p. 286; Snell, pp. 96-7; *Palmerston*, ii. 382-3.

37. *Broughton*, vi. 36; Palmerston to Temple, 17 Aug., B.P.; Palmerston to Shee, 1 Sept., Shee Papers; *Greville*, iv. 417; Lady Palmerston to Lady Holland, 19 Nov. [1841], H.H.P.

KEY TO THE SOURCES
AND OTHER WORKS
CITED IN THE NOTES

The following list is limited to manuscript collections and printed books and articles cited more than once. It also provides a key to the abbreviations and short titles used in the notes.

The list is arranged in alphabetical order by key words. Prefixes and other preliminaries are therefore ignored for this purpose; *Lady Holland*, for example, is entered under *Holland*. Abbreviations in the form of simple initials, B.P., *G.L.C.*, G.P., etc., are separately arranged at the beginning of each alphabetical section.

I have omitted the catalogue or accession numbers of collections in the British Library, Public Record Office and other repositories; the number given is therefore that of the appropriate volume, box or bundle. But for reasons of strict economy I have omitted even these numbers where the arrangement of the collection should permit the specific document to be readily located from the other information given. In some cases, such as the Holland House Papers in the British Library or the Broadlands Papers in Winchester, the arrangement of the papers was not sufficiently advanced to give references of permanent value; but the descriptions promised by the British Library and the Hampshire Record Office should soon make location possible without too much difficulty.

Where, in the notes, a manuscript citation is followed by a printed source in brackets, the latter is either incomplete or inaccurate as to date or content.

In the case of printed books, the place of publication is London unless otherwise stated.

A.P.: Althorp Papers: the papers of the Earls Spencer at Althorp, Northampton. I am grateful to the late Earl Spencer for permission to use these papers.

Airlie: *In Whig Society 1775-1818. Compiled from the Hitherto Unpublished Correspondence of Elizabeth, Viscountess Melbourne, and Emily Lamb, Countess Cowper, afterwards Viscountess Palmerston*, by Mabell, Countess of Airlie (1921).

Albery: *A Parliamentary History of the Ancient Borough of Horsham 1295-1885 with Some Account of Every Contested Election, and so far as it can be ascertained, a List of Members Returned*, by William Albery (1927).

Alder: 'The "Garbled" Blue Books of 1839 - Myth or Reality', by G. J. Alder, *Historical Journal*, xv (1972), pp. 229-59.

Allen's journal: The journal of Dr John Allen among the H.H.P.

Althorp: Memoir of Lord Althorp, by Sir Denis Le Marchant (1876).

Alumni Cantab.: Alumni Cantabrigienses, ed. J.A. Venn (Cambridge, 1940-54).

Alumni Oxon.: Alumni Oxonienses, by Joseph Foster (Oxford, 1888).

Arbuthnot: The Correspondence of Charles Arbuthnot, ed. A. Aspinall (Camden 3rd series, lxv, 1941).

Mrs Arbuthnot: The Journal of Mrs Arbuthnot 1820-1832, ed. Francis Bamford and the Duke of Wellington (2 vols., 1950).

Ashley: *The Life of Henry John Temple, Viscount Palmerston*, by Evelyn Ashley (2 vols., 1879).

Aspinall, *Brougham: Lord Brougham and the Whig Party*, by A. Aspinall (1927).

Aspinall, 'Canningite Party': 'The Canningite Party', by A. Aspinall, *Trans. of the Royal Historical Society*, 4th ser., xvii (1934), pp. 177-226.

Aspinall, 'Canning's Ministry': 'The Coalition Ministries of 1827. I: Canning's Ministry', by A. Aspinall, *E.H.R.*, xlii (1927), pp. 201-26.

Aspinall, *Canning's Ministry: The Formation of Canning's Ministry February to August 1827*, ed. A. Aspinall (Camden 3rd ser., lix, 1937).

Aspinall, 'Goderich Ministry': 'The Coalition Ministries of 1827. Part II: The Goderich Ministry', by A. Aspinall, *E.H.R.*, xlii (1927), pp. 533-59.

Aspinall, 'Last of the Canningites': 'The Last of the Canningites', by A. Aspinall, *E.H.R.*, l (1935), pp. 638-69.

Aspinall, *Press: Politics and the Press c. 1780-1850*, by A. Aspinall (1949).

Aspinall, *Three Diaries: Three Early Nineteenth Century Diaries*, ed. A. Aspinall (1952).

Auckland Papers: The papers of the first Earl of Auckland in the B.L.

B.L.: British Library, London.

B.P.: Broadlands Papers: the papers of the third Viscount Palmerston, the second Viscount Melbourne and the seventh Earl of Shaftesbury, formerly at Broadlands and now in the National Register of Archives, Chancery Lane, London W.C.2. I am grateful to Lord Brabourne and the Broadlands Trustees for permission to use these papers.

BPP: British Parliamentary Papers.

B.P.W.: Broadlands Papers, Winchester: the papers of the Viscounts Palmerston, Emily, Countess Cowper and Viscountess Palmerston, and the Barons Mount-Temple, formerly at Broadlands and now in the Hampshire County Record Office, Winchester. I am grateful to Lord Brabourne and the Broadlands Trustees for permission to use these papers.

Backhouse Papers: The papers of John Backhouse in the Perkins Library, Duke University.

Bartlett: *Great Britain and Sea Power 1815-1853*, by C.J. Bartlett (Oxford, 1963).

Bathurst: Report on the Manuscripts of Earl Bathurst, preserved at Cirencester Park, Historical Manuscripts Commission (1923).

Bathurst Papers: The papers of Earl Bathurst in the collections on loan to the B.L.

Battiscombe: *Shaftesbury. A Biography of the Seventh Earl 1801-1855*, by Georgina Battiscombe (1974).

Bell: *Lord Palmerston*, by Herbert C.F. Bell (2 vols., 1936).

Betley: *Belgium and Poland in International Relations 1830-1831*, by J.A. Betley (The Hague, 1960).

Bindoff: 'The Unreformed Diplomatic Service, 1812-60', by S.T. Bindoff, *Trans. of the Royal Historical Society*, 4th ser., xviii (1935), pp. 143-72.

Blessington: The Literary Life and Correspondence of the Countess of Blessington, by R.R. Madden (3 vols., 1855).

Bligh: This Was a Man. The Biography of the Honourable Edward Vesey Bligh, Diplomat-Parson-Squire, by Esmé Wingfield-Stratford (1949).

Bourne: *The Foreign Policy of Victorian England 1830-1902*, by Kenneth Bourne (Oxford, 1970).

Bowood Papers: The papers of the Marquess of Lansdowne at Bowood House, Wilts. I am grateful to Lord Shelburne and the Trustees of the Bowood Manuscript Collection for permission to see and use some of these papers.

Brock, M.: *The Great Reform Act*, by Michael Brock (1973).

Brock, W.R.: *Lord Liverpool and Liberal Toryism 1820 to 1827*, by W.R. Brock (Cambridge, 1941).

Brougham: Life and Times of Henry, Lord Brougham, Written by Himself (3 vols., 1871).

Brougham Papers: The papers of Henry Brougham in the D.M.S. Watson Library, University College, London.

Brougham Papers, Clements Library: The papers of Henry Brougham in the William Clements Library, University of Michigan, Ann Arbor.

Broughton: Recollections of a Long Life by Lord Broughton (John Cam Hobhouse) with additional extracts from his private diaries, ed. Lady Dorchester (6 vols., 1909-11).

Broughton Papers: The papers of John Cam Hobhouse, Baron Broughton, in the B.L.

Brown: *The Board of Trade and the Free-Trade Movement 1830-42*, by Lucy Brown (Oxford, 1958).

Bruce, i: *Lavallette Bruce. His Adventures and Intrigues before and after Waterloo*, by Ian Bruce (1953).

Bruce, ii: *The Nun of Lebanon. The Love Affair of Lady Hester Stanhope and Michael Bruce*, ed. Ian Bruce (1951).

Buckingham Papers: The papers of the Dukes of Buckingham and Chandos in the Huntington Library, San Marino. I am grateful to the librarian for permission to use these papers.

Bullen: *Palmerston, Guizot and the Collapse of the Entente Cordiale*, by Roger Bullen (1974).

Bullen, 'Portuguese Question': 'England, Spain and the Portuguese Question in 1833', by Roger Bullen, *European Studies Review*, iv (1974), pp. 1-22.

Bury: *The Diary of a Lady-in-Waiting by Lady Charlotte Bury being the Diary illustrative of the Times of George the Fourth interspersed with original letters from the late Queen Caroline and from other distinguished persons*, ed. A. Francis Steuart (2 vols., 1908).

Butler: *The Passing of the Great Reform Bill*, by J.R.M. Butler (1914).

C.H.P.: The papers of the Earls of Carlisle at Castle Howard, York. I am grateful to Mr George Howard for permission to use these papers.

C.P.: The papers of George Canning in the Sheepscar Branch of Leeds Public Library. I am grateful to the Earl of Harewood for permission to use these papers.

Campbell: Life of John, Lord Campbell Lord High Chancellor of England, ed. the Hon. Mrs Hardcastle (2 vols., 1881).

Canning: The Foreign Policy of Canning 1822-1827. England, the Neo-Holy Alliance, and the New World, by Harold Temperley (1925).

Canning and Friends: George Canning and his Friends, containing hitherto unpublished letters, jeux d'esprit, etc., ed. Josceline Bagot (2 vols., 1909).

Cavendish: Society, Politics and Diplomacy 1820-1864. Passages from the Journal of Francis W.H. Cavendish (1913).

Chat. Papers: The papers of the sixth Duke of Devonshire at Chatsworth, Bakewell, Derbyshire. I am grateful to the Duke of Devonshire and the Chatsworth Trustees for permission to use these papers.

Chichester Papers: The papers of the Earls of Chichester in the B.L.

Clanricarde Papers: The papers of the first Marquess of Clanricarde in the Sheepscar Branch of the Leeds Public Library. I am grateful to the Earl of Harewood for permission to use these papers.

Clarendon: The Life and Letters of George William Frederick Fourth Earl of Clarendon, by Sir Herbert Maxwell (2 vols., 1913).

Clode: *The Military Forces of the Crown; Their Administration and Government*, by Charles M. Clode (2 vols., 1869).

Cockburn: Memorials of His Time by Henry Cockburn, ed. Harry A. Cockburn (Edinburgh, 1909).

Colchester: The Diary and Correspondence of Charles Abbot, Lord Colchester, Speaker of the House of Commons 1802-1817, ed. Charles, Lord Colchester (3 vols., 1861).

Connell: *Portrait of a Whig Peer Compiled from the Papers of the Second Viscount Palmerston 1739-1802*, by Brian Connell (1957).

Connell, *Regina v. Palmerston: Regina v. Palmerston. The Correspondence between Queen Victoria and Her Foreign and Prime Minister 1837-1865*, ed. Brian Connell (1962).

Cooper: *Annals of Cambridge*, by Charles Henry Cooper (5 vols., Cambridge, 1842-1908).

Creevey: *Creevey's Life and Times. A Further Selection from the Correspondence of Thomas Creevey. Born 1768-Died 1838*, ed. John Gore (1934).

Creevey Papers: *The Creevey Papers. A Selection from the Correspondence & Diaries of the Late Thomas Creevey, M.P. Born 1768-Died 1838*, ed. Sir Herbert Maxwell (2 vols., 1904).

Creevey Papers: Microfilm copies of the papers of Thomas Creevey in the D.M. Watson Library, University College, London. I am grateful to Major J.C. Blackett-Ord for permission to use these copies.

Croker Papers: *The Croker Papers. The Correspondence and Diaries of the Late Right Honourable John Wilson Croker, LL.D., F.R.S., Secretary to the Admiralty from 1809 to 1830*, ed. Louis J. Jennings (3 vols., 1885).

Croker Papers, Clements Library: The papers of John Wilson Croker in the William Clements Library, University of Michigan, Ann Arbor.

Cromwell, 'P.U.S.': 'An incident in the development of the Permanent Under Secretaryship at the Foreign Office', by Valerie Cromwell, *Bulletin of the Institute of Historical Research*, xxxiii (1960), pp. 99-113.

Crowe: *Reminiscences of Thirty-Five Years of My Life*, by Sir Joseph Crowe (1895).

D.N.B.: *Dictionary of National Biography*.

Dino: *Memoirs of the Duchesse de Dino (afterwards Duchesse de Talleyrand et de Sagan) 1831-1862*, ed. the Princesse Radziwill (3 vols., 1909-10).

Disraeli: *Disraeli's Reminiscences*, ed. Helen M. Swartz and Marvin Swartz (1975).

Disraeli-Londonderry: *Letters from Benjamin Disraeli to Frances Anne Marchioness of Londonderry 1837-1861*, ed. the Marchioness of Londonderry (1938).

Dod: *Who's Who of British Members of Parliament. A Biographical Dictionary of the House of Commons. Based on annual volumes of 'Dod's Parliamentary Companion' and other sources*, ed. Michael Stenton (Hassocks, Sussex, 1976).

Dormer Papers: The papers and diaries of Mrs Caroline Lamb and Sir Augustus Clifford at Grove Park, Warwick. I am grateful to the late Lord Dormer for permission to use these papers.

Dover's diary: The diary of George James Welbore Agar-Ellis, first Baron Dover, in the Northampton County Record Office.

Drummond Wolff: *Rambling Recollections*, by Sir Henry Drummond Wolff (2 vols., 1908).

Dudley to Ivy: *Letters to 'Ivy' from the First Earl of Dudley*, by S.H. Romilly (1905).

Dudley to Llandaff: *Letters of the Earl of Dudley to the Bishop of Llandaff* (1840).

Dupin: *View of the History and Actual State of the Military Force of Great Britain*, by Charles Dupin (2 vols., 1822).

Durham: *Life and Letters of the First Earl of Durham 1792-1840*, by Stuart J. Reid (2 vols., 1906).

E.H.D.: *English Historical Documents 1783-1832*, ed. A. Aspinall and E. Anthony Smith (1959).

E.H.R.: *English Historical Review*.

E.P.: The papers of Edward Ellice in the N.L.S. I am grateful to the Trustees for permission to use these papers.

Easthope Papers: The papers of Sir John Easthope in the Perkins Library, Duke University.

Eden: *Miss Eden's Letters*, ed. Violet Dickinson (1919).

Edgeworth: *Maria Edgeworth: Letters from England 1813-1844*, ed. Christina Colvin (Oxford, 1971).

Eldon: *The Public and Private Life of Lord Chancellor Eldon, with Selections from his Correspondence*, by Horace Twiss (3 vols., 1844).

Ellenborough Diary: *The Political Diary of Lord Ellenborough, 1828-30*, ed. Lord Colchester (2 vols., 1881).

F.O.: The Foreign Office papers in the P.R.O.

Farington: The Farington Diary, by Joseph Farington, ed. James Greig (8 vols., 1922-5).

Ferns: *Britain and Argentina in the Nineteenth Century*, by H.S. Ferns (Oxford, 1960).

Mrs Fitzherbert: The Letters of Mrs Fitzherbert and Connected Papers, by Shane Leslie (1944).

Fitzherbert Papers: The papers of Sir William Fitzherbert in the Derbyshire County Record Office, Matlock.

Foreign Office Records: The Records of the Foreign Office 1782-1939 (Public Record Office Handbooks, no. 13, 1969).

Fortescue: '. . . and Mr Fortescue.' A Selection from the Diaries from 1851 to 1862 of Chichester Fortescue, Lord Carlingford, K.P., ed. Osbert Wyndham Hewett (1958).

Fox: The Journal of the Hon. Henry Edward Fox (afterwards fourth and last Lord Holland) 1818-1830, ed. the Earl of Ilchester (1923).

Fox Bourne: *English Newspapers. Chapters in the History of Journalism*, by H.R. Fox Bourne (2 vols., 1887).

G.L.G.: Lord Granville Leveson Gower (First Earl Granville), Private Correspondence 1781 to 1821, ed. Castalia, Countess Granville (2 vols., 1916).

G.M.: Gentleman's Magazine.

G.P.: The papers of the second and third Earls Grey in the Department of Palaeography, University of Durham.

Gash, *Politics: Politics in the Age of Peel. A Study in the Technique of Parliamentary Representation 1830-50*, by Norman Gash (1953).

Gash, *Secretary Peel: Mr Secretary Peel. The Life of Sir Robert Peel to 1830*, by Norman Gash (1961).

George III: The Later Correspondence of George III, ed. A. Aspinall (5 vols., 1968-70).

George IV: The Letters of King George IV 1812-1830, ed. A. Aspinall (3 vols., Cambridge, 1938).

Gleig: *Personal Reminiscences of the First Duke of Wellington*, by George Robert Gleig (1904).

Glenbervie: The Diaries of Sylvester Douglas (Lord Glenbervie), ed. Francis Bickley (2 vols., 1928).

Glenesk: Lord Glenesk and the 'Morning Post', by Reginald Lucas (1910).

Goderich: 'Prosperity' Robinson. The Life of Viscount Goderich 1782-1859, by Wilbur Devereux Jones (1967).

Goodwood Papers: The papers of the fifth Duke of Richmond in the West Sussex County Record Office, Chichester. I am grateful to the Trustees of the Goodwood Estate for permission to use these papers.

Goulburn Papers: The papers of Henry Goulburn in the Surrey County Record Office, Kingston-on-Thames.

Graham: *Life and Letters of Sir James Graham Second Baronet of Netherby, P.C., G.C.B. 1792-1861*, by Charles Stuart Parker (2 vols., 1907).

Graham Papers: Microfilm copies of the papers of Sir James Graham in the Bodleian Library, Oxford. I am grateful to Sir Fergus Graham for permission to use these copies.

Gran. Papers: The papers of the first and second Earls Granville in P.R.O. 30/29.

Grant: *The Newspaper Press: its Origin - Progress - and Present Position*, by James Grant (3 vols., 1871-2).

Granville: *The Life of George Leveson Gower, Second Earl Granville 1815-1891*, by Lord Edmond Fitzmaurice (2 vols., 1905).

Dr Granville: *Autobiography of A.B. Granville - being Eighty-Eight Years of the Life of a Physician*, ed. Pauline B. Granville (2 vols., 1874).

Lady Granville: *Letters of Harriet Countess Granville 1810-1845*, ed. the Hon. F. Leveson Gower (2 vols., 1894).

Greville: *The Greville Memoirs 1814-1860*, ed. Lytton Strachey and Roger Fulford (8 vols., 1938).

H. Greville: *Leaves from the Diary of Henry Greville*, ed. Viscountess Enfield (4 vols., 1883-1905).

Greville-Reeve: *The Letters of Charles Greville and Henry Reeve 1836-1865*, ed. A.H. Johnson (1924).

Grey: *Lord Grey of the Reform Bill*, by G.M. Trevelyan (1920).

Gronow: *The Reminiscences and Recollections of Captain Gronow being Anecdotes of the Camp, Court, Clubs, and Society 1810-1860* (2 vols., 1900).

Grote: *The Personal Life of George Grote. Compiled from Family Documents, Private Memoranda, and Original Letters to and from Various Friends*, by Mrs [H.] Grote (1873).

Guedalla: *Palmerston*, by Philip Guedalla (1926).

Guizot: *An Embassy to the Court of St James's in 1840*, by F. Guizot (1863).

Gunning: *Reminiscences of the University, Town, and County of Cambridge from the Year 1780*, by Henry Gunning (2 vols., 1854).

H.H.D.: *The Holland House Diaries 1831-1840. The Diary of Henry Richard Vassall Fox, third Lord Holland, with extracts from the diary of Dr John Allen*, ed. Abraham D. Kriegel (1977).

H.H.P.: The papers of the Fox and Fox-Strangways families formerly at Holland House and now in the B.L.

H.P.: The papers of William Huskisson in the B.L.

Hanover: *Letters of the King of Hanover to Viscount Strangford*, introduced by Charles Whibley (1925).

Hardwicke Papers: The papers of the Earls of Hardwicke and the Yorke Family in the B.L.

Harewood Papers: The papers of Viscount Canning in the Sheepscar Branch of the Leeds Public Library. I am grateful to the Earl of Harewood for permission to use these papers.

Harrow Register: *The Harrow School Register 1571-1800*, ed. W.T.J. Gun (1934).

Hary-O: *Hary-O. The Letters of Lady Harriet Cavendish. 1796-1809*, ed. Sir George Leveson Gower and Iris Palmer (1940).

Hath. Papers: The papers of E.J. Littleton, Baron Hatherton, in the Staffordshire County Record Office, Stafford. I am grateful to Lord Hatherton for permission to use these papers.

Haydon: *The Diary of Benjamin Robert Haydon*, ed. Willard Bissell Pope (5 vols., Cambridge, Mass., 1960-63).

Herries: *Memoir of John Charles Herries*, by E. Herries (2 vols., 1880).

Herries Papers: The papers of J.C. Herries in the B.L.

Hertslet: *Recollections of the Old Foreign Office*, by Sir Edward Hertslet (1901).

Hobhouse: *The Diary of Henry Hobhouse (1820-1827)*, ed. Arthur Aspinall (1947).

Hobhouse's journal: The journal of J.C. Hobhouse (Lord Broughton) in the B.L.

Lady Holland's Journal: *The Journal of Elizabeth Lady Holland (1791-1811)*, ed. the Earl of Ilchester (2 vols., 1909).

Lady Holland's Letters: *Elizabeth Lady Holland to Her Son 1821-1845*, ed. the Earl of Ilchester (1946).

Hope of Luffness Papers: The papers of General Sir Alexander Hope in the Scottish Record Office, Edinburgh.

Horner: *Memoirs and Correspondence of Francis Horner, M.P.*, ed. Leonard Horner (2 vols., 1853).

Horner Papers: The papers of Francis Horner in the British Library of Political and Economic Science (L.S.E.).

Howard Sisters: *Three Howard Sisters. Selections from the writings of Lady Caroline Lascelles, Lady Dover and Countess Gower 1825 to 1833*, ed. Maud, Lady Leconfield (1955).

Howick's diary: The diary of Lord Howick, afterwards third Earl Grey (with passages by Lady Howick), in the G.P.

Huskisson: *Huskisson and His Age*, by. C.R. Fay (1951).

Huskisson Papers: *The Huskisson Papers*, ed. Lewis Melville (1931).

Ilchester: *Chronicles of Holland House 1820-1900*, by the Earl of Ilchester (1937).

Jackson: *The Bath Archives. A Further Selection from the Diaries and Letters of Sir George Jackson, K.C.H., from 1809 to 1816*, ed. Lady Jackson (2 vols., 1873).

Jekyll: *Correspondence of Mr Joseph Jekyll with his Sister-in-Law, Lady Gertrude Sloane Stanley, 1801-1838. Preceded by some Letters Written to his Father from France, 1775*, ed. the Hon. Algernon Bourke (1894).

Johnson: *Guizot. Aspects of French History*, by Douglas Johnson (1963).

Jones: *The Nineteenth-Century Foreign Office. An Administrative History*, by Ray Jones (1971).

Jones-Parry: 'Under-Secretaries of State for Foreign Affairs, 1782-1855', by E. Jones-Parry, *E.H.R.*, xlix (1934), pp. 308-20.

Kenin: 'The British Consular Establishment in the United States, 1786-1865', by Richard M. Kenin (unpublished University of Oxford D. Phil. thesis, 1973).

Keppel: *The Sovereign Lady. A life of Elizabeth Vassall, third Lady Holland, with her family*, by Sonia Keppel (1974).

Kingsley Martin: *The Triumph of Lord Palmerston. A Study of Public Opinion in England before the Crimean War*, by Kingsley Martin. (rev. ed., 1963).

L.P.: The papers of the second Earl of Liverpool in the B.L.

Labouchere Papers: The papers of Henry Labouchere in the Perkins Library, Duke University.

Lamb Papers: The papers of the Lamb family in the B.L.

Lambton Papers: The papers of the first Earl of Durham, formerly at Lambton Castle. I am grateful to Lord Lambton for permission to use these papers.

Lever: *The Letters of Lady Palmerston, selected and edited from the originals at Broadlands and elsewhere*, by Tresham Lever (1957).

Lieven-Benckendorff: *Letters of Dorothea, Princess Lieven, during her Residence in London, 1812-1834*, ed. Lionel G. Robinson (1902).

Lieven Diary: *The Unpublished Diary and Political Sketches of Princess Lieven, together with some of her letters*, ed. Harold Temperley (1925).

Lieven-Grey: *The Correspondence of Princess Lieven and Earl Grey*, ed. G. Le Strange (3 vols., 1890).

Lieven-Metternich: *The Private Letters of Princess Lieven to Prince Metternich 1820-1826*, ed. Peter Quennell (1937).

Lieven-Palmerston: *The Lieven-Palmerston Correspondence 1828-1856*, ed. Lord Sudley (1943).

Lieven Papers: The papers of Prince and Princess Lieven in the B.L.

Liverpool Papers, Perkins Library: The papers of the second Earl of Liverpool in the Perkins Library, Duke University.

Londonderry Papers: The papers of the third Marquess of Londonderry in the Durham County Record Office.

Lorne: *Viscount Palmerston, K.G.*, by the Marquis of Lorne (2nd ed., 1892).

Lowry Cole Papers: The papers of the Lowry Cole family (including diaries and letters of the first Earl of Malmesbury and Lady Malmesbury) in P.R.O. 30/43.

Lyndhurst: *A Life of Lord Lyndhurst from Letters and Papers in Possession of His Family*, by Sir Theodore Martin (1884).

Lyttelton: *Correspondence of Sarah Spencer Lady Lyttelton 1787-1870*, ed. Mrs Hugh Wyndham (1912).

M.P.: *The papers of the first and second Earls of Minto in the N.L.S.*

Macaulay's Letters: *The Letters of Thomas Babington Macaulay*, ed. Thomas Pinney (1974-6).

Machin: *The Catholic Question in English Politics 1820 to 1830*, by G.I.T. Machin (Oxford, 1964).

Mackintosh: *Memoirs of the Life of the Right Honourable Sir James Mackintosh*, ed. Robert James Mackintosh (2 vols., 1835).

Malmesbury (Aspinall) Papers: Transcripts made by the late Professor A.A. Aspinall from the papers of the first Earl of Malmesbury and now in the possession of the History of Parliament Trust. I am grateful to the Earl of Malmesbury and the Secretary of the History of Parliament Trust for permission to use these transcripts.

Malmesbury Diaries: *Diaries and Correspondence of James Harris, First Earl of Malmesbury*, ed. the third Earl of Malmesbury (4 vols., 1844).

Malmesbury Letters: *A Series of Letters of the first Earl of Malmesbury, His Family and Friends, from 1745 to 1820*, ed. the third Earl of Malmesbury (2 vols., 1870).

Malmesbury Memoirs: *Memoirs of an Ex-Minister. An Autobiography*, by the Earl of Malmesbury (2 vols., 1884).

Malmesbury Papers: The papers of the first Earl of Malmesbury in the library of Merton College, Oxford.

Marlowe: *Perfidious Albion. The Origins of Anglo-French Rivalry in the Levant*, by John Marlowe (1971).

Melbourne: *The Young Melbourne and the Story of His Marriage with Caroline Lamb*, by Lord David Cecil (1939).

Melbourne Papers: *Lord Melbourne's Papers*, ed. Lloyd C. Sanders (1890).

Middleton: *The Administration of British Foreign Policy 1782-1846*, by Charles Ronald Middleton (Durham, N.C., 1977).

Middleton, 'Backhouse': 'John Backhouse and the Origins of the Permanent Under-secretaryship for Foreign Affairs: 1828-1842', by Charles R. Middleton, *The Journal of British Studies*, xiii, 2 (1974), pp. 24-45.

Middleton, 'F.O.': 'The Emergence of Constitutional Bureaucracy in the British Foreign Office, 1782-1841', by Charles R. Middleton, *Public Administration*, liii (1975), pp. 365-81.

Milton-Smith: 'Earl Grey's Cabinet and the Objects of Parliamentary Reform', by John Milton-Smith, *Historical Journal*, xv (1972), pp. 55-74.

Minto, i, ii and iii: *Life and Letters of Sir Gilbert Elliot, First Earl of Minto from 1751 to 1806*, ed. the Countess of Minto (3 vols., 1874).

Minto, iv: *Lord Minto in India. Life and Letters of Gilbert Elliot, First Earl of Minto from 1807 to 1814 while Governor-General of India*, ed. the Countess of Minto (1880).

Mitchell: *The Whigs in Opposition 1815-1830*, by Austin Mitchell (Oxford, 1967).

Morgan: 'Anglo-French Confrontation and Cooperation in Spanish America, 1836-1848', by Iwan Wyn Morgan (unpublished University of London Ph.D. thesis, 1975).

Morley Papers: The papers of the first Earl of Morley in the B.L.

Murray: *The Honourable Sir Charles Murray, K.C.B. A Memoir*, by Sir Herbert Maxwell (1898).

N.L.S.: National Library of Scotland, Edinburgh.

Neumann: *The Diary of Philipp von Neumann 1819 to 1850*, ed. E. Beresford Chancellor (2 vols., 1928).

New, Brougham: *The Life of Henry Brougham to 1830*, by Chester W. New (Oxford, 1961).

New, Durham: *Lord Durham. A Biography of John George Lambton, First Earl of Durham*, by Chester W. New (Oxford, 1929).

Oldfield: *The Representative History of Great Britain and Ireland: Being a History of the House of Commons, and of the Counties, Cities, and Boroughs, of the United Kingdom, from the Earliest Period*, by T.H.B. Oldfield (6 vols., 1816).

P.O.W.: *The Correspondence of George, Prince of Wales 1770-1812*, ed. A. Aspinall (8 vols., 1963-71).

P.P.: The account, letter and W.O. estimate books of the third Viscount Palmerston, formerly at Broadlands and now in the B.L.

P.R.O.: Public Record Office, London.

Palmerston, i and ii: *The Life of Henry John Temple, Viscount Palmerston: With Selections from his Diaries and Correspondence*, by Henry Lytton Bulwer (2 vols., 1870).

Palmerston, iii: *The Life of Henry John Temple, Viscount Palmerston: With Selections from his Correspondence*, vol. iii by Henry Lytton Bulwer, ed. Evelyn Ashley (1874).

Palmerston, iv and v: *The Life of Henry John Temple, Viscount Palmerston: 1846-1865. With Selections from his Speeches and Correspondence*, by Evelyn Ashley (2 vols., 1876).

Lady Palmerston: *Lady Palmerston and Her Times*, by Mabell, Countess of Airlie (2 vols., 1922).

Lady Palmerston's diary: The diaries of Emily Lamb, Countess Cowper and Viscountess Palmerston, at Hatfield House. I am grateful to Lord David Cecil for permission to use these papers.

Palmerston's Opinions: *Opinions and Policy of the Right Honourable Viscount Palmerston as Minister, Diplomatist, and Statesman*, ed. George Henry Francis (1852).

Panshanger Papers: The papers of the Earls Cowper and the second Viscount Melbourne, formerly at Panshanger and now in the Hertfordshire County Record Office, Hertford.

Parkes Papers: The papers of Joseph Parkes in the D.M.S. Watson Library, University College, London.

Peel: *Sir Robert Peel from his Private Papers*, by Charles Stuart Parker (3 vols., 1891-9).

Peel Papers: The papers of Sir Robert Peel in the B.L.

Perceval: *Spencer Perceval. The Evangelical Prime Minister 1762-1812*, by Denis Gray (Manchester, 1963).

Platt: *The Cinderella Service. British Consuls since 1825*, by D.C.M. Platt (1971).

Ponsonby Family: *The Ponsonby Family*, by Major-General Sir John Ponsonby, K.C.B. (1929).

Powis Papers: The papers of Edward Clive, second Earl of Powis, at Powis Castle, Welshpool. I am grateful to the late Earl of Powis for permission to use these papers.

Prest: *Lord John Russell*, by John Prest (1972).

Pryme: *Autobiographic Recollections of George Pryme, Esq. M.A.*, edited by his daughter (Cambridge, 1870).

Q.V.G.: *The Girlhood of Queen Victoria. A Selection from Her Majesty's Diaries between the Years 1832 and 1840*, ed. Viscount Esher (2 vols., 1912).

Q.V.L., I: *The Letters of Queen Victoria. A Selection from Her Majesty's Correspondence between the Years 1837 and 1861*, ed. Arthur Christopher Benson and Viscount Esher (3 vols., 1907).

I must acknowledge the gracious permission of Her Majesty the Queen to make use of the following three collections in the Royal Archives at Windsor Castle:

RA: The papers of Queen Victoria.

RA, G.P.: The correspondence between the second Earl Grey, Gen. Taylor and King William IV.

RA, M.P.: The papers of William and Frederick Lamb, second and third Viscounts Melbourne. (The third viscount's papers have since been transferred to the B.L.)

R.P.: The papers of the first Earl and the first Marquess of Ripon in the B.L.

Raikes: *A Portion of the Journal Kept by Thomas Raikes, Esq., from 1831 to 1847: comprising reminiscences of social and political life in London and Paris during that period* (4 vols., 1856-7).

Redesdale: *Memories*, by Lord Redesdale (2 vols., 4th ed., 1915).

Reeve: *Memoirs of the Life and Correspondence of Henry Reeve*, by J.K. Laughton (2 vols., 1898).

Ridley: *Lord Palmerston*, by Jasper Ridley (1970).

Roberts: *The Whig Party 1807-1812*, by Michael Roberts (1939).

Robinson and Gallagher: *Africa and the Victorians, The Official Mind of Imperialism*, by Ronald Robinson and John Gallagher, with Alice Denny (1961).

Rose: *The Diaries and Correspondence of the Right Hon. George Rose*, ed. L.V. Harcourt (2 vols., 1860).

Russell: *Life of Lord John Russell*, by Sir Spencer Walpole (2 vols., 1889).

Russell E.C.: *Early Correspondence of Lord John Russell 1805-40*, ed. Rollo Russell (2 vols., 1913).

Russell L.C.: *The Later Correspondence of Lord John Russell 1840-1878*, ed. G.P. Gooch (2 vols., 1925).

Lady Russell: *Lady John Russell. A Memoir*, ed. Desmond MacCarthy and Agatha Russell (1910).

Russell Papers: The papers of Lord John Russell (Earl Russell) in P.R.O. 30/22.

Russell, Recollections: *Recollections and Suggestions 1813-1873*, by John, Earl Russell (1875).

William Russell: *Lord William Russell and his Wife 1815-1846*, by Georgiana Blakiston (1972).

S.P.: The papers of Laurence Sulivan in the possession of his descendants. (One portion of these papers has subsequently been transferred to the British Library and will be found in Add. MSS. 59782-3.)

Scott's Journal: *The Journal of Sir Walter Scott* (2 vols., Edinburgh, 1891).

Charles Scott's diary: The diaries of Charles Scott among the Walter Scott Papers in the National Library of Scotland.

Sedgwick: *The Life and Letters of the Reverend Adam Sedgwick*, ed. John Willis Clark and Thomas McKenny Hughes (2 vols., Cambridge, 1890).

Shee Papers: The papers of Sir George Shee, formerly in the National Register of Archives and now in the British Library. I am grateful to Capt. R. Neall, M.B.E., for permission to use these papers.

Sidmouth Papers: The papers of Henry Addington, first Viscount Sidmouth, and of Henry Unwin Addington in the Devon County Record Office.

Snell: *Palmerston's Borough. A Budget of Electioneering Anecdotes, Jokes, Squibs, and Speeches*, by F.J. Snell (Tiverton, [1884]).

Stafford: *Stafford House Letters*, ed. Lord Ronald Gower (1891).

Stap. Papers: The papers of A.G. Stapleton in the Sheepscar Branch of Leeds Public Library.

Staunton Papers: The papers of Sir George Thomas Staunton in the Perkins Library, Duke University.

Stratford Canning: *Life of Stratford Canning, Lord Stratford de Redcliffe*, by S. Lane-Poole (2 vols., 1888).

Sulivan: *The Letters of the Third Viscount Palmerston to Laurence and Elizabeth Sulivan 1804-1863*, ed. Kenneth Bourne (Camden 4th ser., vol. xxiii, 1979).

Teignmouth: *Reminiscences of Many Years*, by Lord Teignmouth (2 vols., Edinburgh, 1878).

Temperley: *England and the Near East. I: The Crimea*, by H.W.V. Temperley (1936).

Thornton: *Harrow and Its Surroundings*, by Percy M. Thornton (1885).

Tilley and Gaselee: *The Foreign Office*, by Sir John Tilley and Stephen Gaselee (2nd ed., 1933).

Times History: *The History of The Times* (4 vols., 1935-52).

Vereté: 'Palmerston and the Levant Crisis, 1832', by M. Vereté, *Journal of Modern History*, xxiv (1952), pp. 143-51.

'Vyvyan': 'Sir Richard Vyvyan and the Fall of Wellington's Government', by B.T. Bradfield, *University of Birmingham Historical Journal*, xi (1968), pp. 141-56.

W.N.D.: *Despatches, Correspondence, and Memoranda of Field Marshal Arthur Duke of Wellington, K.G.*, edited by his son, the Duke of Wellington (8 vols., 1867-80).

W.O.: The War Office papers in the P.R.O.

W.P.C.: *Wellington. Political Correspondence*, i. 1833-November 1834, ed. John Brooke and

Julia Gandy (1975).

Walker: 'The Rejection of Stratford Canning by Nicholas I', by Franklin A. Walker, *Bulletin of the Institute of Historical Research*, xl (1967), pp. 50-64.

Walpole: *History of England. From the Conclusion of the Great War in 1815*, by Spencer Walpole (5 vols., 1878-86).

Ward: Memoirs of the Political and Literary Life of Robert Plumer Ward, ed. the Hon. Edmund Phipps (2 vols., 1850).

Ward, *Graham: Sir James Graham*, by J.T. Ward (1967).

Webster: *The Foreign Policy of Palmerston 1830-1841. Britain, the Liberal Movement and the Eastern Question*, by Sir Charles Webster (2 vols., 1951).

Webster, *Diplomacy: The Art and Practice of Diplomacy*, by Sir Charles Webster (1961).

Wellesley Index: The Wellesley Index to Victorian Periodicals 1824-1900, ed. Walter E. Houghton (2 vols., 1966 and 1972).

West: *Recollections 1832 to 1886*, by Sir Algernon West (2 vols., 1899).

Wheeler-Holohan: *The History of the King's Messengers*, by V. Wheeler-Holohan (1935).

Wikoff: *The Adventures of a Roving Diplomatist*, by Henry Wikoff (N.Y., 1857).

Wilberforce: The Life of William Wilberforce, by Robert Isaac and Samuel Wilberforce (5 vols., 1838).

Wilberforce Correspondence: The Correspondence of William Wilberforce, ed. Robert Isaac and Samuel Wilberforce (2 vols., 1840).

William-Grey: The Reform Act, 1832. The Correspondence of the Late Earl Grey with His Majesty King William IV and with Sir Herbert Taylor, ed. Henry, Earl Grey (2 vols., 1867).

Harriette Wilson: The Memoirs of Harriette Wilson Written by Herself (2 vols., 1924).

Winstanley: *Unreformed Cambridge. A Study of Certain Aspects of the University in the Eighteenth Century*, by D.A. Winstanley (Cambridge, 1935).

Ziegler: *Melbourne. A Biography of William Lamb 2nd Viscount Melbourne*, by Philip Ziegler (1976).

INDEX

The Index utilizes the capital P as an abbreviation of Palmerston. Ellipses signify the absence of the remainder of a name from the text proper.

P and, 314, 351, 366, 367, 372–3, 464, 482, 489, 492, 493–4, 498, 545, 605, 618, 619, 627
and Poland, 353, 370, 373
and Switzerland, 368, 374
Azores, 390, 394

Backhouse, George Canning, 446, 590
Backhouse, John, 409, 413, 414, 417, 418, 425, 426–7, 438, 439, 440, 443, 446, 450, 583, 590
Backhouse, Mrs, 583
Bad Pyrmont, 3
Baden, 367, 404
Baghdad, 378, 579
Bagot, Sir Charles, 84, 356
Bagration, Princess, 199
Baker, Rev. Robert, 128
Baldwin, Edward, 488
Balkans, 380
Baltic, 353, 383, 559, 565
Bandinel, James, 413, 414, 425
Bankes, William John, 241, 242–3, 245, 246–7, 251
Bank of England, 2, 95, 486
Banks, Army Savings, 147–8
Banks, Sir Joseph, 1
Baring, Alexander, 1st Baron Ashburton, 480, 487
Baring, Francis Thornhill, 415, 581, 582, 592, 602, 604, 611, 615, 631
Barnes, Thomas, 484–5, 489, 490, 600, 615
Barrett, Samuel Barrett Moulton, 264
Barrington, Sir Jonah, 195
Basingstoke, 430
Bath, 1, 167
Bath, Order of the, 352, 435, 453
Bath and Wells, Bishop of, 51
Bathurst, Charles Bragge, 87, 165
Bathurst, Lady Georgiana, 177
Bathurst, Henry, 3rd Earl Bathurst, 244–5, 250, 251, 265, 266, 273, 274, 282, 283, 289, 291, 298
Bavaria, 367, 369, 374, 404
Bayard, 31, 199
Bayly, Lady Sarah, 224
Beauvale see Lamb, F.
Bedford, 124

Bedford, Dukes of see Russell
Bedlam, 160, 459
Beefsteak Club, 41–2
Behan, Thomas L., 480
Beirut, 606, 615, 630
Belgium, 220, 405, 445, 450, 553
question of, 332–49, 350, 351–2, 353, 354, 355, 356, 358–9, 360, 362, 365, 366–8, 371, 372, 373, 375, 379, 380, 387, 388, 389, 404, 407, 408, 419, 421, 429, 430, 431, 437, 448, 460, 491–2, 496, 499, 515, 523, 559, 568, 569, 627, 636
Bengal, Bank of, 3,
Bennet, Charles Augustus, 5th Earl of Tankerville, 200, 445
Bennet, Corisande, Viscountess Ossulston (*afterwards* Countess of Tankerville), 186, 193
Bennet, Henry Grey, 138
Bentinck, Lord William Cavendish, 87, 239, 542
Bentinck, William Henry, Marquess of Titchfield, (*afterwards* 4th Duke of Portland), 84
Bentinck, William Henry Cavendish, 3rd Duke of Portland, 4, 55, 73, 76, 80, 83, 84, 85, 86, 228
Berkshire, 128, 208
Berlin, 359, 360, 372, 373, 404, 431, 567, 596, 615
British representation in, 184, 371, 411, 460, 461, 467, 470, 472, 474, 476, 543, 544
Berry, Agnes and Mary, 4
Bessborough see Ponsonby
Beverly, Algernon Percy, 1st Earl of, 31, 53
Bidwell, John, 413, 416, 446
Bidwell, John, Jr, 440, 446, 449
Bidwell, Thomas, 413, 414–15, 446
Binfield Lodge, 208, 209, 212
Binning, Thomas Hamilton, Lord, 237
Birmingham, 603
Black, John, 485
Blackburn, Edward Berens, 213–14
Blackburn, Elizabeth, 213–14
Blackburn, John Edward, 214, 446
Blackett, John, 490